AUDREY HOWARD

*By Audrey Howard*

# The Mallow Years
# Shining Threads

Audrey Howard

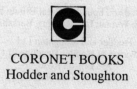

**CORONET BOOKS**
Hodder and Stoughton

*The Mallow Years* copyright © 1989 by Audrey Howard
*Shining Threads* copyright © 1990 by Audrey Howard

*The Mallow Years* first published in Great Britain in 1989
by Hodder and Stoughton Limited

*Shining Threads* first published in Great Britain in 1990
by Hodder and Stoughton Limited

This collected volume first published in Great Britain in 1994
by Hodder and Stoughton Limited,
a division of Hodder Headline PLC

A Coronet paperback

The right of Audrey Howard to be identified as the Author of
the Work has been asserted by her in accordance with the
Copyright, Designs and Patents Act 1988.

10 9 8 7 6 5 4 3 2 1

British Library C.I.P.
A CIP catalogue record for this title is available from the British Library.

ISBN 0 340 62334 9

Printed and bound in Great Britain by
Cox & Wyman Ltd, Reading, Berkshire

Hodder and Stoughton Ltd
A division of Hodder Headline PLC
338 Euston Road
London NW1 3BH

# THE MALLOW YEARS

## Part One

For Marjorie
and Jim
with love

## Author's Note

1. The cotton plant is a member of the mallow family.
2. In 1832 John Fielden and William Cobbett, radical candidates for Oldham township and out-townships of Royton, Crompton and Chadderton were returned as Members of Parliament with tremendous majorities over their Whig and Tory opponents. The addition of Joss Greenwood is purely fictitious.

though these, of course, were long gone. He was, of it ... ... ... He could ... to the ... ...

# 1

The day they were to march was hot and sultry. It was barely daybreak and already Joss could feel the sweat soak into the back of his shirt and collect beneath his armpits. It would be like a furnace by noon when the sun was at its highest but in his enthusiasm he did not really care. He was not yet nineteen years old and about to embark on the most exciting day of his life. The knowledge that he was to tramp twenty miles to Manchester and the same back was of no particular significance to the young man. He was strong and more than a match for a challenge such as this. He had on many occasions walked thirty miles in one day, up on the high moors of the South Pennine Heartland, striding out easily, eating up the vast distances with his long and powerful legs. And today he would be at the side of the man who was, in his opinion, the most dauntless in the world, his own father Abel Greenwood.

Joss Greenwood's grey-green eyes, the colour of wild mignonette in May, became soft with a deep and reverent love and he stood for a moment, one wooden clog on his bare foot, the other still in his hand, looking beyond the small window of the room he shared with his brother, beyond the drystone wall which enclosed his father's small-holding and out to the sweeping folds of moorland and the deep, wooded valleys of the hills which surrounded the cottage that was his home. The building was the last in the row of old 'laithe' houses which were to be found in the hillside valley, half home and half work place with a loom-shop above and stalls on the ground floor for cattle, though these, of course, were long gone. His view of the rugged landscape was uninterrupted. He could see to the top of Dog Hill in the clear morning air and hear the roar of the mountain stream tumbling on to the more placid waters below. But though his eyes encompassed the vast stretches of tussocky grass, the moor heather and blazing bracken of the wild hills, the picture he looked at in his head was that of the man who was his father. Though he listened to the music of the waters which had sung its song for as long as he could remember, the sound he heard was that of his father's voice as he spoke to the men who followed him. He would be downstairs now in the kitchen, putting on his clogs as Joss was doing, ready for the march, watching Joss's mother stirring the pan on the fire which contained the oats mixed with water that was to be their breakfast. His eyes, the exact colour of Joss's own, would be serene, the expression on the passive face uncomplaining. But Joss knew that behind the quiet face and eyes blazed a mind which was sharp and far reaching, courageous and compassionate. Inside the thin, hollow chest, formed to that state by the nature of his work, beat a heart like that of a lion. Though he was no more than five feet six inches tall and weighed only an ounce or two above nine stones, he was a giant of a man, and to Joss and the men who listened to him, only a degree or two below God Himself.

The door opened and Joss turned and the man who was in his thoughts entered the low-ceilinged room. His father smiled the slow, sweet smile which was peculiarly his and his eyes crinkled at the corners and the lines which cut his thin cheeks deepened. His lips parted on big, uneven teeth and he spoke quietly, the broad dialect of the north country-man rich on his tongue.

'Are't not ready, lad?'

'Aye, Pa. I've nobbut me clogs to put on.'

'It's a grand day for it.'

'It is that.'

'Yer Ma's got t'porridge on't table. Men can't march on empty bellies.' Abel Greenwood winked and his son's heart

10

swelled with pride for it seemed his father made no distinction between himself, a lad of almost nineteen and the gallant company of men who had been with him since the hated 'Combination Acts' had been passed in 1800. That was the year Joss was born and though he was not the passionate believer in the righting of the wrongs done his fellowman, that his father was, never having suffered what they did, the prospect of the day's escape from the routine of his life made him willing, eager to march for them. Nineteen years, and before that, and still the battle went on. Today this demonstration by workers from the whole of Lancashire, and beyond the county's borders to Yorkshire and Cheshire, would show those in authority that something must be done to alleviate their suffering and Joss Greenwood was thrilled at the prospect of being a part of it.

'Will they all come, Pa?' he asked, not really caring who came since he would be there.

'Aye. Weather's on our side.' The answer was short. Only when he was addressing a meeting did Abel Greenwood allow his natural gift as an orator to flow from him and even then he spoke quietly so that the enormous crowds who gathered to listen to him stood like silent statues in order not to miss a word of what he said. But at home with his family his remarks were brief, just as though he must save his strength and his eloquence for what had become his life's work.

''Appen they'd not march if it was raining, Pa,' he said scornfully, since he would go whatever the weather.

''Appen not, at least not in such great numbers.'

The younger man's eyes were brilliant in his thin face and his immeasurable enthusiasm for this day's outing put spots of crimson in his cheeks. He was tall, six inches above his father's height and reed thin but he held himself as straight as an arrow. His dark head was proudly set on his broadening shoulders. His hair was thick, tumbling with rich, brown curls on to his forehead, uncut and unbrushed. He wore threadbare breeches and a shirt to match, no stockings and the wooden clogs he had just put on.

'Will there be a great crowd to see us go, Pa?' and pretty girls, too, he would have liked to have said.

'Aye, lad, but that's not the purpose of t'march. We want to show t'maisters rightness o' what we ask for and the more of us go the better they'll see our determination.'

Joss Greenwood looked suitably crestfallen but his father smiled, laying a hand on his son's shoulder. He knew how he felt. He himself had been involved in the often hopeless, sometimes patient but always courageous struggle of the working man for almost twenty-five years. He had fought in the bread riots of Oldham in order to feed his growing family. He had watched helplessly as his own wages declined. He had seen the appalling effect of the 'Combination Acts' which had taken away the working man's right to congregate with others of like mind. But changes had come about slowly. The 'flying shuttle' and the 'spinning jenny' had seemed to him, and other hand-loom weavers and spinners, to be the miracle which would bring, if not prosperity, at least a decent standard of living for them all.

Abel Greenwood, and his father before him, rented the cottage which lay on the hillside of Edgeclough village. It was built on land belonging to the local squire and for the building and the acre of tough-grained soil on which it stood they paid the sum of two guineas a year. It was well built of local stone in the traditional manner by those who had been employed for generations in the spinning and weaving of cloth, first wool and then, as trade increased, cotton. The workroom or 'loom-shop' was on the first floor so that it might obtain the maximum light, with a 'taking-in' door set on the same level with steps on the outside of the building leading up to it from the ground.

They had worked side by side, Joss and Abel Greenwood, since Joss, at the age of eight had proved to his father that he was capable of operating the hand-loom alone, and had been allowed to weave his first 'piece' of cloth. There were

12

two hand-looms, each able to produce a length of cloth measuring forty yards a week, or more, if they wished but the father and son were their own men, weaving when they had a mind to, or working on the smallholding which surrounded the cottage, growing what vegetables the harsh climate of the Lancashire uplands would allow.

It was a good life. Martha Greenwood and her eldest daughter Jenny would often take their spinning jennies — after which the girl had been named — and sit by the cottage door while father and son worked the vegetable plot. Younger children were put to opening the bales of raw cotton, cleaning and carding the fibres and thus the whole family was profitably and satisfyingly employed. The raw yarn was brought to them each week by the merchant from Manchester and the two lengths of cloth which had been woven were sold at the Cloth Hall in Crossfold.

But by this time Joss and Abel Greenwood were among the dwindling number of men who could call themselves independent. The supply of raw cotton on which their livelihood depended was fast disappearing as the factory system, begun in 1806, took a firm hold. Men like James Chapman and his son Barker Chapman, the merchants who had once supplied their yarn for a commission, built their own spinning mill and had not the time nor the inclination, now they were spinning for themselves, to bother with the likes of Abel Greenwood. Those men who had depended on the firm of Chapman for their yarn began now to weave Chapman cloth on an 'outworker' basis but Joss and Abel between them, with a third weaver called Enoch Butterworth, who was also unwilling to give up his emancipation, managed to fetch the raw cotton they needed themselves. One pack pony could carry enough for three weavers, though it was a long trudge to Manchester and back. They took a pride in themselves and in their craft and were determined to manage despite the difficulties.

But many did not and today they were to speak up for themselves through the voices of men like Henry Hunt, John Knight and Abel Greenwood. His eyes softened as they looked into the excited brilliance of his son's and he squeezed his shoulder lovingly, the only demonstration of his feelings he would allow, then he turned away briskly.

'Come, lad. They'll not wait on us if we're late.'

John Knight gave the signal at nine o'clock on that hot and cloudless morning for the columns to swing off Oldham Green and on to the road to Manchester. He had organised the Oldham assembly and Joss Greenwood, as the son of one of the movement's leaders found himself marching directly behind the great man's back.

He looked straight ahead at first for this was the first time he had been so far from his hillside home and the excitement was almost too much for him to contain. He did not look at the thousands of people who lined the route, flinging wide their windows and gathering on their doorsteps to watch the great column of men and women march through the town and out on to the moorland route which led through Failsworth and Chadderton to Manchester. For the first few minutes he stared unseeingly at the low-crowned, broad-brimmed hat worn by John Knight, but he was a young man with a young man's susceptibility to admiration. The shouting, cheering spectators, the joyful sound of the band which kept them in step, the soft excited laughter of the two hundred white-gowned young women, who formed the centrepiece of the procession at his back, was too much for him and he began to smile, then to grin broadly, waving his hand jubilantly at all those who had come to see them off. The white silk banner emblazoned with the inscription "Universal Suffrage", "Annual Parliaments", "Election by Ballot' and "No Combination Acts, Oldham Union' flew high above his head, like a great and glorious bird in the depthless blue of the sky and he knew that by the end of that day, they, the cotton operatives of Lancashire, would have these things. He could see the sprig of laurel in his father's hat, placed there to signify that he was a leader and as a token of amity and peace. The small splash of green gave Joss a

14

feeling of such joy for what it represented he felt his heart expand to accommodate the wealth of his emotions.

They passed through sun-filtered woods, up mossy banks and down into sheltered valleys until they came to the toll-gates at Harpurhey and Joss saw his father stretch up to speak in the ear of John Knight. The distinguished gentleman looked about him as though expecting some mishap for it had been rumoured the magistrates might try to stop them here but there was nothing to be seen except the excited cheering faces of the people.

They had reached Newtown by now and the predominantly Irish population of this worst area of the slums came out to greet them. Row upon row of cheap, back-to-back houses with no visible sign of ventilation or drainage and with every scrap of space overflowing, or so it seemed to Joss, with apathetic, black-haired people. The street through which they marched followed the course of a ditch overflowing with the most appalling mass of human garbage, from the contents of the previous night's chamber pot and bucket, to the remains of dead animals. Children played barefoot, wearing next to nothing in the hot sunshine. Dirty, noisy, quarrelsome, half-starved and half-wild, and strangers, it appeared, to the pump water and privy at the end of the street which was shared by twenty houses. Every patch of land, scrubby and wasted, between the rows of houses themselves, carried a festering heap of filth. There were broken windows mended with oilskin, rotting wood in the doors and frames and the stench from the open drain and underground cellars made Joss Greenwood's head reel.

The men and women who cheered, or stood silently staring, depending on their disposition and state of health, were of low stature, thin and pallid with bowed legs and crooked backs. Their hair was lack-lustre and patchy and their eyes had a curiously dusty look about them as though for want of sleep. They had a spiritless and dejected air but they had been made aware that this blithe company which passed their door was on its way to better their lot and though they had no great hope of it the music and pageantry

15

made a pleasant change in their drab lives and there was a smile or two and even a tentative wave.

Joss held his hand to his mouth as he gagged on the putrid air.

'Look to't front, lad,' his father's voice told him steadfastly. 'Remember 'tis to do away with this that we march.' Joss Greenwood took heart, averting his eyes from the horrors about him, looking to the laurel spray on John Knight's hat and to the bright day ahead it signified.

The band began to play 'St Patrick's Day in the Morning' to please those who stood to watch them pass by and the noise of shouting voices became louder, ringing in their ears until at last they reached the centre of Manchester and their destination.

St Peter's Field!

The marchers were singing now, laughing and filled with spontaneous gaiety, but disciplined just the same. Children clung to their fathers' hands or were lifted on to their shoulders and one might have been forgiven for thinking they were all to attend a country fair rather than one of the greatest political meetings the country had ever known. Joss thought he would burst with excitement and pride to be part of such a good-natured multitude. They were near to starvation, many of them, scarecrow men and women with scarecrow children but still they remained good-humoured, walking the twenty miles, some of them without a shoe to their foot or a bit of gruel in their bellies.

It was midday before the word came that Orator Hunt was to arrive accompanied by the Manchester female reformers, dressed, like the Oldham women, all in white. The sun beat down and the heat became oppressive for no breath of cooling wind could reach the thousands upon thousands who crowded the great field that day. It was estimated later that six per cent of the total population of Lancashire was there, upwards of sixty thousand people and as the massed bands rendered 'See the Conquering Hero comes' sixty thousand voices roared their approval and Joss Greenwood's was surely among the loudest.

At twenty minutes to two the cheering was allowed to die down and Henry Hunt, the great Radical leader whom they all waited eagerly to hear, began to speak.

The Manchester and Salford Yeomanry Cavalry trotted briskly down the length of Cooper Street, intent, as they had been ordered, on arresting the leaders of the seditious meeting which was taking place in St Peter's Field. Henry Hunt's name was on their list, as was that of John Knight, Richard Moorhouse, Joseph Johnson and Abel Greenwood.

The horses of the troopers were restive and hard to control, raw and unused to the field and when the last galloper had gone by, his head still dazed by the amount of ale he had consumed before mounting, the woman and her two-year-old child, who had come to see the procession and with whom his horse had collided, lay still and bleeding in the gutter, unnoticed and unheeded except by those who stood beside her. They were the first casualties of the day.

The first intimation that something was wrong was conveyed to Joss Greenwood by the sudden look of alarm on his father's face. Joss had climbed on to a window-sill, clinging to a drainpipe, which ran down the wall, so that he could see over the heads of the great press of people to where his father stood at the hustings. Abel had been smiling, turning his attention to Henry Hunt, clearly moved by the splendid occasion and the support and loyalty shown by those for whom he had fought so long and hard. Joss smiled too, and hoped his father would be allowed to speak for there was no more fluent and heart-warming orator in the whole of the land. Abel believed passionately in the need for change in the lives of his fellow workers, as did all those congregated there that day, and yet, though his soul burned with it, his way was to speak quietly, simply, movingly and the people who listened to him loved him and did what he told them. No one broke machinery nor wrecked mills in their aim for reform under Abel Greenwood's direction and though he was a fervent radical

17

he did nothing with violence but preached peaceable change through education and the ballot box.

As Joss watched him he saw his father turn sharply away from Henry Hunt, his expression changing from smiling accordance, to dismay and Joss turned also, trying to make out what had alarmed him. He could see nothing but the crowd was beginning to surge and he heard someone cry out ' . . . soldiers . . . there's soldiers . . .' He saw Henry Hunt raise his hands to those before him and the great man shouted something as though beseeching them to stand firm then, surprisingly, there was laughter and Joss relaxed. He saw the soldiers then. They were mounted, appearing enormous above the heads of the people on the far side of the field. Quiet, it seemed to him, orderly and imposing no threat to the bewildered crowd but as he watched, idly wondering if perhaps they had come to join the march, a fine sight in their splendid uniforms, his heart jumped sickeningly to his throat, choking the words of warning he would have spoken. He watched in growing confusion as they drew their sharpened, glittering sabres and began to advance towards the hustings. He found his voice then.

'Pa,' he shouted. He could see the terrified horses begin to rear, surrounded as they were by thousands of men, women and children. The soldiers were trying desperately to maintain order for, at that precise moment, they meant no harm to the crowd. They had come only to arrest those who were breaking the law. The people about them could take themselves back to wherever they had come from for all they cared; but the frightened, panicking multitude did not know this. They only knew sudden fear, the smell and taste and feel of it, which was as thick and oppressive as the mid-afternoon heat. Men and women fell back from the plunging horses, knocking over those behind them and bodies began to go down like dominoes, the first being the cause of the last to fall. The cavalrymen tried resolutely to follow their officers in line abreast but the further their mounts were forced into the solid wall of the throng the

18

less their riders could control them and finally the ranks broke.

Joss's mind became a terrible seething mass of unco-ordinated thoughts but one overruled all others. It was that his father, not afraid as he himself was, but concerned only for those about him would wade into the sea of screaming, panicking women and their children and pick them up in his protective arms, as many as he could carry, taking them to safety and Joss was desperate to be beside him when he did so.

'Pa,' he shouted again. 'Wait for me, Pa, I'm coming.' Many of those between him and the hustings had turned in his direction and away from their leaders, instinct herding them, like sheep, from the approaching danger to the safety of the dozen narrow streets which radiated off the square. Suddenly there were detachments of foot soldiers and Dra-goons blocking their way and Joss found himself held fast in the iron grip of the swaying, panic-stricken crowd. They were packed tight together, as close as matches in a box, gasping and choking. Those women who could draw breath began to scream. Already dozens had gone down as they lost their footing, disappearing beneath the trampling feet of men and horses.

Again Joss was lifted up above the bobbing heads of those still on their feet and he could see the cavalry officer, backed by a handful of mounted soldiers approach the hustings. The officer spoke to Mr Hunt who stepped down obligingly, his hands spread to show he meant no harm but two other gentlemen, Joss could not recognise them, were dragged from the platform with little or no ceremony. One of the ladies with the company tripped and as she jerked herself upwards again a cavalryman slashed across her body with his sabre, for what reason Joss did not know since she posed a threat to no one, and he saw the first blood spilled that day. Of his father there was no sign.

Those who had not yet moved, amazingly unaware that something appalling was happening were standing on tip-toe, craning their necks and asking one another what was to do. However, the yeomanry, having enjoyed a rout of destruction at the hustings and filled with the bloodlust which comes upon those who seek glory, turned their horses in the direction of the silken banners which flew defiantly about the field and within minutes hundreds of those who stood before them were crushed beneath the animals' hooves. They charged again and again, those brave Hussars, their sabres making a fine, flashing sight in the sunlight.

Fresh troops, trained in the removal of the enemy had arrived and at a signal from their officer began the systematic clearing of the square. It was then that the real panic began, the panic of sixty thousand bodies packed tight together and caught in the open with nowhere to go to avoid the stiff-necked, stiff-backed soldiers, the trampling, rearing horses, the flashing, slashing sabres – from where had they come, and why? – were the last thoughts of the bewildered masses as they went down and the sounds grew more appalling with every second.

The dust rose up, drifting beyond the rooftops towards the hot, sun-drenched sky. Those who were still on their feet were forced this way and that in a horrid unison but the piles of bodies, women arched protectively over fallen children, grew higher and more bloody. Joss saw one young woman lift her arm in a mute appeal to a trooper to spare her child and watched, mad with shock and terror as the limb was struck from her body. Though his eyes could not believe the sight nor his mind arrange his thoughts to coherency, instinct had him inching his way towards her over others just as seriously injured and in need of his help. There was blood and soft, damaged flesh beneath his hand, eyes glazed in shock and horror and pain, even death, moans and screams and in the midst of it young Joss Greenwood fought, quite senselessly, to go to the aid of the mother whose body was by now completely covered by others. Men were shouting and pushing, fighting to get out of the square, leaving their comrades, those with whom they had just marched, to lie in their own blood, or crawl desperately to get out of the way of the horses. They were ridden down with as much compunction as an ant's nest which had been kicked over. The soldiers on horseback were screaming as loudly as those they attacked, screaming words of abuse . . .

'. . . damn you reformers . . .'

'. . . bloody radicals . . .'

'. . . the devil take the lot of you . . .'

. . . and the tide of humanity was swept on as relentlessly as waves upon a shore, towards the streets which were their only means of escape and with them went young Joss Greenwood. When they came up against the Quaker Meeting House on the outskirts of the field it was there that those who were still capable of it took a stand. There had been a strong fence about the house made of sturdy pieces of wood and, though he had no recollection of even taking one up, Joss found himself standing, legs braced, shoulders hunched defensively, side by side with the men and women who had survived, swinging a fierce section of timber as though it were a cudgel. The others with him were blood-stained, bruised, caked from head to foot with dust, eyes flaring from maddened faces, mouths opened wide on screams of despairing rage.

For ten minutes they fought, those brave souls, defending themselves and the dream they had set out with that day, unseating several of the yeomanry with sticks and stones and anything else they could lay their hands on and even, though no one could say from where it came, a loud shot from a pistol. But when the Hussars rode in, pushing the defenders back against the walls of the house, the resistance was ended and it was all over.

In twenty minutes the field, which had been thronged with sixty thousand exuberant, joyous, laughing, singing persons, come to show their masters that their cause was just, was emptied.

But for the dead and dying!

Joss Greenwood found his father no more than fifteen paces from the hustings. He lay on his face, his body protecting

21

that of a small boy who cried lustily for his Mam. The child stood up shakily when Joss lifted his father's body from him and began to run, like a small dog after its own tail, in search of his mother and for several moments Joss watched him, his concern for the boy keeping at bay the frightful knowledge of what they had done to his Pa. As long as he concentrated on the boy's distress he could pretend that the heavy body – why was his Pa so heavy? – was no more than knocked unconscious and that soon, when his senses returned to him, his Pa would stand up, a bit shaken and bruised perhaps but whole, and Joss would give him his arm and together they would walk back to Edgeclough, this battle lost but the war still to be won.

'Pa,' he said gently, looking down into the face he loved so well. But his father's eyes stared somewhere over his own shoulder and the blood ran from his ear on to Joss's own bloody hand.

'Oh Pa, please, Pa . . .' Joss lifted the dusty head into his lap and stroked his father's cheek and began to rock him back and forth. For the last time as a boy he wept and it was as his youthful, anguished tears fell on the beloved face that he became a man.

He would let no one help him. They found him, those who had set off with him from the village that morning, those who had survived and crept back to look for friends, and when they would have shared his burden he turned on them, snarling like a cornered beast.

'I'll carry him, damn you. Leave him be.'

Back the way they had come they went, a small band of injured, shocked and dazed men and women, some with silent children, hovering at Joss Greenwood's back, still following their leader even though the one they had begun the day with was dead. Joss stared ahead of him, putting one foot in front of the other, his arms cradling the increasingly heavy weight of his father. Through the long summer evening, warm and sullen with an impending thunderstorm, they tramped until they reached the rutted turnpike between Manchester and Oldham. Some way along was a turning on to a bridle-path, lined on each side with banks of wild honeysuckle and roses. The fragrance drenched the senses of those who had about them the dreadful odour of blood, the acrid smells of sweat-stained human and animal flesh, of dust and smoke and the stench of fear, and of death, and the company stood for a moment, drawing the sweetness into grateful lungs.

It was full dark now and the little band lay down to rest but none attempted to approach young Joss Greenwood whose brain had surely been turned by what he had seen that day. He sat with his back to the broad trunk of a canopied oak tree, his father's body held in fierce, protective arms. He cradled the greying head to his chest and those nearest to him swore they heard him speak to the dead man through the short night though none heard the actual words and not one could guess the depth nor the intensity of his feelings.

The sky became clear and bright with stars towards morning and Joss Greenwood lifted his gaze from the burden in his arms and looked up into the radiance of the fading night. He felt the beauty of it enter his soul and though his heart was breaking in anguish and guilt (for had he not failed to stand by this man he loved?), he held its splendour to him a moment longer before he let the bitterness set about its work. It was then it began to harden within him, like the frill of ice which edges a lake, creeping towards its centre until the whole is frozen, covering the life which lies beneath. Under the ice is the vital force, the growth which will blossom when the thaw sets in, but warmth and the light of the sun are needed and none touched Joss Greenwood at that darkest hour of his young life.

He carried his father into his mother's kitchen at noon and when he laid him gently on the table she had prepared for him, for word had gone ahead of him, Joss Greenwood could not straighten out the arms which had carried his father's body for almost twenty-four hours. They remained bent, held to his chest as though in self-protection and when his mother with a soft cry of grief would have pulled him to her in comfort, he stood stiffly rigid, silent and staring. His eyes had sunk into deep, plum-coloured bruises in his grey face and those of the villagers who had stood respectfully at the roadside to see their leader come home for the last time had not been completely certain that the thin lad who carried him was his son. His face was quite expressionless, indecently so, they were inclined to think, since a show of grief was surely called for. It conveyed neither pain nor sorrow and those who looked into his pale eyes stepped back uncertainly beneath their gaze, for the manifestation of what he was to be glimmered in their cold depths.

## 2

They met for the first time on a stretch of moorland above Friars Mere and though they were alone and unknown to one another she did not drop her eyes when he drew near as young ladies of her age and station were trained to do but stared boldly and with lively interest directly into his face. Her eyes were the blue of the bellflower which grew in the hedgerows and woods surrounding Edgeclough, a violet-blue, shading almost to purple round the pupil and framed by extravagantly long black lashes. Her skin was a pale gold, like honey, pinked at the cheekbones by the biting cold. Her hair, what he could see of it beneath her close fitting bonnet, was as dark as his own with a gloss on it like that of a horse-chestnut and she was tall. He had an impression of colour and vibrant life, of vigour and defiance and a compelling self-esteem which showed in the way her black-booted feet stepped out confidently from beneath the hem of her warm woollen skirt and the determined thrust of her hands into the pockets of her three-quarter length coat. Her back and shoulders were graceful but straight, uncompromisingly so and her head was tilted high and proud. She was obviously not of the labouring class, the quality of her clothes would have told him that, if her attitude had not, and as he stared back at her, astonished at the strangeness of seeing her up here on the wild moorland, alone and so far from anywhere, he was further amazed when she spoke.

'Good morning,' she said cheerfully. 'Is it not a lovely day for a walk?' She stopped, fully expecting him to do the same and he hesitated since he had never in the whole of his life spoken to, or been addressed by a woman who was not of his own class. It was not that he was afraid, nor shy, nor even overawed by the enormous gulf which gaped between them, it was simply that he could see no reason why she should wish to engage him in conversation. Perhaps she imagined it might be intriguing to pass the time of day, of which she would have more than enough to spare, with one of the working classes. One of those strange creatures which crept from their refuge each morning as soon as the sun was up, or before in the winter, to make their way to their employment which demanded they stay there until their master said they might leave which was often after the sun went down again. They were a curious breed, she would think, and nothing to do with her, or her like. A different race one might say, and so, on this cold sunny morning with nothing else to do she had taken a fancy to address one of its number.

'I spoke to a man from the lower orders today,' he could hear her say laughingly to a friend over the teacups, 'and had a marvellously refreshing conversation with him. He was quite ordinary, and clean, with clogs to his feet and could speak the King's English as well as one could expect of such a person. Really, it was *most* amusing.'

His expression of unsmiling contempt did not alter, despite the graciousness of her greeting. He hated with all his heart the class from which she obviously came, the class

25

which had killed his father, and if he could do them harm he would. But this girl was merely a lass trying out her hand at a bit of condescension to, in her opinion, an underprivileged lad, and nothing to do with the concepts which now governed his own life. She obviously thought a lot about herself. One could tell that by the way she raked him with those haughty blue eyes of hers, imagining herself, likely as not, doing him a favour by noticing he was on the same bit of earth as herself, but she was harmless and a touch of mockery on his part would put her in her place. Take her down a peg or two, as they said in his part of the world.

'Aye, 'tis an' all. Fair gives a chap appetite fer 'is snap right enough. Ah trek over yon 'ills every day 'bout this time, or 'appen a mite later. Let streets get aired, like an' t'sun up then ah get mesen out o' me bed. There's nowt like a bloody good walk ter set a chap up fer 'is breakfast and tha porridge tastes a fair treat, tha' knows wi' a reet big plate o' bacon an' eggs ter foller. We 'ave us a clack round t'fire 'til openin' time then a pint or two o' ale at t' "Wheatsheaf" then another stride on't moor an' 'ome fer us tea. Eeh, there's nowt like it.'

He smiled maliciously, watching to see how she would react to his broadly exaggerated Lancashire dialect, or if she would even understand it. Would she perceive his obviously sarcastic jibe at her expense regarding the nourishing breakfast — or lack of it — that a working man could expect, and his election to walk the hills as a form of exercise and enjoyment when he barely had the energy to get himself from his bed to his place of work. Joss was ready to turn away scornfully and continue his journey to the meeting on Friars Mere but without hesitation and with no lessening of her queenly bearing she answered him pertly.

'Yer reet, lad, an' does tha' know summat, I feel exactly t'same. There's nowt like a good tramp on't hills ter perk up a finicky appetite. 'Tis a reet good tonic an' puts roses in tha cheeks. Sets me up fer't day, I can tell thee.'

She began to laugh then. Her eyes sparkled as the sun caught in their depths, narrowing between the tangle of her long lashes. Her lips spread over her white teeth and he could clearly see the quiver of her pink tongue as her mouth opened wide. She threw back her head in an uninhibited way he had never seen before, delighted by his expression of amazement and a certain truculence at being the butt of her humour. But there was no spite in her laughter, just the unspoiled enjoyment of knowing she had been quick enough to see through, and beat him, at his own game. She had realised instantly that he had been 'having her on' as they said in Lancashire and though she did not know why she felt she had evened the score.

'I only bade you good morning,' she went on in her normal voice, 'and you had only to return the greeting and walk on but if you wish to continue in this amusing vein you have but to say so.'

She grinned engagingly and Joss felt a reluctant amusement stir within him, but she had not done yet.

'I don't know who you are or why you are walking up here and I really have no particular interest in either and if you wish to go on, please do so, but really, can you honestly tell me it is *not* a lovely day and that the view at your back can be equalled anywhere in the world?' She turned her astonishing eyes from him to stare out at the splendour of the wide, wild open moors and down to the deep, tree-covered valleys which lay below them. There was an isolated farmhouse far away on the fringe of the moor, smoke from its chimney painting a line of pale grey straight up into the sky and below, huddled against the glint of a river, a small valley town was almost hidden beneath the pall of smoke which covered it. Drystone walls spread their webs across great swathes of green and grey and brown, and the pale coating of hoar frost which had come in the night. The stepped profile of the hillside on the far face of the valley was alternated with bands of tough gritstone and softer shale, and gently on the air was the sound of the tumble of water falling to the valley bottom.

27

Joss turned to look, ready to stress witheringly that he had been nowhere beyond Manchester and could not therefore, like her it seemed, compare what lay before him to any other part of the world, but the austere beauty silenced them both for were they not Lancashire born and bred with a common love of this beautiful part of unspoiled England which was home to them? They shared nothing beyond this but for the moment it was enough and they stood in quiet harmonious contemplation of their heritage. Forgotten was the inordinate cleverness with which Joss had thought to put this lass in her place and her own quickness in answering it. He stood, tall and lean as a young sapling. His clothes were worn and patched but scrupulously clean for water was plentiful where he lived, as was the fuel – peat for the most part – which was needed to heat it. She stood beside him, almost as tall, slender and strong and dressed in the best that money could buy. Stout boots of the highest quality leather, a coat lined with some soft fur against the cold and her full skirt was made from the finest Yorkshire wool.

For a full five minutes they leaned comfortably side by side, their backs against a waist-high rock, absorbing the crisp air into their lungs, delighting their ears with the singing of the streams as they fell from a dozen hidden places into the waters of Hull Brook far below, delighting their eyes as the sun picked up a reflection of itself in the diamond snap of the hoar frost on the peaks.

'You shouldn't be up here on your own,' he said suddenly.

'Why not? Who is there to harm me? I have been coming up here for years now, ever since I was twelve or so.'

'What difference does that make?' he asked scornfully. 'I bet your Pa doesn't know. No man of sense would let a lass of his wander about the moors by herself. It's asking for trouble.' He was mindful of the closeness with which the gentry kept their womenfolk protected but perhaps her family was different. So high and mighty it did not consider any dare harm one of their own. They were like that, the upper classes, capable of believing in their own superiority,

28

their infallibility and even immortality it seemed to him. Look at this girl, strolling about where no girl should be, of any class, for there were desperate folk tramping these hills. Men on the lookout for work, rough men going from town to town, village to village, begging, starving, and likely to strip a lass, especially this one, not only for the fur lining of her coat but for a bit of sport with her slim girl's body. It was well covered, shapeless he would say beneath the layers of clothing she wore but he had no doubt it would be delectable enough to a man who already had nothing to lose. Fourteen she would be, if that, but not unattractive and she was putting herself in the gravest peril by traipsing about on her own along this moorland path.

For some reason the idea made him irritable and he was quite perplexed by his own impatience with her. She was nowt to him, a silly lass, a different and altogether alien species from the one to which he belonged and yet she made him smile with her compelling and quite unquestioning belief in herself and her right to be up here, just as he had and it took him, for a moment, from the deadly seriousness of his own world.

'My father is no concern of yours,' she was saying. Her tone was lofty and her mouth firm, a little prim even, a young lady being taken to task by one who had no right to criticise. She had been about to take herself off in the direction of Crossfold, diverted and intrigued by her encounter with the tall, strange youth on the path to Friars Mere. Until this moment she had imagined the working classes to be inarticulate and stunted creatures with no thought but the contemplation of herself and her family as the providers for their very existence. But this young man had shown her how wrong she had been. Her sharp mind had been stimulated by what she had sensed in his. She had no real conception of what it might be exactly for she had met no one like him before, but his eyes had told her he was quick-witted and shrewd with a reluctance to suffer fools gladly. They had barely spoken. A joke really, a teasing of one another which had been enjoyable, fun, she supposed, and she got little enough of that in her life but his mocking humour had appealed to her own and his love of this land, matching hers, had drawn them close for the space of five minutes.

She whirled about to face him. Her full skirt flared round her ankles and as though she could not bear the obligation to wear it for a moment longer she untied the ribbons beneath her chin and whipped off her bonnet. Instantly her hair fell about her shoulders and Joss drew in his breath sharply. It shimmered in the pale winter sunshine, the light caught in its silken thickness and though it was so dark, chestnut, russet, copper and gold were captured in it, a breathlessly lovely cape almost to her waist, straight and heavy and unmanageable. With an impatient 'tut' she pushed it back behind her ears.

'And what kind of trouble could I meet up here?' she went on. In truth Joss Greenwood did not know since for the life of him he could not remember what he had said to her. He was rendered quite speechless and could do no more than stand and stare at her dramatically altered appearance. With her bonnet ribbons firmly tied beneath her chin and its brim partially concealing her face she had been no more than a personable young girl. Now, in a breathless moment she had changed from a headstrong impudent girl into a woman of strange, almost foreign beauty. There was certainly none like her in the chapelry of Oldham, Shaw or Edgeclough, or none that he had seen and he had for many months now travelled a long road and met a great multitude of his own class and trade in the course of his days.

'Well . . .' he said lamely, '. . . there's many a chap . . . rough and . . .' He had been about to say as tactfully as he knew how, for it was obvious she had been delicately reared, that her contempt for caution might lead her into more trouble than she could handle but as he spoke she pursed her lips and almost soundlessly a whistle escaped from between them. Instantly two large dogs padded silently from behind the rock on which he and the girl leaned, slipping across the frozen ground to stand beside her full skirt, one on either side of her. They were like no dog he had ever seen before, black and sleek with brown markings on the head, and virtually no tail. They were tall, almost on a level with her waist and they made no sound but their eyes stared unblinkingly into his, flat and dark and baleful.

'Bloody hell . . .' he whispered.

She smiled and tossed back her swinging hair, the gesture at once arrogant and yet amused. Her eyes challenged him, filled, not with contempt exactly but with the complete recognition that if there were to be a confrontation, not only between herself and any 'rough chap' she happened to meet, but between herself and him, there was no doubt who would be the loser!

'This is Joby . . .' she indicated the dog on her left, '. . . and this Blaze and though they are friendly enough, when their tempers are not roused, they can be . . . impetuous. I trained them myself. My father gave them to me when they were pups, realising I suppose, that if I were to roam these tops, as I was bound to do, I would need protection. "When they will obey you without question and when you can control them to my satisfaction you may go," he said. It took me six months, in the fields about the house and when he saw what I had made of them he gave me permission to go about alone. I am well aware, as he is, that we are considered . . . unusual, but then we can do no more than make the best of what we are given in life and that is what my father has done with me. He knew the day would come when I would need to get about unescorted and so he has given me the means to do it. If he had not done so I would have found some other way to achieve my freedom and he knew it, of course.' She laughed impishly with a further toss of her proud head. 'We made a pledge, he and I and it had to be honoured and so it has been. He knows I am quite safe with these two. They are completely harmless, believe me, except when I tell them to be otherwise. I have

31

had no cause to do so yet for it seems their appearance is enough to deter the most courageous. I imagine you can see why!'

For the first time in many months Joss Greenwood felt the young and completely spontaneous desire to laugh out loud. He really had very little idea of what she was talking about in her description of her strange relationship with her father but the need to throw back his head and let out the light-hearted merriment this girl inspired in him was more than he could resist. She was watching him, her eyes alight with mischief, knowing perfectly well that she was unique, that her father and the arrangement she appeared to have with him was staggeringly unprecedented in this world of male dominance and female submission to it and her expression challenged him, if he dared, to question it. She laid a hand on each of the dog's fine heads and immediately they turned to lick her fingers, gentle as doves, their eyes worshipping, their bodies straining against her skirt.

'Call to them,' she said to Joss. 'Call them by name.'

'Give over! I don't want me damned hand taken off.' He took a step back, his laughter fading away, his eyes never leaving those of the dogs who had both turned to look at him peaceably.

'Well naturally, if you are afraid.' Her eyes gleamed in the flaunting frame of her gypsy dark hair.

It was a throwing down of the gauntlet, of course, and he was not surprised for this girl was clearly out of the ordinary. Like a boy, she was, a young man daring another to some mad show of courage as he had done many times with his peers in the rough and tumble of play, but this was different. Boys did this, and full grown men sometimes, demonstrating their superiority to one another, recklessly hurling the gage and defying anyone to pick it up. But by God, he'd not be shown up by some slip of a girl, not he! She might turn her bloody dogs on him, with a word or a snap of her fingers, since he was manifestly aware as he looked into her smiling face that she was not to be trusted. She'd win at any cost, her expression told him, but be damned to that, she'd not see him show lack of courage. He *was* afraid since he'd never seen the likes of these animals before, great glowing-eyed beasts who gave the appearance of one moment being prepared to lie down with babes and the next, there was no doubt of it, of tearing a grown man to pieces, and which was it to be with him, he had time to wonder!

'Call them to you, if you are up to it,' she said softly and her eyes smiled, sweet·as you please but her teeth showed between her rose pink lips and he saw her hand move slightly in some secret command only the animals knew.

He drew in his breath, acutely conscious in that moment that it was to be of some strange importance to him. A test he must pass. A test *she* was to set him. A bit of a girl she was, nothing more, but Goddammit, she'd not find Joss Greenwood wanting.

'Joby, Blaze, come here. Come here to me,' and he lifted an imperious hand, his manner implying that there was no question that they would not obey him, indicating to the two dogs that they were to lie at his feet.

Instantaneously, as if they were motivated by one mind they moved gracefully across the frozen ground, standing quietly before him. For a second they had glanced at their mistress and again she made some minute hand movement.

'Lie down, both of you. Lie down, I say.' Joss was aware as he gave the command that it had not come from him but at once the great dogs lay down at his feet. He had seen her control them. They had obeyed *her*, held where they were by her training and if she should tell them they would spring up without hesitation and take out his throat.

He knelt down before them, his face but six inches from theirs, hearing her indrawn hiss of breath. Putting out his hands he laid one on each enormous head, holding them firmly, staring with his own eyes into the black depths of theirs, steady as a rock, his will combating theirs. His fear had gone and his voice was quietly commanding.

'Good boys, good old boys. Now stand,' and at once they stood for him. They looked up at him for a moment, their eyes serene as though to say *this time*, then they turned and padded back to stand watchfully beside their young mistress.

She let out her breath on a long sigh and there was genuine pleasure in her eyes. He had pleased her with his fearlessness, he could tell, and she liked to be pleased. Not many would do so for she would be difficult to beguile or impress, her attitude said. She had questioned his male superiority and he had found approval with her and though he could think of no reason why he should care, one way or the other, he found himself to be quite immeasurably satisfied.

'You are the first person beside myself who has handled them,' she told him admiringly.

'There's nowt to it really.' His tone was self-deprecating, making light of his own bravery and his boyishness shone for a moment from the man he had become on St Peter's Field, ' . . . besides, they were watching out for you most of the time.'

'No, not in the least . . . well, perhaps in the beginning but you showed them you had no fear and they respected you for it.' As I do, her shining eyes said.

'Well . . .' He shrugged, grinning amiably, shoving his hands in his pockets. He was awkward now, unused to decent female company beyond that of his mother and sisters. He had known only the light-hearted women who had, in his past, flirted with him, responded to his own masculine banter. He had no aptitude in the art of small talk and he turned away to stare out again over the valley.

'Do you walk this path often?' she asked, settling herself companionably by his side, quite at ease it appeared in his company.

'Oh aye, when I'm on me way to Saddleworth or Dobens.'

'And what do you do there?' Her face was bright with interest.

'Oh . . . well . . .' She had caught him on the wrong foot again and he stumbled over his words for he had no wish, nor entitlement, to tell her of his movements on these hills of the South Pennines and beyond, nor of the men he met there from the dozens of villages which were scattered over the hinterland. They were secrets which were held close by those who were involved in them and certainly not to be shared with this girl. But he must say something, give her some reason why he was walking this path, some believable reason which would satisfy her sharp curiosity. His brain, sharpened by the years he had listened to, and tramped with his father and those others who even now were awaiting trial for their part at St Peter's Field, sprang readily into action. He was as arrogant and as proud of his heritage as this girl was of hers but he must protect his companions in their great venture. They would be gathering now as they had in the past, illegally, on Tandle Hill and Buckland Castle Moor. Meetings had been broken up in the past when the military had opened fire on them but today they were to be but a dozen or so men, those who were leaders and were to march to York for the trial and if they should be discovered they would all go to gaol. 'The Six Acts', the consequence of 'Peterloo', as it had come to be called, made it illegal for any person to attend a meeting and should he do so and be caught, he and those with him were liable to transportation for seven years.

'Well, I don't always go to Dobens or Saddleworth, or any particular place, really.' He smiled winsomely, allaying her suspicions, if she had any, that he might be lying. He was rewarded by the interest in her face. 'It doesn't make any difference as long as you find a decent burrow.'

'Burrow?' Her voice was sharp.

'Aye. A rabbit burrow.'

'What on earth for?'

'Rabbits! What else?'

'But why should you . . .'

'Have you never heard of rabbit pie?'

'Well, of course, but . . .'

His face became hard for a moment since now he was telling the truth and he did not care to be revealing the domestic deficiencies in his own family but he had no choice. He had started the invention, the only one he could think of on the spur of the moment and the fabrication must be brought to its conclusion if she was to believe him.

'We don't get a lot to eat, me and me family. I have a brother and sister no more than babies. Me . . . me Pa died last year and I'm provider now . . . well . . . main one so . . .' His mouth worked, for the mention of his father still had the power to pain him, '. . . if I can bag a hare or a rabbit for the pot we get a bit of meat in our bellies. Of course, Squire don't like it. It's poaching, you see, and he don't take kindly to having his rabbits snared so I'd be obliged if you'd keep it to yourself.' Better to be caught for poaching, though that could be a transportation offence as well with a severe magistrate, than breaking the law in other, more serious misdemeanours, his memory reminded him!

She smiled broadly, leaning closer to him. He caught the delicacy of some fragrance as she did so, something sharp and yet sweet which drifted from her clothing and though he could not recognise it since none of the women of his association could afford to wear perfume, it reminded him of the woods in summer, of the trees and the tangy smell of grass and new leaves.

'I don't think I have ever eaten rabbit. Is it good?'

'Oh aye, with a few taters and an onion. Ma puts a crust on it . . .'

'A crust?'

'Yes, you know, pastry.'

'Pastry?'

He was laughing now for the very idea that here was a girl who seemed not to know what a pastry crust was, who had never heard of nor eaten rabbit pie or hare stew, was quite unbelievable. It was no lie that if he could snare one or the other he would do so, for food was scarce and expensive as prices continued to rocket and wages plummet, but that was not his objective today though she had been made to believe it was and that was all that mattered.

'Dear God, where have you been all these years? Never eaten rabbit or hare and you a Lancashire lass!'

'We have potted hare for luncheon on occasion but I believe it is not to be eaten after the end of February.'

'Is that so!' He was laughing all the more at her quaintness for really food was food and did it matter what the month was to an empty belly. 'And who told you that?'

'My father.'

'Oh aye, and who's he when he's at home?'

'Barker Chapman.'

The ground beneath his feet seemed to sink quite incredibly and he was afraid he would vomit.

*Barker Chapman*. It was a name which was ever on the lips and in the tortured minds of those he called comrade, a name which was spoken so often by those with whom he associated they felt they knew the man and what he stood for as well as the members of their own families. It represented, more than any other, all the ills of their lives and if the man should ever put himself within the range of their hatred it was doubtful he would survive. And this was his daughter!

He looked into her startled eyes and the revulsion he felt for the name of the man who was her father rose like a bitter tide. He stood up, stretching to his full height and the whiteness of his face and the loathing which flowed from him, must have alarmed not only her, but also the animals. They sensed the sudden change in him and she put out a warning hand to restrain them as they rose slowly, but menacingly, to their feet.

'What is it?' she said, her goodwill dissipating suddenly, the haughty manner of a young woman of the privileged class returning. Her expression said she must surely have forgotten herself for the space of half an hour, forgotten who she was and where she belonged, in the novelty of speaking to this young labouring man, but really, if he was going to act in such an uncouth way, staring and speechless at the mention of her father's name she had best be on her way.

She clicked her fingers to the dogs. 'Come Joby, Blaze. It is time to get on. We have lingered far too long already. Good morning to you. It has been most pleasant chatting.' She nodded imperiously in Joss Greenwood's direction and as he watched her, frozen from head to toe in the implacability of his own venom she put on her bonnet, pushed her hair up beneath it and without waiting for an answer began to walk towards the village of Crossfold.

# 3

Barker Chapman came from a family concerned mainly with banking. A younger son here and there had gone into other businesses, mining, canal building, the constructing of turnpike roads but it was his own father who had been the first to look with interest at the textile trade.

Between 1776 and 1811 there were forty-two cotton mills built in Oldham where the Chapman family lived, the overwhelming majority being put up by men with capital and most had a great deal! James Chapman, son of a banker's son was one. In 1771, Richard Arkwright invented a spinning machine designed to be powered by a horse but quickly adapted to water. It became known as a water frame and he set up his own factory in Cromford, Derbyshire, well away from the troublesome operatives of the Pennine heartland, home of the cotton industry. James Chapman, then thirty years old, was quick to see the potential of such a machine and the means to increase his own already considerable fortune. He built his first cotton spinning mill in Crossfold, a few miles out from Oldham. It was no more than a sleepy hamlet then with two or three cottages, a church and a coaching inn to serve the stage-coaches which passed through from Manchester to Huddersfield.

He brought in whole families from every part of Lancashire, women and children to spin and men to labour, housing them in frail, back-to-back boxes he threw up in a matter of weeks, eight, ten, twelve persons to each, all standing in rows like spokes from a wheel radiating out from his mill and so close together there was scarcely room to walk between them.

He took more trouble with his mill! It was sturdy, six storeys high and the machinery he put in filled every floor. It was set deep in the Penfold Valley, serviced by the plentiful supply of soft, fast-flowing water which tossed and tumbled down the hillside, flooding through the sluices to turn his giant wheel and give power to his machines.

He prospered, he and his son Barker, employing over a hundred persons at Crossbank Mill, as it was called, to spin the yarn which was then 'put out' to hand-loom weavers living and working in their own outlying cottages. Samuel Crompton had devised the 'Spinning Mule', a combination of the old 'Spinning Jenny' which could produce sixteen threads at once and Arkwright's 'water frame' which could spin thirty-eight, and the new machine provided a firm, yet soft, yarn and was capable of operating twice as many spindles as those before it.

James Chapman was one of the first manufacturers to have one in his second mill, built beyond Crossbank and higher up the stream which powered the first and when it was completed he named it Highbank Mill and began to think of not only spinning the yarn but of weaving it as well for he was not a man to put money in another's pocket when it could go just as well into his own. The inhospitable climate of the damp Pennine air which helped the fibres to cling together, reduced the strain placed on them by the new machinery and his production costs fell even lower and his profit grew.

His raw cotton came laboriously from Liverpool by pack-horse on the turnpike roads and by the new canals and was returned by the same method in a 'piece' of completed cloth to Manchester where it was sold.

But James Chapman was never to see weaving-looms in his shed. He died in 1815 and it was his son, an only child, Barker Chapman who built the Chapman weaving-shed on the outskirts of the now bustling township of Crossfold. With the advent of the steam engine and with no need of the water which drove his wheel he could afford to choose a site wherever he pleased and the long tramp his new operatives must take to get to their looms was of no concern to him. He employed in it men who had once worked in their own cottages, and in their own time, weaving a 'piece' as and when they pleased, which did not please *him* and by the end of the year he had forced many of them to give up their independent way of life and become chained, if they wished to feed their families, to his new power-looms. Some chose to remain ungoverned, struggling resolutely for the right to call themselves their own men. They did not care for the factory system, they said proudly, with its harsh discipline, its rules, its fines if they were broken, the peremptory summons of the factory bell and the long hours of labour, as many as seventy or eighty in a week. Mill-master Chapman could afford to let them go their footloose way since he had the vast resources of the unemployed to work his weaving-looms and spinning mules. On this fine day in May when the loveliness of spring was in the air he prepared to set off to the mill to supervise the installation of his latest 'self-acting' spinning mule into his mill at Highbank. It would, without a doubt revolutionise the cotton industry when, set with another in a pair, have in common usage at the same time 2,500 spindles!

Barker Chapman was an impressive man, tall, well built and inclined to overweight, handsome in his youth and living now only to see what he had built carefully placed into hands which would carry on his work, making it grow and prosper as he had, accumulating wealth and prestige for the Chapman name, someone of vision and strength and the dedication to give their life, as he had, to the mills. A son, many sons he had dreamed of in his youth, sons to carry on when he was gone and with this in mind he had married Miss Isobel Townsend, the bonny twenty-year-old daughter of a calico printer from Accrington but in their ten years of marriage he had nothing from her but a string of stillborn infants, one each year until the day she died, delivering to him another.

Not a man to be thwarted he married again. He was forty-three when he took Miss Hannah Baxter, eighteen years old and as healthy and buxom as a farm wench and certain to bear him many fine boys. But it seemed in this one aspect of his life he was to know only disappointment. Nine months after their wedding she gave birth to a girl, as sturdy as he would have wished had she been a boy and encouraged by this sign of his capability to father a living child he and his young wife tried again and again and again until, approaching the age of sixty he faced the appalling truth that he was to have nothing but this one girl child.

Katherine Chapman! Kit! In the far off days of her infancy when Hannah Chapman had been in sole charge of her pretty baby daughter and Barker still had the hope of a son, when she had played with her and nursed her and called the child her 'little kitten', the endearment had seemed appropriate but as she grew it had become shortened to Kit, even by her father. She herself preferred it to Katherine, which in her opinion was formal, whereas Kit spoke of family affection, the fondness of a father for his daughter. She had been disappointed.

On the day he turned his attention to her she was twelve years old, almost as tall as he and quite unremarkable as far as he could determine on the occasions when they met. On this day she was in the garden of Greenacre, walking rapidly across its wide lawn, turning as she came to the high wall which surrounded it in an explosion of movement, then striding back to its furthest corner, her skirts swirling quite indecorously about her ankles. Her bonnet, which should have been on her head was hanging from her hand by its ribbons. Her pace was like that of a man and the little woman who did her best to keep up with her was almost running.

41

He smiled, amused by the sight which reminded him of a tigress, prowling up and down a cage followed by a small and harmless tabby.

It was Sunday. The mills were closed, for on this day his machines were cleaned and oiled, and he was bored. His wife was resting on her chaise-longue in her pretty sitting-room, at thirty-one years of age so delicate and of such a nervous disposition after several failed pregnancies – her only success the girl he now watched – she considered herself to be an invalid. She was of about as much interest to him as were the domestic arrangements of his home.

On a whim he stepped from the french windows of his study and began to walk in a leisurely fashion down the stone steps which led to the lawn, a cigar held in his right hand, his left pushed into his trouser pocket. The sun was warm, it was April and the massed swathes of wild daffodils which crowded the base of every tree were beginning to fade but the fragrance and beauty of a flowering almond, just coming into bloom made a splendid splash of colour against the grey cobbled wall which surrounded the garden.

His movement attracted his daughter's eye as he saun-tered towards her and though he could see the effort it cost her she stopped politely and the round little woman caught up with her, her breath ragged in her throat, her eyes apprehensive in her high coloured face.

'Good morning, sir,' she said and he wondered who she was.

'Good morning,' he answered, not really caring, for he left all household arrangements to his wife, '. . . and good day to you, Kit. You appear to be in a great hurry. May I ask what you are doing?'

'Exercising.' Her reply was only a fraction short of rude and the woman beside her gasped and began to splutter nervously, evidently afraid that his daughter's forthright manner might offend. It did not and Barker Chapman felt a small bud of interest begin to grow in him. She was as strained as a young dog on a leash, her body taut with some passion, some energy which was clamped within her and

42

he wondered quite idly what it might be. He had felt no passion himself for years, beyond that of his business ventures, and he was quite intrigued by this tall and barely contained child, who was his daughter.

'Exercising?' he questioned smilingly. He had breakfast and sometimes luncheon with her on most days of the week and had held short conversations with her on the subject of her studies and had even perched himself on his wife's drawing-room chair and listened to her play the piano. However, when he thought of it, he had never actually *noticed* her before.

'If you can call it by that name,' she snapped and her eyes flashed vividly in the sun's rays and before he knew what she was about she had reached out and clasped his hands entreatingly with her own.

'Control yourself, Katherine,' her governess, he supposed, beseeched her, looking in his direction in such anguish he thought she might be about to weep, but Kit Chapman took no notice.

'Please, Father . . . please let me leave the garden.' Her whole frame quivered dramatically and Barker Chapman felt a great desire to laugh since melodrama had always amused rather than thrilled him, but she had only just begun.

'Can you not see what you are doing to me? Can you not see how insane I shall become if I am not let out of this prison? Do you not realise what I suffer, day after day, walking up and down, up and down within these four walls with no one but this stupid creature for company?'

The 'stupid creature' gave a small moan of sheer terror since it was clear that her control of this girl was small indeed, and what use was a governess who could not keep order, her manner seemed to ask. Barker Chapman turned to consider her as though he was about to agree then looked back at his daughter who, now that she had captured his attention, freed his hands.

'May I not walk some way on to the moor?' she pleaded with him, doing her best to control what she knew had

43

been a quite foolish outburst. 'I will not go far, *we* will not go far . . .' for even she knew there was not the slightest hope she could go alone, '. . . just up on to the moorland path above the house. I long to . . . to stretch my legs. I will be . . . I won't run, Father' – and he knew she was not to be believed for if ever a girl was made to run it was this one – '. . . or speak to anyone we might meet and Miss Strong will be there to make sure I am . . . circumspect . . . Oh, Father, please allow it, let me leave the garden. I am kept all day at the top of the house in the schoolroom and never allowed beyond its door except to walk in this strip of garden with Miss Strong.' Barker Chapman raised his eyebrows, looking about at the 'strip' of garden which covered the best part of three acres and though she saw the direction of his gaze she went on, 'I know nothing beyond how to sew a seam, and that not very well and the names of the flowers you see about you.' She tossed her head and gave them a shrivelling look and her rebellious hair began to slip and Miss Strong put a hand on her arm, evidently with the idea of drawing her away before her father ordered her to be locked up but she shook it off.

'What *is* over the wall, Father?' she beseeched him passionately.

'You know very well what is there, Kit. I have seen you myself go in the carriage with your mother.'

'Oh, I don't mean that! I mean in this land, in the world, in the . . .'

'You are saying you would like to travel?' He sounded amused.

She turned to him and the radiance of her face blinded him. He had it in his mind to wish at that last moment, when it was still possible to draw back, that his curiosity had not compelled him to step out from his french window and that surely he would live to regret the utter boredom which had led him to it on this fateful Sunday. He had lived for over thirty years with nothing in his life but his passion for his mills and the certain conviction that he would pass them on to his son, as his father had to him. Until the day of his death James Chapman and he had shared this expectation, shared their interest, their home life, their journeying to other parts of the country to find buyers for their cloth and it was not until now, in this first strange meeting with his unknown daughter, did he realise how much he had missed that companionship and shared involvement.

He was sceptical at first. She was a girl, no more than a child but who else was there to inherit what he and his father had built? He could marry her to someone like himself in the textile industry but it would no longer be a Chapman concern for on her marriage she would, with all she inherited become the property of her husband. But he was tempted! By God, he was tempted to let her have her head. Just to see if it could be done! What a stir it would make! He had no doubt at all that she could do it for he discovered over the following months that in her female head was a man's brain, sharp, shrewd and devastatingly quick and in her woman's breast beat the heart of a strong man, filled with courage and the ambition to do more than marry and bear children which was her allotted function in life. She became even more impatient with the restrictions placed upon her by Miss Strong, who, now that Mr Chapman had said they might go out of the ordered security of the garden, was afraid her charge might dirty her gloves, or step in some unimaginable horror or even catch a disease from the often quite rough persons they met on the moorland path just above the house. It did not improve matters when Katherine begged to go further than she had been allowed, to stray from the well-defined path and absorb the haunting fragrance of the heather and see the splendid view she was convinced lay just over the hill, and the freedom her father gave her made her yearn for more.

But not even Kit Chapman knew of the turmoil which she had created in her father's mind. The spring and summer had been the most satisfying she had ever known in her young life and the gratifying interest her father seemed suddenly to take in her had awakened all kinds of longings, unnamed and more than likely, she supposed, to be unfulfilled. He had taken to engaging her in conversation, amazingly asking her opinion on many subjects and her own mind, starved and empty, was nurtured by his and she blossomed and grew and though he could not say he loved her, he found he admired her keen, adventurous spirit and even the way she had influenced him.

The dogs decided him. They were a test. One he had devised, God knows why, not only for her but for himself. Take them, he said to her that summer, and make them obey you, make them your protectors against those who would harm you and if you succeed you may go alone to the moor, walk where you please and speak to whom you please for you will have earned the right, as a man earns the right when he becomes a man. It is a risk, but one, if you wish to take it, I will allow. We will make a pact, he told her, watching her soft young face become strong with a beauty and a glow which had nothing to do with her femininity. It will be a pact which we will both honour but first you must let me see your courage, your determination to succeed since these dogs are not for the weak-hearted.

She had done it as he had known she would. She had been twelve when he had begun. She had even then a maturity which had made her an oddity among the young girls which her mother brought to the house and when she begged him, he put a stop to it. The gossip began to bud and grow then but he found he cared nought for it since her future lay not with them and the female lives they would lead but with him and, God help him, in his mills. For the first time in years he felt a surge of excitement.

All that was nearly five years ago, and today, the twenty-eighth of May was her seventeenth birthday and she was to go with him to watch the installation of his new self-acting spinning mule.

She was sensibly dressed as she came down the wide staircase to join him. A plain walking dress in dark green merino since she had been told that the mill floor would be cluttered and dirty. The waist was high and the skirt narrow, the bodice plain and uncluttered with a small, turn-down collar and containing her slipping hair was a small chip bonnet with broad ribbons of the same shade as her gown. Her half-boots were of black kid and her gloves of doeskin and she carried a reticule with a draw-string neck. She was perfectly composed and for a moment he felt a pang of disappointment since he had expected her to be aflame with eager excitement, overawed and trembling with emotion on this incredible day, then she turned to look at him and it was there in her eyes. They were feverish, brilliantly shot with wondrous blue and in them was her deep and ardent gratitude, not love, for it was too late for that between them but an enduring thankfulness which said she would never forget this gift he was about to give her.

His managers and overlookers had been told that Miss Chapman was to visit the mill on this important day and though there was really no need of it – for which among the pale and hollow-chested women spinners and crooked shouldered, bow-legged children who thronged the enormous rooms would dare give offence to their employer's daughter? – they had been warned to be on their best behaviour. They must have a thorough wash before presenting themselves at their 'mules', an insurmountable feat when the water supply in each lane was turned on for half an hour each day, and the smaller children also. Those who worked beneath the machines as 'piecers', twisting together threads which had broken, and as 'scavengers', cleaning up the waste which gathered beneath the mule, were to be made decently presentable.

It was hot in the big room and though Kit had been prepared for it by her father the furnace-like blast which enveloped her the moment she stepped through the doorway brought an instant slick of sweat to her armpits and collected uncomfortably in the small of her back. She was immediately deafened by the noise and could do no more than walk blindly beside her father, his hand guiding her, standing when he did to talk to the manager of the room. Her eyes and mind could make no sense of what she was experiencing for neither had been subjected to what was about her, but gradually some tiny piece of the scene would take shape and become sharply focused, then another and another until she had the whole.

There were dozens of men, women and children working ceaselessly before the machines they attended. The men were clad only in a shirt with the sleeves rolled up and a pair of thin white drawers to the ankle and were barefoot as were the women since they picked up from the floor, with quite amazing dexterity, the threads and cotton waste, using their toes. The women wore a short skirt to just below the knee and a kind of bodice and all had their hair well tied back for there was always danger that it might catch in the frantic machinery into which they leaned. It was ten-thirty in the morning and all of them, she had been told, had already been at their machines for five hours and would continue industriously for another ten or eleven. The spinners stood in the midst of 400 whirling spindles, every thread of which must be incessantly watched and if one should break a shrill cry would go up for one of the smaller children – *children*, my God, for a ghastly moment she had thought them to be small deformed monkeys – would crawl beneath the horrifying wheels and bands and swift-straps, which would, she was convinced, snatch off a limb during a second's careless inattention, to piece together the broken thread. The spinners moved about constantly from one end of the machine to the other, their bare feet sucked into the slick of oil and waste which coated the floor, walking, her father told her, fifteen to twenty miles in each shift, the exercise doing them enormous benefit he added, for it kept their limbs, which were inclined, as he was sure she would notice, to slight deformities, supple and straight.

There were half a dozen 'tacklers', or overlookers, each bearing a thick leather strap who prowled about the long room so that the operatives were constantly under supervision, on the lookout for any infringement of the rules, which were posted on the walls – despite the fact that none could read – and to ensure that there was no time-wasting.

It was not uncommon for a child who had worked for ten or twelve hours or more, to doze off while in charge of a machine and for their own safety these men were here to keep them awake. They were rough often savage these illiterate labourers coming, as many of them did, from agricultural areas where there was no work to be had and from Ireland where it was known insolence abounded. They must all be kept under strict control. They could be violent and had been in the past, rioting and even breaking their own machines which they were convinced would put them out of work, her father said, so low was their intellect! Over all mill-masters hung the spectre of 'General Ludd' and the ordinary folk he had incited until they became a rabble, ripe for revolution and destruction.

But these spinners seemed to have no such thought in their heads as they bent unflaggingly over their machines. The women bobbed an awkward curtsey as she paused to watch their nimble fingers move but they did not stop since it was of the greatest importance, not only to them who were paid for the yardage they spun, but to their master, to keep the spindles turning and the yarn spinning no matter what! A young bobbin-carrier, no more than five or six years old, ran past her at such speed she was afraid he would slip in the oil, taking the roving-bobbins to the mule and bringing away the bobbins of spun yarn, but he did not lift his eyes to look at her. She might have been a fairy princess – if he knew of such a being – or the Squire's lady from Crossfold, it was all the same to him. The overseer's strap awaited him if his slowness caused some holdup in the changing over of the bobbins.

'We will go to Broadbank later in the week, Katherine,' she heard her father shout in her ear, 'to see the weaving-sheds but for now I think a rest in my office,' and she smiled in agreement for really half an hour in this heat and noise and the sudden difficulty she found she had in breathing, were quite enough for one day. She would grow used to it; she knew she would for she must learn all the operations in the spinning and weaving of her father's cotton. But her

49

main purpose was in the office of the mill where the business, the *heart* of the concern, was carried out.

They were seated several minutes later in her father's pleasant office, far away from the noise of the spinning rooms, drinking the coffee which had appeared from somewhere, brought by a clean little woman with respectfully downcast eyes. The room was large, wood-panelled and thickly-carpeted. A fire burned brightly in the hearth. The windows were closed and for a few moments the noise from beyond them did not impinge on their absorbed contemplation of a piece of velveteen which had just been sent over from Broadbank for the master's consideration. Her father was explaining the merits of the cloth, his eyes bright with unexpected pleasure since her fascinated attention gave him a forgotten satisfaction, when the commotion became more insistent and he raised his head to listen.

'It's the new machine arriving,' he said, and he stood up eagerly, surprised by his own enthusiasm and she stood with him, ready to go where he did, wherever that might be, to welcome this incredible innovation which was to make *their* mills the wonder of Lancashire, but he began to frown, moving hurriedly towards the window overlooking the mill yard and she went with him. There were men below, hundreds of them, it seemed to her, none of them with any particular purpose since they milled about like cattle at a market, all going in different directions, getting in one another's way, jostling and pushing and shouting, raising clenched fists and, she could see it now, *fighting*. In the middle of it all on a sturdy waggon pulled by four huge horses was her father's new self-acting spinning machine. Men, strong rough men, with cloth caps and mufflers and all wearing masks on their fâces began to converge on the waggon, held back at first by Barker Chapman's labourers, who had come to unload the machine and place it where the engineer directed them but the interlopers were hazardous in their intention, grim faced and dangerous and when they raised their huge iron hammers, not caring it seemed, whether they fell on man or machine, Barker Chapman's men moved back and stood quietly at the side of the yard since they did not care to be injured in a fight which was not theirs.

There had been reports of rioting in many places during the last two years, of mills and warehouses having their windows broken, of bales of cotton set alight. There was talk of the resurrection of General Ludd, for the gang was organised now and led by a man of control, no longer the shouting, undisciplined mob of rabble-rousers who had once destroyed the machinery which had put out of work the very ones they had pledged to support. It had become an underground revolutionary movement led by masked men. They left alone, as the Luddites had done, the spinning frames and weaving-looms of simple hardworking cottagers and even one or two of the mill-owners, those whose operatives worked in decent conditions and who were paid fair wages. And wherever they went, it was rumoured, they collected money for men who had been thrown out of work and for families who were starving. From Colne down to Oldham they marched and they had begun to be called by a name that was spreading wherever men and women were engaged in spinning and weaving. 'The Onwardsmen' were spoken of reverently, hopefully. From Lancashire, where it had first been whispered, as far north as Glasgow, down to Lincolnshire and Nottinghamshire and south to Somerset, the name, and the men who had coined it, was on the lips of men driven to despair by their inability to earn a decent life for themselves and their families.

Petitions to Parliament asking that a minimum price be fixed below which the manufacturers could not go had been ignored. They had, in desperation, struck work to enforce better wages and even, not knowing of any other way to stop the looms of the mill-masters which had stolen *their* living, taken away the shuttles of those who continued to work in a Rochdale mill but the men involved in the insurrection had been arrested and imprisoned.

Now, it seemed, it was Barker Chapman's turn!

'Father . . .' Kit's voice was but a whisper in the sudden hush but her eyes were on fire with anger. 'Father . . .' Her voice was stronger now, '. . . they mean to break the machine . . .'

'They do, Kit.'

'But are we to let them?' His daughter was surprised by Barker Chapman's acceptance of the destruction.

'How are we to stop them? It seems the men I employ are unwilling to fight and if I was to send for the militia by the time they got here from Oldham it would be too late.'

'There must be men who will stand by us.'

'Look at them. They are in the yard.'

The hammers clanged against the metal of the machine and the men who wielded them, strangely quiet and composed, did not waste a blow and Kit Chapman felt each one as though it fell on her own flesh as she watched helplessly beside her father while they destroyed what was not theirs. She hated them for it and if she could have called down a charge of cavalrymen to slash them to pieces with their sabres she would have done so. If she had a rifle she would have shot each one and should the militiamen come on the scene and arrest each and every one she would have gone gladly to see them hanged. They were not only smashing this splendid machine which belonged to her father and therefore to *her*, but despoiling this day which was to have been the beginning, the foundation on which her life would be built. This was *her* world, to be handed over to her she knew, though he had not yet said so, by her father when the time came and they would not do this to her and what was hers.

*They would not!*

Her feet skimmed the stairs as if she had wings in her heels and her father's warning fell on deaf ears. Her skirt was held high to her knees showing an immodest amount of her leg as she burst from the doorway into the yard and for the space of fifteen seconds they stared in amazement, their hammers poised above their heads. Her hair had, naturally, come down, for unless she sat perfectly still or wore a bonnet it always did. Thus she gave the appearance of some wild, woodland creature in her forest green dress and swirling cape of midnight dark hair. The men did not wish to continue while she screamed some gypsy curse at them for surely, if they did, they would be damned.

'Get away from that machine. All of you. Stand back, I say or I shall call the militia and have you all arrested. Stand away at once and drop your weapons. Do you not know this is a hanging offence, you fools? Now stand away, I say. Go back to your homes and I will say no more about it. But let just one of you touch that machine again and I swear he will live to regret it for the rest of his life which, let me assure you, will be short or spent on the far side of the world in the Australias. I mean what I say. Drop those hammers and be off with you.'

If it had not been for him they might have fallen back, so fierce was her anger, so great her determination, so strong her will. Her nostrils flared and her mouth opened wide on her screams of outrage and her eyes flashed vivid blue sparks at them. One or two, Irish and superstitious, crossed themselves hastily but the one who led them came forward and stood in her path. His face was masked but his eyes were visible and they were scornful, amused, for she was no more than a bit of a girl, the expression in them said. She should be at home with her mother and not interfering in *men's* work.

'Get on with it, lads. It's only Chapman's lass in a tantrum and nothing to us.' He reduced her with those words to a spoiled child who was making a fool of herself.

'Get out of my way,' she hissed, raising her hand to strike this impudent lout who had the effrontery not only to address her in front of these other louts but to make mock of her, of her father's name, but he caught her wrists and held them, laughing, not displeased she could tell, to show the others there was nothing to fear here.

'Smash it up, lads. We'll show him how we deal with men who lower other men's wages so that they cannot

53

even eat. Men cannot live on six shillings a week, and *by God* they *will* not. He takes the bread out of the mouths of our children with his greed but he'll not do it with this machine.'

They broke it up before her eyes and she could have wept for she had loved, if not the machine, the idea of what it meant to her, the symbol of what it stood for in the start of her new life. But the tall and slender young man stared audaciously into her face and she would give no one, least of all this hated intruder, the satisfaction of seeing her humiliation.

'I shall not forget this,' she said to him softly.

'Will you not, Miss Chapman? I certainly hope not. And do not think to frighten us with your threats. We are fighting a just cause, my men and I, and we will win. We are no rabble, but soldiers. Yesterday some of our comrades, Hunt and Johnson, Bamford and Healey were sentenced to long terms of imprisonment merely for meeting and attempting to talk to others who think as they do. That is all, Miss Chapman. Not for thieving or violence, but for talking. So we are done with talking, my men and I. We are to fight now. We are to fight men like your father who are murdering other men, murdering women and *children* in the name of progress. This machine is the first, but tell your father and other men like him that it will not be the last.'

His green eyes gleamed through the slits of his mask, fiercely contemptuous and in some curious way they were familiar to her, as though she had seen them before though she could not have said where. They were as clear and deep as the water which cascaded over the moss into the pool at Sherbrook Falls, but wild, challenging, dangerous.

'I know you,' she said, narrowing her eyes speculatively.

'Do you indeed, Miss Chapman? Perhaps we met at a ball in the Assembly Rooms in Oldham . . .' The men at his back laughed delightedly, '. . . or was it at a dinner party given by one of your father's manufacturing acquaintances?'

'I know you,' she repeated softly, ignoring his men's derision. 'I don't know how but believe me I shall remember and when I do you will regret it. I shall hound you and your . . . your rabble until I see you all hang.'

He laughed and she felt her skin prickle. He was no more than nineteen or twenty but he was evidently held in some respect by these men, many of them older than he. For when he had done he drew them up in formation, called over a roll, each man answering not to his name but to a number, then giving a great shout of triumph they marched off in regular military order with him at the head. And because she was but seventeen, still a child in many ways, as she climbed the stairs to her father's office she hung her head in her curtain of hair and wept.

# 4

They had not gone at once to their homes, his men and himself, for they were still intoxicated with their own success and the ease with which they had achieved it. When they were out of the town and away from the enthusiastic cheers and applause of the labouring poor who lined the streets to see them go, they could not resist all talking at once, laughing and jostling one another like boys let out of Sunday school; all attempt at column and file, which they had drilled, vanishing with their exuberance.

'They'll not find it so easy to displace our womenfolk now, eh Joss? My Janet's spinning wheel's been still these past three years but by God, without this new machine there's bound to be "putting out" again . . .'

'Aye, he'll not manage wi'out . . .'

'. . . our women'll get a look in, 'appen . . .'

'. . . us'll beat 'em now, yer reckon, Joss . . .?'

'. . . 'appen 'e'll think twice about takin' over this valley with his blasted machinery . . .'

'. . . a few more knocks like this 'un an' we'll all be our own maisters again, what d'yer say, Joss . . .?'

'. . . an' just let 'im try bringin' in power driven looms an' it'll be't same fate for them as 'appened with this 'un . . .'

They had climbed the rough track up to the 'Five Pigeons', an inn which was set on the junction of the Lancashire and Yorkshire roads, deep in the moorland. Surely they deserved a celebration, they said to one another and the landlady was a known sympathiser with their cause. Many of her customers worked in the factories in Oldham and along the Penfold Valley and though they had barely enough to feed their children, once in a while they had the few pence for ale and the talk, which went with it, of the good times to come Joss Greenwood had promised them with a fierceness they could not help but believe.

It did not seem in any way unusual to these men, some of whom nearly ten years ago had marched with 'General Ludd' ready to smash and burn, not only in Lancashire but over the Pennines and into Yorkshire in their fight to keep what they cherished, to turn now to Joss Greenwood as their natural leader. It appeared to them as they marched shoulder to shoulder with him, their pale faces flushed with triumph, their narrow backs stiff with pride that the father lived on in a more full-blooded, more *satisfactory* way in the son. They had loved the father, believed in every word he told them, every benefit he had promised them but it had occurred to many as they had stood to listen to him, how much more gratifying it would be actually to *do* something! Most had walked with him to St Peter's Field and not a few had been injured, or even killed and now they were on the move again, done with accepting their lot and merely waiting passively for it to better itself. Joss Greenwood, in these last two years had welded them together with one purpose and whether it be wrong, or even foolish as some were saying, by God it felt good to be

56

in action at last. They were exploited, they knew that, by this new breed of manufacturer, and their women and children more so than they themselves and the injustice of it could scarce be borne. Today had put a stiffener in their spine and if Joss Greenwood, who was the son of the great man himself said it was the only way, then that was good enough for them.

All the men who marched that day had once laboured only for themselves, in a small way, of course, working their plot of land and selling at the weekly market the piece of cloth woven that week, the woman at her spinning wheel, the man, the 'aristocrat' of his trade, at his hand-loom and their children helping in all the processes of cloth making. They had the freedom to decide on the rhythm of their own lives and they were prosperous in their own class.

But the burst of mechanical inventions which had usurped the domestic spinning wheel and the cottage hand-loom had taken their old ways from them and they simply could not understand why they were thrown into such turmoil. Once their families had earned thirty shillings a week and sometimes, when a weaver was involved, as much as fifty and why could they not go on as they had done, they and their fathers and grandfathers before them, they asked? Was there not enough to go round, they asked? But the answer, it seemed, was no for the mill-masters took it all, the spinning and the weaving and all the processes before and after. Unless the women and children, who were quick and nimble and compliant and could be paid less than a man, or any of the men who were prepared to do as they were told, came to work for *them*, they could starve to death in a ditch for all the mill-masters cared. They went, the women taking the children they could not see starve, and so the 'factory', a word which had until the previous century never before been heard of, was begun.

But the men, those who would rather starve than work for another, and those women unmarried and without children, were another matter entirely. Were they not free-born Englishmen, and as such, unable to abide the idea of

57

slavery? For whichever way you looked at it that was what it was. They were not prepared, by God, should the mill-owners have been willing to employ them, which they were not, to work locked up for sixteen hours a day, summer and winter, in a heat of over ninety degrees. It was well known that a man could be heavily fined for sending out for a drink of water, needed in the heat in which he was forced to work, for opening a window, or even for the simple act of whistling, unlikely in the circumstances, as he went about his employment! No, parliamentary reform was called for or, if they were not listened to, a revolution such as had broken out in France. They wanted nothing more, they said, than sufficient money to live decently. They did not enquire too deeply into why they could not earn a living, for politics and the pressures which were arising due to the new 'industrialisation' were beyond their understanding. They had Tom Paine's *Rights of Man* read out to them and societies began to spring up on both sides of the Pennines, for the woolworkers of Halifax and Bradford were in the same sorry state as themselves. Luddism was born and men were executed in its name and political unions were formed and the unrest reached its climax in August 1819 with the massacre which was to be called Peterloo. The 'Six Acts' forbidding such foolishness as had been displayed there were rushed through Parliament and the radical agitation, for the most part, subsided.

But Joss Greenwood and others of like mind fought on. Their women, those who worked for Barker Chapman since children must be fed, were all pale and hollow-chested and prone to complaints of the lung due to the cotton dust they breathed for sixteen hours a day. They were undernourished. They were round-shouldered and had bad teeth caused by sucking the weft up in the shuttle and the surprising fact that they bore a child each year, scarcely stepping from their machines to do so, was due not to their husband's love and desire but because the act of copulation was the only moment of pleasure left to them which cost nothing.

Their children who, from the age of four or five worked

beside them grew hardly at all from their introduction into full time employment, remaining stunted and dwarf-like, their limbs crooked, their joints swollen and deformed through constant kneeling and scrabbling beneath the frames. It was required that they be small, the smaller the better since the space beneath the machines would not allow for a normal, healthy, full-grown child above the age of six or seven and yet they were required to be alert, lively even, for only a child who remained awake, remained alive and uninjured. The mill-owners could not be blamed for it, they said, for did they not employ overlookers to avoid such a catastrophe and if they should need to beat a child, or to kick it even, was that not better than to lose an arm, an eye or even a life?

But working beside the local children were the 'parish' children, brought from all over the country in cartloads and 'apprenticed' as labourers in the cotton mills. No one cared much if an unguarded machine tore off a finger or an arm from one of these children nor if they slept in an exhausted tumble of tormented bodies on a pile of waste in some corner nor if they were fed on a diet of water porridge and oatcake day in and day out. It was of concern to no one that they had a bare ten minutes in the middle of the day to eat it, to relieve themselves, nor in fact whether they lived at all for there was a constant supply from parishes who were glad to be rid, not only of them but of the expense of keeping them. The 'Peel Act' of 1802, the first of the 'factory' acts, limited the working of pauper children to twelve hours a day, later extended to *all* children under the age of sixteen, had done little to assuage the lot of those children for the passing of an act means little when there is no way to enforce it. They cleaned the machinery on Sunday, their day of 'rest' and these infants (for what else were they?) became crippled in body and mind. Nevertheless, as the mill-masters told one another complacently, whenever the subject arose, what greater benefit could society bestow on the poor than to provide them with employment? They were kept from vice and degradation and became useful members of the community in their industry and what could any man ask but that? The factory wages were sufficient, they assured one another, to sustain a thrifty family and though with the passing of the Corn Bill the price of bread was high, causing riots in past years, their own profits were growing and trade had never been better, a matter for self-congratulation, they considered.

Joss had kept his hand-loom working though when he looked back over the two years since his father had died he often wondered how it had been done. Without Jenny, his sister, it would *not* have been done. He had taken his father's pack-pony, tramping miles to the Cotton Exchange in Manchester when he could not get supplies from the merchants of the raw cotton he needed for his mother to spin. He and Jenny worked the two hand-looms, weaving a small piece of cloth each but the work was heavy, a man's work and not meant for a lass of sixteen. Two pieces of cloth, perhaps of no more than thirty yards, would earn him ten shillings and still wages continued to plummet. He worked the smallholding, he and Jenny, cleaned and carded the raw cotton before the spinning and weaving and they did not starve though they came damn near it a time or two.

And at the end of the day he and the Onwardsmen would tramp the moorland, moving unerringly through nights which were thick and dark, drilling their force whenever there was light to see by, into a small but efficient body of soldiers. The soft dash of falling water was in their ears and the soft murmur of men's voices, men they met from other districts who were as swift as they in their retribution against the manufacturers.

He would slip home in the dawn, his tread as light and graceful as his mother's tabby. He could barely see a foot ahead of him when the clouds hid the moon and the stars but he knew every swell and fold, every rock and track and dark tree. The moorland heights were as familiar to him as his mother's kitchen and the men he talked to and planned with were as treasured by him as the members of his own family. They kept the bright flame of his father's memory alive and fed the hatred with which he burned for those who had killed him.

Yes, they said, trade was good, those who were involved with reaping the benefit of it and profits were growing. Oh indeed, and this was the only fact with which the men who followed young Joss Greenwood were in agreement as they sipped the glass of ale they could ill-afford in the tap-room of the 'Five Pigeons'. The air in the room was smoky from the guttering fire and the flames of the candles which were its only light. There were men crowded on settles and leaning against walls, their eyes ablaze with excitement for the whole district knew what had been achieved this day.

'What 'appened? Did you break the machine? Was there any trouble?' their genial landlady begged to know and their tongues ran away with them as they vied with one another to tell her.

'It went like clockwork, Abby,' Tom Butterworth's voice was high with the thrill of it. 'We marched in formation just like Joss showed us, right up to yon mill gates an't machine were there, standing in't middle o't yard . . .'

'Were there no soldiers?'

'Not a one! Well, them what were there to lift it from't waggon were that 'mazed to see us they just stood there gawpin' and we were in and up on it afore you could say knife. They started to jostle us a bit, well, they had to make a show of it, 'adn't they, even if they did agree wi' us on the quiet but it was no contest until . . .' Tom's face assumed an uncertain expression and Abby leaned over the bar counter towards him.

'Until what, lad?'

'Well, there was this lass . . .'

'What lass?'

He turned then to Joss, pulling a comical face. They had talked about Chapman's lass on the way to the inn, the other men and himself, and the remarkable way she had acted, speculating on why she and not her father, as they had expected, had been there in an attempt to defend, or

61

at least protest at the breaking of his expensive machine. The other men had been contemptuous saying they would allow no lass of theirs to act in such an unwomanly fashion and her only sixteen or so. What kind of man was Barker Chapman, they questioned, who could be so brutally hard on those he employed in his mill and yet let a slip of a girl speak for him in a yard filled with rough men? They could find no answer and it appeared Joss Greenwood, who had inherited his father's eloquence and could always find words on other occasions, had none to spare now.

'You tell her, Joss.'

'Nay, it's not important.'

'But she might have stopped us. You saw how she was.'

'Never! A spoiled bairn, that's all she was.'

'Come on, Joss, be honest. She had a . . . a way with 'er.'

'Are you saying she would have prevented you from doing what you had gone there to do, Tom Butterworth?' Joss Greenwood's voice was dangerously low and the men about him quietened, looking at him in wonderment for it seemed he was filled with some strange tension they could not understand. They had fulfilled their mission, had they not and returned safe and sound and proud of themselves as they had every right to be since they had done well. Tom Butterworth was only sixteen but he had proved himself a man today. They were all men in their championship of the downtrodden labouring classes who fought, not only to keep alive but to keep their dignity in employment but they were conscious that Joss was impatient with this talk of some girl who had been part of their day and Abby Hobson, being a woman, could not let it pass.

'Who was she, Joss?'

'Chapman's lass,' he answered shortly, and that's the end of it, his attitude said but she elected not to notice.

'Barker Chapman's daughter!' Her voice was incredulous. 'At t'mill?'

'Aye.' Joss turned from her irritably. The only flaw in the perfection of the day had been the way in which Katherine Chapman had almost turned away the will of the men, *his* men, from the job they had come to do. They had stopped what they were about, ready to drop their hammers at the voice of authority, ready to stand back, he was inclined to believe if he was honest, and doff their caps to the master's daughter so ingrained was their habit of obedience to those who were considered to be above them. If he had not overridden her will with his own, if he had not humiliated her, reduced her to her proper place in the eyes of his men she might have done it, but he was not prepared to say so, for if he should how was he ever to lead these men who followed him as they had followed his father?

'But what was she doing there?'

'How the hell do I know? Making a fool of hersen, I'd say.'

'But what did she . . .?'

'Oh give over, Abby. She was nowt. Nowt! The job's done and we've shown 'em what we're made of and that's all that counts. We mean business and no bloody machine is going to stop us. These new machines threaten our livelihood, we all know that. Look at the miles me an' Enoch have to tramp for raw cotton. Once over the merchants used to bring it to us, begging us to spin it and weave it for 'em. Maybe those days will never come back, Abby. Maybe we'll have to accept the factory system but by God, things will have to be different. We'll have us a decent wage, and conditions, or we'll not work and the only way to let the owners see how serious we are is by serious methods. That's what it's all about, lass. We've to fight, you know that, don't you? We all do, and nothing and *no one* is going to stop us.'

'Aye, tha's right, Joss.'

'Buggers'll 'ave us all under . . .'

'We'll not be stopped . . .'

'Us'll show 'em . . .'

There was jubilation among the younger men, their hot blood deeply satisfied by what they had done, and by Joss's words. The older men smiled, tolerant of them. They had been in the fight for twenty years and more, some of them

63

and had seen many failures but today's success made it all worthwhile.

There was more deliberation on the splendid outcome of the day and of those to come which Joss and his Onwardsmen were planning. They were at ease, the tension, exhilarating as it had been, replaced by relaxed companionship. They were surrounded by the brotherhood of men who were as deeply involved as they and who, if put to the torture would never give them away. It was a moving moment, almost mystical in its significance for now they were no longer rioters, a mob, but a core of hardened fighters, drilled and led by Joss Greenwood into a small army of hit and run soldiers. The moorland was wild and a man could get lost on the desolate stony tracks, the vast outcrop of rocks which could hide a whole battalion, and hostile to those who did not know it. They were safe up here, safe from the militiamen and the troops which had been brought to subdue them and the small inn could scarce contain the triumph of the men it held. They were charged with it, flushed with it and Tom Butterworth who was but a boy and unused to the drink, which was forbidden in his father's Methodist house, could not control his wandering feet nor place them to move in the direction of the path, which led down to Edgeclough. He was a tall lad and, though slender, was heavy-boned. Hard as Joss tried to lift him when the time came for them to leave, Tom slipped through his hands like mist.

'Put 'im on t'settle,' Abby told Joss amiably, her warm, experienced eye studying Joss's tall, graceful body as he struggled, laughing, to contain Tom Butterworth's harmless befuddlement. 'Let t'lad sleep it off there. 'E'll come to no 'arm.'

Her voice was husky and her hand on Joss's arm was warm with a meaning no man could mistake. She had liked the broad sweep of Joss Greenwood's shoulders and the slim length of his waist and hips and legs ever since he had first come up to her inn and her eyes told him so now. His skin was flushed and in the warmth of the tap room he had opened his shirt neck to reveal the brown hollow of his throat and the fine mat of dark hair which led down from it. Abby was a bonny woman, a widow of thirty-three or -four, with a deep breast and fine curved hips, ample and womanly. When Joss turned to her after laying Tom on the settle she was waiting for him, her own buttons were undone to reveal the creamy whiteness of her breasts and Joss sank into them with a murmur of pleasure.

Joss was nowhere to be seen when Tom awoke in the soft dawn, his body cramped from the hours he had spent on the wooden settle. His head ached and his mouth was like the gritty cavity which cut the granite on the moorland. He decided he'd best be off since his father would be waiting for him with his Bible under his arm and a sermon on his lips. He couldn't escape it. He put his head under the pump in the yard, hoping to clear it somewhat for he could remember little of what happened last night or how he came to be on Abby Hobson's settle. Where was Joss, he wondered?

He was quiet as he let himself into the cottage in which he lived with his father and sister. The soldiers who were waiting for him, and anyone else they could lay their hands on in the villages along the length of the Penfold Valley, were disappointed when they trapped only one unsuspecting and confused young lad since they had hoped for the whole gang but he was better than nothing.

He did not see them immediately. His head hurt and his stomach was uneasy and he was thinking of nothing but the comfort of his own bed this Sunday morning and some peace from his father who would be bound to speak, if he learned of it, of the dire sin of drunkenness. The soldiers had hidden themselves in the tall bracken beyond the wall of the laithe house, only one remaining in Enoch Butterworth's kitchen and though at the last minute Tom's sister, Mercy, had shouted a warning despite the brawny arms which clutched her about the neck and shoulders, her young brother walked dazedly into the trap which had been set him. In each of the half dozen cottages which formed the tiny hamlet of Edgeclough a soldier had been posted for it was well known these outlaws hung together and if they were not prevented a villager would be sent to warn them.

Mercy Butterworth wept as her brother was knocked senseless to the floor of her kitchen. She was ready to dart to his assistance but she was held back by the grinning soldier who had her in his grip.

'Fetch the rest of the troop from the cottages, Private,' the Sergeant who entered the kitchen barked. 'I'll watch the lad and the woman. This is all we're to get 'ere, it seems.'

Tom Butterworth was dragged semi-conscious to the door of the cottage. The Sergeant was of the opinion that it did no harm to let the rest of this disorderly rabble of women and children and old men with their lunatic ideas of equality see what would happen to them if they should step out of line as this one apparently had. It would be the penal colony for him, or a couple of years' hard labour, no doubt and if an example was made of him perhaps the rest would toe the line. It gave him a great deal of satisfaction to have netted this one since, to the best of his knowledge not one of the 'reformers' as they liked to call themselves, had ever been caught so great was the conspiracy of total silence among those who supported them. This lad was young and inexperienced, coming in as he had from some obvious overnight wrongdoing but it would be his last fling for the time being, the magistrate would see to that. The spirit of the Luddites lingered on, as the Sergeant well knew for he himself had been involved in taking some of those who had murdered William Horsfall, a hated mill-owner from Huddersfield. He had seen some of them hanged at York gaol, the rest transported, but still the legends of their heroism, as *they* called it, lived on in the songs and stories and secrets of the Luddites themselves. They had been proud men and proud of their involvement in the underground movement which had begun this unrest in the lower classes, but there was one less now to carry on the tradition.

Tom Butterworth's head was ringing from the blow it

had taken and for several minutes he allowed himself to be shoved here and there by the jubilant soldiers. He was aware of a noise somewhere, a woman whimpering and the laughter of men. They had not yet put the manacles on him though he could see through the blood which ran down his face a grinning soldier approaching with them dangling from one hand. He felt quite, quite paralysed, numbed with the sudden horror of what was happening and already he was blindly holding out his hands, prepared to let them lead him away to wherever it was he must go. But the woman — who was it? — had begun to moan in terror and her voice was familiar and he turned in confusion and the blood which dripped from his brow ran hot and mad with outrage. They had Mercy, the soldiers, one holding her arms, the other leering at her uncovered breasts. He had her nipple between his thumb and forefinger and as Tom watched in horror they began to drag her towards the back of the cottage. He looked about him in anguish for the Sergeant, instinct telling him which man to seek for help but he was nowhere in sight.

He screamed then and sprang forward and even before any of those who were watching the 'bit of sport', the soldier was dead, his neck snapped cleanly by the strong right arm of Tom Butterworth.

## 5

Tom Butterworth, just two days short of his seventeenth birthday, was hanged at Lancaster gaol on the twenty-first of July, 1821, for the murder of a soldier.

Though she had sworn to those who had wrecked her father's spinning machine that she would not only see them all hang but would rejoice in it, Katherine Chapman found the day extremely trying to get through. She and her father breakfasted together as usual, served by the same self-effacing maidservants who waited at table every day, but from the moment she walked into the morning room, the door held open for her by the head parlourmaid, she had sensed the tension which charged the atmosphere. There was no apparent change she could put her finger on. Ellen bobbed her usual curtsey and wished her good-morning and Betty and Flora stood ready to offer her collared or potted meats, cold game, poultry or veal and ham pie. There was whiting or herring, if she wished for something hot, broiled sheep's kidneys, sausages, bacon and poached eggs, omelets, toast and muffins, and marmalade and fruit preserve. There were freshly gathered flowers arranged on the table and sideboard, and fat, red strawberries from her father's garden, piled in a luscious tumbling heap on a silver serving dish.

The sun shone in a golden stream of floating dust motes on the shining breakfast table, laying a path across the thick, flower-patterned carpet and she walked along its length to her chair beside her father.

He smiled, not warmly for that was not his nature, but in the pleasantly friendly fashion which had grown between them in the past five years. It was a smile a gentleman will bestow on a lady of whom he approves, not perhaps a lady with whom he is on more than a nodding acquaintanceship, but one he respects and admires. He stood as she approached and asked her how she did on this hot and sultry morning for though it was barely five o'clock the temperature was already rising above sixty degrees. He enquired politely, as he resumed his seat, if she had slept well. As she replied that she had, helping herself to a small piece of whiting from the dish Ellen held out to her, he congratulated himself on the decision he had made five years ago to take her into the business. Though she was a female, his daughter, he had, in all respects given her the rights a man would automatically pass on to a son, and what a success it had turned out!

As he had expected, there had been talk and his wife had sworn that they would be ostracised, cut off from polite society since who amongst it would entertain a woman, a girl yet, but soon to be a woman, who was to mix daily with the riff-raff whom he employed! No ... no ... she would not agree that the men and women in his mills had more respect than to dare address her daughter for she had herself seen them from her carriage in the streets of Crossfold, the women huddled in shawls with sullen faces peering balefully from beneath thin and dusty hair, the men grim-faced and grey and watching her most perilously. And the overlookers were as bad. Though they were forced to keep a civil tongue in their heads in the presence of their master she had seen the way, when they thought themselves to be unobserved, the way their eyes slid about ... well, they were not respectful ... not at all! And her friends, the wives of the bankers and solicitors, of professional men and of other mill-owners would not care to be in the company of a lady, *their* daughter, who must, in the course of the day, put herself forward in a most unladylike manner as she addressed those uncouth persons at the mills.

'She *is* my daughter, as you say, and as such wherever I am received so will she.' Barker Chapman's voice was thin and dry. 'I do business with these men, my dear, and it is to their advantage to know which side their bread is buttered. She is not the only woman to go into business and still be considered a lady. These are modern times, Hannah. The commercial world is expanding rapidly and with it, our outlook on the proprieties is changing. Katherine will conduct herself properly at all times, I can vouch for that and there will be no scandal. She is the most level-headed woman, yes, *woman* despite her youth ... in fact I will go further and say the most level-headed *person* I have come across in business and I assure you she will cause no gossip. She is too ... determined to succeed to risk it. She will go about with me and believe me, there will be no talk, not in my hearing.'

69

'But behind your back, Barker. What of the gossip?'

'They will get over it, Hannah. They will become accustomed to it. They will be forced to if they wish to do business with me.'

She could run it almost as well as himself. Though he had jibbed at taking her into the spinning and weaving sheds at first, she had insisted that unless she learned at least by what means the machines worked and the way in which the operatives *operated* them, how was she to take over the running of the business when the time came.

'Did you take off your coat and roll up your sleeves when you were learning, Father?' she asked impishly.

'Good Heavens, my dear, hardly! I leave that to my engineers.'

'Well then, may I not do what you did which I believe you are telling me was to watch and be instructed by others who *do* such things.'

She could tell a fustian from a velveteen and how each was woven and where the markets were for the finished cloth and like himself and his father before him could shrewdly make one penny do the work of two and, moreover, could pare down production costs until she made a profit of *two* pennies where before there had been only one! She proved to be an able scholar and he was growing confident that when he was gone his mills, under her guidance, would continue to flourish. She still had much to learn in experience and the snatching of opportunities when they arose but she had the best head on her shoulders – Chapman shoulders – since the death of her grandfather. Though she had not had the benefit of a good education, as a son would have, it seemed not to have reduced her capacity to use her brain, quick and lightning sharp, as he himself did. She had no objection to rising at five in the morning in order to be at the mill as the gates opened, nor to working far into the night when necessity demanded and her ability to hold her own in the often sharp practices which were the custom among manufacturers did not go

70

unnoticed by his rivals. She had nerve and was not afraid to speak out if she disagreed with some action he took, but at the same time she was always willing to admit a mistake.

There had been but one truly difficult moment and that had been on the first occasion he had taken her into the Cloth Hall at Crossfold, that innermost and absolutely male sanctum of the cotton industry. They had been met by an appalled silence which had lasted for the space of five long minutes, broken only by the polite greetings Barker addressed to his business acquaintances. They had not exactly turned their backs on her, Barker had far too much influence for them to dare to do that, but their faces were stiff and cold and their voices, when they found them, icy. But Kit Chapman seemed to know instinctively how to conduct herself, keeping well in her father's shadow, speaking only when spoken to and as the weeks went by and they became accustomed to her she was accepted and the day came when it was as though she had always been one of them. She was as wily as her father and grandfather they grudgingly told one another, and they admired her for it since it was the highest praise one businessman could apply to another in these parts.

'Will you read *The Times*, my dear?' he asked her courteously.

'Thank you, Father, no.'

'It seems the Coronation was a splendid affair. Our new King is apparently exceedingly fond of show and pomp and determined his own crowning should outshine anything in history.'

'Indeed.'

'Would you not have liked to be there, Katherine?'

'No, Father. Such things do not greatly interest me.'

'It says here that the Queen looked very fine . . .'

'Really.'

Barker Chapman sighed and folding the newspaper neatly to the precise pattern into which it had been ironed that morning by his housekeeper, placed it beside his plate.

71

He sat back in his chair and regarded his daughter thoughtfully as she picked at the fish on her plate. She had matured in the last twelve months and now, as a woman of seventeen, was, he knew, considered quite a beauty among the gentlemen who had been angling for her hand since she was fifteen years old. She was tall, almost as tall as he, a disadvantage in this era when small and dainty was so much admired, and very dark, when fair ringlets and pink cheeks were the vogue but the gentlemen who had asked for her were prepared, it seemed, to overlook these faults in consideration of the fortune she would inherit. Her wilful hair was brushed into a silken smooth chignon at the back of her head and with the help of two tortoiseshell combs and the lady's maid she had been allowed on her seventeenth birthday, she had curbed the wayward strands which had once slipped about her ears. She wore the gold earbobs he had given her and a soft coffee and cream gingham day dress, very simple and elegant with a long sleeve and a sash of taffeta about her waist and though there was no special gown suitable for a lady to wear in a cotton spinning mill (for who would expect to see one in such a strange place?), she was decently and modestly dressed.

'What is it, Katherine? You seem somewhat preoccupied this morning. Are you not concerned with their Majesties' new state?'

'No ... I ... I cannot seem to find it of particular interest.'

'You mean in general, or merely ... today?'

She looked sharply at him then since they were both well aware of what was to happen today and though the belief that the man should hang for the crime he had committed was shared by them both, he knew and was sorry for it, that it was affecting her more deeply than she cared to admit.

The maids at the back of the room had become still and the tension deepened, snapping almost, for Tom Butterworth was a local man and there would be many who would sympathise with his state today, saying he had been driven to it. His, Barker Chapman's own servants could, no doubt, be acquainted with the man's family, whoever they might be, but that was nought to him and should be nought to his daughter. The man had committed a crime for which the penalty was death, and he must pay the penalty.

'It is to be today,' she said abruptly. 'Seven-thirty, I believe.'

'I am aware of that, Katherine.' At the back of the room there was a small sound followed by a soft flurry of skirts and one of the maids left the room but he did not turn to see who it might be.

'Does it not . . .?'

'. . . affect me?' he finished for her. He paused, looking deeply into her eyes and was quite bewildered by a look of what he could only call confusion there. 'No, it does not. Why should it? Because it was *our* machine the man helped to wreck? Is that what you are asking . . .?'

'No . . . no . . .'

'Then why do you concern yourself?'

'I do not . . . but . . . he is so . . . young.'

'He killed a soldier, Katherine. A man who was doing his duty. The man deserves to hang despite his youth. I heard you say so yourself when they smashed the new machine. You were quite adamant about it then. If I remember your words you swore revenge on all of them, including the lad who is to hang today. Do you now say they were right in what they did . . .?'

'Oh no, Father . . .' Her eyes had become the vivid blue of her anger, the anger she had known then.

'As I recall, you told them that what they did was a hanging offence and you meant what you said. You cannot change your mind because that is now to happen and the one who is to be punished is but sixteen. You are only seventeen yourself and know exactly what you are about and in what you believe. Do you not think he is the same?'

'Yes, of course!' Her chin rose and her colour was high again with remembered outrage.

73

'Then does it not follow that he must pay the penalty if it is proved he was breaking the law. That he must pay the price, the ultimate price for the crime he committed?'

She nodded her head in agreement and though she did not smile for what the man was to suffer was not to be smiled at, in her eyes was the warm and positive belief that what her father said was the truth. She had indeed done all she could, with her father, to get the man convicted for he had been there, it had been proved to the magistrate's satisfaction, when the machine was smashed. Was it not unreasonable now to shrink from the truth, sad, but implacable, that within two hours the man – dear Lord, he was no more than a boy – would be dead! She must not let sentiment, stupid *female* sentiment, soften her otherwise clear-headed thinking. She was her father's heir, pledged to the task of carrying on what the Chapmans before her had built, to defending what was theirs and she must learn to deal with these men, these wicked men who would put the clock of progress back with their destruction and riots. They were no more than rabble, most of them, a mob of base-born, coarse and brutish labourers who could not see that improvement would never be halted and that she, Katherine Chapman, would never be halted either.

They discussed the merits of a new cloth her father was experimenting with as they drove from Greenacres to Crossbank, and the advisability of having troops to supervise the second new 'self-acting' mule they were to install there in the next week or so. The machine which had been wrecked was to be replaced naturally, since nothing must stand in *their* way, the Chapman father and daughter agreed, and though he did not say so to Katherine, Barker Chapman was aware that the young man who was, at this moment, being led to the gallows, was to die for nothing, since his cause had *gained* nothing. They talked of other matters concerning the business. Barker Chapman was not satisfied with the hand-looms which he had put in his new weaving-sheds at Broadbank and what did Katherine think to trying out one or two power-looms now that the steam

74

engine was so readily available to them. Their heads were close together, their rapt attention with their own bright future and that of their mills absorbing them as they drove through the mill gates at precisely five-thirty. The factory bell pierced the air and from every direction scurried frail shadows of men and women and children, running to be through the gate before it was closed to latecomers since, if they did not get through now they would not only be made to wait a further two and a half hours until it was opened again at eight o'clock, but also would be fined for their tardiness. They crowded, women in shawls despite the heat, into the yard, children still half asleep on their feet whose eyes were sunken shadows in their candle-pale faces and men, thin and haunted, but fierce eyed, nevertheless, and bitter.

Without warning, as they packed into the yard with a clatter of clogged feet on cobbles and the soft hum of voices on the air, there fell a menacing silence, a hostile stillness that was louder than the clamour which had preceded it and Barker Chapman and his daughter turned in the carriage to look in bewilderment at their operatives who had suddenly become as frozen as the marble statues in their own garden at Greenacres.

The carriage drew up to the staircase which led to the offices. From inside the mill came the singing of the machinery, the machinery which never stopped except on Sunday for as one 'gang' finished another began and those who had worked through the night came quietly down from every floor, their feet still bare, standing shoulder to shoulder with their companions until the whole yard was a massed sea of white faces. Behind them, their voices raised warningly, their thonged straps swinging, followed a score of perilous overlookers. From the office windows faces stared in amazement as Barker Chapman's managers came to see what was amiss and but for the harsh sound of the overlookers' shouts and the 'thwack' of their straps as they slapped them into their open palms, there was a complete and eerie silence.

Barker Chapman stepped down from his carriage, reaching as he did so for his cigar case. He extracted a cigar, and with the casual air of one who has all the time in the world and is no more than an unconcerned spectator to someone else's drama, he lit it. When it was drawing to his satisfaction, the fragrant smoke curling about his top hat he turned to Kit.

'Will you step down, my dear, and go on up to the office. Tell Mrs Plank to make us a pot of coffee. I shall be up shortly.'

His words could be heard clearly in every corner of the silent yard for even the overlookers, truculent and smarting at this contemptuous disregard for their authority, had ceased to shout orders. Katherine felt her heart fill with some vast emotion which she had never known before. She herself had stood up to a crowd once before. She had been in hot temper, fearing none of the rough men she had confronted and though her father then had known it was useless, accepting that there was nothing to be done to save his machine, she had been wild, undisciplined, giving those men the satisfaction of sneering at her. She would not do so again, nor would her father. He was superb at this moment. He might have been in the tranquillity and seclusion of his own garden, surrounded, not with the hostility and aggression of a silently staring crowd who could, as the expression on their haggard faces seemed to indicate, tear him and trample him, and herself, into the muck of the yard, but among his own rose beds and green lawns. He was smiling imperturbably, his cigar clenched between his teeth and there was no trace of fear on his face. She had never admired him . . . no, *loved* him more than at this moment. She smiled too, and their expression of disdain, of arrogance, was identical. They might be forced by sheer weight of numbers to back away from this confrontation, they said, but they would pick their time to retaliate and they would always win in the end!

As Barker Chapman turned to face the mob, for surely that was what it was, his daughter thought, just like the one which had ravaged France, she stepped deliberately from the carriage, and just as cool as he himself was, opened her cream taffeta parasol and moved slowly and gracefully around the carriage to stand beside him. She slipped her hand through his arm, a gesture which said quite plainly to this riff-raff that if they were to take him, then they must go through her to do it!

'What is the meaning of this gathering?' Her father addressed his remark to a bony-faced, weak-eyed man, tall and quite straight of frame, unlike those about him, who he had decided must be the leader since he stood in the centre of the front row of the crowd. The man stared, not at Barker Chapman now, but over his shoulder directly at the wall of the mill building and Katherine began to realise that not one soul looked at her, or her father, but into blank space, into the air in front of them, into *nothing*. They were expressionless, their eyes clouded now, as though someone had mesmerised every last one of them.

'You all appreciate that you are losing wages by standing here, I suppose?' her father went on, but no one answered him and no one moved.

'I'll get 'em back, Mr Chapman,' a voice at the side of the carriage said and a burly man stepped from behind Barker Chapman's sleek and well-nourished carriage horses, swinging his overlooker's thonged strap gently to and fro. 'A touch with this'll get 'em on the move and I'll guarantee to give you the reason for it before the day's out, so I will.' His tone was perilous, for with every moment the machines were not operating the size of his own weekly bonus was reduced. He had a few nice little sidelines going in the mill, many of which brought him more than his own wage, but he'd not be defied by this motley assembly, and certainly not before the master himself. They were terrified of him, those who worked on his floor, especially the women, and even more, the women with daughters! He began to jostle the drab who stood before him, moving threateningly on the child who was with her but she merely

77

held it closer to her though her face became even whiter in her terror.

'What the devil is this about?' the man began to roar, taking hold of another, pulling and shoving until the man he had picked on fell to his knees, but still no one moved.

'Leave it, leave them be, if you please, Ellis, for I have a few words to say.' Barker Chapman's voice was soft and pleasant but the steel which lay beneath it was obvious to them all, from the oldest there, a mill hand who had come as a parish apprentice with a cartload of others when the mill first opened, to the youngest, a 'piecer' just five years old and with no shoes to his feet. 'If they wish to lose wages they may, and for each five minutes they do not work they shall be fined threepence. I shall go up to my office now and I expect to see this yard empty of everyone except those with legitimate business in it within five minutes. See to it, will you, Ellis.'

The hazy sunshine, yellow and burning above the roof top fell about the yard. The shadow of a vagrant cloud sighed across the metallic blue of the sky and the faces of the men and women who stood passively beside Barker Chapman's spinning mill, darkened, and Katherine felt the touch of an icy finger run across her warm skin. It was unearthly the absolute quiet, and the huge gathering seemed to float like disembodied ghosts, frail, insubstantial, scarcely human at all in their complete silence and lack of movement.

'Come, my dear,' her father said softly at her elbow, bringing her from the strange trance-like state into which she had fallen. 'They will be gone within five minutes, you will see.'

But the silent assembly was still there five minutes later, and ten minutes, and half an hour, and though all the overlookers pushed and jostled and threatened, not one of that vast crowd would move except to fall over when forced to it and Barker Chapman became afraid that serious damage might be done them. Not that he cared a great deal about that, but he had no wish to be held responsible for the mass savaging of his workers at the hands of his incensed overlookers.

He was standing at his office window, watching them, marvelling that a great multitude such as this, without apparent leadership or support could remain so fixed and without movement for so great a length of time. Not one had moved, nor spoken as far as he could tell for more than an hour. They merely stood, each one staring at the back of the one in front or into the space which contained them, until suddenly, as though at a signal, they bowed their heads in complete unison for several long moments then, with a humming like bees which have been stirred with a stick they moved slowly, going quietly towards the door-ways which would lead them to their machines, or, those who had just come off shift, through the gate and into the street. Within five minutes the yard was empty except for the waggons and horses, his own carriage which had been unable to be moved among the press of people, and the labourers who worked there.

It was five minutes past seven-thirty!

'It is because of him,' he said incredulously to Katherine who had come to stand beside him.

'The man who has just been hanged?' She had known it, as he had, though he had not admitted to it, for the past hour since why else would these people, all of them barely above starvation level, have risked all that they had. It had been a demonstration of their loyalty to the men who were fighting, and *dying* for them.

'Yes. They have stood for two hours in his honour. They have each lost four shillings and fourpence, two weeks' wages for some of those children.' He shook his head in wonderment. 'The man murdered another but they have made a martyr of him this day!'

For a moment, a bare fraction of time, Katherine Chapman felt a thrill of awe tingle through her body. She had known no great emotion until this day beyond the single-minded devotion she had begun to give to her father's mills. No one had seemed inclined to show her affection as a child

79

beyond the rough embraces of the woman who had helped in the nursery, and she had given none, for who had wanted it? Today her admiration for her father's courage, her loyalty to him, had turned, she thought, in that moment, to love, but now she had seen something else and it was an emotion of which she had no knowledge, no understanding and she could put no name to it. Perhaps constancy? Allegiance to another? A ruthless discipline to a cause which had given them the willingness and the strength to risk the loss of their jobs in its name, and she found she could only feel a sense of baffled admiration. She did not like it, for these people were rebels who were attempting to upset the authority put over them by the laws of the land. They were trying to stand in the way of progress with their antiquated methods of spinning and weaving and their dogged determination to preserve them. There would be work for all, a decent standard of life for all if they would only allow it to happen in this great industrial age which was to come. One day they would realise it, they must, but today had shown her the true temper, the spirit, if not of this crowd who were but the tools of the movement, but of the men who led it.

Her thoughts seemed to draw her eyes to the gateway which opened out from the yard into Weaver Street and for several seconds the identity of the man who stood there escaped her. He was tall, with a big frame, and thin, almost to the point of emaciation. He had a shock of uncut dark curls and even from where she stood she could feel the compelling fierceness of his eyes. They were filled with a spirit of harsh challenge, a throwing down of the gauntlet at her feet, *her* feet, they seemed to say. Would she take it up? His skin was burned by the sun and his bare arms were folded across his chest. He stood, his legs wide apart, a warrior who has done battle and won, in the exact centre of the gateway and those who were in the yard turned and stood, like him, to watch her. *She knew who he was then!*

Her heart began to pound and though she was acutely

80

aware that she should call her father, who had returned to his desk, she found she could not. They looked into one another's eyes across the width of the yard and the stillness which enveloped them, a stillness which spoke as loud as words, declared their enmity and, at the same time, the curious bond between them which had nothing at all to do with what had just happened here. He lifted his hand in greeting, perhaps a declaration of his dangerous intentions, though there was a certain sardonic mockery in it, then he was gone, slipping into the shadows of the high wall which surrounded the yard.

Katherine Chapman leaned for a long time at the window. There was an emptiness inside her which she knew she must fill and it must be filled with an understanding of what was to happen in her life from this day. She was her father's daughter, a Chapman, and committed to nothing beyond the continuing of his business, to its growth in the industry of cloth-making. The man at the gate was nothing to her. He was from another class, another culture and yet he seemed to acknowledge a link, a binding of their lives which had begun on the moorland path to Friars Mere when they had been scarcely more than children, a boy and a girl, even then on separate pathways. She had been drawn to him, she recognised it. She had seen him only twice since that day and on each occasion he had been the instigator in some dispute against her father and his mills. He was her protagonist in what must surely come, that was beyond doubt, as the mill-workers wreaked their revenge, for surely that was what it was, on her father and other mill-owners, for what they saw as the loss of their livelihood. If that was so, then why did she feel such a sense of loss as she looked at the open gateway where, for the space of a minute, the man had stood?

# 6

Mercy Butterworth was tiny, a dainty flower of a girl, her father called her, like a snowdrop with her pale, luminous skin and silky brown hair. Her eyes were soft and grey, fringed with fine brown lashes and though she was just over eighteen, her figure was as slight as that of a twelve year old. She wore homespun, plain dove grey with a snowy white collar and apron, and though she was a child of Methodism, not given to adornment, she had a natural sweetness, a shining laughter about her which needed none.

Her father Enoch was fifty years of age and a staunch Methodist boasting that he had once in his younger days been present at a fieldside sermon when the great and much loved John Wesley, himself an old man then, had spoken to the massed multitude. He had given each of his sons the name of John before they died as infants, from the mysterious and various ailments which his God chose to inflict on them and it was not until his wife, now dead, had timorously wondered if perhaps they might chance the sixth with another name should a child of his survive. But the child was a girl and he called her Merciful Goodness for that was what his God had shown him, shortened in the first year of her life to Mercy.

His son, named Thomas, since his wife, filled with superstitious dread of the name John, had begged it, was born a year later. He was a merry imp of a child, much loved by his sister and mothered by her as they grew up together. Their mother had died at Tom's birth.

Their cottage was the first in the village of Edgeclough,

as the Greenwoods' was the last and the two families were close. Enoch was a weaver, like Abel had been and between them, Abel, Joss and Enoch, they had undertaken and achieved the task of providing enough raw cotton for Martha and Jenny Greenwood, and Mercy Butterworth to spin the yarn for the three men to weave, thus keeping the two families from the starvation which struck at so many others.

Mercy, with Tom, was a staunch believer in the movement to better the lives of the families who, like her own, were concerned with the cotton trade. Though she did not undertake the walk herself since that was not her way, her heart and soul went with Jenny Greenwood and Joss to wherever there was a meeting, or a march as they walked many miles to support men from towns where cotton was woven or spun. To Saddleworth, to Todmorden and Nelson, to Colne, Burnley and Shaw. They walked the old pack-routes, once known as 'salt-ways' because of the salt which had been carried along them, going by night, and even on one occasion moving by the Long Causeway which led from Burnley down to Halifax in Yorkshire to a meeting of hand-loom weavers in the wool trade.

There had been attempts to form a 'General Union of Trades' with men travelling from Nottingham, those in the lace trade, from Birmingham and Liverpool and weavers from Somerset, and wherever men were exploited. Joss was invited again and again to speak, to take up the leadership as he had before the arrest of Tom Butterworth, of not only the Lancashire Reformers, but of those of many counties.

Wherever he went a thousand weavers and more would be massed to hear his impassioned pleas for the support of their fellow workers who were without work but he would not, though many cried out for it, use force or resort again to machine-breaking. He told them that he was afraid that any such destruction might jeopardise the possibility that Tom would be sentenced, not to be hanged, but to transportation to the penal colonies and surely, Mercy begged him, that was better than losing his young life. He did agree to join a parade which moved through the streets of Black-burn, accompanying three thousand others in protest at the lowering, yet again, of wages, marching in regular order in files of four abreast and though all those in the ragged crowd knew of him and what he had done at the Chapman mill, he was a hero, a legend, the son of the man who had been the symbol of the dream to which most of them clung, and they would not inform on him to the militia.

The mill-owners were saying yet again that power-frames and power-looms alone could save the cotton trade and those who were made to work them longed for nothing but their return to their simple domestic life and both sides were prepared to uphold their own desires and beliefs to the bitter end. But there was to be no more rioting, Joss Greenwood said during that month of June, until Tom Butterworth's fate was decided but that did not mean their protesting voices could not be heard. The machinery which was reducing their wages, or their chances of earning any must not be tampered with, the manufacturers said, or they could not compete in the foreign markets, but the labouring class, those who marched with Joss Greenwood, would not have it. They had been told to 'stand firm, live on air, burn your looms and bear any extremity rather than work for the mill-owners' and that is what they intended to do under Joss Greenwood's leadership.

Enoch Butterworth grieved silently for his son, upheld despite his grief, in the firm conviction of his God's mercy and that Tom, should he be punished in this life for the sin he had committed, would be forgiven in the next. He prayed a good deal in those last weeks of his son's life, more than he had ever done and was filled with sorrow when Mercy would not kneel with him. He could not understand her bitterness, though he recognised that Tom had killed the soldier in her defence.

'He did it for me, Father,' Mercy said passionately. 'He didn't mean to kill him but they had . . . had me by the arms . . . they meant to . . . to harm me . . . you know what I am saying, and to stop him Tom put his arms round

84

the man's neck, holding him . . . tight . . . and . . . his neck broke!'

Her voice which had told the tale a hundred times to others, and to herself became soft with despair and Joss, who sat at the kitchen table beside her, put a gentle hand on her arm. He had seen what flesh she had fall from her small frame in the month they waited for the verdict and the dullness of guilt blight the soft grey of her eyes and he knew that since the day they had taken Tom she had not slept for more than an hour at a time.

'He killed a man, Mercy. There is no excuse for it,' Enoch Butterworth said gravely, his own eyes moist for he loved his easy-going, engaging young son, despite his laxity in the ways of Methodism. 'He has always been a good boy and hardworking. He was abstemious as our religion orders us to be and a good son and brother, but no matter what the cause he had no right to take another man's life.'

'Even in my defence, Father?' Mercy asked wildly, but the father would not agree and when they got word a week later that Tom was to hang on the following Friday and his young and healthy body was afterwards to be delivered to the surgeons for dissection, a custom with dead criminals, Enoch merely picked up his Bible and went out of the cottage door, disappearing along the valley bottom into a stand of trees by the water's edge.

Joss and Mercy stood side by side, the flesh of their ashen faces stripped away from the bones, like the wax of a melting candle, their eyes wide and staring in the black hollows into which they had fallen. The man who had brought the message looked about him uncomfortably, saying nothing more, for what was there to be said? He had been picked by the others to bear the dreadful news and now that he had done so he longed to be away from the suffering that was here.

He had gone when Mercy began to weep. Her rich, sweet mouth opened wide on a cry of anguish and though he felt as though his own heart was being torn, still beating, from his breast, Joss shivered away from the desolation of her.

She lifted her hands to her head and before he knew what she was about to do she had grasped a handful of her own hair and began to tear it, quite literally from her scalp until the blood ran.

'Jesus! . . . aah, don't . . . don't, Mercy . . .' He gripped her arms, appalled, then in the only way he knew how to stop her he pulled her against his chest, holding her writhing body to his own. She would not be still. Her cries were piercing and her face ran with tears and she threw her head from side to side in an effort to be free of him. She would hurt herself if he let her go, for her mind had fallen into a pit of suffering, from which there could be no escape for a long while and so he held her, saying nothing for she was deaf to his voice.

Through the pain, and the disbelief, since surely they would have shown clemency to one so young, another feeling was struggling to free itself from Joss Greenwood, but that was for later, that was for the day when Tom died, that would be brought forth and examined then and he would allow it to drown him in its fierceness. Now he must concentrate on this girl in his arms. That was all he was at this moment, a pair of arms to keep her from falling down and never getting up again. Not the leader, not the son of a mother who grieved for him in his wild ways, not the son of a father who had died for his beliefs but the man who must get this girl, this woman through the days of torment which would follow up to next Friday and beyond.

All night he stayed with her. She swooned against him, her emotions weakening her so dreadfully she could not stand and he carried her slight figure to the small bed upstairs where he knew she slept. He put her on it and lay down beside her, the first time he had held a woman in his arms without lust, and when she finally slept he listened to her ragged breathing and when she woke, crying harshly that was it not enough that they should hang him but they must mutilate his body as well, that he would have no grave, no resting place where she might mourn him, he soothed her again to troubled sleep.

He left her at dawn when her father returned, slipping back after dark to see her, to hold her in his arms, for it seemed only when she was close to him did she get comfort.

She was mindless in her sorrow, doing her household tasks like a machine which has no thought but will, when the correct lever is pulled, go about its function. Her father stayed with her, his face grim and haggard, but in his eyes was the serenity which his religion gave him, the true belief he could not seem to pass on to his daughter. He watched her with Joss in the candlelight, holding his hand, sitting close to him as she had once done with Tom, in the communion of two hearts which feel the same pain and he did not speak now though something would need to be said soon.

And at seven-thirty on Friday, the twenty-first of July, as Tom Butterworth's life was throttled from him, Joss Greenwood stood in her mill yard and stared into the lovely face of the woman who had helped to put the rope around his neck and though he had lifted his hand to her in some greeting, the hatred he felt, the hatred he felt for her and her father and all the men like him who exploited others for gain, hardened, became fast set and unbreakable in that moment.

Mercy was at her spinning wheel when he returned to the cottage that night. The wheel had belonged to her mother and grandmother before her going back to the days of the 'Spinning Jenny', fifty years or more. Her grandmother and mother had spun the yarn on it, with other spinsters for their husbands to weave and the movement of the wheel, the action of the bobbin and spindles soothed her tortured spirit and gave her hands something to do. Tom had worked a hand-loom at Abbotts, a mill-owner in the Penfold Valley, and with the 'piece' her father had woven on his loom on the top floor of the cottage there had been enough to feed the three of them. Like most of the hill dwellers they had a tiny smallholding to augment their earnings and with this they had managed to keep her from the work of a mill girl.

She rose as Joss came quietly into the room and at once he could see the calmness in her eyes. Enoch was there, his Bible on his knee, his pale face coloured to a healthy hue by the glow of the fire. There was fresh baked bread on the table and a pitcher of milk. There was a plate of oatcakes, one of black puddings and another of tripe.

'People have been,' she said simply and he knew that the women, destitute many of them, had managed somehow to fetch the customary condolence on this day of bereavement. It was their way up here in the barren wilderness of the moorland of sharing her sorrow and he could see she was eased by it.

'Sit down and eat. You must be hungry. See, take off your jacket and get by the fire since it's turned cold. And you've a tear in your shirt. Let me have it later and I'll mend it. You can put one of Tom's on. He won't mind, will he, Father?'

And so Tom Butterworth was put to rest, to lie in peace in his sister's heart though his body would never have a resting place.

'I came to see if you were . . . all right,' he said when he had eaten.

'Aye, I'm all right. He's . . . sleeping now and knows no more pain, or fear and it comforts me.' She made a brave attempt at a smile and reached out to touch his hand. Though she was more at peace now, despite her sorrow, knowing that Tom's suffering was done with, she still needed this man's strength. She looked into his lean, brown face, seeing the hard, flat planes of his cheeks, the fierce swoop of his dark eyebrows and deep and complex expression in his eyes, watching as they softened for her and her heart was moved with the tenderness he aroused in her. She was not clever, nor especially pretty though she supposed the velvet grey of the eyes she saw briefly in her mother's mirror each morning were well enough. She was made for the raising and caring of a family, for marriage and children and Joss could probably provide her with neither. He was concerned so passionately with the men and *their* families, with injustice and exploitation, with the cruelty done them and would have no time for what *she* needed but she loved him just the same and would have no other but him.

'Did it go well?' she asked, knowing what had been planned. She had said her own farewell to her brother up on the 'tops' he had loved, alone and inconsolable, not really knowing at what exact moment he had died but with him nevertheless when he did and it had occurred to her afterwards as she walked slowly towards her home that her father's God, a God of love, he said, had separated their family as nothing else could. They should have been together at this moment of grief, she and her father, and yet he mourned alone the son he had lost, as she did her brother. He was a good man, Enoch Butterworth, eager enough to give help to anyone who asked him for it, whatever it might be and yet now, when *she* needed him, he was off alone praying and exorting God to take their Tom into Heaven just as if it wasn't a complete certainty that he would go straight there anyway. The only one, beside the women who had come up quietly to put an arm about her, to help her healing, was Joss.

'Aye, they all stood. Brave they were, Mercy, everyone. The tacklers tried to move them, shoving them, even the children, knocking them down . . .' His voice was harsh with his hatred, '. . . but they wouldn't be moved. How they'll manage, whole families losing more than a week's pay, but they did it, all't same. They're strong, love, just like you an' me are strong when it's needed, but by God, it took a bit o' doing. Sorry, Mr Butterworth, I know you don't take kindly to hearing the Lord's name spoke lightly but sometimes it needs to be remembered that *He* seems to take *us* lightly.'

'Nay, Joss Greenwood, I'll not have things like that said in my house. The Lord is here with us. It's not for the likes of us to question His ways nor what He has put us in this earth for. Tom is . . .'

'Tom is dead, Mr Butterworth, and no matter what the

89

Lord put him on the earth for He had no right to let him suffer what he did. It was not his fault that the soldiers were waiting for us but mine, *mine*. I organised the machine breaking and it was *me* they were there for. Tom paid the price, and Mercy here but you can tell your God the next time you speak to him that they'll not go unpunished, those who took his life. He's a strange God, that one of yours, Mr Butterworth, that lets some men live on the fat of the land while children, no more than babies really, grow old and crippled before they reach the age of ten in the bloody mills. Have you seen them, Mr Butterworth, have you? Little old men and women, they are, with their legs bent under them and their shoulders stooped, coughing their lungs inside out with the dust? Their arms are broken and their eyes taken out and I heard tell of one or two, pauper children nobody gives a damn about, who killed themselves rather than go back to their machines. Little girls get dragged into the machinery by their hair, they get headaches and pains in their bones and all they want to do when the factory bell goes is fall on to the nearest pile of waste and sleep until it rings again to tell them it's time to get back to work. No wild beast treats its young as we treat ours, Mr Butterworth. They are paid, along with the women, wages which have been reduced to starvation level and the pauper children, the "apprentices" as the mill-owners quaintly term them, do not even get that. They work sixteen hours a day in stench, in heat which would fell a grown man, forced by the blows of the overlooker to keep going. They are fed on food you wouldn't give a pig. They try to run away, some of them and so they are chained to their machines, boys and girls alike and I'm sure you are not unaware of the fate of many of the girls. They are slaves, Mr Butterworth, no more than slaves and we should be ashamed that we have allowed it to happen, so I say this to you. Though Tom is dead I know he would be glad, if he had to die so young, that it was in trying to free these children. He didn't die for nothing, I tell myself and I suppose it comforts me to think so. He died to get better conditions for these little slaves, to give them an education so that they can lift themselves up from where they have been kicked, and the men and women who are slaves with them. I could let Tom's death stop me, since, as you seem to think and I agree with you, that I am responsible in some measure for it but I will go on. I will fight and fight and *kill* if I have to, to stop this bloody mass murder, this torture of innocent children and if you, or your God, has anything to say on the subject then let me hear it now.'

His breath heaved in his chest and his eyes glared like those of some tormented beast and Enoch Butterworth stepped back from him, not afraid but astounded to see such passion in a man. Since his father had died at the Battle of Peterloo, Joss Greenwood had become wild and uncontrollable. He had gone about with other fighting radicals, stirring up the people against the manufacturers, speaking of injustice and reform and he had done it hot-bloodedly as one would expect of so young a man and Enoch had not liked it, nor the involvement of his own son. He believed himself in freedom for all men, though he had heard tell that the great religious leader, John Wesley himself had gone so far as to recommend child labour as a means of preventing youthful vice and really, there was something to be said for that.

No, Joss Greenwood was anathema to a man like himself for he seemed in some way, though he fought to right the wrongs done his fellow to go against everything Enoch Butterworth believed in. Joss Greenwood had never worked in a factory and neither had Enoch and so he supposed they could neither speak from first-hand experience as operatives, as men who had suffered the factory system. Joss had worked a hand-loom all his life in his own cottage. They had kept a pig and a few hens and grew vegetables. Martha and her daughter still spun the yarn on their domestic spinning wheels and young Charlie could 'card' now and they lurched, like many families, from crisis to crisis, but they managed. Joss Greenwood had no first-hand knowledge of labouring in a mill when he ranted of injustice and Enoch was not awfully convinced that Joss fought, not for the cause he vowed he believed in, but for the fighting itself. And Enoch did not like to be taken to task by a bit of a lad who knew nowt about 'owt in his opinion. Neither did he like the way he made free with Mercy, his daughter. A good girl, she was, half daft with grief these last few days and not knowing what she was about but he'd not see her handled again by Joss Greenwood like she had been this past week. Not without a ring on her finger as was decent.

Joss had regained his composure now. He had moved to stand at the small window which looked out at the slope of the hillside across the narrow valley. A pack-horse bridge crossed the stream below Enoch's cottage, the track leading from it vanishing into the carpet of heather which climbed it. A blue shadow moved down from the tops, sinking visibly until it reached the valley bottom, then climbing again as a stretched band of cloud moved across the moor. He could hear a dipper call as it circled its nest against a high slab of limestone, alarmed by a buzzard which hung in the sky. He could smell the aniseed fragrance of the Sweet Cicely which submerged the drystone wall which surrounded Enoch's cottage and the beauty and peace almost destroyed the calm he had forced upon himself. Today a young man had died quite savagely at the hands of the hangman. He would never see this again, nor smell the wild flowers nor hear the cry of the bird and it almost broke Joss's heart to think of it. But he must go on. He had been fond of Tom Butterworth in a casual, masculine way and he felt the same way about Tom's sister. His responsibility to them both had kept him here this last week but now it was over and he must get on with his work. He must go wherever he was needed to organise mass meetings and strikes, marches and protests which would lead to the extinction of the system which had created the men, and their mills who were destroying the vast multitude of the working men and women of this realm.

Enoch Butterworth stood up slowly, his great shaggy head of grey hair turning with some deliberation to his daughter. His face was set in a mould of grim determination for though he was not a man with a forceful will, being too engrossed in the unworldly rather than the practical, he could be trenchant on matters which concerned what was right, and decent.

'Go outside, our Mercy,' he said firmly. 'There's summat Joss and I must talk on. See to the hens, now look sharp, there's a good girl.'

'But father . . .' Mercy's face was bewildered.

''Tis man's talk, lass. 'Twill take no more than a minute or so.' His face gentled for the girl, who was as pale as death itself, with great dark, sorrowing eyes sunk deep in their sockets. She was brave, fighting the desolation and harshness of her brother's death. She had got through this day with the steadfast strength of a north country woman who had the capacity to bear all she must. She would recover, he knew that, but he'd not have her trifled with, no, not by his new Majesty himself!

'We have to say a word about the lass, Joss Greenwood,' he said sternly when she had left the room. His eyes followed her as she wandered across the plot of coarse grass to the drystone wall and climbed up to sit on it, gazing sadly across the stream to the hills beyond.

'The lass?' Joss was clearly puzzled.

'Aye. There's been a deal of . . . of contact between the two of you these past few days and I'll have to ask you your intentions, my lad. When . . . when we heard about Tom . . .' he swallowed painfully and a spasm of anguish crossed his face, '. . . well, I'll be honest with you, I was . . . knocked sideways and I . . . I had to get up to the . . . to where I could be on me own with God.' It was said simply and Joss was finally made aware that Enoch's God was as real to him as the girl who sat on the wall outside the cottage, perhaps even more so.

'Well . . . maybe I was at fault, leaving her, but she was with you . . . Tom's friend and . . . well, to tell the truth I wasn't thinking straight. When I got back you were in her bed, Joss Greenwood, and that means but one thing to a

93

man like me!' His voice and face were like granite, accusing, but ready to forgive as his God said he must if Joss was ready to do the right thing.

Joss had an urgent desire to laugh and if the circumstances had been less tragic he might have done so for Mercy Butterworth was nothing to him *in that way*! She was Tom's sister, for God's sake, no more and though he had held her through that dreadful night, soothed her desolation and absorbed her shock and disbelief, she might have been his own sister, or mother or any woman who needed his pity. She was soft and sweet, gentle as a dove, good and innocent as a child and that was all. A child to whom he had given comfort and protection when it was needed.

'Did you hear what I said, lad? I'll not see my lass dishonoured, not by you or any man. They all know hereabouts the way things have been between you . . .'

'Between us?'

'. . . aye and I want to know the way of it before you take yourself off again on your path of violence. I'll admit you're not the man I would have chosen for our Mercy but 'appen a wife and children will take the fire from you. You an' I can make a livin' wi' the looms your father left. With your mother an' sister an' my lass to spin, with young Charlie, an' Daisy, when she's old enough to "comb" and "card" if you shape yersen we can weave a piece or two each week. One of us can fetch the raw cotton from Manchester like we did when your Pa was alive an' take the finished cloth to the Cloth Hall in Crossfold. That young brother of yours is growing and between us we . . .'

Joss began to laugh then. He could see that Enoch was deeply affronted but he could not stop himself. Enoch Butterworth was mapping out the lives of not only Joss Greenwood but his whole family as well and though it was far from amusing he found he could not stop since the sheer effrontery of the man was scarcely to be believed. Marriage! He was talking about marriage between himself and Mercy with the absolute certainty that Joss was bound to agree. And he had not even kissed the girl! He had not even

94

*thought* of kissing the girl, *ever*, when he and Tom had skylarked about the place – a hundred years ago, surely? – and she had watched him with a flush to her cheek and a shine to her eye. He had sensed in a casual kind of way that Mercy Butterworth *liked* him – he would admit to no more than that – and now it was marriage. *Marriage!* It was sheer lunacy. His life could not allow for wife, nor child, not for years, if ever. He was dedicated to . . . Oh Jesus, God . . . he could not be saddled with . . . even if he loved her . . . she was sweet . . . and . . . but Enoch was not smiling and he had, he admitted it, shared her bed with her that night but with what innocence. It had been no more than pity for the terrible grief she suffered, that was all.

'I . . . I'm sorry, really I am, Mr Butterworth. It is no laughing matter . . . but . . . when you spoke of what there was between Mercy and myself, well, I couldn't help myself. You see there is nothing, she will tell you herself. She was distraught, you must understand that, and I couldn't leave her. She was alone, which was your fault, not mine and I couldn't leave her. She was out of her mind, for God's sake . . .'

He found he was beginning to raise his voice for Enoch was looking at him, grim-faced and disbelieving. 'It's true, Mr Butterworth, we did nothing . . .'

'Are you sayin' you don't want my girl, Joss Greenwood?'

'No, I'm not saying that though . . .'

Enoch's face cleared. 'Well then, a day must be set for the wedding.'

'Wedding! Jesus Christ . . .!'

'Now then, lad, before you become a member of this family you'll 'ave to get it into your 'ead that I'll not 'ave the Lord's name . . .'

'For God's sake, man, I can't marry your daughter, or anybody's daughter. I lead the life of a gypsy and that's not for a woman. Tramping from village to village, going to meetings and organising protests and strikes. Living as best I can on the cloth I manage to weave, when I can. My mother will continue to spin what raw cotton I can fetch and with Charlie as he gets older and when I am able, I'll weave a piece. It will keep her and the young 'uns fed but our Jenny'll have to go into mill. Aye . . .' He grimaced painfully and Enoch was made aware of how much it pained him to say it. '. . . She suggested it and she knows that if I'm to carry on then that's what she must do. She's a good lass, a sensible lass and she is helping in the only way she can. But I'm fighting a bloody war here, Mr Butterworth, and don't you glare at me because you know that's what it is, and I must be free to get on with it. Don't you think I wouldn't like to have a home, a wife and family, like any other man but what chance have I of making a girl like Mercy happy? She is . . . the loveliest girl I know and brave too, but I couldn't ask her to come with me. Good God, I'm a soldier and if they catch me I shall go to gaol. I never know from one day to the next where I shall be and it's no way for a woman to live. Not a woman like Mercy who's never been used to . . .'

'I'll live it, Joss, and right gladly.'

They both turned and there she was, smiling shyly, radiant and blushing and it was clear from her expression that she had heard no more than Joss's last words. She moved to stand before him and her eyes glowed with her love.

'I'll go anywhere with you, Joss,' she said simply and put her hand in his.

7

Barker Chapman's spinning and weaving mills were plain and utilitarian, the two spinning mills being six storeys high with small windows of clouded glass. The windows were not for looking out of, nor even to let in much light, the object being to hold within the buildings the moisture and heat needed for their economic running. The buildings existed for one reason only, to make money and were not for show, as some owners made *their* concerns, putting in walls of shining Accrington brick to proclaim their prosperity. The Chapman mills were four square, sturdy and ugly.

His two weaving sheds were of one storey only since the six floors in each mill which contained his spinning concerns fed the appetite of one floor of weaving. Those who were put, as many children were when they grew too big for working beneath the spinning frames, into the weaving sheds were immediately aware of the appalling noise. The spinning frames 'sang' as they performed their function but the weaving looms clacked so loudly they caused actual physical pain, and even deafness. The inability to hear even what one's closest neighbour was saying was overcome by the weavers' knack of learning to lip-read, known locally as 'mee-mawing'. An experienced worker could converse with a friend across a busy shed without uttering a sound, if she could avoid the 'tackler's' eye since the fine for 'talking' was twopence!

There was no heating as none was needed but the sheds were badly ventilated and the reek of the gas from Barker Chapman's recently installed and extremely modern gas-lighting made the atmosphere almost unbearable. It had been known for operatives to bore a small hole in the window frame in order to suck in a breath of fresh air from the outside but when they were discovered, those concerned had been dismissed on the spot.

Barker Chapman had an agreement with his overlookers. 'My daughter is to come down to the workroom tomorrow, Ellis,' or 'Miss Chapman wishes to check that cloth we are weaving, Gribb,' and the men would know to a nicety what was implied. It had begun on the day he had taken her there for the first time, the day on which his first power-frame had been wrecked and had continued ever since. He had more than two dozen of the new machines now, each one operated by a woman for it was they, and their children who were the labour force now in demand. They had more quickly adapted to mill discipline and conditions. They were nimble and quick-fingered, cheap and more easily exploited than men, but the sight of an emaciated, probably deformed child, a gaunt, coughing woman, an almost naked man in the weaving shed was not one for a lady's eyes. On the days she went down there only the sturdiest were presented, women who were young and still bonny, older children who were supple and, not having worked in the mill, like the pauper children, since the age of four and five, had a bit of flesh on their straight limbs. No nasty sights for Miss Chapman, then, but cheerfully smiling like monkeys, presentably dressed and clean, the women told to be respectful and in good humour and the men decent in their dress.

She was at her desk in the corner of her father's office comparing the quality between two pieces of cloth which had been sent over from the warehouse for Barker Chapman's approval. The 'cut-looker' had examined the finished length of cloth, looking for faults in the weaving. These were called 'floats' and any man found to have a float in his work was fined, but this was a splendid piece of cloth and Kit was pleased with it. She would put it to one side for her father to see when he returned from Broadbank where he had been called to look at a loom which the overlooker reported was not working as it should. It was powered by the new steam engine just installed and since it had been put in had to be stopped every few minutes to adjust the threads as they unrolled. The threads were not strong enough to undergo the weaving, her father had been told, and so, saying he would be gone no more than an hour he had taken the carriage to see for himself.

The sharp tap at the door was followed immediately by its opening, as though the man who entered had no time for the courtesies towards his employer's daughter his position as manager demanded. His face was the colour of chalk and his eyes snapped with some nervous tension. He flung himself into the room, turning without closing the door in the direction of her father's desk which had been moved into the bay of the window to make room for the one she used.

'Mr Chapman, sir, can you come at once. The . . .'

He stopped, quite bewildered when he saw his employer's empty chair behind the desk where he was usually to be found. He turned distractedly and as if for the first time noticed Kit. 'Oh, Miss Chapman . . . I was just looking for Mr Chapman . . . I didn't see you there for the minute.' He tried a smile.

'Gribb? Is there something wrong?' She smiled herself, putting down the swatch of cloth she held, straightening her back. She had been at her desk since six o'clock that morning going carefully over the weekly accounting, checking the figures with those for the same week the previous year and feeling gratified by the growth of production and profit. The new power-looms had made an enormous difference to their output of cloth and she really thought it was high time another new weaving shed was built as her father had suggested. There was land and to spare at Broadbank for a third building and now they were to finish the woven cloth themselves they might at last call themselves complete manufacturers. The whole procedure of producing a length of cloth, from the raw bale of cotton which was opened in the blow room for cleaning and blending, through carding, combing, spinning, weaving and now the wet and dry treatments such as bleaching and mercerising was to be done in the Chapman mills and every farthing of profit was to be put in Chapman pockets!

There were almost a thousand cotton mills in the land now and trade was excellent. The machine breakers who had caused so much trouble in the past appeared to have given up the fight and nothing had been heard of them since the murderer of the soldier had been brought to justice at Lancaster. The Manchester cotton weavers had sent a petition to Parliament complaining of the low wages they received, no more than subsistence level they said, and sometimes not even that, but Sir Robert Peel assured the House, after making enquiries, that the weavers lived in comparative comfort. So what had they to complain of, he asked. Those from Stockport, who had sent in a similar petition, had been similarly treated. The machinery was starting a new and prosperous era and now was the time to expand, Kit was convinced of it. There were women and children knocking on the factory gates demanding work, and men too, now that their hand-looms were obsolete. They couldn't keep up with the factories, with men like her father who had cornered the market and though many of those same men were willing to work the new power-looms in Chapman's weaving shed it appeared that strength was not needed, as it had been with the old hand-looms and women, who were more submissive and manageable, might be employed instead. Women who were not inclined to wreck their machines and would be more agreeable to take whatever was offered in order to feed their children!

She stood up and moved round her desk, looking enquiringly at Gribb. He turned about him as though expecting her father to be hiding in some corner then, on seeing she was alone he smiled nervously and began to back out of the room, bowing in a most unaccustomed way as he did so.

'Gribb? What is it? Did you want Mr Chapman?'

'Yes, Miss Chapman, but it can wait, really . . .'

'What is it?' she repeated. 'You seem to be in somewhat of a dilemma. I'm sure whatever it is can be put to rights.'

She waited patiently for the manager to tell her what it was that had him in such an obvious state of panic but he had gained the open door by now and was reaching for it with the manifest intention of going through it.

'Gribb!' Her voice was sharp. 'In my father's absence I am his deputy as you well know. Speak up, man, and tell me what you came to tell my father.'

'Really, Miss Chapman, it is nothing. We can deal with

it. Some small disturbance in the spinning room . . .'

'Then if it is small and you can deal with it why should you come to fetch my father?'

'Well . . . Mr Chapman likes to be . . . told when . . .'

'When what, Gribb?'

'Nay, Miss Chapman. T'isn't for a lass like yourself to be seeing.' The man was so upset he went so far as to forget her position as his employer's daughter, calling her a lass, for that was what she was to him, no more than a lass with no rights to be here in his opinion. If Mr Chapman, who had given strict orders about the state of the working areas, and the women and children working in them when his daughter visited, knew that she had been called there when they were not ready for her, he would fire the lot of them on the spot but she was already walking towards the door, brushing past him and descending the stairs to the yard.

'Miss Chapman, please, there is really no need. A small accident and we can deal with it, really. Do go back to your office, Miss Chapman and as soon as your father returns if you would be so good as to tell him, or better yet, send for me and I can explain . . .'

'Do stop chattering, Gribb. If there has been an accident it must be dealt with and if Mr Chapman is not here . . .'

'Well, he wouldn't necessarily come into the mill, Miss Chapman. Me and the overlookers can tackle it normally, but Mr Chapman has to be told, of course, and then . . . perhaps . . . compensation . . .'

'Compensation! For a small accident?' Kit turned to look at him in astonishment, picturing a bruised shoulder or a cut arm for there was often a minor injury in the huge rooms where machinery was unguarded and children were careless.

The long room was filled in every conceivable space with humming machinery, and it was hot. There were women, drenched with sweat and smelling quite badly, tending spinning mules, and everywhere, small children, almost naked in the intense humidity, ran about from machine to machine, or crawled beneath it. The shrill voices of the

101

women pierced the air with strident urgency, calling to the tiny 'piecers' to mend the threads as they broke. A scrap of humanity, a girl, Kit thought, her face quite blank, her eyes black holes in it, her frame stunted, crept out at Kit's feet, dragging from beneath a machine an enormous pile of cotton waste and oily dust. She did not look up nor get to her feet but crawled along, like a small, wizened animal, between the rows of machinery, pulling the filthy mass behind her until she reached the corner where she piled it on to a heap already begun. An overlooker, unaware that Kit was watching, idly struck her a blow across her narrow back with his thonged strap and she flinched and crawled faster until she was safely beneath the flying shafts and straps of the spinning mule again.

A woman began to cough, her thin figure bent double, her face, suffused with blood, turning to the colour of a plum. Her shoulders shook and she put out a hand to steady herself, lifting the other to rub at her nose and mouth. She tried to spit and Kit felt her own stomach move in a spasm of nausea, then the overlooker who had still not seen his employer's daughter clinging — it was her only means of support just then — to the door frame, pulled cruelly at the woman's arm.

'Get to't corner, yer daft bitch,' and the woman, still crouched almost double, left her machine and staggered to the corner of the room. There was a bucket there, and beside it a jug in which there was a thin, yellow liquid. The woman, still choking and spitting, reached for the jug and began to drink its contents, then, turning hastily, vomited into the bucket. She straightened up, wiped her mouth and sweating face on a bit of waste and, the whole incident taking no more than thirty seconds, ran back to her machine.

Kit turned to Gribb and though she said nothing, her grey-white face and staring eyes asked the question.

'It's the "fly",' Gribb explained apologetically.

'The fly?' Her voice was no more than a whisper.

'It fills their mouths and noses. From the yard. When

102

they can't get rid of it by coughing or . . . well, they drink mustard and water. It makes them sick and . . . they get it up.'

'Dear God!'

'They take no harm, Miss Chapman, none at all. 'Tis better than choking on it.'

She could not answer and the overlooker, the one who had struck the child, came running then, his own face appalled, at what she had time to wonder, for surely he was well used to what had just happened, and for a moment she had the distinct impression he was about to take her arm and bundle her from the room. His face was thunderstruck and he brushed women and children roughly aside to reach her.

'Miss Chapman, really, you should not be here.' It was the man called Ellis, the one who had offered on the day of the hanging to remove the crowd who had gathered in the yard. She had recovered her composure somewhat and though her eyes still darted feverishly about the room, confounded by the sight of so many whey-faced, stoop-shouldered, undernourished and oddly shaped women and children, where once they had been clean, well formed, even managing a smile or two when she had been before, she had found her lost wits, and voice!

'Why not, pray?' she answered him. 'In my father's absence I am responsible for the mill, and, as a matter of interest, may I ask where on God's earth did these . . . these workers come from. None of them look fit to be in charge of a machine and while you are at it please be so kind as to tell me what is going on. I have been told of an accident so I would be obliged if you would lead me to it . . .'

'Oh no, Miss Chapman, no. Your father would not be best pleased if you were to go up there . . .'

'Up where? What has happened?' She began to walk in the direction his vague gesture had indicated and short of laying their hands on her there was nothing the two men could do to stop her. She strode past ceaselessly toiling women who were hard pressed to keep up with the machines they operated for the spindles and bobbins moved quickly and needed constant alertness. Their feet were never still, their hands the same and their eyes appeared haunted for the mules must never stop except for the cleaning of them which took place during their own 'rest' periods. The machines were often turned on early and switched off late, 'cribbing' it was called so that they were forced to work extra, precious minutes for which they were not paid. The spindles whirred and the hot smell of oil and grease clamped shut Kit's mouth and clogged her nostrils and when she came to the end of the long row of machines, turning to the corner of the room where a group of men stood she was not at first certain what it was she saw. She had been told there had been an accident, though not of what kind for the manager and overlooker were afraid to disclose the details. Mr Chapman would have dealt with it, privately, seeing to the family, if the victim had one. A few shillings for tongues that needed to be kept silent, though really none would dare speak up for fear of losing their own job.

'What is it?' she said sharply, moving towards the group, three or four overlookers and another manager. 'What has happened?' As she spoke she slipped in something on the floor and Ellis put out his hand to steady her. It was dim in the corner since the windows were high and let in little light but what there was fell on the floor and she looked down, narrowing her eyes to see what was there.

It was red, bright and shining and thick. A lot of it, seeping into the wooden floorboards along with the oil and sweat and other unmentionable substances which were deposited upon it. She looked at it and knew that somehow she must raise her eyes to meet what was waiting for her. She heard a child cry out somewhere behind her, the voice sharp above the sound of the machinery and a man's voice could be heard telling someone, 'it was for his own good for if he dozed off and tumbled into the machine like' . . . then she lifted her head slowly and forced herself not to flinch as she looked at what they had laid on the blood-soaked pile of cotton waste.

A small boy. Perhaps five or six. His face was like paper, white and fine, the skin clear beneath the grime. His eyes were closed and she could see the blue veins on his lids and the long sweep of his brown lashes. His hair was a soft tumble of baby curls and his small mouth was open, just as though in sleep he dreamed of something which pleased him. He was not, of course, sleeping, for at the end of his thin arms were no hands, just the jagged . . . Oh dear Lord, dear, dear Lord . . . white bone . . . blood . . . blood . . .

She stood rigid and though she felt the food she had eaten at breakfast rise rapidly to fill her throat she made herself, *steeled* herself not to turn away. This was her father's mill, *her* mill and what went on in it was their responsibility. She must not faint or look away. She must not show signs of female weakness or they would shrug their shoulders and ask one another what else could one expect of a woman? She had chosen this. Her father had given it to her and she must accept it. *Every part of it!*

'What happened?' she asked and was quite amazed that her lips, which she thought to be set forever in a clamped line of self-control, could form the words.

The still life group of men sprang to attention together, their astounded expressions slipping simultaneously into ones of horror that she should see this, of dread at what Mr Chapman would say when he heard, not of the accident but of his daughter's witnessing the result, and of anxiety that they might lose their jobs over it. The child had simply been in the wrong place at the wrong time. No one's fault, not even his own. He had slipped on the oil, put out his hands to save himself from falling and . . . well, the machinery had been waiting there, as it always waited for those who were not constantly alert. He had been dragged into it and only for the quickness of his overlooker, might have suffered far worse mutilation than the loss of his hands. He would have still lost his life, of course, since the flow of blood could not be staunched, but . . . well, life was cheap and it was an ill wind for there would be another to take his place before the day was out.

They told her, their tongues clipping their words in their effort to explain what had happened as blame was laid at everyone's door but their own.

'Who is he?' she asked abruptly, allowing herself to look away now.

'Pardon?' they said, not quite understanding.

'What was his name?' They did not know of any since he had come only that week from Liverpool, they said, in a waggon filled with parish children, half of whom knew neither their own name, nor where they had originated. It seemed there was no one to grieve for him.

'Cover him decently,' and when one threw a bit of sacking carelessly over the pathetic body she turned angrily, her eyes ablaze with some emotion even she did not understand. She sent a man to her office, quite astounded he was and when he had put the soft shawl he had brought into her hands she knelt by the boy's side and covered him, gently patting the warmth and compassion about him, perhaps the first his young body had ever known. Then, standing, turning away, she walked past the women who did not even glance sideways from their frames. Past the silent, blank-eyed children, none of whom seemed unduly concerned about the dead child, nor even to be aware that he was dead. They were like ghosts who are forced to haunt the place in which they had met their end, longing to lie down and rest, simply to fade away, but unable to do other than what they did.

A young girl came through the door as Kit put out her hand to open it. The girl stood back, allowing her to pass but she did not hang her head, nor even lower her eyes respectfully as the others did, but stared, quite unafraid it seemed, by the appearance of her employer's daughter. She was slender but her bones were decently covered by her flesh. Her appearance was neat, her hair drawn back into, surprisingly, a cheerful knot of red ribbon. She was dark, her skin fine and retaining a colour which said she was used to the outdoor life. But it was her eyes which drew Kit Chapman's startled glance for they were a shining pearl grey, pale and cat-like, gleaming and bold. She was no more than sixteen or so, pretty, and those eyes bored into hers with unconcealed contempt.

'He's dead, then.' It was not a question but a statement of fact.

'I beg your pardon?'

'The little lad. The one who had his hands ripped off.' It was said brutally, meant to hurt, to accuse.

'Yes, I'm afraid he is.' Why should she feel the need to answer this impudent girl? She had no idea why she did, nor why she had the urge to explain that she had been unaware of the true conditions in which her father's spinners worked. That she had heard of their grievances (as who hadn't?), but she had imagined them to be exaggerated, blown up out of all proportion in their demand for higher wages. Profit must be made. Production costs must be pared down to make it, and if they could not compete in foreign markets they would *all* be out of a job for the mill would close and then what would they do, all those clamouring for a better way of life? Surely any job was better than none and all the time her thoughts fluttered like moths inside her head the girl stood silently by to watch her.

Then, 'I ran to fetch someone. A woman I know. She has a way with herbs, potions, splints and such. I thought if she could stop the bleeding . . . but they said he was gone so I'm on me way back to me machine. Of course, they'll stop me pay an' fine me into the bargain for leaving without permission but I couldn't just stand there and watch the poor little beggar bleed to death.'

'No.'

The girl's eyes never faltered. They were filled with a fierce, quite devastating emotion, hot sparks of it flashing across the space between them, striking at Kit with the force of a physical blow. There was an angry contempt, an animosity, an unwillingness it seemed to Kit even to share the bit of space in which they both stood, so great was her aversion.

'This wouldn't have happened if you'd fenced them machines, you know that, don't you?'

'I beg your pardon?' she said.

'And so you should, or someone's, for you're the one to blame, you and your father. You should certainly be begging that little lad's pardon for takin' his life, not that it was worth much to him, or to anyone else for that matter, since he lived like an animal and was worked like one.'

'I'd be obliged if you would step aside and let me pass.' Her voice was cold. Her own anger was moving inside her, a somewhat guilty anger for should she really be feeling it in the face of what she had just seen? But it was at this impudent girl it was directed. No matter what had happened she was merely a mill-hand and had certainly no right to be laying blame at her employer's door, not if she wanted to keep her job, nor to be accusing her father of neglect. Fencing the machines indeed, when it was well known that the wooden casings which some of the other idealistic mill-owners had considered, were a fire hazard and therefore more dangerous than the machines themselves.

'Of course! I'm right sorry to have held you up. You'll be busy making the funeral arrangements, I dare say, an' havin' a whip round for his family, if he's got any.'

'I fail to see what any of this has got to do with you. Have you no work to go to? If your machine is standing idle I'm sure someone can be easily found to operate it.'

'You don't like to hear the truth then? You don't want to see what's going on in your father's mill, under his *own bloody nose*. You don't want to be reminded that the elegant dress you're wearing was bought with the sweat, aye, an' the blood, of bairns like that one in there.'

'Let me pass.'

'No, I can see you don't, but if you took a stroll round the mills and the weaving sheds now an' again, you couldn't avoid it but you wouldn't like that, would you?'

'I could have you turned off for insolence and . . .'

'Aye, that you could,' but the girl was not afraid, only drunk with her own contemptuous loathing.

108

'What is your name?'

'Jenny Greenwood.'

They separated then, one to her machine and another eight hours of racket and stench and heat, to the bucket in the corner and ten minutes' respite to eat her 'dinner' at midday, the other to the peace and solitude, the comfort of her office, the order of her desk, the coffee served in a china cup by Mrs Plank and the certain knowledge that whenever she chose she could order her carriage and go home.

At the end of the week Jenny Greenwood was surprised to find that her wage, all six shillings and sixpence of it had not been 'docked' of the fine she had expected.

That night Katherine and Barker Chapman had their first argument.

'It cannot be necessary, father,' she finished after she had given him a graphic account of what she had seen that day, and though he had heard it from Gribb, his manager, who had thought it expedient to put forth his own version first, Barker listened politely as was his way.

'Those children were deformed . . .'

'Most are deformed when I take them on, Kit. Their parents are often not as diligent in feeding them as they should. You have only to tour the town on a Saturday night after they have been paid to see them lolling in gutters and on doorsteps. Gin, my dear! That is what they spend their money on and not on nourishing food for their children.'

'But they are so young. Surely they should not be forced . . .'

'Forced! Who told you they are forced?' Her father smiled and his voice was smooth. 'They beat on my gate every day, mothers and their children begging me to employ them, more than I can take, but I let them in, for really, their families need the wages or they would starve . . .'

'But surely . . . there must be some way to allow them to . . .'

She faltered and her hands gripped one another in her

lap but her father reached out and placed his own about them, a rare demonstration of his regard for her.

'To what, my dear?'

'To work, if they must, but in some decent occupation.'

Her father stiffened and withdrew his hands, sitting back in his armchair. His eyes became steely in his grim face and his mouth was tight-lipped with outrage.

'Are you saying that the work I offer these people is disreputable in some way, Katherine. That it is not honest labour for which they are paid?'

'No, no, of course not, but that child . . .' She could not shut out the image of that waxen-faced child, the blue-veined vulnerability of his closed eyes and her own voice was harsh, '. . . the one who died, he came from the workhouse in Liverpool, I was told and really, Father . . .'

'There are hundreds of children who are taken from the workhouse, where, let me assure you, my dear Kit, they are not as well treated as in my mill. Do you not think, if they are to work, and work they must, either here with us, in the mines or up the chimneys, they are not best served in a factory. The work is not heavy. They are warm and fed and clothed. They have Sunday free and many are taken to Church where their religious needs are catered for.' It was evident that Barker Chapman was making a great effort to be patient.

'I know all that, Father, but . . .' She knew what her father said made sense, that it was all perfectly true but she had received a bad shock this morning and she was still flayed by the sights she had seen. They must work, all of them, women and children or they would starve but the look of animal-like docility, the feeling that inside each skull was nothing more than the intelligence to move hands and feet in the necessary operation of the machine; the weariness, the dull acceptance, the very appearance, though she knew her thoughts to be exaggerated, of dying by inches, had harrowed her. Were they alive, but breathing and eating a slow death? Did they long to see, did they even *know* of a flower, the green of the grass, the vast blue . . .

Dear God, she must stop this torturing of herself and listen to what her father was saying.

'Kit, my dear, do not look at me with those reproachful eyes.' He smiled and the face she had come to know so well, was smooth, untroubled. 'Look at it from another point of view. These children are learning a trade. They are apprenticed to us and at the end of their indentures will call themselves spinners, or weavers and, if they wish, will be at liberty to go anywhere they choose, anywhere spinning and weaving is done. They will owe me nothing.'

'Yes, I know that to be true but the child . . .'

'Katherine.' His voice clipped through hers and she looked up, startled.

'Yes . . .'

'Perhaps I have made a mistake.'

'A mistake?'

'In believing you to be capable of running a mill.'

'I don't understand.' Her voice was uncertain and her eyes were wide.

'Yes! You do! If you cannot accept that there will be a certain amount of . . . disagreeable, even distasteful aspects to this business world we are in then perhaps it would be advisable for you to return to the one which is really yours. The one your mother and her friends occupy. I am running a business, not a charitable institution. I must do it in the way which makes the most profit or I will go under. I am asked to employ not only men and women, but their children. No one else is small enough to go under the machines or I would not take them since I care for it as little as you. They are necessary, Kit. The machinery is dangerous, I grant you that but the overlookers are there to ensure the younger children do not fall into it . . .'

'Then what was Ellis doing to allow that child to be so near the machine?' Her voice was passionate and she reached out to him with her hands. She had been appalled by her father's words, knowing that he meant what he said and she could not bear to return to the empty life she had once led but she could not let the horror of this morning

111

go by her without a word. She knew it was true. Profit must be made but not, surely, with the crippling and deaths of young children.

Her father stood up and moved towards the door, his face cold, pinched almost, for he was deeply disappointed. He had known from the start that the mill floor, the weaving sheds would upset her but he had hoped, with time and the growing fascination she found in the business, the satisfaction of knowing that one day it would be hers, she would grow to accept it, as they all did. He went as seldom as he could himself, to the work floors, leaving the managers to see to the running of them. He knew exactly how much each machine produced but he really did not care to see how that production was achieved and Katherine must learn to be the same, or stay away from it altogether.

'If you are to take that attitude then there is no more to be said. I shall go alone to the mill tomorrow and you can remain with your mother and . . . sew, or whatever women do all day long.'

'Father . . . don't . . . please . . .'

'I can see no alternative, my dear.'

'I could not stand it, not again.'

'Then . . .' He shrugged his shoulders expressively, then turned back to her. 'I cannot change the system, Kit, whether you are there or not. The managers run the sheds and I run the business. If you are not prepared to do the same, then you must stay away from it.'

'Father . . . please . . .' She stood up and her lovely silken gown fell about her slender figure. It was the colour of a golden guinea, soft and shining, enhancing the pale gold of her own skin. Her glossy hair was held in place at the back of her head with a looped knot of gold satin ribbons and he thought, for a brief and marvelling moment, what a waste it was to put such splendour in a mill, in the masculine environment his son, if he had bred one, would have taken, since there was no doubt she would be an asset to grace any man's table, his bed, as the breeder of magnificent children. Her face was lit by the intensity of her emotions.

112

'Father, I cannot just ignore what I have seen. It has been a . . . shock. I must be allowed to . . . to consider it. There is the funeral to be seen to . . .'

'Funeral!' Her father laughed harshly. 'What funeral?'

'But the child . . .'

'Is already buried.'

'Dear God . . .'

'As you say, Kit, dear God indeed!' Now, if you will excuse me I shall leave you to . . . consider, was that the word? . . . your future. You must, of course, do as you think best. If you are not in the carriage tomorrow morning at the usual time I will understand but remember, whatever you decide, nothing will change in my mill!'

He closed the door quietly behind him.


## 8


He saw the dogs first. They were lying, one on either side of the path, low in the coarse grass, their ears flat, absolutely motionless, two silent menacing forms barely visible against the harsh black and grey of the winter landscape.

It had snowed in the night, a light dusting which had laid a pattern of lace on the tops but he was below the snowline, half way between the peaks and the valley floor and there was nothing here but tough, gritstone rocks, the harsh remains of summer heather and bracken, brown and snapping underfoot and the endless miles of walls, little more than piles of stones which had come with enclosure when much land along the moorland fringes had been turned into a field system.

It was bitterly cold with an east wind blowing straight from Scandinavia whipping across the Pennines, searching out every patched and thin place in his jacket and breeches.

He shivered and clutched his arms about himself, then beat them fiercely across his chest to get the blood coursing, stamping his feet on the ground as he walked for surely they were frozen solid inside his clogs.

It was steep where he walked and the upland track of causey stones, almost obliterated now, but once used by pack-horses, was slippery, the moisture which coated it frozen during the night. A thin mist lingered in the valley beneath him, wisping about the oak woods, leafless and skeletal and outlining the stately conifers. He could see the roofs of a cottage or two and the shape of Abbott's weaving mill but it was Sunday and, apart from the cleaning of the machinery by the pauper children Abbott employed, there would be no work done this day. In front of him, behind him and above rolled the vast expanse of moor, rising and falling in splendid isolation to the far horizon, its dark and sombre mass flecked with snow. Here and there where water had settled were sheets of ice and down through the mist patterns he could see the dull gleam of the flowing river in the valley.

He hurried on, picking up his heels and stamping down his feet in an effort to warm them, wishing to God he had the price of a new pair of clogs for though Mercy had packed these as best she could, with paper and some cotton waste, they were still as thin as air. He smiled sadly at the thought of her and the frozen skin of his face almost cracked with the pain of it. He had, for the past six months courted Mercy Butterworth with all the propriety a girl of her station deserved, going whenever he could to Enoch Butterworth's cottage at the end of the village street, tolerated as his future son-in-law, and sitting as patiently and decently as he was able under Mercy's loving gaze as Enoch read from the family Bible. Joss was to move into the cottage when they were married since there was more room than in the one in which his mother, his sisters and his younger brother lived and he wondered, as he sat and listened to Mercy's father extol the virtues of 'turning the other cheek' how he was to manage it. Mercy protected him from Enoch as

114

much as she could, knowing Joss's explosive nature and impatience with such beliefs, but her dove-like meekness and bowed head could not always quench his fierce need for action, for the getting up and throwing off of the delicate chains which bound him to her. But how could he? She loved him and thought he loved her. Her brother was dead because of the cause Joss fought for and he felt responsible for it. He owed her something and he was paying his debt as his conscience bade him. But he found it hard. Mercy could not seem to get enough of 'seeing to him', as she put it, mending and washing his meagre wardrobe of clothes, much to his own mother's disapproval making him nourishing dishes to put a 'bit of meat on his bones', fussing over whether he was too cold, or too hot, or tired, and in her new found dignity as his betrothed – he quailed at the word and all it conjured up – she found peace and acceptance as she prepared for their wedding day in the autumn, loving and maternal and yet shy with him in their new roles as man and woman. She would be waiting in the cottage, not far from the window so as not to miss his arrival. On the fire would be a pan of something hot and as tasty as she could make from the scraps she garnered. Carrots, grown in the summer and stored in one of the rooms above the kitchen that had once housed hand-looms, potatoes and an onion or two though these did not keep as well, even a bit of rabbit if Charlie, who was five years old, and handy, had been lucky with his traps.

He loved Mercy, did Charlie and was made up with the coming wedding. Though he spent each day with his mother and four-year-old younger sister, carding the raw cotton his mother was to spin, whenever he could he was up at the Butterworth cottage, doing an odd job or two, those Mr Butterworth found increasingly difficult to do as he grew older, or out on the moor setting his traps or checking to see if a rabbit had been snared. A wiry lad, bright and already longing to follow his brother and dead father in the ways of radicalism, he had the natural independence and plain common sense of the north country lad, a readiness to learn, to 'get on' as their Joss was to do. Mercy's brother had been a martyr to the honourable and just cause in which the Greenwood men were involved and Joss, as its leader, was Charlie's idol. To Charlie he was a warrior who had bested the enemy. Tom had been a soldier too, but he had fallen which did not in any way denigrate him in Charlie's eyes. They were both heroes and Charlie wished for nothing more than to emulate them. To be a spinner, even a master spinner or weaver was well enough, he told Mercy, conscious of the status of her father, but one day he meant to be known as something, *somebody* in this world. He was learning to read and write, taught, as Joss had been, in the village Sunday school, as all the village children were, if they wished it. Whereas most would rather spend their precious free time in more pleasurable pursuits, playing the children's games which had passed from generation to generation, he, and Joss, who had encouraged his younger brother, had persevered.

The dogs rose slowly to their feet as Joss approached. They did not snarl or even move a muscle. Their ears were laid flat and their eyes were still and watchful and their rigid stance warned him that should he make a move they did not like he might have cause to regret it. He stopped and his heart began a sharp tattoo in his chest. His breath shivered in his throat and he held it for several seconds before letting it out. He remained perfectly still for he remembered her words.

'They are completely safe except when I tell them to be otherwise!' she had said, then invited him, challenged him to command them to him, and though he had done so, *she* had allowed it. Two years almost to the day and in that time he had seen her twice. Her spirit had been uncompromising on each occasion, her extravagant courage defying the men he had sent to wreck her father's machine, defying those who, though she had not known of it then, had meant her no harm on the day of Tom's hanging. These were her

116

dogs, Joby and Blaze she had called them, and where they were she would not be far away.

He took another step and one of them growled warningly. Not much of a sound really, just enough to let him know he really was dicing with death and should think twice before chancing another move.

He drew in a deep breath of the lung-searing cold and turned his head cautiously since he had no desire to have it torn from his shoulders. There was a group of stones thirty yards from the track, just on the edge of a drop which went almost vertically down into the valley. 'Badger's Edge' it was called since it was known that a 'badger', one of the men who had once hawked goods about the district, using the pack-way as a means of getting from Edgeclough to Crossfold had gone over the clough in a snowstorm and fallen to his death. The stones were as tall as a man, a dozen of them and they formed a sheltered circle in which anyone seeking solitude could not be seen from the track.

She stepped out quietly from behind the rocks, her back to the edge, saying nothing. She was wearing an outfit which was identical – perhaps it was the same – to the one she had worn then and her hair hung about her face and tumbled down her back as it had on that other day. Her hands were thrust deep into her pockets and beneath her skirt, though he could not see her legs, he knew she stood with her booted feet wide apart. As a man would stand, bold, defiant, declaring that this was *her* bit of earth and what right had he to invade it?

It seemed neither could look away. Their eyes were locked in a strange and cautionary fashion as though each was sizing up the other and yet that was not it entirely for they were both well aware of who the other was, of what the other was and of the antipathy between them. It was more than that, more than the yawning gulf of class, of prejudice, more than the conflict which existed in each of them to fight and wound, to hurt in the protection of what was theirs, he for the people who looked to him for leadership, she for her father's mills. It was, quite simply, the look of

117

a man and a woman taking the measure, *as* a man and a woman, of one another.

She snapped her fingers and the dogs lay down and one yawned. They lowered their muzzles to their paws, giving the impression they were about to doze off but neither took their unblinking eyes from Joss Greenwood.

'So,' she said softly, 'here we are again, Joss Greenwood. I wondered how long it would be before we met up with one another.'

'You have been looking for me then, Katherine Chapman?' His voice was mocking and he felt a surge of triumph as her eyes narrowed in sudden anger. Then she smiled sweetly.

'Only to see you caught and, hopefully, hanged.'

'Like Tom Butterworth?' He felt the acid of his hatred burn his throat and he took a step towards her. The dog, Joby, raised his head.

'Really. Was that his name? I had quite forgot.'

'That doesn't surprise me. What could he possibly mean to you except as some rough, cloth-capped working lad who forgot his place and got his just retribution.'

'Well, so he did. I could not have put it better myself. He killed a man in cold blood and deserved to die.'

'Did he indeed? And were you there to witness it?'

'No, and neither were you or you would have been hanged beside him.'

'*Instead of*, actually, Katherine Chapman, since it was my fault the Redcoat died, not Tom's. He was protecting his sister from the soldiers you sent to find me, damn your rotten soul to hell, and I should have been protecting *him* instead of . . . of . . .' His face worked with something which looked curiously like guilt, guilt and shame, and a deep sadness. 'He was only a boy, trying to do a man's job . . .'

She looked surprised then recovered from it, drawing breath to attack again.

'Really, but then from what I have seen of you, you were ever a violent man. First in the wrecking of my father's machine and then, so you say, in the death of a man who was doing no more than his duty in apprehending a criminal. It appears that you thrive on destruction and interference in the affairs of others.'

'If you mean by that I fight for what is rightfully mine and for those who try to make a decent living for themselves, then you are right.'

'By destroying what is *not* yours. By taking away what will eventually give them prosperity . . .'

'To the mill-owners. Not to those who work for them.'

'It will take time to move from one era to another . . .'

'And what era is that, Miss Chapman?' His voice was cruelly mocking.

'The industrial era. You cannot simply ignore it. You cannot stand in the way of . . .'

'Progress! Yes, I have heard all the arguments the ones who are to benefit from it put forward to justify that claim but I am yet to be convinced.'

'You do not give it a chance . . .'

'Do I not? Perhaps the men who are out of work would like to be given a chance. A chance to feed their children on more than water, oats and potatoes . . . if they are lucky enough to be able to afford even that . . .'

'But they will. If they will accept this changeover from the domestic industry to power looms. A hand-loom weaver can weave only 172,000 picks a week while a power-loom weaver can weave 605,000 on two looms. Does it not seem reasonable that eventually that man will be capable of earning so much more than . . .'

'It is the power-looms that take the bread out of their mouths and it is this for which we are fighting. Not against progress, for any man of sense can see it must come. The men will work at anything for a decent wage, a wage they can *live* on, bring up a family on, but until that day comes I will fight you and your father with every means at my disposal. Did you know that in the barracks at Burnley they house two hundred soldiers, all to keep in order the *dis*orderly populace? Even if the poor weaver dies at his

119

loom, his useless loom, they must maintain the soldiers. There were disturbances there four or five years ago, you see, and so there they sit, doing nothing – unless they have me and my men to chase – ' he smiled maliciously, 'since nothing happens for them to take up arms against, but it will change. I warn you now that though we have been quiet since Tom's death we will come back and if we don't get what we want we will force the mill-owners in any way we can, violent or not, to deal fairly with us. So be warned. Tell your father. I have an army of men behind me and by God . . .'

'Have you no softer side, Joss Greenwood?'

Surprise showed in both their faces, hers at herself as she asked the sudden question for why on earth should she have said that, or even thought it, his at the strangeness of it, but his savage oath, the lunging step he took towards her, the lifting of his clenched fists brought the two dogs to their feet and she raised a finger, no more than that, to bring them to her side.

'A softer side, Katherine Chapman? You dare say that to me?' His face twisted in repugnance and he stepped closer to her and the dogs began to growl deep in their throats. He was no more than ten yards from her. He could see the deep flaring blue flame in her eyes, the outraged dip of her silken brows and the soft pink of her angry mouth, just on the inside of her lips where the moistness was. Her three-quarter length coat was open at the neck and the pale golden smoothness of her throat, the fiercely beating hollow at its base was plainly visible and he felt a tremor run from his belly down the inside of his thighs and he hated her, hated her for it. His bitterness was such that he could have taken told of her, put his hands about that lovely neck and squeezed and squeezed until . . . dear God . . . until . . .

'You speak of softness . . .' His voice was ragged, '. . . you . . . and yours who would sacrifice a child . . . aah yes, I heard of him, Katherine Chapman, from my sister who saw him . . . a baby, no more, being dragged into the frame, and you dare to ask me of softness. How do you sleep

120

sound in your bed at night knowing you are responsible for it . . .?'

'Aah . . . please, don't . . .'

For a moment he was taken aback, not believing what he had heard. He lowered his threatening fists and the shoulders he had hunched, just like those of a bareknuckle fighter about to take on an opponent, slowly fell and the madness in his brain subsided. Without another sound she sank painfully to her knees, an arm about the neck of each dog and her upturned face was anguished and for a dreadful second he felt his heart move in his breast with pity for her. She was so obviously in pain, torn by some great conflict within her and it was almost more than he could do to restrain himself from going to her, putting his arms about her, holding her, soothing away that tangled web of hair from her face, cupping her chin to look into her eyes for the truth. Her mouth was open, so soft and sweet and vulnerable, and her eyes looked up at him, enormous and haunted, begging. Sweet Jesus, what was he thinking of? She was the symbol of all he hated the most. Proud, disdainful, arrogant in her fur-lined coat when his own mother had but a thin shawl, in her expensive leather boots when his sisters trudged the moors in worn out clogs, with her firm golden skin, her fine straight body, her bright-eyed look of glowing health when he moved among men and women every day who were no more than living skeletons, with children who could scarce walk on their stunted limbs. What did she want of him, for Christ's sake, looking at him like that, just as though she was asking him for something? What did he know of the life she led, though he could guess at its splendour. It was evidently one of freedom not known by other women of her class since it was well publicised now that one day she would inherit her father's mills and not only that but would run them, as a son would. She was not a *real* woman, how could she be for she lived the life a man would lead? There was no gentleness in her, no sweetness and soft warmth as there was in Mercy, and yet . . . and yet there was something, something as basic as the earth on which they stood, as deep rooted as the trees in the valley, as unyielding as the moorland itself. She was not feminine as Mercy was feminine, but by God, she was all *female*.

He turned away from her, afraid if he remained he might go to her, put out his hand to help her to rise, and that, he knew, must never happen.

Kit felt the dogs as they licked her face and hands, distressed as her strangeness conveyed itself to them and she stood up abruptly, steadying herself on their strong backs. She flung up her head, pride stiffening her spine for was she to let this . . . this stranger see the secret guilt she had carried for the past week since the death of the boy? She had gone back to the mill with her father the following day, telling herself that she would, somehow, do it differently, that she would convince him that, surely, there was some way to replace the children, but when she had tried he had taken her down to the gate, rough with her in front of the men who watched, and begged her, if she could, to inform these women, indicating the patient, shawled creatures who stood there that from now on there would be no more work for their children.

They had set up such an outcry, beseeching the 'maister' to reconsider for they had other bairns at home to feed and if these they had brought were not suitable, too big perhaps, they could fetch the others. Their men had no jobs, they cried, not for a year or more, some of them longer, and if the children did not work how were they to manage? She had seen their eyes, those haunted eyes for even as they spoke they had hated themselves and her for forcing them to it, in offering these scraps of humanity as the only providers of the family, but what else could they do, those eyes pleaded to know.

She attacked with venom. 'You go about the country preaching your sermons on justice for the labouring man, on a fair wage for a fair day's work but you know nothing about the *real* working of a mill . . .' Her voice was harsh, unforgiving.

122

'Damn you, my own sister works in your father's mill. Don't tell me I know nothing of what goes on there.' The pity was gone as if it had never been and he turned gladly, ready again to fight her since that was safe and all he knew how to do, all he could allow himself to do.

'I have seen your sister. She looks none the worse for working in my father's mill.'

'That's no thanks to your father. It was a man like him who abandoned her . . .'

'Abandoned her . . .?'

'Aye. She was what's known as a pauper brat. I'm sure you know what that is, Miss Chapman. Brought from some poorhouse to work in his mill and when she didn't suit . . . My father found her on the moor. She was holding the hand of another child, a girl about six years old, my father said. She was dead. Her legs were deformed, stunted and weak. Some mistake had been made at the poorhouse, deliberately, to get rid of them. A mill-owner who couldn't be bothered with a crippled child and another who was too young to work. Jenny . . . she was only about two years old, my mother said, and they had been abandoned, like a couple of unwanted pups . . . She was sixteen when my father died and . . . she was kept at home before that . . . with her mother . . . safe. She had food . . .'

Dear God, why was he telling her this, explaining the roots of Jenny's beginning and the reason for her look of good health . . . 'just as you do, Katherine Chapman. Your father, as a father should, provided for you, as mine did for us . . . as is their right as fathers. But the men I know cannot provide for their own, *as is their right,* with decent work, *as is their due . . .*!'

They glared at one another wildly, gripped tight in the madness and inevitable clash of their single-minded wills. There was nothing more to be said. They had fought and neither had won and what was the use of going over and over the same painful conflict. She knew, he had seen it in her eyes a moment ago that the employment of children, and their mistreatment, was wrong but it seemed she was

123

prepared to turn a blind eye to it, for the sake of her father, he supposed. She was not without feelings for he had heard of the incident with the shawl, but perhaps that made it worse. To know, to sympathise, to bear compassion and yet to go on must surely be more wicked than to be as her father and the other mill-owners who genuinely believed they did no wrong.

But they might stand here forever and spit at each other. He might sense her indecision, her uncertainty but there was no getting away from the truth, that she, or her father and the rest of the mill-owners had killed Tom Butterworth. He must cling to that for it was a fact. He must not let her pain, if that was what it was, deflect him from the hatred he felt for the system her father and others like him and through them, *she* had created.

'Your father is the murderer, Katherine Chapman, and should have been hanged in Tom Buttworth's place.' He said it quite without emotion, passionless and therefore more chilling and rejoiced to see the hot flame of her enmity, her hatred of him and her loyalty to her father burn in her eyes.

'And what of you, Joss Greenwood? When are you to hang? The militiamen cannot seem able to catch you or your men as you go about looting and burning and destroying. Well, you can be sure I shall tell them it was you who wrecked my father's machine. It seems you are quite elusive, but one day you will make a mistake, or perhaps one of those underdogs you champion will give you away. You cannot win, you know. We are too strong for you, or perhaps it is you who are weak and not quite the man you seem to think yourself.'

She laughed and tossed her head and her hair flew back and rippled almost to her buttocks. She placed her hands on her hips and the bitter cold flew ribbons of scarlet in her cheeks. 'I despise a man who promises much but cannot seem to carry out what he declares so loudly he will. Fight you, say, and win, you say! How, and with what? You cannot return your followers to their rural activities since

124

time will never march backwards. There are laws to restrain you, made by those who rule the land. There are those who are meant to rule and those who are meant to be ruled . . .'

'So you see yourself as Queen, then, Katherine Chapman, and we are your humble subjects to be ground beneath your . . .'

He stopped suddenly and his panting breath clouded about his head. His chest heaved and his fists clenched yet again by his side, but slowly his brain cleared, then he sighed slowly, sadly, and the madness left his eyes.

'Really, I do not know what I am about.' It was as though he spoke to himself. 'I stand here in fierce argument with a woman who knows nothing of the distress and disaster in this land. She is like a child in a tantrum. She is as ignorant as the rest of the country to the true predicament we are in. All these years, fifty nearly, since the first water frame was invented we have tried. They have banned us from meeting together, from forming a trade union to protect ourselves and still we fight on.' He laughed softly and she found herself listening to him as she had not listened to him when he shouted. He spoke well, with little of the broad dialect of the north countryman. She was not to know of the hours he had spent in teaching himself to erase it, since, when he addressed the crowds, not only of his own Lancastrians, they must understand him. He must be understood by the gentry, the squirearchy, the millocracy, and even those up in London when the time came for him to go there.

'I need my head seeing to.' He shook it gently, as though at his own folly, turning away, ready to set his foot on the track again, ready to deliver himself to Mercy's loving arms and sweet and modest kisses for she understood him, and the passion of his work, as this woman did not. Then he looked back at her, grinning quite good-humouredly over his shoulder.

'Go back to your playing, Katherine Chapman . . .'

'Kit,' she said unexpectedly.

'Pardon!'

125

'My name is Kit.'

'Is it indeed! Well then, *Kit* Chapman, go back to the toy your father has promised you if you do as he says. That is what you want isn't it? If you are a good girl and behave yourself and close your eyes to what is distasteful, you might even be as rich and successful as he is, though I doubt it. I doubt you have the stomach for it, since that is what you will need. A strong stomach!'

He tipped his cap impishly and in that moment she forgot the ideal for which they both struggled, so diverse and yet, though neither was aware of it, the same, and, marvelling at the light of laughter in his eyes, the engaging tilt to his dark eyebrows, wondered how they would have been, Kit Chapman and Joss Greenwood, if they had known one another in different circumstances.

She heard him begin to whistle as he stepped out jauntily on the path and she could have sworn that the violent exchange they had shared had done him the world of good!

# 9

The three men sprang to their feet when she entered the room and for a second she was startled since she had thought her father to be alone. She hesitated at the door, raising her eyebrows enquiringly in his direction and her father moved round his desk and came across the carpet to take her arm.

'My dear, I was under the impression you had gone to Crossfold with your mother. Did I not hear her say something about a new gown for your birthday?'

'It did not take long, Father. Miss Cavendish is clever and knows exactly what I require.'

'Well then, in that case, come and meet an old friend of

mine.' He turned, leading her forward, his face reserved, his smile cool and Kit Chapman received the distinct impression that she had caught her father off guard. She had indeed been into Crossfold, spending an hour of her precious time, time when she might have been more profitably employed going over the monthly accounting, listening to her mother and the rest of the clientele who crowded the salon owned by Miss Cavendish, gush approvingly over the high waisted, ivory silk gown which was being created for her to wear at the ball her father was giving to celebrate her eighteenth birthday the following week. It was a lovely dress and the occasion would be splendid but she really did begrudge the time that was needed to be pinned and prodded and told to stand this way and that, when Miss Cavendish knew her exact measurements and requirements and could so easily make and deliver the gown without Kit even having a fitting!

Her mother had been most put out when she had said so, telling her she was unnatural and really, she should have been a man since she had never yet met a girl who was so disinclined towards pretty clothes. It was not exactly true for Kit dressed well. She had a talent for creating a look of understated elegance, a simple, uncluttered style which made the decision of what to wear each day so easy. Day-dresses of white French lawn in the summer, with gigot sleeves, which were then fashionable, and a sash of soft apple green, of lemon or biscuit or rose pink, and of long-sleeved gowns of cashmere or merino in winter. Simple lines, pleasing colours, misty blue, poppy red, crisp lime green, with her straight and shining hair arranged in an Apollo knot. Many ladies were forced to add false hair of plaited loops to thicken the effect but Kit's abundant hair made this practice unnecessary and with a jewelled comb to hold it in place the style made her look even taller and her pale golden neck long and slender.

The man who was appraising her with a cool and interested expression was half a head taller than she was. His fair hair was cut short and brushed smoothly about his head and his eyes, a deep and chocolate brown, narrowed for a moment before they began to smile. He had a self-assurance of manner that suggested he had generations of gentlemen behind him. As though his ancestors had been among the privileged, a condition which had continued until it reached him, but Kit was not taken in by the charm of his smile which revealed his fine, white teeth, nor the courteous bow he inclined towards her. She had met many gentlemen just like him in the course of her new business career, and at the functions she attended with her mother and father and she had very quickly come to recognise an opportunist when she met one. Those who believed that an heiress was fair game, and this was one of them!

'My dear,' her father was saying, 'may I introduce Mr Samuel Atherton. Samuel, this is my daughter, Katherine.'

'Mr Atherton.' She extended her hand and the older gentleman took it, bowing gallantly, but in his eyes, as brown as those of the younger man, was an expression of quizzical interest.

'Miss Chapman, this is a delightful surprise.'

'Surprise, sir? Did you not expect to meet me, then?' The gentleman faltered and shot a strange look at her father, then smiled suavely. 'We hoped to, Miss Chapman, we certainly hoped to, but first, may I present my son, Harry. Harry, this is Miss Katherine Chapman.'

'Miss Chapman.'

'Mr Atherton.'

His manners were exquisite, his education obviously expensive and despite his air of superiority, which, she supposed was one that all men of his class had, she found she could not help returning his smile for it was impudent as though to say he knew his own worth and how could she fail to recognise it.

For several moments there was a small confusion of who was to sit where and which of the gentlemen was to be allowed the honour of holding her chair, but at last they were all seated.

'Mr Atherton and his son are staying in the area for a week or two, Kit. They are . . .'

'Kit?' Harry Atherton leaned forward, interrupting her father, then turned to him swiftly. 'I beg your pardon, sir. Forgive me but I was intrigued when you called Miss Chapman . . .'

'Kit? Yes, somehow my wife and I . . . well, a pet name, you understand, and it has become a habit.'

'And I prefer it to Katherine, Mr Atherton.' He turned instantly to her, his eyes glowing.

'Do you indeed? What a pity. Katherine is such a pretty name. One of my favourites if I may say so. How did you come to be known as Kit?'

Harry Atherton crossed one immaculate leg over the other and sat back in his chair. On his face was an expression of the keenest interest. He smiled encouragingly.

'Well, I hardly think our family idiosyncrasies can be of the slightest concern to someone like you, Mr Atherton.' Kit felt a small kernel of irritation bud inside her. Only the need for good manners in the presence of her father's two guests kept her from telling this arrogant stranger to mind his own damned business, but he merely grinned imperturbably and as though they were alone, leaned forward once more to say quietly, almost conspiratorially, 'Oh but it is, Miss Chapman. Anything you do would concern me and I would dearly love to know how you came by the . . . endearment!'

She turned, quite astonished, to her father, for surely he would not care to have his daughter spoken to in such a . . . a familiar manner but the two older men were smiling paternally. She felt the irritation become a prickle of anger, and something else, she could not really put a name to it, came to keep it company and she knew a decided longing to attack what was evidently this man's inflated sense of his own self-esteem. What was her father thinking of, letting this . . . this upstart speak to her as if they were old friends. How dare he question her on what was a private family matter, but her father interrupted smoothly.

'Come, Harry! You are teasing my daughter and she does not like to be teased.'

She turned to stare in amazement at her father for in all the years she had known him and she could really only count the last five or six, he had never once been jocular. Her mouth popped open quite foolishly and the three men began to laugh and for the first time in her life she wished she was one of those women who could command a man's thoughts with the teasing and pert ways of a pretty flirt. Some had the knack of being able to divert with a capricious look, a fluttering of eyelashes. To turn what might become too serious into something amusing. She was at a disadvantage and she did not like it, nor did she care for the way her father had placed her there!

'I hardly know Mr Atherton, Father,' she protested, conscious of the amusement with which Harry Atherton was regarding her.

'Come, my dear, do not upset yourself. Harry did not mean to embarrass you. He has always been known as a tease.'

'Has he really?' Her manner was disdainful as though the very last thing she wished to be acquainted with was Harry Atherton's teasing and she could sense her father's sudden disapproval, and wondered at it, for he, like her, did not suffer fools lightly. These men must be important to him or he would not act so strangely, nor so out of character. She had never heard mention of the Athertons, father or son, and yet it appeared that Samuel Atherton was an *old* friend of Barker Chapman's. In what way she could not imagine. Certainly not in business for he was a product of the class known as gentry and her father was not. Perhaps they had gone to school together but whatever their connection it seemed they were pleased with one another now, smiling and nodding benignly, smugly even, she would have said.

'Are you visiting friends in the district, Mr Atherton?' She directed her polite social question at the senior gentleman, hoping to amend the somewhat bad impression she had made, since the indolent smile of the younger made her decidedly uncomfortable.

'Why no, Miss Chapman. Your father and I were discussing the possibility of . . .'

'Mr Atherton and his son are here to . . .'

'Yes?' She looked from one to the other, quite perplexed since it seemed to her there was some flickering undercurrent here, into which, in a moment, she was to be flung. Her eye caught the polite smile, the amused eye of Harry Atherton and her heart missed a beat for she knew quite suddenly that the tension was to do with him.

'Would you think me rude if I were to ask you if this is a social call, Mr Atherton, or does it concern the mills?' Her voice was cool, imperious, 'Because if it does, as I *feel* it does, then I think I should be consulted.'

Her father answered. 'It does concern you, my dear and believe me I would have talked it over with you but you seemed intent on the dressmaker and your new ball gown . . .'

'*Father*, please, you know that is not so!'

'Katherine, can we not continue this when Mr Atherton and . . .'

'Of course.' At once she turned courteously to Samuel Atherton. 'Forgive me, sir. My manners are appalling. May I give you some tea, or perhaps coffee. You and your son will have a long drive, no doubt. I do beg your pardon but I cannot even claim to know where you are from, or where you are to travel today . . .'

'We are come from Cheshire, Miss Chapman. My family have a property there, and no, we will not take tea though it is gracious of you to ask.'

'A property in Cheshire, really? You are in business there?'

Samuel Atherton smiled. 'No, we have . . . land, an estate, farming land and a bit of shooting, you understand, but with four sons . . .' He shook his head and his smile deepened, '. . . that is why your father's offer was so welcome.'

'My father's offer?'

'To take Harry into the business.'

She felt the air about her move, lightly brushing against her, cold and quite painful. The smile she had pasted on her face to accommodate her father's guests remained there but the coldness in which she sat chilled her to the bone.

'Into my father's business,' she said and her voice was light, the voice of a lady holding a conversation with a gentleman, one she did not know very well but to whom, nevertheless, she must be polite.

'Yes. That was what we were discussing when you came in,' rudely, he might have added, she could see it in his face, and where you have no real right to be but his mouth smiled urbanely and she continued the charade, for that was what it had become.

'In what capacity, may I ask?' She did not look at Harry Atherton, nor Samuel Atherton but at her father and her eyes, though *she* still smiled, were like chips of blue diamonds.

'In the capacity in the first place as . . .'

'I do not think I should be given a title, sir. Not until I have earned it.' Harry Atherton lifted his well bred head to smile at Barker Chapman. 'I have a lot to learn, I am sure.'

'Indeed you have, Mr Atherton.' Kit's voice was soft, but not at all warm. 'The work of a mill-master is not for the weak.'

'Oh, not mill-master, Miss Chapman.' He put his hand to his brow languidly. 'Heaven forbid!'

'What will you be then?'

'Really, I cannot say. I shall be an apprentice. What do you think to that?'

The picture of the 'apprentices' in her father's spinning mills flashed vividly across her eyelids and for a moment she had the most unladylike desire to scream with hysterical laughter. The last apprentice she had seen had been dressed in nothing more than cut-down ragged breeches, no shirt, no shoes . . . not even hands! She remembered the smell,

132

the unbearable heat, the veil of cotton 'fly' which hung in the air and crept into the mouth and blocked the nose, the damp which had come through the soles of her shoes, the noise of the machines, the shouts and the sharp crack of the overlooker's strap. Where would this handsome, this faultlessly dressed gentleman fit into that picture, she thought frantically.

'You are familiar with the cotton trade then, Mr Atherton.'

'Oh hardly, but I have some skill with figures and, which is more to the point for that is what your father needs, I am rather good at selling whatever you have to sell to those who do not always wish to buy it. I remember once at school I had a number of . . .'

'You are not at school now, Mr Atherton.'

'How perceptive of you, Miss Chapman, but please, allow me to tell you what I am to be employed in. You and your father are, I have been told, completely indispensable at the mill.' He looked as though he found this hard to believe, in her case at least, but he continued smoothly. 'Someone must find new markets for your cloth, would you not say?'

'Really, Mr Atherton?'

'Really, Miss Chapman.'

'Are you accustomed to working for sixteen hours each day, whatever else may come along to distract you?'

'I am sure if you can do it, Miss Chapman, then so can I!' He smiled engagingly. 'It seems we are entering an age of machinery and if one is not to be left behind, one must accept it. My eldest brother does not require me to help him collect the rents from our tenants on the estate which will one day be his, nor does he need the services of my two brothers who are already become soldiers. I must support myself, Miss Chapman, and your father being good enough to come forward with an offer of honest employment . . .' he bowed in her father's direction, '. . . I seized the opportunity.'

And what other opportunities are you likely to seize,

given the chance, Kit Chapman thought as she looked at the quite calculating, completely agreeable smile of Harry Atherton.

'You do not trust me,' she said to her father when the carriage bearing Samuel Atherton and his son had been politely waved down the drive. They had taken tea with Hannah Chapman since, as hostess she had insisted, and had promised, as Kit had known they would, realising bitterly it must have been arranged beforehand, to attend the ball for her eighteenth birthday the following week. Samuel would bring his wife and daughter and . . . well . . . if Mrs Chapman insisted . . . really, it was most gracious of her . . . they would be delighted to be weekend guests.

Harry Atherton had smiled, tilting a sardonic eyebrow in her direction as though admitting quite blatantly – to her – that he was thoroughly enjoying himself, at her expense, she imagined since why else should he keep grinning at her like some supercilious cat. A cat from Cheshire which had just been allowed to lap the dish of Lancashire cream which had *her* name on it!

She had waited, her nerves frayed to raw and painful edges until she and her father were alone, her mother gone to summon the housekeeper since, with important guests to be prepared for and with no more than a week in which to arrange it, Hannah Chapman would be hard pressed to spare an hour even to lay her head on her pillow.

'Of course I trust you, Katherine. You are being foolish . . .'

'Foolish! I imagine if I had been your son and not your daughter you would not have used that word.'

'Katherine . . .'

'Please, Father, let me speak. I had supposed, as I am one day to be your successor, indeed I had been led to believe I was to run the mills, as I am well able to do, whenever you are absent, that all decisions, all actions to be taken to do with the mills would be shared with me. Does this not predispose one to imagine that if this was the case I should be consulted, not only in the manufacture and selling of

134

our cotton, but also about the men we employ to achieve it. I am acquainted with all our staff, all the overlookers and managers, the factors who buy our raw cotton, who ship it from America, the agents in Liverpool, in fact *every man* concerned with the spinning and weaving of our cloth. If that is so, why was I not informed of this . . . this Harry Atherton?'

She threw up her head and was quite mortified when the splendid Apollo knot which her maid, Janet had devised for her, began to slip, and a smooth strand of hair fell across her cheek. She brushed it back angrily, her hands going to the back of her head to adjust it and her father smiled.

'My dear, you speak of sons and daughters and your rights as my successor but really, one can never forget you are a woman!'

He had meant it kindly, a compliment, but her face blazed to crimson fury and her eyes glittered ominously.

'For all your bold comments about my fitness for the role you are preparing for me, you do not really think me able to do it, do you? You are to put in this popinjay to supervise what I do . . .'

'Come now, Kit. You already know more than he will ever learn. How can he possibly supervise . . .'

'Then why is he to be employed, and, more to the point, Father, why did you not tell me?'

'Katherine . . . Kit, sit down, please and do me the honour of listening to me without jumping down my throat every time I open my mouth to speak. You are hot-headed, daughter, and must learn to control your emotions or you will never make a business man. You allow everyone to know exactly what you are thinking and that will never do.' He sat back and studied her and though she lifted her chin in that haughty way she had, like a princess who is to inherit the crown which was no doubt the way she saw herself, he knew she was paying attention.

'Harry Atherton will be very useful to us in our business, Kit. He knows nothing about commerce and less about the

135

manufacture of cottons but he has something which you will need . . .'

'I?'

'Yes, when I am gone!'

'Good Heavens, Father, how can you . . .?'

'Do not be foolish, Kit. There, I have used the word again and if it offends you then I must apologise but let us be realistic. You are to take my place, my business, my *mills* when I am dead, Katherine, and that is why we are preparing you for it. You will do splendidly or I would not allow it. I would sell the lot to George Abbott or Albert Jenkinson, both of whom would give me a good price but, quite frankly my dear, we do not need the money. I hate to seem . . . mercenary but if I were to die tomorrow, mills or not, you and your mother could live in style and luxury for the remainder of your lives. But you see I have this hankering to think of my mills, *our* mills, spinning and weaving and turning out the best velveteen and fustians for another generation, and even beyond. But there is a new age coming, you know that. Harry Atherton knows it, too, and it is to be the age of the machine. It will be, quite simply, an industrial revolution. We shall be turning out more cloth in one day than my father did in a week, a month! And that cloth has to be sold! Markets must be found, all over the world, and someone must find them, and get our cloth to them.'

'Harry Atherton?'

'Harry Atherton.'

'But he knows nothing about it.'

'We shall teach him, you and I, and when he knows *almost* as much as we do we will allow him to work for us.'

'I still do not understand why you told me nothing of this.' Her face had cleared and returned to its normal colour but her eyes were still watchful for she had the feeling there was something her father was holding back. She had known a sense of discomfort when Harry Atherton had teased her about her name, a sense that there was more to him, more

136

to the words he spoke, than was apparent. Her father had been . . . strange, unlike himself and Mr Atherton senior, positively arch in the way he had studied her.

'I wished to sound out Samuel, and Harry, before putting the proposition to you. They are not "trade", you know, as you and I are considered to be.' He smiled at his own small joke. 'The Athertons are landowners near Chester with three hundred years of privilege and authority behind them. They do not work, my dear Kit, and though I was at school with Sam Atherton, we do not quite come up to their considered opinion of what constitutes a gentleman.'

'Rubbish!'

'Rubbish indeed, but then you and I are practical people and have been brought up to believe in the satisfaction of a full day's work, and the profit it brings us. We live a satisfying life, in our eyes, but they, of course believe theirs is better than ours and that we are mad to do it, particularly as there is no need of it since I am an independently wealthy man. But now they are forced to reconsider. There are four sons, you see, and the estate can only support one so, Harry Atherton, being a sensible and ambitious young man must look elsewhere for the wherewithal to support the expensive tastes he has been reared to consider his due. And, my dear, I think he will earn his keep. He is a personable young man, do you not think so?'

Barker Chapman watched his daughter keenly. He did not appear to be doing so as he lifted the lid of his silver cigar box and selected a cigar. He took his time lighting it, studying, or so it seemed, the smoke wreathing slowly to the ceiling, but his heavily lidded eyes watched and waited for her reaction to his question. He and Sam Atherton were both opportunists, in a completely different way, naturally, and the delightful solution to both their difficulties was an opportunity neither could ignore. Though Barker Chapman could quite easily have the pick of any young buck in the county for his lovely and wealthy young daughter, he knew the man must be exactly the right one for his Katherine. She was self-willed and self-opinionated and would need a strong man, if not to steady her, for the man who could do so did not exist, at least to pull in the same direction as herself. He must be a gentleman, naturally, but one prepared to realise that *she* was the 'mill-master'. There would be a pre-marriage contract to ensure this for Barker Chapman's mills must remain *Chapman* mills. No fortune hunter would get his hands on them, or on Katherine, but *somebody* must be found to marry her. Despite his quite liberal ideas, his madness, some would say in allowing his daughter to inherit and run his mills he believed that she must be married and before he died. A woman not married was an unnatural thing, in his opinion, but he must choose, as far as he was able the man who would be Katherine's consort in marriage. He must supervise its setting up, train the man who was to stand beside her, or more probably, if he knew Kit, just *behind* her, since, though he would not admit it to anyone but himself, to put a vast fortune in the hands of a woman, even one as shrewd as Kit, was not *quite* like leaving it to a son. Not that she would squander it for that was not her style, but with someone standing, looking over her shoulder so to speak, she would more carefully guard it.

And Sam Atherton's Harry was the perfect man, with the added bonus of being a superb salesman. Had he not sold himself as husband for Barker Chapman's daughter? Sam needed the generous amount of money Barker was prepared to put into his estate. Harry required some activity into which he could funnel that bright and enormous energy, that self-seeking ambition, greed, if you like, which was the reason Barker Chapman approved of him, and the rewards he knew would be his if he kept his nose clean!

Kit shrugged carelessly, apparently unimpressed with Harry Atherton.

'I suppose he has a certain . . . style.'

'Style? What does that mean?'

'He will appeal to those who like to be flattered.'

'Then he will do well since who does not? Is that all you can say about him?'

'What else is there to him?' She turned away, uninterested

in Harry Atherton's charms but Barker Chapman was not deceived. An attractive man, not only to women but liked by other men was an asset to any concern, and Kit was not as immune as she pretended to be. He had seen her confusion under Harry's teasing scrutiny, her concern with her hair and the smoothness of her gown, all indications of a woman's interest in a man. She had not perhaps been aware of it herself but to a man of experience it had been there to see. No, Barker Chapman was quite satisfied with it all and with the way in which she had been distracted from her original question. He had not told her about Harry Atherton because, despite his protestations to the contrary, quite simply, being the man he was, he told *no one* everything he did!

He came from a family which had for generations been in banking, but was still considered 'trade' by polite society. He owned spinning and weaving mills and all the processes associated with the textile industry. His father had been a wealthy man when he built his first spinning mill at Crossbank and in the past fifteen years or so the Chapman family fortune had grown to such a size Barker could count himself one of the wealthiest men in Lancashire. He owned land in both his own county and in Cheshire, farming land, mining ventures, a share in the family banking concerns in Oldham, Manchester and Liverpool.

But his heart, if he could be said to have one, was devoted to his mills, and now, surprisingly, to his only child.

# 10

Barker Chapman, it was well known, was not really a gentleman. Like most of his family, and indeed, many another with wealth, had married wisely, love rarely being a matter for consideration, following the trend of the gentry, aristocracy and royalty.

Barker had loved neither of his two wives. What regard he had now went to his daughter and on this day which was her eighteenth birthday his expression might almost have been described as fond as he watched her open the gifts she had been given.

A gold filigree necklace linked with pearls and earbobs to match. A ring set with amethysts and a bracelet of the finest opals. Mother of pearl combs for her hair inlaid with tourmaline, satin slippers and a butterfly brooch created in turquoise and an aquamarine.

She smiled, composed and unastonished, since she had been used to seeing such jewels on her mother and now that she herself was a woman it was her turn.

'Thank you, Father. They are delightful.'

'The slippers and combs are from your mother.'

'I shall thank her later.'

'I have another gift for you, my dear.' Barker Chapman smiled and there was a gleam of gratified approval in her eyes as he placed the slightly worn velvet jewel box on the table in front of her. Really, she had done so well since the unfortunate incident of the child killed in the mill six months ago, putting it behind her with a resolution which he had hoped, but had not been absolutely certain she possessed. She no longer went into the spinning-rooms and weaving-sheds without prior warning to the mill-manager which was only sensible, leaving the running of the machinery to those in charge of it and when Harry Atherton came into the mill, as he was to do within the month, there would be no need for her to venture any further than the office block, perhaps the warehouse or into the design room where he himself and more lately, Kit, worked on experiments with new cloth. Harry would stand as a buffer between her and the rougher side of the work for Barker still harboured a seed of doubt about her . . . well, he could only call it her womanly sensibilities regarding the conditions of the work force.

He watched her as she opened the box.

She moved through the evening on a drifting cloud of enchantment which turned her from an attractive young girl into a creature of radiance and light, her happiness blazing from her like the hot, golden flames of a furnace and those from Crossfold and Oldham and Manchester who had come to celebrate her eighteenth birthday told one another they had never before realised what a beauty Barker Chapman's girl had become. She wore the ivory silk Miss Cavendish had made for her, a clinging, high-waisted gown as light as thistledown with a low neckline and a tiny sleeve and scattered on the bodice with cream silk embroidery. Janet had dressed her hair into a heavy, intricate coil in the centre of which she had placed half a dozen ivory silk rosebuds and around her neck was the magnificent rope of ivory pearls, given to her by her father.

'They were your grandmother's,' he said 'and worn by no one since.' From that she deduced that neither of her father's two wives had been considered worthwhile enough to wear them but that she, his daughter, was! 'I saw your gown and . . . well, can you deny that they are not the perfect match?'

He led her out in the first dance, to the astonishment of those who knew him, since Barker Chapman used occasions such as these, not to be sociable, though he was never less than the perfect host, but to do business with many of the manufacturers who were his guests. Of course he took his wife on the floor and then the wife of the gentleman who was his house-guest, as was only polite, but his face as he presented, as it were, the treasure of his daughter to those who had come to celebrate her birthday was really almost fatuous, they thought.

She danced every dance. Squire Longworth of Longworth Hall, set between Shaw and Oldham – the Squire only consenting to mingle with the manufacturing classes on account of Barker Chapman's house-guests, with whom he was acquainted – took her from her father's arms with an eagerness which, as the ladies watching agreed, was unseemly in a man of his age, whispering in her ear and most reluctant to let her go when some young sprig came to claim her.

There was Jonathan Abbott, the son of George Abbott, who had spinning mills over Edgeclough way, ready for a flirtation, ready to make love to her if it could be managed and she was willing, but, prodded by his father, who could make neither head nor tail of Barker Chapman's madness, in letting this lovely child anywhere near his mills, really ready to marry her.

'By God, you look fine,' he said, his eyes undressing her, his florid face pressing close to hers, his heavy body blundering most uncomfortably against her own and his polished boots crushing her satin slippers.

'Thank you, Jonathan. You are most kind.' She tossed her head and smiled so brilliantly, for was she not worthwhile in her father's eyes and what else mattered? He missed a step as he whirled her about the floor and, no longer obeying his father in his instructions to 'make himself pleasant to the Chapman girl' he began to do it for his own sake, for really, Kit Chapman would be more than adequate in any man's drawing-room or in any man's bed!

He had no time to expand upon his sudden realisation of her charms when she was whisked away once more, this time by Ritchie Jenkinson, the son of another mill-owner, Albert Jenkinson, a baize and dommet manufacturer from Rochdale, who was for several minutes struck quite speechless as the delightfully bubbling Miss Chapman captivated him with her sparkling wit.

'May I take you on the floor, Miss Chapman, before you are carried off by another of your admirers. They are like bees to the blossom this evening and who can blame them!'

It was Harry Atherton. She had seen him earlier, of course when he had arrived and been installed in the luxury of the guest rooms Hannah Chapman had had prepared for them, with his parents and sister, Diana, a well-bred, languid young lady of her own age who, though her father had barely a shilling to his name, knew her own value. A thoroughbred then, Miss Atherton and quite ready to be bored with the bourgeois 'tradesmen' with whom, for her brother's sake, she was to mingle. Mrs Atherton, an older version of her daughter, said quite clearly by her attitude that the idea of her son going into the business of cotton spinning and weaving, despite its financial rewards, would bring nothing but dishonour to the family name, since she herself was niece to a baronet!

They took the elegance, the comfort, the hospitality of Greenacres quite for granted, summoning maids at all hours of the day and night for hot water, hot towels, tea trays, supper trays and anything their aristocratic minds could devise, and here they were, the masculine Athertons quite prepared to be gracious if that was what it took, the females, ordered by their menfolk, doing their duty.

'Your sister does not care for dancing, then?' Kit said sweetly as he whirled her beneath the chandelier which held forty candles.

'Why yes! She loves it the best in all the world, after hunting.'

'Is that gentlemen, or the fox?' Her smile was malicious.

'Miss Chapman!' One fair eyebrow arched and his eyes gleamed with sardonic amusement. He was taller than she was by eight or nine inches and as she looked up into his handsome face she could feel his warm breath, wine- and cigar-scented, fan her own. His eyes were dancing now, a warm brown dancing that said how immensely he was enjoying himself, enjoying the luxury, the superb food her father's chef served, the warmth and the comfort and the beauty of her father's home, and ready to enjoy her, like Jonathan Abbott, if she were willing.

'You really are an attractive woman, Kit Chapman.'

'And what is that to you?'

'Can you not receive a compliment without beating a man about the head with it?' He leaned nearer to smile more warmly into her face.

'It would depend on the man, naturally.'

143

'You know how to wound, Miss Chapman. Come, accept what I say as nothing but the truth.'

'Not from you!'

'And why is that?'

'Because I wouldn't trust you to the top of Friars Mere, that's why. There is some reason for this . . . this claptrap and I have a fair idea of what it might be.'

'Have you indeed, Miss Chapman. Could it not be that your charms have quite bowled me over and, as a man, I cannot help but spill out my innermost dreams to you when I have the chance.'

'Fiddlesticks!'

He threw back his head and roared with laughter and every head in the room turned to stare.

'I like you, Kit Chapman.'

'And you are showing me up with this silly exhibition. Furthermore, I do not care to be held so tightly.'

'Ah ha! You are afraid of me, then?'

'Don't be absurd and if you don't stop this . . . this stupidity I shall walk off the floor . . .'

' . . . and insult your father whose hospitality mine is enjoying. Why, Miss Chapman, where are your manners?'

'And where are yours? I was given to believe you were a gentleman.'

'And so I am, so come, smile at me and at least pretend you are enjoying my company.'

She drew in a deep, infuriated breath.

'What is it you want, Mr Atherton?' she asked him as they floated for the umpteenth time by her father and his father, standing side by side in communal gratification to watch her and Harry Atherton take the floor.

'I really don't know what you mean, Miss Chapman.'

'You know exactly what I mean. You have insinuated yourself into my father's good graces . . .'

'Insinuated! Good Heavens, what a dreadful word, Miss Chapman, or may I call you Katherine?'

'No, you may not and insinuated is the word which describes exactly what you are doing, not only with my father but with me. I do not come with the deal, you know, Mr Atherton.'

'Miss Chapman, *the deal*, what a way you do have with words. My, my, you really are rather . . . what is the word I search for?'

'Inaccessible I think would describe it precisely.'

'Oh, I don't know.' He narrowed his eyes, letting his gaze linger on her mouth and she felt the flush of warmth begin somewhere in the region of her knees and move upwards until her whole body, including her face and neck was rosy. His lips curled in an amused smile over his white teeth and she prayed the music would not stop at that precise moment, for if it should and she was forced to walk coolly across the floor to her mother she was absolutely certain her legs would not support her. On and on they went, round and round, their eyes locked in a clash of wills. He was a superb dancer, holding her firmly, guiding her expertly in the precise steps of the dance and she began to respond to it, to sway when he did in the lilting rhythm which had somehow got inside her head. Dip and sway, her dress flowed about her as smoothly as water and though it appeared she had no room in her head for thought it occurred to her that she could float on like this forever. His eyes smiled warmly into hers, holding her glance, his smoothly brushed head nodded slightly in time to the music.

Suddenly people began to clap, a gentle and polite coming together of white-gloved hands, then, as the music played on and she and Harry Atherton swung round and round beneath the sparkling chandelier, it became more enthusiastic and a man's voice cheered. There was laughter and colour, dazzling light and soft shade, and to her horror she became aware that she and Harry were the only couple on the floor.

'Bravo, bravo . . . how enchanting they look . . . what superb grace . . . she is a credit to you, Barker . . . indeed . . . what a lovely couple . . .'

There was nothing for her to do but to curtsey, first to

145

the grinning Harry Atherton and then to the applauding spectators who crowded the edge of the floor, to affect a blushing modesty and embarrassment at her own boldness when really all she wanted to do was to stamp her feet and smack Harry Atherton's silly smirking face with all the strength she could muster. She could tell by their faces what her father's guests were thinking. What else could they assume when Samuel Atherton and Barker Chapman stood side by side smiling like two old foxes who are in the hen house, their children, she and Harry Atherton, so evidently made for one another and so obviously approved of. So that was the way of it, they would be saying, Barker Chapman's girl spoken for by the son of an *old* family, and what chance had their sons, their expressions said quite clearly.

'I'll never forgive you for this,' she hissed through clenched teeth and brightly smiling lips.

'I? What can I have done now, I wonder?' Harry's warm, carressing hand held her elbow as he guided her politely back to her mother. His arrogance and high-toned opinion of himself was beyond believing and her own body's response to *his*, appalling! She didn't even *like* him, for Heaven's sake and as for being paired off with him, as seemed likely by the look on the face of her father and Samuel Atherton, she would see him in hell first. Not a word had been spoken about marriage, ever, by her father, nor even hinted at and she had been glad of it. She supposed one day, when she had achieved her dream of running her father's business concerns, of being free and independent *as men were*, she might consider marriage, children, providing neither interfered with her professional life. She was lucky, she knew that, for women were not considered in this man's world, did not exist above a certain level, had no rights, no responsibilities, no obligations except in the home, no entitlement to property, no claim on society bar what their menfolk felt was proper. She, if her father had considered it more beneficial to himself, might have been married at sixteen to a man of *his* choice, but she had been allowed to leave the secure and protected world of a lady and move into the exciting, challenging, quite relentless world of a man, and she was not, absolutely not going to put what she had been given into the hands of this fortune-hunter at her side.

'If you will excuse me . . . I must . . .' She pulled her arm quite rudely away from his restraining hand and turning swiftly to avoid both her mother and *his* mother, who sat together with the precious Diana, whose airs and graces had frightened away a score of young men who had approached her. She moved as quickly as was circumspect from the salon, and along the gallery which was thronged with guests, down the stairs and through the first door which opened to her hand.

It was her father's study. It was empty and she sighed with relief. Thank God, just a minute was all she needed, a minute to get over the swell of rage Harry Atherton had aroused in her and then she would go back and face them all, her father, his father and the fool who thought she should not only be glad to receive his attention, but also honoured by it.

She wandered towards the window, drawn by the shaft of moonlight which lay across the terrace and which bathed the whole garden in a sheen of misty silver. It was almost the end of May and everywhere shrubs and trees were budding riotously in the eagerness they showed each year to be out of the hibernation winter cast over them. She could see the shadows on the rippling bark of the trees, and even the separate leaves, lovely and ethereal, on each bough. Her hand reached for the catch of the french window and in a moment she had stepped stealthily, smiling and quite ridiculously pleased with herself, down the stone steps of the terrace and on to the lawn.

He saw her coming and the torch of wood he had ready in his hand felt foolishly heavy and out of place and without his being consciously aware of it, it fell from his hand on to the uncut grass behind the summer-house. The reason he had come slipped easily out of his head, like the hard ice on the moors which must give way to the warmth of the sun. What possible purpose could such things have on a night like this, his bemused senses begged of him, with the loveliness, the grace and sheer magic of the woman who walked across the grass in his direction. His eyes saw her and were dazzled and his heart saw her and grew grave with the truth of what lay there and his mind saw her and was filled with the despair of it for what could she and Joss Greenwood ever share, beyond the enmity of that which lay in the past and the violence which would come in the future. The summer-house had been his target. Just a small reminder on this day when the big house was full of guests that his people were still here and when the time for it came round, as it surely must for the manufacturers would not listen, they would strike, not merely at their playthings as this summer-house was, but at their mills and their looms and their warehouses, until they *did* listen.

But tonight it was out of place. It was her birthday, he had been told for he had spies everywhere and the present he was to bring her seemed somehow inappropriate now. No longer as clever as he had thought it. His own personal gift, he had imagined from his world to hers, but it would not do now.

He stepped out of the shadows and let her see him. She was not afraid, though tonight she had no dogs to guard her.

'What do you want here, Joss Greenwood?' she challenged him but there was nothing in her voice but a strange softness and he felt himself sigh sadly for what might have been.

'God knows now. A present for your birthday.' He bent to pick up the torch and held it out to her. 'I was to light it. Set fire to the summer-house but I give it to you unlit, so, my birthday present to Kit Chapman.'

She looked like a statue carved from marble but her eyes were alive and in them, as though she had sensed what was in him, was a curious expression, one which he thought he recognised.

'Why did you not do it?'

'Again, I don't know. I saw you there. It no longer seemed appropriate.'

The silence was long then, and somehow speaking, threading them together quite naturally though neither would ever be able to explain it.

'We have not heard from you for some time.' Her eyes held his and still he felt no amazement at this that was suddenly between them.

'No, but you will.'

'I suppose so.'

The darkness away from the house enclosed them in a world far from the one they both knew, a fresh and quite separate world in which only the two of them existed. The house at her back was soft with light from every window and it flowed out over the heath garden and the flower beds close to the wall, but here only the stars lit the space about them. Two silhouettes cut out of the darkness, no more than a yard or two between them, each face straining to the paleness of the other.

'I don't quite know what to say, not that it makes much difference. I didn't expect to see you, or anyone out here. The music . . . the noise, it's from somewhere I've never been, another world really, so I stood for a moment to listen, I don't know why . . . and then you came.'

'I was escaping . . .'

'You like to do that.' She saw the gleam of his teeth in the darkness as he smiled.

'You know I do. And don't you?'

'I am not . . . captured.'

'Not even by the life you lead. The things you do for those you . . . fight for.'

'I choose to do it . . . but let us not . . .'

'No.'

There was silence again, but it was not repressive. For that time in which fate had decided to bring them together, not as enemies but in a tentative curiosity in one another as individuals, they were without animosity.

149

'You look . . .'

'Yes . . .?'

'You look well in your frock,' he said lamely, quite unable to turn his gaze away from her, awkward, almost a boy again in his bewitchment.

'Thank you, Joss.' She was grave, completely without artifice as she spoke his given name for the first time.

'Do you still walk up to Badger's Edge?' he asked softly.

'Sometimes.'

'It is on the track to my mother's house.'

'I know.'

It seemed the magic would never be broken and they took a step towards one another then from somewhere a man's voice called her name and a wide path of light shone through the window of the room from which she had come, not quite reaching them.

'I must go.' His voice was almost regretful.

'Yes.'

'Goodbye, Kit Chapman.'

'Goodbye, Joss Greenwood.'

## 11

He was waiting in the same circle of stones, his back to one of them, his arms folded across his chest, his face serious as he stared out over the valley. Almost at his feet was the edge of the cliff face going down and down to the swathe of grass and the scattering of rocks far below.

He heard her call to the dogs, her voice clear on the quiet air and he swung round immediately. As she walked towards him the dogs bounded in great joyous circles about her, quite unconcerned by his presence because she was the same and he found he was aware of every turn of her head, of every breath of air she drew into her lungs, every movement of the muscles of her face and neck as she smiled at him and each sound and intonation of her voice as she called to the dogs. It was completely segregated from the logic and plain common sense with which he addressed himself to life but somehow he accepted it as part of the strange fascination she seemed to hold for him. The glow in his heart when he looked at her was simply there. One moment it had not been, now it was. Beyond reasoning so why try to explain it. Irrational, he knew, just as he knew what he felt for Kit Chapman was madness and that he should throw on his cap and without another glance, nor even a greeting, stride off in the direction of Edgeclough and sanity, but of course he did not.

There was mist up here and she had appeared out of it like a blurred and dissolving shadow. The damp had traced itself about her uncovered hair, decking it with dew-drops and loosening the usual flowing strands of it from her chignon. She pushed it back behind her ears and came to stand beside him, looking out over the misted landscape, the gully below into which the traveller had fallen, or so it was said, hawking his goods to the remote cottages in the area. Here and there the top of a tree protruded through the drifting grey, the breeze moving the mist about in wisping strands, like her hair and they could hear the everlasting music, which was never far away, of the mountain streams.

'Good morning,' she said after a moment. 'A splendid day for a walk,' and because his heart hammered at her closeness and he was suddenly afraid of her and of himself, he was sharp.

'What's good about it?'

'My word! What a grumpy lad he is then!' She was laughing but he could see quite clearly in her eyes that she was as afraid as he was.

'Why did you come?'

'I often walk up here. I told you that the last time we met on this path. And I might ask you the same question?'

151

'I am on my way to a meeting.'

'Really.'

They both knew the other was lying and without conscious thought they leaned side by side against the tall rock and both sighed in unison.

'I didn't want to come, no, that's not right. I wanted to come but I knew I shouldn't. I have been here an hour, telling myself with every minute that passed that I must get on, that I had things to do, that there was no sense to it. You do see that, don't you?' He did not turn to look at her as he spoke but he could feel her eyes on his face.

'I know. I said the same thing as I walked up. I could so easily have gone the other way, up to Sherbrook Falls, anywhere but here but . . .' Her voice tapered away, almost sadly and he turned then to look at her. She was eighteen, not a beauty certainly, but beautiful nonetheless. Her mouth was wide and strong, but there was something about it which said it could so easily slip into laughter if allowed. She had been brought up a solitary child and from the age of twelve, she had told him, trained to take over her father's business. His heir, a wealthy and much sought after young woman and it had made her serious, intent on only serious things, not much given to the giggling to which young girls of her age were prone. Her eyes looked dubiously into his, uncertain and not awfully sure she approved of this strangeness between them. They were enormous in the dampness of her pale golden face, brilliantly blue, the violet in them washed out like the skies above. Her dark eyebrows dipped in a frown, almost of annoyance and she bit her lip.

'I think I had better get back,' she said, trying so hard to be the haughty Miss Chapman, daughter of Barker Chapman who was unused to speaking to rough fellows such as he.

'I think so too,' but still they continued to look at one another. The dogs had lain down, several feet away, but something of the tension between the two people conveyed itself to them and one – was it Joby or Blaze he remembered thinking dazedly – began to bristle.

'I can't seem to think straight,' he said, running a distracted hand through the rough, damp tangle of his curly hair and as he did so her own hand lifted, quite involuntarily to his forehead, smoothing where his had just been and he took it and very gently put his lips to the inside of her wrist and she felt the touch of them move through her whole body.

'Joss . . . I'm scared . . . I do not understand . . . all my life I've known exactly what I've wanted. I've understood what . . . my feelings were about . . .' She took a deep breath, '. . . about life and . . .'

'About men?' He smiled deeply into her eyes, his hands still holding hers.

'Well no, not really, but . . .'

'You don't want complications.'

'No.'

'Then you must turn round and walk away right now, Kit Chapman. We are not meant for one another, you and I. Dear God, there could not be a more mis-matched pair. Our background, our beliefs, our needs are as different, as separate as any two species of animal could be. I hate you, you know that. I hate your people, your class, your careless unconcern with . . .' He stopped and threw back his head and his laugh was false and strident. '*Complications*. Dammit to hell . . . what are we doing here . . .?' His voice was shaking now and, her heart going out to his pain for it was answered in hers, she leaned against him putting her forehead to his lips to stop the flow of words which hurt them both.

'Don't . . .' she said sharply, seeing the working of his mouth and throat, so near to her own and without thought, as naturally as she had known, deep down, that it would be with him, she lifted her mouth for her first kiss. Their lips dovetailed, cool and damp from the misted air, sweet and soft and when he lifted his head to look into her face the sharpness, the rough and spiky corner of his anger had gone and they both smiled in delight.

153

'Do it again,' she whispered and he did and this time it was longer and deeper and she leaned into his arms, wanting more, though she did not know then what it was.

'Kit . . .' he said and his voice was shaking and he held her close, his cheek against hers and she knew what it was, and so did he.

'We should run away from one another as quickly as we can and not look back, you know that, don't you?' he said softly.

'Yes, but it seems I cannot.'

'I know.'

'What are we to do?'

He put her from him, smiling ruefully. 'What do you suggest, Kit Chapman? Just look at us.' He held her arms out wide and his eyes swept over the rich soft wool of her three-quarter coat. It was a lovely blue, with deep pockets, simple but serviceable enough for walking. Her skirt was of the same colour, wide and also easy to walk in and her boots were of a supple leather, black, highly polished. He could see a froth of lace at her throat pinned with a brooch in which some jewel flashed and he marvelled at her folly in coming up here alone, despite the protection the dogs afforded. He found he was suddenly afraid for her, afraid she might be hurt, accosted in some way, insulted by some rough fellow and he was quite amazed by the overwhelming sense of protectiveness he felt towards her. Some rough fellow . . . dear God . . . could not that description apply to him when put beside the elegant, expensively dressed Miss Katherine Chapman?

'Look at us, Kit,' he repeated and her eyes now roamed over him, over the worn and patched breeches which had once been his father's, the thick woollen socks his mother had knitted, his wooden clogs, well made and serviceable but the mark of a working man, the cap he had thrown on the rock beside him.

'What do you see?' he asked her gently.

'Joss . . . don't . . .' since how could she deny it?

'We must. We must look at what we are.' His smooth

brown face, freshly shaved since he had known she would come, his warm, firm, sweet lips curled up at the corners even in repose. The deep, cat-like green and grey of his eyes, the wings of his eyebrows tilting up towards the rough tumble of curls on his forehead. She looked and he watched her and saw her eyes become soft and dreaming in contemplation of him and he wondered where the wild Kit Chapman, the one who had threatened to see him hanged on the day he had wrecked her father's new machine, had gone. She was surely not this soft, sensual woman who was looking at him with her whole female yearning in her eyes for him to see.

'Sweet Jesus . . . we must be mad. We have nothing to give one another.'

'No . . .' and her mouth found his again, carefully, like a child experimenting with something new and exciting, something which grown-ups did, but the feel of her body under his hands was not that of a child, nor the taste of her lips and her tongue.

They spent an hour, dazed with the wonder of it. They stood, her back to the rock, sheltered from the wind and the rain which came down to blot out the valley beneath them and when they were both wet through, laughing, kissing the rain from eyes and mouth and chin, they parted, the dogs padding after her, turning all three again and again to look at him until she disappeared into the mist from which she had come.

They met almost every day at some time, marvelling on how each mind knew when the other was there. No matter what time of the day it was, he or she, would be at Badger's Edge.

'Have you been here long?' he would say, sweeping her into his arms.

'I have just this minute got here,' she would answer, her lips reaching hungrily for his.

The next day or the next he would be leaning against the same rock his face peaceful and as she ran to him she would ask, 'Have you been waiting long?' and his answer, 'No,

155

I've only this minute come,' did not surprise her. There was something in her, and in him, some magic which spoke over the miles so that quite often, when she was with her father or Harry, their commercial minds deep in profit and loss, in turnover and yardage she would lift her head and smile, then shake it in amazement.

'What is it, my dear?' her father would ask, a smiling question in his eyes but she would shrug her shoulders and pretend a forgotten errand, some female excuse to put him off and within the hour, for perhaps no longer than five minutes, she would be in Joss Greenwood's arms, desperate for the feel of his body and his mouth against hers.

'Those dogs of yours get an inordinate amount of exercise these days, Katherine,' Harry remarked lazily as she whipped them through the back gate of the mill yard one morning and up in the direction of the moor. 'They must be the healthiest beasts in Lancashire and why have you suddenly decided they must come to the mill with you.'

'Not that it's any business of yours, Harry, but I feel it does them no good to be shut up in the stables at home all day.'

'Could not one of the grooms exercise them?' He tilted his fair head in her direction whimsically, 'not that it is any concern of mine, as you pointed out, but it seems to me . . .'

'It seems to me, Harry Atherton, that every time I turn round to do something I find you looking over my shoulder. Have you nothing else to do but spy on me?' Her colour was high, unusually so and her eyes glittered in a quite amazing violet flame. The skin of her face was smooth and had become tinted in the summer months to a deep wild rose on her cheekbones, the rest a delicate golden amber. She looked quite lovely, alive and glowing, more than he had ever before noticed and he looked with renewed interest at her.

'I? Spying on you? My dear Katherine, perish the thought!

156

I have more than enough work to do in my day without keeping an eye on your comings and goings.'

'Well, do it then, and let me get on with mine.'

Each time they met Joss demanded, and took a little more of her until they were both like the dry, crackling, sun soaked bracken in which they lay, ready to be consumed by the slightest spark into an inferno. Their passion for one another was slow burning, barely discernible on the surface of their separate lives, well tamped down with only a wisp of smoke and a strange warmth to warn those about them that there was some difference in them and yet underneath it raged, in Kit more slowly since she was untouched, inexperienced. But Joss was a man well used to satisfying his physical needs. From the age of twenty when he became acquainted with Abby Hobson's welcoming body and since then with more than a few willing young working lasses he had met on his travels, his body had been pleased, pleasured as often as he desired. Now he was in love. He loved Kit Chapman. He wanted no other and he could not have her! She allowed him small liberties, afraid, so afraid not of him but of herself. This was so new, this delicate unfolding of her woman's desires, her delight in her own body's response to his. She did not know where it would lead, indeed if it should lead anywhere. She did not know where she *wanted* it to lead. It was as fragile as the cloudberry which made a sweet pillow for her head, and as fragrant. She wanted, at that moment, to do no more than hold it to her, to savour it, to take it out in the dark of the night and marvel at it, but she needed to keep it secret, in a place of concealment until she had grasped the implications of her love for Joss Greenwood.

Yes, she loved Joss Greenwood and it terrified her.

'I want to make love to you,' he said to her on their third meeting. They had moved away from the track which ran along Badger's Edge, walking hand in hand, a man and a woman accompanied by two dogs, in the vast, empty stretches, for as far as the eye could see, rolling hill upon rolling hill, of the South Pennine moorland. There was

157

nothing. No cottage, nor farm nor shelter of any description, just the sudden winding of an old pack-horse track leading to Denshaw and on to Huddersfield, or a turnpike abandoned with the coming of the new canals. It seemed as endless as the ocean, an ocean without sailing ships, divided by the deep troughs of gulleys, steep cloughs and the gentle flow of a stream which became a roar as it cascaded over a ledge to become a waterfall.

They were content then, as they walked, their faces turned to the sun, or to one another which was the same thing. They shared little in their lives, not heritage, class, culture or beliefs, little but this, this love of the 'tops', the rugged, rocky hills, the deep, sheltered, wooded valleys. It was harsh, the upland climate at times, waterlogged in winter, scourged by winds and snow, gripped by ice that crackled underfoot, fog-ridden and desolate, but now as summer laid her gentle, sometimes treacherous hand upon it, it was majestic, shaded by a dozen colours from palest green, lavender, gold and bronze, softened by trees in the valleys that were a carpet of multi-coloured lace from this height, but this man and woman who had been born to it, who had known it in every shade of temper, loved it and in it their love for one another flowered, not softly, nor slowly but with the vigour which marked them both. They would lie in the bracken hidden from everything but the skylark above their head and their ardour grew at each encounter. His hands could not be restrained from caressing the smooth skin of her face and neck. His lips explored the curve of her ear, his tongue its inner softness and his teeth its lobe. He became bolder, more peremptory, more challenging in his eagerness knowing she was as willing as he, since he was a man used to women and her body told him she was not prepared to wait. His fingers were restless, ardent, moving to the buttons of her bodice then turning ill-humoured when they did not open easily.

'Help me, dammit,' but she would sit up and toss back her hair which he had loosened and her rosy face would become pale and strained for how was she to allow him what he wanted, what *she* wanted at that moment more than anything, *anything* she had ever before wanted in her life? They were Kit Chapman and Joss Greenwood. They lived both of them, *now*, for the hours they stole from their separate lives, nothing in the past, nothing in the future but could she take that final, irrevocable step, which would change her from what she was, *just*, a marriageable young woman, a virgin, which a husband would require, into this man's mistress. She loved him. God, how desperately she loved him but the risk she took was appalling for what could he give her? What could she give him?

'I want to make love to you.'

'I know.'

'And you do not?'

'Joss . . . dear God . . .'

She left him, running, the dogs at her heels, her face wet with tears, the content, the sheer joy of living gone, it seemed forever, for this must stop.

But the next day, or the next, she would be there at Badger's Edge and so would he.

'I know nothing about you,' she said on another, quieter occasion.

'Nor I, you.'

'Tell me.'

He turned to smile at her. The sweetness, which had almost soured in him, shone in his eyes for her. They sat on a flat rock above Friars Mere, shoulder to shoulder, their minds and hearts and bodies gentle on this day. It was almost the end of the summer and it was in both their minds that with the coming of the winter they would be faced with the impossibility of meeting up here on the winter moorland which had been their sanctuary for over three months.

'What d'you want to know?'

'What did you do as a boy?' she asked with the eternal feminine yearning to know the boy who had become the man she loved.

'I worked with my family. My father was a weaver and my mother spun the yarn for his loom. I did the cleaning and carding . . .'

'By hand?'

'Of course by hand. There were no machines to do it then. I picked the bits out of the raw cotton and untangled it ready for my mother to spin. When I was big enough my father let me use the hand-loom which had been his father's.'

'And were you a good little boy?'

'I don't suppose so,' bending to kiss her.

'And your sister, the one I met in the mill. How old is she?'

'Jenny's nineteen and should have been a man.'

'Really! Why do you say that?'

'She is like you. Though she does as she is bid, a woman who has her place in the order of things.'

'Like we do in . . .'

'In your class, yes. There is the same set of rules among our women too.'

'Really, I did not know.'

'Oh yes, and though Jenny abides by them she is as rebellious as I am underneath. In a way she is stronger than I am for where I have thrown off the conventions because I am a man and I am allowed to do it, she is forced to stay in her place. A woman must have strength to do that. She would dearly love to come on the tramp with me to . . .'

'Yes?'

'Wherever I go.'

'Aah . . . yes . . .'

He told her about the days when his family had been independent and free, secure and confident in the knowledge that they were craftsmen who counted for something. He described to her the day on which his father had died and of his own devastation, making the massacre at St Peters Field come alive for her, nurturing the seed of doubt which had been planted in her on the day the child had lost his hands in her father's mill and she became quiet then, lost and uncertain, the grand beliefs with which she had grown, which her father had bred in her that profit was a virtue of which to be proud, that loss was a mortal sin, sitting uneasily on her shoulders.

She told him about Harry and for the first few moments as she spoke he felt as though she had flung him into a lake, deep and dark, its bottom wild with weeds which grappled to hold him down. He could see the light on the surface of the water and hear the sound of the life which was above him but as he struggled madly to get back to her, to hear what she said, he could not catch his breath.

'. . . as a salesman originally,' she was saying. 'There will be markets all over the world for the cotton which is manufactured in Lancashire and someone must travel to them and find the buyers. I was scornful, really I was for he is . . . his father is of the landed gentry and his mother, well, one might have been forgiven for thinking her to be related to His Majesty so imperious was she, but for some reason my father believes that Harry is the man to expand our growth.'

Her voice was lazy, her eyes dreaming in contemplation of the pure pale blue of the sky above them. Her head was on his chest and she could not see his face.

'He came to us just before my birthday and I must say I was suspicious. It was so evident that his father and mine were up to something so naturally I began to imagine they were making a match between them. For Harry and me. My mother would love to be allied to a family who can claim kinship with nobility, even the minor kind and it would do my father no harm for it to be known he was related to the niece of an Earl or whatever he is. He is a mill-master, an industrialist so of course they would not receive him at the moment but if I were to be married to one of them, who knows what contacts might be made. But Harry is an idiot, really. So charming, so completely a member of the privileged class one wonders how he can bear to consider a union with one of us, but he loves money

161

and sadly, his family has none. Land, oh yes, for shooting and hunting and whatever else they do in season, and a bloodline which goes back into eternity, but he would dearly like to be rich, one suspects. I suppose he could be considered good looking and his manners faultless but I am pleased to say he has made no move to which I could take exception and I suppose when he has learned the textile trade, as I learned it, in the factory for twelve or more hours a day . . .'

He sat up so violently she was thrown to the ground and her expression of amazement might have been amusing in other circumstances. She looked up at him, ready to smile with her skirts above her knees and the sprig of heather which he had laughingly, lovingly put in her hair fell over her eyes.

'Joss?' she said, leaning on her elbow, shading her eyes against the lowering sun but he sprang up his whole body snarling with the force of his emotion and the two dogs rose to their feet, catching his fierceness, beginning to growl in the back of their throat.

'Joss . . .?' she said again. She sat up and arranged her skirts more decorously as though instinct told her this was not the moment to be seen as a hoyden. She watched him warily.

'Dear sweet God,' he hissed, his back to her, unable to turn to look at her as he spoke. 'Do you ever listen to yourself, do you? Have you no idea of the world outside the bloody gates of your fine house and your splendid mills? Do you give a thought to the men and women . . . and children too . . . who are killing themselves . . .' He turned on her then, his eyes dark with his jealous hatred, for that was what it was, '. . . yes, my fine lady, killing themselves quite literally so that you can . . . what was the word . . . *expand* your growth! Thousands and thousands of them marching to London with bleeding feet to hand in petitions which no one reads, or if they do declare as rubbish. Starving, deformed children . . . Jesus, I must be mad to sit here with you . . . lolling in the grass . . .' He was in torment with his guilt and his shame and the blazing inferno of his jealousy which he loathed himself for feeling.

She stood up slowly and the expression on her face began to harden into the same one he wore.

'. . . and so they are to marry you to this . . . this sprig of a gentleman, are they? who is to work in the factory for twelve hours a day. Poor sod, one wonders how he will manage it!' His voice was a parody of her own, '. . . but then if he is to dip into your fortune and into your . . .' For a sick moment he nearly used the coarse expression men use among themselves for such things and doubtless if he had she would not have understood but in that moment he stopped himself with an effort which was so violent she could visibly see the sinews of his face and neck, his arms and hands, struggle for self control.

'You are all the same, all of you, scrabbling for every penny . . .'

'And you do not? Why are there strikes and . . .?'

'They need to eat to stay alive, damn you.'

'Dear God, are we always to have this . . . this diatribe on every occasion that we meet. Starving children, unemployed men, women who are forever producing children so that they might put them in the mill. Why do they not contain their families to one or two so that they do not go under in the deluge of babies they have year after year . . .'

'It is the only pleasure they have, making love to one another but then you wouldn't know about that, would you? You're keeping that fine body of yours for someone worthy of it, I suspect and it must be given where it will do most good for your father. Christ, do you and your kind ever do anything just because you want to or must every-thing be bought and sold to the highest bidder . . .'

She sprang at him then, reaching for his face but he knocked her away with the back of his hand and without the slightest sound both dogs leaped at him together and he saw it in her face, the longing to let them tear him to pieces. It lasted for no longer than a second but it was

163

enough to carve itself into his mind with an anguish which he could barely withstand.

'Joby . . . Blaze, down, down, I say,' and immediately the dogs reared back, dropping one on either side of him, each muzzle lifting a little to reveal their bared teeth, each head that had allowed him to fondle it affectionately during the summer months stiff with hatred.

'You had best take yourself off, Joss Greenwood,' she whispered, 'before they do you an injury.'

'So I had.'

'I shall not come this way again,' she said but in her eyes was the beginning of something which begged him not to let this happen, not to let her go. God knows what she wanted of him, her own mind agonised since this madness must finish but the endless days before her without him in them could not bear thinking about. She hated him for what he had said to her, for what he believed in, but how could she live without him? It was as simple as that, her eyes told him.

He looked at her and he saw it and the violence left him. He felt it drain away in the hopeless dread which her going would leave and though he simply could not bear the hurt he must inflict on her he knew the time had come when he must. She was so young, surely, his desolate heart said, she would get over this. She would marry this man her father had picked for her. She believed she could resist it, she pretended it was nothing but a business arrangement but deep down she knew it was not. They were alike, despite the difference in their class, this man whoever he was, this man and Katherine Chapman. The bridge could be crossed between them as it never could between her and Joss Greenwood. Though he longed for it, demanded it, had taken masculine offence when she had hesitated, though he would have carried the picture of it forever in his heart, he had it in him to give thanks she was to leave him as she had come. He had loved her, loved her now and always would and the gift he had given her, reluctantly, was the gift of her virtue. For a whole summer they had pretended, perhaps built fantasies in their innermost hearts, of marriage, of children, of the years ahead together, but that was all they were, fantasies, dreams which children dream and now the time had come to put an end to them.

'Joss.' She could see the indecision in his eyes and the true power of his love for her and her heart lightened and her eyes became soft for a moment before he delivered the thrust.

'You must go back to your father, Kit Chapman.'

'Joss . . . please . . .'

'I cannot meet you here . . . again . . .'

She stepped back from him, her body sagging though she was upright. She did not know what was to come but the pain of it hit her even before he spoke.

'There is a girl . . . you see . . .' he continued agonisingly.

'Please . . .' She put out a hand as though to stave off a blow.

'. . . and I am to be . . . married to her next month.'

It was as though her body had become filled with some substance which ran along her veins to limbs which had been weak, to her shoulders which had drooped, to her head which had wilted on her neck and she stood tall, erect, proud of who she was with no need of the support, or love of any man. Her eyes darkened to a sombre purple and though every scrap of colour receded from her face, it was alive, vital and threatening.

'Then you had best get back to her since you are not needed here,' and with a click of her fingers she called the dogs to her and strode away towards the track which led to Crossfold. Her steps were firm and her head high and as he watched her go he had never loved her so much as he did at that moment.

Joss and Mercy were married on an autumn day on which the sun shone from the pale sweep of an eggshell blue sky, over the moors, which fanned out from the tiny Methodist Chapel, where Enoch Butterworth and those of like mind worshipped, laying a great slumberous haze of warmth and lassitude. It would be the last of the summer, they said, those who had come to fill the Chapel and the surrounding burial ground and beyond that even, spilling out on to the moor itself. They could smell the winter in the air, they said. It was the middle of October and amazingly warm but it would not last, for these parts were well known for the ferocity of the weather from now until April or May.

There were more than a hundred there, the men and their wives, those who followed Joss Greenwood on, some said, his violent path of destruction or, as was more likely, they were inclined to believe, those who had known him four years ago, of revenge for the death of his saintly father. It was well known he had no interest in politics before then. He had been no more than a lad, skylarking about, often seen in the company of a pretty lass or two and though he had done his work as conscientiously as any father would like he had certainly not appeared to have a serious thought in his head. His eyes had always been laughing with more than a hint of impudent mischief curling the corners of his mobile mouth and his mother had loved him more than she should for how could anyone resist his merry and engaging flippancy?

Now he was a leader of men, a challenger of authority.

He had lost that jaunty charm which had endeared him, not only to pretty girls but to all those who had seen him grow up in the village of Edgeclough. It had been replaced by a bold defiance of authority, a dangerous shortcoming which, though it brought chaos to the mill-owners, often frightened those who sympathised with his beliefs. The Onwardsmen were known now from Liverpool to Halifax, from Glasgow to Somerset and their name had only to be mentioned in the presence of a mill-owner and he was putting up his barricades, calling in the soldiers to protect his mills and his weaving-sheds and his machines. Surely, they asked, those who wanted an end to it all and a return to peace and some decency in their lives, it must be resolved soon?

Mercy Butterworth, Mercy Greenwood now, left the Chapel to no joyous pealing of bells since such frivolity was frowned upon by those who worshipped there, her hand through the arm of her husband, as lovely and serene as a spring snowdrop, her head shyly lowered as a snowdrop should, though her face was radiant. She wore no bridal gown, nor her husband a bridal suit but in her hands and in the buttonhole of his frayed lapel was a mixed spray of freshly picked wild flowers, red and white Campion, Maiden pinks and white Rock Rose, tied with a delicate froth of white ribbon. Her family, her new family clustered about her and Charlie, greatly daring kissed her cheek, making her blush and then her new husband did the same, deepening the colour in her cheeks to flame and they all agreed they had never seen a prettier bride. There would be no wedding feast, how could there be? It had taken many weeks to scrape together the fee for the parson since even a shilling was hard come by these days. Many of the men and women who had come to wish them well had probably never been legally married since the finding of the fee was often beyond them and anyway, what did it matter? They had no property to leave their children, should they have any and should those they have survive, so why go to the bother of legalising a union which was much more convenient to consummate in the simplicity of a bed?

He kissed his mother goodbye and promised her he would see her the next day since, though he was to live with Mercy and Enoch now he would continue to weave on his loom which had once been his father's and grandfather's before him. Mercy would spin for as long as there was raw cotton available but it was getting more and more difficult to come by, as the machines of the mill-owners, Barker Chapman, George Abbott, Albert Jenkinson and half a dozen others in the town and along the valley ate up the supply. The raw cotton was brought by canal from Liverpool and on to Manchester and as far as Saddleworth before the waterway carried on through Standedge tunnel to the other side of the great Pennine chain to Huddersfield. It came in great quantities, swallowed up by the factories to feed their power-frames and power-looms, stored until they needed it in vast new warehouses, stored, the woven cloth, in other warehouses just as enormous ready to be sent on the same route back to the great seaport and across the oceans of the world to the buyer. Calicos, ginghams, fustians, sateens and velveteens, thousands upon thousands of yards of cotton cloth, making the North, the whole of the country one of the most prosperous in the world and though a great number of the population were at or below subsistence level, those who were not were intoxicated with it.

Joss Greenwood took his new wife to their marriage bed that night as gently as he knew how. He was twenty-three, a man who had been offered and taken more than a few women in the past three years. Abby Hobson, who still good naturedly accommodated him whenever he was in the region of the 'Five Pigeons' had taught him what pleased her and what she liked he had found was acceptable to all women. A bit of decent wooing, kisses and soft laughter and the belief he gave them that they were worthwhile to him, not just their female bodies but in their complex female minds which needed so much more understanding than many men knew of. He had loved many women in the fleshly sense and liked some of them too, particularly the brazen-hipped Abby who asked nothing of him but that he gave her as much enjoyment as she gave to him.

Of the other one he would not allow the smallest whisper of thought to infiltrate his mind for she no longer existed. She had been an abstraction, a shadow without substance, which had, for a lovely moment delighted him, dazzled him but, like illusion, had vanished with reality.

Mercy loved him. Her eyes adored him through the soft candlelight as they and Enoch ate the simple meal she had prepared early that morning. She knew nothing of men beyond the gentle and modest kisses they had shared and the almost brotherly embrace he had enfolded her in as he left at night. He did not love her. He did not desire her and had found the idea of undressing her, of laying her on the bed and covering her naked body with his own, quite unnerving, since she was like a child to him. Just eighteen and virginal as a nun and he was to take that from her.

She began to tremble quite violently as he closed the bedroom door. They were to sleep in the bed Enoch had shared with his own wife since it was the largest in the cottage, and this was enough to alarm Joss Greenwood since the idea of Enoch who was never parted from his Bible, doing to his wife what Joss was about to do to his daughter, and in the same bed, was enough to douse the fiercest passion!

He took her clothes from her one by one, not allowing her to slip into a dark corner and undress herself as she would have preferred since if they were to be man and wife they must know one another's body, take pleasure in it and in the act of love, and this, as he had learned, was the sweetest way to start it. She allowed it, standing like a forlorn child in an agony of embarrassment as he slowly took her garments from her one by one, kissing her frail white skin, here and here, his hand lingering at the curve of her small, exposed breast, smiling as fondly as he knew how, allowing her to know he held her, and her woman's body in the highest esteem, taking his time in bringing her to the rightness of her own desire. Her long fine hair drifted

169

in a soft cloud about her face and shoulders and she shivered at his touch. She hung her head, her eyes staring at her own feet through it all, not once raising them as he shed his own clothes and when he finally put his arms about her she became rigid. He soothed her gently, putting his lips again to her ear and neck, finding the places where experience had shown him a woman is most vulnerable, responsive, smoothing his hands down the length of her narrow back, pressing her tiny body close to his own. She made no protest when he laid her on the bed, lying beside her, careful with her, taking his time in his inspection of her smooth flesh, her tiny pink-tipped breasts, the satin of her inner thighs, with his hands and his lips and his own strong male body. He was mindful not to bear down upon her too heavily for she was as light as thistledown, as insubstantial as a handful of air and he was afraid to hurt her. She cried out sharply as he penetrated her and his mind was so fixed on her frailty it almost unmanned him.

When it was done he lay back with relief. The next time, he told himself, would be easier since she would know him and what was expected of her but in the days and weeks that followed it was always the same. She loved him so much in the day, following him with eyes which shone with a light which said he was the centre of her world, that he *was* her world but at night she withdrew herself, not bodily but in her mind, from his rough demands, his coarse and inexplicable ardour, the strange sounds which came from him, only holding him tenderly when it was done with and the stranger he became for those few minutes, was her Joss again. He was patient. He made love to her so gently, so delicately, he often found he could not himself become a man, to love her as a man loves a woman, and so he began to try less and less. Her sweetness defied him for how could he hurt it? Her gentleness overpowered him since he felt himself to be less than a man in their bed but she was his wife.

It was April now. He and his men had been meeting regularly with other members of radical reform societies, mainly at the 'Five Pigeons' which along with other public houses was being used more and more as a meeting place. Trade Unions were under the ban of the law and though frightened Tories had tried to put a stop to it, denouncing the inns as places where the lower orders talked sedition and mill-owners had called upon the authorities to punish publicans for allowing the illegal trade unions to collect there, Abby Hobson was afraid of no one and was certainly not concerned with the possibility that she might lose her licence. Every night they crowded there, the men who had nowhere else to go bar their miserable hovels and the everlasting sight of downtrodden women and starving children. They could do nothing about it, though it broke their hearts, so they escaped it by mingling with other men in the same condition but with the hope Joss Greenwood and other militant radicals put in their heart. They often did not drink since they had no money. Sometimes, when the 'Benefit' clubs or 'Thrift' clubs of which 700,000 of them were members, gave them a 'hand-out', or the poor relief, the outdoor relief some of them were granted, contributed a small amount to the family welfare, they might have the price of a jug of ale and it was not unheard of for the open-hearted landlady to slip a jug over the bar counter to a man who had nothing but the company of other men to comfort him.

They had all gone. The night was very dark, the thick, low cloud cloaking the moorland in a blackness which could almost be felt, but it was mild. The air gently caressed the cheeks of the flushed men as they stumbled away in every direction, cheerful most of them for they had been uplifted by the plan Joss Greenwood had outlined to them, excited with the prospect of being about something after the long torpor of the winter months. Abel Broadbent fell into one of the cold little moorland streams which tumbled noisily down the hillside to the valley bottom where it met the River Penfold and there were a few amiable curses mixed with their high laughter since, for once, they felt optimistic and what did a dousing in the water matter?

Joss watched them go, his own face softened with a smile for he had grown to love these hapless men who looked to him for leadership. He was younger than most of them but the last four years or so had matured him, made him into a strong and compelling man, a man accustomed to being obeyed, to have other men follow him without question. He went to meetings in Halifax and Huddersfield to hear Mr Richard Oastler, a man involved in the abolition of colonial slavery and now taking up the cause of factory children, to Blackburn to listen to William Cobbett who had been imprisoned after the massacre at St Peters Field and as far south as Nottingham to sound out the ideas of others who thought as he did. He was much respected though still far too wild for some of his followers. He was about to threaten Barker Chapman again and though what he had said made sense and had the majority mad with excitement, one or two of the older men had it in them to wish he was a little more like his father. He had incited the younger men this evening, promising them with fire in his eyes that the blow they were to deliver the Chapman mills would be repeated up and down the Penfold Valley and into Crossfold and Oldham itself. Fine talk and bold, but that was his way.

He was still rangy without an ounce of spare flesh on his big-boned body and his shaggy hair was cut only when his wife could get him to sit still long enough for her to get at it with the shears. There were fine lines in the skin around his eyes and the shadows of clefts beginning on either side of his mouth. His skin was brown, even in the winter since he walked for miles in all weathers across the moorland paths and his step was springing and graceful. He had a magnetism now that was undeniably male, arrogant and headstrong for his authority had for so long been unchallenged, drawing not only the appreciative eyes of the women, most of them young and fancy free and ardent in their support of the cause, and ready to show it to the one who led it, but also Joss had the championship of the men.

Abby Hobson was stirring the fire with the brass poker

172

when he returned to the tap room. Her movements were slow and unhurried and as she turned to smile at him the weight of her splendid breasts fell forward, straining against the fabric of her bodice. Her nipples were peaked and brazenly full and as he watched she undid the top buttons one by one, allowing him to see the magnificent valley of fine white skin which divided them. Instantly he felt himself become erect as he had not done for months in his bed with Mercy and the cloth of his tight breeches was uncomfortable against his thighs.

'Tis 'ot in 'ere, lad,' she said, 'and that there smoke don't 'elp none. Mind, I do like the smell of tobacco and brandy. Will you 'ave one fer the road, Joss?' She smiled, offering him more than a glass of brandy if he cared to take it and if he did not, letting it be known he would not give offence. A woman of ease, of comfort, a woman made for pleasure, not only of herself but of the man of her choice. She gave the abundance of herself, the bounteous goodwill of her body where it pleased her to give it and woe betide any man who tried to help himself, but of all the men she knew and had known, none moved her like Joss Greenwood. He was ten years her junior but he was a man for all that, and not since Matt Hobson had she recognised such a man. Her husband, the publican of the 'Five Pigeons' had died some years ago and she had taken the inn over, keeping order when men grew unruly, as easily as he, a bareknuckle prizefighter, once had done. She had loved him well and been faithful to him while he lived but she was a woman of appetite and liked to eat when she was hungry.

Joss sighed and shook his head though he ached, quite literally in the region where Mercy's submission could not touch him, to take what he knew Abby offered.

'Nay, lass, I must be on me way. It's an hour's walk and Mercy'll be waiting.'

'Aye, 'appen it'd be best.' She smiled quite gently at him and her great dark eyes, gypsy eyes from the man who had probably fathered her were filled with compassion. 'You'll not want ter be worryin't lass.'

173

'No . . .' but he did not turn away from her.

'She's a lovely little thing, Joss,' she said sincerely, but not giving you what you need, her eyes continued and though she made no movement her body seemed to sway a little and the lift of her breasts drew him another step towards her.

'Abby . . .' His voice was thick and a fine film of sweat broke out on his face.

She sighed deeply. 'Eeh my lad, there's no need to be uncomfortable with me. I've seen it all and there's many a young girl needs time . . .'

'She cannot . . .'

'Joss, there's no need, not with me.'

She opened her arms and he sank into them, pressing his aching flesh against the warm softness of hers. She raised her rosy face and his lips found hers, moving hungrily from them to the flesh beneath her chin and the hollow of her throat. His hands rose to take her bodice from her and the chemise she wore beneath it and his hands cupped the magnificence, the lovely rose-tipped bounty of her breasts. But it was not enough. Tipping her back until her buttocks rested on the table beside the fire he lifted her skirts until they were bunched about her waist and with a swift move-ment undid his own buttons and in a moment he was inside her and wave after wave of giddy-paced excitement thrummed through him and into her until she cried out and so did he. It took no more than a minute or so and when it was done he stood between her legs, his breath ragged, his face like that of a mad man, his eyes savage.

At last she pushed him away and stood up, her naked breasts swaying an inch from his chest. She put her hands to the fastenings of her skirt and in a moment it was round her feet and the gloriously female splendour of her was there for him. She reached out and began to unbutton his shirt and when he was as naked as she, she leaned into his arms and began to lick his skin, just below his chin, follow-ing the strong line of his throat, the sweat-dewed mat of his chest hair and down to his flat stomach and he groaned

174

with delight, grasping the entangled mass of her hair.

She looked up at him and smiled and her eyes were black in the firelight. 'That was for you, Joss Greenwood, and now this is for me.'

'How did you know?' he said, hours later. She had been, one moment, like mother earth, basic and honest and understanding, allowing him the great and plentiful goodness of her heart and the next, a wild woman, demanding, showing him the secret delights of her body and how best he might please them and only when her pleasure had been attained, and his again and again did they lie in peace together before the dead fire.

'Nay, don't ask me, lad. I'm a woman and I know what drives men. Some men have needs which others don't, and women are much the same. I could see what you were missin' 'cos it was in me an' all.'

'I cannot . . . seem to make her love me.'

'She loves you right enough, Joss, what woman wouldn't?'

'Oh I know what she feels for me, Abb, but she's so . . . so little, no more than a child and I'm afraid to hurt her.'

'Women like to be 'urt a bit . . . now an' again. You weren't exactly gentle wi' me a time or two tonight, my lad.'

He leaned on his elbow and smiled into her face. Her hair was a rich and glowing red, like the pelt of a fox and it was snarled about her head, burnished by the firelight almost to gold. Her eyes were understanding, the eyes now of a friend, the eyes of a woman, complete and uncomplicated. A friend!

'I have a great deal of affection for you, Abby Hobson.'

'So I noticed in the last hour or two, but what else ails you, Joss Greenwood? 'Tis not just that little wife o' yourn, is it?'

'No.'

'Perhaps . . . a woman?'

He sighed and his eyes looked into hers, seeing the

175

wisdom and tolerance there and putting his cheek to her full breast he told her of Kit Chapman.

'She's no good for you, lad, heartless, like the rest of her . . .'

'I know, Abb, but who has made her so?'

'You're defendin' her.'

'Aye, she's his child. She has no say in what happens at that mill.'

'You love her then, Joss Greenwood, or you'd not be takin' up for 'er. You really love 'er.'

'Aye.' His voice was sad and empty.

But as he walked home his face was calm, his body at peace as he listened to the sounds of the moor at night. The soft splash of water against the stones, the squeak of some small creature in the budding heather, the rustle of another as it crossed his path at a run. He had not felt so content since before his father died and he wondered why that was. He had been a callow youth, carefree, careless, ready for any prank his own or his mate's brain could devise and though they had known hard times his childhood had been secure. He had been aware that other children, factory children, pauper children had not been so lucky for he had gone about with his father and listened to men who told them so, but he had not really *known*.

He was a man now with the knowledge burned deep inside him of the desolation which was creeping over this northern land he loved so well. He was a man of responsibility, with a wife at home and his mother and her family to help support. He did not know where he was to get the next supply of cotton for his wife and his mother to spin in order that he might weave his piece but somehow, just at this particular, bewilderingly contented moment, it did not seem to matter. Was it just because his body's hunger had been assuaged – surely not – or was it because he had allowed Kit Chapman into his heart again when he had spoken of her to Abby Hobson?

Mercy was waiting for him when he got home, her face rosy from the heat of the fire. Though coal was readily available, and cheap to all those who could afford it, most of the cottagers cut peat from the bogs which stretched for miles across the moorland basins and which, when they drained, compacted into the fuel which was a substitute for coal and had the advantage of being free. It burned just as brightly and warmly and the cottage kitchen was cosy as he stepped inside.

Mercy smiled, standing to move across the room, lifting her lips for his kiss as sweetly as a child. Her eyes were clear and innocent and if he had not himself taken her as his wife he could have well believed she was no more than fourteen and virgin. His heart was soft for her, protective, but his manhood folded itself away, knowing sadly she was not a complete woman, nor probably ever would be. She was a lovely young girl, eager to help him in his work. Her heart was filled with her love for him and for her father, her dead brother and her new family but physically she was as immature and as naïve as a child. She imagined that she fulfilled her role as his wife, that she did her 'duty' though she would not think of it quite like that, in his needs as a man, and she was happy despite her repugnance for it.

'You shouldn't have waited up, love,' he said, no sense of guilt or remorse for the past hours he had spent with Abby coming to trouble him.

'I wanted to hear how the meeting went,' she replied, bustling about the kitchen, a wife now, as she saw herself. A woman in her kitchen seeing to the requirements of her husband. This was where she felt at ease, washing and ironing his shirts, mending them, creating tasty meals from nothing and watching with great pleasure as he ate them.

'Well, I think, though some of the older men were not convinced.'

'Would you think me disloyal if . . . if I said I felt the same, Joss?' She carefully put the pan she had filled with water on the fire, then stood back to look anxiously up at him. It was a wife's job to support her husband, her expression said, but this one of hers was sometimes an enigma to her. She knew he was fighting for the oppressed and the starving folk who were her neighbours, many of them, but he frightened her sometimes with the intensity of his recklessness, of his daring.

'No, Mercy, you may say what you please. But talk does not always bring about the reforms we need. We must often resort to other means.'

'I know . . . but to . . . well, suppose someone is hurt?'

'We shall make sure no one is.'

'Oh Joss, sometimes I wish . . .'

'What lass?' His voice was patient.

'That there was some other way.'

'Well, there isn't, so how about getting me something to eat? I've been on the tramp all day and I'm fair clemmed. I've had nothing since me breakfast and porridge and treacle doesn't stick to your ribs like . . .' He stopped as she turned away in confusion and what appeared to be distress. Instantly he was contrite since she did her best with what little he could give her. Enoch put the few shillings he earned directly into her hands each week but the hens from which they sometimes had an egg or two had long since gone into the pot and with winter just behind them, the store of vegetables was finished. Of course she could not give him a hearty breakfast and he had not meant his words as a criticism but as a joke. Now she was close to tears and he sprang across the room to hold her in his arms.

'Don't fret, sweetheart, please . . . don't cry. The porridge was well enough and I'll not be wanting to get far, will I?' He smiled and kissed her cheek, bending to look into her eyes. 'Give me some bread and . . . whatever you've got and we'll be away to bed . . .' but the tears still fell and she hung her head as though in deepest shame.

'What is it, Mercy? For God's sake, tell me.'

'Oh Joss . . . I'm sorry . . . but . . . well . . .' She lifted her tear-stained face, her eyes agonised with guilt. 'There's nothing to eat, Joss. I tried to manage, really I did. I went up to your Mother's to see if . . . well, perhaps . . . sometimes Charlie's had a bit of luck with his traps, but there was nothing, and Martha . . . they had nothing either.

178

Oh, I'm sorry, Joss . . .' She might have been frittering away the few shillings a week he earned on gee-gaws and bon-bons, so pitiful was her expression but it was nothing to the despair in his own heart. His wife, and apparently his own mother, were harrowed by the emptiness of their own larders while he himself had been concerned only with the frailties of those others in Lancashire who were in need, who were starving, the men ready to commit murder, the women to go on the streets to earn a shilling to feed their families. Now, at last, that spectre had come to stalk his own family and he had nothing to offer his wife but words. He stared over her head and the glow of exhilaration he had felt as he walked across the tops faded away, going out like a torch leaving nothing behind but a wisp of smoke and he knew, at last he finally *knew* what it was he fought for. All these years he had fought. He had protested and marched, wrecked power-looms, for if the power-loom was broken and the spinning frame was left untouched did it not follow that the manufacturers still producing yarn would send it to the cottagers for weaving? He had broken windows and a few heads. He had put his name to a dozen petitions, preached what was called *sedition*, attended illegal meetings, drilled men in the use of weapons to fight for what was rightfully theirs and now what was rightfully *his*. He had been shouting into the wind, he realised that, liking the sound of his own voice, enjoying the power he had and the splendid way men jumped to do his bidding, but he had not really *known* but now it seemed he was to experience it at first hand. He could not stop now, even though his own wife and mother were in the same plight as the others. He could not stop *because* they were in the same plight as the others.

Now, finally, their fight had become his fight!

179

# 13

They were silent as they streamed down the hillside, no more than a dozen of them since that was all that would be needed for what was to be done. They had kept to the wood which sloped down the hill since it gave them good cover, a rush and blur of dark shapes, dropping over the rough wall and into the grassy ditch beyond though there was no one to see them since the watchman was at that moment enjoying the young girl Ellis, the overlooker in the spinning room, had supplied him with. It had cost him sixpence, of which the girl got nothing, beyond the keeping of her job but it was well worth the money for though she had struggled somewhat at first it being her first time, and was painfully thin with no breasts to speak of, being only twelve, she was female, cheap and clean. He never knew what hit him as he slumped across her white body.

'Dear sweet Jesus . . .' someone said, his voice sounding abnormally loud in the dense black silence of the night and for several minutes there was complete confusion since Joss Greenwood had not allowed for this predicament and not being there to ask, those who milled about waiting for him had no idea what to do with the silently weeping child. They covered her decently, averting their eyes, ashamed most of them of their own maleness, wondering what the hell to do with her but, sniffing dolefully she took matters into her own hands, and vanished, it seemed, to wherever it was she slept when she was not on shift.

It was Saturday night and the weaving-shed, for the first time since last Sunday night, was shut down, the machinery switched off and idle, ready and waiting for the factory children, including, presumably, the one who had just been outraged by the watchman, to clean it the next day.

He was there then, quietly appearing from nowhere, a slightly darker shape in the darkness, tall, easy, soothing their jitters just by being there. They grouped about him, unnerved by what had just happened, longing to unburden themselves to him but quelling their instinct to shout about the obscenity of it. They had heard of course, about the plight of many a young girl and of the use the overlookers made of them, those who had no home to go to and no man to defend them. They were often offered to other men who came to do business in the sheds, it was said, an added inducement to the closing of a better deal. Naturally, it was well known that the heat in which these girls worked hastened the process of female development so that in some cases a girl of eleven years might have the breasts of a fully mature woman so who could be blamed, those who took advantage of what was offered them said, when they took it? The girls were clean, free from disease, at least for a while and, if they did well and made no fuss could be rewarded with a penny now and again to spend as they liked.

It was almost midnight, an hour when those who had beds to go to were in them, and only those who screamed and fought and fornicated about the gin-mills of Pig Lane, Boggart Hole and Lousy Bank, tore the peace of the spring night to shreds with their wild cries and their howls of drunken laughter. The bulk of the warehouse stood between the men and the town and only the odd hoarse cry or the wail of some woman, rose above its high roof and they took no notice. It was well known that Crossfold was no place to be on a Saturday night and those who took no part in such goings on stayed in their villas and mansions and kept their doors and windows locked.

The glass made no more than a tiny shattering sound as Joss put the stone through it and when he had wriggled inside the men were eager, ready now to show what they were made of in this war they fought. They were ordinary men, labouring men who asked no more than a decent wage and a dignified way of life but they had been forced to take on the role of soldiers and not all were cut out for it. Joss's white teeth gleamed for a moment in the darkness of his face when he opened the enormous door to them, wide enough and high enough to accommodate the horses and waggons which came to take away the velveteens and fustians so beautifully woven by Barker Chapman's operatives.

The warehouse was stacked high. Roll upon roll of carefully wrapped cloth waiting to go to many parts of the world, ready to be put on the canal barges which would carry it away, first on the Huddersfield canal to Manchester and then on to Liverpool by the Bridgewater canal. Barker Chapman's wares would go by 'narrow boat' beyond Old-ham up and down a dozen locks before they reached the sea but these would not make that journey for Joss Greenwood had other plans for them.

The first smoke was no more than a trickle, a vague wisp sneaking through a crack in the brick wall. There was the merest flicker of a flame, not ready yet to take good hold, smouldering and whispering among Barker Chapman's splendid cloth. The men stood uncertainly, the empty oil jars in their hands, quite fascinated really, forgetting for a moment where they were, watching, as small boys, the mishap of another, then Joss's fierce whisper had them on the move, their clogs fetching sparks from the cobbles of the yard, clattering out and into the street and in a moment they were over the stone wall again. Even then it seemed they could not tear their excited selves away but must stay and watch, kneeling to peer over the wall at their own handiwork.

They had wanted to wreck the power-looms Barker Chapman had put in but Joss had been against it. Though he was aware of the logic of their thinking, their belief that if the Chapman weaving-sheds could not weave who else could Barker Chapman turn to but themselves, he himself had begun to doubt it. In theory it was sound, their thinking, but this time he wanted to get at the mill-owner in another way. Those operatives who worked the looms would be thrown out of work if they were destroyed. With the woven cloth itself burned to a crisp, Barker Chapman would have no option but to begin again, with work for carders and spinners, for weavers and finishers and nobody thrown off. And when this was safely alight, burning so fiercely it could never be put out, they were to march on to Abbott's mills, to the Jenkinson mills and as many more as they were able, and do the same there.

They were half way up the hill, their jackets streaming behind them, their arms flailing enthusiastically, their shouts of triumph not pleasing him much since it was not the action of a band of soldiers but of children who have just tied two door-knockers together. But he supposed that sometimes they must be allowed this outlet for their frustration and bitterness or they would go mad with it.

It was then he heard the scream. It was high and desperate, lifting the hairs at the back of his neck and for a moment they all stopped, the memory of the desolate child fresh in their memories. Surely to God she had not gone into the warehouse ... Dear God ... suppose Barker Chapman put the children in there to sleep ... Sweet Jesus ... but then their faces cleared for they were conscious that no man and certainly not one as careful as Chapman would allow a group of children to roam about in a shed containing thousands of pounds worth of cloth.

'Who the hell ...?' one whispered though if he had shouted it is doubtful his voice would have been heard above the increasing roar of the flames. The fire had taken hold with a will now, leaping up above the roof of the warehouse, fed by the easily devoured provender of the fabric within, lighting up other buildings set apart from it since by keeping his sheds well spaced Barker Chapman had thought to avoid the very disaster which was now taking place. Glass was beginning to shatter in the windows and tiles popped and again the scream rang out, nearer this time and it was then he saw her.

*Kit Chapman!* It was Kit Chapman. A vividly illuminated figure set against the lurid wall of the warehouse, running, tripping, picking herself up, turning about again and again and so close to the burning building he could well believe he could see smoke coming from her clothing. She seemed not to know what she was doing, to be unaware of everything but the flames, uncaring of her own safety, desperately seeking something which eluded her.

They all watched, paralysed with shock, himself included since they had dragged away the unconscious body of the watchman and had believed there was no one else who could possibly be injured. The warehouse was empty except for the cloth, they had been told by Jenny who was an experienced spy for the movement by now, going often where she had no right to be to gather information. The apprentice children slept where the bales of raw cotton were stored and there was no one on the site but the watchman since, it had appeared, no disturbances were expected at Barker Chapman's mills and weaving sheds. Many mill-owners had asked for troops to protect their property in the scattered outbursts which had rippled across Lancashire but Barker Chapman in his insolent belief in his own superiority needed no one to guard what was his!

His daughter darted suddenly to one side, foraging under the disbelieving gaze of Joss Greenwood and his Onwardsmen, among a pile of what appeared to be rubble, then finding what she sought she ran like the wind, carrying something towards a trough which stood by the gateway. It was a bucket. *A bucket.* Swinging it wildly she filled it from the trough, set there to water the horses of her father's callers and, her mission clearly understood now by those who watched, she began to wobble lop-sidedly towards the open doorway of the burning warehouse. Surprisingly there were as yet no flames coming from it, but inside it was an inferno, savage, loud and hungry and she was going in to douse it with a bucket of water!

The others, still frozen in horror, did not even see him go, the first they knew that he was no longer with them was when they saw him from their elevated position above the street, racing across the yard, his long legs eating up the distance from the gate to the warehouse doorway. She had just reached it when he dragged at her arm and even then, with her skirt beginning to smoulder she swung the bucket at him, screaming wildly, maddened, her eyes like those of a warrior defending his territory, cursing and dangerous.

'Leave go, you fool, the warehouse . . .' Her voice screeched insanely with the need for speed and for a moment he thought he could not hold her or, as seemed more likely in her furious strength, she would take him in with her. He held her with both hands now, dragging her, screaming and kicking, spitting in his face, the bucket gone, thank God, or she would have brained him with it. Still she would not let him take her. Her nails raked at his eyes and his cheeks, drawing blood. Her knee came up, ready to plunge into his crotch and he had time to wonder where she had learned that trick then he struck her, not a violent blow but enough to stun her and he caught her in his arms as she fell.

He was half way up the hill, Kit Chapman mumbling against his chest, her hair all over the place, her arms hanging limply when he realised his men were still there at his heels.

'Get home, for God's sake,' he shouted, '. . . we'll have to leave the rest. Go on, they'll be here in a minute, you bloody fools . . .' and in the space of thirty seconds they were all gone and he was alone with Kit Chapman in the blessed peace and coolness of the woods.

He laid her down on a pillow of mosses. There was a thick carpet of dead leaves, dry now since there had been no rain for several days. There was a dense layer of wood sorrel, nourished by the leaf mould, delicate pale green upside down parasols with yellow-centred white blossom. There was a ring of beech and hornbeam about them, all in new leaf and he could hear the whisper of the breeze in the canopy above him and smell the delicate fragrance of new growth.

She sat up slowly and in the pale glow from the burning buildings down the hill he could just make out the blur of her white face and the glitter of her eyes. She put her hand to her jaw where he had hit her and he heard the sharp intake of her breath as she winced. He knelt by her side, his knees deep in the softness of the moss and waited.

She turned her head then, bending it a little to look into his face and though he could see no change in her expression, indeed no expression at all, there was no mistaking her venom.

'You set it, didn't you?' Her voice was like a razor in her throat.

'Yes.' He could certainly not deny it.

'You bastard.'

'No doubt, but it had to be done.'

'*It had to be done!* A week's work . . . a *month's* work. Hundreds of yards of expensive cloth and it all had to go up in flames! Why, dammit? For God's sake, why?'

'You know why, Kit Chapman.'

'Do I? Do I? My God, if I live to be a hundred the logic of this . . . these outrages you commit will continue to baffle me. They spun it, weaved it, these . . . these people of yours. They worked and were paid for that work and in a moment's insanity you have destroyed it.'

'As you are destroying them.'

'Destroying them? . . . We employ them . . . give them work when there is no other to be had . . .'

He stood up, sighing wearily for what was the use? They were saying the same words they had said when they last saw one another nearly nine months ago, which they had said a dozen times before and still it was the same. Both looking at the coin from opposite sides and though it was the same coin they each saw a different face to it.

'Are you all right?' he asked, ready to walk away since what else was there to do. He felt his arms ache with the need to put themselves about her, just once, sweet Jesus,

186

just once more, to hold her as he had last summer, in love, but he must get away from here before they caught him, before *she* caught him again in the deep netted trap of love.

He was half way across the tiny glade then he stopped, taking a step or two back towards her. She was still crouched upon the ground, her arms draped across her drawn up knees, her head bent on her arms.

'It just occurred to me . . . an idle question really since what is it to do with me, but what the hell were you doing at the mill alone at this time of night?'

'You're right.' Her voice was muffled in the crook of her arms. 'It has nothing to do with you.'

'I'll leave you then but perhaps it would be a good idea if your father kept a stricter watch on his daughter in future. Crossfold is not exactly the place to be on a Saturday night.'

'Damn you, Joss Greenwood, damn you to hell! What business is it of yours?'

'None whatsoever, but had you not perhaps better get down there. They will be looking for you. The warehouse is a holocaust now and I presume, if you are missing they will imagine you to be in it.' He kept his voice neutral, without expression.

'My father knew I was in the . . .'

'Where?'

'In the design room. I drove the phaeton in. There was something I wanted to finish. So I left the dogs in the stable . . . then I smelled smoke . . .'

'You drove yourself! My God, he must be mad.'

'He trusts me. I am his son.'

She lifted her head then, proudly and even in the dim light, illuminated now by the flames from down the hillside, he could see the satisfaction that simple statement gave her. 'He allows me to do exactly what a son would do. He knows I will come to no harm with Joby and Blaze.' She made a contemptuous movement with her hand. 'What do I want with dinner parties and evening concerts. I had a problem to be worked out so I changed and came down.'

'You still like to take risks then?' His voice was low almost as though he did not want her to hear.

'And you do not?'

'I am a man.'

'So?'

She tossed back her hair and a sudden explosion of flame lit up her face. There were black smudges on it and her hair was wild. The gown she wore, a riding habit of dark cloth was fitted tight to her body, sculpting it, displaying the lift of her breasts, the narrowness of her waist and the lovely curve of her hips. She was quite magnificent in her newly won womanhood, violent in her rage, dangerous but proud, proud to be who she was and of what she did, hating Joss Greenwood still for what he had been to her.

He grinned sardonically since she must not see into his heart and his white teeth slashed his face. 'You don't look like no son to me,' he said, and his eyes roamed insolently over her body.

'You filthy bastard,' she shrieked and leapt forward, reaching again for his face, for any part of his flesh from which she could draw blood, for his eyes to blind him so deep was her hatred but he caught her wrists, laughing now and in a moment he had her backed up to the wide trunk of the tree under which he had laid her minutes before.

'You see how easy it is to overpower you, my lass? You are a woman, *not* a man and any man who has a fancy for it could take you, and your fine ideas and reduce you to what you are. A *female*! a *woman*! Your father might call you his son, God damn him, but look at you, *look at you*, you are helpless in my hands, in any man's hands . . .'

'If I had my dogs . . .'

'Do you take your dogs to your bed with you, my fine lady, for that's what you need to make you see what sex God made you. A man to tame you, to make you into the woman you are . . .'

'And you are that man, I suppose? Well, you were not man enough up on the moors that summer, Joss Greenwood, so tell me what has changed?' As she finished speaking she spat full in his face but he did not release her to wipe the saliva away. Bending his head he put his face against her straining breasts and with all the time in the world, or so it seemed, rubbed sensuously against them, with his cheeks and his mouth until he felt her nipples harden, then swiftly, as she gasped in outrage he lifted his mouth to hers, taking her lips beneath his own. Brutally he captured them and they trembled and though for the space of a heartbeat she would have turned her head away, they opened under his and the softness, the fire, the sweetness surprised neither of them.

They were both breathing hard, both fighting, though neither of them could have said why, or for what since they were both fully aware of what they wanted.

'Don't . . .' she whispered against his mouth and he let go of her wrists and felt her hands lift to cling to his shoulders.

'Oh Jesus . . .' His mouth slipped down her arched throat and her eyelids fluttered in the straining pleasure of her body's response but from down the hill the sound of men's voices drifted on the tide of flames and billowing smoke and as they at last penetrated her bewitched mind, she stiffened and her eyes opened wide. His dark head was beneath her chin, his lips warm at the hollow of her throat and he was whispering her name.

'Dear God!' Her voice was a shriek of pain, of horror, of abhorrence and he fell away from her in confusion. 'Oh dear God . . . you bastard . . . get away from me . . . get your hands off me . . . my father will have you horse-whipped for this . . .'

He was stunned, overpowered by the strength of his need for her which he had thought to be dead, of the dangerous emotion she had disturbed in him. His senses were as sharp, as raw as though they had been exposed to the fire down the hill. His breath hurt his chest and every part of his body was acutely aware of hers but she was looking at him with such loathing he could not bear her to know it. His face strove to smile coolly for she must *never* know it.

189

'Your father, my dear Miss Chapman, would be wise to have you locked in your room for if you are to go about bestowing your favours on all and sundry as you did with me, and delicious they were if I might say so, well . . .'

He managed a smile of amused contempt, feeling at last the black, snarling anger he needed to expunge the memory of her body and her lips and sweetness of the moment from his brain.

'You . . . devil . . . I'll see you hanged . . .'

'So you have been telling me for the last three or four years and yet I am still here, my lass.'

'Not for long . . . dear God, if I have anything to do with it, not for long. No one has known who it is that leads this mob which goes about burning and looting, and raping for all I know . . .' `

'Oh no, not raping, Miss Chapman.' He raised a sardonic eyebrow. 'I had no need of rape here tonight for you were more than willing, I would say, wouldn't you?'

She struck him full in the face and, unprepared for it, it rocked him on his heels but he only laughed and she thought she had never hated any man as much as she hated this arrogant devil.

'You are as foul in your mouth as you are in your deeds and if you cross my path again I will kill you . . .'

'Really, Miss Chapman, such melodrama. Come now, a little kiss! Where was the harm in it? You were not unwilling the summer before last as I recall, and don't tell me you didn't enjoy it tonight?'

'Don't . . . don't push me too far . . .'

'I have no intention of pushing you anywhere, nor will any man from what I have learned of you. A man likes a woman to *be* a woman, you see, and you . . . well . . .' His dark eyebrows tilted wickedly, '. . . but I really must go since I hear a hue and cry coming up the hill . . .'

'I know you now, Joss Greenwood, and your family since your sister works in my spinning mill . . .'

Instantly he had her in the vice of his two hands again, holding her wrists agonisingly in front of her face and she was afraid then, shrinking back from him. He was black-faced with anger and his eyes beat her down and his voice was icy, chipping away the apparent amusement he had felt, telling her that what had gone before had been no more than child's play.

'You threaten my family, you bitch ... you touch my family and you won't be the only one to talk of killing. Do you understand? They have nothing to do with this, nothing, and if a hair of their heads ... any one of them is harmed I shall know where to look.'

'Go ... oh for dear Christ's sake ... go ... I cannot bear you ...'

He threw off her hands, then turned slipping away through the trunks of the trees without a backward glance and she leaned against the tree, her face quite blank, her eyes empty and staring, though her mind was alive and crawling with the imagery of her thoughts. She hated him and all his kind and no matter what they did she would not give in. She would punish them and through them, *him* and if it took her to the end of her days she would make sure he was hunted down, imprisoned, transported if she could arrange it so that she might never see his face again. She had known some sympathy for their plight, those frail children who worked in her father's mill and had wondered in the secret recesses of her mind whether, were she to be in the place of those women who put them there, might she not feel the same sense of grudge, the same sullen resentment. Might she not have fought beside the man who had just, she realised now, saved her from an unthinkable death, clawing for the right to share in what the mill-masters had? She had heard them say so often, these faceless men and women that if the manufacturers tried to increase their own profits through wage cuts and sweated labour, then, through machine breaking, they would make sure there *were* no profits. It had a certain plausibility but why could they not see that if the mill-masters closed their mills, as they would be forced to do, it would be the labouring man who would suffer. Why did they not accept ... Oh dear

God . . . it was *him*, that damned radical reformer . . . *Joss Greenwood* . . . Joss . . . aah . . . how she . . . no . . . no . . .! At each confrontation he made her think, made her wonder and question and it did no good. She had a mill to run, a profit to be made, workers to pay, a responsible position in the economy of the country. She was part of what made the country great, and he was no more than the breaker, the destroyer, the instigator in the tearing down of what men like her father and grandfather had built up.

Her body was still in a tumult, fiercely consumed with the energy she remembered so well and understood so little, an energy she had known only with him. She wanted to stretch langorously and at the same time beat on the trunk of the tree at her back with angry clenched fists. There was something stirring in her body's core, something she did not recognise but which she was desperate to discover and her lips still burned with the touch of his. She rubbed them frantically with her hand and her heart was dazed and despairing.

'Kit . . . Katherine . . . Katherine . . .' Her father's voice, almost unrecognisable in its desolation, floated up from the road and there were other voices, hoarse and urgent and getting louder. She turned to look dully and on the slope of the hillside, coming up towards the trees, were the figures of men, dozens of them.

'Kit . . .' Her father, still dressed in evening clothes was in front of them, shouting to them to spread out, to go round the back of the buildings and in a moment she knew she must go to him for he was distraught, believing her, perhaps, to be in the burning warehouse.

'Get the dogs . . .' she heard him shout, '. . . they'll find her if she's . . .'

She must face him, make up some story to explain how she came to be up here, so far from the mill site, dirty, dishevelled, but unharmed and as the hurried speculation of what she must say slipped through her tired brain, her heart grew still and cold for she had realised that, without conscious thought she was preparing, quite instinctively to protect Joss Greenwood.

She turned her face to the rough bark of the tree and wept.

# 14

Harry Atherton watched his employer's daughter cross the mill yard, admiring the way in which her skirt swung, almost but not quite brushing the cobblestones. Though he knew she would not do it deliberately, for it seemed Miss Katherine Chapman was impervious to a gentleman's admiring glance, her hips moved in a way that was infinitely sensual, and her arrow-straight back constrained her to lift her breasts quite splendidly. She had left her bonnet in the office and her hair caught a sultry beam of sunlight, turning it to the superb glow of a chestnut, so shining it looked as though it might just have been polished. She stopped to talk to one of the workmen, the foreman who was in charge of the rebuilding of the new warehouse and her face was impatient and her hands lifted, cutting through the air, and presumably his excuses, as though to pour scorn and disbelief on whatever it was the man said, and Harry chuckled. She would, no doubt, be telling the poor beggar his own business, demanding to know why since it had been a week ago that the first brick had been laid, the building was not complete. Already the foundations were down and the walls waist high and it would probably be no more than a week before the roof was ready to go on since Katherine Chapman seemed blindly determined, almost obsessively so, he thought, to have the new building filled with finished cloth as it had been before the fire.

His sharp brain wondered why. There was no doubt that

the Chapman mills stood to lose an enormous amount of profit, not to mention the cost of rebuilding the warehouse but it did appear to him that this was not the only concern on Katherine's mind. It was as though the horror of the night of the fire could only be scourged from her by the act of replacing what she had lost, and as quickly as possible, just as though she must have everything exactly what it had been before.

It was a puzzle which set his alert mind humming. He had not been present at the dinner party held that night at Barker Chapman's home. There had been his employer's bank manager and his wife, so Harry had heard, the owner of the local newspaper, *The Crossfold Observer* and his wife, a business acquaintance from Germany who was interested in Chapman fustians, and Albert Jenkinson, his wife and daughter – brought to balance the party.

Harry realised quite early in his new position – and smiled to himself – that Barker Chapman, though the arrangement he and Harry's father had made was firm, would allow no liberties to be taken, not until the final event had been legalised. Harry Atherton had been given the chance, but he must prove himself capable of grasping it before he could consider the Chapman wealth at his disposal. He was Barker Chapman's insurance, if you like, on his daughter's future. He could do her no harm, nor any good, really, since she was completely able now to run the mill alone but he was her *bulwark*, her shield between herself and her fortune, and the rest of the hunters who crowded about her at every function she chose to attend. He was a gentleman. The 'right sort'. He would ensure that the dynasty – of mill-owners, for God's sake – would not die, in fact he was to inject it with some decent blood!

And he would enjoy the task immensely, he told himself, since Katherine Chapman was – apart from the misfortune of her birth – an ornament splendid enough to decorate any gentleman's home, particularly one as luxurious as Greenacres, which would, naturally, come to him. She was bright and had a malicious wit which would add spice to their partnership. She was elegant and ladylike, quite lovely to look at, and very, very rich. Not for a moment did it occur to him that he might fail and when Kit entered his office he smiled, at his most amiable for the pictures in his head were more than pleasant.

'And is it to be finished by lunchtime then?' he asked, raising a good natured eyebrow and though often he irritated her beyond measure with his flippancy, Kit could not help but smile back at him.

'Perhaps not, but if I have anything to do with it, Harry Atherton, it should be no longer than the end of the month.'

'My heavens, you can get more work out of a man than my old schoolmaster who used to beat us unmercifully if we were not word perfect in our French conjugation.'

'No doubt, but then I should imagine that is the only way to get work out of you,' and she looked pointedly at his immaculately trousered legs, crossed at the ankle, which were propped on his desk.

'How sharp you can be, my dear Katherine. So cutting, my heart is in tatters. And so serious. Do you never relax for a single moment?' His smile was silky and innocent.

She sighed and shook her head. 'Everything is a joke to you, isn't it? I am trying desperately to replace the yardage we lost in the fire, to make up the orders which were to go out the next day while you sit about on your . . . chair, smiling and talking nonsense and getting nothing done. Can you not . . .?'

Quite lazily he picked up a sheaf of papers and moved them towards her. His eyes narrowed almost dangerously but his voice was pleasant.

'Before you dress me down as I have just seen you do that poor chap in the yard, take a look at these will you? They are letters from customers, those whose cloth was lost in the fire. Where do you imagine I have been these past weeks, my dear? Down to Leicester to the hunt . . .?'

'I wouldn't be at all surprised . . .'

195

'Now then, Katherine, that is not at all polite and quite unworthy of you and if you read these letters you will see you were mistaken in me.'

'Oh for Heaven's sake, Harry . . .'

'All right then, listen to this. Do you imagine I am happy to invest my time and my energy and my considerable talents . . .' he grinned disarmingly, ' . . . into this business of yours if I am to get no return? Hardly, my dear. I have been to call on every man, in England at least, who has lost cloth in our . . . your warehouse, at considerable cost and taking up an enormous amount of my time, assuring each and every one of them that Chapman's, despite this slight setback, will have a new consignment ready for them by the end of the month . . .'

She gasped. 'The end of the month! Harry, for God's sake, you know that's not possible . . .'

'Your father does not agree.'

'But the operatives cannot possibly manage to produce that amount by the end of the month. Two months, perhaps, since we shall have to have somewhere to store it . . .'

'I have rented a warehouse from George Abbott.'

'Very commendable of you but how are we to fill it?'

'Extra hours, extra shifts, seven days a week until we have made up what was lost.'

'Seven days a week! But the machines must be cleaned and oiled and the children cannot . . .'

He sighed deeply and stood up, brushing down the faultless creases in his dove grey trousers.

Harry Atherton had done well in the year he had worked at the Chapman mills. He had not, as Barker Chapman had, been brought up in the cotton industry. Where he came from the manufacturing classes were held in contempt and though a chap would not be censured for marrying where money was, far from it, they could not understand, and said so, why he should choose the daughter of one of those upstarts, who thought themselves to be as good as they. And on top of that he was to learn, so he said, every process of cotton manufacture, the skills, the difficulties, the stratagems that the damn class got up to! He accompanied Barker Chapman on his daily rounds of the mills and the weaving-shed and was shown the intricacies of the machinery, to the counting house to learn the intracacies of profit and loss. He went often to the Cloth Hall in Crossfold mixing most agreeably with the commercial gentleman who admitted to each other they had not expected him to stay the course as long as he had. He was an 'easiful' man which was not something to be said in his favour since the textile trade was cut-throat and if he should cross swords with one of his competitors, many of whom would slice a bean in half if it could make a profit, it would be interesting to see how he would fare then.

'Look, Katherine. Your father has told me of your . . .'

'My what?' Her expression was perilous since she had found on several occasions that her father seemed disposed to talk of her to Harry Atherton behind her back and it alarmed her since she had not forgotten her eighteenth birthday when she had been quite certain that it had been his and Samuel Atherton's intention to pair her off with Harry. Nothing had been said since and Harry had kept his distance, communicating with her only in the course of business and on the one or two evenings he had been invited to dine with the Chapmans. Then there had been other guests and not by word or deed had there been an indication that he was anything but her father's employee.

'My what?' she said again.

'It does you justice, really it does since it is well known that ladies, or most of them, have tender hearts . . .'

'What the devil is that supposed to mean, Harry Atherton?'

'That you do not care for your operatives to be worked too hard. That you would prefer not to employ children despite the fact that their families cannot do without their wages and the work they perform can be done by no one else for it needs tiny bodies to . . .'

'Stop it. Not another word. How dare you and my father discuss me behind my back, how dare you? I am fully aware that children must be employed and I have said nothing about . . . turning them off. I appreciate that the work they do is important . . . necessary. It was just that . . . well . . . I just felt . . .'

'Yes, Katherine?'

But she would not let him see the slightest sign of weakness in her. She must not allow any of them to say that she was a woman and therefore could not discharge her duties as a man would. Her father, this man, all of them had no qualms about employing children and if she was to compete with them, as her father's heir, then she must do what *they* did.

'I shall speak to the managers this afternoon. Let me know what you need exactly, to make up the orders and I shall see that it is done. Now, if you have nothing further to tell me I must be about my business.'

'There is just one more thing, Katherine.'

'What is it?' she asked defensively, turning back to him.

'You look quite incredibly lovely today, my dear.'

The slamming of the door as she left the room could be heard in every part of the counting house and so could his following laughter.

Barker Chapman's dwellings to house the families which flocked in ever-increasing numbers to beg work at his mill spread like a weed round the factories and to pay for them and for his new warehouse, for someone must, his spinners and weavers had their wages reduced once more by three-pence a cut.

Those who lived in Pig Lane, Boggart Hole and Lousy Bank and were already at starvation level in their Chapman-built terraces of 'company houses' became even more sullen.

'We won't stand for it,' they said and their angry mutterings grew louder and could be heard even above the sounds of their neighbours' brawling, their lust, which they all shared in the back-to-back intimacy which was thrust on them in their one up, one down dwellings. They could be seen in groups of four or five at the tap which was shared by twenty cottages and was turned on for an hour each day, or at the communal privy, used by the same twenty families. Their pinched faces were set between crooked shoulders, their hands thrust deep in trouser pockets or tucked inside the wrappings of a shawl.

'We won't stand for it,' they said, and there was despair and violence breeding in the slums Barker Chapman had created. Those in Pig Lane and Boggart Hole and Lousy Bank and the squalid alleys behind them became surly, knowing as they sipped their water porridge and treacle that, though there was not much they could do about it, since they must work to earn even what little they had, they did not like it at all. They watched the manufacturer, Mr Barker Chapman and his daughter, the fine Miss Katherine Chapman, the mill-owner Mr Albert Jenkinson and the weaving-shed owner Mr George Abbott ride down Jagger Lane in their carriages, their glossy carriage horses better fed than they themselves were and word was carried up to Joss Greenwood at Butterworth's cottage that it was time to be on the move again, to make bloody Barker Chapman hurt again in his pocket, to burn something else he valued, like his mill, or his weaving-shed, or his house.

'We won't stand for it,' they said. They had been promised better things, by Mr Hunt at St Peters Field, four years ago now and still they were starving, still the men were forced to watch their women and children flock to the mill to bring home the wages which fed the family, or not! The price of bread had gone up again and were they to stand for it, they asked one another, when their wages, or more precisely the wages of their women and children had been cut?

Gangs of youths roamed the streets, playing at 'Onwardsmen', looking for mischief and when they found it in the shape of Mr George Abbott they threw stones at him, hitting him on the head, and in Mr Albert Jenkinson's weaving-shed where they smashed his windows, every last one of them. They were men, they said, weren't they, not bloody animals to be worked until they dropped. They wanted the old system back with their wives at the spinning wheel and themselves at their hand-looms and in their own homes and if they could not have it, why not?

'It won't come again, that's why,' Joss told them unsparingly, 'and it's no good shouting for it and saying you won't have anything else. It's gone, can't you understand it? There are power-frames and power-looms and that's the end of it but we'll find something to take the place of what we've lost, don't you fret. We might not work for ourselves any more, we might not even work any more but we'll bloody well fight until we've got a life that's fair and decent. A fair day's pay for a fair day's work . . .'

'It's a bloody long time in coming, Joss Greenwood. They're making us work even 'arder and longer than what we were since that bloody warehouse fire *and* for less wages. What 'ave you ter say to that, then?'

'I know that, Isaac Pickering, but by God if we stick together and wait it out we're bound to win. That's the answer, can you not see it? Fight and more fighting and even more, and when we can say we won't work for what they're prepared to give us, and mean it, then we've got a chance. We need to close ranks, let no one part us for only in strength can we fight with strength. One day we mean to have the vote for every man . . .'

' . . . and woman, eh, Joss . . .'

'Aye, Sarah, for with the likes of you to put in your fourpenny worth how can we fail?'

He and Mercy, Jenny and Charlie had gone up to Ravenstone Brow above Saddleworth, the green and gold and purple infinity of the moorland stretching out for miles on all sides of them and the men had come to listen to him and to other reformers who had come to talk to them. This last blow struck them by Barker Chapman had flung them low and they needed the hopeful words Joss and the others gave them to lift them up again. They had crept up from as far away as Oldham and Bury, from Rochdale and Todmorden and Bacup, the women bringing sickly infants and younger children. The older ones, those who worked in the mill for six days out of seven fell into their beds on a Saturday night and did not get up until Monday.

It was Sunday, high summer and everywhere heather and gorse and bracken bloomed about the knees of those who walked in it. Lapwings beat over their heads, stirring the still air with their wings and the heat wrapped itself about the great crowd, lulling them to somnolence for it was not often they could sit and do absolutely nothing. They were tired, those who had walked ten miles here and must walk the same back and many simply lay down and went to sleep, pillowing their heads on soft grass and sweet smelling clover, shielded by bracken fern and ling and purple moor grass, their eyes closing on the sight of tiny, quite beautiful cloudberry.

But the men did not sleep. They milled about Joss Greenwood and the two who had come to talk to them, remembering Abel Greenwood, the martyr, and Tom Butterworth, who, though he had not died for the cause but in defence of his sister was a martyr nonetheless, looking to the man who was now indisputably their leader. He was speaking of forming a union even though it was illegal, as this meeting was illegal, and of wrecking not the power-looms which were taking their living, but of the wisdom of attacking Barker Chapman and George Abbott and Albert Jenkinson and the other mill-owners who were bringing their trade to the Penfold Valley, where it would do them the most damage – in their pockets! As they had done in the burning of the Chapman warehouse. All along Hull Brook and the waters of the river which had once driven the wheels to power the machinery, these new men were building and if the textile trade was to survive in Lancashire, men like themselves would be needed to ensure that it did. It could not be done without them and the manufacturers must be made to see . . .

They had crept up between the drowsing women and children, slipping past on their bellies like eels, hidden in the waist-high summer bracken, even their red coats invisible in the dense foliage. Joss was standing on a rock, head and shoulders above the hundreds of men about him. He had seen the movement of the bracken, taking no particular notice for there were dozens of children about. Young lads delighting in the hidden depths of the undergrowth, playing the games young lads love so well.

His voice was powerful, mesmeric and the men understood and believed what he said. It made sense and they cheered and clapped one another on the back, saying it would not be long now, surely, since how could they fail to overcome their destitution and misery with a man like Joss Greenwood to lead them?

They rose from the bracken at their very feet, not children but soldiers, no more than two dozen but enough to move in a tight circle towards the ringleaders. They let the others go, those on the edge of the crowd who panicked and ran, stopping some of them to pick up a crying child or a bewildered woman. Those close to Joss, Abel Brigden, Jack Akroyd, stood by him for even if they had been inclined to it they could not have run with the others. They were radicals, leaders of men in other parts of the country where cotton and wool and silk were manufactured and workers were exploited, brothers in arms against oppression, who had come to speak today to Joss Greenwood and his Onwardsmen, to tell the Lancashire spinners and weavers to keep a stout heart and a hopeful one for they were supported by those of Yorkshire and Nottinghamshire. These men and others had marched beside Joss in protest, their faces masked as his had been, but they were not masked today and neither was he and the soldiers had the three of them by the arms, knowing them, it seemed, before the horrified crowd had realised what was happening.

'Run ... take your families and run,' Joss shouted at the top of his voice and so used to his authority had they become they were away, pushing and shoving and jostling so that the six soldiers who held Joss and Abel and Jack had to be protected by their comrades. They drew their muskets, and the officer-in-charge, his sabre, standing about the three captives, ready, should it be necessary, to shoot anyone who dared a mischief against them or the three men they had captured.

Half a dozen of Joss's men, those who had come alone and were without a family, hung about thirty yards or so from the troop of soldiers, ready to make a dash for it but willing, if Joss gave the word to take on the armed soldiers.

'For God's sake, run! If they get us all there'll be no one to . . .' and they watched helplessly as the butt of a rifle at the back of his head brought Joss to his knees. They went then, hundreds of them, streaming across the moorland like the waves of the sea and the soldiers watched them go impassively since they had the ones they had come for.

It was then Mercy began to scream. She had stood, quite paralysed, beside Jenny and Charlie, unable to comprehend what was happening. The sight of those red coats had plunged her back into the terror of that day when . . . when Tom had . . . when the soldiers . . . when the soldiers . . . had . . . She pulled frantically at Jenny's restraining hand and Jenny was not certain whether it was to run to Joss or away from the soldiers. Charlie, fleet as the rabbits he snared, darted towards the circle of soldiers who were keeping a close guard on their captives until the hostile group of their followers decided what to do.

'Charlie . . .!' Jenny's shriek drew the attention of one of them and before the lad could reach his brother the man had scooped him up, kicking and swearing, under his arm. He ran like the wind, carrying him back to where Jenny and Mercy hovered, his long legs leaping like a hurdler and though the boy still struggled, begging to be let loose, tears streaming across his ashen face, the man would not release him.

'Come on,' he said roughly to Mercy and Jenny, grabbing Jenny's arm with his free hand since she seemed to be the one most likely to respond. Joss's wife was still screaming, her voice shrill, demented but beginning to fade into the moan of an animal in shock and when Jenny was dragged along so was she.

'We just can't leave them,' Jenny agonised, but the momentum of the slope of sweeping moorland, down and down and down, carried her with the others until the little scarlet-splashed group behind them was no longer visible.

'Please . . .' she cried to the unknown man, her breath breaking in agony from her tortured lungs, '. . . please . . . can't we . . .?'

'There's nowt to be done, lass, nowt . . .'

'But . . .'

'They've got bloody muskets . . .'

Within five minutes the stretch of moorland beneath Ravenstone Brow was empty, every man, woman and child who had come to hear Joss Greenwood, Abel Brigden and Jack Akroyd, gone and all that was left was the bright splash of colour where the soldiers still stood defensively about their captives.

The officer lowered his sabre then returned it to its scabbard, his careful eyes still sweeping the moorland about him. There was nothing to see but the miles of empty bracken, the stretch of the hills above and the long decline below him into the Penfold Valley. The sun which warmed his back painted a blue shimmering haze above the long and lovely sweep of the heather which minutes before had made a fragrant bed for those who had the stink of the factory in their nostrils for six days a week. There was nobody, nothing but a bird rising from the shadow of the far side of the valley and the sound of its cawing.

'Right, sergeant' he said smartly. 'I think we may proceed now. They have all gone.'

'Aye, lad, 'tis safe to move on as you say. They've all gone now. It would look bad to be overcome by women and children, fine soldiers like you.'

Jack Akroyd suffered the same fate as Joss Greenwood as his laconic, smiling remark reached the ears of the officer and he fell against Joss who was still struggling to rise. Blood flowed from behind Joss's ear, dripping on to the whiteness of the shirt Mercy had ironed for him the night before and his head rang with pain but he was determined to stand. With a great effort, his thoughts jagged and piercing, the swiftness of the attack still dazing him, he stood straight, his hand reaching to help Jack.

'Get your hands off that man,' the sergeant barked but Joss took no notice, stooping a little now to raise Jack to his feet. Abel took his other arm and at last all three stood tall, staring boldly, arrogantly, the officer would have said, at the circle of soldiers.

'You are under arrest,' he said arbitrarily, 'for contravening the Combination Acts of 1801 and 1819, one of which states that a seditious meeting such has been taking place here today where more than seven persons have gathered is illegal. You three, as its leaders will be tried and sentenced. Right, sergeant. Manacle the prisoners, please and we will get them down to the lock-up at Oldham.'

Jenny Greenwood stared into the dying embers of the fire in Enoch Butterworth's grate. She leaned forward in the chair, putting her elbows on her knees and cupped her chin in her hands, her eyes unfocused, her face strained and weary. Upstairs, induced by the draught of valerian which Sarah Pickering, one the village women, had brewed for her, Mercy slept at last, still trembling fitfully as her dreams carried her back to the moment earlier in the day when she had seen her husband clubbed to his knees and to three years ago when she had seen her brother knocked almost senseless in the same way. They would hang Joss just as they had hanged her brother, she had screamed again and again until Martha Greenwood, the mother of the captured man but herself composed had sent for Sarah who knew every herb which grew and what each was capable of.

'She will do herself an injury,' her mother had said when Jenny had turned on Mercy, shouting at her to be quiet. 'You have not loved a man yet, Jenny Greenwood and cannot know how she suffers. Her brother was hanged and it has . . . made her . . . delicate . . . more anxious.'

'We are all anxious, Mother. Good God . . . oh dear God, what are we to do?' It had been the turn of Enoch then, reprimanding her sternly for taking the Lord's name in vain, telling her it was possible to save her brother only through God and prayer and to get down on her knees and beg His forgiveness and to intercede for the life of the man who, in his own opinion had lived lawlessly, mocking God in his . . .

'Oh for Christ's sake be quiet, old man,' Jenny had shouted nearly off her head with worry and Enoch, bitterly offended, had left the cottage swearing he would go up into the hills to speak on her behalf and on her brother's behalf to his God. He had known of Joss Greenwood's disposition when he had married his Mercy and the hopes he had nurtured that the love of a good woman and the begetting of a family, which he had prayed would bring an end to the violent ways of his son-in-law, had come to nothing and now look where he was. Rotting in Oldham gaol with others like him and with transportation staring him in the face and what was to happen to his young wife, Enoch's daughter then, he asked?

The cottage was quiet. Charlie and Daisy had been put in with Sarah's young ones, though Charlie at seven years of age had protested wildly, asking why they could not go, all of them, all of Joss's men and break him out of the gaol like they had done for others, who had been taken? Jenny had been inclined to ask the same but Martha had soothed them both, begging Jenny to be cautious, to wait and talk to the others for no good would come of breaking the law a second time that day.

'What will they do to him, Mother?' she asked now and Martha leaned into the firelight, her own face drawn and haggard for she had known this upheaval so many times since she had married Abel Greenwood. So often he had been apprehended, fined, once three months in prison for 'disorderly conduct' though a more peaceful man had not existed. Her son was violent, disregarding the peaceful ways of his father, marching, drilling the men who followed him up to the moors, breaking machinery and, she was well aware, though nothing had been said to her, that he had

206

been involved in the burning of Barker Chapman's warehouse.

'I don't know, lass.'

'What will they do without him?'

'They'll manage, Jenny, same as always. Like we've managed since they brought the first power-looms into the valley.'

'But they depend on him. They look to him for leadership and a bit of hope.'

'There'll be others to carry on.'

'Dear God, Mother, he's your son. Are you not concerned that they might send him to the colonies?'

'He'd still be alive.'

Jenny sprang up, her hair springing up with her and her mother marvelled that these three children of hers could be so wayward for even their Charlie, at his age, was heading the same violent way.

'I'll get the men together. There's a hundred of them'd be willing. We'll have the three of them out of that gaol by nightfall tomorrow. It's been done before . . .'

'And have him a wanted man, on the run for the rest of his life.'

'I'll go down now to Isaac Pickering's. He'll fetch the others.' She reached for her shawl throwing it like the wings of a bird across her shoulders her face vivid now she was on the move. She had gone as far as the door when Martha's voice stopped her.

'You'll do no such thing, my girl. You'll sit down and stay here with me.'

'Give over, Mother. I can't hang about and do nothing . . .'

'Why is it always what *you* can't do, or what *Joss* can't do? Why is it that whenever there is trouble, whenever someone is *in* trouble, the pair of you must be off somewhere, doing something regardless of what the one *in* trouble needs?'

Jenny hesitated then, looking back at her mother, her eyes saying she could not bear to sit here doing nothing, begging her mother to let her go, and yet, admitting in her heart that she could not, that she *should* not go, that Martha Greenwood was right. She wanted to be off for her *own* sake, because *she* was frustrated and needed to be doing something. If Joss was freed by his men, which it was more than likely they could manage, since there would be no more than half a dozen soldiers guarding the gaol, he would not be free at all. He would be a man wanted by the law, his name on the magistrate's list as a criminal and what good was he to them then? He would be unable to move about freely as he did now. He would be forced to hide, to dodge and run at every alarm, disorganised, hunted, never able to stop in one place long enough to speak to anyone, let alone the crowds who came to drink up his strength, to take hope from his power. He must be a free agent and if he must go to goal to be free again, then so be it.

She moved back slowly, her feet dragging on Mercy's well-scrubbed floor. She sat down again in the chair from which she had just risen and putting her face in her hands began to weep.

They were shut up, the three of them together in a slip of a cell scarcely big enough to house one. There was no window, no light nor air and the stench of other men who had been there before them was so thick Joss thought he would choke on it for it got in the way of each breath he took. He was afraid, more afraid than he had ever been in his life for wherever he had rested in the past, he had been free, out in the open where the sun was, or the gracious beauty of the moon and the stars. He was to stand trial at Lancaster at the next Quarter Sessions before the magistrate, for conspiring with Abel Brigden and Jack Akroyd, to raise the wages of those employed in the cotton industry, which was against the law as set out in the Combination Acts.

The learned counsel said so at his trial three weeks later, remarking sharply that any assembly which endangered the peace and security of other men could only be looked upon with great anxiety, particularly as the object of the gathering was an impossible one. The new machinery, without which there would be no foreign trade had reduced the wages of the labouring man but that gave him no right to disturb the peace of others. The acts of Joshua (Joss) Greenwood, Abel Brigden and Jack Akroyd, the accused, amounted to an expressed and avowed determination to destroy the most fundamental freedom of a man to employ men and to pay wages as he chose. It attacked the very foundation of the government itself and was not to be borne at any cost.

The accused were each sentenced to a year's hard labour.

## 15

Martha, Jenny and Mercy Greenwood moved wearily up the track leading to the moorland path which would take them to Edgeclough. Jenny carried Daisy who was soundly asleep, her small head lolling against Jenny's shoulder like that of a broken doll. Some way behind them Charlie limped, his feet dragging, his face drained of colour or expression, his eyes staring ahead of him and Martha turned jerkily, clutching at Mercy's arm as though to keep her balance.

'Come on, love, it's not far now,' she called to him anxiously but he just went on putting one foot in front of the other, like a sleepwalker, giving no indication that he had heard her.

'Wait for him, Jenny, or he'll not catch up,' and Jenny stopped obediently. They stood, patient as oxen, almost mindless in their exhaustion, Martha clinging to Mercy until Charlie came abreast of them, then they resumed their journey, not speaking again for it took what little strength they had left just to keep going.

It was distressingly hot and the three women had tied their shawls about their waists, the weight of them too great to be carried. Their wooden clogs made a hollow sound on the stony track and their tread was heavy and flat. Martha slumped against the fragile figure of her daughter-in-law and it was evident in the way Mercy leaned towards her that even Martha's light weight, since she was painfully thin, was a burden to her. Martha's head hung down as though the effort it would take to lift it and look ahead was beyond her. Her face was a pasty grey, lined as the bark on a tree. She coughed continually and when they reached the gentle brow of the hill which led on to the moor, she stopped, gasping for breath.

It was almost dark. The sun was a livid ball of fire in the sulphurous sky, its lower curve already dipping below the horizon, the vast space about it the colour of a hot coal. There was orange and gold and apricot fading at its edges to the palest lemon and in the far distance a tiny star or two pierced the pale pearl grey.

'I'll just sit for a minute, lass,' Martha said when she had got her breath. 'It's that damned "fly". I just can't seem to clear it from me chest. I've been sick three times but it'll not be gone. See, put our Daisy down, love. She'll be all right on the grass,' she said to Jenny, 'an' we'll wait for our Charlie. Poor lad, I'd carry him meself but he's that big.'

'I'll try if you like, Martha,' Mercy said tiredly, but Martha shook her head.

'Nay, love, you can't manage him. 'Appen a minute's rest will perk us up.'

They sprawled on the tufty grass beside the track like so many marionettes whose strings have been cut and Jenny eased her clogs from her bare feet which were as black as the fireback where the soot settles. She wriggled her toes, sighing with relief, then stretched her shoulders trying to ease the agonised muscles.

It was almost nine o'clock and since five that morning

they had all been on their feet, she and Mercy and her mother at their spinning frames, Daisy 'piecing' broken threads and cleaning waste from beneath the machines and Charlie as a bobbin boy. Fifteen hours in Chapman's frantic determination to make up the woven cloth that had gone up in flames in the warehouse which her brother had burned. Not that she blamed Joss or regretted for one moment the destruction which must have cost Chapman dearly but by God it seemed sometimes that she, and all the others who worked for him were paying for it. The machines were never still, twenty-four hours a day, even on a Sunday, and the only time they were cleaned was during the few minutes in which the operatives were allowed to eat their food and relieve themselves at the tub in the corner of the yard. It fair turned your stomach taking away any appetite you might have had, up to your elbows in muck and grease, oil and cotton waste but it had to be done.

And how long could they go on like this, her mother and Mercy and the children, she asked herself? She had begged Ellis to allow her mother to sit for five minutes when she had almost fainted in the desperate heat and had been told viciously that if her mother wanted to sit down she was welcome to do so outside the factory gate where three dozen other women were waiting to take her place.

She put a protective arm about her mother's shoulder, hugging her to her. She bent her head to look into her face and her own was worried. Martha Greenwood was in her forty-ninth year, an old woman who should by rights be taking her ease, at time of life, by her own fireside. She was strong, or had been, since she had lived all her life on the high moorland in good clean air and had fed on vegetables from her own garden, on fowl she had fattened herself, pork from her own pig and when she was a child, milk from the cow her father had kept. A hard life certainly, from dawn to dusk and beyond, but a healthy one, out of doors in the shelter of the cottage wall spinning in the sunshine and though she had lost seven of the ten children

211

she had borne, they had all been healthy at birth. Now, in the three months since Joss had been imprisoned they had all been swept into the factory system, either that or starve, she had aged ten years. It had nearly broken her heart to take her young ones into the mill, against which for so long her husband and son had fought but she had simply no choice.

Enoch Butterworth had died the week after Joss was sentenced. He had taken it hard, fretting on the shame of having not only a son hanged for murder but a son-in-law imprisoned for sedition. It seemed to take the heart from him, rendering him suddenly rudderless without a course to put his feet, a course approved by his God. It was not that he no longer believed in Him but that He seemed to have become disapproving of Enoch Butterworth and it was more than he could bear.

'I'm tired, Mercy,' he said one Sunday afternoon. 'I'll go and have a lie down,' and so he did and never got up again. Mercy, too anguished on the fate of her husband and how she was to manage without his strength, violent and destructive though it had been at times, to spare any for her father, buried him quietly in a corner of the yard of the Chapel where he had worshipped, closed up the cottage where generations of Butterworths had been born and took herself, her furniture and her father's hand-loom up to Martha's, putting the loom in beside those which had once been worked by Joss and his father. It made no sense to pay rent on two cottages, she said tiredly so if Martha didn't mind . . .? Martha had welcomed her daughter-in-law, taking her into her own bed and comforting her when she cried for her husband in the night, wondering as she did so on the mystery of her son's attachment for this delicate little wife of his who never seemed to grow from a girl to a woman.

'Come on, my lasses, we'd best be off,' her tone was cheerful, her face determinedly bright, 'or we'll not be home before dark.'

'Nay, Mother, let's sit for a while. It's nice up here, cooler and the view's lovely. We should've brought a picnic.'

Martha smiled at her daughter's small joke, thanking God for her since she was the life-line to which they all clung now that Joss was not here. She was a strong one, her eldest daughter and with her help Martha knew they would manage until Joss returned. By God, they'd have to! The memory of the day she had just gone through and the anticipation of the one she must suffer tomorrow, and the next day riveted itself into her mind but she tried to ease her daughter's worried expression by standing up and straightening her shoulders, just as though they really had done nothing all this day but enjoy a picnic amongst the sweet grass and heather of the moor. 'Nay, we can't loll about here, can we, lass?' She turned to look at her daughter-in-law, surprised somehow to see her rise to her feet, for if anyone looked as though she could be knocked sideways with a feather it was Joss's wife. Her face had a bleached, quite lifeless look about it, the pale prettiness of her cheeks gone with the appalling smell and atmosphere in which she worked and though she had never been robust what flesh she had had been burned away from her in the mill. Only Jenny looked capable of doing a full day's work without too much trouble and that, her mother decided was because the girl was so like Joss. Tough-grained and ruthless in her determination not to let the mill-master bear her down. Like a tiger she was in her defence of those who worked with her, defiant even of Ellis who was no less than the devil in man's clothing. She had earned herself many a clout with his leather thong though it was in reality only meant to keep the younger children awake and at their employment and to prevent them falling into the unguarded machinery.

'Thought you was about to drop off there, lass,' he would say spitefully, 'so don't look at me like that. And none of yer lip, neither, or you'll be out of that door and on the street with all them others looking for a job. There's plenty more where you came from, tha' knows, aye, and work a damn sight better an' all,' which was not true. Jenny

213

Greenwood was one of the best workers he had and on *her* and all the other women who worked beside her depended the amount of the wage *he* took home at the week's end. The 'tackler' or overlooker might have as many as one hundred and sixty women and their spinning frames, or in the case of the weaving-sheds, their looms in his charge. His wages were assessed on every pound, collectively the operatives earned and so it was in his own best interest to keep them hard at it. An overlooker was very often a man who had been a weaver himself and he was able to strip and re-assemble a Lancashire spinning frame or a hand-loom with ease, though power-looms needed that new breed, an engineer to serve them, but it was on Ellis's efficiency and those of the rest of the overlookers that Barker Chapman's profit depended. The tackler was the most hated and feared man in the factory since his job was well paid and secure and he could do as he pleased with the labouring women and children provided he produced the weekly yardage of cloth his employer required.

'I don't wish to know *how* you do it, Ellis. You are in charge of the machines and I leave it to you and the managers to get the best results,' Barker Chapman had told him. 'I do not employ managers and overlookers and then expect to do the job myself. Do you understand?'

Ellis did, perfectly!

Daisy and Charlie slept curled about one another like puppies in a basket, their heads pillowed on the springy grass and Mercy, who had sat down again abruptly, seemed to have dropped off into a light doze. It was still very warm though it was almost full dark. The sky had cleared of all but a blurred pink smudge over Badger's Edge and a tiny sliver of moon no bigger than a child's finger nail lifted serenely into the pearly grey. The stars had brightened and the smell from the heather curled about the two women who crouched shoulder to shoulder against the sun-warmed face of the rock. It was quiet, so peacefully quiet a small moorland creature ran madly across the bit of ground in front of them, quite unaware of their presence and Jenny sighed. They still had a couple of miles to go to reach the cottage in Edgeclough and when they got there they must turn round and tramp three back to the mill for five o'clock starting. The children would be difficult to wake and even more difficult to persuade to the walk and as she watched her mother's head nod to her chest she knew that they couldn't go on like this any longer.

For almost three weeks since Joss had been imprisoned they had trekked back and forth, back and forth, at first quite strongly since they had been fresh and determined to manage until he was home again but increasingly these past few days she and her mother had been forced physically to manhandle the children from their beds, pushing and shoving and coaxing until they were on the path to Crossfold. Daisy would grizzle until Jenny felt like landing her one, but the little girl was bewildered, frightened, exhausted to a point beyond her own childish strength. The soft flesh had been scraped from her and she already had the shrunken look of the typical factory child and Jenny was ashamed of her own frustrated anger. Charlie did his best, once they had him out of his bed, declaring stoutly that he could easily do the walk there and back but his eyes had become strangely unfocused lately and his submissive manner was so unlike the bright and cheerful imp, who had talked of nothing but following their Joss. He had taken it badly when his brother was sent to Lancaster and though he worked hard, having no choice, he was curiously lifeless.

It's this bloody walk, Jenny admitted to herself as she sat among her sleeping family. The work was killing but she reckoned they could manage it, all five of them if they hadn't this three-mile trek at the beginning and end of each day. It put two hours each morning and the same in the evening on the strain of the already punishing work day. They were allowed no more than four or five hours in their beds each night and the limit of the children's endurance had been reached. What they were being forced to do was more than could be managed by a grown man let alone a child. Her mother would keep going until she fell dead at

215

her machine and Mercy, frail as she was at least understood the necessity of it but Daisy, and Charlie to some extent, were stupified by the sudden and quite terrible change in their young lives.

'Are you awake, lass?' her mother's voice interrupted her thoughts.

'Aye, Mother.'

'We'd best get on, Jenny. It must be nearly ten.'

'I suppose it must.'

'Well then, you get Daisy up and me and Mercy'll give Charlie a hand.'

'No, Mother.'

'No! What d'you mean?'

'You put your head down and go back to sleep.'

'Jenny! Don't be daft, girl, we can't stop here.'

'Why not? It's mild and dry and that grass is soft. Spread your shawl out and get some rest, Mother.'

'Nay, love, we can't . . .' but the argument had gone out of the older woman's voice for the idea of simply going to sleep, of waking up in the morning and having no more than a mile to walk to the factory, perhaps six hours of rest, was very tempting but . . .

'We've got to feed the children, Jenny,' she said, her voice weary and discouraged. 'They can't do a day's work with nothing in their bellies.'

'I'll walk up to the cottage and get something.'

For a moment Martha Greenwood allowed herself the relief and wonder of letting her daughter trek up to Edge-clough while they all settled here in the softness of the bracken which lined the track then she shook her head.

'Nay, you can't do that. It's not fair on you. You need a . . .'

'Come on, Mother, why should we all get no sleep? I'm strong and really not tired' – which was a lie – 'and I'd have to walk it anyway. No, you four stay here. I'll be back in an hour or so,' which was probably true for the weaknesses of the other four held her back. 'I'll fetch something. It'll have to be cold but the sleep will do the

216

young 'uns more good.' Her voice softened and in the darkness she found her mother's hand. 'It makes sense, Mother, you know it does.'

'Aye, lass.' Martha sighed and for the second time that night thanked God for this good girl of hers. 'You're right but I hate to see you go off in the dark on your own.'

'I'll be all right, Mother. Now put your head down and before you know where you are I'll be back. Go on, love, go to sleep.'

They moved into a company cottage in Lousy Bank at the end of the following week, one up and one down, the agent for the landlord cheerfully called it, and to excuse the smell but a family of twelve had been evicted the previous day for non-payment of rent and he had had no time to get it cleaned. He winked at Jenny as he spoke but his little joke fell on deaf ears since they were all too stunned to even notice it. They stood, Martha and Jenny, Mercy, Daisy and Charlie in the doorway of the cottage and behind them was the handcart overflowing with Martha's few pieces of good furniture and what Enoch Butterworth's wife and then Mercy, had cherished, and a place must be found for them and for the one loom they had been able to fetch for when Joss came home he must have some means of earning a living. He might be able to struggle on with a bit of hand-loom weaving though Martha had heard that a 'piece' of sixty yards which once had fetched ninepence a yard in his father's day and for which Joss had last been paid only three shillings had been reduced to a mere ninepence for the whole length, and that was when the work was available which was certainly not a guarantee! The new sophisticated machinery, which was to bring prosperity, was certainly doing just that, but only to those who were already prosperous. There were select committees pondering even now on why it was. Benefit societies had put petitions which argued their common cause and begged the support of men of affairs, before them but still they did nothing. Relief committees gave out rations to those most hard pressed but the textile workers of Lancashire did not want *relief*, they wanted decent wages for decent work done.

Though Martha had lived in the area all her life she had never ventured into the heart of Barker Chapman's network of company houses until this day and though Jenny had assured her that they would not be here long saying it was but a temporary stay, close to the factory and easy for the children, she had been quite appalled as they had walked through from Jagger Lane, which was the main thorough-fare of Crossfold into the maze of Boggart Hole, Pig Lane and Lousy Bank. A dense cloud of smoke pressed down on their heads penetrating the honeycomb of back streets through which they had trundled the handcart, borrowed from Isaac Pickering and to be returned the next day, and the jumble of the hundreds of hovels which lined them. Each house had no foundation and therefore no ventilation or drainage and the walls, what the builders called 'brick-noggin' were no more than half a brick in thickness, giving little or no privacy. They had been flung up overnight, making quick and easy money for the builder and looked – and were – as if each one was on the point of collapsing. The gutters of the streets were thick with some abomination. Children, those who had the will and physical capability for it, swarmed like flies over mouldering heaps of refuse, the odd dead cat or rotting carcase of a dog, the ash heaps which were carted away once a week, or not if the carrier failed to come, screaming obscenities at anyone who passed by, or chucking stones, or mud, or any foulness which came to hand.

'I want to go home,' Daisy wailed and Charlie ran a bewildered finger along the frame where once there had been a door, trying to hold his breath for as long as he could since the rotting floorboards gave off a reek of the previous occupant's careless sanitary habits and he felt his head reel with it. They stood in a tight group, their faces clenched, their muscles rigid, their faces the colour of the ash which spilled from the grate across the sagging floorboards.

'Martha . . .' Mercy whispered, her little work-roughened hand reaching for that of her mother-in-law.

'I know, love, I know,' and what else was there to say. They had been brought down to this now, forced by circumstances beyond their control from the cottage up on the clear, sharp-scented moorland where the wind blew sweetly and the smell of heather and gorse and lavender filled and delighted the nostrils. Brought down to the reality of Boggart Hole, Lousy Bank and Pig Lane where the alleys fanned out like the spokes of a wheel from the factories which grew in Crossfold, over a hundred now, where once there had been green meadows and grassy tracks, weathered cottages snug against the hillside, a church or two alongside a coaching inn and the Cloth Hall. Now there were mean rows, hundreds of them, of what Barker Chapman and the rest of the manufacturers just like him called 'workers' cottages', built to house the operatives who toiled round the clock, day shift and night shift, in the making of his cloth. Each week, or so it seemed to those who remembered Crossfold when it had been a pleasant country town, more were thrown up as out-of-work agricultural labourers and out-of-work weavers flooded down from the hills to find work and now, Martha Greenwood agonised, it was the turn of her family.

But that must be left until later. It did no good to dwell on it. Somehow they must manage here, the five of them and first they would have to set about the task of making this stinking pig-pen habitable.

Far into the night they worked, scouring the cottage from top to bottom so that they could at least put their beds down on a bit of clean floor. They had scrubbed until the standpipes had been turned off at three o'clock and there had been no more water to be had to heat on the fire in the newly cleared grate. Jenny worked like a being demented scarcely able to contain the heat of the thoughts which scorched her brain. Though she had worked for twelve hours or more, scraping filth from walls and floors, shaking rag rugs vigorously in the alley to the blank-eyed amazement of the slatterns who were to be her neighbours, carrying dozens of buckets of water from the standpipe at the corner of the passage, watched by women who did not even *own* a bucket, she had not flagged. There was a trembling to her shoulders and a dark stain beneath her eyes. Her face was pale and strained but there was a look about her that swore she could go on for another twelve if she had to, and in her brain was the resolve that she did this not for herself, nor her family but for her brother and those he fought for. She was a fanatic, as militant as he in the fight for the betterment of her fellows. She hated the tyranny of the mill-masters, the harsh treatment rendered the children who worked beside her, the very concept of children *needing* to work beside her. She was strong and could labour hour after hour beside any man. She was unafraid, reckless some said in her defence of the underdog, in her defiance of the overlookers. She hated them for the vicious thugs many of them were. She hated the repression and the reduction to less than beasts of the women beside whom she spun and had it not been for her mother for whom she was responsible as Joss carried on the fight, and for her brother and sister, she would have become a soldier in his brave army of men, with his Onwardsmen. She would have tied up her skirts and her hair and marched beside them, burning mills and breaking the machinery which, though it gave a meagre wage to many, brought untold wealth to the few who were at the top.

But she would fight on in any way she could while Joss was in gaol. She was a woman and often filled with a humour which she thought to be frivolous but she would fight on until they had the better of those who exploited them. For every step they took forward it seemed two were taken back, but by God it would not always be so. The working class were surfacing through the muck and the filth in which they had drowned for so long, becoming aware of their own identity, of their own importance and Joss had told her that when they understood it they would be a force to be reckoned with, through their unity and by the sheer weight of their numbers. Even now the benefit societies were helping to get many through the hard times and if they could just stick together, hold on, they would win and houses like this one and all its neighbours would be a thing of the past.

Mercy was asleep in the bed by the wall, looking as though she was dead as she lay neatly on her side of it. They would have to be careful with Joss's wife, she mused, as she watched the shallow rise and fall of her sister-in-law's chest. She was not right. There was something gone from her, leaving her as dependent as Daisy, a child lost and frightened and needing to hold the hand of the nearest adult, but that must wait. She had enough to worry about without worrying about Mercy.

She rose from the chair before the fire and her mother awoke from the light doze into which she had fallen.

'What time is it, lass?' she murmured.

'Time for bed, Mother, or we'll miss the five-thirty bell.'

Mercy Greenwood's mind was as simple, as guileless as that of a child. A child brought up in a kindly fashion by an elderly father to believe that the reward for obedience, purity, kindness and generosity to one's fellowman, was a contented, work-filled day and a dreamless, peace-filled night. She had lived by this creed for the first eighteen years of her life and it had proved to be true.

The first crack in her equanimity, no more than a hair-line, fine and noticed by no one, even herself, began on the day they hanged her brother.

She could remember, she was sure, though she had been no more than a baby herself, the day Tom was born. She had not, of course, at the time known how he came to be in her mother's arms, she only knew that the wonder of him, the joy of him in the years that followed was like a gift from the God in whom she implicitly believed. She must have been worthy of Him to be so well rewarded, she told herself when she was no more than a child. She tried to do all the things her father told her were the aim of a good Christian girl, a good Methodist girl, marvelling on how

221

easy it was, not aware that the simple goodness of her own soul, the innocence of her heart were the real cause of it. She was happy. She could imagine no other way to be. She could imagine no other way to feel and in the isolated cottage in which she lived with her father and Tom, in the small community of the village where there was really no opportunity for wrong-doing she met nothing to change her conception of how life was for the rest of the world. In her simplicity she imagined that everywhere were villages and towns, though she had never seen a town, where people worked hard, where sometimes they might be one family with less than another but which, when it became known, was helped by those who had more until the bad times were over.

Of course she knew that there were rich people, grand people, a King even in London, who lived impressively splendid lives though having nothing with which to compare it, she could not even imagine what that meant. The word 'wealth' had no meaning. She had all she wanted, so was that what it was? She thought about it as she lay on a carpet of clover and watched a butterfly drift across her vision, a fat bumble bee flounder from flower to flower. The sky was a ceiling of blue above her head, the liquid cry of the curlew filled her ears with its melody, her bed was soft, her body whole and healthy, filled with well-being and only ten yards away her young brother hummed a tuneless song as he dug down between the roots of the bracken for the rabbit he was certain lay waiting for him.

He was ten years old then and she was nearly twelve and surely life would go on forever like this. They worked hard, she and Tom, helping her father with his piece which he took each week to the Cloth Hall in Crossfold, spinning the cotton he brought back into yarn so that the cycle could go round again and her world was secure, protected from anything which might shatter her tranquility.

It was Joss Greenwood who pulled the soft, fleecy, ever so cosy wool from her eyes, but even then it did not harm her, for was not Joss and others like him to put it right?

She had never heard of a knight in shining armour, nor of the white horse it was rumoured he rode, since her only knowledge of words came from her father's Bible, but if she had, it was certain Joss Greenwood would have been one! The mill was a dreadful place, Joss told her, where people worked for long hours in appalling conditions. Where children laboured with little hope of escaping it, but when Joss said it she could tell by the flash in his eyes and the strong and determined way in which he set his mouth that he would soon put it right and she was comforted. If she could help in any way she would, she told him shyly and he had said that any help they could get was more than welcome.

His smile when he looked at her made her heart leap like the fish Tom went after in the river which ran through the valley, and she loved him. She longed, though she knew she would never have been brave enough to go through with it as Jenny Greenwood did to stride out with Joss and Tom and all the others who were to free the overburdened mill-workers from their bondage, to meetings up on the moor, to listen to Joss speak as she had heard he did, to listen to others from Yorkshire and Nottinghamshire, who it seemed, were as badly off as the Lancashire weavers and spinners but she knew she would be afraid, even with Joss and someone must stay at home to spin, to cook and clean and mend. That was *her* job, she told herself, her contribution to the cause they fought for, to look after those who fought in it.

She was afraid when the soldiers came. She had not understood what it was they wanted. She had done no wrong. Her family had done no wrong. They lived by the word of her father's Bible, those which said that the meek would inherit the earth and which were, of course, unquestionably true. She was alone and though she longed to run up to Martha Greenwood's cottage, for Joss's mother always gave her a sense of security the soldiers would not let her.

The next few hours were difficult to remember. She had

223

seen a bird once, a wheatear which had built its nest in a clump of gorse, close to the ground and while she watched, dozing a little in the absolute stillness and quiet which existed nowhere else but high on the moor, a hawk had flown over. Instantly the small brown bird which had been busily mothering its fledglings, fluttering and twittering as mothers do, became as immobile as the rock against which Mercy leaned. The hawk hung lazily in the sky for many minutes, its eyes seeking for any sign of movement far below it but the wheatear had not winked its eye, nor ruffled one feather and the hawk had gone on leaving it unscathed.

Mercy Butterworth did that on the night the soldiers came and it was not until she felt the large sweaty hand of the soldier at her breast did she begin to scream and when she stopped they had gone, the soldiers and Tom.

And they had hanged Tom. Her good, honest Tom who had been hers from the moment of his birth. A soft-eyed, soft-fleshed baby whose hands had reached for her own infant curls, a merry tumble-legged toddler, an engaging, mischievous boy who, though he was never bad, did not always follow the teaching of her father's Bible. An eager, fresh-faced youth, dazzled by Joss Greenwood's ideals, longing, as Joss attempted to do, to ease the suffering of the 'afflicted poor'. A young man then, who had harmed no one in his life. And they had hanged him!

The tear in the fabric from which Mercy Butterworth was fashioned widened a little more on the night of her wedding to Joss Greenwood. She loved him. Oh, how she loved him and the wonder of discovering that *he loved her*, that they were to be married was a joy which almost healed the desolation of losing Tom and would have if Joss had not done to her what he did on her wedding night. It was so *violent* and Mercy found she really could not cope with violence. He became someone else when he climbed into the bed they shared, wanting to look at her shrinking body – as the soldier had – demanding that she should do the same to him. His face became red and dangerous and his eyes wild and the noises he made terrified her. Afterwards, when the dreadful thing he did was over, he was *her* Joss again and she loved him then, and during the day when his tall body was calm and his kiss soft and his eyes kind and gentle, she felt a return to that warm safety of her childhood, her girlhood and the peace of it lapped about her.

It was shattered on the day, when persuaded by the sunshine and the companionship of her family to walk up to Ravenstone Brow and listen to Joss speak to the mill-workers, the soldiers had come again, to arrest her husband, they told her, for the gathering together of a crowd for an illegal meeting as laid down in the Combination Acts. He was put in gaol for it and not long afterwards the last guardian of her childhood, when goodness had been rewarded by happiness, was taken from her when her father died. She knew then that somehow, in some way, she had been so grievously wicked that she was to be punished until she repented of it. Her punishment was the work she was forced to do, by Martha, her mother-in-law, by Jenny her sister-in-law at the spinning frame in the Chapman mill.

'We all have to do it, even Daisy,' Jenny told her.

'But Daisy's done nothing wrong, Jenny.'

'Of course she hasn't. What's that got to do with it?'

'Then why has she to work in the mill?'

'Because we *all* have to work in the mill. Because we have no other way to stay alive, that's why.' And Jenny had cried that night though no one had heard her but Mercy.

She hated the spinning room but she accepted it as her punishment for the badness she must have done. She accepted it and the black exhaustion of the long walk from Edgeclough to Crossfold and back again. She clung to Martha as the only steady, unchanging reality in a world which had gone mad, a world from which everything she had loved, everyone she had loved, except Martha, had been taken from her. There was no stability except Martha and the only way to escape from where she had found herself was to shut it out. It was easy when you learned the knack of it. By concentrating hard on the little brown moorland bird, by pressing the picture of it firmly into her brain, everything else faded away and the hawk passed over. She could do this at five o'clock in the morning when she stepped up to her spinning machine and when the engine was switched off fourteen hours later she would be bewildered but immeasurably relieved to find the day had gone by without her suffering it.

The day they went to live in the cottage in Lousy Bank had been too much, even for the little moorland bird which was her friend and it refused to come and help her. The stinking, decaying refuse-heaped alleyways through which they had walked with the handcart to Lousy Bank had terrified her. The sore-eyed and misshapen children who screamed abuse had her shrinking against Martha for protection. The slatternly women, who had given up the fight against the filth, which lay not only on the rutted track but also on their own children, their homes and themselves, since water was needed to keep them clean and they had none, leaned indifferently in doorways, waiting for the standpipe to be turned on in order merely to drink. They watched her, it seemed to her, knowing she was sinful, their eyes following her progress through the filth which oozed up over her clogs and when she had passed by they would tell one another she was suffering only what she deserved.

'I want to go home,' she wept, when Daisy did. 'I don't want to sleep upstairs in that dirty room with Daisy and Charlie. Please don't make me. If I must stay here and I suppose I must, please let me sleep down here with you and Jenny . . . please . . .'

Martha, too appalled by her own and her family's misfortune to see the strangeness which was developing in her daughter-in-law, perhaps too close to it and its day-to-day familiarity, sighed impatiently.

'See, take this bucket and go to the standpipe at the corner and fill it. Charlie, you see to the fire and we'll get some water heated when Mercy comes back and start scrubbing out the . . .'

226

'Martha . . .' Mercy whispered, the thought of going out alone among those dreadful people who would jeer at her, too awful to contemplate and Martha, seeing the blankness settle in her daughter-in-law's eyes, took pity on her.

'I know, love. It's a bit strange . . . never mind, Charlie will go and you can do the grate . . .' and when, hours later, it was done she had allowed Mercy to share her bed the little bird came to comfort her. It was all right then.

## 16

They were walking across the yard the next day. Jenny had Daisy by the hand, and Mercy and Martha, with Charlie, were close behind. She was one woman among hundreds who moved in their shawls and wooden clogs, their rough homespun skirts, to their spinning frames, but those about her bowed their heads and shuffled, their hands folded patiently, while she strode out like a man, her uncovered head held high, her riot of curls spangled with raindrops, her breasts thrust proudly beneath her shawl and the man in the office saw no one but her. He liked the way she looked about her as though she owned the place and was considering what she could get for it, the way her glance passed over every man in the yard, all those who were looking at *her*, as though they simply did not exist, and he liked the way her hips swung and her breasts peaked and the strong straight arrow of her back. His eyes narrowed speculatively. He drew on the cigar which was clamped between his strong white teeth and he began to smile.

Though he stood in the bay window of Barker Chapman's office with all the assurance of the man who owned the mill, though he was in charge of Crossbank, of Highbank and Broadbank while Barker Chapman and his daughter travelled about the country on business, Harry Atherton was not exactly satisfied with the position he held and though he fully expected in the near future to start on the wooing of Katherine Chapman now that he had insinuated himself into her father's good graces, he was restless, a mite irritable, for the damned mills and the weaving-sheds did not really seem to have need of him. They ran themselves in fact, with the excellent managers, the engineers and overlookers that Chapman had put in and Harry realised sourly that what he had thought of as a position of some importance, of responsibility with the authority to make decisions during the weeks Barker Chapman was away, was no more than that of a figurehead, a man at the top who had no function at all and that Chapman had known of it when he left his mills, supposedly, in Harry's charge.

Harry Atherton was bored and when he was bored he was inclined, as his mother well knew, to get into mischief. He turned away from the window and the now emptied yard and shouting for his clerk told him to look sharp and fetch Ellis the overlooker, from the spinning room at once.

Ellis was all smiles and good humour when he entered Mr Atherton's — Mr Chapman's office in truth. He had obliged Mr Atherton — the young Squire as those in the mill called him — with what he wanted several times in the past. He liked them young and free from disease of course and Ellis had the pleasant task of ensuring that they were both. He kept the best for Mr Atherton, wondering quite often why a man who was wealthy — or would be, for they all knew which way the wind blew — and handsome and presumably well able to obtain his own women, should trouble himself with mill girls. Still it took all kinds to make a world, as Ellis well knew and some men had strange tastes and it was nothing to do with him. He was well paid for what he did and if a girl refused, as some did, it was no trouble to get rid of them and set on one who was more willing. He was always amazed by those, not many it was true, who showed independence, shouting they would rather starve, but if that was what they wanted, to hell with 'em.

Mr Atherton raised an imperious head as Ellis stood before his desk. He had never in his life spoken to someone in trade and certainly not to their underlings until he had been introduced to Barker Chapman. Ellis was an unknown quantity to him, a servant and yet not at all like the servants, as one of the landed gentry, he had known all his life. They were something he understood, voiceless unless addressed but at the same time members, in a curious way, of his family. Old retainers who had served his family, *their* forebears serving *his*. This kind of man, this overlooker, the managers and engineers with whom he worked, were a breed unknown to him and he found it hard to address more than a clipped word or two to them. Still, this one was very useful, and discreet too, which was convenient.

'Yes, sir?' he said.

'There is a particular girl I wish to speak to.'

'Speak to, sir?' Ellis was clearly bewildered.

'Indeed. I saw her in the yard just now. I will describe her and you will bring her here.'

'Nay, I don't even know their names, sir.'

'She is quite distinctive . . . tall with short hair . . . curly, quite . . . unusual . . .'

Ellis's face cleared and he beamed for the description could fit only one girl, then it clouded again and he pulled at his lip with grubby fingers. He shook his head doubtfully, for if there was one girl in all of Barker Chapman's mills who would spit in the face of the young Squire, soon as look at him, it was this one. Blast her eyes and blast the eyes of this young fool for fancying her since it was going to be difficult to get her to comply and Ellis did not like the taste of failure. A proper firebrand, she was and if she had not been such a tireless worker, earning money for him he would have got rid of her long since. Always taking up for someone, she was, giving him a mouthful if she saw him so much as raise his strap to a child. Not that she could do

229

much on their behalf and if he wanted he could have her out in a jiffy but if he were honest he supposed he would have to admit that he quite enjoyed the exchanges he had with her and if he could find a way to do it, which meant if *she* was willing, had meant to have her for himself.

'Well, sir, much as I'd like to oblige I'm afraid this one might be difficult.'

'Difficult! Don't be ridiculous,' but there was an excited gleam in Harry Atherton's eyes.

'No, sir, really. She's a . . . well, if you'll pardon the expression . . . a hellion . . .'

Harry Atherton began to smile and Ellis smiled with him for he could see the way of it now. He was not a fanciful man, brutal and coarse, taking his pleasures where and when he pleased for the most part. He exploited the children, the girls in his care, the mothers who would do anything to feed their children, telling himself that most of them would finish up in a brothel or on the streets in any case and if they were to do it they might as well do it with the commercial gentlemen he sold them to. Some preferred the independence of prostitution to the discipline of the mill but as he watched Harry Atherton's face he was aware that this one had a partiality for the . . . well, he could only call it . . . the unusual!

'She'll not come willingly, sir,' and he knew the statement had pleased the man on the other side of the desk.

'Fetch her.'

She was at her frame when Ellis walked towards her down the length of the noisy room. She wore nothing but a sleeveless bodice and her skirt was tied up in a way which, should she slip in the oily filth on the floor, would not hamper her movements nor catch in the machine. She was bathed in sweat, her bodice soaked in it and the round aureoles of her nipples were clearly visible through the wet fabric. Her feet were bare, and her ankles, and they were slim, neat and the skin where the muck had not reached was white and fine. She darted up and down the long frame, her eyes constantly on the look-out for broken thread,

230

moving the carriage by turning the driving wheel, her whole body always in motion, graceful as a bird and yet without a single wasted movement. There was a child beneath her machine, deftly avoiding the whirling straps and wheels as she swept up the waste and he saw Jenny Greenwood lean down and smile at her.

'All right, Daisy,' she said, 'that'll do,' and the girl crept out and for a moment leaned against Jenny quite fearfully.

'Go on, love,' he heard Jenny say, 'go and do Mercy's machine. You know you can't stop with me.'

She whirled about when he tapped her on the shoulder and when she saw who it was her expression of surprise turned to one of truculence.

'She's new,' she said defiantly, 'but I'll see she does her work.'

'You know 'er then?' he asked pleasantly.

'Aye, she's my little sister but she'll do well as a piecer. We're used to hard work in our family.' Her manner was proud and though she held a conversation with him not once did she still her hands or her feet and he was forced to move up and down the machine with her.

A boy darted up to them with a creel of bobbins. He was too big to crawl under the machines and would, in a month or two be taken on in the weaving-sheds where a loom would be found for him but in the meanwhile he would work as a bobbin carrier.

'Thanks, Charlie,' Jenny said and Ellis was struck by the likeness between the boy and the girl.

'It seems your whole family is employed here, Jenny Greenwood.'

'Aye, and all doing a good day's work, Mr Ellis.'

'Of course you are, lass.' He grinned maliciously, 'But there's another way for you to earn a few bob if you've a mind. Want me to tell you about it?'

She turned and her machine fell idle. She put her hands on her hips and glared at him, her lip curling distastefully as though he was something unclean she had narrowly missed stepping in.

'You can take your foul mouth and your foul ways and get out of my sight, Mr Ellis. There's many a poor lass with no one to defend her gets dragged into your filth and if there was something I could do about it I would, but I'm not one of them! One day buggers like you'll be strung up for what you do and it's not far off, believe me. Until then, leave me alone for you'll not terrify me into messing with your sort, or the men who pay you.'

'Will you not, Jenny Greenwood?'

'No, now leave me to get on with my work.'

'Oh no, lass, you can leave that for now. Put your clogs on for Mr Atherton'll not like his good carpet messed up.'

'*Mr Atherton!*'

Her heart, pumping vigorously in her outrage, missed a beat but she was not afraid since what could *he* want with her. She worked well, she knew she did though everyone knew whose sister she was and whose daughter she had been. They did not believe her to be involved with the Onwardsmen. So what did Mr Atherton want, her quick mind asked and the answer was so ludicrous she began to laugh since she was nought but a common mill girl with dirty feet and a sweat-stained bodice and he was a fine gentleman who was, if the rumours were correct, to marry the mill-owner's daughter.

'Go on, Jenny Greenwood,' Ellis was saying softly, 'and don't bother to get cleaned up. It seems he likes 'em rough!'

On the night before they were to go on their travels Barker Chapman and his daughter Kit had dined Harry Atherton at their home, discussing prior to his arrival his fitness to undertake the running of it in their absence.

'Do you really think he is capable of managing it all, Father?' Kit asked anxiously.

'I should not be going if I had any doubts, Kit,' her father replied mildly, drawing on his cigar. Harry was to dine alone with them that night, Hannah declaring petulantly that she could not abide the boredom of listening to them

232

discussing the mills and the frames, the weaving-sheds and the looms, the rising cost of coal and all the trivia of business which seemed to be of such vital interest to her husband and daughter. How any woman could bear to think of such things, was even *capable* of thinking such things when there were so many other quite fascinating pursuits available to her was a constant source of wonder and irritation to Hannah and she said so constantly. As a result Barker and Kit were not a little relieved to dispense with her company on their last evening.

They dined on vermicelli soup followed by a superb salmon with turbot and lobster sauce. There was a choice of trout or whitebait, no more than a sliver on bone china so fine and fragile it was possible to see the pattern of the white damask tablecloth through it. There had been a roast saddle of lamb, larded quail, roast duck and turkey poult, whichever was preferred and Harry Atherton wondered at the magnificence of the food which was barely tasted by the master, which one assumed was eaten in the servants' hall. A green salad followed with mayonnaise of chicken, tomatoes and green peas *à la française, suédoise* of straw-berries (from the Chapman hothouses, naturally). Charlotte Russe and compôte of cherries, Neapolitan cakes, pastries and Madeira wine jelly and all to cater to the appetites of three people. Harry, accustomed, despite his family's pen-ury to the superb tables found in his mother's dining-room and in those of their friends thought it all to be somewhat ill-bred, a little too vulgar and ostentatious and though the thought of the enormous waste did not trouble him unduly since if one had money it was only sensible to spend it, it really was unforgivable to feed one's servants, who came from the lower orders after all, on such delicacies.

Barker Chapman's wine cellar was just as magnificent, old and venerable and exceedingly rare, each bottle chosen by his butler, whose excellent training had taught him to complement each course. There was brandy and cigars and when Harry had stood, expecting Katherine to withdraw as was the custom at the end of the meal to take her coffee in solitary ease in the drawing-room, he had been quite amazed when she shook her head.

'Sit down, Harry. I'll take a brandy with you but I think a cigar would be beyond me, and don't look at my father like that, either, since I have no intention of leaving you and he knows it. Really, Harry, you are so hidebound in your ideas of what constitutes good behaviour in a lady. I had no idea you were so conventional.'

She said it mockingly, laughing at his upbringing and for a moment she saw the longing in his eyes to order her from the room, as his mother would her own daughter should she be impertinent enough to wish to remain with the gentlemen.

He smiled disarmingly, quickly hiding his expression, reaching languidly for his brandy glass and shaking his head as though she was a child who was up to some mischief and of no concern to her elders, quite innocent, of course, as children are but in need of a good spanking just the same.

'Really, Katherine, where on earth do you get your ideas? I am the most unconventional of fellows . . .'

'Where *fellows* are concerned, I suspect, but not the ladies.'

'How . . . charming you are,' he murmured and she knew that though he smiled sweetly it was not really the word he would use to describe her. Wilful. Wayward. Arrogant. Self-opinionated. Obstinate and damned exasperating, but not charming!

'I am afraid you must blame me for her impudence, my boy.' Barker watched the smoke from his cigar which his butler had just lit for him, drift to the ceiling. 'She is as I have allowed her to be, in fact, as I have made her, are you not, Kit?' and you will just have to make the best of it, his eyes said as they met Harry's. '. . . And she is more in touch with what goes on in the mill than I am,' which was not true for nothing went on in Barker Chapman's mills that he did not know of, nothing! He was well aware of Ellis's little sidelines, those involving girls who were in his charge

234

and of Harry's involvement and as long as it did not interfere with the smooth running of his mills he turned a blind eye to it. Ellis was an excellent tackler and he knew where to find men like himself who were needed to keep it all in order and running as efficiently as it did. If he made a few shillings on the side, good luck to him and if Harry liked a bit of sport with young women it was only natural. He was a man after all with a man's needs. It was what Barker Chapman would have done in his place.

Harry had gone, murmuring his hopes that their journey would be not only delightful but might reap rich rewards in the obtaining of orders for their mills. They were not to worry about the business, not at all. It was in his good and careful hands and though Kit was doubtful about his choice of words since his facile good humour was to her not the characteristic best suited to run a mill, to deal with managers and overlookers and customers since it spoke of a careless disregard, a flippancy which did it no good, she must take her father's word that Harry would be equal to it.

'Come, my dear. We have taken him on to help us build our overseas markets and that is what he will do when the time comes. But he must know the cotton trade to be able to convince potential buyers that what we are selling is the best and the ideal way to do that is to be in charge of it, to manage it himself. He is keen and intelligent and has learned quickly. Believe me, my dear, Harry Atherton will rise beautifully to the occasion. He wants to make money, Kit. That is his most important quality. A man who is as ambitious and as ruthlessly determined to have wealth as he is will not let us down. Now, shall we retire? We have a long journey ahead of us tomorrow.'

And now they were home again and at the ball Barker Chapman had given to celebrate their successful venture Harry watched Kit Chapman from where he leaned indolently against one of the fluted columns in the ballroom. She was surrounded by a group of ladies and gentlemen, friends and business acquaintances of her father who thought it expedient to keep on his right side by deferring to his daughter and who all, without exception had the glazed look of a congregation which is burdened with a long-winded parson. One or two of the ladies tried to turn the conversation to other more feminine matters, concealing yawns behind their fans for really this constant talk of warp and weft was most unladylike and the gentlemen, who wanted nothing more than to retire to Barker Chapman's study and the secluded masculine environment to be found there, tried desperately to edge away from her, wishing to God the blasted band would resume playing so that they might give the excuse of waiting partners.

What a bore she is! What a pompous bloody bore on the eternal subject of the textile trade and but for the fact that she was one of the wealthiest heiresses in Lancashire he'd pack his bags and go back to Cheshire, Harry thought. She looked magnificent, of course. Though a lady never exposed her skin to the sun, since to be freckled or brown as a gypsy was quite unacceptable, her already golden skin had been tinted by the sunshine in which she walked on the Pennine moorland to a glowing, peached amber. Her gown of aquamarine silk was cut on simple classical lines and it fell from her gleaming shoulders to the floor in a fluid sculpting of her body, lovingly accentuating her breast and hips. She wore sapphires at her neck and wrist and in her ears and her dark hair was unadorned, dressed to the back of her neck into a heavy coil which tilted her head to a proud and haughty stare.

Dear God, what a woman she would make if only she were not so obsessed by her mills, by the spinning and weaving of cotton, which though it had made the fortune she would get, was driving him quite simply to the mad-house. He must get away soon. He had learned all he needed to know to sell Barker Chapman's piece goods and now, after nearly two years he was ready, and entitled, surely to get into those rich markets, those luxury hotels, those splendid cities in which beautiful women were lavish with their favours to the man who had the money to buy them. And he would sell Barker Chapman's velveteens and fustians, make no mistake. He would do well for him, make him another bloody fortune. That was his game, his function in this ill-bred process of manufacturing, not addressing himself to profit and loss, to the stink of machinery and weaving-sheds and the mass of sweating humanity who worked in them. He would travel, like a young lord he would travel but first he must guarantee his place in Barker Chapman's world of commerce by marrying his daughter.

The buffet supper table was still buzzing with dozens of the hundred persons who had been invited to the ball, heaping their delicate bone china plates with lobster salad, roast fowl, garnished ham, ornamental tongue, roast pheasants, trifle, fruited jelly, charlotte russe and custard in crystal glasses. There were two enormous epergnes weighted down with fruit, bowls of flowers, candles and the tables were draped with ivy in which pink rosebuds and white satin ribbon were threaded.

'Katherine, you have not eaten yet. Let me fill a plate for you.' They all turned as one as he approached, their faces slack with relief and bowing their adieus, for the moment, they said, they each found they had some urgent matter to which they must attend, a chignon to be rearranged, a flower come loose, a lady who really must not be left alone for another second.

'What a lovely time you are having, Katherine. I declare you really do enchant everyone with your splendid achievements in the cotton exchange in Manchester and Liverpool and your description of Mr Whitney's gin-mill, which is used so extensively in the cotton trade had me quite spellbound. I had no idea the seeds of the cotton were such awkward little devils and how much of a boon it was when he invented it.'

He grinned audaciously and raised his eyebrows and Kit Chapman drew in a deep breath, her face taking on the bright glow of the rosebuds decorating the table. Then she began to laugh, a deep and merry laugh, throwing back her head, careless of the lively shining knot at her neck and the scattering of a pin or two.

'You are saying I'm a bore, Harry Atherton.'

'Heaven forbid that I should be so rude.'

'You are the only man who tells me the truth and so you shall take me to supper. I have not yet begun on the system of cotton planting an American gentleman, whom I met in London, told me about and I mean to share it with someone. While we drink champagne and sample some of those strawberries for which I have a fancy I shall tell you all about it.'

'You will do no such thing. I want to hear . . . other things about you. But you shall have your strawberries and champagne, and more if you wish.' His mouth curled in a rich and sensual smile and the deep brown of his eyes whispered something to her, something which had nothing to do with food and she felt a small spring of curiosity well in her to find out exactly what it was. If she liked it she would taste it, if not she would discard it, spit it out laughingly, pulling a face as she had once done as a child over a dish of prunes.

'Go and sit in that little alcove by the fireplace on the landing and wait for me and if anyone else should try to sit beside you tell them . . .'

'What?' she asked laughingly, quite intrigued by this new and boldly masterful gentleman who had, it seemed, replaced the carelessly indifferent one she had known for over two years. His indifference had not annoyed her, in fact she had found it reassuring after her first fears that her father might have organised him as a husband for her. But he had quite done away with her suspicions in his obvious concern for the mills and his eagerness to learn the trade and with the hours, as many as herself and her father, he had put in each day. And now, if she cared to, she thought she might find him amusing, perhaps a pleasant way to make her forget . . . someone else . . . and she could hardly come to harm on the landing of her father's house in the company of a hundred guests!

He was quite a fascinating man, she thought, an hour later as he regaled her with humorous tales of his boyhood

238

and the – to her – quite ludicrous code of conduct imposed by the landed gentry. She listened to his recounting of glorious days in the saddle, of men called whippers-in, of earth-stoppers and coverts. Of what it cost – dear God she could scarcely believe it – for his father to keep his own personal stable and private kennel, of his home which had almost gone with Cromwell since, naturally, his own family had been for the King, of the long gallery and the medieval great hall, of his own 'Grand Tour' which his father had managed somehow, putting her own quite ordinary trip about the country in the shade.

They sipped champagne, a whole bottle and more, glass after crystal glass and she felt the lovely peaceful warmth slip through her body and her head told her heart, quite bemused by the wine that she really did not care what happened since Harry Atherton's eyes, brown and smiling and his lips which were an inch from her bare shoulder were really very nice indeed.

'You are quite delicious, Katherine, when you can be winkled out of that commercial shell of yours. There's not a girl here who wouldn't be in your shoes and not a man who wouldn't be in mine and those eyes of yours! They remind me of a jewel my mother has, not blue nor purple but somewhere in between and your skin is . . . it brings to mind a golden retriever I once had, golden and smooth as cream . . .'

'Come on, Harry, can you do no better than that,' she said lazily though she had to admit that he excited her with the closeness of his warm lips.

For an instant there was a curious prick of light in his eyes, an almost fox-like fierceness, then reaching out quickly he drew the curtains across the opening of the alcove and before she could protest, should she have wanted to which she was not even certain of, he placed his lips lightly on hers, moving them just a little, breathing his warm, wine-scented breath against them until, quite amazingly she felt her own open and his breath was in her mouth. Only one man had kissed her before, like this at first, then fiercely, hungrily and she had responded as naturally as the earth opens and takes in the rain. This was nothing like it, nothing at all since she knew enough now to recognise the difference between love and simple lust, but it was decidedly pleasant, none the less. His mouth slid effortlessly across her neck and with an expertise which told her he had done it a time or two before, explored the curve of her ear, the small hollow beating beneath it and the smooth line of her jaw. He did nothing to which she could take exception and when he stopped and lifted her chin to smile at her she smiled back quite naturally.

'Did you like that, Katherine?' he asked impishly.

'I must admit I did.'

'Would you like to try something else?' His smooth face was confident, telling her he was quite sure of her answer.

'I don't really think so, Harry. I have had enough excitement for one evening. Now if you will take me back to my mother I must fulfil my duties. There are a dozen men with whom I must dance. Oh, and thank you, Harry, for pointing out to me how tedious I am becoming. It is a lesson I have learned well. I shall not repeat it, believe me.'

Harry Atherton was smiling as urbanely as only he knew how as he seated her next to her mother in the ballroom. There were rows of delicately carved, gilt-legged chairs on which those disinclined, or not invited, to dance might take their ease and though Hannah as was her duty made certain that no young unmarried lady was a wallflower for long, she did love to exchange gossip with those of her neighbours and acquaintances who had marriageable girls like her own. She could not help but preen as Harry bowed to her and the rest of the ladies when he returned her daughter to her and her sharp eye noted the glow and sparkle which emanated from the girl. She looked meaningfully at her friends, Mrs Abbott and Mrs Jenkinson, who both had girls in the marriage market, her expression asking triumphantly could they not see which way the wind was blowing for if ever a girl had the look of someone who had just been kissed it was Kit Chapman. Of course it was quite scandalous that

240

she should have allowed it but the fact that she had could signify only one thing. Penniless he might be, her expression said but they could not help but agree he was a catch for a mill-master's daughter. They were of the industrial classes, many of them only a generation away from a weaver's loom in a moorland cottage and he was of the landed gentry and she meant to have him, one way or the other, for her daughter. She might, if she had been an astute woman, one who was not blinded by the outer trappings and background of Harry Atherton have had some reservations if she had seen the peril in his eye as he sauntered in the direction of her husband's study where the serious drinkers, all male naturally, were gathered.

'He wants our girl, Hannah,' Barker Chapman informed his wife the next day in the privacy of Hannah's bedroom, a place he rarely visited. 'He says he has served his apprenticeship and feels he should now be given the chance to present himself as a serious suitor to Kit. He has fulfilled all the conditions of the agreement made between his father and myself, so he tells me and the time has come to honour it. He even went so far as to tell me of the feeling which our daughter had aroused in his breast, quite filled with ardour he was, and which has grown over the months and he feels it is not quite fair to expect him to wait much longer. Most forthright, he was and quite determined that Kit returns his devotion though I must admit I have seen no sign of it myself . . .'

'But I have, Barker.'

'Really, my dear.'

'Oh yes, last night at the ball they were missing for at least an hour and when he returned her to me she was . . . well, I can only describe her as . . . glowing . . .'

'Glowing. Good God . . .'

'Indeed, Barker. I was seriously disturbed, not only by the embarrassment but by the knowing looks which were exchanged between Sarah Jenkinson and Emma Abbott. Things like that can ruin a girl's reputation, you know that, Barker. But let us give thanks that the announcement of

241

their betrothal will subdue any gossip which might have arisen.'

'Betrothal! I did not mention the word betrothal, Hannah, though I am seriously disconcerted by what you have just told me. Why did you not say something before? If I thought he was taking liberties . . .'

'Oh no, Barker. He is too much of a gentleman to . . .'

'And knows which side his bread is buttered, by God.'

'. . . but do you not think it might be wise to speak to her. Let her know what you have in mind.' Hannah could scarcely contain herself, rehearsing already the way in which she would tell, no, not tell, *hint* at what was afoot when she took tea with Sarah and Emma Abbott tomorrow afternoon. She would be very secretive, letting drop a snippet here and a snippet there, just enough to have them pleading to be told what it was that delighted her so but she would smile and shrug her shoulders and shake her head and beg them not to press her further for really it would be no more than her life was worth if it was to get out before . . .

She was deep in her day-dreams of a wedding in spring attended by the aristocratic relatives of Harry Atherton, scarcely hearing her husband's answer.

'Certainly something needs to be said and I shall see to it immediately. I cannot believe that Kit would act in a manner which would bring discredit to her or her family. To be truthful, my dear, I find it hard to conceive of her . . . er . . . dallying with Harry Atherton at all. She is quite scornful of him, when she speaks of him at all and seems completely preoccupied with the business.'

And high time she became preoccupied with something else, his wife thought, though naturally she did not say so.

'. . . but if there is something afoot I wish to know of it. I would be delighted with a match between my daughter and Samuel Atherton's boy but if she is not willing, Hannah, I would not try to force her.' The lie sat easily on his lips and he believed it. 'We employ Harry in the mill, pay him handsomely too and one day soon he will be off to sell our

242

piece goods in many parts of the world where previously there has been no market. I have trained him myself and he will be an asset and, I must admit, more concerned with making a profit if he were married to Kit. So we will see. I shall speak to her tonight and find out what, if anything, is going on between them.'

Kit Chapman dined with her mother and father that evening and her attention was captured at once by the curious undercurrent, an air of something not quite as usual between them. Her mother appeared excited, her father rather more severe than he normally was and when Hannah excused herself the moment she had eaten her iced pudding, fluttering like an overweight butterfly from the room, Kit turned questioningly to her father, her eyebrows raised.

'What on earth is wrong with mother this evening? She seems to have an exciting secret which she is determined to keep to herself.'

Barker smiled, nodding to the butler to light his cigar. When it was drawing to his satisfaction he stood up and held out his arm to her.

'Shall we go into my study? There is something I want to discuss with you.'

She began to laugh when he told her. He had seated her before the fire, poured her coffee which was unusual, asked her if she would care for a glass of madeira, perhaps a brandy since, though it was not the drink for a lady he knew she liked a sip now and again. He took a moment or two to let the masculine calm of the study, the completely male surroundings which they both enjoyed, lap round them, then, knowing there was no need to beat about the bush, told her what Harry Atherton had asked for.

'My God, he doesn't waste time, does he?' she said when her laughter had subsided. 'He kissed me . . . oh yes, Father, why pretend it shocks you since you know very well it meant nothing to me, or to him, just a bit of mischief which, as an unmarried girl I am not supposed to indulge in, but that was all it was. He is a rogue, a charming rogue and . . . well . . . we drank champagne and . . . he kissed me.

243

There was nothing more to it than that. I'm afraid I laughed at him a little, but really, the idea of marriage is ridiculous. I will admit that when you first introduced him and his family I was afraid that was what you had in mind but the last two and a half years seemed to have proved me wrong. Nothing was said. He got on with what he was taken on for, worked well and he surprised me with his conscientious attention. But as a husband . . .' she began to laugh again. '. . . really, I would rather take Jonathan Abbott or Dick Jenkinson . . .'

'You may have either.' Her father's face and voice were quite serious and she became still for it appeared there was no room for laughter here.

'I want neither,' she said quietly.

'Then whom?'

'Father, I cannot believe what I am hearing. You know I do not want marriage . . . children . . . at least not yet . . .'

'A woman must be married, Kit.' His voice was gentle. 'I am not telling you that you may not run the mills when I am gone but you would do better as a married woman than as a . . . spinster. If you married you would have status, protection, a security from the attentions of other men, a position in society . . .'

'I have that now.'

'My dear, as long as you remain unmarried you will be at the mercy of every fortune-hunter from London to Edinburgh. You will be an enormously rich woman and they simply will not let you alone. While I am here you are under my protection. I stand between you and them but when I am gone . . .'

'Dear God, Father, you have years . . .'

'I am sixty-four, Kit. I am no longer young.' He was being enormously patient with her.

'But . . .'

'Harry is my choice but you may have any of the . . .'

'Please, Father . . .'

'Katherine, listen to me. Let us approach this in an intelligent and practical way. You are not without

244

judgment. You have a cool head on your shoulders and you have an understanding of business I have met in no one before. We are to do great things now we have got those damned radicals behind bars and the constant threat of machine breaking and burning lifted from our shoulders. Believe me, my dear, it has been a constant worry since the warehouse was destroyed and the cost of guarding the mills ate seriously into our profit. Things will die down now, there will be a steady pattern of growth and an increase in our production which will need our . . .'

His voice moved steadily through her head. She could hear exactly what he was saying and if it had been demanded of her could have repeated his words to the letter but ask her what they meant and she could not have said. The last understanding she had ended at the precise moment her father said, '. . . behind bars.'

*Behind bars! Behind bars! Behind bars!*

'. . . and so you see, Kit, it would really be to your advantage if you were to . . . well, shall we say, not exactly encourage Harry Atherton's proposal but at least do not turn it away out of hand. He is very useful to us, or will be. He is a very pleasant, personable young man and it is known he comes from an excellent family. He will give a good impression among business men abroad. He will know how to make buyers feel important since he is well-mannered and well-bred. He knows the cloth now and really, when you consider it, is quite an asset to us in the business. Heaven knows how he will take it if you turn him down without hope. That is all he wants, I believe, the hope that you will consider him. Is that too much to ask, my dear?'

'No indeed, Father.'

He looked slightly surprised since his daughter was well known for her argumentative turn of mind. He had expected somewhat more of a show of opposition from her so perhaps she really did have a fancy for the boy, despite her earlier laughter. Females really were so unbelievably hard to understand, even Kit Chapman whose mind was more masculine than many a gentleman he could name.

'You will . . . take him, then?' he asked tentatively, 'or at least listen to what he has to say?'

'Yes . . . but . . .'

'What is it, my dear?'

'You mentioned that . . . you said some radical reformers had been . . . imprisoned . . .'

'Did I?' He looked perplexed.

'You said that with these . . . these men behind bars . . .'

'Oh yes, I remember now. It was while we were travelling. I myself have only just heard. Three were captured at an illegal meeting up on Ravenstone Brow, I believe. They were tried for sedition and convicted . . .'

'Convicted?' Her face was as white as his own shirt front and her eyes stared into his with such . . . well, he really could not describe how they looked, they were so strange, so wild, so . . . then he remembered! She had been there on the day one of them had smashed his new spinning frame. She had been consumed with rage then, threatening to see them all hang, violent in her hatred of them. Now she must feel a sense of triumph, of elation that at last they were being brought to justice and he could not blame her for they had been a thorn in the side of the manufacturers for years. Onwardsmen, they had called themselves. Well, they would be broken up now for their leader languished in gaol, he had been told, and two others, and if they hanged them it was no more than they deserved.

'Who . . . do you know who . . .' Her voice was no more than a thread of sound in her throat.

'No, I did not concern myself with names, Kit, though I believe one came from Edgeclough which has long been known as a hotbed for their particular brand of nonsense.'

'They . . . they are to . . . hang . . .'

'No, but by God . . . Kit, my dear, you look . . . what on earth . . .'

'I am perfectly well, Father, really.' She looked at him and her eyes were steady and quite without expression. 'I will have that brandy now, if I may.'

246

'Of course. Now, may I send Harry in to see you. He is waiting to . . .' He was at the decanter and did not see the violent shudder which passed quickly through her body and when he turned, though she was still pale she was perfectly composed.

'Why not?' she said and raised her glass to his.

# 17

Jenny Greenwood walked along Jagger Lane, the springing step with which she usually moved quite gone. It was January. The new year had just begun, coming in with a bitter cold which had frozen the standpipe at the corner of the passage and hung icicles from every rotting roof-top in Lousy Bank. All along the foul street and in every back alley people were freezing to death. There were bodies propped against doorways, those who were homeless, new ones every day waiting for the watch cart to come and haul them away to their paupers' grave. The rutted lane which led from Lousy Bank to the main thoroughfare was all white with rime, hiding pleasantly with its thick hoar frost the unmentionable substances which with the coming of summer would fill the nostrils with its stink.

It was a glorious morning. Sunday and the belching smoke which formed an arch above the town on every other day of the week was gone today to reveal the high clear blue of the sky, shading from delicate pink in the east to the deep winter blue above the town.

Jagger Lane was empty. The shops in which the wealthy purchased their goods, which came each day on the coach from London, were all closed and shuttered. Where the street ran out from the town's centre to the long winding lane of the residential area, those who lived there, managers, solicitor's clerks and the more prosperous shopkeepers in their villas and smart terraced houses, were still in their beds.

Jenny pulled her threadbare shawl more closely about her. She had her riotous halo of curls well covered today and her arms were crossed over her breast, hugging her body. Her woollen skirt though patched in many places, very neatly with material of several colours, was clean and her bare feet encased in their wooden clogs had been washed only that morning in the ice she had melted and heated over the fire. She had washed as much of her body as she could beneath the silent gaze of her mother but it had been difficult with no more than a panful of water and no soap.

'Where are you going, lass?' her mother asked and not for the first time and Jenny gave the same answer as she always did.

'Don't ask, Mother.'

'I must. You're my daughter. Can I let you go out each Sunday, aye and at nights an' all and not fear for you? Tell me, girl, where are you going?'

'I can't, Mother.'

'Let me come with you.'

'You must rest, Mother. You need your rest.' Her voice was calm and expressionless, as it had been for weeks now just as though the vivid, resolute light which had burned fiercely in her had been blown out, to be replaced by something which was just as strong, just as determined but with no warmth in it. Her movements were unhurried. They seemed to indicate that she had all the time in the world to go wherever it was she went each Sunday and Martha Greenwood, from the warmth of the hollow of Mercy's back against which she slept, felt the dread creep over her as she knew the cold would creep over her, and all of them, as soon as she got out of bed. The icy air hurt her face and though there was a small fire in the grate which Jenny had lit half an hour since, the dank frozen chill had not yet dispersed. There were rags to the windows to give some privacy but she knew beneath them the small panes of glass would be a solid mass of ice.

She buried her head more deeply into the pillow and the dread grew. Something terrible was happening to their Jenny, draining the compelling life from her and though she defended them all just as fiercely and worked just as hard as she had ever done, she was not the same girl who had moved with them into Lousy Bank. Perhaps it was that? Perhaps the hovel into which circumstances had forced them to live was too much for a girl brought up in the clean, sweet air of the moors but Martha knew it was not that. Her girl was too strong for that. She had questioned her daughter, sharply at first suspecting a lad but when she had asked her Jenny had laughed, quite hysterically, until the tears had wet her face, denying it and telling her mother she was not to worry, everything would be all right and to go back to sleep.

'Let the fire go out, love. We'll stop in bed today.'

Jenny Greenwood turned then, almost a dancer's pirouette, a gypsy dancer Martha had once seen and for a moment Jenny's face came alive, looking as it had done months ago. It was flushed with emotion, warm with her love for her mother, and the headstrong resolve which Martha had seen on the occasions she had followed their Joss. She lifted her head, tossing her curls, lifting her hands to them in a gesture of defiance, or so it seemed.

'No, you'll not, Mother. Keep the fire in today. Have a bit of comfort for God's sake and to hell with it. See, I'll put a shovelful on . . .' and taking the bucket from the side of the grate she threw some coal on to the smouldering fire watching with immense satisfaction as it caught hold and flared up into a bright warmth which they had not seen for a long time. She stood for a moment to watch it, her hands on her hips then turned again to Martha.

'Now keep it like that, d'you hear and eat those tripe bits you were saving. Give some to the children and Mercy, but eat them all, every last bit. I'll bring something for you to eat . . .'

'Dear God, Jenny . . . where . . .?'

'Don't ask, Mother,' and she was gone.

She turned at the corner where Jagger Lane met Reddygate Way, stopping for a moment or two to watch the frosted sky over the brow of the hill which led out of town to Edgeclough change imperceptibly from oyster to pearl grey. Her face, strong and infinitely enduring, softened as the memories flooded into her mind. Of days, warm and secure in her father's protection, of strong arms and a serene face, of Joss who rotted in prison but who had once carried her 'piggy-back' up this same brow, of her mother, her apron clean and starched, her hands steady as she brushed the long hair which Jenny had cut off. Days of childhood, but now she was a woman with a family who depended on her.

She breathed in the iced wine air and smiled and felt the tension drain away and it was almost with relief that she turned to walk up Reddygate Way. The houses which lined it on both sides were just as substantial as those in Jagger Lane but there was an air about them which spoke not of families and children's laughter, but of well scrubbed commercialism, of better times, of genteel poverty perhaps which had not gone under. Here there were rooms to be had for those who did not care to be put up at the local hostelry, of varying degrees of comfort according to the means of its tenant and it was to one of these that she went.

Harry Atherton's rooms were very comfortable indeed. His landlady had been the daughter of a parson brought up to be a gentlewoman and with no accomplishments beyond a talent for playing the piano, sewing a fine seam and directing her servants in the provision of her father's comfort. When he died he left her a small legacy, not quite enough to live on so, being a lady of some independence and strength of mind and unwilling to take on the only respectable employment open to her, that of governess in someone else's home, she decided, and beggar society's opinion, to take gentlemen lodgers into her home. Respectable only need apply, her advertisement said. She kept her servants, who now cooked and cleaned for three very reputable gentlemen, serving them in their own suites of rooms and keeping to hers, seeing them once a week to collect their rent. Providing they were discreet they could do as they pleased, though not in so many words.

'Come in, Jenny,' he said and she did, stepping boldly into his comfortable drawing-room and before she could lose the resolve which had hardened in her that morning, she threw off her shawl and strode defiantly to the fire-place in which an enormous fire blazed. She stood with her back to it for a moment absorbing its heat, then with steady fingers she began to undo the buttons of her bodice.

Harry watched her with disbelief at first for it was many weeks since that day last October when he had first whispered in her ear what they might do together if she was willing. Then she had turned on him like a wildcat caught up an alley by a prowling tom, spitting her disgust, ready he had believed to scratch his eyes out. He had loved it and almost in his heart loved her for he had always treasured that which was hard to come by and this woman would be that. Since then he had forced her to him many times, threatening if she did not come he would fire her, and the whole of her family and he had meant it, she could see it in his eyes.

'Rape me then,' she had said, 'and be done with it. I'll not be the first mill girl to be taken down by the maister, nor the last.' She had lifted her head in that arrogant way she had, daring him, defying him and he knew, by God, that his days of boredom were over with for the time being. 'Go on,' she had continued contemptuously, the first time he had summoned her to his office, 'take what you want and I'll be on my way and be quick about it for I'm losing money while my machine lies idle.'

'Dammit, Jenny, but you're a rare one,' he said admiringly. 'Are you not afraid of me?'

'What's there to be afraid of? You're a man, I'm a woman. I know what happens and if that's what I have to

do to keep my family from starving then get on with it.'
Her lip had curled in contempt.

'You have done it before then?' he asked later, in the
comfort of his rooms, lounging against the fireplace in the
indolent pose of a young gentleman quite at ease and why
should he not, for was that not what he was? He wore
immaculate dove grey trousers, a coat of claret and his shirt
frill was white and crisply pressed. His fair hair was brushed
smoothly and his brown eyes were warm and approving in
the well-shaved symmetry of his face. The contrast between
them was quite startling and she could not help but marvel
that this handsome, faultlessly tailored young gentleman
should want her. She was not even particularly clean since
it was hard to be fastidious when the water was turned on
only once a day and that when she and her family were at
the mill.

'What I do, or have done in the past is nothing to you,'
she went on scathingly.

'Oh but it is, Jenny, and please feel free to call me any
name you care to lay your tongue to. I can see you are
longing to. I must say I find this highly diverting. The . . .
the others . . . were so . . . submissive . . .'

'Oh for God's sake, let's get it done.'

'No, oh no, my dear, not like that. Not at all like that.'
He smiled disarmingly then reached for a cigar, lighting it
lazily, his eyes never leaving hers and for the first time she
felt uncertain. She had come, that first time, to be used
against her will by this man who Ellis had told her liked a
bit of 'rough'. He had said many other things to her on that
day concerning how she might best please a man such as
Harry Atherton and her flesh had crawled and the inner
core of her woman's body had shrank from it for she had
known no man's touch, but she had come. She had no
choice.

'You see, my dear,' he went on, casually letting his eyes
roam over her, 'I want you to enjoy it also.'

'Then you'll have a long wait.'

'I don't think so.' He grinned and she was quite fascinated

252

by the glowing firmness of his well fed flesh and the whiteness of his teeth. When he smiled two deep creases appeared in his cheeks, dimples they would have been called on a girl.

'What d'you want with me?'

'I've just told you.'

'You're mad.'

'Only for you, Jenny Greenwood,' and his smile broadened.

'Then get on with it.'

'Only if you're willing.'

'Well, I'm not.'

'Then when you are we will enjoy it all the more. Until then you will come here when I tell you.'

And now that time had come for she could no longer stand against him. She would not waste herself though, nor the indignity, the humiliation she was to suffer. She would get everything she could from him, make him pay for what he was about to do to her, make him *sorry*, by God, in the end that he had done it. She would not sell herself lightly. She would earn it, the money she meant to obtain from him would buy food and warmth for her family. Week after week she had spat in his face, clawed his face in her effort to madden him into *taking* her for then she could have told herself that what was done, was done against her will but now she was to be forced into offering herself. To be shamed like any street whore. Well, so be it. He could try, he could damn well try to cheapen her but by God she'd lead him a merry dance before she was through with him.

When she was completely naked she stood before him, without shame, without humility and when he touched her she did not flinch. Her eyes locked with his, savage and bitter and for a moment he hesitated, not unwilling, far from it, but not convinced that she was.

'What are you waiting for, Mr Atherton?' she said silkily. 'Here I am just as you said I would be, offering myself to you. Let me see what you have to offer me.'

They were sitting by the fire, her mother and Mercy, Charlie and Daisy when she arrived home. The room was warm, almost cosy by the standards they had known during the past weeks. Daisy leaned against her mother, her sunken face quite rosy in the fire's glow, languid with the warmth. Martha had been cleaning, polishing with the last of her home-made beeswax the incongruously lovely blanket chest, the table which had been her mother's and the dresser which was stacked with the crockery they had brought from Edgeclough. The room smelled of it. On every side was the stench of years of filth, seeping through cracks in the walls, through broken and split doors and windows and up through the rotting floorboards and by the end of the day the smell of the beeswax would be gone but for just that moment it brought back memories to Jenny of the kitchen in the cottage which she still called home.

They turned to look at her when she entered the room, bringing in the raw chill of the January day and her mother's eyes questioned her sadly but she avoided them. She put the basket she carried on to the table, turning to smile brightly and the children stood up expectantly for she had a look about her that said something unusual was about to happen.

'Now then,' she said, 'who would like a piece of . . .?'

'What . . . what, Jenny?' Daisy's face flowered with excitement.

'A piece of custard pie?'

The child's face fell for their Jenny's joke was unforgivable, but her sister lifted the cloth from the basket and reaching inside brought out a plate on which was an untouched tart. Daisy's eyes grew enormous and her mouth popped open and a small dribble of saliva ran down her chin. Charlie, older and wiser than she, looked suspicious, since when could they afford such delicacies as this. He knew it took his mother all her time to put the porridge and treacle, the plain boiled potatoes, the stale bread bought when it was almost a week old, the tripe bits, into their stomachs. The rent on these homes was not cheap, despite their appalling state of repair, and with the wages of the three women, himself and Daisy who earned one and sixpence a week, they managed, just, to exist above starvation level. But he was a boy, a boy who had seen nothing like this for a long, long time and when Jenny cut him a large piece and put it in his hands he fell on it, stuffing it in his mouth, laughing with excitement, watching, as the lovely pastry flaked about his chin, the appearance of a jug of milk, a packet of tea, a loaf of crusty bread, cheese, a green cabbage and a ham bone with only a slice or two cut from it, the results, though he was not to know it, of a raid on the larder of the parson's daughter.

'Where . . .?' he managed to say but Jenny shook her head laughing with delight, her heart soft and at peace with herself, everything she had done that day made insignificant by the look in the boy's eyes.

'Ask me no questions and I'll tell you no lies,' she laughed but he was not satisfied. He was the man of the house while his brother, his leader, was in prison and he could not have one of the women in his charge going about alone and coming home with an unexplained basket of food which he knew full well they could not afford.

'Now then, our Jenny,' he said, his seven-year-old voice stern, 'our Joss wouldn't like it if . . .' but Jenny laughed and ruffled his hair then bent to kiss his awkward cheek.

'Don't worry, lad, I've done nothin' illegal. There's this lady in Reddygate Way, a parson's daughter she is. Well, I've been working in her house and I was given this basket of food in payment.' That was the exact truth. No lies and she could look her young brother in the face and say it without shame, without remorse, without regret and the delight, the joy, the look of well-being which was already alerting the faces of her young sister and brother made every moment of it worthwhile. She *had* worked hard today, pleasuring young Mr Atherton and the things she had done and had done to her . . . she could hear his voice yet . . .

' . . . stand just there, with the light falling on your . . .

255

yes, yes . . . that's right . . . now drape this shawl about you . . . no, leave your breasts uncovered . . . put your hand . . . there . . . now, if I lean a little you can reach . . . now turn with your back to me and put your . . . lovely . . . aaah . . .' and when it was done and she had been dressing beneath his satisfied gaze he had said to her carelessly, '. . . and the next time, don't bother to wash before you come. I want to see you just as you are at your machine, do you understand?' She did!

She looked away from her young brother then, the rosy glow of her face not entirely due to the warmth from the fire and her body, aching though it was, throbbed with a curious feeling which was not altogether displeasing.

'Come on, Mercy, don't sit there with your mouth hanging open. Put the tea in the pot and we'll have us a nice brew and a ham sandwich an' all and don't stint because there's plenty more where that came from. I'm to go each Sunday and perhaps a couple of evenings after work so tuck in, oh and Mother, order some more coal, will you. With what we save on food we can manage a bit of a fire now.'

They were in bed, the children as Martha called them, including Joss's young wife among them, the intense joy giving way to the exaggerated weariness of the undernourished, and she and Jenny sipped a last cup of the delicious tea. She felt it put warmth in her and the good food in her belly had strengthened her but her old heart was frail and hopeless, helpless with pity as she looked at her girl. Jenny would not meet her eyes but stared into the fire, sipping her tea, seemingly absorbed in her own thoughts.

'Who is he, lass?' Martha said at last. 'One of the managers?' for who else had the money to give food away such as they had just eaten.

'No one, Mother.' Still her girl did not look at her.

'I'm not daft, Jenny. It must be someone with a bit of cash to send that basket of food.'

'Don't ask me, Mother, for God's sake leave it alone.'

256

'I can't, lass. I can't bear to think of it but I must.'

'Does it matter who it was?'

'No, I suppose not.' She sat up suddenly. 'Dear God, it's not Ellis, is it? I couldn't stand to think . . .'

'No, Mother, it's not Ellis. He'd not be so generous.'

'Thank God . . .!' She was silent for a moment, watching her daughter, surprised somehow to see the . . . well, the girl did not look chastened, not particularly ill-used. There was a drag of strain about her mouth but her eyes were calm, steady and certainly not harrowed as you would expect those of a girl who had been 'taken down' to be.

'Do you . . . love him, Jenny?' The words sounded ludicrous in the circumstances but they popped into her head of their own accord, just why she could not have said but her daughter looked up and her whole face split into a shout of laughter.

'Love him? *Love him!* Dear sweet Jesus, are you mad? I hate his guts and one day I'll make him pay for what he's done to me but in the meanwhile my family'll eat well and something'll be done about this place too, or I'll know the reason why.'

But in her eyes still was that strange, quite unexplained glow, mysterious and troubling to her mother who had once known the joy of physical pleasure herself.

Kit Chapman lay in her bed and stared up at the lazily dancing shadows on the ceiling. Her maid had built up the fire since the night was as bitter as any they could remember, or so the older servants were saying in the kitchens, and the rosy flames tinted the white paintwork to apricot and gold. It was reflected in the black panes of the window where Janet had drawn back the curtains and in the polished surfaces of the furniture and Kit watched them, her mind empty, quite blank of everything but the stray darting thoughts of the events of the day. Blurred, thankfully and vague and she hung on to the feeling, the insubstantiality of her mood for only in its merciful oblivion could she cope with it.

257

She breathed lightly, taking in shallow sips of the warm air, afraid to disturb her own mindless tranquillity, the measured pace of her heart, the heavy stillness of her body. Janet had brushed her hair, excited and longing to talk, as she had thought her mistress would, of what had happened this evening since it had been all over the servants' hall within five minutes, but her chatter had trailed away on the wave of Kit's silence and her young face, looking at that of her mistress in the mirror had become sad, compassionate and wondering at the same time on why it should be, since surely this was, *should* be the happiest day in the life of Barker Chapman's daughter.

'Thank you, Janet. You may go now,' Miss Katherine had said, her face set and . . . and lost, somehow, though surely that was fanciful, Janet told herself.

'Will I make up the fire, Miss Katherine?'

'What . . . oh, yes . . .'

'Good-night then, Miss.'

'Good-night, Janet.'

*Good-night* . . . would she ever know that again? The awful thought was in and out again before she could stop it, just as though it had slyly opened the door for all the others to follow, they flooded in on a torrent of anguish and despair and she sat up in bed. Her hair fell about her in a great silken shroud and she clutched her bent knees with desperate arms, hiding her face in them but still she could see what was there. The peace, the false serenity was gone in a blinding current of pain and she called his name.

'Joss . . . Joss . . .' Her voice caught in her throat, trapped there in silence and there was no sound but the gentle ticking of the clock on the mantelshelf above the fire. Where was he? Please, dear Jesus, tell me where he is. Let me be with him, let me see him, let him hear me, let him know that I am in his heart as he is in mine. Give him strength, give him *my* strength, keep him safe, bring him back.

She lifted her head, then pushed back the covers, padding silently across the carpet to the window. The skies were clear in the frost-trapped harshness of the night and when she pressed her face close to the window she could see the outline of trees and shrubs, each one clothed in a thick hoar frost, white and exquisitely beautiful against the blue-black eternity of the sky.

'Joss . . . Joss . . .' Her mind could not get beyond him, beyond his name, beyond her body's pain and longing and the room she was in, warm, comfortable, soft, could not contain her. In a moment she had flung off her nightdress and her mind still functioning on the level of basic needs, she dressed in the warmest clothing she had, thick boots and woollen stockings, a shawl of cashmere about her long, unbound hair.

The dogs greeted her in silent delight, snuffling ecstatically against her hand. They padded quietly beside her as she let herself out of the stable yard and their noses were a mere inch from the hem of her skirt as she strode up the pasture at the back of the house and on to the track which led to the moors. There was no moon as yet, but the stars clustered thickly in the velvet darkness of the night and they lit her way between crisply frozen bracken and the stiff and cracking carpet of the grass.

The cobbled track once used by pack-horses, was slippery with white rime and she could easily fall and break her ankle, she thought dazedly, left to lie here and freeze to death but what did it matter? Would *he* be warm and so should *she* be?

The track wound in long curves up the steep slope and as she went higher, wrapped in the vapour from the mouths of her dogs and herself, she could see nothing of what was below in the valley for it was Sunday and the mills would not yet be firing up for Monday's first shift.

It took her an hour to reach it, the circle of stones at the top of Badger's Edge and when she did she was gasping for breath in the lung-searing pain of the cold but her body was warm and her muscles had lost the cramp of the despair which had held her since that tangled moment in her father's study. What had gone before was a dim memory, difficult to recall and not important, never important now, and what had come after drifted vaguely, trifling, insignificant, barely remembered through her confusion. Up here she could mark it out, pick the essentials from the turmoil of what had happened, distinguish what was of concern to her and what was not. Up here she could think.

She leaned her back against the same tall rock, imagining that she could feel the warmth that he had left there. She let it in then, she let *him* in, opening the closed doors of her mind which she had slammed shut, forever she had thought, on the night of the fire. They had scarred one another quite disastrously on that night and on others but could she say those scars had healed, that her wounds were gone, that she was whole again, delivered from her deep love of Joss Greenwood? She had told herself that it was so and pretended that she believed it but now, facing the truth, the honesty she prided herself in, she knew she had lied.

She loved Joss Greenwood. Then she had loved him and now she loved him and sadly, could she really envisage the day when it would end? She sighed, somewhat more at peace, accepting the inevitability of it, of him, and of their love. Oh yes, she knew he loved her despite the wife he had and the life he led. It was as certain as the stars which came each night to pierce the dark heavens, as the sun which rose each day and fell each night, hidden many times behind a cloud of confusion but always there nevertheless.

She pulled off her mittens, putting her hands to her face, cupping it as he had once done, then blowing on her cold fingers for even the soft wool could not keep out the bitterness of the January night. The ring slipped round her finger, the enormous jewel which adorned it catching on the knuckle and she became still then, quiet, hiding herself suddenly from the strange unfamiliarity of it, quite bewildered for a fraction of a second on where it had come from, for she had never before seen it. Not that she could see it now, in the pale darkness which fell about her but she could feel its weight, its dreadful weight and as she did, her mind scurrying to hide from the knowledge – too late, too late –

she remembered Harry Atherton's smilingly satisfied face, her father's formal kiss and the ecstatic fluttering of her mother and as she did so she felt the frozen tears slip painfully across her cheeks and the whole horror of it came flooding in on her bent head.

# 18

'An April wedding, I think, do you not agree, Kit?' her mother said and her father nodded his approval. The sooner the better in his opinion for she had had a strange reckless look about her recently which he did not particularly care for. He could not put his finger on exactly when it had come about or what had caused it, but he had a definite feeling that he would like to see her married by Easter, perhaps a couple of children to steady her in the next two years, sons preferably while he himself was still here to supervise their upbringing. Then, with the foundations of her life securely cemented and herself well protected in the safety of marriage and motherhood she would be a splendid rock on which to continue the growth of his empire. He was fast becoming the most important manufacturer in the South Lancashire textile trade with his three mills, his blow room, his combing and carding mill, his fine new warehouse, big enough to hold miles and miles of cloth; his finishing shed, design rooms and dye-house. And he meant to build again this year. Another spinning mill and weaving-shed, expanding to employ over a thousand workers, since among them Albert Jenkinson, George Abbott and himself hired the near majority of the textile workers in the sixteen square miles of the Oldham chapelry.

'That sounds reasonable, my dear,' he said to his wife, 'then if Kit and Harry are considering a wedding journey,

France perhaps, or Italy, they might spend the summer travelling. I think I could manage without them for a while.' He smiled, one might almost say twinkled if such a word could be used to describe Barker Chapman's serious visage, over the humorous notion of Barker Chapman being unable to run his mills alone and his wife laughed politely, looking to her daughter and her daughter's new fiancé where they sat side by side on the elegant sofa in the drawing-room.

They had dined in the usual sumptuous manner, Kit picking at her food in the way her mother had wished to see her do for years, in the way a *lady* should. She did not look at anyone, her eyes fixed on her plate or the tablecloth or the window opposite. She spoke only when a remark was addressed particularly to her and if one did not know better one might have believed that Harry Atherton was some business acquaintance of her father's, a stranger to whom she had just been introduced and whom she did not care for. And yet she wore his ring. His grandmother's ring, he had told them, bequeathed to him when she died, for his own bride. It was heavy and old-fashioned, of no special value except that of great antiquity and the knowledge that it had been worn by innumerable ladies of the family of gentry.

'Kit?' her father said. 'We are speaking to you.'

'Yes Father, I heard you. I do apologise and must beg you to excuse me for I have a headache.'

'A headache, my dear.' Both Hannah and Barker Chapman echoed her words in amazement since neither had ever known their daughter to suffer a moment's sickness in her life. From the day she was born she had thrived, quite excessively so, her mother had often thought when it was considered well-bred to faint now and then. But now it seemed she was ailing and Hannah looked at her sharply since young women who suddenly developed unusual symptoms were instantly under suspicion. She *had* been alone for more than an hour with Harry, her betrothed, on the night of the ball and heaven knows what had taken place.

Perhaps it might be expedient to bring forward the date of the wedding . . .!

'Really, Father, I am quite well but . . .'

'Katherine, please do go and lie down. I cannot bear to think you are suffering on my account. If I were not here I am sure you would have retired by now.' Harry was possessively smug in his newly created role as her husband-to-be and Kit felt the revulsion rise in her as his hand reached out to touch hers. It took all her self-control not to snatch it away in disgust but instead she stood up abruptly and moved away from him, ready to dart to the door if he should offer to . . . to kiss her goodnight. It was hardly likely in front of her mother and father but when had Harry Atherton ever been bound by rules that, in his opinion, which was that of a gentleman, were those composed by the industrial classes and therefore not worth considering?

'Very well, my dear,' her father said, rather displeased his expression telling her since this was not the stalwart Katherine who had stood among men in the mill and matched her will against theirs but he was willing to allow it this time since the situation was new to her. In his private heart where no one could see but himself he admitted quite frankly that he had pushed her into it with less of a fight than he had expected but it was done now and there was to be no retreat. A betrothal was almost as binding as marriage with contracts and signatures which, without a great deal of inconvenience, could not be rescinded. She had accepted it quietly enough and he would not put up with any female vapours, should she feel inclined to produce any. She would not, of course. She was his daughter, trained to do what was necessary in the world of commerce, to put business before any personal matter and this was a business transaction and well she knew it. It had been explained to her on the night Harry had proposed to her and she had not refused. Now the next step must be taken and this curious pose she had effected must be discarded at once.

'Very well, Katherine. I'm sure Harry is right. You must retire if you are feeling indisposed. We cannot have you drooping at the party, can we?'

'Party . . .?'

'Come now, Katherine.' He was becoming irritated. 'Have you not been listening to *anything* we have talked about this evening? The party on Saturday night for our close friends and relatives. To celebrate your betrothal to Harry. The invitations have been sent out and already your mother has received several acceptances, have you not, my dear?'

'Indeed I have, and Harry's family have consented to be our guests for the weekend. My word, we shall be a houseful! Not that I mind, you understand,' turning hastily to her future son-in-law, 'in fact I am looking forward to it immensely, introducing our family to yours.' More than she could describe, her joyful, triumphant heart sang, for this moment was the pinnacle of all her most treasured dreams, the pinnacle of *all* mothers' most treasured dreams, she was certain. Her daughter was to be allied in marriage to a son of one of the most privileged families in the north and she could hardly wait until Saturday to display it all, to the mothers of girls who had not yet been selected, to her manufacturing friends who had not quite believed her secretive, preening charade of something stupendous to come, to her own relations who, though they were high in the millocracy of Lancashire had not yet achieved an association such as the Chapmans were to be rewarded with.

'I had not realised . . .'

'What, my dear?' Barker Chapman's voice was silky but beneath the benign concern was the rough grit which said she must stop this nonsense at once.

'I'm afraid . . . my head aches so . . . I confess I did not hear your . . . the plans for . . .'

'For the betrothal party?'

*Betrothal party!* Oh dear God, what was she doing? How had she become entangled in this farce her mother and

264

father were planning so joyfully? What had happened to her? Why had her sharp, quick-thinking brain, her normal ability to be three steps ahead of anyone else's mental processes let her down? In the space of a week, or was it two – Lord, what was wrong with her? she could barely string two intelligent thoughts together – she found she had become engaged to marry a man she scarcely liked, let alone loved. A man who amused her, at times, with his impudent wit, who made her smile and shake her head as one would at the antics of a precocious child, but certainly not someone with whom she could get into bed. She had allowed him to kiss her ... was that how it had happened ... as an experiment really, a test for herself to see if she could erase the memory of the kisses of another man, but as he had kissed her, her inner self, the one that loved Joss Greenwood, had shivered away from it. He was a self-seeker, an opportunist, doing business with her father, selling his family name, but more importantly to Barker Chapman, the manufacturer, his own charm and talent for convincing men that Barker Chapman's piece goods were the best to be had. He could mix at any level with men of the business world and over a glass of whisky, or a magnum of champagne, whatever it might take to clinch the deal, he could and did sell her father's cotton. Already he was moving about the country, Manchester, Liverpool, London, using the contacts he had built up, selling the Chapman cotton goods and business was booming. Her father was gratified, she knew, by the success of his plans, those made on her eighteenth birthday, she realised that now, the business deal he had struck with Samuel and Harry Atherton and now it had come to fruition. Everything was flowing as Barker Chapman had intended and on Saturday night, before the whole of the Penfold Valley, and no doubt half of the Cheshire gentry, she and Harry Atherton were to be put on show, the achievement complete, the dream come true, the pinnacle climbed and won.

'My dear, are you to go or are you to stay?' she heard her father ask, his mouth smiling but not his eyes and she

265

knew quite suddenly that she must tread very, very carefully now. He would not take kindly to having his plans destroyed nor allowing the rest of the world (for who in the valley was not aware of his success?), to smirk and whisper of pride going before a fall as that girl of his flung his glory back in his face. The triumph he had accomplished, not just in his business but in his forthcoming connection with a family who had known privilege and authority for hundreds of years, had been worked for, sweated over and should she dash it from his hand it would be the end of her career, her hopes of carrying on his mills, *her* mills then, when he had gone. She would no doubt be given in marriage to a somewhat lesser gentleman in the industrial world and breed a child each year, the mills sold or bequeathed to a cousin, a male cousin, her father's favour in which she had basked for nearly eight years withdrawn coldly, implacably, *finally*.

So, she must play the game, pretend, act out the charade, be as clever and devious as he as she looked for a way out of this dilemma since there was nothing more sure in this life than the certainty that Kit Chapman would never marry Harry Atherton!

She felt the sluggish blood begin to surge through her veins, hotly, defiantly and colour pinked her pale cheeks. Her eyes grew calm, the haunted look of a wild and cornered animal slipping away to be replaced by an almost imperceptible cunning. She felt strong, invincible, her wits returned to her, those that had been swept away when her father had told her of the three felons, one of whom was Joss Greenwood. She would smile, she *did* smile now, and smile again and again as she planned her plans and schemed her schemes and the time to begin was . . . well . . . what was wrong with right now?

'Father, Mother, Harry, I am so sorry. I really do not know what came over me. It was unforgivable of me to be so rude and on such a momentous occasion as this. Perhaps it was the excitement after all since a girl does not become engaged every day and I suppose the sheer . . .' – could she say 'joy' or was that going too far — 'the sheer singularity of it went to my head. I shall go and ask Janet for a draught to clear it and then I shall come right back and we can continue with our plans for Saturday night. No, do not argue with me, Harry, I insist and you should know by now how I do love to have my own way.'

She smiled silkily, her old self again to all intents and purposes and she saw the two men relax and look at one another, visibly relieved by her manner. They were both astute, not easily hoodwinked. They must have been both bewildered and alarmed by the shocked state she had been in — though without it she doubted if she and Harry Atherton would have now been betrothed. Perhaps it was as well for she would have fought her father into the ground and lost what she had anyway. Now, with guile and stealth she would have it all and see Harry Atherton go to the devil!

She dreamed of Joss that night. He was clamped to a wall which sweated damp and his face, haggard, gaunt, thin, was turned up to the light which fell from a barred window. In his eyes was an expression which, though she puzzled and puzzled over it she could not understand. It asked her for something and though she called to him, beseeched him to tell her what it was it seemed he could not speak. He turned to look at her and his eyes, a cloudy mixture of grey and green were dull with misery and pain. Tell me, Joss, my love, my love . . . tell me . . . tell me and the words still whispered in her throat when she awoke.

She smiled and wished her father 'good morning' as Ellen opened the breakfast-room door for her. She discussed the coming day's business, the economic condition which was so good, the possibility of parliamentary reform and the guest list for her betrothal party on Saturday. Through it all she ate a splendid breakfast as she always did, smiled cheerfully and was as matter of fact as her father was used to seeing her.

She had her own suite of offices now at the mill for as her duties and responsibilities had increased and with it the paperwork she must apply herself to, the ones she had shared in the first months of training with her father had not been big enough to contain them both. Harry had his own – just one large room for he was seldom in it – next door to hers and in which he kept his samples, his orders and all the paraphernalia he seemed to require as Barker Chapman's salesman. He was concerned, he said, with fulfilling the constant demand for new products and designs, needing clerks and office boys to run here and there on his business, making a great show of doing it, but doing it nevertheless, and selling Chapman cloth by the thousands of yards.

But she was restless, her mind still dwelling in that dream prison cell with Joss, still haunted by the strange plea which had been in his dream eyes. She prowled about the room, moving from her desk to the window to watch the unloading of bales of raw cotton and the loading of dress goods on to the waggons pulled by huge and patient Shire horses. She played with the ring on her finger, finding it heavy and unwieldy, ready to take it off and put it in her reticule with the excuse that it was of too great a value to her to risk it in the hurly burly of the day. As she watched a girl came out of the spinning mill, tall and fine looking, with well set shoulders and a straight back. Her hair was a cloud of tossing dark curls about her head and though it was still cold and the contrast great between the humidity of the spinning room and the chill of the yard, her shawl was merely draped carelessly across her shoulders, trailing its fringed edges almost in the mud of the yard. It was pretty, the colours of scarlet and rose and deep claret, not at all like those worn by the women in her father's factory and she wondered idly how such a girl had come by it. The girl walked with a springing jaunty step, so different from the rest of the female workers Kit had seen creeping submissively about the place, looking about her with all the indifferent hauteur of a young queen. She cared for no one, her attitude said, and if she wished to loiter in the yard as she was doing, then what was it to anyone else?

Strangely, she turned and lifting her hand to shade her

eyes from the smoke-hazed winter sunshine, which was low above the mill roof, she stared directly up at the office windows, almost as though she expected to see someone she knew. Instantly Kit recognised her and as she did so her heart banged furiously against her breastbone, hurting her. Her dream came back to her with the force of a blow and in it Joss's pleading eyes looked straight into hers and she thought she knew at last what it was he asked of her. This was his sister who stood in the yard so challengingly and somewhere his mother, his young brother and sister were waiting for his return, *and his wife*, her shrinking mind said and how were they dealing with this tragedy which had come into their lives. They lived in a cottage at Edgeclough, Joss had told her, spinning what they could, living on what they grew and what Joss could weave and now, for the past weeks, how long exactly she did not know since she was afraid to arouse suspicions by questioning her father, they had been without his support. What was her name, his sister . . . Jenny, that was it, was a spinner in the factory, he had said and Kit remembered her on the day the child had lost his hands. She had been younger then, three years younger, both of them girls and now they were women, sharing somehow, a common bond of love for the same man. She remembered the way Joss had described his sister, the affectionate humour in his voice when he said she should have been a man, and even this, for should not Kit Chapman have been born a son, gave them unity.

Jenny Greenwood did not see her for her eyes were looking for someone else and later, when the mill-owner's daughter came into the spinning room, standing in the doorway, a lovely bright flower against the drab uniformity of the rest of the room she looked at Kit Chapman with contempt, a sneering look which asked what in hell's name had brought *her* to look them over. She herself must be on the alert, scarcely able to glance up from her frame since if she missed a broken thread leaving the two ends loose she would be in a great deal of trouble.

Miss Chapman walked slowly up and down the

enormous room, waving imperiously away the darting figure of Ellis who had appeared immediately she had come through the doorway, his own face wary for what the hell did this mean? It was three years since she had been here on the day the boy was killed and there had been many accidents since but in that time he had run his one hundred and sixty frames just as he pleased, and the women who operated them. Now here she was poking about again and he'd best look sharp and report it to Mr Gribb, the manager who would pass it on to Mr Chapman. He couldn't have her nosing about not with things the way they were. Some of the lasses, with her on the spot, might take it into their head to speak up, her being a woman.

Calling to a lad who carried a creel of bobbins to 'drop that and run and fetch Mr Gribb,' Ellis watched Miss Chapman's progress.

Kit felt the spongy mess on the floor, cotton waste, fluff and oil, squelch around the soles of the soft leather boots she wore and knew that the hem of her fine woollen dress, a pale harebell blue, would be ruined but she continued regally between the hissing, singing machines, drawn with a fascination she did not try to analyse to find the family of Joss Greenwood. Somewhere in the village of Edgeclough was his mother and his wife. Would she herself be able to look her in the eye, to regard dispassionately the woman with whom he had shared, if not his love, then his fine body, the one she herself had coveted almost from the first day they had met. She did not know! She had been no more than a young girl then, fifteen, sixteen but she had been pulled towards him by invisible threads of need. She had grown to love him, to want him desperately but she had withheld herself and in all of her life she had regretted nothing more.

None of the operatives looked up from their machines and again she was struck by the ill-used, worn-out demeanour of the women who could never, not for a moment, stop their endlessly restless hands and feet. Their backs were permanently bent across the frames of their machines and as they leaned over the hems of their short skirts rose up to reveal the grey white sticks of their legs. They were barefoot, of course, in the sweating heat and filth, forced to keep up with the speed of the machines for while the engine ran so must they. All they needed were 'hands' which is what they themselves were called, and brains sufficient to guide the hands and the wit to keep themselves out of danger. Their minds had no stimulation, stagnating in their aching heads, beyond the care those with their own children about them tried to exercise. Twenty to thirty miles in a day they would walk following the mule carriage and all in the space of twenty feet.

At last she saw the girl from the yard and drawn again by some strange compulsion she stopped, and bewildering herself for what could she say to her, reached out and touched her arm. The girl turned instantly, her hand still hovering about the machine for left to itself it would ruin the yarn she was spinning, then she turned back and with a swift and practised hand, switched off the machine. She stood, head up, eyes gleaming, awaiting her master's, or in this case his daughter's command. She did not bob a curtsey as many would in her place but stared straight into Kit's eyes, revealing nothing of her thoughts, her own face expressionless.

For several seconds Kit was at a loss for words. Indeed she had no idea why she had stopped the girl, nor even why she was here. What should she say to her? What indeed? And what had brought her here? What indeed?

'Excuse me . . .' she said, groping for words, for something to say, well aware that Ellis was watching at the end of the room, that Gribb was moving towards her between the rows of machinery, that Jenny Greenwood's was lying idle, losing money not only for her, who could, she was certain, ill afford it, but for Ellis and Gribb, who she was equally certain, would not care for it.

'Yes?' Jenny Greenwood said. Just that one word. Yes! Her face was quite blank but coming from her was such a strong wave of resentment Kit could feel it wash against her and she flinched a little, stepping back in confusion.

'I wanted to ask you if . . .?' What? for God's sake. What could she say to his sister? What could she ask her? How is your brother, Jenny Greenwood? Have you heard from him? Of him? Does he still live even? Does he survive wherever he is? Does he eat, is he warm, is he injured, does he still love me, when will I see him again?

'Yes?' Jenny said again, coldly, waiting, as all those of her class were expected to wait on those above them and Kit knew she must move on.

'I wished to examine the work you are doing,' was all she could think of to say, coolly, employer to employee.

'There's nowt wrong with *my* work.'

'I'm sure there isn't so in that case you will have no objection to my examining it.'

Why was it that every time she and this woman met they were instantly ready to be at each other's throats, like two bitches neither of whom cares to lie down with the other. Snapping and snarling their black temper, neither prepared to lower their eyes and be the first to step away. Jenny Greenwood was nothing to her, beneath her interest as they all were in the spinning room except as 'hands' to run her machines. She merely wished, in some vague and unthought-out way, to help the family, if it was possible, of Joss Greenwood, to put out a hand, not of friendship exactly, for could they ever know that, but of assistance. But of course it would be taken for patronage by this irritating girl who would rather starve than eat what Kit Chapman might provide.

Jenny Greenwood stepped back resentfully, aware that there was nothing she could do to prevent Kit Chapman from studying the yarn she was spinning, indeed from ordering her out of the mill if she chose, without reason nor reference. She was her 'master'. She owned her. She could lift her up or fling her down, whichever she fancied, and her proud spirit longed to spit in her face, to strike her down contemptuously and grind her into the muck and oil and waste which they were forced to endure for the best part of sixteen hours a day. She glided about the counting house, the spinning and weaving-sheds, the mill yard, scarcely noticing the human ants which scurried madly beneath her feet and certainly not noticing if she crushed one or two in her careless indifference to them. She had the power of life and death over them, the right, if she chose, to end the existence of whole families if a member of one should offend her, or for no other reason than they were surplus to her needs and Jenny Greenwood hated her for it.

'Can you find any fault, madam?' she asked, her insolence making the women about her gasp.

'If there is one to be found I will find it.'

'I've no doubt you would if there wasn't.'

'You step dangerously, Jenny Greenwood,' and they took a stance face to face, both frighteningly close to blows, Kit's former compassion flown away in the teeth of this girl's enmity but a movement at her back drew her away from the confrontation and she turned, finding Gribb at her elbow, Ellis behind him.

'Is everything in order, Miss Chapman?' the manager asked smoothly.

'Of course, Gribb,' she managed to gasp. 'I was merely questioning this girl on the quality of the yarn and I am quite satisfied with it.'

'Thank you, Miss Chapman. Will there be anything else?'

'No thank you,' and without another glance in the direction of Jenny Greenwood she swept from the room.

She waited until the following Sunday slipping from the house as a pale dawn edged the peaks of the hills behind Greenacres. Many of her father's guests had only this moment left, others just fallen into their beds after the party which, in the way of things where young bachelors were present, and ladies retired, had ended in horseplay and a certain amount of cheerful drunkenness, the young gentry the worst of them all. Harry Atherton, assured now of a grand future in what would one day be *his* house had been carelessly attentive for an hour or two to his new fiancée, then gone to join them, believing, it seemed, that as she was now almost married she would be glad to sit and gossip among those who were.

It was splendid up on the moors, not as cold as at the beginning of the year, with a light dusting of snow capping the hills. As usual on a Sunday the air had cleared and the higher she climbed the headier it became and when she reached the hill overlooking the village she could pick out each individual chimney and the pencil straight line of smoke which came from one or two. Eleven there were, eleven cottages and in one of them Joss Greenwood's family lived and again, as on the day last week when she had accosted Jenny Greenwood, she had not the slightest notion of what she would say to them.

They had gone, she was told by the astounded woman who answered her knock on the door of the first cottage she came to.

'Gone . . . gone where . . .?'

'Why, to Crossfold, Miss,' the woman said, eyeing incredulously the fine warm wool of Miss Chapman's clothing – since who in these parts did not know the daughter of Barker Chapman – the stout cut of her leather boots, her shining hair which slipped in a most unladylike, undisciplined manner about her face and shoulders, the healthy flush on her smooth cheeks, the sleek beauty of the two dogs who clung to her skirt, wondering speechlessly what on earth their employer's daughter would want with a family who worked in her own mill.

'But I was led to believe that they lived in Edgeclough.'

'No, Miss, not any more. They couldn't make the walk, yer see, not t't mill an' back, not wi't little 'uns.'

'The . . . the little 'uns . . .?'

'Aye. Daisy's nobbut a baby really and though Charlie's older 'e's not that strong now . . . since . . . well. T'were a bit of a hike after sixteen 'ours in't mill so they left an' rented t'cottage in Lousy Bank.'

'Lousy Bank?' She whispered the name just as though to

274

speak it out loud might somehow taint her lips with its foulness. *Lousy Bank!* Along with Boggart Hole and Pig Lane it was spoken of as the centre of the dens of vice, of the harbourage of disease, where the homes of those who lived there were foul and damp, rat-ridden, with tunnels leading into a labyrinth of alley-ways where danger and even death lurked for the unwary.

'When ... when did they leave?' she asked and the woman sniffed, somewhat offended to be asked to give out information to a woman who was, choose how, one of the enemies of Joss Greenwood. What did she want with them, her suspicious eyes asked, sorry now she'd divulged as much as she had. She'd half a mind to call Isaac and get him to order this hoity-toity piece from *their* bit of land but common sense prevailed since she *was* Barker Chapman's lass.

'I can't remember,' she replied tartly.

'Could you ... do you see them?'

'No.'

'I was wondering if a message might not be got to them.'

This was too much for Sarah Pickering who had watched with tears in her eyes the departure of the woman she called friend, the mother of the man who was rotting in gaol, put there by the likes of this madam, for trying to better the lot of the labouring poor. It was all their fault, this disaster which had fallen on the spinners and weavers of Lancashire and Yorkshire, their greed which had aggravated it, their callous disregard for the working man's dignity and self-respect and she'd be damned if she'd stand in the cold on her own doorstop answering her foolish questions.

'They work for you, all on 'em. Give 'em bloody message thysen.'

# 19

He blinked in the sudden blaze of sunshine, blinded by it, shielding his eyes with his arm but blessed by its golden haze and the soft heat which enfolded him. His body felt as though it would never be warm again. The damp and the chill of his prison cell had crept into his bones and even now as he stepped out on the road from Lancaster to Clitheroe with the warm sun on his right shoulder he could hear the crack of his knee joints and wondered if he would ever lose the ache in them. He had been out of the prison on many occasions, of course, for hard labour meant just that and the local quarrymen were glad of the convicted felons to do the work of breaking up the stone. Day after day, week in and week out, in sun and rain and driving gales, in the bleak winter of the north where the cold had entered into his soul, in the fragile spring which had come so late, taken with faceless others to break stone, and his back and almost his spirit, but he had survived and now he was to go home. He was hardened and older. His face was thin and gaunt, he was semi-starved and had been made to pay dearly for his 'crime' but now, with the repeal of the hated 'Combination Acts' he would begin again.

They had got word to him in gaol, those men who had dreams in their heads, as he had, of an immense exchange of ideas and ideals and who needed a man who could put those aspirations into words. Men like William Cobbett and John Fielden, the radical politician Francis Place who believed in one vote one man and who had asked him if he would care to write, being something of a notability now, an article or two in the pamphlets and newsheets which the working man was likely to read. He was a man well known for his sympathies towards those crushed beneath the heel of the new industrialists they said, and might he not have a contribution to make in *another* way beside that of violence towards their cause? Cobbett's *Weekly Register* which had been published for the past twenty odd years was one, and though Cobbett himself wrote most of it himself he would be glad, he said, to print Joss Greenwood's ideas among his own.

The *Poor Man's Advocate*, published weekly, condemning many individual cotton firms, though they could not pay him much, would gladly include anything he might have to say on the matter of reform, which, with his experience and knowledge of the working man, they were certain would be considerable.

And so he was to become a writer, to earn his living at it if it was found he had the knack. A journalist, though this description made him smile as he stepped out towards his home.

He walked five miles that day, following the turnpikes and the pack-horse trails below Tarnbrook Fell, stopping to rest, to sleep uneasily beneath a sweet smelling hedge of hawthorne, waking a dozen times, unused to the night-time peace broken only by the squeak and rustle of small animals, missing, incredibly, the grunts and snores of his cell mates.

There was a farm just off the road, no more than a smallholding, a cow, a pig, geese, reminding him of the cottage in Edgeclough and though the farmer, a dour north countryman with no time for the vagrants and tramping men who roamed the Lancashire uplands told him to be off, he traded a glass of milk and a hunk of stale bread and cheese for two hours' work cleaning out his pig-sty and a pile of logs chopped.

He crossed the River Hodder just before nightfall, thanking the fates for the kindness they bestowed him with the warm weather. Impulsively he stripped off his clothes, jumping naked into the breathtaking iciness of the water, his milk white body like a thread of yarn beneath the clear, silvery grey surface but his teeth shone in a grin of pleasure in his startlingly brown face. Though his clothes were stale when he put them back on he felt exhilaratingly clean, tingling from head to foot and glad to be alive. He was going home!

The restrained grandeur of the hills of Bowland, the forests, the sunken trails waist high in Sweet Cicely were not unlike the spread of hills surrounding his own home and he longed for the miles to be eaten up so that he might be there. He slept the second night in a bed of hedge parsley not having eaten that day and when he arrived in Clitheroe he knew he must find work to buy food.

For sixpence he cleaned out the stables of a coaching inn, sweating and faint as he did it but his handsome smile and courtesy pleased the landlord's wife and she gave him an enormous bowl of thick soup and a heel of bread to go with the money.

He bought bread and cheese, some oats and potatoes and, strengthened, he managed almost ten miles the next day crossing below Pendle Hill and on into the forest towards Burnley. He knew the country here for he had attended many meetings and had marched in protest with the weavers who worked in the northern Pennine heartland. He slept in a bed for the first time that night since he had left Lancaster gaol, the six children who normally crowded together in it swept unceremoniously aside to accommodate the great and glorious leader of their cause and though he had protested to their father, a known sympathiser on whose door he had scratched, it was insisted upon. They had nothing but porridge and treacle bubbling on the spluttering peat fire but what they had was his they told him and were big-eyed, scarcely able to believe it when he brought out the bread and cheese. Their appetites, fed for so long on bland, tasteless food which was cheap, craved a taste of something sharp and they fell on it with such delight, tears pricked his eyes and he pressed them to eat it up unconcerned with how he would manage the next day.

278

It took him another three days to get through the Forest of Rossendale, working whenever he could for what anyone would give him to eat, sharing what little they had with the men and women, who all knew him now, who had waited, they said, for his return. What would it mean to them, they asked him eagerly, with the repeal of the Combination Acts? Surely things would be better now that it was no longer illegal to meet, to 'strike' or 'turn-out' as it was called in their struggle for wage increases. Food prices had risen again, they said, and something must be done and they looked at him trustingly for they knew whatever it was, Joss Greenwood would do it.

He was growing stronger now. The sweet, wind-ruffled air of Brandwood Moor, north of Whitworth filled his lungs as he tramped and still the sun shone on him kindly and he took off his shirt, letting it warm and brown his prison-white skin.

He stopped a dozen times in those last few days before he began to smell the air of home, to soak and splash in the torrents of clear, stinging water which cascaded down the hillsides and crags into the steep cloughs.

They were waiting for him at Rochdale, word having been sent ahead of his return, gathered in groups at every cottage door and field gate, not speaking much for they were filled with emotion and some of the women wept. They were a scarecrow assembly, thinner than they had been a year ago, with the fight scraped out of them by hunger and sickness, their children listless, not knowing nor caring who this man was, and he nodded and shook each outstretched emaciated hand unable to speak for he was overwhelmed.

It was almost dark when he began the climb from Cow Heys up to Badger's Edge but he could see her waiting as he had known she would be. The stones were shadowed on their eastern side but where she leaned, her head turned to watch the track up which he would come, the lowering sun struck brilliantly, bathing her in its golden light. She wore a light gingham skirt and bodice to match of pale apple green, simple and uncluttered and she had rolled up her sleeves and taken off her shoes and from a distance might have been some barefoot country girl waiting for her man. Her hair was fastened back carelessly with a dark green velvet ribbon and it was the first thing he took from her as she swayed into his arms. His hands buried themselves deep in her hair before his mouth took hers and for a long, long moment their lips clung together. Their bodies met in enchantment, breast to breast, thigh to thigh and when he released her mouth his eyes met hers, asking the question before he did.

'How did you know?'

'I have come each evening. A year they said, so . . .'

'I knew you would be here.'

'I knew you would know.' She laughed softly and her lips lifted to his, greedily, and her hands went to the buttons of her bodice, some of which were already undone.

'Let me,' he whispered, pressing her back against the tall stone. Slowly he undressed her in the pale blue half-light of the summer evening, each silky shoulder studied and murmured over, kissed with lips which were smooth and increasingly passionate until the bodice lay discarded in the grass and her breasts were cupped, one in each of his hands. The nipples, already hard and thrusting, pressed eagerly into his palms and he took them between his thumb and forefinger, rolling them until she arched her back and her throat and he bent his head, putting his lips beneath her chin, smoothing them down her flesh until his tongue tasted the swollen pink tips, taking each one in turn into his mouth. He pressed his face between her breasts, rubbing his cheek against their firm, soft fullness and in his throat a sound began, a longing, aching sound which was echoed in hers. He knelt then and with the patience and pleasure of the true lover he drew down her full skirt and petticoat, placing his parted lips on the white skin of her belly, moving them delicately across every inch of it, slowly, slowly and when he reached the downy bush of her pubescence she cried out harshly. She was naked, the soft pale gold of her

280

skin glowing in the last rays of the sunlight. He pulled her down to him and her back scraped against the rough stone but she did not feel it. She had but a moment to wait and then his flesh was against hers and the sweetness of the clover-studded grass was beneath them. He raised himself above her before he penetrated her and the tiny budding core of her womanhood throbbed and expanded, glowing and growing until she cried out to him again for she could not wait and he looked down at her, male triumphant and his eyes were the gleaming green of a hunting leopard.

'I love you, Kit Chapman, dammit but I love you,' he cried and then he was inside her and she cared for nothing but the pain of it and the sweetness and rapture and the sudden shivering delight which touched every part of her body. She felt it in her thighs and her belly, in her breasts and straining nipples, down each arm in a languid bonelessness and when he fell on her, shouting his own masculine pleasure she caught him to her, holding him in possessive arms, showering his face and neck with a score of butterfly kisses and stroked his back with trembling butterfly hands.

It was full dark when they dressed one another, laughing softly as they struggled with petticoats and clogs, ribbons and breeches, the smoothing of tangled hair, taking a long time, lingering fingers unwilling to leave soft breast, hard muscled thigh, mouths unwilling to give up the smoothness of long silken back or strong throat. The stars came out to lighten the patch of moorland and the stones of Badger's Edge. They could not bear to part and would have started again but from somewhere close the dogs rose soundlessly and became restless. He stared in amazement, first at one black and almost invisible shape and then the other.

'Good God, where did they come from?'

'They've been here all the time.'

'I should have known you would not come this far without them. I'd forgotten about them in my eagerness to . . .' He pulled her against him, his passion for her growing again and she laughed softly, delighted, but the dogs would not be still now, as though they scented danger in the deepening dark of the wild hills.

'I must go, my darling,' she said wistfully. 'I have taken to my bed with a sick headache but if anyone should feel the need to knock on my door and enquire of me, my maid will have a hard time explaining my absence.'

'She knows where you are?'

'Oh yes, but not who I am with. She has been with me for years and is well used to my mad habit of walking with the dogs. She thinks I am quite out of my mind but I fear if I do not return soon she will be alarmed and alert my father. She is devoted to me but she will safeguard her job, and my safety, if it came to the choice.'

'Kiss me again.'

'Just once . . . oh, how I love you. How have I managed all this time without you?'

'I cannot imagine, now kiss me again and while you do it put your hand just there . . . aah . . . and this button appears to have undone itself . . .'

It was half an hour later before she asked the question she had dreaded. She stood within the strong circle of his arms. He was excessively thin, thinner than she had ever known him but he was as hard and strong as a length of steel, the work he had done wielding a pick in the quarries of northern Lancashire fining him down to nothing but skin and bone and hard muscle. They were quiet now. They had known the depths of anguish in the months they had been apart, a great wrenching of their senses that had brought turmoil and disorder to their separate lives. And now they had known love, a supreme physical love which had brought them together in just as complex an emotion as any they had known. It had uprooted all their previous ideas of class and culture, of loyalty to others, of the hopeless past and the unknown future, but now as their bodies rested against one another in a peace which clung about them, soft as mist but strong as the stones against which they leaned, they could speak of it at last.

'Are you to go home now, Joss?'

'Yes. I am anxious about my family. God knows how they have managed without me. But Jenny is a fighter, always has been and will have seen them right. We have friends . . . it is at times like this that we gather round each other . . . our people. They are all hard workers, my mother and Jenny and . . .'

' . . . And your wife?' There was no censure in her voice, only understanding of how it was since had she not herself been pressed unwillingly into the arms of another man.

'Yes . . . she is frail though . . .' He stared out over her head into memories of Mercy, then looked down into the face of this woman he loved, smiling, '. . . but they have good neighbours in Edgeclough. They will have . . .'

'They are not in Edgeclough.' She made the statement flatly not knowing of any other way to tell him.

'What . . . I don't understand. How do you . . .'

'They had to move. The children could not manage the walk from Edgeclough to Crossfold each day.'

'But why should they need to walk to Crossfold each day?' He was clearly bewildered.

'They had to work, Joss, all of them.'

'But . . .?'

'What did you imagine would happen to them while you were in prison?'

'I don't . . . I had thought they would . . .'

'Would what?'

'Isaac sent a message. He would try to get some raw cotton to them for my mother to spin. With Jenny at the mill and Charlie weaving a piece . . . I was not told . . . A message or two saying they were all right . . . Goddammit to hell . . . why was I not told . . .?'

His throat worked and his hands gripped her shoulders as he stared down at her, his fear beginning to snap and snarl at him, like an animal of prey which circles another. He shook her, his increasing terror for his family making him careless but she stood her ground.

'Where the hell are they?' he demanded, just as though *she* had spirited them away while his back was turned.

'They have a cottage . . . in Crossfold.'

'A cottage? What sort of cottage?' since it was well known what kind of cottage was going begging to the likes of factory hands in Crossfold.

'A company cottage, they are called.'

'A bloody company cottage, is it?' he snarled and her head snapped on her shoulders as he thrust her away from him and despair settled quietly, like vultures in a tree, about them. It had been so short, the joy, the love, the understanding and now came the reality. She had him back, whole, strong and it seemed, once again to take up the sword in his fight for those he loved as much, perhaps more, than he loved her. They were his family, as his wife, his mother, his brother and sisters were his family. They needed him where she did not and when they suffered he blamed her. She was one of the other side, one of the 'maisters', the manufacturing class who made millions over the bodies of the labouring poor, *of which he was one*.

'Where in Crossfold?' he demanded to know harshly, not looking at her.

'Lousy Bank.'

'*Jesus . . .*' He lifted his face to the dark blue of the night skies and gripped his thick hair with desperate hands and she could see the glitter in his eyes which she suspected were tears.

'They work in my father's mill,' and her voice could not somehow sound anything but disinterested as though it was really nothing to do with her since she was only the messenger. Inside her chest the pain was almost more than she could bear and she wished she could weep away the tears which threatened to drown her.

'All of them?'

'Yes.'

'Oh dear sweet Lord . . . Daisy . . . Charlie . . .'

'Yes.'

'And you made love to me knowing . . . knowing my family . . . my little sister . . . you bitch, you cold-hearted bitch . . . she is only a baby . . . a baby . . .'

284

He turned on her then and lifting his arm struck her full in the face, leaving an imprint on the smooth cheek he had just kissed so gently, then, torn to shreds by his devastation, by his love and hatred of her he turned on his heel and began to walk in the direction of Crossfold, not looking back and she watched him, holding the dogs lest they go for him. He disappeared into the night and she sat for an hour, dry-eyed, for she had sworn she would not weep for him again.

His mother opened the door to him, her face peeping out suspiciously and when she saw him standing there she let out a shriek of such pure joy, Mercy mistook it for terror and knocked the pan of mutton stew she was stirring into the fire and over the highly polished black-leaded hearth.

'Joss . . . Joss, my son . . .' was all his mother could say over and over again, drawn into the circle of his arms, then they were all there with the exception of Mercy who was weeping, not knowing which way to turn as the lovely stew smouldered on the hot coals and her husband mumbled against his mother's shoulder. Daisy had him by the legs and Charlie held him round his waist, his tear-stained face pressed into the curve of his brother's back and for several minutes nothing was said that made sense. His mother gave up her place in his arms, reluctantly, for his wife but Mercy hung back, confused and when Joss kissed her gently he felt her flinch beneath his touch.

But at last he could look about him, dreading it but knowing he must face what his family had been brought down to because of him.

The room was warm, excessively so, for it was high summer but there was a decent fire in the neat and tidy hearth. The walls had no cracks in them nor mouse-holes, and had been recently whitewashed. The frames of the door were sound, as was the stout door, newly painted and glass in the windows had been mended and were whole with shutters to protect them. Pretty curtains were drawn across them, and on the scrubbed floor were his mother's rag rugs, colourful, warm, clean. Most of the furniture come from Edgeclough had gone to the pawnshop in the first weeks, but what was left was polished with the familiar – he could smell its fragrance – beeswax his mother made herself.

He turned about, looking at the comfortable room, his face bewildered, stunned, then at his family and his bewilderment grew. He had seen too many stunted bodies and haggard faces, those of the work-worn scarecrow poor who never in the whole of their lives had enough to eat and he had expected to see it here. His mother had never been plump for she had worked hard all her life but she had been strong. A handsome girl grown into a mature, not unattractive woman with a clear, well-scrubbed skin and a steady gaze, and now in her fiftieth year she was just the same. The strain was there, the strain and worry of a mother with a wilful son who had fetched up in gaol for his troubles but nothing more. She was an elderly woman, past her prime perhaps, but serene now that her lad was home, and in good health. He turned to Charlie, to Daisy, wondering at the firm flesh on their straight limbs, again not plump but far from the undernourished, malformed scraps of humanity he had seen in the mills and weaving-sheds during the past six years and which he had agonised over as he stumbled from Badger's Edge to Crossfold.

Mercy smiled at him tremulously. Her face was still pale as it had always been but she had recovered somewhat from the shock of seeing him, finding comfort as she always had in the simple domestic tasks Martha set her. She was shy now under his gaze and she turned away to the spoiled stew showing herself in the only way she knew how by beginning the preparation of a meal for her returned husband.

'Get me some water, Charlie,' she said and Joss, still standing in the middle of the room, his head almost touching the ceiling watched, speechless still, as his brother opened the door into the alley and with the jug he had picked up, ladled some water from the rain butt which stood just outside the door. He carried it carefully to Mercy who poured it into a bowl and began to clean up the burned stew.

'I'll have something for you to eat in a minute, Joss,' she said and Martha Greenwood smiled, then unable it seemed to stay away from her son for a moment longer, put her arms about him and laid her cheek on his chest. She looked up into his eyes, studying them, studying the lines of his face, the strain about his mouth, the perplexity, the anxiety which had settled on him as he entered the room and which had nothing to do with his previous torment. He answered her gaze with a smile and a gentle kiss dropped on her brow.

'Are you all right, Mother?'

'Aye, son, and you?'

'Aye.'

'Then sit. You must be fair clemmed.'

They ate fresh bread and slices of ham with pickles, Mercy apologising that she could not give him something hot, consumed with distress at the spoiling of the stew, he thought, and nothing else, and all the while they talked, telling one another how lovely it was to be together again there was a strange unease, a slight air of tension which sat on his mother's shoulder and it told him he must not ask what had happened until he and she were alone. It was understood, the look which passed between them and he waited patiently, wishing Charlie and Daisy would get to their beds and yet dreading it for there was something wrong here and he knew he must face it when they were gone.

He was quite amazed as his mother kissed the children goodnight to see his wife lean over Martha's shoulder and receive a kiss too and when the three of them had climbed the narrow staircase, looking back to him to say good-night again he could not believe his own eyes.

'Mercy?' he said questioningly and she turned back obediently.

'Yes?' Her face was wary. She had only just become used to sharing a bed with Daisy, with Charlie on the other

287

side of a blanket strung across the room, and she seemed suddenly afraid she was going to be asked to do something she did not quite like. Something she had found distasteful in the past though she could not really remember what it had been.

Joss felt his mother's hand on his arm, telling him something, and he understood since he too remembered.

'Good-night then, sweetheart,' was all he said and Mercy smiled like a child.

'Good-night then, Joss. It's lovely to have you home.' He might have been *her* brother too.

'It's good to be home, lass.'

They sat, one on either side of the fireplace, his mother and himself. They had cleared the table and cleaned the dishes, carrying in the sweet rainwater from the butt and it was not until they were settled that he began the questions.

'Where's Jenny?'

His mother stared him straight in the eye as though daring him to dispute her answer.

'She's working.'

'At this time of night?'

'Aye. She cleans for a lady in Reddygate Way. A parson's daughter. She goes a couple of nights and on a Sunday.' And still her eyes looked defiantly into his, why he did not know, since there seemed nothing wrong with extra employment, particularly with a parson's daughter.

'So that's what pays for all this, is it?' He looked about the comfortable room, indicating with his hand the luxuries which he was sure none of the other inhabitants of Lousy Bank enjoyed. Though his mother's room smelled of fresh bread and beeswax, his nose could detect very faintly, now that he had grown accustomed to it, the stench which lay over the whole area in which the mill-workers lived. He had gagged on it as he strode through the alleyways and back passages to this house, asking his way in the maze of streets through which he walked. He had leaped over great stretches of slimy water in which objects not for the squeamish floated, across evil-smelling heaps the contents of which

288

he could not recognise and did not linger to find out. The air was heavy, foetid, so thick he had found it difficult to breathe and his heart had hammered in his chest, with the heat and the effort it took to wade through it and with fear for what he would find at the end of it.

Now, it appeared his terror had been for nothing since his family looked better than they had done since before his father died.

'When will she be home?'

'Soon, but promise me something, Joss. You'll not scold her.'

'Why should I?'

'Well, takin' on another job . . .'

'I don't know how she does it, working for fourteen hours and more in the mill then cleaning in what spare time she's got left, but it's only what I expected of her, knowing the way she is.'

'She's strong, lad. We all are.'

He smiled and leaned forward to touch her hand affectionately.

'By God, you must be. When I see the children who work in the mills about here, poor little sods. I fully expected our Charlie and Daisy to be the same but now I find . . .'

'Who told you they were in't mill?' His mother's voice was sharp.

'Oh . . . a woman who works there. I . . . I met her on the way home. She told me you'd moved . . . Jesus, I nearly went off my head . . .'

'Nay, Joss, you shouldn't 've worried. We're grand, grand.'

'I can see that, but are you not ready for your bed? The factory bell goes at five, not that you'll be there by the end of the week with me home to do some weaving . . .'

'Nay, we've all got part-time, well, me an' Daisy, and Charlie puts in no more than . . .'

'*Part-time.*' He looked incredulous since he and his On-wardsmen with others like John Fielden had been petitioning for part-time, or a shorter working day for children and the age at which they might start work, for many years. The legislation had already been passed by Parliament but with so few factory inspectors the law was difficult to enforce.

'Aye, me an' Daisy work six hours and Charlie does ten.'

'And the rest?'

'What d'you mean, the rest?'

'All the other children?'

She looked saddened, putting out her hand to placate him for his expression said that though he was glad for his own family, he wanted the same humane treatment for *all* of them and why should the Greenwoods be given what the others were denied?

It was like a light seen at the far end of a tunnel when it came, far away and puzzling. He knew what it was, of course he did but he had to distinguish the shape and size of it before he could recognise it clearly for exactly what it was.

He had hit her! He had blamed her for what had happened to them, shedding his own guilt by placing it on her shoulders. She and her father and all the other manufacturers had created the system, helped by men who had invented the machines to make it possible, and thousands had been dragged down with it, his own family, so he had thought, included. But while he had been imprisoned she had protected them for him. He did not know how she had done it, contrived to influence the working hours, the overlookers, the manager of the spinning mill, for though she was entitled to do as she pleased with the men and women and children in her employ, working them for as *long* as she pleased, her father would certainly not have agreed with what she intended for the family of the felon, Joss Greenwood. Jenny and Mercy, young and with good food inside them would be able to manage the work and so she had not drawn attention to them but his mother, too old really to be in the mill at all, and Daisy and Charlie whose soft young bones could so easily be bent or broken, as happened to thousands upon thousands of children, had been spared.

'And . . . this cottage?'

'Nay, some workers came. Said they were doing repairs to Mr Chapman's property but to tell the truth, Joss, they only did this one. They brought the water butt and threatened all them in Lousy Bank with dismissal, or eviction, or both, if they interfered with it, God only knows why,' though of course she was certain she knew in her heart. 'We're not liked round here, Joss, since we've managed where the others haven't, but nobody bothers us and with the extra Jenny fetches we've got through it.'

It was gone midnight when Jenny Greenwood let herself into the cottage and she almost screamed out loud as the figure in the chair by the fire rose to its feet, tall, standing, head touching the ceiling, hands outstretched to take hers. She was still glowing, her hair tumbled about her head, her manner languorous, stretching, sighing, a slow graceful turn of her shoulders, a slow drooping of her long eyelashes and for a moment Joss Greenwood's skin prickled and his heart hesitated uncertainly for he had seen this look before on a woman . . . then the sense of disquiet vanished like smoke in the wind as Jenny's face lit up and her eyes were bright as candles in her joy.

'Jenny . . . Jenny, my lass . . .' and could not speak so great was his emotion.

'Joss . . .' and neither could she. The memory of the man with whom she had spent the last two hours was dashed away as she sank thankfully into her brother's arms.

Martha Greenwood watched them from the bed which she shared now with Jenny. She wore a white cotton nightgown, the one into which she had modestly changed behind the sheet Joss had put up to screen her only half an hour since. She had worn it as a bride over thirty years ago, spinning the yarn herself, her husband-to-be weaving it for her on his own hand-loom. It had stood the test of time as she had, durable as she was and strong. She had not let that strength be taken from her ever, and she had reared children, who were the same. They were alike in their beliefs, in their powerful and unyielding refusal to give in. She had known from the start what Jenny did, Sunday after Sunday and on two or three nights a week and she had not blamed her, knowing, if she had been the right age, she would have done the same herself to feed her children. But she had seen the girl bloom in beauty, an insolent beauty which said she cared for none of the folk who wondered how she came by it. Bold and defiant, careless, for what did it matter, her attitude said, since she had what she wanted, which was security, for her family, tenuous perhaps and not to last forever, but better than most. Someone protected her, and them. Someone had made this home habitable and Martha had a good idea who it was since it must be someone with power. Not enough to let the world see what he did for he had his way to make, but someone influential enough to whisper in the right ear, to grease the right palm when it was held out to him.

And now he was home, her son the fighter and what was to happen? It would not be long before he worked it out for himself and got the name of Jenny's lover out of her. Not for a moment did it occur to her that the man, gentleman she supposed, careless, charming, indifferent to everything but his own needs, was not their protector.

# 20

'Katherine, I will not be put off again. The summer is nearly over and still you will not decide on a date for your wedding. Your father is not going to like this at all. He allowed you to persuade him that you needed more time to get your work up to date at the mill before taking a wedding journey during the summer, now you are making further excuses and all amounting to nothing. You are not indispensable at the mills, Katherine and well you know it and so does Harry and believe me he will not wait forever. Your wedding dress has been made for months, *and* those of your attendants. People are beginning to talk, indeed Mrs Jenkinson went so far as to ask me if Harry, *Harry*, mark you, had other plans and intimated that now he had become so invaluable to your father he had no need to marry you! I could not refute it, naturally, without telling them that my own daughter was darting from side to side like a rabbit in a cage in her effort to avoid taking that final step. I am at my wits' end to know what to do or say to my friends. Six months' engagement is perfectly acceptable but after that people begin to wonder. I realise that some girls, though not many I do assure you, are not … concerned with marriage. That some will remain spinsters but they are usually young women with no dowry, no looks and unless they will take a shopkeeper or a tradesman are doomed to remain unmarried. But not you, Katherine. You are the most sought after in the county of Lancashire and cannot escape it. Believe me, you *will* marry and what your apparent objection to Harry Atherton is, I cannot for the life of me imagine. He is of the finest family. He is agreeable, well-favoured and his charm is undeniable. Really, I do not know what is the matter with you …'

Kit was lounging on the window-seat of her mother's sitting-room which led from her bedroom at the front of the house. It was high and airy with furniture of a gossamer fragility, spindle-legged chairs, small velvet sofas of the palest rose, silk curtains of ivory and a carpet to match. The ceiling was picked out in rose petals and acanthus leaves and straying tendrils of gold and each of the two bays had deep-cushioned window-seats.

Kit leaned her head against the window-pane and stared out across the rolling stretch of smooth lawn towards the towering oak trees, planted centuries ago, the tall pines, the yew trees, the sycamore which had once been part of the vast forest covering the Penfold Valley. The house had been planned and built to stand among the trees, only taking out those which had been necessary. It was as though Greenacres stood in an enormous forest glade, the garden at the front cut in two by the long and winding drive of plane trees.

It was August and the flowering season was at its peak. Great swathes of roses of every shade from palest pink to deepest red crammed beds around which gardeners worked, weeding and taking off the dead heads for Barker Chapman demanded nothing but perfection. There were dahlias, begonias, fuschia in profusion, all surrounded by immaculately trimmed bushes of every shade of green imaginable. A boy was carefully sweeping the stone steps which led down from the entrance porch to the gravelled driveway and two more were on their knees in the hazy sunshine clipping the lawn, watched by the eagle-eyed head gardener who supervised and criticised every snip and cut.

It was Sunday and when her mother had finished lecturing her on the subject most dear to her heart which was Kit's forthcoming marriage to Harry Atherton, Kit would slip away to change from her light morning gown into clothing more suitable for walking, collect her dogs and stride out . . . no, run every step of the way up to Badger's Edge. September, Autumn, then winter would soon be here and what would they do then, she wondered mournfully as her mother's voice droned on at the edge of her mind. She could still walk up there and indeed saw no reason why she should not for the whole household was accustomed to her love of ranging the high moorland and would be surprised if she should stop but soon it would be too cold, too wet for her to show her love, to take his, in the arms of Joss Greenwood.

Her eyes clouded and became unfocused, not seeing the trees nor the garden and the men working there looking instead to the memory of that day, a week after Joss had come home when she had gone, unable to stay away, up to Badger's Edge. It had been grey with a fine drizzle which had shifted in the smooth wind, blurring the track and the shape of the standing bracken, hiding the tops of the hills and the undulating stretch of the moorland on every side. It was a day come suddenly in the middle of weeks of sunshine, when a man could get lost in the wildness, on the faint, almost obliterated tracks, through gorse and heather and strange groups of lowering rock piles. It was a day for staying at home by the fireside, not cold, quite warm in fact with the heat of the summer ground taking the chill from the rain which fell on it, but cheerless in its melancholy.

She did not see him at first. The grey of his clothing blended into the grey of the stones but the dogs' hackles rose warning her that she was not alone and she whirled about expecting some vagrant, some wandering itinerant, homeless as thousands were, sheltering perhaps in the lee of the stones.

He simply stood there waiting for her to speak. The fine drizzle had soaked into his clothing and plastered his hair in dripping black curls to the shape of his head. His hands were stuffed into his jacket pockets and his collar was turned up. As she stared at him he pulled his cap from somewhere and wiped his face with it, still not speaking, his eyes clamped to hers. The dogs stood between them, waiting for her command to attack or to drop down into the heather, ready to do either for though they knew him well it made no difference. They were growing older now, eight years she had been protected by them, but they were still as strong, as defiant, as savage as she had trained them to be if needed.

'Call them off, Kit,' he said at last, softly.

Still she stood, her face as hard as granite. She was hatless but her full length coat covered her from neck to ankle and her stout boots were warm and dry. Her hair, like his, was painted to her skull, but straight and heavy, accentuating the beauty of her high cheek bones, the strength of her firm jawline. Droplets of rain beaded her lashes and her lips and her eyes were narrowed and cold.

'Please. I have come to apologise. Call them off.'

At last she spoke, her voice as cold as her eyes.

'How did you know I would be here today?'

'I have come every morning . . . and waited. I could not let you think . . . I was made aware of what you had done for my family as soon as I got to Lousy Bank. I had to tell you . . . to thank you. That is all. What I did was unpardonable. Not just in striking you but in believing you capable of . . . of . . . being with me while you let my mother . . . my family starve. Will you forgive me? I ask no more of you. I could not rest . . . I must get on with what I do now that . . . well, you will have heard of the repeal of the Combination Acts . . .' He raised his hand wearily to brush back his wet hair which dripped across his face, his smile hesitant, rueful, '. . . I'm sorry, you do not want to hear that and I had not meant to mention it but I could not leave without . . . I had to see you . . . to thank you. I will go now . . .'

But still they stood, face to face with the dogs between them, a strange tableau should someone have passed by to see them. There was a straining tension, a leaning of one towards the other though there was five or six yards between them. The rain misted about them, growing heavier now, sliding in rivulets across each desolate face, then he groaned harshly in his throat.

'For God's sake, Kit, put me out of my misery one way or the other. Go, or stay, as you must, but do something. I love you, dear God, how I love you. I don't want to and if you tell me to clear off I will, but do it quickly for I do not think I can manage this much longer.'

'Joss . . . my love . . . aah . . . my love . . .' and with a soft cry she stepped over the crouching dogs, her hand giving them some automatic signal which they obeyed without question and flung herself into his lifting arms. They were about her then, straining her to him and the rainwater in his clothes were squeezed out against his body and ran down it and he began to laugh and weep at the same time.

'I thought I had lost you. I thought I had lost you,' he said over and over again and her tears and his, and the soft raindrops mingled together in joy and sorrow since this was their life and always would be.

'Forgive me,' he mumbled into her wet hair and her face turned up to his and the brilliance of her smile blinded him for a moment before their rain-wet mouths met, warm, slippery at first but clinging. He cupped her face in his hands, smoothing the cheek he had struck, kissing it in a fever of remorse but she took his hands in hers and put his arms about her again unable to get close enough to him, it seemed.

And so they had begun again, those ecstatic encounters on the 'tops', the top of the world in a world peopled by just the two of them, uninhabited but for the stoat and rabbit and weasel, by cole tit, wheatear and blackbird. Whenever they could they met in that magical August month, unaware of what was to come. Their love was looked kindly on by the gods, they thought, impregnable, unassailable, strong, proved so by the years and by the disasters through which it had come. Days might go by before she could get up to Badger's Edge for as a 'fiancée', her status had altered. She was Harry Atherton's future wife now and he was not awfully sure she should be allowed to roam about in the company of only her dogs. She was to marry into one of Cheshire's oldest families with a tradition of greatness behind it, from the battlefields in which Cromwell took a stand against their King to the latest at Waterloo only several years ago.

'What has that to do with walking my dogs on the moors, Harry?' she asked patiently. She tried so hard to be patient with Harry, she really did, nipping and darting like a hare avoiding a greyhound, diverting his plans for their marriage into other, less explosive channels, making promises which she did not keep, avoiding his sometimes amorous advances though these, surprisingly, were not as demanding as she expected. He was good humoured with her, sure of her she supposed, since there was no way Barker Chapman would allow such an advantageous contract to be broken, allowing her to be foolishly female, allowing her to be somewhat evasive in her last days of freedom. She would be his wife this year, of that he was positive, or early next. His father was becoming as pressing as her own, demanding to know when that 'damned girl' was going to set a date which would not, at the last moment, be postponed, amazed at the indulgence shown her by her father, and by Harry, but Harry had his own diversion which he was not quite ready to give up and it suited him, just for now, to allow Kit her prevarication.

There were times when, running like a child, skipping across the browning bracken, the fading heather, she would arrive to find Joss not there and her heart would falter, beating on his name, anguished sometimes beyond all reasoning since she was well aware he was engrossed now with the forming of a legal trade union to speak for, to act for 'the deluded people' as the labouring poor were called, those who, oppressed by hunger listened to any doctrine which they were told would redress their grievance. He was one of the 'politicians' who were to tour the country, taking up issues which the aristocracy, the squirearchy, the millocracy believed he really did not understand, stirring up the rabble, they said to violent action. She had refused to discuss it with him, refused to let it into their lives which, she said, existed for no more than a few hours each week and what he was to do, what *she* was to do, was separate, apart from what they were, what they did in the sheltered beds of heather and clover they made for themselves in the deserted expanse around Badger's Edge or Friars Mere.

'They will catch you, put you in prison again,' she had wept in a moment of weakness against his sun-browned chest, since it was well known now that Lord Liverpool's government was fearful of an insurrection which it might not easily be able to master. There was a limited number of troops in the Oldham area but she had heard her father say that £500,000 had been raised for the purpose of creating an efficient repressing force, thirty thousand men, he had been told, to protect the district. Parliament had just passed a new Combination Act which permitted the existence of trade unions like the one Joss was forming but strictly limiting their ability to strike, and with the unusually high rise in food prices, the people, the poor deluded people were stirring uneasily once more.

'Don't sweetheart, don't . . .' and he held her close and kissed her passionately for he had never seen her weep before and he was dismayed that he had weakened her. 'They can do nothing, not by themselves. They might catch a man here and there but they will never break the organisation . . .'

'I don't give a damn about the organisation, only you,' but he had kissed her wet eyes and cheeks, smoothing her throat with warm lips which dipped easily into the neck of her bodice. His hands were gentle, then strong as they took her breasts, and her melancholy would fade away with her garments, the argument, the anxiety and the great partition which was erected about each of them when they were apart.

'Harry and I are to go to London for a few days, Kit. I want to introduce him to . . . well, you know them all, those with whom we do business but I am anxious they should become familiar with him before you are married,' her father told her the following week. 'You can manage without me, I know that, my dear but . . .'

'Don't worry, Father, please. I have been your deputy for so long now I am well able to continue while you are away. The mills will not fall down about our ears on account of your absence, not for a few days at least.' She paused, smiling, then sat down in the chair which was drawn up to his desk. Her father had the weekly statement of accounts in his hand and his face looked troubled, the first time, she realised, surprised, that she had ever seen it so. There had been a great many rumours in the newspapers and on the lips of their manufacturing acquaintances of bank failures, of stock exchange collapses, of businesses going bankrupt, the great 'boom' as they had called it in the commercial world of Britain about to languish. They blamed the

299

government, they said, for there was certain to be great privation among the lower classes who were always the first to feel the sharp cold when the trade winds changed. London, Manchester, Birmingham and the agricultural areas of the country were showing already the familiar fruits of distress and, it was whispered, machine breaking was being revived by those radical political societies who had caused so much disruption a couple of years ago.

'Is there to be trouble, Father?' she asked calmly.

'I fear so, my dear. There is a slump coming in the textile trade and only those with the strength to ride it out will come through it, and those with cash behind them, needless to say.' He smiled thinly, for was he not one of those and would manage, but some who worked on a tightrope budget from raw cotton to the sale of their woven cloth would have a hard time of it.

'So you are to go to London . . .?'

'Yes, as I told you and to ensure that our markets are safe. We shall start in Manchester and then go on to the capital. I have many acquaintances in the government who will let me know which way the wind is blowing and how I may keep myself protected until it is over. But it may be a while, Kit, before we see trade become as splendid as it has been these last few years.'

He reached into his pocket and drew out his cigar case. Taking a cigar from it he lit it, then when it was drawing to his satisfaction, he leaned back in his chair, studying her closely.

'And that brings me to another matter which has been troubling me for the past few weeks and I think you know to what I refer, do you not, Kit?'

For a second her heart stilled in her breast, then leapt like a salmon trying for a waterfall up the river. Dear God . . . surely . . .? but he was smiling, coolly but smiling and if he had known of her association, the last only yesterday in the darkening autumn evening of Badger's Edge, with Joss Greenwood he would certainly not be sitting there discussing trade with her.

'I am not . . . sure . . .' she said hesitantly, knowing of course, exactly what it was.

'Come now, Kit, let us have done with this maidenly reluctance and get this union with Harry Atherton finalised. You have prevaricated for long enough and I have allowed it since you were . . . well, he was not your choice but mine. But you seem to be fond of him as he is of you and his family are eager, as I am, to see you married. Before I leave for London, and, by the way, I shall be spending a couple of nights at Harry's home in Cheshire where his father will press me, I know, I would like to have a date to give him. Shall we say an October wedding and then in the spring you and Harry can go to Italy as I promised for a month or two. The crisis should be abating by then and . . .'

'Father, I had rather hoped to be a spring bride . . .'

'You had a chance for that this year, Kit.' His voice was crisp and quite determined.

'But the dress, my wedding dress. The one Miss Cavendish made for me, and those of the attendants, will not be suitable since they were made for a summer wedding and it will take time to . . .'

'Nonsense! I am sure Miss Cavendish will manage admirably with others, suitable for winter.'

'Really, Father, the expense . . .'

'Since when did expense bother the likes of you and me, Kit?'

'Well . . .'

Barker Chapman stood and with a swift and surprising movement gripped her forearms, lifting her from her chair. He held her before him, showing his physical superiority for the first time in her life. He had always controlled her before with his quick mind, his sharp intelligence and because, quite simply, he was her father and the only one who could give her what she wanted. Now he held her with hands which hurt.

'It is to be the first week in October, Katherine. I am determined upon it. I have arranged it all, the church and the parson and your mother is to have Miss Cavendish here in the morning for the fitting of a suitable gown and all the other garments you might need. The marriage contracts have been drawn up and agreed, by Harry and his family and by myself so all it needs is the wedding service. You do understand, do you not? Now I shall say no more so you may fetch Harry in here and take a glass of sherry with us. We shall tell him together. The first week in October and no delays.'

Joss was not there on the next three evenings she walked up to Badger's Edge and in her heart, though she was in almost physical pain with her need for him, she had it in her to be glad he had not come for what would it achieve to pour out her desolation to him when he could do nothing to help her. He knew of Harry Atherton, of course and must suspect that her father had some role for him in her life but while it was not mentioned, as *his* wife was not mentioned, Harry had no part in theirs. For three days and nights her mind had twisted and turned, doubling back on itself in an effort to find some plausible reason why, for the moment, she should not marry the man her father had duped her into accepting. She could, of course, refuse point blank to go on with the wedding but as she thought of the consequences her body trembled. Her father would instantly return her to her mother's drawing-room where she would again take up her embroidery and fine sewing and her painting in water-colour, which was the employment of all of the young ladies with whom she had mixed as a girl, those who were not already married. She was twenty years of age, an old maid in many people's eyes and would probably remain so, a 'daughter-at-home', a companion for her mother, unless she married, there to remain until her father's death when she would pass into another man's guardianship, no matter what her age, the guardianship of a relative her father thought suitable. Four weeks, she had little more than four weeks before she became Mrs Harry Atherton.

She leaned back on the stone where so many times she had been taken in love by Joss Greenwood and tried to imagine the supreme act, not between herself and Joss but between herself and Harry and even before the images of it could become properly focused in her mind's eye her female body, that which loved Joss and *his* body, recoiled in revulsion, even the thought of it too appalling to contemplate. But that was only a small part of it, an important part indeed, but the worst was the certainty that she would never see Joss again. He was not a man to share his woman with another man. He had a wife and God knows if he made love to her, for she had no idea and had not asked since she did not want to know, but that would not signify with Joss. *Kit* was his and if he could not have all of her, even for a few hours a week, he would have nothing of her. She knew it. The moment she became the wife of Harry Atherton she would lose Joss Greenwood. She was trapped. Her clever, imaginative mind which had been arrogant enough to believe that somehow she would get out of this, that she would have it all, the mills, her own life to lead as she pleased, and Joss, had been caught in a web from which, no matter how she struggled she could not escape. To have the mills she must take Harry. To have Joss . . . well . . . was there any way in which she and Joss could share a life? Was there?

She felt the hysterical laughter rise in her throat since she knew that whatever she did, whichever way her life went, she could never entirely possess Joss Greenwood. He belonged to so many people, to all those men and women, the children who looked to him for salvation, but most of all he belonged to, was tied forever to . . . his wife!

Turning in a circle, her mind a boiling ferment which somehow she must calm before she reached Greenacres she called to the dogs and walked up to the path which led to Crossfold. She had taken no more than a dozen steps along it when, with a sharp snap of impatience she reversed her step, leaving the path and began to climb towards the higher land above Badger's Edge. It became more barren the higher she got but the landscape suited her mood, desolate, wild and as rebellious as she herself would like to be but knowing in the midst of it all she had no choice. She was her father's child. He approved of her. He approved of what he had made her. He had given her freedom but when she had run, enchanted with it, into the wide open spaces in which men were allowed to range free, she had found, to her dismay, that she wore a rein, a long rein but which could, nevertheless, be pulled short if she went too far. Her father had told her she was to be his son, to inherit his mills and run them when he had gone. It was to be her role but now he had another for her and how was she to play both these roles without being torn in two? She was to be Harry's wife, the mother, she supposed, of his children and yet, her father told her she was to . . .

She threw back her head in a gesture of hopelessness. Dear God, how was she to do it? She could feel the hysteria begin to rise in her and she stopped, her back to the steeply sloping stretch of moorland she had just climbed. She was almost at the highest point and it would be dark soon. It was nearly autumn, the long days of summer almost gone and soon, she knew, she must accept that with the summer would go her love.

She turned wildly, almost overbalancing, her arms flailing about her, ready to scream that she could not, simply *could not* do it, when her eyes caught the flickering movement of a figure on the edge of her vision. A slowly moving figure draped in some brilliant colour which stood out sharply against the windburned green of the grass. She watched it curiously, becoming still, her voice silent in her throat, momentarily diverted from her own despair, trying to distinguish who is was so high on the moorland tops.

At last she could make out the form of a woman. She was some way off, her face indistinguishable in the gathering gloom, but where she had come from, or where she was going, Kit could not imagine since there was no track up here. It was too high for the pack-horse routes which stayed below a thousand feet – and the clouds – so what was she – if it really was a woman and not a figment of Kit's disordered imagination – doing up here?

The woman stopped when she saw Kit, as surprised as she was and Kit lowered her arms, still in the desolate state into which the prospect of her own future had plunged her, willing to believe that this was just a ghost. She had agonised for so long on the dear images of Joss and the living death his loss would bring her that now it seemed that she had conjured up the picture of his sister for that was who the vision was moving towards her through the knee-high bracken. It was Jenny Greenwood.

They looked at one another, each unwilling to be the first to speak, each unsure that they even wished to speak. Jenny was dressed in an ankle length skirt of homespun cotton, a soft grey, serviceable and meant to last. Her bodice was of white cotton and she wore clogs but round her shoulders was a slipping shawl of the finest cashmere in shades of rich red and claret. It was a lovely garment, not something a mill girl would normally wear and Kit could have sworn that in those first moments of awareness Jenny Greenwood blushed as deep a red as her shawl.

She has a lover! How else could a girl who worked in a factory own a garment as fine? And the man was well-to-do, that was obvious and, one supposed, not likely to marry a mill girl. She would dearly like to engage the girl in conversation, to find out his name since the possibility was that it would be one of the sanctimonious gentlemen with whom she herself did business and who considered *her* no better than she should be. How pleasant it would be to sit down with her and pass the time in some . . . well . . . she could only call it *gossip*, the kind of conversation women like to indulge in now and again. Not women like her mother and her mother's friends whose sole interest was fashion and the latest Penfold Valley scandal, but someone with her own heritage and view on life. Why she should imagine that person might be Jenny Greenwood, she did not know but at the back of her mind was the impression that in different circumstances they might have been friends. Or was it, if she were absolutely honest, that she was drawn like a magnet to the irresistible lure of this woman because she was Joss's sister, because she knew him, had known him since he was a boy, and the enchanting possibility that his name might be mentioned?

'You're a long way from home,' she said coolly, wondering as she spoke why she should do so and apparently Jenny thought the same for instantly the uncertain expression on her face changed to one of truculence.

'What's that to you? You don't own the moor as well as the mill.'

There was a familiar tightening of the air between them and Kit felt the hard shell of irritation begin to set about her. It seemed she could do or say nothing which did not immediately raise this girl's hackles. Not that it mattered to her, but really she had meant no offence with her simple remark. Perhaps it was the way she had said it then?

'You seem bent on quarrelling with me whenever we meet,' she said, surprising herself.

'Quarrelling? Is that what we're doin'? Nay, it's nowt to me what you say for the likes of you an' me can hardly *quarrel*, can we? In the first place, you've to be friends to fall out and we're certainly not that and never will be.'

'My word, how touchy you are, Jenny Greenwood. Do you have no conversation that does not involve discord and provocation?' She managed to sound amused as though at the squabbles of a fractious child but Jenny's face remained set in her cold enmity. 'Whenever we meet which I agree has been on two occasions only, you seem intent on attacking me.'

'Don't be daft, woman. You mean *nowt* to me. It's your *sort* I despise and always will so if you'll get off the path I'll be on me way.'

'Certainly. God forbid I should hold you up. You must be on some errand of great importance so you had best be about it. You should not be up here anyway.'

'I see, you're ordering me off your land, are you, an' I suppose if I disobey you'll set those damn dogs on me.'

'Good God, Jenny, I only meant . . .'

'What?' Jenny's eyes were like those of a cat, narrow and venomous.

'That there are ruffians roaming these parts and you are a woman alone. They would have that pretty shawl from you in . . .'

'My shawl's nowt to do wi' you . . .'

'I'm not implying it *has*, only that there are men on the tramp all over these hills who would steal it from you and . . . other things besides . . . They aren't fussy since they've nothing to lose, whereas you . . .' Kit felt the old exasperation, for that was what it was, push them apart, but something led her on. This was the sister of the man Kit loved. If there had been more she could have done without stirring up further speculation, for his family, she would have done so. She had been surprised, pleasantly so, when there had been no repercussions from her reckless interference in the running of Ellis's spinning machines when she had spoken to him privately on the matter of part-time work for Martha Greenwood and her children, telling him nothing, naturally, of her reasons. She had no need, her expression had told him, but he would not be forgotten when promotion, or perhaps a rise in his wages, was proposed. She had been in fear for many weeks afterwards that her father, or Harry might notice the three hands who were employed on a part-time basis but Ellis appeared to be a wise man who could see the prospect of advancement when it was offered him, and when to keep his mouth shut. No doubt she would be made to pay for it at a later date but she would face that when it happened. She had not particularly cared for his conspiratorial smile when he had agreed, but that did not matter, nor the way his eyes seemed to watch her as she crossed the yard when he happened to be there.

There was a long uneasy silence while Kit racked her brain to think of some subject, easy for them both, on which she might address Jenny Greenwood.

'You . . . walk up here often?' she said at last.

'No. I haven't the time.'

'Of course not,' and how would she, or the energy, after sixteen hours at her frame but still Kit persisted.

'I love these moors. I find great solace . . . peace up here.' She looked about her, her eyes soft now and dreaming as though her communication with Joss Greenwood's sister had calmed her. 'It is so empty with nothing to . . . disturb you, nothing but the silence and the stillness . . .'

'I know.'

'Do you feel the same?' Kit lowered herself into the glowing bracken until only her head and shoulders were visible. She looked down the great sweep of the moorland into the deep wooded valley of the Penfold and Jenny Greenwood watched her with bewilderment. This was Katherine Chapman. This dreaming woman, whose face, moments ago, had been strained with some deep unhappiness, was the daughter of the most hated man in the chapelry of Oldham. She was the fiancée of Harry Atherton. They were to be married next month, Harry had told her and he was not awfully sure that he and Jenny would be able to continue their . . . association, was how he carelessly put it. It would be difficult, he said with a wife to consider and she must expect to support her family without his help from now on, his attitude said. There would be no more baskets of food and, she supposed, the protection and upkeep of the hovel in Lousy Bank would end as well for who else but he would have ordered the repairs to it, the sturdy water butt which was for their exclusive use. He had no further use for her now, though he had not said it in so many words, and suddenly, in the space of time it took for Katherine Chapman's eyes to turn smilingly to hers in some strange communion, Jenny Greenwood saw the opportunity she had been waiting for since that first moment in the spinning room when Ellis had told her that Harry Atherton liked a bit of 'rough'.

Moving with the slow, cat-like grace which had brought her to Harry Atherton's notice she walked over to Miss Chapman and sat down beside her.

'I have always loved it,' she said, then turning to her, she smiled.

# 21

Barker Chapman was extremely gratified with the success of his journey and even more so with the way in which Harry Atherton had conducted himself among the manufacturing gentlemen to whom he had been introduced during their stay in London. Not by the slightest raising of his often insolent eyebrows had Harry conveyed to them that, though he was of the landed society to which they themselves could never aspire, they were anything but exceptionally fine fellows. He and Barker had dined with several Members of Parliament, those who could be of use to Barker Chapman in the foretold slump in trade, but naturally, these were gentlemen, as Harry Atherton understood the word, for only those of *his* class, at the moment, could hope for such giddy heights.

They had stayed a night or two at Atherton Hall in Cheshire before the run to London since Mrs Atherton had been most insistent that she must return Mrs Chapman's superb hospitality in some small way, even if Mrs Chapman could not personally avail herself of it.

And thankful she would have been too, Barker thought sourly, if she could have seen the massive stone pile which was the ancestral home of the Athertons. Stone walls, stone floors with a medieval hall in which the whole of Greenacres would have readily fitted. Hundreds of portraits of Athertons past staring gloomily at this upstart from the trading classes, a bed hard and smelling of damp despite the fire which burned in the grate and food he would have been ashamed to put before his own servants offered him with an air of supreme indifference, an arrogance which said quite plainly that to be any other way must surely have the stamp of the ill bred. They had drunk an inferior wine, the money which had gone from his own pocket into that of Samuel Atherton obviously not spent on such foolish nonsense as comfort for himself and his family but on the magnificent hunters in the stable, the hounds which were housed more comfortably than Barker himself, but they had drunk the health of Harry and his absent fiancée who would, the following month become his wife.

They had taken the 'Manchester Telegraph' coach from London heading along the miraculous North Western coaching road which led to Northampton and Leicester. It had been much improved by the immortal Thomas Telford and the first leg of the journey, starting at the 'Bull and Mouth' at St Albans and ending at Derby where they were to spend the night took only a splendid eleven hours. They breakfasted at Redbourn and lunched at Market Harborough, staying overnight at a comfortable post-house, dining on roast duck and on the following evening after travelling eighteen and a quarter hours all told, entered Barker Chapman's own coach in Manchester for the twelve or so miles from there to Crossfold.

It was almost dark as they began the stretch of slowly climbing turnpike road beyond Oldham. The summer had gone now as September gathered momentum in its dash towards winter and the road ahead was a grey misted length of ribbon edged by banks of windblown wildflowers which were retreating as winter advanced. It was bleak country to right and left and up ahead, studded here and there by the pinpricks of light where a village huddled against a hillside, or a lone cottage braved the coming winter in solitary isolation. There would be snow up here, drifts of it twelve feet deep into which carriages and waggons, animals and even humans had been known to be stuck fast, but now, though the hint of the cold to come was in the air it was warm in the carriage and both men dozed a little since the two-day journey had been long and tiresome.

Another hour would see them back at Greenacres and comfort, thought Barker thankfully after the spartan ordeal he had suffered at Atherton Hall, and Harry was busy with pictures of Jenny Greenwood and what he would do to her on the following evening.

They were both considerably startled when the carriage came to a violent stop, swaying most alarmingly as the coachman struggled to bring the frightened horses under control. One wheel almost went over into the ditch at the side of the road and Barker was flung against Harry and both fell into the corner.

'What the devil is it?' Barker shouted to the coachman, though the windows and curtains were drawn.

'God knows, sir. Perhaps highwaymen,' and Harry grinned not at all afraid, finding as always something amusing to say though Barker Chapman did not smile.

'Frederick, what's to do?' he shouted again, considerably annoyed, letting down the window and stretching his head out into the cool air, ready to berate the careless fool who had thrown them into this predicament but his voice died away in bewilderment when he saw them. No more than a dozen, a silent circle of pale-faced men, one at the tossing heads of the horses, the rest, like nightmare figures, merely standing, saying nothing, simply there!

'Now then,' Barker said sharply, not afraid but seriously displeased by this inconvenience. 'What is the meaning of this? Stand aside at once and let me pass,' for you all know who I am, his manner said, but they did not move. They were working men, of the labouring class which was causing such trouble at the moment and would, when the slump really began to bite and the price of bread rose again, cause more.

'What do you want? Why have you stopped my carriage? You realise, I hope, that you are breaking the law, gathering like this. Now stand away or you will be arrested. The penalty for such insolence as this is transportation . . .'

One man stepped forward, a tall man with a thatch of dark hair and an air of assurance about him and the others

311

seemed to sigh thankfully, looking to him to tell them what to do.

'Not any more, Barker Chapman,' he said clearly. 'Have you not heard that the Combination Acts have been repealed? Aye, it's allowed now to gather in groups and talk about how we can manage to get our wages raised by the likes of you. We're not breaking the law any more, are we, lads?'

'No . . .' There was a muttered response from those about him and a voice at the back of the group, well hidden by the others and by the darkness could be heard grumbling sullenly of justice. There was some shuffling which seemed to imply they were not in complete accord with the first man who had spoken and Harry Atherton stepped down from his side of the carriage and walked round it to face them and he was the sum and substance of all they hated most, a gentleman, brushing an imaginary speck of dust from his immaculate trousers, yawning a little behind a languid hand as though the bleating of sheep, or the squabbling of children bored him to the point of tears. They and their forefathers had whipped off their caps to men like him and for a moment the habits of generations swayed them to move back respectfully from him but the man at the front, aware that he was losing control, leaped forward decisively and as he did so Barker Chapman stepped down from his carriage, exasperated beyond measure by this foolishness.

'I've had enough of this. Now stand away at once or I shall be forced to send my coachman for the militia . . .'

'The militia is it? They'll do you no good, Barker Chapman, for they're all over at Crossfold where there's talk of burning your brand new warehouse . . .'

'Who the devil are you, you insolent swine? I'll see you behind bars for this.'

'Will you indeed? There's a hell of a lot of us to imprison. The Onwardsmen are growing stronger with every day that passes and bastards like you will be made to realise that we won't be beaten.'

Harry Atherton's face became taut then, the amusement he had shown at the appearance of this animal-like band of men, slipping away as his outrage grew. How dare they, was the expression, quite amazed, on his face, just as his grandfather and great-grandfather might have looked if one of their peasant labourers had had the gall to address them.

'Stand away from this carriage,' he said, fully expecting to be obeyed at once, but the man braced his long legs and his smile was insolent, swaggering.

'Try and make me,' he taunted.

'Stand away at once or I shall give you the biggest thrashing of your life.' Harry raised his cane and the expression on his face was ugly, dangerous. The crowd of men fell back then and the man who held the horses' heads slipped to the back of the group wishing to be as anonymous as the rest, but still the man laughed and Harry's eyes narrowed to black slits of rage. He moved his hand, his thumb slipped along the cane, there was a sharp click and the cane was no longer a cane but a rapier!

'Now then, Harry, there is really no need for that, my boy.' Barker Chapman was sighing in irritation as he stepped between Harry's snarling violence and the dark haired man. His back was to him and when the man drew the knife from beneath his coat Barker did not see it and when it entered his back, and his heart, the last thing he did see was Harry Atherton's incensed face.

She did not seem able to settle anywhere. All through that first oppressive night when they had put her father's body, not knowing where else to lay it, in the depths of his own curtained bed, when the doctor had gone and her mother lay sleeping beneath the draught he had given her, Kit wandered from room to room trying desperately to escape the horror, not only of his murder, but of who had murdered him. Her mind dipped in and out of it, fascinated, repelled, in and out like a heron's beak into water, studying first one horrendous thought and then another, unable to stop, unable to determine between them for they were all beyond comprehension. There was blood still, on her dinner gown for she and her mother had been still at table when they had carried Barker Chapman across his own threshold, on her hands and on her face where she had scrabbled at it in her anguish, blood from the gaping wound in her father's back.

'It was the Onwardsmen . . .' Harry had told everyone at least a dozen times, his face excited, she thought, by the evening's work and certainly not unaware, even then, of what it would mean to him when he married her. 'A dozen of the swine attacked the carriage. I drew my sword, naturally, but they closed in and . . .' He had bowed his head in remembered despair, a man who had done his best to protect the father of his bride-to-be but overcome by sheer weight of numbers.

She had not spoken since her mother had needed immediate attention, the faint she was in deep and endless. The servants, every one it seemed, had screamed and milled about the hallway, drawn there by the drama, causing more confusion until her mind went quite blank, unable to function without the complete neutrality that was most needed. She moved in a dream world where she was able to fill her role, and did, at a certain level of consciousness, giving rise to the rumour that she was a cold-hearted woman who had neither fainted nor shed a tear at the sight of her father's mutilated body.

She sat by the fire in the kitchen for several minutes, not awfully sure where she was or how she came to be here since she had never been in this part of the house before. She was watched by the bewildered, excited servants, those who swore they could not sleep this night and could they be blamed for their reluctance to go to their beds, they asked one another.

'Will you change your gown, Miss Katherine?' Janet had wept, weeping not for Barker Chapman but for this frozen-faced woman who had shown her maid a careless kindness during the years she had served her, but Kit Chapman, though she heard the voice buzzing like some persistent fly trapped inside a window could make no sense of it. Within ten minutes though they had pressed a cup of tea into her hand which was left untouched, she had risen from the chair, turning her head to look for the way out.

'Come, Miss Katherine dear,' Janet said, 'let me put you to bed,' but ignoring the hand of her young maid, Kit followed the walls of the room until she came to a door and opening it stepped through to find herself in the stable yard. At last, her shocked mind registered thankfully, at last a place which was familiar, and crossing the yard watched by the hovering servants in the kitchen doorway she opened the door to the stables and went inside. The dogs rose to greet her, the stumps of their tails moving in delight but when she dropped down between them, an arm about each strong neck they became quiet, licking her cold face with their warm, loving tongues.

The night went on and on forever. Her whole life was lived in it, lived in tiny, vivid snatches which did not last long enough for her to examine them properly. She found herself on the driveway in one of them, walking determinedly towards the gates which stood open – going where? – to allow entrance to the men – who were they? – who came and went regularly throughout the night. Where was she going, one of them asked most respectfully since Miss Chapman must surely be in shock and should be taken back to her maid, but she had shaken off the restraining hand, turning off into the black void of the garden. Only it was not black for it seemed every window in the house was lit by a hundred candles and the light fell through them in neat oblongs on to the lawns and flowerbeds. Her body was painful, the skin tight and hot to the touch and her eyes ached with tears she could not seem to shed and she prayed that the dawn would come so that she might be released from this silent, bitter grieving.

They all slept now, Harry she supposed, one of them, dreaming of the wealth his bride was to bring him, the wealth which would be unfettered, free for himself to do with as he pleased now that Barker Chapman was dead.

315

Kit Chapman felt the warmth of her body drain slowly from her, taking with it the finer feelings Joss Greenwood and his family had awakened in her. Taking the girlishness, which, though she was a woman of twenty still lingered in her, an inclination to laughter, innocence, trust, love, filtering away as dawn ended the night on which her lover had murdered her father, leaving nothing but a coldness setting her in a place in which no one would ever reach her again.

She would see him hang, of course, he and as many of them as could be identified. Harry would know them and Frederick the coachman and she would ask if she might be there when they did it. She had said it once before, a hundred years ago now, a young girl screaming at a young labouring lad of how she hated him because he had wrecked the machine she loved. He had killed it before her eyes and now he had killed her father, the man who, if she had not exactly loved him, had been the pivot of her life, the centre of the world she was to inherit. Her father had given her the promise of freedom, given her what no other man had ever given her, even Joss Greenwood, which was a belief in her own self, in her own existence and now he was dead and the man who had killed him would pay with his life.

At last it was done. She was sitting on a low wall at the back of the house when the first pale tinge of pink and gold told her that day was approaching. She saw the sky lighten along the high line of the South Pennine hills in the east and the dogs who were lying at her feet stood up and shook themselves. She could smell the dampness of the soil and the dewed grass and the pungent aroma of the compost in the far corner of the vegetable garden. She was cold and her gown, a simple, highwaisted sheath of pale gold satin was damp and clinging to her body.

She sighed deeply and the rage which had blasted at her in spasmodic waves throughout the night was no more than a cold, hard, tenacious knot inside her, held firmly under her control, holding *her* firmly in control. Her mind was clear and sharp, her thoughts well ordered and presently she would go indoors and change into the black of mourning which was required. There would be many things to order, to plan, the first, of course, her father's funeral.

The thought no longer agonised her. He was dead, her father, and his going, the *way* in which he had died though it had presented her with her first sorrow had also given her an uncompromising strength of will, a powerful resolve that said there was nothing left in her life now but her mills which she must keep running, and the bringing to justice of her father's murderer. She had got through it alone, this night. She had needed no one, only her dogs' company and she had got through the worst. She might have fainted away in sheer horror as her mother had done, as it might have been easier to do, slipped away in a draught-induced trance, letting Harry, or George Abbott, or her father's brother come from Oldham take charge but that would not do. She had known from the first moment that it would not do. She was Kit Chapman, of the Chapman mills. Not Barker Chapman's daughter any more but Kit Chapman of the Chapman mills.

The thought was kind to her. She liked it. She studied it with increasing pleasure, aware suddenly that in all this long night no one had come to her insisting, however pityingly, that she must return to the house. Not one person had been to fetch her, to tell her, to *order* her that it was high time she stopped this nonsense and behaved in a manner befitting her station. No one had followed her, servant or family, to beseech her to come in out of the cold, to take this shawl, to get some sleep, to have a sip of this or a bite of that, to tell her what was best for her!

And they never would! Not now! Not on this day or on any other!

She stood up and smoothed her hands down the skirt of her gown, then lifted them to her hair, habit and the memory of her mother's voice making her fiddle with pins and combs, then, with a defiant gesture which spoke louder than any words she might have uttered she pulled them all

317

out and with her hair in a long, heavy cape, silken and straight about her shoulders she walked quietly back towards the house. The dogs padded at her heels and when she reached the stable yard and the side entrance to the house she did not send them to their usual place but with a click of her fingers called them to her. They were somewhat hesitant for neither had been inside the house before, but obediently they followed her along the passage and into the wide hallway. At the foot of the curving staircase they hesitated again.

'Joby . . . Blaze, to heel,' she said softly and with their cold, black noses pressed to the hem of her skirt Katherine Chapman climbed the stairs of her house.

The funeral, as was expected, had been attended by a great many gentlemen of the manufacturing classes, some from as far away as the Midlands and even Scotland, but what was more gratifying to Hannah Chapman, at least, was the unusually large group from the gentry. Naturally Harry's family was represented, by Samuel Atherton and by his wife and son, since Harry was to marry the bereaved widow's daughter when their period of mourning allowed it, but even the Squire had been there, the dreadful circumstances of Barker Chapman's death, one presumed, requiring his presence at the graveside. Most kind of them to attend, she had murmured into her black-edged handkerchief taking each hand which was held out to her, to steady her, one thought, since she was exceedingly frail beneath her widow's weeds. The Penfold Valley had been shocked and horrified by the event, Mr Abbott and Mr Jenkinson knowing quite well it might so easily have been one of them in the splendid coffin or any one of the industrialists who did business in and around Oldham, and they took their leave of her telling her and Katherine that the bereaved ladies had only to send a message and help with the business of the mills or indeed with anything financial or commercial would be immediately made available to them. Yes, yes, Harry Atherton was able, very able indeed, they said to

Hannah, when his back was turned, but he was not *really* one of them. He looked simply splendid in his well cut, well bred coat and trousers of black, his top hat and black gloves and there was no doubt he had a way with him which was inordinately pleasant but could he manage the *mills*? He could sell Barker Chapman's velveteen and fustian and the muslins with which Barker had been experimenting – a new market again – and had already done so beyond all expectations, but could he *manage* those mills and if he could not, what was to happen to them? He and Barker's girl could live very handsomely with or without them, it was true, but there was intense speculation even as the first spadeful of earth fell on the coffin on what Barker Chapman, and now his daughter, was worth.

Kit had stood next to her mother, her head bowed meekly, shrouded from her bonnet to her boots in black, her eyes shadowed behind her mourning veil, her expression unreadable. She listened, when her father's coffin had been put in the ground and the mourners had returned to Green-acres for refreshments, to the flow of conversation around her, to the conjectures and calculations of what her fortune might be, becoming louder as the gentlemen relaxed with a welcome glass of madeira, or even whisky inside them. She did not smile, not even to herself, on how surprised they were to be over the next few days for she did not find their remarks in any way amusing, though she promised herself the pleasure of doing so on the next occasion when they should meet, possibly when one of them needed some small favour her father would unquestionably have allowed them.

She was at the mill the next morning at five o'clock sharp. From head to foot she was in unrelieved black and when Harry arrived five hours later, riding lazily into the mill yard on the bay he had bought himself recently, he was startled to see her carriage in the corner of the yard and her carriage horse in the stable when he threw the reins of his animal to the lad whose job it was to see to them.

'Katherine, my dear.' His face was solicitous and his

hands reached out for hers as she stood by the window, a sheaf of papers in them held to the light but she avoided him, returning to her desk, putting the papers on a neat pile in front of her before she sat down.

'Are you unwell, Harry?' she said coolly.

'Why no, my dear. Should I be?' He smiled his charming smile, seating himself indolently on the corner of her desk. 'Why do you ask?'

'Merely that as it is ten o'clock and you are five hours late I presumed you to be ill.'

'Katherine.' His smile deepened at her small joke. 'I must admit to a distinct reluctance to rise from my bed this morning after . . . well, after yesterday and to a certain concern to find *you* here at all. I had thought a month, perhaps two, before you returned . . .'

'There are mills to be run here, Harry. Business to be transacted . . .'

'I realise that. What do you imagine I am here for, my pet? You can leave it all to me.'

'I do not think so, Harry. A mill cannot be said to be well run if the one who is to run it arrives five hours after the engines are turned on.'

'Katherine, really, is this some kind of a joke because if it is I am not amused. I can only suppose you to be still distraught after your father's death, and who could blame you? Why do you not return home? Take at least a few days, my dear, and then . . .'

'I am perfectly well, Harry, and perfectly well able to run the mills. Now if you wish to continue in your present employment you may do so for you are good at it. I need someone to sell my piece goods but if you do not work to my satisfaction I will dismiss you as I would dismiss any man who does not come up to my standards. They are high, Harry, as my father's were high. I will not put up with latecomers in the mill and I will not put up with it here. The factory bell goes at five and I shall be here before the operatives come on for the first shift. See that you do the same.'

He stood up slowly, straightening his tall and graceful body, lifting his arrogant head in total disbelief. He was still struggling to hold on to the hopeful notion that Katherine was joking with him, teasing him, that in a moment she would smile and make some remark about new brooms sweeping clean and had he really believed she meant it. She would laugh and call for coffee and they would talk, make plans for the future and he would put one or two ideas to her that he himself had devised like the one regarding this nonsensical fancy that he and she should be at the mill at the godforsaken hour of five o'clock when they had managers who were paid to arrive at that time. He had spent several hours in the arms of his sweet Jenny last night and her lusty demands had drained him to the last drop of his considerable virility. He had almost decided to stay in his bed for the remainder of the morning since Gribb and the other managers who had kept the mills going for the past week were well able to do the same for another day. He really had not expected to see Katherine here, not for weeks and he deserved a day off after all he had been through. Perhaps he would ride over to Greenacres after lunch, he had thought, to enquire on the state of mind of his beloved, dinner at the Old Bull in Crossfold and a game of cards. A pleasant day and one which a gentleman of means could well afford. Only the fancy to sit in Barker Chapman's chair which he meant to be his, had brought him here, and then only for half an hour or so, he had told himself.

He kept well leashed the explosion of anger which grew inside him.

'I cannot quite understand your meaning, my pet,' he said.

'And I should be obliged, Harry, if you would refrain from calling me your pet.'

'Katherine! Have you lost your senses? I can only assume that the events of the last week have shaken you more than we thought. Will you not go home and I think it might be advisable if your mother called in the doctor. You cannot be well, indeed you cannot.'

321

'Harry, for God's sake sit down and listen to me. I have something to tell you and you will not like it.'

'I do not like *this*, Katherine, and I do not care for your manner. I think it is high time you went home and I suggest you go straight to bed.'

'Don't be ridiculous, Harry.' Her face was still pale but her eyes were clear and lucid. 'There is nothing wrong with me. I have nothing to keep me at home and this past week has not been . . . easy.'

'No indeed, that is obvious from your manner . . .'

'Stop it, Harry. Stop treating me as though I was a foolish child who has not the wits nor the experience to decide for itself. There is something to be said here so sit down and let us be honest with one another.'

'Honest!' His face was white with fury and he lifted his hand and pushed it through his smoothly brushed hair. His mouth curled in snarling temper and his eyes were a hot, hating brown. 'Are you suggesting I have done something *dishonest*?' He put both hands on the table and leaned across until his face was close to hers, his attitude asking quite plainly who the hell she thought she was and how she, no more really than a factory girl, had the gall to question a gentleman's honour. His mask had slipped quite badly and his true feelings were showing and Kit was made to realise how far he had been forced to stoop in marrying her to get what he wanted. But she was not dismayed, rather she felt as though a great load had been lifted from her mind for it made the task ahead of her so much easier. She had felt nothing but contempt for him during the past week, when she had time to think of it. On the night she had met Jenny Greenwood she had known a vast and thankful relief that it was over, the charade her father had pressed on her. It was finally done with when Jenny had told her of the events of the past year and she had been waiting only to tell her father of the true colours of the man who stood before her. She had been too late for her father had died but it was not too late for her.

Now her hostility towards this man who had mocked

322

not only her father and herself but the virtue of a woman who could not defend herself showed in the disdainful curl of Kit Chapman's lip, the haughty lifting of her head and the expression on her face which said she despised him.

'Do you not think it dishonest to make love to one woman when you are about to marry another. Not only that but to take advantage of someone who has not the authority to refuse what you demand of her. For a basket of food you forced yourself on a girl . . .'

'*Forced*. I have no need of force with women, my girl.'

'Then you admit you have been this woman's lover.'

'I admit nothing. I do not even know which woman you speak of. Who is it who has told you these lies about me? You are talking nonsense, Katherine, and I can only assume you are seriously deranged. Your father's death . . .'

'. . . has set me free, Harry, to do exactly as I please. I may marry, or not, as the fancy takes me and I have chosen *not* to marry you.'

His eyes were almost black now and deep with his hatred of her but in them was a recognition of the dilemma he was in and the care he must use to get out of it. He had allowed her to see, just for a moment, the true Harry Atherton, the one which could when it was needed charm the birds from the trees but who, deep inside him where it had been bred, believed in his own superiority and rank and who meant, when she and her money were well and truly tied to him, to return her to her mother, to her middle-class, industrial background and take up again the life of a landed gentleman. There was enough money to ensure that he lived in luxury for the rest of his life and, his contorted face and bleak eyes said, he was not about to give it up.

She watched him in faint amusement and sudden admiration as he fought to control himself.

'Katherine, my dear, let us not get this . . . this affair out of proportion. I am afraid you have caught me out in a small pecadillo, but really, can you seriously believe that it means anything to me? Gentlemen, my dear, are . . . well, you are a lady and innocent and when I tell you that we have . . . appetites . . . there, I have shocked you, but you will see that it means no more to us than . . . than eating a meal when we are hungry. This girl, she flaunted herself somewhat in the yard, attracting my attention and . . .' He smiled ruefully, a small boy caught with his hand in the jam pot, ' . . . well, I'm afraid, just once I promise you, I could not resist temptation. I was flayed with guilt afterwards, Katherine.' His face was flushed and earnest and his eyes begged her understanding and forgiveness, ' . . . not only for your sake since you know my feelings for you but towards the girl so, knowing how hungry they always are, or so they say, I gave her food . . . sweetmeats. She came to no harm, Katherine, since no doubt it was not the first time . . .'

'It's no good, Harry.'

'What do you mean? I am telling you the truth.'

'I am afraid I do not believe you.'

'Katherine! I cannot understand you, really I cannot. Some slut has been to you crying rape, I suppose, and you are prepared to take her word against that of a gentleman.'

'A gentleman, Harry? Is that what you are?'

'Watch your tongue, Katherine, or I will . . .'

'Will what, Harry? Have me flogged at the cart-tail, or dismissed without a character reference?'

'See here, Katherine. This has gone far enough. You are impugning my word as a gentleman and I demand an apology. I have told you the truth about this . . . this girl . . .'

'You had no option.'

'Blast you, I will not have this. It must stop at once. You are not yourself, Katherine and I insist you allow me to return you to your mother. I will look after the business while you have a couple of weeks' rest and when you are recovered we will set a date for our marriage and no more will be said of this. Come now, where is your pellisse? I will call your carriage . . .'

'No, Harry.'

324

'See here, my girl. I have had just about as much as I can take . . .'

'Then there is the door, Harry. You have but to walk through it and I think after this conversation I will reconsider my offer of employment. I cannot put the sale of my cloth in the hands of a man I do not trust.'

'Do not be more stupid than you really are, Katherine. *We are to be married.* The marriage contracts have been drawn up and agreed by my father and yours . . .'

'Who is now dead.'

'It makes no difference.'

'But it does. My solicitor informs me that as my father did not sign them and as I am his sole heir I may do as I please. And it does not please me to marry you.'

He lost his control then.

'You bitch. You low class, common bitch . . .'

'Thank you for that, Harry. It confirms that I am doing what is best for us both. Now, if you will excuse me I have a lot to do today. If you call at the office you will be given your wages up to yesterday . . .'

'You have not heard the last of this . . .'

'Oh I am sure I have not, but really, I should not waste your time. It is over, Harry, so I will bid you good-morning.'

## 22

He thought there had been an accident, or a fight, one of the daily incidents which occurred in Boggart Hole, Pig Lane and Lousy Bank when tempers flared over who was next at the standpipe, a domestic quarrel, a drunken brawl, a dozen urchin children in a flurry of fisticuffs, of no particular interest or concern to those who watched indifferently but this was not like that. There was an air of tension,

325

of something nasty afoot, venomous and threatening and most of the protagonists appeared to be women.

'What's going on here?' he shouted as he turned the corner of the alley into the narrow passage of Lousy Bank. His heart began a rapid tattoo against his rib-cage and his long legs felt curiously weak for the disturbance appeared to be right outside his own front door.

'Get out of my way.' Joss Greenwood's voice was wild with sudden fear and he elbowed aside the sullen women who jammed the passage.

The first thing that caught his eye was his mother's lovingly polished table standing upside down in the pool of water from the overturned butt. There were other objects which he recognised, a rag rug made from odd pieces of cotton, dyed in different colours and sewed together by his mother's careful hand. There was a large white milk jug, smashed into a dozen pieces, a cushion, fashioned again by his mother from what she could salvage from worn out clothing, stuffed with heather and lavender, a framed sampler proclaiming that Sarah Greenwood, aged nine, had embroidered it in the year 1788, several pans, a lovely bright shawl of red and claret and a Bible, the only book his father had ever owned.

'What the hell is happening here?' he demanded to know roughly, pushing his way through the jeering crowd and some woman, without turning round to see who it was who had spoken, unwilling, one suspected, to miss a single moment of what was happening, answered him cheerfully.

'It's them bloody Greenwoods. Bein' thrown out, they are and not afore time an' all. Jumped up hoity-toity besoms . . .'

The room seemed to be filled with shouting, pushing people and somewhere a child sobbed quite piteously. He could make no sense of it, nor of the men who were lifting this and that, a chair, a bucket, whatever came to hand, ready it seemed, to chuck them out in the passage in the wake of those already there and which, not surprisingly, were fast disappearing. A woman hung on the arm of one man who was cursing her obscenely while a second attempted to drag her off. A boy was kicking and biting in the grip of a third and against the wall his mother stood, her eyes enormous in the grey despair of her face. She held Daisy against her breast while her other arm was about Mercy who appeared to have become almost senseless, slumped against Martha's shoulder.

'Put that down, you bastard,' the woman was screaming and with a thrill of horror Joss saw that it was Jenny. Her face was scarlet with outrage and her foot rose again and again as it tried to find a vulnerable place in which to kick the man whose arm she held. He swung her off her feet, aiming a heavy fist at her head and the second man was grinning now, ready to enjoy what had started out as a routine eviction but was promising to become, with this spirited hellion, a bit of sport.

'Hold her, Ned. Get her arms lad, and I'll tak t'other end. Yer little bitch. Like a bit of a fight, do yer . . . see, Ned, 'old 'er properly or she'll 'ave me in't . . .'

The third man put down the trinket he was fingering, turning to watch with growing interest the manhandling, no more than that at the moment, of the girl they had been sent to put out on the street. Her and her family, they had been told by the Chapman manager, and they had no reason to doubt his word, for non-payment of rent. The old woman and the younger one, a good looker an' all, seemed to be out of their minds, senseless with terror, though the lad was a plucky little bugger. It was taking all his own considerable strength to hold him now as he shrieked the girl's name.

For a moment or two they thought the roof had fallen in on them. Indeed the man who held Jenny Greenwood's arms, twisting them cruelly behind her back while the second fumbled at the neck of her bodice, suffered a broken collar-bone as he was flung from the cottage into the alley, landing in the pool of water from the butt and for good measure, splitting his head on the wall of the house opposite. The second and third men, quite bewildered by the

327

explosion which erupted about them and from God only knew where, were convinced at least two, perhaps even three men had attacked them and throwing caution to the wind, darted through the broken doorway and off up the alley, scattering the delighted crowd as they went.

Jenny cried sharply then, her face pressed tight against his chest and the others huddled beside him, finding a small measure of comfort in his presence in this new catastrophe which had come to engulf them. None could speak coherently at first, indeed they had to put Mercy to bed with an infusion of valerian to make her sleep before sense could be made of their weeping, their jumbled lamentations.

'What is it, Mother?' He turned to the one who had recovered first. Jenny still trembled before the fire for though she had fought wildly, bravely, had, while the need was there, defended her family courageously, now that Joss was here and the crisis temporarily averted, she could not pull herself back together again, nor forget the rough handling the Chapman bully boys, those kept for occasions such as these, had subjected her to, nor the terror of what might have happened had Joss not come home when he did. She watched him, seeing the deep grooves which had recently been chiselled in his dark face, the strain about his strong mouth and even, she noticed, the threads of grey in his thick, curly hair. He was only twenty-five and yet he had the quiet maturity now of a man ten years older, all the hot-headed violence of his younger days scourged from him in gaol. He was beginning a new era in his fight for his fellow-man and though he often met with the Onwardsmen and talked to them, sharing his experience and giving his advice he did not always agree with their constant talk of machine breaking, of mill burning, of window smashing. It did no good for the mill-masters merely re-built their mills, or their warehouses, replaced the broken machines and windows and put wages even lower to pay for them. Only by parliamentary reform could the conditions of the poor be improved and to achieve that they must be represented by their own Member of Parliament up in London. Each man, irrespective of his class, his wealth, or lack of it, must be allowed to choose. Each man must have a voice and that could only be made possible when each man had a vote.

'They said we had not paid our rent, son,' Jenny could hear her mother saying, 'but you know that's not true. We shut the door in their faces but they broke it down.' She looked towards the doorway where Joss had propped up the door. 'They began to throw our things out into the street . . . they were all laughing, them out there. They can't abide to see decent folks make something of themselves . . .'

'No, Mother, you know that's not true. They try hard but circumstances are against them. We've been lucky with . . .' He stopped speaking abruptly since he had been about to say her name, to tell his mother who it was who had been their benefactor but she was not really listening. Her face, gone suddenly old, was turned towards the grate. Her shoulders slumped and her hands rested limply, hopelessly on her clean white apron.

'Why have they done it, Joss? We've done nothing to them, the Chapmans. It wasn't one of us . . .'

The voice from the corner was hard and bitter.

'No Mother, it wasn't but that bitch up there thinks it was. They've been here looking for you, Joss. The militia and then a troop of special constables. Quite gave the whole street something to talk about for days and what a thrill, watching them take this place apart and then there's our jobs . . .'

'Your jobs?' His voice was quite bewildered. 'What about your jobs?'

'We haven't got any. The lot of us were told last night we were to find other employment.' Jenny did not add that Mr Gribb had remarked brutally that they wanted no family of murderers working in the Chapman mill.

'But what . . .?' He could make no sense of it, she could see and when Jenny stood up her voice was harsh as she spoke.

'They think you did it, our Joss.'

329

'Did what, for Christ's sake?'

'You knew Chapman was killed?'

'Aye. By footpads, I was told.'

'No Joss, Onwardsmen, and the leader was Joss Green-wood.'

He began to laugh then, his whole face working in some strange frenzy.

'Dear God, does no one commit a crime which is not blamed on us?'

'They themselves said they were Onwardsmen.'

'Well, I wasn't there and I can prove it. For the past week I've been in Yorkshire talking to men there . . .'

'Working men?'

'Of course! Who else?'

'Will they be believed?'

'Richard Oastler will. I was with him for the whole week, and others who speak for reform . . .'

'Then go and tell them, for God's sake. Perhaps we'll get our jobs back. How are we to manage? Where are we to live? Dear God, I can't stand much more of this, lad. I've twisted and turned, like a bloody vixen with the hounds after it, trying to hold this family together. I've done things I'm not proud of, to feed them while you were in . . . in gaol. When's it going to end, Joss? When?'

'I don't know, lass, but we'll not give up . . .'

'*You'll* not give up! What about me? I'm twenty-two years old and for the past six years while you've been marching here and there, waving your sword in protest at what's been done to the working man, I've been clinging on to what we've got, fighting too, but for the survival of your family. Don't they say charity begins at home, our Joss? Well, how about some for me because I bloody well need it . . .'

'Jenny . . . lass, come on . . . don't weep . . .' He had risen to his feet, moving towards her, his face alive with his compassion but she turned away from him, putting her face to the wall and her voice was empty and quite without hope.

330

'I've kept us fed and dry and warm but I've worked hard for it, Joss. Hard and dirty.'

'I don't know . . .'

'I'll not tell you in front of the children, nor soil my mother with it, but I'm not ashamed. I'd do it again if I had to. I'm strong, Joss, stronger I think than you are and though I could just give up right now, put my face to the wall like this forever, it wouldn't do me any good, nor the child I'm carrying.'

'The . . .'

'Aye, so what are you going to do about it, Joss Greenwood, because I've had enough.'

He was put in the prison barracks at Oldham until they could check his story that on the night that Barker Chapman was killed he was in the company of Richard Oastler, and other men of repute who were fighting for the strange and seemingly amusing belief that children should work for no longer than ten hours in one day. It took a week and when he was released, with no apology or compensation, merely a strict admonishment to keep out of trouble in future, he walked the five miles to Crossfold, just as he was, dirty, unwashed, unshaven and as grim as the prison cell he had just left.

She was sitting in her father's office, *her* office now, her face absorbed as she studied some papers on the desk before her. The two men who had run after him when he passed through the ante-room, through the enormous counting house where her clerks worked, were hot on his heels but he threw them off with a flick of his wrists, his strength, it seemed, as powerful and undefatigable as his rage.

She stood up and the chair in which she had been seated crashed backwards to the floor. Her pale golden skin lost every vestige of its colour and her eyes were a vivid, vicious blue in her alabaster face.

'Miss Chapman . . . he walked past us . . . we did not know who he was . . . took us by surprise . . .' They were only clerks, their faces said and they eyed his menacing strength with some alarm, not really quite sure that even with two of them they could physically manhandle him from the building. 'Shall we call a couple of the yard men . . . ?'

'No . . . thank you, Chambers . . . you may go . . .'

'But Miss Chapman . . .'

'You may go.'

They did not speak for a full thirty seconds, each of them consumed with the heat of their enmity. It was almost a month since they had seen one another. They had made love, then afterwards leaned into one another's arms in peace and the lovely aftermath of it, dreaming together in the last warmth of the dying day. They had known that the time they had been allowed together must surely come to an end soon, but they had not known, on that last day, that it was ending then. They had kissed softly, lovingly, their mouths smiling against one another's, their hands clasped, unwilling to be parted, sighing, smiling again, returning for another kiss, then laughing with the joy of it.

Nothing of that day remained, here in this room as they eyed one another with a hatred as great as their love had been. She was the first to speak.

'Why are you not in prison?' she hissed. 'I know they arrested you. How did you get out? Tell me and be quick about it for you will be back there by nightfall.'

'For what reason should I be in gaol?' His voice was as malevolent as hers.

'For the murder of my father.'

'I did not do it.'

'Liar! You were seen there.'

'No.'

'You and your . . . Onwardsmen.'

'Perhaps them, but not me. I was in Yorkshire with a man whose reputation is above reproach.'

'It makes no difference. The results were the same. You and your . . . rabble. They and you are the cause of my father's death and I shall not forgive you for it.' Her voice was filled with her loathing of him and all he stood for. 'I hate you now, Joss Greenwood, with all my heart and if I can harm you I will. You are a murderer, no matter what your . . . your friends say, if they are to be believed . . .'

'It has been checked and found to be correct.'

'You and they are liars.' Her voice rose in an anguished scream and she threw back her head in pain for she knew he told the truth, but she would not, could not again be at peace with this man and so she chose to disbelieve it.

'I did not come to explain my whereabouts to you, madam.' His voice was as cold as the white hollows of snow which already were beginning to form in the 'tops' as winter approached and his spleen was as great as hers. 'I meant to give you the biggest thrashing of your life, as I would a man who had been as vile as you. That is what you deserve for what you have done to my family, but I . . . cannot. You are weaker than I and could not fight me as I need to be fought so I will content myself merely with saying this. You are not a woman. You have no warmth nor compassion. You have no humanity nor even the mercy of an animal which will put another out of its misery with one quick blow. Because of what you imagine I did to you, you have, without thought, thrown three women, one of them elderly, one pregnant, and two children on to the streets of Crossfold. You have taken away their employment, for what it was worth and consigned them to the workhouse, to poor relief for that is all they can expect now. Because of you and your kind they are to live on hand-outs, on charity, no more than the animals which are put on the earth for you to eat and to work to make you wealthy . . .'

'That is your fault, not mine. If you stayed at home and provided for them, as any decent man should instead of propping up your own arrogance with the "cause" you fight, they would not be as they are . . .'

She could see she had wounded him then and she pressed her advantage home eagerly.

' . . . you go about playing at soldiers, doing good, you tell yourself, stirring up those who know no better, to rebellion, while at home your own family starve for want of a man who is more concerned with his own triumphs than their needs.'

'You . . . bitch . . .' There was a terrible and quite unforgiving blankness in his eyes, a look that said that though he hated her for it, what she said could only be the truth and he was devastated by it. She could feel her own triumph flood through her veins, the joy which had replaced the despair when he had told her his wife was carrying his child. She allowed the strange thought, that which marvelled that in all this chaos, the enormity and strength of their need for revenge, the thing that had crucified her more than any other was that while he had been making love to her, he had obviously given the same pleasure to his wife who was now to bear his child. And *she*, Katherine Chapman, was not, and never would! She could feel the wound going deeper and deeper and even, she suspected, beginning to bleed and she turned the knife a little more in his flesh for he must suffer as she did.

'You call yourself a leader of men, probably a philanthropist, even a saint in your championship of the poor but you do no more than build up your own image playing at soldiers on the moor, killing men like my father . . .'

'I did not kill him.'

'Perhaps not, but your *men did* and that is all the same to me.'

'And so you take your vicious revenge by turning off my mother and sister, my wife . . . by putting two children into the streets to starve. Punish *me*, damn you, not them. If I had not come home when I did they would have raped my sister . . .'

'*Raped* . . . who . . .' She became still then, her face suddenly uncertain.

'Those thugs you sent to throw them into the street . . .'

'Thugs. I . . .'

'Don't pretend you know nothing about it. There were three of them, helping themselves not only to my mother's things but to my sister's . . .'

334

'Jenny . . . ?'

The virulent flow of his hatred was diverted for a moment, veering away from the narrow gully through which it ran towards only her. His voice faltered as she spoke his sister's name. With it she had brought a new dimension into their conflict and Jenny's voice rang cruelly, as hers did, asking for God's sake, where it would all end? He could feel himself grow weak, brought down, first by his sister, for her words had had the ring of well grounded truth in them, and then by this woman, who did no more than repeat it. But it made no difference. He must go on. He had given as many years as Jenny to this fight for what was rightfully his and theirs and no matter what it cost him he must continue. They *did* weaken him, the women he loved, all of them *because* he loved them but he must not let them divert him from what he knew to be right.

'Yes, Jenny,' he went on. 'They were about to have some sport with her. You see she is no more than a factory girl and who would blame them. As such she would be available to any man who had a fancy to take her down. Now no one would dare lay a finger on Miss Chapman or Miss Jenkinson for if they should it would be a hanging matter. And yet you are all women, all defenceless, the same under the skin and just as easily hurt or humiliated, but they have no defence, you see, the girls in your mill, or anybody's mill for if they should complain they would be turned off to starve. Ask Ellis, Kit Chapman. Ask him how he manages to live as high on the hog as he does and ask yourself how he managed it under your father's sharp eye without being dismissed himself. Ask yourself a lot of questions and you will find the answers in your own weaving-sheds and spinning rooms. Now I say this to you. Leave my family alone. If I find them harmed again I shall know where to look to find the culprit.'

He turned then, leaving her office so quietly those in the ante-room were not aware that he had left and when he was gone she turned blindly and stood for ten shaking minutes with her face pressed close to the wall, just as Jenny had. She did not weep for it was too deep, too shocking for that but her heart wept and indeed every sense in her body, every pulse and muscle and bone ached with the torment of it. He was gone forever from her life since what had been torn open so savagely could never be mended. He would never forgive her for what she had done to him and his family in her madness and in truth she could never forgive him for what he had done to her in his carelessness. He had every right to make love to his wife since she *was* his wife, but not while he was making love to her, her woman's illogical mind screamed. And he certainly had no right at all to incite men to murder others in a cause which though it might, some thought, be just, was definitely not rational.

But she would not dwell on it, she told herself doggedly since she must get on with her life, with the life she had fought so hard to retain for herself. She would not pine nor languish for something which, from the first had been frail and doomed to be short-lived. She had allowed herself once, years ago, nearly three now, to day-dream, but Joss had married and she had been forced on to other realities which had nothing to do with her love.

No, she would stiffen her spine and lift her head and do what she had always intended. She would run her father's mills ... *no, her* mills and it would be enough, she told herself.

She picked up the papers she had been studying when Joss had burst into the room, making a note here and there but all the while she trembled so violently her teeth chattered and the marks on the paper were no more than an illegible scrawl. The sense of betrayal and pain was so fierce it hurt her to breathe, the air about her taut and hopeless and difficult to drag into her lungs. She could not dispel the nightmare pictures from her mind of Joss Greenwood removing his wife's garments one by delicious one – as he had done with her – until she lay against him, her naked body trembling and ecstatic beneath the touch of his hands and lips – as hers had done – and quite simply she could not bear it.

336

But they would not go away, those pictures, remaining inside her head with a vividness which made it ache badly, pressing against her eyes so that the figures on the papers before her ran together. She felt she had lost weight and colour and substance within the last hour, everything she held dear draining from her and leaving her hollow.

A child! They were to have a child, Joss and Mercy Greenwood. Another woman was to give him what she never could and it would bind them together, he and his wife as no wedding vows could, or had. A son perhaps, to be led lovingly, for Joss would love his son, along the paths of reform all the Greenwoods seemed determined on.

She considered it. Joss and his son, and her mind began to slip away from reality, seeing them hand in hand, the smaller figure a replica of the larger and holding the child's other hand was his mother. Joss's wife, the woman who had given him the boy and therefore, dear to him.

The sense that Joss had broken a promise, though he had made none, been faithless, though she had no claims on him was so strong she bent over her desk, winded and gasping and she wished quite coldly that she could die of the pain.

There was, creeping over her, a terrible numbness and she was grateful for it. It would not last, of course but at that moment she welcomed its benevolence. She was suspended above the devastated, deceived woman at the desk, quite amazed by her calm but glad of it as picked up her pen and began to write.

Joss knocked on Sarah and Isaac Pickering's cottage door where he had left his mother and his family on the day he was taken to Oldham. He had not been able to think where else to put them, short of the workhouse and they had all, including Jenny, been in a trance-like condition of hopelessness which seemed to say quite plainly that they did not care *where* they went. A dangerous state of mind which he did not like but Sarah would look after them, she had told him compassionately until a place could be found

337

for them. A bit of a squash but Charlie could go in with her boys next to Isaac's hand-loom and the rest wherever there was a bit of space to put a pillow. He was not to worry, she had said stoutly, though she was glad of the few shillings he put in her hand. Isaac would go to Lousy Bank with his hand cart for the rest of their things, those Joss had not been able to carry and he was not to think about it. What were friends for, besides it would be grand to have Martha back. By, she'd missed her and their Jenny, but her eyes had studied Mercy somewhat warily for there was something not quite right about Joss's child-wife. A right pretty little thing she had been, still was for that matter, but her vulnerability, her strange air of having slipped away for a moment, inside her own head, was quite unnerving.

It was Sarah who opened the door to him and her gaunt, granite face, quite indomitable despite what life had heaped on her strong shoulders, smiled in pleasure. She was not much given to gestures of affection but she had a special place in her heart for the family of this man, and for the man himself since where would they be, all the working families of the cotton trade of Lancashire without the hope first Abel, then his son had given them.

'Nay lad, you're a sight for sore eyes an' no mistake. Come away in an' tell me't news. We'd 'eard you were to come 'ome today an' yer Mam's that excited she's bin backwards and forwards to't end of t'village looking for you. Your Charlie's only just this minute gone 'ome for 'is tea an' you should see't rabbit he caught. Well, your Jenny 'ad it skinned and in't pot before dratted thing was cold. She sent 'alf over to us . . .' She shook her head, marvelling on the generosity of those who, having barely enough to feed themselves will share what they have with others, seemingly unaware that she fell into this category herself. ' 'Ave yer been 'ome yet . . . well, no, you wouldn't, would yer, not knowing . . . eeh, Joss, what a miracle . . .'

He stood just inside the cottage doorway bending his head to avoid the low frame. His face was bewildered and his eyes roamed about the room. There was no fire for fuel

338

must be saved for the winter and the room was cool and empty. Sarah had four living children, those who had survived the 'fevers' which weeded out the weak from the strong but none were in evidence, nor was Isaac and there was no sign of his own family.

Sarah began to laugh then. 'Eeh lad, your face is a picture and well it might be for we all 'ad a look just like yon when the chap came ter fetch yer Mam.'

'Fetch my . . . ?'

'Aye. On the day after you'd gone. 'E 'ad the key an' a bit o' paper which said the rent was paid an' if yer Mam wanted any 'elp she'd only ter say so.'

'Sarah . . . I don't quite . . . who . . . ?'

'Nay lad, no one knows who sent 'im nor why but yer Mam was made up with it an' I don't think she cared. She grabbed that key an' my mop an' bucket and was up the street like a girl. Your Jenny was still standing there, her gob open and Mercy . . . well . . .' The less said about Mercy Greenwood the better so she hurried on with her tale. 'We all went up, me an' Annie Bottomley, Ellie Aspinall an' 'elped yer Mam . . . Well, the place 'ad been empty for a long time an' it was a mess. Isaac made up a bit of whitewash and repaired a broken frame or two. Charlie an' my Jem went up to't tops an' cut some peat, fetchin' it back on't 'andcart an' . . .'

'Sarah . . . Dear God, Sarah . . . ay up . . .'

'I know, it 'ardly seems possible an' what they'll live on God only knows but *He* provided them with a roof over their 'eads so I reckon the rest will come . . .'

'No . . . not God, Sarah . . .'

'What d'yer mean, lad?'

'It wasn't God who gave my family back their home.'

Sarah put out a work-scarred hand and touched his grooved cheek. Her eyes were soft and compassionate. They all went hungry. They were cold and desperate and their men tramped miles across the moors looking for work. They accepted poor relief, many of them, and the benefit given them by the societies set up by the reforming men, a

339

hard and bitter pill to swallow for men who had known independence and freedom. They did not like it and there was trouble coming again it was said, as trade worsened. But this man would not give in! Isaac and many of the others who congregated up at Abby Hobson's place on the moors, lost heart and became sullen, muttering of their grievances, their repeated disappointments but they had not suffered as this man had. He worked tirelessly, sacrificing his own family for theirs. He had gone to prison for them. He held them all together best way he could and never gave up hope that one day he would get for them what his father had told him they should have.

'Nay, Joss, no one's askin' who did it. Same one as dismissed them from t'mill and turned 'em out o' Lousy Bank, I reckon. We all do things in temper, say things we shouldn't when we think someone's done the dirty on us. After a bit we see sense again, when the madness leaves us an' then all we want ter do is make amends. We're sorry! We accept that we've made a mistake an' we try ter put it right.'

She looked at him and her wisdom was infinite and pitying. Throw no stones, Joss, she was saying, not until you're sure some have been thrown at you.

He could see Kit Chapman's face as he strode up the village street towards his old home, his *proper* home, his mother's home and for a sweet moment he allowed his love for her to flow over him and through him, cleansing him of the bitterness and the hatred. She had let him revile her, knowing as he did so that what he said to her was untrue, but she had not told him. She had given his family back their cottage, a place to shelter while he was away. She was a mill-owner now, one of the hated industrialists and as such could never associate herself again with a man like himself but she was fair and just, with pockets of goodness in her which would not allow his family to suffer because of him. She would never, could never allow the fragile emotion which had grown between them to remain, let alone blossom and so she had cut it out quite drastically.

340

She was *his* enemy but, her action said though *she* had not, that she would not, make war on his family.

His mother was at the cottage door and when he opened his arms wide she ran like a girl straight into them and her tears of joy were enough for him . . . *then.*

## 23

The man standing on Miss Charlotte Burton's doorstep was soberly dressed in good black and he was clean. His manner was very respectful. He had whipped off his hat when the door was opened to him and the parlourmaid had no reason to disbelieve that he was anything but what he said he was, an associate of Mr Harry Atherton.

'He's not here,' she said politely as Miss Burton required her servants to be.

'When will he be back,' the man said and it was then that the girl felt the first prickle of alarm, well, not alarm exactly, but disquiet for she was not accustomed to men of Mr Atherton's standing, and those others who 'resided' with Miss Burton, allowing their eyes to roam over her body quite so openly.

'I don't know. I think . . . perhaps you had better speak to Miss Burton, sir.'

'Perhaps I better had. Will you tell her I'm here.'

'Who shall I say is calling, sir?'

'Nay, she'll not know me, lass. Just show me in.'

'Well, Miss Burton likes to know who . . .' but the man had stepped inside the hallway, turning round quite boldly to stare at the heavy, old-fashioned furniture, the pictures Miss Burton's father had considered suitable for his wife and daughter to see, the fading splendour of what had once been the parson's fine residence.

341

'Please to wait here, sir,' the parlourmaid said nervously, not awfully sure she cared to leave this stranger in the middle of Miss Burton's hallway and not a man in the house to protect them should he prove awkward. She did not like the way his eyes assessed Miss Burton's possessions, nor the way they assessed herself since she was not unused to gentlemen's glances and this one was . . . not nice!

'Miss Burton says she can spare you five minutes, sir,' she told him a moment or two later, not adding that her employer had told her to stay within earshot.

'How may I help you, Mr . . . er . . . ?'

'I'm looking for Mr Atherton, Miss . . .'

'I am Miss Charlotte Burton, Mr . . . er . . .'

'Good day to you, ma'am,' and he looked pointedly at the chair by the blazing fire, opposite the one in which she sat but Miss Burton did not invite him to join her. She was a lady and knew instinctively, despite his fine clothes, that this was no gentleman.

'I'm afraid Mr Atherton no longer lives here,' she said distinctly, her hand hovering no more than an inch or two from the bell which would summon her parlourmaid to her. Like the girl, this man made her uneasy though he was polite enough. It was in his eyes, she thought, as though there was nothing he had not witnessed and nothing he would see that would ever shock him.

He looked surprised and then disbelieving, disposed, she thought, to swear, or ask her peevishly if she was quite certain and her hand moved to touch the bell on the table beside her.

'Where's he gone then? I only saw him a couple of days ago.'

'Perhaps you did, Mr . . . er . . . but he is no longer living here.'

'Well, that was quick. When did he leave?'

'See here, Mr . . . er . . . What has Mr Atherton to do with you?' for *he* was a gentleman, her attitude said.

'I worked for him, in a manner of speaking and we had

a bit of unfinished business to attend to. I hadn't expected he'd take off so soon or I'd a' bin round earlier.'

'Really! Well, I'm sorry I cannot be of more help to you.'

'Well, you can, I'm sure. He probably left his address. Gents like him always do, so if you'll write it down I'll get in touch with him.'

'I am afraid I cannot do that. I had no instructions from Mr Atherton to give his address to anyone.'

'No, but you know it though.'

'Of course, since he asked me to forward any mail.'

'Right, hand it over then.'

'I beg your pardon.'

'I think you heard what I said, Miss Burton. I want to write to Mr Atherton on a very urgent bit of business so if you'll give me his address I'll be on me way and leave you in peace. No harm done and no one any the wiser and if you touch that bell you'll wish you hadn't, believe me.' The last few words were uttered with such smiling geniality Charlotte Burton could only think that she had not heard aright but the man took a step towards her, his highly polished boots making no sound on her threadbare carpet. His eyes narrowed menacingly. They were the palest grey she had ever seen, almost without colour and in the dim light of the afternoon they looked almost white between his lashless eyelids.

'I don't like your tone, my man and I must ask you to leave my home at once or I shall be forced to send for the . . .' Her voice trailed away breathlessly as he put both hands on the arms of her chair, leaning so close to her she could smell the onions he had eaten for his dinner.

'No, I don't think so, Miss Burton, really I don't. Mr Atherton'll be well pleased to hear from me and wouldn't thank you if he heard you'd stopped us getting together. An' neither would I, see?'

Harry Atherton was at breakfast a week later when the letter arrived. It had been a period in his life which he would not like to re-live and as he slumped at the table, alone since the rest of the family had not yet risen, he gloomily contemplated his future. What the hell was he to do, he asked himself, as his father had asked him, snarling, a dozen times since he had arrived at Atherton Hall with, as Samuel Atherton described it, his tail between his legs! He could not believe his ears, his father said over and over again in that first hour. A girl, a bloody mill girl had turned him down, turned him *out*, told him she no longer required his services, not only in business but as a husband. What the hell were you thinking of, boy, letting a woman of her class tell you what you should do, he had thundered. You were engaged, dammit, the contracts drawn up – dear God, the contracts which had stated in black and white exactly how he, Samuel Atherton was to benefit and through him the land which had been held in trust for his eldest son. They had been agreed, by himself and Barker Chapman and though at heart he had despised the man and would not in more favourable circumstances have given his girl a second glance, what that girl now had was morally theirs! And now Harry had allowed her, that was what galled him, *allowed* her to send him away like some mill-hand who had worked for her but no longer suited.

It had gone on and on, round and round in circles until it arrived back where it had begun, and then round again until Harry could willingly have put his hands about his father's throat and strangled him. His brother had been the same. The eldest son who was to have returned his birthright to its former glory with the money Barker Chapman was to pay them for what they had sold him. Now it was in ashes, the grand future, the lives they were to lead, the dowry his sister was to receive to tempt an impoverished but landed gentleman of their own kind into marriage. And his father, it seemed, could simply not get it into his head *how* it had happened, just as though Katherine Chapman was some foolish child, some pretty ninny without two words to say for herself and certainly not the gumption, nor the wit to see through the masquerade which was his son. Harry had sworn, in the heat of his almost senseless rage that he would not let it rest, that she would be sorry

344

at she had crossed swords with him, that he would find some way to repay her and as he opened the letter, idly scanning its ill-written contents it seemed that in his hand might be, must certainly be, the way to do it.

Kit Chapman and her mother were dining in almost complete silence. They had little to say to one another these two women who, though they had been brought up in the same surroundings with the same background of the solid industrial middle class, were so vastly different. During the day, and when the meal was over and she could retire to her father's study – still called that more than two months after his death – Kit could absorb herself in the minutiae of the working of her mills, studying accounts and patterns, balance sheets and designs, but during this trying hour or two in the evening she must do her best to hold a conversation with this woman. She was her mother and Kit had a responsibility to her, a certain fondness but apart from that biological fact they had nothing in common. Her mother was tearfully bewildered by her daughter's stubbornness in running the mills alone and, worse still, her declaration that she was not to be joined in marriage to Harry Atherton after all. It was a bitter blow from which Hannah Chapman could not recover and she was inconsolable. Her mourning allowed her to hide from many of the, she was sure, horrid innuendos which would be bandied about the chapelry of Oldham but her close friends and relatives were understandably concerned at her sorrow, not only for Barker and the dreadful way in which he had died, but for the loss of the splendid son-in-law of whom she had been so proud. Katherine was a heartless, perfidious daughter and disloyal to the memory of her father who had arranged this great match for her and could anyone blame her mother for the unforgiving disappointment she showed.

And so they lived uneasily together, each knowing they had no alternative, and when the butler informed Katherine that Mr Atherton was in her father's study and would be grateful if he might have a word with her when she had finished dining, naturally, their reactions differed so greatly, they each might have been given a different message.

'Mr Atherton! Good God, what on earth does he want after all this time? I thought I had heard the last of him,' from Kit, and

'Mr Atherton! Oh, my dear, it is Harry. How wonderful . . . oh, how wonderful . . .'

'Tell him I will be there shortly, Winters,' from Kit, and

'Show him in immediately, Winters,' from Hannah and the flustered butler looked from one woman to the other, uncertain which he was to obey. Mrs Chapman had been mistress of the house for over twenty years and he had been here when she came, but Miss Chapman owned it all, and him, down to every last cup and saucer in the kitchen cupboard.

Kit sighed. 'Oh very well, Winters. Ask Mr Atherton to join us for coffee in the drawing-room.'

He was dressed, as they were, in the deep black of mourning and Kit felt a surprising bubble of laughter rise in her throat for really he was the supreme showman, acting the part of the young gentleman of breeding, which he was, still grieving, his demeanour said, which he was not, the loss of a man who had been not only a friend but one who he had hoped, in the future, to call 'Father'. He stood in the doorway of the drawing-room, his hand not exactly on his heart but very near it and Kit had again that strange desire to laugh. He really was absurd and could anyone take him seriously, she asked herself? She forgot the menace of their quarrel on the day she had dismissed him, was ready even to forgive his dalliance with Jenny Greenwood since it no longer had any connection with *her* life, willing to believe his story that – perhaps – Jenny had tempted him for she was an extremely striking young woman and irresistible to a man of Harry's self-indulgent nature. On that day she had been still raw and vulnerable, grieving her father, hating Joss Greenwood, eager to sever her connection with Harry himself and be on her own. She had been abrasive, unsure of herself, wanting to have them all swept away, Joss, Harry and the gentlemen of her father's acquaintance who were resolved to steer her where they thought she should go.

Now, with two months of calm, of running the mills as she wanted them run, of seeing the success with which she did it, she was softer, more forgiving, ready to smile and enjoy his amusing banter. No more than that, of course. She must admit to a certain surprise at seeing him but then he had always been of a shallow nature and quite unmoved by the darts of irritation she had often thrown at him.

'Mrs Chapman, my dear Mrs Chapman. It is unforgivable of me to impose myself upon you in your time of bereavement but I really could not leave the district without calling on you. I had unfinished business . . . a small matter and was about to board the coach to Chester but something held me back. Do say you are not offended.'

'Harry, my dear boy. How could we be offended? Indeed, any offence we might feel would have arisen if you had *not* called to see us. Would it not, Katherine?'

Indicating at once her firm resolve to draw her daughter to the attention of Harry Atherton, and of Harry to Katherine, Hannah allowed him to kiss her hand before almost pushing him towards Kit.

'Katherine, what can I say? These weeks must have been quite dreadful for you.' Her hand was in his and his eyes were brimming over with his concern but about his mouth played a small, disarming, quite impudent smile which was meant to tell her that really, she must not take him quite so seriously as her mother appeared to do. He was, of course, enormously sympathetic towards her in her sorrow and the devastation she must find in running the mills single-handed but if he could lighten her load, her day, this hour with his own brand of sly humour, he was more than willing. His eyes touched briefly, admiringly on the smooth gloss of her chignon and the stark black silk of her gown which, despite its severity was as fashionably elegant as any she wore. A simple sheath, highwaisted, banded just beneath her breasts with a thick cluster of black jet, her pale golden shoulders rising from it, a black velvet ribbon round her slender neck.

'But may I say that your beauty has not suffered from it . . . oh my dear, I do beg your pardon. I realise I should not be so forward now that we are no longer . . .'

Did his wicked eyes gleam with unshed tears, she thought, or was that a twitch of amusement curling his well shaped lips, and the laughter which had bubbled in her rose to the surface and erupted in a most unlady-like chuckle.

'Oh Harry, will you never change? Why do you persist in this charade of sorrow for my father when the only regret it has caused you is the withdrawal of his money.'

'Katherine. You wicked, wicked girl, how could you?'

'Oh Harry knows what I mean, Mother and is not offended, are you Harry? It took a great deal of resolution to bring himself to work for my father and to engage himself to me but he applied himself to it with great courage. So what could a gentleman such as he, who would make a sacrifice so extraordinary, find offensive in a little honesty. No, Harry, do not look so humble, it does not suit you, nor so aggressive since I do not like it. Tell us what you want and let us have done with humbug.'

'You have not lost your capacity for sharpness, Katherine.' His smile was just as amused, with no glimmer of the affront he must surely feel and she was surprised for the words spoken on the day that they last met were coming back to her. He had told her then that she had not heard the last of him, calling her a bitch and worst of all in his eyes, no more than a factory girl, so why, eight weeks later should he be here, smiling, kissing her mother's hand – herself a factory girl, one presumed – and making himself generally pleasant to one and all. It made no sense for surely he was not naïve enough to imagine he could ingratiate himself back into her good graces after what had passed between them. Perhaps he wanted his job back since he must know he would never get *her*. And what of the 'business' he spoke of? With another mill-owner perhaps? As a salesman?

'So what are you doing back in Lancashire, Harry?' she said as she handed him a cup of coffee. 'Surely the delights of the hunt have not palled already.'

'No indeed, though I must admit to a certain boredom with a life of indolence after being so strenuously occupied in your father's mills.'

'Really.' She smiled disbelievingly.

'Really, Katherine.' He smiled sweetly at her over the rim of his cup. 'When one has been fully employed for as long as I was . . .'

'And well paid for it into the bargain.'

'Indeed, as you say. I found it hard to do nothing but merely drift through the days seeking one pleasure after another to alleviate the tedium.'

'Really Harry. You do surprise me.'

'I surprise myself.'

'And what are you to do about it?'

'That rather depends on you, Katherine.'

'I? What have I to do with it?' A small knot of tension had twisted itself beside her left temple since she did not care for the bright gleam of triumph . . . was that what it was? . . . in his eyes. He lounged carelessly beside her mother on the rose pink velvet of the sofa. The lamplight burnished his fair hair to gold and turned the healthy warmth of his face to a dark brown. The black of his coat seemed out of place on such a glowing, handsome young animal and yet its severity only served to enhance his masculine beauty. He was confident, sure of himself and she wondered uneasily what it was he wanted for his manner said he was perfectly certain he would get it.

Her mother yawned behind her hand, then apologised profusely.

'Dear me, these late nights really do not suit me any longer. I am long past the age when I can stay out of my bed beyond ten o'clock. Would you think me rude if I were to retire, Harry? I know it is not quite the thing but . . . well, you and Katherine have known one another so long I think I might be forgiven for overlooking the niceties.

You are . . . I feel as though you are . . . almost a member of the family . . . well, I'm sure you will know what I mean.'

There was much hand-kissing and bowing, of murmuring of how lovely it was . . . how charmed he was . . . of please *not* to be a stranger, and Hannah was escorted from the drawing-room to the foot of the staircase where her maid waited with a lamp.

'Good-night, dear boy,' she said, archly.

'Good-night, dear Mrs Chapman,' his eyes assuring her that everything would be all right and Hannah went to her bed that night for the first time since the murder of her husband, a delighted and hopeful woman, murmuring in her excitement that she would never be able to sleep.

'Now then, Harry,' Kit said when he had seated himself opposite her again. 'What is it you want?'

'How hurtful you are, Katherine. Why should I want anything? Can I not merely be a caller come to see how you, and naturally your mother, are doing.'

'No, not really, not Harry Atherton.'

'Yes, very hurtful indeed, as you were on the occasion of our last meeting.'

'We both said things in the heat of the moment but they cannot be taken back and nothing has changed.'

'My ambition to marry you has not, Katherine. I will give up the pretence that I have an all abiding passion for you although I cannot deny I find you a very desirable woman. I won't pretend, as I have pretended in the past because you are too intelligent, too shrewd to be taken in by any great spectacle of undying devotion but we could be very affectionate with one another, friends perhaps, lovers, of course and I would not stand in your way in the matter of the mills. They are yours and always will be. Come now, Katherine, admit we would do very well together, you and I. I make you laugh, can you deny it? I am . . . amusing and would make a good host at your table, a shield and protector . . .'

'My father said those very same words . . .'

'There you are, you see,' he said eagerly, 'and you set great store by your father's wisdom, did you not?'

'Harry, please, this is . . .'

'This is right for us, Katherine, you know it is. I am a superb salesman. Your father would not have employed me, had he not thought so. You need a man like me . . .'

'And you need a woman like me . . .'

'That is what I am saying, Katherine . . .'

'It's no good, Harry. I told you weeks ago that I did not want to marry and nothing has changed.'

His expression did, right before her eyes, so quickly she could hardly believe it. From eager, boyish charm to a rigid and absolute oppression which said that Harry Atherton had done his best to be reasonable and if she was not prepared to deal with that he could quite easily turn it about.

'Has it not, Katherine?' he said quietly. 'Are you sure?'

'Oh come on, Harry. How you do love to be mysterious. A boy playing games . . .'

'Not any more, Katherine. I have tried to be reasonable, to bring to you what can only be advantageous to us both, to point out to you in a friendly, gentlemanly fashion that really you are foolish to attempt this . . . this whim of being your father's successor alone. You need me, Katherine, and I intend to show you just how much.' He stood up, the charade of the young and amiable gentleman of breeding, minding his manners in the presence of a lady, slipping away at a quite terrifying speed and the true and dangerous face of Harry Atherton was revealed. His eyes became quite black as the pupils dilated and his face took on more colour with the sudden rush of angry blood to his head.

Why, he is mad, she thought dazedly, wondering why she had not seen it before. How has he kept it hidden so well for all these years unless it was that he had all he wanted, all that he had been promised and so had no need to let it be seen.

'Harry.' Even yet she did not acknowledge the danger she was in. 'What on earth are you talking about? I told

351

you the last time we met that our relationship had ended. My father was the one who wanted this marriage between us, not I, and now that he is dead I am able to decide for myself . . .'

'No, my dear Katherine, you are not able to decide for yourself. I think you do not realise how much you need a man to guide you, to protect you . . .'

'Harry. If you continue to talk this way I shall be forced to ask you to leave. In fact I think you should go right now. We really have nothing to say to one another, have we . . . ?'

'Not even about Joss Greenwood?' His smile had become less of a wolf's grin now. He had her, it said, in a situation which had taken her by surprise and the knowledge had given him the strength to shrug off the rage to which he had momentarily succumbed. It pleased him to see her incredulous face, the shock in her eyes, the colour drain quite dramatically from her cheeks. It gave him a feeling of power and he loved it and quite pleasantly now, just as though the wildness she had seen in him had not occurred, he continued smoothly.

'You have heard of him, of course, Katherine, the reformer who is willing to suffer so dreadfully for his belief that the lower orders are equal to other men. To gentlemen, in fact, and that they should have what you and I have. A lunatic, in other words, who should be incarcerated in an asylum, or transported. What do you say, Katherine?'

'I really . . . I had not . . .'

'Come Katherine. You have such forceful opinions on everything from the morals of your own mill girls to the sorry notion that a woman is able to arrange her own life. Surely you must have considered this rebel who has gone against your own father, I believe. A machine wrecked, a warehouse burned down and if I am not mistaken, Barker Chapman's murder . . .'

'No . . .'

'No, Katherine! I was there! I saw the man and though this radical has drummed up the names of men who will give him an alibi, questionable in my opinion since I could never bring myself to take seriously those who are forever championing their "fellow-man". I do not trust them, nor do I believe that this Greenwood was with them on the night in question. I shall say so . . .'

'No . . .'

'Again no, Katherine. Can you have some information the authorities do not, perhaps?'

'No . . .'

'Then it is for some other reason that you deny his complicity, at least in your father's murder. What can it be? Come Katherine . . .' His tone was silky and as she struggled to regain her composure she could see the frenzy of his joy, the joy which knew no bounds as he took his revenge for her own mockery, her own contempt of him eight weeks ago.

'You know this man, do you not, Katherine? Rather better than you are willing to admit. There is something between you which you thought you had kept secret but you see, my dear, whatever you do, no matter how careful you are, there is always someone who notices that your actions, unremarked by most, are unusual.'

He was completely self-possessed now, in control of himself and her and the enchantment of it had him in a thrall. Katherine Chapman, at whose hands he had suffered humiliation after humiliation was looking at him with eyes in which there was nothing but a dreadful blankness.

'It's true, is it not, Katherine, go on, admit it. He is your lover, is he not? Joss Greenwood. A common labouring man has . . .' Here he spoke words of such obscenity her mind reeled with it, retreating into a place where she could not hear them, could not have him tarnish the most precious things she had known and though his voice went on and on and she could hear the sound and see his lips move, the words were unintelligible. She must pull herself together. She must gather her wits from every scattered corner of her trembling mind, gather them and piece them into a whole, into coherent thought since she must not only defend herself from this madman she must attack him so that he could not do battle again. He had shocked her, stunned her, but not for long . . . oh no, not for long.

She could actually feel the warm blood begin to course through her veins, rushing strongly to her heart until it beat in a tattoo of rage equal to his own and her eyes glittered savagely. As her head snapped up, bringing his words to a sudden halt she had time to realise, and even smile a little inside herself, for was she not as wild as Harry Atherton?

'How did you come by this foolishness, Harry? Who was your informant for indeed he is as mad as you.'

'*He!* I did not say it was a man.'

Dear God, not . . . not Jenny? It could not be Jenny . . . and then her mind cleared and was brilliantly sharp again. Jenny Greenwood knew nothing about herself and Joss and if she had it was not likely she would put the information in the hands of this man who had seduced her. In that first week after her father had been killed and Kit had thought Joss had killed him, her desire for revenge had included his whole family. She had put them out in the street, taken their work from them but she had regained her sense of justice, become aware of her own wickedness and arranged for them to have their cottage returned to them. She had compensated them for her brief lapse into the bitterness and hatred of those first few days, tried to help them in different ways and she was certain Jenny Greenwood would know of it. So who? Who had put her in the hands of this man? Who?

'It does not matter, man or woman. You can go to hell and take your foul tongue with you.'

'Oh ho, my fine lady. So that is the attitude you are going to take, is it? And if I put it about the district that Joss Greenwood has his hand up the petticoats of . . .'

'Stop it, you bastard . . .'

'You don't like that, do you, or at least you don't like to hear it spoken of by me. Well my dear, unless we come to some arrangement, you and I, it will be spoken of by every

354

mill-owner in the Penfold Valley. They will not take kindly to the knowledge that one of their own is consorting with a man who is doing his best to put them out of business . . .'

'What kind of arrangement would that be, Harry?'

'Why, exactly the one we had before your father died, I think.'

'You are willing to take on the well used goods of a working man. A woman who has . . . what was the phrase . . . had the hand of a labourer up her petticoats?'

'If she is as well placed as yourself, Katherine. I am not overly particular . . .'

'You must be insane.'

'No, but you will be if you do not do as you are told.'

'Get out of my house, Harry. Now! Or I will have you thrown out.'

'The wedding I think, next month, but I will return to the mill tomorrow and go through the books with you. We can put it about – I'm sure your mother will help us here – that you have suffered a nervous disorder brought on by your father's death but you are recovered now, your old self again and that you and I are re-united . . .'

She began to laugh then. It was so dreadfully absurd. Could he not see she really did not care what he did, or said? He could do nothing to hurt her. She was not concerned with what people said of her. They had talked about her ever since she was thirteen and her father had allowed her out on the moor with only her dogs for company. She was one of the wealthiest, most influential women in South Lancashire and not one of her business associates could afford to get on her wrong side. She was the foundation on which many of the smaller mill-owners had built their businesses. Dozens of them owed her money and if she called it in they would be unable to carry on. It was a practice her father had begun years ago, astute, shrewd, knowing that a man who is owed money has the loyalty of those to whom it is loaned. She had position and if not exactly the respect of other mill-owners, men of authority in the chapelry of Oldham, for they could make no sense of her determination to run her father's mills, at least she had their ear. They might not care to know that she and Joss Greenwood were more to one another than adversaries on two sides of a battle but there was nothing they could do about it, whether they were to believe it, or not. They could not ignore her, certainly, if she were to make a complaint – defamation of character, was it called? – against Harry Atherton, that is if she cared to, despite his breeding. He was not a Lancashire gentleman, not one of them and though his word might be listened to, would it be heeded? Would they believe, could they really believe that, despite her strangeness Miss Katherine Chapman, daughter of Barker Chapman, would associate in *that* way, in *any* way, with a man such as Joss Greenwood. It was a chance she must take. She must find out where Harry had obtained his information and it would not take long for his accomplice must be silenced too. A man in her own mills to know so much about her – and her connection with the Greenwood family. A man in authority. That must be it, that must be the source of Harry's information and if she put her mind to it there was no doubt that by the end of the night she would have his name.

She turned to Harry who had moved to lounge insolently against the fireplace. He was at home, his manner said, back where he belonged and reaching inside his jacket he brought out his cigar case. Selecting a cigar he lit it without asking her permission, blowing smoke agreeably into his own air, in his own drawing-room, looking about him at his many splendid possessions, not least of all, the woman who sat on the sofa.

He smiled when she told him that if he did not remove himself from her home and her life within the next thirty seconds she would call her men-servants and have him flung into the driveway. He was still smiling as she reached for the bell and even when she told the butler, smoothly, to bring Dick and Jack and Robert for Mr Atherton was leaving and seemed in need of assistance in finding the front door.

356

He was not smiling as he flogged his bay down the gravelled driveway towards the gate.

# 24

'You're ter go up ter't "Five Pigeons" but not until after dark, Mr Greenwood,' the urchin said, grinning amiably despite the temperature which was several degrees below freezing, the rag or two he wore for modesty's sake, and his bare, chilblained feet.

'What for, lad?'

'Nay, I dunno. Lady said it were urgent and you was ter tell no one.'

'What lady?' but could there be any other 'lady' up there on the bleak and windswept moorland except Abby Hobson, two years older now but every bit as bounteous and blooming as she had been when she had drawn him into the comfort and release of her body when he had needed it. Not that her favours were in any way directed at him these days, though he dared say they might be if he was to ask. She was not a woman to live the life of a nun though she must be approaching forty and would be taking what she needed, giving what was needed, good-natured and uncomplicated, both in her sexual nature and appetite, and her feminine wisdom.

'I dunno. She gimme sixpence an' said you'd do't same.'

'Don't go, Joss. I don't like it. What's that woman up at the inn want wi' you. There's all sorts go there, thieves and vagabonds, tinkers and wanderin' vagrants . . .'

'Now mother, there's no such folk drink at Abby Hobson's place for she'd not allow it.'

He smiled to himself as he remembered her, openhearted and generous with the occasional free jug of ale to a man

357

who had not two halfpennies to rub together in his trouser pocket but who had come, nevertheless, to listen to the hope, the optimism, the despair, the anger of others like him in the fight for a decent life. Militant radicals. Men like himself who put heart in them. A meeting place then for those who would, had it not been illegal, have formed a trade union, and Abby had allowed it, as many publicans did for were they not of the working class themselves? But thieves and vagabonds, tinkers and wandering vagrants, indeed any man Abby did not like the look of would be shown the door for she'd have no 'riff-raff' in her place.

'Happen there's some trouble. The Onwardsmen would meet there and if they wanted me in on it what better way than to put the name of Abby Hobson on the boy's lips. They could hardly send a message to say *they* wanted to see me, could they? If the lad was questioned and mentioned *her* name they would only smile and take me for one of her . . .'

'Joss! There's no need for talk like that, not in front of your wife.'

They both turned to look at Mercy Greenwood who sat in the chimney corner playing with a marmalade kitten, holding it to her breast, then to her cheek, crooning a little song, her eyes shining in delight, her smooth cheek rosy in the firelight. She looked exactly like some small girl who has been given a gift and cannot express her joy in it. The kitten jumped suddenly from her lap, its sharp claws catching the threads of her skirt, then skittered sideways as she bent to retrieve it.

'Naughty kitten. You mustn't do that or you'll hurt yersen,' she laughed and held the struggling animal to her in a passion of love.

Joss and Martha sighed simultaneously as their eyes met. Not in front of Mercy, she had said, just as though his wife would know what he meant, should he have told her, that once Abby Hobson had been for a short while, his lover.

'I was only implying that to give the child such a message was . . .'

358

'I know, lad,' and his mother sighed again for really it was almost more than she could bear at times, this creeping about after dark, the mysterious callers her son had and journeys he made to God only knew where. She had hoped after his spell in prison that it might, with his grand new job of journalist, all end and she could sleep snug in her bed knowing all her family were safe where they should be, snug in *theirs* but it seemed her hope was forlorn.

'Give the lad a bite, mother . . .' he turned to the boy who had edged closer to the warmth of the fire and the fascination of the leaping kitten, ' . . . see, here's another sixpence.'

He stepped out across the moor, rough and pitted with rabbit holes into which he might stumble, scattered with rocks on which he might turn his ankle and the icy, moorland streams hidden in the coarse frosted grass which, if he did not move warily would soak him to the knees freezing his boots to his feet and his trousers to his calves.

There was a pallid moon moving in and out of a thin veil of cloud but he could still scarcely see his hand before his face. He walked quickly for, despite his protestation to the contrary to his mother, there *were* beggars and ne'er-do-wells wandering these hills and possibly special constables sworn in to capture those impudent working class men, his own Onwardsmen, who had the ridiculous notion that they were as good as any other man and drilled up here on every moonlit night, forming themselves into an army to fight for it!

He felt a strange sense of urgency, a prickling, crawling sensation at his back and once or twice he looked over his shoulder as though he was being followed, smiling as he did so at his own fancifulness.

The wind got up and he shivered. It was January and as cold as charity up here. There would be snow before the night was out, he told himself as he breasted the brow of a hill and began to descend into a hollow at its foot. There were high, natural stone walls about it, thrown there by

359

the elements and as he reached the bottom the wind parted the clouds, the moon shone brightly and in that moment, a brief moment before the darkness covered them again, he saw them.

Six of them. Big, huge shouldered men, men probably from one of the 'navvy' camps which surrounded each town and sprawled across open countryside where the railway tracks were to run. Men used to manual labour, wielding picks and shovels, with calloused hands and fists, thick, muscled legs. Troublemakers for the most part who would kill or maim, whichever was asked of them, for the price of a jug of ale.

The moon came sliding out of the cloud again and stayed there, hanging in the purple-blue sky, illuminating the moorland and standing some way to the left, his back against a tall rock, indolent, a gentleman smoking a gentleman's cigar, was a man Joss had seen several times in the vicinity of Chapman's mills. An arrogant man with a haughty lift to his head, the hair on it shining a pure silver in the moonlight, his well-bred countenance smiling a little as the six men began to close in on their prey.

'Take him,' he said casually, drawing again on his cigar, settling himself comfortably to watch just as though he was a spectator at a boxing ring where bare knuckle prize fighting was to take place.

Joss knew he must get his back against his own rock. Some protection at least, as the men began to circle him slowly, their eyes gleaming, slit-like in their anticipation of the blood they would spill and the bones they would crack. He felt the stone at his back and his last clear image as he went down was of Kit Chapman's face.

There were too many of them, of course, for as he turned to one or two, the other four or five came at him from his blind side. The fist which crashed against his temple was as big as the hooves of a cart-horse. There was nothing to be done but try to protect his vital parts, his chest, his eyes and his brain, to curl up into the position in which he had come from his mother's womb and hope to God they did not mean to kill him for if they did there was little he could do to prevent it.

There was nothing, once he was down for them to get their fists to so they used their boots instead, not hastily or even with any passion, but in a leisurely fashion which said they knew they would not be disturbed, systematically laying their steel-tipped toe caps from one end of his body to the other until he knew, as his mind slipped away he must look like nothing less than a bundle of bleeding rags. His ribs had gone for his own breath was agony as it scraped in and out of his tortured lungs and the last thing he heard was the well-bred voice of the lounging gentleman.

'Leave him now, lads. That will do. I will pay you . . .'

She was at dinner when the message was put into her hand. It was brought in on a silver salver, a scrap of paper which looked as though it might have passed through several hands before it reached hers.

'This was delivered a few minutes ago, Miss Katherine.' Winters' tone was haughty and not at all pleased for he was not accustomed to having such things thrust at him at the *front* door, mind, by ruffians like the one who had delivered it.

'What is it, Winters?' She put down her wine glass aware that her mother had raised a wisp of scented lace to her nose as though the grubby piece of folded paper was sure to carry some dreadful disease.

'Indeed I could not say, Miss Katherine, but the . . . man who handed it to me was most . . . definite that you should have it at once. Quite . . . offensive, he was, even threatening.'

'Threatening, Winters? Good heavens . . .' and she was smiling as she read what Harry Atherton had written. The blood drained away from her face quite dramatically and Winters told Mrs Batty later that he thought she had been about to faint, indeed he did, and as for Mrs Chapman, well, she began to utter small cries of fear and had it not been for Dorcas, a sensible girl, thank God, would have fallen herself into her bowl of soup.

She was out of the room and up the stairs, the note still clutched in her hand and all the while she was ripping away her lovely evening gown and replacing it with the sensible woollen dress – no petticoats for they would weigh her down – her walking boots and a black, fur lined cloak with a hood against the splinters of snow which were already beginning to fling themselves at the window, she did not once let go of it. It was her link to Joss, one which she dare not break nor cast aside for if she should, might she not lose her sense of direction, the sure instinct which would take her to the exact spot described in it.

No carriage then for the track was narrow, hard and stony and the coachman, a sensible man with concern for his horses, she thought, even more than for his mistress, would probably refuse anyway. She would walk it, run it, fly the distance if she only could, for if she did not get to him in time the cold would finish him off should his injuries have not already done so.

'He has taken the beating for you though I am sure you will suffer just as painfully,' the note said. Dear God, let him live . . . and she had laughed at him, thinking he could not harm her, that there was nothing she cared about that he could destroy. Let him spread his rumours and gossip about Kit Chapman and Joss Greenwood, whisper in the ears of her business associates of her love for the son of a weaver, a convicted felon, a troublemaker, what did she care for none of them dare cut themselves off from her. She was too strong, too wealthy, too influential for him to do her harm. So he had found another way to punish her for what she had done to *him*.

Dear God, let him live, she prayed as she let the dogs out of the stable for even she dare not go up alone on to that sinister night-time moorland which must surely contain in every hole and ditch hungry men who would slit her throat for the boots on her feet. The dogs sensed her fear and clung about her skirts, silent and menacing, protecting her, their attitude saying, from anything which might leap at them from the shadows and which they would quickly dispose of.

It was two hours before she found him, exactly where the note said he would be. A place, if she had not known the moors as well, possibly better than the garden surrounding her own home, she would never have come across. God knows how long he had been there and for an agonised moment she thought he was dead. She could see the congealed and frozen blood on his mauled face, so dark with bruises and whatever other injuries he had received it was difficult to distinguish against the black and frozen ground on which he lay curled. The snow, whipping in hard pellets about her crouching figure had not yet got a hold but she knew that if she did not get him moving in the next few minutes he would die.

'Come alone,' the note had said, 'or the next time it will be worse . . .' *The next time* . . . Oh dear God . . . Dear God, let him live . . .

'Joss, get up, Joss,' she snarled in his ear since this was not the time for patience and sympathy.

He was scarcely conscious and did not know her, or care to be bothered in any case.

'Get up, damn you,' and she pulled violently at his arm, glad in every part of her frenzied mind of his terrible scream.

He began to moan, moving feebly, begging her to let him alone, to let him lie still since the agony was too great to be borne.

'You will have to get up because if you don't you will die, Joss Greenwood. They will be here soon, the men who roam the hills looking for anything that will give them a square meal and a jug of ale. They will have heard you, or sensed you, as animals do the wounding of one of their own kind and they will gather to take their share of the kill. They will not need to choke you to death for the cold will have finished you off. Get up, damn you or I swear I will leave you to them.'

'Leave me then,' she thought she heard him say and again

she tore at his arm, hearing the awful sound of bone grating on bone and the shriek of his pain carved her to her own bone but she would not let him be.

'Get on your feet, you coward. Stand up for I cannot carry you, nor, if I had the strength for it, would I. Come on, Joss Greenwood. They told me you were a leader of men. *You* told me you were a leader of men but I can see no sign of it now since it seems you are prepared to lie here and die like a rabbit in a trap.'

'Kit . . . for God's sake . . . I cannot . . .' it sounded like, but his mouth was torn and a strip of flesh was frozen to his bloodied lips.

'Give me your good arm, dammit.'

'I . . . cannot move . . .' and at her back one of the dogs began to snarl at something, his hackles raised, his head flat, his eyes looking into the darkness which contained a scent, or a movement which he did not like. It might be no more than a moorland animal hunting its prey but it frightened her and her fright gave her strength.

'I don't give a damn how much it hurts you, Joss Greenwood,' she hissed through clenched teeth, '*You will get on your feet.*'

It took ten long minutes to half-lift, half-lever him on to the waist high rock at his back, his own efforts a little stronger now. She took off her warm, fur-lined cloak and wrapped it about his shivering, groaning body, careless of the blood which his movements had started flowing again, feeling its warmth soak into her bodice and drip on to her shaking hands.

'Come on, stand up. You're a hero, you are, to all those men who follow you so let's see your bravery. Stand up. Put your good arm about my shoulder and one step in front of the other. Joby . . . Blaze, to me . . . that's right . . . careful, lean on me . . .' which she really had no need to tell him to do for he was like some man the worse for drink, his weight dragging her down, straining her muscles to the point of agony.

'Let . . . me . . . rest . . .'

'No, keep going, damn you . . .' since she knew that if she put him down she would never get him up again.

'Kit . . . please . . .'

'No . . .' and it seemed to occur to neither of them to wonder, he that she should be there at all; she that she had not hesitated to come.

The path was no path at all, merely the most direct route to Edgeclough, and she took it, her instinct telling her that that was where help would be. She dragged him on to it, that unsteady, hole-riddled, rock-strewn path, making no effort to go slow and steady, no effort to spare him pain since she was shivering violently now without her cloak. *She* was the crutch on which they both depended. *She* was the eyes to lead them to safety and if she fell by the wayside they would *both* go down.

On and on and on. Hours of it, days of it, weeks, and their breath, hers as well as his, rasped, burning excrutiatingly in their throats.

'I . . . can't . . .'

'You . . . can . . . and you . . . bloody well . . . will . . .'

A rock turned beneath her foot and for a despairing second she knew she was about to fall but somehow, though it tore her arm and wrenched a moan of pure and exquisite agony from Joss, she righted herself.

And then there were lights. Just a pinprick or two in the dark fabric of the night. The smell of peat smoke and the drift of pale grey against the blackness, coming from a chimney, a baby crying behind some cottage door and they were at Martha Greenwood's garden gate.

They took him from her, his mother's cries echoing about the cottage kitchen, his sister giving her a look of pure, venomous hatred, knowing somehow that this was to do with *her*. There were half a dozen people, it seemed and an urgent voice telling Charlie to ' . . . keep Mercy upstairs, for God's sake lad, or she'd go out of her mind if she sees this . . .' *And a pregnant woman might miscarry with the shock of it!*

Another, a woman, barked out orders to run and fetch

this, or that, to put that there and hold that here, and to be careful with that hot water, for God's sake and to watch his arm since it looked broken to her.

They did not take him up the stairs to the loom-shop where, apparently, she gathered from the garbled conversation, he slept, since the task was beyond them all but brought down some sort of a truckle bed and without another glance in her direction, stripped him naked, cutting away most of his garments, and laid him on it. His mother wept silently over his white body which, for the most part, was now red and black with bruises.

She stood like some frozen statue, nailed to the door through which they had half-dragged, half-carried him and watched while the woman – dear God, it was the one she had spoken to . . . when was it? . . . who had told her the Greenwoods had left Edgeclough – bathed and stitched him together, cleansed and soothed with some liniment almost every inch of his mangled body, strapped his arm and his chest so tightly she heard him curse her and finally when it was done, kiss him soundly on the cheek.

'I reckon thee'll 'ave a right shiner in't mornin', Joss Greenwood,' she told him fondly, 'but thee'll live.'

'No thanks to you, Sarah Pickering,' he whispered faintly. 'I feel a bloody sight worse than before you got your hands on me.'

'Who did it, lad?' They hung about him; the woman called Sarah, his sister, his mother and his brother and with Mercy off to sleep again, Joss said breathlessly, 'Some gang of footpads, I reckon, who fancied having the gold rings off my fingers.'

'But what of the message from Abby Hobson?'

'I never got to find out.' His voice was fainter now and his glance which had caught hers, slipped away but not before it had told her that this was between the two of them and not to be spoken of now.

'Abby Hobson? What would she want with our Joss?' Jenny Greenwood reared up from the protective position she had taken up beside her brother but the older woman,

366

Sarah, was spooning some liquid into Joss's torn mouth and indicated vigorously that they were all to step back from her patient.

'Let 'im rest, Jenny. 'e can answer all yer questions tomorrow. 'e'll sleep now wi' this I'm givin' 'im, 'appen for twenty-four hours, so leave 'im be an' get to your beds. The mill gates'll be open in a few hours . . .'

It was as though the words reminded them that the owner of those very mill gates was still standing where they had left her at the cottage door. She was not important. It was because of her, and others like her that Joss Greenwood was lying as he was, mauled almost to death by men who surely must have something to do with opposing the very things *he* fought for, since they had not believed the statement about the footpads for a minute. He had been savagely beaten by men who knew him since *someone* had sent the false message to get him up on the moor in the dead of night and *she* was involved for how else had she known of it and brought him home?

But she *had* brought him home and would you look at the state of her. They did, now that their Joss had been seen to. She was wet through to her undergarments, which would be of the very finest there was no doubt of that, and all over the front of her, down her bodice and dark grey skirt were brown stains which could only be Joss's blood for she herself was not injured. Her long hair had come down and was snarled in a wet and filthy tangle about the chalk white blankness of her face and she shivered so violently the door at her back rattled in its frame.

'Sweet God, get 'er t't fire before she teks a fever. See, Jenny, run up an' get some blankets . . .'

'Not me, for it's her fault our Joss is . . .'

'Don't answer me back, Jenny Greenwood.' Sarah Pickering's voice was like thunder in the small room and already Martha had her arm about Kit's unresisting shoulders, leading her to the warmth of the fire. 'Fetch me them blankets or I'll fetch you a backhander you'll not forget in a hurry.'

367

Charlie was sent to bed since he had to be up at four, they said, and he could do no good hanging about their Joss who was fast asleep anyway under the influence of the herb potion Sarah had given him, and with Jenny holding a blanket to the fire to warm, she was stripped as unceremoniously as Joss, placed in the rocking-chair without words since they'd none to give her, only the impersonal benevolence they would give any hurt creature which happened by their door. Hot tea was poured down her throat and her flesh rubbed until it was raw but the blood flowed again beneath her skin, tingling until she could have cried out with the pain of it.

'Will you tell us about it, lass?' Sarah said at last, more forthright than Martha, more forgiving than Jenny who could not even bring herself to look at this woman she hated above all others.

'No.' It was only a whisper in her throat but they heard it.

'What were you doin' up theer at this time o' night? Not walkin' them savage beasts beyond yon door, I'll be bound.'

'I had a . . . message . . .'

'Who from?'

'I cannot say.'

'Come on, lass, we weren't born yesterday. Why should someone knock the livin' daylights out o' Joss Greenwood and then send for Katherine Chapman to carry 'im 'ome? You an' Joss are on opposite sides in this bloody war.'

She stood up suddenly, her manner imperious, despite the tangle of her hair and the grey blanket which she held close about her, or perhaps because of it for it was like a Queen's mantle.

'One wonders why anyone bothers to try and help you people,' she said, her voice high-toned and disdainful, 'if this is the thanks one receives. Really it is beyond belief. I drag that man miles over the moor at great inconvenience to myself and instead of a bit of decent gratitude that he has been returned to you in a *curable* condition, perhaps a word of thanks which would not be out of the way, I am

368

cross-examined on my reasons, not only for doing it but for being on the moor myself. Perhaps I was there to meet a lover.' Her eyes flashed blue sparks and even Jenny Greenwood was impressed into silence. 'Or perhaps I was not but whatever it was it has nothing to do with you. I may have been walking my dogs, or myself, or I may not, but whatever the reason for my being there be thankful I was for it saved the life of . . . of the man on that bed. I was there. I came upon your son, madam . . .' this to Martha, '. . . and I brought him home as I would *any* wounded creature I found. That, I'm afraid, will have to satisfy you. Now, if I might have my things I will be on my way. No . . .' this to Sarah, ' . . . I do not need an escort since I have two outside. It would take a brave man, or a very foolish one, to tackle them.'

'They say t'best defence is ter strike first,' Sarah murmured when she had gone.

It was three weeks later – a Sunday and there had been a fresh fall of snow during the night making walking difficult but she managed to get as far as Friars Mere. The dogs had floundered beside her, thrusting their heavy black bodies through a foot of snow, blundering occasionally into a deeper drift, their expressions comical in their amazement and her laughter was the only sound in the vast, white emptiness. She wore trousers beneath her skirt, the fullness of it tucked up into her waistband and though her boots were often up to their tops in the soft and powdery snow she was exhilarated, feeling easier and less prone to the bouts of anxiety with which she had been harried since the night of Joss's beating. She had longed to go down to the spinning room and accost his sister, beg to be told how he was a dozen times each day. To call up her dogs and stride out to Edgeclough, to hammer on his mother's door and beg to see him, to be reassured that he was not permanently damaged, that he was healing, that he was not blind, or crippled but she knew she must not. He was with his family, his wife and she must leave him there now. She had done what she had to three weeks ago for what had happened to him had been *her* fault. Now she must continue in the only way she could for him, for his wife and unborn child and leave him to get on with his life, as she must get on with hers.

The sun shone on the rolling beauty of the white hills, criss-crossed with the tops of crumbling dry-stone walls and in between each stone the snow had blown, making patterns of crystal mosaic. There were shadows cast by the skeleton trees and scattered rocks, blue-smudged, from the paleness of a bird's egg to the deep purple-blue of an amethyst, and the air was so clear and sharp it went to her head like champagne.

She saw him coming up the snow covered track, trudging slowly, his head down, his arm bound tightly beneath his jacket, one sleeve of which dangled empty. His breath curled about his dark head and she could hear it quite clearly in the still air as it moved in and out of his lungs. He was nearly half a mile away and had not seen her but she knew, unamazed by it, as she knew all his thoughts as though they were her own, that he was on his way to Greenacres to see her.

'Joss.' Her voice lifted his head. 'Wait there, I'm coming,' and the snow no longer impeded her as she flew across it, leaping and laughing, her heart singing, her sad intentions all forgotten in the joy of seeing him.

He stopped and waited for her and she could see in his face the effort it had taken for him to walk the two miles from Edgeclough across the wilderness of the snow covered moorland. His still swollen eyes were ringed with deep purple bruises and though the contusions were fading and almost healed his face was pallid with the look of a man only recently risen from his bed.

Her joy brought forth his own, reluctantly.

'I know. I look as though I have just done a dozen rounds in the boxing ring, and lost the bout.' He tried to grin.

'How are you?'

'Healing.'

'Your arm . . . ?'

'Will be as good as new, Sarah tells me, and who am I to argue with *her*. Fortunately it is not the one I use for writing.'

'I'm glad.'

'I had to see you,' he said simply.

Could she turn from him as her betrayed heart had told her, weeks ago, that she should, when they faced each other like this, the simplicity and the truth of their love shining between them. She sighed sadly, knowing she was tied to this man and his destiny with bonds which might be invisible but were stronger than the binding of the rocks to the ground on which they stood. But he had not come to smile and gaze at her, as he was doing, she knew that, but for another reason.

'I would have died but for you.'

'I can't tell you, Joss,' she said, knowing what he would say next.

'You cannot expect me to let this pass, Kit. He nearly killed me and I want to know why.'

'You . . . saw him?'

'Oh yes, and saw him smile before I went down.'

'Dear God!'

'Why, Kit?'

'Because of me, Joss. Because I sent him away. He swore then he would make me suffer for it and, having learned somehow about you and me, he did it in the surest way he knew.'

'I cannot let it go, you know I cannot. I am not fit yet but when I am . . .'

'No, Joss.'

'No man does this to me, Kit Chapman. No man, least of all your . . .'

'Please, you know . . . I was forced into it by my father. The moment I was able I told him I wouldn't marry him. He made threats but I laughed at him . . .'

'Where does he live?'

'Let it go, Joss, for God's sake . . .'

'*Let it go!* He damn near crippled me and you tell me to let it go.'

'I know it can't be easy for you simply to ignore it. To pretend it didn't happen, or at least to try, but I will not let it continue . . .'

'*You* won't let it continue.'

'No.'

'Where does he live? If you don't tell me I'll find out somehow.'

'His family is powerful and if you were to harm him they . . .'

'It's all right for *him* almost to kill a man from the lower orders, is that it, but not for that man to seek justice?'

'Joss, he would deny it and he would be believed. They would ask themselves why a man of his . . . standing should bother himself with a . . .'

'With a man of *mine*, is that it?'

They were both breathing hard and she could see the pain it caused him, the simple act of drawing the cold air into lungs which might have been damaged. But she could not tell him. Would not, for if he was to go to Atherton Hall and confront Harry Atherton, which was probably what Harry hoped for, he would arrange it somehow for Joss to spend the rest of his life in gaol.

She turned away from him, her face quite expressionless for he must not see how much it cost her.

'I cannot tell you where he lives, Joss, and I never will. If you wish to do yourself further damage then you must do it without my help. And now, do you not think it wise for you to return to your wife and . . . She will be worried about you. Joby, Blaze . . . to me.'

And with the tears which he did not see, freezing on her pale cheeks, she walked away from him.

# 25

Jenny Greenwood had worked until the day her son was born, not caring very much if she harmed him, or herself, at her old machine in Chapman's spinning mill. Surprisingly, when she had asked at the gate for work, having been told by Isaac Pickering that they were 'taking-on', a fortnight after they had returned to Edgeclough, she was told that there was and that if she knew of someone who could 'doff' there was a position vacant in the carding room. A strong boy was looked for, one who was not afraid of hard work, which had amused her for where in the mill was hard work not done? They were 'thronged' at the moment, run off their feet with work, she was told, so the hours would be five in the morning until nine at night, but later, when the work load eased he would work only until seven in the evening. Did she know of anyone who would suit?

Of course she did, surprised that anyone with the name of Greenwood should be considered fit persons to work in the Chapman spinning room for the Greenwoods, after the Chapmans, were perhaps the best known family in the district. Everyone had heard of Joss Greenwood who had led the men of the Penfold Valley in their fight for reform. It was known that his family had, when her father died, been victimised by Miss Katherine Chapman; that they had been evicted from a company cottage and dismissed from her mills but it seemed the persecution was over since it had been put about among the managers and overlookers that should any of them require employment it was to be given to them.

Charlie and Jenny had walked each day from Edgeclough to Crossfold, a good breakfast of oats and milk inside them, their 'baggin' of cold tea, bacon and wheaten bread to sustain them during the day. Charlie, as a doffer was employed to stop the spinning frames and take the 'flyers' off, remove the full bobbins and carry them to the roller, replace the full bobbins with empty ones and set the frame in motion again.

There were a great many frames, all moving so quickly it took dozens of children to keep them in motion and the overlooker's strap made of black leather with six separate thongs, each eighteen inches long and heavy enough to break a child's arm, was very much in evidence. The dust was like a cloud, settling on machines and 'hands' alike, drifting insidiously beneath shirt-collars and waistbands and into tender young ears, irritating the skin and inflaming the eyes, clogging the lungs so that every man, woman and child coughed continuously. The bobbins were tipped into baskets which were dragged the length of the room by the smaller children, a basket which stood taller than a table, large, and when full of bobbins, exceedingly heavy. Many of the children pulled their soft bones out of place, shoulder bones over which their ribs grew until they were so deformed they were forced to adapt strips of canvas to tie about their bodies in the form of a corset in order to stand upright.

But Charlie, despite this, knew he was one of the lucky ones. As he and Jenny walked home together in the black pitch of the winter night he knew he went to a warm kitchen, a soothing bath before the fire if he wanted it, a secret kiss from his mother, a bowl of hot broth with wheaten bread and a restful sleep of six or seven hours in his own clean, warm bed before he need rise again the next morning. He had Jenny to walk beside, to listen to his dreams of working with Joss one day; to get out of the mill before the brutalising effect of the work and his environment crippled him and his young mind. He did not use words such as these, naturally, for his mind was that of a

374

boy, immature and confused, distressed by what he saw and was forced to accept. He knew that their Jenny carried some man's baby, that she was unmarried, not that anyone cared, particularly among the de-humanised men and women with whom he worked. She would work for as long as she was able and again after the child was born, he supposed but it was up to him to bring home what he could – at the moment one and sixpence a week – to feed his mother and Daisy. Joss earned money, he had been told, with the articles he wrote for *The Republican* newspaper and the *Weekly Political Register* but Joss had Mercy, who was not fit to be let out alone, to support.

Jenny's son was born on the day the Power-Loom Riots began. He was a fine healthy boy with his father's fair hair but thick and curling like her own. His eyes, right from the start, were a deep and melting brown and though she had carried him for nine months cursing the day he was conceived, she loved him from the moment her mother put him in her arms.

'A fine lad, our Jenny,' Martha said softly, hesitantly, while in the background Sarah watched closely as she cleared away the detritus of childbirth. The two women were well aware that Jenny had not wanted this child and if she were to reject him now what would become of the bawling scrap of humanity?

It took no more than a trembling, anxious sigh from her mother's throat and the feel of her newly washed son in her arms and the bond was formed between Lucas and Jenny Greenwood. She forgot the days of disillusioned anger, the months of hard and grinding labour when her back had seemed about to break and her spirit weaken. The nights of silent weeping for something she had lost and which was now miraculously replaced, whole and sweet in the form of her child. He cried loudly and when his demanding lips closed over her nipple and silence spread itself about the room, the voices downstairs could clearly be heard. Jenny was engrossed and deaf to what was being said but Martha and Sarah exchanged glances and when Sarah

375

nodded to some unspoken question from Martha, her mother slipped down the stairs and was just in time to hear the words of the lad sent with the message.

There was trouble in Bolton, it seemed, where, as a result of the slump in the cotton trade, foretold by Barker Chapman a few days before he died, several manufacturers had cut their weavers wages by fifteen per cent. The weavers, men whose patience was finally at an end, without waiting for their leaders, one of whom was Joss Greenwood, had begun what was later to be called 'the most controlled riot in history'.

Their targets were the new power-looms which were taking their livelihood from them.

Mr Greenwood was to get to Blackburn as quickly as he could, the excited lad announced, for the hand-loom weavers, some twenty thousand of them, had assembled there. 'They've got pikes, Mr Greenwood and firearms too, I were told to tell thi', some with gret 'ammers an' every-one's got a weapon o' some sort. They mean business this time, sir. Every power-loom in't valley's ter go, they say. They'll not touch t'spinning' frames 'cos if t'manufacturer spins 'is yarn an' 'e's no looms ter weave it on e'll 'ave no choice but ter send it to us. It meks sense, don't it, Mr Greenwood?'

The lad, no more than thirteen or so, hopped from one foot to the other, eager, one supposed, to be off to march with all the other young boys, flushed with the idea that at last they were to be about something worthwhile instead of sitting on their arses talking about it.

'Right lad,' Joss told him quietly. 'Off you go then.'

'Are thi not ter come then, Mr Greenwood?' the boy asked, disappointed, for it would have been grand to march into Blackburn by the side of one of their leaders.

'I'll be along presently,' Joss told him and the lad turned away, quite bewildered, not only by Mr Greenwood's less than fervent acceptance of his message regarding the upris-ing since, if he didn't look sharp and do something it would all be over before he even got there, but by the sad and weary look of the old woman who had crept down the stairs to join them.

When he had gone Martha looked bleakly at her son.

'So it's to begin again, lad?' she said tiredly.

'It seems so, mother.'

'Will it never end?' Her voice was despairing. For over thirty years she had lived with it, first the father, then the son, two sons for there was no doubt Charlie would follow his brother as soon as he was old enough.

'One day it must.'

'I wonder if I'll ever see it, my son?'

'Perhaps not, but your grandson will.'

Though he and Isaac, and the other Onwardsmen they picked up on the way, marched through the night the great multitude of men had already destroyed almost every power-loom in the weaving-sheds of south Lancashire. The weavers had marched in lines of four abreast, a great long trailing procession of men and boys, and some women, singing one of the popular ballads of the day. 'The Hand-loom Weavers Lament' which told of their poverty, of having nothing to eat, nor clothes to put on their back; of their broken clogs, ending in the downfall of the tyrants of England whose race would soon be run.

Only the power-looms were destroyed that day, the spinning machines left untouched. Nothing was stolen, so controlled were the men and when one over-enthusiastic lad was seen to remove a strap from the gear he was told firmly by the rest of his group that he was to put it back for they had not come here to plunder.

They were striding out across Rake Head towards Higher Mist on the way to Burnley when Joss caught up with them and their joy knew no bounds for though their success had gone to their heads like the finest French brandy, he was their leader, their spokesman, the man who had fought on their side for nearly six years and how much more satisfying it would be to have him with them. When it was done with, he would be able to tell the rest of the country about it in the grand newspaper he wrote in, and then everyone would know of it and how the men of Lancashire had stood up for their rights against the oppression of the masters. They would all be working at their own hand-looms again by the end of the week, they told one another as they marched with light step, fed a constant stream of the yarn the mill-owners would spin but would be unable to weave and their troubles would be over.

They cheered and clapped him on the back as Joss strode past them, making for the head of the column and the men at its front. It took half a mile to bring it to a halt, just near the 'Towneley Arms' inn and those with a penny in their pockets drank the landlord's ale until it ran out.

The man in charge of the column, or so he said, had a strange likeness to Joss. About his age, he was, with a great thatch of dark hair and sliding grey eyes. He was thin, awkward, with elbows which seemed about to break out of his jacket sleeves and two inches of wrist showing beneath. But he was good-humoured and ready to pass over his command to Joss.

'We've bin waitin' on thi, lad,' he said genially, leaning against the wall which surrounded the inn and those about him nodded in agreement. 'We can tek no more, Joss, not after . . .'

'Who are you?' Joss asked quietly.

'Name's Ted Earnshaw. I bin wi' you from't start but we've . . .'

'I don't know you.'

'I reckon yer don't know three-quarters o't lads 'ere today.' Ted Earnshaw looked back to the long, sprawling column of men, the end of which could not be seen on the track as it dipped beyond the brow of the hill. 'Yer away a lot now, Joss and them what followed yer reckoned yer'd fergotten 'em.'

'And you're saying they'll follow you instead?'

'Nay lad, I'm not out ter tek your place. All I'm sayin' is that wi' you so busy wi' yer grand job on't newspaper an't like, 'appen they're glad to 'ave someone give 'em a word or two o' advice now an' agen. Tell 'em what ter do, like.'

378

'And perhaps lead them into doing something foolish. Something that'll bring our cause into disrepute . . .'

'Nay, give ower, Joss. I were only tryin' ter . . .'

' . . . like waylaying the coach of an important man. Like committing a crime which can do none of us any good. In fact doing so much harm that the names of these men, the Onwardsmen, is spoken of with contempt and outrage.'

'I don't know what yer on about, Joss Greenwood.' Ted Earnshaw straightened up his spiky body, ready to bristle up to Joss in a pose of injured resentment. His pale face had gone even paler and his eyes had a habit of slipping away, then back again to Joss's, never still for a moment.

'I think you do, Ted Earnshaw, and when this . . . this disturbance is done with and the men dispersed, you and me will have something to say to each other. It seems you've a mind to take over my role in this fight we've started and that you'll go to any extreme to get what you want, including blackening my name. But do you and me want the same thing for these men, tell me that? Are you doing this for them or have you some other motive? There is always a troublemaker in every gathering. Men who love violence for its own sake. Men who will inflame a crowd to do something it really has no stomach for, then stand back to watch as heads are broken and buildings burn. I have it in my mind to ask if you are such a man, Ted Earnshaw. That's what I'd like to know and I mean to have the answer. The name of the man who killed Barker Chapman would interest me, or the one who put him up to it, but this isn't the time, nor the place.'

The men who stood about, crowding in closer in an attempt to hear what Ted Earnshaw and Joss Greenwood appeared to be arguing about, looked at each other in stupified silence as the name of Barker Chapman was spoken. One or two nodded, thinking they knew the reason for it since the dead mill-owner had always fought their cause. They turned to speak to those behind and like a darting swallow, the words winged back to those in the column, garbled and senseless, that Joss and Ted were

379

discussing the wickedness of Barker Chapman, though why they should do so at this particular moment was a mystery.

'These men must be turned back,' Joss said, his eyes like flint as they held Ted Earnshaw's.

'They'll not be stopped now, not by thee nor anyone.' Ted Earnshaw's eyes gleamed, strangely pleased, and daring Joss to deny what he said.

'I can try. This isn't the way to go about it. The newspapers will condemn them for it, radical and conservative alike and it will do our cause no good.'

'Mebbe, but we've bin tipped ower th'edge wi' this last cut in wages and these lads are bound on their course. Destroy't power-looms an' we'll get us liveli'ood back.'

'You know that's not the way, not any more. The masters'll only fetch in new ones. You can't stop progress, you know that.'

He turned his back on Ted Earnshaw and began to speak. Great was his magnetism, a quiet thing now but all the more impressive for it. His eloquence was a glorious ribbon of words as he spoke and every man pressed about him in his shadow. They gathered, those who could get near, to listen and as his words reached them they began to hesitate for what he told them made sense and they trusted him. Almost he had them for they were not violent men, just hungry and desperate, exploited even beyond their forebearance and they were ready, if he could have had their attention a moment longer, to follow him back the way they had tramped, to wait again, to trust him to speak for them of the vote for every man, but Ted Earnshaw leaped up on to the wall which surrounded the inn.

'Lads, listen to me. We've come so far, don't let's turn back now. Think, think what we've done today and what it'll mean to us . . .'

'What's 'e sayin'?' The words went along the track from mouth to mouth, each man telling the man behind him that Ted Earnshaw was praising them for how well they had done today and telling them how they would do better tomorrow.

'Is Joss with us?' they asked, for so great were their numbers no more than a hundred or so had heard him.

'Must be. He's standin' at the lead with Ted,' and so they picked up their pikes and their hatchets, their hammers and iron bars, like boys off to a parade, stamping their feet in unison, beginning to move forward in their march to victory and as Joss ran along the line begging them to re-consider they cheered him, thinking he was rallying them on.

'It's no good, lad, they're set on it,' Isaac said to him. 'You'd best fall in an' when we get to Burnley p'raps yer can make 'em see sense.'

So Joss Greenwood 'fell in' with the men who loved him and would, if they had but known it was his intention, turn about and follow him back to Crossfold and Edgeclough and the dozens of towns and villages from which they had come.

The crowds grew bigger as they approached Burnley, thousands and thousands of men and in the centre of it Joss Greenwood was like one droplet in a bucket of water, hemmed in by the men who, gathering about him, thought he was part of it. There was a rumour that troops of cavalry were in motion, being fetched from one place to another, that they had been stoned and that strangely, they had wielded only the sides of their swords and shot only above the heads of the crowds.

'They're on our side, lads,' one marcher chuckled and so it seemed for as they commenced their destruction of the power-looms in the weaving town of Burnley, though the cavalry troops were seen and heard shouting to the men to stop what they were doing, when they were ignored they did little to carry out their orders. Joss stood to one side, a silent despairing figure as doors were broken down and windows smashed and the men swarmed through the factories, leaving alone the singing frames on which the yarn was being spun, the yarn which next week, or the week after at the latest, they themselves would be weaving on their own hand-looms. Their great hammers flew through the air, shattering power-looms and when the foot soldiers arrived, just too late, the weavers escaped through windows on the far side of each building.

Joss tried again when the swelling sea of men came to rest on Dog Hill. He could see his own cottage below him and the straight line of cottages dropping down the fold of the slope which was Edgeclough. His mother was at the door with an arm about the shoulders of Daisy and Mercy and at every doorway and gate women and children gathered for never had they seen so many men in one place. They and Joss had been making their way steadily southward, going wherever a power-loom was used. They were tired and hungry for they had little to eat except what was given them, but the feverish excitement which had burned in them at the start had corroded into their hearts and souls, branding them with a need so great they were no longer men with a mission, but machines, like those they had sworn to destroy. They were quiet where once they had cheered and sung and whistled. They had been harried by soldiers, too few to make much difference and other men had stood in their way, come from the magistrates, it was said, to read the Riot Act but they had been brushed aside like so many quarrelling children.

Joss, exhaustion showing in the slump of his tall, fine body, in the deep lines which ran from his nose to his chin on either side of his mouth, in the frowning eyebrows above deep, sunken eyes, moved about the crowd, crouching to speak to a man, a group of men, to men who dozed or even dropped off to sleep as he begged them to go home.

'You've shown them now that you mean to take no more cuts in your wages. Stop now and go home before the soldiers begin arresting you . . . Oh, I know they can't take you all but they'll not let you go on, lads. You've destroyed hundreds of looms but they'll not let you get away with it . . .'

But Joss knew as he spoke that these men could not stop this clamour they had begun and could not be asked to stop it. They were beyond reason, beyond hope, probably beyond caring. They had begun with the enthusiasm which had believed that with the destruction of the hated power-looms they themselves could be restored miraculously to their former standards and if they could not achieve it, their expressions said they might as well die swiftly by the soldier's sword than by the slow process of starvation. They had contained, fed by the fine beliefs injected into them by their leaders, a brave assurance they would win this campaign but it had dribbled away, bit by forlorn bit as they had tramped, footsore, weary, starving through Blackburn, Burnley and half a dozen cotton towns along the way and now on to Crossfold where there would surely be soldiers waiting for them for property must be protected. The authorities were organised now, the first shock of suprise worn off and the magistrates were taking action. But they could not stop. Not now. They had begun it, the weavers of Lancashire and the movement had gathered speed until it could not be stopped.

'Are thee not wi' us then, Joss?' the men asked.

'Aye lads, every step of the way.'

'Chapman's next, then,' the cry went up and they marched shoulder to shoulder, like soldiers now, their hammers and pikes carried bravely as they had seen the military men do.

She was there at the gate. Kit Chapman. Joss was at the head of the column of men. He carried no weapon. He had broken no windows, no machines. He had destroyed nothing, but, as he had promised he had stood by his men and when she saw him her eyes narrowed for a moment, their message of despairing love extinguished to be replaced by the blazing defiance he knew so well. She held a pistol and the soldiers who flanked her on either side and behind her in the mill yard carried muskets.

Joss stopped and so did the men who marched with him for the sight of a woman, even the hated and feared Miss Chapman was something for which they had not allowed. Men, a man with a weapon, they would rush him without thought, without fear for they were beyond such consideration as death now, but this was different and it brought them to a halt.

'Good morning, Miss Chapman,' Joss's voice was polite. 'We would be obliged if you and your men would step aside. We mean you no harm.'

Her eyes flared into the snapping sheen of ice when the cold winter blue of the sky is reflected in it. Bright and angry flames of scarlet burned in her cheeks and she straightened her shoulders.

'You must kill me if you mean to get in here,' she said clearly so that even men far back in the line could hear her words.

Joss sighed. He was bone weary, desperate to have this over and done with. No one had been hurt. Not one person injured, mill-owners and manufacturers alike, standing aside, some of them in sympathy for the plight of the weavers, as their power-looms were destroyed. There would be consequences, to himself and to the other leaders, that much was certain but the men's determination was petering out and after this he knew he would surely be able to convince them that they had made their voices well and truly heard. This must be the last. It was as though destiny had brought Kit Chapman and himself together for this one last time, to destroy her mills as their love had been destroyed by the vast gulf which yawned between them. It was deep and wide, deepening and widening with every moment they stood, eyes and wills locked at her mill gate and for him to hesitate was foolish.

'Miss Chapman. It might be advisable if you let us through. My men are weary and want nothing more than to do what they came to do and go home. For your own sake call off your soldiers.'

'You must be mad if you think I will allow you to walk in here as you have done throughout Lancashire and break my machines.'

It was as though they were alone, the vast crowd at Joss's back, the soldiers at hers fading into a fine grey mist on the edge of their vision, blurred and silent and still, shades of

384

grey and red with no function but to wait patiently for the outcome of the conflict between this man and this woman. Whoever lost it would step aside, taking those who were with them, allowing the winner to do what must be done.

'You cannot stop us now.' Joss's voice, though quiet, was clear and the men about him lifted their weapons and shuffled their feet, ready to shoulder their way through this woman and these soldiers the moment Joss gave the word.

'I can try,' and he knew she would. If they trampled her into the ground she would not move before their onslaught. She would stand her ground, *her ground*, her head held bravely, her feet planted firmly on her bit of earth and not until she was under their feet would that proud and lovely face lose its challenging courage, would those brilliant eyes become dulled. She would, quite simply, die before she gave an inch of what was hers.

Her eyes glared into his, not wavering to look at those about him. This was a struggle, a clash of wills between just the two of them, a deadly state of war in which there was no one but Joss Greenwood and Kit Chapman. She was the most courageous, the most dangerous woman he had ever known and for a split second he saw what might have been between them if they had been friends and not enemies. The lovers they were meant to be. She was strong and wilful but her femininity was beyond question. She was dressed from head to foot in unrelieved black and yet she was glorious, the vivid colour of her face, the slipping darkness of her hair enhanced by the austerity of her mourning. He had never loved her more than at this moment, the moment in which, to protect her, he must humiliate her.

He moved slowly towards her, his step unhurried, his smile gentle. He kept his hands well away from his sides and though she lifted her weapon, pointing it at his chest, the soldiers did not move and neither did his men. They seemed to know that they really had nothing to do with what was happening here. It was between this man and this woman.

When the firearm was touching his chest he stopped, still smiling but his heart ached painfully for her. Her mouth worked savagely and her teeth showed like those of a cat which is cornered but in her eyes was the desolation of love which knows full well that it cannot kill, no matter with what loathing, the object of that love. Though she died of her hatred of him at that moment she was as incapable of pulling the trigger which would end his life as he was of turning the weapon on her.

At the last moment she made a token movement, her eyes dying a little, the pistol wavering, not towards him but away and when he put his arms about her it was as though she thanked him. She began to kick and scream and bite at his hands but he lifted her easily from her feet carrying her to one side beyond the gate post and behind the high wall of the factory.

'Righto lads,' he called out as he went and with a great cheer his men surged forward, bearing the unresisting military with them and within seconds the clang of the hammers on the power-looms rang out from the broken windows through which the younger men had chucked anything they could lay their hands on.

'Dear God . . . I hate you . . .' she whispered.

'I know . . . I know . . .' and their eyes spoke the dreadful truth of their living love which both had declared quite dead. Then he smiled and she was never to know the effort it took to speak without his voice shaking, to inject that touch of flippancy which was needed if they were both to recover from this.

'I'm afraid I must leave you now, my dear Miss Chapman.' He almost faltered over her name for her eyes which had once been luminous with her love, with the sweetness she held for Joss Greenwood, turned to black hatred for the enemy who had this day defeated her in battle. It was what she needed.

'You can go to hell, Joss Greenwood,' she hissed and her long nails reached to tear out his eyes but he stepped aside, his step jaunty, his grin impudent and daring.

'And you too, Kit Chapman. Perhaps we shall meet there,' as he fell into step with his jubilant men.

The following day, Joss Greenwood, though he had sworn he would get his men home, for enough had been done to bring to the notice of all the land the distress in the Lancashire textile trade, had failed to persuade them and had gone with them to Chadderton where they attacked the factory of Messrs Faulkner, destroying forty looms. So far the rioters had proceeded without opposition but intelligence of their intent – from someone who was never named – had been conveyed to the military who were guarding factories in the town. A party of twenty riflemen and the same number of dragoons, more serious and without the sympathy aroused in the breasts of previous soldiers, probably Lancashire men themselves, and within ten minutes of the Onwardsmen and their followers entering Chadderton seven persons lay dead and dying, one of them a woman.

It was finished.

In Blackburn and in an area of six miles around not a single power-loom survived. A thousand looms amounting to thirty thousand pounds, and the hand-loom weavers in the South Pennine Hills and valleys cleaned and oiled their hand-looms in readiness for the work which would now, surely, come their way, the work for which they had fought so hard to achieve, their objective won it seemed.

Of the sixty-six men arrested for their part in the riots, one was Joss Greenwood. Another was Ted Earnshaw. A third was a man called Paddy Kelly who, when he was threatened with transportation begged to be considered for a lesser sentence if he should turn King's evidence on the matter of the murder of Barker Chapman.

The case quite overshadowed the trial of the rioters, for when the man who was to have been Barker Chapman's son-in-law was brought to identify the accused murderer, Ted Earnshaw, Mr Atherton emphatically denied on his word as a gentleman that this was the assassin, affirming again and again that the prisoner Joss Greenwood was the man he had seen cut down Barker Chapman.

'But the man has an alibi, Mr Atherton,' the magistrate protested, for dearly as he would have liked to oblige a fellow gentleman, it was not in his power to do so. 'Vouchsafed by gentlemen of impeccable character. Not one, but several and at the very hour of the murder which you yourself verified was actually speaking to no less than two hundred people at a meeting in Bradford.'

'They were mistaken, all of them.'

'Come now, sir. Two hundred people cannot make such a mistake.'

'Are you calling *me* a liar?' Mr Atherton was incensed and the crowd was delighted, and so were the gentlemen who reported it in the newspaper the next day, particularly when Ted Earnshaw, who was by some curious mistake put in the same cell with half a dozen of Joss Greenwood's followers, confessed the very next morning to the murder and a month later was hanged for it.

# Part Two

It was two years and he was to be freed from gaol today, she had been told by the Squire who was also the magistrate, when he dined with her that week, but this time she would not be there to meet him when he passed by Badger's Edge. He was no longer a part of her life and, she told herself, she scarcely gave him a thought these days. Now and again, during her working week some stray event, one that had nothing to do with Joss Greenwood might bring him back for a hurried moment, before she had time to set her mind against it, at first vividly, achingly, as though he stood there with her to witness it but as the months passed, moving to twelve and beyond, crossing the anniversary of the day on which she had last seen him, his memory was beginning to fade . . . she told herself.

She had replaced the power-looms his men had destroyed and to house them she had built a splendid stone weaving-shed, strong enough on its four floors to stand the weight of a hundred, two hundred power-looms. Steam engines provided the power, the engine house erected at right angles to the main building with great arched windows like those of a chapel. It faced north to obtain the best light and had a tall chimney on which the name Chapman was painted, discharging a continuous and massive cloud of filthy smoke over the town.

The machines she put in were of the very latest design, William Dickinson's 'Blackburn Loom' which introduced picking sticks to drive the shuttle backwards and forwards. The mechanism was such that one weaver could attend to two machines without assistance and could weave a million 'picks' a week in contrast to the 605,000 on the old machines, almost doubling production and halving her wages bill! She had begun to experiment with printing her finished cotton, bringing in a cylinder machine which could print almost five hundred pieces a day, designing many of the patterns herself.

She was busy. She was Miss Katherine Chapman, owner of the Chapman Spinning and Weaving Concerns, Katherine Chapman, the innovator who employed a thousand men, women and children in her spinning rooms, her weaving-sheds, her carding rooms, in her finishing and printing processes which were growing in the centre of Crossfold. Her days were filled, satisfying the part of her which had resolved, years ago, that she would be the son her father had wanted her to be. She was a respected business woman, known to be shrewd, hard-headed, with the ability to make a profit before most of her competitors were out of their beds in a morning. She dined with gentlemen of influence and was much sought after by hostesses with sons, even among the landed society of south Lancashire.

Though there had been curious rumours whispered about the valley before the Power-Loom Riots of 1826, ugly rumours gathering momentum of a strange liaison between her and the felon, Joss Greenwood, started by God alone only knew, they had been seen to be the laughable nonsense they were when her weaving-shed was destroyed by the very man whose name was coupled with hers, along with the many others on that dreadful day. Would she have suffered as they did, those with sense said to one another, the gentlemen in the Cloth Hall, the ladies in their drawing-rooms if they had been ... whatever it was she and Joss Greenwood were supposed to have been to one another? Hardly, and whoever it was who had begun the rumour should be horsewhipped.

Kit had smiled when she had seen their speculative glances, for there was no smoke without fire, was there? –

but it had passed over, the riots turning the mill-masters' thoughts to more important matters than fools' gossip. But she had never discovered the name of the man who had given the information to Harry Atherton, nor how he had come by it, since she could hardly call each of her employees to her office to question them on such a delicate subject without letting everyone know of it! It had irked her and for weeks she had imagined knowing eyes watching her, waiting for her to fall as obviously Harry had hoped but as time passed and her mills continued to flourish she put it from her mind.

She travelled, to America and to the European continent, looking for markets for her piece goods and her name was known for honesty, value for money and reliability. She employed men she could trust, managers and overlookers and had engaged and trained a young man, brought up in his father's textile firm in Rochdale but wishing to make his own way in the world, to replace Harry Atherton. Though it had caused talk – but when had she not? – she had moved about the country with him, accompanied only by her maid, Janet, introducing him to men with whom she did business and had sent him, once she was convinced of his worth and integrity, to buyers found by Harry Atherton in other countries. Her cotton, her velveteens and fustians, her new muslins and piece goods went to a dozen places worldwide and the mistrust with which once she had been treated had vanished.

Yes, her days were splendid, just as she had always imagined they would be. From four-thirty in the morning when she rose from her bed in order to be at her mill gate by five-thirty when the bell was rung, until that moment when, her hair rippling down her back, brushed until it crackled by Janet, she was left alone to face the night.

He came to her then, his grey-green eyes gleaming between narrowed, smiling lids, his mouth curling humorously. Come with me, he would say, up on to the moorland we both know so well. We will follow a track which will lead us to some secluded place where the winds blow soft and free, where the skylarks sing and the scent of the heather will make us tipsy with joy. Leave this burden which you have taken up and I will leave mine and we will be as unfettered as the creatures who roam there. Cut the knot, as I will and come . . .

He would hold out his hands, those strong brown hands and take hers and draw her up into the magic circle of his arms, his beautiful masculine body against hers and her heart would go soft, weak with her need, her love, her anguish. She would move from the chair by the fire, her feet bare, the hem of her nightgown trailing across the fine, rich depths of the carpet to stand before the window, to stare sightlessly across the pitch-black of the night garden where nothing could be seen beyond the dark outline of the hills against the lighter hue of the sky. Her mind, so filled during the day with profit and loss, with production and patterns and yardage was empty and into the emptiness poured the dangerous, tormenting thoughts of Joss Greenwood.

They had given him two years this time. Sixty-six offenders, ten of them, those arrested with weapons in their possession, sentenced to death, the sentence later commuted to transportation and it was said among the manufacturers that one of them should have been, the leader of the mob, Joss Greenwood. Mind you, they said, he was known to have friends in high places who, it was suspected, had spoken out for him and he had been sentenced merely to two years' hard labour in Lancaster gaol.

Two years! She had held her head high, a victim as hundreds of other mill-owners had been victims of the Power-Loom Riots of April 1826 and agreed with them that it was scandalous and that the £126,000 raised by sympathisers in London, not for them, the ones who had lost, some of them, their whole livelihood but for the distressed and afflicted poor of the north, was really beyond belief. She had stood among them, one of them of course, and as she dined on pheasant and salmon and drank the very best French champagne, as she moved in the pleasant and convivial company of the fashionable and expensively dressed; as she carelessly ran up bills for swansdown muffs and lace fans, for velvet cloaks lined with soft fur, fine white kid boots and delicate creamy parasols, she could not, no matter how she laughed and chatted, no matter how she danced, and attended musical concerts in Crossfold, rid her mind of Joss Greenwood in his cell in Lancaster prison. Each night he escaped from that cell and came to claim her. In her mind he was still laughing and reckless, dashing, like a gypsy with his brown tumble of curls and his eyes bright with his hunger for her. Would he still be the same, her mind begged to know and the answer was, of course, that he would not. She remembered the last time he had been released from Lancaster and the shock she had suffered when she had seen the fine bones of him outlined beneath his white flesh, the grey in his hair and the lines about his eyes and mouth. He had suffered cold and damp, gaol fever and a rat-ridden cell, hunger, and had been worked unmercifully, but he had survived; *just!* His robust constitution had served him but he had not learned from his confinement. It had not, seemingly, taught him that his way was wrong. He had taken her looms and smashed them. He had taken her love and smashed it, throwing it insolently back in her face when she allowed him to reach for it. He had humiliated her, not once, nor even twice but time and again and though she felt the ravaged pain and anger of it, she could not use that emotion to stifle the other. The loving would not be destroyed by the hating. It came again and again in the night. As Janet closed the bedroom door softly so would Joss Greenwood open it again.

On some nights she could not withstand it. Tearing the nightdress from her she would fling on her plain woollen walking dress, her stout boots and coat and call up the dogs and walk the moors in the dead of night, her cheeks wet with tears, her heart beating fast with the exertion of climbing up and up to the high point above Edgeclough and the village which sheltered his family. She would crouch on her haunches, her chin resting on her knees and wrap her arms about them as she probed the dark roofs of the cottages, searching for God alone knew what. Peace? A calmness, which came only to her in her work, comfort . . . but from what? Down there lay his wife and the child she had borne him. A son, perhaps who would be walking by now, growing and unseen by his father.

And at five o'clock, as the last of her 'hands' flowed in through the gates in an endless wave of patient be-shawled women, submissive and bowed, with cloth-capped men and children clinging to other children she would be there, ready to close the gates on latecomers who would be forced to wait until they were opened again at eight o'clock.

She would move about her counting house and her design room, confer with her managers, her book-keepers and clerks, attend to overlookers who needed her advice, study patterns and quality, orders and consignment notes, receive business men, lawyers, bankers and all the gentlemen with whom she had dealings and who, knowing her value, no longer required *her* to go to *them*. She was calm then, at peace then, comforted then as the day flowed smoothly over her. She did not *ever* go into her spinning rooms, her carding rooms, her weaving-sheds when the machinery was in motion, nor when her operatives were employed there. She inspected the frames, the power-looms when it was necessary after the engines were turned off and the rooms were still, empty and silent, leaving the hiring of the hands, the management of them to the tacklers who were, after all, employed for that purpose.

She saw Jenny Greenwood that day, with a boy who could only be Joss's brother, walking beside her, her heart lurching at his likeness to Joss. He was tall, fine boned and slender and walked with the same grace. It was June and the sulphurous yellow sky was cast over, pressing down on the town with the smoke and steam from dozens of chimneys. From her office window on the top floor of the building she could see over the high mill wall to the sprawling labyrinth of houses which surrounded it and in which her workers lived. There were blackened church spires standing up here and there, the whole crusted with the soot and filth which poured from the chimneys. There was nothing as far as the eye could see but drab streets, smoky skies, a thick polluted air, the grim monotony of a mill town but she was accustomed to it and did not even see it. Her whole attention yearned towards Jenny Greenwood and the boy, longing to open the window, to call out to them as they crossed the yard and for a dreadful moment her hand actually reached out to the sash, but they turned suddenly, speaking to a girl behind them, a weaver by the look of her. She had bad teeth, caused by sucking the weft up in the shuttle, called by the weavers themselves, 'kissing' the shuttle and Kit knew that soon, when the boy who worked, she had heard, in the weaving-shed, had been there long enough, he would look just like the girl. And yet he appeared healthy enough. He was not round shouldered as many of the weavers seemed inclined to be, nor sallow and afflicted with chest complaints as the carding room lasses were, nor bleached of countenance as those in the spinning rooms became.

How did his family manage, she wondered, as she watched him disappear into the weaving shed, with Joss Greenwood in gaol? What of his mother, of Jenny, the younger one whose name she did not know . . . and of his wife and child? Did they eat well? Did they eat at all? She raised her head suddenly, stepping back from the window, moving to seat herself behind her desk. Dear God, what was wrong with her? It was nothing to her what his family ate, or did not eat and she'd be damned if she'd spend another minute of her day thinking about them.

Charlie Greenwood had a headache. Everyone in the weaving-shed had a headache but they were well used to it by now for the pollution which ravaged the town, the stifling, breathless, airless heat of the sheds, the humidity which sapped the strength of the strongest, spared no one, man, woman or child. He could hear the sound of the engine wheels and the hum of the machinery as it was set in motion. He had removed his jacket and trousers and his clogs, placing them safely out of the way of the flying straps beneath his machine and, barefoot, rolled up his shirt-sleeves and the legs of his thin drawers. He would, for the next fourteen or so hours, apart from two ten-minute breaks be required to tend to two clattering looms with shuttles making two hundred 'picks' a minute, in a steamed atmosphere and a din so horrific the operatives could go deaf with it while at any minute a rebellious shuttle might shoot forth and take out the operative's eye. For fourteen, fifteen, sixteen hours he would not be allowed to sit down since it was necessary while he ate his 'baggin' to sweep beneath and to clean and oil his machine. While it ran he must stand, for the motion of spindles and shuttles cared nought for human pain and woe, nor for the heart and soul of the operative which must be left at home. Hands, and enough intellect was all that was needed to keep the body out of danger for it must keep pace with the machine. The weaver must always be alert for a fault since the loom would go on weaving it continuously until the error was corrected. The looms were packed, as many as would fit into the smallest space, leaving just enough room for the operative to walk sideways between whirring belts and wheels and the ferociously moving picking stick. Each loom had a gas light, the gas turned on at a central point, coursing through considerable lengths of piping while the overlooker walked along the alleyways with a taper, lighting the mantles in an atmosphere that was already thick with escaped gas.

Yes, Charlie Greenwood had a headache but it was not allowed to stand in the way of his joyous thoughts for today Joss was coming home and this time he was not to tramp it as he had done three years ago but would have his fare paid on the coach which would fetch him from Lancaster to Oldham. It had been put up by those radicals, journalists and men from many walks of life who were working for reform and by the Union which had been created as a result of the repeal of the Combination Acts. Tonight when

Charlie returned home Joss would be there and the great burden which had been carried by young Charlie's shoulders as the man of the house these past two years would be lifted. He had worked in Chapman's spinning mill and weaving-shed for over four years now, always with the dream that he would be able to escape it and work with Joss and men like him in the struggle for a decent wage for a decent day's work, one following the other as naturally, as properly as day follows night. He wanted, when he was old enough, to become a member of one of the many committees established in the hand-weaving district of Lancashire for the specific purpose of campaigning for legislation to regulate wages to protect the hand-loom weaving industry. There was a man in Manchester, one John Harvey Sadler, an inventor and engineer who was attempting to contrive machinery which would enable one man to operate two hand-looms at the same time so that he might compete in his own cottage with the power-loom such as the one Charlie ran in Chapman's mill. Charlie would dearly love to see this happen for it would mean that with Mercy and Daisy spinning he might return to the cottage industry that had once been the life of his own father.

He heard the child scream, even above the sound of the machinery. It was a thin scream, like that of a rabbit caught by the stoat but Charlie had heard the frightened, painful cries of children many times before. He knew he could do nothing about it so he gritted his teeth and got on with his own work. One day, he said to himself, one day, repeating it over and over again. One day, one day, one day . . . ! It was something he had taught himself, a kind of hypnotism he put himself under to block out the sights and sounds which went on about him every day. Some of the operatives, after several months, grew hardened to it, too debased and dehumanised themselves by ignorance and by their own poverty to care much for the sufferings of others. Their own domestic comforts were non-existent, their own families as lacking in morals and dignity as animals in a shed. Unlike Charlie, they had nothing with which to compare this existence to the one they left in the morning and to which they returned each evening.

The child cried out again, a long wailing cry of such utter despair and hopelessness Charlie felt the hairs of his arms and legs and on the back of his neck rise stiffly. His scalp prickled and he swallowed several times but his mouth had dried up and his tongue stuck to the roof of his mouth. Still he knew he must not look round. If he so much as turned his head away from his loom, not only could a fault develop but there was a strong possibility he might be fined.

One day . . . one day . . . one day . . .

He heard a man laugh and again the child wailed in anguish, the sound suddenly cut off and as it stopped it seemed to Charlie the absence of it was worse than the sound had been. He could bear it no longer. He was almost a man wasn't he and though he knew he himself would surely suffer for it, since it was known he was the brother of a 'reformer', and as a 'meddler' himself in what did not concern him for he had spoken up in a child's defence before, he deliberately switched off his machine before he turned to see what was happening in the far corner of the weaving shed. All about him operatives, most of them women and children since they could work a power-loom as easily as a man and were willing to work for less bent industriously over their close-packed machines. Not one turned, through fear or indifference, or usage to what was being done to the child who had cried out.

She was no more than three or four, a frail thread of a child wearing a boy's underdrawers and nothing else. Her dirty skin was as thin as parchment and her bones threatened at any moment to break through it. Her head appeared to be too big for her tiny body, ugly somehow and out of shape and Charlie had time to consider that she must be one of the 'idiots', put in a consignment of twenty sound 'apprentice' children, a practice much used by the parishes from which they came. Charlie's face moved in pity and anger at what he saw.

There were three overlookers engaged in their 'bit of fun',

400

known, all of them for their brutality and for their ability to wring every last scrap of labour from those operatives, and children, in their charge. The child had been gagged. A piece of tow had been twisted into the shape of a cord, put in her mouth and tied at the back of her head and with his leather thonged stick the tackler was 'persuading' her to run round one of the machines which was part of his 'concern'. She was on her knees, her poor vacant face twisted in bewilderment and pain, her narrow back already showing the weals of the thong across it.

'Gerrup looney an' let's see yer run,' the man was mouthing for through the din of the machinery his actual words could not be heard. 'Gerrup on yer feet, yer daft little bugger. I'll teach yer ter fall asleep whilst yon machines goin'. It's the strap fer you an' anyone else who thinks she can . . .'

He got not further as the full weight of Charlie Greenwood took him from the side. They both landed heavily against the wall of the room and it was doubtful who was more surprised, the overlooker or the two who stood, open-mouthed and disbelieving, watching him. The child had scrabbled out of the way, having enough sense to recognise her opportunity to escape the cruelty of the men who owned her and they let her go, ready, as they came from their stunned trance to tackle this new potential for some sport. One of their own 'hands' attacking an overlooker! It was a case for dismissal, naturally but before that they would teach him a well deserved lesson. They didn't hold with rebellion, not among this cringing workforce over whom they had complete authority and this one would really be worth it. He'd given them a bit of 'lip' before, in defence of someone or other, as had his sister who worked in the spinning room and it was well known his brother was a radical who was at this moment serving a sentence in Lancaster for disturbing the peace.

They both began to smile as they pulled Charlie Greenwood from their fallen colleague.

* * *

401

They were at the end of the village street, every last one of them, to meet him, all the cottagers and even men and women from further up the Penfold Valley and higher still from the edge of the moorland.

His mother had him fast in her arms for she had been uncertain whether she would live to see him again since two years is a long time when you are beyond fifty. They held one another tightly for a moment, mother and son, both without words, her face pressed to his chest, his cheek resting on her grey hair. Those about them became silent, their sympathy reaching out to enfold this man who had suffered so much for them, and for his mother who had, in her way, undergone as much as he. Most of these women about her, though they might go hungry and had often been cold and weary, had a man to give them a hand, to smile grimly with them in the past as they shared a crust of bread among those of their children who survived. They had the comfort of a shoulder, perhaps not strong, nor even broad to weep on when the day just gone could scarcely be borne and the one to come was sure to be worse. But Martha Greenwood had lost one man, a man whose crusading spirit had been snuffed out in the campaign against oppression and she looked to be in the process of losing another if the state of Joss Greenwood was anything to go by. A walking skeleton was a kind description of him and would she ever put a bit of flesh back on his bones, they asked one another, shaking their heads sadly. What was he . . . twenty-eight, twenty-nine and the streaks in his brown curls were thick and white, not unattractive, one or two of the younger women agreed, but where was that glowing, brown-skinned gypsy look he once had, the engaging brightness of his grey-green eyes, the springing, cat-like grace of his long-legged walk?

But he turned to smile and his teeth were still white and whole between his curving lips and his eyes lit up with pleasure as he recognised face after face. He waved a thin hand, then had it taken by a moist-eyed man, then another and another. They followed him down the rutted street, jostling one another to be near him as he walked, one arm about his mother, the other about his childlike wife who acted, they whispered, as though she had no idea who he was but in that sweet way she had was willing to welcome anyone who was kind to her. His young sister, Daisy, ten years old now and, miraculously a kitchen skivvy at Edgeclough Hall with the Squire's family, for which her mother gave thanks on her knees each day, opened the cottage door wide to reveal its spotless, if spartan, homeliness and those who had accompanied him fell back for he'd want a bit of peace and quiet with his family now.

He was seated before the small peat fire, what small store of energy he had spent on the walk from Oldham to Edgeclough, his face almost grey in the last fading shadows of the evening sun. He had managed as much as he could of the appetising rabbit stew his mother had coaxed him to eat and drunk almost a pint of the foaming milk, sent over by a grateful weaver. He had marvelled at the pies, the black puddings, the 'fatty' cake, all prepared by women who had cause to be grateful to Joss Greenwood for the growth of their children in the last two years and though he swore it was none of his doing since he had merely been caught up in the events of that fortnight he, and the other sixty-five who had been sentenced, were venerated as near saints by those who were certain at last, that what they had fought for was surely accomplished. They had their bit of spinning, a 'piece' woven each week, or more if they could manage it and the prospect, now that John Harvey Sadler, the clever young inventor, had promised it of a hand-loom which could do what a power-loom did.

Joss leaned his head on the back of the chair, his two year old nephew on his knee and the last of the suns rays fell about his head. His mother watched him thankfully. He looked right 'peaky' but she'd soon alter that, somehow or other. They had a few pence put by, what with Daisy up at the Hall and no longer in need of feeding and their Jenny and Charlie earning enough to keep the four of them, which reminded her, where were they, her eldest daughter

403

and younger son? It must be gone half-past eight and she had expected them home earlier tonight. Running, they would be, despite the long and unmercifully hard day they had put in, eager to get home to see their Joss. He'd not noticed how late it was becoming, poor lad, his head drooping above the curls of Jenny's Lucas, his hands limp and big knuckled about the sleeping child, as he dozed himself.

She rose to her feet and treading lightly so as not to wake him moved across her kitchen, peering anxiously from the open doorway and along the village street. Long shadows lay in strips across it, banded with muted shafts of sunlight as the lowering sun poured its last rays between each cottage. The slopes of the hills directly to the front of her were a dusky purple, their rims edged with gold and the sky shaded from them, to yellow and peach and the final pale summer blue of the evening.

Martha shaded her eyes, looking in the direction of the track which led from Crossfold to Edgeclough. It curved down through waist high bracken and gorse and she could still see the dark line it made through the vegetation.

'What time is it, Mother?' Joss's voice was drowsy and in the quiet his mother jumped nervously.

'It must be nearly nine.'

Joss sat up stiffly, lifting the sleeping child and placed him in the chair opposite. His body still ached with fatigue but his eyes had become alert and there was a questioning expression on his face.

'Shouldn't they be home by now. Didn't you say they finished at seven today?'

'Aye. I don't know what's keeping them.' She turned abruptly, then seeing his expression of unease, her own face tried a smile of unconcern.

'They'll not be long, lad, don't you fret. 'Appen the overlookers found them something extra to do. You know what they're like. It's nothin' to them if young 'uns are fallin' asleep on their feet. Nay, don't get up, our Joss, rest yourself . . .' but Joss had risen from his chair and come to stand beside her. He followed her gaze up to the Crossfold track, then his eyes swept the length of the soft valley along which it ran, past his own front door and then up again to the far side. The hills were banked all about him, high sweeping moorland, the edges of it starting just beyond the village. It was a lonely place to some, a vast emptiness, a threat to those not used to it but he had lived for the past two years in a cell barely bigger than his mother's larder and he welcomed the feeling of it stretching away on either side with nothing in it but space. He let himself drift away for a moment, breathing in the sweet warm air, the scent of many things, of foxglove and heather, of yellow broom and purple clover and he felt the headiness of it lap over him in healing waves. The stillness, the peace, the calm after the clangour and cries of his imprisonment, rested gently in his heart and he gave silent and humble thanks for his survival and return to it. It sustained him, this often barren and inhospitable land, gave him life and hope and the surety that . . . what? What was it, that feeling of certainty which steadied him to the path he would move along tomorrow and the next day and the next. It was bred in him as it had been bred in his father and grandfather. They were men of the north, a hostile country sometimes but it was their country and they would have it free for the men and women who lived in it.

'There they are . . .' His mother's glad voice brought him from his deep musing. He turned, smiling his pleasure, eager to be re-united with these two who, more than any others knew him and his purpose, his dream, who shared them, who had stood beside him so many times, in adversity and suffering, and in joyful triumph. Jenny. The mystery of Jenny and the baby she had borne. So much to talk about, to tell her and to ask of her, surely, to discover the name of the father of her child. And Charlie. Almost a man now and he would be a fine man, a brother of whom any man would be proud. Despite his extreme youth he had kept faith with Joss, taking on a burden a boy of his age should not have been asked to shoulder, working as a man would work, caring for his mother and sisters in Joss's absence, in a sense *being* Joss.

They were both smiling, Joss and Martha Greenwood, as they watched the two figures come slowly over the brow of the hill. They were too far away as yet to make out their features, just two figures close together, moving down the stony track, leaning together in an extreme of weariness so great it seemed neither would make it to the first cottage.

'Let's walk to meet them,' Joss said stepping out into the last mellow shaft of the sun which showed but a third of its orb above the hills. As he spoke he put up a hand to shade his eyes, looking towards his brother and sister, narrowing them slightly in puzzlement. He put out his other hand to his mother who was following him as though to stop her and she turned to look at him, her expression questioning.

'What is it?' she asked.

'I . . . I don't know.' He had moved to the gate, his eyes still intent on the two figures who had reached the first cottage and as they did so a man and a woman came out of it and hurried down the short path into the street. The woman put her hand to her mouth and quite distinctly on the quiet air Joss heard her cry out. The man, it was Adam Cartwright, took hold of . . . who was it? . . . Jenny? . . . Charlie? . . . and the one remaining sank slowly, quite gracefully into a crouching position against Adam's garden wall.

Joss began to move, first slowly and then, as his heart beat quickened, more rapidly until he was running. Behind he could hear his mother calling his name and on either side of him as he ran cottage doors were opening and heads looked out, voices enquiring what was to do? His feet, he suddenly realised, were bare since he had removed the boots he had worn on his journey from Lancaster and he could hear the slap of his soles against the causey stones which lined the street and the sharp sound of his own breath in his throat. Adam was gently lowering the thin form of the boy he held to the grass verge outside his own garden gate. His face was contorted with horror and his wife was weeping. She didn't quite know what to do in that first moment of shock and kept circling her husband and the figure he held in his arms.

'Oh Lord ... Oh dear Lord ... Oh my God ...' she kept saying over and over again.

'Give over, woman ...' Adam said roughly, ' ... and go and get some help. Fetch Martha and ...' He had not seen Joss who had stopped just behind him and in his compassion he could do no more than rock his burden back and forth, like a mother with a child.

Joss fell to his knees beside them and the groan which wrenched from him brought all those who had followed him in wonderment, to a halt. His mother was among them, her face white and terrified and against the wall where she had fallen Jenny Greenwood lifted her head. She was as grey as the stones she crouched beside. The sweat ran down her face from beneath her hair and dripped from her chin and her bodice was wet with it. She seemed unable to move her arms which were bent awkwardly and there was blood on her. On her breast and on her shoulders, on her arms and staining her skirt and some had even dripped on to her feet.

'Oh sweet Jesus ...' Joss's voice was no more than a whisper in his throat. He did not turn to look at his sister as he spoke since his eyes were nailed to what had once been the engaging face of his brother Charlie. ' ... Who ... what ... who did this to him?'

'His overlooker ... and two others. His arms are broken ... and ... don't let me Mam see his back.'

Martha Greenwood began to scream.

'Oh God ... Oh God ...'

Jenny's voice was like a razor. 'He's got nowt to do with it, nor with anyone round here, I reckon.'

'How did you get him home.'

'I carried him.'

# 27

He was waiting at the mill gates when her carriage drew up to them, standing, like a statue carved from granite, directly in the horses' path. She heard her coachman shouting and cracking his whip, telling someone to 'get out o't road or 'e'd run 'im down' and was almost thrown from her seat to the carriage floor as it came to an abrupt halt. There were voices yelling and the carriage horses were whinnying and she could hear the crash of their hooves on the cobbles. The carriage rocked again and the commotion outside it grew greater. There was a surge of men and women about it and she could see cloth caps and heads draped in shawls just above the level of the window, a sea of faces swamping the area about the open mill gates all looking in one direction, and hear the sound of the factory bell calling them to work.

'What on earth is going on?' she heard herself say out loud, irritably, since it was almost five thirty and the engines would have been turned on and these operatives who were milling about the carriage and restless horses should by now be at their machines ready to do a day's work. The carriage window was already open for the day promised to be hot again but when she put her head out she did not immediately see what was holding her up. The shuffling feet of her workers had lifted the dust which lay on the road and a fine cloud of it floated on to her horses, her coachman and laid a coating on to the pale green sprigged muslin of her summer gown.

'What is it, Frederick?' she called out.

'Some lunatic in the road, ma'am.'

'What lunatic?' she asked, squinting through the dust and it was then that she saw him. Though her eyes looked at him, a tall, emaciated figure, dressed in breeches and an open-necked shirt, a shaggy mane of greying hair, unkempt and dusty falling in his eyes, they did not immediately recognise him though naturally her heart did. Would it ever forget that familiar beloved outline, the shape of him, the way he stood, the tilt of his arrogant head, for it was still there, the sum and substance of the man she loved, emanating from this man who stood in her path. But this man was – must be – well over thirty years of age. There were lines of weariness and strain about his tight clenched mouth, a mouth which gave the appearance of cruelty, a bitter and menacing threat and surely it could only be directed at herself? This man's eyes were like pale green chips of ice between his narrowed lids and his face was so grey and sweating it might not have seen sunlight, daylight even, for months on end. This man's hands were big, raw and his fingers were like claws, flexing and unflexing. This man was a stranger to her, one she really did not wish to know, and yet, it was he. Her heart told her achingly that it was he.

'Katherine Chapman,' the man, Joss Greenwood, said, and though his voice was not loud it was clear and everyone of the throng about her carriage, slipping through the gateway, milling about her yard, reluctant it seemed, to enter the mill and miss this confrontation, heard it. They knew, of course, all of them, why he was here for those who had witnessed the appalling beating of Joss Greenwood's young brother had told others, who had in their turn spread it about the town, but it had not reached Greenacres, not yet. There would be trouble, those who watched were well aware, for Joss Greenwood, just freed from prison, a fighter in his younger days, a believer in the equality of all men and a detester of oppression would not let it pass.

'Katherine Chapman. Step down from that carriage, if you please.'

The coachman snapped his whip above Joss Greenwood's head but he did not even flinch. The horses pawed the ground restlessly and tossed their heads and though he seemed in imminent danger of being trampled, Joss did not move.

'Get out o't way, yer damned fool,' the coachman cried, his own face indignant for he was severely put out by this defiance of his authority. He had driven Barker Chapman and now his daughter to the mill and back for the past twenty years and always the men and women who jostled the streets of Crossfold, stepped back, some respectfully, some perhaps resentfully, but they had given way to him just the same.

'Step aside at once,' he roared.

Kit Chapman lay back against the velvet upholstery of her carriage and felt the blood drain away from her head. Her pulse beat was thick and heavy at her wrist and temple. She had been busy inside her own active brain planning the installation next week, if she could arrange it, of the new machine which would print the cloth she produced. Simple designs they would be just now but an engineer she had met only last week at the dinner table of Mr Graham, who was her bank manager, had told her that the mechanised roller printing she was to use, though still in its infancy, would by the end of the decade become so sophisticated she might print any design or colour she had a fancy to. The challenge was immense since it would enable her to open up new markets with not only the plain, unpatterned cloth she now manufactured, but light, prettily printed muslins and ginghams, beginning with the raw cotton and finishing with a fabric which would be complete, ready in fact to be made up into a morning dress of the very latest fashion.

She could not seem able to gather the scattered fragments of her pleasant thoughts. Could not even collect her wits to enable her to face this dangerous crisis, whichever way she turned. Scurrying hither and thither, trying to put them into some sort of order, they disintegrated again and again into chaos and confusion. What was he doing here the very day after, she had been told, he had been released from prison? What was his purpose in taking up this challenging stand between her mill gates, his face thunderous, his eyes betraying the enormity of his rage, his finely strung body trembling with it? What had she done since yesterday that had driven him to this madness since, being an ex-convict he would be under the eye of the authorities and one step off the path of lawfulness and the proper behaviour required of him would have him back behind bars before he had time to lose that dreadful prison pallor he had acquired in the past two years. But she could not sit here in the dim warmth of her carriage forever, pondering on the reason for it. She must at least enquire of him the purpose of it. Naturally everyone knew of his championship of the 'distressed and afflicted poor', that was why he had been imprisoned, and, she supposed wearily, he was to be about that championship right away, pressing his ideas of wide-ranging political freedom on to the common man. A militant man, then who had caused, she had heard, the dreadful Power-Loom Riots of two years ago, a man concerned with the repeal of the Corn Laws, of the ten-hour bill for factory children, *any* kind of bill, or law in fact, that would make life easier for the common man and stand in the way of profit for those who employed them.

But her heart plunged and bucketed in her breast at the thought of stepping from her carriage and looking into his face again. She had imprisoned her feelings for him tight inside her, tamed them, forced them, subdued them to manageable proportions, told herself that her life was good now, believed it, and now, with one glance from his piercing eyes and the sound of her own name on his lips it had exploded inside her, firing up and burning as fiercely as her own furnace in her mill. But he'd not see it! By God, she'd not let him know of the tumult inside her. If he wished to roar like a lion, to make a show of his own rage, whatever it was about, outside her own mill then let him, but she would not participate in that performance for all to enjoy.

She would be cool, disdainful, contemptuous. She would let him see how she despised him and all he stood for, by God she would.

She opened the carriage door and stepped down into the dusty area before the mill gates. Lifting her pale green silk parasol she put it up languidly, a lady protecting her fine skin from the already steaming rays of the sun's heat. Her bonnet was held high, a pretty froth of silk and tulle tied beneath her chin with wide silk ribbons and she wore white gloves and white kid boots. She was elegant, stiff-necked with pride, a high mettled, fearless lady who, scarcely able to believe the audacity of this man who was barring her way, was forced to enquire of his purpose in doing so.

'May I ask what you think you are doing? You realise that you are trespassing on private property and that if you do not stand aside and let me pass I shall have no recourse but to summon the constable and have you arrested. Surely you are not so eager to return to gaol. I believe you have only just been released.'

'You bitch! You filthy, vindictive bitch.' His hatred and rage was so great, so malevolent, the words of scorn dried up in her throat and she took a step away from him, not afraid as yet, but considerably alarmed and bewildered. Merciful God, what was wrong with the man? He appeared to have taken leave of his senses, to be quite mad and certainly beyond understanding the words of contempt she had meant to heap on his head. His face was contorted, almost unrecognisable in its loathing and though she was well aware that this scene, these feelings were nothing new between them, that they would never reach a point where either would be in agreement with the other, this was different. This was the roaring of a wounded, tortured animal, an animal that has been ill-treated again and again until at last it can stand no more, until it turns on its tormentors and is ready to tear them to pieces in its agony and violence.

'Joss . . . what is it . . . ?' The crowd were amazed to hear her say. It was uttered uncertainly, every grand resolution she had nurtured flung to the winds in her concern for him, but it was obvious that he did not hear it.

'You are not fit to be called a woman.' His voice was muted as though somewhere deep in his throat he had tamped it down for fear it would escape him in a scream. 'An animal has more compassion than you and I am cursed to have known you. These people are forced to share in your viciousness, most of them unable to stand against it and I do not blame them since they have no alternative but you are a monster, a vile and profane monster who should have been drowned at birth . . .'

'Now look 'ere, you . . .' the coachman began, his face quite scarlet with his outrage. He put his foot on the step of his high seat at the front of the carriage, ready to climb down with his whip and clear a path for his mistress. Already the crowd about them was becoming so enormous it spilled out into the street as far as the corner and in the yard several managers and overlookers were trying to force a way through to the gate. Children and frail women were being pushed to one side, several had fallen and the situation was becoming dangerously out of hand, but Joss Greenwood did no more than turn his eyes on him, a look that said it would be unwise to interfere and the coachman stayed where he was.

Kit stepped back again as Joss moved towards her and her heart banged frighteningly in her breast. The parasol trembled in her hand and for a moment she thought she would stumble as her high heel caught in the hem of her gown.

'Joss . . . for God's sake . . .' she began, her back against the door of her carriage. She was hemmed in, surrounded by the hundreds who longed in some way, in *any* way to see her downfall, whatever that might be. They had all suffered at her hands, at her father's hands, not personally, of course, but at those of the men she employed to subjugate them in the spinning rooms and weaving sheds where conditions crippled them, maimed them, afflicted them with disease and illness, *killed* them sometimes, made slaves of

413

their children and all for wages which barely kept them alive. If they could see her humiliated, perhaps beaten by this man whose brother, it was said, was at death's door, by *her* orders then some quality of redress would be returned to them.

'Don't foul my name by speaking it, you hell-kite and you may do away with the concern for it does not suit you. You would kill a child as we well know to make a profit of sixpence and to carry out your obscene intents you employ men who are as evil-minded as yourself. Or perhaps you had a hand in it. Perhaps you laid on the lash yourself . . .'

In his pain and blind, unreasoning rage he said things which he knew to be foolish, untrue, exaggerated since he had loved her once and perhaps still did and in his anguish over it he was doing his best to trample it into the dust at their feet. She would not personally have supervised the beating his brother had been given and, if he could have blown away the black fog of hatred which befuddled his brain he would have seen the truth but it was doubtful he even wanted to. Someone must pay for it. She was the one who, at best, had turned a blind eye to it, at worst, ordered it and so he was here to collect what was owed him.

'I do not know what you are talking about, Joss Greenwood, and if you think to frighten me with your ravings you are mistaken.'

'Is that so? Then how is it that every man and woman in this town knows of it. Every cottage I passed on my way here had someone at the door asking after him . . .'

Almost he had begun to weep, his pain more than he could contain, the memory burning in his brain, and his heart, of what he had left in his mother's cottage in Edgeclough.

'For God's sake, Joss . . . please . . . what has happened to . . . ?' She put out a hand to him, appalled, but he struck it brutally from him as though her touch might coat him with filth.

'Don't put your hand on me, you she-devil. How you can stand there with that . . .'

'For pity's sake, speak more plainly.' She was no longer afraid, nor even concerned for him. Her own rage was rising to meet his, as it had always done, the spark from his igniting the dry kindling of hers. They were like two sticks which, when rubbed together caused such friction everything about them, including themselves was consumed in the blaze.

'I do not intend to speak at all, Katherine Chapman, except to say that your corruption and greed, and that of all the others like you will find its true level one day when you all go to hell. Your inhumanity to those of your own kind . . .' The tears blurred his eyes and again she was pulled towards him for surely he was in need of a hand to steady him but again he stepped back from her in revulsion.

'What in God's name are you talking about?' she cried. 'For a man who swears he does not mean to speak you have a lot to say and I have yet to understand what it is . . .'

'I will show you what it is. Get in your carriage.'

'You cannot order me about like one of your followers. Now, for the last time get out of my way . . .'

'Get in your carriage at once or I shall throw you in. I have but to reach out my hands and put them about your head and within thirty seconds you will be dead. Melodramatic, you say, smiling, but if those men back there, undoubtedly among them the ones who almost killed my brother, should try to stop me, I will do it . . .'

'*Killed your* . . .' Her face had gone paper white and her voice was incredulous. 'Charlie . . . ?'

'Aha, you even know his name.' His voice split on his pain. 'You can look the other way when they beat him almost to death . . . and you know *his name*. Now get in that carriage for I mean you to see what you have done. You sit in your splendid office . . . oh, I know you don't go in the spinning room, or the weaving-sheds . . . they tell me so, those who work there, for though you gloat over the profits you make from them you cannot bear to afflict

415

yourself with the pain they suffer. It offends you to see them, to smell them, to hear them cough their lungs up, to pull out their soft bones, to have them broken and deformed. Your conscience might trouble you, if you have one which I doubt and then it would not be quite so easy to enjoy the wealth you make on their broken bodies. *Now get in your carriage.* We will drive to the edge of town and then we will walk the rest of the way. Call off the men behind me, call them off, Katherine Chapman for though they might kill me, by God, you'll go with me.'

He would not get in the carriage, unable to compel himself to be so close confined with her and when they reached the end of Reddygate Way, he strode out ahead of her, stopping only as she gave instructions to her coachman to wait for her here. Frederick was white-faced now, afraid up here alone on the moors with a madman who was abducting his mistress but help would not be far behind for the managers would have the special constables up to Joss Greenwood's cottage almost before he himself got there.

She was not dressed for walking the three mile track to Edgeclough. It was full summer and the bracken was high and thick, growing across the pathway until it almost met in the middle and the skirt of her gown was full and wide with deep flounces edged in emerald green ribbon. Her boots were soon torn and scuffed and before she had gone half a mile the heel of one snapped right off. It was still early but the heavy yellow sky pressed down on her head. She did not call out to him to slow down to allow her to rest a moment, to gather her breath for her stays were tightly laced, but strode along behind him just as though it was a cool spring morning and she herself was dressed in stout walking boots and skirt. His hostile back moved ahead of her and he did not once speak nor look back to see if she was still behind him.

They lined the streets of the village to see her walk by and though her feet were blistered and bleeding she did just that, her back straight, her head high for even now she had no conception of what she was to see nor of what depths it would plunge her. She was appalled, more by Joss's pain and anger and hatred than by what he had actually said. By *his* suffering and not that of his brother for she had known, naturally, that boys in her mills must receive a flogging or two if they were to be kept in line, or so the tackler told her.

None of the cottagers uttered a sound as they watched her go by but their eyes were bright with their curiosity. They were still, quite unmoving, looking at her as though she was some creature they had heard about but had never seen before, something strange and quite revolting, not of their race and therefore not one with whom they would like to be acquainted.

The small kitchen seemed to be full of women. Joss did not go in but merely indicated with a contemptuous hand that she was to enter. Jenny was there, her face inscrutable, her eyes hot and loathing. There was a slip of a girl, perhaps fifteen, with silken brown hair and confused grey eyes — who was she? — who shrank behind a chair in which rocked an older woman who did not even glance up at her. Joss's mother? And another older woman, greyer, granite faced, tall and stern, guarding this family from further cruelties, it appeared.

And on a truckle bed, face down, was the slight figure of a boy. She moved across the room until she stood over the bed and at once Jenny was there, a sentinel to protect her brother from this woman whose fault it was that he lay there at all. He had a light cotton sheet pulled up to the back of his neck but the left side of his face could clearly be seen against the white sheet beneath his head. At least she thought it was his face! It was so swollen and bruised, so laced with cuts and abrasions it was difficult to tell where his mouth and nose should have been, where his eye actually was in the slitted mask of what had been his face. So deeply imbedded in his swollen flesh, his long eyelashes could not even be seen and but for the breath which whistled between his broken teeth and lacerated lips she could not have said that the hole through which it came was actually a mouth.

417

'Dear Lord God . . . ' Her voice was no more than a light breath, unheard by them all but Jenny.

'And that's not all, Miss Chapman.'

Jenny gently lifted the sheet from her brother's back and actually smiled, her eyes cold now with hatred as Kit Chapman turned away, white-faced, sweating and sick, sagging against the wall behind her.

'Look at him again, Miss Chapman,' she murmured softly. 'Look at what your men have done to my brother. Three of them there were, two to hold his arms after he had been stripped and one to flay the skin off his back. Then those who held his arms broke them, I was told, quite deliberately before they started on his face. That mark there . . . no, perhaps you cannot see it among the rest of his injuries but it is the mark of a hob-nailed boot. It took Sarah two hours to sew up his face and another two to put splints on his arms but they can do nothing for his back, naturally. And all this for trying to protect a child, an *idiot* child, who had no right being in the mill in the first place.'

Kit's teeth began to chatter and her whole body shook from head to foot as she slipped into shock. She pressed her face to the wall and put her hands to her face, trying to shut out the sight of the red squashed pulp of the boy's back which moved excruciatingly, shallowly with each desperate breath he took. In and out it rasped and in his semi-conscious state he moaned and instantly they were about him, his mother and Jenny, the third woman, each willing, eager to take on his pain, their hands hovering helplessly, their eyes beseeching one another to tell them what to do to ease his agony, their loving pity and helplessness a palpable thing in the kitchen. She turned back to the group then, with all her soul longing to help, to ease the boy's suffering, their suffering, anyone's suffering who should ask it of her and her eyes met those of Joss Greenwood as he hovered by the open kitchen door and she saw in them the reluctant recognition of what was in her heart.

'I did not know,' she said thickly.

'You should be aware of everything that goes on in your mills. You are responsible for this.'

'I did not know,' she repeated.

'You knew of the child who died and you did nothing.'

'Sweet Jesus . . .'

'I cannot ever forgive you and neither will He.'

'I know that. I cannot forgive myself.'

'You should go now.' His face was hard and implacably cold and as he spoke the fragile girl moved from behind the chair and ran to him, her face crumpled in the easy tears of the young.

'Joss, will Charlie get better?' she said, moving trustingly into the outstretched shelter of his arm. 'I cannot bear to see him hurt so.'

The change in Joss was quite dramatic and to Kit, devastating. His eyes warmed and became soft and his mouth curved into a smile of infinite tenderness. He kissed the girl on her cheek and she sighed as she rested like a little bird against his chest.

'Of course he will, Mercy. He is strong and Sarah and Jenny will make him better. Go and play out for a while, sweetheart. Why don't you pick some flowers so that when Charlie wakes up he will be able to see them by his bed, and when you come back Martha will make us all some dinner.'

He kissed her again and she smiled eagerly.

'Oh yes, I know just where there are some lovely violets . . .'

'But don't go far, sweetheart.'

'No, I won't,' and she darted from the kitchen out into the sunshine and as she went Kit heard her begin to sing.

Their eyes met across the room and his answered the wondering question in hers.

Yes, they said, she is my wife and I love her, and the wintry expression in them challenged her to remark on it if she dare.

His wife! Her eyes were huge in her ashen face. His wife! The girl who she had thought to be no more than fifteen,

419

timid and made afraid by what had been done to Charlie Greenwood, perhaps the daughter of a neighbour, *was Joss Greenwood's wife.* And where was the child, the son she had imagined these last two years while Joss had been imprisoned, *his* son. Surely that sweet-faced woman, since she was that, that simple child could not be the mother of a child, the mother of Joss Greenwood's son? The woman she had feared and hated and envied. *Go out and play* he had told her and she had gone, singing as artlessly as a seven year old. Her eyes returned to his and the questions and answers which flowed despairingly, contemptuously between them told her it really made no difference. Not now. He would not allow Kit to come near him again, she could see it in the coldness which had replaced the violence of his rage. This was his home, nothing to do with her, as his wife was nothing to do with her. Her overlookers had almost killed his brother and he had blamed her, brought her to see what had been done, and that was all, and what did it matter now. It was finished. There was nothing more to say, or to be done between them. They were enemies, bitter foes in the war *he* fought and she must accept the fact. She must return to Crossfold, to her mill where the weft and warp of her life lay before her to be woven. This day must surely alter its construction and certainly some good must come of it, or her life up to this day would have been for nothing. She could no longer sit in her ivory tower, a princess who did not recognise the minions who served her, aloof and distant from the men and women and children, the overlookers who had them in their charge and the managers who came each day to tell her how much profit she had made the day before. Her father had been wrong. The other mill-owners of her acquaintance were wrong when they left the management of their sheds and spinning rooms to others.

There is no advantage in employing them to see to these things and then doing it oneself, George Abbott had said to her on numerous occasions, and as long as I get the yardage I want I leave it to others as to how I get it! She had followed the same path, the path her father had set her on. She had not known, had *forgotten*, made herself forget, the two occasions on which she had gone into the spinning room, telling herself that such things were happening all over the country where factories, mines, chimneys were swept, establishments where children were employed, so what could *she* do about it? There was no other way.

But was there? Was there?

She put out a hesitant hand to Jenny Greewood who knelt beside her brother's bed, longing to lay it in sympathy on her shoulder. Her eyes lifted to Martha Greenwood but his mother was consumed with her son's pain and she did not look up from her frantic clinging to the hopeless belief that her closeness to him might ease it. If she could have changed places with him she would have done so, joyfully, her face said as she bent over him.

'Go home, lass. There's nowt yer can do 'ere,' the stony-faced woman bade her, the same one who had mended Joss when Harry's bully-boys had beaten and broken him. How strange it is, she thought, that I should be so closely involved with this family, not only with Joss but with his sister, his brother, and now, in an abstract, quite curious way, with the child he calls wife. I cannot seem to shake myself loose from them, from a concern about them that has nothing at all to do with Joss. There is something in Jenny and Charlie that arouses my admiration and in another time, and place, I might have found affection, friendship, something I have never had before.

She moved from the dim warmth of the kitchen and out into the late morning sunshine and was surprised to see that it was still daylight. What time was it? What *day* was it, her confused and aching heart asked for it seemed an aeon since she had stepped from her carriage in front of her mill gates that morning.

She stopped before the tall figure of Joss Greenwood. His back was to the warm, sun-coated wall of the cottage, his eyes closed, his face held up to the sun and when she put her hand on his arm he jumped guiltily as though he was not accustomed to standing and doing nothing. His face closed up when he saw who it was and he straightened his thin frame to his full height.

'You have had enough then?' he asked harshly.

'They do not want me in there. I am in the way, and besides you have done what you set out to do.'

'And what is that?'

'You have punished me.'

'Is that how you see it?'

'Oh yes. There is no use my saying what I feel inside me here . . .' She struck her clenched fist fiercely against her own breast and her voice was thick and strangled in her throat, ' . . . you would not believe me if I did, so I will . . . will leave you.' She paused, her eyes which she felt she could never raise to any member of his family again, somewhere on the shading of brown hair in the opening of his shirt and was ashamed at her own longing, even then, to put her lips there. 'Would you allow me to send up my own doctor . . . or anything you might need . . . I hesitate . . . I do not wish you to think I am offering charity . . .'

He began to laugh then, a hoarse and anguished laugh, disbelieving, and she felt her heart shrivel up in pain but she did not flinch from him, or from her own desolation.

'You can go to hell, Katherine Chapman, and take your bloody concern with you. My family need nothing from you. None of us need anything from you but justice. Can you give us that?'

# 28

It made a small sensation when Jenny Greenwood was summoned from the spinning room to Miss Chapman's office and those about her wondered what trouble the family were in now. It was no more than two days since Charlie Greenwood had been flogged by the overlooker in the weaving shed and the lad only alive by the skin of his teeth, what were left of them, they had heard. And nothing had been done about the men who had beaten him, it was said, not even a reprimand, and the three of 'em walking about like 'cocks 'o the north', worse than ever in their brutality.

'Make yersel' tidy, my girl,' Ellis told her, smoothing his hand over her slender buttocks as she leaned across her machine to switch it off. He grinned lasciviously, darting out of the way of her upraised hand, admiring the sweat-stained outline of her pert breasts, telling himself that he would find a way to get her on a pile of cotton waste before long. She might be the leavings of Harry Atherton but what did that matter? The trouble was, she didn't give a damn about anything he might threaten her with. Nothing frightened her and when he thought to control her with the promise that he would tell the world who the father of her child was she had laughed in his face and told him to go ahead. Pity that bit of business with the young Squire had come to nothing but it seemed the high and mighty Miss Chapman was as unafraid as this one and cared nought if her good name was fouled on the lips of the whole valley. It would have been grand to have been carried on the coat-tail of the man who married her. Still, he did all right on the whole, busy with his finger in this pie and that and he'd a few bob put away for a rainy day. He wondered what it was Miss Chapman wanted this slut for. Happen she was in trouble again for there was no doubt the whole bloody family had a talent for it.

Kit rose to her feet when Jenny entered her office and as the stale smell of sweat and oil and the odour which was peculiarly that of a factory in which every window is tight shut, came in with her, Kit resisted a strong urge to put her lavender scented handkerchief to her nose. The girl was unkempt, her hair wrapped about with a strip of torn cotton, her bodice so damp with sweat the circle of her dark nipples were clearly visible. Her skirt was tucked up at one side into her waistband and she wore nothing beneath it but a pair of men's underdrawers. Her calves and ankles were filthy and the clogs into which she had carelessly pushed her feet were crusted with muck and oil.

They studied one another across the vast stretch of deep velvet carpet, across the shining surface of Kit's desk, across the enormous chasm which divided them, not only of class and of privilege, but of the wounds inflicted by Kit Chapman on the family of Jenny Greenwood. They might have come from different continents, worlds even, so great was the contrast between them but as Kit looked into Jenny's eyes she allowed the thought to flit into her mind that if she herself had been born to a cottager, a weaver, to the life Jenny led, to the slavery of a spinning frame or a loom, to a six-mile tramp each day from the mill and back, might she not look as Jenny did, and could not the same be said of Jenny? Put her in a silk gown, perfumed and elegant and might not she and Jenny Greenwood change places without a great deal of bother? Jenny was not coarse featured, nor stunted as many of her contemporaries were. Her hair when it was washed and brushed as it had been on the day they had met on the moor was as dark and glossy as the wing of a blackbird. Her eyes were a pale silken grey, not at all like those of Joss or Charlie and her skin was fine and creamy beneath the layer of oil and filth which now coated it. Her teeth were white and straight, whole and undamaged. She held herself erect and her body was small boned, slender and tall.

She watched Kit now with an expressionless face, standing still and quite relaxed, her hands hanging loosely at her side, no sign of strain or of nervousness, nor of being overwhelmed by her surroundings, by the strangeness of the circumstances, nor of Kit herself.

'How is your brother?' Kit asked quietly.

'Which one?' Jenny smiled slyly and Kit's heart lurched uneasily.

'Charlie, of course?' she answered, hoping that Jenny would not hear the awkwardness in her voice, nor the sudden bumping of her heart.

'Why should you care?'

'There is no reason for you to imagine that I do, but I should like to know just the same. You sent away the doctor so I have . . .'

'He'll mend.' The answer seemed careless, heartless even but Kit had seen the solicitude with which Jenny had leaned over her brother in the kitchen of her home and she was well aware, as who was not, for it was a prodigious feat, that she had well nigh carried him the three long miles from the mill to Edgeclough on her back. A strong young woman, her strength forged in the fierce heat of the fire of life. A loyal, trustworthy woman who would give her life for those she loved, for that in which she believed.

'May I ask how his injuries are healing?'

'What the hell's it to you, for God's sake. You gave him them, more or less.'

'You must believe that, of course, and I make no attempt to defend myself. There is no defence and I will carry his scars to my grave . . .'

'Will you indeed?' Jenny's voice was mocking and she laughed abrasively. 'So will he.'

Kit sighed, watching the amused contempt brighten the deep smudged eyes of the woman by the door. Of course she would act this way. What else had she expected? Her brother beaten to within an inch of his life, his young blood soaking into her flesh as she carried him home, his broken arms dangling about her neck, his screams of agony in her ears as he wandered in and out of the fog of consciousness. And she had been forced by sheer necessity to return to work in the mill of the woman who, in her eyes, indeed in everyone's eyes who worked there was the cause of it.

'Will you sit down, Jenny?' she said, indicating a chair placed before her desk, sitting down herself, smoothing the fine silk skirt of her honey-coloured gown.

Jenny Greenwood was, for the first time since she had

425

entered the room, at a loss. Her eyes widened in astonishment and her lips parted. She moistened them with the tip of her tongue and Kit saw the uncertainty shadow her eyes.

'Sit down, Jenny. I want to talk to you.'

Jenny laughed then and into her eyes came an expression of malicious enjoyment. Her mouth widened on a huge grin and her eyes glowed.

'Sit down! In that chair? Shall I tell you something, Miss Chapman? I've been in this room before. Did you know that?' She swayed a step or two closer swinging her shortened skirt, almost performing a clog dance in her glee. 'Yes, someone else called me up here once. You and your Pa were away somewhere at the time. I told you about him up on the moor, d'you remember. He did me down, that grand fiancé of yours, on that very table, once he had me . . . where he wanted me. He liked to do it with the door unlocked, just as though the idea that anyone could walk in and find us, me with my skirts up and him with his breeches down gave him an added . . . what's the word . . . zest! Ha, you might well look amazed and so was I, I can tell you. Strip off, he says, that first time I was sent for but I wouldn't, so he never let me alone after that. You'll give in, in the end, he says, and d'you know what, in the end I did. When your little sister's crying for something to eat and your mother's so cold she can't sew on a button, you give in, in the end. He wanted *me* to say I wanted it, you see. He wouldn't force me, he said, but there's forcing and forcing, wouldn't you say, Miss Chapman? After that he'd have me on the desk with the clerks outside . . .'

She bent her head suddenly but not before Kit had seen the desolation in her eyes but she knew better than to sympathise with this proud woman. She wanted no sympathy, no charity. What she had done, what she had taken had been not for herself but for her family, and still her family were persecuted, the cause of it, without doubt, herself.

Jenny lifted her head again and her eyes were proud now, and joyful.

426

'But it was worth it in the end . . . for the boy. They say good comes out of everything and . . .'

'The . . . the boy . . . ?' and Kit's heart began to pump erratically.

'Aye. He was two in April and . . .'

'You have a son by . . .'

'Yes, and I'm not ashamed of it.'

'Then there are . . . two children . . .'

'What are you talking about?'

'Your . . . your sister-in-law . . . your brother's wife . . . she has . . .'

'What?'

'A child of the same age . . .'

'Mercy . . . good God . . .!' Jenny's face was incredulous and in that moment Kit Chapman felt the joy, the shameful joy race through her and she began to smile, to lift her face to the ceiling ready to shout it out loud but Jenny Greenwood had had enough and she let it be known by the sudden impatient movement of her whole body.

'What is this all about? Whatever it is let's have it over and done with. What do you want with me? Surely not to gossip about my family?'

'No.'

'Then what? Is it the sack, or a fine for missing two days work? There was no need for you to take the trouble to send for me to tell me. Ellis could have done it just as well. Or is it my turn for a flogging? Come on, let's be done with it and let me get back to my machine. I'm losing money while I'm standing here jawing with you, money I can ill afford. There's only me and our Daisy working now until Joss gets going again.'

'I know. It was through me Daisy got her job. I'm not asking for thanks nor gratitude only the recognition that, despite your belief to the contrary, I am not . . .'

'You got Daisy her job at the Hall.'

'Yes.'

'But how . . . ?' Jenny's face had become still, her eyes

wary, just as though the ground on which she had thought herself to be safe, had begun to shake.

'Does it matter?'

'No one said.'

'No one knew, except myself and the Squire's wife.'

There was a deep and shocked silence and into it Kit allowed herself the small flickering hope that a step had been taken to bridge the steep 'clough' that stood between herself and this woman. Jenny's hands clenched against her stained skirt and she looked about her quite wildly since it appeared she did not know exactly what to do with the news she had just been given, and wished in a way that she had not. She hated this woman, though she was aware that in the past they had owed her favours which she had shown them. She had taken a liking to her, reluctantly, on the day they had spoken on the 'tops' but she had not allowed that liking to grow, for Katherine Chapman was the culmination of all that Jenny Greenwood hated most in the world. She had shown no concern for the rest of the multitude who worked in her mills and who lived like wild animals in the squalid houses she, or at least her father had built for them. The Greenwood family had been singled out for consideration others had lacked and why, now that she was here was this woman asking her to sit down, for God's sake, just as though they were two ladies about to take afternoon tea.

'Will you not listen to what I have to say, Jenny Greenwood. You and your brother are forever mouthing vilifications of the injustices done by myself and the other mill-owners, to the men and women we employ. Your brother goes from one end of the country to the other, I believe, begging men of conscience to listen to him and you, I presume, support him in this. You demand to be heard, you radicals. You do not ask, but demand that you be listened to. Now I will do the same. I demand that you listen to me.'

'What the devil can you say to me that I might be remotely interested in?'

428

'Sit down and find out.'

'No, not in the same room as you.'

'And I took you for an intelligent woman. Very well, but I shall speak just the same.'

'You're the maister in this factory.'

'So I am, and in that case I am within my rights to dismiss you from your work as a spinner in my mill.'

Jenny's face drained of all the colour it contained and her eyes died a slow and hopeless death. Kit felt a great wave of pity engulf her for it seemed a cruel way to make this woman stand down from her blind, deaf attitude of hatred.

'So . . . that's it, is it?' Jenny whispered and though she tried hard to keep the strength of that hatred within her for it supported her, Kit saw the bleak despair gnaw at its base, taking the straightness from her back and shoulders, the proud lift from her head.

'Yes, that's it, Jenny Greenwood. I have plenty of spinners. Enough to fill another spinning room if I wished, but what I have not got is an assistant. A woman to help me in my office, a woman I can trust, a woman who knows the mills as well as I do myself, but from a different point of view. A woman who knows what the other women feel who work for me. What they need, what the children need. Someone quick to learn, eager to learn, shrewd, intelligent, brave, bull-headed. One who knows what is wrong *and can help to put it right*. A woman who is not afraid, of me, of the managers, of hard work and of what people will say about her . . . Jenny? For God's sake girl, sit down before you fall . . .'

She hurried round the desk, her distaste at the unwashed smell coming from Jenny Greenwood gone in her concern. Jenny had put her hands flat on the desk, swaying slightly, her chin on her chest. Her eyes had closed and her breath hissed from her open mouth as though her lungs had deflated in shock. Kit put her arm about her shoulders and led her to the chair and this time Jenny sat down willingly.

429

'I'm sorry, Jenny, if my manner of offering you a job seemed cruel but I could think of no other way to rip apart that caustic shell of hatred you had built around yourself. Forgive me, but I had to reach you somehow.'

Kit shook her head, then walked briskly back to her chair, giving Jenny a moment to recover her badly shaken composure. Then, impulsively, she rang a small bell on her desk and when the black-gowned little woman who, from a tiny but compact kitchen down the hall, dispensed tea and coffee to Kit's visitors, or even a light meal should Miss Chapman require it, entered the room, ordered, 'tea for two, if you please, Mrs Plank,' just as though Jenny Greenwood was the usual caller Mrs Plank was accustomed to serving. Mrs Plank stared, open-mouthed, quite unable to shift her feet, as she said later to her husband, looking at Jenny Greenwood slumped, all covered with muck and stinking like a pig pen on the green velvet chair she herself had brushed and dusted that morning and it was not until Miss Chapman cleared her throat saying, 'At once, Mrs Plank,' did she find the wits to stagger from the room.

Jenny drank the tea silently, her face turned away from Kit. It was quite blank, pallid with the shock which had her in its grip, but slowly, as the flavour and strength of the beverage she had never before tasted from a china teacup, with milk *and* sugar, penetrated her frozen mind and brought a faint colour, a mere hint of cream in its chalk whiteness crept beneath her skin. For ten minutes neither spoke. They could hear the sound of the engine, the clatter, even through the closed windows, of the looms across the mill yard, the shouts of men loading and unloading waggons and the crash of the hooves of the great Shire horses which pulled them. At last Jenny spoke.

'What makes you think I can do this grand job?'

'I know of no other woman who could.'

'Why?'

'You are Joss Greenwood's sister.'

'And if I say yes . . . what of my family?'

'You will be in a position to safeguard them and their

430

future. You will have a salary sufficient to see to their every need.'

'And my son?'

'Bring him with you.'

'Where to?'

'To live with you at Greenacres.'

'Greenacres . . . ?'

'Why not? You cannot walk from Edgeclough each day with a two-year old strapped to your back. It is, of course, your decision but it would be more practical, I think, if you were to live with me for the time being. There is an empty nursery and more servants, nursemaids I suppose, than I can count. He would be educated, brought up in any way you want. The grammar school at Crossfold . . . but I am getting ahead of the matter in hand. It is your choice, Jenny but before you make it remember that it will benefit not only you and your family but every person in my employ.'

Charlie was awake when Jenny crept into the silent cottage. He was still flat on his face but he could lift his head a little in order that the cheek on which he rested might be turned so that the flesh would not stick to the sheet. His splinted arms lay awkwardly along his body and he could do nothing for himself but with the resilience of the young and the nourishing food which his mother spooned tenderly into him whenever he would allow it, uncaring of the pennies she spent on procuring it, those put by so laboriously over the past two years in readiness for a rainy day, (since was this not *it*?) he was beginning to heal. He could open his swollen eyes to thin slits and Jenny's heart turned over with her love for him as he tried to smile when he saw her.

'Hello love,' she whispered, kneeling beside him. 'D'you want a drink?'

'Yes please, Jen,' he mumbled and when he had sipped awkwardly through the thin bit of tubing Joss had devised for him, for though he could manage to eat from the spoon his mother put in his mouth, whatever cup was put to his lips the liquid it contained merely ran away on to the sheet.

'The others in bed?'

'Aye. Mam wanted to sit up but she was tired and I made her go to bed. Mercy went with her.'

'Aye.' Nothing more was needed to be said between them about Mercy since it was taken for granted that wherever Martha went, Mercy went too, clinging like a child to her hand, weeping piteously when they were parted.

'And Joss?'

'He's gone.'

'He'll do well in that grand job. He's a way with words, has Joss.'

'Aye.'

'And what will you do, my lad, when you're better?'

Charlie's face, though it could not have been said to change expression since there was none to start with in its ferociously distended state, revealed a great sadness.

'I dunno. Not the mill.' He spoke only in a staccato paucity of words.

'You're right there, love.'

'What d'you mean, Jen?'

Jenny leaned her back against the table leg. She was sitting on the floor, her face no more than a foot or so from Charlie's. The fire's glow played on her pale face, giving it a false impression of well-being and in her eyes was a dawning, growing excitement, a spark of something which Charlie found he liked, though he had no idea of what it could be.

'There's to be changes, Charlie, for thee and me.'

'Changes?'

'Aye.'

'What sort of changes?'

Jenny's eyes dreamed into the future only she could see and Charlie felt the gladness, whatever it might be for, pump vigorously through his battered body.

'How would you like to go to school, Charlie Greenwood? Joss isn't the only one to be offered a grand new job.'

\* \* \*

Katherine and Hannah Chapman dined, as they always did when they were alone, at seven-thirty. Kit often brought home reports, accounts of profits, or a sheaf of papers which she had not had time to glance at during her busy day and she would retire afterward to her study for an hour or so. She rose at four-thirty each morning, winter or summer and therefore she liked to be bathed and in her bed by ten o'clock and even then she might sit up among her pillows and study her weekly profit sheet, often falling asleep with the papers in her hand and the lamp still burning. Her mother had grown accustomed to it since the death of her husband three years ago and had learned, as indeed she had learned while he was alive to amuse herself, playing endless games of patience or having her companion, a well-educated, but impecunious, lady named Miss Fryer, slightly younger than herself and of excellent family, read to her from one of the delightful romances of Sir Walter Scott, his very latest published only that year, *The Fair Maid of Perth* being her favourite.

They had eaten a simple meal of salmon trout with parsley-and-butter, tiny new potatoes freshly picked that day from the garden, roast fillet of veal with peas, and gooseberry sorbet to follow. Superbly cooked as Barker Chapman had always demanded, efficiently and effacingly served by Ellen the head parlourmaid and Betty, watched over by the white gloved and critical personage of the butler, Winters, and Kit had seen no reason, because the master was dead that she should not be similarly obliged.

'We are to have a house-guest, Mother,' she remarked casually as she and Hannah sipped their coffee in the drawing-room. Winters had drawn the curtains for though it was midsummer a swirling mist of light rain laced itself against the windows and the evening light had faded early over the almost invisible hills at the back of the house. Kit had ordered a small fire lit, two or three branches of candles cast a pale peach glow over the two women and the room was soft and lovely, feminine with its fragile chairs and

433

delicate figurines, its velvet sofas and dainty, spindle-legged tables.

'Really?' Hannah stirred her coffee glancing with bright interest at her daughter for it was a long time – surely it must have been the Athertons? – since guests had spent a night at Greenacres. 'And who is that, my dear?'

'You have not met her, Mother.'

'Who are her family then? Are they in cotton?'

'You might say that. Yes, I think you might say that.' Kit smiled over her coffee cup and her mother wondered at the small warning prickle which seemed to run down her own back.

'From where? Are they a Lancashire family?'

'Oh indeed. Born and bred for many generations in Lancashire.'

'How interesting, Kit, and yet you say I do not know them. Now that is odd because I could have sworn I knew all the mill-owners and their family connections from Blackburn to Manchester. Where do they live?'

'In Edgeclough.'

The prickle skimming Hannah Chapman's back became decidedly stronger. 'Edgeclough?'

'Yes, you know the village a couple of miles west of here . . .'

'I know the village, or shall I say I have heard of it as who has not, for it is where that troublemaker lives . . . what was his name? . . . the one who went to prison for inciting the riots a couple of years ago?'

'Greenwood?'

'Yes, that is the name. Dreadful man, but really Kit, I cannot recall a property of any size in that direction.'

'There is none, Mother. My guest lives in the village itself.'

'In the . . .'

'Yes.'

'But there are only weavers' cottages there.'

'That is true.'

'Kit, you must be more explicit since I cannot imagine

what you are talking about.' Hannah's face was quite red now and though she really could not believe – it was far too preposterous – that Kit meant to bring someone who was not of their rank to be a guest in *their* home, she felt the prickle in her spine become a painful tremble, almost a palpitation to which she was prone when she was upset, in the region of her heart.

'Very well, Mother. I am to employ a young woman to help me in the mill . . .'

'Not as a clerk, Kit. The men would not like it.'

'No, not as a clerk, Mother. Her precise duties at the moment are vague, but she will work with me. In my office. I intend to train her myself . . .'

'As what, my dear Katherine. There are no women employed in the mills except as machine operatives and you would hardly be . . .' She stopped and her mouth began to tremble. She put her hand to it and that shook too and she placed her coffee cup carefully on the table beside her.

'You cannot mean what I think you mean! I will not have a girl from a weaver's cottage in my home, Katherine, if that is what you are trying to tell me. Do what you like with her at the mill, which I know you will despite what people say about you for you are well accustomed to it, but I will not have her at Greenacres.'

'She will be my assistant, Mother. She is intelligent, ambitious and though she has not been brought up to it, she will learn . . .'

'Not in my house.' Hannah's voice was implacably hard.

'No, not in your house, Mother, in mine.'

'Katherine! How dare you speak to me like that. Though your father in his wisdom, of which, now, I am seriously beginning to doubt he had any, left the house and indeed everything he owned to you, I am mistress here . . .'

Kit's voice was gentle. 'No Mother, you are not.'

'Katherine! How can you be so hard?'

'I had a good teacher, Mother and he taught me how splendid it is to get one's own way. And that is what I am doing now. Our guest . . . my guest, if you prefer, will be to me what Miss Fryer is to you, though I would wish her to dine with us so that she will learn to . . .'

'Oh no . . . oh no, Katherine.'

'Then she and I will dine alone.'

'You are saying I must eat in my room?'

'No, I am not, but if you do not care to share a table with your daughter and her companion, then you are at liberty to eat where you wish.'

'Merciful Heaven, what is the world coming to? To eat with a servant! Your father did not mean this when he left his mills in your care. He would no more have invited one of his mill-hands into our dining-room, into our *home* than he would some Irish peasant from Pig Lane. You must be mad, absolutely mad! What am I to say to our friends? And . . .' Her elderly face crumpled as she dissolved into the easy tears of a woman who can think of no other way to get what she wants, ' . . . are we to include her in our guest list when Emma Abbott and Sarah Jenkinson dine with us. She will not even know which knife to use, if she has even *seen* a knife . . .'

'She will learn. I will teach her.'

' . . . and her nails will be dirty . . .'

'Don't be ridiculous, Mother.'

' . . . and what of her family? Will I be expected to entertain them as well?' Her weeping became more liquid and she reached for the wisp of handkerchief in her sleeve.

'No, you will not. They would not wish it . . .'

'*They* would not wish it! And who are they to say . . .?'

'Their name is Greenwood. The woman who is to assist me is Jenny Greenwood. She and her son will live here in my house . . .'

'Her son? And is her husband to come too?'

'She is not married.'

'A . . . widow . . .?'

'No.'

'*You are bringing a whore and her bastard to live in our home?*'

436

The silence which followed dragged painfully from second to second. Kit watched her mother's face disintegrate into lines and sagging flesh which had not been there before and she was sorry. Hannah Chapman was forty-two years old, a pretty woman who spent hours in front of her mirror with her maid and the lotions and unguents she rubbed into her fine skin. Youthful, plump, and even yet looked at admiringly by many gentlemen of her own generation for she would be a fine catch for any man with the wealth of her dead husband behind her. Now, in the space of ten seconds she had aged to a woman of sixty and her voice was the hissing of snakes in her throat.

'If you imagine I will sit down with a woman who had an illegitimate child and who is a member of the family who murdered your father you must be insane and I shall consult my brother to use his influence to have you put away.'

'Mother.' Kit's voice was endlessly patient. 'It was proved that . . . that Joss Greenwood had nothing to do with Father's murder. Do you think the man would be walking about unharmed if he had? And his sister is a clever woman, strong and trustworthy. She is not to be blamed for . . . her child. She was . . . seduced by someone who had a hold on her . . .'

Hannah Chapman stood up. Her tears were gone now and in their place was the dislike she had always known she felt for this unconventional, independent, obstinate and in her opinion, quite freakish daughter of hers. Years ago when Kit had been a girl and, Hannah had hoped, malleable, she had run to her father and spurned Hannah's hopes that they might be as other mothers and their daughters were. Kit had taken up the pursuits of a son, become Barker Chapman's son, scorned the dictates of polite society and become, Hannah privately thought, the laughing stock of Crossfold. She had carried on, after her father's death, with the running of his mills and had, her mother was told by the gentlemen with whom they dined, made a success of it, but in the past year or two there had been no more offers

437

for her of marriage. No man wanted a wife, no matter how wealthy, who was a successful *business man!* They had hoped, after her father's death, to see her falter a little, perhaps slip and fall so that one of them might pick her up, kiss her better, send her home to the nursery, and put back to rights the business her father had, foolishly, left in her hands. But she had not fallen and Hannah would never forgive her for it.

And now this! A mill girl, a factory girl with the morals, so it appeared, of an alley-cat, and in *her* home. It was not to be borne and though Hannah Chapman knew she had no choice but to bear it she would let it be known, in her own home and in the Penfold Valley that Katherine Chapman was no longer her daughter.

'You will, of course, do as you please, Katherine. This is your house, as you point out and you may entertain whom you like in it. But not in my presence. I would be glad if you would arrange for me to have my own suite of rooms, my own servants, and only those I invite shall enter them. Good-night, or perhaps it is goodbye.'

## 29

The town simply rocked with it and Hannah was most gratified by the strong support she received in the beginning from the ladies of her acquaintance who thought they had nothing to lose by giving it. They were unaware of the dreadful position in which she had placed their husbands, most of whom did business with Katherine and who knew it to be only expedient to stay on her right side.

'Dammit, what will the bloody woman do next?' George Abbott thundered to his wife in the privacy of their bedroom, not really distinguishing between Hannah and

Katherine since it made no difference to him who was to share Katherine Chapman's home with her, nor who worked in her office, his only anxiety being the awkwardness the whole foolish situation would create in his world of commerce. Of course, what else could you expect when women were allowed to meddle in the affairs of gentlemen, he begged his wife to tell him? Their damned female emotions were bound to get in the way of their judgment. And did Katherine Chapman have any?

Was that emotion or judgment? His Emma wanted to be told since it was well known that Barker Chapman's daughter had spurned the splendid hand of Harry Atherton, a gentleman of great position, if little actual cash, and anyone could see how much he had been devastated by it and by her coldness to him. Which, to Emma, showed a lack of emotion *and* judgment on Katherine Chapman's part since any girl, particularly of their class would have snapped him up and had him to the altar before the year was out. And now, it was rumoured, he had married a great heiress from Guilden Sutton and Katherine Chapman had lost her chance for good.

'Well, she could finish the Abbott Mills if she had a mind to it,' George said, irritated beyond measure by his wife's female ramblings on a matter which had not the slightest bearing on his dilemma. He couldn't afford to offend Katherine Chapman whatever Hannah might demand of him in the way of loyalty, and there were many gentlemen of Crossfold who were in the same tenuous position. She had only to call in a note or two here and there and not a few men of the textile trade would find it hard to continue so what the hell was he, and they, to do now, he asked Emma to tell him?

'But we can't dine with Hannah in a separate part of the house one week, and with Katherine the next,' his wife wailed. 'Hannah would be affronted though I doubt if Katherine would care. She has no heart at all and no concern for anything but those mills of hers . . .'

'As I have for mine, woman, and that is why you will

continue to call on her and to entertain her in our home and if Hannah doesn't like it then I'm sorry but there's nothing else to be done. I have relied, first on Barker, and now on his daughter for a loan now and again and one does not displease the man, or in this case the woman, one owes money to.'

'But that . . . that factory girl might be there . . .'

'Then we shall just have to grit our teeth and make ourselves pleasant to her.'

'*To a mill girl?*'

'Aye, and don't forget, my lass, your grandmother was nought but a spinner in her father's cottage, as was mine so there's no need to put on that grand air with me. There'll be more than a few gentlemen, and their ladies too, who'll have to toe the line with Katherine Chapman from now on and if that means being pleasant to a mill hand then we'll bloody well have to do it.'

'We must get some clothes for you, Jenny,' Kit said to her briskly on the day it had begun, 'and to do that I think we will travel to London for I mean you to be as elegantly gowned as any of the ladies of this town. Miss Cavendish is all very well but it will take too long for the fabrics and all the rest of the things you need to arrive so we will have a small holiday and fetch them ourselves. It will be an opportunity to get to know one another without . . . other factors intruding.'

'To London?' Kit might have suggested she and Jenny were to go to the Americas to hunt for bearskins to dress themselves in, so confounded was she, and besides, who did she think she was, telling Jenny she was not dressed as she should be? She had on a perfectly decent skirt and bodice, clean and made by her mother only three years ago when there had been a copper or two to spare from Harry Atherton.

'Yes, why not? Don't tell me you have some objection to being fitted out with a fashionable gown and perhaps a bonnet. You will pay for them yourself in the end, you know.'

'Then in that case there's nowt wrong with what I've got on.'

'And that's another thing.'

'What?'

'You really will have to make an effort to stop using the word 'nowt'. I appreciate that many of the men I do business with are only a generation away from weavers' cottages themselves but they have learned to speak, or been taught at the grammar school, the language of a gentleman.'

'Meaning I'm no lady. Well, I never pretended to be and if how I speak, *and* dress don't suit, then p'haps you'd better get down to the spinning room and pick someone else for your fine job. I'm a mill girl, Kit Chapman. That's what I *am*, and learning to wear fine clothes and say *nothing* instead of *nowt* won't change it . . .'

'There you are, you can pronounce the word if you put your mind to it. Just listen to the way I speak and watch what I do and you won't go far wrong.'

'Is that so! Well, you may be interested to know that I think *nowt* a pound to dressing and speaking like you and if it wasn't for being able to give my lad and my Mam a bit of comfort I'd tell you to take your bloody job and . . .' The words were hissed through clenched teeth.

'But you won't, will you, Jenny Greenwood?' Kit smiled sweetly. 'You haven't quite the nerve to go that far, have you?'

'It's got nowt to do with nerve and well you know it. I'm doing this to try and get a bit of food in them bairns' mouths down there and a decent roof over their heads, *and for no other reason*. D'you think I want to spend my days, aye, and every spare hour it seems, in the company of Barker Chapman's lass, do you? I wouldn't spit on you if you were on fire, only for *them*.'

'I know that and I must admit the thought daunts me too. But you can be of use to me, you see and so I will make the best of it and you must do the same.'

Jenny had walked from Edgeclough to Crossfold that morning as she had done every morning, leaving the cottage at four o'clock just as the sun was showing its rim above Dog Hill. Lucas was to remain with Martha for the time being but only until Jenny was settled at Greenacres and the nursery had been prepared for him. He was a brown-eyed, sturdy-legged replica of Harry Atherton, with his father's devilish smile but a certain sweetness in his expression which reminded his grandmother of Abel Greenwood, which was strange since they did not share the same blood.

The parting from her son and her mother had been hard, for Martha seemed to think she was to go to the ends of the earth – which was what this new position with Katherine Chapman appeared to her to be – and that she would never see her girl again. She had clung to her fiercely, afraid suddenly since she herself was not young and with Charlie helpless and Mercy no more than another child to be cared for alongside Lucas, how was she to manage?

'It's all arranged, Mother,' Jenny told her lovingly. 'Sarah's to come up each day until Charlie's on his feet again . . .'

'But Sarah can't afford to sit about here all day with . . .'

'Sarah *can* afford it, Mother,' and she was delighted with the grand feeling she had when she added, 'I've seen to that.'

'You . . . ?' Martha's face was bewildered.

'Listen Mother, this new job I'm to do . . . it's responsible work . . .' She tried to remember the exact words Kit Chapman had used when Jenny had told her, brusquely, that she would be willing to take the position offered her. She would give it a try. Yes, she would live up at the big house, she had told Miss Chapman, though God knows how she would cope with it, the stares of the servants, the gossip, the contempt and rejection and loneliness she would suffer, but by God she'd manage it somehow. She could hardly trail each day in her grand frock across the open moorland from Edgeclough to Crossfold and back, could she? Besides Miss Chapman had said she must learn not only the workings of the mill and the changes Miss Chapman envisaged and which Jenny was to supervise, but how to mix with the ladies and gentlemen of Miss Chapman's business and social acquaintance.

'It will take a lot of hard work, Mother,' she continued, holding her mother's hands across the kitchen table, then turning to smile at Charlie who was, as his back healed, almost ready to sit up now. 'I'm to take on duties which need constant watching and can only be given to someone trustworthy.' Could she be blamed for feeling a little bit flattered at that, she had asked herself privately? 'That's what *she* said and if I'm to do anything to help to change what's going on I've no choice but to trust *her*. I can afford to keep you and Mercy, and Charlie *and* pay Sarah to help you . . .'

'Dear God in Heaven . . .'

'Perhaps He is at last, Mother.' She turned to Charlie and leaned forward to touch his still badly swollen face. 'And when you're better . . .'

'Yes Jenny?' He held his breath and his eyes glowed between his slitted eyelids.

'You're not to go back to the weaving-shed . . .'

'No . . .'

'No lad. What would you like to do more than anything else in the world, Charlie, apart from working with Joss?'

'You know, Jenny, you said I could . . .'

'Aye, and I'm to keep my promise. You're to go to the gammar school in Crossfold,' and her voice was hopeful, joyful for had not Joss said that only through education could a man better his station in life and now *she*, Jenny Greenwood, was to give Charlie that chance.

'Will you like that, love?'

'Oh, Jenny, just wait 'til our Joss hears about this.'

'Aye, I wish I could be here when you tell him.' Her face crumpled for a moment since how was she to leave this loving circle which had sustained her for as long as she could remember, then it brightened. Joss had said it time and time again that only through moving on could progress be made and by God she meant to make progress now.

She'd been given a chance, a bite at the good things which were set out on the tables of the privileged and if they should seem sour at first then she'd keep on tasting until she found what she liked. The rest she'd spit out or overcome somehow.

'Watch out for Lucas for me,' she said at the last, burying her face in the soft, sweet smelling flesh of her son's neck, then she was gone.

She was standing silently in Kit's office when she arrived, looking out on to the hurrying crowd of men and women, the fretful children, listening to the incessant sound of their wooden clogs on the cobblestones, watching, remembering, her heart sad for those who were slipping patiently into the sheds and the spinning rooms, there to stay for the next fourteen, fifteen, sixteen hours. She saw Kit at the gate, ready to shut it on the latecomers, then moving across the yard, nodding to a man who touched his cap, a woman who sketched a curtsey and bitterness soured her throat for it seemed, despite Kit Chapman's fine words; that nothing had changed.

'Aah, Jenny, good morning. I won't be a moment and then we can . . .'

'They can't help being late sometimes, you know. They don't do it on purpose. God knows, they can't afford to lose their wages in fines. They've got sick children at home, many of them and have you any idea how hard it is for a woman to leave a child . . .' her face worked briefly in a spasm of pain before she could speak again, ' . . . in the care of another who's probably only a year or two older, or even on its own? They have to work to feed them and so they're left alone and yet when they're a minute late you shut the gate in their faces and make them wait until eight o'clock.'

Kit stood quietly, her face expressionless, her first instinctive anger – since when did anyone take Kit Chapman to task about *anything* – dying away, her hands which had been reaching out to some papers, still hovering above them.

444

'Of course, you are right,' she said at last. 'It has been done for so long it just never occurred to me to stop it. Latecomers have always been fined and I merely carried on what my grandfather began years ago. What do you suggest?'

'Me?' Jenny's mouth dropped open in surprise.

'That is what you are here for, Jenny. To assist, to advise, to help me contrive a business which will still make a profit without exploiting my employees. You see I *must* make a profit or there is no use in manufacturing my cloth for if I lose money I shall lose the mills and those people out there will be without work. Over a thousand of them. I have the expertise. I know *how* to make a profit, but *you* are a spinner, you are a woman of . . . well . . . a woman who has . . .'

'I'm one of the "distressed poor", is that what you're saying? There's no need to mince words with me. Well, so I am, or was. I know how they live and how they suffer in these mills of yours to earn a few bob a week. Well, I suppose you and me, being two sides of the same coin, so to speak, could try to solve not only their problems, but the ones *you* are going to have because you're going to have some, make no mistake about it, Kit Chapman. You'll be despised by everyone in the valley but then, so will I for they'll say I've gone over to you for more money. Well, let me tell you now that I haven't. I'm willing to trust you, for a while at any rate. There will be those who say I'm in it just for what I can get, and I admit that's partly true. Why shouldn't me and my family be warm and well fed, have pretty things and learn our letters like you and yours, but I'd not give you the time of day, never fear, if I didn't think I could do some good for those poor beggars out there. My brother's been doing it for nearly ten years and my father before him. My younger brother nearly lost his life for it. There's not a lot a woman can do but now I'm to be given the chance and I'll take it. So first off, we'll have those gates open again and every one of them outside who has a genuine reason for being late will be allowed in. I can tell a man who's been on the gin and too befuddled to get out of bed on time though he'll pretend it's for some other reason. They can wait until eight o'clock for I'll not stand for them kind of tricks.'

They moved through the spinning mills together on that first day, a strange and unbelievable sight to the spinners and tacklers who stared with mouths agape at the two young women. Kit wore a harebell blue gown of gingham, the bodice high to her neck with small puffed sleeves to her elbow. The skirt was wide and quite unsuitable for negotiating the narrow spaces between the machines and each operative was forced to stand hastily to one side to allow her employer – and her skirt – to pass by. Her half boots were of white-laced kid with high heels and around her slender waist was a wide satin sash the same colour as her dress. Her hair had been arranged by Janet, as it always was, into the style which suited its heavy straightness, an 'Apollo' knot at the nape of her neck and secured with a froth of blue satin ribbons. The use of rouge which had once been fashionable was now declining, since the style was to be languid, listless and pale causing many a gentleman to remark that there seemed to be no healthy females about these days, and Kit's golden skin, peach tinted at the cheekbones was considered to be quite odd. Tight-lacing was the mode but Kit, having no Mama to press her and no concern in the rivalry for a gentleman's interest, did not observe it, indeed had no need of it.

Jenny had washed her abundant hair the night before, taking the scissors with which her father had once trimmed his 'piece' of cloth, and cutting it as she did about once a month until it was no more than three inches from her white scalp and it rioted all over her head in thick, glossy curls. Her plain grey bodice and ankle length skirt were completely unadorned and her feet were pushed stocking-less into her wooden clogs. Her eyes were smudged with weariness since she had slept little during the past week but their colour, not unlike the grey misted skies above Dog

446

Hill, was clear and lovely. She was clean, decent but beside Kit, a plain grey pigeon next to the brilliance of a peacock. She spoke to Kit almost constantly, pointing a rough, broken-nailed finger to a dozen things in every row of machines and Kit nodded and was seen to touch Jenny's arm, to talk close to Jenny's ear, to stop when she did and examine a pair of the new 'self-acting' spinning mules only recently installed which could spin not only the very finest of threads but double the number spun on the old machines. They tested together the quality of the yarn spun, rubbing it between experienced fingers, both of them and making comments which none could hear. And those about them were quite mesmerised to see Miss Katherine Chapman, their employer, the owner of the mills and of the machines they themselves operated go down on her knees in her beautiful blue dress, just as though the garment meant nothing to her, with Jenny Greenwood, whom they all knew as one of themselves, and draw out a small child who cowered beneath a spinning frame. A little girl of no more than three or four who was plainly more terrified of the creature, beautiful and unimagined in the child's mind, than anything she had ever known in her short life. She was familiar with nothing but the colours of black and grey, with obnoxious smells, which she did not know were obnoxious, with dirt and filth, bricks and smoke, angry faces and the feel of the strap and had not known anything else existed.

She was set on her feet and in her fear her bladder emptied itself down her thin grey leg and when they led her between the rows of machinery, a skeletal hand held in each of theirs towards Ellis who had been stamping his feet in obvious pique at his employer's presence in 'his' room, the child might have been going to the gallows so great was her despair.

No one could, naturally, hear what was said between Ellis and Miss Chapman but those close to them declared later that if looks could kill Jenny Greenwood would have dropped dead on the spot. He had argued hotly, even forcibly with his flint-faced employer, attempting to take the

447

almost senseless child from her but another overlooker was brought over to take his place and the women, those who had the strength to bolster up their usual indifference to anything but the earning of their wage and the feeding of their children, watched furtively as the two women, the man and the child walked out of the spinning room.

'Now then Ellis,' Kit Chapman said crisply when the four of them had gained the privacy of her office. 'I would be glad to hear your version of the event which took place in the weaving-shed a few days ago. I appreciate that you are overlooker in the spinning room and that you are in charge of one hundred and sixty frames there but on this particular occasion I believe you were absent from your work. While you were absent – and I know exactly when that was – this child here . . .' She pointed to the girl who crouched, like some small, dazed night animal caught in the full glare of sunlight, against the wall of the office, ' . . . was considerably abused by an overlooker in the weaving-shed, in fact *two* overlookers, while another looked on. She was gagged, I was told by an observer and whipped round a machine. A young boy who came to her aid had both his arms broken and was so badly flogged it was feared for a while that he might never recover.' Her voice dropped almost to a whisper. 'If he had died, Ellis, those three men would have been hanged for murder. I, personally, would have seen to it. For some reason this child, the child in question, perhaps to hide the evidence, has been transferred to the spinning room and is now in *your* care . . .'

'Now see here, Miss Chapman, if those two in the weaving-shed said I had anything to do with it they are lying. I admit I . . . well, I never laid a finger on the kid, or the lad. It was them that strapped her and flogged the lad . . .'

'Their names, Ellis?'

'Well, I don't know as . . .'

'I wish to know their names, Ellis, so that they may be charged.'

Ellis began to smirk and finger the full moustache he now

affected, believing thankfully that his part in the affair was to be overlooked if he played informer. He lied when he said he had not helped in the beating Charlie Greenwood had received, since he had long harboured a grudge against Jenny Greenwood for her refusal to allow him the liberties he had, if he was honest, almost begged her for; for her scorn, her contemptuous treatment of him as a man; any member of her family would do to work off some of the rage she invoked in him. He had lusted after her for a long time but when Harry Atherton had laid his claim to her Ellis had been forced to relinquish his quarry to a stronger, more authoritative beast of prey. But he had not given up and when Atherton had gone, still swearing revenge on the woman, Ellis's employer who, it turned out had spurned *him*, Ellis had renewed his chase after Jenny Greenwood. Her refusal had made her even more desirable, her contempt more vulnerable, for though he had been hot for her body, his hatred of her had become a cold thing. She was no more than a spinner, a factory girl who he could have dismissed whenever he wanted to, but his resolve, like a certain other part of his body, had hardened each time he caught a glimpse of her as she leaned over her machine.

Now she was watching him, her expression one of withering hostility and he could hardly wait to get her back at her machine for by God she'd pay for this. No doubt she had come running to Miss Chapman, defending that spineless lout who was her brother, demanding that the men involved be punished. It was well known that Miss Chapman was a mite squeamish when it came to the factory floor and it was just like her to pick on this one incident to ease her conscience. For years lads, and lasses, had been flogged in the mill yard for stepping out of line, children strapped to keep them awake and she'd never opened her damned mouth, but, it was rumoured, she had a soft spot for these Greenwoods because of her fancy for Joss Greenwood, he supposed. It was strange how these high and mighty ladies and gentlemen, such as her and Harry Atherton liked to bed with a class inferior to their own, but that was life and

449

nowt to do with him, except when he could make a guinea or two out of it. *He* didn't care who he tumbled, except for Jenny Greenwood. Now she was a bit special and when he had the chance, willing or unwilling he'd have her drawers round her ankles and her skirts over her head and she'd pay for this humiliation she had heaped on him. It was strange the way Atherton had run off three years since, especially after what he himself had told the man about Miss Chapman and Joss Greenwood. Still, he, Ellis had a good spot here in Chapman's mill. A position of responsibility, a decent wage since all his girls worked hard to provide him with it, and as much wenching as he could handle from the fresh girls as they came in. He'd been a bit of a fool to get involved with the flogging Jim and Alfie had given young Greenwood but he'd smooth it over, like he always did. Pity about Jim and Alfie, but then they were nowt to him, were they?

'Their names, Ellis.'

'Jim Briggs and Alfie Jackson.'

'Thank you. I will send for them at once and I would be obliged if you would step into the outer office where the Peace Officers are waiting for you.'

The smirk dropped from Ellis's well-fed face and his mouth gaped to reveal the poor state of his teeth. He'd kissed the shuttle a thousand times before he became an overlooker and those at the front were no more than rotting stumps. The amazement on his face might have been amusing if the situation had been less serious, but it was replaced just as quickly with an expression of such malice Jenny felt her stout heart quail. She had worked in the mill for so long the complete authority of the overlooker had been bred in her and though she had defied more than one they still had the power to frighten her, even if she had not let them see it.

But not Kit Chapman. It was *her* authority which counted here and since the day her father had died she had been opposed by no one. She was in command, supreme and all powerful. They all belonged to her, these men, women and children and they were here because she chose to allow it. She could hire them and fire them at will and her haughty disdain for this one, her absolute belief that, should she want to and she did, he would be behind bars by nightfall was explicit in her face.

'I've done nowt . . .' he began to bluster, remembering at the last moment who she was, remembering that she was no submissive spinner he could have cringing over her machine. 'I was there I'll give you that and happen I should have stopped it but it weren't my place. He was in their charge and he'd taken a swing at Jim. Knocked him to the floor. Like a madman he was and we had to control him . . .'

'An eleven year old boy and *three full grown men*. Tell me, Ellis, who held his arms, who *broke* his arms . . . ?'

'Not me, Miss Chapman. It were nowt to do wi' me.'

'We shall see then, Ellis, when you come before the magistrates.'

'Now look here . . .'

'No, Ellis, you look here. I am the master in this mill and I'll not have my operatives half killed by . . .'

'You weren't so bloody fussy in the past,' he roared, all constraint gone. 'You did nowt when that brat 'ad 'is arms ripped off, did yer? No, you steered clear of t'spinning room when it suited yer. There's dozens . . . hundreds feel t'strap, week in an' week out but you shut yer bloody eyes to it until this bitch 'ere put 'er two-pennorth in . . .'

The child in the corner turned her face to the wall and Jenny called out in a high, appalled voice. The door burst open and in a moment the Peace Officer had him by the arms, manhandling him towards the door. Several clerks craned their necks to see better and Mrs Plank hovered hesitantly at the end of the hallway. Kit Chapman felt her legs give way beneath her. She sat down slowly and her breath sighed out from her in a long expulsion of guilt.

'It's true,' she whispered. 'What he said was the truth, but from now on it will be different, I promise you.' She was looking at no one in particular and Jenny was made aware that she was talking to no one but herself since she was the only one to blame for it and she was the only one to put it right.

'What will you do with the child?' Jenny asked softly after a moment or so. 'The poor thing's terrified out of her wits. Will you leave her for the kitchen maids at Greenacres to fetch up. Or are you to turn her into a skivvy instead of a piecer?'

'No, of course not. She can . . .'

'What?'

'Well, what do you suggest?'

'She could go to . . . in the . . .' Jenny gulped for the word was unfamiliar on her tongue, ' . . . in the nursery with Lucas.'

'Good God!'

'Why not?'

'Well, no reason, I suppose.'

'Poor little beggar will probably feel more secure with another child.'

'Do you think so?'

'Have you no imagination, Miss Chapman, except that which you put to work in the making of profit each week?'

Kit chose to ignore the question, saying instead. 'We are to go on a journey.'

'Where are we going?'

'Home first, and then to London. But you are right. Flora will look after her. She has, I believe, ten brothers and sisters, all younger than herself so she should know how.'

They spent five days there. In a borrowed gown of Miss Chapman's and with Janet, her maid to accompany them, Jenny Greenwood rode in a carriage for the first time in her life, from the mill to Greenacres, which, if she were to be asked, she could have described to no one since her fevered gaze fell on so many beautiful and bewildering objects they all ran together in a kaleidoscope of colours and shapes and she saw none of them. She was vaguely aware of the disdainful faces, of skirts being drawn aside as she passed, of whispers behind gloved hands and the disapproving sniff

452

of the girl called Janet when she was asked to find a gown suitable for *Miss* Greenwood, but it all hurried by on the periphery of her conscious mind.

She stepped, this time in a dark blue travelling outfit which fitted her rather well, and a bonnet to match, a shade too large and quenching the bright, excited spirit of her eyes and tumultuous hair, into the coach for London and shrank for several hours into the protective silence which allowed her to appear composed, unmoved by the desperate speed at which they went. Ten and a half miles an hour, Miss Chapman told her imperturbably, appearing quite unconcerned by it all, but anyone who had been to London before, (as Jenny had been told Miss Chapman had) must find the journey most ordinary.

They reached St Albans the next day, the whole journey from Manchester to London, not counting the night they stayed at the pleasant and comfortable coaching inn at Leicester, taking no more than an incredible eighteen and a half hours. The coach, a beautiful thing in Jenny's wondering eyes was of a dull, black leather with broad, blackleaded nails tracing out the panels. Above these were four oval windows with leather curtains. Upon the doors were displayed in large characters the names of the places from where the coach started its journey and where it would finish it. Jenny read the words carefully each time they came to a post-house where the horses and sometimes the drivers, were changed, marvelling at names such as Portsmouth, Bath, Holyhead and York, Shrewsbury and Dover and where they might possibly be! She tried not to stare too blatantly at the multitude of travellers moving from one part of the country to another as though it was commonplace to them, an everyday occurrence which happened to all, gentlemen in full-bottomed cloaks, beavers and mudstained boots, ladies in wide skirts, wide bonnets, laughing, flirting, drinking, gambling some of them on how long it would take to get from here to there.

The inn at which they were to spend five nights was quite splendid with broad corridors and stairs, elegant drawing-rooms and four poster beds hung with silk, their sheets smelling of lavender. Miss Chapman ordered three bedrooms and a private sitting room since she did not wish to be pestered by bothersome gentlemen, she said and still Jenny Greenwood seemed unable to unclench the tight snap of her jaw, merely nodding and smiling as best she could, trembling at every strange sound, of which there were many, jumping at every loud noise, of which there were even more.

But by doing exactly what Miss Chapman did, by copying every move, every step she took, her smiles and 'good mornings', her courteous 'good evenings', her confident walk and interested gaze, Jenny Greenwood began, little by little, hour by hour, to relax, hesitantly to look about her and actually *see* what went on.

They strolled the length of Oxford Street, Janet a pace or two behind them, boiling indignantly, Jenny was well aware of being made to feel a lesser personage than a mere factory girl. They looked in the splendid shop windows, their facades brightly lit by gas-lamp, their doors open, they were told, until ten o'clock at night. There were shops selling watches, fans and silk, china and glass, crystal flasks every shape and size and colour, the likes of which Jenny had not even known existed. Behind handsome glass windows were pyramids of pineapples, figs, grapes and oranges and when she asked Miss Chapman tentatively what they might be she heard Janet snigger behind her hand. There were shops selling lamps of crystal, silver and brass, slippers and shoes and boots and on Greek Street beyond Soho Square, the magnificent showrooms of Josiah Wedgwood where tables were laid out as though a dinner party was expected at any moment and salesmen hovered discreetly between columns which rose from the polished floor to the plastered ceiling. It was, one of the young gentlemen told them politely, Mr Wedgwood's declared aim to 'amuse and divert, please, astonish, nay, even to ravish the ladies with his display'.

They toured Woburn Walk in Bloomsbury, spending a

day in the first shopping centre designed purposely as a shopping street and at 'The Royal Opera Arcade', a setting of superb shops at the back of the Haymarket Opera House.

But it was in the salons of the great dressmakers and designers that Jenny was made truly speechless. She had, up until then, managed a word or two with Miss Chapman even going so far as to venture an opinion on this or that, but as they ascended the gilt and mirrored splendour of the pale beige carpeted staircase of Monsieur Antoine, just come, they were told, straight from Paris to dress the ladies of London, that she almost lost her nerve.

'We shall have you suitably attired, Jenny and I must admit these peignoirs are quite delicious.' Miss Chapman studied a delicate foamy creation which Jenny could not even recognise as a garment for any woman to wear, or hazard a guess at *when*. 'I should feel decidedly wicked sipping my early morning tea in one of these.'

Sipping tea! Is that what they were designed for, Jenny had time to marvel before being led on to study pelisse-robes and morning dresses, lace petticoats and round dresses, with or without a train, walking dresses trimmed with swansdown, black kid sandals, small black beaver riding hats, York tan gloves, white kid gloves, dresses with 'demi-gigot' sleeves, 'marie' sleeves and 'imbecile' sleeves and evening dresses of satin and gauze with no sleeves at all, and available in Madam's size and any colour Madam might care for, by the end of the week.

And in one of the new evening gowns of which Miss Chapman insisted she needed at least half a dozen, on their last night in London, she and Miss Chapman sat in a private box, as Miss Chapman called it, at the 'Prince of Wales' theatre to watch a performance of 'The Corsican Brothers', a romantic drama adapted from the French, Miss Chapman said. It was, Jenny thought, the most magical moment of her life and she would never, if she lived to be ninety, forget it.

The next day they boarded the coach at St Albans, Janet a mite more respectful of the elegantly dressed young lady

455

who had once been Jenny Greenwood, spinster, from Edge-clough but who was now, it seemed, ready to tackle any-thing from the high-toned butler at Greenacres who had turned up his nose at her five days ago, to the reformation of the whole town of Crossfold and every cotton mill in it.

'And what did you make of London then, Jenny?' she heard her mistress ask her new assistant as the coach pulled out of the mill yard.

'It were all right, I suppose, if you like that sort o' thing but there's nowt to beat a good country fair or a Whit Sunday walk in Oldham.' And her eyes had smiled ma-liciously as she turned her fashionably bonneted head to stare – bored to death with it all, she would have them believe – out of the coach window.

## 30

They did not recognise her on the first day she appeared at the mill gate with Katherine Chapman and it was not until one of the managers, a young man of about thirty-five who had often admired the flaunting strangeness of Jenny Greenwood's short, glossy curls, remarked on her resem-blance to the mill girl, that it was realised this *was* the mill girl.

'Shall I shut the gate now, Miss Chapman?' the yard foreman said as the clock on the counting house wall struck five thirty, but Miss Chapman shook her head briskly.

'No Sam, not yet. I shall return to my office now but Miss Greenwood will tell you when.'

The man went so far as to utter, '*Yer what . . . !*' before he remembered to whom he was speaking and even then, when Miss Chapman had walked away, her own bare head shining in the early morning sunshine, he found he could scarcely control the habit of a lifetime, his hands fingering the large key, putting it in the lock, edging the stout gates to a slow closing against half a dozen hurrying women whose thin faces shone with relief to see them still open.

'Let them in, Sam, if you please,' Jenny Greenwood had the bloody nerve to tell him and if she didn't watch out he'd clout her one despite her grand frock and the dainty leather boots she had on feet which had known nothing but clogs.

'Who the 'ell d'yer think you're talkin' to, my lass? Dressed up to the nines yer might be but you're still nowt but a factory girl and no right to throw yer weight about at *my* gate.'

But Jenny had taken up a stand in the centre of the arched gateway, addressing a remark to, being answered hesitantly by the dozen or so women who hovered there, smiling, nodding in agreement, touching a sympathetic hand to a bowed shoulder, allowing the women to slip inside the gate and he could hardly shut them with her between them, could he? She was sharp with Jacob Smith, the smell of the gin he had drunk the night before still on his breath and told him to stand aside before she called a man to eject him since only genuine latecomers were to be let in, and surprisingly Jacob Smith did so and at forty minutes past five the gates were clanged shut, not to be opened again until eight o'clock and as Sam crossed the yard he was heard to mutter that old Mr Chapman would be turning over in his grave this day.

'Was there any trouble with Sam?' Miss Chapman asked Jenny as she walked into her office.

'Not really. He would have liked to shut *me* out and make me wait for three hours and see me fined for my cheek but I stood in the gateway and he could do nothing about it.'

'And the women?'

'Most of them had sick children to see to before they left.

One of them, her husband or that's what she calls him, though I doubt they're wed, had had an accident and she had to help him out of his bed. Oh, all legitimate reasons for being late so I let them in. It was . . .' She had been about to say that it had been a joy to her to see the slack relief on their poor pinched faces but she could not seem to let herself be natural with this unusual woman. She had begun, at last, to believe that Katherine Chapman's intentions were to be trusted. That she meant what she said, but though they had spent almost a week in one another's company, it did not get any easier. Too much stood between them. They could not, despite good intentions on both their parts, immediately become friends, if they ever would. And if they were to become working partners, for they both wanted this revolutionary idea to succeed, they would have to put aside their past relationship and try very hard to forge a new one for the future, if it could be done.

Kit Chapman leaned forward, resting her elbows on her desk. Beside it, making it double the length, had been placed another which was, for the time being, to be Jenny's. They were to sit side by side and every transaction, every concern to do with the business, every commercial intercourse recorded, profits, loss, meeting agendas, shift rotas, the state of trade, each negotiation Katherine Chapman conducted would include the presence of Jenny Greenwood and all would be explained to her as it happened. She already knew all there was to know about the technical side of spinning and would be invaluable in the organisation of the new work system and the rates of wages which would not only be fair – a decent wage for a decent day's work as Joss Greenwood had dreamed of – but would provide a higher standard of living for all her operatives. But for now the relationship of Katherine Chapman and Jenny Greenwood must be worked out satisfactorily.

'Sit down, Jenny,' she said, her face unsmiling. She watched as Jenny carefully negotiated the wide skirt of her gingham gown round the corner of the desk holding it gingerly until she was sitting down. It was in fine stripes of cream and white with a wide cream satin sash. The bodice was neat, the sleeves close fitting to her wrist, modest and serviceable once she had mastered the art of walking in it, though she had thought the colours chosen by Miss Chapman to be far too light for the walk she intended each day about the mill. It was to be her job to reorganise the placing of the machines so that each operative might have more room and so be exposed to less danger. There was to be stout fencing put about the moving parts of the machines to safeguard against accidents. The windows were to be reconstructed in order to allow for ventilation . . . oh, she could go on all day about the plans she and Miss Chapman had discussed and over which her heart rejoiced, but still, when she lay sleepless between the fine sheets on the bed Miss Chapman's housekeeper had told her roughly was to be hers, the doubts still plagued her for it all seemed too good to be true.

'We must trust each other if we are to make a success of this new venture, you know that, don't you, Jenny?' Miss Chapman was saying, and Jenny nodded brusquely, wishing it was as easy as that.

'I cannot imagine the kind of life you and others like you have known, but neither can I imagine how the King up in London lives for I have never seen it, nor suffered it. Try as I might I can only see your old life through your eyes and because of that you must be patient with me if I seem . . . unsympathetic. I have never known hunger, or cold or discomfort and though I can try hard I do not know what it is like to suffer any of them. I have lived a life of privilege but that does not mean I am without . . . emotion. I suppose I must be honest and tell you that I knew there were young children working in my mills and sheds. I was told by my father that the work they did could be done by no one else, that there was no one small enough or nimble enough to do what they did, that their families would starve if I did

459

not employ them and if you are honest you will agree that that part is true.'

Jenny nodded her head again but the expression on her face was still coolly impassive.

'Until your brother was so cruelly beaten and I was forced to see the results I turned my face from the truth of it. I pretended to believe that it was necessary and could not be changed, that if it were, there would be no profit in it for me. If we work together, you and I, we must be able to devise a way to run a business, make a profit, without killing children, maiming them, turning them into grey-faced, elderly ten- or eleven-year-olds with bowed legs and hunched backs. I don't know how to do it. I need help. I need someone who knows what I am talking about. I need someone to talk *to* and I cannot deal with a woman who I know holds me in contempt in her heart, who does not *believe* I mean what I say. I want you to work as hard as you have ever worked, in becoming that person, for really it is in the best interests of your family, your friends and those you have worked with in the past. Does that not make it worth your while?'

Jenny studied her, her face quite unreadable and Kit felt her heart sink since her expression, or lack of it, seemed to say it did not.

'I will do the best I can,' she said after a long pause, 'but I really can't find it in me to take pleasure in it.'

'Take pleasure in it? For God's sake don't tell me you would prefer to be back in the spinning mill with those . . .?'

'Those what?' Jenny's voice was dangerously quiet.

'With those women who do nothing but move parts of a machine about all day long and whose brains have become dormant because of it. Here you can *use* yours in work that is stimulating, exciting, challenging. Make decisions, when you have the experience, give orders and see them carried out *and* be exhilarated by the results. Does that not excite you?'

'This is your mill and you are the one to benefit from the excitement.'

'But it's not just that, is it?'

'No.'

'What then?'

'I've despised you for so long, I will be truthful, that I cannot get out of the habit. You, and men like you, have been detested by men and women, like *me*, for so long we can't just put it aside because suddenly you say you are different and, because of it, so must we be. You tell me I am to be your 'right hand' in turning this mill into a place where them down there can earn a decent wage and live a decent life. Now *why*, I ask myself, and how long will it last? Is it because of what was done to our Charlie? You say it was. You didn't know what was goin' on, you tell me, but how do I know that's the truth? *I don't know you*, only as a mill-owner and I've always reckoned them not to be worth a great deal. I can't *take* to you, is what I'm saying, and I don't know if I ever will. Happen when you've *proved* to me you mean what you say and this isn't just summat you fancy doing to ease your guilty conscience which, after a while might ease itself anyway, then I might believe what you say.'

'I have the greatest desire to fire you right now.'

'Aye, happen you have, but you'll not find another woman in that mill that'd do what I'm willing to do. I'm not afraid of you, you see, and they are.'

'I might have bitten off more than I can easily chew, you're saying?'

'Summat like that.'

'Why don't we spend the day together on Sunday and discuss it without the work at the mill to distract us. We could take the dogs and walk across the moor . . .'

'No thanks. I like to spend Sunday with Lucas and my family.' She stood up. 'Will that be all then?'

And Kit was dismissed as carelessly, as contemptuously as though Jenny Greenwood was the 'maister' and she no more than a 'little piecer' who had needed a reprimand. Jenny had made it obvious that her privacy and solitude were her own and not to be tampered with by Kit Chapman.

461

When the day was over, when the nerve-wracking choice of knives and forks and spoons, of glasses and all the paraphernalia the wealthy middle classes seemed to find necessary to eat a simple meal, was done with, her greatest pleasure was to retire to the lovely rooms she and Lucas shared on the first floor at the side of the house and be alone with him. She would sit, peaceful and at rest, her son in her arms, her mind empty and receptive to his child's prattle, and look over the long sweep of the sloping hills in the misty distance.

'I thought you might like these rooms, Jenny, since they have such a pretty view,' Kit had said carelessly, but Jenny had not known they had been given her so that she might look out on, not the immaculate gardens, which were alien to her, but the majestic splendour of the South Pennine heartland she loved so well. She would take her small son from the newly decorated nursery where he spent the day and where already he was the darling of his nursemaid's heart and after she had listened to his amazing accounting of his day among the luxuries he now took for granted, and then tucked him up in the small bed next to her own, she would wonder if she had done the right thing. He was her son, despite the man who fathered him. His family was working class, no-nonsense north countrymen and though her own parentage was not known there was no doubt in her mind that she had the same ancestry as the Greenwood family. Peasant stock, working their land and their looms, the backbone of England and was it right, she agonised, to deny her son his simple, untitled but honest heritage? Or, now that she had the chance for it, would it be right to deny him the privileges he would undoubtedly receive under the patronage of Katherine Chapman? An education, that of a young gentleman, an upbringing that would surely lead to some position of importance perhaps in the Chapman mills.

She was inordinately homesick. It was an ache in her which clawed incessantly, even the 'singing' of the spinning machines as she walked through the mill filling her with a

462

desire, incredibly, to get her hands busy about the flashing spindles, to leave the confusing world of figures and trade and percentages, of business meetings and commercial transaction Kit loved so well, the formal etiquette and stylised way of living at Greenacres.

She would put her arms about her mother almost before she dropped her baskets, in a long, trembling embrace, stubbornly checking the easy tears, rejoicing each time at the improvement in Charlie. His arms were mending and the good food and fresh, clear air of the moorland where he walked each day were restoring him to the robust health and natural high spirits of an eleven-year-old. He would stand awkwardly as she put her arms about him, almost as tall as she was, and would in a week or two take his place beside the young gentlemen at Crossfold grammar school. He had his first, brand new jacket, not one handed down and made over by his mother, new breeches and boots and his books, purchased secondhand from the shop in Crossfold, were already packed carefully in his bag. The moment Sarah told him he was fit to have the splints removed from his arms, he was to be off and he could hardly wait. Joss had promised him a grand job with the newspaper when he was sixteen, or perhaps, with an offer from Miss Chapman if he did well in his studies of a place in her mill, the boy could scarcely wait to start this wonderful life that was to be his. The only smirching of the fresh start he was to have was the giving of his evidence at the trial of Jim Briggs, Alfie Jackson and Arnold Ellis who were all three in Oldham gaol.

Mercy, with eyes for no one but Lucas would reach out hungry arms to him; calling him Tom as she had always done, seeming to confuse him with her dead brother and the boy, cheerfully accepting it for she had called him that since he was old enough to notice, would run to her, loving her, Jenny knew, as much as he did herself. Mercy was endlessly patient with him, absorbed by his bright interest and his tales of what he did at 'home', her own sweetness enfolding him and quietening his vivid excitement to the

463

peaceful contemplation of every fascinating object in the garden from the scattering of the corns to the chickens, the picking of daisies to make a chain for his golden curls, the planting of seed for next year's potatoes, the un-hurried pastimes of a country life with which she filled her day, her life, her very being. She would sing songs and tell him stories and only reluctantly allow Martha to nurse her grandson, and when the time came for he and Jenny to return to Greenacres, would weep piteously for her 'Tom' whom she could not bear to lose again.

The whole of Crossfold was astonished the next week when an army of workmen, Irish most of them and glad of the work, any work which would feed their starving famil-ies, began the renovation of the Chapman mills. Kit and Jenny had discussed at length on whether it would most benefit her employees to have their homes or the place in which they worked improved first. Kit planned to com-pletely demolish, row by obscene row, the mean, ram-shackle houses her grandfather had built for his workers and replace them with small, solid buildings with a bit of garden attached to each, a drain for carrying off every sort of filth and a constant supply of water to everyone from the river, its need gone now with the advent of the steam engine. There would be a parlour and a decent scullery and two or three bedrooms and a privy in the yard, one to a family.

'If they are decently housed and decently fed it follows that they will have the strength and will to do a decent day's work,' Jenny said, 'but put them in new houses before they have a chance to get used to the idea that their station in life is not only to be improved upon but also changed completely and they'll not know what to do with it. They need to be re-educated before they are rehoused or they'll have the new lot as bad as the old. First their conditions and working hours at the mill. A rise in wages, no more slave labour for their children and their outlook will change quite radically. They must be made to see that this is no fraud to trick them into working harder for the same wage, but a genuine consideration of how we can *all* work together to achieve one aim.'

'So, the mills first and shorter hours for better wages. But they must be made aware that I want value for money, Jenny. No more than ten hours a day for each child under ten years of age . . .'

'Right, and a proper dinner hour when they can stop to eat their baggin . . .'

'Whatever that might be. Is it a Lancashire dish?'

Jenny laughed grudgingly. 'No, it's anything you bring to eat at "baggin" time. Dinner time. Or I suppose you'd call it luncheon.'

'We shall have a proper dining-room and . . . what else, Jenny?'

'Special rooms for the female operatives to change their clothes in, proper clothes for them to wear, aprons and such, a washroom with water and conveniences with sewerage to carry off the waste. Proper ventilation . . .'

'And a schoolroom . . .'

In her wildest dreams it had never occurred to her that a decent education for the children might be one of them. And in her eyes was the beginning of a curious expression which might have been an unwilling reluctance to believe that Kit Chapman really *did* mean to do what she *said* she meant to do. 'But if they are to work . . . ?'

'They will be given time to attend classes in the evening. I read about it somewhere, I can't remember now, but it is called the "monitorial" system by which one teacher educates a number of monitors, perhaps among the older children who will in turn teach another group. The system is simple and economical . . .'

'And will they all be able to go, even the "apprentices"?'

'Naturally, and they shall have a proper house in which to live with a housekeeper, boys and girls separately, with decent clothes and food . . .'

'Treat them right and they'll work. My father used to say that, and right willingly . . .' And almost she was ready to believe in it at last!

465

But of course this happened over many months, months in which Jenny Greenwood declared a hundred times to herself that she could put up with it no longer. Her head ached every night as she laid it on her pillow, crammed to its capacity with the knowledge with which Kit burdened it each day. Her body longed for the physical exercise which it was accustomed to, straining inside the elegant gown and petticoats it was forced into each morning, longing to clothe itself in a simple, free moving skirt, a cool, easy, short-sleeved bodice, the homely cosiness of her shawl and clogs. She was a mill girl, brought up to hard work in a hard climate with others like her. She understood that, it was her life but this with Kit Chapman was as foreign to her as though she had been set down at the court of King George. She was neither of one class nor the other and the woman who had put her here, though she was carelessly kind, treating her not as a servant, but neither as a friend, seemed to find nothing strange in the situation. She was talking of entertaining some businessmen and their wives, influential gentlemen from the south who might be of use to her, and she to them and the hardship – and foolishness that it was necessary – of finding two gentlemen to make up the numbers since it seemed there must be an equal ratio of ladies and gentlemen in any party. It was all so . . . unimportant when put beside the genuine hardship Jenny had known all her life.

Though she and Kit had formed a workable relationship based on common need they still moved about each other with the delicacy of two cats tip-toeing across an acre of broken glass. In the three months since Jenny had moved to Greenacres she had not seen Mrs Chapman and had not considered that it was required of her to ask after her. She had known full well what had happened when Kit had told her mother that a factory girl was to be elevated to the position of assistant to the mill-owner and not only that but was to live in the house with them. It was obvious from Mrs Chapman's continued absence from the dinner table that she was living in another part of the house and Jenny smiled wryly when she thought of the upheaval there must have been when Kit announced it, even among the servants. She could see it in their faces when they waited upon Kit and herself. In the insolent slant to their watchful eyes, eyes that told her that they were only doing what they did because Miss Chapman was present, because they had been ordered to do it, but if they had the chance with no risk to themselves, they would not hesitate to insult her. She was a working class girl with no rights to be sitting in the candlelight at the beautifully polished table, in a silken gown, perfumed and elegant as Miss Chapman herself. They watched her, she knew, their eyes malicious, waiting for her to use the wrong fork, or even her fingers but she did what Kit had told her to do on the first night that they dined together and waited until Kit had made a choice, then did the same. Knife, fork, spoon, napkin, wine glass and after a while she no longer had any need to copy her employer. Quite simply, whatever Kit did, Jenny followed suit and even her broad Lancastrian accent began to mellow somewhat, as her brother's had done when he mixed with men of a different class. She would never completely eliminate it but she learned to sound each word separately, not running them together, nor clipping the ends off them. She studied hard to understand and use many words she had not even heard of until she met Kit.

'I have an inordinate amount of paperwork to complete before we can go home, I'm afraid, Jenny. You have a consummate head for figures so shall we go through them together. We will accomplish more in an hour together than I could in three.'

*Inordinate! Consummate! Accomplish!* They were words no simple, forthright working lass could even get her tongue round, let alone understand but Jenny Greenwood, allowed the full use of Barker Chapman's splendid library, made it her business to find out, and even to try them out, on her own, naturally before her bedroom mirror but it was not until Kit began to laugh, not unkindly one day that she learned that not only must one know the meaning of a word, the spelling, but also the pronunciation!

'Jenny, I am sorry, I am not laughing at you for really, I have nothing but admiration for the way in which you are getting to grips with your new situation and surroundings. If you were not such an intelligent and determined woman you would have given up before the first week was out, would you not? I am not blind, you know, though I might appear not to notice what goes on, unless it is on a balance sheet or a spinning frame. You really are very clever, Jenny and I do not say that in a patronising way, as though I am adding "for a mill girl". You have a good brain and you are using it and you are not afraid of me, or the servants. Oh yes, I have noticed that too, but I decided at the beginning that you must learn to manage them yourself. They will do anything I order them to but you must learn, and they as well, that you have as much right to give orders as I have. You are not a servant here, nor are you a guest. You are a resident . . . no, that is not the word . . . an inhabitant, perhaps . . . *you live here* as I do so you must deal with that role. Now then, these words you are determined to learn. I think it is commendable of you to try, there, you see . . . *commendable*, another one. Do you know what . . . ah, you do, good . . . well, any word I use which you do not understand, stop me at once and ask. That is all there is to it. You must be able to hold your own in the society in which I move, business and social, and only if you have confidence in yourself will you succeed.'

'If Joss can do it, then so can I.'

Kit felt the painful lurch of her heart at the sound of his name on Jenny's lips. It was the first time she had mentioned her brother and though Kit had prepared herself — she thought — for the moment which was sure to come since it was only to be expected that Jenny would speak of her family, the shock was enormous. And she must contain it, not allow Jenny to see that it had affected her in any way. The day, three months ago when he had forced her to see what her overlookers had done to his brother was as alive and agonising as it had been then, and the bitter hatred in his eyes, the contempt, had burned its way into her soul. She should not speak of him, not really, for surely Jenny would hear the strangeness in her voice but she could not stop herself. The yearning to know where he was, what he was doing, was too great to be subdued.

'Your brother is . . . he is living . . . at home . . . ?'

'Good God, no.'

Kit's face was expressionless as she picked up her wine glass and took a sip from its pale golden contents and though her hand trembled a little Jenny was too intent on her own social graces to notice.

'What does he do now? Forgive me, I do not mean to pry or open old wounds but . . . I suppose he still works for the reform he was so vociferous . . .'

'Vociferous?' Jenny looked enquiringly at Kit.

'Yes . . . to utter words . . . clamorously . . .'

'How do you spell it?'

'Really, does it matter . . . ?'

Jenny stared, surprised by the impatient tone in Kit's voice, ready to tell her not to bother with her damned explanations of the big words she used if it was to make her irritable but Kit pulled a face and smiled, replacing her wine glass beside the others.

'I'm sorry, Jenny. I didn't mean to snap but to tell the truth your brother and I have crossed swords on a number of occasions. He was a wild young man, you must admit, and in this valley the manufacturers, including myself had cause to curse him for the damage he did, but surely after being in . . . well . . .' She toyed with the fish on her plate, prodding it with her fork, not looking at Jenny, but Jenny finished the sentence for her.

'In prison, you mean. You reckon it should have knocked all that nonsense from him, is that what you're saying?'

'No, I'm not. But since the Power-Loom Riots the cotton industry has been relatively peaceful and I wondered if he was to . . .'

'Stir it up again?'

'Yes.'

'Well, I'd hardly be likely to tell you, would I?' Jenny smiled in the first genuine moment of shared amusement between them. '. . . and now that he knows what you are planning to do, your mills would not suffer, if he were planning anything, that is,' she added hastily. 'He is very impressed, you know.'

Kit's heart plunged again and the pleasure surged through her, though really, she thought frantically, what was it to her? What did it matter what *he* thought? She was doing this for *her* sake, not his, for her own peace of mind so why should his approval mean anything to her? But it did. It did! The accusation in his face, that grim, relentless face, the curl of contempt on his mouth, the ugly aversion even to sit beside her in her carriage, just as though he could not bear his flesh within touching distance of hers, had been the hardest thing she had ever had to bear in her life. That snarling malevolence had gone with her wherever she went in the last three months. It had hounded her dreams, turning them to nightmares, sat on her shoulder in her counting house, sneering that the profit she made was more to her than the soft flesh, the soft bones of the children she employed. It dogged her footsteps, each one she walked on the moorland up beyond Friars Mere to Moorcroft where she often climbed now since she no longer went to Badger's Edge. It followed her in her loneliness, for she admitted she was lonely, jeering at her, telling her she was fast becoming the old maid Crossfold firmly believed she was to be. She had loved no man but him, and never would, she acknowledged to herself and for the most part she accepted her loneliness, her solitary walks with her dogs, four of them now with the two young ones she was training, and her solitary bed. She found, though it was no surprise to her, that she enjoyed Jenny Greenwood's company but they talked of little else but business, their separate personal lives, their angry past, too fragile to be spoken of between them. Jenny was understandably eager, whenever she could to spend every moment of her spare time with her son and with her family at Edgeclough.

'What is he engaged in then, if it's not a secret?' she went on trying her best to appear only casually interested.

'He has a job now.'

'A job?'

'Aye . . . er . . . yes. He writes for *The Republican*. They pay him a wage,' she said as though the wonder of it could scarcely be believed. 'He's a journalist.'

'How . . . grand.'

'Yes, and he writes articles for Cobbett's *Weekly Political Register*. Have you heard of it?'

'I believe I have. What does he write about?'

'Well, can't you guess?'

'The oppression of the poor. The wickedness of the industrialists. The horror of Lousy Bank and Pig Lane. Low wages. Long hours. Exploitation of children. Am I right?'

Jenny did not smile and her eyes retained that cool speculative look which said though Kit Chapman might have set about the task of transforming her mills, which she undoubtedly had, it did not necessarily follow that the lives of her workers would improve. It stood to reason that should the conditions in which the operatives worked become bettered, their output of work would naturally increase and in that case would not Kit Chapman make even more profit. It certainly did not, in her opinion, make any difference to the relationship which existed between them which was that of employer and employee, cool, impersonal and with not a great deal of trust on her part. She would wait and see, her attitude still said, for was not the proof of the pudding in the eating, and the damn thing not even in the oven yet. She had begun, surprisingly, to find a quiet satisfaction in the work she did, discovering in it, as Kit had said, a certain challenge, but she was not happy, and neither, she knew, was Kit Chapman since she was going against her own class, her own kind, men who believed her to be a traitor, a viper in their bosom which, if they had been able, they would dearly have loved to fling off and trample on, but she was too powerful. They said she was mad, that she would surely lose her fortune, that her workers would loll about all day in their new homes, if they ever got them, that they would make their new homes into *old* homes before the year was out for they knew no better, that they would idle the hours of business away, gossiping with one another in their new *dining-room* – had anyone ever heard of anything so disgraceful? – that their children, with hours in the day in which they had nothing to do, would run wild in the streets and cause untold trouble to those forced to put up with it.

And as for educating them, well, they all knew where that would lead, didn't they? They would get ideas above their station, would begin to believe they were as good as any man, a˜ that fool Joss Greenwood assured them they were. God had put them all on this earth, the Lord in his castle, the parson in his church and the peasant in his cottage.

Somewhere in between stood the wealthy middle class, that new breed known as the industrialist, the manufacturing mill-owner, created not by God but by himself and if he had anything to say on the matter it was that Katherine Chapman must surely soon see the error of her foolish ways. How that was to be accomplished they were not awfully certain, since she was the wealthiest of them all, but if she carried on as she was doing, flinging her father's hard-earned cash about as though it grew on bloody trees, she would not be that for long.

And in the meanwhile Kit Chapman and Jenny Greenwood existed uneasily side by side, not at all sure that even, should their grand new experiment succeed, they themselves could do the same.

# 31

It was one of those glorious winter days when the eye is drawn constantly to the window to look out again and again at the blue of the sky, a clear and depthless blue that stretches forever with nothing to mar its perfection. When the book one reads or the papers with which one should be engrossed no longer have the power to hold the attention, when the head lifts constantly, when one stretches and yawns and knows finally that there is no further use to try despite what is still to be done and that with the eager enthusiasm of a child shut up too long in the schoolroom, an escape must be made.

Such a day called to Kit Chapman. It was almost Christmas, a dreaded time for her since it was a day when families were re-united, a day of joy and merriment, of presents given and received, of smiles and kisses and, perhaps only once in the year, of goodwill towards one's fellowman. One day of blessed rest for those who worked the other three hundred and sixty-four, a day not to be spent alone but which she knew she would do since her mother, who did no more than nod coolly to her should they meet in the garden, had said in a note delivered by Miss Fryer that she was to share Christmas with her dear friend Emma Abbott.

But that was six days away yet and Kit Chapman had learned that, except for the planning she must of course organise for the future sale of her cotton, it was sometimes a relief to live only for today. And today told her she was a fool and a madwoman to sit behind this desk with her nose in her papers when she could be out striding across the tops with her dogs. She had work to do, she was well aware of that but nothing which could not wait until after dinner this evening, nothing with which, in an emergency, Jenny could not deal. It was not often that she allowed herself the indulgence of kicking up her heels and acting like a young girl but today was so beautiful, so special, surely she could afford to please herself, to gratify this whim which had come upon her, to throw the whole blessed business in Jenny's lap, call up her dogs and just go. Of course she took long walks each Sunday, often staying out from dawn until dusk with nothing in her pocket but an apple and a piece of cheese but the winter days were so short and once a week was so little. Today was Wednesday, a working day and her manufacturing father and grandfather would turn over in their manufacturing graves if they knew but it called to her, the biting, frosty blue day, the crisp champagne air which would fill her lungs on the top of Moorcroft and Broad Head and she could not resist it.

She stood up abruptly, so abruptly Jenny jumped and dropped her pen.

'Good Lord, you gave me a start. What's the matter? You look as though someone's put a mouse down your back.'

'Not a mouse down my back but wings on my heels. Dammit, I cannot stand this office another minute. I cannot see much of it from here but what I *can* see of the sky tells me the moors will be splendid on such a day. I don't often do it but I am going to play truant. I'll catch up on those papers tonight.'

'You don't have to make excuses to me. You're the "maister" here and if you can't please yourself, who can?'

'You're right. Can you manage without me for an hour?'

'I beg your pardon. Have you not noticed how capable I have become? Say the word and you can take a week off should you care to.'

'Hold on, my lass. You may be pretty good but you're not indispensable yet.'

It had taken years for Kit herself to learn to run the

enormous and complicated concern which was the Chapman Spinning and Weaving Mills but Jenny Greenwood, she had to acknowledge, had assimilated in six months what had taken Kit twelve to do. Admittedly Jenny's experience in the spinning rooms had given her a head start on the seventeen year old Kit Chapman but her mind was receptive, just as though it had been empty for years of everything but the mental processes needed to run a machine, dry and thirsty for knowledge and now, as Kit poured it in, it drank it up greedily, always ready for more.

'But that day is not far off Jenny,' she said quietly, then, spinning round with her skirts dipping in excitement she strode towards the door and the carriage which always stood waiting.

She crossed the wooden footbridge which spanned the stream at noon, climbing steadily on the other side of the valley beyond Crossfold. She had put on a rough woollen skirt of dark red, deep and glowing against the winter's day. Her three-quarter coat was of the same shade but checked in shades of cream and white and on her head was a white tam o' shanter. Her black boots were stout and snug, especially made for her for walking and round her neck was a vivid red scarf. She looked magnificent, her eyes a delighted blue, like that of a harebell with a sparkle in them which was brighter than the sun reflected ice which coated every blade of grass, every dried frond of bracken. The blood surged beneath her golden skin, gathering on her cheekbones.

The track up to the high moorland, the *real* moorland which even in summer was dark and rough and uneven, was white with rime and slippery and the stones scattered over the surface made walking difficult. The rough grass was heavy with frost so fine it was like spun sugar and here and there where water lay in the dark, peaty soil, ice gleamed brilliantly. Her old dogs stayed close to her side, still supple and active for even when she had no time to roam the hills with them, one of the grooms had orders to exercise them daily. But the young ones, not yet a year old, frolicked together in the unexpected joy of being out with her, their high spirits and youthfulness making them impossible, just at that moment, to command. But she knew exactly how they felt and she had not the heart to call them in. Let them caper like fools for that was how she felt. She wanted to run across the open spaces, to climb rocks and to jump from them and shout aloud in an exhilaration which was sweet and fast flowing in her blood and which she had not felt for many months.

The sun was not very high and the far side of the valley was in shadow, smudged here and there by a huddle of buildings, isolated weavers' cottages and a farm or two. She could see the glint far below of the river, circling between scattered black patches of leafless trees and where it turned, winding away behind a hill, the tall chimneys of George Abbott's mill. She kept to the faint track for a while, winding in long curves up the steep slope. Hard gritstone bands protruded like a man's ribcage along the hillsides and water dashed over them in great falls, so loud she could no longer hear the excited yapping of her young dogs.

She followed the pack-way, its old flags set deep in the thick, peaty layers of grass, the inheritance of the upland forests which had once thrived here. The pack-horse route had probably been used to carry salt in the old days, and lime which was needed to improve the acid soil of the farmland. A 'white way' it was known as, just as the route which had carried coal was a 'black way' and those along which clay or pottery moved were 'red ways'.

The air was colder up here and she pulled her coat and scarf more closely about her as she reached the highest point at Friars Mere. There was a tumble of stones, the ruins it was said of an old chapel, used by the monks. The ice crackled about her feet and her breath wreathed about her head. She leaned against a massive stone and looked across the vast expanse of moorland, rising and falling in weathered nobility, dissected at a lower level with the regular landscape caused by the encroachment of enclosure. Rectangular fields and orderly access trackways, straight walls which created from this distance an image of a chequerboard of black and white, flecked as it was with snow. Farms crouched right up to the moorland's edges, smallholdings, no more, with a few cattle, a 'laithe house' which included under its roof a barn for storage, a mistal or cow house, space for a horse and cart and living quarters for the hardy moor dwellers.

She noticed the movement just as she was about to turn away. It was too cold to stand and the blood which had coursed through her veins in a hot tide as she had climbed was beginning to slow. The dogs stood quietly now, the two young ones leaning against her skirt, Joby and Blaze in a phalanx of protection a little way out, one to her left, the other to her right, scanning the distance and it was the faint growl deep in Joby's throat that warned her.

The figure was no more than a dark smudged shape against the grey-white background of the winter vegetation, with a thin shadow following, moving slowly, stopping now and then to stare about but as it came nearer Kit could see the slight swing of a skirt and knew that the person who approached was a woman.

'To me Joby, Blaze, lie down. Prince, Barny, stay, stay boys . . .' and all four dogs lay down obediently. It took more than fifteen minutes for the woman to reach the ruined chapel. She appeared either uncertain of her direction, or, like a child, uncaring, stopping to touch this and that, to examine a rock or a frozen plant, her voice, as she got nearer, soft and enquiring as she spoke, addressing her remarks to whatever it was she touched. There was a fey, ethereal quality to her, not quite of this world and Kit felt the hairs on the back of her neck rise as she recognised Joss Greenwood's wife. The last time she had seen her she had hidden herself behind a chair, then, at Joss's bidding had run out to 'play' while the women tended to Charlie Greenwood's wounds. The lad, healed now and completely well apart from the scars on his face and back which would be his for life was attending Crossfold grammar school where he was gaining, besides a fine classical education, a grounding in writing, arithmetic, mathematics and modern languages, a little out of his depth, as yet, among the sons of mill-masters and manufacturers but already showing that ingenuity of which some boys are blessed, gaining a reputation as quite a celebrity by the simple method of revealing to his awestruck peers the scars on his back. An up and coming young man then with the sense to take advantage of any weapon to hand in the battle of life, a fighter like his brother and sister and this elf-like creature who, in a moment or two would stumble over Kit's dogs, was his sister-in-law.

Strangely, after the first warning growl the dogs made no move to bar Mercy Greenwood's way as she came over the lip of the hill. It seemed they recognised this child-woman was no threat to them, or to the one they guarded, and the old dogs merely laid their muzzles on their paws, while the young ones waved a friendly tail.

'Oh . . .' she said, with a little start, not afraid of them, Kit realised and when her eyes rose and found Kit's she smiled in a friendly fashion, the anxiety she had shown on the day at the cottage not apparent in the cold emptiness of the moors. She was warmly dressed with a shawl about her head and crossed over her breast, tied at the back as one would a child. There was another wrapped about her shoulders and her grey homespun woollen skirt was of good quality. She wore stout clogs and heavy, hand-knitted stockings. Her fine skin was flushed with the warmth of her climb, her cheeks pink and like satin but it was her eyes which were her greatest beauty. They were enormous in her tiny face, a soft and velvet grey, set in long brown lashes and in them was a glow of pleasure, of trust, a delight which spoke of her love for the moors in which she wandered so far from home. There was no fear, no hesitancy in her movement. This was her land, her manner seemed to say, her place where there was nothing to hurt her, nothing to fear up here where no people came. Where there was no dirt, no smells, no rotting obscenities to bar her path, no noise but the sound of the water and the call of the raven.

478

Up here she had no need of her little 'bird' and this lady, these dogs gave off no warnings of the perils which lay below.

'Good morning,' she called out. 'It's a grand day,' just as though there was nothing unusual in finding a well-dressed lady in the isolated spot.

'Indeed it is,' Kit answered, not awfully sure what to do or say for the girl . . . woman really . . . seemed so normal, but Jenny had intimated that their Mercy was not quite . . . well, as a grown woman should be. She had given no details, naturally, her loyalty to her family allowing no outsider to pick at its shortcomings but Kit's rebellious heart had missed a beat, glad and ashamed of its gladness, as she had been when she had learned that Joss and Mercy Greenwood had no child, at the hint, not spoken aloud, of course, that Joss and Mercy were not husband and wife in the true sense of the word.

But what the devil was she doing out here, miles from Edgeclough and all alone? The weather had winnowed out the usual itinerants, the wandering, out of work Irishmen, farm labourers, weavers, *any man* and his family who roamed these hills going from town to town looking for work but there was still the chance that some ruffian might happen along, not caring where he slept or how he ate as long as he could find the means, lawful or not, to obtain it. She saw such men herself now and again but they gave her a wide berth at the sight of the snarling teeth of Joby and Blaze and the increasingly protective fierceness, inclined now and then to slip away as their attention wandered, of her new dogs. But Mercy Greenwood had no such protection. What was Martha Greenwood thinking of, allowing her out of her sight for it was clear the girl . . . woman . . . had no idea of her own danger. Jenny had told her that Mercy loved her mother-in-law and never strayed far from her side and yet here she was, on Friars Mere with the look of someone out for a stroll in her own garden.

'Are you alone?' she asked carefully, then drew in her breath sharply, about to cry out a warning, a sharp command to Joby as Joss Greenwood's wife kneeled down beside him, trusting as an infant and laid a small, mittened hand on his smooth head, but the elderly dog merely blinked a tolerant eye in Mercy's direction and allowed her to stroke him, to fondle his ear, as amiable as a cat curled up on a rug before the fire.

'What a lovely dog,' Mercy said smilingly, 'and the others,' looking around. 'Are they all yours?' and then, as the two young ones bounded over, she fell in a laughing jumble of black stockinged legs, skirts and warm petticoats, entangled with the smooth black bodies of Prince and Barny.

'Stay Prince, stay Barny.' Kit laid a restraining hand on the quivering rump of the nearest dog but he was too enchanted with his new friend and it took several minutes before Mercy could stand and the dogs would obey their mistress and the two women were laughing, tidying their hair which had come loose in the tussle, eyes like stars, cheeks flushed.

'I'd love a dog like that,' Mercy said wistfully, eyeing Barny who still could not resist the temptation to lick her hand.

'Will Joss . . . your family not get you one?' His name slipped out before she could stop it but Mercy turned eagerly.

'You know Joss?'

'Well, yes. We have met a time or two.'

'Well, that's grand. I'm his wife, Mercy.'

'Yes, I know.' Kit's voice was gentle for really this child, she was only that, was the most innocent creature she had ever met. 'I saw you on the day Charlie was hurt . . .'

Instantly she could have bitten her tongue for Mercy reared back, her face whitening in fear, just as though Kit had raised a fist to her.

'It's all right, really. He's better now and going to school, so there is no need for you to worry,' Kit gabbled, desperate to take that look of horror from Mercy Greenwood's face and slowly the girl's colour returned and her body relaxed.

The dog nuzzled her hand and she looked down at it and the last of the strain left her. Kit felt her own rigid shoulders settle more comfortably and the breath sighed out of her. Dear God, what *was* wrong with the woman? She was as highly strung as a young colt. A simple sentence, a few words which had no harm nor threat in them had nearly had her over the lip of the mount on which they stood and even yet her hand rested as though for reassurance on Barny's head and Mercy was still not the eager young woman she had been fifteen minutes ago. She watched Kit warily as though she was afraid she might say something else to frighten her, ready to dart away should Kit threaten her peace of mind again.

She shouldn't be here, Kit thought, searching for some innocuous remark, about the weather, or the dogs, anything which had no peril in it for the disturbed child who looked at her from the face of Joss Greenwood's wife. How had she got up here? She was cosily dressed just as though someone had got her ready, put on her shawl and tied it at her back. But she must get her home to her family at once and though she was reluctant to return to that cottage in which there was so much remembered pain, she must. The memory of Joss was there. His eyes hating her, filled with his revulsion for her and what she had allowed to be done to his brother. The memories haunted her still, no matter how hard she tried to erase them, no matter how much profit she ploughed back into the improvements for her work people, his eyes would never let her alone, the expression in them would glare in the night for as long as she lived.

She had done her best, arranged for the youngest girl to work at the Hall, for Charlie to go to school and of course Jenny was invaluable to her, but . . . and here her breath slowed painfully as she prepared to take Joss's wife back to him . . . she really did not think she could fight the despair, the pain, the torment of loving this woman's husband for much longer. She was safe in her mills, in her weaving-sheds and up here on the moors where nobody came but the birds and the moorland creatures, the occasional far off figure of a wandering vagrant but in the village of Edgeclough was the aching, the slow and tortuous death of the ephemeral dream she had once known as a young girl. They had both been young then and filled with the joy of one another. Before Harry, before this woman, before the insurmountable barrier of hate had reared itself between them.

'Would you like to walk with me and my dogs?' she asked at last and even to her own ears her voice was harsh but Mercy's face smiled in pleasure and she looked down, stroking first one affable head then another, first Joby, Blaze, Prince, then Barny, who seemed to be her favourite.

'Yes, if it's all right.'

She went wherever Kit led, amenable to anything Kit might suggest. She threw a stone for the dogs, delighted when the two young ones raced to bring it back to her.

'Tom and I used to come up here,' she said suddenly, stopping to peer at a hollow where the frost lay so thickly it might have been snow. 'Of course we don't now because he's not old enough yet but when he's five or six Jenny'll let me fetch him, won't she?'

'I'm sure she will,' Kit said soothingly. They were at the top of Dog Hill now and far below was the village of Edgeclough. She could even make out the roof of the laithe house in which the Greenwoods lived and she thought of leaving now, of saying to Mercy Greenwood, 'See, there is your home, go on, go down to it . . .' but how could she trust her to do it. She was kneeling as Kit stopped, her gentle face, her soft eyes close to the dogs, waiting to be told what she must do next, quite unaware that she had only to run down the steep hill and she would be home.

'Come on, Mercy, let's get on. I'm sure your . . . your husband will be anxious about you.' Her throat almost closed on the last words and as she heard her own voice speak them she had the urgent need to bend herself double to ease the pain but again Mercy cringed back from her, her eyes flaring in panic.

'Oh no ... he's ... no ... he's away. Martha said he wasn't to be back and really ... I would rather sleep with Martha ... please ... please ...'

Dear sweet Lord ... Kit felt her lungs close on the desperate breath she tired to force into them as the pictures which teamed into her head almost paralysed her. Dear God ... what was this child saying ... what did she mean? What had he done to her, what had *someone* done to her to make her so afraid of almost everything, and yet so trusting with a complete stranger? She was afraid of hurt and pain, it seemed, of violence, her reaction to the memory of Charlie told Kit that. She was afraid of ... of the passion ... was that it ... of love ... the strength, the lusty sweetness of sexual excitement. Kit had seen her run trustingly into his gentle arms on that same day so ...

So what did it matter to her, her mind demanded brutally to know? What did anything to do with this woman and her husband matter to Kit Chapman? They had their life, whatever it might be, and she had hers and what they did with theirs, *in* theirs, did not concern her. She had come to return this poor demented child, this gentle little sparrow who had flown high today among the dangerous hawks and when she had seen her to her doorstep she would be off. Just a simple return of a wandering child which Martha Greenwood would surely understand. But why was no one looking for her then, her logical mind asked, if that was the case, but she refused to answer it, merely taking Mercy Greenwood's hand in hers and leading her down the steep slope towards her home.

He opened the door when she knocked and the shock to them both was so great neither could speak. Eye clung to eye, appalled, both of them refusing to acknowledge that first initial explosion of gladness which came and went before it could be dwelled upon. Mercy still clung to Kit's hand, the dogs to her skirt, ready, should it be needed to defend both these weak females to the death but the two young ones, sensing the lessening of animosity in Joby and

Blaze who recognised the man, snuffled about his knees and hand, willing to be friends if he was.

'Joss . . .' Mercy's soft voice was nervous and she leaned against Kit's shoulder, partly hidden by it. He dragged his tight clenched gaze from Kit's for a moment, staring at his wife as though he had never seen her before and had not the slightest notion of who she was.

'What the devil . . . ?' but his voice, loud, harsh with shock made Mercy flinch and Kit could see him visibly make an effort to calm himself, saw the effort he took to soften his voice and his expression and all the while her eyes filled themselves with him, storing the image of his brown face, the thick familiar swathe of his curly hair on his brow, the shape of his smiling mouth, smiling tenderly now for his wife, the deep clefts one on either side of his lips, his lips themselves . . . aah, Joss, my love, my love . . .

He put out a hand to draw his wife across the step and his expression of gentleness, the soft clasp of his fingers reassured her and she went to him, leaving Kit on the outside, alone, but for her dogs.

'Lass,' he said to his wife and the compassion he showed for this damaged woman brought a lump to Kit's throat. 'Where have you been? How did you . . . ?' He turned to Kit and his eyes became distant. He was in control of himself. The shock he had known when he opened the door and seen her there had subsided and his concern was for his wife, not the woman who had brought her home.

'I found her on the moor. She seemed . . . lost.'

'I hope she was no trouble to you.' His politeness was chilling.

'None.'

'My mother is . . . a cousin in the next village is unwell, so she has . . . She left a note that she had sent Mercy to a neighbour. Obviously she did not go. I'm sorry you have been brought out of your way.'

By looking slightly to the left of his face while he did the same so that their eyes did not once meet they were able to pretend that they were no more than two strangers, one who had done a kindness to the other and must be thanked courteously.

'Not at all,' she answered and though it had all been said and she knew she should move she simply could not. She wanted none of this. She wanted none of him, ever again for the pain was so great she really could not stand it. Just to be near him, though three feet of solid, heavy air stood between them, was the most exquisite agony she had known and she could not, not yet, give it up. A moment more, dear Lord. A moment more to breathe in the scent of the cold air about him, to sense the rapid beat of the pulse in the hollow of his throat, to see from the corner of her averted eye the tight held grimness of his mouth, knowing he meant it for her, but not caring, not caring just as long as she could be here, in his presence for a moment longer. It must last for a long time. It must last forever!

'I'm cold Joss,' Mercy said, shivering a little in the shelter of his protective arms, her head resting against the strong curve of his shoulder and suddenly Kit hated her, hated her, would dearly have loved to smack her silly, simple face, to scratch her gentle dove's eyes, the childish pout of her pink mouth, for she was his wife. This woman was his wife, entitled to share his bed, to love his body, to bear his children. She could, if she had a mind, lean sensuously against him when the door closed and shut out the rest of the world, put her mouth against his, tease him with her tongue, whisper in his ear of what she would do to him and his hard, long man's body, of what she would like him to do to her soft willing woman's flesh if he would care to climb the stairs with her. But she would not. She could not and neither could Kit Chapman and the knowledge tore at her, slashed through the hard shell of the composure she had layered about herself, tore it from her in a severance of agony and her eyes looked directly into his.

She felt the flagged stones of the path tremble beneath her feet as the earth tilted and her own pain overwhelmed her but she could not look away. She felt no shame in allowing him to see her love since she felt none. Her pride,

485

the arrogant pride which had hugged to itself the knowledge that at least he was unaware of the love she could not seem to kill, which he himself could not seem to kill, no longer cared that it was flaring from her eyes, on the breath she forced out of her lungs, from the very pores of her skin for him to see. What the hell did it matter, the defiant lift of her head said? Let him laugh, let him pour scorn on her, let his mouth curl in contempt and revulsion, she loved Joss Greenwood and she always would and there was nothing any longer that she could do to hide it.

But he did none of these things. His whole body became unnaturally still and she watched, wonderingly, the slow, quite incredible chink of light prick the ice green and grey of his eyes. His breathing quickened on the gradual parting of his lips and warm blood ran beneath the brown flesh of his face. His eyes narrowed a little as though at the last moment he would hide it from her, then it came, glowing for her, brought painfully from the place where he had hidden it, buried it, smashed it down into a hole and buried it and was there where she could see it at last, whole, sweet, undamaged, *his love for her*.

She felt the tears brim from her eyes and begin to run down her face and inside her, where the rock had been for six months, the ice riven rock he had put there on the day Charlie was beaten, she felt a gentle warmth dissolve it into her body, releasing it into her arms and legs, her mouth which began to smile, her hands which would have reached for him, her heart which did.

'Joss.' His name was a balm on her lips, a soothing salve which smoothed away the pain.

'Kit,' and it was the same for him as the forgiveness healed him.

They seemed to find no other words necessary, nor to wonder at the strangeness of declaring their renewed love before the sweet and empty woman who clung on his arm and who was his wife.

'Will you come in?' he said, opening the door to her now.

'Thank you.'

'You must be cold,' and I would that I could warm you here, right now, his eyes continued.

'Yes.'

'Mercy, sweetheart, when you have taken off your shawl make Miss Chapman a cup of tea, will you?' and Kit found no hatred in her now for the woman Joss Greenwood called 'sweetheart'.

## 32

It was easy now for them to become lovers again since what was more natural than that Joss Greenwood should visit his sister, his nephew who had taken up residence at the home of Miss Katherine Chapman? And it was well known that Miss Chapman was a radical sympathiser for why else would she flatten row after row of the perfectly adequate houses her grandfather had built for his workers and, it was rumoured replace them with others which were, in their opinion, those who criticised, far too good for the common man.

He dined with them a week after Kit had returned his wife to him, walking the three miles from Edgeclough to Crossfold in his wooden clogs which he still found more comfortable than the boots he now wore in his daily life. He took them off under the cover of darkness at the gate which led to the driveway of Greenacres, hiding them under a bush, pulling on his boots before beginning the walk up to the front door and when Winters opened it to him he might have been any one of the number of well dressed gentlemen who called on Miss Chapman. A dark green coat, plain, well cut but serviceable buff waistcoat and trousers. His long military boots were of well polished, good quality brown leather and his hat which he handed to Winters as though he were well used to a butler to wait on him, was what was known as a 'Wellington', the crown curving outwards towards the top and the narrow brim curled up at the sides. His greatcoat, ankle length and of good Yorkshire wool was black. It was very evident from his attire that Joss Greenwood was a man of some standing in his own community and though he had, and still did, called himself a working class man, he worked now with his pen in the telling articles his clever brain devised and which were printed in *The Republican* and similar radical newspapers such as Cobbett's *Weekly Political Register*. His wages were small but enough to support himself and his wife, and contribute towards the upkeep of his brother's schooling.

He had been condemned by many for trying to turn simple folk into dupes for his own political ends since it was well known that he had leanings in that direction but men of conscience such as William Cobbett, Richard Oastler and John Fielden held him in high esteem and he was welcomed to speak on the platforms of the meetings he attended on behalf of the working man he still fought for.

But it was not that, nor indeed of anything to do with reform that he thought as Kit Chapman walked across the brightly lit hallway to greet him, her hands outstretched to his, her eyes shining with joy. They might have been alone so vividly did they let their emotion be seen, their love for one another a living glory. They seemed careless of who saw it among the servants who hovered respectfully in the background and Jenny Greenwood who had followed Kit from the drawing-room to welcome her brother when the door bell rang, felt the shock of it hit her just below her breasts in the region where a body blow was most telling.

Their hands clasped, their flesh softly touching and caressing, fingers entwined for a long, long moment, not like acquaintances, nor even close friends but as lovers, reluctant to let go, to part, to become separate again.

'Miss Chapman.' He spoke her name softly in a tone of voice Jenny had never heard him use before, even with Mercy, breathed it through lips that curved in a tender half-smile and yet his expression was serious, frowning almost, just as though this was the most important moment of his life and must not be treated lightly. She saw him lean forward, his head bent to Kit's, lifting her hands in both of his and for a fascinated moment she thought he was about to bring them to his lips before the quite spellbound gaze of the deferential gaze of the butler who waited to pass Mr Greenwood's greatcoat to the footman, and the housemaid who had no particular job but to see that the downstairs fires never went out.

It was as though no one would move, could move, not until the mistress of the house gave the order and Kit, Jenny became aware in the midst of the breathtaking silence, was not even conscious that anyone else was there beyond Jenny's brother, Joss Greenwood.

Winters waited, Joss's hat in his hand, his face quite expressionless, his eyes clamped on the portrait of James Chapman which hung above Joss's head. The footman's white-gloved hands waited to receive Joss's greatcoat which was still slung about his shoulders, his eyes, not quite so well trained as those of the butler who had more experience of such things, sliding curiously from the face of the woman whose servant he was to that of the man at whom she gazed so strangely.

Dear sweet Lord! It was all Jenny could do not to spring between them with her hands ready to strike out at their silly faces. She stood in the doorway of the drawing-room, the smile of welcome, the smile of greeting for her brother beginning to turn into an unbelieving, incredulous flare of outrage for it seemed everyone from herself to the influential mill-owners of Crossfold had had the wool firmly pulled over their eyes by this couple. *Joss and Kit Chapman!* Her brother and her employer. It was inconceivable and yet the evidence of it was here right before her eyes. They were standing like ... like two lovestruck youngsters, starry-eyed, flush-cheeked with the servants looking on, servants who would in the next few minutes be racing back to the kitchens, vying with one another to pour out the details to the rest. It was beyond belief, she could see it even now in the face of the housemaid, she could feel it in her own stunned mind, and how the devil they had managed to conduct what was so obviously an affair of long standing in a community as insular as this was beyond understanding, but that was not the issue causing anxiety here. It was, at this precise moment the delicate task of parting Joss Greenwood from Kit Chapman in the swiftest possible fashion and at the same time making the whole situation seem not at all out of the ordinary. *She* was his sister and therefore should be the one to receive his affectionate embrace, not Kit Chapman who, everyone in the valley had believed until quite recently was the sworn enemy of the radicals. Of course they did not say that now, now that she was taking the working man's side in the fight for what he called justice but that did not concern her at the moment. All that mattered was that Jenny Greenwood loved her brother and must defend him from the gossip which surely must come of this.

'Joss, my word but don't you look grand,' she said loudly, so loudly Winters and the footman and the housemaid who had quite forgotten that she was there at all, jumped guiltily and turned to look at her as she leaned against the door frame.

She wore a simple, long-sleeved afternoon gown of cream muslin edged at the neck and hem with cream challis work. The broad sash was of cream satin and on it she had pinned half a dozen cream rosebuds grown specially in the Chapman hothouses. They had decided, she and Kit, knowing that Joss had no evening suit, indeed had been anxious that he might have no suit at all for neither had seen him in anything but a jacket and breeches, that they would wear their simplest day dresses and not don one of the dozen splendid evening gowns they each possessed. But Joss Greenwood mixed with gentlemen now, with men of good family who, though they were of a higher social class, thought as he did. He appeared on platforms, an uneducated man who had educated himself, through his reading, through communication with men who *were* educated and was respected as an eloquent, plain speaking, forthright and intelligent man. A man of the people then, but one who was rising above his own humble birth. He had skills they could use, the men of reform, skills which were needed when there were elections to be won. He had the mass of the working man behind him. Not that they, any of them, had as yet, the right to vote, but one day they would and Joss Greenwood told them so and they loved him for it and for the education he promised their children. Food for their bellies and food for their minds, he said. Revolutionary ideas certainly, but ones which appealed to those who lived in Lousy Bank, Pig Lane and Boggart Hole.

He turned now, still dazed it seemed, still drowning in Kit Chapman's glowing brilliance, bewildered and not awfully certain who it was had spoken to him. His eyes met Jenny's then and he saw the warning in them and the love she bore him and when she looked away, inclining her head in the direction of the servants, his gaze followed hers and instantly he was aware of what he was about. Kit was still swaying towards him, her face possessed enchanted, ready to sink into his arms if he should hold them out to her, to lift her mouth for his kiss, to lay the length of her body against the length of his. She appeared mindless in her joy, her expression telling him she could not believe that they were together, their minds in harmony and at peace, that after years of hatred and bitterness, their love was holding them in beauty again.

He placed her hands carefully at her sides, letting them go reluctantly and stepped back, clearing his throat which had become clogged with emotion. Turning, he threw his greatcoat from his shoulders and handed it to Winters who passed it to the goggle-eyed footman, then he lifted his arms to Jenny and without a word she flew into them.

The servants all twitched into action, moving towards the back of the hall, disinterested in the public demonstration of the feeling shown by these two who were, in their opinion, completely out of place in Miss Chapman's home. Pearls before swine, they told one another for had they not been born in a weaver's cottage, the pair of them and what Miss Chapman thought she was doing was beyond them. It was bad enough having Jenny Greenwood, no more than a spinner, a factory girl, ordering them about as though she had been born to it, now it seemed they were to serve her brother, a radical reformer and an ex-felon.

Not one of the three could have said what they ate that night. Kit had ordered a simple meal, again considering Joss since she had no wish to embarrass him with a complicated menu to which he might be unaccustomed. It saddened her that she knew so little about him, that in the years they had known one another they had never once sat down to eat together, that they had done none of the simple, ordinary, everyday things which friends, lovers, husbands, wives do together. She had no idea of his tastes, his likes and dislikes, the colours which found favour with him, the books he read, the flowers, the food, the weather, hot or cold, summer, winter, spring, he preferred. They had talked over the years of their respective childhoods, of their love for one another and for the sweeping hillsides and moorlands of the Lancashire Pennines but beyond that she knew little about him. Of course she was only too well aware of his political beliefs and his conviction that all men were equal but now, she prayed fervently, now they surely must have the chance she had waited for to get to know one another, not as lovers but quite simply as a man and a woman.

They talked, he and Jenny, about the startling changes Kit was making in the factory, the better conditions she was creating for her operatives, the new houses which were already being erected for them to live in but Kit just listened, not really hearing what they said, content merely to watch him through the candlelight, to bask in the approval she saw in his eyes, to see the warm smile curl his lips, the constant turn of his gaze to meet hers.

' . . . naturally we did not make the profit we had in the past . . .' Jenny was saying to him seriously, just as though *she* and not Kit were the mill-owner, ' . . . since with fewer hours being worked by each operative and a higher wage given to them, it could not be achieved but the amazing thing, now that a rota has been worked out that is fair and well within the capacity of the women and children, profits are beginning to rise again. They still work damned hard, Joss, but it is as though the . . . the concern Kit has shown, the better conditions, the humane treatment they receive has given them a new optimism, an inducement, even a pride in what they can achieve. Kit has devised a bonus scheme and you could scarcely believe the competition which goes on to win it. And the children . . .' She leaned forward into the light cast by the candles and her face glowed, ' . . . to see them gradually lose that look of . . . of old men and women, to see them begin to smile, to look about them without fear and their faces, when they sit at their desks and suddenly, like a candle lit in a dark room, understand what the teacher is explaining to them, to see their minds *wake up* . . .' She shook her head at her own fanciful description and Kit watched Joss's hand go out to her, then as he turned towards herself, feel the lovely warmth of his love, his respect and admiration flow over her and knew she deserved it. It had taken a great deal of courage and resolution to go against her own kind, against what her own father and grandfather had contrived in the past thirty years or so, but for this man who had shown her how to go about it, she had done her best to enrich the lives of those who worked for her. Would she have acted as she was doing if she had not been so closely involved with the Greenwood family, would she have *cared* about the Greenwood family had it not been for her love for Joss, she had asked herself a hundred times in the six months since Jenny had come to work for her and the answer had

493

been that she did not know. How could she say, she only knew that her involvement had opened her eyes, and her heart. There was a way to run a business, to employ men, women and children fairly, and still make a handsome profit, despite what other men of commerce said, and she and Jenny were finding it, but it was this man who had led her to the start of it.

They drank coffee in the drawing-room and Joss was offered a brandy and cigar by the high nosed butler. He seldom drank brandy since it was beyond his means and had never tried a cigar but now, winking at Jenny, he took both and when Winters lit the cigar with the disdain of an aristocrat forced to wait upon his own servant, he coughed and choked and spluttered and declared he was amazed that anyone could do it for pleasure and that presumably one had to be born to such things since he was not.

But at last the laughter, the conversation, even between sister and brother ran out and the tension, soft and breathless which joined Kit and Joss, the tension of a man and a woman completely aware of one another and of no one else began to invade the room. Jenny could feel it wash against her own flesh, and it prickled, and her woman's body remembered what she had known with Harry Atherton. Not love certainly, nor even liking, but the desire which is born between male and female, a physical attraction which takes no heed of the mind, nor even the heart, but only of the senses. Their eyes were fixed upon one another with a longing so great, so powerful she felt a great need to get up and run from the room, to leave them, she was sure, to fall into one another's arms the very moment she had gone. Should she say something, she agonised. Let them know she had seen – as who had not – what was between them. The atmosphere, with the silence, became more strained until at last she could stand it no longer.

'You would not believe how Lucas had grown since last you saw him, Joss,' she said quite wildly. 'He already knows his letters though he is not yet three years old. I'm sure he will be asleep but perhaps you would like to see him.

Mother would be hurt if she thought you had been here and not visited her grandson . . .'

She was babbling and she knew it but at last she had caught the attention of her brother and filled with some sound, the silent and charged vacuum in which he and Kit were held fast. Immediately, as though he was glad of the diversion, not from Kit herself, but the pressure in him her closeness had created, he sprang to his feet.

'Of course. He must be getting quite a lad now. Three years in April, is it? But I don't want to wake him.'

'No really, I'd like you to see him.' Her face softened. 'He's a lovely boy, Joss, sweet natured, not like . . .' She stopped abruptly and her cheeks flamed and both Joss and Kit held their breath for she had almost spoken the name of the man who had fathered her son and Kit, who had guessed long ago who it was, was well aware that if Joss knew he might be tempted to take his revenge on the man who had not only given him a vicious beating but had 'taken down' his sister. But Jenny turned away, moving towards the door and Joss and Kit followed her, their hands brushing, their shoulders touching, their bodies waiting impatiently for the moment which surely must come.

The nursery was a soft and golden haven of warmth, the light from the glowing fire and from the night candle which stood on a low table filling it with a gentle soft-hued peace. Flora, once parlourmaid but now in charge of the nursery, sat beside the fire, some small garment in her hands and as they entered she rose hastily to her feet, sketching a curtsey, not only to her mistress, Miss Chapman, but to the mother of the boy in her charge who, for tonight, while *Miss* Greenwood entertained her brother, was to sleep in the nursery. Jenny Greenwood, named whore by those who did not know her, had gained the respect and obedience of many of the servants at Greenacres, not just because it was expedient, but for the resolute way in which she had tackled her new life, for her fairness in dealing with them, and others, for her plain speaking and plain common sense and by her refusal to be intimidated by those who considered themselves to be above her in the social structure of the house. It was well known what she was doing for her own class and though some, like Mr Winters, thought she should have remained in the station of life in which she had been placed since her reforms did not better *his* way of life, there were many with relatives in the textile trade who had cause to be grateful to her.

'Don't get up, Flora,' Miss Greenwood said now, putting her fingers to her lips. 'My brother has come to peep at his nephew. We won't wake him . . .'

'Nay Miss Greenwood, t'little imp's awake. 'Tis just as if he knows you've got a visitor an' can I get him to sleep, not on your life! See, will you look at him . . .' she said fondly as the bedclothes on the small bed in the corner of the room heaved convulsively and two shining eyes in a face crowned with a thick mop of fair curls peeped mischievously over them. There was laughter bubbling from the curl of rosy lips, and baby teeth gleamed in the candle-light. The boy sat up, then, enchanted with his own daring, stood up in the bed and began to bounce excitedly, his little nightgown riding up his sturdy legs to reveal his tiny male genitalia which bounced joyfully as well.

Joss and Kit stood side by side as Jenny moved across the room, her whole face wide and smiling her delight. In a moment she and the boy were engaged in a game which consisted of much kissing and hugging, of giggling laughter and rolling on the rumpled bed, oblivious it seemed, to those who watched. The love which bound Jenny Greenwood and her son was like a beacon in the warm room, a lovely thing to see and Joss was reminded of her misery when she was carrying this child who was now the very centre, the pivot on which her world revolved and the strange irony which had decreed such joy should come of so much wretchedness.

He turned to smile at Kit, to share with her his pleasure in his sister's happiness but the expression on her face wiped his smile away and he almost, only the watchful eyes of the nursemaid stopping him, drew her into his arms. He had no need to ask her why her face was so curiously still, so flat and empty, so lifeless and without hope. His love was sensitive now, sharp and wise to her despair since he himself felt it. They were never to know what Jenny knew. He and Kit Chapman. They were never to treasure the joy of a child as his sister did. Never to feel their own son wriggle and squirm in play against them as Jenny's son was doing, never to hold the flesh of their own flesh in loving arms and in that moment, as she looked up at him, her face quite dead, her eyes bright with unshed tears, he felt her desolation mingle with his own. She would never marry, and he, Joss Greenwood, was married to a woman who was and would be forever a child herself and would never conceive one of her own.

The nursemaid had turned away, lifting the poker to stir the glowing embers of the fire, busy with tongs and the coal scuttle. Joss put out his hand, cupping Kit's cheek, caressing it with his thumb, his eyes deep and sad as he looked into hers. There was nothing to say, it was there for her to read in his face, as he read it in hers and she turned her lips into the palm of his hand, kissing it passionately, declaring with that gesture that it did not matter, that as long as she had his love it was enough.

From the corner of his eye as he still looked into Kit's face he caught a movement from the other side of the room where he had noticed there was another small bed. It was tidy, made up, he had thought for the nursemaid to sleep in but as he watched the flat surface moved and on the pillow a small head turned, then rose up for a moment and two eyes peeped over the bedclothes at him. As he stared the eyes vanished and the head seemed to shrink beneath the covers and the bed was still and almost flat again.

'Who's that?' he asked curiously, still holding Kit's hand but the nursemaid appeared not to notice as she looked towards the bed in the corner of the room. Kit had turned to look as well and they both took a step or two in the direction of the bed.

'Nay, don't go too near, sir,' Flora said warningly, 'or you'll scare't poor mite to death.'

497

'Scare *who* to death, Flora,' Kit asked questioningly. 'Who on earth is it?'

'Eeh, I don't know her name, Madam. Nobody does.'

'But who is she? How did she get here?'

'Why, don't you remember? You brought her here yourself.'

'I did?'

Jenny had turned to watch as Kit and Joss, with Flora hovering anxiously at their backs, stood a yard from the bed. Her son was curled on her lap, his bright head on her breast, his eyelids drooping in sleep and for a moment the contrast between the secure, loved, contented boy, safe in his mother's arms and the terrified child in the other bed was quite dreadful.

'She's been here over six months, Kit. She came when Lucas and I did. You brought her from the mill on the day Ellis and the others were arrested. You and I were off to London so you left her with Flora. She's been here ever since.'

'Good God! I'd quite forgotten about her. But why is she so afraid? No one harms her here.'

'Wouldn't you be afraid if you didn't know what was to happen to you next? I suppose she came with a waggon-load of children from somewhere . . .' she shrugged, ' . . . only Gods knows where, or what happened to her before Ellis got his hands on her. She's known nothing but change and fear, hunger and brutality probably since she was old enough to stand, or even before. Can you wonder she trusts no one. She allows Flora to bathe and change her and has been taught how to use a spoon to eat her food. She's put on weight, you'd hardly know her from the child we brought in here six months ago but no one can get near her, not even Lucas. She's been abused not only by adults but by other children as well so . . .' Jenny hugged her own child to her, concerned evidently for the plight of all the children who had known the dreadful life this one had, her expression giving thanks that Lucas would never know the suffering of the child in the other bed.

498

Kit let go of Joss's hand at last, intrigued, why Jenny or Flora could not have said, and moved towards the bed in which the child cowered. They watched her as she drew back the covers and all of them, with the exception of Flora who was used to it by now, gasped at the rigid, unfocused look of terror in the child's eyes. A little girl, she was, still thin and pale, but quite normal in stature, the dreadful look of the undernourished, the unusually large head, the indecently protruding bones gone with the diet of good food she had eaten for the past six months. Her hair was thick and glossy, a lovely russet with a tendency to curl and her eyes were a soft sea green. But the look in them was appalling, so filled with unimaginable horror both Joss and Kit gasped out loud.

'Good sweet Jesus, what the devil has been done to her?'

Flora bristled. 'Why nothing, sir. She's been as well looked after as Lucas here. She gets the same food and Miss Greenwood has the seamstress make her little clothes just as she does for Lucas. She's warm and cosy but . . .'

'What is it, Flora?' Kit turned to look into the kindly face of the nursemaid.

'She'll not let me cuddle her, Miss Chapman. I've tried times to get her on me knee. We all have. Well, we feel so sorry for the poor little mite but she just goes as stiff as a dead rabbit. Quite give us a turn it did, the first time it happened. She stopped breathing, ma'am. Blue in the face she was, so after a bit we were afraid to touch her. She's no trouble as long as no one touches her, 'cept me when I wash her, like, an' you'd hardly know she was there . . .'

'Does she not speak?'

'Oh no, madam, not a word.'

Kit turned to Jenny. 'Did you know of this?'

'Of course, I'm in the nursery every day.'

'And you didn't tell me?'

'I'll be honest, Kit, but it never occurred to me. You had given her a home, good food, warm clothes. I didn't think you would be . . . be concerned beyond that. Besides, we thought she would come out of it.'

'Well, she hasn't.'

'No, but perhaps with time, and Lucas . . .'

'Has she not been given a name?'

'Well no, poor little poppet . . .' Flora's face was filled with sadness.

'Indeed . . .' Kit leaned over the child and with a gentle hand brushed back the soft hair from her forehead. The gesture brought no response. Kit stood up, her hand still fondling the little girl's cheek, then she turned to the nurse-maid.

'I'll come up again tomorrow, Flora and we will see what can be done. I'll not have an unhappy child in my mill and I'll certainly not have one in my home.'

Jenny said she would stay with her son until he slept and then take him to his own little bed beside her own. Joss was to give her love to her mother and tell her she and Lucas would be over on the following Sunday. They embraced affectionately, the sleepy child between them as Kit and Flora watched and as they left the nursery she and Joss heard her begin to sing a lullaby to her boy.

They stood just outside the nursery door in the darkened corridor and as it shut behind them they were instantly enclosed in the world each had waited impatiently for since he had invited her into his mother's cottage in Edgeclough. For over three years they had waited, not consciously perhaps, since neither had believed that it would come again, but their bodies, each one awakened, would not forget, could not be made to forget and they came joyously together now as she took his hand and began to lead him towards the staircase which went down from the nursery floor to her bedroom. When they were inside her last coherent thought was that although they were in a house filled with people not one of them knew exactly where she was – except perhaps Jenny! Winters had seen them all go up to the nursery and Flora had seen her and Joss go down towards the drawing-room. Janet would not come until she was summoned and until then . . .

She sighed as he placed her on her own bed, her mind

dwelling sensuously on the hundreds of times she had imagined this moment.

'You break my heart with your loveliness,' he whispered as he put his mouth to her naked breast.

'You soothe my soul,' she breathed as she held his head more closely to her.

'You bring me such joy . . .'

'You always have.'

## 33

The series of strikes which whiplashed through Lancashire began in Hyde, near Manchester, the leader a thirty-year-old Irishman called John Doherty. Wages had been cut again and though there was talk of militancy and holding out forever, the strikes failed. There was starvation stalking the county since they were out of work for six months, many of them, but the bleak struggle, though it caused hardship and poverty never before known in that part of the land did more to unite the working man than at any other point in his past history. A new militancy appeared, a new sense of defiance and purpose and a new fellowship between the working man's leaders. Francis Place, John Fielden, John Doherty, Joss Greenwood and others were agreed that a National Union, with Doherty as secretary, should be formed. A weekly levy of one penny per head on each working operative was willingly paid, producing a sum which went towards a 'benefit' of ten shillings a week for each family unemployed. Not much, Joss agreed, when Jenny questioned it, but enough to keep starvation from the door and surely a beginning in the great social service which he envisaged for those suffering hardship.

He was often at Greenacres in the spring and summer of

that year, going ostensibly to visit his sister and nephew though there were those who whispered that that was not his only reason for calling. Kit Chapman had been seen with a lean, dark man who looked suspiciously like Jenny Greenwood's brother, striding across High Moor to Badger's Edge with her four ferocious dogs running beside her and what were they doing up there, those who heard the rumours asked each other? And what was Kit Chapman thinking of mixing with the likes of him, a man who had been imprisoned for machine wrecking and mill burning, a man who was the opposite to every conviction her own father had believed in. Turn over in his grave her father would if he knew what was going on and surely it must all be to do with her close association with the Greenwood family? All of them!

There was Jenny Greenwood, tricked out like a lady in her silks and satins, giving orders to men like Ernest Gribb who had been a manager at the Chapman mills for over twenty years. You would think she was the mill-owner the way she went about the newly renovated spinning room, nodding and smiling at the women who worked in it, stopping to speak even, uncaring it seemed of the minutes wasted when the spinning frame was turned off. There was space enough between each machine to hold a dance in, it was said, and a new system of windows which let down from the top providing fresh air into the room and on the side where the sun struck, blinds were put up to shield those who worked there from its heat, and though the children still crawled about beneath the machines to 'piece' and collect the waste, those same machines were so hedged about with guards it was a wonder they could be made to function. And the hours they worked! No child under ten years of age employed and those that were did no more than eight hours at a stretch. *Eight!* Could you believe it and how on earth was Kit Chapman to make a profit, they marvelled, in those circumstances?

But that was not all. At the back of the mill she had

erected an extension in which there was a *dining-room*, warm in winter, wide open windows in the summer, with tables and chairs in which the operatives could sit for half an hour and eat their 'baggin', that which they could now well afford to be nutritious and filling on the incredible, ridiculously high wages she was paying them. There was piped water, clean and cool, brought from the river which ran beside the mill and separate privies for the men and women to use, *whenever* they wished to. No rules, nor fines. Like a bloody rest home, it was and no wonder there were always dozens at her gate clamouring to work there.

And at the end of their eight-hour shift, broken at midday for half an hour, the children of her operatives were given two hours' schooling in the back of the warehouse in a space she had cleared for them, and the new schoolroom and dormitories she was having built – these for her apprentices – were almost ready for them to move into.

In the weaving-sheds another agitator and radical had been made up to overlooker. Jem Pickering, son of Sarah and Isaac Pickering, had organised the same kind of madness as Joss Greenwood's sister in the spinning rooms, treating his operatives as though they were civilised human beings and not the slow-witted, shambling and stunted dwarfs most of them were. They had the same consideration given to them, the same incredible privileges as those in the rest of the Chapman factory, his authority complete, it was understood and him not yet nineteen! It was said he could take to pieces the Lancashire loom and put it together again in the space of an hour. He understood the weaving trade as well as any in the Penfold Valley since he had worked on his father's loom from the age of six. He had devised a method of threading the shuttle by hand, doing away with the arrangement of 'kissing the shuttle' which had lost so many operatives their front teeth. He was a good 'tackler' and they had come to depend on his skill and knowledge. He had a feel for the correct delivery of the cloth and the proper flight of the shuttle but that made no difference to those who were of the opinion that he should be kept in his proper place which was at a loom until he was well in his twenties, as the rest of the overlookers had been. And those who whispered of these things to one another in the drawing-rooms of Crossfold, in the counting houses of the other mill-owners, in the Cloth Hall and 'The Old Bull' in Jagger Lane were bitter and resentful, not that Kit Chapman was doing these things but that she was apparently making a success of them. But then, they comforted themselves, she was mad, out of her mind and what else could you expect of a woman? They forecast it would all turn sour on her, just wait and see and those who were in her debt and had no recourse but to put up with her nonsense, waited.

They moved into their new houses, her pampered operatives, in the new village she had created just on the outskirts of Crossfold where she had bought land. Well lit streets, they had, paved and with adequate gutters to take away rainwater. The rubbish cart came once a week to remove their refuse, for there had been cholera in town that year and it appeared that Miss Chapman was of the opinion that where there was filth and bad water, there could be sickness.

What the community did not know and it was doubtful they could have kept quiet about it if they had was that besides the resident teacher Katherine Chapman employed to educate the children in her mill and the resident physician she retained to improve their health, was that the same doctor, young and with liberal ideas, was instructing the women in a method of contraception which would keep their families to manageable proportions!

The Penfold Valley buzzed with talk. Those manufacturers and their wives who were accustomed to dining with Miss Chapman and her protégé, Miss Greenwood, who had been forced upon them against their will, declared that really, they did not think they could abide it much longer. They had been quite taken aback on the first occasion Miss Greenwood, *Miss* Greenwood, if you please, had been

504

introduced to them by Kit Chapman as her colleague and friend, but short of turning on their heels and walking from the house which Hannah Chapman would have been delighted to see them do, they had no option but to take her hand and smile frostily.

George Abbott, seated next to her at table, told his wife later he had fully expected her to eat the excellent duckling, Kit Chapman had served, with her fingers, but it appeared Miss Greenwood had picked up more than the knowledge of how to wear the exquisite rose-pink silk gown she was in, which any pretty woman could have been put in to resemble a lady, for she used the correct knife, fork, spoon at the correct moment and even congratulated Kit on the excellence of the wine served, just as though she had drunk it all her life.

'You are in the business of spinning, I believe,' she said to him in a voice from which the broadness of Lancashire had not completely gone.

'Indeed Miss Greenwood.' He could not bring himself to say more and his wife, who sat opposite looked as though she might become stuck in the frozen pose she had taken when Jenny Greenwood had the audacity to address a remark to her husband. Put up with her they were forced to do, but converse with her, *never*, but Jenny Greenwood knew her own worth by now and she saw no reason to efface herself in the company of these men and women whose grandparents had been no better than her own.

'And what do you think to the Bill for introduction of the ten-hour working day proposed by Mr Michael Sadler, Mr Abbott?' she asked.

'I think it to be no more than foolish nonsense, Miss Greenwood.'

'Really. Do you not agree with Mr Richard Oastler that our children should be free?' Her face was as innocent as a babe.

'Free, Miss Greenwood. I'm afraid I do not understand you.' His good-natured face, heavy and well fed was turned slightly away from her as though only courtesy to his

505

hostess — and the five thousand pounds he owed her — kept him seated beside Jenny Greenwood.

'You have heard of Mr Oastler, Mr Abbott, and his fight for the abolition of colonial slavery?'

'Indeed. Who has not?'

'You think him an honourable man then?'

'Naturally.'

'Then you would believe his word when he spoke it?'

'Of course.'

'Then what of the letter he wrote in the *Leeds Mercury* several weeks ago regarding the slavery of thousands of children in our very own mills?'

'Come now, Miss Greenwood. You cannot possibly mean it. Those children are free as air itself. They are not forced to work in our mills. They may do as they please, as their parents please . . .'

'And free to die of starvation if they please.'

It was as well that Kit stood up at that moment, signifying that the ladies should retire, leaving the gentlemen to their cigars and port, for George Abbott, as he proclaimed furiously to his wife later, might have thrown caution to the wind and told Jenny Greenwood to take herself off back to the hovel she no doubt came from. It was more than a gentleman could stand and his wife, a lady, agreed with him quite tearfully since her friendship with Hannah Chapman was put seriously to the test by the dreadful strain of being forced to remain on good terms with Katherine. Hannah was cool with her and bitter on the subject of the lower orders who tramped through her lovely home and gardens. Though she was not in the habit of walking in them herself she was often disturbed by the sound of *that child* who romped and squealed on the lawn with his nursemaid and by the sight from her window of *that woman*, his mother and the rest of her horrid family, enjoying what had once been hers alone. She could see her own daughter consorting with a class inferior to her own, laughing and chatting with the woman and more often now as the weather improved, with the one who was her brother.

The very one who had once destroyed dear Barker's machines and burned his warehouse for which crimes he had served two terms of imprisonment. Dear Barker's daughter brazenly flaunting herself, she was, with those to whose level she had sunk and if poor Barker could see what the wealth, for which he and his family had worked so hard, was being squandered on, it would surely kill him all over again.

Kit Chapman was happier than she had ever been before. She would look back to what she had imagined then to be days of perfection. Like the first time her father took her to the mill. The day on which he told her she was to be his sole and complete heir. The day she had been allowed to walk alone for the first time up on the moorland accompanied only by her dogs, but none of them could compare with each lovely day to which she now awoke. She was fulfilled in every need she had. Her mills ran smoothly and efficiently, not as yet making the profit they once had, though her reputation for the best quality cotton was still upheld. Her mind was sharp, her heart content, her conscience clear as she watched the miraculous improvement in the people she employed. They were gaining confidence in her now, realising that this 'experiment' she was proving was no nine days wonder to impress the factory inspectors when they came, but an on-going improvement in their own lives.

And her body glowed with the physical fulfilment Joss Greenwood gave it in her bed, and her heart was tranquil with the emotional fulfilment he gave her every moment of her waking hours. He came to her as often as he was able, sometimes no more than once in two weeks for his work took him all over Lancashire and Yorkshire as he reported on the conditions of those in the textile trades. Though he still wrote articles for several working class newspapers his time was being given up to an increasing demand for his presence at political rallies and meetings. He could command a mighty gathering wherever he went since the men for whom he fought revered him, trusted him, looked to him still as the man who would better their lives. Perhaps not this year, or even the next but one day his revolutionary ideals would come to fruition. Whenever there was a meeting involving a Whig or Tory supporter there would be a great deal of rough heckling, shouted abuse, fights and even garbage chucked indiscriminately, but when Joss spoke they would listen quietly, almost with love, for he was one of them despite his obvious rise in the world.

'You will go to Westminster one day, my darling,' Kit told him.

'And your mother will invite me to dine with her.' He laughed softly, sitting up to look at her in the half light of the candles which stood on the table beside the bed. They had dined with Jenny who had, as usual, excused herself on the grounds that she wished to look in on her son, all three of them acknowledging now, though not openly, that Kit and Joss were lovers and when the servants had withdrawn, told that they would not be required again that night, Joss and Kit had gone up the wide staircase to her bedroom. Though he did not spend the whole night with her, much as they both longed for it, since his mother and Charlie would both expect him home after dining with his sister, they would share an hour or so in the dangerous but enchanted world which was, as yet, just their own, before Joss mounted the rather elderly mare he had bought to move more easily about the immediate vicinity of his home. They were both aware that such a relationship as theirs, carried out in a house where the servants could not fail to realise eventually that Joss Greenwood was more to their mistress than merely Jenny Greenwood's brother, must surely become common knowledge in the community but as yet they were unable, and unwilling to look for some other way to continue it. They would not be parted again, they had both sworn it, but how they were to manage it without destroying not only Kit's reputation which was already a matter for conjecture in the community, though as yet only on the subject of her sanity, but Joss's credibility with those who trusted him in their fight for justice. And how would Martha Greenwood face the truth, if it should come out? She and Kit had met only once on the day Charlie was beaten by Kit's overlookers but Kit knew from Jenny that she was held in grateful esteem by Jenny's mother. Everything they had, the Greenwoods, and many of *their* social group, they owed to Kit Chapman. Not given, most of it, but earned by them because she had allowed them the chance for it and her name was spoken of almost reverently now on the lips of all those who had cause to thank her. But Martha loved her son and her son had a wife who, though she was not as she should be, was still his wife and very dear to Martha. Marriage was marriage, good or bad, in health *and* sickness and what else could you call Mercy's affliction but a sickness? And despite her gratitude to Kit Chapman and Joss's avowed belief that all men were equal there was still in Martha's heart the feeling that the Greenwoods and the Chapmans were not of the same social position. The classes did not mix, not in Martha's world, they did not marry and though she did not consciously consider it, not knowing the situation existed, they certainly did not become lovers.

Kit's golden skin was the rich colour of honey in the warm light of the candles. Her hair a dark and tangled mass on the pillow and she had flung one arm above her head. The movement lifted her breasts, peaking her nipples, amber tinted against the whiteness of her skin and Joss's hand reached to caress each one in turn. Her free hand absently stroked the hairs on his chest and he bent to kiss her, brushing back the hair which drifted across her face. Her lips were warm, parting a little beneath his but it was clear her thoughts which only minutes before had been wholly concerned with his hands and his mouth and what they were doing to her naked body, had flown away to some other place which demanded her attention.

'A fine thing,' he grumbled laughingly, 'when a man cannot capture the interest of his woman when he lies naked in the same bed with her. He pleasures her until she cries

509

out with it then when she has done with him her thoughts instantly wander to other things. What must he do to re-capture her notice, d'you think? This perhaps . . . ah ha . . .' as Kit squirmed with delight, ' . . . or this . . .' and she stretched and sighed languorously beneath his delicately probing finger, turning to him at once for there was never a moment when he did not bewitch and enchant her with his touch.

She was watching him dress when she spoke again. The words of love and delight, the whispers and soft laughter, the joyous sounds of their lovemaking were still drifting sensuously about the shadowed room but her head was clear now.

'I meant what I said, Joss.' Her voice was low.

'About what?' He was busy with his boots, his mind concerned with the half hour's ride he must undertake, with the time he must give to his mother, his brother and his wife before he journeyed the next day to Manchester where he was to speak to a gathering of cotton workers, sharing the platform of John Doherty, the secretary of the newly formed trade union. He was torn, not into two parts, but into three or even four, with the commitment he had towards Kit, towards his wife and family, the men who were loyal to him and those who urged him to further his career in the political arena.

'About Westminster. There are to be elections in a year or two and what better man to represent the people than you?'

His hands stilled and he stared blindly into the corner of the shadowed room. It was as though she had read what had been in his mind for many months now. It was believed among his fellow radicals that they could win control at the forthcoming elections even though the right to participate at the polls was restricted to property-holders and ratepayers. The townships of Oldham, Royton, Crompton and Chadderton and the newly created constituency of Crossfold were to be formed into a three-member parliamentary borough and the registered electorate was limited by the

510

property qualification to no more than one thousand five hundred out of a population of just over fifty thousand. But four-fifths of the electorate were composed of men in small businesses, shopkeepers, men who owned smallholdings with a cow or two and all dependent on working-class custom. And the working-class man was solidly behind Joss Greenwood and the other radical reformers. If they were to take it into their heads, as well they might, to boycott these same shopkeepers where else could they sell their milk and their butter, their bread and oats and the goods the working man purchased. Joss Greenwood, if he chose, could become one of the radical candidates for this borough, and he knew it.

He jumped to his feet, stamping them into his boots which had been flung willy-nilly about the room in his eagerness to love Kit Chapman an hour ago. He appeared not to have heard her, or if he had was not prepared to listen.

'Did you hear me, Joss?' she said quietly.

He became still then. 'Aye, I heard you, lass.'

'It's the money, isn't it?'

'Nay, I've no mind to be a Member of Parliament, nor to live up in London. I'm a Lancashire lad and I love a Lancashire lass and I'll not be parted from you, nor my family and besides, there's nothing I can do . . .'

'That's not so, Joss. You've proved time and again just what you can do for these people of yours. They love you. They rely on you. They trust you above everyone because you have never let them down, and because you are one of them.'

'Say that's so, I still couldn't go.' His voice was harsh.

'Because of the money.'

'Aye, because of the money . . .' He turned to her swiftly, his face truculent, arrogant, filled with his frustrated pride, but beneath it in the depth of his clear eyes was the longing. ' . . . and don't you go saying you'll give it to me because I won't have it. You know yourself what the property qualifications are for a Member of Parliament. I've no personal income so how would I live? I'm nought but a hand-loom weaver . . .'

'No, no! It is an honourable trade but that is not all you are.' Her voice was high and defiant and she leaped from the bed, glorious in her nakedness, truly a woman now in the mature roundness of her breast and hip but she might have been fully clothed for all the notice either of them took of her body. 'You are a leader, Joss. There are not many born to be such but you are one of them. You told me your father was one and perhaps he was, but you have drawn these men of the cotton industry into a force to be reckoned with. Only you! And it should be you who speak for them up at Westminster. Let me help you, Joss. Please let me help you. I have more money than I know what to do with. I am spending it now on houses and schools and all the things you have told me they need and what I have come to believe in myself, through you. How much better it would be if you, with your eloquence, could make *others* see it too. Those in Parliament who have the *real* power to change things. Don't let your pride stand in your way, in *their* way. Would you have them go on as they are just because you were too puffed up with your own feelings to consider theirs. You are a bigger man than that, Joss Greenwood. You know it and I know it.'

She could see it in his eyes then. The belief that it could be done. The realisation that what she said was the truth. There was a sudden excited lift to his head and a squaring of his broad shoulders. The very idea that he, a weaver's son, could sit up there with sons of gentlemen, a working-class man, perhaps the first to do so, to speak on behalf of his own. It was so heady he could get drunk on it, his expression said and yet that was surely not what this was about. For a moment he had been carried away with his own joy, his own self-satisfaction, but then was he not human? Was he not allowed to revel for a moment in the pride any man would feel in what he had achieved, what he could achieve in the future if he allowed it to happen? It was his decision and he must make it alone, without the distraction of this woman. She was *his* woman and he loved her for what she was, for what she had done, for what she had already given him of herself but she was bewitchment and he must not be beguiled by the magic she held out to him.

He took her in his arms and held her in a way which had nothing to do with sexuality despite her nakedness. He leaned on her strength, depended on her now, he had come to realise, not just for his bodily easement, for the comfort and joy her love gave him, but for the power of her woman's wisdom, the surety that she was always waiting here for him, for her patience when it was needed, for her stubborn resistance, the ability she had to exhilarate him, to anger him sometimes, to make his life whole. She was his life and without her he would be nothing but this must be considered, not with her to influence him, but on his own. He must decide the rightness of it. There would be no doubt in anyone's mind where the money had come from to send him to Westminster, should he decide to stand for the candidature and those whom he represented must be made to see that he did it for them, not for his own splendid ends which is what would be said of him. A kept man they would call him, and worse. There was his mother, and Charlie, who would have to know. Explanations would have to be made and though Miss Chapman's benevolence, directed at *all* her workers now, and not just the Greenwood family, was an accepted fact surely it would not extend to supporting a man, a grown man, *keeping* him, feeding and clothing and housing him, they would be bound to say. It would not take either of them long to understand the implications. He was a man with a wife, who was *not* a wife. A man, with a man's needs. Kit was a woman, a strong, self-willed woman who also had needs and he and she were together more than was usual. Could he put that burden of shame on his mother, for that was what she would be? Shamed! And yet she was a compassionate woman. Perhaps she might be an understanding woman also, and young Charlie, though still a boy, was mature, experienced, not in the ways

513

of love, but in life. He was a scholar now, with a flair for learning, which was astonishing his tutors, and in his maturity was old enough to know the truth and ready, surely, to accept it. For the sake of the men and women he had always supported, would he not accept it?

'Will you do it, Joss?' she said, her cheek pressed into the curve of his shoulder. 'God knows how I will manage without you if you go to London. I cannot bear the thought and I'm sure I will regret it the moment you are gone but you know it is right for you. I am trying hard to tell myself that I am doing this for the men and women you love so well but if I am honest that is only partly the truth. I love you, Joss, more than any other in the world and whatever I say it will sound priggish, pompous even, but you were meant for this and I am willing to . . . to . . .'

'Let me go despite the pain it will cause you?' He bent his head lovingly to hers. 'Kit. Katherine Chapman. Do you know what you are to me? Do you? Inside you is a fire which warms me, a light which shines from you so that I can see. You are so fine, so good and if that makes you sound saintly that is not how I meant it. I cannot count the times you have tried my patience with your devilish ways until I could take a whip to you. No, you are no saint, my lovely Kit, but you have a good heart. It has been burdened by what your father put in it but you did not allow it to become callous as the rest of the mill-owners in the valley. You are a business-man whose sole aim is profit as your father's was but you have brought a woman's compassion to it, proving something of great importance to the men and women of Lancashire. That fair treatment brings a fair reward, not just for them but for you.'

He threw back his head and laughed. 'By God, will you listen to me sermonise. Saint Joss now, alongside Saint Katherine and the pair of us with more sins on our souls than Enoch Butterworth could shake a stick at.'

'Who's Enoch Butterworth?'

'Someone I once knew. It's a long story from a long time ago but I think old Enoch would approve of my taking this

514

step to help his fellowmen, though not the way I'm to go about it!'

# 34

Jenny and Charlie noticed the three men on Easter Sunday. She and Lucas had walked the three miles from Crossfold to Edgeclough as they did every Sunday, the small boy running ahead for he was always in a hurry to get to his grandmother's cottage, and to Charlie. He was three years old tomorrow and Charlie had promised to take him up on the moor to show him the warrens where Charlie caught the rabbits which went into grandmother's pot. He was well aware that grandmother had no need of the rabbits Charlie caught, not like she had in the old days his mother had told him about. They had almost starved then, before Aunt Kit had become a 'reformer', though he was not at all sure what that was, and had given the workers, of which his mother and Charlie had been but two, a lot of money, again he was not certain of how much. But the rabbits Charlie caught could be given to other, poorer families who lived in the village Charlie told him.

His mother spoke to him at great length on the wickedness of wrongs done to the 'poor' by the 'rich', among which he often thought they must be numbered since they lived in such a lovely house, and his grandmother did not – so was she not poor? – but his mother said not. It was really too much to understand and though he was well aware that he was better off than many of the boys with whom he played in the village what did it matter when they all had such fun? Sunday was the best day of the week.

He suffered his grandmother's embrace, wriggling like a rabbit himself, but good natured with it, the only characteristic he had inherited from his father, for which his mother gave daily thanks, apart from his handsome face. Aunt Mercy kissed him and would have sat him on her knee, calling him 'Tom' as she always did, why he did not know since that was not his name but he evaded her strange grasp and her strange vacant stare and ran straight to Charlie. They began to wrestle in the way all men did, to show one another their love, and he certainly loved Charlie.

Charlie Greenwood was twelve years old now, growing into the frame which was a replica of his older brother's. Tall, lean, all arms and legs and elbows still, growing out of his breeches as quickly as his mother put him in a new pair, and despite the scarring of his engaging face, agreeable to look on. There was a line across his lips, well defined and deep where Arnold Ellis's boot had split his mouth but already, as he filled out from a scrawny boy to a well set up youth, beginning to fade and as his mother said, he was always laughing these days so you'd hardly notice. The pucker above his left eyebrow, sewed up as best she could by Sarah Pickering, lifted it into an expression of quizzical amusement, of wry humour at the world which Charlie Greenwood now found so much to his liking and fortunately the teeth he had lost were at the back of his mouth, the gap left not visible except when he yawned. He was not much given to yawning since, being a strong and wiry boy he was rarely tired and never, never bored. He had followed his brother and the rest of the Onwardsmen, when he could escape his mother's vigilance as a young boy, but now he was the pride of his family in the grand school at Crossfold and his brother had told him his talents would be needed in other directions as the thinking man he was to be. A lawyer perhaps, but that was in the future and this small scrap who tried to climb his leg and who Charlie loved inordinately, he did not know quite why, was claiming his attention, demanding to be off, like the two men they were, up to the tops to inspect Charlie's traps.

'You'd better not let the Squire hear you say that, my

lad,' Jenny heard him say to her son as they walked up the path towards the track which would lead them to Dog Hill, and the inevitable questions . . . 'Why Charlie?' . . . 'What for Charlie?' . . .'How Charlie?' followed on the air. It was an easy enough climb for the three-year-old boy who had been taught almost from the time he could walk, as they all had as children, the meaning of striding out, of simply going on and up, without whining.

She turned back to her mother, no longer bearing the baskets of food she had once brought for they were not needed. She was proud of her own ability to provide for her family. The soft-hued warmth of the clean, white-washed kitchen, the bright fire in the hearth, the dresser lined with her mother's crockery, the brass candlesticks and herb jars, the rugs, the fresh curtains at the window, the comfortable, highly polished furniture and the saddle of lamb she could smell roasting in her mother's blackleaded oven. Upstairs were three bedrooms made over from what had once been the loom-shop worked by her father and Joss, with comfortable beds and good woollen blankets and white bed-spreads crocheted by her mother and Mercy during the winter, bright rugs and curtains. Daisy slept in one on her rare night off and her mother in another with Mercy, while the third was Charlie's. In the stall at the side of the house was the mare that Jenny had bought for Charlie so that he might ride the three miles to school each day and stored beside it was the coal which was delivered now that Charlie could no longer collect the peat for his mother's fire.

It was a joy to Jenny and her heart was filled with it as she looked at Mercy, marvelling at her mother's forebearance with this pretty child who was her brother's wife. She was twenty-six now and looked scarcely older than Charlie. Bonny she was, the firm flesh on her golden with the sun, her brown silky hair springing in fine curls about her smooth face. She had become fuller bosomed in the plenty which had come with Kit Chapman's reforms and Jenny's own elevation in life, a fit wife for any man, one would think and it was only when you looked into her eyes that the emptiness there was revealed.

'And how is Miss Chapman, lass?' It was the first question her mother always asked.

'She's well, mother and sends her regards.'

And perhaps for the very first time since they had met in the doorway of the spinning room on the day the child had lost his hands in a machine, Jenny Greenwood's mind dwelled softly on the woman who was her employer and probably, though she admitted it only to herself, becoming her friend. Certainly the friend of those men, women and children in her mill who had cause, *now*, Jenny acknowledged truthfully, to give thanks for the improvement she had brought into their lives.

'The proof of the pudding is in the eating' she had told herself sourly. Well, she had tasted the pudding and it had proved to be delicious and though she had not yet come to terms, and probably never would with the recognition that her brother and Kit Chapman were lovers, could she really blame Joss when confronted with the woman who was his wife? So, she would try to keep to the adage, held dear in these parts where privacy was valued, that it was 'nowt' to do with her. It seemed to hurt no one, she was the first to admit, indeed Joss had never looked better and as for Mercy she felt no lack of affection in this family where she was treated as a well-beloved child.

They spent a pleasing hour or two on subjects dear to her mother's heart. Country matters, simple and unchanging. Events which had happened during the week, events which happened every week in the uncomplicated and contented life Martha spent with her daughter-in-law, while Mercy busied herself about the kitchen, dusting and polishing objects which she had dusted and polished only an hour since, basting the saddle of lamb in the oven, declaring she would make an apple pie for Charlie and Tom's return, running to the window a dozen times to look out for their coming. Jenny felt her nerves tighten as she watched the constant movement of Joss's wife, wondering how her mother could stand it but Martha seemed not to notice beyond a motherly admonishment to 'watch that oven, lass, 'tis hot', just as though Mercy really *was* no more than a child.

Charlie got out the mare from the stall at the side of the house where once his forebears had housed their few cows, and she and Lucas were lifted on to the animal's back for the journey home as they always did. Strong her son might be but Charlie insisted upon it, walking beside them to Greenacres and then riding back since it was a long walk for the boy who was by now, half asleep against his mother. She leaned down to kiss her mother and Mercy and their affectionate farewells fell softly in the darkening yard as they turned out into the village street. Sarah was at her door, outlined against the soft glow of her fire-lit kitchen and she waved before going inside and the clip of the horse's hooves sounded loud on the quiet cobbled street.

It was at the top of the brow which led out of the village when they saw the men. Three of them striding away in the direction of Beal Moor just as though they had come from Edgeclough. They were no more than dark grey shadows against the pale grey of the evening sky, their faces a white blur as they turned to look over their shoulders at Jenny and Charlie.

'Who are they, d'you think?' Jenny mused. 'They look as though they've been visiting someone in the village.'

'Nay, I don't know.' Charlie stared after them but the men did not look back again, disappearing into the growing darkness of the moorland. He turned again just before they began their descent on the long, winding track to Crossfold but there was no one to be seen.

The lad came to the Greenwoods' cottage door at just gone half past seven the following Sunday morning. He was decently dressed, ready for church, he said, which the Squire insisted upon each Sunday for his servants, but they had all been thrown into confusion when the accident happened and . . . well . . . if Mrs Greenwood didn't come at once there was a chance she might not see her daughter alive again.

'Daisy . . . oh dear God . . . dear God . . .' Martha reeled against her son, her face ashen and it was Charlie who read the note. Written on the Squire's own notepaper it was, and though he did not recognise the handwriting, never having had a letter from the Squire before, there was no denying the authenticity and gentlemanly hand of the letter. Daisy had fallen, it said, down a flight of stairs. The Squire's own physician had been called but the girl was unconscious and in the physician's opinion, though he did not wish to alarm Mrs Greenwood, her daughter's condition was critical.

'I'll saddle the mare. She'll take us both,' Charlie said, his own face like death and the boy watched interestedly as the mother and son whirled about in the first muddled moments caused by shock before they steadied themselves.

'Mercy . . . Oh dear Lord . . . Mercy . . .'

'Get her up . . .' for Joss's wife was still in the bed from which Martha had just risen.

But Mercy Greenwood would not be 'got up'. She was alarmed by *their* alarm, frightened by Martha's frantic exhortations to be a 'good girl', distressed by the impatience of the woman who had shown her nothing but love and tolerance, whose even temper and steadiness had given Mercy a lifeline to which she could cling.

'Please . . . Martha . . .' she whimpered, cowering beneath the covers, her eyes enormous in her pale face, ' . . . I would like to stay in bed today . . .' for sometimes when her little bird failed her Martha allowed her to lie in the soft feathered security of the bed they shared, to lie and watch the clouds drift serenely across the blue of the sky, to see the wind ripple the tall bracken and the pretty yellow gorse, until she felt the tranquillity soothe her.

'Mercy lass, you must get up and go to Sarah's . . .' Martha was savage now in her anguish for her youngest daughter, pulling at Mercy's shoulders, tugging at the bedcovers but Mercy held on.

'Come on, Mother,' Charlie was shouting from below. 'The mare's saddled . . .'

'She won't get up . . .'

'Leave her then. She'll be safe enough in her bed . . .'

'Please Mercy . . .' Martha tried one more time but the girl was nearly demented now in her distress.

'Will you go up to Sarah's, please Mercy . . .' but blood was thicker than water and this girl was no blood of Martha's and though she knew Mercy should not be left alone since she was incapable of intelligent thought and that given time she should have sent Charlie up the street for Sarah, there *was* no time, and so the choice was made.

The four men watched impassively from the shelter of the little spinney at the back of Martha's cottage as she and her son moved off slowly for the mare carried a double load. Charlie had tried to persuade his mother to ride the animal while he ran beside it for it would have been quicker but she had never been on a horse's back in her life and so, with her arms tight about him they began the seven mile journey to the Hall which lay on the far side of Ashton.

When they had disappeared up the back track which went, not through the village, but in the opposite direction, the men slipped, like silver grey shadows, down through the neat rows of seedlings Mercy had planted the week before and into the cottage, closing the door behind them.

Jenny had stopped for a moment to have a word with Sarah as she and Lucas walked down the street two hours later, remarking on the coldness of the day and the certainty that it would rain before the hour was out.

'Aye, back ter winter it is, that's fer sure. Best round t'fire on a day like this, my lass, an' that's where I'm off right now.'

Lucas was darting ahead, eager to get to Charlie to show him the rough wooden musket, that Dick, the stable lad, had carved for him for his birthday. They could have a good game up on the top of Dog Hill for though Charlie was almost grown up he did not mind playing the games dear to Lucas's three-year-old heart. He lifted the latch, his

521

face, still that of baby, rounded cheeks wreathed already in the joyous grin he reserved just for Charlie, prepared for a moment or two, but no more, to suffer the fond embrace of his grandmother and Aunt Mercy before the serious business of the day began. His mother was but a step or two behind, shaking out the folds of her long, serviceable cloak for the rain which had threatened all the way up from Crossfold had begun, clinging in fine droplets to the fabric.

She felt herself begin to apologise for in her confusion she was convinced she had come to the wrong house, though in her mind of course, she knew she had not. She was ready to back out again, to scream to the three men who stood about the kitchen that she was sorry, really she was, that this was not her house, nor even her mother's and she would tell no one, no one in the whole wide world of what she was looking at, no matter if she was put to the torture if they would let her go, if they would let her son go, if she could be allowed to return and wipe out the last thirty seconds, make them vanish as though they had never been, never happened. If she could be allowed to pick up her big-eyed, open-mouthed boy, take her hand from the latch where it still rested, pull the door to and simply go back to the time, two minutes ago now, when she and Lucas had still been at her mother's front gate. But it was too late. Her eyes had seen what was there, what had been done and it was too late.

Too late for her, and far too late for Mercy whose resting place on Martha's newly scrubbed kitchen table would be her last. Her naked white body appeared to be without bones, her head hanging over the edge of the table until her tangled hair swept the floor. She was on her back. Her tiny breasts were flat, like those of a girl-child and on them was congealing blood about the nipples. She had bruises on almost every part of her body, scraped raw where vicious hands had grasped her tender flesh. Her legs had been held apart so violently she gave the appearance of being almost torn in two and Jenny's demented mind, unwilling to deal with the horror, could not seem to get past the problem of how her mother would remove that vast pool of blood from the table.

'Good morning, Jenny. Come in an' close t'door, lass. 'Tis right cold out, for' time o't year and we'd hate to lose the warmth of yer Mam's kitchen. Please . . .' the voice became sharp, ' . . . close t'bloody door for we want no nosy parkers pryin' in what's not their concern, do we?'

She closed the door, moving automatically closer to her son, her mother's hands pulling him to her, her arms encircling him in a gesture which was already hopeless. Her face was the grey of the pale ashes spilling into her mother's hearth and her firm flesh had fallen in, deepening her eye-sockets to black pits. The bones of her face stood out like a bleached skull as she tried hard not to look at what had been done to her brother's wife.

'Take off yer cloak, my lass, an' come to't fire,' but she shrank back against the door and Arnold Ellis smiled. The year he had spent in prison had stripped the loose flesh from him, revealing his angular frame, the big bones of his hands and wrists, accentuating the cruelty of his thin-lipped mouth. The boy cowered from him in her arms, burying his young face in her skirts and she stroked his fair curls in an effort to soothe him but her eyes would keep straying to what lay on her mother's kitchen table and her terror drove out all thoughts beyond the one which searched for a safe way out for her son.

'Put t'lad to one side an' come 'ere, Jenny,' Ellis said, 'or one o' these lads will tek 'im from yer and they're not over gentle.'

'No . . . please . . . don't hurt the boy . . . please . . .'

'He's a bloody Greenwood, in't he?' Ellis's expression was mild, interested, as though he and Jenny were discussing a diverting fact in the genealogy of Jenny's family, ' . . . as you are, as yer brothers are, both of 'em.'

'I don't know what you mean. Why are you here? What do you want with us?'

'I'm 'ere ter collect summat what's owed me, Jenny Greenwood.'

'I owe you nothing . . . nothing . . .' She was babbling, she knew it as Ellis gestured to one of the other men who began to saunter across the kitchen towards her.

'No . . .' Her voice was ready to rise into a scream and instantly the third man who had slipped up behind her, clapped his hand across her mouth, silencing her. She could smell him, she could smell them all and her stomach rose in horror but she knew she must make no noise . . . Why? . . . Dear God, why not? for a scream would bring the men of the village but there was Lucas . . . Lucas.

'But you do, Jenny Greenwood, you an' that bitch we worked for, me an' the lads. We was doin' no more than givin' that precious brother of yours what he deserved, what many a lad got in the mill yard for giving a bit o' lip, but Charlie did more than that. He struck Alfie 'ere, didn't he Alf, and so we give 'im a licking which was no more than 'e deserved, but what 'appens? You go runnin' ter high and mighty Miss Katherine Chapman an' me an' Alfie an' Jim get a year's hard labour, which we didn't much like, ay lads? But it wasn't until a certain . . . well, shall we say someone else who 'ad a grudge against you and Miss Chapman, came ter me an' . . .'

There was a stirring at the back of the kitchen, just beyond the heavy chenille curtain which her mother drew across the scullery door on a winter's night to keep out the draught, and Ellis stopped speaking abruptly as though he had said too much. Jenny strained her eyes and her ears, for surely there was a fourth person hovering there, but the man holding her pulled off her bonnet and, getting a savage grip in her short hair, forced her eyes back to those of Ellis. They glowed like the coals in her mother's fire, his hatred supreme, his triumph dominating the room. The other two men did not speak but merely stood, watching her, enjoying it, enjoying Ellis's game of making it last for as long as he wished before the final act, whatever he wished that to be.

'So yer see, Jenny Greenwood, me an' the lads're going to punish you for what yer did to us. We're going to punish you and yours because through the Greenwood women we'll get back at the Greenwood men. Both of 'em. Revenge, that's all that kept me goin' in the last twelve months, my lass, an' when I met up with ... well ... the idea was thought up an' 'ere we are. That brother of yours, the one what thinks he's Jesus Christ saving his flock and stirring up folks so that a man can't carry on with a bit of business when he's a mind to, will p'raps think twice afore he goes sticking his nose in where it din't belong, an' as fer Charlie Greenwood, he'll wish he'd died under the lashing we give him last year when he sees what's bin done to his sister. We'll break them both, through you and the other bitch, Chapman. The idiot was a bit of a bonus ...' He indicated the still figure of Mercy Butterworth, 'we'd forgotten her but while we was waiting for you we 'ad us a bit of entertainment, like, but Alfie 'ere was a bit rough, or was it you, Jim? I forget.'

'No ... no ...' Her head moved from side to side, denying what he was saying, denying the evidence of what had been done to Mercy though the appalling truth of it was sprawled on Martha's kitchen table. Her eyes rolled in her head and the man's hand dragged at her hair, pulling the skin back from her forehead and the smell which was in her nostrils was not of them but of her own terror, for herself, oh yes since her mind and weak woman's body knew exactly what they had in store for her, but for her son, her beautiful boy who was her life.

'Take the lad.' Ellis's voice was a razor slashing her to pieces for she had heard what men did to small boys. They were looking at Lucas, beginning to smile. In his hand was the pitiful lump of wood with which he was to play at 'soldiers' with Charlie and his stunned face, his deeply shocked, mercifully dazed eyes stared back at them. His golden curls gleamed in the firelight and his cheeks were tinted by it to a lovely, rose pink. He was a handsome child, still with the beauty of babyhood on him and Jim Briggs smiled. Jenny saw it and her frozen mother's heart died.

'Don't hurt him,' she whispered. 'I'll do anything you want but don't hurt him. He's only three years old,' but the inert figure of the boy was dragged from her arms, leaving them empty and lifeless. The man who held her breathed some obscenity in her ear, his breath foetid, and pushed himself against her back but she was conscious of nothing but the small figure of her son, his face like a mask, too terror-stricken even to cry.

But the man was becoming impatient. She was quivering against him, just like the other one had and he was ready to start again. He dipped his hands inside the bodice of her dress, gripping her breasts, squeezing until she cried out in pain and the others turned to look at her, speculatively, gloatingly, obscenely, waiting it seemed, but not for much longer, for some signal which would tell them they might begin their sport.

Ellis had turned to look at the child, his face suddenly watchful, the expression on it curious as though something had stirred in his mind, something which chaffed a chord, a memory perhaps, one he could not quite recall. He moved across the room and looked down into the boy's blank face, into his flat brown eyes, then, with a muttered oath he took the boy's arm and began to drag him towards the back of the room.

'No . . . Dear sweet Jesus . . . oh please, don't hurt my baby . . . please . . .'

'What is it?' the quiet voice but sharp now, from behind the curtain said.

'I thought yer'd like ter tek a good look at this lad, sir.'

'Why? What's the brat to me?'

'Can yer not see it, sir?'

'See what, for God's sake?' but the voice had a hesitancy about it which said its owner had suddenly become aware of something quite remarkable in the boy's appearance.

'What d'yer think, sir?'

'I think . . . I think you may have something, Ellis. Something which needs looking into, and I mean to . . .'

Ellis turned back to the men in the kitchen who had begun cruelly to handle Jenny Greenwood's cringing body.

'Right lads,' he said casually, 'she's all yours but

526

remember what Mr . . . er . . . what you was told. We don't want no 'arm to come to 'er, not like the other . . .'

'Wait.' The voice was soft but peremptory and Ellis turned his head, frowning a little for it was hard to hold back these men of his once they'd got the feel of a woman in their hands. Like dogs they were who have the scent of the bitch, and just as violent if they are thwarted, ready to tear himself and each other into pieces, snapping and snarling over who was to be first.

'Yes sir?'

'I need a moment to think . . .'

'Right sir, but can we get on with . . .?'

'I said wait, man. Tell those . . . ruffians of yours to wait until I give my permission.'

'They'll not like it, sir.'

'I don't give a damn what they like. Have they not had enough?'

'No sir.'

'Tell them that unless they do as I say I shall report the murder of that woman in there to the magistrate and that within the day they will be back in gaol, and you too. You know I mean it, don't you, Ellis?'

It seemed Ellis did.

The man who stood in the shadow of the scullery stared into the mindless brown eyes of the boy. His own were icy and cold, like frozen brown water.

'How old is this boy? Ask her. Tell her not to lie.'

She told the truth. He was her child and she would have said anything, or done it to save him.

'He's three years old, sir, she says.'

'What month was he born?'

She told the truth again. The cruel eyes of the man studied the boy who hung between him and Ellis like some limp doll, his hand still holding his musket.

'Shall me an' the lads get rid of 'im, like we was goin' to, sir?' and in the kitchen Jenny Greenwood began to scream.

'Tell her to be quiet,' he said, and she bit her lips until they bled.

527

The men moved menacingly at Ellis's back and he repeated his previous question. They couldn't hang about here much longer. It was a bloody wonder no one had come to investigate that last scream and if they didn't get going soon, someone would.

'No, I think not.' The man spoke thoughtfully and his voice had softened strangely. He put his hand on the boy's head.

Ellis began to lose patience. 'We'll 'ave ter look sharp, sir, if we're ter catch t'other 'un up on't tops. We're not sure she'll even go ter Friars Mere so it might tek a bit o' time ter locate 'er. The lads'll not be long in there with that bitch, but beggin' yer pardon, sir, I want my turn an' all. I've waited a long time fer this day an' I'm not bein' done out of it,' not for you or anyone else, his suddenly cold eyes said.

'Very well. I must admit to fancying a "turn", as you so quaintly put it, myself but I think I'll forgo the pleasure in view of . . . this new development.' He placed a gentle finger on the boy's rounded cheek. 'I must get right away from the district immediately.' He began to fondle the boy's curls and there was an expression in his eyes which, in any other man's might have been described as proud. 'When you've done, get out of this area, all of you. Forget the Chapman bitch, and remember what I said to you. I do not make threats I cannot keep, Ellis, something you'd best impress on those thugs of yours. One word of this and I shall have the three of you back in gaol, and for so long you will all be too old to ever enjoy a woman again. Do I make myself clear? And tell that woman in there that if she wants her boy to live she'd best do the same.'

'Right sir, we'll not be far behind yer,' and already Ellis's hands were at the fastenings of his trousers for he meant to be first. He turned back to the homely kitchen in which so much violence had been done that day, not even seeing the man and the boy slip from the back of the cottage. He watched greedily as Jenny Greenwood's clothes were torn from her body and her mouth was bound with a strip of cambric from her own pretty petticoat. She struggled so hard one of the men was forced to club her with his fist and the other two held her, almost senseless, between them. When she was completely naked Ellis signalled with his hand and Mercy Greenwood's tiny body was tipped carelessly to the floor and Jenny was laid down in her place on the table.

## 35

The funeral drew the biggest gathering of mourners ever before seen in the Penfold Valley. They came for miles, from Yorkshire and Cheshire, from Derbyshire and Westmorland, from wherever the name of Joss Greenwood was known, from weaver's cottage and from the Hall in which the Squire's family lived. From the working man in his clogs to the black-suited, immaculate gentlemen of the squirarchy, arriving on foot, on horseback and by carriage until the whole area about the small hillside Chapel was black for a hundred yards in every direction with grieving men and women. The horror of it had drawn them all together, high and low, as nothing else had ever done, the Squire feeling himself to be in some way involved as his own notepaper, somehow, had been used, in the carrying out of the crime.

It was said of Martha Greenwood that she would not be long behind her daughter-in-law in her own coffin, but she was the only member of the family to stand with her head held high at the graveside. It had been whispered in the drawing-rooms and factories of Crossfold, of what had been done to Mercy Greenwood before she died, the appalling details spared them in the bare, quite formal announcement of her murder in the newspapers but no one knew exactly what it was, though the men could guess.

Charlie Greenwood was no longer the cheerful, light-hearted young boy who had set his school friends laughing in the classroom. His face had always been good-humoured with a glint in his eye which said it did not take a great deal to turn to easy laughter. Easy going then, and, since he had recovered from the injuries he had received at the hands of the overlookers in the Chapman weaving-sheds, looking forward to his grand future. He would get on, there was no doubt about it, under the patronage of Miss Katherine Chapman, his benefactor. Three or four years at the grammar school, it was foretold and then on to the University for it had been discovered he had a clever mind and an aptitude for learning which was quite extraordinary in a weaver's son and there was talk he might make a teacher, or even a lawyer. A matter of great pride he had been to the Greenwood family and would you look at him now. The anguish in his face was there for all to see since he was the one who had found them, his brother's wife quite naked, it was whispered, his sister tied to a table leg and in a frenzy, and would either of them ever recover from it, they asked one another and the sad answer seemed to be no. He was like a boy grown into a man overnight, supporting his mother and younger sister, she whose imminent death, it was reported, had taken him and Martha Greenwood from their cottage on that fateful day. He was white-faced and sick, standing to attention at the graveside as they shovelled the dirt on to the coffin but surely the worst sight and one the men who followed him could hardly bear was the complete breakdown of Joss Greenwood who was to be, it was rumoured, radical candidate for the constituency of Crossfold.

And but for the quiet presence and continuous support of Katherine Chapman might not the whole family have gone under for it was said Joss Greenwood's grief was terrible. She and Sarah Pickering were the only ones on their feet and in their right minds on that day and it was they who had made Mercy Greenwood presentable enough to be viewed by those who came to pay their respects. Besides the family she and Sarah were the sole persons to have seen what had been done to her and the picture which would be carried with her to her dying day had been savagely locked away in Kit's mind. It would be brought out and grieved over at a later date but quite simply there was no time for it now since somehow she and Sarah, for whom she gave thanks in a hundred ways must get the family through the pain and the horror and the anger until it could be controlled.

Charlie had screamed, she had been told, over and over again, being still a boy then, until every man and woman in the village had stood in the space before his mother's cottage. His mother, thankfully, had lost her senses and Charlie for more than half an hour would let no one in until Sarah and Isaac had overpowered him and Isaac had run all the way to Crossfold for her, with Sarah, almost senseless herself, keeping the doors locked and the curtains drawn for Charlie and Jenny could bear no one to see what had been done to Mercy.

And Jenny, poor frenzied Jenny, still wandering the moorland looking for her son. Calling his name again and again until she could no longer speak, raising the hairs on the backs of the necks of the men who searched with her. She had run out of the cottage, past the weeping women and ashen-faced men and on to the moors behind to look for him, saying only that the men who had killed her sister-in-law had taken him. She was still looking for him three days later, dry-eyed and staring, too desolate even to attend the funeral of her brother's wife, indeed to care that she was dead.

Mercy Greenwood lay by herself at last, dressed in a simple white dress, her face, thankfully unmarked, washed, her hair brushed in soft curls about it, her expression peaceful with no trace left of the violent way in which she had died. She had been tenderly placed on the trestle table the men had put up in the room which had once held Abel Greenwood's weaving-loom. White sheets had been placed at the window and candles lit at the four corners of the room, replaced as they burnt out by others, flowers, masses of them brought up from Greenacres in an effort to expunge the horror of her death with the sweetness and beauty of life, a peaceful haven for her last resting place on earth.

And when he came from wherever it was he had been brought, Joss would not be stopped, though Isaac and the constable had tried, from seeing what had been done to his wife and to hear in a voice which was dead and hopeless, of the abduction of his sister's son.

His cries, like Charlie's were unendurable and the women of the village, as they mourned, covered their ears and drew their children indoors and thanked God it was Sarah Pickering and Miss Chapman and not themselves who had to deal with it. Anything the two women needed in those days before the funeral, they had only to ask for, they were told, just as long as it was not to be with Charlie and Joss Greenwood for the two brothers could not contain, nor control the virulent hatred, the savage and violent pain, the guilt and shame and horror, for surely there was nothing worse a man could suffer than to see the violation and abuse of a woman he loved.

'Thank God Mercy's dead,' Joss cried harshly, the only words he spoke before he ran off into the dark and no one had the heart at the moment, nor the courage to tell him of Jenny Greenwood's missing son. They had searched, hundreds of men from all over Lancashire, from Yorkshire where Joss was known and respected, even loved by those who called him brother in the fight, moving across the moorland from Hind Hill as far south as Tintwistle, from Edgeclough across Saddleworth Moor to Broadhead Moss and west to Tandle Hills but no trace had been found of the boy. Perhaps he was dead, they said but why should the murderers take the body with them? How many men had there been? Jenny Greenwood would not say. More than two was made evident by the nature of Mercy's injuries but why? For God's sake, *why*?

At first it had been thought that a band of passing ruffians had chanced upon the two defenceless women, taking their pleasure, but when Charlie Greenwood became coherent and was able to speak, it seemed a note purporting to have come from the Squire, had been sent to lure him and his mother away. When they had found their Daisy hale and hearty and uncommonly perplexed, as had been the Squire when he was called and shown the note, though he had been inclined to blame practical jokers, *then* Martha and Charlie had ridden home again, the bewilderment and irritation turning slowly to dread, then a cold creeping fear, for the note had been sent for one purpose only; to remove them from the cottage.

'It's too well thought out to be chance, and too well planned to be chance,' the magistrate, accompanied by a Peace Officer told Katherine Chapman, she being the only one with any sense remaining, in his opinion. 'Someone deliberately wanted to get one of those women, or perhaps both of them alone. Why? What reason could they have for wreaking such ... well I can only call it revenge, Miss Chapman, for what else could it be? It was not chance. There is nothing stolen as far as we can tell so ...' He shrugged, ' ... do you know of anyone who could have reason for doing such a thing?'

But Kit had to admit that she didn't and indeed had no time even to consider such a thing. She moved through those heart-chilling, mind-chilling, bone-chilling days before the funeral with an unhesitating willingness to be what anyone asked her to be, to do what anyone needed of her. She had sent a message to Greenacres for Janet to pack a box with clothes suitable for a lady in mourning, plain and unadorned, with necessary undergarments. The gown she had worn on the mad journey up to Edgeclough and in which she had tended to Mercy Greenwood had been burned. She did not sleep except for a light doze in the chair beside the fire and when she did Sarah was there to watch them. She administered the valerian Sarah infused, to Martha, to Daisy who was allowed home by the Squire's lady, distraught and difficult to handle in those first few

533

hours. She lay down beside Charlie and held him in her arms, calming him without words in the way Joss had once calmed Mercy Butterworth when her brother was hanged. He was wild, off his head, talking of revenge and how, if it took the rest of his life he would find the men who were to blame, of what *he* – a twelve year old boy – would do to them, whoever they were, when he did. He was quite inconsolable, his face ugly and swollen, his eyes slits of pure hatred in his once young face for he could not get the picture of that violated body out of his young mind, but when she put her arms about him, giving him what at the moment his own mother was unable to give, pulling his head to her breast as his mother had done when he was a small boy, he slept fitfully.

She held the hand of the dazed and frozen woman who, though she had not given birth to her, was the mother of Jenny Greenwood, who loved her and her son as deeply as though they were her own flesh and blood. Held fast in shock, she was; the potions Sarah administered to her gave her peace. But though she seemed to be far away in a place where the hurt could not reach her she must not be left alone and the women of the village, with Kit and Sarah sat with her in turns as she rocked slowly in her chair, staring out of the bedroom window at the moorland where her daughter roamed in search of her boy, waiting for her to come home with him. Her daughter who had gone quite mad, wandering in circles like a wild woman, dressed in the same garments she had worn for days. Her daughter who could not sleep nor eat but kept up with the men who searched for her boy, unwashed, wild-eyed, snaggle haired, and lost it seemed just as surely as he was.

And Joss? What could Kit do for him, say to him, to bring him from the frenzy, the crazed and dangerously unbalanced state into which his grief had tipped him? He disappeared for hours on end, not looking for the boy as the others were but for the men who had taken him, and the life of his wife.

He sat far into the night before the day of the funeral, in the chair that had once been his wife's, staring sightlessly into the fire, his face black and brooding, his hands hanging limply from the arms of the chair and Kit wondered on the strangeness of the brother and sister, so close in all these years and yet now, in death and sorrow, so far apart. They seemed unable, Jenny and Joss Greenwood, to sit together in the same room, to share their pain and loss as those of a family will for whenever Jenny wandered back to the cottage, which she did now and again to see if there was news of her son, Joss would leap up and go outside, waiting until Jenny had blundered off again into the night, before he returned. What was it, Kit wondered that made them afraid to be alone together, to comfort, if only with a loving hand, the pain they both endured.

Kit knelt before him on that night, saying nothing, offering him her loving compassion putting her hand gently on his arm but he flung it off, flung *her* off and rising, stamped out of the cottage as though it could not contain him, nor he what was within it.

And now she was in her grave, his sweet child-wife and the vast multitude come to mourn her, come to mourn with the man she had loved, had drifted away, reluctantly it seemed as though they would like to offer, if they could, something more to the suffering family, but what was there to give? There had been no gathering at the cottage after the funeral as there would for a death under normal circumstances, no funeral feast to refresh those who came to mourn, to sustain them on their journey home. Kit and Sarah had discussed it and had decided it would not do, for they, the family of the murdered woman, had gone temporarily to another place though they were present in body, staring at nothing, saying nothing, four black figures hovering uncertainly about the cottage kitchen. They could not be expected to receive callers, to chat softly, to go through the pattern of bereavement which gave comfort to those who had decently laid away a loved one. It was too soon. Indeed would it ever be the right time? They waited,

535

for Jenny, for Lucas, for release from their suffering, and Kit waited with them. Sarah found nothing strange, it appeared, in the daughter of the great house of Chapman, the owner of the Chapman mills, the wealthiest woman in South Lancashire, taking on the supervision and care of a lowly weaver's family. None of them, and none of the men and women, who had appeared from nowhere to see what they could do when the news got about, questioned it, nor seemed to wonder at it, for Miss Chapman was not out of place in the cottage kitchen. She was not grand, nor overbearing, nor patronising. She offered herself simply as another pair of hands, another heart to grieve, another back upon which burdens could be laid, another mind to solve the problem of how to ease the anguish.

'I'll be off then, Miss Chapman,' Sarah was saying softly when the cottage door was flung open and Jenny Greenwood stood there swaying wildly in the doorway. They all sprang to their feet in confusion, even Martha, badly frightened by the violence, for had they not known her well it was doubtful they would have recognised the woman who stood there.

'It was Ellis . . .' she screeched, ' . . . Ellis and the others who were sent to gaol for beating my brother. They did it, they took my boy but it was not them who thought of it, oh no it was not them, for they had not the wits. There was someone else there, I know it . . . behind the curtain, someone else who hated me . . . and her . . .' she pointed a trembling hand at Kit, ' . . . enough to set them on me.' She laughed wildly and Sarah moaned in her throat for surely they were forever cursed in this house. 'Guess, Kit Chapman, go on, guess who it was who had a reason to believe he was badly done by . . .'

'Harry Atherton.' His name was but a whisper on Kit's lips but they each heard it and already Joss and Charlie were reaching for their coats.

'Aye, that's who's got my son . . . *his* son. By God. I've searched these moors, my mind in a turmoil knowing there was something . . . something but not being able to catch it. I was . . . my brain wouldn't function. I didn't care what they had done to me . . . I'll mend, for women do, but my boy . . . they have taken my boy . . .'

'We'll get him back, Jenny. Me and Charlie. You stay here with Mother and Daisy and me and Charlie will take the coach to . . . where does he live . . .?'

'I don't know but she does.'

They all turned to look at Kit, even Martha whose poor mind could not even grasp what they were about and Kit took a step back from the awful snarling hatred which glowered from the three faces of Martha Greenwood's children. Joss had heard Jenny admit to the fatherhood of her son but he didn't care, if he had even noticed. He cared for nothing, not Lucas Greenwood, not Martha, his own mother, not what had gone before which was good in his life, nor what would come when this tragedy was decently buried; not forgotten, but accepted. He wanted revenge, he wanted to expunge his own guilt and shame and here was the opportunity, an opportunity to use his fists on the man who had done this to his family. Not once but twice to beat him into the ground, to do to him, and the others what they had once done to Charlie.

'Where does he live?' He did not use her name and his eyes, though they looked at her face, avoided hers.

'I . . . I can't remember . . . It has been a long time.'

'Where does he live? We can easily find out.'

'Then you must.'

'Tell me or I'll . . .'

'Joss, for God's sake, don't do this. Tell the Peace Officer. Go to the magistrates, but don't . . . please . . .'

Sarah Pickering huddled against the fireplace, afraid as she had never been afraid in her life. There was so much badness here, such malevolence and yet these were decent people and they loved Kit Chapman, all of them. In the past few days she didn't know how they would have managed without her. Once they had called this warm-hearted woman a "stuck up bitch' but she had been a rock to them all and when they were themselves again they would realise it. A good friend to Jenny Greenwood and more to Joss, it was rumoured and by God, she herself had thought in the past few days, if she could give him a bit of comfort now, in any way at all, poor devil, then good luck to her and to him for he'd had a rough time of it with the sweetly vacant woman he had married, God rest her soul. If anyone could pull them all together again it was her for she'd the strength and tenacity not often found in the gentry. Soft they were, most of them, but not this one, no, not this one, and now they were all three of them advancing on her, threatening her as though she had something to do with it, whatever it was they were talking about. God in Heaven, if somebody didn't do something soon they'd be about her and have it out of her one way or another and she'd not stand by and watch it, not Sarah Pickering.

'Stop it,' she screeched, 'stop it, yer daft beggars. What the dickens d'yer think yer doin'? Sit down, all of yer, an' pull yerselves together. Hasn't there been enough violence in this 'ouse . . . Dear Sweet Jesus . . .'

'I only want the address of the man who took my sister's boy, and by God, I mean to have it.'

'How do you know it was Harry Atherton? Jenny didn't see him . . .'

'I know . . . I know, I tell you . . .'

'Jenny, sweetheart, you're not in a fit state yet to . . . make a decision. See, why don't you and your mother come home with me? I'm going back to Greenacres this afternoon but you could come with me, you could all come with me and then, when you are . . .'

Joss Greenwood's eyes narrowed in his ravaged face, grey and lined like that of a man twice his age. They had sunk deep into his head and there was no trace of the handsome good humour, the quizzical interest, the expression of intelligence and compassion which had grown as the boy became a man. There was hatred there and bitterness, a souring of his spirit, a tainting of the goodwill he had cherished towards the men he had led. He had been wild and disorderly in his young manhood, but never brutal. The very air about him had crackled with his anger and contempt for men who had exploited other men but he had always retained his humanity. Now his face was cruel, sullen, baleful with the lust for vengeance which was eating his mind and soul and Kit recoiled from it.

'Joss, for God's sake . . .' Sarah's voice softened as she remembered what he was suffering. 'Joss . . . see, sit down, lad and . . .' but he turned on her so savagely she shrank back against the chimney breast.

'Sit down, *sit down*, with them bastards out there . . . and Lucas . . . they've got her lad and God knows where he'll end up. Let's hope he's dead in a bloody ditch since we all know what happens to pretty little boys, don't we . . . don't we . . .?'

'Dear God . . .' Sarah's voice hissed in her throat and Martha moaned feebly, turning away for she could not bear the expression on her son's face.

'I'll kill them, every last one of them, so help me . . .'

'No, Joss, leave it to the law . . .' Kit's voice was high and wild.

'Bugger the law,' he said, quiet now and all the more menacing for it. 'I've another score to settle with Mr Harry Atherton, an old score . . .' His voice trailed away then he turned to his sister and brother.

'Jenny . . . Charlie . . .?'

In the chair by the fire where she had fallen his mother began to weep.

They had gone, the three of them, striding away up the track which would lead them to Crossfold. Jenny had washed herself and changed the torn and filthy dress she had worn for almost a week, brushed her hair and put on her bonnet and they looked like any normal, decently dressed family, she and Joss and Charlie Greenwood. Charlie, a boy only a day or two ago, his face that of a man now as he took up the sword his brother pressed into his hand, ready to use it though he was no fighter and, if he was honest, badly frightened by what he had heard and witnessed this day in his mother's kitchen.

Martha sat in the same chair not moving until Kit knelt before her.

'What will you do, Martha?' she asked.

'Nay lass, what can I do but wait for them.'

'Will you not come back with me. I could look after you until they return.'

'It's kind of you but this is where I belong. We should all stay where we were put on this earth.'

'No, you're wrong, Martha. We can all move on if we have the wits for it. Charlie will be a great man one day when he has finished his schooling and . . .'

'Joss? Aye, if he can get over this. He's not in his right mind just now, and won't be for a while but he's strong and he'll survive.'

'I'm afraid for him. If he should find Harry Atherton . . .'

'It's not likely a nob like him would be mixed up in the . . . death of . . . well, you know what I mean. And why should he take our Jenny's lad? No, they'll be home soon but they need to be *doing* something, him and Jenny, looking somewhere and Jenny's living on nothing but hope. They'll be home directly and I must be here when they do for I'll be needed. Charlie has to get back to school. To get on with his life. He's only twelve, Miss Chapman and can't be looking back forever, nor our Joss.'

'No . . .'

'He's work to do and he knows it, when the anger's gone. Them words he said . . . he'd not mean them, you know that. He'll not kill anyone . . .'

'No . . .'

'He's wild, hating, and I don't know how long it will be before it leaves him. He loved Mercy, you know that?'

'Yes.'

' . . . and he needs to avenge her, he thinks, being a proper man but when the sense returns to him he'll see that it must be left to the proper authorities.'

'I know.'

540

'You must be patient, lass,' and with those words Martha acknowledged the bond which existed between her son and this woman.

'Tell them both . . . that I'll be waiting for them . . . when they are ready . . .'

'I will, lass but I can't promise either of them ever will be. They've both suffered a loss, more than they could bear, really. Joss feels . . . well . . . Mercy's brother died because of him, he thinks, and now Mercy . . .'

'I know . . .'

'And my Jenny, she's strong but she loved that boy. I don't know if she'll ever . . .'

'Don't say it, Martha.'

'No. You're a good lass, Kit Chapman, but . . .'

'I know, but I cannot . . . I will wait for them . . . tell them.'

## 36

It seemed, though she had never in her life worked so hard, that she had more time on her hands than she needed that summer. The summer of waiting. She went alone each day to the mill, working in her office from the time the factory bell rang until seven or eight, nine or ten in the evening, poring over pages of accounts, profit sheets, invoices and bills – dozens of those – from builders and carpenters, engineers and architects, those involved in the construction of her new dwelling houses. She was busy, riding in her carriage out to the almost completed village, inspecting the neat streets in which sturdily built cottages stood, shops, an inn, for the men must have their ale, a church for those of a religious nature, a school, and even a Mechanics Institute which was to provide lectures in technical and scientific subjects, and a reading room and library. There was a vast range of broadsheets and tracts available, pamphlets and popular radical newspapers with a weekly circulation reaching twenty to thirty thousand. With a growing number, already, of working men able to read them; these would be made readily available to those who could not afford to buy them. There was to be an assembly room where functions might be held, a public bath and wash house and a hospital and all to be surrounded by a park, green fields and open spaces where those who worked confined in the mill all week might take the air on Sunday.

But she still had time in which her head was not busy, when her hands were not busy and her thoughts took her over the hills to the village of Edgeclough. They had come home, Jenny, Joss and Charlie Greenwood, she had been told, a week after they had left in the search for Jenny's missing son, Lucas, but they had come without him. Sarah sent word with her son, Jem, who was manager now in Miss Chapman's weaving-shed, that Jenny was grieving, still wandering far and wide in her search, taking no heed of what they told her, going God knows where, disappearing for days on end, turning up only to change her clothes, to kiss her mother and her brother who had returned to school, then to be off again, following the desolate path which led to nowhere, it seemed. Of Joss there was no word for Sarah had none to give.

So time hung heavily and hopelessly on Kit Chapman's hands and there were only so many hours she could put in at the mill. She walked the hills and moorlands with her dogs close to her heels, her only companions these days, they said of her, going nowhere near the village where the Greenwood family lived for something told her not to. She did not know what it was, perhaps a sense, which said they needed to be without her until they had come to terms with their dreadful loss. Not recovered, for would they ever be that, but accepting, and still Joss Greenwood had not come home.

It was September before she went up to the nursery. The

day was wet and her spirits could not face the drifting mist of rain which sighed against her window, the thought of the weary and ever increasing reluctance to confront the lonely walks, the reality that this was to be her life from now on. Without Jenny whose friendship she had come to value. Without Joss whose love slipped through her fingers like water, refreshing and necessary to life but as elusive as the wind. She must have something beside her mills which once had seemed to hold everything she had ever needed. She must or she would become as dry and withered as the leaves which already were falling from the trees beyond the window.

She was drawn that day by some curious impulse to see the child who was alone there now, forgotten, watched over by none but Flora. Flora who still went about the place with a wan, tear-stained face, mourning the boy she had loved as her own and had no time for the silent child who, against Flora's will, was still in her charge.

She rose from her chair and bobbed a curtsey as Kit entered the room. It was quiet now where once a mischievous imp called Lucas Greenwood had romped and roared and stolen the hearts of all the housemaids, empty somehow, and yet did a small ghost still hang about to break hearts as he once had?

Kit felt the tears catch her eyes and a lump she could not swallow come to her throat.

And there was the child.

She remembered the last time. All she had been aware of then was a shadowy face, a mop of hair and two deep set eyes before the sheet had been drawn up to cover them. A small trembling mound cowering away from the danger, the abuse, the harsh words, the careless violence which had been turned on her by all the tall beings she had known in her short life. Instinct, and self-preservation had given her the animal-like reflex that told her that they were to be avoided at all cost. She had been comparatively safe from them beneath the wheels and straps and spindles of the spinning frame, in the dark and filth and waste which, when she heaped it up about her kept her from their frightening eyes, the sounds with which they reviled her, and the lash of the giant's stick. They had caught her though, three giants and after that she couldn't remember what had happened until she had found herself in some strange thing which had contained water. Water like that in which she had often been tipped upside down when she had fallen asleep. They were going to do it again, she realised that of course, and so she had simply sat and waited for it, knowing there was nothing to be done for they always won, always.

She was sitting mutely at the nursery table when Kit entered. Her hair which had been recently brushed was a soft mass of red-gold baby curls and Flora had tied a white length of ribbon to one of them, not very expertly for none of Flora's sisters had ever had such a thing. She wore a little white dress and frilly drawers, white stockings and shoes. She was spooning quite delicately, a rich creamy porridge into her mouth, licking her pink lips with a tongue which flicked in and out like a little cat's. Alone and withdrawn to some place where no one else could reach her, steadily eating the food, the food which had transformed her from a tiny and grotesque parody of an infant human being into a delightfully pretty, still slender but charming little girl. She might have been accustomed to such surroundings, such lovely clothes, to the good food all of her young life, so serene did she appear as Kit opened the door and entered the room but as she did so, beginning to smile wonderingly, for in six months the child appeared to have recovered completely, the little girl's eyes became quite blank, the spoon clattered into her empty plate and she simply slipped downwards until she was completely out of sight beneath the table and the tablecloth which hung almost to the floor.

'Oh no, sweetheart, no, I'm not going to hurt you,' Kit cried out at once, hurrying across the nursery to the table which was placed near the window. She lifted the cloth, smiling, her heart, quite amazingly, warm and gentle for the frightened child, ready to draw her out, to stand her up on her feet, to lead her across the room to the nursery fire and even to lift her on to her own lap, to hold her in arms which had never before held a child. She had known no child but Lucas. She had been carelessly fond of him since he had been a part of Jenny but he had been an exceedingly masculine little boy, spoiled to distraction by Flora and the other maids, loved by his mother whose joy he had been and taking for granted his male dominance of all the women in his young life. But this . . . was different.

She put out a hand to the little girl who was grovelling, her face to the carpeted floor, her hands sweeping wildly, just as though she was gathering the patterned roses with which it was strewn. Sweep and sweep and when she had it all, whatever it was she had gleaned to her, she began to back out, dragging it with her from beneath the table. It was heavy, whatever it was she imagined she carried in her arms for her little face strained and even sweated and Kit could almost smell the fear on her.

'Dear God,' she whispered, 'what is she about?'

'Gathering waste, Miss Greenwood said.' Flora's voice was quite matter of fact. 'She always does it when she's frightened or when she sees someone she doesn't know. Reckons its a new "tackler", I suppose and she'd best be about something before he straps her.'

'But it's been over a year. I thought by now she would be . . . well, I don't know . . . happy, normal . . . She certainly looks it. I don't think I have seen such an attractive child and with a bit more flesh on her bones . . . Oh Lord, now what . . . ?' She stepped back as the little girl scampered from the far corner where she had evidently put the waste and dived back beneath the table.

'She's getting some more,' Flora said. 'Busy as a little bee she is sometimes, fetching and carrying and sweeping, just as though she thinks if she stops she'll get a clout, which she probably did,' she added, 'poor little beggar.' Flora turned to the fire and reached to put on some more coal, evidently so accustomed to the child's ways they were no longer of much interest. ' 'Course she's no one but me to . . . to give her a bit of company . . .' It was said not only sadly, with a threat of tears, but also accusingly, letting Miss Chapman know that Flora could not be blamed for the child's lack of intelligence.

'Well, something must be done. She cannot go on like this. My God, more than a year and she's still living in that awful, fearful world. One would think the kindness you and the other servants have shown her would have made her realise she no longer has anything to fear.'

' 'Appen she needs more than that,' Flora said cryptically, daringly, but Miss Chapman appeared not to hear.

'How old do you think she is, Flora.'

'Nay, it's difficult to say. They all grow at different rates and one child's not like another. Four or five, 'appen.'

'Well, I cannot have this,' Kit said, just as she might to some awkward manager who had gone against her in her own factory. Moving slowly towards the little girl, who was crawling along the floor dragging some unimaginable load behind her, she put her hand on her arm. Immediately the child ceased all movement. Still, still as a wheatear when the hawk flies over, still as a rabbit when the stoat goes by, her silky lashes fluttering in an orgasm of terror as she waited for the blow.

Kit lifted her gently to her feet, then took her hand. It was so cold she gasped but without conscious thought she drew the small, beautifully dressed child towards the nursery fire and the child went blindly, obediently, mindlessly, her fear so great she emptied her bladder into the freshly laundered softness of her frilled drawers. Kit sat down in the chair and the child stood before her, like some sacrificial lamb which knows full well its fate but awaits it stoically since what else can it do? Kit held her cold hands, chafing them between her own warm ones, watching for some change in her expression but there was none.

'Sweetheart,' she said softly, not knowing herself in this new role which the child's despair had cast her in. 'There is nothing to fear here. You are safe with us and always will be. See, there is Flora who looks after you and soon we will have a governess, a kind lady to teach you your

546

letters. Will you not like that?' The child's eyes stared sightlessly into hers and her hands tried to draw themselves from Kit's restraint. But Kit would not let her go. 'See, come and sit on my lap before the fire. You are so cold and we will get warm together. Come, sweetheart, climb on my lap and we will be quiet for a moment.'

The little girl continued to stare, eyes wide, at Kit's moving mouth, a small terrified animal hypnotised by a snake and even when Kit patiently lifted her, placing her awkwardly onto her lap, the little girl sat, stiff as a wax effigy and just as still.

'T'will do no good, Miss Chapman,' Flora said wisely. 'We've all tried it an' all she does is wet her drawers. 'Appen she'll come round after a while when she begins to understand no one's going to beat her or stick her head in a bucket of cold water.' She saw Miss Chapman wince and could have bitten her own tongue because everyone knew such goings on were a thing of the past now at the Chapman mill but Miss Chapman only held the child closer, to no avail, Flora could see. 'Pretty little poppet though, isn't she?' she added.

She was a pretty little poppet and all during the following week, whenever Kit had an hour to spare she went up to the nursery. She would sit at the table and draw the child's attention to the books and games and toys which were scattered carelessly about since Lucas had been considerably indulged by his mother and the little girl would stare at them, politely it seemed to Kit, doing as she was bid when told to sit, to stand, to look at this or that, to hold the 'dolly' or the 'teddy', to put her hand in Kit's, to sit on her lap, obedient as she had been made to be in the factory, but not trusting, ever. She never spoke, or if she did no one heard her and Kit wondered at the hopelessness of employing a governess for she was at a loss as to how the woman could teach the child. She had tried a time or two herself, reading to her out of a book, telling her the tales her own nurse had told her, of elves and fairies, of little people, of magic and far away places, of lovely angels and cheerful animals but the little girl seemed unimpressed until Kit began to see that it all meant nothing to a child who had known only hobgoblins and demons, haunted places where evil lurked and the filth, not only of the mill floor but that in men's minds, but she continued to try, for what else was there in her barren life?

It was several weeks later when she went up to the nursery on her now daily visit, her step slow, her feet dragging and when she opened the nursery door, her determination to break through the child's wall of silence and fixity was missing. She felt low today, her woman's body, it seemed, drying to a husk without the sustaining love Joss had fed it. Five months since she had seen him and she scarcely dare think of him and his hard male body, so great was her longing.

The little girl did not even turn her head to look at her, let alone greet her and Kit sighed in the renewed melancholy which had come upon her today. Five months since the dreadful events at Martha Greenwood's cottage and in all that time there had been not one word of Joss Greenwood. Sarah had told her through Jem, that his mother had received a note or two to say he was well but there had been no clue as to where he was or what he was doing, of how he was living or supporting himself. The fine political career which was to have been his was in tatters, they all recognised, and even his fight for the betterment of the men who had followed him for over ten years seemed to have been swallowed up in his own personal fight for survival.

Parliamentary reform had been called for all over the country and the Prime Minister, Wellington was to resign over it, they said, so opposed to the idea was he, but Lord Grey, heralded as the next Prime Minister was pledging that if he was asked to form a government he would propose a Reform Bill. Joss, she knew, would have been jubilant, since it would transform the franchise in the boroughs and counties and it was calculated that the total electorate would be doubled. Where was he? Did he know of it? Did he care any more?

Kit sighed again as she looked at the child. She was becoming sturdier with every day, the flesh on her limbs glowing with the sheen of good health. Her short crop of curls had grown longer and today Flora had tied it with a blue ribbon, more experienced and with more concern now that Miss Chapman was showing some interest. The dress the child wore, a pretty blue sprigged muslin was already too short as she grew taller. She still collected 'waste' beneath the table, or did when anyone other than Flora entered the nursery, but the unchildlike obedience, the wariness, the rigid acceptance of the kiss Kit gave her, the embrace which she seemed not to understand, indeed to consider threatening in some way, were becoming an irritant to Kit.

'Good morning, Miss Chapman,' Flora said.

'Good morning, Flora, and how are we all today?'

'Champion, thank you, ma'am.'

Kit turned to the little girl, making herself smile, wondering for the umpteenth time why she continued to come up here to the nursery since the girl was unconcerned whether she did or not. Feed her, clothe her, leave her to live in her own private dream world where nothing troubled her and the child would know no difference. She admitted to herself that she had become fond of her but perhaps it was merely because she had no one else to give her affection. Perhaps it was pity, if she were honest but it seemed not to matter. Possibly it would be kinder to let go of her, let her develop, or not, in her own time. She was not educable, that was certain in her present state, and she realised that the secret idea she had carried inside herself for the past few weeks, that she could make this child, her *own* child, the one she would never bear herself, was really no more than a fantasy.

'I think I'll leave the lesson today, Flora,' she said. 'I feel like a walk with the dogs. Those old ones of mine need a bit of exercise,' just as though she needed to excuse herself to Flora. Guilt, she supposed. The guilt of not being able to bring life to this little girl who had been so damaged in her own mill. Who had never been taught to love and so could not accept it. Guilt that she, Kit Chapman, was so soon to give up the idea of trying to teach her. She turned abruptly, on an impulse.

'Put her some sturdy boots on, Flora, if she has any . . .'

'She hasn't any, Miss Chapman. There's only some . . . some belonging to . . .' She could not go on.

'To . . . Lucas . . . ?' Kit's voice was filled with sadness. 'Yes . . .'

'He wouldn't mind, Flora. He was ever a generous little boy.'

'Aye . . .' Flora wiped away a sad tear and neither questioned the way in which both took for granted that the boy would never return.

They walked out of the side entrance into the yard, both of them blinking in the vivid sunlight of the bright autumn day. Kit held the little girl's hand in hers, limp and chill, even in the warmth. She had removed the hat which Flora had jammed onto the child's head, throwing it carelessly to a chair in the passage and the sunlight struck fire from her hair. Their boots grated on the cobbles which lined the yard and the sound carried on the air and from the open stable door on the far side four black bodies hurtled, low and fast, close to the ground, their faces grinning in delight, the stubs of their tails moving furiously. They came towards her, ready to leap and jump, idiotic in their joy, the grace and dignity with which they were normally imbued, lost in their clumsy cavorting.

'Merciful Heaven . . .' One hand shaded her eyes and the other held fast to the child's and she had no time for the hand signals with which she normally controlled the dogs.

'*Down* . . . down I say . . . Barny . . . stop it at once . . . wait a minute . . . Joby, you fool . . . *Stay* . . . stand . . . lie down . . . down Blaze . . .' In her fear for the girl the words tripped incoherently from her lips, making no sense to the dogs who were used to her clear, crisp commands. They were confused, blundering heavily against her skirt, prancing this way and that, rearing up on their back legs, meaning no offence, offering no danger but big and heavy and quite, quite terrifying in their fierce black beauty. Barny, three years old and the buffoon of the four, the clown who loved to play, aware that no danger threatened his mistress turned to the little girl, offering her his laughing face, his sharp white teeth, his drooling tongue, ready to accept the friendship of her hand on his head but she stood as though transfixed, her eyes empty, just as though she could bear no more and had simply gone away.

'Lie down, boy,' Kit said quietly and he did, and so did the rest, settling obediently about the feet of herself and the child and the silence stretched on and on. Across the yard the stable lad stood in anguished misery, telling himself time and time again that it was not his fault. He hadn't been told the little girl was to come with Miss Chapman or he would have held those beggars back until *she* had control of them. Sweet Jesus, that poor little kid, how would she react to it? They all knew her, of course. They had seen her walk beside her nursemaid a hundred times in the garden and sit quietly on the lawn while Lucas, God bless him, played merry hell with Mr Smith's flower beds but Miss Chapman had left instructions that the dogs were to be kept locked up while the children were about.

'Take the dogs away, Dick,' Miss Chapman called carefully, her voice quite controlled, hardly daring to rumple the air which moved about them for fear of sending the little girl further into her trance-like state. If she could just edge her back into the security of the porch, with the door between them and the menace of the dogs, no menace at all really, but horrendous surely to the child, she felt she could encompass her terror. Perhaps she should pick her up and cradle her in her arms, comfort the stiffness of her but that had never worked before and she was afraid to disturb the stillness which had fallen about them.

To her horror Barny stood up. Never, since he was a young puppy had he disobeyed her command. Told to 'stay' he would remain there until he died of it. Through storm and thunder, starvation or a sound thrashing she could guarantee nothing would move him, or any of them, until she gave the command but now he ambled across the few feet which separated him from the little girl and with the unerring sixth sense an animal seems to possess and which told him of her misery he lay down before her and as gently as thistledown nosed at the small hand which hung limply at her side. He licked it, the tip of his tongue just touching her fingers. Not enough even to stir them but her hand jumped and stiffly, probably the first time it had ever done so to another living thing, lifted until it rested on his broad head. It seemed not to know what to do next, lying there like a wilting flower, white against the black, then Barny stood up and his rump moved from side to side and her hand fell off his head so he nosed it again and this time she placed it palm down on his nose, stroking it back across his shining eyes to the top of his head, then, more boldly, across the polished softness of his broad shoulders. She turned her face up to Kit's and smiled. 'Barny good boy,' she said, just as if she was admonishing Kit for reprimanding the dog. 'Barny good boy.'

Kit began to weep. The tears ran across her face and dripped on to the crisp cotton of her bodice and on the other side of the yard Dick felt his own throat close up as the 'poor little beggar' took her first hesitant step from the black world into which she had been born.

Kit was on the lawn, the dogs about her, the child on her lap when Jenny came out of the side door. Someone hovered at her back, a servant eager to announce her, but Jenny waved her away high-handedly, shading her eyes against the sun until she caught sight of Kit. She was wearing blue. A lovely flaunting blue the colour of a forget-me-not and her silk bonnet was a rose garden of cream and palest pink tied with a blue silk ribbon.

She stepped out boldly, knowing quite well every servant in the house had been informed she was here and that all those who could get to a window were staring in horrid

552

fascination at a woman who had been raped, the word only whispered naturally, not by one man but by three. Disgraced she should be since it was well known that only women who encouraged that sort of thing, endured it, and if she had any sense of decency at all she should at least have removed herself elsewhere, or, as most would, have committed suicide.

Her face was not that of the Jenny Greenwood Kit knew. It was a thin wedge, pale and harrowed with the shining grey of her eyes dimmed and sunken into dark, shadowed caverns but the set of her mouth was firm and unyielding. It said she would not weep again, or if she did no one would know of it. That though she had been badly beaten, she was not down and should she ever fall, which was unlikely, she would damn well pull herself up again without any man's hand to help her.

Kit placed the child on the rug then stood up slowly, her heart beating fast, her own face, had she known it, like tallow.

'Jenny?' she said softly, enquiringly, welcomingly.

'I need to work.' Jenny said abruptly and her eyes stared unblinkingly into Kit's begging her to say nothing of the past, not yet, and Kit understood.

'And I need you to work, by God.'

'I can't sit about at home and do nothing, but I want you to understand . . . I might have to go away . . . now and again . . . at a moment's notice . . .' if there should be any news, her eyes said, of the boy.

'I understand. When would you like to start?'

'My boxes are in the driveway.'

'The driveway?'

'That bloody Winters didn't want to let me in.'

'But you came in just the same?'

'Naturally.'

They both managed a tremulous smile.

'May I . . . may I greet a friend, Jenny? I've missed you so much.'

The servants were all made quite speechless by the

spectacle of their mistress enfolding and being clasped in the arms of the woman who had once been her sworn enemy.

# 37

They settled back together into the companionable routine they had known six months ago, nothing changed it seemed in Jenny Greenwood's sharp and lucid mind, nothing altered in their splendid partnership except that now it was Kit who went up to the nursery instead of Jenny.

'What's she called?' Jenny had asked abruptly on that first day as they shared a cup of tea, still beneath the fascinated gaze of the servants, while the child leaned trustingly against the panting black side of Barny.

It was one of those lovely September days which linger sometimes as autumn moves gracefully towards winter. As warm as June but clear and burnished with a sharpness to the colours which comes at no other time of the year. Up on the hilltops there were shades of gold and red and brown, deepening into purple grey shadows as they ran into the valley. The horse chestnut tree which shaded the two women from the bright sunlight was still green and vigorous and hung all about with fruit and the flower beds were filled with the vivid mass of chrysanthemums, yellow, bronze, crimson and white.

The little girl stood up and ventured a step or two on to the grass, her small feet hesitant, almost as though she was afraid she might damage it in some way. She was still by no means the noisy, carefree child that Kit wished her to be but her curiosity, come suddenly, timidly to life, led her to place an experimental hand on the pattern of Kit's gown, the smoothness of the soap Flora bathed her with, the roughness of the bark on the twisted trunk of the chestnut tree, the softness of her own curls when they were brushed. Looking enquiringly at Kit, still not absolutely convinced that this loveliness about her might not be wrenched from her should she displease, she held Barny's collar and while he slowed his pace to hers, trotted down to the lake to gaze in speechless wonder at the swans which moved serenely on its surface. Since that first incredible moment when she had reached out her hand to the dog she had become a human being, a child with a child's needs and a child's growing trust. Kit did not think she would ever be lively. Perhaps it was not in her nature, even under normal circumstances. How was Kit to know? But she smiled joyfully, her sea-green eyes shining, her gaze marvelling as though the things she saw, she saw for the first time. She loved the flowers and the soft glowing flames of the nursery fire, the lively kittens who lived in the stable, the white clouds, the blue of the sky, the silver moon and stars and the golden sun, the colours and movement of Kit's lovely gowns, the stretch of moorland, the sweep of heather beyond the walls of the house, and Barny!

Kit took her to Jagger Lane to visit Miss Cavendish to be fitted out for new winter dresses, giving rise to another great and overwhelming wave of gossip since what would Barker Chapman's daughter do next, they wondered, and could the child be hers for they seemed extremely close and Kit Chapman held the child's hand, proud as a peacock, just as though she *was*, but those who remembered the incident of Charlie Greenwood's beating, remembered also the child involved and besides, had you ever seen a Chapman with hair that colour?

'Do you know, I cannot seem able to find a name suitable, Jenny. We call her "poppet", Flora and I . . . an endearment, you understand.' On dangerous ground for did not Jenny Greenwood, a mother grieving her son, surely dead, and if not that, lost forever, know only too well about endearments for had she not called him her 'sweeting'?

'Yes, but she must have a proper name.' Jenny's voice was stony and she kept her eyes averted just as though she could not bear to rest them on a child which was not hers. 'Will you adopt her?'

'I had not thought of that, either. This transformation has come about so recently I have still not got a grasp of it. I was . . . it sounds so selfish, so self-absorbed, but I . . . missed you and, to pass the time, I suppose, I began to take an interest in her but it was not until she took a fancy to Barny, and him to her that I was able to reach her . . . but a name? . . . yes, you are right . . .'

Kit watched the child reach out to a leaf which had just detached itself from the branches of an oak tree, drifting lazily down above her head and on to the grass. It might have been some winged being from another world she was so absorbed and she squatted down to study it, the dog beside her, the other three eddying about her in a protective circle. Kit's face assumed a musing expression and her eyes were soft and unfocused.

'A name . . . ?' she said again, ' . . . but what . . . ?'

'Have you not a family name?'

'I don't think so and I can hardly ask my mother. It takes her all her time to nod in my direction if we should cross paths on the driveway.'

'No, I suppose not.'

'It really is curious. There is surely one that is appropriate for her . . .'

'Did you know that in the old days of the movement . . .'

Kit turned to look at Jenny and her eyes were clear and interested.

'What movement?'

'The movement my family is involved in.'

For some reason it seemed Jenny was unwilling or unable to mention her brother's name. It was as though the past, the immediate past was too painful a subject to dwell on, that the future was all that concerned her, the present and the future and nothing else.

'Please tell me.'

'It was the day my father was killed at Peterloo. They marched, all the men of the village and many women too.

Charlie and Daisy were babies and my mother needed me at home. I was fifteen and though I longed to go, I couldn't. But they had an emblem . . .' The pain had receded from Jenny's face and her expression was soft, proud. 'They wore them in their hats, the men . . .'

'What?'

'A sprig of laurel. It signified peace and harmony. Perhaps . . . one day we will all know it. Perhaps this child will bring you . . .'

'Peace . . .' Kit sampled the word slowly, a little sadly for it was an elusive thing, her eyes seemed to say. 'Laurel for harmony and peace.'

As she spoke the child turned, holding out the leaf with fingers which said it was the most amazing thing she had ever laid eyes on. She smiled, sharing her amazement with them and even Jenny felt her heart move a little at the child's delight.

'Laurel. That is lovely, Jenny. Laurel.'

And Laurel Chapman walked across the smooth grass towards the two women.

But it was almost the end of October before Jenny spoke of her brother. Though Kit was busy, busy with her mills where she and Jenny went each day, busy with the plans for the opening of her new hospital at which, to the consternation of Crossfold, the Squire himself had agreed to officiate, busy with the employing of a governess for Laurel, there were hours, days even, when Jenny was aware that there was a growing despair in Kit Chapman when Joss Greenwood still did not come home. A grief and loneliness in her that was as great as Jenny's own, a quiet sinking into a kind of apathy which frightened her.

'Tell them both I will wait for them,' she had said to Jenny's mother, and Martha had repeated it each time Jenny came home from her searching, her desperate wandering from town to town.

'Tell them both I will wait for them,' she had said, and she, Jenny had come – for what else was there for her but this woman and this work? – but Joss had not. Kit Chapman was a woman in the shadows. A woman who had remained after Joss Greenwood had left her to go God knows where. Drifting, she seemed to be, waiting for someone who never came, listening for a voice which never spoke, going to her mills each day, moving slowly through the day with often little to say to herself but 'thank you' and 'just as you please, Jenny' and at the end of it, 'good-night' as she languished her way to bed. Ever since Jenny had returned she had been the same and Jenny had been patient with her grieving (for did she herself not know its tearing pain?) until one night at the dinner table, after asking the same question twice with no answer, she had been able to stand it no longer.

'He's not dead, you know,' she said abruptly. 'He's not in his coffin beneath six feet of earth.'

'I beg your pardon.' Kit's eyes had been clouded, her gaze bewildered.

'He would be disgusted if he could see you now.'

'I'm not sure I understand.'

'You know exactly what I mean and this . . . this self-pity is not worthy of you. I thought you were strong, tenacious with the backbone and single-mindedness which would not let you simply . . . give up but I see I was wrong.'

'Jenny . . . !' Her voice was anguished and her expression said she could scarce believe the cruelty of the words Jenny spoke. They were friends and sympathy between friends was taken for granted. Hers for Jenny in *her* heartache and the certainty that Jenny understood Kit's grief. But now it seemed Jenny was ready to turn the knife in the eternally aching wound which Joss's desertion had caused.

'Don't "Jenny" me in that whining voice, Kit Chapman. You knew he had to go, to come to terms with the way in which Mercy was killed, in her death for he sincerely loved her despite her . . . deficiencies. She was like another sister to him and after what they did to her . . . it would not have been . . . decent to turn immediately to you. Give him time . . .'

'I know ... I know but dear God, I can hardly stand it ...'

'He is doing what he needs to do ...'

'*But what is it? Where is he?* My life without him is sterile ... Dear Lord, if I had realised ...'

'Stop it! Stop this caterwauling this instant or I swear I will leave this house and find myself a cottage somewhere. You are not the only one to suffer a loss, you know. I have not seen a sorrier face since one of Pickering's lasses lost her kitten in the stream. Wailing and weeping she was, and her a child of eleven and it was not until Isaac promised her another did she wipe her nose and stop her blubbering ...'

Two pink spots appeared on Kit Chapman's cheeks and she squared her slumped shoulders.

'Are you suggesting I should find myself another lover, Jenny Greenwood?'

'Of course not, but I am suggesting you look about you and see what is needed here and it is not a drooping, miserable creature with a face as long as a fiddle and not a damn word to say for the cat. That child of yours could do with some attention, not to mention the final stages of the hospital. That builder has been to see me a dozen times this week and the draughtsman swears if you do not give him an answer by the end of the week he will take his talents elsewhere.'

'An answer to what?'

'Nay, don't ask me. You're the "maister".'

There was silence then, a silence still quivering with the hurt Jenny had inflicted but there was a feeling of something else apart from that of resentment at being brought to task by a woman who was, though very close to her, surely not qualified to criticise. How dare she intrude on Kit's grief and physical loss of the man she loved? How dare she speak as though that grief was no more than ... than a child's tantrum at the loss of a kitten, had been her first reaction but creeping into her misery and growing bitterness and indignation was the voice of reason and compassion for Jenny was right and Jenny *did* have the right, as someone who also suffered, to reprove her. Kit's life, and her bed, was vast and cold and empty without Joss in it but it was the life she must lead for now, and she must not inflict her wretchedness on a woman who had enough of her own.

'Where is he, Jenny?' she said quietly at last. 'You must know since you were the last to see him.'

'Aye . . .'

'Can you not tell me what happened? I have not questioned you. I did not want to . . . probe your wounds . . . to make them hurt again . . .'

'They will always hurt until I find my son.'

'Of course . . .' hastily, ' . . . but you are . . .' Kit cleared her throat, aware that what she said might sound trite, patronising and really, could she say she knew the agony of loss Jenny must be suffering, despite her own, but she was constantly amazed at Jenny's composure.

'You are very brave, Jenny,' she said in a low voice.

'No, not at all. I am simply determined. I mean to find Lucas and I cannot do it if I fall to pieces, if I sit down and simply fade away, if I retreat from life and pain and decision making as I often long to do. It would really be very pleasant to just fold my hands and stare off vacantly, as Mercy did, so that I no longer feel anything but who would find my son for me then? And I need money so I must work. I have men to be paid who are searching . . . the factories . . . the mines . . . places where . . . where sweeping boys are employed . . .'

'Sweet Jesus . . .'

'He's small, Kit, so they could use him . . . they could have sold him to . . .'

'*Sold him* . . .'

'Aye, Ellis and the other men . . .'

'Jenny . . . surely not . . .'

Jenny's lip curled scornfully and the look she turned on Kit was filled with contempt.

'You've never really been able to face up to the realities in life, have you, Kit Chapman? Paint it up in pretty colours and what's underneath won't be seen. You know damn

560

well from your own experience that children are used for every purpose under the sun . . .' She threw her head back and her throat worked in a violent contraction as the pictures the words evoked crowded into both their minds. 'I sometimes . . . God forgive me . . . wish I could hear that he is dead so that I should know he is not being . . . abused . . . Dear God, oh dear sweet God, he is only three years old and so . . .'

She swallowed and swallowed, putting up a hand to cover her eyes and Kit stood up violently, barely able to stand the suffering at the other side of the dining table. They had eaten a succulent saddle of lamb, or was it veal, perhaps chicken, neither woman could have said and the silently staring figures of Winters and Ellen still hovered at the back of the room but Kit dismissed them with a movement of her hand and they went gladly ready to spread the news in the servants hall that that hussy had broken at last.

'You went to Harry Atherton's then?' Her voice was harsh and her face as white as the tablecloth, with shock, with pity and with self-disgust at her own stupidity. She had not thought, not in detail of what might truly have happened to Lucas Greenwood. He was dead, she had presumed sadly for why would three ruffians such as Ellis and his cronies spirit him away? Simply for money it seemed. They had wanted revenge on Jenny, and presumably on Charlie for his part in their conviction and to kill her child was surely a cruel enough way to get it, but how much more terrible to take him away and leave Jenny to agonise for the rest of her life on his fate.

Jenny lifted her head and her eyes stared back into the past.

'Yes. We found out where he lived. It wasn't hard, a well-known family like his . . . Atherton Hall, just outside Chester. We went, the three of us, me and Joss and Charlie. The butler ordered us round to the back door. Oh yes, he knew at once we weren't gentry but Joss pushed him aside, you know what he's like. They came into the hall, him and his father and another chap, his brother, I think and when

561

Harry saw me he smiled just as if he knew what I'd come for. Give me my son, I said. Your son? What on earth are you talking about, woman? he said. I know you were there when they raped me and murdered Mercy, I was screaming, and I saw his father give him a funny look but he was still smiling, enjoying it. Rape! he said. Murder! My dear woman, are you mad? And his father stood there, and his brother, their faces ... odd, somehow, but behind him, you could see that. You took my son, I said again. Your son, Harry Atherton and I'll have him back if I have to kill you for him. I went for him then, tore his cheek to the bone before they dragged me off. But he hadn't finished with me. I have no son, he said. My wife and I have a daughter, yes, three years old and called Elizabeth after my mother. Let me see her, I screeched, beyond reason ... they had the three of us surrounded by manservants, waiting for the Peace Officers but he only laughed again, holding his hand to his face where the blood flowed. Indeed I will not, for I believe my wife has her in the drawing-room with our guests, and besides she has nothing to do with you. And that was that, as far as he was concerned. Joss was ... uncertain. He did not know him, you see ... not as I do and he knew I had been out of my mind ... and Charlie ... poor kid. I knew he must not be made part of this again. It made me realise what I was doing to them, to both of them. They took us to the gaol in Chester but the Athertons made no charge and we were released the next day. But I ... I wanted to be sure ...' Her eyes had become hooded, withdrawn and strange and Kit felt the prickle of disquiet run down her spine.

'We went back the next day, me and Joss. He was humouring me really. We left Charlie at the coaching inn. They were there ... in the paddock at the back of the Hall. We had to climb the walls and walk up through some woods ... the child was on a pony ...'

'Lucas ... ? Dear God ...'

'No. It was a little girl. She had fair curls under her bonnet. I could see nothing of her face but she had on a little dress . . . and her drawers were . . . were . . . She was the same size . . . shape as . . . as . . . but of course . . . being Harry's daughter and half sister to . . . well . . . it was not . . .'

'So you left?'

'What else were we to do? Joss was . . . distraught. I think if we had found Lucas he would have been able to . . . it would have made up in some way for what . . . I had gone through . . . and for Mercy.'

'Why does he feel himself to blame so?'

There was a long and harrowing pause in which Jenny strove to regain her composure, badly shattered by the reliving of that day. Her hands shook and the sweat stood out on her face as though she had been running and she took out a wisp of lace to wipe it away before speaking.

'He was a . . . happy-go-lucky lad. Always laughing and having a joke. Not at all serious like Father. Not a wicked bone in his body but a bit wild, high spirited. He hadn't a lot of time for what my father did. He was enjoying himself too much to be bothered by what others did. He had a way with the girls and as long as he slept in a warm bed and had a good dinner once a day he cared nought for nobody. That is until my father was killed. It changed him overnight. At least, he tried to change into the man my father had been, what my father would have liked *him* to be. I'm not saying my father didn't love him. He did, he loved us all. He loved *all* men and when he went Joss felt the need to take up where he had left off. But in a way he was warring against his own nature. It was in him to be light-hearted and yet he couldn't be. Not with what he took on. And so he became violent, doing what he thought to be right when he wrecked machines and burned warehouses. But he began to realise it wasn't the right way to go about it. And he began to see what it was doing to us. What *he*, with his wild ways, was doing to us as a family. And it nearly defeated him. Perhaps it *has* defeated him . . .'

'Oh no . . . no . . .'

'He doesn't know who he is anymore, Kit. To understand

that his wife was murdered by men who ... because of who we are, because of him, and you, and Charlie and what we are trying to do for all those poor beggars in the factories and mines and sweat shops up and down the country, because of that they hated him and so they got back at him by abusing the women in his family ... and ... taking my boy ...'

'So what is he doing ... what did he tell you ... ?' Kit's cry echoed devastatingly about the elegant dining-room. 'Where is he ... where is he ... and Lucas ... ?'

'Only God knows, and he's not had a lot to do with us for a long time.'

There was a letter the next day come by the stagecoach from Preston to say that a boy answering the description of Lucas Greenwood had been found sweeping chimneys and would Miss Greenwood come at once for the child was barely alive and if he should be her son he would immediately need a mother's care.

She was back within the week, hollow-eyed, thinner somehow, Kit thought, alone and desperate.

'It was not ... ?' she asked fearfully as she led Jenny to the fire in the small back parlour where they increasingly sat as the autumn turned cold and slid towards winter, less formal than the drawing-room.

'No, thank God ... and yet ... if it had been he I could have ... nursed him until he died and known, finally, where he was.'

'Dear God ... what ... ?'

Jenny shivered and put her hands to the cheerfully blazing fire, glad of the warmth and the comfort of Kit's presence.

'I thought the mill children were badly done to, Kit, but this ... this baby, for he was no more than that ... God ...' she covered her eyes, ' ... how we can call ourselves human beings, *human* and, one presumes belonging to *humanity*, of which there is little in the world. If he had lived I would have brought him home ...'

'Of course, we would have found a place for him.'

Jenny turned then to look at her and suddenly her eyes

564

filled with tears and she began to weep. She shook her head from side to side and Kit, thinking she wept for her son would have gone to her, would have held her, would have done anything to ease her pain for she loved this woman now as she would a sister but Jenny put out her hands and through her tears a smile trembled.

'No ... please, no, it's all right, really ... I swore I would not weep again until I found him and then it would be for joy. These are for you, Kit Chapman.'

'Me! I have no need of your tears.'

'I know. It is just that, after all these years, after all we have said about you, I recognise you, at last, as a truly good woman.'

'Fiddlesticks.'

Jenny went each Sunday to visit her mother and Charlie, striding off alone in the warm woollen dress with a shawl thrown about her as once she had done as a mill girl. She had taken to wearing vivid colours, scarlet and a green like that of an emerald, violet and lavender, lovely as the flower of that name, cornflower blue and turquoise. She flaunted them defiantly, and herself some said, just as though she made the statement her son was not dead; that though he had been taken from her he would soon be back. *She* would find him and bring him back and in the meanwhile she would not wear the drab of mourning. Crossfold said she was mad now, gone off her head after what had been done to her, and most probably, her baby son, charging about the north country at a moment's notice it was rumoured, examining every young boy who came to light and none of them him, of course. But not so daft that she didn't know how to keep on the right side of Kit Chapman, who was also a crank, a childless crank and no doubt Jenny Greenwood was thinking of her young brother, Charlie, for where else had Kit Chapman to leave her mills.

Jenny regained some of her weight when Kit pointed out to her she was no good to anyone if she melted away to nothing in her restless searching, not only for her son, but the return of her peace of mind. She worked hard and late, very often missing her evening meal and picking at a tray the housekeeper left out for her.

'Come home with me, Jenny,' Kit begged her that night as she herself left the mill. 'You should eat properly or you will be ill and then who will look for Lucas?'

'Joss.'

It was so unexpected Kit felt the blood rush savagely to her head, then drain away and she put out her hand to the door handle to steady herself. She had called her carriage and it stood in the yard waiting for her but at the last moment she had gone to Jenny's office to try and persuade her to put away her ledgers, her swatches of the new design John Bamber was to take to London the following week, to turn off the lamps and come home. They could eat a companionable dinner as they seldom did these winter nights, and talk.

'Joss . . . ?' Her voice was low and hesitant for it was many weeks since Jenny had spoken of him and the events which had taken place at Atherton Hall. 'You have heard from him?' Her heart hammered painfully and she had a great desire to press her hand to her breast as she had seen her mother do on many occasions.

'He . . . has been home.'

'Dear God, and you did not tell me.' She whirled about just as though she would dash from the room, fling herself down the stairs and into her carriage and gallop, yes, gallop all the way to the edge of the moorland and then run, skim over the dark, rough, uneven surfaces of it straight into his arms . . .

'Kit, don't . . . don't go . . .'

'I must see him . . . how he is . . .' She turned back, her face quite breathlessly beautiful in her joy. 'How is he, Jenny . . . is he well . . . has he recovered . . . what did he say . . . where has . . . did he speak of me . . . ?'

'Yes.'

'Then I must go . . .'

'No.'

'No, Jenny . . . don't tease me . . .'

566

'No, Kit, no! He does not want to see you.'

Jenny stood up, then moved quickly round the desk to Kit. She put out a hand for Kit Chapman no longer looked beautiful, nor particularly well.

'Please ... sit down, sweeting.' In her compassion for the stricken woman she called her by the endearment she had reserved only for her boy.

'I don't want to sit down.'

'Let me tell you ...'

'You have just told me.'

'He ... he has taken up his work again. He is so busy. I had meant to tell you more gently but when you said ... well ... sit down ...'

'Stop telling me to sit down.'

'Then I will come home with you and we will eat dinner and talk.'

'What of? He does not want to see me ...'

'Perhaps if you gave him time. He has lost so many months. He has searched for Lucas ... he has many ac-quaintances all over the north, men who make it their business to look out for abused children, where they can. That is what he has been doing ...'

'You knew?'

'Yes.'

'And you said nothing?'

'He asked me not to ... and I did not want to distress you ...'

'He will not see me then?'

'I ... fear not.'

'Then he is a coward and I am better off without him.'

'He has things which must be done ...'

'Things ... ?'

'Yes.'

It came to her blindingly.

'It's the new Reform Bill, isn't it? I have read about it in *The Republican*. They say that Lord John Russell speaks of converting the House of Commons from an assembly of representatives of small classes and particular interests into

567

a body of men who represent the people. It will mean half a million more people on the national electorate. That there will be an election soon.'

'Aye.' Jenny held her head high and there was a pride about her which Kit had never seen before.

' . . . and they want him for candidate?' she finished softly.

'Aye.' Jenny's voice was sad.

It was clear at last. All these months he had kept away from her. She had grieved for him, mourned him as a wife mourns the loss of a husband and it was his pride, his damned, awkward, stubborn, *male* pride which had kept him from her since he knew they would say he wanted her only for what she could give him with her wealth. The wealth which would allow him to become the man the people wanted him to become. The man to speak for them up in Westminster.

'He is not only a coward, Jenny Greenwood,' turning against even this woman who was his sister, 'but a fool and does not deserve the loyalty his people give him,' she said bitterly. 'I want nothing to do with such a man.'

# 38

They did not speak of him again and the slight strain which had flared up between them making them polite with one another for a week or two after Jenny's revelation soon ceased in the growing affection and dependency the two women had on one another. Their common interest in the splendour of their new village, already unofficially named Chapmanstown, drew them there whenever they had a moment, to watch the occupancy of each cottage taken up by her mill-workers, to see the well-lit, well paved streets, to visit the school where already those first pupils of her classroom at the mill were teaching others in the 'monitorial' system which worked so well. They were both overcome almost to tears by the bright-eyed, lively interest their visit caused the giggling children, still admittedly, some of them, bearing the humped backs and bowed legs which their introduction to a better standard of living had been too late to eradicate. They were clean, decent, curious to see these two great ladies, not many of them awfully sure who they were but happy to recite their 'adds' and 'take-aways', to sing a song, or show off their new reading skills. There were older boys attending the Mechanics Institute after their day's work, straining, now they had the chance, to 'get on' and over all was a warm air of hopeful prosperity and goodwill.

'Good morning, Miss Chapman,' the women called from their newly 'donkey-stoned' doorsteps, sketching a curtsey some of them for old habits die hard, their eyes placid, their shrunken frames beginning to put on unfamiliar flesh, their children high-spirited, their menfolk men again, and on the site where their old homes had been, Pig Lane, Lousy Bank and Boggart Hole, buildings were being erected, a spinning mill crammed with the new 'self-acting' mules, a weaving-shed with the very latest of power-looms, a carding room, warehouse and printing room where, it was said, Miss Chapman would employ another five hundred or so people when it was complete. She was one of the largest manufacturers in Lancashire now, far exceeding the goal her father had envisaged and they spoke of her with wondering voices since how had she done it with the wages she paid and the subsequent loss of profit she must have suffered?

She spent time in the nursery, getting to know the small girl, Laurel, who, though she could not as yet be said to answer to the name, turned eagerly to Kit when she entered the room. A governess had been employed, a kind woman of thirty or so who had been taught at home by her brother's tutor, well educated and intelligent in a day when women were taught to do nothing but obey their masculine guardian, be he father or husband. She had been faced with the life of the poor relation in her brother's home now that her family was scattered and her parents dead, subject to his wife's whims, or the opportunity to support herself in the only way open to a gentlewoman. She chose the latter.

'Slowly, I think at first, Miss Copeland, for I fear she is somewhat timid.' Miss Copeland had been told the sad story of Laurel Chapman as she now was. 'It is a lot to expect of a child who has been so sadly abused.'

'I'm sure we will manage very well together, Miss Chapman. She has a bright look about her and ... well ... I am very fond of children ...' which proved to be true.

But they did not really need her, Miss Copeland and Laurel. The child became absorbed in the world of learning with which her governess surrounded her. Flora, who had grieved so keenly for her Lucas, now found, just as she was beginning to 'take' to 'Laurel', the child was being possessed by another woman; one over whom she had no authority and though she sat about during lessons, her face truculent, since how that woman expected the poor little poppet to read and learn from such amazingly curious books about flowers of the garden, about trees in the woods and birds in the sky was beyond her. What *good* did it do? As for French, well, the child could barely speak her own language. She was to do arithmetic and to use a globe of the world so that she would know where each country was situated, and what was she, Flora, to do while all this was going on, pray? Sew the child's little dresses, torn hems and such and darn her socks, bathe her and see she was fed and then what?

Kit drifted through the days, busy, always busy from morning until night, up at half past four in the dark cold of the winter's morning, already at the factory as the gate was opened at five-thirty for the first shift workers. And when she arrived home there was an hour in the nursery, coaxing Laurel to accept a hug, a kiss, begging a smile in the slow process of gaining her trust and affection, being ready always to give her own. She would consult with Miss

570

Copeland, conscious of Flora glowering at their back, on the child's progress which was slow but steady, to listen to the sensible woman's plans for the future and to turn her mind to the increasingly irritating problem of Flora who, after almost two years in the nursery, imagined it to be her personal domain. A schoolroom must be contrived, away from Flora's influence and Flora herself must be found something and soon she would do it, when she could force her mind to let go of the misery which blocked out everything else.

It was some weeks later, a Saturday and at six o'clock the factory bell had sounded its message to those who operated them that it was time to close down the machines until Monday morning. She and Jenny dined in almost complete silence. Jenny appeared to be preoccupied with her own thoughts, her mind far away, Kit supposed, on some increasingly fruitless errand to Liverpool, Manchester, Leeds or Bradford where men still sought her son. She had taken the coach from Oldham half a dozen times in the past three months, on a wild goose chase Kit had heard Flora say quite tearfully to Miss Copeland who had been made aware – by Flora – of the dreadful events of last year.

'Will you be walking tomorrow?' Jenny asked her suddenly.

'I don't know. It depends on the weather. I heard Dick and Frederick discussing the possibility of snow,' but her vague and quite disinterested answer seemed to indicate that really, what did it matter, rain, snow, thunder, if she wanted to walk she would let none of them stop her.

'I'm going to my mother's.'

'Really?' Kit's face was stiff, set away from Jenny, for the mention of Edgeclough was painful and embarrassing to them both. 'But what is unusual about that? You go every Sunday.'

'Yes, but I thought . . .' Jenny shrugged. 'I was merely making conversation, Kit. Both of us are . . . distracted with problems which beset us and really, we should . . .'

'What Jenny?' Kit stretched out her hand to Jenny's

571

where it lay on the polished table and her thin face softened. 'I know I am not a great deal of fun at the moment but . . .'

Silence fell again and Jenny addressed herself to the splendid turbot and lobster sauce on her plate prepared by Kit's chef. They ate without speaking, sipping pale golden wine from crystal goblets, smiling, murmuring to the servants who waited on them, gazing both of them into the candleflames in the centre of the table.

It did not snow as Frederick the coachman had forecast but the next day was grey and cheerless with a low, leaden sky which promised it would do so before long.

'Will you go to your mother's, then?' Kit asked at breakfast.

'Aye. I'll not stop for long if it looks like coming down. She had a cough last week and I want to see how she is or I'd not chance it. And neither should you. Look at that sky. It's as black as the inside of a parson's hat.'

'Oh, I don't know. I fancied walking as far as Besom Hill with you. It's only an hour's . . .'

'Kit, you can't. It would be madness.'

'Besides,' she was saying, 'you are always telling me you should spend more time with Laurel . . .'

'I intend to. As soon as the winter ends I am going to start taking her out with the dogs. I was hardly older than her when I first went out with them . . .'

'Rubbish! You were thirteen or more. You told me so.'

'Jenny! I have not known you in such an argumentative mood for a long time. If I want to go I shall and if I want to stay by my fire, I shall. You should know by now I shall do exactly as I please.'

Jenny sighed as she pulled her thick woollen shawl about her.

'Aye, I suppose so. You were always an awkward beggar.'

It was no more than an hour later when the doorbell rang. She had one foot on the bottom step of the staircase, ready to go up, a book in her hand, one she had loved as a young child and which she thought she might read to

Laurel. She had decided to take Jenny's advice — because it suited her, she told herself — and spend an hour or two before the nursery fire, take the child on her lap with the increasing pleasure both of them were beginning to enjoy in one another's company.

She waited a moment as Winters made his majestic way towards the heavy front door, pondering on who might be calling on her at this hour on a Sunday. At the last moment before the world fell in on her she was tempted to signal to the butler that she was not at home, but then she heard his voice and she could not have moved if a fire had been lit beneath her feet.

'Is Miss Greenwood at home?' he said, and the frozen mantle of paralysis fell about her, shrouding her eyes so that all she could see was darkness, covering her ears so that all she could hear was the thunderous roar of her own heartbeat. Her mind locked itself on the last coherent thought it had, closing about the picture of herself with Laurel settled comfortably on her lap, the lively fire, the pretty kitten, soft and grey and frivolous which was Laurel's dearest possession and which would certainly be expected to share the delight.

He was standing in the hallway when she finally turned, sick and shaking, white-faced, and in the midst of the chaos, curiously angry. Winters still held the door open, his face red and indignant since the visitor had been told *Miss* Greenwood was not at home and yet had still been ill-bred enough to force his way in. The effrontery of the working class was really unbelievable, particularly this family who had been, in his opinion, quite incredibly indulged by Miss Chapman. First the woman and her bastard child, then the boy who was getting above himself, and his betters, Winters had heard, at the grammar school, and now this one, no more than a convicted felon, coming to the *front* door, if you please, like a gentleman caller and asking for his sister, just as though they were as good as anyone.

She said the first thing that came into her head.

'How dare you come here?' Her eyes were a hard and

bitter blue. The aching, anguished recollection of the past months (or was it years, for so it seemed?) pressed against her in great waves of blackness and she wanted to hurt him, hurt him as he had hurt her, over and over again. For on all the joy he had given her he had heaped misery so that the joy was buried, stamped down and extinguished. She had loved him so. Loved him in every way a woman could and when she had held out a hand to him in his desolate loss he had struck it aside and told her, told Jenny to tell her, she meant nothing to him.

'He does not want to see you', Jenny had said and now he was here, like any casual caller, indifferent to her feelings, asking to see his sister.

'Believe me,' he answered her coldly. 'Had I known you were here I would not have come. I wished to see Jenny but she is not here.'

'I live here. Would you not expect to find me in my own home?'

'I was told you walked the moors on . . .'

He turned to go, his eyes blind it seemed, for he almost fell against Winters who still held the door open for him. It had begun to snow and a handful of flakes flung themselves through the open doorway, causing Winters to blink his eyes and step backwards his expression saying quite plainly that it was high time this foolishness was done with. Could the fellow not see that Miss Chapman wanted nothing to do with him and yet he was blundering about like a blind man, unable, it appeared, to get himself through the open doorway. Should he call Dick and Robert, his eyes signalled to Miss Chapman but she had her own fixed on the man's back and on her face was the strangest expression he himself had ever seen. What it meant, he was unable to say but whatever it was it gave her a kind of . . . glow! A moment ago she had been consumed with anger, now, all of a sudden it was gone to be replaced by something Winters did not recognise. Fanciful, he knew it, as he told Mrs Batty later, but he had never seen his employer look quite so lovely.

'Joss,' she said very gently, and their visitor stopped, his face quite blank, not more than six inches from the door frame which he gave the appearance of studying.

'Thank you, Winters. You may close the door and go,' she said, ' . . . no, with Mr Greenwood on this side of it, if you please.'

Winters was tempted to hang about, just on the other side of the door which led to the kitchen for there was sure to be something of interest to tell Mrs Batty. It was nearly a year since the fellow had been here . . . and why? Where had he been and doing what . . . and with whom? But something, some strange feeling in the air prickled the back of his neck and instead he closed the door softly and left them alone.

There was a long and solid silence and somehow she knew it must be broken. Fragments of thought slipped into Kit's head and out again. There was one. It was to do with Jenny; and Lucas! It must be. Nothing else would get him here to this house when the chance that he would see *her* was high. He had come and he had been devastated. He was *still* devastated. Though his voice had been ice-covered, cruel even in his stony politeness, there was in him a volatile tension which had him groping about at the door as though his senses were stunned, *as hers had been.*

She could feel the bubble of joy just beneath her breastbone and a pulse fluttered delicately at the base of her throat, but she must contain it all, hold her breath, scarce move unless she disturb the fragile emotion which struggled to endure in the hallway, the very feeling from which Winters had just hurried away.

'Why have you come, Joss?' She savoured his name in a voice which was velvet soft, light as air, letting it rest inoffensively inside his head.

'Jenny said she would be here.'

'You have something to tell her?'

'Yes, but it can wait until I see her.'

'Does it concern Lucas?'

'Yes.'

575

'Joss . . . please . . . can you not tell me?'

He spoke harshly, the effort it took to compose himself very evident.

'I had word of a child . . . she wanted to go herself but she is . . . very tired. I persuaded her to let me go alone. There have been so many disappointments. It was in Clitheroe, a mill child . . . from the poorhouse they said, who matched the description of . . .'

'Of Lucas?'

'Yes . . . It was not him. I came to tell her.'

'I'm sorry.'

Still he kept his back to her, stiff and furious, violent somehow as though his pain and fury might unleash something he wished to keep well hidden.

'Will you not turn round, Joss? Take off your coat and come to the fire. I will order some coffee, it is a cold day and . . .'

'I must be on my way. It is an hour's ride to . . .'

'Please . . .'

'I cannot . . .'

'Why . . . ?'

He turned savagely then and his pain flung itself across the space between them but she did not flinch.

'Because I am afraid I have not the strength to . . . damn you, damn you, Kit Chapman, you are . . .' He bit off the sentence, already revealing too much and she rejoiced but she must not allow him to fight his way through her vulnerable defences and escape again. She had let him go once, told him she would wait for him but he had not come. This time it would be different. This man was hers. She had fought, been wounded and bled for him and by God, *now*, she meant to have him. He loved her still, exultantly she knew he loved her still, but his foolish masculine pride, his passionate certainty that they could never be together, that there was too much standing between them had kept him from her. Curiously, now that she was dead, because of the way she had died, his wife held them apart more certainly than she had alive. But it would not do. He was strong and might fight her, but she was stronger. He was resolute, determined, but she would be more so.

'Please come and sit by the fire. It is only the small parlour. You can tell me what you were to tell Jenny and I will pass it on. Let me send for coffee . . .'

'I cannot stay. My mother is expecting me . . .'

'No, she is not. You know full well she is not.'

His eyes gleamed for a moment in the dim, fire-lit hallway but he lifted his head menacingly.

'You still like to give orders then, Kit Chapman, but I do not take them.'

'So I see.'

She stepped down from the staircase, the book, picked up so long ago – when was it? – still in her hand, and he moved an inch or two from the door, his face guarded but with something in it which was eager to escape, to be let free.

'Jenny was right. She said you were still . . .'

'What, Joss?' Her eyes narrowed and the fire's glow put a softness in them which was exquisitely familiar to him and he moved, mesmerised by her as he had always been ever since he had known her, taking another step towards her.

'Pigheaded!' and incredibly there was a small lift to the corner of his mouth and she smiled too.

'I know, and there are those who call me worse but I have a tough skin and a strong back.'

His eyes drifted over her involuntarily, slowly, and with infinite care she held her breath, wishing in the way of a woman that she had worn a prettier gown, dressed her hair more carefully, not realising that her air of slight informality, unconcern, the drift of loose tendrils about her face and ears, the simplicity of her apricot morning gown gave her the look, not of a lady of fashion, but of soft, careless womanhood.

He turned away from her abruptly. 'I must be going.' He began once more to fumble with the door catch. 'I have to get back . . .'

'Joss, for God's sake leave that damn door alone and turn back to look at me. Let me see what's in your face. Look at mine, I beg you. What we had . . . what we still have cannot . . .'

'Nay, I'll not live on you, Kit Chapman, for that's what you're asking and I'll not turn round and look at you again for if I do I'll be lost,' then he was gone.

She had worked so hard for it and now it no longer mattered. That was the irony of it. No, that was not strictly true for what one had created, built up and strengthened with one's own blood and sinew, like a child in the womb, can never be discounted, nor be considered of no matter. But the mills were a distant hum in her head, a vague, barely distinguishable sound which was drowned by the noise of the pain of her loss. She did not want to listen to it, to any of it, longing to escape from her life for the first time since she had grown to womanhood. And her business was running smoothly and could safely be left in Jenny's capable hands. She might do as she pleased, go where she pleased, walk the moors each and every day, stay in her bed until noon if she so desired for she could now indulge in that wondrous thing known as 'time to spare', 'slippered ease', 'leisure', should she care to take it, but it was strange to her after nine years, unfamiliar and she could not find herself comfortable with it.

What to do then to fill her empty days? What next to strive for? Always there had been a goal. Some objective towards which she must strive. At first it had been her father's attention. Not his love exactly but the need to see approval in his eyes, or even just to make his eyes look at her. She had achieved it. She had become the son he had longed for, that she had longed to be, working beside him and then when he died, in his place at the mills, her mills.

And then Joss. What could she say to herself about Joss that was not already known, loved, longed for, grieved over? She had known hope in the months after Mercy Greenwood had died that somehow, in some way he would

578

turn to her, that at last they could know the peace, the comfort, the joy, the partnership of a true marriage but the very thing which was so dear to her, which she had sweated and wept over was to keep them apart. Was she to choose? Give all she had away so that Joss would not have the barrier of her wealth between them. Could she live on fifty pounds a year in a cottage, could *they*, their love, survive it and she knew it could, but that was not *her* destiny, nor was it Joss Greenwood's. He spoke to many men with his words which were printed in their newspapers but he could speak *for* them in Parliament if he would swallow his damned pride and take what she offered.

In March she went to Southport, spending a lonely few days walking the promenade, staring for hours on end at the wide golden sands and watching the tide come in and out. She drank afternoon tea on the glass covered verandah of the comfortable hotel and ate dinner in solitary splendour, listening quite intently to the small orchestra which played for the entertainment of the diners. She breakfasted on fresh caught Lytham herring, afterwards walking again, wrapped up in her elegant sable-lined coffee coloured cloak, the raw March wind pinching her face, watching the gulls wheel and dive, listening to their lost-soul cries and by the afternoon was on a train heading homewards.

'I thought you were to stay a week,' Jenny said, her eyes careful, hiding the compassion she felt for this pale-faced, sad-eyed woman who had spent her adult life *giving* and had received nothing in return.

'It seems I am not cut out for holidays. I can't quite get the hang of them.'

She lost weight and could not sleep.

'Why don't we have a few days in London?' Jenny suggested in June. 'Perhaps this time we might find it possible to enjoy it.' She smiled, they both did, remembering those days years ago when they had struggled and fought against liking one another, determined both of them, to stay loyal to their own class. 'I really am in need of a new bonnet,' she added, 'and that Monsieur What's-is-name 'might be glad of our business. What d'you say? Gribb can manage for a day or two without us.'

They bought day dresses with low draped bodices and imbecile sleeves, and evening gowns of extreme *décolletage* with enormous gathered skirts. Pelerine mantles of rose-coloured velvet and peignoirs of silk and gauze, bonnets of *poult-de-soie*, jewelled combs, and Jenny, a *ferronière* which was a narrow gold and jewelled band to be worn low, daringly, about her head and which Monsieur said would be magnificent with her short curls. Shoes and slippers with square toes and rosette trimmings, laced boots of black velvet and satin, coloured stockings and embroidered gloves.

'God knows when we'll wear them,' Jenny said as she preened before her mirror, a green velvet bag with a gold cord dangling on her right arm, and though Kit knew they went through the motions of enjoying this mad spending, the luxury of their smart hotel, the evenings at the theatre, neither of them could wait to get home.

'What is he doing?' she asked abruptly, in August.

Jenny did not pretend not to know who she meant.

'He addresses meetings and political rallies. He writes articles for the newspapers . . .'

'And the candidacy?'

'Is still his if he can . . .'

'Find the money to support himself?'

'Aye . . .' Jenny sighed.

'All that he wants I can give him but he won't let me.'

'It seems not.'

'Then he is a fool,' and her voice was bitter, hopeless.

'I'll tell him so next time I see him.'

'Don't trouble yourself.'

She was sitting on a flat rock, her arms hugging her knees, her eyes staring sightlessly at the valley stretched out below Friars Mere when she heard his voice behind her.

'You were walking here the first time I saw you.'

She whirled about, her face which was already pale

580

and shadowed, losing the last of its colour, only her eyes retaining their striking blue brilliance. They were wide, startled and her first words were concerned, not with the wonder of his presence but the laxity of her dogs.

'How in damnation did you creep up past Joby and Blaze?' she snarled since it seemed that only in anger could she conceal her joy.

'I knew I could count on you for a warm welcome, Kit Chapman, and as for your dogs, they are getting old now, and besides, seemed to find me no threat to you. Indeed they wagged those ridiculous stumps of tails as I walked by them.'

'Damned dogs! I don't know why I keep them . . .' but the colour had flooded now to her cheeks, a rosy glow of something which could only be called hope, surely, for why else would he seek her out, if not with hope for *them*?

But she could not be gracious about it, even as it flooded every hollow space in her body, bringing to life the dreary, twilight world in which she had existed for so long.

She turned away from him as she spoke.

'And what brings you here, Joss Greenwood?' she said, just as imperiously as she had done ten years ago on this very spot.

'You do, Kit Chapman.'

'Really, and what have I to do with you anymore?'

'God only knows, but it seems you do. The truth must be faced that we cannot live apart so if you will be good enough to look at me . . .'

She turned back to him and it shone between them with such brilliance they both gasped with the wonder of it. He held out his arms to her.

'I cannot escape it, my darling. I will have to marry you if only for the sake of those poor wretches down there who depend on me, you know that, don't you?'

'Oh yes.' And with a sigh of thankfulness she moved into them, bringing to life again the warmth and colour of the great, endless fabric of their love.

# SHINING THREADS

Again,
for Howard and Janet,
with my love.

She was like a young queen in her hauteur. The warm honey of her skin, the pale, cat-like grey of her eyes, the sweeping burnished darkness of her hair which flowed unconfined down the length of her straight back promised a stunning beauty to come. She had on a white cambric shirt, frilled down its front, with full sleeves which were caught in a narrow band at the wrist, and, amazingly, pale buff riding breeches of the finest doeskin. Her knee-high boots were brown and of the very best leather, polished until they gleamed, and she wore brown kid gloves and carried a riding crop.

Had it not been for her hair and the knot of scarlet ribbon with which it was carelessly tied back she might have been taken for a boy. She sat astride her small chestnut mare with the regal grace which spoke of generations of majesty, of the divine right to rule stretching back into eternity, and yet her grandfather had been no more than a humble hand-loom weaver.

Her two companions were as attractive as she, with the same magnificent seat in the saddle. Dark as gypsies with eyes as blue as a cornflower with a touch of violet in them, they possessed the wide, laughing mouth which was so eternally female in her, but which in them was firmed into masculine arrogance. Their hair was thick and curling, tumbling in boyish disorder above fiercely swooping black brows. They were dressed just as she was but where her breeches were buff theirs were dove grey, clinging to their strong young thighs and buttocks.

It was a bright and pretty day. The sky was a high, placid blue and the sun fell in a brimming haze on the three young riders. They were laughing. Their heads were thrown back, their brown throats arched and smooth and the noise they made disturbed a scatter of magpies. The birds scuttled about a stretch of tussocky grass for a moment before lifting above the bracken and into the air, drifting away on almost motionless wings.

The slight breeze was warm and soaked in the fragrance of heather and gorse. It moved the shadows cast along the track by the shoulder-high bracken and rippled through the hair of the riders. A curlew took flight in alarm, its liquid, bubbling song rising into the clear air, and the high-stepping, mettlesome mounts rolled their eyes and tossed their fine heads. Around their feet quarrelled a pack of dogs, tall and black with brown markings and no tail to speak of, glossy and well muscled and as healthy and vigorous as the youngsters and the horses they rode.

'Do you think my mother believed you?' the girl said. Her voice still quivered with laughter as she spoke. She lifted her gloved hand to push back the heavy weight of hair from her forehead, an impatient gesture implying she would dearly love to be free of it, as she was free at this precise moment of every other female constraint which hampered girls of her age and obvious station in life.

'Lord, I don't know, but what could she do about it? It's not the first time we've made that excuse to Aunt Jenny but short of sending a message to old Wilding to check that he had actually summoned us to the schoolroom she was forced to accept our story. Anyway, what does it matter? We're out now and it will be worth the flogging we're bound to get from Charlie when they discover where we've been. And we did ride into the schoolyard and out again so we're not lying when we say we've been there, are we?' The boy who spoke grinned impishly. 'And, by God, I would submit to half a dozen beatings to get away from that damned mill for an hour. We'll be there soon enough one day, I suppose,

8

when we have done with lessons. But now we are on holiday and I fail to see why we should be forced into the weaving shed, don't you agree, brother?'

He turned to laugh in the direction of the second boy and he might have been looking at his own reflection in a mirror: the same arrow-straight back and broadening young shoulders, the same eyes and smiling mouth, firm white teeth and tenacious jaw, the same look of sleek and graceful high spirits, and it was plain there was no more than a minute or two between them in age.

'But what did she say?' the girl demanded to know.

'Oh, the usual stuff. She could quite believe our school-master was not satisfied with our performance as scholars and that we needed to do extra schoolwork to help keep up with the rest but that in her opinion we were wasting our time and his.'

Drew Greenwood grinned broadly and his boyish face glowed. 'Aunt Jenny's not taken in by us, you know. She realises that if we can manage it we'll not go into the mill with her and Charlie. She understands too, whereas our mother doesn't. Mother believes that anyone with the blood of Chapmans and Greenwoods in their veins could not fail to be intoxicated with the idea of being a millmaster, as she was, but Aunt Jenny's a good sort and she'll not press us yet.'

The girl sighed. 'I wish she was the same with me. I had to slip out of the side door while Laurel's back was turned. Then Walter refused to saddle my mare saying he'd been given orders not to and that if I showed my face in the stables he was to send for Miss Copeland at once.'

Tessa Harrison's face was indignant. Her clear skin flamed to poppy at her cheekbones, the reminder of the stable boy's outrageous behaviour so incensing her she moved her mare to a faster gait as though to escape it.

'What did you do?'

'I had to saddle her myself.'

'Did Walter try to stop you?'

She turned to grin lazily, lifting an amused eyebrow.

'Oh, come now, Drew Greenwood, would he dare lay a hand on *me*?'

'No, I don't suppose he would. Silly question, really.'

The three young riders had reached the summit of Badger's Edge where, it was said, a 'badger' or travelling salesman had fallen to his death in a snowstorm many years ago. With fluid grace both boys sprang from their saddles and with a word to their horses, two tall bays with impeccable bloodlines, to stand, they sauntered across the uneven spiky grass to stare, shoulder to shoulder, over the sprawling town which lay far below in the valley. The girl dismounted more slowly, speaking softly to her mare, rubbing its nose affectionately with a strong, slender hand before moving to join the others.

All three were tall. The girl was a bare six inches shorter than her companions who were exactly the same in height and size and colouring and so compellingly identical it was impossible to tell them apart. Pearce and Drew Greenwood then, twin sons of Joss and Katherine Greenwood, and beside them their cousin, Tessa Harrison, only daughter of Jenny Harrison, their father's sister, and all three of them would inherit a share in the fortune, the great estate, the mills, the railway stock and every other asset which made up the wealth of one of the most influential and affluent families in south Lancashire. Endowed from birth with not only the shining good looks of the superior beings they so obviously thought themselves to be, they possessed too the glorious belief that they were unique in their world, and in every other come to that, and had the financial provision which made other, lesser mortals reluctant to disagree.

'They should have let us go away to public school at Arnmoor with Nicky Longworth and Johnny Taylor instead of to that damned grammar school in Crossfold.' Pearce said moodily, flicking his riding crop against his leg. 'We might have been taught something other than two and two makes four and how much profit a successful manufacturer may

10

realise before breakfast, which, as far as I can make out, must be at least double what *other* manufacturers are capable of. Mother can't see it, of course, nor Father, as we are to spend our lives in the mills, they say. What use would the education the *Squire's* son receives be to us, she asks, for we are to be industrialists and not landed gentry as Nick is. Our grandfather and *his* father before him did not slave to make money merely for Drew and I to spend. I nearly said "why not?" I'll tell you this, if we *are* to be cotton manufacturers as she says, I'll not do it without a fight.'

Pearce Greenwood shaded his eyes from the sun, looking towards the west and the thick pall of smoke which lay like a sour blanket over the town below. A great sweep of wildly rolling moorland stretched between, rough and uneven, patched with wide folds of growing bracken, gorse and heather which, in a few weeks' time, would be thick and verdant with colour, yellow, green and purple, as summer reached towards its peak.

Tessa stood between the two boys, all three with their backs against a grey-veined rock. A skylark sang high above them and they turned to stare upwards into the great vault of the blue sky until their sharp eyes detected the black speck which was the bird. She sighed gustily then lowered her gaze to scan the familiar landscape which lay at her feet and stretched as far as the eye could see on either side of her and high at her back where the south Pennine heights rose up and away towards Yorkshire. She had roamed these hills with her cousins ever since she had been able to sit a horse, trailing far behind them at first since she was younger and had not the strength nor expertise to keep up. But it had not taken her long to be as swift and as skilful as they in guiding her mount across streams with dangerously unstable wooden footbridges, following narrow lanes winding in long curves up steep slopes and on into the misty distances of the packhorse routes which had once carried goods to outlying hamlets and isolated farmhouses. She learned to go over stony paths which led nowhere but to

11

huge outcroppings of rock, stretches of moorland which were steep and identical to a dozen others and in which a man could lose himself for days, or forever! It was damp for the most part, with grey-topped hills reaching into the clouds, peopled by none but the starving, itinerant families who moved from town to town looking for work, or mischief, and often not caring which they found, ruffians some of them who would knock a man senseless on the chance of a farthing.

'What *will* you do then?' she questioned her cousins. Her eyes were half-closed against the brightness of the sun. 'Aunt Kit has set her heart on at least one of you going into the mill. She doesn't much care which as long as there is someone to carry on the dynasty as she did.'

'Like hell she did! She got married and passed it over most conveniently to your mother and Charlie and followed Father up to Westminster as fast as the coach would take her. She doesn't really give a damn about any of the mills as long as there is enough money to support him as a politician. I can scarcely believe the stories we are told about her when she was a girl. Obsessed with the mills and as determined to do with them as a son would, they say. Learning to be a manufacturer just as though she was a man, and making more of a success of it than any other millmaster in the valley, we're told. Can you imagine anyone, man or woman, being consumed with the tedious task of spinning and weaving cotton when one could be far more enjoyably employed elsewhere? And yet Mother did it until she was twenty-five or six and married father. Can you believe it?'

Tessa found she couldn't, really. Joss and Katherine Greenwood were notorious in the Penfold Valley for their absolute devotion to one another, to the exclusion of everyone, even their own sons. Some would have it that there had never been a more mis-matched pair: Joss Greenwood, a radical, a revolutionary in his younger days, it was rumoured, much concerned with strikes and machine breaking; and Kit Chapman the daughter of the very mill-owner whose machines he had wrecked.

Pearce Greenwood lowered himself to sprawl on the springing turf, his back resting against the grey-pitted rock and the other two did the same, stretching out their legs and crossing them at the ankle.

From behind them there was a sudden snapping of dogs quarrelling amongst themselves. They were only half-trained and excitable, curiously like their young owners, ready enough, it seemed, to be amiable providing no one interfered with them but with a snarl of temper just beneath the surface. They lay down, lowering their splendid heads until their muzzles rested on their paws, but their eyes were never still as they kept watch against anything they might not greatly approve.

They all lounged indolently in the early summer sunshine: healthy, thoughtless young animals, sleek, graceful, high-spirited, dangerous when crossed, with very little difference, it seemed, between the well-bred horses, the magnificent dogs and the handsome young people. They were arrogant in their complete belief in themselves and their place in life, which was privileged and secure. They were defiant of fetters which might attempt to bind them to a life which was safe and tedious. They cared only for freedom, the freedom to go where they pleased, to do as they pleased, a desire which was, as yet, sufficiently met up here on the high moorland.

They did not speak for several minutes. Drew held his face up to the sun, his eyes closed and the luxuriously thick fan of his eyelashes forming a shadow on his brown cheek. Pearce chewed a blade of grass as he gazed reflectively at the slender ribbon of the river which could just be made out through the thickening foliage of the trees in the valley bottom. The dogs moved restlessly: one stood and lifted its leg against a rock, while the others sauntered across to sniff where he had left his mark, then lay down again waiting for the signal which would herald the wild race across the tops

13

in which all such days ended. Minutes passed and still nothing was said. They all dozed in the soft spring sunshine, the dogs' eyes opening and closing in that half-sleep into which animals fall, the youngsters graceful and lounging, even the horses, heads drooping, seeming to nap a little in the peaceful warmth.

'I wonder if the millhands are to have a day off next week when the branch line from Oldham to Crossfold is opened?' Pearce's voice was lazy, quite unconcerned, really: *he* was to see the celebrations so what did it matter if the lower orders did not? In fact he, his father and brother were to ride on the railway train from Crossfold to Oldham and even on to Rochdale, if they had the fancy for it, since Joss Greenwood, as Member of Parliament for Crossfold and a man of substance in Lancashire, was to be one of its most important guests on the occasion of the opening. There was to be champagne, Pearce had been told, bunting and bands playing, the train filled with the town's leading industrialists, those who were to make even *more* profit with this marvellously rapid method of speeding their cloth and their piece goods to the Exchange in Manchester. It was 1853 and the age of 'railway mania', it was called. Each week new railroad schemes were announced in the Press. So far there had been 357 of them, inviting subscriptions from 332 million pounds' worth of stock. Many of them were entirely bona fide, and astute men of business such as the Greenwoods had made themselves even wealthier: but some who had invested in companies which had been floated merely for the purpose of extracting money from the gullible, had subsequently gone under in their eventual collapse.

But none of this concerned the Greenwood sons. What was it to do with them, they asked each other, since they cared nought for the slightly distasteful business of making money?

'Why should they?' Drew grunted, settling his back more comfortably against the rough rock. 'They can't afford the price of a railway ticket so what difference will it ever make to them?'

'Oh, I don't know. They are saying there will be track laid all over Lancashire and even over the Pennines into Yorkshire. Many believe that railway travel will become cheaper and that eventually everyone, even the poorer classes will be in on it.'

Both boys sat up and their young faces glowed with interest. They had been to London once, by coach on the rutted, bone-shaking turnpike roads. Though the onset of the journey had been of great excitement to them as young boys, twenty-four hours later it had become so tedious to their restless minds and bodies they had decided it was of no interest, nor the several days they had spent in their father's company being shown the 'sights' of London. Give them the open moorland, the excitement of being part of a walking line of guns every autumn, shooting the grouse, the pheasant, the young birds hand-reared expressly for the purpose of a gentleman's sport. The thrill of Squire Longworth's hunt was what they enjoyed, leaping hedges and ditches, wild gallops across open fields, the fox no more than a breath away, the hounds giving voice on a frost-bitten winter's morning. They wished to be gentlemen, in the company of other gentlemen, following the fine and gentlemanly pursuits their pedigreed friends followed.

But the railway train! Would that not make a difference? The idea of moving at great speed, to Liverpool where no doubt there would be fascinations dear to the hearts of the young men they almost were; to Manchester, now that Oldham and Crossfold were *connected*, and whatever heady temptations lay there, and even, as the men of steam predicted, through the tunnel they were to dig beneath the Pennine chain and on to the 'other side' where God alone knew what delights might await them.

'It might be worth seeing, brother, what d'you think? When Father said we were to go I was not particularly

15

concerned but it might be fun, you know. We've never been to Rochdale.'

'Yes, we have. We went with Mother once to see some dreary Chapman relative, don't you remember?'

'No, I can't say I do.'

'Of course you do. My God, Pearce, your memory is as bad as some old woman's.'

'And who are you calling an old woman?'

'If the cap fits . . .'

'Would you like to stand up and say that?'

'With the greatest of pleasure. A bloody nose would look well on you next Wednesday.'

'And a black eye for you, brother.'

The quick, snarling Greenwood anger slipped its leash and lifted both boys to their feet, their eyes flinty blue, their black brows dipping furiously as they clenched strong brown hands into fists, ready, each one, should it be needed to kill the other to prove himself right. But Tessa sprang up, stepping between them as she had done a hundred times – when it suited her – before a blow was struck.

'And what about me?' she snapped. 'Why can't I go with you on the train? Who declared it should be you two and not me? I'm just as interested in the railway train *and* in travel and would dearly love to go to Rochdale. Miss Copeland told me it is situated in the most beautiful valley and that the manor of Rochdale was once owned by Lord Byron.'

Both boys looked confused, not perfectly certain who Lord Byron was though they had an idea he might be some sort of literary person and as such surely of no interest to their cousin who held books in as much contempt as they did. But she was merely clouding the issue and well she knew it.

'You can't be serious.' Pearce lowered his fists as Drew did.

'Why not? Why can't I go if you can?'

'There are to be no ladies included, that's why.'

'And why not?' Her eyes snapped furiously.

16

Drew shrugged. 'I suppose because the gentlemen imagine they will not be interested.'

'Mother is, and Aunt Kit and they haven't been invited either, have they? Oh, they can go and stand on the platform and watch the gentlemen have all the fun but they are not to ride on the train. It simply isn't fair,' Tessa declared as she did at least once a day. 'They are both concerned in the business world, just as Mr Abbott and Mr Jenkinson are, so why shouldn't they go? Tell me that.'

Drew scratched his head wonderingly then looked at his brother for really they had given it no thought. Indeed, they had given little thought to their *own* inclusion in the great event. Their father would no doubt officiate at the splendid moment when the engine had got up steam and was ready to head off on its journey. They themselves would certainly share in the excitement, watched and admired by the ladies who would come to see them off, but, as usual, this cousin of theirs was not satisfied with her own *female* part in it.

She had begun to whirl about in her indignation and the dogs milled at her feet, moving excitedly as her fierceness communicated itself to them. She turned to face her cousins, hands on her hips, legs apart, chest heaving and her expression was bright and furious. Her eyes snapped, the pale grey velvet shaded, like a stormy sky, to the tints of slate and charcoal, deep and threatening. She could scarcely contain herself, not, as they thought, in her rage, but in fear.

Tessa Harrison by, in her opinion, a fluke of nature, was born a girl and for as long as she could remember, though she defied authority and her own femininity, she had resented it. Whenever she could throw off the reins her governess slipped about her, the bridle which convention and her mother put on her as the gently reared daughter of a wealthy middle-class family, she had escaped from them, riding about with her male cousins and their friends wherever they went. She would put on a pair of their outgrown breeches and riding boots, leap on to the mare's back and gallop away exultantly, as they did, knowing that she would be punished later for it, not caring, for that would be *later* and this freedom and excitement was *now*. But lately, as they had begun to move away from boyhood, she had sensed that her cousins were ready to leave her behind, that her participation was accepted somewhat reluctantly, that they were a trifle *irritated* by her female presence as they went off on their completely masculine jaunts with Nicky Long-worth and Johnny Taylor. They wouldn't tell her where they were going sometimes, which was worse, saying carelessly that she was not at all likely to enjoy it, eluding her grasp and her furious demands to know what they were up to, and she had become increasingly alarmed. She had not accepted it, naturally, begging them to wait for her, declaring that she was not going to be left out of it, whatever it was, but they had gone off nevertheless, and she had become even more afraid. She could ride and even shoot as well as they, for they had taught her. She had been given permission by her mother to ride to hounds with the Squire's hunt, for were they not gentry and therefore, in her mother's eyes, responsible and understanding of the need to protect a young, unmarried girl's reputation? But that was not enough for Tessa Harrison. She wanted to go wherever her cousins went, illogical and absurd as that might seem, and she would tell them so. What else was she to do with her life if she could not be with *them*, she asked herself, do as they did, laugh with them over the foolishness of those who were fettered to rules, risk herself in the hazards they were to know? What would her life be without them in it?

'I'm going with you next week. I want to ride on the train just as much as you do and I shall ask Mother and Uncle Joss to let me go. Why should you go and not me? I can do anything you do, cousins. I can ride, yes, *outride* the pair of you and you know it. I could race you both from here to Greenacres and be home five minutes before you. Don't you dare simper at me, Drew Greenwood, or I'll take my crop to you. I could open your cheek to the bone and then that cheeky little dairymaid ... oh, yes, I've seen you

18

hanging about, both of you, outside the dairy. Well, she won't smile so sweetly at you then, will she? I can do anything *you* do and I don't mean to sit at home next week and sew on my sampler whilst you enjoy yourselves...'

'*Sew! A sampler! You!* Now that *would* be a sight worth seeing, don't you agree, brother?' Pearce stretched his growing body, throwing back his head in a shout of laughter.

'I would have to see it before I'd believe it.' They were both laughing now, taunting her, for there was no finer sight than Tessa in a rage. They all had hot tempers, they were the first to agree, especially themselves, snarling, knife-edged tempers which could flare in a minute from mere irritability to a rage from which the servants fled in alarm. Their Aunt Jenny, who had them in her charge whilst their father was at Westminster, refused to become involved with what she called their childish squabbles.

'Let them fight it out between them, preferably in the stable yard,' she would say wearily, eyeing their bloody noses with distaste, her attitude perhaps the result of the accidents, some of them leading to death, and the floggings she herself had witnessed as a young spinner in the mill she now managed. It had not been unknown for an overlooker to break a child's arm with his leather thong, and her nephews' bruises inflicted on one another seemed petty indeed when compared to the suffering, the real suffering which had once prevailed. Her own brother Charlie had taken such a beating when younger than they. It had almost killed him and he bore the scars on his back and face to this day.

'I can do anything I have to, Pearce Greenwood,' Tessa remarked loftily, '*anything*, and that includes sewing a sampler if I put my mind to it, though I must admit I'd rather fight a game-cock.'

'Perhaps, little cousin, but you cannot beat me or Drew in a race to Greenacres. That little mare of yours is game but no match for my bay, or Drew's.'

'Fiddlesticks! I'm not talking about keeping to the tracks,

19

you know. I mean whichever way any of us cares to take and if that frightens you then you have only to say so and we will forget the whole thing.'

'Now hold on, Tess. You cannot mean to gallop across the moorland. It's as rough as hell out there and if one of the animals should put a foot in a rabbit hole or be faced with rocks which...'

'Well, of course, if you are not up to it...'

'Of course we are, but...'

'Then what are we waiting for?'

Pearce shrugged, then turned to grin at Drew who leaned indolently against the rock, his eyes half-shut against the sun, seemingly oblivious to the wrangling between his brother and cousin. He was well used to this throwing down of the gauntlet by one or the other of them – a challenge which must be taken up if the scorn of the others was not to be endured. They loved the friction which set the blood tingling, the dare which must be accepted. Wild as young colts, all three of them, daring and reckless, they gave no thought to danger, to risk, beyond a care for their nervous, high-stepping mounts, to anything which might smack of caution. The brothers, young as they were, defied all comers at school, fighting back to back for the sheer joy of risking their handsome faces, their fine young bodies against boys older and heavier than they, often over nothing more serious than the sorry cut of a fellow's jacket.

'What d'you say, Drew? Will we take her on? I know it's a shame to risk her mare against our bays, but if she's mad enough to do it who are we to deny her?'

The stretch of moorland from Badger's Edge to Greenacres lay to the east of Crossfold and Edgeclough. It was rough terrain and uneven, about three miles mainly downhill and inhabited on the 'tops' only by rabbit and stoat, curlew and magpie and wheatear. It was fit only for small animals and birds but within ten seconds of the signal, which was the dropping of Tessa's scarlet ribbon, they were all three soaring away from the sun which was beginning to lower itself towards the hills on the far side of the Penfold Valley.

Tessa could feel her mare start to take charge and she let her go, trusting her instincts, guiding her only generally in the direction of Greenacres. She could feel the intense excitement vibrate through her own body and she knew she communicated it to her mount for the mare surged on as madly, as blindly as she herself did, not caring what came up before her, not seeing it, only sensing the rapid approach of the scattered rocks, the dips and folds and hollows which must be traversed before she and the mare clattered into the stable yard. At no time did she even consider that she might not get there, nor be the first home.

The mare nearly pulled her arms from their sockets and she flew like a wild bird, a bird knowing it should be alarmed at its own height and speed, and yet unwilling to return to earth and safety. On and on, and at her back she could hear the frenzied yelping of the dogs, the thunder of her cousins' mounts as they dashed over the stretch of grey rock. For a moment, as the mare turned instinctively to avoid an outcrop of tumbled rocks higher than a man's head, the sun was in her eyes and she was blinded but she let the animal take her round the rocks.

They came to a dry-stone wall, then another as they reached the lower ground for it was here that enclosure had made inroads upon the edge of the moors, and the mare rose lightly over each one, her hooves not even clipping the crumbling stones. There was a cottage or two clustered in a hollow, sheltered from the cruel Pennine winds, and women and children stopped to stare in amazement, then shook their heads and turned away since it was only the wild Greenwoods trying to kill themselves as usual.

Drew and Pearce raced a scant yard behind her, watching her back with fond pride for, really, was there another girl like her in the whole world? Her hair streamed out three feet behind her, a banner of dark, burnished chestnut in the late afternoon sunshine. They were so close they could see

21

the sweat stain the back of her shirt and hear her breath, ragged and urgent in her throat. She was fearless, leaping shoulder-high rocks and wide, quite appalling chasms cut in the rough ground in her determination to be first home. She did not even look back so convinced was she that they had been forced to drop behind, unable to keep up with her.

'Shall we let her do it, brother?' Pearce shouted, for really she deserved to win, but she heard him and her outrage exploded in her, flowing madly to every part of her body. With a fierce shout she urged her mount on until the animal's legs were no more than a dark blur against the grey and green of the moorland. The smell of gorse was everywhere and she thought she had never been happier in her life. The wind created by her own speed and momentum slashed at her face and plastered her shirt against her chest. She could feel the animal beneath her strain harder and harder. She could sense the heartbeat, like a rapid tattoo on a drum matching her own, and she threw back her head in joy, catching for a moment a glimpse of the tiny speck in the sky which was the skylark wheeling in perfect grace above her. It was free, as she would be free, always. It flew high and wide allowing no man's hand to capture it, filling its days with no employment other than the ecstasy of living, being, breathing, its existence tied to nothing other than the next moment, and she would do the same.

She could hear the explosion of hoofbeats at her back and the sound of Drew's voice, breathless and frantic as he realised that she might win, not by his allowing it but by her own efforts, and a great shout of triumph erupted from between her lips. She could see the chimneys of Greenacres ahead of her among the magnificent trees which clustered about the house. Then she was in them, galloping, moving as precisely as the bird in the sky as she guided her mare expertly between their enormous trunks. For a moment she had been sightless, coming from the brilliance of sunlight into the dim and dappled softness of the trees, then she was

22

through and beyond them was the gate into the stable yard at the back of the house. Walter, the stable lad, had heard her shout and was running across the yard to open the gate but she could see he would not get there before she did. Not for a second did she hesitate. Up she went, she and her mare, up and up, high as a man's head. She was over with no more than an inch to spare, landing on the other side as lightly as drifting thistledown. There was the smell of steaming horseflesh and the sound of the animal's laboured breathing, the ring of its hooves on the cobbles, and for a timeless moment she was alone in the magic world she and the mare had just shared. Then they were there, Drew and Pearce, crashing about the yard, their faces red and sweating, their eyes admiring, bestowing on her the accolade of acknowledging she was as good a horseman as any they knew, including themselves.

Walter hovered on the fringe of the mêlée caused by the three overstrung horses, joined by Thomas and Jack, ready to lead the animals away when they were told. On the faces of all three grooms was an expression of resigned acceptance which said quite clearly they were of the opinion that none of the young people would make old bones! They strode off laughing, arm in arm, and though Drew and Pearce were taller than she was, and six months older, they looked considerably younger. They were boyish, their faces almost formed in that curious way of males who are not quite men. Tessa, on the other hand, though only sixteen, was completely a woman, even if her appearance at the moment belied it.

Charlie Greenwood glanced about the dinner table at his family. They were all there this evening. His brother Joss, down from Westminster, splendidly handsome in his evening black and white, his hair still thick and curling about his head but where it had once been dark as a gypsy's, now it was threaded generously with white. Commanding of eye and well used to moving amongst all classes of men from

23

the operatives in the mill to the Prime Minister, the great
Lord Aberdeen himself, Joss was as usual no more than an
arm's length from his serenely smiling wife, Katherine, their
hands, or so it appeared to Charlie, to be forever hovering,
each ready, should it be needed, to give loving support to
the other. Their devotion had once been the talk of the
Penfold Valley; anyone in their company was immediately
conscious of their apparent inability to be more than a yard
or two apart and of the secret and sometimes disconcerting
smiles they constantly exchanged, but now, after twenty
years of a marriage which most had said would not last,
their passion for one another was unabated.

Kit Greenwood turned to her husband, her own glossy
hair slipping from the intricate chignon her maid had
devised, as it had done for as long as Charlie could remember, and his brother put out a tender hand to tuck the
straying tendril behind her ear. Her eyes, the same violet-
blue as her two sons', softened as they looked at Joss, as
they did for no one else, and her silken gown, simple, stylish
and extremely expensive, Charlie knew, matched their
colour exactly. She had amethysts in her ears and at her
throat and looked ten years younger than her actual age
which Charlie knew to be forty-eight. Indeed, her own
daughter, Laurel, who was Charlie's wife and in her twenty-
ninth year, they calculated, looked scarcely younger. Of
course, she was still grieving the loss of their fifth child and
could not be expected to be as sleek and glowing as her
mother, who was not really her mother for Laurel had been
adopted, as had his own sister, Jenny, as a child of four or
five.

Poor Laurel, though a stranger looking at Laurel Greenwood would be hard pressed to understand why Charlie
should think that about his wife. She wore a gown which
was fashionable and obviously expensive. There were pearls
at her throat and in her ears, lustrous and costly, and in the
room about her were the luxurious trappings bought by the
wealth of which she was a part. But she was a part only by

24

adoption, which was where the trouble lay. Until she was five years old or thereabouts she had laboured in the Chapman mills, abused and starved, and indelibly printed in her mind was the memory of those years though she did not consciously recognise it. She had longed all her life, from the day she had been old enough to shape the thought, to be as *they* were, to be *them*, if you like. She yearned to be as carelessly confident of the security which was theirs as were her brothers and cousin, to have a *proper* place in the order of things, not by gift but by *right*. She felt she had not and it had eaten into her so that she was tense and insecure, afflicted with the deadly and completely irrational fear of a return to the terror she had known as a child. It made her sour, envious and uncomfortable to live with. Charlie loved her, made allowances for her and wished his niece and nephews could do the same.

What a labyrinth of relationships his family was, Charlie thought, as he watched his sister, who was not really his sister, lean forward into the candlelight, emphasising a point she was making with the flat of her hand on the polished table-top. Joss and himself were true brothers, but Jenny was a foundling and, like her daughter Tessa, whom he and Joss called niece, and Laurel, his wife, was no blood relation at all.

But Drew and Pearce Greenwood were. They were true Greenwoods for all to see. Not quite seventeen years old and from the moment they were born they had been thorns in the flesh of everyone – as they had been today, he had been told – from the lowest scullery maid who had the continual scrubbing of the muddy tracks they made wherever they marched their imperious boots, to their own father who was as determined to make businessmen of them as they were to avoid it. Lusty, brawling babies they had been, terrifying their nursery maids with their devilment from the moment they had been able to get up on their sturdy, well-fed legs and strut like young lordlings doing whatever *they* wanted to do. Laurel had been eleven or so at the time, a quiet child as he remembered, made that way by her beginnings in life, at peace in the schoolroom with Miss Copeland and in the nursery with Flora who had once been her nurse. It had been as though a whirlwind had descended, since Tessa Harrison was born only a scant six months behind them. New nursery maids and a full-time nanny had been engaged to order them about, and Flora too, who had not cared for it after seven years with the placid Laurel, nor for the constant demands, arrogant and made with the utter certainty that they would be immediately attended to, of one wilful girl child and two rowdy boys who were as alike as two leaves on a branch. The noise and complete devastation had driven Laurel and Miss Copeland to shut themselves up, to *lock* themselves up in the schoolroom, but even there, a year or two later, her brothers and cousin were knocking on the door demanding to be let in, saying this was *their* schoolroom, *their* house, *their* pencil and ruler and book. What a trial they had been, the three of them, and still were to her, Charlie knew, as she did her best to run the household with the same precision he and Jenny ran the business.

His sister, Jenny Harrison, was a widow now though to look at her one would not have thought so. Years ago when she was a spinner she had cut her hair short and it still swirled in loose curls about her head, dark and glossy and springing. A brazen girl, it had been said of her, who cared nought for convention, which perhaps explained her carelessness with her own daughter's upbringing. She had ignored the observance of the standards of her own class, flaunting her beliefs that all men were equal in the radical cause.

Charlie believed that the only reason Jenny married the man she did was that he was as weak as she was strong. Joseph Harrison was not a man who had it in him to command his wife to stay at home where she belonged, to mind his hearth and the girl child he gave her, and it was precisely this quality in him which made Jenny choose him. The son of a weaver the same age as herself, he was the shadow who followed her footsteps wherever they led but without the spirit to challenge her will, let alone the congestion in his chest which carried him to his death. It was as though he had never existed, Charlie considered, if it were not for the vital daughter he left behind and who was cast, thankfully, in her mother's image.

Tessa Harrison. She wore the simple white tulle which was considered suitable for a young unmarried lady, chosen for her by Laurel, no doubt, since Tessa herself showed no concern for the gowns and ribbons, the embroidered fans and shawls, the frilled parasols and flowered bonnets which were considered to be the sole interest of young ladies. She was heiress to her mother's fortune, made in service to the mills, a girl who, when it suited her, could be as docile as a kitten, as sweet as a gillyflower, but who, as everyone from the maidservants to Joss Greenwood himself knew, had the wildest temper, the most self-willed and obstinate disposition of any of them. The trouble was, of course, that her own mother was seldom at home and whilst she was absent, Miss Tessa Harrison, determined to follow the path along which her male cousins walked or ran shouting with high-spirited laughter, simply ran with them.

The house in which they all lived was named Greenacres for obvious reasons. It stood in a splendid twenty acres of land some miles north-east of Oldham. When it was built almost eighty years ago by Kit Greenwood's grandfather it had been surrounded by woodlands and, at its back, the magnificent hills of the South Pennine chain. Since then the industrial factories and chimney stacks, the dwellings built to house the millworkers had fanned out from the centre of Crossfold which had then been nothing but a cottage or two, a church, a forge and an ale house, until they reached almost to the high stone wall which surrounded the Greenwood estate.

Greenacres was built of stone, mellowed now to a soft shade of silvered grey. The windows at ground level rose from floor to ceiling allowing in the luminous northern light. Some were flat to the wall, others had deep bays, the rooms they illuminated richly panelled and high. The roof was steeply sloped with two dozen tall chimneys and on the south-facing wall was a conservatory, burgeoning from glass wall to glass wall with gardenias, orchids, magnolias, camellias, all mixed with cascades of trailing ivy and tall ferns. There were hanging baskets of verbena, fragrant all year round, singing birds in cages and wicker chairs stuffed with fat cushions in which to sit and enjoy it all.

The house was square and solid, with a look of permanence and steadfast reliability, but though it lacked the elegant lines of houses built in Georgian and Regency times, it had a pleasing symmetry overall. James Chapman had liked what he called a bit of 'style' about him and had commissioned delicate rosewood for his hallway and staircase, soft, glowing. Yet in comparison the fireplace was enormous, burning great logs on most days of the year for he also liked warmth and comfort. The drawing-room had not been changed since the day he and his son, Barker, had filled it with comfortable velvet sofas and chairs, rich, deep carpets of Axminster, oil paintings and water colours, porcelain of Sèvres and Meissen, Wedgwood and Spode, Chinese screens and grandfather clocks in lacquerwork cases. There was silk damask upon the walls and crystal chandeliers, and in every room in the house lovely furniture by Chippendale, Sheraton and Hepplewhite. There was a dining-room, a morning room, a 'back' parlour, a study and a library containing thousands of books. The bedrooms were large, airy, most warmed by fires in winter and summer for the northern climate was not known for its hospitality. On the first floor there was a gallery which ran round three sides of the house, filled with paintings of lovely women, handsome men and splendid horses, with sofas and armchairs, and flowers everywhere. Beyond it and entered from one end, seldom used now, was a 'large salon', furnished with spindle-legged chairs in blue velvet, inlaid rosewood

28

tables and screens of delicate Chinese lacquer, all of which could be moved out so that the room could be used for a concert or a dance.

The house was set in what had once been nothing but woodland. Removing only enough trees to clear a space for it, and an acre or two of undulating lawn, the oak, the ash, sycamore, pine and yew stood all about the grounds, and flower beds, planted with dahlia, chrysanthemum, rose and fuchsia, glowed like jewels amongst them. Rhododendron and hydrangea grew, not formally but arranged to harmonise with the splendid backdrop of the hills and moorland. There was a driveway lined with plane trees, winding from the gateway to the entrance porch and then round the back of the house to the extensive yard and stables. There was a small lake on which swans glided and crocus, hyacinth, snowdrop and wild daffodils clustered thickly about it and starred the lawns in spring, and a heath garden lay at the base of the walls of the house. It had a quiet and informal beauty, which, at the back of the house, spread out into paddocks filled with splendid thoroughbreds, an orchard or two, vegetable gardens, until it reached the high wall which enclosed it.

'Well, I'm for a stroll round the garden,' Charlie declared suddenly. 'It's a lovely night and I reckon a bit of fresh air would be very welcome before we turn in. Will you take my arm, my love?' he said to his wife.

Instantly, like three lamps which have just had their wicks turned up, Drew, Pearce and Tessa came alive, and when Charlie and Laurel walked down the worn stone steps of the terrace and on to the dewed grass, his niece and nephews were already running like wild colts down the slope of the lawn, Tessa with her skirts bunched up high above her knees.

Charlie Greenwood walked between the rows of well-spaced machines which filled the enormous room, stopping every now and then to speak to a spinner or to watch the smooth movement of the spindles on the mules. Kit Chapman had installed 'self-actors' almost twenty-five years ago, the mechanised spinning frame replacing the old manual machine where the spinner had to move the carriage by turning a driving wheel. It had been a heavy and exhausting task, usually done by a man. Now the operative, without touching the fly, just turned a guide, a movement needing no more than the lightest pressure which instantly set in motion the spindles and took in the heavy carriage. It was so easy and light to use that a woman with the help of one 'piecer' could manage not one machine, but two.

It was twenty years since the first effective Factory Act had come into force, with an Inspectorate which was legally empowered to enter any factory it so desired. Children under the age of nine were not to be employed, it stated, and those under the age of thirteen were to be at their machines for no more than twelve hours a day. Of course, these same children and young people had no way of proving their age, should they have wanted to, since the compulsory registration of births was not enforced until 1837. It was doubtful their own mothers, who bore a child regularly every year, knew the exact age of each of her offspring, having neither the strength nor inclination to be concerned. The employers had one yardstick: if the children were the right *size* they were considered fit to be employed in the mill, and one did not ask for sight of a birth certificate.

The Act also declared that regular meal-times were required for the children who worked at their mules and looms and provision must be made for two hours' schooling each day but when a 'hand', which is all they were to unscrupulous millowners, was at its desk and not 'minding' its machine, little profit is made, and besides, what does a man who is to spin or weave for the rest of his days want with reading and writing?

Of course, Charlie Greenwood's sister-in-law had attended to all these matters twenty years ago at the Chapman Spinning and Weaving Concerns, her new mill at Chapmanstown, and, as far as possible, at her four older mills which her grandfather had built in Crossfold. She had begun her enlightened, some said lunatic improvements in the conditions of her operatives' lives with the renovation of her factories and the building of new houses on the land she purchased on the outskirts of the town. They were sturdy little dwellings with a parlour and a scullery, two or three bedrooms, a bit of yard at the back and a privy for each family. There was piped water from the clean, fast-flowing river and allotments, one to each man, so that he might grow his own vegetables. A church, an ale house, a school, a library were also built and a Mechanics Institute where sturdy young lads, eager to 'get on', were learning things which would surely lead to revolution among the lower orders. What would it be next, the stunned inhabitants of Crossfold and Edgeclough, and indeed the whole of the Penfold Valley had asked, and more to the point, where was the profit in it? But twenty years after the Act in many of the mills it was *still* the practice to employ children under the legal age, many of whom were worked until they fell asleep at their machines. Only last week, Charlie had heard, a little lass who swore she was nine years old but who could have been no more than six or seven was half-scalped at Jonathan Abbott's mill when her long hair – which should have been tied up in any case – became entangled in the machine, still

31

moving, which she was cleaning. She had been dragged clear by her demented mother for whom she was 'piecing' and taken to the infirmary in Edgeclough to be stitched up. It seemed it was of no concern to her employer when she had turned up for work the next day at the customary time of five thirty for her twelve-hour shift – in need of her wage one presumed – the bandage on her head already grey and stained with the filth with which she and her family were in daily contact.

Despite the open windows, the long room with its rows of clattering machinery was fearfully hot. Scores of women and older children attended the mules whilst others ran from machine to machine piecing the broken yarns, sweeping up the cotton waste, the smallest clambering beneath dangerously moving straps and pulleys, chains and wheels, all fenced off, to get at the oil-coated waste which collected there. Some carried empty roving bobbins, taking them to the machines and bringing away the full bobbins of spun yarn which were placed in a huge basket and dragged away by a sturdy and cheerfully whistling lad. The air was thick with 'fly', specks of cotton fibre and dust which, despite all efforts to dispel it, still hung in a mist about the workers' heads.

Charlie did not expect to find anything amiss in his spinning room. Nevertheless, it did no harm to let the overlooker see that he was on the alert for any infringement of those rules made to protect, not exploit the operatives. This was part of his daily round and though today's took place as usual it was at a quicker pace than he would normally proceed. As soon as he had finished his inspection he was off to Crossfold's new railway station to join his brother and nephews, ready to take his seat on Crossfold's first train, by invitation only, and ride the exciting ten or so miles from Crossfold to Rochdale. His carriage was even now waiting in the mill yard, the horses' hooves striking sparks on the cobbles in their eagerness to be off.

A young boy of ten or eleven drowsed over a snarling

machine, his head drooping since it was almost the end of his twelve-hour shift, and Charlie tapped him lightly on the shoulder. The overlooker, who walked at Charlie's heels, snapped his malacca cane angrily against his own leg, his expression revealing that left to himself he would have used it on the boy. He regretted the loss of the customary 'tackler's' thong, several straps of leather six inches long, but which Mr Greenwood, as daft as his sister and the rest of the Greenwood family, would not allow in his mill. Edwards was a good overlooker with many years' experience as a spinner until he had been 'made up', and knew as much about the machines as the engineer in whose charge they were. He could get more yarn out of his 'girls' than any other tackler in the factory but he did regret the reducing of his own authority by the ... well, he could only call it the *softness* of the Greenwood family with their refusal to allow him to discipline his young charges. Children were beaten in factories. They were beaten on farms, in mines and indeed everywhere they were employed, but the floggings, the dousing in cold water and all the other necessary punishments which kept children up to the mark were frowned upon here.

Mr Greenwood stopped at the end of the row of machines, smiling at a cheeky-faced young boy who had just emerged from his 'scavenging' chores beneath a machine. The child was far from plump but his bones were straight, his flesh firm and his eyes were bright. He was dressed in the usual fine cotton drawers and sleeveless shirt with no shoes on his dirty feet but his grin was impudent and carefree.

''Ow do, Mr Greenwood,' he said.

'How do, lad.' Charlie grinned down at him.

'Grand day, Mr Greenwood.'

'It is that.'

'Sorry about that, sir,' the overlooker said through gritted teeth, feeling in some way that his authority had been again undermined by the child's cheek in addressing one of the

33

managers of the mill, but Charlie shook his head smilingly.

'It's all right, Edwards. I like to see a child with a bit of spirit.' He took out his wrap-reel and began to study the 'wrapping' of the yarn as the carriage on the machine was drawn out. At his back the overlooker fumed silently. It was like this every day when Mr Greenwood inspected the spinning room and but for the splendid wage he earned and, as an overlooker, the neat little villa he rented so cheaply from his employer, he wouldn't take it. Interfering in what he considered to be *his* duties. The supervision of the spinners, the piecers and scavengers, *and* their chastisement if he felt they needed it, was *his* job. Of course, he had heard of the family's squeamishness before he took up employment with them but sometimes when he saw the, to his mind, *free* way in which their workers were allowed to approach them if they considered they had a grievance, it was almost more than he could take. What was the world coming to when a lad could address the owner's *brother*, for God's sake, and get no more than a friendly greeting in return? Naturally, when Mr Greenwood or Mrs Harrison weren't about he'd fetch a lad, or a lass if it came to that, a clout or two, not hard like, for it would be more than his job was worth, since it had been known for a 'rough' overlooker to be dismissed on the spot.

Charlie looked about him and sighed in satisfaction. He was pleased with the general air of cheerfulness which lay over the room, the smiles the women and children gave him as he passed and the sound of a man whistling nearby. Years ago a man could be fined for whistling at his work though Charlie often wondered what any man had found to whistle about in those days. The greatest boon, in his opinion, of the 1833 Factory Act had been to open a window to the rest of the world on the industrial conditions which existed in the mills, though it seemed to him that not a lot of good had come out of it in many of them, despite the reports of the Factory Inspectorate. Tales of abuses had shocked the world and there had been outcries from a great number of people on how conditions should be changed. But poor building materials had produced unsafe buildings, bad ventilation, suffocatingly high temperatures in which the hands worked. Very few millowners were prepared, as Mrs Jenny Harrison and Mrs Joss Greenwood were, to spend money on renovating factories which quite satisfactorily produced the required yardage each week. Long hours and the increasing speeds at which the machines went exhausted the operative, but she turned up for work each day so what was the millowner to do but allow her to do it? Disease thrived in the overworked and undernourished bodies and adults who burned themselves out were easily replaced by others. More, not fewer children were employed since the new machine did not need the brute force of a man to run it, and besides, was not a child's wage a quarter of that paid to a man?

Nine years ago a further Factory Act had reduced children's working hours to six and a half each day with a half day's compulsory schooling. However, what was known as a 'relay' system was introduced by unscrupulous millowners, the factory day stretching over fifteen hours, from five thirty in the morning until eight thirty at night, making it almost impossible to detect whether the new law was being observed. The Act, passed to protect the overworked and underpaid labourer, mainly children, not only in the textile trade but in all forms of employment, was once more obstructed by the unprincipled employer. Children continued to work for fourteen hours a day, and profit, the god, the duty, the right of the master, grew a hundredfold.

John Fielden, supported by Joss Greenwood, continued to press for the 'Ten-Hour' Bill, a ten-and-a-half hour day from six in the morning until six at night with one and a half hours for meals, and in 1847 the Act had been carried for young women and children. This further incensed the millowner since, if he was to turn off his engine for two-thirds and more of his workers, it was scarcely profitable to keep it running for the remaining third. But again, with a series of shifts and overtime, which could be checked by no one, the Bill was got round and women and children laboured, just as they had always done.

'Mr Greenwood'. A light touch on his arm made Charlie turn but before he could speak the overlooker at his back, his face thunderous, began to bluster, attempting, without appearing to, to hustle away the girl who stood there. She wore only the briefest of skirts and a scanty, sleeveless bodice. Her feet were bare but she was sturdy enough, with the wiry look of a young greyhound.

'Get back to thy machine, my lass,' the overlooker hissed, 'an' don't thee be mitherin' Mr Greenwood. Can thi not see 'e's busy? If there's 'owt wrong I'll see to it mesen directly.'

'No, let her speak, Edwards. What is it, lass?' The overlooker was forced to stand back, his face red, his eyes snapping with vexation, his expression conveying to the unfortunate girl that she'd be sorry for this, really she would. Charlie frowned, a feeling of unease evaporating his former sense of satisfaction.

'What is it?'

'Oh sir . . .' Though she seemed somewhat overcome at her own daring now that she had his attention since he was *manager* of this mill in which she was nought but a humble spinner, her chin lifted stubbornly and there was a resolute gleam in her almost colourless eyes. She had never spoken to Mr Greenwood before, indeed it was not her place to address anyone higher than the tackler who was over her, but this was an extreme circumstance and extreme circumstances made for extreme measures.

'Yes?' he said kindly and she took heart, despite the tackler's steely expression, looking directly, bravely into Mr Greenwood's eyes. They were a greeny-brown, she noticed, surprised that she should observe such a thing, the state she was in, but they were smiling encouragingly at her and he bent his head a little the better to hear her in the clangour around them. He was not a tall man. In his early childhood there had been poverty in the textile towns of Lancashire.

36

His diet had not encouraged the building of sturdy limbs and firm flesh, but later, when his family's circumstances had improved, so had his physique. He was not handsome really, but with a nice face even though the scars on it, one across his mouth and the other above his left eye, gave him quite a rakish air. She had heard, though perhaps it was just a rumour, that he had been a 'piecer' himself once and had been beaten within an inch of his life by a bullying over-looker for defending a little girl who was the butt of the overlooker's ill-temper. It was hard to believe when you looked at the smooth, beautifully tailored cut of his coat and trousers, the immaculately ruffled white of his shirt front, the gold tie-pin and cuff-links and the impression of superb good health which glowed about him. And even harder to believe was that the lady who was his wife, Mrs Laurel Greenwood, was that very same small girl he had rescued. It sounded very romantic, if you believed in such things, which *she* didn't, and anyroad she was not here to speculate on the past of this man who was in charge of the whole of the spinning side of Chapman Manufacturing. Really, how she had got up the courage to speak to him at all, she didn't know, but speak she must, choose how.

She drew in a deep breath.

'It's new under-tackler what's bin took on, sir. 'Im as come from Abbotts.'

'What about him?'

She bared her teeth for a moment as though she would like nothing better than to sink them into the new tackler's neck. Mr Greenwood was waiting patiently and though she was well aware that the overlooker at his back was warning her with narrowed eyes that she had best know exactly what she was doing since she was going over *his* head, she continued courageously.

''E's got our Nelly in't tackler's room, Mr Greenwood.' Her voice held a note of apology as though she was sorry to be bothering him over such a trifling matter and him so important, but there was defiance in her since it was her *right*, her eyes said, to speak up when an injustice was being done. And there was fear too, for though such things were rare in the Chapman mills one did hear of such terrible happenings, especially to young girls, in other mills in the valley. 'She's bin in theer ower 'alf an 'our an' ... well, tis a long time, sir. 'E said as 'ow she were cheeky an' needed a talkin' to but that be a long while talkin' to a little lass, an' anyroad ... well...' She squared her thin shoulders obstinately and her pugnacious little chin lifted, 'I reckon someone ought ter fetch 'er out.'

Charlie Greenwood straightened up and looked beyond her in the direction of the tiny office at the end of the room, the door of which was closed, and the overlooker behind him stirred uneasily. He too had heard, aye, even witnessed some of the ... well, to give it a *kind* word ... the mistreatment of little lasses in the industrial areas of the country. Though he himself was not slow to give a child, *for its own good*, a lick or two with his overlooker's cane, since many a time it could save that child's life by preventing it from falling asleep and into the moving parts of a machine, he didn't hold with interfering with young girls.

'Lead on, lass,' Mr Greenwood said ominously and the overlooker added 'aye' just for good measure.

The girl turned thankfully, light as thistledown in her relief, running on bare and filthy feet between the neat rows of machines all set in pairs and at each pair a woman and child. It was very hot, not a dry heat, but humid like some tropical jungle, and every man, woman and child in the room was dewed with perspiration. The heat brought out a variety of smells from the cotton itself, from the oil-soaked pinewood floor and from the mahogany carriages and creels. Above it all was the whirr of spinning spindles, the shriek of tortured leather straps and the thump of carriages 'letting-in'. At the door to what was known as the 'little cabin' the girl stopped, with Mr Greenwood and the overlooker directly behind her. It was a small room opening off the main spinning room, used as an office, and in it the overlooker kept his equipment, usually no more than a simple balance and wrap-reel, a quadrant-type yarn tester and a ready reckoner. With these he checked the yarn from each mule at regular intervals and ordered gear changes to be made whenever his 'wrappings' indicated a departure from the required count.

It was somewhat quieter here away from the vicinity of the clattering machinery and Charlie could hear the echo of his own and the overlooker's boots on the floor of the main passage along which they had just hurried. This part of the flooring had been overlaid with maple to withstand the relatively heavy traffic of shod feet. Only the overlookers, of the work force, wore boots. Everyone else was barefoot and it was common practice among the operatives to pick up waste with their toes which became, in a sense, a third 'hand'.

From the office came no sound at all.

'Oh, Mr Greenwood, tell 'im to give ower. Tell 'im ter let our Nelly out.' The girl, whose protective instincts were savagely alert put her hand to her mouth, her eyes huge and desperate in her chalk-white face. She was afraid now, not of the sound of anger, or even the dreaded overlooker's strap, but by the absence of any sound at all.

'Out of me way then, lass,' Mr Greenwood said menacingly, putting his hand on the door-knob, turning it, ready to thrust himself into the room, surprised when he met resistance since there was no lock to the door. It was unnecessary as there was nothing of value worth stealing. His face darkened as his frown drove down his fierce eyebrows and the girl edged up to his back, as eager as he to get inside, willing, it seemed, to lend a hand in the breaking down of the door if it should be needed.

'What the hell's going on?' Mr Greenwood roared and the sound of his voice lifted every head in the lofty room, turning each one avidly towards him. They had all been aware, of course, that Annie Beale had accosted their employer; most had been keeping half an eye on the small drama but they could afford no more than that since each operative spinner was paid a sum directly and precisely related to the amount of yarn she had spun in the preceding week. Besides, if a thread should break in the fraction of time it took to glance away and the yarn end be lost in the machinery, it would take valuable time they could ill afford to find and repair it.

'Open this bloody door.' Charlie Greenwood's voice was dangerous now and even Annie was alarmed since she'd never seen such a killing rage in anyone's face. His eyes were slitted and gleaming, the whites suffused with blood, and his big hands had formed into fists which threatened to smash through the door-panels, indeed through *anything* which stood in his way. But the door remained shut though on the other side could now be heard small scuffling sounds and a child whimpered.

'Nelly...' Annie Beale whispered and before the name had sighed from her anguished throat Charlie Greenwood's sturdy frame had smashed against the door taking it from its hinges as though it was made of cardboard, sweeping it into the cabin. The chair which had been placed beneath the door-knob went with it.

The man was still fumbling with his trouser buttons when Charlie fell on him. He was a thin, sallow-hued, round-shouldered little man with a hank of dusty hair who, if something was not done to stop it, would be snapped in two like a bit of dry stick in Charlie Greenwood's maddened grasp.

'You rotten bastard ... you filth ... you stinking piece of filth ... I'll kill you, kill you for this, d'you hear?' Charlie was yelling, out of his mind, it appeared, his face white and sweating, his eyes staring at something which surely, thought the overlooker who had followed him in, had really nothing to do with what had been done to the frightened child. He seemed to be looking at and acting upon images of such horror and obscenity, awakened by the scene in this room, that Edwards knew that if he himself did not act quickly, Charlie Greenwood would commit murder.

40

Nelly Beale stood against the wall, her eyes wide and shocked. She was fully clothed but down the inside of her bare, grubby leg ran a dribble of blood. She was nine years old and almost at the end of her own six-and-a-half hour shift as her older sister's 'piecer'. When it was finished, when she had washed herself in the women's washroom Kit Chapman had installed twenty-five years ago, when she had eaten her 'baggin' in the dining-room provided for the workers, she would spend the afternoon doing her sums, reading her book from which over the weekend she had learned by heart a whole passage to 'say' to the teacher. She would be a little girl in a normal little girl's world, singing, playing a tambourine, giggling as little girls do with others. But now, in a moment of animal lust, her young innocence had been cruelly taken from her.

Her sister ran to her wordlessly, swift in her need to remove her from the violent destruction which threatened. She put her arms about her and led her from the room where, it seemed to her, not only rape but murder was to be done today.

'Mr Greenwood, sir ... Dear God in 'eaven ... Mr Greenwood ... leave 'im be ... Christ man, thee'll do fer 'im ...' Edwards was grunting, his own considerable strength unable to control Charlie Greenwood's killing rage. The molester of the child was screaming like a pig with a butcher's knife to its throat and in the spinning room women began to cry out, their machines coming to a standstill, threads snapping and children running this way and that for want of direction.

There was a cracking of bone and the sallow-faced undertackler went as limp as an old dish-rag in Charlie Greenwood's grasp and as he slid, like water which can be held in no man's hand, to the floor, Charlie regained his senses. Edwards, who had grasped him fiercely from behind about the arms and chest, slowly, carefully, stepped away from him, hardly daring to look at the crumpled heap on the floor, though it was nowt to him if the man lived or died.

The heap stirred and groaned, then was violently sick and Mr Greenwood inched away from him looking as though he could quite easily be sick himself. The man fumbled his way to his feet holding the arm which Edwards had heard snap, shivering and sweating at the same time, and when Mr Greenwood lifted a hand to wipe his own sweating face, recoiled away from him.

'Nay, I'll not touch you again, man,' Mr Greenwood croaked. 'I'm only sorry I soiled me hands on you in't first place. I thought never to see the likes o' this again, not in *my* mill, anyroad, but it seems I was wrong. But you'll not satisfy your perversions again in this town, no, nor in bloody Lancashire, if I've 'owt to do wi' it.' In his distress Charlie Greenwood had begun to revert to the broad northern vowels of his youth. 'If I could have you clapped in gaol or flogged at the cart-tail, by God I would, but I know the magistrates in these parts, aye, an' the rest o't country an' all.' His voice was bitter. 'Throw up their hands they would if it were one o' their own but some poor workin' lass'd be nowt to them. So get yer gone before I have yer thrashed in't yard fer all to see. An' don't go lookin' fer work in south Lancashire fer I'll make sure you find none.'

The man had gone and Charlie and Edwards stood uneasily side by side in the cabin.

'I can't abide that sort o' thing, Edwards,' Charlie Greenwood said at last.

'Nay, sir, tha don't 'ave ter say 'owt ter me,' Edwards protested. 'I can't say as 'ow, if I'm 'onest, I agree wi' all tha methods in't mill but I don't like ter see a lass taken down, especially as young as that 'un.'

Charlie looked surprised at Edwards words. 'What is it you don't agree with then?' He was calmer now, glad it seemed, to talk of normal, everyday things.

'I don't reckon it 'arms some o' them bigger lads to 'ave a bit o' discipline now an' again.' Edwards stuck his chin out. 'I 'ad a few thrashin's in me life an' it did me no arm.'

'Happen not, but I'll not have it in my mill, think on. And

42

you're not the only one, lad, to have been given a beating. Where d'you think I got this face of mine? Not in the prize-fighting ring, I can tell you.'

'Aye ... well ...' Edwards cleared his throat and moved towards the smashed doorway. He'd said his piece though much good it would do him. 'If that'll be all, sir, I'll get back ter me work. Them women out theer are runnin' about like 'eadless chickens and the machines all tangled up. It'll tekk the best part of an hour ter sort 'em out. Oh, an' I'll 'ave to 'ave another chap ter take place o't ...'

'Right, Edwards ... and thanks for stopping me from killing that ... bastard. He deserved it but I wouldn't like to swing for him, just the same.'

'No, sir.'

He was still brooding, lounging against the cabin wall, his narrowed eyes staring at where the child had stood but seeing pictures which seemed to grieve him when Annie Beale slipped across the threshold, pale as wood-ash and just as insubstantial.

'Thanks, Mr Greenwood,' she said quietly.

'Nay, lass. I'm only sorry that it happened in my mill and that we didn't get to her in time to ...' He struggled awkwardly with the words since he was a man and ashamed of his own masculinity at that moment. 'Why didn't you report him to Mr Edwards as soon as the bugger took her into the cabin?'

'It's not my place ter tell one tackler what t'other's up to, sir, you know that.' She looked quite shocked and he was saddened that even now, after all these years of enlightened treatment, this girl was still afraid of a system which might lose her her job if she 'spoke out'.

'But ...'

'Anyroad, sir ...' she interrupted smoothly, seeing no need to dwell on something which could not be undone. 'I've cleaned 'er up an' she's back in't jennygate ...'

'Good God!'

43

'Aye, well there's bread 'as ter be found an' only way ter pay fer it is wi' brass what we both earn.'

Charlie sprang away from the wall and almost lifting her from her feet led her from the office. His face was contorted with anger, not at her but at the circumstances which forced this girl, scarcely more than a child herself by the size of her, to accept not only what had been done to her sister but that she must be prepared to 'clean her up' and return her to her work as though nothing untoward had happened. And this was *his* mill, known throughout Lancashire as a *model* mill; a model mill built on the spot where once had stood row upon row of mean hovels thrown up by Kit Greenwood's grandfather to house his own operatives. She had razed them to the ground and in their place had erected the factory which had become the talk of the textile industry. Six storeys high, the site covered several acres. The rooms in which the work was done were high and spacious with windows which opened – as the old ones had not – in order to allow in what fresh air there was, and blinds were put on those which faced south to keep out the heat of the sun. The machines were set, in pairs, at a decent distance from one another, most of the moving parts well guarded. At the back of the building was a separate room with tables and chairs where the workers could eat their 'carrying-out' in peace instead of beside their machines as they did in other factories. There was piped water, brought from the river, clean and cool, and separate privies for the men and women. Insanity, those millowners with whom Katherine Chapman had done business called it, sheer madness and where the hell would it lead? Might not *their* workers want the same thing, indeed were they not already grumbling about better conditions and higher wages?

Charlie Greenwood looked down at the girl who was apologising to him for causing a disturbance, assuring him, *him* who had defended girls just like her, and children too, all his life, that she and the child would soon have the machine going again. She was anxious to let him know, just

44

as though he was as unrelenting as any other millowner, that he would lose no profit over this little commotion. Did she not know that his own scarred face had been given him by an overlooker in circumstances very similar to those in which her sister had been involved? Had she not heard of Joss Greenwood, his own brother, now up to Westminster as radical Member of Parliament for Crossfold, who had caused such trouble and aggravation on behalf of the working class in his younger days he had been put in prison for it? Was she not aware that his father, Joshua Greenwood, had died for his belief, aye, given his life at St Peter's Field in the massacre which took place there?

'Nay, lass ... what's your name? ... Annie Beale. Well, Annie, thi shall have thy bread and a bit more besides,' he went on, deeply moved, 'if I've 'owt to do with it, and as I'm bloody maister I reckon thee can count on it. Now get thissen home, you and the child an' when *she* feels up to it, you an' her come back, d'you hear? Send someone to collect thy wages an' you shall be paid. Now, don't you argue wi' me, Annie Beale, for I'll not 'ave it. Dear Lord in heaven, what next ... no, please ... I want no thanks ...'

He could do no more, he told himself; it wasn't much but still a damn sight better than she could have expected in any other mill in the Penfold Valley, for despite his family's efforts to improve the lot of the workers in the textile industry there were still tens of thousands in the land who suffered under the tyranny of profit-mad millowners.

He shook his head sadly as he walked out of the spinning room and into the bright, sunlit yard, since their dream of equality was as far off as it had been over thirty years ago when his father had died for it.

'Mr Greenwood's not here just now. He had some business to attend to up at the Cloth Hall later on so happen he's gone straight there. Unless it's some family thing which has held him up, as is more than likely. There's always something with them Greenwoods. If it's not them wild lads who should be here in this very room right now as ordered by their father – and the Lord only knows where they've got to – it's the lass. She's as bad as them, let me tell you. Why, only last week we heard she'd been seen over at . . .' The man who spoke turned his head to look back at the long passage which led into a room where a dozen clerks employed in the main counting house of Chapman Manufacturing had their heads bent industriously over their tall desks. Satisfied that he could not be overheard he beckoned to the large man who blocked the doorway and automatically the man bent his head to listen.

'She'll not be told, you know, and her no more than sixteen,' he continued importantly, implying that he was privy to the Greenwood's most private family business, indeed, his manner seemed to say, had been asked on more than one occasion for his advice. Will Broadbent straightened up distastefully, unwilling to listen to gossip.

'Have you no idea when Mr Greenwood will be here?' he asked curtly, letting the clerk know he was not concerned with tittle-tattle about the girl of whom, he had heard, the whole valley gossiped, nor indeed of the family who owned the mill. He was aware, as who was not, of the tales of the wild Greenwoods: the woman who had begun the legend over thirty years ago, the man she had married and whose involvement with the outlawed radicals, as they had been then, was still spoken of with some awe by those he had fought for, and now their sons who were if anything, it was rumoured, more rebellious than both of their parents put together.

'No, and if you ask me . . .'

'Yes, yes,' Will interrupted him brusquely, then looked about him as though searching for someone to tell him what to do next.

'You had an appointment with Mr Greenwood then?'

'Aye, at eight thirty sharp.'

'Well, I can't help you and if that will be all I'll get back to me work,' the clerk said, implying that if this chap had nothing better to do with his time than hang about gossiping, he had.

'Thanks.'

Will turned away and walked down the steep flight of steps, hesitating on the bottom tread to gaze out into the yard. It was bustling with activity. There were enormous waggons pulled by enormous horses, all loaded with Chapman goods ready to be taken to the new railway station in Crossfold. Men grunted as they shifted huge sacking – wrapped bales of the finest fustians, velveteens, sateens and muslins, all to be despatched to the warehouses of Piccadilly and Portland Street in Manchester where they would be stored awaiting shipment to every corner of the known world.

Against a building at the far side of the yard other men unloaded bales of raw cotton each weighing 500 pounds, just come from the southern states of America by way of Liverpool. The Chapman enterprises were situated in five mills in different parts of the town, two concerned only with spinning, two with weaving and this one which combined the two processes and all the other processes connected with the manufacture of cotton cloth. It was huge, six storeys high and covering many acres. On the ground floor, where

47

the humidity was the highest, were power looms since the weaving process must be done in a damp atmosphere to prevent breakage of thread, and the heavy beams on which the warp thread was wound were of too great a weight for the upper floors. Here also, and on the first floor, were carding, drawing and roving rooms and above them spinning was done on the top four floors.

The men were hot and sweating from their exertions and their brawny muscled arms rippled in the smoke-hazed sunshine. There was a clatter of horse's hooves on the cobbles and a chestnut mare galloped dashingly into the yard, scattering the men and boys who were about to address themselves to the task of moving the bales of cotton to the blow room where they would be opened and the raw cotton cleaned and blended.

The men might have been a pack of dogs for all the notice the rider took of them. They were useful, naturally, for the work they did, but not to be spoken to, nor any particular care taken to avoid them since they were expected to get out of *his* way. He threw his leg over the horse's back and leaped lightly from the stirrup to the ground and with a shock Will realised that this was no arrogant lad, but a girl, a girl like none he had seen before. He could do no more than stand and stare, mouth slack and eyes wide with astonishment, since she was wearing a shirt and breeches more suitable to a male than a female.

'Where's that boy?' she shouted, her clear voice carrying above the crash of hooves on the cobblestones, the cries of the men and the creak of the pulley which was being used to winch some machinery to the first floor of the mill.

From across the yard a young lad darted amongst the activity, avoiding men and carts and horses until he reached the girl, catching the reins as she threw them at him, pulling the peak of his cap as he did so.

'Give her a good rub down, Sam. I shall be here for about half an hour and she's hot. We've been out since dawn up to Longworth Moor."

'Yes, Miss Tessa.'

*Miss Tessa!* Miss Tessa Harrison! He should have known, of course, for who else could it be? This was the girl about whom the manufacturing class of the whole of the Penfold Valley whispered and, by God, he could see why. He stared quite openly, unable to do anything else since she was undeniably the most magnificent young woman he had ever seen. Any female so dressed would be bound to attract attention but it was not just her clothing which drew every male eye in the yard to her, though that was indecent enough. It was the way she tossed her imperious head, the defiant stare which did not really *see* the low-born beings about her, the square and challenging set to her shoulders and the graceful way she strode across the yard towards him, masculine in its arrogance and yet eternally female in its fluid movement. There was insolence written in every line of her taut young body but its symmetry was spellbinding to these men whose own wives revealed little of their bodies to them, and then more than likely only when the candle had been blown out. Her young breasts, unbound beneath the silk of her shirt, bounced joyously as she walked and Will felt his breath catch in his throat.

Bloody hell! How did she get away with it? She must be no more than sixteen – that was what the clerk in the counting house had told him – the daughter of a well-known and well-regarded woman, the niece of one of the wealthiest men in south Lancashire. A female of her class could lose not only her reputation but with it the chance of a good marriage which was her destiny in life, so he had heard, if she were to be seen talking, unchaperoned, to a man who was not a close relative. Not a whisper of gossip, even of the most innocent, must touch her. She would be guarded like a precious jewel, always accompanied by another lady and never, never allowed to be alone with a gentleman, not even the one she would marry. Dressed like schoolgirls in modest gowns were the ones *he* had seen in their carriages, usually in white, bonneted, gloved, every inch of flesh which might

49

be considered indecent hidden from sight and not even the turn of an ankle revealed to any man until they were married.

But Miss Tessa Harrison's legs, the soft curve of her booted calf, the long, firm muscles of her thigh, the twin globes of her buttocks, all rippled beneath the fine stuff of her breeches and her eyes looked challengingly into his, not caring, or so it appeared, for her own reputation, nor indeed considering whether she had one.

When she reached where he still stood rooted to the bottom step of the stairway which led up to the counting house, she stopped. There was a deep silence for several tense moments as she waited for him to move aside. Her gleaming grey eyes, or were they silver he wondered in awe and confusion, cat's eyes, the pupils outlined with a thin black line, stared directly into his. In that first fleeting moment he felt a strong urge to step hurriedly out of her path, to fumble with his forelock as the inferior orders were expected to do to those above them, to go bright red and mouth some humble greetings – but something in him would not allow it and his eyes refused to drop away from hers.

'What are you staring at?' she asked rudely, her eyes pale and dangerous. The small riding crop she carried slashed against her leg and he had the distinct impression she would like nothing better, indeed would have not the slightest hesitation in using it on him or on anyone who stood in her way, but he did not move. His mouth curved in an amused smile.

'At you, my lass,' he answered softly, watching the hot colour flood beneath her white skin. 'As is every man in this yard and can you blame them?' Deliberately he let his gaze travel down the length of her body.

'You insolent . . .' Her mouth gaped in amazement and the scathing words with which she obviously longed to flay him lodged in her throat. Tessa Harrison was not often lost for words of any kind, and she knew many more than a lady should, but it seemed they had become misplaced some-where between her brain which leaped wildly to consume this presumptuous millhand, and her mouth which hung foolishly open. Her eyes blazed into his whilst her furious mind considered some way in which she might reduce him to his proper and inferior place in life. But even whilst it did so, some tiny core of her woman's sensibility, indepen-dent and extraordinarily wilful, pondered on the pleasing shape of his hard mouth, the smoky brown depths of his eyes which had the most curious amber flecks in them, the brown smoothness of his freshly shaved face and his smile, an odd slanting smile which gave him a decidedly whimsical expression. He was a head taller than she was, with wide muscular shoulders and yet his waist and hips were slim. He leaned indolently against the door frame, his manner saying quite plainly that it was of no particular interest to him whether he had offended her or not and it was perhaps this which intrigued her the most.

'You are unforgivably rude,' she managed to say, foolishly, she realised.

'Mebbe I am.' His smile deepened into an amiable grin. 'But you can't expect men, if they are men that is, to be unaffected by the sight of such . . .' Again he let his gaze wander speculatively up and down her lovely, quite aud-aciously displayed body, 'such splendour,' he finished softly.

'I could have you flogged for this, you know that, don't you?' she said, just as softly, and somehow, though the words they were saying were quite clear in their meaning, their expressions seemed to imply something else, something which neither could quite grasp.

'Nay, hardly. If you don't want to be looked at, my lass, then you shouldn't make a spectacle of what no sane man could resist taking a peep at, or even two.' Will's grin became even wider, showing the strong white teeth which were a legacy of the pitchers of milk and lumps of cheese he had consumed as a boy and she found herself watching his mouth with a surprising intensity. 'You mun be used to

51

taking offence, I dare say,' he went on engagingly, meaning no impertinence now since what he said must be the truth. 'Dressed like that every man between here and Oldham would be hard pressed to keep his eyes off you.'

'Who the devil are you to air your views on my appearance?' she managed to gasp. 'What I wear is nobody's business and certainly none of yours, whoever you are.' She had recovered herself now, the hot flash of her temper exploding quite visibly. 'And I should be obliged if you would stand aside and let me pass.' Her face had gone strangely white, a pale translucent white as her fury increased, and her eyes had become almost transparent. She lashed her riding crop about her leg, in danger of hurting herself so menacing was her rage. Her nostrils flared and her soft pink mouth had thinned into a hard line, straining to find the words to punish him, to spit them out and turn them on him, whoever he might be. No one, except perhaps her Uncle Joss and he was hardly ever at home, had ever defied her dangerous spirit, had even had the courage to try to curb it. From the first nanny in whose arms she had been put at birth when her mother had hurried back to the mill which was her greatest concern, to the last young governess who had been employed to educate her, not one had had the resolution which was needed to discipline Tessa Harrison and so she had come to young womanhood believing herself to be infallible. She pleased herself, barging her way through whatever obstacle was put in her path. Her cousin Drew was the same, knocking aside or breaking any opposition which threatened him. Pearce, though just as bent on his own way, was a shade more subtle, perhaps a shade cleverer than they. He had a knack of climbing *over* a hurdle, of getting exactly what he wanted but with less wear and tear on the nerves, the temper, the peace of mind and sanity of everyone involved in their upbringing. She and Drew often admired the way he did it, watching as he teased and cajoled until he had what he wanted, marvelling at his patience but not caring to try it themselves. She had moved, as they did, through sixteen years of her life expecting and getting everything she had ever wanted from it. It might be a nuisance in the evening when her mother insisted she wore a dress instead of her customary boots and breeches to the dinner table, but it was worth the bother for the freedom she was allowed at other times. She did not know, and did not care to ask lest it be curtailed, why her mother was so liberal, so different from the mothers of other girls of her acquaintance. It was enough for Tessa that she was: she took advantage of it and of every moment of liberty she could, blessing the mills which kept her mother so preoccupied.

'Get out of my way, you ill-mannered lout,' she hissed now, 'before I take my crop to you and wipe that foolish grin from your face. I don't know what you are doing here loitering in the doorway when you should be about some labour, but I intend to let my uncle know and you will be fired immediately.'

'Now then, lass,' Will said mildly, 'there's no need for that. I were only telling you the truth and well you know it, else why should you get in such a tantrum? Any lass who dresses . . .'

'By God, I won't stand here to be insulted by some . . . some yard labourer in my mother's mill. Are you to leave now or am I to have you thrown out?'

Will's face hardened and the amused and perfectly amicable expression in his eyes disappeared. He moved down from the bottom step and out into the yard. The sunlight fell on the short, rough cap of his hair, shading its pale brown to a pleasing, glinting fairness. He wore plain kersey breeches of good grey with stout black knee-boots and his jacket was of dark green corduroy. His shirt was a paler grey than his breeches and in the open neck was knotted a jaunty, freshly ironed red neckerchief. He looked just what he was: a labouring man who had come up in the world and certainly not the yard-hand she had thought him to be. He was a man who had, by hard work and self-education, risen from the thousands of faceless, nameless operatives who minded the mules and looms in the cotton factories of Lancashire; a man who could claim a position of responsibility, perhaps not yet of the manager class but not too far below it. He was about twenty-seven or eight with a look of good-natured tolerance, an easy-going man and yet there was a keen intelligence, a tough-fibred shrewdness about him which said he would be a hard man to take advantage of.

'Well?' Miss Harrison of Greenacres demanded loftily. 'Shall I call these men to throw you into the street or will you go unaided?' But her eyes studied his height and width somewhat uncertainly for now he was out of the shadows she could see he was taller, heavier, stronger, than any man in the yard.

'I think I'll stay just where I am,' he said softly.

'Very well.' She turned away from lifting her chin with the disdain of the young thoroughbred she was. She raised her hand and beckoned to four brawny men who had stopped work to watch, giving their undivided attention, as did every man in the yard, to the scene at the foot of the counting-house stairs.

'I would be obliged if you would throw this man into the street at once,' she told them imperiously. 'See, you four over here, if you please.'

'I'd save your breath if I were you, lass,' Will said pleasantly enough. 'You don't want to make more of this than you already have. I am here to see Mr Greenwood and I doubt he'd take kindly to a brawl on his counting-house steps.'

'*You!* To see my uncle? Rubbish.' She did not even bother to turn her contemptuous glance on him but continued to gesture towards the four men who were reluctantly moving towards her, their eyes on the uncompromising man who stood at her back.

'They will not take me on, lass, believe me.'

'They will if I tell them to and when my family hears of

54

the insulting way you have addressed me my cousins will give you the biggest hiding...'

'Lass, lass, give over. You're only making a show o' thissen. I meant no harm when I said every man in the yard was looking at you, nor offence. I was merely stating the obvious and surely to God you must know it, if that's the way you always dress. What man could resist it? They've never seen such fine...' Despite himself he could not help but grin and she turned, her expression menacing and her crop darted towards his chest, snapping against the knot in his neckerchief.

'Yes? Fine what?'

Will pushed his hands through his hair in exasperation and wondered how in hell he had got into this ridiculous situation. Why had he even bothered to speak to this girl when all he had to do in the first place was step aside and let her pass? She evidently believed she was above every consideration, every rule, every discipline with which life was ordered. It was nowt to him what she wore, how she spent her days or into what trouble, as a rebel, they led her. He had meant no disrespect, none at all. He had been amused and strangely stirred by her appearance, as any man would be, but she had turned on him like a wildcat, creating this explosive situation in which not only he and herself were involved, but every damned man in the yard. There was not one moving, from nine-year-old boys, delighted by this diversion in their humdrum day, to older men who should have known better.

'Miss Harrison, will you not lower that riding crop?' He grinned for it was all so foolish, so childishly foolish. 'I'd not want to have to take it from you.' Instantly he could have bitten his tongue for it seemed she could resist no challenge; that everything said to her which she did not care for, must be opposed.

She grinned.

'Try! Go on! Take the crop and I shall say nothing to my uncle or my cousins of your insolence.' The end of the small whip just tickled his cheek and he felt the irritation in him stir to something else. He was a man slow to anger, equable, since his size and strength made other men reluctant to tackle him. But this bloody girl was like a persistent wasp: nothing to be afraid of but ready to sting if she could, to hurt him in any way she could, and no matter how many times he waved her away, she buzzed in again and again to attack wherever she found an opening.

'Oh, for God's sake, lass, be off about your business and let me take care of mine...' The whip lashed out to sting his cheek sharply. She smiled brilliantly, her eyes vivid and mocking, her lips curved maliciously over her white teeth as a trickle of blood ran down his face.

'You were saying...?' She danced away from him, her pert breasts lifting delightfully against her shirt.

The smoky brown softness of his eyes darkened dramatically. He put up a hand to his cheek, then looked at the blood on his fingers. His voice was ice cold and round the yard there was a concerted hiss from a dozen or more throats as the men pressed in closer.

'You need a good thrashing, Miss Harrison, and have done for a long while, that's what I'm saying, and if you were mine I'd see you had one before this day was out. And every day until you had learned some manners.' Before she could close her astounded mouth or blink her incredulous eyes he had taken her crop away from her and with a gesture of contempt snapped it in two over his bent knee. He threw it to the ground and her gaze followed it, the expression on her face quite unbelieving.

The yard was as silent and still as the cemetery on the outskirts of the town. There was no movement beyond that of the horse's tail as it swished at the flies which tormented it. The men waited, stunned by the big man's impudence. They waited for Miss Tessa to erupt into the savagery of which they knew her to be capable but the sound of another horse entering the yard turned all heads except those of Will Broadbent and Tessa Harrison, who continued to stare

56

challengingly at one another. Not until Charlie Greenwood spoke did Tessa Harrison tear her gaze away.

'Tessa, what are you doing here?' He threw the reins of his horse to the waiting boy and walked tiredly towards the doorway, his eyes somewhat vague as though he had things on his mind other than his mill and was merely being polite.

'Charlie, this man has . . .' She turned angrily to him.

'Not now, sweetheart, I have been . . .'

'But, Charlie, you cannot mean to let this pass. He has . . .'

'What pass, Tessa?' He had reached them by now and as though he had only just become aware of the tension in the yard he turned to look about him and at once every man and boy sprang into action and the yard became alive again.

'What's been going on here, Tessa?' he asked, but his slumped shoulders and strained expression said he really did not want to know and at once, to Will's surprise, she went to him and took his hand.

'It's nothing, Charlie, really. Some small disagreement, resolved now but what . . . ? Is there news of . . . ?' Her voice was soft, amazingly so, Will thought, the flashing eyes and furious clenching of her jaw completely gone as her concern for her uncle showed in her face.

'Aye, two hours since . . . but . . .' He sighed deeply.

'Not . . . ?'

'Yes, dead, poor little mite . . . a girl . . .'

'Oh, Charlie, I'm so sorry. And Laurel . . . ?'

'Sleeping now. I stayed with her. That's why I'm late.'

He turned away from her abruptly and found himself face to face with Will Broadbent. Conscious suddenly that he was saying more than was decent before a stranger, his voice was sharp.

'Do you have business here, Mr . . . er . . . ?'

'Will Broadbent, and I believe we have an appointment, Mr Greenwood, eight thirty sharp, but I can come back, sir, if you're . . .' Will was polite and yet he showed no humility for he was a man who knew his own worth. He was courteous as a man should be, not just with this man who he

57

hoped would give him the vacant post of under-tackler, but with anyone who, in his opinion, deserved it. Unruffled, honest of expression and sure of himself, but in his eyes was a look which conveyed his sympathy, the sympathy one man shows another who is grieving. Mr Greenwood was not himself and though Will had taken precious time to come to see him, it would not be right to press the man at this moment.

Tessa Harrison might no longer have existed for all the notice he now took of her. He was here by appointment, one made by Mr Greenwood only yesterday when Will had approached him in the yard. Naturally, he was well aware that employment at the Chapman factory was hard to come by for every job which fell vacant had two dozen applicants waiting to fill it. It was like working in heaven, it was said, compared to the dozens of other mills in the valley. Besides the decent working conditions in their mills the Greenwood family had built a school and all those who worked here, into the second generation now, could read and write, were well set up, healthy and cheerful, with none of the deformities which were to be found in the mill where Will presently worked. That was one of the reasons he wanted to leave it and be decently employed without the dreadful necessity of trying to get a day's work from operatives who were underpaid, underfed and exploited by the unscrupulous owner.

The repeal in 1846 of the hated Corn Laws, which had made rents high and living low, had alleviated matters somewhat for the lower classes as the price of bread came down, but there was still hunger, disease, squalor, long hours and hard labour in most textile mills. There were still strikes in which strikers' families starved and men, maddened by despair, ran amok, smashing, killing. But the 'hungry forties', as they were calling them, were surely done with now as trade boomed, mills prospered and unemployment was on the decline. The cotton towns, though they were for the most part a hideous, unplanned sprawl of delapidated cottages, broken pavements, rutted tracks and open drains, would surely improve with the Greenwood family's living example of how things might be done. A decent day's work would be rewarded with a decent wage.

'You're after the job in the spinning room?'

'Aye, sir. I want to work decent and ... well, where I am now ... it's not to my liking, but if you're ... I can come back ...'

'No ... no, come up, Broadbent, and we'll talk about it.' Charlie Greenwood turned to his niece who still held his arm. 'You'd best be off home, sweetheart. Nay, don't pull your lip at me, lass. You shouldn't be here in the first place, you know that.' He smiled affectionately, then without allowing her to speak again turned away and, indicating to Will to follow him up, began to climb the stairs.

He was on the top road which led from Crossfold to Edge-clough where he had lodgings, when she rose from the spiky bushes of gorse which lined the track and amongst which she had been sitting, coming, it seemed to him in that moment, from the very ground beneath his feet.

It was almost noon and the sun fell directly on the glossy cape of her dark hair which had escaped the chenille net. The beauty of it caught his breath, then his irritation, at himself for being so affected by it and at her for her fool-hardiness in being here, alone, sharpened his voice.

'Good God, Tessa Harrison, what the devil are you doing up here by yourself? Don't you know there are all manner of ruffians on these moors? Have you no sense? And what is your family thinking of to allow it?'

She shook her head and shrugged as though to ask what that could possibly have to do with him.

'Did you get the job?'

'Why should you care?' His voice was set and closed.

She smiled and he felt his heart lurch against his breast-bone; then he turned away so that she might not see his face. It appeared that she bore him no ill-will for what had happened in the yard, indeed, now that it was over and done

59

with, she found it amusing. She had a quick, hot temper, her smile said, but she was not one to harbour a grudge nor to sulk over it, as many women would, and her refreshing candour moved him in some strange way.

'It's nothing to me, really,' she answered lightly. 'Just put it down to curiosity. There were fifteen applicants, you know. I wondered what you had that they hadn't.'

'And have you decided?'

'I was hoping you would tell *me*.'

He sighed and turned back to her. 'Don't you think you had better get on your horse and go home as your uncle suggested?'

'I rarely do as people suggest, as you must have noticed.' She lifted her autocratic head then grinned impishly and he could not help but smile back.

'That's true, and yes, I got it. I start next Monday. Nice chap, Mr Greenwood.'

'I know. We all are in the Greenwood family.'

'Really?' His smile was rueful now and he raised his eyebrows.

'Mm. Though I'm not related by blood, of course.'

'Oh, aye. How's that then!' He found himself responding to her completely natural manner. It seemed not to occur to her that they had met for the first time only that morning, or even that he was to be employed in the family mill. She found him intriguing. He interested her and so she satisfied that interest in the only way she knew how. She asked questions regardless of his station in life, or hers.

'My mother was adopted. She has no idea where she came from.' She sat down on a sun-warmed rock indicating that he should sit beside her and again it seemed an entirely natural thing to do.

'Oh, aye.' His eyes were very soft as he studied this amazing girl who could in one moment be a bold-faced minx, and the next almost demure. He hesitated for a moment as though debating with himself on whether to speak, then:

'I was t'same,' he said quietly.

'The same?'

'Aye. Came with a cartload of others to Abbotts when I was no more than a nipper and I've bin there ever since. Mind you, I was a strong lad. God knows where I'd come from but wherever it was they'd fed me well, so I survived. I think that's why I love these hills so well, this moorland . . .'

'Why, Mr Broadbent?' She was quite enthralled and again he was bewildered by the mercurial changes in her moods. He felt a thrill go through him to have captured her complete attention, then a surge of irritation at feeling it, but he went on nevertheless for it was delightful to have those incredible eyes gazing so earnestly into his.

'Because we were shut up so much. It wasn't until I was a man grown that I could please myself, you see, then I discovered all this.' He waved a hand in the general direction of the great sweeping moorland which lay all about them and her own eyes followed the gesture. 'When I was a child I spent my Sundays, first at church where the millmaster's wife seemed to think it her duty to send me and my companions, then cleaning the machines on which the following day we were to labour. We had no time for tramping the moors, I can tell thee, even if it had been allowed, which it wasn't, or we'd the strength, which we hadn't. Apprentices, as we were called, were not well fed, Miss Harrison, and we had to be in the loomgate or jennygate from five in't morning until eight at night. It was a long time for a child.'

'You seem to have done well on it, Mr Broadbent.' It was not meant as a criticism, merely a statement of fact. Her eyes ran over his broad shoulders and the long strength of his limbs and as they did so they narrowed approvingly and she felt a not unpleasant flutter in the vicinity of her throat as the pulse there quickened. He really was a most unusual man with his strong, good-humoured face, his lazy, slanting smile. He had a way of talking, articulate and open, and though now and again he fell back into the way of speech of the working man he appeared to be, he was what she supposed would be called well educated. He was looking at her now in that gleaming, speculative way which she recognised, despite her youth, as the admiration of a man for a woman. He liked her, she could tell that, despite the battle they had fought in the mill yard. And that was another thing. Not many men would have had the daring – which she admired – to stand up to her in that way.

'Aye, well...' He grinned disarmingly and she leaned closer to him, her eyes filled with her curiosity. 'If you promise not to send for the nearest constable I'll tell you how I came to thrive where others didn't.'

'Oh, please.' She hitched herself even closer and he wondered at the trust and confidence of this girl. Though he was to be an employee in her family's mill, like hundreds of other men, he could very easily mistake her friendliness as an invitation for something else, which would not be hard to do, he admitted. A man might take advantage of what she seemed to offer and though it was doubtful any man would achieve much with this fireband, he thought wryly, she would be seriously offended. And yet why should it concern *him*, he asked himself as she smiled winningly up at him, her eyes like grey crystal in the vibrant beauty of her face, and he did not know the answer.

'Should you not be getting home?' he asked, suddenly aware that he himself was not immune to her attraction, to the interest she showed and the pleasure she seemed to find in his company. What man can resist a pretty woman who hangs on his every word? Though he knew it was probably only the reaction of a girl bored with her own class and curious about his. *He* could not resist *her*.

'Oh, no, please go on.'

He allowed himself to smile again, his eyes on her curving mouth. 'Well ... I used to steal from the larders of those who had more to eat than I did.' His face became serious and her soft ... dear God ... soft pink mouth dropped open in awe.

'Where ...?'

'Every place I could find with a window I could open. Not the poor, of course, since they had nowt worth stealing anyway, but on most nights I would slip out when the others fell into their exhausted sleep and find a house which looked as though the occupants fed on more than cold-water oats and pigswill.'

'*Pigswill?*' She shuddered and pressed her shoulder against his.

'Aye, for that's what the others ate, lass. At first I'd hardly the strength to walk the necessary miles, for these houses were not close to the mill, as you can imagine . . .'

'No, indeed.'

'. . . but gradually, with the food I ate, and I only stole what was nourishing, and the milk I drank, I became stronger and could go further afield. I was a very resourceful lad, Miss Harrison,' – and you are a resourceful and strong man, Will Broadbent, and will go far, she had time to consider – 'and I meant to survive. I used to enjoy those walks, striding out in the summer night when it was warm and all scented with the aroma of wildflowers, or the heather drifting down from the hills. I had known only the stink of the mill, you see, and the spinning room and all the unwashed people who worked there.'

'Of course.' Her eyes were enormous in her pointed face, a face bemused and wondering, and he had the most overpowering inclination to place his mouth on the one which parted in fascinated interest as he told his tale. He tore his gaze away to stare into the sunlit valley below, then he grinned.

'Promise me you won't breathe a word to your uncle or I'll lose me grand new job afore I start?'

'My uncle? Why?'

'One of the larders I robbed was at Greenacres.'

'Oh Lord, you didn't?' He could see he had impressed her enormously, as would anything which was out of the ordinary, different, or smacked of defiance of authority.

'I did, Miss Harrison. I helped myself to a turkey leg which

I knew would not be missed, a lump of the most delicious cheese which I have since discovered was from our own Lancashire, drank a pitcher of milk, thick with cream, and some plum pudding. It was Christmas, you see.'

He had not said it to gain her sympathy, just to demonstrate why he had remembered the exact meal on which he had dined that night in the house in which she herself was probably upstairs sleeping. But somehow his words moved a soft and dangerous thing inside her and she took fright at it since this man was a stranger after all.

She cleared her throat and blinked her eyes as though to clear the fog of curious emotion which blurred them, then stood up quickly and turned away for she did not want him to see and wonder over her sudden agitation. In her mind's eye she could still visualise the tiny scar he had on his chin, no more than a small indent, and she wondered wildly how he had come by it in his deprived and loveless childhood; then, even more wildly, why it should concern her.

'I'd best get you home, Miss Harrison,' he said abruptly.

They were the exact words needed to release her from the strange enchanted spell his voice had cast about her. She was no weak girl who needed a man's help to get her from one place to another. She was Tessa Harrison who could ride gloriously to hounds and keep up with the best horseman in the county. She could leap the highest hedges and the widest streams. She could shoot fifty birds with fifty shots and had been known, though her family were not aware of it, to dress herself in her cousins' clothing and frequent a bare-knuckle prize fight and even a bear baiting with Drew and Pearce and Nicky Longworth. She had not enjoyed either, but she had *seen* them, had proved herself as strong and resolute as any man and she did not need this chap to escort her home.

'I need no help to get me home, Mr Broadbent,' she said sharply, her eyes flaring in a burst of annoyance which came from nowhere to attack him.

'As you like, Miss Harrison.' His voice was just as curt for he had found himself to be quite devastated when the softness, the sweet womanliness of the past few minutes was dashed away coldly as the affronted Miss Harrison leapt lightly on to the back of the small mare she whistled up.

'Safe journey, then,' he could not help adding for it seemed to him it was a long, hard road she was to take.

'Heavens, Mr Broadbent, I am to go but to Greenacres, after all.'

'I doubt it, Miss Harrison.' Turning swiftly away from her, his face curiously stern, he strode off in the direction of Edgeclough.

## 4

They stood in the office of the spinning-mill manager, their faces set in identical expressions of boredom, young gentlemen impeccably suited in the sober uniform of a businessman: black frock coat, light grey trousers, plain grey waistcoat and a shirt front which was immaculate. Each wore a pearl tie-pin in his neck cloth, a present from their mother on their seventeenth birthday, just gone. Their loathing of commerce could not have been more evident and Mr Wilson sighed, for what was the use of it? They wasted *his* time, which was valuable, and their own, which was not, but Mr Greenwood had insisted upon it and there was nothing the manager could do. He had worked at Chapman Manufacturing for nearly twenty years, starting as a spinner, then overlooker, a promotion to foreman, then manager of this mill two years ago, answerable to Mr Charlie Greenwood himself.

For the past few months, ever since they had left school,

the twin sons of Mr and Mrs Joss Greenwood, who owned Chapmans, had been coming to the mill each morning at five thirty. Slowly, week by week, they were moving through the whole process of preparing and spinning yarn, starting in the blow room where the bales of raw cotton were opened, cleaned and blended ready for combing. Here the impurities and short fibres were removed until the cotton was ready for spinning. There were five more procedures to be gone through – winding, knitting, warping, sizing and drawing in – before the spun yarn was ready for weaving and the cloth finished. All must be thoroughly learned by Masters Drew and Pearce, and though they presented themselves each day and were seen to be there in the flesh, so to speak, it could not be said that either of them had the slightest notion of how the simplest process came about, nor the slightest desire to be told.

They had been lounging against the stable-yard wall, just beyond the laundry, when nemesis had fallen. A pretty laundry maid stood between them, all three giggling over some nonsense the boys were pouring into her willing ear, when Joss Greenwood had come across them. He had arrived at Greenacres unexpectedly, perhaps for a purpose, who was to say? Certainly not the two boys whose eyes had widened in alarm as his hands fell on their shoulders, the expression on his face freezing the blood in their veins.

'You will settle down to some decent occupation,' he said when they stood before the desk in his study, 'and that means, naturally, in the trade which employed your maternal and paternal grandfathers. Your place is in the mill. You are to be commercial gentlemen as not only your father, your grandfather but your great-grandfather were before you, not young squireens like Nicky Longworth or Johnny Taylor who were born to it. Do you understand?'

They said they did.

'*You* were born to be manufacturers and manufacturers you will be. That is why you were educated at the local grammar school and not at public school as your friends were, so that you might get something in your heads other than a bit of Latin and Greek. Do I make myself clear?'

They said he did.

'Now I appreciate that you have no particular aptitude for it; that you have no inclination towards machinery, nor the adding up of profit and the subtraction of loss. But you will learn, for that is what you are to do with your lives now that your schooling is ended. Is that clear?'

They said it was.

'You will accompany your Aunt Jenny and Charlie to the mill each day, starting at five thirty, as they do, and you will learn to get on with those about you. To start with you will go with Wilson on his daily round of the mill at Chapmanstown, since it is the largest, and make yourselves conversant with all the processes of spinning, and work with Aunt Jenny in the counting house getting to know the overall business strategy. You will travel to Manchester with Charlie to acquaint yourselves with the trading side of the business, see to the purchase of raw cotton, learning from him, and others, how to judge *when* to buy and how much to *pay*. There will be the organising of credit to our customers, the collection of trade debts in world markets and the proper knowledge of how to husband your resources. You will agree, will you not, that there is a lot to be learned and the quicker you get started the sooner you will be able to take over when the time comes. Is that understood?'

They said that it was.

'You will go to the Cloth Hall each week, or perhaps more often, depending on trade. Your lives will be controlled, not by your own whims and fancies but by the factory bell. There will be no galloping off to join the Squire's hunt at the first hint of autumn. You will work in the spinning rooms and weaving sheds and get yourselves dirty, as I did, as your Aunt Jenny did, as Charlie did, as your own mother did, and you will become millmasters, the manufacturing gentlemen you were destined to be. Do you understand? And if I hear you have disobeyed me I shall have you whipped into the mill yard and keep you permanently without money until you stay there.'

Mr Wilson was droning on and Drew yawned.

'. . . designed to spin and wind automatically. It will also make the necessary adjustments between successive draws to take account of the growing size of the cop and the decreasing length of the bare spindle blade, as you will see when we go into the spinning room . . .'

What is the old fool blethering on about? Drew's eyes signalled to Pearce. God knows, he was answered, and could you care less? The two handsome boys, just seventeen years old and destined never to go to Cambridge, never to go on a Grand Tour as Johnny Taylor's father had promised *him*, never to go *anywhere*, their despairing expressions said, but across the yard and into the spinning room, or to Broadbank and the weaving sheds, stared desperately into one another's eyes.

'Now have you any questions before we go into the spinning room, young sirs?' Mr Wilson asked genially, shortsightedly, hopelessly, since he knew there would be none.

They said they hadn't.

'Right, then if you will follow me we will step across the yard and Broadbent will show you the self-actor in motion.'

Pearce told himself that this time it would be better. No one had warned him on that first day two months ago when they had entered the spinning room, and so the shock had been all the greater, and he had felt that he could not really be blamed for the way he had reacted then. He and his brother had been reared like the young colts up in the paddocks of Greenacres and the contrast had been appalling. Suddenly they had been transferred from the lush meadows where they had bucked and kicked their high-spirited heels since the day they were born. Taken from the sun-dappled freedom, from the joy of being skittish with their own kind, it had seemed to Pearce, they had been put, like the pit-ponies they had heard about, in the black confines of the underground mines. That was how the spinning room had appeared to Pearce, used as he was to wild moors, high-vaulted skies and the pungent smell of heather and gorse in his nostrils.

There had been a general darkness at first, a lack of the fresh air and sunshine to which they were both accustomed, though the windows of the mill stood wide open. The noise was indescribable; clatter, rattle, bang, the swish of thrusting leavers, the crash of carriages 'letting in', the shouts of the minders as they summoned a piecer or a scavenger. What seemed to be hundreds of people crowded down the long rows of spinning mules with literally thousands of spindles and the heat was such he could distinctly see the oil bubble from the pinewood planking of the floor. Little piecers ran barefoot repairing broken threads, skidding and slipping, some of them, with the speed they went, rolling instinctively to avoid the gliding carriages, well aware of the consequences should one of the advancing monsters catch them.

A film of flock, or 'fly', as it was called, immediately settled on the fine coats of the two young gentlemen and dusted their smoothly brushed hair. Pearce felt it invade his mouth as he took a deep breath, settling in his throat and drifting into his nostrils. His stomach lurched uneasily and the breath became trapped somewhere in his lungs. He knew himself to be suffocating. If he did not get out of here he would either vomit the substantial breakfast he had eaten all over his new, pale grey waistcoat, or faint right away like any languid maiden. The mass of interested faces, the noisy spinning mules, the straps and belts and wheels, the constant movement of women and children and machines all ran together, blending into a misted haze which floated before him and about him, and he had time only to fling himself backwards, down the steps and into the yard before nausea overtook him. He clung to the wall, watched by men who nudged one another slyly, their prediction that these two fine young gentlemen would never last the course becoming true on their very first day, it seemed. His face sweated and so did his body inside the immaculate crispness of his clean shirt. He felt dirty and wretched, a sensation he had never known before and he had not liked it. But he had been forced to go back, time and time again, and it had never got better. Never. The walls closed in on him; the machines appeared to glide towards him the moment he entered the room, hemming him in between their lethally moving parts. He swore he would overcome the sensation and was ashamed when he could not. He was afraid of nothing, just like Drew. They had ridden frighteningly wild horses ever since they had been big enough to climb on their backs. They had jumped hurdles higher than their own heads. They had gone out with the hunt and taken many a tumble, broken a bone or two, clambered back on and continued as though nothing had happened, smiling through the pain. They had fought boys bigger and stronger than themselves, had their eyes blacked and blacked a few in their turn, bloodied noses, and known no fear. The bleak, open barrenness of the moorland, vast and empty and cruel at times, an enemy of those who did not respect it, was their territory, a place he loved and roamed with Drew and Tessa, but it held no terror for him, unlike the hot, clammy, airless hell of the spinning room. And his terror grew with every visit, a terror he was forced to hide from everyone but Drew, and it shamed him.

On this day, as he followed Drew inside, the din and confusion which met him at the door instantly stunned him, taking his mind and his determination. His step faltered. His eyes went black and sightless and but for the broad back of his brother ahead of him he would have lost his way. He was like a sleep-walker, but some tiny, still-intelligent part of his mind told him he must just follow that back wherever it went: hang on to that thought, to that solid, dependable shape ahead of him, the brother who had never in all their young lives together let him down or deserted him, who had been his other half for sixteen years and who would lead him from this place which, with every second, was closing in on him.

But it was no use, his last desperate thought told him, as the greyness about him became black. He felt himself slip on the oil-soaked floor, his stomach heaved and the blood began to drain away from his head.

'Just bend ower, lad,' a light voice said and he felt a pressure on his arm and across his back and though it was not forceful he found himself obeying. He was hanging, head down – how in hell had he got here? – over a motionless machine. He could see nothing but oil and cotton-waste and the face, young and cheeky, of a little piecer who had crept beneath the machine to get a better look at him. There were bare feet everywhere, dirty and splayed, ugly some of them with swollen veins and joints, but the pair nearest to him, though just as dirty, were small and fine, narrow and really rather shapely. He sensed dozens of pairs of curious, probably amused eyes on him; then he was gripped again in a violent spasm of nausea.

'Come on, old chap,' a gentle voice said and familiar, strong brown hands, duplicates of his own, grasped his. He clung gratefully to them as they began to lead him, blind and ill, towards the doorway at the end of the interminably long room and out into the yard.

'Fresh air'll see 'im right,' a voice said briskly, as though the owner of it really had no time to be wasting on him, then he was out ... thank God, thank God ... out of the smell and the din and the enveloping walls, the hellish confusion, and at once he was recovered.

He lifted his head and looked into Drew's concerned face, which grinned at once, letting him know that though he did not really understand what ailed his twin he was quite willing to try, and to stand shoulder to shoulder with him should anyone turn awkward over it. There was a girl there, small, light-boned and thin and yet giving the impression, strangely, that she was as sturdy as the weeds which grew in the hedgerow. Her face was pale, and plain as a bleached yard of cotton. Her eyes were a sharp and almost colourless blue and her fine, mousy hair was dragged back from her face into what must surely have been a painful knot at the back of her head. Her bare feet stepped without concern on the bare cobbles and he knew that this must be the person who had, with her quick thinking, saved him from losing consciousness.

'Tha'll be reet now. Tek a few deep breaths,' she ordered, wiping her hands down her sacking apron. She did not look away when his eyes met hers, nor shuffle about awkwardly as the lower orders often did in the presence of their superiors, but met his glance steadily. He had never seen a girl less comely and yet she had a quiet dignity which was unusual in someone of her age and class. 'Tha'll get used to it, like we all 'ave to,' she added ready, now that he was recovered, to get back to her work.

'Like hell I will,' he answered harshly, wiping his arm across his sweated face. 'I'll run away to sea before I'll go in there again.'

'Hold on, brother.' Drew's lazy drawl and narrowed eyes indicated to him that the undertackler, Broadbent, was not far away but Pearce was beyond caution.

'No! You hold on, brother. It's not you who turns faint like some puling woman...'

'I never 'eard such nonsense in me life. Turnin' sick ower a bit o' stink. We none of us like it, Mr Greenwood, but we've no choice. It's work or starve wheer I come from an' let me tell thi, we're glad o't work. 'Ave thi ever bin in Abbotts mill or any on 'em in this valley? 'Ave thi? Conditions 'ere are like a palace compared to t'other 'uns. Thee'd 'ave summat ter be sick ower if thi 'ad ter work theer.'

Both young gentlemen turned to stare at the girl who spoke. She might have been some creature from another world, or a gatepost which one does not, naturally, expect to speak, so deep was the amazed consideration they gave her now. Indeed, despite their close proximity to them, the two boys had never actually *noticed* an operative in the weeks they had been working in the mill. The girl stared back at them grimly, such a plain, drab little thing, resembling nothing so much as the sparrows which nested in the ivy on the walls of Greenacres, a sparrow which, nevertheless, was prepared to take on two magnificent soaring eagles. Her expression asked quite plainly what else could you expect of these pampered young fools who were playing, reluctantly she had heard, at being commercial gentlemen. Their aunt and uncle knew exactly what she and the hundreds of others in the mill endured day after day, though this was a good mill. Both of them knew the meaning of *work*. These two young bucks, quite evidently, would soon tire of the discipline, the sheer physical discomfort of the factory floor and take themselves back to their old pastimes of shooting everything that took wing and riding like madmen with others of similar inclination, chasing the fox through the farmer's cornfield.

'I'll get back ter me machine, then,' she added coldly. 'Time's money ter me, an' I've already lost 'alf an 'our wi' thee.' With that she turned on her heel and walked away, her thin back straight, her narrow shoulders squared.

'Sorry about that, Mr Broadbent,' she said to the overlooker who still leaned in the doorway. He was watching the two young men. They were laughing now, quite amused, it seemed, by the strange girl who had given them the sharp end of her tongue but not the least offended since, really, did she matter? They had got themselves, through her, out of the damned spinning room and why not take advantage of it? They strolled towards the gate with the appearance of gentlemen who, having done their day's work, were off about more important matters, though it was barely seven o'clock.

'Nay, Annie, don't fret, lass. It's not the first time it's happened and it'll not be the last.'

'Does't tha think they'll come back, then?' she asked, surprised.

73

'Oh, aye. Their father's set on it, it seems. It's to be their mill, after all.'

'God 'elp us, then.'

'Happen he'll get over it, the sickness.'

''Appen, but that'll not mek 'im into a millmaister, Mr Broadbent.'

There was a sudden commotion at the closed gate and the man who had charge of the key ran frantically across the yard to unlock it. Every morning the gate was locked on those late-comers who had no legitimate excuse, such as the illness of a child, and not opened again until eight o'clock, but the girl who was shouting to be let in was not one of those and the gatekeeper knew better than to keep her waiting. The mare was restlessly sidestepping, catching her rider's impatience, and the gatekeeper fumbled with his keys whilst the voice on the other side urged him to get a move on. At last he had it open and in she came, hair flying out in a banner behind her, scattering the same men and boys Will had watched her disperse a few weeks ago. He had not seen her since that day but she was just the same. Heedless of those who got in her way, she went straight as an arrow towards her target, her two cousins who had turned to look at her.

She did not dismount. Drew put up a hand to her mare's nose as she leaned down to him. All the men in the yard, grumbling beneath their breath, had turned to look at her, as Will was sure she intended. Her mare moved sideways again, nervously shying away from the enormous waggon which was just entering the yard, but she held it in expertly, her gloved hands firm on the rein, her slim, muscled legs strong and lovely in their dove-grey breeches.

Her eyes narrowed as she caught sight of him across the heads of the men and there was a burst of laughter as she said something to her cousins. All three turned to look at him and he could feel the hard knot of anger tie itself beneath his breastbone. The two young men lounged indolently against the mill wall, their hands shoved deep in their

74

trouser pockets, their dark eyebrows arched, their eyes gleaming in identical amusement. He saw their good white teeth flash in their sun-darkened faces and then, with the insolence of the lordly young gentlemen they considered themselves to be, they turned away. He was nothing to them, merely that breed known as overlooker in their mill, a man *under* the man who was in charge of the spinners, but not of *them*. Pearce left the other two for a moment, making some sign to the boy who hung about the yard and whose job it was to attend to the horse of any caller. In a moment the boy returned, leading the two restive bays which the brothers rode. They all three turned to look at Will again, the girl grinning now to let him see that this was really *her* doing. The boys mounted gracefully and one turned to him, grinning, his voice flippant since they all knew he was lying.

'Some urgent business. Tell Wilson, if you please.' With their coat-tails flying and the girl's hair and ribbon streaming out behind her, they galloped madly from the yard, down the street towards the edge of town and the wild moorland which was the only place they really wished to be.

Mr Wilson came slowly down the steps from the first-floor spinning room, his face resigned but not unduly concerned since they were not *his* problem, thank God.

'Where the devil have those two gone now?' the men in the yard heard him say out loud, shrugging, for what else could you expect? It was no good trying to tame a bird which has flown free since it came from the egg and in their opinion, their good-humoured north-country faces seemed to say, best save your breath to cool your porridge. It was too late. A flogging once a week starting in the nursery was what those two had needed, her an' all, really, then happen they might have shaped themselves. Too late now, they repeated as they resumed the work which had been so violently disrupted, bloody glad it was nowt to do with them.

'Urgent business, they said, Mr Wilson,' Will answered

him, eyebrows sardonically raised, and was not surprised when Mr Wilson swore quite rudely beneath his breath before turning back to the stairs.

## 5

She had given her mare her head, letting her go flat out over the rough stretch of moorland known as Besom Hill, seeing the coarse grass blur beneath the animal's hooves. Her face was pressed close to the mare's neck as she bent down with her into the wind. Her dratted hair had come loose as usual, whipping about her head and eyes, blinding her for a moment, and she did not see the half a dozen rabbit holes until her mare swerved to avoid them. She felt herself move forward over the animal's neck, her co-ordination gone completely with her balance; when she hit the ground, though she landed in a clump of heather which broke her fall somewhat, the breath was knocked from her body. She lay for a minute or two, gasping for air, watching the sky swing in sickening loops above her, then as it steadied and became still and serene again, she sat up, looking around for her mare.

She was high up here, almost at the top of the moorland sweep with a splendid view of the rock-strewn stretch of moor which went on endlessly as far as the eye could see. It was bleak and treeless, rough ground pierced with moss-covered boulders, submerged in gorse and bracken, with a dozen shades of green from the paleness of the ferns which sheltered by a dry-stone wall, to the dark, cloud-shadowed foliage on the far side of the deep clough which split the land. A soaring, grey-green landscape, hard and enduring, cut with water and rocks, where a bird or two wheeled above her head, and nothing else.

There was no sign of her mare.

'Damnation,' she said softly, swinging back her mane of hair. Then, feeling for the ribbon which confined it and finding it gone, she pulled her scarf from around her neck and carelessly bound up the troublesome locks. She stood up and dusted off her cream, doeskin breeches. Shading her eyes from the sun, she looked about her, her eyes penetrating the vast landscape for a sight of her mare. There was nothing to be seen, no movement of any kind beyond that of the birds above her head.

It was not cold and the clouds were broken and low, some enfolding the top of the highest peaks. They moved quickly allowing the sun to show through, and for half an hour she sat on a rock and stared out across the tops, to the next and the next, whistling now and again to attract her mare, should she still be in the vicinity. But the mare was not inclined to show herself and would, no doubt, be well on her way to the stables at Greenacres by now. There was no alternative but to walk: almost five miles, she reckoned, skirting Edgeclough and Harrops Edge and following the rough moorland track to the back of the Greenacres parkland.

It was warm walking but very pleasant. She removed her jacket and was tempted to hide it under a rock, picking it up the next time she came this way for it was cumbersome to carry. She draped it over one shoulder, climbing steadily up the next rocky incline until she reached the brow, then, carried by her own momentum, almost running down the far side.

Her boots began to chafe her heel. She was used only to riding in them; in fact, come to think of it, she really had no footwear suitable for striding out across the hills since she rarely did it. She walked over the Squire's moor when she accompanied Drew and Pearce on one of his shoots but that was in a much more leisurely fashion, more of a stroll than a walk.

She skirted Edgeclough an hour later, clambering over a dry-stone wall to walk on the rutted path, once a 'salt-way', she had been told, which led past the town, or hamlet as it had been in the old days. The clamouring of factory bells and whistles announced the changing of shifts and far below she could make out the patient crowds of ant-like men, women and children streaming through half a dozen factory gates.

The moors were deserted, achingly empty, and the sun had gone completely as the summer's day began its slide towards twilight. Her boots were really rubbing now as she began the descent from Edgeclough towards Chapmanstown. Damn it, she would have to stop a minute and take them off. She must have blisters the size of a guinea on her heels. But if she took them off would she be able to get them on again, she wondered? Well, she'd rest for a moment and then go on. Her mare would have reached home without her by now and Walter would be running round the stable yard raising the alarm. There'd be a search party out in half an hour and she wanted to be well on her way before she met up with it. How very demeaning to have taken a tumble on this relatively easy stretch of moorland! Drew and Pearce would crow over it, saying she was not fit to be let out alone, which would bring the whole matter to her mother's attention. There would be hell to pay, probably an ultimatum to take Walter with her on future rides or some such nonsense.

They came over the brow of the hill just as she stood up, half a dozen or so of them. The man was of medium height but painfully thin and a washed-out, ferret-faced woman shuffled behind him pushing a broken-down hand-cart on which rattled and shook a festering pile of what Tessa could only describe as rubbish which threatened to fall off with every turn of the wheels. Slung out behind was a miscellaneous rabble of children of various ages and sizes, all

78

scratching and picking at themselves, with sore eyes and no teeth to speak of in their wizened, little old men's faces, small and stunted with rickety legs and no shoes to their dirty feet.

They all stopped when they saw her, as though she was some mirage shimmering ahead of them, which, in a way, she was. Who would expect to see a girl such as herself alone up here, a girl in a pure silk shirt, in breeches of the finest quality doeskin and boots of the finest quality leather, all of which would fetch a decent price in any market?

The man's eyes, which had been vague and empty, sharpened to flint. He did not turn to the tribe behind him, merely put out a hand which said 'leave this to me, we'll have us a grand supper tonight', and they all stood obediently, well used to taking his orders, it seemed.

'Good day to yer,' he said cheerfully, his Irish brogue so thick it was difficult to understand. '"Tis a great one, ter be sure.'

'Indeed,' she answered guardedly, beginning to walk towards him for he stood on the track down which she must go to reach Crossfold.

'Could yer spare a copper or two fer a starvin' family?' His eyes ran over her like the fleas which so evidently swarmed on himself and his family, to judge by the way they were scratching, and she dug her fingers into her own suddenly prickling scalp.

'I don't carry any money with me,' she said shortly, wishing to God she'd brought the dogs with her, cursing her own stupidity in leaving them at home. She'd imagined, as she had always done in the past when she had come across a vagrant or a tramp or one of the itinerant families she met, such as this one, that she had only to touch her heels to her mare's flank and she could outrun any man with dubious intentions towards her.

She began to edge past them. The man made no move to stop her, merely watching her with the child-like curiosity of someone set down amongst beings he had never before

79

clapped eyes on, and she began to breathe a little more easily. The woman even sketched a curtsey, though there was no respect in it, and it was not until she reached the last figure, a weasel-faced, cross-eyed, runny-nosed lad somewhat bigger than the others, that the whole family moved. The man must have made some signal behind her back and as she passed the boy, trying hard not to look into the nastiness of his face, his foot shot out and neatly inserted itself between her boots, bringing her down with her face in the dry-baked hardness of the track. They were all over her then, like a pack of squealing rats, hands and small, filthy feet pressing her down until the man's voice, harsh and expecting to be obeyed at once, shifted them all.

'Turn 'er over an' let's see what we got,' he commanded and several pairs of hands obliged until she was glaring up into the dirt-ingrained face, the cunning, jubilant eyes, the mouth in which there was nothing but blackened stumps, of the head of the family. For several minutes they all laughed and chattered evidently unable to believe their good luck and though Tessa struggled wildly, threatening them with everything from a flogging to transportation, even the gallows, they took no notice. In her heart where up to now there had been no more than outrage, alarm began to grow. She had believed that though they might take her boots, her beautifully cut and tailored tweed jacket, she had nothing more to fear than that: they were a family and therefore, though they might be thieves, would not use violence. But the man and the boy who had tripped her were looking at her in a nasty way, licking their cracked lips, their eyes on her freely moving, almost exposed breasts which strained through the silk of her shirt. The woman had become uneasy, shifty, watching her menfolk with the resignation of one who has long given up defiance or argument, and when told would obey without question.

The man did not speak, just lifted his eyes to those of his son and smiled. The boy smiled back at him and when the man, with a curt movement of his head to the woman and the rest of the group indicated that they were to move on, the gesture saying that he and the lad would be along presently, they obeyed at once.

Tessa began to scream. It was no more than the shrill cry of a rabbit when faced with a stoat, a despairing cry, but the woman turned back, her woman's sensibility giving her, for a moment, the pity one female feels for another who is to suffer as perhaps she once had done, as perhaps her own female children had done, despite their age.

'Get on, woman, 'tis nought ter do wi' you,' her husband, if that was what he was to her, said and struck her across the face. For a second, only the boy held Tessa; he was looking away towards his parents, waiting eagerly for what he was to share with his father, impatient for his mother to be dealt with as he had probably seen her dealt with a hundred times before.

Tessa was up then, and free of his grasp, pushing him out of her way since she was stronger than he was, bounding in terrifying leaps down and down the steep stretch of moorland, tearing herself on the spiky gorse, banging her ankles on angry rocks, her breath hot and cutting in her throat and chest, her back cringing away from what was behind her, her flesh flinching, expecting at every step to feel their hands. There was another wall ahead of her, higher than she was, dangerous with loose stones, crumbling and waiting only for an unwary hand or foot to bring it down. She had her fingers on the top cam stones, pulling at them to lift herself up and over, but her pursuers were at her back now, their hands reaching for her. She could smell their foul, unwashed bodies, the stench of the rotting teeth in their opened mouths, then she was carried backwards, flung into the waist-deep fern and bracken and her cry, her feeble cry of anguish, was strangled by a cruel hand.

The roar of rage could be heard as far away as Edgeclough, or so she believed later. Now she was conscious of nothing but a great, heavy shadow looming over her, of hands which she tried weakly to resist: then air and space

81

and light, emptiness, no sound but that of men's voices and men's bodies blundering away into the distance, becoming fainter and fainter, a blessed 'nothingness' which wrapped itself about her peacefully. She dared not look, of course, for fear she had imagined them to be gone and they would be standing over her, grinning, taunting. She curled herself up, her arms wrapped about her knees, pulling them high to her breasts, her head tucked into her shoulders, prepared to stay there until Drew or Pearce, or even Walter came for her, but a voice spoke up sharply.

'Nay, they've gone now. You've nowt ter be feared of. Mr Broadbent'll mek mincemeat of 'em, tha'll see.'

She peeped out from beneath her folded arms. A young girl was peering over the wall at her with an expression of disapproval which seemed to ask what else you could expect of a lass who wandered the hills all by herself, dressed up like she was, and if she had her way, a good thrashing would not go amiss. She was about her own age, a girl whom you'd not recognise tomorrow if you spoke to her today, so colourless was she. A girl with a pale face, pale eyes and pale scraped-back hair, wearing a clean, drab shawl and a bodice to match. The rest of her Tessa could not see.

'Are yer ter stay theer all day, then?' the girl asked tartly.

Tessa stood up slowly, turning anxiously towards the steep incline where, she supposed, the men had gone, then back to the girl.

'Who was it?' she quavered, a violent fit of shocked trembling beginning to shake her from head to foot. Even her teeth chattered.

'Come over't wall,' the girl ordered and Tessa obeyed without question. She was wrapped snugly in the girl's shawl. Her flowing hair was tied back again with the scarf, the hands which performed the task strangely gentle. She leaned gratefully against a shoulder which was thin but apparently strong and when the girl began to walk in the direction of Edgeclough, still with her strong young arms about her, Tessa went with her.

82

'Tha've nobbut thissen ter blame, tha' knows,' the girl said crossly, just as though Tessa had become involved in a minor tumble brought on by her own foolishness, as in a way she had. 'Theer's nowt in't world'd make me cross them moors on me own. Mr Broadbent lives up near me so me an' 'im always walk together, but if 'e's on different shift I wait while Aggie or Rose is ready. I used ter walk wi' me Mam but she ... well...' She shook her small head fiercely, not prepared to reveal anything more of herself to a stranger, it seemed. She continued to scold Tessa in the sharp voice of one who is used to being in command of others, taking no 'lip' but at the same time patting her shoulder awkwardly, giving her time to pull herself together, soothing her, not with obvious sympathy but with her own sensible belief that there was no use in crying over spilt milk so best get on with mopping it up.

They came to a small house in a row of similar houses: all neat and tidy, decent, with a bit of garden in front, the windows polished and the steps donkey-stoned. There was an air of spartan cleanliness about the one her rescuer entered. It smelled of carbolic and beeswax. The hearth was freshly brushed, the brick floor freshly swept, the table all set out with decent crockery, and floating out to greet them the smell of something cooking on the sparse fire. At the table sat four children. They all turned expectantly as Tessa's friend opened, then shut the door firmly behind her, the gesture saying quite clearly that what was done inside these four walls was no one's business but *theirs*.

'This 'ere young lady 'ad an accident so put kettle on't fire, our Nelly,' she said brusquely. Tessa found herself placed with little ceremony in the rocking chair by the fire, a cushion at her back, a buffet at her feet and all done with the minimum of fuss and no regard at all for her higher station in life. She might have been a casual acquaintance, perhaps another mill-hand, but made *comfy* just the same.

She still shivered and shook and when the tea was put in her hand she could scarcely hold it. She was settling into a badly shocked state now and the girl looked anxiously at her and kept going to the window to stare out into the darkening street.

'Get on wi' thy tea, our Polly,' she said to one little girl who was inclined to stare in awe at Tessa.

'Are tha not 'avin' any, our Annie?' the third girl asked. 'I put a bit o' scrag end in wi't carrots. Do thi good,' she added with the same business-like air of their Annie.

'Aye, but I'll wait while Mr Broadbent gets 'ere, Gracie.'

'Where is 'e then, Annie?'

'Never you mind. Get yer tea down yer. There's many a lass'd be glad o' that, so shut thi trap and gerron wi' it.'

When the knock on the door sounded she was there to answer it at once, apparently having seen the caller come up the garden path. She flung it open with evident relief and the enormous man who entered smiled at her for a moment, telling her, since she was really no more than a child herself, that everything was as it should be. He turned instantly to Tessa, squatting down on his haunches before her.

'Lass,' he said softly. They all gathered round, the scrag end forgotten in the wonder of the moment: Annie, the one who had brought her home, their Nelly who had made the tea, Polly, whose endeavours with the scrag end were being so ungraciously ignored, Gracie and a boy who looked to be a year or two younger than Annie. Their expressions were solemn, their faces as plain as their older sister's, but sharply intelligent.

'Are you ... did they ... hurt you, lass?' the man asked, putting up a hand to smooth back her tangled hair and was relieved when she did not shrink away from him, though she did not answer.

'Are you all right, Tessa?' he went on and at the sound of her name she turned and a faint semblance of sense began to show in her empty grey eyes, the first Annie had seen since she had ordered her to climb over the wall.

'Yes, thank you,' she said politely.

84

'They ... they didn't touch you?'

'No ... only ...'

'Only what, Tessa?'

'They knocked me down.'

'They'll not do it again, my lass.'

'Oh ...?'

'They'll be half-way to Leeds by now, I shouldn't wonder. I gave them a helping hand, like. But if they've hurt you in any way I'll fetch them right back and hand them over to the constable,' – but not before I've given them summat they'll not forget in a hurry, his bleak expression said.

'Oh, no, don't bring them back.'

'No, that's what I thought.'

He stood up then and looked about him, so tall and broad he seemed to fill the scrupulously polished kitchen from wall to wall. He said a word or two to the boy who nodded his head in understanding and after flinging a cap on his pale hair, left the cottage at once.

It was then Tessa recognised him. She had last seen him in the mill yard when her cousins had run off with her to the moor. They had all three laughed at him since he had Drew and Pearce in his charge that day and their defiance of him had excited them. He was watching her steadily now, his soft, smoky-brown eyes concerned, with no hint of the coolness with which he had looked at her then, and not only then but the first time they had met when he had threatened to put her over his knee and spank her, like a naughty child.

'I've sent Jack to let your family know where you are. When you're ready I'll take you home ...'

'That you'll not. Not while you've summat inside thi, both o' thi.' Annie began to crash plates about, sending their Nelly to stir the stew, their Polly for some peat for the fire and their Gracie to bed.

'Aah, Annie ...' It was not often anything as exciting as this happened to the little girl, '... can I not stop up ...' Gracie began but Annie, whose word, it seemed, was law, would brook no argument and the child, taking a candle from the dresser, went obediently up the stairs.

Tessa was put on a bench by the table, shoulder to shoulder with Nelly. A plateful of stew with the precious scrag end plainly on view – most on *her* plate though she didn't notice – was set before her and she was told sharply, as the child had been, to 'eat up, lass'. To her surprise she found the food quite delicious.

She was feeling better now. No one took any notice of her. Polly was telling the big man, Mr Broadbent, they all called him, apparently well used to his company, about some wondrous thing she had become acquainted with at Sunday school the day before. Annie moved briskly between the table and the hearth in which an iron basket, fixed to the back of it, held the open fire where the cooking was done. When the meal was eaten Polly and Nelly took up a bit of plain sewing, mending what looked like a cotton sheet, whilst Annie moved about, performing tasks the function of which were a mystery to Tessa, with the energy and vigour of a whirlwind. Mr Broadbent lit his pipe. The room was peaceful, warm with nothing of tension in it and Tessa looked about her with growing interest.

She had never seen a room so small and cluttered and yet so achingly clean. Where did they get their water, she thought, and how did one cook on that . . . that contraption in the hearth? And what on earth had been in the tasty meal she had just eaten? Who were these people, the girl and her family who, now that they had become used to her presence, acted as though she was one of them? Where was the mother, the father, and what was Mr Broadbent who was an overlooker at the mill doing here? Surely *he* could not be the father? The girl, Annie, had said he lived up her way which did not seem to mean with her. She studied the tall oak settle to one side of the fireplace, used as a seat but with a cupboard underneath. There were barrels against the wall and stoneware storage jars and on a shelf what looked like wine in glass bottles. She watched Annie take a spoonful of salt from a pinewood box mounted on the fireplace wall, then select a few dried mushrooms from a net which hung from the beam above the fire.

'Isn't bread done, lass?' she asked Polly and when the girl nodded, as sparing with words as her sister, Annie opened the door of the baking oven beside the fire. She nodded her head approvingly in Polly's direction, apparently well pleased with the girl's efforts and Polly, perhaps six or seven years of age, though she did no more than nod her own head, looked gratified; Annie's unspoken praise was something to be treasured.

The clock on the wall struck seven; they all turned to look at it and as they did so the boy returned, nodding in Mr Broadbent's direction.

'That lass'd better be gettin' off 'ome, Mr Broadbent,' Annie said firmly as she pushed her brother into a chair and put a plate of the stew in front of him. When she was satisfied that he was filling himself in what she considered to be an adequate manner, she turned in a bustling, efficient way to Tessa, her attitude so completely like Nanny in the nursery of her own younger days that Tessa began to smile. 'See, put that there shawl about thi ... no, give over arguin' wi' me. I've another. It were me ... me Mam's.' Her voice was almost ungracious but Tessa was getting the measure of this Annie by now and did as she was told. Nor did she say much in the way of thanks for somehow she knew Annie would not care for it.

'I'll si thi in't mornin', Mr Broadbent,' Annie said, wiping her hands on her coarse apron.

'Aye, lass. Five sharp at the top o't street.'

'Right. Well, good night then,' she said and before Tessa and Will Broadbent were hardly over the doorstep the door was shut resolutely behind them.

They walked in silence for five minutes or so. Tessa was inclined to look stealthily over her shoulder, keeping close to Will Broadbent's strong left arm and when she stumbled he took her hand and tucked it into the crook of his arm.

She clung to it gratefully, still fragile in a way that surprised her. She was a young woman, tall, and strengthened by the hours she had spent in the saddle, by the outdoor life she had led. She had been afraid of nothing in all her life since, she supposed, nothing had ever threatened her until today; but the ordeal she had suffered, though no harm had come to her, had for the moment sapped her confidence in herself and she was glad of this man's quiet, unflaunting strength beside her.

'You're not to come out alone again,' he said definitely, another who believed he was not to be disobeyed, apparently.

'Indeed I won't,' she answered readily enough, not adding that from now on, when she was not with her cousins, she would bring the dogs, knowing that was not what he meant.

'Good lass.'

There was silence again for another few minutes, then she broke it.

'Who is that girl, Mr Broadbent?' In the darkness she did not see 'Mr Broadbent's' smile at the sound of this imperious young girl, who thought herself to be only a stratum or two below the Queen up in London, addressing him so respectfully.

'She's called Annie Beale. She works in the spinning room at Chapmans.'

'Really? She doesn't seem very old.'

'They start young, lass. She's been a piecer, then a spinner since she was nine. Their Nelly pieces for her now. I think Annie's about sixteen.'

'But why are she and her family alone?'

'Her mother died a while since. I don't know what happened to her father. Annie never speaks of him. She and Nelly are the only earners.'

'How on earth do they manage?'

'They rent that cottage from Chapmans. Your mother lets her have it cheap, and they live off the land. Jack goes full time to the school at the factory. He's a clever lad and Annie wants him to have his chance. You saw the peat they use on the fire? Well, he collects that from up on the moor. Coal's too expensive, you see. He has an allotment and grows potatoes and onions, carrots and such.'

'But how can they afford wine?'

'Wine? Dear God, they only just scratch by as it is. What makes you think they drink wine?' He was laughing out loud and she felt the strength of her recently wounded spirit return to her.

'I saw it in the bottles on the shelf.'

'Nay, Miss Harrison.' At his words she realised that though she clung to his arm in the most intimate way he was telling her that they must now resume the relationship they had known before the attack. 'That wasn't wine, t'was cordial. Nelly and the others gather field and hedgerow fruits, cowslip and sloe and elder, and Annie makes them into . . . well, what you thought was wine. She's a grand lass. She made up her mind when her Mam died she'd keep her family together and she's doing it. It's a bit of a tight-rope at times, one slip and they'd all be off, but she works hard and gets on with life especially when you consider what happened to Nelly . . .'

He stopped speaking suddenly, his face expressing his irritation at himself, it seemed, and even in the enveloping darkness she sensed it.

'What is it, Mr Broadbent?'

'You'll not want to hear it, Miss Harrison, not after . . .'

'Oh, please, I'm all right now, really, I am.' Something told her that whatever it was that had happened to Nelly had a connection with today's events.

Will hesitated, evidently made uneasy, not only by speaking of such a thing on this occasion, but of perhaps revealing a confidence which was not really his to disclose.

'It was your uncle told me . . .'

'Charlie?'

'Aye. He was involved . . . well, not involved but it was brought to his notice. He didn't like it, you see, not in *his*

mill and I think he felt responsible. That's why he asked me
to keep a ... well, you might say a *brotherly* eye on Annie
and the children.'

'Yes?'

'Nelly's only a little lass. You saw her. An overlooker took
her into the cabin ... a few months back ... you know, the
one in the spinning room.'

She didn't since she had never been in the spinning room
but she nodded just the same. The skin on her arms and the
back of her neck began to prickle.

'I'll not go into detail, lass.' Will's voice was quiet and he
put his other hand over hers where it lay in the crook of
his arm. 'But ... well, Mr Greenwood didn't get to her in
time. Nelly wasn't as lucky as you.'

'Dear God ...'

'I reckon *He* was looking the other way that day.'

'Yes.'

'But Annie cleaned her up, made no fuss, nor did Nelly
and that's what infuriated Mr Greenwood, I reckon: that they
should just accept it as though they'd no rights to be
defended and must take whatever life chucks at them without protest. They would have been back on their machines
a few minutes later if Mr Greenwood hadn't sent them
home. He paid them while they were off an' all. A grand
chap, Mr Greenwood.'

'Yes, yes, he is. Thank you for telling me, Mr Broadbent. It
seems you are meant to reveal a side of life I know nothing
about. First yourself and how *you* survived ... no, indeed,
I had not forgotten ... and now about Annie and Nelly.'

'You'll not let on I told you, Miss Harrison? Annie doesn't
even know your uncle told me. She'd not like her private
family business discussed, even by those who mean her no
harm. You saw how she was?'

'Indeed. She is a ... proud person, I'd say.'

'You're right there so we'll say no more.'

They had reached the outskirts of Crossfold by now, just
where Reddygate Way led out on to the bit of moorland

90

between there and Edgeclough. There were lights and a carriage or two, the beginning of paved streets and Tessa halted, turning Will towards her. Her face was earnest in the street light.

'Do you think she would be offended if I ... took her something. As a thank you, I mean?' Her eyes were deep and shadowed but he could see a pinprick of light in each one, like a tiny star and he felt that sweetness, that lurching tenderness she had awakened in him the last time brush against his heart.

'I think she might, Miss Harrison.' His voice was soft.

'I would like to show my gratitude, nevertheless. She was very kind.'

'I imagine the only thing she would take from you would be your friendship, Miss Harrison, if you could spare it. Why not start by returning her shawl next Sunday?'

She looked up at him, astonishment plain on her face, even in the shadowed darkness.

'My friendship?'

'Aye, for she's got little enough of that and it'd cost you nowt. And, by the way, I sent a message to your Mam to say there was nothing to worry about; you'd had a tumble from your horse and you'd be late home – that Will Broadbent'd be bringing you. I knew that'd satisfy Mr Greenwood and it's the truth.'

He was sitting by the fireside reading from a book, the three girls at his knee, when Annie's astonished face peered at Tessa through the open door. Somehow she was not surprised to see him and was glad that she had tied up her hair with a bright knot of scarlet ribbon before she left Greenacres. The ride over, with the dogs, had put colour in her cheeks to match the ribbon and her silvery grey eyes were brilliant as they searched out his. With an effort she dragged her gaze away from him and back to Annie.

'I brought your shawl,' she said awkwardly, standing on

91

the doorstep. Her usual high-handed assumption that she was immediately welcome wherever she went was sadly lacking this day.

'You've not come on yer own, not after what 'appened t'other day?' Annie gasped, her disbelief in this girl's daft and foolhardy ways taking her breath away. 'I've never known 'owt like you, really I 'avent.' She peered over Tessa's shoulder as though fully expecting to see a complete battalion of soldiers guarding this feckless girl; when none appeared she 'tcched-tcched' angrily, reaching out to draw Tessa in before she was attacked by some dreadful mob which must have followed her across the moors. 'And I 'ope that animal out theer won't eat me daisies,' she added crossly, referring to Tessa's mare, 'an' them dogs 'ad better not mess me clean step, neither, or I'll tek me broom to 'em. Look who's 'ere, Mr Broadbent, an' after all as we said to 'er.'

She shook her head, shoving Tessa quite rudely into the chair opposite Will, taking the neatly wrapped, freshly laundered shawl from her and throwing it impatiently on to the table where she was evidently making blackberry pies.

'Tha'd best pour thissen a cup o' tea for I've no time ter bother, what with them childer ter see to an' pies ter get in th'oven . . .' Without further ado, just as though Tessa was the last person alive she could do with right now she continued, with a curiously delicate hand considering the noise she made with pots and rolling-pin and dishes which all got in her way, to roll out the pastry. But in her cheek was a touch of colour and her eyes were soft with pleasure.

Tessa chanced a swift glance at Will and her insides turned right over in the most unusual way as he winked at her.

# 6

She sat on the round-topped stool in front of her dressing-table and stared at her own reflection in the mirror while Emma brushed her long, difficult hair. At each stroke her head snapped back on her neck and the maid watched her anxiously. Miss Tessa's temper was always uncertain: she could be sweet-natured and generous, carelessly bestowing ribbons and lace-trimmed handkerchiefs on her maid when she was in the mood. Lately she had been somewhat softer, dreaming and seemingly unaware of Emma's presence, allowing her hair to be brushed and brushed for the required five minutes without uttering a word of protest, her face absorbed, deep in some reverie. Emma was grateful for a moment's respite in the drama that was often enacted in the dressing hour before dinner.

It was almost dark now as autumn took hold. Emma had lit the lamps and stoked up the fire for as the nights drew in it was becoming colder up here in the harsh northern climate of the Lancashire Pennines.

A great flock of blackbirds prepared to roost for the night in the depths of the rhododendron bushes which grew wild amongst the trees, making an enormous clatter as they imagined all kinds of danger menacing them. Sparrows squabbled over possession of a cosy niche in the ivy growing against the walls of the house and the noise of the birds seemed to bring back her mistress from the daydream in which she was enveloped. She jerked her head irritably and the maid sighed knowing the moment's peace was over.

'That will do, Emma. You'll have it out by the roots if you go on much longer. Fix it up anyway and quickly, if you please. I'm in a hurry.'

'There's plenty of time, Miss Tessa. Dinner's not for another hour yet.'

'Oh, I've something to do before dinner so do hurry. Tie it up in a ribbon and then pass me my breeches.'

'Your breeches! For dinner! Dear Lord, your mother will . . .'

'I'll be back in time to dress for dinner, Emma, but I've somewhere to go first. I hadn't realised the time and you let me sit here daydreaming . . .'

'Not me, Miss Tessa. I was only brushing your hair as I've been told to do each night and morning.'

'Oh, for God's sake, girl, give me the brush and a bit of ribbon and I'll do it myself.'

'Oh, please, Miss Tessa dear, be a good girl. You know your mother likes to see you dressed nicely with your hair done properly,' and not in the outfit of a bold lad with your hair hanging down your back like some gypsy. The unspoken words hung on the warm, scented air but Tessa did not appear to notice, or if she did was so accustomed to the maid's silent accusations they no longer troubled her, if they ever had.

But Emma meant it this time and meant to have her own way. Usually she merely stepped aside and shut her mouth and allowed her young mistress to do exactly as she pleased. It was easier that way with less damage to her own nerves and to the many pretty ornaments in the bedroom. What did it matter anyway, for when her mother was at the mill no one questioned what Miss Tessa did or said or where she went, so why should Emma wear herself to a shadow trying to make her into an elegant young lady? That, of course, is what she had been employed to do. Emma saw that her mistress was clean and tidy; that her clothes – mostly shirts and breeches, for heaven's sake – were neatly pressed and mended, and then sat back and enjoyed the peace and comfort of the pretty room without Miss Tessa Harrison in it.

But Mr and Mrs Joss Greenwood were home again now that the House was no longer sitting, and would be at dinner and all three of them, Master Drew, Master Pearce and Miss Tessa, would need to be on their best behaviour. She had laid out her young mistress's new dinner gown, a white muslin this time, pretty and trimmed about the sash with white satin rosebuds, slightly off the shoulder but with a modest sleeve. All of Miss Tessa's gowns were quite lovely, in Emma's opinion, and very expensive but she had a way of throwing them on hurriedly, irritably, since, her manner said, it would be so much easier simply to go down to dinner in her breeches, as her cousins were sometimes allowed to do when their parents were absent, with her hair tied back in a careless knot of ribbons.

'No, Miss Tessa, no!' the maid continued. 'I am to do your hair and put you in your new dress, your mother said, otherwise your uncle will naturally be upset and questions will be asked, and you know what will happen then.'

Tessa scowled and thrust back the flowing cape of her hair with both hands, knowing that her maid spoke only the truth. No one, not even her cousins, knew of her 'brush' as she casually called it *now*, with the tinker family. Should they find out – and might not her uncle do so if probing questions were asked? – her freedom would be severely curtailed. All her family were considered quite appallingly unconventional by the rest of the Penfold Valley and though her mother and Uncle Joss, as head of the family, were aware that she rode astride like a man, if they should discover that she had been in *danger* because of it, a vastly different attitude would be taken. They had all been rebels in one way and another, Jenny Greenwood, Joss Greenwood and his wife Kit, earning themselves reputations as trouble-makers in their defence and support of the exploited operatives, the brutalised children, scandalising the Penfold Valley with their carryings-on. Perhaps because of that they had

95

understood, and allowed her own fight for a measure of freedom but she was certain they had no idea of the jaunts on which she accompanied her cousins, or even that her cousins *themselves* participated in such activities, and she had no wish for them to become acquainted with the true picture of her life.

'So we'll brush your hair and dress it at the back of your head with your new tortoiseshell comb, Miss Tessa,' her maid continued slyly, 'and your mother will be so pleased with you. Now, sit you down again while I get the pins.' Tessa had no choice but to grit her teeth and place herself before the mirror again.

Emma brushed back the hair which was as rebellious in its disorder as her mistress. When it was as smooth and tangle-free as she could get it, she began to pin it up on each side of a centre parting, then brushed it into a huge and intricate coil at the back of Miss Tessa's head. But it seemed the style was determined to be awkward tonight and the maid clucked her tongue irritably, pulling quite forcibly at her mistress's head. The trouble was that the hair was so thick, so straight and slipping; no matter how she struggled, strands of it would keep escaping out of the coil and hanging down Miss Tessa's back in the most wilful fashion. The maid's face was red, her mouth full of pins as she patiently adjusted the tortoiseshell comb for the third time but the girl had had enough and she sprang up, scattering pins and combs and the hairbrush about the bedroom floor.

'Oh, for heaven's sake, Emma, does it really matter *what* style you achieve as long as it's tidy? Won't a simple knot on the back of my neck do? You could put some rosebuds in it like you did the last time,' she wheedled, genuinely trying to be helpful. She really did want to slip down to the stables, for a minute, no more, to join her cousins in what was happening there. She had never seen a foal born before, nor indeed any animal, not even one of the dozens of kittens which skittered about the stable yard. She knew she might be prevented, not by her family who, due no doubt to their working-class, down-to-earth, no-nonsense *practical* heritage would see no harm in it, but by the stable lads and grooms, the coachmen themselves who would be shocked to have a female amongst them on such an intimate, *physical* occasion. And if she told Emma where she was going there would be such a caterwauling the whole estate would hear of it.

'You must be fashionable, Miss Tessa,' the maid said sternly, quite enjoying this momentary power she had over her young mistress. 'This style is right up to the minute and your aunt is bound to notice coming straight from London as she has.'

'Dear God,' Tessa moaned, sitting down again obediently, but before Emma could lift the brush to begin all over again, she turned and smiled. The maid's heart sank for she knew that smile so well: it meant mischief, there was no doubt of it, and the often wicked temper which followed if she was not allowed her way.

'Why do we not cut it, Emma?' she asked vividly, her eyes joyous in her expressive face, an expression which said she wondered why she had not thought of that before. It was such a simple solution to a tangled problem since Emma would have no further need of pins and combs and she would really have no further need of Emma.

'Cut it?' the maid gasped.

'Yes. Why not? Mother has short hair and she is not thought to be unattractive. Aunt Kit and Uncle Joss are used to seeing her as she is, as we all are ever since I can remember, and they find nothing strange in it. Uncle Joss wouldn't mind at all, nor Mother since I have heard her remark a number of times on how easy it is to manage.'

'Oh no, Miss Tessa, oh, no, I cannot allow it.'

'*You* cannot allow it? And what has it to do with you, pray?'

Tessa's face had turned truculent and she stood up, a head taller than her maid and not at all sure she might not strike her for her insolence.

'Please, Miss Tessa, don't, don't, I beg you. Your beautiful hair . . .'

'Mother's hair is quite beautiful, in my opinion.'

'Maybe it is, Miss Tessa, but your mother is an elderly lady and a widow. She is allowed to be . . . to be eccentric and no one notices any more but if you were to do it, a young, marriageable lady, how will you ever attract the attention of a husband . . .'

Tessa turned away in disgust, her still-maturing body somewhat brittle and vulnerable and yet eager, for though she had no intention of marrying, not for years yet, she wanted to live life to the full, its joys and triumphs, even its disasters should they come, and how could she if she was perpetually harassed by those who would stop her getting at them?

'Where are the scissors, Emma?'

'Oh, please, Miss Tessa dear, don't, I beg you . . .' Emma was almost in tears now and wishing in her heart, as she had done a hundred times in the last couple of years, that she had been given any job other than this in the great house of Greenacres. It was simply impossible to mould Miss Tessa into a young lady of fashion. She had been allowed to run wild for too long, you see, making it extremely trying not to say downright *punishing* for those who had her in their charge. As Emma was fond of telling her own mother who had once been in the service of the Chapman family but was now pensioned off in one of the Chapman alm-houses, she felt she had aged ten years in the two she had served Miss Tessa.

This house had once belonged to the great Barker Chapman who, with his father, had begun the Chapman Spinning and Weaving Concerns. When he had died, murdered it was said by a group of rioting men calling themselves the 'Onwardsmen' who had fought for better conditions and wages for themselves and others in the textile trade, the great wealth he had left, his mills and weaving sheds and many other business concerns, this house, had all come to his daughter, this girl's aunt. Emma's mother, who had been parlourmaid then, had often spoken of the scandal which had set the Penfold Valley aflame when Miss Chapman had married the man some said had been involved in her own father's murder: Joss Greenwood, no more than a working man himself, a hand-loom weaver, a radical and a revolutionary and now a Member of Parliament. He and his wife spent most of their time up at Westminster, coming home only when the House was not sitting.

Firebrands, both of them, and so was this girl who was no blood kin, which was strange. She was stamping about the bedroom now with every appearance of darting off to the kitchen to fetch a bread knife to her hair if the scissors did not immediately come to hand. Dear God in heaven, what was she to do? Doubtless she would be the one to get the blame should Miss Tessa arrive at the dinner table with her hair cut like that of a child from the poor house.

Emma looked desperately about the room as though searching for something which might distract her young mistress from the course she was set on, but there was nothing forthcoming.

It was a lovely room situated on the first floor of the house, on the corner with windows on two sides facing south. The furnishing of it was completely feminine, expressing not Miss Tessa's taste but that of her aunt's mother who had, years ago, decorated and furnished it for her own sixteen-year-old daughter. The furniture was of glowing rosewood; slim-legged tables, a rococo desk, though Emma had never once seen Miss Tessa so much as write a note at it in the two years she had been with her; low, rosewood-framed chairs, armless and with the backs and seats embroidered in delicate pinks and creams. There was a dressing-table softly swathed in white muslin, a rosewood chest and the walls of the room were lined with blush-pink silk. Ornaments were grouped tastefully on tables and shelves; ivory combs and silver-handled brushes, a manicure set of mother-of-pearl, a jewel box of engraved gilt with a Sèvres china plaque set into the lid, cut-glass toilet bottles and jars with silver-gilt tops.

The stuffily draped four-poster of the beginning of the century had been replaced by the half-canopied bed with a high, prettily draped canopy and curtains at its head only. There was a feather quilt and a silken counterpane and enormous white pillows edged with lace. At the windows behind pelmets trimmed with ball-fringes hung lavishly draped damask curtains matching the colour of the walls, and the light from the windows was further softened by swathes of white muslin. The predominant colours, even of the huge carpet which covered the whole floor were cream, white and blush-pink, delicately lovely as Mrs Hannah Chapman, now dead, had once been, restful and dainty and not at all suited to the temperament of Miss Tessa Harrison who was neither.

Emma tried again.

'Come now, Miss Tessa dear, sit down and I'll dress your hair in a simple knot.' Her voice was coaxing for anything was better than a shorn head. 'And when you see your mother tonight you can ask her permission to cut your hair like hers. See, it won't take but a minute . . .'

'But it will all be over if I don't go soon.'

'Only a minute and I promise you you'll be off to wherever it is you're going.' And the sooner she went the better in Emma's exasperated and nerve-torn opinion. 'Your dress is laid out and Polly will be up in a minute to lend a hand with your stays and it will take no more than a second or two to get you into it. Now, will you have the white rosebuds in your hair, or the satin ribbons?'

'Dear Lord, will you stop babbling and pass me my breeches and boots. Surely even you will agree that white muslin is hardly fit attire for the stables and . . .'

'*The stables!* Merciful heaven, what d'you want in the stables, Miss Tessa?' Emma was immediately suspicious since it was not unknown for her young mistress to say she would be only a second or two, promising to be back in time for dinner and then simply to disappear, and them lads with her. It was rumoured she had been seen at a cock-fight, wearing her cousin's jacket and top hat with her hair pushed up inside it, but Emma, even knowing Miss Tessa as she did, found that hard to believe since their father would have skinned them lads alive if it was true.

'Oh, damnation, I had not meant to . . .'

Enlightenment dawned on Emma's face. 'It's that new animal, isn't it? The one that's in foal. Percy told me it was ready . . . You're not going there, my girl, you can take my word for it.' In her agitation Emma went so far as to forget her place and the respect she had been taught to show her betters. She had an 'understanding' with Percy, the head stable lad at Greenacres, who had told her in a discreet way, of course, for even servants, particularly of the superior kind like Emma, were treated with a bit of common decency, of the foal's imminent arrival.

She began to flutter about the room, wringing her hands. Tessa hesitated for though she knew she was a trial and a tribulation to her maid and had seen her near to tears a time or two, she had never seen her quite so badly distressed.

'Look, Emma,' she said irritably for really the girl was a damned nuisance and time was pressing if she was to get to the stables and back before the dinner gong sounded. 'Why don't I just tie my hair up for now as the girls in the mill do, and then when I get back you can dress . . .'

'Because you're *not* a mill girl, Miss Tessa, that's why.' Emma rounded on her, goaded beyond endurance, her face a bright pink in her effort to restrain herself from smacking this silly child's face.

'Mother was once and she's allowed to wear her hair anyway she likes and I don't see why I shouldn't. All this dressing up . . .'

The perilous sound of her voice was interrupted by the resonant noise of the dinner gong from the hallway downstairs and the relief etched on Emma's face was quite comical. Thank God, oh, thank God, she repeated over and over

101

again to herself as Miss Tessa sighed in heartbroken resignation, or so she would have her maid believe, and began to move dejectedly towards the bed and the inevitability of the pretty gown which lay there. She'd put her in the damn dress *without* her stays, for where was Polly? And do her hair in a simple coil on her neck. Make her presentable for a family dinner. But if she brought up this ridiculous notion of cutting her hair again Emma would go right to Mrs Harrison and ask to be relieved of her duties, really she would. The privilege of being a ladies' maid was not worth it, not to this one, it wasn't, and if it came to it she'd rather scrub the bloody scullery floors than go through what she suffered day after day with Miss Tessa, really she would.

The foal was on its feet, its shy, liquid eyes, fringed with deep brown lashes, looking anxiously at the entranced group of humans who hung over the stable door. The mare was inclined to be despotic in her protection, tossing her head challengingly and Tessa laughed with delight.

'Is she not brave? I do believe if one of us was to go in there she'd kick and bite until we took ourselves out again. And what a little beauty her baby is! Look at those legs and the colour of her. She's like the mahogany table in the hall. Honestly, I could cry when I think we might have been here to see her born had we not been made to eat dinner at the prescribed time that every one else in the valley dines. Would you not think that just for once we might have been allowed to absent ourselves so that we could have seen her born? Percy could have come for us ... Oh, look at her, will you? She is going to – what is the word, Walter? – suckle. There is no need to blush ... and see how she goes at it. Even with those fragile legs she can stand to do it. What was the exact time of her birth, Walter?'

She turned to the stable lad who leaned with them over the loose-box door, the expression on his face as foolishly doting as a mother with her firstborn, his head to one side, shoulder to shoulder with the Greenwoods, social position forgotten in the wonder of the shared moment.

'T'were just gone eight, I reckon, Miss Tessa.'

'There, you see, we were half-way through the soup.' Her expression was dramatic.

'Well, *we* were here for almost an hour before dinner, but you didn't show up.' Drew's voice was scornful. 'I suppose you were preening yourself in that delectable creation you have on and had not the time for something of *real* interest. Your own reflection in the mirror must have been altogether fascinating...'

'That's not true, damn you.' Tessa's face had turned a furious red and her raised voice caused the new mother to stamp her feet in anger and alarm.

'Keep your bloody voice down, cousin. If you make her nervous she'll lose her milk. And it doesn't really matter to anyone whether you came or not since we all missed the big event.'

'I tried to come, I really did. It was all the fault of Emma and her absolute refusal to allow me to cut my hair.'

'Your hair, Miss Tessa?' The stable lad was clearly mystified.

'Oh, take no notice, Walter.' Pearce's eyes were narrowed in admiring contemplation of the mare and her foal, and not a little envious of Drew to whom they both belonged. He had won the animal in a bet, a wager with Nicky Longworth. Drew had declared his bay to be capable of jumping higher than Nick's magnificent roan and since the bet had been Drew's bay against Nick's mare which had been in foal, they had set up the practice fence in the Longworth paddock immediately. The great deal of money his father had paid for his bay did not even cross Drew's mind and if it had there was little doubt he would not have allowed himself to be concerned over it. Nor did he consider that if he lost he would be without a decent mount. He *would* win, whatever the cost, to himself or his animal. A wager was a wager and a gentleman would honour it, as he would any challenge.

'How high shall it be, Drew?' Nicky had enquired lazily.

'As high as you please, old fellow.' The pole had been at its highest, just over seven feet when the hooves of Nicky Longworth's roan had clipped it, sending the Squire's son over its head to hit the ground with a force which stunned him.

Without a moment's hesitation, ignoring the Squire's grooms who had been about to dash across to the lad who was, after all, the son of their master and should be checked for damage, Drew thundered towards the pole, lifting his bay over it with half an inch to spare, narrowly missing Nicky Longworth who had the presence of mind to roll out of the way.

The handsome little mare was in the Greenwood stables by nightfall but the talk was that Joss Greenwood had better watch that touch of instability in his sons or they would not survive to see twenty. They were all wild, the young gentlemen who rode hard and took no heed of danger to themselves, but the Greenwoods had something about them, particularly since they had begun work in the family mills, which was more than foolhardiness. They seemed ready to fling down a challenge on the slightest provocation, strung high on nerves which surely would snap one day.

But the mare was lovely, and so was her foal. Pearce watched them together and though he was not awfully sure *he* would have attempted such a height, unless dared by his own brother, he would dearly love to own her.

'It's true, Pearce. It was all that damned arguing about my hair and how it should be dressed. Would I have rosebuds or ribbons and on and on until I could have struck her. Left to myself I would have tied it up and been down here at least half an hour before the dinner gong.'

'You still wouldn't have seen her born, just as we didn't.'

'I know, but I would have been here with you and witnessed some of it. She must have been nearly ready to give birth...'

104

'Oh, for God's sake, shut up, Tessa. It's done with now so what does it matter?'

'I'm only explaining why I didn't come.' Tessa gritted her teeth: it was most unfair of them to take this attitude just as though she hadn't tried and tried to get down to be with them. They had no idea how difficult it was to be a *girl*. 'It takes Emma *hours* to decide what I should do with my hair and then hours actually to *do* it. Plaited or coiled...'

'Christ, Tessa, all we ever hear from morning till night is you moaning about that bloody hair of yours. If you are so persecuted by it why don't you do what you are always threatening to do and cut it off?'

'No one will do it, damn you.'

'I'll do it.'

They all turned to look at Drew, even Walter who had no idea what they were talking about and, really, was it any wonder? Their minds were like the sleek and beautiful blood animals they rode: fast, complex, skittish when checked, moving too quickly for him. Though he spent some time with them each day in the stables and paddock and was as adept as they in the saddle, he could never follow where they went.

'*You?* What with? The gardening shears?'

'If you like.'

'Don't be a bloody fool, Drew.' Pearce's voice was rough.

'All right, then. If Tessa runs back to the house for her scissors I'll cut it for her with those.'

Tessa looked into the indolently smiling face of her cousin. There was nothing she wanted more – was there? – than to be rid of the fuss and bother attached to getting herself ready for the day and how much time and argument she would save if she were not subjected to Emma's ministrations, yet she hesitated. Drew was such a devil you were never quite sure where you were with him. He had a way of looking at you that dared you to gamble – which was how he had won the mare – if you had the nerve. His violet-blue eyes were clear and innocent but his mouth slanted in a sardonic smile which she did not quite trust.

But she was a Greenwood, brought up as one anyway, and when had any of them ever turned away from a challenge?

'Wait here,' she said turning towards the door which led out into the dark stable yard and she knew by the way his eyes gleamed and the broadening of his smile that she had won his admiration.

'Don't be stupid, Tess.' Pearce tried to put a hand on her arm but she shook him off. He shrugged and turned away so that neither of them could see the doubt in his eyes. Though she might be as undisciplined as himself and Drew when the opportunity offered, including herself in all the light-hearted escapades they thought up, she was still a *girl*. Despite the breeches she wore and her desperate attempts to follow wherever they went, one day she would be stopped and that day must surely be soon. She was almost seventeen years old and ripe for the pickers in the marriage market. What the hell would her mother do with her, and *them*, if she turned up at the breakfast table in the morning with her hair cropped like a man's?

The scissors were in Drew's hand when Pearce turned back to them. Walter, knowing at last what they were about to do, had reared off, his hand to his mouth, his face white, his horror so great Drew might have been about to plunge the blades into Tessa's breast.

'Eeh no, Master Drew, you don't mean ter . . . ?'

'Be quiet, Walter, this has nothing to do with you.' Tessa's voice was feverish as she placed herself within the reach of Drew's hands and the snip-snip of the lethal scissors.

Walter moaned deep in his throat as the first gloriously shining strand, so thick and lovely he felt the urge to beg if he might have it, fell to the cobbled floor of the stable. Another went and another until all about the recklessly laughing young girl was a carpet of hair, the rich chestnut glints in it quite extinguished as though they had derived their life from the girl herself.

'Dear God, you'll catch it from Aunt Jenny,' Pearce said softly and, like Walter, his young heart ached with something he could not describe as his cousin was stripped of her most obvious claim to femininity. What was left of her hair stood out in differing lengths, tufty, like the shorn skin of a rabbit, and beneath it her face had become as pointed and fey as a pixie's. Her cheekbones appeared to have widened and become higher and more pronounced. Her eyes were enormous, glittering, so clear and pale a grey as to be almost colourless, piercing the semi-gloom of the stables like two of the new 'electric rays' which were, Pearce had heard, being used to illuminate Vauxhall Gardens up in London. Not that he had seen them, you understand, but surely they could not be more brilliantly lovely than Tessa Harrison's eyes? Her small chin thrust forward challengingly and she laughed.

'Well?' she said, tossing her head which felt so light she thought she might float away.

'Jesus . . . !'

'Aah . . . Miss Tessa . . .' and Walter looked as though he might weep.

'Just a shade more here, I think,' Drew said cheerfully, 'and then under the tap with you.'

'The tap? What on earth for?'

'Trust me, little cousin.'

He towelled her wet hair with a bit of old horse blanket rubbing the short stubble which suddenly, miraculously, was no longer stubble but a moving cap of smooth darkness, clinging about her head, not in curls as her mother's did, but in short and springing waves. They fell over her forehead and about her ears, hugging the nape of her long and shapely neck, outlining her neat head and producing in her a strange and bizarre beauty the likes of which had never before been seen in the Penfold Valley. It accentuated the width of her forehead and the delicate strength of her pointed chin, the pretty shells of her ears and the pale velvet-grey of her eyes.

107

'Bloody hell, it actually suits you,' Pearce blurted out in amazement and the curious and speculative expression on his face was mirrored in that of his brother. It was the look of a man confronted, for the first time, by a new and exciting woman, a look which says quite plainly that he is intrigued and more than a little willing to get to know her, to have her look at him with as much interest, and if she did not, the added thrill of persuading her to do so.

She did not see it, only the approval written on his face and that was all she wanted.

'And what about you, Walter?' She grinned at the stable lad who was staring, open-mouthed and slack-jawed at this dashing young lad who was very definitely *not* a young lad. Though her hair was shorter than his own, its boyishness merely served to emphasise the thrusting peaks of her high young breasts, the smooth white skin of her shoulders above the disarranged neckline of the dinner-gown she still wore, the slender shapeliness of her bare arms which he had never really noticed before, and the sight of it all took his breath away.

'By gum, Miss Tessa,' he breathed admiringly, letting his masculine appreciation show in the way his eyes ran over her, then blushing furiously he turned and blundered from the stable.

'Well, cousin,' Drew's voice was somewhat husky and his fingers gripped the scissors fiercely, 'it seems you have at least one admirer should the rest turn tail at the sight of you.' They wouldn't, of course, his eyes told her.

'Fiddlesticks! I want no admirers.' Her heart beat fast and joyously as she ran her hand through the delightful softness and lightness of her hair. 'Come on, let me slip inside and up to my bedroom before Mother sees me or I'll be for it. I'm sure you will want to ride over to the Hall tomorrow to tell Nicky Longworth of your new foal and I want to come with you. We'd best lie low until then or we're bound to be stopped.'

For a second only she lost her nerve at the thought of her

mother's dark anger, then she tossed her head again as another thought followed, much more exciting.

What would Will Broadbent think? Would he look at her as approvingly as her cousins and Walter had done? Would his eyes warm with admiration, then narrow in that quite thrilling and masculine way which happened sometimes? Or would he laugh, treat her as an enormously amusing child, naughty and wilful and deserving of a spanking?

Well, what did it matter what Will Broadbent thought? His opinion meant nothing to her, she told herself, and if he so much as smiled when next she saw him she would . . . what would she do? As she lay in her bed, having avoided the servants and her family and gained the privacy of her room quite safely, she grinned wickedly in the dark at the thought of the fun there would be tomorrow.

7

The fox, being a night feeder, provides no sport early in the day and it would give her the greatest satisfaction, she decided, to arrive at the Hall amongst the Squire's Friday-to-Monday guests before they set off in its pursuit. There would be aristocratic ladies and gentlemen, manorial families from Lancashire, Yorkshire and Cheshire and perhaps even further afield come for the start of the hunting season, booted and spurred, languid and bored and ready to be amused by anything for a lark, particularly the gentlemen who would approve of her own boldness in defying every convention enforced by society. It would give her even more satisfaction to see their faces when she whipped off her top hat to reveal the splendour of her new hair style which nobody but Drew and Pearce and Walter had yet seen.

No, she wouldn't wear a hat. She would gallop up to the Hall with her short hair all about her head as she had seen her cousins do and would enjoy the vast consternation and be as outrageous as she pleased. She would ride with the wind intoxicatingly in her face and hair, through farmyards and over fences, showing them her daring and endurance, showing them that she was as able and strong and durable as any man there. Why she should want to do so never crossed her mind.

It was a clear and glorious day. The trees were almost naked now and the fallen leaves made a dry, rustling sound beneath the hooves of the horses, a splendid carpet of red, gold, green and brown. The fields had been harvested, then ploughed and the long, neat furrows reached into the distance, orderly and somewhat business-like. Bright-eyed jackdaws disappeared in and out of them, hopping up and down with sprightly steps, and on the edge of the fields stood trees holding the former spring nests of rookeries.

The mellow October day was perfect, acting as a barrier between the last of the autumn and the bitter weeks of winter to come. There were still wild flowers bobbing their last blooms in the cool sunshine: the yellow buttons of tansy and orange of toadflax, the deep pink and white of fumitory, its fern-like leaf so fragile it looked like smoke from a distance.

Though she rode like the wind, leaping and diving, the thundering explosion of horses' hooves in her ears, flat on her mare's back across pasture and meadow, her companions close about her, hounds ahead, the clarion call of the horn, the spray of mud and river water, the scatter of earth thrown up by their passage, she was scarcely conscious of it, or them, as she moved through the day in some dream world, their noisy presence jostling about her like discordant ghosts. Her cousins were nowhere to be found when later the stable yard at the Hall was filled with the wild-riding end of the hunting party, hoof-beats erupting against the cobbles, the smell of steaming horse-flesh, the well-bred shouts of the fox-hunting set applauding the success of the day. Her own cheek carried the brown stain of dried fox-blood for she had been the first lady to reach the kill. There was to be champagne and they pressed her to stay but, for some reason, she found that the great and glorious sparkle with which the day had begun had evaporated. She could not have said why since she had been a huge success, showered with compliments on her appearance, her bravery and the glory of the kill, but really, she said politely to the Squire, who could not take his eyes from her flaunting and extra-ordinary beauty, she must be getting home since her 'people', speaking as *they* spoke, would be expecting her.

She was on the top road which led from Longworth Hall to Crossfold and Greenacres when he rose from the flat stone on which he had been sitting. It seemed right, some-how, as though everything had been moving towards this moment: the frustration of yesterday, the cutting of her hair as an act of bravado which had been a statement of some pressure within her; the dream-like quality of today, leading up to her meeting with this man who had trembled on the edge of her conscious thought ever since she had opposed him in the mill yard.

She reined in her mare, ready to smile, the afternoon, though drawing in towards nightfall, brighter suddenly. She had her back to the lowering sun which shone directly into his eyes and she could see the expression in them, warm, glad, she knew, to see her, as she was to see him.

'Miss Harrison.' His uncompromising jaw which told the rest of the world of Will Broadbent's intention to succeed, to get on with his life in whichever way it took his fancy, softened for her. She felt herself become disentangled from the complexities which seemed to beset her, and life slowed down and simplified to this moment, to this quiet stretch of moorland and she knew he made it so. She sat for several long, tension-free seconds, looking at him, at the under-

111

standing he had of her which showed in his quiet smile, glancing away smilingly, then back at him, recognising that there was no need for haste nor impatience.

'Will you not get down?'

'I think I might.'

'I hesitate to help you.' He grinned, absurdly pleased with himself for some reason which seemed not to matter in the lingering end of this lovely day, though she guessed it had something to do with her.

'Perhaps I might not mind today.'

'Miss Harrison! I can hardly believe my ears. Have you lost your senses?' He was still smiling and warm. 'Where is the independent young lady who needs assistance from no man, or so she told me?'

'I . . . I found that to be untrue, Mr Broadbent, if you remember . . . ?' Both their faces darkened suddenly as they were reminded of her encounter with the tinkers from which he had saved her. She still woke in the night, her body drenched in sweat, crawling with the memory of those filthy hands, the rank stench of unwashed bodies and decaying teeth in her dreaming nostrils. Only the deliberate bringing back of this man's controlled strength which he had shown her twice now, could dissolve the nightmare.

The quiet, almost tender moment shattered and his face closed up.

'Aye, I remember it and it occurs to me you made me a promise on that day. Have you no concern for your own safety, girl? At least when you came over to Annie's you had the sense to bring your dogs but now I find you riding hell for leather along a lonely track which no sane woman would attempt. Have you no sense at all?'

'Apparently not, Mr Broadbent,' she began, ready to smile, to soothe his sudden irritation with an unusual apology, a warm glance, a reference to Drew and Pearce who could not be far behind her. But the image of her as he had seen her then, fragile, defenceless, made him harsh in his fear for her, careless of the lovely moment they had just created.

'You did not mean to keep your promise then?'

'Yes, I did, but ...'

'Then why are you here completely alone, with no one, not even those dogs to protect you?'

'If you will allow me to speak ...'

'To make further promises which you have no intention of keeping?'

'No, I would just like to ...'

'You are like a child who must be forever watched ...'

'Dear God!' She was as maddened as he now without really knowing why. The strange sense of unhurried tranquillity, the smiling calm he had instilled in her had gone and she felt her resentment rise sharply to swamp her previous pleasure. What right had *he* to tell *her* where she might or might not go, and with whom. She was at liberty to please herself how she went about, her haughty expression said. To tell the truth, in the excitement of the last twenty-four hours she had given no thought to the danger which could stalk these moors and which recently she had been careful of. She had expected to ride home with Drew and Pearce, later on, much later on, and it was only her own curious unease which had brought her home early.

But that had nothing to do with Will Broadbent. Just because he had rescued her from those Irish tinkers – whom she had now convinced herself she could have dealt with on her own anyway – he imagined he owned her. Well, he didn't and she would tell him so. Sensing her anger, her mare began to move restlessly, stepping sideways in a circle round the standing man until the sun which had been at Tessa's back now fell on her face.

'I would be obliged if you would get out of my way,' she said, high-toned as any of those with whom she had hunted that day. 'You are making my mare nervous,' which was not true. 'I cannot imagine what you can be doing hanging about on this path like some wandering vagrant ...' Her voice, which had been loud and defiant died away slowly as the expression of ill-humour on his face drained away and the corners of his mouth twitched. His whole manner altered miraculously. His eyes became warm again and alive with amusement and his mouth stretched in a wide smile over his white teeth.

'What the devil have you been doing to yourself, lass?' he laughed, shaking his head in disbelief. 'My God, if there was another girl like you in the whole wide world I'd eat me damned cap. Peak an' all.'

For a moment she felt her anger dissipate and pleasure moved in her again for she took his words as a compliment. But he had not done yet. 'If you were mine I'd take a strap to you for you're surely the most contrary female in Christendom. There must be a thousand women in Lancashire primping and preening with the curling irons, or whatever it is you women do in an effort to catch the eye of us men, and they would all, like as not, give their souls for hair such as you had. But you! You have to throw it away like some unwanted...'

'It *was* unwanted and is none of your business besides,' she said tartly.

'Dear God,' his eyes had lost their glow, 'd'you think I'm not aware of that?'

'Then why is it that every time we meet you find it necessary to threaten me with a thrashing and spend all your time lecturing me on how foolish I am?'

His voice snapped in exasperation and he made a sudden movement towards her mare, catching the bridle and bringing the animal to a halt. He was breathing hard and his face had darkened.

'Because that is the feeling you arouse in me with that capricious and flighty manner you have. *And* the careless way you put yourself in danger. And for God's sake get down off that damned animal: I've a crick in me neck from looking up at you.'

'Again I say what I do does not concern you and *no*, I will not get down. I am on my way home so let go of that bridle before I am forced to lay my crop about you.'

114

He sighed and stepped away. His face was without expression now, the warmth and laughter she always seemed to have the power of inspiring in him, emptying from him.

'You're right, it's nowt to do wi' me so I'll move on and you can do the same, Miss Harrison.'

He watched her turn, ready to guide her mare away, her head, so strangely defenceless in its short, close-fitting cap of tumbled waves, held in high disdain. He was struck by the way the loss of her hair, which was said to be a woman's crowning glory, had made her somehow more and not less feminine and the words were out before he stopped to think about them, or the effect they were to have on his life.

'It suits you like that. I don't know why it should, but it does.'

'Your approval is of no concern to me, Will Broadbent. I'm sure you know that?' Her lip curled disdainfully but she did not move on.

'Indeed I do, Miss Harrison. You don't give a damn what anyone thinks, or so you keep telling me and who am I to argue?' His mouth began to twitch again and she looked at him suspiciously, not at all sure whether to be offended again. He smiled as his eyes went to her hair, but they admired it now, and *her*, and she was somewhat mollified.

'Well, then,' she said, not quite sure what she meant by it.

'Come on, get down and let me look at you properly. I'm certain there must be some quite fascinating explanation on how it came about and, really, I can't wait to hear it.'

'If you're going to make fun...'

'No, really. I would like to know how you persuaded your mother, who must be a remarkable lady, to let you have it cut, and besides, we cannot be at each other's throats every time we meet. I thought we were to be friends when we were at Annie's ... No, no...' He stood back, his hands uplifted in a placatory manner, his grin broadening, '...I'm not going to lecture you, really. If you are intent on risking yourself...'

'Mr Broadbent...' Her voice had a warning in it, but she swung her leg over her mare's rump; then, fastening the bridle to a clump of gorse, she moved to stand beside him, looking out over the darkening valley.

There was a mist coming off the river, tinged a soft rose-pink by the last of the sun's rays, and further along the valley bottom was the dark smudge which was Crossfold. Lights pricked the smudge but up here they were still in full daylight. They had moved together, sauntering towards the flat rock on which he had previously been squatting, lowering themselves into the same sitting position with their arms about their drawn-up knees. Neither spoke as they allowed the soft-hued ease of mind which Will Broadbent seemed to generate, to slip comfortably over them again. It was satisfying, tranquil, with no need of words to fill the silence and yet they were both aware, Will more than Tessa, that there was more to it than that. He acknowledged her as she was, awkward, stubborn, wilful, and did not judge her nor condemn her, for he understood her striving nature which in many ways was like his own. And sensing his understanding and acceptance she was untroubled, with no need of the defiance she showed to others. She could be herself, perhaps the self no one had ever seen before, allowing the friction with which she challenged life to be gladly set to one side.

'I really *do* take the dogs with me when I ride out alone, Mr Broadbent, and having seen them that day at Annie's you must realise that I am quite safe with them. But today, though I set out with my cousins I decided to come home early. We had been with the hunt...'

'So I see by the blood on your face.'

'You don't approve?'

''Tis a cruel sport, lass, and the custom of rubbing the brush of the poor little beggar on your face ... well, it's what I would call barbaric.'

116

She bristled and he put a hand on her arm. 'Nay, don't let's start again. See, wipe that mark off your cheek...' He pulled a clean white square from his pocket but instead of handing it to her he turned her face towards him with a big, gentle hand and rubbed at the dried blood which had turned a rusty brown on the smooth skin of her cheek. It was stubborn and he clicked his tongue, his eyes engrossed with his task. She watched his face with an odd breathlessness and a feeling of expectancy, her eyes bemused, and as he felt her gaze on him his breath shortened. He cleared his throat.

'It doesn't seem to want to come off.' He tried to sound casual. The hand which held her chin trembled.

'Try a bit of spit.' Her voice was soft and there was a quiver in it and he knew he must be very careful with her. She was a woman, but yet a child: innocent and trusting with him, but not, he was sure, ignorant. She was of an age when most girls were thinking of marriage, but still a child and he must be careful.

He made his voice merry though the effort was great.

'A bit of spit! Miss Harrison, whatever next?' She smiled then put out her tongue and when he had rubbed his handkerchief across its pink moistness, he carefully cleaned off the offending stain, not meeting those incredible eyes which were looking so earnestly into his.

'What do you do on your day off?' she asked him presently and though he had resumed his contemplation of the shadowy valley he was aware that she was still studying him.

'Nowt, really. I walk across the hills if I feel like it or go to political meetings, but there's not a lot to do in these parts when the mill's closed. There's talk of forming a football team in the mill but they'll not want me in it since I've never played the game in me life and I'm too old to start now.'

'How old are you, Mr Broadbent?'

He turned to smile at her and watched the corners of her

mouth lift in answer to his. 'I must be twenty-eight or nine, I suppose.'

'Really!' and her sixteen-year-old face conveyed pity. 'What else do you do?'

'Sometimes I take the train to Manchester and then in the summer there's the fairs. I read a lot but more often than not after I've been in the mill all week I feel the need to get out and let the wind blow in me face and even the rain . . .'

'I know.'

'Oh, aye.' He turned to her in surprise for though she was a forthright, independent and, some said, entirely too free a young lady for her own good, he had not realised that she shared his own deep attachment to this bleak environment which was their heritage.

'Indeed. I can think of nowhere I would rather be.' As she spoke she felt a sense of surprise for she could clearly hear her own voice, accompanied by those of Drew and Pearce, bemoaning the fact that they were forced to remain here, tied to the family inheritance. It really was amazing. What was it about this man which brought out something in her which she had not even known was there? That made her say things which were sometimes insolent, disdainful, mocking as only she could be and the next moment seduce her into a state of well-being in which she brought forth statements she had certainly not meant to make, nor even knew she had believed? And yet she *did* love this high patch of Lancashire despite her constant reiteration to Drew and Pearce that she wanted only to get away with them to some magical world which she had convinced herself existed beyond it.

She turned to look at him, a large and personable man, smiling, his expression steady, interested, humorous, concerned with what she had to say and finding it worthwhile. 'But that doesn't mean I wouldn't like to travel, to see some of the world beyond the Penfold Valley, as long as I could come home to it.' As she spoke she knew that what she said was the truth though she had not been aware of it. Her voice

118

had become somewhat defiant again, irritated with herself for allowing him to glimpse a part of her which was not really meant to be seen.

'No indeed.' His voice was grave.

'Don't smile, Mr Broadbent.'

'I'm not smiling, lass, but do you think you could bring yourself to call me Will?'

The fire had been built up, the logs crackling and fragrant, the flames glowing into the high ceiling and casting shadows on the rich rosewood panelling as she entered the hallway. It was quiet and deserted, warm, secure and so ... so *homely* she felt her heart wrench and she stopped, one foot on the bottom tread of the stairs.

She turned and looked about her, studying this home of hers which she had never before really noticed. A hundred hundred times she had raced up and down these stairs; skated along the tiled floor in pursuit of, or pursued by her cousins. She had laughed and cried, screamed in temper and skipped for joy. She had toasted marshmallows in the flames of the fire, sat on a stool and dreamed into it, played all manner of games and tricks and all the time the house had been here, as steadfast and reliable as ... as Will – now why had she thought that, she wondered, confused – or her mother, always here when she really needed her. As safe as houses, that was what they said, and that was exactly what she felt here. She always protested that she didn't *want* to be *safe*, but she realised in that moment, perhaps just for that moment, that everyone needed a place, or a person, in whom they felt secure. There had always been this house *and her mother!*

And tonight she knew she was going to distress her mother, take from her the pleasure her brother's visit brought her just as surely as if she were to strike her full in the face. And all for a childish whim. No more. That was what it had been, an impulsive, infantile caprice which was not worthy of her mother's daughter. Her mother would be

119

upset, she knew full well she would when she saw the state of her hair; she had known full well when she had allowed Drew to cut it, but it had not stopped her.

And that was what had taken the lovely glow, the excitement of the day from her when the hunt was finished, that and the unspoken regret in Will Broadbent. Though he might tell her she looked well with her hair shorn like a ragamuffin – and perhaps she did, perhaps it suited her in its strangeness – but she had sensed that he deplored the loss of the long, shining splendour of the hair which she had discarded so lightly last night. As her mother would. No doubt Drew and Pearce would be back soon for not even they would dare risk their father's displeasure should they not be home for dinner. Drew would defend her, try to take the blame; he would say he had encouraged her, own up to his share in the horror for it had been his hand which had held the scissors.

She could hear Uncle Joss's laughter in the drawing-room. It was almost dark. They would be having sherry perhaps, Charlie and Laurel, her mother, Aunt Kit and Uncle Joss, her family, before going upstairs to bathe and change for dinner. The mills would have closed at six the night before, the boilers not to be fired up until five tomorrow morning, Monday. She and her cousins had been invited to ride to hounds any day they pleased now that the season had begun and she had heard Drew promise carelessly, thoughtlessly – since when would Uncle Joss allow his sons to hunt on a working day? – that they would all be at the Hall tomorrow. Between then and now she must try . . . try to explain – was there an explanation? – to her mother; make an effort to clarify . . . well, demonstrate to her mother *why* – was there a logical reason? – she had acted as she had. To say she was sorry. That she hadn't given it any *real* thought. That she hadn't really *cared*, at the time. To plead with her mother to understand.

In that moment Tessa Harrison began the difficult process of growing up. For the first time in her young life she felt

120

compassion for *someone*, an adult, not a sickly kitten or an orphaned puppy or a rabbit caught in a trap, as children do, but a person who, by *her* action would be wounded. Somehow she must let that person know that she was sorry; not sorry that her hair was cut short, but that the cutting of it should cause her mother distress. And now was as good a time as any to begin. She knew quite positively that this remorse on another person's behalf would not last, that it was not in her to bend her will to another's, to put the wishes of someone else before her own, to curb the wilful need to get away from the restrictions her sex, her age and her class put upon her, but right now she was experiencing these emotions and she must do what her often-stormy heart told her before she changed her mind.

She did not fling open the drawing-room door as she normally would, noisily, a child still in her exuberant need for life and excitement, but moved into the room in a manner so sedate it would have gladdened Miss Copeland's heart.

They all turned to smile, her family, welcoming her and had she not, for the moment anyway, been this new and strange Tessa she would have laughed out loud as their smiles slipped away like ice melting in the sunshine. They sat like figures carved in stone for several moments then very slowly her mother put down the glass she was holding, not once taking her eyes from her, and raised a trembling hand to cover her mouth. She seemed unable to move beyond that, her eyes enormous in her bone-white face, her body still, her brain atrophied and unable to function, or so it appeared.

'Tessa ... child ... have you had an accident?' her Aunt Kit faltered and her Uncle Joss rose slowly to his feet, ready, should he be needed, to move rapidly across the carpet to catch his niece when she fell, as fall she undoubtedly would.

'Dear God ... sweetheart...' Charlie sprang to life, pushing aside Laurel's trembling hand, striding with his great long legs after his brother until they both stood before

121

her their hands lifted, eager to comfort, to support, to hold, but not sure where to lay them since they did not want to cause further damage.

'What happened? Jesus, lass, what happened?'

'Nothing . . .'

'But look at you. Your riding habit is covered with blood or . . . or is it mud? And your face . . . you're as white as a sheet. What the devil . . . who . . . ?'

Slowly her Uncle Joss's eyes rose to her hair and she became aware that her unkempt appearance . . . yes, she remembered now, she had come off her mare in the ditch beside Jenkinson's oat field . . . well, it would be the Squire's oat field since Jenkinson only rented it from him – her appearance, stained, muddy, bloody from the fox had somehow distracted them from the real injury of the day. The injury to her beautiful hair.

'Who did it?' Charlie whispered, his mind racing to all kinds of horror, to vagrants and gypsies, tinkers and ruffians, rapists and those who . . . who . . . and surely this child had been in some pervert's hands for who else would take from her her lovely hair, and if they had taken that, what else had she lost?

Her mother's face floated, she could think of no other words, towards her, stationing itself besides Charlie's shoulder, grey and amazingly agonised and for a moment Tessa was confounded by its strangeness, its utter, utter horror.

'Now, Jenny, it's all right, lass,' her Uncle Joss said, moving rapidly to take her mother's arm and Tessa was made aware that there was something in her mother's absolute terror that had nothing to do with her. 'Tell us who did this to you, Tessa, tell us . . .'

'I did it,' she protested harshly and again they were all struck dumb. And all the softness, the love and remorse with which she had been going to approach them evaporated in her own terrified distress for matters had all gone so horribly wrong. 'I was tired of having Emma forever nagging me to have it brushed and washed . . . and pinned up . . .

122

put into nets ... and things. Well, I asked her to cut it ...'
Her voice had become high, childish in her defiance.

'Are you saying Emma cut your hair?'

'No, oh, no, Uncle Joss, no, she wouldn't so ...' boldly,
'... I did it myself.' She lifted her shorn head, 'And I like it
even if no one else does.'

'Well, no one else does, that's a certainty,' and Charlie,
her beloved Charlie on whom she had always counted
to defend her when no one else would, turned away in
disgust.

There was a clatter in the hallway and a cheerful voice
shouted that it was going to see if there was a chance of a
drink in the drawing-room. The door burst open and with
all the enthusiasm of two boys let out of school, Drew and
Pearce Greenwood catapulted into the room, just as mud-
spattered, just as tumbled, just as wild-riding and wild-
natured as she herself had been, and in their path stood Joss
Greenwood and his sister, Jenny Harrison.

'Whoops,' said Pearce frivolously, still laughing from the
overflow of champagne which had run like water from a tap
in the Squire's great hall and of which he and Drew and
several other of their young companions had drunk deeply.

'You have been at play with the young lordlings, then,'
their father asked ominously, 'and have just this moment
decided to grace your mother's drawing-room with your
presence?'

Drew laughed and swaggered, somewhat unsteadily, in
the direction of the nearest chair but his father's voice cut
about him like a whip.

'Stay where you are, lad, unless you want to feel my hand
in your face.'

'Joss ... darling ...' Kit murmured but her husband for
once did not listen to her voice.

'I would like to know, and by God, one of you had better
be quick in telling me, what has been going on here today.
First we have missy here,' he waved a heavy hand in Tessa's
direction, 'coming in looking like some waif from the

bloody workhouse, frightening everyone into thinking she had been robbed or . . .' he shook his head like some beast tormented by three troublesome flies, 'or worse, and then you two swagger in as though you were lords of the bloody manor, and as drunk . . .'

'Joss . . .'

'Don't Joss me, Kit Chapman,' he roared and the wild temper which none of them, including his wife, had seen for years, made them all wince. 'What's going on here and what's this damned girl had done to her? Because if you think for a moment I believe she cut her own hair just for the hell of it . . .'

'I did, Uncle Joss.'

'No one asked you to speak, girl,' he thundered, turning on her, and Jenny put out a hand to him, the first stirring of alarm, not for her daughter but for him, moving in her. Now that she had determined that Tessa was not physically hurt, she could feel her own outrage growing: an inclination to drag the girl upstairs, put her across her knee as she would a child and give her a long-overdue thrashing. What she had done was childishly defiant and though she herself had cut her own hair short against all the then rules of decency, it had been done for a completely different reason.

Or had it?

Jenny Harrison looked back for a moment to that wilful, resolute girl she herself had been more than twenty-five years ago. Resolute in her determination, she had told herself to protect and support her mother, her younger brother and sister whilst Joss had been fighting the injustice inflicted by the oppressive millowner. She had been forced to go into the mill when her father was killed at Peterloo and her brother had gone out on the rampage, wild with grief and his need to take Joshua Greenwood's place. She had been the only wage earner in the family and the responsibility had made her strong, self-willed, defiant of convention. She had told herself that to cut her hair was a measure of safety in the spinning room where machinery was waiting to drag

124

in any careless hand or unbound length of hair, but, if she were honest, had she really cared about that when she had taken her father's shears to her own waist-length mass of curls? Had she not been impatient of control – as her daughter was – the control that said that whilst Joss might spend his time marching with the rioting men, smashing machines and windows in his challenge of the masters, she must stay at home and guard his family? It had been no more than a display of her own revolution and when it was done and she had enjoyed the shocked stares and whispered disapproval she had had no choice but to leave it as it was.

The memory brought a measure of understanding.

'Go upstairs, girl,' she said quietly to her daughter. 'I will be up directly.'

When Tessa had gone she turned to the tableau which still stood, tense and ready at any moment to explode into a scene of great violence. The two young men had somehow arranged themselves shoulder to shoulder, not exactly with their fists up and clenched, but giving the impression that they were prepared to fight should they be pushed to it. Her brother, she realised with something of a shock, was no longer taller than his two lean young sons, and she recognised, if he did not, that though they were no more than seventeen they were at that inevitable stage in a man's life when he is no longer prepared to be dominated by his father. They were young men now, the two of them, each a part of the other, a double commitment of conflict; young cubs yet, showing their teeth to the old lion but not prepared for much longer to back away from his superior strength.

'Leave it, Joss,' she said.

'No, by God! These two have been inciting that lass of yours for years now, dragging her along on their wild skylarking . . .'

'She'd not need much dragging, Joss.' He took no notice.

'. . . treating her as though she herself was a young lad and this is the last bloody straw . . .'

125

'Joss, Tessa is my responsibility . . .'

'As these two are mine and it seems to me that I've been sadly lacking in that direction, but I mean to change that right now. They've been up at the Hall drinking, aye, seventeen years old and carrying on as though they were the Squire's sons and with a perfect right to live the lives of landed gentlemen. I'll have a word or two to say to Longworth the next time we meet. *His* son might be allowed to act the rake-hell if he wishes but mine certainly will not. Don't think because I'm in London I know nothing of how you joy-ride about the countryside on those damned thoroughbreds of yours, which were bought, by the way, from your Aunt Jenny's and Charlie's efforts on *your* behalf in the mill. And now Tessa is becoming the same. It's time all three of you settled down to the realisation of who you are: the sons and daughter of a *millowner*. You drift in here as though you're doing us a bloody favour by bestowing your company on us. Your mother has been most upset,' – which was not true for Kit Greenwood, though she loved her sons, barely gave them a thought as long as her husband was with her – 'and I'll not have it. Now I don't know whose idea it was to crop that child's head like some sheep at shearing time but I've absolutely no doubt that one of you or both, had something to do with it.'

He passed a hand over his eyes and there was a visible tremor in it. Jenny frowned, for suddenly something seemed not quite right about the shape of her brother's face, and the smooth amber of it, the look of glowing health which had always been his, appeared to be draining away, leaving it grey and clammy. He put out a hand, blindly seeking some support and in that moment before they began to move towards him in alarm, he seemed to shrink so that not only were his young sons as tall as he but exceedingly taller.

'Joss!' The scream which came from his wife's throat had all the despair and terror of a child who has been confronted with a dark, unimaginable nightmare. It was heard quite clearly in the kitchen, freezing every servant to immobility, and up in her room where Tessa sat disconsolately on her dressing-table stool, sighing over the punishment which was surely coming, the sound brought her to her feet.

Drew and Pearce Greenwood, with the rapid reflexes of the young, had their father by the arms, one on either side of him, their own faces as pale as death itself, their strength the only support which kept him from crashing to the floor like some poleaxed animal. They were quite appalled, panic-stricken, for it seemed their reckless insolence so evident in the unabashed rebellion they had shown, was killing their father before their very eyes.

'Father ... ?' Pearce's voice, no longer that of a man but of a frightened young boy, followed close on their mother's scream. They loved him, their distraught young faces said; they were sorry, dear God, how they were sorry, and if he would just stand up straight and give them both a good hiding they would never defy him again. But as their mother flung herself across the room, her arms outstretched to hold him, not only upright but in this world since she could not live without him, her expression said, he slipped quietly from their grasp into a crumpled and surprisingly small heap on the carpet.

The doctor had gone, swearing that if Mr Greenwood put a foot out of bed within the next month, Mrs Greenwood would surely be a widow. He would call the next day, he said; a light diet, perhaps a bit of fish or chicken, and certainly, now that he had been bled he would improve. Mrs Greenwood was to take this potion to make her sleep, or *she* would be his next patient. Yes, undoubtedly Mr Greenwood had been overworking but it was only a slight inflammation of the head and, given time and rest, he would recover.

Kit Greenwood was drifting protectively over the still-sleeping figure of her husband, her violet-blue eyes enormous in the suddenly old and waxy pallor of her face, ignoring the doctor's advice regarding herself with the con-

127

tempt it deserved. *Sleep*, when the only person who had ever meant *anything* to her in the whole of her life, might slip away whilst she closed her eyes! Was anything more ridiculous? She attached herself to his bedside, not quite touching him, but certainly willing into him the very breath of her own lungs should his not prove adequate.

They sat in the drawing-room, none of them speaking for what was there to say? It was their fault, of course, his sons and his niece knew, for had he not been so goaded by their waywardness, he would undoubtedly not be lying inches from death at this very minute. Laurel held Charlie's hand, badly frightened and in need of comfort, blaming them as much as they did themselves. She was seen to lean her bright head against the sombre darkness of his shoulder, sighing tearfully, for though Joss Greenwood was not her father by blood, she loved him dearly.

They were side by side on the sofa, the three culprits, Drew and Pearce with Tessa between them, still in the mud and muck of the hunting field and they all jumped guiltily when Jenny spoke.

'This is not your fault, you know.'

'Oh, Mother, it was, it was.' Tessa began to weep noisily, no longer, now that the crisis was over somewhat, able to contain herself.

'We've always made him wild, Aunt Jenny, and now look what we've done.' Pearce's voice was distraught and Drew put his head in his hands, filled, it seemed, with the deepest shame.

But Jenny Harrison, though she recognised this as an ideal opportunity to hit them with the stick her brother's 'turn' had presented to her, was too honest a woman to use it.

'No, lad. Joss has always had a quick temper. We all have, let's be honest, and if it were that which had cudgelled him as it did, he would have been struck down years ago. Your father has driven himself for the last thirty years doing what he set out to do when your grandfather died on St Peter's Field. He swore then he'd take the fight wherever it was needed to try to get a decent living for the "afflicted poor", as we were called. Aye, I say "we" because he and Charlie and me were among them when the hand loom became obsolete. He fought himself to a standstill, did your father. He went to gaol twice, as you know, and for the past twenty years he's never given up hope of a fair deal for the working man. Twenty hours a day he's worked and I reckon he's just paid the price for it. He wanted to see the rest of the men he fought beside get a vote of their own, you see, not just those with property and influence, but it's not come and I think it's taken the strength from him. So you're not to blame yourselves, any of you. But that's not to say you've no need to mend your ways. I want to see you two at the mill gate at five thirty sharp tomorrow morning and as for you, miss, you'll go nowhere without a bonnet to cover that head of yours until your hair's a decent length. D'you hear?'

Tessa said fervently that she did but even as Jenny Harrison looked into the tearful face she was aware that though her daughter meant what she said, and honestly meant to obey her, it would not be long before she forgot her bonnet, or lost it, or simply threw it away, since she was *her* daughter after all.

That night as Tessa lay restless in the tangled covers of her bed, the house hushed and uneasy about her, she brooded on the shape and colour of her own nature. Why had she done it? Why did she do so many wild and challenging things? There was no need. She was allowed so much more freedom than the girls of her acquaintance and yet she abused it, gambled with it, risked losing it just for the sake of some excitement, which, after all, caused nothing but sorrow to her family whom she loved dearly. That moment of reflection in the hallway before she had entered the drawing-room had been, probably, the first feeling of uncertainty she had known in her life. She had found it uncomfortable and so had ignored it. But perhaps they were right, those who bade her shape her restless activities into a more lady-like pattern. Perhaps she should stay at home

129

and ... and ... *what?* What should she do? Sew and paint, play the piano and write interminable letters ...? Oh, dear Lord, the thought appalled her. She couldn't do it but she really would try to be a little more as her family wanted her to be. She would ... she ... would ...

# 8

They were seventeen years old when they really *saw* her for the first time and strangely, or perhaps not in view of their closeness, they did so at exactly the same moment.

'I think we'll give a big Christmas party this year,' Laurel said, 'not just the family but friends as well. We could empty the salon and line the walls with chairs, put a dais at one end and engage a small orchestra so that we might dance. Not a grand ball since we haven't the space and not a dinner party either but something in between the two.' She turned anxiously to Charlie who was studying a newspaper whilst coffee was being served after dinner. 'Do you think it might be possible to invite the Squire, darling?' She sat down beside her husband and looked up entreatingly into his face, begging his support, her tense look implying how dearly she would love someone to show some interest in this splendid idea of hers. There was nothing she feared more than being overlooked in this family of arrogant males – except Charlie, of course – and self-possessed women and yet, unless she stamped her foot and pouted, made a great to-do, that was exactly what happened.

'There's no reason why he shouldn't be sent an invitation,' Charlie answered her absently, 'though whether he accepts is an entirely different matter.'

'Drew, Pearce and Tessa are frequent guests at the Hall so do you not think he might be persuaded to allow us to repay his hospitality? It would be only good manners on our part after all.'

'Nothing ventured, nothing gained, sweetheart.'

'We might even make it into a fancy-dress affair, everyone masked until midnight. That might tempt him,' she continued, for she was desperate to get into what she called 'good' society. If she did she was convinced she would be more ... well, more ... assured and less prone to this foolish – she knew it – belief that she was going to be, that they were *all* going to be, flung back to the old days when the Greenwoods had been nothing but lowly weavers. If she could just claim the patronage of the Squire and his lady, if she could drop it casually into the conversation of her afternoon callers that she had more than a second-hand acquaintance with the leading family of the Penfold Valley, how grand it would be and how special she, Laurel Greenwood, would feel.

'It sounds delightful, Laurel,' Drew yawned, then turned to look at his brother for he was well aware of his sister's longing for social recognition in the gentrified class of Crossfold. He raised an enquiring eyebrow at Pearce asking if it might be possible for the two of them to slip away to some more congenial surroundings but Laurel intercepted the look which passed between them and her face became thoughtful.

'Why don't you put it to Nicky Longworth?' she said after a moment. 'The three of you have been thick as thieves for years.'

'You mean ask Nick to ask his father and mother if they would kindly agree to attend my sister's party?'

'Oh, Drew, you know what I mean.' She sighed tremulously. 'Naturally you and Pearce will be there...'

'Are you certain, my pet?' Pearce grinned amiably.

'I am *positive*, Pearce Greenwood, am I not, Charlie?' The dreadfulness of their father's collapse, though he had

131

recovered now, still remained vivid to both young men and they became instantly restrained.

Her husband laid down his newspaper and turned politely to her. He was always polite to his wife.

'I beg your pardon, dear?'

'I am begging your support, Charlie, in the matter of my Christmas party and I must insist that you compel Drew and Pearce to be there. Aunt Jenny ... ' She twisted anxiously in the direction of her aunt who glanced up reluctantly from some papers she was studying. Tessa watched her mother's eyes turn from warm interest to cool appraisal of her brother's wife. Her mother always looked like that when she was brought face to face with Laurel's hunger for social advancement: cool, expressionless, disinterested as though the trivia with which Laurel concerned herself was mindlessly tedious.

'. . . you do agree with me, don't you?' Laurel was saying, apparently unaware of her aunt's slightly jaded opinion of her, and Tessa wondered at Laurel's absorption with her children, her husband, her position in the society of Crossfold and the Penfold Valley to the complete exclusion of anything else.

'Agree with what?'

'That Drew and Pearce must be made to attend my party and to use their influence and advantage as friends of Nicky Longworth in persuading the Squire to accept my invitation to it.'

'What party is that?' Tessa felt a surge of interest for was there to be an argument to alleviate the boredom of the hours between dinner and bedtime?

'Oh, Aunt Jenny, please listen. And you, Charlie. It will be Christmas in four weeks' time and I would love to give you a Christmas party – something entirely different from the usual family affair, particularly as Father and Mother will be unable to attend. Mother tells me Father is settling down nicely in Italy but the journey back for Christmas so soon after arriving there is completely out of the question.'

132

'I appreciate that, Laurel, but what is wrong with just having family for Christmas dinner?' Jenny said suspiciously. 'It is what we have done for the past twenty years and I see no reason to change. The children enjoy it and it would be a shame to have a party which excluded them.'

'They could still have their party on Christmas Day but we could have *ours* on Christmas Eve. A Christmas Eve fancy-dress ball with masks ... a champagne supper ... decorate the salon. Heavens, it must be years since it was used. It would be when Father was re-elected in ... when was it? Ten years ago. Oh, please, Charlie, you must say yes.' She turned to him, her white skin flushed with a lovely rosy glow, her green eyes sparkling up into his, her whole body surging enchantingly towards him. Tessa saw him soften and lean somehow towards her, the movement at once conveying something which made her look away awkwardly and her cousins exchange knowing glances. A promise between them, from her to him, something she pledged to give him if he would back her up on this against Jenny who was bound to be awkward on general principle. Not that Charlie ever denied his wife anything. She had a way with her sometimes that was hard to resist, so soft and pretty and gentle, and Charlie viewed it fondly. Or did he just do it for the sake of peace? A peaceful man was Charlie, who hated discord and loved his wife.

Tessa grimaced in embarrassment and turned away from them and at that moment both Drew and Pearce looked at her. To her amazed bewilderment, instead of grinning and pulling a face as they would normally do when confronted with one of Laurel's little play-acting performances, they continued to stare at her as though they were hypnotised. Two pairs of vivid eyes held some strange expression in them, unreadable in the soft glow of the lamplight and she felt the discomfort rise up in her until it reached her heart which began to thump against her breastbone. What was the matter with the pair of them? Had she grown another head, or was it her hair which Emma had arranged with a complicated array of pins and a knot of bright ribbon in an attempt to disguise its short and springing growth? It had increased by an inch or so in the last month and could now be pushed behind her ears but it was still difficult to contrive a style which could in any way be called normal. She knew her mother sighed when she looked at her but then she had never been a young lady concerned with fashion, had she? She was too tall for one thing, where small and dainty was the vogue, with a long-limbed grace which was quite delightful had she but known it. She had broad shoulders, a bosom which had continued to bloom until it was quite splendid. She was dark with what she knew was a big mouth, when fair hair and rosebud lips were considered the thing. Tall, dark and well-rounded, then, with a comical hair style, but that did not give her cousins the right to stare at her as she had seen them stare at many a pretty girl. She was *not* a pretty girl: she was their cousin and companion of many years. To show her disapproval, first making sure no one was watching but them, she pulled a face and poked her tongue out at them.

At once they folded into silent laughter, both of them spluttering into their after-dinner port and a great wave of relief washed over her as Pearce winked and inclined his head in Laurel's direction, sighing dramatically.

Drew, however, turned courteously to Laurel.

'I think it is a splendid idea, big sister, and I for one am all in favour of it.'

'Why, thank you, Drew. There you are, you see.' She turned in triumph to Jenny. 'Someone else is on my side.'

Pearce, knowing instinctively that Drew had some reason, which no doubt would be revealed in a moment, for this turnabout, spoke up in his support.

'I am with you, too, Laurel. It would make a splendid change to have a party to which one could invite one's friends.'

'Really! You mean it?' Laurel was enchanted. 'And you would sound out Nicky Longworth?'

'Oh, indeed. I dare say all our acquaintances' – meaning, of course, in the fox-hunting society of the Penfold Valley, which he knew quite well was what Laurel referred to – 'would be delighted.'

'It sounds daft to me,' Jenny muttered irritably, turning back to the report she was reading, 'and if you think I'm going to dress up as Good Queen Bess or Mary Stuart, you can think again.'

It was plain from Laurel's face she cared not a jot or tittle what Jenny Harrison did, nor even if she attended *her* Christmas party at all. Important people would be there, people with whom she longed to mix, people of fashion and good breeding, considered to be gentry in the Penfold Valley. For most of her life she had been on the same footing as the local towers of trade and commerce, rich and powerful men, many of them, but it was the 'ancient' families of south Lancashire on whom she had her sights, those who were not merchants, shopkeepers, industrialists; whose money had come to them not by way of anything which could be bought and sold, but was inherited wealth. And the head of the local society, of course, was the high Tory Squire Longworth, the greatest landowner in the district. The only way the new railway route to Crossfold could effectively proceed was across the Squire's vast estate and by allowing it he had become almost as wealthy as the Greenwoods themselves. The Squire had never accepted an invitation to any of the homes of the local millocracy but if Laurel Greenwood, through her younger brother's connections with them, could coax him and his lady wife to hers, what a feather in her cap that would be. A triumph indeed for would she herself not have a foot in the door of Longworth Hall, and where, her excited thoughts wanted to know, might that lead her?

'So it's settled then?' she asked breathlessly, her hand gripping Charlie's arm in a passion of joy.

'Indeed it is, if Aunt Jenny agrees.' Drew sipped his port peaceably.

'It's nothing to do with me, lad.'

'Well, then, all we have to do now is to decide what we are to go as. I must admit I can quite see myself as a Regency buck: I would look well with a powdered wig. As for Tessa, what would suit her more than one of those delectable, high-waisted draperies of shimmering fabric I am told the Empress Josephine used to wear? I can quite see her . . .'

'Yes, yes, how splendid.' Laurel was not really listening though both Jenny Harrison and Pearce Greenwood turned to look at Drew with narrowed, uncertain eyes. 'What will you wear, Charlie?'

Laurel's delight was very appealing and Tessa saw Charlie's hand go out to touch the back of her neck, resting there in a warm caress, and again, when she looked away, her eyes met those of both her cousins who had also seen it. Their expressions, so similar it was quite uncanny, were speaking of something which caused a strange but not unpleasant fluttering in her throat.

'And what will you go as, Pearce?' she heard herself say, surprised at the ordinary sound of her own voice.

'I had not thought . . .'

'Oh, come on, Pearce,' Laurel was laughing now, animated and lovely, looking no more than nineteen again in her excitement. 'How about Henry the Eighth?'

'Please, Laurel . . .' He tore his eyes away, reluctantly Tessa thought, from her own, his face a warm brown, his mouth beginning to curl in a familiar, whimsical smile, 'I have hardly the figure to play Henry the Eighth. But we shall see, shall we not, brother, what the evening will bring?' There was something in his voice which seemed to say he was not referring to costumes.

She wore a dress of incredibly light chiffon, high-waisted with satin ribbons tied beneath her breasts, as Drew had described so accurately. The narrow skirt fell in straight folds to her sandalled feet and she floated all in white like a wisp of swansdown, the hem of the dress drifting and fluting about her naked ankles. Her arms and shoulders were bare though her mother insisted that the deep plunge of the neckline be draped to hide the swell of her smooth white breasts. Her hair was brushed up on her head, arranged with false pads and curls into a reasonable copy of a Grecian hairstyle, an intricate arrangement of glossy swathes and ringlets threaded through with white satin ribbon.

'Who are you supposed to be then?' her mother asked, quite amused now that she had ensured her daughter was as decorous as propriety demanded, though what Crossfold would make of it she could not imagine.

'I am a Grecian lady of great renown.'

'Dear Lord, who's that then?'

'Diana the huntress.'

'Didn't she have some kind of an animal?'

Tessa's face fell. 'Yes, she did. Do you think I could take one of the dogs?'

'Now Laurel *would* have something to say about that.'

Tessa laughed, then turning abruptly, leaned down to kiss her mother's cheek hurriedly. They were not given to demonstrations of affection, but she felt a great flow of it well up in her for this woman who, she was fully aware, had always gone against the code of her society in allowing her daughter so much freedom.

'Thank you, Mother.'

'For what, child?'

'I don't know, really, I just want you to know . . .'

'I *do* know, Tessa. Now come on, lass, we don't want Laurel to steal all the limelight. Not that she's likely to, the minute those downstairs clap eyes on you.'

Even now it was uncertain whether the Squire would attend. He had answered Laurel's invitation with a brief note to say he had a prior commitment on that date but if he could manage it he and his family and Christmas guests might look in for half an hour to wish the Greenwood family

137

seasonal greetings. It was almost in the style of a manorial lord bestowing a visit on a deserving tenant.

Laurel was delirious with joy, almost insufferable in her pride. She was unaware that had it not been for Nicky Long-worth who had reminded his father of the charm, the wit, the good looks and good manners of the three Greenwood youngsters who were often included in the Squire's hunt, he would have thrown the invitation to the back of the fire where it belonged.

They went downstairs together, mother and daughter. Jenny, who vowed she was far too old for dressing up, appeared serene and elegant in stark black velvet, relieved only by a magnificent diamond choker about her smooth neck and long earrings to match. She made the perfect contrast for her exquisitely, simply dressed daughter and the two young men who watched for her at the foot of the stairs were bound in her spell, caught in the shimmering magic of her.

'Drew, Pearce, good evening,' their aunt said to them, offering a cheek to each in turn, which they kissed without once taking their eyes from Tessa. 'You both look very dashing. And what a cold evening it is. I do believe it might snow before morning. A white Christmas would be lovely for the children.'

'Indeed.'

'Where are Laurel and Charlie?'

'In the drawing-room. The first guests are due to arrive any moment.'

'Well . . .' She glanced from one entranced face to the other and a small pang of misgiving struck her. She had seen that look on a man's face many, many times, directed not only at her daughter as now, but at other women, including herself. It came in different guises from pure lust to the deep and endless love, strong, steadfast and beautiful to see, that her older brother felt for his wife, the mother of these two young men. And if it transpired that one or the other of her brother's boys should make up with *her* girl she would have no objection. They were wild and reckless, hot tempered and arrogant, but good-natured withal. And her girl was strong, stronger than both of them, though that was not yet immediately apparent; she would tame and control, shape into a steady man, the one who would be her husband. It would be a good match, but with which one, for God's sake? They were both looking at Tessa as though she was the Christmas fairy come to life.

Jenny shook her head, smiling at her own absurdity, for they blew hot and cold, the pair of them, changing their minds as often as they changed their splendid jackets. Tessa looked superb tonight, older than her years and eternally feminine, and would not any man with a drop of red blood in his veins stare as these two were doing?

'I'll join them for a sherry, then,' she said, wondering why she bothered, and left the three of them knowing that none had even noticed she had gone.

The young men were dressed identically in tight black riding breeches and a white frilled shirt open at the neck. Their tall boots reached their knees and they wore gold earrings looped on thread about their ears and a red bandana most rakishly tilted over one eye. Their brown skin and white teeth added to their startlingly effective appearance, as did the mock cutlass they each wore at their belts. Laurel had decided against masks as she wanted none of the company to be in any doubt of the identity of the peerless guests she hoped to entertain this night.

'Pirates or gypsies?' Tessa asked impishly.

'He's a pirate and I'm a gypsy.'

'How clever.'

'We thought so, but not half as clever as you, little cousin,' Drew stepped away from Pearce to stand in front of her as she moved down from the bottom tread of the stairs. Pearce frowned and fingered his cutlass, ready to plunge it into his brother's back, but she stepped lightly between them, moving towards the towering Christmas tree which stood at the foot of the stairs, adjusting a strand of tinsel on its bough, allowing them to study her whilst she stood gracefully on tip-toe to reach the branch.

'You *have* grown up since we saw you an hour ago,' Pearce murmured, his eyes narrowed, 'and in a most delightful way. Mind you, we have noticed for the past week or two that you have become quite the young lady, have we not, Drew?'

'Indeed we have.'

'And in what way is that, Pearce?' she asked innocently, immensely pleased with her own womanhood which had come on her so suddenly and so splendidly. She smiled over her shoulder, scarcely troubled, as she had been on the night the party had been discussed, by their speculative glances, for did she not know what scamps they were? Charming scamps who would flatter any pretty woman, and she knew now, and was pleased with it, that she was pretty. And she was almost in her eighteenth year so why should she not try out this amusing pastime of mild flirtation, even if it was only with her cousins? They were exceedingly handsome, both of them, and quite willing, it appeared, to go along with the game.

'Come over here and we will show you.' He grinned wickedly and a small shiver of delight ran through her. His teasing eyes were so lovely and blue, so blissfully familiar, and this nonsense made her feel so grown up.

'My turn first, I think, brother, since I am the oldest,' Drew said softly and there was something in his tone which was not teasing at all. He had followed her as she drifted away from the Christmas tree, leading her resolutely in the direction of the mistletoe which hung by the drawing-room door. When his cool hand fell on her arm she turned, smiling and ready for her very first kiss, glad that it was Drew – or was it Pearce? – then realised that it made no difference. His lips were warm as they rested on hers and she could taste his wine-scented, cigar-scented breath and the sharp smell of his freshly shaved skin.

'Merry Christmas, sweetheart,' he whispered amazingly,

his cheek against hers. Then before she could open her eyes which she had closed in pleasure at the loveliness of it, he kissed her again, a delightful repetition of the first time. His hands were firm on her upper arms and she felt herself sway for an instant against him, then he was gone. She opened her eyes and knew they were shining as she waited for Pearce to take his turn, as he surely would, wondering if his kiss would be as pleasant as Drew's. But he was standing next to his brother, shoulder to shoulder as they always did, grinning audaciously.

'Well, then, little cousin, which one did you like the best?' they teased, but in both pairs of enquiring eyes and about each smiling mouth was that strange expression she had seen a month ago and she knew they were in deadly earnest, in deadly contention as they so often inexplicably were.

'Which ... but I thought ... I did not know that you had...'

'What are you trying to say, my pet?' Pearce's eyes wandered to her mouth and with a sense of amazement she understood that she had been kissed by *both* her cousins and, amazingly, their kisses had been identical, so identical she could not have said which was which. Or perhaps it was that way with all men. A kiss was a kiss, no matter who gave it to you. But Pearce was waiting for an answer and she must cover her confusion for she did not want them to think her a silly female flustered by her first encounter with a male.

'That you are both exceedingly impertinent and I cannot for the life of me understand what all the fuss is about.' Her voice was teasing. 'Both were quite ... pleasant,' she tossed her head to show her supposed indifference for it, 'but that is all.'

'So you are saying you do not care for it, then?' Drew's mouth opened on a shout of laughter, then he stepped forward and, as the cousin he was, kissed her soundly on both cheeks. 'Well, then, we shall have to wait until you are a bit older,' he declared from the elevated position his six months' seniority gave him, 'shall we not, brother?'

'Merry Christmas, Tessa, and a happy New Year,' Pearce offered her his arm and they were as they had always been, impertinent and infinitely dear to her, both of them.

The evening was a huge success, Laurel positively purring as she moved amongst her guests for they were all aware that the Squire had favoured her with a promise to "look in' on her small party. The house was luminous with candle-light and fragrant with blooms from the greenhouses at the back of Greenacres, hundreds of flowers lining the stairs which led up to the gallery and salon, and in the lovely room itself great swathes of ivy, garlands of mistletoe, holly and red satin ribbon.

There was chilled punch and chilled champagne, claret, Madeira and sherry; salmon and game, lobster and pigeon pie, oyster patties, mayonnaise of trout, paté and prawns; tipsy-cake and fruited jellies and mountains of ice-cream mixed with almonds and cherries, the laden tables decora-ted with a dozen epergnes burdened with fruit and edged with trailing ivy and pale pink rosebuds from the Greenacres hothouse. Quite, quite exquisite, everyone agreed. Had not Laurel Greenwood done well? the whispers echoing about the salon hissed as she came in on the arm of the Squire, his lady behind them with Charlie.

'Dear God, there'll be no holding her now,' Pearce draw-led as he lounged indolently on one side of Tessa against the tall windows looking out on to the icy winter garden. Drew, from her other side, sipped his champagne and agreed lazily, his eyes not on his sister as she was led out on to the floor by the man she obviously considered her own personal endorsement of having 'arrived', but on his cousin. They had taken it in turns to dance with her though they had been forced, when it could not possibly be avoided without a scene, to allow Nicky Longworth and one or two others to take a turn round the floor with her. They had vied with one another to make her laugh out loud, causing heads to turn to see what Jenny Harrison's undisciplined daughter was up to now. And that 'get-up' she had on was

142

scarcely decent. Her ankles were on display for all to gawk at and it was obvious to anyone with eyes in their heads that she wore no petticoats beneath that shockingly diaphanous gown. It was well known that Jenny Harrison was an un-orthodox woman, capricious in her own youth, it was said. Well, weren't they all? Kit Greenwood had been a law unto herself from the day they killed her father and it seemed her sons and their headstrong cousin were to be the same.

And yet when the Squire favoured her with a dance, taking her in a graceful dip and sway about the room, evidently as intrigued with her as her madcap cousins appeared to be, she was as demure and modest as any sixteen-year-old should be, smiling innocently, speaking, one supposed, when spoken to, her eyes, on a level with his, cast down quite shyly. He was so delighted with her, remembering her skill and bravery on his own hunting field, that he took her round again, returning her to her mother most reluctantly. He had a word and a smile for Drew and Pearce who sprang to attention respectfully as he approached, his own son with them, and though Laurel was none too pleased at the amount of time, almost twenty minutes, he then spent chat-ting with them, it really was a triumph for the family.

The Squire and his lady had been driven away in their carriage when Pearce took Tessa's arm and drew her to one side.

'Meet us at the bottom of the stairs in ten minutes,' he whispered.

'What for?' she whispered back.

'Never you mind. It's a surprise. Just be there.'

They were there waiting for her. They led her along the back passage to the side entrance of the house, one carrying her warm, fur-lined cape, the other a stout pair of boots, and when she was snugly bundled up they opened the door with a flourish.

'Just for you, little cousin, and a very happy Christmas from us both,' Pearce said softly, revealing the magical garden beyond. It had been snowing for more than an hour.

At first small, frozen pellets had stuck fast to the lawns and paths, turning within half an hour to huge, soft flakes which had laid themselves, like the swansdown which lined the edge of her hood, three inches deep in a smooth and silent layer across the estate and the moorland beyond, transforming it into a world of such perfect, unspoiled beauty she drew in her breath with delight. It was eerily quiet. The lamplight stretched out in a pale yellow path across the glistening snow, gold and silver shimmering where the light reflected from it. The sky was a deep, mysterious purple and from it tumbled and whirled enormous fat snowflakes. Trees and bushes were captured in their dazzle, stretching out graceful arms to take on the shape of smooth, white, diamond-studded statues. It was all glitter and dazzle and when she stepped out in it, a hand in each of her cousins', it closed in around her, caressing her with the infinite tenderness of a lover.

They were quiet at first, almost reverent, stepping softly across the wide lawn beneath the salon window, looking back at the three sets of footprints they had made, those in the middle blurred by the dragging of her cloak.

But the peace did not last. How could it? They were young and in love with life and enjoyment and their own immortality, and when Pearce picked up a handful of snow and moulded it into a hard, round ball, warning his brother to beware, it did not take long for the other two to respond. Their shrieks of joyous laughter were heard even above the sound of the orchestra, drawing an amused crowd to the window. Within five minutes Laurel Greenwood's salon was emptied of every gentleman under the age of sixty, her own husband included, and even a dozen of the most daring young ladies, those who could escape or ignore their mamas' eagle eye.

It was said by many of the young guests to be the best party the valley had ever known, with the snowfight allowing those young ladies who had the inclination for it, more freedom than their mamas – or husbands – would have thought decent. More than a few lovely gowns were ruined and satin dancing slippers in tatters. Cheeks were rosy and warm despite the snow which danced against them and the laughter and shouts of triumph rose as snowballs found their mark. When it was done and a smilingly frozen-faced Laurel, who had declined to go outdoors and make a fool of herself, served hot coffee and mulled wine to those gentlemen who remained, Tessa curled herself up under her quilt, the firelight picking out the snowflakes which still floated against the window, and tried blissfully to decide which of her cousin's warm, Christmas kisses had pleased her the most.

## 9

Will Broadbent's tiny house, rented from the Greenwoods when he had begun work at the Chapman Mill as an over-looker, was set in a bit of garden at the end of a row of similar houses. Each had a parlour, a back kitchen which led out into its own yard, two bedrooms above, a good dry cellar beneath and a privy to each family.

Will's cosy parlour in which he had placed a couple of comfortable wing chairs, one on either side of the fireplace, and a round table covered with a red chenille cloth, was as warm as he could get it on this cold, snowy Christmas Day. The shelves in the alcoves beside the chimney breast were filled with books and the fireplace had a cast-iron surround with a brass fender and gleaming fire-tools. The polished floorboards were partly covered by a square carpet and before the fire was a hearth rug. There were curtains at the windows, red chenille again with a fringed pelmet, and on the walls were several commemorative plates, one produced to mark the 1832 Reform Bill and another the Chartist Movement of 1838. Will had been no more than a lad at the time of the first event but he had grown up with tales of the daring and recklessness of men of the Radical movement which had aimed to help other men, like himself, women and children too, to work with dignity and fulfilment in the cotton mills of Lancashire and, indeed, in many other parts of the country. Deeply interested in reform, though not perhaps with the fervour of Joss Greenwood or the late William Cobbett, he attended political meetings, union meetings, liking to hear an argument from every side before making up his own mind and went each week to the library in Chapmanstown, erected by Mrs Joss Greenwood for the betterment of the minds of her workers, to read the national newspapers from cover to cover.

Sir Robert Peel, the greatest of all English statesmen in Will's opinion, had died three years ago when he was thrown from his horse, and his death had affected Will deeply. Indeed, the whole nation had mourned the great man. It was due to him that the hated Corn Laws had been abolished, thus alleviating to some extent the conditions of the poor, though the deed had lost him his own office in government. An enormous loss to his country, Will had read, and he agreed with the statement wholeheartedly.

He sat before his own cosy fire, aware at the back of his mind that he was lonely, acknowledging to himself that man was not meant to live alone and that he should be thinking of taking a wife. For twenty or more years he had lived in the Penfold Valley and for the past six months, ever since he had gone to work for Chapmans, he had lived in this little house, his first home and one that could so readily be shared with the right lass, perhaps children. And he had made it what it was. Unlike most men who would have been content with a bed, a chair and a table under which to put their feet, he had found a great deal of satisfaction in turning it into his own place.

Feeling somewhat foolish at first, he had scoured the

second-hand furniture shops of Crossfold and Edgeclough, sorting through the sad treasures of women who, perhaps, had fallen on hard times, finding pieces which pleased his eye. Knowing nothing of craftsmen such as Hepplewhite or Sheraton, nevertheless Will recognised a decent bit of polished wood when he saw it. The lustre of mahogany and rosewood and walnut, the glowing colours in the tapestry of his wing chairs, gave him immense pleasure. The hard-wearing Brussels carpet, made in Halifax, though worn in places was swirled in patterns of faded rose and sage, and the hearthrug, come from somewhere in the Orient he had been told by the owner of the pawn-shop where he had bought it, was soft and warm to his stockinged feet.

In the small scullery behind the parlour was a pine dresser on which he had set out dishes, plates, cups and saucers bought at the Crossfold country fair during the summer. There was some durable pewter and a copper pan or two and he had smiled as he placed them on the shelves, chiding himself for an old woman, but pleased, just the same, with his first *real* home, his kitchen, simple in pine and deal. The bedroom upstairs he had furnished in what was, to him, luxurious comfort: a big brass bed with snowy linen and warm blankets covered with a splendid Welsh quilt stitched in hearts. Again he had laughed at himself, glad that the men with whom he worked could not see his pride and pleasure in what, surely, was a woman's domain. The fact was, he liked beautiful things. He didn't know why and certainly did not disclose the fact to anyone, even though his handiness with his fists and his great strength, well known and appreciated in the mill, would have discouraged any man from making a disparaging remark about it.

They were well built, these houses, he mused, as he strode for the third time to the window to peer out at the snowy world beyond, aware that he was becoming increasingly restless. The road outside his gate, though knee-deep in snow at the moment, was paved and well lit on a dark winter's night. There was an air about the houses not exactly of prosperity, for none of the Chapman employees could be said to have wealth, but of care, pride even, in each well-maintained, well-polished cottage. The windows shone, the gates were intact and oiled, there were curtains, mostly clean, and steps which were donkey-stoned each Saturday. Gardens in the summer produced a flower or two and at the back was a row of allotments where men like himself grew cabbages and potatoes. The privies stood by the back gates of the yards, the cleanliness of each depending upon the family it served. For the most part, they were scrupulous, since every house had its own piped water and the sewage was adequately taken care of by the splendid drains.

He sat down heavily in the chair and picked up a book. He put his stockinged feet on the fender, lit his pipe and prepared to have an hour or two with Mr Charles Dickens' *David Copperfield*. It had come from Mrs Greenwood's library in Chapmanstown, where the many young men and women who could read and write were allowed to borrow books.

But it was no good. Somehow David and Steerforth and pretty Dora could not hold his attention and he knew it was because, today of all days, Christmas Day, he was alone. Why should it concern him now, he wondered, when for the past seven or eight years, ever since he had left the apprentice house, he had been on his own, living in lodgings, without family or friend?

His eyes drifted to the holly he had hung above the fireplace and the mistletoe pinned to the door-frame between the parlour and the scullery. He smiled ruefully, asking himself which young lady he had hoped to catch in a Christmas kiss when not one soul had crossed his threshold since he had taken up residence here. That was not to say he did not enjoy the company of a pretty woman. He was friendly with the landlord's wife at the Dog and Gun, a bonny woman a year or two older than himself with a husband of almost fifty who had lost his appetite for his wife's curving flesh. Strange, since she was extremely obliging – to Will and, he suspected, to several others whom he was certain shared her favours.

He nearly dropped his pipe when someone hammered on his door and was severely handicapped for a moment or two as he attempted to brush away the hot ash from its bowl which had fallen on his cord trousers. His expression was quite foolish as he stood indecisively on his own hearth rug, wondering who it could be when all it took to find out was a stride or two across the parlour and the opening of the front door. Of course, he could peep from behind his chenille curtains to see who was mad enough to wade through the drifts which were certain to have piled up where the wind had blown them. It had snowed heavily many times in the past for the winters up here on the edge of the Pennines were fierce and stormy and those of the spinners and weavers who lived in Chapmanstown and must trudge up to Crossbank, Highbank and Broadbank had tales to tell of finding themselves up to their armpits in snow banks. Mrs Harrison, a woman of ingenuity he had heard, and to be admired, had organised them into groups so that they travelled together, and if one got into difficulties the others could form a rescue party. It had been quite hilarious, it seemed, and certainly a novelty, especially as Mrs Harrison had arranged for them to have a bowl of hot soup to restore them to a working condition before they switched on their mules or looms.

And last night there had been just such a blizzard.

She was on his doorstep when he opened the door; not Mrs Harrison of whom he had been thinking but her daughter. She was dazzling, brilliant with delight, like a child who has achieved the impossible. Her eyes glowed into his, her mouth wide and sweet, parting over her white teeth in a huge grin. Tessa Harrison: the young girl who had, in the last few months, become his friend.

Friend! Dear God, if anyone of her family became aware of it, particularly those reckless cousins of hers, he would be hounded not only from the mill, his job there and this snug cottage, but from Lancashire itself; and yet their relationship was completely innocent. It had begun on the moor, on the top road from Chapmanstown to Edgeclough. It had begun an hour or two after she had snarled her wild Greenwood temper at him in the mill yard. It had begun when he found her waiting for him to enquire whether he had got the job he had asked for. It had begun when she had shared her family history with him, who had none, and had been enthralled by the tale of his sad beginnings. It had begun and flourished on the few occasions they had met when her cousins had ridden off without her, she said mutinously, refusing to include her in some wild and reckless folly. He had walked the moors every Sunday, not looking for her since she was no more than a child, he told himself, and a child of the class to which he, as a millworker, had no access. When they met it was by accident, an encounter neither looked for nor planned, but which both enjoyed; perhaps for only a few moments in which she enquired of his job and his progress in it, he to admire her growing hair, to joke about her cousin's cutting of it, to ask politely after her uncle's health. After the incident with the Irish tinkers he had been somewhat short with her, subconsciously recognising that his exasperation was more than one human being's concern for another, but she seemed not to notice. Sometimes they sat on the rough grass together, saying nothing, at ease in their silences with no need to make the small talk they both found so irksome. He was often amazed that he found such pleasure in the company of a young girl, one in whom, he told himself, he had no physical interest, nor shared interest at all, really, for she was no reader and had neither heard of, nor was concerned with what he read. He did not care about the hunting of the fox, nor the shooting of game birds, which it seemed she did and was good at, she boasted, but somehow they met on a bit of common ground, neither realising what it was, relishing one another's company. They had come across one another at Annie

Beale's cottage, sharing a cup of tea and a joke, easy with one another, and with her, as a mutual friend.

But there was something different about her today.

She was beautiful: not in the way a child, or even a young girl, was beautiful, but as a woman. Alive, vibrant with her own joy of getting here against almost overwhelming odds, the tenacious hold she had on life which gave her the strength and courage carelessly to thrust aside whatever obstacle might be thrown in her path. There was not another female in Crossfold, in Lancashire, he believed, like her. Not one of them would have tackled the walk from Greenacres to Chapmanstown, a distance of more than three miles, on foot over ground which, though it was not exactly high moorland, was rough and hazardous with deep hollows and sharply rising inclines, and in three feet of freshly drifted snow.

'Look,' she beseeched him before he could speak, lifting her feet, first one then the other, on which she had strapped what looked like a pair of round, flat, mesh sieves, something the gardener would use to riddle his soil free of large objects. They had a handle protruding from somewhere at the back, made of wood, clumsy and comical, but she was clearly beside herself with her own ingenuity.

'What the devil are they?' The delight, the wondering emotion, intact and perfectly shaped and which had become quite clear to him at that moment was mercifully hidden from her by the obligation to admire what she obviously considered her due.

'They're bats of some sort. I found them in the cupboard where Drew and Pearce keep their cricket things, fishing tackle, walking sticks, stuff like that. I think they play tennis with them. You know tennis, don't you? The Squire has a covered court ... Anyway, when I was deliberating on how I might get here I saw these and remembered a picture in a geographical magazine, in Canada or North America I believe it was, and the man in it had these on his feet so I thought what a splendid idea to strap them to my boots.

Briggs found me some leather straps ... the mesh is ever so strong and when I stepped on to the snow – well, you could see the servants all expected me to vanish from sight or at least sink up to my waist but I walked on top of it. Can you imagine? Lord, it was wonderful. I've never been out before, not on the moors, I mean, when it was like this, and if you could have seen it! Oh, Will, I wish you could have seen it ...' Dear God, so did he, so did he ... Her voice became hushed and her eyes were like crystal, a clear-cut grey with a darker grey rim and around the iris the most incredible white, as white as the snow over which she had just tramped to come to *him*.

He felt the pain spear him in his fierce masculine need to sweep her off those ridiculous things she had on her feet and into his arms. Into his heart, for that was surely where she would be from this moment. He could feel his arms begin to lift and his body sway towards hers. Though she was tall her head would fit neatly beneath his chin and her long body curve itself snugly against his. He could feel it there already and his rose to meet it, his maleness instantly knowing the rightness of it and demanding to be recognised. Dear, sweet Lord, but she was beautiful and no matter what they said of her in the valley, her heart was good, her nature warm for who else had taken the trouble to remember Will Broadbent on Christmas Day?

'It was like magic, Will,' she was saying, 'or like poetry, not that I really know any, but what I imagine it must be to those who do. You know the feeling you get when a song is sweet? Your skin prickles ... it was so ... so pure and clean, untouched white everywhere, and if I had not known the landmarks I should have been lost.'

He felt the familiar anger ... no, it was fear ... for her rise in his chest. She was so dear and the risks she took, the risks she was allowed to take, were almost more than he could bear. Was there no one to watch over her, to care as he did, for her safety? But as he gazed, quite bemused, absurdly so, he knew he could not approach her, not now, not today.

'And yet there were great patches of blue where the shadows lay. A landscape of pure, sparkling white and blue and the trees were like ... like filigree, like lace almost, against the snow and the sky, and there was nothing else. There were patterns in the snow where the wind had moved it as though someone, a child perhaps, had tried to draw a picture...'

'Should you not come inside, lass?' he interrupted gently.

'Oh, Will, do you not think you could fashion another pair like these,' she asked, lifting her feet clumsily, 'then I could show you? It's like walking on clouds ... yes, that's it...'

'I've never walked on clouds, my lass, and I reckon I never will, nor anyone, so perhaps ... But come in first and have a cup of tea, then we'll see. You must be cold.'

'No, I'm not, that's the wonder of it. I'm as warm as toast, feel.'

She put the bare palm of her hand against his cheek and without thought, since he was beyond it, he turned his warm mouth into it, moving his lips softly along the base of her thumb.

Her words froze on her lips. She simply stood there, her hand thrilling to his touch. Something as vivid and as simple as a flicker of lightning seemed to shiver between them. Her eyes were big and wondering, her lips still parted in startled delight, and when he drew her inside she took her marvellous footwear with her, scattering snow across his carpet. She made no objection when he sat her in a chair, nor when he knelt at her feet and removed not only the 'bats' but her stout black boots as well. She held out her feet to him, obedient as a well-brought-up child, her eyes on his bent head, waiting, just waiting for the next step in this delightful condition which had sprung up between them.

But when he had removed her boots he stood up abruptly since he found his hands were inclined to linger caressingly about her shapely stockinged foot and ankle. He made him-

153

self busy with the coal-scuttle and fire-tongs, heaping up the already dangerously high fire, arranging her boots to dry. She wanted him to turn and look at her again, to lap her about in that amazing but delicious sense of expectancy she had felt when he kissed her hand, but he moved away and she felt an illogical wave of disappointment wash over her.

'I'll put the kettle on,' he said, in what he hoped was a normal tone of voice, conscious that she was looking at him, conscious of her stillness, her breath held in, for she was a young girl with no experience of such things and the kiss he had placed in her hand had been a mistake, an impulse a man of his age should have resisted. She was not sure of it, or of him, or of what was expected of her, so she was waiting for him to take the lead in whatever was to happen, if anything *was* to happen. It was up to him to return them to the casual friendship which was all that could ever be allowed between Tessa Harrison and Will Broadbent.

He tried to keep up what in other circumstances he would scornfully have deemed 'small talk' and when he came back from the scullery, bringing teacups and milk, she was stretched out with her feet on the fender, her toes wriggling in the warmth. He placed the kettle on the fire, careful not to touch her, keeping a wary distance, his chest filled with the distressing weight he carried within him.

She took the cup of tea he handed her looking about her curiously at the cosy room, this parlour which was that of a *working* man, just as though it was the most natural thing in the world to be doing, the most natural place to be on Christmas Day. She was the daughter of a wealthy millowner, he was an overlooker in that same mill, twelve years her senior, a man from only God knew where, and yet she seemed to be conscious of no disparity in their hugely different circumstances, nor of the impropriety of being here in a bachelor's home, alone and unchaperoned. He had, he admitted to himself, not worried unduly over it in the past months when they met on the moors or at Annie's where the artificiality of social conduct seemed so trivial. He had

154

been attracted to her. She was a lovely young woman and there would have to be something wrong with him had he not been, but now in the short time it had taken him to open the door and look into her enchanted, enchanting eyes, all was changed.

'It was good of you to come,' he said formally and she turned to look at him, surprised by his tone.

'Don't be silly, it's Christmas Day. I knew you would be alone so when Mother and the rest started a game of whist and Laurel's children were removed to the nursery I slipped out of the side door. I knew no one would miss me.'

'What about your cousins?' His voice was curt for though their father's collapse earlier in the year had made Drew and Pearce Greenwood, for a short time at least, more conscientious in their duties, it had not taken them long to fall back into their old ways. They turned up at the mill long after the factory bell had rung. They were missing, one or the other of them but more likely both at the same time, just when they were supposed to be busy at some task in the spinning room, the carding shed or the counting house. Long before the appointed hour at which Mr Greenwood or Mrs Harrison left the mill, they were reported to have been seen riding off on their fine bays, doubtless in search of mischief. On some days they simply didn't turn up at all. It did not unduly interfere with Will's work as an overlooker but Mr Wilson was often put in a most embarrassing position when some business gentleman with whom one or other had an appointment was left high and dry with only Mr Wilson – which was really quite adequate – when he had expected to be greeted by the son of the owner. It was said in the mill that they might as well let them do as they pleased since they did it anyway, and if they were no longer to come to the factory at least everyone would know what to expect. Now the foreman and managers with whom the young sons of the business were relied on to co-operate, were all at sixes and sevens, calling them a damned nuisance and wishing their father would give them leave to spend their days with the hunt, or whatever it was young squireens did with themselves.

'Oh, they took themselves off as soon as Christmas dinner was eaten. God knows where they've got to since they don't always tell me these days.' She sighed, exasperated by her cousins' defection but then she turned to smile at him, making his heart turn over, letting him know that right now she didn't really care. 'They'll be back by tea-time and the opening of presents, which brings me to . . .' She grinned and getting up to move to where he had hung her coat on the back of a chair, reached into her pocket and drew out a small package. It was roughly wrapped in some bright paper and tied with a length of scarlet ribbon.

'Happy Christmas, Will,' she said cheerfully and handed it to him, putting into his suddenly trembling hands the first gift he had ever received. He stared at it, quite numb, unable to speak or even to think clearly, unable to look up into her face lest she see what was written in his.

'You're supposed to say thank you and then open it, Will,' she said impishly, sitting down opposite him again, clearly delighted by his reaction.

'Aah, lass,' he managed to mumble, the package resting in his big hands which were reluctant to disturb its loveliness.

'Will, for heaven's sake open it. I'm sorry it's so poorly wrapped but I'm not much good with things like that. All fingers and thumbs. I'm just the same with sewing and paint-ing. That's why I never do any.'

It was a scarf. Bright red, wide and long and hand-knitted, the pattern of it was complicated and skilfully done. He allowed himself a quick glance at her face, his own bemused, and she laughed.

'No, I didn't do it, Will. Miss Copeland, who used to be my governess, or one of them, I had so many, knitted it for me last Christmas and I've never worn it. I hope you don't mind but it seemed just right for you. And perfect for this weather.'

He shook his head, beyond words, appalled by his own

156

inclination to weep like a baby, studying the scarf as it glowed richly across his hands, unable to move or even glance at her lest the tears pricking his eyes should escape.

'Let's see how it looks, then.' When he made no move to put it round his neck she took it from him, standing before his seated figure while she wrapped it about his neck, tying the fringed ends beneath his chin, unaware of the rock-like stillness of him.

'There, that looks splendid,' she said briskly, 'and now I really do think I should be going. It will be dark by four.'

'I'll walk with you ... an' wear me new scarf.' He grinned. 'I'm only sorry I've nothing for you. I didn't know, you see ... I'd no idea ...'

'Rubbish. I've got heaps of presents at home.' She reached for her boots and coat and though he would dearly have loved to help her with them he knew quite simply that it was impossible now. That everything was impossible now. All that had been sweet, and, he realised, precious to him, was clearly out of the question, for the person of Miss Tessa Harrison was beyond his reach. She appeared to have regained her composure which had fled away with his unexpected kiss, but she was not aware that the last half-hour had separated them as sharply as the sudden closing of a heavy curtain separates an audience from the players on the stage. He must avoid her; keep out of her way, treat her as the young mistress, daughter of his employer when encounters at the mill, for instance, were unavoidable. She would be bewildered by it since he knew she had taken their strange companionship for granted, but if it hurt her so much the better for she would keep out of his way then. But today, this last day as her friend, must be allowed to continue in its magic for a little while longer.

'Oh, I forgot to tell you about the ball, Will.' She whirled to face him, her eyes eager and excited, and he stepped back from her for surely she would sense the need in him?

'So you did, lass. Was it a huge success and did all the

157

young gentlemen fall swooning at your feet when they saw you in your splendid frock?'

'Frock!' She laughed, still holding her coat before her, waiting as young ladies did, for the gentleman to assist her on with it. 'What a word to use! It was not just a frock, Will, but the most enchanting outfit, all gauze and satin ribbons, and everyone simply stared when I entered the ballroom. Well, you will have seen the pictures of Diana the huntress in one of those books you forever have your nose in...'

Yes, he had, and the thought of her in a flimsy garment like that the goddess of Roman mythology wore, made his skin tingle and his breath shorten and he felt the need to smash in the face of every man who had seen her in it.

'... and I had nearly every dance with Drew and Pearce who simply wanted to fight every gentleman who approached me, even the Squire, I suspect, though they were forced to let him take me on the floor. Heavens, it was like being in a magical world and when those wicked cousins of mine whispered to me to meet them at the side door...'

He felt his jaw clench and knew he really must get her coat and her boots on her and open the door to the world outside. Dear Christ, she was a child, prattling on about a party with no thought in her head but what fun she had had. No more than a young girl and should be left that way.

And yet she seemed to have gained something since he had last seen her up on Badger's Edge; an indefinable impression which was probably an illusion, a trick of the firelight and the snow reflecting through the window, but which seemed to say to him that she was not *quite* the girl he had chatted with amongst the winter bracken of the tops. What was it? What was in her eyes, the flush of her cheek, the soft turn of her lips as though she smiled at some secret memory?

She was looking at him strangely too, assessing him in some way, her gaze reflective, a glow of something in her eyes which were a pale grey velvet now, the crystal gleam gone all of a sudden.

'We went out into the garden, Drew and Pearce and I,' she continued, her voice almost a whisper so that he had to lean towards her to hear it. Dear God, what was she saying?

'We walked, the three of us, across the snow when, all of a sudden, everyone was there. They had seen us from the window and came out, dozens of them, throwing snowballs, the gentlemen pushing one another about in the drifts which grew. It was glorious, quite glorious. There were gentlemen kissing ladies . . .' She stopped and waited, smiling, then, 'It was Christmas Eve after all, Will. It's allowed, you see, particularly if there is mistletoe.'

Her eyes drifted from his to the small green bough which was just above his head in the doorway.

'A merry Christmas, Will,' she said softly, still smiling. She put her coat on the chair and, quite deliberately, moved across the small room towards him. When she was directly in front of him she lifted her hands, resting them on his shoulders.

'Well, are you not going to wish me the same, Will Broadbent?'

'Lass,' and his eyes narrowed, 'you don't know what you're doing here. I'm no lad to giggle with under the mistletoe.'

'I'm not giggling, Will. '

'What the hell's that got to do wi' it?' he said roughly, since he knew exactly what she meant.

'Drew and Pearce kissed me, Will. I liked it.' Her smile deepened.

It was perhaps this, the knowledge that some other man had sampled what he was so busy denying himself, that shattered his control and his voice was beset with peril.

'I'm not Master Pearce, Tessa Harrison, nor his brother. Are you sure you want to continue with this game?' But his hands were about her waist now, big and gentle but ready to be rough since she felt so lovely beneath them. He wanted to grip her tightly, perhaps hurt her a little though he didn't

159

know why, to savour the warm smell of her skin and hair against his face, to blend her limbs into his. But she was only a girl testing her female strength and power over the male and he did not care to frighten her. She knew nothing of passion, true passion, nor what she did with her light-hearted flirtation and he must put a stop to it . . . he must . . .

'It's only a Christmas kiss beneath the mistletoe, Will,' she breathed, her soft young face lifting to his, her eyes beginning to close in what she thought to be the accepted fashion.

''Appen it is,' his voice was husky, 'and 'appen it isn't . . .' Then her mouth reached his and he took it as gently as he knew how. Her lips were trusting, innocent, and he held back, desperate not to offend her in this game she was playing, appalled at the back of his mind by his own behaviour, but her lips parted and clung and her arms crept about his neck. She shifted her body, drawing it closer to his and his mouth became more urgent, more demanding since, *his* body said, he was a man holding a woman who was willing in his arms. He crossed them at her back, lifting her up against him, feeling the roundness of her breasts press against his chest and when she seemed not to mind he lifted his hands to the back of her head, his will beginning to master hers, his male body to dominate. His hands moved to her neck, caressing the soft flesh of her throat beneath her chin and his mouth travelled about her face, warm and moist on her cheeks, on each closed eye, her jawline.

'Oh, God,' he moaned in the back of his throat, pleading with her to stop him, for someone must.

'Will . . .' Her breath was warm on his brow and her own mouth found, somehow, the tender place beneath his ear, and the hot desire which might have been stopped, flowed madly through him. She was so lovely; her skin was smooth, like satin and smelling of wild flowers, and her shoulders which were revealed . . . somehow . . . Oh, Christ . . . were a pale golden silk in the fire's glow. Her breasts . . . her breasts . . . her nipples round, sweet, pink and hard with her longing, swelled into his hands which closed eagerly about them. She arched her throat and small sounds of delight came from it. He pressed his mouth against it before moving down to take her peaked nipple between his lips.

'Tessa ...' Her name was sweet and soft on the air, 'I love you, girl ...'

'Love me ...'

Her clothes lay in a feverishly abandoned heap about her feet. Her body was a pale amber column and for a moment he stayed his demanding, compelling hands, and hers, to look in wonder, his eyes worshipping the beauty of it. Her splendid shoulders, smooth, womanly and yet strong; the high peaks of her young breasts, rosy and eager and full. Her small waist and slender hips, her long tapering legs between which was the dark, flowering centre of her and which she was, though she was not quite sure how, longing to give him, longing for him to take from her. She was one of those rare creatures of her own sex, he realised, marvelling, who are ready for love, for loving, with no need of the complexity of wooing, of coaxing; a freely giving, enthusiastically taking woman who would match his own ardour once he had taught her how.

'Will ...' Her naked body swayed towards him, enclosed his like a flower clinging to the trunk of a tree. His own emerged quite miraculously from its wrappings, beautiful, hard, the muscles of it standing rigid beneath his brown skin.

'Sweetheart, sweetheart,' he heard himself murmur, terrified somehow that this loveliness, this forbidden sweetness would be snatched from him. He was beyond reason, beyond any thought, any concern other than that he must have this girl, this woman, wherever he could lay her.

'I love you, Will,' he thought he heard her say as they clung together and then the worn fabric of the fireside rug was beneath them and when he took her they both cried out with the pain and joy of it.

They lay for a while in silence, the firelight dappling their entwined limbs to gold and amber and rose and he heard her sigh in pleasure.

'I do love you, Will,' she said, in that natural, free-spoken way she had. She had not learned to be subtle or artful, and all her life had said exactly what she felt or meant, and it seemed she could see no reason to be different now.

He lifted himself on one elbow and looked down into her rosy face. His heart was straining to free itself of his love for her, to pour it over her in endless waves, to wrap it about her, to hold her within it, with him, for the rest of their days and his eyes were deep, filled with his pride in having her love. He cupped her cheek with a gentle hand and smiled.

'Aye, I reckoned you might, after what we've just done. There was no holding you, nor me neither, for which I make no apologies. But what's done is done, lass, and there's no turning back now.' He turned to look about him at the room which was no longer just a room but a shrine – dear God, what had she done to him, to make him so fanciful? – a shrine to their love. He let his eyes study each piece of furniture, each picture and ornament, before he brought his gaze back to her. She lay against his arm, her eyes unfocused and dreaming, the short crop of her hair in a cloud about her head and he put up a hand to brush it back from her forehead.

'There'll have to be a few changes but I've got a bit put by so you must get whatever you need to make this place just as you want it, sweetheart. I know it's not what you're used to but you an' me'll be happy here.' His face was very serious. 'I'll make you happy, Tessa Harrison, I swear it, for if ever a lass was loved it's you.' He grinned and ruffled her hair again. 'But do one thing for me, will you? Grow your hair for the wedding. I'd like to see it a bit longer, maybe with a flower in it, you know, like a proper bride ...'

She had been smiling, still woven in the fabric of love, not really listening to what he was saying, just the pleasant sound of his deep voice, but gradually through the languor-

162

ous mist she distinguished a word or two. 'Wedding' was one; 'bride' was another.

She sat up slowly and his eyes dropped to the soft weight of her breasts as they fell forward. He raised a hand to cup first one, then the other, but she pushed it away.

'What did you say?' she asked him warily.

He looked momentarily perplexed, the hand she had refused hovering somewhat uncertainly as though her rejection of it had sown a sudden seed of doubt.

'Say?' He tried a smile but even then her expression alarmed him. 'What about?'

'You ... you mentioned ... a wedding.' She drew away from him a little, shrugging off his arm and his alarm grew stronger, surging quite sickeningly through him, seizing him by the throat. Really, this was mad, for had she not just ... well, any girl of her upbringing ... she would hardly have allowed him ... encouraged him, surely, if she did not mean to ... she had said she loved him ...

'That I did, sweetheart.' He forced his voice to be steady and put out a hand to draw her back into his arms. 'We must be married now. I want it more than anything, Tessa, and so do you, else why should you ... ?'

'Married!'

'Aye. As soon as she'll see me I'll speak to your mother, or should it be your Uncle Charlie, seeing as how he's the man of the family?. They'll not like it ...' His face became anxious then. 'You don't think they'll refuse, do you? Make you wait until you're of age ...'

'Married,' she said again. Her enormous eyes left his and wandered about the room. In them was such a look of terror he reached out to her, not certain what was frightening her so but ready to protect her from it with his life.

'Aye, what else? We're handfast now, my love. More than that, I reckon. It'll be hard but your mother was a working lass once, and Charlie Greenwood came from ...'

'*Married! To you!*' Before he could stop her she had scrambled to her feet, reaching urgently for her clothes

163

which she began to drag about her. Her eyes were haunted, her face so drawn she might just have been recovering from some dreadful illness.

He stood up slowly, magnificent in his manly beauty but her eyes would not look at what had, only minutes before, delighted her. His voice was harsh.

'You'll not marry me then, Tessa Harrison?'

'I don't want to marry anyone.' She began to laugh, the sound tearing hatefully through the small room. In his agony he did not recognise the panic in her, the desperate beating of her wings against the bars which he had imperiously put up about her, the bars which were closing on her freedom. He only heard what he thought to be her amusement, her scorn, her rejection of the gift, the precious bounty of the love he had for her.

She had gone, blundering blindly into the snow when he himself began to laugh, the sound gaining volume, on and on until it died away into the empty lonely silence her going had left.

The snow had nearly gone when she came back, the sudden, almost spring-like sunshine clearing it from rooftops and garden walls and revealing the track between Greenacres and Chapmanstown.

'Will . . . ?' Her eyes were enormous in her hesitant face and she tried a tremulous smile.

'Yes?' he replied coldly, but already he was opening the door wider the more quickly to have her over the doorstep. The book he had been reading fell to the floor as his arms lifted to take her inside and he groaned as her body nailed itself to his.

The lead up to the big strike was long. Wages had been cut in the recession of seven years ago but promises had been made by the millowners to return to the old levels when trade improved. Trade was improving, the operatives said, but against a background of rising food prices and the non-appearance of the increased wage they had been promised, in March 1853 a general wages campaign began. There were mass meetings and parades to rouse and mobilise those who were unorganised and the resolution was formed to demand nothing short of an unconditional advance of ten per cent in their weekly wage packet.

In October of the same year employers in Preston locked out their entire workforce and in many other places 'short time' was introduced. The lock-out in Preston began to create hardship and anxiety, not only in the town itself but amongst many of the people not actively engaged in dispute. Most had become involved without really understanding what their union leaders told them, willing to obey since the hardships of the 'hungry forties' must not be repeated. If they were told this course was best for them, that this was the only way to show the masters that they were a solid, unbending army, no longer prepared to be trampled beneath the millowners' feet, then they would obey; but they had not known, they whispered to one another, that the struggle would take so long.

Six months had passed now and each week the benefit they lived on, collected from men and women still in work, not just in the textile trade but in many others, including the shopkeepers who if they did not keep the millworkers' custom would go down with them, was reduced and men who had earned two pounds a week were trying to keep a family on no more than ten shillings.

Every man who still worked in a strike-bound mill, and there were a few, was branded with dishonour; not a man, but a 'knob-stick' who was subjected to the most harrowing forms of intimidation. Many of them sincerely did not believe in the strike, and said so, and the tales of beatings and other brutalities were reported each week in the newspapers. Often the 'Bashi-Bazouks', as the gangs of youths who perpetrated these outrages were called, had been arrested and charged not only with criminal assault, but conspiracy. They roamed about in groups of thirty or forty, under the guise of 'body-guards' but in reality terrorising any man or woman who tried to work.

In February 1854, the masters said they would re-open their mills if the workforce would be prepared to accept the wages they had earned before the start of the lock-out in the previous October, but when the mills were opened none of their operatives reported for work.

Agents were sent to Ireland and to various agricultural areas of England to fetch men and women who were starving and would therefore be glad to do anything to put food in the mouths of their children. Thousands arrived by train and were then carried in covered carts to the factories of Lancashire, escorted by police constables.

Again arrests were made as many of the strike leaders tried to stop these new hands from entering the mills and taking the jobs they themselves were trying, or so they said, to protect. Lord Palmerston had been appealed to by the striking men but he could do nothing to help them, stating that their employment was still available to them if they cared to take it up again.

The situation was becoming more ugly as each week passed and now it was said that the union tax, 'voluntarily' paid by those in work to support the strikers, was to be put as high as eightpence a week on each loom or mule. The rumblings were beginning to be heard as far away as Colne or Burnley and indeed in all the towns where cotton was manufactured. Families, hard up themselves, were forced to support what they had begun to realise was not a just cause.

A young widow with two children and not a penny to spare had refused to pay last week at Abbotts when the collector came to her loom-gate. When she returned to it after her breakfast she found her shuttles had mysteriously vanished and when she complained those about her merely looked away, saying it were nowt' to do wi' them. She was now out of work and on 'relief' and the unions were not collecting for *her*.

Written threats had been nailed to walls where any operatives not complying with the union men could not miss seeing them.

'IF THAT OILER AT CROSSBANK MILL DOES NOT PAY UP A CALLER WILL BE OBLIGED TO COME AND PUT HIM IN THE COUNTY COURT.'

'IF THOSE HANDS AT ALLSOP AND GREENS DO NOT PAY UP THEY WILL GET SOMETHING THEY DO NOT LIKE.'

'IF THE BLOW ROOM HAND AT BRIDGEFOLD MILL DOES NOT PAY UP "PUNCH" WILL SEND A FINE TROOP TO HIM.'

There were men, women and girls in many mills with a will on them like iron, short of cash and not a little impatient with those who were on strike for no good reasons that they could see, and who would be bound to say so, and refuse their eightpence a week to those who demanded it of them.

It was a week later when the first of the bad troubles began. Chapmans had not experienced any problems since the unions had scarcely a toe-hold there. For twenty years the operatives had held themselves apart from other mills, their better working conditions, shorter hours, decent wages and the neat and sturdy company cottages most of them occupied instilling in them no desire, or need, to associate with those who wanted what they had. They were content with their labour and what it brought them and like those who believe that another man's fight is best left alone, especially if that fight made no sense, they walked by when the street-corner meetings, and the men who formed them, demanded they fight the injustice which was being done to their fellows. The unions had become strong with spinners' unions, weavers' unions, combers' unions and in the past twenty years many wrongs had been put right but the Preston operatives' strike was a hardship of their own making, so most of those not involved believed.

It was said that young men and boys were turning to petty crime, stealing and getting into fights which were more than youthful squabbles, with nothing better to do than roam the streets and look for mischief. Young girls might be had at any street corner for the price of a loaf of bread. These girls had no other way to keep themselves alive and some, finding they had a taste for such a life, were unlikely to give it up when times were better. They were innocent, most of them, when they began their new trade, inexperienced, and when the strike was finally over and the cost of it counted the number of illegitimate babies was found to have increased and who was to pay for their upkeep? Certainly not their mothers who were little more than children themselves, and so they fell on the parish like hundreds of others whose lives were drastically changed by the lock-out.

Annie Beale was at her mule when the man approached her. It was three years since her mother had died, taking the child she had just borne with her, leaving Annie to support the four she left behind. And she had done so uncomplainingly for they were her responsibility. A great one for responsibility and duty was Annie and if, with hard work and an obsessive sense of loyalty, she could give them a bit of decency and a start in life, then she would. There was Jack, three years younger than herself, and bright and he'd make more of himself than her own father had, wherever he was, for he'd run off and left them when his wife had told him he was to be burdened with yet another child. Nelly, who was eleven, had never been 'right' since she had been interfered with by the overlooker but she worked besides Annie without complaint. The two youngest, Polly and Grace, not yet old enough to work, were champion in their tireless and sadly mature preoccupation as guardians of their home in her absence and somehow or other the family managed. She was proud of her honest, independent, hardworking brother and sisters. They were obliged to no one, paying their way as decent folks should, but only just.

On that day she was blind and deaf to all but the movement and sound of her two machines, keeping an eye on Nelly, who was piecing for her, and when the man touched her arm she was disposed to be irritable for she had neither the time nor the inclination to turn and gossip.

'Will yer support t'Preston strikers, lass?' The man mouthed genially. He was a working man, dressed as one, since he did not want to be thought of as a cut above those from whom he collected though it was plain from his confident, swaggering manner that he considered he was. His teeth glittered in his full, red face – no hunger there – as he showed them in a false smile. 'Eightpence a mule, that's all, an' the men an' women o' Preston will bless yer for it.' He shook his collection box persuasively but when she turned to look at him his eyes were cold, ready to be hostile if she refused.

'I can't. I've four childer ter support,' she said curtly and turned back to her machine, the matter done with as far as she was concerned.

But not to him. He touched her bare arm again, only lightly, but she flinched away for though the room was hot his hand was like hard ice against her flesh.

'Now then, lass, yer wouldn't turn yer back on those in need, would yer? You're a spinner thissen an' will know the history o't cotton trade. Maisters 'ave trodden down t'workers long enough in our opinion an' must be taught that us'll not 'ave it.'

'I've no time ter stand an' argue. I've nowt ter give yer. I just told thi, I can't afford it.'

Her face was expressionless. Indeed, she felt nothing, not

169

pity for the workers, many of whom in her opinion were too bone-idle to get out of their beds in a morning; nor even resentment, for all her emotions were concentrated on her need to get on with her work, her resolution to support her family, not those of another. If everyone was the same there'd be no need for all this hullabaloo, and if she had had time to turn off her machine and tell him she would have done so.

But his face had become set in a perilous smile and it was clear he was not prepared to be brushed off as if he were of no more importance than a troublesome fly.

'Come now, my girl. Yer mun 'ave a bit put by fer a rainy day an' them in Preston are sufferin' it now. Share it wi' 'em an' when 'time comes, an' it might, when yer in't same plight, they'll do it fer thee.'

Annie could feel her irritation growing, thrusting through the layers of attention she must pay her labour since she was on 'piece' work and every minute she lost would mean a smaller wage at the end of the week. She could feel her hard-won equanimity slipping away and her pale eyes narrowed.

'I've none ter give,' she threw over her shoulder, 'an' if I 'ad I'd think twice about it. They've only themselves ter blame, them as is locked out. Most on 'em was offered a rise last year but unions forced 'em ter stay out, goin' on about a standard rate o' pay, whatever that might turn out ter be. They've 'ad chance ter go back last month an' they turned it down. I've no time fer 'em, nor yer collection, so clear off an' let me gerron wi' me work.'

Her face was cold and tight, and around her women were peeping furtively over their shoulders at her, wishing they had her nerve. Most had paid the 'tax', though the eight-pence they had been 'asked' to hand over could be ill-afforded. They were frightened by the tales of what had happened to those who didn't, of beatings and harassment, of women being jeered at by alarmingly large gangs of youths, and even physically assaulted, and they did not want

170

their own families to suffer. Surely to God it would soon be over, they whispered to one another, and in the meanwhile best tighten belts and pay up.

From the end of the room where he stood in the cabin doorway Will watched carefully, ready, should he be needed, to intervene on Annie's behalf. He'd not have his operatives intimidated by this new breed of union men who were really no more than troublemakers, denouncing tyranny and yet, in their own way, upholding it with their menace.

'You've no call ter talk like that, my lass. Yon are thy people an' they depend on't benefits they get given by their own kind. If yer can't find it in yer 'eart ter support 'em, there's them hereabouts what'll reckon yer as bad as them "knob-sticks" in Preston. Will yer not, me lasses?'

He whirled about and smiled at the mass of women who had turned to watch Annie, and in his corner Will took a step forward, then another, waiting for some sign from Annie that she was being harassed, reluctant to interfere since the man had a right to go about the cotton workers as he chose; but he would have no violence.

The man smiled smoothly at the nervous women. He spoke in a voice just loud enough for them and Annie to hear above the noise of the machines.

'Thee thissen'd not like ter work beside a "knob-stick", would thi?' His meaning was clear and they all looked away from him quickly, though one or two shook their heads in sympathy with Annie. He turned back to her. 'So will thi change thi mind, lass, an' give ter them what's in need?'

'No, I won't,' and she turned a contemptuous back on him.

'Right, lass, I 'eard yer,' and he smiled at the back of her head before moving on to the next machine where the spinner already had her eightpence in her hand.

'IF THE SPINNING HAND AT CHAPMANS DOES NOT PAY UP CALICO JACK WILL SEE TO HER.'

It was pasted on the wall by the side of the gate the

171

following week, along with a dozen others, for Annie was not the only one to refuse to pay her 'voluntary' contribution in aid of the Preston strikers. In the worry of how long it would take her to save up for a new pair of boots for their Jack who was shooting up like a weed, it had little impact on her. She lived from day to day in her practical way, ekeing out her wage to feed hungry mouths, making do and putting a bit by when she could. Nothing much mattered beyond getting from one pay day to the next; beyond the necessity of completing at the end of her ten hours the household tasks which were too much for her young sisters; of seeing to the children; of listening to their Jack telling her of the clever things he learned at school where he went *full time*; worth every minute of her precious time for he'd make something of himself, would Jack, or she'd know the reason why; and of cobbling together all the bits and pieces of her life which were so fragile.

They were hanging about on the edge of Chapmanstown when she finished her shift. The last houses were at her back and the empty track which curved over the moor towards Edgeclough lay before her when she saw them. Half a dozen or so young men, brawny and brash, larking about, laughing, jostling one another as young men do, nothing to do with her, and her heart did not even miss a beat as she strode past them.

It was March, cold and blustery, the clouds torn into long shreds by the wind, and through which a thread of blue tried to creep. The newly budding heather and bracken was caught by the gusts, bending earthwards, and her fine hair was torn from her shawl, whipping about her head like pale fibres of cotton. She pulled her shawl more closely about her, tucking her arms inside it, and stepped into the teeth of the wind which met her as she climbed higher.

She was glad their Nelly was not with her. She'd caught her finger on a 'picking stick' last week and it had festered and swelled, making it impossible for her to piece, so Annie had made her stay at home today. Best place for her on a day like this and Annie wished with all her heart she could stay there for a couple of years more. She was so little, thin and quiet, without the stamina she herself had, especially since she had been abused by that bastard of an overlooker.

Badger's Edge came up on her left and soon she would be in the lee of Besom Hill and just half-way home. It had begun to rain, spilling in a cold sheet directly into her face. She wrapped her shawl more closely about her head, bending down into the face of it, hugging herself as she quickened her step. She could still hear the shouted laughter of the men whom she thought must be drunk, the way they were carrying on, and she wondered where they were going. She had never seen them before but she supposed they could live in Edgeclough. For once she had not waited on Will since there were others on the track with her, turning off to Dingle, Moorside and Linthwaite, small villages in which some of them lived, but suddenly she was alone and she heard the men coming up fast behind her.

They were still laughing as one fell against her, not hard enough to knock her down but with a force which sent her staggering almost to her knees. She regained her balance and her pale, pointed face became a vivid, indignant flame and her eyes narrowed angrily.

' 'Ere, what d'yer think your up to?' she cried, rounding on him fiercely. 'Why don't yer look where yer goin', yer great oaf? Just come from 't Ship, 'ave yer . . . ?' But before she could finish she was shoved from another direction, propelled quite violently towards the man who had first pushed her, his grinning face thrust into hers as he caught her arms.

'Well, if it ain't little lass as what refused ter support 'er brothers an' sisters in Preston,' he smirked. 'Look 'ere, lads. Look what we 'ave 'ere.' He turned her about so that she faced the rest of them, holding her for a moment before shoving her towards them. Her shawl remained in his hands but he threw it to the ground and trampled it into the muddy track. When the next one caught her he tried, leering and malevolent, to kiss her before she was pulled from his embrace.

For five minutes they pushed and shoved her from one to the other, laughing at her anger at first, becoming more dangerous as her anger turned to fear and they sensed it in her. She broke away once and began to run, in which direction she didn't know, anywhere to get away from the mauling hands, the loose, open-mouthed laughter, the mud with which they had daubed her, the rain running down her face and through her hair wetting her to her undergarments.

They watched her go, still shouting with laughter for she was headed back in the direction from which she had originally come, and when she had gone fifty yards they started after her. Her skirt, heavy with water and mud held her back and her scattered, frantic thoughts dwelled for a moment on simply stepping out of it and running like the wind in just her drawers, for she was sure she could outrun them then. She was fit and strong, used to exercise, but what if she should fall and they should catch her without her skirt, in nothing but her sodden drawers and bodice? Would not their thoughts turn to something of a more menacing nature than a 'bit o' fun'?

'Calico Jack's right be'ind yer,' a grunting voice said. 'Yer should've paid up, lass, when yer 'ad chance. 'Appen tha will when't collector comes round next week, ay?' and a foot tripped her. She landed flat on her stomach with her hands stretched out in front of her as she tried to save herself and for several moments she lay on the spiky wet grass, completely winded. They were all about her again, their heavy clogs moving and slipping on the grass, their laughter loud and ugly. She could see those clogs fidgeting as the men moved from foot to foot, waiting for her to get up so that they could knock her down again, so that they might devise some way to humiliate her further, to intimidate and frighten her, a lesson to others who would not comply with the rules which they had written. Her head reeled and the horizon lifted in a sickening motion and on her right the stones of Badger's Edge seemed to move towards her.

They had her by the arms then, picking her up to dangle both feet off the ground, between two of them. She was coated from the top of her head to her bare feet in mud. It stuck to her wet body, outlining her small, peaked breasts, her nipples, the thin but shapely length of her legs and she felt the fear paralyse her as the laughter died away and they fell silent as every pair of eyes ran down her body.

One licked his lips. Dear God, is he Calico Jack? was her last despairing thought, then the world exploded about her and she fell like an empty sack to the wet earth. There were shouts and the movement of enormous shadowy figures, the vague and quite senseless sound of a woman's laughter, dark shapes so big and filled with vigour, with colour and movement, she could make no sense of it. Something crashed within an inch of her face which was pressed to the pulped grass and a voice told someone to, 'watch that bloody horse of yours, brother'. Then there was quiet, an absolute stillness and calm, and all she could hear was the soft patter of rain against the rocks which littered the ground where she lay.

The peace went on and on, how long she did not know. Five seconds, five minutes, five hours perhaps, she did not care in the wondrous release from the terror which had been forced on her. Then the thunder came back, moving the ground on which she lay and she cowered away from it, unable to lift her head to see which one it was who had come back to torment her.

'Dear, sweet Jesus,' a voice said, soft and filled with compassion.

'The bastards! I've a good mind to go after them again.'

Men's voices but not like those who had brought her to this. Voices she had heard at the mill. Cultured and yet harsh with the anger of young men who would not damage a woman, any woman, for they had been brought up to protect those weaker than themselves. To be gallant and courteous, to honour a woman's virtue, to take it, certainly, if given

175

permission, to take it willingly, merrily, but with sweetness, not violence.

'Put my cape about her, Drew.' A long, flowing garment was placed over her as four strong young hands lifted her to her feet.

'Let me have her,' a girl's voice said and she went willingly into the curve of strong, female arms. She was held fast against a tall, slender, woman's body, safe, familiar and infinitely comforting for she could still feel those hard masculine hands and hear the sound of hard masculine laughter.

'Are you all right, Annie?' the girl's voice said quietly in her ear, meaning have they interfered with you as men do? She spoke so softly the young men could not hear her and Annie was grateful for she did not wish to be burdened just yet with such thoughts.

'Yes, they did not ... hurt me.' Her voice was muffled against the girl's shoulder and she clung to her for a moment longer, then stepped back and looked up into her face: Tessa Harrison and at her back would be Drew and Pearce Greenwood.

'Thanks.' She had recovered somewhat and her voice was brusque.

'Are you sure?' Tessa smiled and in her vivid face still lingered the excitement of the last few minutes, the enjoyment she had known as she chased the attackers across the moorland, and yet there was understanding, sympathy, for had she not suffered what Annie had, in the grasp of the tinkers? 'We were up on Badger's Edge and saw them chase you. We weren't certain whether it was ... well, what it was they were after. From up there, covered in mud as you ... sorry, Annie ... we thought you were...' She shook her head and became brisk. 'But really, should we not be getting you home? One of my cousins will take you up, will you not...?'

She turned to the young men who stood awkwardly at Annie's back. They were not quite certain how to treat this child they had just rescued, this poor, bedraggled, mud-

176

spattered little rabbit, and were only waiting for orders from Tessa who seemed to have taken command.

'Pearce.'

'Of course.' Pearce leaped forward and in a moment Annie was in his arms, the mud which rubbed on to his fine woollen jacket of no consequence as she was lifted to sit before him on the back of his tall bay. She did not know which was worse, the ordeal through which she had just gone or the dizzying heights in which she now found herself and the restless movements of the horse beneath her. Then he sprang lightly up behind her, placing his arms on either side of her to take the reins. She shrank from his touch and he was most careful with her as they walked gently in the direction of Edgeclough as Tessa directed them.

The small cottage seemed about to burst apart from the press of people who crowded within it. Nelly, Polly and Grace fluttered about like three pale moths, appalled by the sight of their sister, whom they had never seen other than calm, unruffled and immaculate, in such a sorry and mindless state, whilst Jack, not yet a man but no longer a boy, seemed undecided whether to weep or go and fight the devils who had done this to their Annie.

Pearce and Drew shifted from foot to foot, ready to do anything which might be asked of them, for Annie was not herself at all, as anyone could see, since she clung to Tessa in a most unusual way.

The men were got rid of, the tin bath lifted down from the scullery wall and filled with hot water by the three frozen-faced, tearful little girls. It was warm and quiet. Female hands washed her hair and soaped her back whilst Tessa's soft voice chatted of this and that and nothing at all, as though she knew that, at this moment, this was what Annie needed most. Female things, female voices, soft, gentle, the faint perfume of her own skin, the fine silk of her shirt, the commiseration of her sisters, the friendly, almost casual attention which asked nothing of her and brought the familiar order which was the stuff of life, back to her. Tessa watched the strain leave Annie's face and when she began to give instructions to her three young sisters, it left theirs also since they recognised that she was herself again and the tension in the room eased.

'Are you feeling better?' Drew enquired politely, as young English gentlemen are trained to do with a lady. They were all drinking tea, cramped together in the tiny room for Annie would not hear of them leaving without 'sumat inside 'em'.

'Aye. I weren't 'hurt. They was just lads ... bullies...'

'Tell me who they were and we will deal with them.' Pearce moved to lounge against the table, standing close to her, towering protectively over her slight figure.

'Nay, I don't know their names.' Annie was alarmed by his nearness and masculine aggression, of which she had had more than enough today, and edged away to a safer place behind her teapot. 'They belong t't union, sent ter frighten me an' t'other lasses inter payin' towards Preston strike fund. I were tellin' Tessa about 'em only last week...'

Pearce turned to stare, bewildered, at Tessa, for how did this factory girl come to know his cousin and, more to the point, have the privilege of calling her by her Christian name? But Tessa frowned and shook her head, indicating that she would explain later, wondering as she did so why she had not spoken of their acquaintance to her cousins, or even her mother who would surely have understood. The reason probably had something to do with Will: they were sometimes together in Annie's cottage and the secret part of her life, with Will, seemed inexplicably linked to Annie and the friendship the three of them shared.

Annie was clattering about the kitchen now, awkward and ungracious, tidying away the pans which had heated the water for her bath, waiting for them to take themselves off and leave her to recover with her family with whom she was at ease. The bath stood before the fire, the cooling, muddied water still in it, embarrassing her. Her sisters were inclined as yet to cling about her impatient figure and when Tessa nodded towards the bath Pearce and Drew instantly sprang forward to lift it, laughing now that the drama was done with.

'Where . . . ?' they queried, for really, what did one do in these circumstances, since they had known only the comfort of an upstairs bathroom, with hot and cold piped water.

'The back door, you idiots,' she mouthed at them and as they tussled with the bath between them even the children began to smile despite the god-like proportions of these two gentlemen, circling about them as they edged towards the door.

'Sit down, Annie,' Tessa beseeched her, 'just for a moment.'

'Give ower, lass. I've them childer ter see to . . .'

'Oh, sit down and tell me all about this union thing. I'm sorry to say I didn't take much notice last week when you and . . .' she turned round to make sure they were not over-heard, '. . . when you and Will were talking about it.'

'No, I didn't think you was listening,' Annie replied dourly but there was a glint of amusement in her eyes.

Her cousins, returned from their mastery of the bath water, listened, fascinated for the first time by this aspect of mill life of which they had previously known nothing. They had heard it mentioned a dozen times around the dinner table but what had it to do with them, they had asked one another, yawning? Now they had an almost proprietary interest in this quaint thread of a girl who was as sharp of voice as she was sparing of words.

When they had gone to fetch the horses Tessa took Annie's reluctant hand and from her own superb height and splendid good looks, smiled down into her face.

'You have nothing to be ashamed of, you know,' she whispered, 'and nothing to fear now. My cousins will see to that. Something like this appeals to the gallant in them.'

'Aye, so I noticed,' Annie answered shortly.

'Will you be all right now?'

'O'course. I've got ower worse n' this.'

'Would you like me to . . . ?'

179

'Nay, you gerron 'ome.'

'I'll call to see how you are.'

'Give over, there's no need.'

'Nevertheless, I will. We *are* friends you know, Annie, though you make it very difficult at times.' She smiled to take the sting out of her words.

''Appen yer right,' Annie agreed grudgingly, the light in her eyes soft.

Tessa lifted her head in that haughty gesture Annie knew so well as though to say that all was now settled to her satisfaction.

'I shall come on Sunday on my way to ... well, on Sunday.'

She had explained to her cousins, to her own satisfaction at least, how she had become friendly with Annie, leaving out all mention of the tinkers who had frightened her last summer, and naturally, of Will Broadbent.

'I visit her now and again,' she said airily, 'and take a few things for the children. Well, you can see how they are placed,' she added, making it sound as though she was the lady of the manor distributing munificence to the poor and they seemed to find no reason to question her further.

They rode home companionably side by side, the three of them taking up the width of the rough track which led over Besom Hill and beyond Badger's Edge to Crossfold. Those they met on the way were forced to step off into the grass to let them go by, but it is doubtful the three riders noticed or, if they did, thought anything much about it.

There would be no more collecting in the mill, Pearce said ominously, for the out-of-work operatives at Preston. Besides, had he not been told that they were slowly drifting back to work, those who had been on strike for the best part of thirty-six weeks? They had won nothing beyond a long, hungry winter. The strike leaders, it appeared, had no option but to capitulate and the masters would soon be celebrating a victory. It was being said that labour, as a commodity, could obtain no higher price than the purchaser was willing to give for it and the strongest party would, in the end, win.

The March wind ruffled through Tessa's growing hair, flicking a damp strand across her mouth. Her eyes were a soft grey velvet musing on the plight and appearance of Annie Beale, and her thoughts were full of admiration. A nasty experience, but Annie had made herself recover, for the sake of her family. Not many young girls in factory life today would have had the strength, of mind and body, to evade those bully boys, for so long, as she had, and then pick herself up and reassure her sisters that she was not in the least hurt, just madder than a wet hen, or words to that effect.

Tessa smiled, then glanced down at her own slim legs which were becoming wetter every minute in the persistent drizzle which fell. She had flung her cape about her, fastening it carelessly as she left Annie's cottage but it had become loosened, riding back over her shoulders, allowing the damp to penetrate her clothing beneath.

'Just a minute, you two,' she said, falling back a pace. 'I want to fasten my cape. This drizzle is getting heavier and I'm going to be wet through by the time we reach home.' She made her horse stand whilst she undid the cloak, lifting and whirling it about her head and shoulders, allowing it to settle but not before the two men who had halted obediently had seen the joyous lift of her breasts, very obviously unconfined, the dark and peaked circle of her nipples through the damp silk of her shirt. Two pairs of vivid blue eyes narrowed. Two brown throats dried up, the breath within them becoming trapped, and when they each turned away and their eyes met it was with the murderous rage which springs up between two dogs who covet the same bitch.

'What the devil are you staring at?' Drew snarled, just as though Pearce had been found ogling Drew's woman. His hand closed viciously about the crop he held and it was quite certain, if he had been within range, that he would have sliced it across his brother's cheek.

'I might ask you the same question.' They drew their horses up hard against one another, nose to tail, and as Drew lashed out with the crop, Pearce caught his arm. The bays, unused to such rough and menacing handling, reared and pranced, their thoroughbred eyes rolling in fright, their long and fragile thoroughbred legs clattering across tumbling stones and treacherous rabbit holes. But still they came at one another, their well-muscled arms and strong brown hands looking for a hold, for something to hit, to damage, to destroy, in their mindless, unreasoning jealousy.

A sharp lunge brought Drew from his mount and he slid beneath the belly of Pearce's kicking, enraged animal, but in a second he was up, his arms reaching for his brother, his feet digging into the soft ground, finding enough purchase to heave Pearce down with him.

'You filthy bastard ... you filthy bastard,' he was snarling, his eyes slitted with rage, his mouth hard and cold and cruel. His arms were about his brother, lifting him bodily from the ground; then they both went down, rolling against the legs of the screaming horse, sending it, and the other, racing away in terror in the direction of Crossfold and the safety of the stable.

'I'll kill you,' Pearce sobbed in the back of his throat, his hands reaching for his brother, his teeth searching for his jugular, his booted feet for anything, preferably in his breeches, which might do him the most harm.

'Drew ... oh, dear God ... Pearce ... Stop it, stop it. What is it? ... Dear Lord, what is the matter? Stop it, stop it ...' She tried to get between them, her cape hampering her so she flung it off. She had done no more than secure the top button when her cousins had, unaccountably, gone for each other's throats, and it came undone easily. The rain was coming down harder now and she slipped in the wet grass, falling heavily on her back, drenched to her skin, her bold breasts almost naked, but the two men who fought

182

over her were too concerned with killing one another to see. Splattered with mud and blood from a wound one had inflicted, they grappled fiercely, flinging unco-ordinated blows, some of which found their mark but most ending ineffectually in the ground. If they could have kept their feet, face to face, doubtless they would have half-killed one another since, both being skilled at bare-knuckle fighting, they would have fought to a standstill, but scuffling on the wet and slippery grass as they were they did little damage.

During the five minutes the fight lasted Tessa did her best to stop them but it was they themselves who ended it.

They rolled away from one another as though sense and reason and sanity infiltrated their fevered minds at the same moment. Slowly they sat up, several feet apart, their heads bowed on their arms which were draped across their bent knees. They did not look at one another, nor at her.

'Well,' she said indignantly, 'what the devil was that all about? You realise you have terrified your horses into stampeding, I am wet through and covered in mud and one of you, or both, is certain to have a black eye or a bloodied nose. What happened? What were you fighting about? Did one of you say something the other did not care for, was that it? You're like a couple of schoolboys, always ready to scrap over nothing. One of these days those tempers of yours will get you into serious trouble. Oh, I know I've a temper too, but nothing like the exhibition I've seen here today. Now you'll have to walk home and I hope to God those bays of yours have come to no harm or Charlie will . . .'

'Go home, Tessa, there's a good lass.' Pearce's voice was drained of all expression.

'*Go home!* Don't you start ordering me about, Pearce Greenwood. Just because you and Drew have had a spat it doesn't mean you can . . .'

'*Go home, Tessa!*'

'Dammit, I will then. Why should I stay, or even concern myself with either one of you?'

'Quite, cousin, so go home.'

She had gone, her cape enveloping her from head to toe when Drew spoke.

'What are we to do, brother?' he said softly, still staring at the ground between his legs.

'God knows, for I don't.'

## 11

'We can't go on like this, dammit, and well you know it. It's nearly six months since we became . . .'

'Lovers. Is that the word you hesitate over, my lad?'

Tessa rolled on to her stomach, draping her arms across Will's broad, naked chest, smiling languorously into his face. Her eyes were soft, filled with the sighing warmth of the aftermath of their love-making and he felt a great desire to shake her, to fling her off and climb out of the vigorously crumpled depth of the feather-bed, to stand up and bellow his frustration, to stamp about the small room and bang himself against the walls, to hurt himself physically, as his sore heart was hurting now.

'Don't turn away from me, Will,' she said plaintively, moving herself up his body until her lips were an inch from his. She put up a hand to his face, forcing him to look at her then took his bottom lip between hers, sucking it gently into her mouth, tracing her tongue along the inside of his lips in the way he had taught her. She smiled into his eyes, inviting him to begin again, then lifted herself on to her hands until her breasts touched his face, each nipple brushing sensuously across his parted lips.

184

'Open your mouth wide,' she ordered breathlessly and when, unable to refuse, he did so, she pressed each one in turn between his lips, the rosy peaks finding his tongue. He licked them slowly, rolling his tongue about the soft flesh which hardened and filled. He felt his body begin to respond to her, as it always did, rejoicing in the way hers pleased it, again as he had taught her, and inside him something tore loose and broke away in pain. Whore's tricks, his anguished mind told him before he could stop it, then it thought of nothing as the wicked skill she brought to his bed overcame him. She was expert in the art of love-making now, bringing him and through him, herself, to peaks of glorious, shouting delight, not once, not even twice, but several times at each encounter. Sometimes it was a quiet, shivering, almost lyrical experience. A soft rejoicing in the way their bodies met and joined, so perfectly balanced in their need and fulfilment, he felt a great desire to weep at the beauty of it. Then she was tender, as gentle as a dove on his hand, submissive and willing, he thought, to be anything he wanted her to be.

'Marry me,' he would say then, even as he spoke the words knowing the foolishness of them, and he would watch her, hopelessly, as she became restless beneath his gaze. 'Marry me and we'll go away. Emigrate to the colonies. They want strong, healthy men and women to begin a new nation in Australia . . .'

'Among the felons?' she would laugh.

'There are men of importance there now. Land to be had for those prepared to work. You'd love it there, sweetheart. There'd be no restrictions on you as there are here. An outdoor life in a world so big and empty and free you could ride that mare of yours for evermore and never meet another living soul. A farm of our own . . .'

Her gaze avoided his, or worse still, to him, became filled with a mischievous gleaming, that look of smiling ardour, of passion which would, without question, render him to the depths and heights where her need took him. Always it was the same. She answered his questions, his pleas, his demands with the certain persuasion of her body, diverting his masculinity to the attention, not of their future, but to the rapture of now.

From the day it had begun she had set the pace, the rhythm, made the rules, giving him everything he wanted of her body, taking everything she needed of his, fulfilled to such glowing beauty he had been amazed, on the next occasion he had come face to face with her mother, that she had not approached him on what he had done to her daughter. She was seventeen now and certainly ready for marriage and her body, nourished by his, for as the saying goes, 'man feedeth woman', became a woman's, magnificent and proudly flaunting. And each time he tried to speak of the future, even though he knew inside himself where practical common sense lay that his hopes were forlorn, she would fling herself upon him, her mouth reaching greedily for his so that the words were kept locked inside him. She made *his* body desire *hers*, filling his mind not with what he recognised as a pathetic dream of the future, but with forthright and lusty desire.

But not this time. This time he would not be seduced into that mindless abandonment of thought and sense which her magic wrought in him. This time her body and her use of it would not come between him and what he had to say to her. He meant to make her understand that he wanted to be not her lover but her husband. He could not go on like this, week in and week out, hiding away in this cottage the love he had for her, delightful though their hours together in this bed were. It was a marvel to him that their relationship, which surely to God must be known to those who lived nearby, had not yet reached the ears of her family. She was discreet, too discreet for his liking since if it became generally known that she was seeing one of her uncle's employees in secret, would it not force the confrontation he hoped would end this deceit and make her his wife? They would not like it, especially those two lordly cousins of hers, but the Greenwoods had come from working stock and might that not incline them to look more kindly on him as a husband for the daughter of the house! He was strong. He had a good brain and that most driving whip of them all, ambition. He would be more than overlooker or foreman in someone else's mill, by God, he would. His clever brain, and he knew it was clever, would find a way to make him his own master one day. He wanted none of their money and, if he were honest, none of it for Tessa though he supposed he could not deny her her inheritance. It was only recently that he had been made up to foreman with a decent wage to suit his new position. He could afford to rent perhaps a small villa on the outskirts of Chapmanstown, or at least something a bit better than this cottage. He was realistic enough to know that Tessa was used to luxury beyond his imagining but if she loved him, and she told him over and over again that she did, she would be prepared to make some sacrifice, surely? He would even try to get in a girl to help with the heavier housework. Allow her to have more freedom than the wives of other foremen. Freedom to ride her little mare up on the moorland road and . . .

Here his thoughts became confused for how was he to afford to feed and stable a horse, and besides, would he care to have his wife galloping about the countryside as Miss Tessa Harrison did? He knew he wouldn't and if that was the case, could he hold her to him, reined in and locked in a cage, which is how she would see it, if he dared not allow her the freedom she needed? Was he being selfish in asking this child-woman, since that was what she was despite her sexual maturity, to set herself down into the life a woman of his class must live?

He turned away from her then. Easing her body to one side, he slipped out of the bed and strode to the window, staring blindly out into the pale spring sky. The candle on the small bedside table which she had insisted upon lighting so that they might study one another more intimately, turned his hard, muscled body to the colour of amber, the light

187

emphasising the broadness of his shoulders, the lean beauty of his narrow waist, buttocks and shapely legs. He did not look back at her but he was conscious of the tight-clenched impatience and distinctly heard, as her breathing slowed, her long drawn-out sigh of resignation.

'What are you doing over there?' she asked softly, knowing quite well what was coming for had it not happened a dozen times before, but attempting to avoid it with lightness. 'Come back to bed, sweetheart. I shall have to go soon if I'm to be home for dinner and you know we won't see one another until next weekend. Come here, Will, and put your arms . . .'

'Stop it, Tessa. Stop wheedling like some sixpenny strumpet. Don't demean yourself, or me, or what we feel for one another with these . . . these silly games. Get up and put your clothes on.'

He turned without looking at her and began to fumble his own way into the trousers she had removed from him two hours since, the shirt which, playing the temptress, she had insisted she would unbutton, slowly, one by one, her mouth on his chest and shoulders, his flat stomach and strong thighs. A witch and a wanton, if he were honest, she had lifted him to a groaning, quivering summit of joy.

'Oh, Will, don't . . .'

'Put your clothes on, Tessa. We must talk.'

'I don't want to talk, Will. I want to . . .'

'I'll be downstairs so be quick about it.'

Her face was sullen as she entered the parlour, still buttoning up her shirt. Her hair lay in a gloriously dishevelled cloud about her head, dark as the midnight sky. Her breeches were crumpled from the careless disorder in which they had lain for the past two hours and in her hand she carried her riding boots.

'I don't want tea,' she said coolly, 'so don't bother with the kettle. Besides, I thought on an occasion such as this a lady and gentleman were supposed to sip champagne from a crystal slipper, not drink a mug of tea round a . . .'

Before she could finish the sentence he had stepped

dangerously across the room. The palm of his hand, when it hit her, made the sound of a pistol shot and her head rocketed to one side with the force of it. Her hair lifted and flung itself in a shimmering curtain across her face and when she turned back to him her eyes burned through it, as fierce and baleful as those of a tiger in the night.

'Don't ever speak to me like that again, my lass,' he said, his voice warning her to be careful. But this was Tessa Harrison and should he not have known she was a woman, no matter who struck her, who was not to be intimidated by it? She sprang for him, her nails reaching for his eyes, her bare feet flailing at anything they could find for a target.

'You bastard,' she hissed. 'I thought you were a man but it seems you are no better than those louts who pick on anything smaller and weaker than themselves. But I should have known. I should have known from the first that you could never be anything but a product of your own upbringing, a bully and a tyrant who would hit a woman . . .'

'Stop it, Tessa, don't be any more foolish than you already have been.' He had her easily in his grasp, his arms pinning hers to her side, his body forced against hers so that she could not move. Her face was just beneath his, white with rage except for the flame print of his hand across her cheek, her eyes brilliant, like sparkling, lamp-lit crystals between her narrowed lids.

'Let go of me, let go of me,' she spat at him and when he did she almost fell. He pushed her unceremoniously backwards until she was forced into the wing chair by the fire, keeping her there easily merely by holding her shoulders with both hands and placing his knee on her lap to prevent those lethal feet from finding their target between his legs.

'Let me up. I wish to go home.' Her face was set against him, cold and expressionless now, the hot fury turned to ice and she no longer struggled.

'Not until you have heard what I have to say.'

'Nothing you have to say is of the slightest interest to me

189

and I would be obliged if you would take your hands off me at once.'

'My dirty, working man's hands, you mean?' He smiled grimly.

'Something like that.'

'You were happy enough to have them on you half an hour since.'

'That was different.'

'Of course. Then I was what you wanted me to be.'

'And what is wrong with that? You made no complaint then, as I recall. You were more than happy to let me . . .'

'Stop it. Let's have no more of this. You know what I want to talk about but you're afraid of it so you divert me with . . . with whore's tricks . . .'

'So I'm a whore, am I? No wonder you have been so willing to let me into your bed. Not only a whore but one who costs you nothing. You don't even have to walk down to the nearest inn where I believe such women are to be had. You have one come to you. How convenient . . .'

'You're doing it again, Tessa. Listen to yourself. You know you're talking rubbish, I can see it in your eyes. You know what you say is untrue but you're so afraid of the truth you're prepared to tarnish what is precious, good, between us so that you don't have to hear it. Go then, if you must . . .' He stood away from her abruptly, lifting his hands to show that he would not try to prevent her. 'Aye go, but if you do, don't come back.'

She had stood up as he moved away from her, her bare feet whispering on the carpet as she strode across to where she had dropped her boots, her face stormy, every line of her offended body telling him in what she hoped was no uncertain manner that it would take a lot of coaxing on his part to make her forget this. But his words stopped her and for several moments he watched her haughty back as she struggled with the hope that he was bluffing. She wanted desperately to pull on her boots, to shrug into her jacket, toss on her tall beaver hat and without looking at him again, sweep disdainfully from the house. She wanted to, oh, yes, she wanted to, but he could see the indecision, not in her eyes, since her face was turned from him, but in the slight tremor of her shoulders, the clenching and unclenching of her fists.

She turned then and he felt his heart move painfully with his love and thankfulness. She *did* care. Despite her restless changes of mood, the fidgeting with which she treated his attempts to find some bedrock on which to stabilise their relationship, she was not, thank God, reckless enough to walk out on it. She was ready, albeit reluctantly, to hear what he had to say.

'Sit down, lovely girl,' he murmured softly.

'Tell me what you have to say,' she said but her eyes had melted, despite herself, at the endearment, and her love shone through them.

'Sit down, please.'

The delicately woven, fragile stuff which bound them together was stronger now and he grinned ruefully, boyishly, the breath he had been holding sighing out of him as she sat down in the chair she had just left. Her face was still truculent, her mouth mutinous, but she turned her smoky grey eyes on him, watching him warily, waiting for him to speak.

He picked up her jacket which lay on the table and held it to him, looking down at it without seeing it, stroking the rough tweed with patient hands, strong hands, a working man's hands, and she found herself watching them, remembering their smooth and erotic passage over her own body. She shivered and looked away.

'What is it, Will?' she asked, though, of course, she knew.

'We must be married, lass.'

'*Must?*' He saw that she was offended again and his own hard-won patience stretched itself uncomfortably. She was like some prickly hedgehog which, at the first hint of threat, thrusts its spines to hurt the hand which meant none. He sighed and bent his head, his strong face soft with his love.

'I love you, Tessa, and you say you love me.'

'Don't you believe me?' She threw back her head defiantly.

'Sometimes.'

'Only sometimes? Why do you think I come here and get into your bed?'

'Aaah . . . !'

'And what is that supposed to mean?'

'Only that a woman does not have to love a man, or indeed the other way round, for them to . . . to please one another in a sexual way. There would be few partnerships if it depended only on love, Tessa.'

'I *do* love you, Will, and I don't know what you mean.'

'I mean we must move on. We cannot stand still like this. Dear God, for nearly six months now every time I've spoken about it you've shied away like some nervous colt. You're young, I know . . .'

'I'm seventeen . . .'

'And I reckon I'm twenty-nine or thirty and I want a wife . . .'

'So I'll do, is that it?'

'No, it's not. Why the hell must you turn everything about the way you do? I believe it's meant to put me off but this time I'll not be denied my say. I love you. I want you. I want to wed you, lass. Bloody hell, is that not clear enough? You've been my . . . my mistress, there, does that satisfy you since you seem to like to use the right words? . . . for long enough and I'll wait no longer. And the risk . . .'

'What risk?' Anything, *anything* to sidetrack him.

'Don't be childish, Tessa. You know you take a risk every time you leave that blasted animal of yours tied up in my back yard. D'you think no one notices? It will come out soon enough and then you'll have no reputation left at all. Not that I care about that. You'd be my wife and there's not a man in the valley would dare say a word about you, to me or to each other. But there's other risks, lass. What if you should conceive? I try to be as careful as I can but sometimes you're a bloody challenge to any man with your wildness and I'm put to ... well, you'll take my meaning.'

'No, I don't.'

'Never mind, then, but it's bound to happen and I want us to be wed when it does.'

There was a deep, endless and, to Will, quite dreadful silence. That was what he felt. *Dread*. She continued to look at him, her expression unreadable, saying nothing, and the misery began in him then, the sheer, bloody, hopeless misery which lapped through the layers of his skin. It not only racked him from within but surrounded him like a black shadow through which he could hardly see her. She did not answer and he knew it was because she didn't know how.

He answered for her.

'You can't bring yourself to do it, can you?' His voice was harsh and she felt a great longing to go to him then, to put her arms about him and draw his head to her shoulder, to comfort him in the only way she knew how. They were lovers. She had spent the last months in the most delightful occupation of being loved, of being made love to by Will Broadbent and she had gloried in it. She loved him, or at least she thought she did, and she did not want to lose him. She could not bear to consider the prospect of a life without him in it but she was not at all sure she wanted to be married. Not yet. Not to Will. Not to anyone. She was quite old enough for marriage and motherhood but it was not for her, not yet. She had thought about it in the quietness of her own bedroom, away from the hard beauty of Will Broadbent's body which delighted her so and which she must have, but the prospect of living in this tiny house, in the primitive conditions which, when one was not compelled to it was *fun*, simply appalled her.

And yet, could she live without what he gave her, not just with his body but his loving spirit? So was *that* love? She knew she was treating him as some men treat certain women, as a diversion, a sweet and thrilling pastime which had nothing at all to do with her real life. She was not sure

whether it was Will she wanted ... loved ... or what he could give her, and she was desperately afraid to set herself the task of finding out. Now he was determined on marriage and she knew she could not go through with it. Perhaps when ... well, in a year or two ... or when ... when...
*When?*

It was no good and she knew Will could see it in her face. He picked up her jacket and held it out for her. She slid her arms into the sleeves, then, as he reached for her boots, stood like a child as he eased each foot in turn into them. He brought her cloak and tucked it about her shoulders, then stepped back from her, unsmiling, his eyes unreadable.

'Goodbye, lass.'

'Will, don't send me away. I do love you and one day ... when ... Dear Lord, I cannot bear to let you go ...'

'Then don't.'

'Let me have some time to ... Oh, surely there must be something, some way ...'

'You know what I want.'

'But, Will ...'

'Nay, say nothing more. It's in your face. Don't come back unless it's to tell me we'll be wed. I love you, Tessa, and I'll wait for a while. You're young ...'

It began to rain, a soft spring rain as she rode along the track which led from Chapmanstown to Edgeclough, the freshness of it sliding down her cheeks and mixing with her warm and anguished tears.

The knock on the door startled Annie. She had not been expecting anyone this late in the afternoon since Tessa usually came earlier, and she had been hoping to get the last of her spring cleaning finished before the children came back from Sunday school.

'Oh, it's you,' she said tartly when she opened the door, then stood back to allow Tessa to enter. 'Wipe yer feet. I've just done that there floor,' she added and was mildly surprised when Tessa meekly did as she was told. Tessa's face which was always a clear, creamy white had an overtone of grey in it and her eyes were shadowed. Annie studied her carefully.

'I'll put kettle on,' she said moving towards the fire and when she had done so she returned to her scrubbing of the deal table, treating it with the demented fervour which she gave to every job of cleaning she tackled. From the corner of her eye she watched as Tessa picked up first a teacup, then a spoon, putting each back where she found them without seeing them, then flung herself into Annie's rocking chair, her unfocused gaze on the dancing flames in the grate. She put one foot on the fender. Her head was slumped between her shoulders and she did not speak, even when Annie put a mug of weak tea in her hand.

'What's up?' Annie said, sparing of words as always.

'Nothing.'

'Then get out o' me road an' let me gerron wi' me spring cleaning.'

Tessa looked up in surprise, then sighed deeply.

'I'm sorry, Annie, I know you have things to do but I just didn't know where else to go.'

'Thanks.'

'No, I didn't mean it like that, it's just . . .'

Annie watched Tessa brood silently on whatever it was that troubled her, though she knew she'd not have far to look to find the reason for it. The whispers were already rustling like the wind through the bracken on the tops, going from machine to machine. Whispers about their newly made-up foreman and – they hardly dared breathe her name – this young woman who was crouched in Annie's kitchen chair. Annie had given the spinner who had hissed of it into her ear a withering look and told her sharply not to be so daft and to mind her own business, but it'd not stop there. Just let Mr Greenwood or Mrs Harrison hear of it and Will would be out on his ear quicker than you could say 'picking stick.'

'Best tell me, lass.'

Tessa sighed again and Annie shifted impatiently, banging

her mug of tea down on the newly scrubbed table. Some of the tea slopped over the rim of the mug, staining the fresh surface and Annie stamped into the scullery, tweaking the wrung-out cloth from its nail by the scullery door where she had just hung it up to dry. Muttering darkly she wiped up the tea, returning the table to its immaculate condition, then stood back to admire it.

Tessa watched her, then began to laugh for, really, was there another like her?

'Oh Annie, you'd make some man' – probably the one I've just left, she thought sadly – 'a wonderful wife. You're sensible and ... and domesticated with no longing to ride over the brow of the next hill just to see what's on the other side.' She stretched out her hand to touch Annie's arm but Annie drew back, uncomfortable with demonstrations of affection, though she would give you her last farthing even if it meant she herself would starve.

''Ow d'you know what I want?'

'I'm sorry, you're right. How do any of us know what ... what others want and if we do, it's not always possible to give it to them. How can we ... ?' Her voice drifted away uncertainly.

'Nay, don't ask me. Yer talk in riddles sometimes an' if yer've nowt better ter do wi' yer time but sit about and gossip, I 'ave.' But Annie's plain face was soft with compassion.

'Life's a bloody riddle sometimes, Annie.'

'An' I'll 'ave no bad language in my kitchen neither.'

'I don't know why you put up with me, Annie, I really don't.'

'Nor me neither. Reckon no one but me'll 'ave yer.'

'You're right.' They smiled in perfect understanding at one another.

'It's Will, isn't it?'

'Yes.'

''E's ready fer marriage an' you're not, is that it?'

'Yes.'

'Not good enough for thi, is that what yer sayin'?'

'No, Annie, oh, no. You know I'm not like that.' But Annie was not so sure. Tessa was 'gentry' and spent a large part of her life with gentry. Could she give up the social position she had, which was bound to happen if she married Will? Mrs Will Broadbent would be a considerably less important person than Miss Tessa Harrison.

'Then what's ter stop yer?'

'Annie, I don't want to get married. I'm not even eighteen and the thought of living for the rest of my life . . .'

'In a foreman's cottage, is that it?'

'No . . . well, yes, up to a point though I'm sure if we were married Charlie would promote him to something more suitable to . . .'

'To'th'usband o't millowner's daughter. D'yer know, Tessa Harrison, I can't fathom you. Social position, or so you say, don't seem ter bother thi'. I'm a spinner, wi' clogs an' a shawl an' yet yer seem ter like me company, so why, when yer love the man, a man what's the same class as me, will yer not wed 'im . . . ?'

'I do love him, Annie, at least, I think I do . . .'

'Then wed 'im, fer God's sake.' Annie sat down and hitched her chair closer to Tessa's, her sharp little face a bright pink in her earnestness. 'Can yer not see what a good match it'd be . . . ?'

'*A good match!*'

'Don't tek that tone wi' me, lady. 'E's as good as any man in't valley. An' when yer Mam's gone, an' yer Uncle Charlie, who better ter run them mills than a man what's bin fetched up in cotton?'

'And what about Drew and Pearce? Are they to be disinherited?' Tessa drew back abruptly, deeply offended by Annie's contempt for her cousins' capabilities as millowners. 'They'll take over when . . . well, when they're ready.'

'Give over.'

Tessa stood up. 'If you're going to insult my family then

197

I think it's time I left. Thank you for the tea. And I don't think I shall be able to call next week.'

'Suit thissen.'

But as Annie watched Tessa ride away her face was sad and filled with pity, not only for the girl – for what else could you call her? – who seemed unable to reach out and hang on to the happiness which was offered to her, but for the man who offered it.

## 12

The first awareness Tessa Harrison had had of the 'trouble' which existed between Russia and Great Britain was last November when the newspapers reported that the Russian fleet had fired on seven Turkish frigates and three corvettes at Sinope – wherever that might be – and nearly four thousand men had perished. She couldn't understand it, really she couldn't, she had said to her mother who had read the account out loud to them. Why should the sinking of Turkish ships and the killing of Turkish sailors have anything to do with them, for heaven's sake? But everyone seemed to think it did and it was apparent the British public was highly indignant. Now it appeared the French and British had declared war on Russia and troops had embarked for Varna.

The news about the war excited Drew and Pearce. They had known from the start that there was to be one, Drew said, and naturally, Britain should be drawn in if she was to protect her interests out there.

'Out where?'

'In the Balkans.'

'Well, it's a mystery to me and I can make neither head

nor tail of why Britain and France should declare war on Russia over it.'

They were all three sprawled before the drawing-room fire. Laurel and Charlie were dining with commercial acquaintances and as always when Laurel was absent they all took advantage of it, even Jenny, turning up at table in whatever they had worn during the day. They were relaxed, quiet, a family with no need of the bright social conversation which Laurel insisted upon.

'They've made their camp on the northern slopes. The French have 15,000 men and 520 guns. It says the Russians have already retreated from Silistra and the British and French have pitched camp at Varna. It's rumoured to be quite a glorious sight: white tents and green fields, broad sweeps broken by a great many fine trees overlooking a shining lake, or so the papers say, and all surrounded by meadow land and backed by the rugged outlines of the Balkans.'

Pearce's soft voice trailed away and his eyes seemed to gaze, not at the valley he described but at some image only he saw. His brother looked away, his own eyes shuttered.

Jenny lifted her head from the newspaper and her voice was startled.

'You sound as though you'd like nothing better than to be there, lad?'

'The thought had occurred to me, Aunt, that it might be rather splendid to see something other than mill chimneys and loom-gates before I die.'

'You've been to Italy to visit your mother and father. Why should you wish to see ... where was it? ... Varna? I don't even know where it is.'

'Varna is on the Black Sea, Aunt Jenny, half-way across the world and a long way from Chapmans mills.'

'But your life is in those mills, Pearce, you know that.'

'Indeed. I am only too well aware of it.'

'And what is that supposed to mean?'

'Why, nothing. Only that Pearce and I are not the stuff you

199

and Charlie are made of, Aunt Jenny.' Drew's voice was smooth as he stepped in quite instinctively to support his brother. 'We are neither of us, or so it appears, naturally cut out to be industrialists, as you are, as our own mother was. Father became a politician, despite his humble beginnings...'

'Humble beginnings, is it, Drew Greenwood? And don't we all come from those, you included?'

'Oh, indeed we do, Aunt Jenny, but I hardly think Tessa, Pearce and I fit into the...'

'Oh, don't talk daft, lad. Your grandfather and your father planted taters to see them through the winter and even in 1826 during the power-loom riots they brewed nettles to make a bit of nourishment for Charlie and Daisy who was our sister. They were only children then...'

The three faces about her had taken on that faint and uneasy look of the young when confronted with the awkward and tedious reminiscences of the old. It was all history, their expressions said, and nothing to do with them and their generation. But she had lived through those times, riots and machine-breaking and the fight for a decent standard of living for the working man. And the father and mother of those two young men who were staring so irritatingly at her, had been in the forefront of that fight. Yet here their sons sat, careless, restless, ready, it seemed, to take a ship, if they had the choice, to some far-flung spot on the globe just for the hell of it. Just as though they were Nicky Longworth or Johnny Taylor, with no other obligation but to amuse themselves.

'Don't you care?' she asked coldly.

'About what, Aunt Jenny?' Drew's voice was polite, genuinely puzzled she could see.

'About what happened to your family. To all the families around here thirty years ago.'

'Really, Aunt Jenny, it is all so long ago. The future...'

'Depends on the past, my father always said.'

'How very quaint.'

Drew's face had assumed the haughty expression of a young prince and her own became a bright pink in her anger.

'You supercilious young devil! Your grandfather was a great man with a wisdom and a feeling for others which I suspect you wouldn't recognise. He was a working man, as I am a working woman, as *you*, both of you, are from a working-class family, and you will not expend your so-called humour at his expense. You really do amaze me, yet I don't know why you should for you've always shown a marked reluctance to take up your responsibilities in the mill. And I suppose you feel the same, do you?' She turned savagely on Pearce. 'About ... what were the words your brother used? ... the need to see something other than mill chimneys and loom-gates before you die?'

'Well, it would be splendid to travel but I don't know whether I'm prepared to go all the way to the Balkans to ...'

'To escape your heritage, is that what you're saying? To live like young lords without having to do a day's work in your lives? Shooting grouse over the Squire's moor ...'

'The Squire works hard, Aunt Jenny,' Drew protested angrily. 'He is busy from morning till night seeing to the needs of his tenants, just as you do your operatives. His people, he calls them. He is Chairman of the Bench at Quarter Sessions, a magistrate and is always occupied about the estate ...'

'Oh, that.' Jenny Harrison's voice was contemptuous, reducing Squire Longworth's busy day to the proportions of a tea-party which, if he did not care for it, he had no need to attend.

'Yes, that!' Drew was beyond caution now and though Pearce made a movement towards him, one that said he should take care, he chose to ignore it. 'And, I can tell you, the life would suit me admirably. Out in the sunshine instead of inside that ... that ...' It seemed he could find no word strong enough to describe his detestation of the mill. 'In the rain, if you've a mind to, not bound by clocks or bells but merely the seasons, the needs and desires of one's own inclination which certainly would not include the amassing of more and more money which one can scarcely need, surely?'

'That's because you have plenty already which others have worked for.'

'But there is no need of it any more. There is enough and to spare for us all. We can live in luxury for the rest of our lives . . .'

'And what happens to your workers? Are they to be thrown out like old bobbins, or will you keep them in this luxury as well?'

'They would not lose their jobs. If we were to sell the business whoever bought it would continue to run it just as it is.'

'Really! So you would cast off your responsibilities just as though you were talking of a herd of cows or a flock of sheep to be sold to the highest bidder? These are people you are concerned with: men and women who have worked loyally and faithfully for your family, some of them for over twenty years; young men who are beginning to make something of themselves because of the chance they have been given. Your family have shown all these people the opportunity to move forward, to find a change of place, each generation taking another step up. Yet you want to throw them all away so that you might walk in the rain whenever you have a fancy for it.'

'You will not understand, will you, Aunt Jenny? You will not even try to see what I am, what Drew Greenwood is. That we are not all the same. You are one of them . . .'

'And proud of it, lad.' She stood up and with quiet dignity walked from the room.

'Well, you have put the cat amongst the pigeons,' Pearce said softly, wondering how the war in the Balkans had led to the passionate argument between his brother and his aunt on the eternally recurring theme of the trials of the working 'poor'.

The scene between Jenny Harrison and her nephew was not spoken of the next day or the next, and by the end of the week Drew and Pearce had convinced themselves it had been forgotten. The weather had turned quite glorious. It was almost the end of May, Whit Monday and a holiday, and they with Tessa were to stroll down in the bright sunshine to watch the Whit walks.

Tessa had seen nothing of Will and made no attempt to. She missed him quite dreadfully. Her body, now that of a woman with the needs of her awakened sexuality, was even more restless than usual and she rode the moorland with all the wildness which had always been in her, but doubly so now without Will to soothe her to peace. She startled many a tramping family as she flew past on her fleet-heeled mare, her dogs about her feet, her unconfined hair growing longer now and streaming about her head like a dark and whipping pennant. At night she lay in bed, tossing her stimulated body from side to side, or fidgeting at the window for the rose-flushed dawn to break over the hills.

He had steadied her, she was aware of that now, making her think of things which had nothing to do with the wild excitement which had once been important to her. Now, without him, she needed it, or him, again. Several times during the week, as the spring evenings drew out towards summer she had been tempted to ride over to his cottage. She longed to fling her arms about him in a passion of love, to declare that she would marry him, despite her doubts, since she really could not manage without him and his quiet strength. Perhaps, in a week or so, if she still felt as miserable, she would drop by and talk to him, ask him to be patient with her, give her time to think. The thought heartened her, glowing like a tiny candle flame in the surprising darkness his absence left her in. Drew and Pearce had grown somewhat cool with her in the months she had known Will, going, she thought sadly, knowing nothing of their secret, on their own masculine and hell-bent pursuits from which she was firmly excluded. She had ridden to hounds in season, the last hunt in April, and joined the Squire's shoot over his moorland during weekdays when her cousins had been forced to the mill, accompanying them when they managed to elude her mother's and Charlie's disapproving eye, but they were different with her now. They had their share of milliners, dressmakers, actresses and parlourmaids, those who were fair game to young gentlemen such as they, and appeared to be completely preoccupied in their man's world in which, she was aware, she no longer had a place.

On the day of the Whit walks the houses in Jagger Lane and Reddygate Way were decorated with flags and banners, with mottoes which read 'God save Good Queen Victoria'. There were processions of Sunday school children in their Sunday best, the girls in white starched pinafores, the boys in white starched shirts and all provided, to those who could not afford them, by the ladies of the many church committees formed to help the deserving poor. Those who could pay for the new outfits of their children, a custom at Whitsuntide, did so, naturally, and even put a ribbon on the end of a glossy plait, or a rosette in a buttonhole.

The Mayor and Corporation marched manfully into the market place. When silence was obtained and the children, who were inclined to be boisterous on this day of freedom from loom or mule or schoolroom, were hushed, the Mayor said a prayer for Whitsuntide, since Pentecost was a religious festival after all.

The bands, of which there were at least half a dozen, struck up 'God Save the Queen' and when they were done the children who had been practising for weeks sang it in piping voices, most out of tune and not one finishing at the same time as his neighbour.

Led by a marshal on horseback supported by two stalwarts with spears, both on foot, the procession moved on then for it was felt that some of its members were becoming restive. It must have been two miles long, Tessa grumbled to Drew, and did they really need to stand and watch this endless assembly of Wesleyan, Methodist, Primitive

Methodist, of Latter Day Saints, Catholic and established religion as church after church went proudly by carrying its own treasured banner? There was to be a fair on Crossfold green with stalls, dancing and puppet shows, prize-fights and side-shows, a fortune teller and later, when it was dark, a display of fireworks.

There were three or four annual fairs held at Crossfold, where trading took place, where household goods were bought and sold, where menageries and travelling shows drew folk from miles around, and the excitement was intense. There would be clowns, they had been told, acrobats, peep-shows and freak exhibitions. Percy had whispered to Emma who had breathed of it to her young mistress as she brushed her hair – almost back to its original length, thank God – that there was to be a goldfish pulling a boat in a glass tank, could you believe it? Oysters smoking a pipe apiece just like a man, and, giggling, dancing girls exposing themselves to the public gaze for money.

Tessa had lately taken, much to the surprise of the Penfold Valley, to wearing an elegant gown when she was seen about Crossfold and had even been noticed coming out of Miss Maymon's dressmaking establishment, her mother's coachman behind her staggering beneath an armful of packages. They could not, of course, explain it and neither could Tessa herself, seeing no connection in her new preoccupation with how she looked and her love for Will Broadbent. It was as though that part of her which had been subdued for years as she rode madly at the heels of her cousins had begun to drift lightly, awakened by his hands and lips, to the surface of her woman's sensibilities. Now that she was a woman in the truest sense of the word, she needed to look like one, even to act like one at times.

She had gone a time or two to Annie's cottage in her new, stylish gowns, and to the Hall with Laurel, who had been invited to tea by the Squire's lady. Stepping down from the carriage in crimson taffeta, amethyst silk, honey-coloured velvet, turquoise satin; in cashmere of the softest hyacinth blue, tarlatan of palest peach, as bewitched by exotic and glowing colours as her mother, it seemed, she appeared as an elegant, suddenly fashionable young lady when it pleased her to be, delighted by the sensation she caused.

Now, on this annual day of celebration she wore a gown of rich cream, simple and beautifully cut, fitting closely to her breast and waist, the skirt so full it had filled the carriage. Her hat was like a flower garden of cream and apricot rose-buds, made from silk and lace. Her gloves were cream and so were her high-heeled kid half-boots and the dainty, lace-trimmed parasol it amused her to carry. She was playing a game, as both Drew and Pearce were aware, delighted with its novelty, basking in the admiration which turned every head in her direction and brought an appreciative gleam to each male eye which fell on her. When she was tired of this part she played she would discard it.

The green at Crossfold was an enormous pasture on the edge of town, reached by walking up the steep slope of Reddygate Way. It was packed from fence to fence with hundreds of tents and side-shows, with stalls selling every-thing from sweetmeats to the very latest Bowie knife, made in Sheffield but fashioned, it was advertised, for American and Indian fighters. Painted and gaily dressed clowns tumbled about the spaces between the tents. Acrobats per-formed the most amazing and seemingly impossible contor-tions with their elastic bodies. Jugglers juggled and showmen screeched of the wonders of fat ladies and thin men, of sheep with two heads and a fish with a woman's body. Bands played and the sky was blue and cloudless and when she saw him she felt her spirits lighten and her curi-osity sharpen but she would not, of course, show him that for one didn't with a *real* gentleman.

'There's Nicky Longworth and Johnny Taylor,' Drew said.

'Who's that with them?' Pearce asked.

'I don't know,' she murmured and it was not to Nicky and Johnny that her eyes were drawn but to the indolent figure of the man who strolled beside them. He was looking at her with the exaggeratedly cool expression gentlemen of his class always seemed to assume when presented with a pretty woman but there was a leap of pleasure in his eyes which she knew was answered in hers. He was tall, loosely put together, half a head taller than she, with crisp fair hair cut short and brushed smoothly about his well-shaped head. His eyes were a deep chocolate brown, narrowed and speculative in his bronzed face, and when he smiled as he did now his lips parted on teeth which were white and perfect. His manner said quite plainly that his ancestors, like those of Nicky Longworth and Johnny Taylor, had been of the privileged class, generations of them stretching back into time, of landed gentlemen, great soldiers, men of superiority and honour, but his whimsical smile told her that it did not matter since what was it to her, whoever she was, and to himself at this special moment?

'Drew, Pearce, good to see you,' Nicky Longworth said enthusiastically, just as though he had not drunk himself into a stupor with them the night before, pumping their hands, terribly glad to have them for his friends, it appeared.

'And Miss Harrison ... Tessa. How splendid you look, doesn't she, Johnny?' But Tessa, her hand bowed over by both her cousins' friends, had not yet torn her eyes away from those of their companion.

'Oh, do forgive me. May I introduce an old school chum of mine ... well, we were at the same school though Robby was at the end of his learning as Johnny and I were just beginning. He was somewhat of a god to us, I can tell you. He has come up for the ... Oh, I do beg your pardon, Tessa, here am I rattling on ...' To tell the truth Nicky was quite bowled over by young Tessa Harrison's striking beauty. He was accustomed to seeing her in her riding outfit, mud splattered and a bit of a tomboy, really, and now here she was looking as elegant and ... well, there was hardly a word to describe her radiance as she waited for him to complete his introductions.

'May I present Robby Atherton? Robby, this is Miss Tessa Harrison . . .'

'Miss Harrison.'

'Mr Atherton.'

He bowed over her hand, his manners exquisitely good humoured, his education obviously expensive, as the Squire's son's had been, his air superior but his impudent smile irresistible.

'. . . and her cousins, Drew and Pearce Greenwood.'

For several moments there was well-bred confusion as introductions were completed and it was perhaps this which kept concealed from Drew and Pearce the attraction which had flared up between their cousin and the gentleman to whom they had just been introduced. The polite conversation, the charming smiles and meaningless small-talk, hid the tension. Then Mr Atherton turned courteously to Miss Harrison, drawing her a pace or two away from the rest.

'You have been acquainted with Nick and Johnny long?' he asked her, placing a confident hand beneath her elbow, leading her even further ahead of the others with the manner of a gentleman who has the perfect right to do so if he wishes, but without being in the least discourteous.

'For quite some time, Mr Atherton. Squire Longworth has been kind enough to allow my cousins and myself to join his hunt.'

'Really? They are a charming family. Mine have been on friendly terms with them since before I was born, I believe, though this is the first time I have visited this part of the world.' But it certainly will not be the last, his admiring eyes said. I have never seen such beauty, such style, such splendour and having found it I do not mean to give it up lightly.

'Oh, and why is that, Mr Atherton?' She could feel the excitement effervesce inside her, foolishly perhaps, even dangerously, for such headlong and immediate attraction could not possibly survive, but when had Tessa Harrison ever considered danger?

'I have been in the army, Miss Harrison, and away from home since I was eighteen. A death in the family, my father's brother, brought me home and I was compelled to give up my commission. The estate, you understand.' He shrugged his shoulders on which, his manner said, the whole burden of his family inheritance now rested. He was sure she would know what he meant. 'And then there is the hunt in Leicestershire, and my own in Cheshire. The grouse, of course, and we have a lodge in Scotland. Deer stalking, you know?'

Oh, yes, she knew, for was it not the life she herself admired and should she not have known that this man was the kind to lead it? He was so amazingly handsome with his long and elegant mouth and that whimsical half-smile lifting the corners, the smiling brown gaze from eyes that said everything his words, so polite, so correct, could not say, not to a lady such as she was.

'My word, you must lead an active life.' Her own trite answers were just as hidebound.

'And you, Miss Harrison? What do you do with yourself? I know you ride to hounds for you have just told me, but surely that does not occupy all your time?' So could not you and I be somewhat more enjoyably employed away from these people, somewhere quiet and sun-filled, song-filled, and suitable for the delights we could show each other? But naturally, a gentleman conversing with a lady to whom he had just been introduced could not speak the words out loud.

Her smile was dazzling. 'No, indeed. I fill my days most pleasurably.' But not, of course, as they were meant to be filled, the slanting, cat-like grey of her eyes told him.

'I'm sure you do. Painting and fine embroidery.'

'Not particularly.' Her eyes dropped of their own volition to his curving mouth.

'My word, Miss Harrison.'

'Yes, Mr Atherton?' she said breathlessly.

'If we carry on like this for much longer I swear I shall be forced to believe you are as foolish as the rest of the young ladies whose aims and conversation are all the same and to whom I have been introduced by the score, and I know you are not. So why are we conversing in this absurd manner, do you think?' He grinned down at her engagingly, wickedly, then winked and her heart soared with delight for it seemed his wit matched his looks and breeding.

'You are teasing me, Mr Atherton.'

'Am I, Miss Harrison? I believe I am, but please, my name is Samuel Robert Atherton, Robby to my friends and if I may I shall call you . . . ?'

'Tessa.'

'Tessa . . . Tessa, may we pretend we were introduced, let's say three months ago, and are well acquainted. So well acquainted your cousins are looking at me with the obvious intention of calling me out or beating me to death with their bare fists . . .'

She turned, startled. 'Drew and Pearce?' Why should they be concerned since she was so evidently accompanied by a gentleman of the highest pedigree, a friend of the Longworth family and surely in safe hands? Then her enchantment with this new feeling was too strong to let her attention wander for another moment and she turned her brilliant smile back to him.

'. . . but I'm sure they will not mind if I snatch you away and escort you round the fair. Now tell me what you would like to see first, Tessa . . .' His voice deepened on her name and his eyes assessed her in that completely male but gentlemanly fashion he had been brought up to assume with a lady. His admiration was very evident. He was quite old, she thought, twenty-eight or nine, with wide shoulders which fitted his elegant coat with that perfection such English gentleman seemed so easily to achieve. His face was finely chiselled and his body delicately balanced, every portion of him matching exactly every other. Moulded by the same culture as Nicky Longworth to repress embarrassing emotion, nevertheless his interest, his approval, the warm excitement with which he regarded her, the open-hearted,

210

light-hearted charm, a touch perhaps of complexity, a boyish air overlaid with the maturity of an experienced man, was overwhelming.

'Tessa,' he said again, quite urgently, 'call me Robby. Say my name.' She knew precisely what he meant.

'Robby . . .' Her eyes smiled into his. Then, for the first time in her life, Tessa Harrison looked shyly away from a man.

'We are to dine with the Squire tonight, Tessa,' Drew said casually the next morning but his eyes were careful and Pearce's, who had followed him into the breakfast room, were the same as though, curiously, they were both waiting to judge her reaction.

She kept her face somewhat averted, pretending a great deal of interest in the fruit on her plate, making a determined effort to calm the tumult of her nerves, the exultation which surged through her at the thought of seeing him again so soon. Of course, this was *his* doing, she knew it. It was he who had instigated, somehow, this invitation to the Hall, and though the three of them dined there quite often, the suddenness of this command had surprised Drew and Pearce.

'Well, and I may not be able to attend,' she said airily, foolishly, for nothing in the whole world would keep her away, she knew, so why had she said it? She could find a dozen reasons to stop her from going, couldn't she, she asked herself, for even now something inside her called to her to halt this startling thing which had happened to her. It told her to be patient and wait. Yet it was not like her to hesitate, to be cautious, particularly when it was something she wanted so desperately. It had caught her off guard, probably because it was so soon after Will, she told herself, and really, should she not restore her heart to a sound and carefree condition before risking it again?

No such thought was in her head as she sat next to him that evening. Though they were the conventional distance

211

apart at the dining table she could feel the warmth of his body strike hers, smell the fresh, lemon-scented aroma of his shaving lotion and was acutely aware of the texture of his brown skin, the movement of his muscled shoulders beneath the well-fitting evening coat, the shape of his smiling mouth from which came the courteous and correct words a dinner guest is expected to address to another and the fierceness of his desire which lay deep in his brown eyes.

They met again the following weekend when the Squire ended the season with a hunt ball to which Miss Harrison and her cousins were invited.

She had marked time all that week, chafed by her need to see him again, to see if he was as she remembered him, consumed by the span of the days which dragged from second to everlasting second, from hour to endless hour. She had been unable to sit still for longer than thirty seconds, to sleep for longer than an hour, her mind dwelling on the colour and shape of his eyes, the tilt of his eyebrows, the soft brushed gold of his hair and the absolute certainty that when his mouth found hers, as she knew it would, she would know the absolute and supreme truth of life itself. She rode for hours on the tops, demanding of her mare impossible speeds, then standing, shivering, as the animal did, in a fit of remorse. She could not understand the way that she felt, nor, if she was honest, did she care to wonder about it since it could not be altered by wondering and marvelling. She fretted through every long hour which kept him from her.

She wore an evening gown of stark simplicity, a sheath of poppy-red taffeta, cut so low there had been a murmur as she entered the ballroom between her cousins. She wore no jewellery though it was known there were many fine pieces in the family, owned by her aunt, and her aunt's mother, Hannah Chapman. Since Drew had cut her hair so dramatically, it had grown again and she wore it now low on the nape of her neck in an intricate coil in the centre of

212

which was one enormous red silk poppy. Drew and Pearce were elegant at her side in their black evening attire, handsome and superior as thoroughbreds and glaring about them, those in their vicinity declared, as though they might strike any man who so much as spoke to her, though why they should since they were known to be light-hearted themselves, was quite an enigma. But it was agreed that they made a most arresting trio as they stood at the top of the Squire's splendid staircase waiting in line to be received by him and his lady, their commercial background scarcely showing.

He was at her elbow almost before her hand had been released by the Squire's and for the next three hours, to the chagrin of every lady present, to the swelling, dangerous, and surprising resentment of her over-protective cousins, and to the mortification of the Squire's lady who could not understand how a gentleman of such impeccable breeding could be so ill-mannered as Robby Atherton, they danced every dance together, ate supper together; bemused, bewitched, the Squire's lady said acidly to her husband, raising pained eyebrows as they floated past her once more, and, really, if her husband did not intervene and remind their weekend guest of his obligation in return for their hospitality, she would.

## 13

She thought about Will in those weeks of enchantment more than she had ever done since their last bitter quarrel and she wondered on the reason for it. Was it because in this new and rapturous love, this giddy joy she knew each time she and Robby Atherton met, she could at last understand what Will had felt for her and, in a strange way, sympathise with him? How would she feel if she were to be deprived of the man, the handsome, complex, lovable man who was Robby Atherton? Would she not have felt and acted in exactly the same way? Would she not have been empty of hope and joy, as Will had been? Would she not have been angry and bitter because the love which had filled her days, and her life, had been savagely ripped away from her? As Will had been. But surely Will must have known that eventually what they had must end, for how could he, an employee in her family's mill, hope to become the husband of one of its daughters? He would have known in his head, where reason and logic was, that one day she would marry one of her own class, or even above it, for she was a woman not only with physical attraction but a splendid dowry which would be enough to earn her a grand catch in the marriage market. She was, if not by name then by birth, a Greenwood, a member of a family which had clawed its way from weavers' cottage to what it was today, and certainly she could not be expected to go back a step, which was what she would do if she married Will. That is, if she had wanted to!

She looked back curiously to that period in her life, no longer than three or four months really, in which she had been bewitched, she could think of no other word, by the splendour, the hard masculine beauty of Will's body. Though she tried to tell herself that it had been no more than the awakening sensuality of young womanhood – since she knew about that now – an inherited recklessness which all the Greenwoods seemed to possess and which she had been unable to deny, she was honest enough to admit that it had been more than that. True, she had been delighted with the amber glow of his smooth skin, the steady gaze of his smoky brown eyes, the warm strength of his firm mouth. She had desired only to be across the threshold of his cottage with the door shut firmly behind her; shut herself and Will Broadbent on one side of it, leaving on the other reason and sanity; shut out the world which, she admitted to herself, she wished to remain ignorant of what she did with a man who was no more than her uncle's overlooker. All she had wanted, desperately needed, was to have her arms about his neck, to be clinging to his strong shoulders whenever they met. It had been a folly in which she had indulged herself, a folly she had thought never to undertake. She had wanted him. She had wanted his brown and muscled body, the hard yet tender love he had offered her. She had wanted it and she had been prepared to do, or say, anything to have it.

But there had been another side to their relationship and she must not scorn it. Will Broadbent was a man who had been given the ability to sharpen his own intelligence. He was keen, shrewd and with a warm spirit to add balance. He had possessed the knack of giving her, as she knew he gave others, not self-esteem exactly, since she had that, but a worth which had nothing to do with how she looked or who she was. He had argued with her, naturally, since they were both stubborn with a belief in the rightness of their own opinions, but he had given her the realisation that her mind and her emotions were as important to him as her fine body. He had made her laugh, his wit often audacious and irreverent. He was well read and had told her tales she had never heard from Miss Copeland, adventures of men like Columbus and Marco Polo and more recently of the great David Livingstone and his discoveries on the continent of Africa, holding her in his arms in the deep feather-bed until other, more pressing matters had overtaken them.

So, a man worthy of loving was Will Broadbent, but not to be compared with the dazzling splendour of Robby Atherton.

He called the following Friday, giving the appearance of a man who has been hard pressed to contain himself for the required period polite society demanded of a gentleman, arriving in the Squire's carriage which he had borrowed, he told her, since he could hardly carry 'these' on his roan. 'These' were roses, masses of velvet-textured, heavily perfumed buds of every shade from the palest cream through delicate pink to deepest scarlet, a carriage-full begged, he said ruefully, from the Squire's garden. Not to be compared with *her* velvet-eyed beauty, of course, his eyes told her, smiling down at her with that easy, lounging charm she found so irresistible. She was so indescribably happy she could barely speak.

'I know I should not have called unannounced but I thought if your mother was receiving ... well, I would dearly love to ...' he shrugged his shoulders, telling her without words that her family was of the utmost importance to him now. As the astonishing image of her mother 'receiving' slipped in and out of her mind, the roses were placed carefully in her arms, thorns catching in the fabric of his superbly cut, superbly tailored coat and in the soft ivory muslin of her afternoon gown, fastening them together for a breathless moment, his mouth close to hers, his hands hovering as he delicately disentangled them.

'My mother is not at home but I believe Laurel ... my cousin ... is receiving callers. That is if you would not mind ... well, there are other ladies ...'

'I should be delighted to meet Laurel,' he said gravely.

The ladies, wives of manufacturing gentlemen, naturally, for Laurel had not yet been successful in enticing those from the gentry on whom she had set her heart – the Squire's lady, Mrs Celia Longworth, related to a minor earl, it was said; Sir Anthony Taylor's wife, Lady Prudence, a lady in her *own* right – were flung into an absolute turmoil of genteel confusion at the arrival of such an obvious member of the ruling class. So well mannered, they observed, so well bred, so patently interested in Jenny Harrison's girl it was almost indecent. And would you look at her with her arms full of roses and her eyes with stars, and which way was the wind blowing *there*, they wondered to one another.

'Laurel, may I introduce Mr Atherton? He is a guest at the Hall.'

At the Hall! Did you hear that? The ladies were positively

agog, casting sidelong, knowing glances as he bent his head courteously over each hand. As for Laurel Greenwood – well, if she had been a dog she would have wagged her tail, so great was her satisfaction. He sat amongst them, perfectly at ease as he balanced a fine bone-china teacup and saucer in one hand, a fine bone-china plate on which Laurel had placed a dainty macaroon, in the other. He listened to every word they each addressed to him. They were delighted with him and his pedigreed presence in their midst and when he begged Tessa if he might be shown the gardens, they watched, with sighing regret, as he went down the steps from the drawing-room and on to the wide green lawn.

Tessa felt her face soften with blissful satisfaction. She had known from the first, of course, but it was miraculous to realise that her instinct about him had been right. He was not only handsome and charming, he was amiable. He was kind. No sunshine had ever been so warm and bright, dancing on her skin as she walked beside him on that afternoon – a bright blue afternoon shading into a golden evening and the dazzling prospect of what was waiting for them, though not to be spoken of yet, naturally. How did she know? What was it about him that was so in tune with *her*, with the intricate bone and muscle, tissue and nerves of Tessa Harrison? Why did she feel so at *one* with him? She neither knew nor cared. It was there, it had happened and why should she question it? What did they talk of that afternoon, she wondered later? They laughed at the same absurdities, she did remember that, until, with a suddenness and a fierceness that surprised her, Drew and Pearce were there, like two boisterous, roistering, foolish schoolboys, or so they seemed in contrast with the complete man who was Robby Atherton. They invaded the magic circle which had wrapped itself around them; became surly when she was disinclined to notice them, her haughty manner telling them quite plainly to take themselves off, for could they not see that just for this one time, this enchanted moment, she could well do without their presence?

They only scowled, placing themselves on either side of her.

'You're in these parts again I see, Mr Atherton,' Drew said, rudely, Tessa thought. 'Or have you been a guest at the Hall since last weekend?'

'Please, call me Robby. And no, I have been home but the Squire invited me to meet some friends he has coming for the weekend.' And what has it to do with you? his coolly arrogant expression asked before he remembered that these were Tessa Harrison's cousins of whom she was, presumably, fond, and therefore must be treated politely, difficult though that might be. He knew, naturally, being a man, what caused their antipathy.

'Indeed.' Drew sounded as though he couldn't quite bring himself to believe him.

'Indeed. A champagne picnic is planned for tomorrow afternoon, and a party in the evening. But are you not invited?' he asked somewhat urgently, turning to Tessa, his whole demeanour implying that if she was not he could scarcely be expected to attend himself. 'I was given to believe that you . . .'

'Oh, yes, we shall be there, shall we not, cousin?' Pearce took Tessa's arm quite savagely, much to her surprise and annoyance. 'We shall *both* be there, Mr Atherton.'

'I believe you had a gentleman caller this afternoon, Tessa?' Her mother's look was keen and Tessa turned eagerly to her, her radiance shining about the candle-lit drawing-room, her expression that of all those who love and long to talk of the beloved.

'Yes, did Laurel . . . speak of him?' She and her mother had dined alone that night, Drew and Pearce galloping off into the darkening night, only they knowing where they were going and why they rode at such a breakneck speed to get there.

'No. She and Charlie had already left for the Abbotts when I got home. It was Briggs who told me. You know what an old gossip he is. Quite beside himself with it, he was. A gentleman caller, he said, making sure I knew exactly what he meant.' Her mother smiled for there was no worse snobbery than that which existed amongst servants. 'Who was he, lass?'

For some reason Tessa turned awkward, assuming the casual air of a hostess who has been called upon by an acquaintance of no importance and who is really not worth the mentioning.

'Oh, no one really. A friend of . . . a mutual friend of Nicky Longworth's and, I suppose, of Drew and Pearce. They were here to greet him.' It was almost true.

'Someone I am likely to know?'

'No, not really, Mother.'

'Is he likely to call again, d'you think?' Jenny Harrison was intrigued by her daughter's capriciousness. As far as she knew, Tessa had shown an interest in no man beyond a willingness to engage in flirtation of the very lightest kind with her cousins' friends, and here she was fidgeting about the room, restless as a colt and with a flush on her cheeks to shame the almost overbearing show of roses which stood in the hallway.

'Heavens, how am I to know? Why do you ask?'

'Charlie and I are to go to London for a week or so. There is to be an exhibition and Charlie is eager to see this new combing machine designed by James Noble. We are off first thing in the morning. It is said to be . . . but there, you are not interested in that, I'm sure. I did tell you we were to go several days ago,' she added gently, for she could see her daughter was not really listening.

Tessa was not. Already she was dreaming against the window, gazing down the dusk-filled garden with the air of someone who has been transported to another world, one in which less fortunate mortals such as her mother were certainly not included.

Jenny smiled.

\*    \*    \*

They had met a bare two weeks ago and when he moved urgently towards her as she entered the Squire's ballroom she was touched with an almost unimaginable terror. It was too soon; it had happened too quickly. Then he smiled and her terror fled away as though it had never been. She was dizzy and bemused with love for him. She adored him. There was nothing she would not give him, or do for him. Nothing.

'Come into the garden with me. The moon is shining and if you promise not to scream I shall kiss you,' he teased, but their desire tightened the air about them with such force they were both overwhelmed by it.

Her eyes were twin stars, brilliant, the expression in them letting him know how very willing she was. She had waited for him for so long, since when one was deep in love an hour is forever. Each time they were apart she was in turmoil until she saw him again. Had she imagined him, she agonised, endowed him with graces which existed only in her mind? But as she took her hand from the Squire's and put it in his, he was exactly as she remembered him, knew him, wanted him to be, his eyes were almost black with his love for her, his mouth smiling, not just at her, but at himself and his own eagerness to take her in his arms before the whole company, for what else could it be but a declaration of his intent?

And they had not spoken a word as they glided away from the suddenly silent group of watchers for they had been dazzled, mesmerised by the enchantment of being in one another's arms.

'Why, Mr Atherton, you are no gentleman to say such a thing to a lady. If he were here I would inform my uncle who would certainly take his whip to you, but since he is not I may be forced to ... to allow it.'

'It would be worth it if he took the skin from my back.'

'And if he did I would ...-soothe it with ... salve.'

'Tessa.' His breath was sweet on her upturned face. 'You really are ... you must be a witch. Before you left home this evening admit you brewed some potion which you have slipped into the champagne I drank, for I believe ... yes, I believe ...'

'What do you believe?' Her lips were no more than an inch from his and the Squire's lady declared to her husband that she really meant it when she said she would *never* allow that hussy in her home again. Her husband pointed out drily that she would have to ban the whole Atherton family who had been landed gentlemen for as long as his own, for if he was any judge young Atherton would be making an announcement before the week was out, if he had not already done so with his behaviour tonight.

'That I am falling in love with you.' Robby Atherton told Tessa Harrison.

'Mr Atherton, how you do go on ...'

'Stop it, Tessa.' His voice was sharp suddenly and his face had lost its smiling impudence and for a strange moment she was struck by a feeling of familiarity, a feeling that she had seen that expression somewhere before, a likeness to someone she knew. But the sensation passed in the bewildering, overwhelming emotion which fevered her skin and prickled her spine. His hand was hard on her back and the one in which hers rested gripped it cruelly.

'Robby ...'

'Go to the ladies' room ... for God's sake, make some excuse. Dammit woman, can you not see I am serious? I will meet you ...'

He bowed her off the ballroom floor, evading politely the hand of the Squire's lady, the beckoning finger of Nicky Longworth, the restraining clasp of old friends and over-enthusiastic mamas with daughters in tow.

She thought she would have a fight on her hands, not certain whether it was to be between herself and them, or just between the two enraged young men themselves as her cousins accosted her, surrounded her it felt like, in the quiet passage which led from the main hallway to the ladies' retiring room.

221

'What the hell d'you think you're up to?' Drew hissed menacingly, his hand hot and vicious on her arm.

'Making a bloody show of yourself.' Pearce was just as violent and for a moment she felt the ominous shadow of something cold and icy pass through her, then her heart reminded her that her love waited and she had no time to bother with her cousins' tantrums. God only knew what had got into them now, and she really didn't care. She only knew she must get rid of them as carefully as she could before their ugly mood erupted into the ballroom and stopped her escaping.

She made her voice aggrieved. 'Drew, Pearce. Where have you been all evening?' And before they could answer, taken aback by her tone, she hurried on to the room set aside for the ladies and where they could not follow, calling over her shoulder, 'Wait for me at the entrance to the ballroom. I'll be about five minutes. The hem of my dress is torn.'

She left them and when they had gone, slipped back to the side door, fleeing beyond the lights of the Hall, beyond the formal garden and across the smooth lawn to the summer house, led there by the absolute certainty that that was where he would be, and she was not surprised when she found him waiting there for her.

'Tessa . . .' He seemed uncertain now, no longer the hard and masterful man who had ordered her to meet him here.

'Robby, perhaps we should go back?' In her new-found maturity and bountiful love, since she *did* love him, she gave him the opportunity to draw back while there was still time from this confrontation which he had demanded.

'Tessa, you look so beautiful. The moon has taken your colour and made you into a silver maiden.'

'I don't quite know what that means.'

He took her hands in his and with a simplicity which was astonishing to her in a man of his years, his experience and knowledge of life, he told her, 'I'm so much in love with you.'

'Robby . . .' She could not speak for the tears in her throat.

'Could you love me, d'you think?' It was so different from what she had expected she could not answer. His words were quiet with a gentle sincerity in them she could not have believed existed in this mature, complex, quite dazzling man. She had thought he would sweep her off her feet, run with her exhilaratingly across the dewed grass, perhaps barefoot, plying her with champagne. Kiss her until her head spun, demand, take, his masculinity assertive, but he was trembling with need, his hands lifting to her shoulders. She was a lady, his manner said, and he was a gentleman. He had been made as he was by traditions which told him a gentleman treated a lady with respect, courtesy, chivalry, gallantry. Beneath his well-bred, well-polished shell was a virility which was without question; which seethed to escape and crush her to him, to take her since she was so lovely, so willing, so exactly what he had always wanted, yet he would not. Ladies such as she, despite her wicked humour which delighted him, had a purity not just of the flesh but of the mind, an innocence which must be protected from the coarseness of the male until her husband, the man who loved her, himself in fact, taught her with gentleness the meaning of desire.

'We'll go back now, my darling,' he said quite sternly, holding out his arm to her. 'I will call on your mother next weekend, if she will allow it, but until then I think it best that you be returned to where the Squire's lady, and your cousins, can see you.'

Blindly, her will for the first time submissive to another, she took his arm but at her touch he trembled violently. She heard his breath rasp in his throat and he groaned.

'Bloody hell . . .' Then, 'Forgive me, my love, but I just can't do it. I meant to take you back to them. You're so sweet, so lovely. I only wanted to hold you for a moment. Just one kiss, but then I was afraid . . . of you . . . and what I might do to you. You're young, inexperienced,' he laughed shakily, 'and have no idea what I'm talking about or what you're doing to me but I'm damned if I'm going to let you go in without one kiss to ... to mark the ... we will be married soon...'

He put his arms about her, crossing them at her back and drew her softly against him, his love so strong and glorious she would have gladly died for him then and there, if he had asked it of her.

He placed his lips against hers, their first kiss, and liquid honey ran hot and fierce and sweet along her veins and into every part of her awakened woman's body. They breathed their longing into one another's mouth, tongues touching, lips clinging, then parting reluctantly.

'I love you.'

'Oh God, and I love you.'

And several miles away, in a candle-lit cottage, a man lifted his head from the book he was reading and shivered.

They saw each other every day. He took rooms at the brand new Station Hotel, built to accommodate those who now rushed about the country by the comparatively new method of travel, the railway, whilst he awaited her mother's return.

'I cannot impose on the Squire, my darling, not without telling him of my intention towards you and I must speak to your mother first. You cannot, of course, come into the hotel but I can hire a carriage and take you driving. Your reputation may be somewhat damaged, I'm afraid, but as we shall be engaged by the end of the month and married by the end of the year it can hardly matter.'

She wore her most elegant gowns and extravagant French bonnets, brought at great cost from London, lovely colours of pale amber, peach, apple green, cream and cornflower blue, white lace and white silk rosebuds on her parasol, as dainty, perfumed and feminine as she had ever been in her life. A female, submissive and obedient to male dominance, catching her breath at the almost primitive, animal-like docility she knew.

They left the carriage and walked, moving slowly, dream-like, smiling at her strange awkwardness in her cumbersome petticoats and wide skirts, her high-heeled white kid boots, Tessa Harrison who had strode these moors in breeches and a man's shirt, hands clasped, hearts clasped.

He kissed her many times, each one becoming sweeter and more difficult to end, hurting her sometimes in his passion for her. His body trembled against hers, and hers responded and when he stood away from her his breath would be short and harsh, his eyes a deep, deep glazing of brown.

'Dear God, I cannot ... I shall do something damnable if I do not take you home,' he whispered against her throat, and she could barely stop herself from pulling him down into the waist-high, sweet-smelling fern. Only the awareness that he would be appalled, much as he wanted it, stopped her since she knew that to him she was as white and virginal, as untouched and innocent as a newly budded snowdrop.

On the day before her mother was to return he had business to attend to in Manchester. Restless and impatient without him she called for her mare and rode over the moor to see Annie.

## 14

' 'As tha told Will?'

'I have not seen him.'

'Tha owes it to 'im, Tessa.'

'Dear God, Annie, are you my keeper? It does not matter what I do or don't do, there you are, an expression of disapproval on your face, telling me where my duties lie.' Her guilt made her sharp. 'What have I to tell Will? What is there I can tell him?'

'Eeh lass, I knew thi ter be 'eartless at times but never cruel. This is cruel and well yer know it especially after what's bin between yer. D'yer love this chap? If tha does, yer mun tell Will. Are thi ter wed this chap? If tha is, tell Will an' let 'im gerron wi' 'is life...'

'Don't keep calling him *this chap*. He is named Robby Atherton. You speak of him as though he was some fortune hunter who is merely after my wealth. He has money and land and ... and he wants to marry me. He is to speak to Mother tomorrow.'

'Tha's in a rush, the pair o' yer. I thought you said you met 'im at Whit walks. Tis only a month since...'

'I know, oh Annie, I know, but we love each other so.'

Tessa stretched her tall, slender body in an ecstacy of joy, her arms above her head, ready to soar up to the ceiling and beyond, away from the earth which bound her, dipping and swaying the full skirt this new Tessa Harrison felt the need to wear, about Annie's stone-floored kitchen, rapturous as Annie had never seen her, her face lit in a way Will Broadbent had not, it seemed, been able to achieve. Poor Will, and yet what a pitiful word to apply to the quite devastated strength, the clench-jawed, savage-eyed pain of the man who had snarled his way about her kitchen only last night, very much as Tessa was doing now, but for a very different reason.

'What the hell's she playing at, Annie? Christ, it's been weeks and she's not been near me. Oh, I know I told her not to come back until she was ready for marriage but I thought she would realise ... I was convinced she loved me, you see. That given time ... she is so young ... I stayed away from her ... Dear God, Annie, I love her. That is all there is to me...'

'Give over, Will Broadbent...'

'It's true. She's had me in a thrall since the very first time. I wouldn't have her unless she married me, I told her,' he laughed harshly, 'so she came to my house and made short work of that statement. You understand what I'm saying?'

She did. She had known from the first of the physical nature of the relationship between Will and Tessa but he was not a man who would go in for 'dallying'; a steady man who would give his heart wholly to one woman and love her until the end of his days. He was strong, self-reliant, enduring, but Tessa Harrison had brought him to his knees, taken what she wanted from him for as long as it pleased her, then drifted on to the next sensation, the next adventure, the next pleasure to take her fancy and this time his name was Robby Atherton. The son of a gentleman and therefore much more acceptable to the Greenwoods and their status, to Tessa who could now, if she chose to it seemed, live the life of a gentleman's wife, shooting and hunting in season, parties, the hunt balls, all the exciting pastimes the gentry got up to and which Will Broadbent's wife could never have.

'I asked her every time she came to me to let me speak to her mother, her uncle, or her cousins, or whichever male relative their class insist on, but she put me off. Mr Greenwood has promised me manager of the spinning mill at Highbank when old Fishwick retires at the end of the year, aye ... me ... a pauper child, a little piecer and scavenger to be manager at Highbank. There'll be good money, Annie, and a fine house. There's a plot of land out New Delph way that I've got my eye on. We could build ... anything she wants. She loved me, Annie, else why would she ... ?'

His voice was harsh, no longer caring about any finer feelings Annie might have, nor of the children upstairs who could hear what he said, '... else why would she come to my bed? You've not loved a man yet, lass, but I reckon you'll know what I'm talking about when I say that woman is my life and without her I'm nothing. Now there's talk of her ... of her making free with some chap up at the Hall ... in a red dress and walking the moors dressed like a bloody lady, hand in hand with ... but that I'll not believe. Not even of her, wild as she is. Dear Christ, she was in my bed only a

227

couple of months ago. It's said she was ... that he ... that they are lovers ... but she'd not do that, would she, Annie ...?' Annie had shaken her head numbly, horrified to be the witness of such suffering, unwilling to be made a part of this turmoil and yet how could she avoid it, for they were both her friends.

Now, the very next day, here was Tessa floating about on air, it seemed, over some haughty, self-opinioned gentleman of enormous superiority, an aristocrat of the highest order. Handsome, oh aye, and oozing charm and wit and, by God, Tessa was dazzled by it.

But this Robby Atherton wanted to marry her she said and was to knock at the door of Greenacres tomorrow and tell her family so.

'Is 'e thy lover an' all?'

'That is none of your business.' Tessa was appalled.

'I reckon it is when it were only a month or two back you were in Will Broadbent's bed.'

'Who the devil told you that?'

'Will.'

'He's no damn right ...'

'It's true, in't it?'

'It makes no difference.'

'It does if tha's sharin' thissen between this chap an' Will.'

'How dare you, how dare you?' Tessa's face was white with rage as she turned and strode from Annie's cottage without another word. How dare Annie besmirch her love with comparisons to what she had done with Will? How dare she speak so coarsely about the miracle which was softly curled inside her, the feeling she held to her, within her, silent, sweet, secret? She was in love this time. Not in the way she had once loved Will for that had been strong and lusty, a pure, white-hot passion that in no way could be compared to the delicacy and fragrance of what she and Robby felt. She and Will had suited one another, she told herself, taken one another as one does a meal when one is hungry but he was not a man she could marry, for God's sake. She wanted, as Robby did, to place her body against his in some private world away from this one, to discard the wrappings, one by one, of their clothing, to gaze with awe and rapture, to touch and hold and finally possess. Robby had not said so, naturally, not yet, but she had seen and recognised it in his eyes. But they were to be married first. She was to be his wife and one paid respect to the lady one was to marry by taking her virgin to the altar.

She had agonised over this, her memory scalded by the touch of Will Broadbent, wishing with all her heart that she could have given Robby this gift which men seemed to set such store by but it was too late to worry about. She had not loved Will as she loved Robby, so surely it did not count?

She was still seething with indignation, swearing she would not go near Annie Beale's cottage again as she urged her mare up the slope towards a great outcropping of rock. She crossed a shallow, slow-moving stream which, when it reached the bottom, would wind along the valley floor. She paused for a moment on the old wooden footbridge, then cantered along the narrow track before she moved on to the rough, uneven surface which led to Badger's Edge. The bracken stood tall, nearly as high as her mare. There was a mist moving in the hollows below her, but the sky was a delicate pink on the hills shading to a pale blue vault above her head.

The sun was low since it was late and would soon be setting on this early summer's day. The air was sweet, smelling and tasting as sharp as wine, and she dragged great mouthfuls into her lungs, leaning back in the saddle, allowing her mare to go as she pleased as she fell into a daydream.

Her eyes were vague as she looked towards the trees carpeting the valley below her. As the shadows lengthened their shaded green turned slowly to a smudged and darkening grey. Her dogs padded silently beside her, accustomed to her changes of pace, ready to slow, to stop and doze or, almost beneath the mare's belly, to race with the wind as she did. Soon, too soon, it would be high summer, then autumn with winter not far behind, the cruel Pennine winter which prevented only the most foolhardy from venturing out in it, but what did she care now? Long before that, long before the month of June was out, as she and Robby eased themselves further into the deep, soft-textured rapture of their new love they would move on to the next step in their delicate courtship. They would inform her mother and his family that they loved one another. Long before the snows came she would be married to Robby and living far away from here in Cheshire.

But before then she would become his 'fiancée' and once she was that, she would be changed into the young lady Samuel Robert Atherton of Atherton Hall, a gentleman, was to marry. She would be a valued possession which must be guarded every minute of the day and night, a treasure which would be prepared, wrapped up in its wedding finery and given to him in the sanctity of the great wedding ceremony for all to see. A virgin bride in her white, *his* bride, and though it was himself who would take that virginity from her, until then, innocent. She was his lady and though she knew he was mad to possess her, his reverent love made him draw back. She was not to be treated like some obliging wench from his mother's dairy and he would wait, as a gentleman should, until she was his wife.

How she loved him. He was her 'parfit gentil knight', the man most girls dream of, so dashing, so gallant, handsome and strong but with a wit which delighted her, a mind which somehow had the keenness of her own north-countrymen, despite his upbringing. He had a contempt for the often shallow and superficial qualities of his own class which surprised her. He worked hard, he said, on his grandfather's estate which would one day be his since his father's older brother had died childless and his own father had died when he himself was a boy. He took it seriously, hunting and pursuing the activities with which gentlemen of his class amused themselves but only when his duties allowed, he told her earnestly.

They loved the same things, shared the same interests. He was, in a way, her cousins all over again, rolled into one man, but without their wildness, quite amazingly appearing to know who the person inside Tessa Harrison was, and what she needed. He was the other half of her, fitting her and she him as though they had been made each to complete the other.

He rose almost from the ground at her feet, making her mare shy so that for several moments it was all she could do to stop the animal from bolting. The dogs snarled menacingly and her voice was high as she called them to her. The alarm she felt gave her reason to be sharp and she was glad of it for the unexpected sight of him on this weekday evening badly frightened her.

'Will, for God's sake, you really should not leap out from behind a rock like that. You know my mare is nervous and the sudden ... Why did you not ... well ... stand out where you could be seen?'

'Would you have ridden over to greet me or would you have turned round and pretended not to see me, avoided me as you have done these last few weeks?'

'Don't be silly, Will.'

'Silly? what does that mean, Tessa? But perhaps you're right. Happen it is silly for a man to hang about hoping to catch a glimpse of a woman he thought had some feeling for him.' His voice was toneless, his face quite without expression but in his eyes was the flare of madness which comes to a wounded beast when the hurt is almost too much to bear. His face was drawn, looking older than his years. He had not shaved and his shirt was creased as though he had put it on several days ago and not removed it since.

'I've not come to harm you, Tessa,' he said at last, when the silence in which she fidgeted nervously seemed long enough, 'so you can get down off that animal's back.'

'I ... well, I really cannot stay, Will. It will be dark soon and ... well, Laurel is ... another child, you know, and there is so much to attend to ...'

'And you are to attend to it, is that it?'

'Well . . .'

He sighed deeply and passed a hand across his pale, shadowed face. 'Don't lie to me, Tessa. Not now. Let us be honest for this one last time together.'

'What . . . ?' Still she did not dismount and he smiled wearily.

'Don't fret, my girl. I've not come to hurt you though the devil knows you deserve it. I said last year that a good thrashing now and again in your childhood would not have gone amiss but I'll not give it you, nor take, as you seem to think I might, what now belongs to another man . . .'

'Will . . .'

'Don't Will me. The whole spinning room is whispering about you and that popinjay up at the Hall . . .'

She sprang hotly to her love's defence. 'He's not a popinjay . . .'

'. . . and we all know what goes on up there amongst the gentry.'

He straightened his back as though for the past few weeks it had been bowed with the weight of a heavy burden which he was about to throw off. His eyes were like granite now, cold, the smoky brown humour gone with his love. They were filled with his contempt for her. His lips curled and the expression on his face told her he despised her whole class which treated so lightly men such as himself. 'It seems you have found some other man to warm your bed . . .'

'No . . .'

'Aah, so you have not yet played the whore for him as you did for me . . .'

'It's not like that . . .'

'Dear me, Miss Harrison, has he been able to withstand your charms as I seemed unable to do? Of course, he is a gentleman, they say, so perhaps he is made differently from the rest of us.'

'Will, please . . .'

'I don't want to hear what you have to say, Tessa. I would

have listened to you if you had come to me and told me honestly that you no longer ... that you and I ... that your feelings for this ... him ... were stronger. I might not have liked it, nor understood it, for I truly believed there was something fine between us but I would have respected you for being truthful. I might not have given you up easily...'

He bowed his head and she could see the tremble of his powerful shoulders and the working of the muscles in his throat. 'You were so young but time would have remedied that and when it did I thought ... hoped you would recognise what we could do together, where we could go together. I'm not a man to be content with the place in life the parson tells me God meant me to have.' He lifted his shaggy head, uncut and unbrushed, and stared at her as he might at some creature which he had found beneath a stone. 'I meant to move on and *up* and I would have done it with you since it would have been *for* you. But it seems I didn't recognise you for what you are. How foolish I was! I could have enjoyed the simple and uncomplicated use of your body without the agonies of remorse I suffered after we had made love. I idolised you, could not believe my good fortune in having you love me. I did not realise that you were simply amusing yourself with me, passing time which must hang heavily on ladies of your class in the tedium of the day. Most paint water-colours, I believe, or do fine embroidery but it seems you like to...' Here he used a word she had not heard before but whose meaning she instantly understood, an obscene word so coarse it was spoken only between men. 'You *are* a whore, Tessa, and even that insults those who go by that name for they are at least honest in their profession. You are a liar and a cheat and I am saddened to think that I spent useless hours longing for you, loving you, weeping ... oh, yes, I wept for you. So go back to your latest lover' – his face jerked in pain but his eyes still dwelled on her face in contempt – 'and tell him from me that I can recommend you as a splendid...' Again he used a word she did not know but whose meaning was clear. 'But your morals leave much to be desired. It's a long and vexed road you tread, Tessa Harrison. I shall get on with my life now and you get on with yours, whatever it might be. And God help you when you fail to find what you look for, since no one else will.'

He turned then and began to stride away across the springing turf, his own step light, as though he had freed himself from the load he had carried and laboured under for so long. He did not look back. His head was held high and proud, almost jaunty, and Tessa felt her heart move painfully beneath her ribs, aching with some strange and sad emotion in which shame and sorrow were mixed. Why had she been afraid of the steadfast man who now walked away from her and their brief life together? That was what had kept her from him, she realised now. She should have gone at once to him and told him of Robby since it was his right to know but the fear of hearing the words he had just spoken had held her back: the fear of seeing on his face the scorn and disdain he felt for her, the knowledge that he found her worthless. She had dreaded it, avoided it by avoiding him, and as she turned her mare towards Greenacres her face was wet with tears.

The expedition to invade Sebastopol led by Lord Raglan reached the Crimea at last. He had been informed that a safe and honourable peace could be obtained in no other way. The nation thought so and the government thought so and he was not to delay his decision to attack. Despite the sickness of the troops and their complete lack of preparation for war, he set forth bravely to do as he was bid.

The first mistake was caused by the misunderstanding between the systems of the French and British armies. The British, as Wellington had always done in France, were prepared to purchase at a fair price the carts and bullocks they needed, having brought no transport of their own, from the simple country folk who came into their camp. The French, on the other hand, believing that stores belonging to the government of one's enemy are a fair prize, entered and plundered villages within the British lines, abusing men and even women, and like snow before the sun the supplies on which they had counted simply melted away.

That was the first mistake but certainly not the last as Lord Raglan looked about him for the transport needed to carry the expedition consisting of 61,000 soldiers and 132 guns. Somehow it was accomplished and on a soft and sunny day a week later, they prepared to set off but, staggeringly, it was found that the British were not ready. They should have been in lines of seven and where was the delay, they were asked. No answer seemed to be forthcoming but at last they were prepared for the daring exploit of invading the Peninsula. They marched gloriously towards the banks of the Alma where a great battle was fought and despite the initial blunders, was won in triumph and the Russians were forced to retreat.

Pearce Greenwood read the account of it in the news-paper and his eyes gleamed in his sun-browned face. He savoured phrases such as 'irresistible vigour in all parts of the field', 'immediate advance' and the words spoken by Brigadier Sir Colin Campbell: 'It is better that every man of Her Majesty's Guards should be dead upon the field than that they should turn their backs upon the enemy.'

What splendour! What magnificence, the newspaper reports declared. Did it not describe exactly what every right-minded Englishman, if he had hot blood in his veins, which Pearce did, was thinking as he ate his bacon and eggs that morning? The names of the divisions of which the British army was composed were enough to make any man reach for his rifle and his horse and travel immediately to the Crimea to see for himself what was going on: the Light Division', 'the 2nd Battalion Rifle Brigade', 'the Grenadiers', 'the Fusiliers', 'the Coldstream Guards', 'the Light Dragoons', 'the 11th Hussars'. They painted pictures of flags snapping in the breeze, the sun reflected on polished sabres and boots; the flare of the kilt above brawny knees; scarlet coats and sleek, well-bred horses and the roar of battle-hardened men, the cream of Britain's finest, for surely that was what they were, as they whipped the enemy from the field.

He sighed forlornly as he lowered his newspaper and looked about the room. Briggs and Dorcas, one of Mrs Shepherd's clean, respectable and efficiently trained parlour maids, stood to attention by the sideboard, their eyes somewhere over his head, their faces expressionless. He wondered what the hell they thought about as they waited for him to tell them what he would eat for breakfast, if he would eat anything at all from the dozen silver platters which stood under their silver covers on the sideboard.

He was alone at the table. Laurel ate breakfast in the peace of her own small sitting-room and his Aunt Jenny and Charlie had gone to the mill an hour ago, as he was only too well aware. His brother ... well, God knows where his brother was at this moment. Some actress in Manchester, he had said vaguely, as he had ridden off into the night, and to expect him when he saw him.

The door opened and the subject of his thoughts lurched across the threshold, dressed as he had been last night before he took the train to the charms, one supposed, of the actress. It was obvious to Pearce and to the servants that he had been drinking heavily, and alone, by the look of sullen oppression which hung about him like a mist. Pearce, in his own misery, recognised his brother's, and the unhappiness was made worse by the knowledge that for the first time they could not share it. How could one console a man who suffered the same malady as oneself? In one way he did not care about Drew since his heart ached only for himself and yet, in this ludicrous situation, they were the same person.

The thought gave him the strength to speak sympathetically to his brother. Really, he thought, with a sardonic twist of his young mouth, one could almost laugh about it had it not been so painful.

'Do you want something to eat?'

'No.'

Drew sat down heavily and stared moodily at the empty coffee cups in front of him and the two servants exchanged glances which asked quite clearly what the devil the young master had been up to now? If he had nothing better to do than fiddle with a teaspoon all day, they had, and if he was not to break his fast why didn't he beggar off and get changed for his day's work at the mill and leave them to theirs?

He lifted his head suddenly as though seeing them there for the first time. 'You two can go,' he muttered. 'If I need anything I'll help myself.'

The servants, all bustle and activity now, left the room smiling, relieved to escape for the time being the uncertain tendencies of the Greenwoods' volatile nature which could, at a moment's notice, turn from the blankness of utter boredom to the sheer exuberance of some anticipated escapade. God knows which would take shape today with the pair of them looking as though they'd lost a guinea and found a farthing.

They sat for five minutes without speaking, then Pearce cleared his throat painfully.

'What are we to do, brother?'

Drew laughed harshly. 'Only God knows and He's not speaking to me.'

'Perhaps not, but we must speak to one another.'

'Oh, absolutely.' He twisted round in his chair to stare blindly out of the window. 'Do you know, when I was having a quiet drink with myself last night – I couldn't face the actress, you see – out on the moor actually, I had the strangest thought.'

'Oh, yes, and what was that?'

'What would have happened if she had chosen one of us?'

'The irony of it has not escaped me, either.'

They were silent for a distressing moment while Drew blinked rapidly.

'I would have killed you for her.'

'I know, so at least that has been averted.'

'Yes.'

'One must try to see the bright side, I suppose, or so they say, but I'll tell you this. I'm not hanging about to see her go up the aisle with that bloody . . .'

'You think it will come to that?'

'He's calling tomorrow, isn't he, with the express purpose of seeing Aunt Jenny. What else could it be but . . . ?' Pearce could not continue and felt his heart constrict with angry pain. My God, was this what it did to you? This raging, savage jealousy which ate into him. It had him in such a damaged state he could not think beyond the desperate certainty that he could not stay here to see her married to another man. And the laughable thing, the almost hysterical thing that had him nearly in tears was that he was suffering it *twice*, for himself and his brother, and he knew Drew felt exactly the same. They had shared most things: their hatred of the mill and their hopeless attempts to escape it; their love of this land, this harsh north-country land which had bred them; their light-hearted disposition, their arrogance, their hot heads and warm hearts which had fallen in love a dozen times, often sharing the favours of the same pretty girl. And now, irony upon irony, they were in love, both of them, with Tessa Harrison.

'Seen the newspaper?' he went on curtly.

Drew turned to stare at him. His face was drawn, unshaven, his eyes quite blank, dead somehow, and yet in them was a prick of bewilderment as though his brother's question was beyond him just at the moment. His shoulders sagged.

'I can't say that I have. Is there something interesting in it?'

'Read that.'

'I don't think I can drum up a great deal of concern.' Drew turned away again, then stood up and walked slowly to the window. Putting a hand on either side of it he leaned against the frame and stared down the long sweep of lawn towards the lake and the trees on the far side.

'I love this place, you know,' he said almost dreamily and Pearce knew, with a kind of surprise, that his brother was near breaking point and that it was up to himself to provide the answer for both of them; that for the first time in their eighteen years, one of them must take the lead.

'Listen, Drew,' he said quietly. 'Listen to this.' And he read the report of the Russian defeat at Giurgevo.

There was a long, almost death-like silence. Then Drew turned to him and this time Pearce knew he had his attention.

'Stirring stuff.'

'You know what I'm saying, don't you?'

'Oh, yes.'

'An adventure at last. We have always, since we were boys, dreamed of one but we were forced into the mill. Made to see where our duties lie. And for the past year we have done it. Now, for a little while at least, I think it is *our* time. It might put Charlie and Aunt Jenny in a bind but I'm certain our combined contribution to the running of the mill could be easily taken care of by one little piecer! There will be someone to take our place for a . . . well, however long it takes. A month or two, perhaps . . . until the . . . wedding is . . .'

'Don't.'

'It has to be faced, dammit.' Pearce's voice was hard and angry. He was suffering pain for the first time in his life and he was angry. He did not know how to deal with it beyond getting away as far as possible from its source.

'How are we to manage it?' Drew's voice still dragged but he had straightened up. There was a look almost of hope about him, as though the torpor had shifted somewhat like a mist when the breeze touches it, revealing a path which might be explored, a path which might lead to a way out of it.

'Get on our horses and simply ride away.'

*     *     *

239

It was, strangely, Will Broadbent who drew to the attention of their uncle when he returned from London that Drew and Pearce Greenwood had not been seen for a couple of days.

'Maister says 'as 'ow he wants to see them lads of 'is,' the young lad who had been sent to deliver the message, told Will.

'Well, they're not here, tell him,' Will answered flatly, not at all sure he wanted to be involved with *any* of her family just now. 'I was told by Mr Wilson they'd gone away.'

'Gone away?' Mr Greenwood repeated to him ten minutes later. 'Gone away where?'

'Nay, don't ask me.' Will's voice was short, curt even, but Charlie did not notice as the first trickle of annoyance ran through him. 'Who told you they had gone away?'

'Well, I suppose it was Mr Wilson, but he'd been told by ... Nay, I don't know. It seemed to be just sort of ... accepted...' To tell the truth he could not for the life of him remember how he had come by the knowledge, or the rumour, if that was what it was. It seemed that all those in the manager's office, each one assuming it had come from the other, were convinced those 'damned lads' had been given permission to absent themselves and yet here was Mr Greenwood looking madder than a wet hen. Perhaps this time he'd give 'em what for.

'Have they not been home, sir?' he said calmly. Dear God, they'd bred a pack of wild cats, untamed and unreliable, this family of decent, hard-working, *working-class* folk, for that was what they were. Yet from them had come these uncontrollable lads and that ... that lass whose claws had raked his own heart almost to shreds.

'I've not seen them, Will, but then they often don't dine with us, or breakfast either, come to that, so I wouldn't expect to. They come home late...' He shook his head in exasperation. 'Has no one seen them at the mill?'

'Not that I know of, Mr Greenwood, but I expect they've

240

gone off on some junket ... some adventure which has taken their fancy...' He stopped, realising who he was talking to, realising that he was talking about two young men, eighteen years old and no longer schoolboys who were expected to indulge in such nonsense. They had never grown up, never come to the maturity expected of most men. For the past year they had been made, half-heartedly, to present themselves at the mill and it was a wonder to him that they had lasted as long as they had. No doubt they were in London or Paris, living high and dangerously, recklessly risking their young lives on anything which seemed foolhardy. And so he was not surprised a week later to hear that those 'damned lads' had fetched up with Lord Raglan's army in the Crimea.

## 15

She was at the door to meet him when Briggs opened it. Her mother waited in the drawing-room, promising nothing, she said, for it was far too soon, declaring she would reserve her opinion on this 'Robby' her daughter spoke of, until she had met him. Tessa was seventeen, ready for marriage and, from the look of her, rapturously in love with this man she had met on Whit Monday and, she admitted, a time or two at the Hall. She would see him first, a proper introduction, question him about his intentions, his family, his suitability as a husband for her daughter, and Tessa had her permission to ask him to call.

Briggs took his top hat, bowing reverently for this was a gentleman and not many of those stood in this hall, not real gentlemen. Then obeying Miss Tessa's instructions, he left them alone together. There had been talk about her – when had there not been? – and the Squire's Friday-to-Monday guest, which had reached the servants' hall, and now, it seemed, there was more to it than talk for as he closed the door behind him Miss Tessa flung herself into the gentleman's eager arms.

'There's something in the air, Mrs Shepherd,' he told his only confidante in the kitchen, the housekeeper, 'and I wouldn't be surprised to see a wedding very soon and on a very grand style. A gentleman, this one.'

Tessa wore a day dress of muslin in a tawny shade of amber. The skirt had a dozen flounces, each edged with black velvet ribbon; the pagoda sleeves were frothed beneath the wrists with a mass of lace; the bodice was tight and plain. Her hair was smoothed back into a glossy chignon, unadorned but for a tawny ribbon of velvet. Emma was delighted with her for it seemed her young mistress was a lady at last, a lady who cared about fashion and elegance and the need to allow her maid to take as long as was necessary each day to groom her, to change her as many times as was necessary from one outfit into another.

'Darling, you look beautiful,' Robby whispered.

'And so do you.' Her breath was sweet on his lips. He was correctly and immaculately dressed, his olive green frockcoat exactly the right length, the lapels wide, the collar high. His dove-grey trousers were tight to his long, lean legs, clinging to the calf muscle, his boots polished and his frilled and pleated shirt-front ironed to perfection. He smelled of lemon soap, his face freshly shaved, glowing and brown with health, and his gold-blond hair was smoothly brushed, not a curl of it out of place. His brown eyes worshipped her and she thought she had never been so exquisitely happy in her whole life.

He grinned engagingly. 'Do I look good enough for the daughter of the house?'

'She will simply fall in love with you, just as I did.'

Her answer was still on her smiling lips as he opened the

drawing-room door for her, stepping back a little to allow her to enter before him. Her mother stood up, her face serious for this was a serious business. She had never met this young man and she would not be charmed by any facile and good-natured fool who thought he might get his hands on her daughter's inheritance, since one day she would have one. It looked somewhat suspicious to her that this gentleman who had only just come into her daughter's life was already making his intentions known having swept her off her feet, it seemed, in a matter of weeks. She would size him up, as she sized up any man who came to do business with her at the mill and draw her own conclusions. That was why she had not wished to hear any of Tessa's gloriously coloured notions on what a paragon of virtue he was, what a marvel, indeed a miracle of perfection, and from such a splendid family, or so Tessa would have it. She would decide what he was when she met him: from long experience she could read a man, his motives, his beliefs and values, his pedigree and breeding as easily as she could read a balance sheet.

He walked towards her, coming from the past as savagely as the fist of a pugilist swinging up from nowhere, the blow hitting her between the eyes with a force which took her senses, her breath from her lungs, the strength from her legs. She could feel the movement inside her head as her mind began to go round and round, darkening the space about her, blinding her eyes, reeling and dipping, flinging her about sickeningly, nauseously, as though she was a child on a swing which goes far too high. She put out a hand to ward him off, both hands as she felt herself fall, and her last thought as the blackness slipped mercifully over her was that she had burst her heart and would be dead before she hit the ground.

'Mother ... Dear God, catch her, Robby, she's fainting. Mother, what is it? Ring the bell, Robby ... Dear God, Mother ... Robby ... ask Briggs ... fetch Emma ... smell-

243

ing salts in Laurel's drawer, she always has them. Mother, oh, darling ... speak to me ... tell me what ... ?'

She could hear her daughter's voice spiralling down the length of the tunnel which led into her head, the words hollow and echoing, and even see her terrified eyes peering through the darkness. She was sorry she had frightened her. She had never, in the whole of Tessa's existence been anything but calm, unruffled; not the perfect mother, perhaps, since she spent all her days at the mill, not always there when Tessa had needed her in her childhood, but never anything other than perfectly controlled. She had left this girl to others to bring up, hoping it would be all right, not knowing how to do anything else, not being awfully sure she could be anything else. But she had always, always been strong, steady, and had never swooned before in her life. But the sight of the man her daughter loved had taken away the props, the crutch on which she herself was balanced, and somehow she must find it again, or make another.

He was looking at her, concerned, his eyes bewildered, his face just as she remembered it, his expression telling her that he was willing to be anything she wanted him to be for as long as it suited her, the young and endearing manner she knew so well. His mouth slanting into a smile of encouragement, his hand on her arm, ready to lift her wherever it pleased her to go, a gentleman at the disposal of a lady, and she did not know whether to love him or hate him.

Her face was the colour of putty, somewhere between beige and gunmetal, it's youthful elasticity gone, the flesh drooping, sweating, and she trembled violently. She was on the sofa, her head propped on a cushion, her skirts bunched uncomfortably beneath her as though she had been picked up quite urgently and bundled on to the nearest resting place. Tessa knelt beside her, chafing her hands anxiously. The room seemed to be full of people: Briggs hovering distantly as he always did by the door; Emma, her daughter's maid, wringing her hands, and Dorcas, a sensible lass and the only one to show calm, holding the smelling salts which a moment before had brought her back to her senses, and *him*, the man her daughter wished to marry – which, of course, was impossible now.

'I'm all right,' she managed to whisper but her eyes could not tear themselves away from him. He stood to one side, a visitor, a stranger, really, who had been involved in a small family emergency, had helped out but who, knowing his place, had moved away to give the family, her daughter, some space and air to breathe.

'What happened, Mother?' Tessa continued to worry her with her hands.

'I ... I would like to go to my room, lass.'

'Of course, Mother. Emma and Dorcas will help you but ...' Her gaze turned, radiantly, even now, towards the man she loved ... Oh, dear God ... dear, sweet God ... 'may I not introduce ...'

'I'll go now, daughter.'

'Please, Mother ...'

'If you will give me your arm ... see, Dorcas, lift me up ...'

'May I help, madam?' A true gentleman, he was beside her as she tried to rise, offering her his arm, his support, anything she might need as a lady and which he, as a gentleman, was willing to give her.

'No, no ...' She broke the spell she herself had made, the link her eyes had forged with his, by turning abruptly away, rudely the rest of the assembly were inclined to think, particularly her daughter who loved him. He fell back, startled, genuinely puzzled by her apparent distaste for him, then bowed, his impeccable code of conduct keeping his face politely expressionless.

He had gone, she had been told an hour later as she lay in her darkened room, not undressed for she simply could not face the task. He had sent his good wishes for her speedy recovery, Tessa said coolly as she sat beside her, and the hope that they might meet again to discuss his and her daughter's future, when she was feeling better able to manage it. Perhaps the next day, if she could spare him an hour, since he wished to get the matter settled before he discussed it with *his* family.

'He loves me, Mother.' Her daughter's voice came to her out of the darkness and she thought her heart would break, just as she was about to break this child's. All these years and the past dead and buried, she had thought, hopelessly at times, but more easily as the years moved on and now, on an explosion of anguish and joy, of despair and winging ecstasy, it had come back to destroy them all.

'I can see that, lass.'

'Will you meet him tomorrow, then? If you feel better that is. He has to get back ... the estate ... his grandfather is not well so he cannot remain here indefinitely. I want to ... we both want to make plans and there is his family. If I bring him up to the mill, to your office ... or perhaps here if you feel up to it?'

'No, my lass. I'm afraid not.'

She saw the shadow who was her daughter lift herself from the chair in which she had waited, keeping quiet with a great deal of self-control until her mother was herself again. She moved across the room, graceful and lovely in her tawny gown, her face bewildered, her eyes mutinous, her expression saying she would have this man no matter what her mother said, or did, to try and stop her. She stood beside the half-drawn curtains, then flung them open with a great clatter and moved back across the room to stare with narrowed eyes into her mother's. She found them steady and unflinching, clear and honest as they had always been with no inclination to look away.

'Why? What's wrong with him? He comes of a good family and ...'

'I know that, Tessa.' She saw the startled movement of her daughter's arms, both lifting fractionally, almost a shrug as if to say she wished she could understand what was in her

246

mother's mind for, really, this was so foolish when anyone in their right minds could see how perfect she and Robby Atherton were for one another.

'How do you know?'

'Would you obey me if I told you that I didn't want you to see him again?'

'Of course not.'

'Could you not trust me to know that he is not the man for you, Tessa?'

'You know I could not. Do you expect me to give him up without any explanation? To give him up *at all*, with or without any explanation, a reason? There *is* no reason. Mother, please, Mother, will you not tell me what happened in the drawing-room? I have never seen you faint, or even be ill. Heavens, I don't think you have had a day off from that mill since the day I was born. You were yourself when I left the room to greet Robby, even as I returned, but suddenly you keel over like a ... Why, what was it? It can have nothing to do with Robby since you have never met before so ...'

'Tessa ...'

'Mother, I must insist that you see him tomorrow, or if not then, as soon as you feel well enough. We are to be married and there is a lot to do.'

'You must never see him again.'

Tessa whirled away in exasperation, sensing her mother's urgency but refusing to accept it, throwing it back at her forcefully since it made no difference. She would marry Robby Atherton, with or without her mother's consent or approval. She would not listen a moment longer to this foolishness, this stupidity, this *insanity*, this unbelievable refusal of her mother, not only to accept her love, but to give an explanation for her opposition. She would leave now. She would go ... somewhere ... Robby would find a place for her ... and as soon as they could they would be married; not with all the pomp she knew would have been the choice of his family but in a little church somewhere.

247

Her mother could disown her, disinherit her, what did it matter? She had only one life, one chance, and this with Robby was it. They were so alike, so perfectly in accord, some lovely bond between them making them the one spirit and flesh the Bible talked about though they had not as yet made love in the full sense of the word. But they would. Tonight. She would go now. Let herself out of the small side door and ride over to the Station Hotel where Robby was . . .

'No Tessa, you can't do it.' Her mother, it seemed, had read her mind, but it didn't matter. If they locked her up, which was unlikely, her mother knew she would escape. A hundred times in the past she had climbed down a conveniently placed tree, swinging from bough to bough to join her cousins in some wildness and she would do it again if she must. Put on her breeches and boots and . . .

'I can see I must tell you the truth, girl.' Her mother's voice was harsh and grating, just as though with the prospect of telling what was to come her mouth and throat had dried up and become like the sands of the desert.

'I wish you would, Mother, then perhaps I can give Robby a decent explanation of why we must marry without you.'

'No, lass.' And now she was gentle, her disciplined, composed mother, so gentle Tessa was suddenly very afraid but still she fought on, for what else was she to do? She would have Robby Atherton.

'Mother, please understand. I don't care *what* you say about him. Tell me he is a . . . a murderer, a . . . a . . .' What was worse than murder? She couldn't think, but if Robby had done it, she didn't care, she would still have him.

'He is, I'm sure, a perfectly acceptable young man, with no criminal record. He will make some woman a good husband one day but it cannot be you, my darling, not you, ever.'

'My darling'. Her mother had called her 'darling'.

'Please, Mother . . .' Her voice was the voice of a fright-

248

ened child, frightened by some unknown monster which hid in a cupboard and was about to leap out on her.

'Robby Atherton, as you call him, has another name, Tessa. Once, long ago, until he was three years old he was known as Lucas Greenwood.'

'Lucas Greenwood ... what ... who ...?'

'He is my son, Tessa, and your brother.'

She lay in the dark, in the complete and utter dark which was her hatred, her despair, her hopelessness and fear. Her mind seemed to be infested with the words her mother had spoken, senseless, of course, but making perfect sense when you saw the picture her mother painted. She had refused to believe it, naturally, screaming out that same hatred – of her mother – the despair and hopelessness, the fear in which she now lay. But then there had also been the enveloping belief that her mother was lying to her, that she was mistaken – for how could she tell after all this time? – that she was out of her mind. Indeed, she grasped at any explanation which occurred to her to prove her mother was quite mad.

She could hear her mother's voice now, patient, kind, filled with sorrow and yet there had been a kind of joyousness she had not understood, had been crucified by, and she had said so in her dementia.

'He is my son, lass. Would not any mother's heart be glad to have her son, who she had thought to be dead, returned to her? I am torn between grief for you and gladness for myself. Dear God, there is a great need in me to run after him and turn him about to face me, to look into his eyes and tell him who I am.'

'How can you be sure?' Her voice was flat and toneless for she knew her mother told the truth.

'He is exactly as his father was at that age.'

Her mother had been a spinner, long ago when times were hard and the poor oppressed. That was what they called them, her mother said: the oppressed poor. And it was for his efforts to help them, to win them a decent life, that her Uncle Joss had gone to prison. His family had survived. Tessa's mother. Charlie, no more than a child. Daisy, the younger sister now dead. Their mother had starved, and to keep her family warm and fed Jenny Greenwood had contrived, that was the word she used, to get what they needed from Harry Atherton, a manager at the mill and to whom, for a while, her Aunt Kit had been betrothed.

'It's a long story, Tessa and I'll not bother you with it now. He was a scoundrel, charming and ruthless in the pursuit of what he wanted. He wanted me. I was pretty then, and strong, so I gave him what he wanted in return for the things my family needed. You understand what I'm saying? He went away. Kit sent him. I was never quite sure how she did it . . .' her mother's voice was vague as she lived again in that haunted past, '. . . and I bore his son.'

'Why did you . . . give him to his . . . father?' Her voice was flat and lifeless.

'He stole him from me. He came to the house when I was alone and took him.'

'And you let him?'

'Things . . . were done to . . . to me. There were . . . other men. Afterwards Joss and Charlie and I went to Atherton Hall. We were deceived. We saw a child, a little girl Harry said was his. She wore a bonnet . . . I couldn't see her face. She was the same age as Lucas . . . I thought . . .'

Hope shone for a moment in Tessa's eyes, then was extinguished.

'I was . . . I did not know for certain Harry had him. I thought he might have taken him somewhere else . . . revenge, you see, for what he thought had been done to him by the Greenwood family. Put him to a chimney sweep or . . . but now I know. My son was here today. If you cannot accept it we will . . . I will question him. He must have some memory. We will go to Atherton Hall. But don't you see, he believes he is the son of a gentleman, the heir to a great tradition. This will not . . . not please him. It will inflict great pain on him and you will still not be able to ... to marry him. But we will do it if...'

'No.'

'How will you explain your decision not to marry him?'

'I shall not.'

'Something must be said to him.' Just as something should have been said to Will Broadbent, a voice inside her head whispered, and wasn't, and here was her punishment. She could not stop loving him, her 'parfit gentil knight'. Her mind might know he was her brother, but her heart and body did not and they would mourn his loss, grieve for him and ... dear God ... long for his touch just the same. The flesh was no different, the mouth she had kissed, her flesh, her mouth which did not recognise that it was a sin now even to *think* of, what they had almost done and what, God help her, she still wanted more than anything. What was she to do? Where was she to go? The rest of her life lay before her without him in it and how was she to manage travelling through it alone?

She tried to weep for perhaps it would relieve the heavy weight of suffering which rested in her chest, crushing her and her shallowly breathing lungs, the pain which twisted viciously about her heart and head and indeed in every part of her tortured body, burning her eyes which would not see him again, her ears which would never hear him whisper her name, her fingers which would never clasp his.

And there was so much hatred in her. A hatred of the fates which, smiling slyly and nodding at one another years ago, had brought her and Robby to this. On the day her mother had met his father how the gods must have chortled knowing the devastation that encounter was to bring, not only to her mother but to the children she was eventually to bear. And her mother. She hated her mother with a frantic loathing which filled every cavity in her body, oozed from every pore of her flesh. It had been her, her carelessness, her disregard for the consequences, despite her protestations that she had done it for her starving family, which had

251

brought this on them, this agony of spirit, this poison which was festering into her soul, this grief which would never be assuaged since Robby *was* her spirit and her soul.

The tears would not come. She sprang from her bed where she had lain fully clothed, motionless for the best part of the night. The dawn was near for she could hear a sleepy bird-twittering close by her window where the sparrows nested and there was a thin line of light along the top of the hills in the east to the back of the house. She could see the two dark and towering pine trees outlined against the pale sky. She did not think now for the part of her which could reason had closed down, deep in shock and no longer able to cope with logical thought. The world had gone mad, her world which had collapsed about her in a lunatic fashion and left her marooned in some place she did not know, in which she was alone. She must escape from it and she must do so in the only way she knew how. Her mare ... up there it would be clean and empty ... her mare would take her and if she should not come back the animal would, eventually, find its way home, or someone would take it in ... steal it, sell it, what did it matter? Her breeches ... but that would take too long ... a saddle ... but that would take too long ... How had she got out here? As she crossed the stable yard the stray thought penetrated her mind, fragmented with no meaning nor answer so she cast it away. She threw her leg across her mare's back, the skirt of her tawny gown bunched up about her thighs, her bare feet and legs not feeling the chill of the early morning, her hands gripping the mare's mane to guide her.

She rode through the trees, moving across the thick green carpet of dewed undergrowth. The full weight of summer foliage brushed her head and a squirrel darted amongst the leaves, abusing her angrily before dashing back to shelter. As she came out of the spinney and started up the track towards the high moorland, a breeze blew into her face the smells of yesterday's summer sunshine, a hint of the warmth that was to follow but which had not yet risen from the misted ground.

Her mind was quite empty now, pain and pleasure gone, hate and love gone, perhaps a beginning of acceptance though no such thought entered her head. Her mare was nervous, not caring overmuch for the feel of her rider's gown about her flanks, the bootless feet and bare legs, the absence of rein and saddle and stirrup, of not being guided in the way she was accustomed. She shied at everything in her path from the moving, breeze-blown bracken to a harmless clump of heather which had rooted in the hollow of a rock.

Where was she going? Not to Friar's Mere, nor Dog Hill nor Badger's Edge for these were places where she had known happiness, laughter, companionship, love and what had they to do with her now? Great hills stood around her, their flanks clothed in a tapestry of purple and gold and green. The faint track on which she moved, trance-like, was no more than deep ruts and pot-holes but she did not see them as her mare picked her way around them. She came to a place where on one side the track had collapsed in a torrent of rain and it fell in a scree over the precipitous slope. The animal, with an instinct of its own, clung to the bracken on the opposite side.

She had no idea where she was when she finally slid from the mare's back. Not that she coherently thought about it. There were stones, a jumble of them on the top of a barren fell, wild and with a thin, whining wind which found its way beneath her dainty afternoon dress and touched her skin unkindly. She sat down, mindless, senseless, looking out over but not seeing the thickly wooded vale far below through which the glint of water shone. She leaned her back against the rock and the veil, dragging and thick and cold, fell over her and she could neither see nor hear.

# 16

'I must see her, Mrs Harrison, really I must. There is something strange here and I will not go away, as you say I must, until you have told me what it is. I must apologise for my obstinacy but ... well, she will have told you, Tessa and I are very much in love. I am not a boy, madam, in the first flush of calf love but a man of nearly thirty ...'

'I know that ... Mr Atherton ...' Jenny's voice trembled and almost broke.

'You know?' He looked surprised.

'I ... I had guessed you were ... older than ...'

'Then you will know that I do not take my feelings for your daughter lightly.'

Dear God, he was just as she had known in her heart her son would be, had he lived. Though his father was Harry Atherton, a man who had given thought to no one's needs but his own, who had been greedy and cruel, heartless and dealing only in easy charm, this man, her son, had a strength, surely, at least a stubbornness that would not easily be turned away from the woman he was certain he would marry. He had waited a long time for the right, and fit, bride to come into his life, his haughty manner said, and no one would deny him. But she, Jenny Harrison, must, and do it in a manner that would give no hint of his true birthright. He was to lose his love and though it broke her mother's heart and put an almost intolerable ache in her mother's arms that longed to lift and enfold this son of hers, she could not take his life away from him as well. Somehow he must be made to return to the world he knew, to pick up the living he knew, to resume without Tessa, what he had before he met her.

Her daughter was not in the house. Her mare was not in the stable. They did not worry unduly for it had always been her habit when she was unhappy to take to the moor and stay there all day sometimes, returning calmed, perhaps not accepting whatever troubled her but better able to bear it. That was where she would be now, up on the tops weeping for her lost love and when she was ready she would come home and somehow she would survive. As her mother had survived.

There was some fuss in the house over the non-appearance of her nephews, her tired mind had registered, not caring overmuch for when had those scamps not caused trouble? Really, she had enough to grieve her without worrying where *they* might have got to.

'She is not here, Mr Atherton.'

'But where is she? Surely she would not have gone away on this day . . .' on this special day when she and I were to be betrothed, his bewildered face asked. 'She must have known I would return to see you, to ask you to consider me as . . .'

He pushed his hand through the bright tangle of his unbrushed hair and she watched him hungrily, glorying in his masculine beauty, the way he lifted his head, the turn of his smooth jaw, the slender strength of his horseman's hands. She would not see him again after today and though the thought was a pain barely endurable there was a tiny floating joy in her which told her that she had been returned from the dark place into which his kidnapping years ago had flung her. He was a man now and she knew it. He was alive and healthy and she knew it. Another woman's son, but Jenny Greenwood knew, at last, at last, he was here on this earth still, not dead as she had thought, not murdered or maimed as young boys were in the mills and mines and chimneys where she had feared he might be. He was *her* son, though he did not know it and never would, for the

255

knowledge would torment him, cause chaos in his life which would be hard enough to bear, for a while, without her girl.

'I think she may have gone to visit a cousin in Liverpool. Yes, I believe that was what she had in mind. She was under the impression you were to go back to Cheshire and decided to go and stay for a while. She won't be home for ... well, I cannot really say. They are very sociable there, parties and such ...'

His eyes turned a cold, putty brown and he straightened slowly.

'You are lying, Mrs Harrison. I don't know why but, by God, I mean to find out. A cousin in Liverpool! After what happened yesterday you expect me to believe a tale such as that? You took against me from the start and somehow you have persuaded Tessa ...' A look of confusion shifted across his face and Jenny Harrison felt the tears seep to the back of her eyes and knew she would weep soon for her son, and her daughter, and their broken hearts.

'But how ... why ... ?' he continued helplessly.

'Really, Mr Atherton, I must ask you to leave my house.' If he didn't go soon she would break, break up into a thousand pieces as she was hurled hither and thither by their separate and yet bonded pain. 'It really does no good ...'

'Mrs Harrison.' He sat down in the chair close to the fire, his face, had he but known it, looking as hers did when she was absolutely determined on a course of action which nobody but herself considered right. His voice was quiet and very polite. 'Mrs Harrison, I shall not leave, you know, until you tell me the truth. I shall sit here in this chair until Tessa returns from her trip to Liverpool, if necessary.' He raised sardonic eyebrows. 'And I shall have the truth from *her*. She will not lie to me.'

Jenny Harrison sat down in the chair opposite her son knowing that something fine and ... yes, the word was 'sweet' was to be taken from him in the next few minutes. And she herself was to lose the last, the very last slender belief that there was goodness somewhere in the harsh world around her. She had tried to spare him, her son, her beloved son, but even that was to be taken from her in the bewilderment, the disbelief, the amusement, she supposed, that he would feel at first before she convinced him. Then would come the horror, the total horror and loathing as she stripped him of all he loved in his life; of his life itself, really, for how would he bear the destruction of the man he thought himself to be?

She tried one last time.

'Believe me, Mr Atherton, when I say I am sure Tessa will contact you when she returns from . . .'

'Mrs Harrison.'

There was silence for a moment as the mother looked for the last time into the still dauntless eyes of her son.

'I will tell you the truth now, Mr Atherton,' she said hopelessly.

Her mother was in the stable doorway as she clattered into the yard, a darker shadow in the darkness of the night which was illuminated by the myriad of stars in the navy-blue sky. They did not greet one another. Her mother moved to one side as Tessa led her mare through the doorway, watching silently as she rubbed the animal down. When all was done Tessa turned and began to move towards the stable door, brushing past her mother as though she was not there.

Jenny put her hand on her daughter's arm, feeling it flinch away and her own heart recoiled from the rebuff.

'Tessa, you must speak to me, lass.'

Tessa shook off the restraining hand and continued to stride towards the side door of the house. Jenny thought she would crumple up and die with the pain of it, and indeed wished she could as it hit her again and again. Then anger stirred.

'He's my son, damn you,' she called after the retreating back of her daughter, following her across the yard. 'Do you think you are the only one to hurt? You have not borne a child, Tessa Harrison, and so you cannot know the strength

257

and the agony of a mother's love when she loses that child.'

But Tessa walked on as though she had not spoken. When she reached the door her hand did not seem able to turn the door-knob, but fumbled with it blindly. Jenny opened it for her and they moved into the dimly lit quiet of the passage which led to the main hallway and staircase.

'Tessa . . .' She took her daughter's arm, firmly this time, driving down the anguish which came to her. 'We must speak to one another. We cannot go on as though this had not happened. I . . . have never said this to you before . . . but I love you, girl, and . . .'

Tessa whirled about violently, flinging her mother against the panelled wall and Jenny was frightened by the expression on her face as the lamplight fell on it.

'Do you think I care about that? Do you? Do you imagine that your . . . your love . . . can make me feel better again? Pick me up, brush me down . . . kiss where it hurts . . .'

'No, no, lass. I didn't mean that . . .'

'At this moment I feel I will never be well again, Mother. I will never recover. That is what I feel and how *you* feel means nothing to me. My head tells me that you're not to blame, but my heart' – she struck her chest violently with her clenched fist and her mother winced – 'says it will never forgive you for what you have done to me and Robby.'

'Darling . . .' Her mother's voice was an anguished whisper. 'I'm sorry, dear God, I'm sorry . . .'

'Leave Him out of it, and leave me alone. Let me go . . . now.' She made a huge effort to control herself. 'Perhaps later . . . but for now. Leave me alone.'

They sat in different rooms, the two women, but in exactly the same attitude as they mourned the same man: a rocking chair by a window moving slowly backwards and forwards, heads back against a cushion, hands folded, eyes staring out towards the east as a pink dawn crept along the tops and the sun rose on another day.

\*      \*      \*

The sun rose earlier in the Crimea than it did in England that day. The dawn of the twentieth of September was soft, balmy and sunny, glowing from behind the snows of the Caucasus at about five o'clock, outlining the fleet of war steamers, eight French and one British which sailed towards the mouth of the River Alma. Their guns opened fire with the ferocity of ravenous beasts about to fall upon their prey and the two young men who stood beside their horses recoiled sharply, trying to hold the bridles of the animals which reared in fright. It took them several minutes to calm the terrified beasts, then with the fluid grace of born riders they mounted them, turning this way and that indecisively.

'It's started, Pearce. By God it's started. We missed the scrap at Giurgevo but we're to be in on this. Where the hell should we go, d'you think?'

'Where the hell will they *let* us go? Surely to God you don't intend to climb to some vantage point and watch as so many seem to be doing? That chap we spoke to yesterday had brought his mistress to see the spectacle, I was told. Anyway, in this smoke we should see nothing.'

'They are to go up to the plateau which stands above the valley, so I believe, but I should like to be closer, wouldn't you?'

They were yelling at the tops of their voices as they galloped away, manoeuvring skilfully to avoid soldiers who darted everywhere, tents, carts, guns and the chaos which had sprung up as bugles sounded from every quarter.

'D'you think we'll get any breakfast?' Pearce shouted jubilantly, not caring whether he did or not.

'Well, the troops certainly won't so really we shouldn't either, old man. It's only fair.'

'You're right. Now where should we go first? No one seems to mind our presence and perhaps we may be able to help in some way. We are both good shots.'

'Indeed, and excellent horsemen so I suggest we follow the cavalry.'

'Dear God, this is better than the mill, wouldn't you say, Drew?'

'You never spoke a truer word, brother, and won't we have something to tell them when we get home?'

The smoke had cleared somewhat when the great Lord Raglan arrived and as he rode off with his staff along a pathway leading round the western side of the heights, Drew and Pearce Greenwood removed their hats respectfully, as they had done for no man before. He was calm and steadfast, it was said of him, his resolution higher when danger pressed. He and his soldiers were children of a proud and obstinate race and would advance through the jaws of death if needs be.

'He's bloody marvellous, isn't he?' Pearce whispered reverently.

'They say he's waiting for three more battalions to arrive but due to the rain in the night it will take some time to get them here. They may be glad of us yet, brother.' Drew's face was tense and boyish in his excitement.

His words were drowned by the sudden thunder of the guns from the artillery of both sides. Two eighteen-pounders had been brought up and as they beat on the senses, the eardrums, the blood and flesh of every man within a radius of ten miles, order and sense was blown away. If either of the sons of Kit and Joss Greenwood had been asked to describe that day they could not have done so with any coherence. They had begun it as two excited schoolboys out for a spree, a lark, something to describe to those back home, an adventure which they had both craved. They ended it as men, frightened, sickened, devastated, but men at last.

The allied armies spent two days on the battlefield of the Alma. When it was done the dead and wounded lay within a space only a mile and a half square while about Telegraph Hill the bodies were piled so high it was impossible to see over them. No one alive on that bloody field had ever seen such a spectacle, except perhaps Lord Raglan himself who had fought and lost an arm at Waterloo. Men, seasoned soldiers, fell ill when they looked about them and the effect on Drew and Pearce Greenwood was to shape them for the rest of their lives. They had become separated from each other as the first sweep of men and horses pushed them apart. Pearce's horse was shot from under him as he turned it about, his face ludicrously bewildered, wondering where he should go in this mad world which had suddenly erupted about him.

When he got to his feet, already quite deep in shock for despite his declaration to the opposite he had not really meant to *fight*, he found himself defending his own life with no more than the shot gun he had brought with him, the one he used against the grouse on Longworth Moor. An instinct for self-preservation luckily took over what was left of his senses. Finding, first a musket, then a sabre, each clutched in the hand of a bloody and quite-dead soldier, for an hour he parried and shot wildly, carried along blindly until the man beside him began to shout that 'they were on the run now'.

It was then, as he staggered along behind the retreating Russian army, so stunned he merely did what others did about him, he realised what he had done, where he had been, how he had spent the past few hours of his life. He had seen men, *real* men scream and crumple in front of him. He had felt the steel he held slide sickeningly into other men's flesh. He had seen blood, torn flesh, shattered bone, and worse, erupt from bodies broken and mutilated. The images penetrated his clouded mind – he sank slowly to the ground and began to vomit.

They stepped over him, still chasing the Russians, cheering now for they had won a victory, but Pearce Greenwood wept for he had lost his brother and how was he to live without him?

'Pearce . . .'

The voice brought him back, a hand lifted his face from his own vomit and the blood-soaked earth on which he lay. He turned slowly but there was no one there he knew, only a soldier in a blood-stained tunic, his eyes staring and haunted in a blackened face.

'Dear God, Pearce . . .' The soldier held out his arms and they both began to weep.

# 17

She sat by the tightly closed window of the pretty bedroom, a soft white shawl about her thin shoulders, another thrown over her legs. A fire burned brightly in the grate, its flames heaped with an abundance of coal, and on the white ceiling and rose-silk walls shadows danced and wavered. Outside a flurry of hard-pelleted snow flung itself against the window but when Tessa turned to look there was nothing to see but a wall of whiteness, shifting and leaping, slowing as the wind died down, then hurtling as fast as one of the railway trains which ran through the valley bottom, across her vision as the wind sprang up again.

She was impassive now, dry-eyed and silent in her self-induced calm; rigid of mind and body, free for the moment of the punishing memories which came so often to devastate her as she gathered her small reserve of strength together. If she concentrated hard on the top of Emma's small, frilled cap as it bent over some mending in her lap she could empty her mind of everything but the will, the resolution, the absolute effort that was needed to drive Robby Atherton's face from every corner of her mind.

But she must have Emma's cap on which to set her mind. It was a trick, of course, because anything would do really: the Meissen figurine on the mantelshelf, the silver candleholder by the bed, the gilt-framed miniature of her cousins as children. But somehow Emma's cap, simple, pretty, fluted, quite foolish, really, but always the same, seemed to have the knack of emptying her mind of the pain.

She had flung herself about at first in the dangerous rage which had come to consume her, just as she had once done as a child. She had frightened poor Emma as she had fought, time and time again, to live without his memory inflicting its vicious pain upon her.

'I cannot bear it another moment. I must go ... I must and no one will stop me,' she had screeched in her anger at what had been done to her and her mother had sat beside her, for the first time in living memory leaving her mills to manage as best they could without her. She would not lose this child, not this child as well, her terrified mind had implored some god, her own face pale as the death which threatened her daughter. Tessa had taken a fever several weeks after Robby Atherton had gone. The heat of it had burned her flesh away like the tallow of a candle and Jenny had despaired for the child no longer cared to live, it seemed. But she was strong and she had recovered to make the lives of those around her more miserable than they cared to contemplate.

'Let me get up, Mother. I cannot stay here with nothing to do but think.'

'Be patient, Tessa.'

'Let me at least walk out to the stables and see my mare.' This, when she could barely sit up.

'Be patient, child.' Her mother's reply was laughable really, if it had not been so sad.

But she wouldn't be told. She fought them all violently, hurting herself, breaking everything she could lay her hands on as she threw exquisitely fine figurines at those who tried to stop her. Emma had the feeling in the back of her mind that it was not all to do with the fever which for weeks had brought her so low; this was a weakness not just of the body, but of the heart, or Emma missed her guess. They'd all seen, or been told of, the handsome young gentleman who had come a'calling and Miss Tessa's happiness had shone through the house, affecting them all for, really, it was true what they said about 'laugh and the world laughs with you, cry and you cry alone'. They'd heard her laughing and singing for days on end before he'd called on Mrs Harrison. Then all of a sudden he'd gone tearing down the drive on Mr Greenwood's horse, sent off with a flea in his ear, though God only knew why, a fine, well set-up gentleman like him, and *she'd* gone off her head because of it, if you wanted Emma's opinion. It was a mystery, it really was, and Emma almost broke her heart over the state of her since.

But her temper, unpredictable and dangerous, was back with a vengeance now as they all knew to their cost for they suffered it at close quarters.

'She threw the teapot at me, Mrs Shepherd,' Emma sobbed. She had thought Miss Tessa to be a hellion before her illness but it was as though those days had been all sweetness and light compared to now. 'If the tea had run on me I would have been scalded. As it was a bit of broken china hit me on the hand, see, just there.' She pointed to where a trickle of blood ran. 'If it goes on much longer I'm giving in my notice . . .' This was a drastic thing to contemplate in the climate of unemployment which prevailed in the valley.

'Now, Emma, don't be daft, lass,' Mrs Shepherd said sharply.

That was how their young mistress was now. Tormented, that was the word which came to Emma's mind, one minute and then the next staring vacantly at nowt, not even answering when she was spoken to. Aye, had they not all suffered in one way or another at the hands of the three wild youngsters who had dominated this household in the past? Though they were sorry for the plight of the poor lass since she'd been so badly, the girl could be a danger, now that her mother had returned to the mill, a danger not only to herself, but to the servants who had been left to look after her.

'I don't care what you say, Mrs Shepherd, if she don't get

out soon God knows what she'll do. She's as wild as an animal in a cage at times.'

Emma had been to the Zoological Gardens at Liverpool once when her family had stopped there for a while on their way from Ireland and the famine which continually seemed to rage there, before moving on to Crossfold. The restless padding and infuriated snarls of some beasts, the listless apathy of others had made a great impression on her and had lingered in her young mind. Miss Tessa reminded her of them. Not the padding, of course, since she could do no more than stand weakly by her chair as yet, but the snarling, the wildness, the sudden, depthless silence were enough to make your blood run cold.

And Miss Laurel did her best, poor thing, and her with another little one to see to.

'I do wish you would stay in bed, Tessa. Don't you think it would be wiser to rest instead of ...'

'Taking up everyone's time and energy with my constant demands? It would be so much simpler if I were to remain here, mim as a mouse, hidden away and a nuisance to no one, wouldn't it? It must be so peaceful at table now without Drew and Pearce and myself to ...'

'That is not what I meant. In my opinion, this determination of yours to leap out of bed so soon after what has been a very serious illness ...'

'*Leap?* If only I could! Why am I so weak?'

'It cannot be good for you, all this anxiety to be on your feet. Why don't you stay in bed and I will fetch you a book from the library?'

'A book! Dammit, Laurel, I don't want a book. I want some excitement, some noise, something going on. Why don't you send the children down to see me?'

'They would jump all over you, darling.'

'I don't care. I want them to.'

'Now, Tessa, you know what the doctor said. Besides, Robert and Jane are at their lessons and Nanny would not like it if I woke Henry and Anne from their nap. And baby is too young...'

'Laurel ... please...'

'Just rest, Tessa.'

'*I don't want to rest!*'

It was March before she was completely recovered, nine long months before she was able at last to walk with her usual proud carriage and not just the lurching stagger from one piece of furniture to the next, with Emma and Dorcas hovering at each elbow. At last she could pass out of the bedroom which had been her prison for so long; away from the cosy, fire-warmed comfort, the feather quilts and lace-edged pillows, the soft carpets and soft voices, away from safety and into the wide hallway towards the stairs.

'Let me do it alone,' she begged Charlie who would have held her arm.

Down the shallow steps of the stairs, one by one, she went, her hand refusing the banister, her legs like jelly but her face hard and determined in her triumph. She wore a pretty gown of scarlet delaine, the colour giving her a bold and gypsy look which belied her fragility. It had been made to fit her new slenderness and the bodice clung to her small breasts. The skirt was full and plain with fifteen feet of fabric round the hem. And beneath it were half a dozen fine cambric petticoats, each flounce edged in white French lace. Fastening back her flowing hair was a scarlet ribbon.

The front door stood open to let in the sunshine and she stepped through it into the fresh light of spring. Gardeners raised their heads from their planting and touched a finger to their caps and she nodded to them, but it was not them who held her attention.

On the gravel driveway, stamping and blowing through her nostrils as though she knew what a great day this was, stood her mare, saddled, her coat glowing, her mane tossing, her eyes rolling in her mistress's direction. Walter held her bridle, beaming from ear to ear, his face as red as Tessa's dress.

266

'She's ready for thee, Miss Tessa,' he said, then wiped his nose on the back of his hand.

She walked down the steps, her legs no longer like jelly but strong and sure and when she put her face against that of the animal's she was smiling since she knew she would survive now.

'Give me a week or two, Walter.'

'Happen less, miss?'

'Aye, happen . . .' and they both grinned.

The valley of Balaclava lay desolate and melancholy. The road to the camp was a track of liquid filth. The town itself was as muddy as the plains which surrounded it. The tideless harbour was no more than a common sewer in which floated not only the waste of the bodies of thousands of men but the carcasses of soldiers, horses, dogs, cats and every other discarded and decomposing matter which could be found no other resting place.

For weeks now those who still survived had been without proper clothing, fuel or food and to worsen matters further in this vast and mystifying war, the reason for which the soldiers themselves were not fully aware of, there was a virulent outbreak of cholera. In the camp hospitals the men lay down to die upon the bare ground and in the hospitals themselves, ignorance, dirt and confusion prevailed for want of doctors, blankets, medicines, bandages, fresh water, beds and space to put beds. Even had these been available, there was still the need for someone with the sense and energy to arrange them all together.

The weather was appalling. There were heavy squalls with winds so strong they brought down every tent on the plateau. No fires could be lit and no food cooked and the sick and wounded lay exposed to the elements which were no respecters of rank. Generals, officers, soldiers, sick, wounded, hale and hearty lay together in the deluge and when the rain turned to snow 300 men died in one day.

But worst of all, far worse than anything which had previously befallen them, four steam transports, ten sailing transports and four freight ships, caught by the violence of the weather were dashed to the bottom of the harbour.

And those who were left, without blankets or rugs, socks, boots, biscuit, salt beef, or even corn for the horses which survived, must face the winter in the liquid mud on which the camp floated. Every victim on the muddy and half-frozen plains of the Crimea sent home doleful and angry accounts of his own and his brother soldiers' suffering. It was always the same. They lived from hand to mouth with the minimum of ammunition to keep them safe from the enemy. Their lives were unendurable and when they lost them it was from overwork and exposure, not as soldiers in the heat of battle but like deserted children abandoned by cruel parents. In two weeks the number of sick increased from 13,000 to 16,000. What had become of the fine army, they asked one another, sent off so dashingly, for no other reason, it seemed, than that there had been no war for forty years and it was time for another?

It was about this time that Miss Florence Nightingale arrived at Scutari and the hospital there.

The two young soldiers had, with what remained of their strength, dug a hole in the hard ground, just deep enough and wide enough for them to sit, or lie side by side, drawing over it a sheet of canvas from another such hole in which four soldiers of the 2nd Hussars had frozen to death several weeks before. Thousands of men had died but the loss of life had become a condition of life itself and they concentrated the whole of their physical energy, which was scant, and the whole of their mental energy which was not much better when there is nothing to do all day but turn their minds to their memories.

'Do you remember the day she' – they never mentioned her name by unspoken mutual agreement – 'challenged us to a race from . . . where was it? . . . Badger's Edge or Friar's Mere? . . . I forget, to Greenacres? She jumped that bloody gate as though it was no more than a foot or so from the ground then turned to grin at us. It was May. The sky was so blue that day and it was warm . . .'

'Warm? Warm? What the devil does that mean, d'you think, brother? How does it feel? It is so long since we enjoyed it I have forgot. To be warm and dry and clean . . .'

'And can you remember the time we went with Nicky Longworth and Johnny Taylor to that dog fight at the Craven Heifer?'

'She didn't like it, as I recall . . .'

'No,' the voice was soft and smiling, 'and, really, would you have expected her to? She only went because we did.'

'The poor brute was nearly disembowelled . . .'

'And she brought her dinner back and then tried to pretend she had eaten something which had disagreed with her.'

'Eaten something! What do those words bring to mind, Pearce? To eat something. Actually to put in your mouth some delectable, tasty, delicious, *palatable* food. What, though? What would you order if you could have anything you wanted?'

'Roast beef.'

'Yes, yes, or smoked salmon with . . .'

'No, a saddle of lamb with mint sauce . . .'

'Pheasant done in . . .'

'Followed by . . .'

'Washed down with a good claret . . '

'And then a warm, clean bed . . .'

They fell silent. Their shoulders touched and they huddled in the faint and grave-like light cast through the heavy canvas, their backs to the wall of the dugout. They had a candle which they did not light, ever, except in the emergencies created by Pearce's nightmares where he dreamed he was buried alive beneath a growing mound of dead and injured soldiers, as he had been at the tail end of the battle of Alma. Drew had been beside him for they had made sure as the frenzied day had eased towards nightfall that they did not become separated again. When the bursting shell had lifted a dozen or more soldiers, shredding them to an assortment of bloody torsos, arms, legs and heads, and threw them by some strange chance over Pearce, burying him for ten appalling minutes with the softness and wetness and obscene weight, it had been Drew who had dug him out. Pearce dreamed of it often, screaming as he had done then, clinging to his brother until the candle was lit and sanity returned.

They had a blanket between them, their most treasured possession since not many were so lucky. They had an upturned wooden crate on which stood the pathetic bits and pieces so dear to a soldier far from home and which once they would have laughed over: a miniature of their mother as a girl, a few letters from their aunt and Charlie, a length of satin ribbon with a faint smell of some woman's perfume and which neither would acknowledge to be hers, a box with brushes and a comb, razors and a tiny, prized sliver of soap.

They each wore mud-stained breeches, knee-length boots, an army greatcoat and a peaked soldier's cap. They were dirty with a sour odour about them for neither had washed, let alone bathed, in weeks. Their beards were dark and stiff and their blue eyes, once so vivid, clear and devilish with merry arrogance, were dulled and staring from faces old and tired beyond their years. They had seen and heard sights and sounds they would never forget. They had lost their horses and every fine thing they had brought with such high expectations from England and in each one was the common longing to survive and get home. Nothing more. To survive the cholera and the dysentery, the shot and shell the enemy rained upon them, the siege and the enemy which besieged them. Somehow to get up that invisible track to Balaclava and on to the first transport they could arrange to England. They had been taken for soldiers and had not argued since that was the only way to be fed. They existed, when they were on the duty they were forced to do, in the mud and rain and bitter cold of the trenches, returning to sleep in wet clothes on the wet ground of their dugout.

'D'you remember the fatty-cakes Cook used to make for the servants? We used to turn up our noses at them as some quaint dish of the working class.'

'They'd be bloody welcome now . . .' But the rest of what Drew Greenwood said was cut off by the clear call of a bugle and with a muffled exclamation both young men leaped to their feet, threw aside the canvas of their 'home' and with a hundred others began to move towards the source of the sound.

Tessa read Drew's letter again then stood up and strode towards the door, gathering up her crop and jacket as she went. She would ride over to Edgeclough and visit Annie. It was a week since she had seen her and in that time she had done nothing but tear about from one place to another in search of some occupation which would keep her from going mad with boredom . . . and grief. There were, after all, only so many hours in which one could ride to hounds, and besides the season had ended with the coming of early summer. She had ridden for hours across the burgeoning moorland grasses, called time and time again at the Hall with the excuse that she brought news of Drew and Pearce and though the Squire and his friends welcomed her warmly, the Squire's lady could not quite forget Tessa Harrison's behaviour at the ball last year. She and Robby Atherton had been the talk of the community then and after all it had come to nothing.

March had seen the allies making preparation for the bombardment against Sebastopol. In April there was what Pearce called a 'skirmish' at a place called the Mamelon. In May an expedition was despatched to Kertch with the express purpose of seizing the strait which led into the Sea of Azoff through which the Russian supplies were sent, and in June the Mamelon described by Pearce was captured. In July and August the Allies crept nearer to victory, and on

271

the 'glorious twelfth' Tessa accompanied the Squire and his guests, shooting grouse, partridge and pheasant, drifting very pleasantly through the late summer and autumn days, the depth of her sadness hidden away beneath her wild, high-strung laughter. It was a pity about her cousins, they said, still, for some reason known only to themselves, out there fighting in the Crimea when they might have been having such fun with them, but they had Tessa to amuse them. She was so exhilarating, reckless and willing to do *anything* they did in her search for pleasure, careless and indifferent to the opinions of others. She wore her new outfit, designed by herself and made up for her by a disapproving Miss Maymon who had never created such garments in her life, of black riding jacket, sleek, skin-tight breeches and a white, watered-silk waistcoat. She wore a black top hat, a white frilled stock and black riding boots and was vastly amused, she told an admiring Nicky Longworth, by the consternation of the commercial and manufacturing society of the Penfold Valley who had, no doubt, thought her roistering days had come to an end with the departure of her cousins for the Balkans. She caused a sensation on the hunting field at the start of the new season, in the company of the wild and, in her mother's opinion, unstable fox-hunting set of Crossfold who were, they thought, beyond being amazed at anything Tessa or her missing cousins did.

She was herself again, in other words, arrogant, conceited and charming and the harsh desolation of her nightly weeping was known to no one. They were not aware, those who condemned her wildness, that only in such desperate frivolity, the light-minded and heedless search for 'fun' which was the sole aim of the set of which she was a part, could she momentarily displace her deep unhappiness. The despairing misery which washed over her when she was alone was held at bay only by the total abandonment with which she flung herself into their giddy lives. What else was she to do, she asked herself hopelessly, when she was alone with her ghosts? The brief fling she had enjoyed with Robby Atherton, who had not been seen at the Hall since, was over with neither the worse for it, they were saying, though of course *her* reputation would never be the same again. Only *she* knew that *she* would never be the same again.

In short, she fitted again into the world of the squirearchy, the gentry and the lesser aristocracy as she and her cousins had always done, preferring ploughed fields and recklessly taken ditches, damp drizzled mornings of moorland, wind and foul weather to the polite and civilised world of dinner parties, soirées and evenings of culture which her aunt by marriage, the socially ambitious Mrs Charles Greenwood, thought she should favour. She was known quite definitely to join the gentlemen in their after-dinner billiards and claret and to have won quite a large sum of money at some card game at the Hall. A restive colt again, she appeared to be, impatient of all restraint, though those who spoke of it agreed that at almost twenty she was long past the age to be coltish.

'She's trying to kill herself,' they said, not at all surprised for it was known they, meaning herself and her cousins, had always been mad.

'She *will* kill herself,' Laurel declared when the wild, hell-raking stories of Tessa Harrison's disdain for her own life and limb became common knowledge and her mother grew old before their eyes, agonising not only on the peril to her daughter's physical safety, but on that to her mind.

'Why don't you come to the mill with me, lass?' she asked carefully one day in September. 'Come and see what you make of it.'

'Drew and Pearce made nothing of it, Mother,' she answered in that coolly impersonal voice in which she addressed Jenny Harrison, 'so why should I?'

'You have more sense than the two of them put together, if you'd care to put it to some use.'

'At the mill, you mean?'

'Aye, why not? It helped me when I was ...'

'What, Mother?'

'When I needed my mind taking off things.'

'And is that what I need?'

'You are still ... still not yourself, lass,' she said awkwardly. Neither am I, she thought and can you wonder after what has happened to us both? The very foundation of their lives had been disturbed, roots which they had thought to be securely settled almost torn out, roots which were still shaky and prey to any stray breeze which might blow against them. It was as though the rock to which they had both thought themselves firmly fastened had become dislodged and they must take care, in their fragile relationship, not to tumble down the scree which loomed beneath them.

'I didn't hear you come in last night, Tessa, and I was awake until past midnight. I know it's the acceptable thing for young men to go skylarking into the early hours, but it won't do for you.'

'It's a bit late to be concerned about my reputation, Mother, if that's what's bothering you, and I was not out all night. And besides, Nicky and Johnny are as good as brothers to me, just as Drew and Pearce were, and until they return home I'm quite safe with their friends.'

'That's as maybe...'

'We only rode up to Friar's Mere to see if the ghosts of the monks really do walk as they say they do when the moon is full.'

'Why, in heaven's name?'

'Why not, Mother? It is no more senseless than your going each day to the mill to watch cotton being spun and woven.'

'That cotton buys the fine blood horses you ride and that outrageous outfit you wear.'

'Mother ... if you don't mind I am due at the...'

'Lass, I'm only trying to help you. To give you something ... a purpose, a road to set your feet on again.'

'Really, Mother, I have a road...'

'No, you have not. A wild track, that's all, and where will it lead?'

'Can you honestly see me doing what you do all day? Sitting at my desk planning business strategy, dealing with commercial gentlemen from Manchester or wherever it is they come from? I would not know a bale of raw cotton from a ... from a carding machine, nor a mule from a loom, and as for the financial side, well, it's as incomprehensible to me as how to sew a fine seam.'

'You could learn, child, and it would give you some diversion other than riding about the countryside with that wild pack of your cousins' friends. You need something else besides ...'

'I have something else, Mother. I have been invited to go down to Leicestershire with the Longworths. The Squire's lady seems to have relented and pardoned me my lapse of good manners of last year. She seems to be of the opinion that having been ... been jilted by a gentleman whom I, a member of the manufacturing classes, should not have had the ill-breeding to monopolise in the first place, I can now be forgiven. I can consider myself under *her* patronage, she says, providing I don't try to marry her son.'

The young soldier lay on the narrow cot. Every time he twisted his racked body the blanket which covered him was thrown violently aside and each time it fell, the second soldier who sat by his bed patiently recovered it and patted it tenderly back into place.

The enormous room was filled with the subdued murmur of men's voices, some, like this soldier, babbling in delirium, others whispering, mumbling, staring upwards into the high, vaulted ceiling, some perhaps praying, others on the road to recovery or not so badly hurt or ill, talking quietly to one another.

There was a mixture of odours, the overall stench of putrefaction and vomit, of blood and excrement, almost but not quite masked by the smell of good carbolic soap and antiseptic.

A nurse stopped and put a hand on the brow of the

soldier in the bed, smiling at the man who sat beside him. She was decently dressed in a neat grey gown over which she wore a huge white apron. Her hair was confined in a white cap and she reminded the soldier of a capable nanny he had had as a child. There were a dozen or more just like her, moving from bed to bed; others were scrubbing floors, up to their elbows in buckets of lye-soap as they patiently attempted to keep at bay the cholera, the typhus, the dysentery and the half a dozen other diseases which were killing more men than had been cut down in battle.

The war with Russia was almost over. Sebastopol had finally fallen but out of the 405,000 men committed to the Crimean War by the British and the French, almost 26,000 were killed on the field and a staggering 39,000 from disease.

'Does your wound need dressing again, Mr Greenwood?' the nurse said gently to the man by the bed.

'No thank you, nurse. It's almost healed now. You have been most kind.'

'You really should go back to your lodgings, you know. Your brother is in good hands and should there be any change I will send an orderly for you.'

'I would be most grateful if I might be allowed to stay for a while longer. We were ... are ... very close and if he should ... Well, we are twins, you see.'

'Yes, that is very evident, Mr Greenwood.' The nurse smiled and hesitated, her kind eyes studying the thin, paper-white face of the young man by the bed, then the flushed and hectic one on the pillow. 'Very well, a few more minutes, but the surgeon will be here soon and...' She hesitated again as though weighing her words before speaking. 'I ... well, I'm sure you are aware of the seriousness of your brother's condition.'

'Yes.'

'The stump has not healed and is ... I'm so sorry, Mr Greenwood, but I'm afraid the gangrene has taken a firm hold and the surgeon is certain we will have to ... cut again.'

The young man bowed his head, no immediate expression of any sort crossing his young/old face and the nurse felt an urge to put out a hand to him for he was no more than a boy. He raised his head and smiled as though he was trying to spare her pain and she felt a hint of the charm he must once have possessed in another world than this, shine through to please her woman's heart.

'Yes, I understand, nurse. I will remain, if I may, until the surgeon has been.'

The soldier on the bed began to fling his arms about and his hands clawed desperately at his face. His head moved frantically from side to side on his sweat-stained pillow.

'Get them off me ... Sweet Christ, I can't breathe ... please, oh, please ... I can't breathe ... heavy ... get them off me ... Jesus, oh, Jesus ... It's the mill all over again, the bloody mill ... suffocating ... I won't go in again, Charlie, I swear it ...'

His voice ended on a despairing scream and the nurse looked about her hurriedly, for the morphine with which he was drugged was evidently wearing off and some more must be administered by the doctor.

'And you shan't, old fellow, you shan't. Do you think I would let them take you in there again, knowing how you hate it?' The young man's voice was soft and filled with love. The soldier calmed somewhat as his brother's hand smoothed his hair back from his fevered brow and his eyes, almost submerged in the swollen flesh about them, opened a little.

'Brother ...' He managed the semblance of a smile.

'I'm here, lad, I'm here.'

'I was having one of those damnable nightmares.' His expression was apologetic.

'I know.'

'I'm ... glad you're here ...'

277

'You can't get rid of me, lad. The proverbial bad penny...'

'I'd ... I'd have liked to see her again.'

'You will, old chap, just as soon as we get you on your feet.'

'You'll make sure she knows I love her.'

'You'll tell her yourself...' But the soldier's vivid blue eyes had become unfocused again and the brightness of delirium had returned as his voice rambled on about the loveliness of the golden bracken and the swiftness of his bay which would take him to her. He did not want to spend his life in that accursed weaving shed, he declared irritably, when there were so many other more pleasurable things to do. The fox ... it was away...

He was drowsy now as the drug administered by the doctor took effect and it was only then that the man beside him broke down. What fools life made of us, was his agonised thought, when his brother's life could now be measured only in hours.

It was to Annie that Tessa first spoke of Will Broadbent.

'What of Will?' she asked carelessly. 'Does he still call on you?'

'Aye, whenever 'e can.'

'And is he well?'

'Champion.' And nowt to do with you, her manner said but Tessa was never one to be put out by Annie's close-mouthed asperity.

'Is he ... did he become manager? There was talk of it the last time we met.'

'No.'

'*No?* Then who got the job? And why didn't he?'

'It weren't for 'im, 'e said. 'E were after summat else an' so 'e 'opped it.'

' 'Opped it? Whatever does that mean, for God's sake?'

'Look, my girl, I don't press you ter tell me what came o' that chap you was to wed and then never, so don't you go pokin' yer nose in Will Broadbent's business. It's nowt ter do wi' you.'

'Annie ... Dear God, don't ...'

Instantly Annie was sorry. She had not meant to be so unkind. Had she not been aware that though Tessa had spoken not one word about the surprising disappearance of the man she was to marry, his going had devastated her? She had been ill and Annie had made enquiries about her and had even sent a note but she had received no reply. Not that that concerned her but she had never quite forgiven Tessa for her indifference to Will Broadbent last year. Now here she was asking casual questions just as though he had been no more than an acquaintance.

''E's gone.' Her manner was short, since, like affection, humility was hard to demonstrate.

'Really, Annie, if you don't stop this ... this foolishness I swear I'll throttle you. Can you not just answer a simple question with a simple answer instead of all this evasiveness?'

'I don't reckon I know what that means but 'e's gone an' I were told yer Mam an' Mr Greenwood were right upset when 'e went. 'E's an 'ead on 'is shoulders 'as Will and Mr Greenwood told 'im so 'an all.'

For some unaccountable reason Tessa felt her heart begin to thud in her chest and she was reluctant to let Annie see the awkward and stiff set of her shoulders. She stood up and moved to the window, staring out into Annie's scrap of garden.

'What is he doing then?'

''E's gone up Rochdale way. 'E's brought the Chadwick spinners and weavers together to form a co-operative and run their own industrial enterprise. Will set up a committee, apparently with 'imself as chairman. They've found t'capital, Will said, by selling shares at five pounds each an' all't shares were sold within't week.' Annie spoke with the care of a child who repeats some passage she has learned by heart but does not really understand.

279

'They bought some land at a penny a yard, close to't railway where there's a siding an't mill were built an' in business in six months. There's 400 looms fer weavin' and 20,000 spindles fer spinnin'. Will ses that at the first 'alf-yearly meetin' of't company an' the 450 shareholders, they'd already med a decent profit an' look set fer a prosperous future. Will's managin' director an' the last time chap what I were talkin' to saw 'im he were ridin' in a carriage wi' a pretty woman at side of 'im. Whether it were 'is carriage or 'ers I couldn't tell thi. Now then, did y'ever think ter see't day when a pauper's brat, fer that were what he was, could rise ter such heights? Mind, he were a good tackler, were Will. 'E knew engines an' e' knew cotton from't minute it come from't bale right through t't piece goods. An' 'e were fair wi' people. Now it seems as 'ow 'e's got a feel fer business an' all.'

Annie turned triumphantly to Tessa as though to say, "There, see what can be done with what you considered a mere working-class man not fit for the likes of you," but Tessa was staring out of the window, her mind far away, scarcely listening and Annie sighed heavily.

Later Tessa rode down the long slope from Badger's Edge to Crossfold. The sun was red as it sank over the Pennine hills. There was a great stillness in the air, as there was in her heart and she wondered about it: was it a sadness about what might have been, or was it indifference to what had been?

She could hear a dog bark at the back of the house as she rode towards it and some bird singing in praise of the beauty of the autumn day. For a moment in the poignancy which drifted like cobwebs about her, through which, if she was not vigilant, she might have to fight her way, she let Will's face etch itself sharply on her mind. A strong face and arrogant. Not with the arrogance of Drew and Pearce Greenwood nor of Nicky Longworth who all considered themselves to be somewhat above the rest of mankind, but with the sureness of a man who knows his own strength and what he will do with it. Not a handsome face. Vulnerable at times in his love for her since she admitted now that he had loved her. Smoky brown eyes flecked sometimes with green and at others with amber. Curling hair, ordinary, cut short to his head so as not to cause him any trouble. A slanting, humorous smile to his curving mouth, a sardonic twist to it, a lifting of his heavy eyebrows, a smooth and freshly shaved brown cheek.

Will Broadbent, then. A man she had admired and in a physical sense of the word, loved. A dependable man, truthful, sensuous, gentle, all these words described him and once, years ago it seemed, all this had belonged to her. She had turned away from him, chasing a dream of her own, careless of his hurt and the days which would be so empty for him without her. There were other women in the world for him to love, she had told herself as she had wound herself into Robby Atherton's arms, and now he had found one. What was so bewildering was the hard knot of something in the middle of her chest which she could not identify and which would not go away.

# 18

The tall, extremely thin young gentleman had changed trains at Manchester and Oldham on his long journey from London. His bearing was very evidently that of an army man though surprisingly, since he *was* a gentleman, he was not an officer. He was dressed in a motley collection of clothing: the peaked cap of a soldier of the line with the greatcoat of a foot guardsman. His boots were of the Household Cavalry but they were unpolished. There was an air about him of indifferent disregard for his appearance as though that morning he had taken the first garments to hand, whatever they may have been, and flung them on his uncaring body.

He got off the train at Crossfold and walked slowly along the platform. The station clock was five minutes fast, for every village and town in Britain kept its own time, several minutes before or after that in London, and idly he wondered why.

The journey had been comfortable. Despite his extreme shabbiness he had travelled first class in a coach which was based on the style of the old stage coach. Through his inertia he had felt a slight pang of pity for those who had travelled third class for the weather was wet and extremely cold. The poor devils had sat in waggons which, unlike some which had sides and seats, were open to the elements and any stray spark from the engine was a definite threat. Passing through tunnels which poured down floods of dirty water, they must have arrived so wet, bedraggled, and begrimed it was a marvel to him they travelled at all.

The station was almost deserted. A trolley heaped with trunks and boxes indicated that someone of importance had arrived while another was piled with milk churns which a porter was trundling briskly towards the goods van. The gas lights had been lit for it was almost dusk. Soon spring would be here but this March day reminded him of the winter he had spent – was it only a year ago – on the harsh Crimean plains with . . .

His face moved jerkily and his hand was seen to reach out as though to some unseen companion but he continued his slow and steady pace towards the ticket collector. He handed the man his ticket and briefly their eyes met. The man had seen a hundred such as he in the past six months, dragging themselves back from the Crimea, many worse than he with no coats to their backs, no boots to their feet, no feet, unemployable and bitter. This one, however, he knew personally. Well, not personally, but who in the Penfold Valley was not familiar with the Greenwood brothers?

Those blue eyes which were said to have dazzled and charmed the ladies from here to Burnley, were not so bright now, and not so insolent as once they had been.

'Mr Greenwood, sir,' he said respectfully, for they were all aware that these two lads had fought for Queen and country and were to be recognised for their bravery.

*Two lads?* Then where was the other? He stared after Mr Greenwood's retreating back, arrow-straight and with not so much meat as it had once carried, and wondered which one it was who had been left behind. Not that it mattered really, for there had not been much to choose between them for devilment.

It was dark when the hansom cab he had hired reached Greenacres, the early dark of a dismal March day. As he stepped from the cab he could smell the rich, damp earth and the faint aroma of daffodils. Daffodils have no perfume, he thought wonderingly, and perhaps it was his imagination but he knew he could smell them just as clearly as he could see them in his mind's eye, bobbing and dancing merrily in the wind which whipped straight down from the bleak moorland.

Light streamed from every window of the house, lying in bands across the garden: lamps lit in rooms in which no one would sit, fires glowing where no one would linger. So it had always been since he was a child and before, he supposed, in this household where once there had been no mistress to supervise what the servants did and so they had done what their previous mistress had told them. There was comfort and warmth, always, and an abundance of good, splendidly prepared and cooked food which the servants ate too, naturally, and he pondered on it for the first time in his life.

The great oak door opened when he rang the bell and Briggs was there, his face smooth and expressionless, though it was certain that in his mind was the disapproving thought that it could be no gentleman calling, unannounced, at this time of the evening.

His jaw dropped and he put a hand to his own heart and for a moment there was a warmth in his eyes, almost, one might say, a hint of moisture.

'Sir ... oh, sir ...' he gabbled, ready to move forward, to grasp the young gentleman's hand. Then he remembered himself. He straightened and stepped back, his duties recalled but the gladness still gleamed in his eye.

'Welcome home, sir. It is indeed a pleasure to have you home.'

'Thank you, Briggs. It is good to be home.'

The butler waited for a moment, holding the door wide open as the young gentleman stepped inside, smiling, looking beyond him to the porch, the beginning of bewilderment on his face as the hansom disappeared into the darkness of the drive.

'Master ...? Er ... you are alone, sir?' he ventured, slowly closing the door on the cold and windy darkness, reaching out to his young master, eager to take the shabby army greatcoat from him, to relieve him of the quite battered cap and his one piece of pitiful hand luggage. Beneath the greatcoat he wore the torn and mouldering battle-dress, once a brilliant scarlet, with one epaulette missing, of a common soldier of the line.

In Briggs' eye flashed the picture of the last time he had seen Joss Greenwood's sons, immaculately dressed then in expensively tailored coats and breeches, fine cambric shirts and peacock, watered-silk waistcoats, with boots as superbly polished as the tall bays they rode. Their faces had been dark and dashing, excited by something known only to them, laughing, heedless and reckless as they galloped off madly down the drive intent on some mischief, he had thought sourly.

And in the two years they had been away something dreadful had happened to them. Here was Master Drew – or was it Pearce? – looking as though he had had the stuffing well and truly knocked out of him, and where was Master Pearce, or was it Drew?

'Is my aunt at home, Briggs?'

'Indeed, sir. She and the family are at dinner.' He was about to ask should he announce him, for really he was a stranger but this was his home and he was at liberty to go where he pleased.

His master swayed slightly and Briggs put out his hand solicitously.

'Miss ... Miss Tessa...?' he whispered so softly Briggs could barely hear him.

'Indeed, sir.'

Master Drew – or was it Pearce for heaven's sake? He must ask him, Briggs thought irritably – continued to stand in the middle of the hall, quite incapable, Briggs thought, or so it appeared, of deciding whether to go or stay.

'Are you unwell, sir?' he asked, wondering whether to offer his master a seat.

'Miss Tessa, you said...?'

'Yes, sir.'

'And her ... is she alone?'

'Alone, sir? I'm afraid I don't understand.' Dear God, surely he had not been ... well, damaged in his head? He seemed quite dazed, and yet so quiet no one could be afraid of him.

'Has her ... is her...?'

'Yes, sir?'

'Is her husband with her?'

'Husband?' Briggs' mouth fell open. 'Why, sir, Miss Tessa has no husband ... Dear me, what made you...?' Then he stopped for it was not his place to question the son of the house on his obviously confused state of mind.

The young master began to walk unsteadily across the hall. 'I'll go in then, Briggs.'

'Very well, Master ... er ... I'll fetch Dorcas out, sir, for you and ... you'll want to greet your...'

They all stood up, pushing back their chairs quite violently. Dorcas sketched a frantic curtsey as she passed him in the open doorway, her own face wet with sudden tears.

Then Briggs closed the door quietly behind him as he always did.

There was complete silence for the space of ten seconds, though it seemed longer, then Tessa's voice murmured something in a hushed whisper. It was not clear what she said, even to herself, for it had been no more than a devastated recognition, a wailing cry of torment deep inside her at the realisation that whereas two of her beloved cousins had gone to war, only one had come back.

'Charlie ... Aunt Jenny...' He stood, like a small whipped boy, not awfully sure what he should do to get himself across the vast expanse of carpet to the comfort he so desperately needed, the haven from the pain, the hoped-for refuge in which to hide whilst he attempted the healing of the part of him which had been torn away at the hospital in Scutari.

'Oh, dear, sweet Lord...' Charlie began to walk towards him and Laurel sat down again abruptly, her eyes enormous and glittering in her ashen face. His Aunt Jenny put her hand to her mouth and for the first time in his life – another first, he thought dully – he saw her weep. She seemed to be incapable of movement, standing beside the table in her elegant silk gown, crucified, it seemed to him, by some dreadful emotion which surely could not have been aroused merely by his homecoming.

'Oh, my sweet boy...' he heard her say, amazingly, then he saw nothing else, felt nothing else but the strong, steady, infinitely loving, endlessly compassionate arms of Tessa Harrison as she put them around him, enfolding him in the first scrap of peace he had known since his brother had died in his arms. His own arms were about her, clutching desperately, for surely the strength which had held him upright from Scutari to this moment was about to slip away, finally, and only she could keep him on his feet.

'Tessa ... Tessa ... Tessa...' he said over and over again, his face buried in her shoulder, the soft, sweet-smelling curve of her neck, her gown already wet with his agonised tears.

'Sit down. For Christ's sake, sit him down,' Charlie was saying harshly, his own arms ready to support him should Tessa's prove inadequate.

'Darling, come ... let me hold you...' He felt her turn for a moment, frantically, to Charlie who hovered beside them, bidding him open the door ... the morning room ... more comfortable ... more coal on the fire ... hot coffee ... Then he was in the depth of the soft sofa, the fire warm on his bare feet – he had no socks, of course, but where had his boots gone? – and her arms were still about him, her shoulder there for him to lean on. His aunt's hand, steadier now, was holding a cup of something hot and delicious to his lips, while Laurel ... and Charlie ... were weeping and all the time he shook like the trembling aspens which lined the lake. He must pull himself together, regain his composure for at least as long as it would take to tell them of what had happened, and suffer again that frozen state of senseless, unfeeling shock he had known for the past eight weeks and in which he could endure the telling. Then, and only then, would he let it all wash over him, re-live it, fall into the nightmare which, when it was told, would surely once and for all be done with.

'Darling, can you speak of it now?' Tessa said, her lovely grey eyes as soft and shadowed as the drifting veil of the mist which so often covered Friar's Mere. There was a lingering desolation in the expression on her face, as if she knew what he was to tell her and was not certain she would ever recover from it, but it must be said. 'We are not sure...' Her voice was but a whisper. She looked up swiftly at her mother, not smiling for that would be impossible now, but with a memory of the past when Drew and Pearce Greenwood had played boyish pranks, changing places as easily as two coins from the same mint. They had relished the confusion, or sometimes the lack of it for quite often no one was aware that a trick had been played.

So, who was this in her arms? Which loved man? No matter which one, she would mourn the other until her dying day.

'Which ... who ...?' Her voice cracked with the depth of her sorrow.

'Pearce died in the hospital at Scutari.'

It was said and she could not bear it, and neither could he.

They sat for almost an hour with their arms about one another, saying nothing. On the other side of the fireplace Jenny Harrison sat in a low, velvet, button-back chair, a ladies' chair in a ladies' room, and watched them compassionately. Charlie had his arms about Laurel who was weeping as though her heart was broken. The morning-room had long been a family room, less formal than the drawing-room where guests were received, and it seemed appropriate now that the family should begin their grief here. The room had a lived-in air, homely and slightly untidy with books lying about, today's newspapers crumpled on a low table, sheet music standing open on the piano, playing cards in a box, not opened since Pearce and Drew went away. It was here that Drew Greenwood began to feel the emptiness, the dead and sterile shell which had been left when Pearce died, begin to fill with what he knew would be his own agony. He must speak of it before the pain became too much for him.

'We were in the last bombardment of Sebastopol,' he said simply, staring into the fire, his eyes far, far away on the barren plain which they had come to know so well. 'What a lark, we thought, on that first day. What fun to be there, amidst the excitement and adventure, away from the mills and the deadly boredom of the hours we spent in them,' and away from you whom we both loved, Tessa Harrison, though he could not say it, of course. 'We couldn't wait to leap on our mounts and follow the soldiers, the cavalry, to fight in the glorious battle we were convinced it would be.'

He paused, capturing that unbelievable, almost forgotten,

carefree youthfulness. 'We lost our horses on that very first day. Do you remember them, Tessa? Such lovely animals who had not been trained for ... They were terrified ... We killed them, Pearce and I, just as surely as if we had put a revolver to their heads. It would have been more humane if we had done so. Mine got a sabre thrust in his belly ... he was screaming. I don't know what happened to Pearce's: I didn't ask. You got like that, you know. You never asked anyone what had happened to them. At the end of the day you simply slipped into your tent and if the next time you were mustered there was a face missing, a dozen faces you had known the day before, you didn't ask.'

'No ...' Tessa's hand soothed his forehead.

'I saw Lord Raglan once, you know.' His voice was soft, his thoughts not marshalled into any particular order, just uttered as they came into his head.

'Did you, darling?'

'We were always wet. For months we were wet. In the trenches ...'

'Why were you in the trenches, Drew? You were not soldiers.'

'No ... I don't remember now.' He passed his hand over his face as though in a dream. How could he tell them the reason he and Pearce could not come home? How could he tell them the reason they went in the first place? 'It was ... there was nothing else to do. They thought we were soldiers so they fed us what there was.' He looked down at the odds and ends of his uniform. 'We lost all our clothing ... a shell, and the dead have no use of ... what they wore. Those boots belonged to an officer. I did him a kindness so ... as he lay dying he said I must have them. A decent fellow. From Norfolk I believe.'

'And then ... Pearce ... ?'

'Yes. Well, we survived two years almost though thousands and thousands didn't and then ... there was to be an attack on the Redan. There were 12,000 men there to defend it, we were told and we were to send only 4,000 stormers and supporters. If it had been ... different, we might have laughed. A handful of men expected to take and hold an open work defended by thirty-two battalions of Russian infantry! But we did it ... we did it. The Light Division and the 2nd Division. We got in but instead of storming on after the retreating Russians we were ordered to extend on the parapets and begin to fire ...'

His voice tailed away as in his memory he re-lived that fatal day, that fatal hour, that fatal order which had, finally, cost his brother his life.

'They came back at us. They pressed us closer and closer. We ran out of ammunition and were forced to throw stones ... stones against bullets and shell and sabre and bayonet ...'

There was a long and dreadful silence as the five people in the pleasant room observed quite clearly the pictures one of them had conjured up.

'We were forced over the parapet and into a ditch, every one of us who was left. Those who could, scrambled up, running the gauntlet of fire, of grape and musketry. The Russians were cheering, manning the parapets which we had just left, firing into the chaos of bleeding, falling soldiers, into the heaps of our men who lay in the ditches unable to crawl out. They even brought up two field-pieces and ...'

Again he fell silent, his mind beginning to close instinctively against the pain of what came next, knowing he must tell it, but not sure that he could finish.

'Leave it, Drew. Let it rest now. Let us get you to bed ...'

'I felt a blow to my arm. I thought ... I didn't know I'd been hit until I fell. There were dozens of us there ... one on top of the other, dead and wounded. Pearce was shouting that we should make a run for it but something pinned me down. I didn't seem able to extricate myself though I felt no pain. I didn't know I'd been hit, you see. "Come on, brother," he shouted again. "Don't just lie there or must I carry you, you lazy devil." He was grinning, you know how

'... he was. He had bent down, ready to heave me to my feet when the shell hit the ... a dozen yards away. He caught the full blast ... his legs ... were ...'

'Oh, God, oh, dear God ...' Was it Tessa or her mother who cried out?

'When I came to I couldn't find him. I went crazy, I think. My arm ... my arm was ... I don't know ... bloody and ... somebody held me down while they dressed it. Then I ran from man to man ... hundreds of them lying on the bare ground. It was a lovely day ... autumn. The sun shone on them ... Dear God ... I found him two days later. They were about to put him on a ship for Scutari. His ... feet ... please, Tessa, hold on to me ... his feet were gone, both of them, and ...'

'Drew ... oh, Drew ... please, I cannot bear it ...'

'... so I went with him. I stayed with him on the hospital ship but ... the surgeons tried ... he would not heal ... the gangrene had ...'

Tessa wept blindly, clinging to him now, tortured by the picture of handsome, dashing Pearce Greenwood brought down to the pitiful agonised creature, dying by inches in a foreign land with no one but his brother to care what happened to him. And yet, who else would he have chosen, had he had the choice, but this man who was part of him, who had shared the same womb, the same cradle, the same rip-roaring childhood and reckless youth? This brother he had loved and who had loved and comforted his pain until the end.

'He died in November. It took him two months. They kept ... taking off a bit more. But I was with him, he was in my arms when he went.'

His voice was spent, his head drooping, his face quite blank, empty of pain, of regret, of everything but the need to fall, for the moment, into oblivion.

'What have you been doing since then, lad?' Charlie's voice was neutral as though he was holding himself, and Drew with him, by a tight and tenuous thread to the world of reality, to this world in which they now were and in which they must spend the rest of their days without Pearce Greenwood.

'Nothing much, really. We buried him . . . the nurses were kind. They came to his funeral. Then I stayed on. I could not bear to leave him, you see, by himself in that land which had killed him. I helped in the hospital . . .'

'Why did you not write?'

'I wanted to tell you myself . . . about him.'

'We were so anxious. Your mother was . . . and your father tried to find out what had happened to you . . .'

'Did he? How strange.'

'Why do you say that? You are his . . . were . . . his sons . . .'

'He took no great interest when we were here.' It was said with no rancour, just a great and engulfing weariness. He sighed, his face grey like the ash in the fireplace, his eyes deep in liver-coloured hollows.

She heard him screaming from his room along the corridor. She had fallen into a light, haunted doze, the night almost gone, exhaustion and grief overtaking her at last, and when the sound began she sat up in bed with her heart pounding, disorientated, with the tail end of the dream she had been in still lingering in her frightened mind.

They had been up on Badger's Edge, the three of them, sharing the easy laughter which was part of their companionship. The horses had cropped the grass close by, their reins dangling and the dogs sprawled about them, dozing with their muzzles resting on their paws. How lovely it all was, she had been thinking, as Pearce's eyes, as blue and brilliant as the turquoise in the necklace her aunt wore, smiled into hers, when the sky, the great familiar vault which had hung over them all their lives in every colour from the palest oyster to the deepest purple, simply erupted, emptying hundreds of bodies from its glorious arch, pouring them down upon their heads, flinging them willy-nilly about the plateau until they were heaped in great obscene piles. Heads and limbs were twisted in unnatural angles from their torsos, flaccid and writhing, and from beneath them, sticking up into the soft summer air, was one living hand. It clenched and twisted, begging to be let free and she could hear his voice ... Pearce's or was it Drew's, from somewhere beneath ... Pearce ... ?

Oh, God! Oh, dear God. It *was* Drew and his voice was becoming more shrill with every passing second.

She bumped into her mother on the landing. The night was as black as pitch, no light filtering through the heavy curtains which shrouded each window. Briggs, as was his duty last thing at night, had extinguished every lamp and the corridor was like a long, dark tunnel. There had been no thought in her mind of lighting the candle at her bedside nor any of the lamps which stood about her bedroom, since her instinct had been to get to him as quickly as she could, to extricate him from the mass of corpses which were slowly burying him alive and under which his mind was slipping into madness.

How did she know? *How did she know?*

There were tables along the passage, each with its own lamp, and after crashing into her mother, no more than a pale, shapeless shadow against the open doorway of her own bedroom, her hip caught one, sending it in a spray of splintered glass to the floor.

'Sweet Jesus,' she heard her mother gasp and from some dark place above them came the sound of quavering female voices asking what was to do and a deeper one, male, ordering them to be quiet and get back to their beds where they belonged.

He was still asleep when they stood over him, she and her mother, his mouth a blacker hole in the blackness in which he lay. He was clawing at his bedclothes, his hands tearing and twisting, his arms pushing at something, his head moving frantically from side to side as he gasped for air. The screaming had subsided to a low, frantic moaning

293

and when her mother lit the lamp at his bedside his eyes flew open and stared up into the flickering shadows the light cast on the ceiling. He became perfectly still, not even breathing for a moment, then his head turned slowly on the pillow, so slowly and carefully it was as though he was desperately afraid of what he might see.

Tessa knelt down beside him and put a hand on his cheek, stroking it, brushing back his sweat-drenched hair, making small noises in her throat, the noises all mothers make to frightened children, saying nothing which made much sense, but soothing him with the sounds, calming him.

'Tessa, oh Tessa...' His breath shuddered violently in his throat.

'Yes, darling, I'm here.'

'I was...'

'I know...' With delicate tenderness she put her arms under his head and drew him towards her, cradling him against her with a little sigh. She put her lips gently to his brow and he lifted his own arms and clung to her, his face in the soft, sweet-smelling division between her breasts, her hair falling about him like a protective shield. She felt his stiff body fall slowly into peace and his breath drift from his mouth against the curve of her breast. He was thin, frail, and his bones felt brittle beneath her hands. Her heart was squeezed with love and pity and on her face was a look her mother had never seen before.

She watched them for a moment, Jenny Harrison, then, making a decision which even then she was not sure was right, turned and walked from the room, closing the door behind her.

for their own person will remain by a mad a place
she would she walked up into the darkness, shadows the
light cast on the ceiling becoming indistinct, her rather
breathing for nursing on the her head ticked she was on the
pillow, to whole bed for a full of true as a snicker, the expres-
to be and when he overhead cooperating reminded of the
eyes blind soul setting looking down guilty with cheeks as
obscurely negating as a child, Beside her had more those
when her less ever had been born, perhaps otherwise have

## 19

Laurel watched them anxiously as they walked hand in hand
from the terrace and down the smooth sweep of lawn which
led through a series of terraces, flower beds and smoothly
clipped box-hedges; beyond the massed rhododendrons
and ornamental rose beds to the rougher grass which surrounded the lake. Her face was creased with doubt and in
her eyes was an expression of unease.

'Really, Aunt Jenny, do you not think it is time Tessa put
away those extraordinary garments she insists on wearing
and dressed in a manner more suitable to her station in life?
I had hoped she might be going to do so recently but since
Drew returned she is as improperly dressed as ever. She is
nineteen now and surely too old for such things.'

She stood at the window of the morning room. It was
Sunday and breakfast, a leisurely affair on this one day of
the week when the mills were closed, was almost over. She
would go up to the nursery floor soon to direct the activities
of her nursemaids, of Nanny who was in charge of baby Joel,
of Henry and Jane, of the governess Miss Gaunt who gave
lessons to six-year-old Robert and five-year-old Anne, of Miss
Copeland who had been her own governess, and Tessa's,
and still helped out in the schoolroom. Miss Copeland was
over sixty now but still very useful in her own supervision
of the young woman who had come to take her place and
Laurel would not have dreamed of pensioning her off to
some cottage on the estate. Anyone who was able to perform
some task which would leave Laurel with more freedom for

her many social obligations would always be found a place in her household.

'What were you saying, dear?' Charlie was deep in yesterday's newspapers and did not even look up. He was well accustomed to his wife's anxiety over almost everything her cousin did, or said, and was once again reminded of the deepseated and strange feeling of insecurity she had unconsciously acquired as a child. It made him gentle with his wife, perhaps more indulgent than he might otherwise have been. He held her in considerable affection, a protective and obligatory affection which had never faltered. He made love to her when she would allow it, not often for she had conceived six times in nine years, bearing five live children, and she wanted no more. He knew she did her best, running this house ~nd her children with efficiency and a certain good humour; this was what she wanted and was a way of life she understood. But, and he knew he must be honest about it, she was somewhat jealous of Tessa Harrison, and it soured her life.

'I was remarking to Aunt Jenny that it was time Tessa grew out of the notion that she is a boy and not a young woman and gave up wearing those ridiculous breeches. Will you look at her . . .'

They made a stunning couple, there was no doubt about it but Charlie could see what it was that made his wife so uneasy. Tessa simply drew every male eye to her wherever she went. She had become a gloriously sensuous woman, there was no other description for her, and yet she was still no more than an innocent girl. Where did she get that flaunting, outrageous, and fascinating – and Charlie was aware that there was not a man who came within a hundred yards of her who was not fascinated – magnetism? He drew in his breath sharply, then looked away, not wishing his wife to see him admiring such splendour. He caught his sister's eye and grimaced, aware, awkwardly, that she knew exactly what was in his mind. She did not blame him for it since, though he was Tessa's uncle, he was still a man.

296

'She does no harm, Laurel,' Jenny said mildly, folding her own newspaper and standing up to move towards them. 'You must admit she has done wonders with Drew in the last three months.'

'But everyone is talking about them.'

'I can't see why. They have done nothing they have not been doing all their lives.'

'But alone. Just the two of them.'

'What are you suggesting?' Jenny's voice had become cool.

'I am suggesting nothing, Aunt Jenny, I am only repeating what has been implied to me in every drawing-room in Crossfold. They are never apart. He clings to her hand wherever they go for everyone to see and she makes no objection.'

'He is her cousin. His brother died in harrowing circumstances. He is only just beginning to recover. And who else would he turn to but Tessa? She is the closest to him after Pearce.'

'Oh, I know all that, but I must say I find it extremely embarrassing having to listen to my friends, not in so many words, naturally, for they are ladies, but intimating nevertheless that there is more to it than cousinly affection.'

'Fiddlesticks.' Turning on her heel Jenny swept from the room but not before Charlie had seen the uncertain expression on his sister's face.

'And shouldn't he be back at the mill by now?' Laurel continued, allowing her voice to rise plaintively now that there was only her husband to hear it.

'He'll go back when he's ready.'

'Heavens, he's been home three months already. How much longer is he going to lark about like the young squire?'

'He needs time, Laurel. You know how close he was to Pearce.' Charlie tried to be patient, realising that Tessa, and now Drew, threatened Laurel's security in some curious way which was not even clear to herself.

'I think he is making it an excuse not to go back to the mill.' Charlie thought so too, but with far more understanding than Laurel since he had seen his nephew's distaste for the work they had been expected to do there. Neither of them had been true 'commercial men' as he and Jenny were, and he tried to imagine how he would feel if he was forced to work at something he loathed. But then hundreds and thousands did so for it was that or starve and not many were as privileged as Drew Greenwood.

Drew had changed quite dramatically from the pale, devastatingly thin and hollow-eyed shadow he had been on his return. As handsome and strong as ever, his old audacity showed in the brilliance of his vivid blue eyes when he and Tessa rode to the top of Badger's Edge, the ghost of Pearce Greenwood always at their shoulders, to look out on the lovely stretch of summer moorland which swept down to the busy valley, the chimneys of the growing town. It showed in his eagerness to do what he, his brother and Tessa had always done: in their search for anything which might erase the memory of the past two years. But only with her. She was his 'partner', a 'steadier' to the other self Pearce had taken away from him. For three months no one had spoken of the past, nor of the future, knowing his loss and suffering, allowing him to do as he pleased, what best suited him, what best mended him.

Tessa protected him fiercely. He was not to be pressed to resume his duties in the mill, she commanded. Indeed, no one was to mention the mill. They rode out when and where they pleased as the weather improved. He had quickly recovered his boundless health and the humorous, engaging charm he had shared with his brother. Country life, country pursuits that had nothing to do with warp and weft, with yardage and quality, with frames and looms, boilers and steam engines, these were what he sought. He had not survived the hell of the Crimea to spend his days in the hell of his family's mill, his manner said, though he did not voice such an opinion out loud, and no force, no coercion was put on him to do so.

The peace treaty with Russia had been signed at the end

of March and guns were fired in all major towns of Lancashire to signal the end of the hostilities. The armies of the Allies were to return to their own countries as soon as possible, they were told, and there was to be great rejoicing and fireworks on an enormous scale in London.

A naval review by Her Majesty the Queen at Spithead, one of the finest sights the country had ever witnessed, those who saw it reported, showed exactly what England could do in times of war. The fleet was so large it extended for several miles across the Channel and people travelled on the new and exciting railway trains from all parts of the country to see it.

It was not until the end of May that a day was appointed as a national holiday to celebrate this new thing called peace. Hardly before the day had started the guns were booming from Oldham barracks and in every church tower bells rang, fit to wake the dead, Briggs remarked gloomily, and what was the point of it when the war had been over since September? There was to be a celebratory procession with bands and flags, banners and mayoral speeches and Tessa spoke to Charlie on the advisability of risking Drew in the intense fever of patriotic joy which would undoubtedly abound there.

'I don't know if he'll be up to it, Charlie. All the hurly-burly, the noise and confusion, all those people celebrating what was to him ... well, you will know what I mean. The memories ...'

'You can't go on cosseting him forever, lass. You know, you're like a mother cat protecting her kitten whenever anyone threatens his peace of mind. He's bound to think of Pearce, as we all will, but sooner or later, preferably sooner, he must rejoin the world. You and he spend all your time up on the tops, playing with those thoroughbreds of yours in the paddock and racing that curricle you've acquired. Just the two of you, lass, and it really won't do. He's a man and must mix with other men, do what they do. These months have been good for him and have returned him to full health but he needs other things now. All men do, Tessa.' His voice became very quiet. 'And no matter how you both refuse to face it, one day he must return to the mill. It will all belong to him, and when the time comes he must be able to run it alone. With Pearce gone he has no choice but to learn how to go about it.'

'Charlie...' Tessa's face was soft with pity.

'No, lass, he must face up to life again. Take him to the celebration. Put on your prettiest gown' – and let him see you as you are and not as a replacement for Pearce Greenwood, Charlie thought – 'and go and have some fun. I'm sure the Squire's lad will be there.'

'Drew, my God, old chap, it's good to see you. We had heard you were back and have been looking forward to...' Nicky Longworth, with more sensitivity than Tessa would have given him credit for, said no more than that, pumping Drew's hand enthusiastically, terribly glad to claim him for a friend, for was he not something of a hero amongst those with whom he, and Pearce, had once roistered?

'And Tessa. How absolutely splendid you look, doesn't she, Johnny? Why have we not seen you both at the Hall? Why don't you come over...'

She held Drew's arm protectively, waiting for the sudden trembling to subside, and when it did and his face broke into a tentative but pleased smile, she relaxed her grip somewhat. His right hand, when it had been shaken by several more of the 'fellows' who had come over to see the fun, closed over her own where it rested in the crook of his left arm and he squeezed it gently to let her know he was all right.

And they did indeed look splendid, both of them. She wore blue, a lovely cornflower blue that was almost violet. Her jacket fitted neatly to the sweet curve of the bosom she had regained when her flesh returned after her illness, and her enormous skirt was looped about its wide hem with tiny bunches of silk cornflowers. Her bonnet was the same colour, decorated under its brim with masses of white tulle and her blue lace parasol shaded the grey velvet of her eyes.

Drew's face, in the sun-warmed breezes of the days spent in the saddle, had regained its brown smoothness. His dark curly hair was cut short, glossy and thick, tumbling across his wide forehead. His eyes narrowed in a deep and brilliant blue as he smiled at his friends and his mobile mouth curved across strong white teeth. He wore dove grey with a well-cut watered-silk waistcoat. His shirt front was snowy and his boots polished. He had removed his top hat and his tall frame was straight and yet easy, graceful. He looked quite beautiful, she thought proudly as she looked up at him, just as though it was all her doing, and in a way it was. She was the one who walked with him through the tortuous memories which harrowed him, who shored up and filled the gaping hole left by his brother's death, who held him in her arms in the black of the night when his cries brought her from her bed. She it was who had coaxed him to eat, to rest, to doze in the sunshine with his head in her lap, to get up on the new bay he bought and ride again as he had not done for two years. She had brought him back to this hesitant willingness to be a part of life again and she felt a most proud and proprietary self-esteem settle about her.

In the weeks they had been alone together, he talking, weeping, but speaking at last of what he and Pearce had seen in the battles they fought, she listening, weeping with him, he had finally asked her about Robby.

'When Pearce and I left . . . you were to be married,' he said diffidently. Just that, nothing more. A few words which invited her to speak of it if she wished.

'Yes.'

'He . . . you changed your mind?'

'I . . . I was ill.' It was no lie and yet not the full truth. Her face was averted from him and she knew he could not see the expression of pain which flickered across it. Robby Atherton still lay uneasily in her heart. A hard and often despairing desolation struck at her when she least expected

301

it. She loved him still: that was a fact of her life which would not change. How could it? Her mother had told her, from experience she said, that time would heal her, would lessen the ache in her heart, and during the last three months with Drew she had found a certain measure of content. His need had overridden hers. His pain had pushed hers to the back of her conscious mind, tamped it down to bearable proportions in her breast, not lessening it, as her mother said, but easing it somehow as she poured what Robby had left into her compassionate love for Drew. What a tortured pair they were, she and Drew Greenwood, she thought as she turned back to him, the sharing of their misery perhaps making it more bearable.

'I had a fever. I was ill ... off my head for weeks. You know about it, don't you?'

'Yes. Aunt Jenny told me.' His expression was gentle, steady, with something in it which invited her to confide in him, if she wanted to, as he had done with her. They were friends as well as cousins, it said. He was not the young man he had been when he rode away, not yet, but he was more than willing to give her a hand to cling to, if she had nothing else. But somehow, despite his dearness, she could not tell him the whole truth.

'I was not myself. At times it seemed I was not to recover and he did not ... return.' Dear Robby, forgive me for the lie, she whispered in her heart, but it lay easily on her conscience for what else was she to say?

'When you were recovered, you did not let him know?'

'No.'

'Why not, if you wish to tell me?'

'I ... it seemed we were ... no longer suited.'

She looked up and smiled and was startled by the intent expression in his eyes as they stared into hers. A deep and concentrated watchfulness showed there and waited for her answer as though its meaning, the content of it was of the utmost importance.

'You love him still?'

Again there was that breathless attention to her words, a diligent alertness which placed a faint prickle of surprise in her. His eyes studied her minutely, blue, she had never seen them so blue, and he seemed to hold his breath. And she knew, suddenly, though she could not have said how she knew, that her answer was vital to him and for his peace of mind it must be the right answer.

'One must have a love returned for it to flourish, Drew,' she said softly, knowing as she said it that he was satisfied.

They began to widen their activities. He took her to see a play at the assembly rooms in Crossfold, *Richard III* which was staged quite splendidly considering that it was not put on at an established theatre such as those in Oldham or Manchester. He was quite shaken by the press of his family's acquaintances who rushed to shake him by the hand, expressing their joy in seeing him 'himself' again, not mentioning Pearce, perhaps warned against it by the savage look on Tessa Harrison's face. She held fast to him like a tendril of clinging ivy, they noticed, those mamas whose daughters might, now that he was home and apparently settled down from the hellion he had once been, be pushed in his direction. Was there any truth in the rumours that circulated about them, they wondered to one another? True, they had always galloped wildly about the countryside ever since they had been children, but there had been three of them then, which made a difference, one must admit, from just one man and one woman! And they did seem completely wrapped up in one another since it was noticed that his eyes followed her every movement. Was Jenny Harrison keeping something from them, they asked one another? But the question was still unanswered.

Nicky Longworth remarked to Johnny Taylor as they discussed it over a bottle of his father's best claret that there really could have been nothing in the rumour that had circulated some time ago that Tessa Harrison and Robby Atherton were to be married. And if there had been she'd damned soon recovered from it. Most women went into a decline when they were jilted but there was no sign of it about Tessa. What a splendid creature she was and if she weren't so firmly attached to that lucky cousin of hers he wouldn't mind giving her a whirl himself.

At the start of the hunting season, when he had been home for six months, they rode over to Longworth Hall. She was dressed in the superb outfit which had been made for her by Miss Maymon and which had caused such a commotion last season, a magnificent study in black and white. But for the high swell of her breasts, she and her cousin might have been the two brothers, one of whom lay in his grave at Scutari.

She was instantly surrounded by admiring gentlemen the moment she put her booted and spurred foot to the ground and none of them noticed the ominous clenching of Drew Greenwood's jaw. She was breathless with laughter, swaggering amongst the men, one of them, it seemed, as she accepted a glass of punch. She was completely at home in their company, unaware, as indeed were they, of any gulf between them. She had been welcomed here, despite her commercial background, from an early age. She had dined, with her cousins, in the medieval great hall, had watched them play wild games, and even joined in on occasion, down the long gallery lined with ancestral Longworth portraits. She had danced with them at their last Christmas party before Drew and Pearce rode away and dreamed here in the arms of her love, before the great darkness had fallen in on her. Now, it was as though she had come home.

'Tessa.'

His voice was like a whip, snapping about her and the group of laughing men. They all turned, their faces still wreathed in merriment, their eyes glowing with that particular look gentlemen bestow on a pretty woman, especially if she is as spirited as Tessa Harrison. He could see it in their eyes, that slight hint of coarseness only another man will recognise, a look of speculation as these boisterous and brash young gentlemen eyed the long and lovely body of his cousin.

'It's time we were mounted,' he said harshly. His voice sounded strange even to himself for he could not bear, simply could not bear her even to speak to these men who were clustered about her. He was eaten up with jealousy and had not the least idea how to cope with it. She must come to him, she must come at once, his arrogant manner said, or he honestly thought he might break down in some way. His legs which had so easily swung him on, and then off his new bay were rigid with the necessity of keeping himself upright. But at the same time he could feel that familiar snapping rage, that savage temper, the Greenwood temper, the Chapman temper, he had been told, that had been his mother's, begin to race through him. *She was his*. Tessa Harrison had belonged exclusively to Drew Greenwood for the past six months. She had folded herself in all but the physical sense about his wounded soul and body and had begun the process of healing within him.

She knew, of course. Though he said nothing more and they were all looking at him in amazement – for had not Drew Greenwood always been the most amiable of fellows, except in a fight? – she knew, and miraculously she put her glass in the nearest hand and came to him.

'I'm ready, cousin, if you are.'

That night, just as though the terror he had lived in for several minutes that day had awakened the sleeping beast of his nightmare, he screamed for her, calling her by name, urgently, though he still slept.

Jenny Harrison stood by the door of his bedroom watching the now familiar scene as Tessa rocked him against her breast. Laurel was at her back, and Charlie, and over Laurel's head their eyes met in understanding. Jenny closed the door quietly.

'You're not going to leave them there alone?' Laurel was aghast, genuinely shocked by her aunt's attitude towards something which was not at all proper. Both Drew and Tessa were in their nightclothes, almost lying together on the bed, and how could Jenny Harrison countenance such a thing, turn a blind eye to what was becoming a scandal in the Penfold Valley? It must be stopped, this gossip which was on everyone's lips and which might affect her own standing in the community. It must be put an end to, preferably, in Laurel's opinion, by sending Tessa to her own mother and father in Italy for a few months until it had died down, and returning Drew to the mill where he belonged. This attachment between her brother and her cousin had begun to frighten her as she recognised its potential for dislodging her from her present position as mistress of this house. One day, of course, Drew would marry, some shy, submissive sixteen-year-old who would be safely and easily managed by someone as proficient as herself. But if she and Tessa, who was headstrong and wilful, were bound together in the running of Greenacres, how could Laurel possibly retain the control which had been hers for so many pleasant years?

'Well, you might be able to overlook such behaviour, Aunt Jenny, but I certainly cannot, not under my own roof with innocent children sleeping in their beds not a dozen yards away.'

With a crash she flung open the door, her hand which held the doorknob losing its grip so that the door hit the wall violently. A draught of air eddied in with her, lifting the lace curtains at the open window, whispering about the quiet room and making the flame of the candle dance and flicker, casting dreadful shadows on the ceiling and walls. Before Jenny could stop her, or even catch her breath to speak, Laurel strode into the room, her small figure casting a huge shadow.

Drew had begun to move slowly away from the horror of the bodies which clutched at his own, from the weight which he knew was his brother Pearce, his brother who had no feet, indeed no legs; away from the tortured screams of men and horses and into the warm, scented presence of the woman whom he knew would be there, ready to welcome

306

him back. His breathing had slowed to a peaceful calm, his turbulent body becoming quiet, and he sighed thankfully. He did not awaken, merely moved from one level of sleep to another, from the nightmare into the state of dreamless peace she brought him.

He awoke to confusion: to wildly dancing shadows, huge and distorted, to harsh cries and angry voices. There were people struggling. He did not know who they were in that first awareness and for a few moments he floundered, ready to call out to Pearce to come and give him a hand, or to Tessa to gather him into her arms; one of them, either would do, to be there for him, as there had always been someone. He struggled to sit up, to make some sense of it and he felt a calming hand on his shoulder, hers, and in that moment he knew what he must do to make himself complete again, secure again.

'What the devil's going on?' He was ready to leap from his bed though he had on only a nightshirt, and casting modesty to the wind he threw back the bedclothes and stood up. Charlie, incredibly, was struggling with Laurel who was beseeching his Aunt Jenny – dear God, it was like a bloody circus – to do something before the good name of the family was completely ruined. It would be best, really it would, she cried, if Tessa went to Italy – couldn't she see it? – and later, when Drew was settled in the mill, perhaps with some suitable young lady, Tessa could come back and . . .

'For God's sake, Mother, will you tell her to be quiet before I smack her silly face?' Tessa was furious. 'How dare she come in here with her vile insinuations, upsetting Drew . . .'

'I'm not upset,' he said and he meant it. For the first time since he and Pearce had left this house two years ago he felt filled with well-being, eager to fight with anyone who cared to take him on. He had no idea what was happening. He knew he had been dreaming, well, having one of his night-mares, and that for an awful moment his dream world had followed him from sleep, creating a fog of swirling shadows about his bed. Now he saw it was only Aunt Jenny, patient and enduring, Laurel and Charlie having some kind of argument, familiar and everyday ... and Tessa.

'You won't be satisfied until you have driven us all to the point of madness with your stupid and quite unbelievable implications, will you?' Tessa was shouting. 'Have you no humanity in that self-centred mind of yours, or does the whole universe begin and end with what you consider proper? You listen to those feather-brained friends of yours who have nothing better to do than gossip over their tea-cups, ruining reputations with as much compunction as swatting a fly. Dream it up, if it does not exist, as you have decided to dream up this fantasy that Drew and I are ... well, whatever that nasty mind of yours ...'

'Charlie, are you going to let this niece of yours insult ... ?'

'Insult? That is where *your* talents lie, Laurel, that and your gift for seeing villainy where there is none ...'

'I really believe you are quite mad, Tessa,' Laurel said coolly, raising a fastidious eyebrow. She had decided, it appeared, to treat Tessa's outburst with the disdain one shows to a child in a tantrum. Her husband's reluctance to support her in this was really unforgivable and she would not forgive him, nor Tessa, her manner said. It was not in her nature to brawl like a fish-wife, particularly with the servants within earshot, as they were certain to be. But Tessa, driven at last to lose the patience and temper she had sworn to keep under control at least in Drew's presence, had no such compunction.

'I must be to have lived in the same house as you for nearly twenty years, and if I am you have driven me to it with your double-faced, double-tongued hypocrisy ...'

'How dare you.' Laurel was white-faced, her eyes pure green slits of outrage but still her training as a lady, which Tessa surely was not, held her in check.

'Tessa, I will not have this,' Jenny said, trying to signal to

Charlie to get his wife out of the room. 'It cannot be good for Drew and it certainly makes me feel...'

'... and if you think I shall allow you to...'

'*Tessa*, that is enough.' Her mother's voice was like a pistol shot for though Tessa was perhaps only voicing Jenny's own thoughts it did no good, none at all, to bring them to light now. Not now.

'Thank you, Aunt Jenny. She really does deserve a good thrashing and if she were mine she would have one.'

'That is for me to say, Laurel, not you.'

'A baggage such as she is deserves...'

'And what does that mean, Laurel Greenwood? What are you implying now, pray? That I stand on street corners like any common...'

'*Tessa!*'

'I do not imply anything, my girl.' Laurel was incensed beyond care now, ready to say anything, anything, regardless of the truth: to wound her cousin in any way she could, and the more painful it was the better. 'Dear God, it is no more than two years since you were disporting yourself all over the valley with that gentleman, if one can call him that, from the fox-hunting set of the Squire's. God alone knows what you got up to with him but whatever it was, it surely must have escaped no one's notice that he did not offer marriage. Really, Tessa, one can only hope that there is someone somewhere who has not heard of your reputation since the likelihood of your marrying seems very remote.'

The silence which followed was like the endlessly grey, endlessly deep waters of the lake in winter. Small, cruel ripples washed against the stricken girl who drowned in the centre of it. Her face was as white as her demure lawn nightgown, rigid, clenched with anguish, and she seemed unable to move, to speak, to defend herself. Her fiery temper, the strong and heedless defiance she had shown had been defeated, blown out like a candle, her vividness quenched, her spirit torn from her.

'I would be most obliged, Charlie old chap, if you would

remove your wife, my sister, from my room.' Drew's drawling voice was insolent in its intention to insult. 'She really does need taking in hand, you know, and if you have not the backbone to do it, I would be delighted to give her the beating she deserves. One would think a woman of her age – what is it now, Laurel, thirty-two, thirty-three? – would have learned tact and indeed some common sense. And she is quite mistaken, you know.'

He moved lightly across the space which divided Tessa and himself, turning her to face him. He cupped her face gently with his hands, looking down into the deep, glacial grey of her stricken eyes. In his was the warm certainty of his intentions.

'She is quite wrong, my darling,' he said, heedless of the three people who watched. 'I have known you and everything there is to know about you from the day you were born and it would be my joy and my honour to marry you. That is, if you will have me.' Then he grinned impudently, just as once he had done, his humour and charm concealing from her the urgency with which he waited for her answer.

They saw the wretchedness leave her. They watched the stiffness, the awful steel-edged tension drain away and with a sigh of thankfulness she simply leaned into the arms which were held out to her.

20

'You don't have to marry him if you don't want to, lass,' her mother said to her, her expression one of gentle understanding for only she knew of her daughter's anguished love for Robby Atherton. To the rest of the household and community it had been no more than a girlish romance, the short-lived excitement of a gentleman whose curiosity and attention had been aroused by a pretty girl somewhat beneath his station in life; a restless, spirited girl who should not have been put forward, nor attracted his notice in the first place if she had been properly brought up. And the whole thing had come to naught, as these things have a way of doing, but leaving Tessa Harrison with a reputation irretrievably tarnished, which was why this marriage to her cousin was so timely.

'I want to marry him, Mother. I love Drew, you know that, and he needs me. And I have no one else in my life, no one else I could share my future with. What better way to spend my life than with a man I have loved ever since I was a child? There is nothing else for me, Mother, *you* know that.'

'But that is no reason to marry Drew, child. He is recovered now.'

'That is because he knows I'm here to ... protect him.'

Jenny looked surprised, then disbelieving.

'No, Tessa, you mustn't think that. If you believe that he can only live his life with you by his side then you are being ... well, I was going to say coerced into marrying him. Oh, I know not deliberately since Drew wouldn't do that to you, but unwittingly. You have been his ... his crutch – no, don't argue with me for that is the right word – ever since he got home. You have taken Pearce's place by his side and have helped to heal him. Now I'm not saying I'm against the marriage, but I don't want you to do it for the wrong reason. Drew is ... a wild young man and you're no meek and mild miss yourself, my girl, and I reckon when he gets over this gratitude he feels towards you and you overcome the sense of responsibility you seem to have for him, there'll be fireworks. You're a strong girl ... woman ... Tessa, and you'll not take kindly to bonds ...'

'*Bonds?* Drew would not bind me.' The uneasy calm which existed between Tessa and her mother flared up instantly into the tense friction left over from the grief they

311

had shared two years ago. She was polite with Jenny, enough to hide the rift between them from the rest of the family, but the ease had gone from their relationship and would never be as it once was. She was aware that the devastation, the desolation had not been caused by her mother, just as the shell, aimed by a soldier's hand, which had killed Pearce, could not be blamed for his death, but the bitterness remained in her heart just the same.

'Drew is a man, child, and has all the male characteristics of possession, pride and pigheadedness. And you are a beautiful woman, yes, you might well stare and smile, but there is something about you, not just to do with the way you look, that men like.'

'Oh, come now, Mother. When I'm Drew's wife I'm hardly likely to attract men to my side.'

'Why not? You have always been ... different from other girls, mixing with that free and easy lot up at the Hall. Oh, yes, I hear about the goings on ... Now don't pull your face at me, my girl, since I know you, and I know you wouldn't do anything to shame your family or yourself...'

Tessa turned abruptly away so that her mother could not see, and wonder at, the expression on her face.

'... but your name is linked with it just the same. Drew is a friend of Nicky Longworth. The Squire seems to have taken a fancy to you both and at the moment, with Drew not entirely himself yet, there has been no discord. No ... problems, shall we say. But let me tell you this: when you are his wife things will be very different. He is his father's son with a capacity for enormous emotions, whether love, hate, jealousy or rage, of the most red-blooded kind.'

Tessa listened to her mother with every appearance of disbelief but her mind returned to that moment when she had been laughing with Nicky Longworth and the others at the Hall as she had done a dozen times before in the past. They accepted her cheerfully, as they had always done, seeing her not as a girl when she had tagged along with them, but as an appendage of Drew and Pearce. But she was a woman now and she had sensed the change in them, the speculation in their eyes. Admiring certainly, and still respectful for dare they be anything else in the company of Drew Greenwood? But assessing just the same, since she was an unattached girl whose reputation was somewhat questionable.

And Drew had not liked their recognition of her attractions, nor the way she had responded to it. It had amused her and, if she was honest, pleased the female in her, that was all, but he had not known that and his displeasure had been very evident. She had thought at the time it was his own fragile condition and state of mind but now, as she listened to her mother she recognised there had been something else there, something she had seen once before.

On the face of Will Broadbent!

'I cannot let him down. He does need me, Mother.'

'I think it might be you who needs him, Tessa. I think that is what you are saying. You have made up your mind there is no one else for you and so, because he has asked you and you feel beholden, you will marry him. To comfort yourself as well as him.' Her mother's voice became urgent. 'But there will be someone for you one day, lass. Don't rush into this thing because it is expected of you.'

'Don't be ridiculous, Mother.' Then her manner softened somewhat. 'Don't you see it would be suitable for both of us . . . ?'

'Suitable! That is no reason for marriage, not in my opinion, though I daresay there are those who would argue with me over it.'

'I only mean Drew and I really are alike. We are suited by our temperament and upbringing. We admire the same things, activities and . . .'

'Yes?'

'He knows I cannot abide housekeeping and doing all the things Laurel does . . .'

'And what about Laurel? You and she do not get on. Are you prepared to live under the same roof with her for the

313

rest of your days? This house is Drew's inheritance and will one day be his. Laurel has run Greenacres for a long time now, and very competently, if we are to be fair to her. She looks on it as her home and unless you and Drew are prepared to ask her and Charlie and the children to find other accommodation you will have her at *your* dinner table, which she will consider to be *hers*, forever.'

'I will not interfere with her. She is mistress here.'

'No! You will be mistress. Your husband will be its master, *is* master now with Joss and Kit permanently abroad. You would do better with a housekeeper who could run the place, and Laurel in her own home elsewhere. Charlie could afford to buy a grand house where she could be in complete charge but it would mean you would have to settle to domestic duties...'

'Good God, I couldn't bear it. I'd rather have Laurel queening herself about the place.'

'You could perhaps share the responsibility...'

'Merciful heaven, how appalling. No, she does it so well, as you say, and I should be bored to death within a week. Besides, I want to help Drew.'

'To do what?'

'Well,' she shrugged her shoulders since she was not sure, 'in whatever it is he is to ... to do.'

Jenny looked at her sadly, not awfully sure her daughter knew what marriage to Drew Greenwood entailed, and not awfully sure she wanted to tell her. He was a complex man, particularly since the death of his brother, always youthfully self-willed and ready to challenge any opinion which opposed his own. Now that he was a man would he not be doubly so? Pearce's death had shattered him in a particularly subtle way, for they were not only brothers but twins. And the manner of Pearce's death had been harrowing for in the back of Drew's mind was surely the thought that his brother had died from wounds sustained as he rescued Drew from the Redan at Sebastopol. What nightmares dwelled in the mind of Drew Greenwood? What frailties remained to bring him down? What weaknesses which he might be unable to withstand? He had, almost overnight, become himself again, confident, positive, audacious even, his wit and charm a delight at the dinner table. He had even apologised to Laurel and Charlie, begging their forbearance, claiming the strain of his recent illness, for what else could it be called? His good humour, at least to Charlie, proved irresistible, though his sister was less inclined to be forgiving.

The three months betrothal was something which must be got through with the best possible grace, he said to Tessa. It was expected of them. They were members of a family with obligations not only to each other, but to his father and mother, to her mother and to their position in the community. There would be parties and dinners in their honour and it would be churlish not to comply. Joss and Kit Greenwood were to come home at once, to see their only son married and also to attend to several legal matters which now arose because of it. There were many preparations which must be attended to, not the least Tessa's wedding outfit and trousseau for her mother declared, despite the peculiarity of the betrothal, her daughter would not go to her marriage without a new shift to her name. And Laurel, her mouth grim, her face set in a mould of cold disapproval, was nevertheless determined to snatch every advantage she could from her brother's connection with the gentry and would entertain as many as could be crammed into Greenacres in the three months prior to the wedding.

They had ridden that day up to Friar's Mere, guiding their mounts amongst the browning, mist-soaked bracken which dripped about them. It was cold that autumn, almost winter though September was barely done with, and they both wore warmly lined capes and gloves. Their own breath wreathed with the horses' about them and when they dismounted to look over the shaded valley, she shivered suddenly, not with cold but with some sudden disquiet which came from nowhere to trouble her.

He draped a companionable arm across her shoulders,

wise in the ways of women. Best not to startle her too soon with his own needs, and so he remained, despite the magnificent diamond on her finger, just as he had always been, cousin, companion, friend.

'Are you cold, sweetheart,' he asked lightly, 'or just contemplating the future as Mrs Drew Greenwood and finding it somewhat daunting?'

She looked up at him sharply. She was not always sure lately when he was teasing. In his new role as her 'fiancé' she supposed he had the right now to be somewhat more ... familiar with her, not intimate, for that was reserved for their wedding night, but not exactly the same as he had been as 'cousin'. But he was just the same. Both of them had suffered a great loss. They had been bruised and lonely, needing, probably, to be loved and they had given something to one another on the day when he had asked her to marry him and she had accepted gratefully. She needed warmth and some emotion he seemed to be offering. She rested easily when she was with him, trusting him as implicitly as she had always done and she was aware that in her he found something he had lost with Pearce.

'Oh, really, Tessa, don't tell me you don't find this somewhat strange?'

'Well ...' She knew what he meant and was grateful that he was treating it with humour and lightness.

'It is new to us both, this "betrothal".' He grinned down at her, making her smile as he exaggerated the word.

'I'm not afraid, Drew Greenwood.' Immediately she began to bristle, shying away from him indignantly but he pulled her back, laughing, his eyes narrowed and shining.

'Yes, you are, just a little bit. Afraid that things might be changed between us because of ... well, because you will be my wife, but I promise you they won't.' He grinned wickedly. 'Would you like to try something?'

'What?' she said suspiciously.

'Well, we are betrothed, as they say, so surely it would be allowed?'

'What?' she said again.

'A kiss to seal our ... pact.' He smiled even more engagingly, turning her so that she faced him. He reached up to tuck a damp strand of hair behind her ear, his gaze moving across her face, resting on her smooth brow, the puzzled depths of her eyes, the touch of rose in her cheeks put there by the cold, and finally, her soft, parted lips.

'What pact?'

'To marry, of course, and besides, it won't be the first time. Remember that Christmas when Pearce and I caught you under the mistletoe? We each stole a kiss from you. In fact, I do believe we had no need of theft.'

Her mouth curled up in a wide smile and as it did so he placed his own carefully against it. It was a smiling kiss, light as thistledown with no more in it than a friend might give to another. He tasted the sweetness of her breath and felt the warmth of it drift into his open mouth. She leaned against him, willing to go on, her eyes so lovely and trusting told him, and he caught his breath.

'Did you know that in this light your eyes have the palest, softest blue in them?' he said wonderingly. 'Like the smoke you see against a summer sky. Transparent almost.'

'Oh, Drew, stop teasing.' Her arms crept up behind him, her hands gripping one another in the centre of his back. His were across her shoulders and he pulled her into them, tucking her head into the hollow of his neck.

'I need you, Tessa,' he said quietly, his breath moving her dark hair.

'I'm here, Drew,' she answered and when she looked up at him, smiling, his face was serious. He held her gaze for a moment, then bent his head and took her lips again and this time it was different. For a moment she wanted to draw back for this was how Robby had kissed her. This was warm and filled with desire and she was not really ready ... no ... not with this man who was her cousin. She closed her eyes so that Drew could not read the expression in them, the expression which surely would reveal to him that ...

317

that other kisses had been left there, and in her heart, and that no one, no others could replace the ones she had lost.

But when she opened her eyes again there he was, Drew Greenwood, her beloved cousin, grinning delightedly, dashingly handsome, familiar, loved, winsome and dear.

'There you are,' he said, 'how was that?' Taking her lead from him, she pretended to bob a curtsey, dimpling in laughter.

'Very nice, thank you, sir.'

'Have you another to spare, d'you think, since I must admit to finding it very pleasant myself?'

He was breathing rather more heavily than usual when he drew away, but he merely looked into her face as though to check that she had not taken fright and when he could see that she hadn't, he pulled her gently back into the circle of his arms.

'That's enough for today, cousin,' he said, his voice soft and inclined to tremble over the top of her head.

The next time was a week later. They had dined with the Longworths, just the two of them invited, much to Laurel's chagrin since she had expected, as Drew's sister and closest relative until Joss and Kit returned from Italy, to be included in any celebration given for the newly engaged couple.

They had drunk an excellent wine with dinner, and champagne to toast the happy pair who really made a splendid picture, everyone agreed. That girl of Jenny Harrison's was quite superb in her white lace gown, and the effect of the broad scarlet sash wound tight about her slender waist and the matching ribbons in her dark hair, dressed in tumbled curls, was simply stunning. She was almost as tall as her bridegroom-to-be in her white satin high-heeled slippers, and he was immaculate in his black and white evening clothes, a perfect contrast in his male beauty for her loveliness. How magnificent they were, how handsome, and could anyone fail to believe that they were not made for each other and that their future together could be anything less than perfect?

318

They had held hands in the carriage on the drive home, still laughing and inclined to fall against one another in the hilarity produced by several glasses of champagne. Like children they were, giggling over the rather pompous but kindly speech the Squire had made in their honour, and the number of times they had been told how well suited they were, perhaps, as Drew remarked gleefully, because they were both from the class known as 'trade' and therefore, one supposed, to consummate the perfect union.

It was dim in the hallway. Briggs had left one lamp at the foot of the stairs before retiring, as he had been ordered to do since they were to be late. The logs in the enormous fireplace had smouldered down to whispering ash, a golden flame here and there, and a curl of smoke. It was warm, intimate, a place where they were both relaxed, at home and secure.

'I think I'll have a brandy before I go up,' Drew drawled. 'Would you care to join me?' An eyebrow arched questioningly.

'Why not?' She was light-headed and pleasantly tired, ready for bed but unwilling somehow to let go of the content that lay about her.

The brandy made her gasp and the heat of it rose from her stomach where it had found the champagne, and put flags of scarlet in her cheeks to match the ribbons in her delightfully tumbled hair.

'Slowly, cousin,' Drew laughed, putting an arm about her shoulders as they sat side by side on the sofa before the dying drawing-room fire. 'Sip it slowly and then, when you are almost asleep, I shall take you up to bed.'

The words meant nothing to Tessa beyond what they said: it had not yet occurred to her to think of her cousin in 'that way', and the implication which sprang instantly to Drew's more sexually alert mind completely escaped her. She felt a quiver run through him and the clear image of Will Broadbent came surprisingly to her mind. Why, she thought, at this particular moment, should she think of him? Then she was conscious of the suddenly taut presence of Drew beside her, his arm rigid across her shoulders.

'What is it, Drew?' she asked though really she knew. How could she not when she had been loved by Will Broadbent, who had caressed every part of her, sweet and secret parts which had set her on fire for more?

But Drew, though a man too, was her cousin, and had been all her life. That was who he was.

The simple and, to her, quite logical thought slipped into her mind, to be followed by the equally logical and obvious reply that they were to be, not just cousins, but man and wife. In that moment she knew they must take that next step *now*, before she had time to dwell on it, before she had time to consider the *mechanics* of it, before she had time to jib at it, to get cold feet and turn away from it, since he *was* her cousin, dammit. It must be done without thought, without design. It must be done *now*.

Blindly she turned to him, not knowing where to begin, and as swiftly as he had come Will Broadbent winged away, and her heart, on which he was still engraved, was filled with Robby Atherton. Kisses ... oh, Robby, Robby, my love, that was how ... how it had begun ... sweet, warm ... Dear God, how she loved him still, but she loved Drew ... she did ... she did, but not, sadly, in the way she had loved Robby ... Robby, Samuel Robert Atherton ... and with none of the passion she had given to Will Broadbent.

His mouth was there waiting for hers and wisely – how did he know her so well? understand her as he did? – wisely he let her take the lead, sitting almost passively, there, his arm relaxed now about her shoulders, waiting. She was aware in that moment that if he had responded eagerly, attempted to move at a faster pace than she could manage, she would have let Robby Atherton into her soul, and refused him.

She could taste the brandy on his lips. They were warm and very soft, moist on their inside. They moved with hers in little butterfly motions, soft and fluttering, waiting, smiling, she could see that, in pleasure.

'You are very dear to me, Tessa,' he murmured, again the right words, with no mention of love. He put up a hand, a brown, familiar hand which she had known all her life and placed the palm against her cheek. He began to guide her then, holding her cheek gently as he kissed her, his fingers warm against her skin. Sighing, his lips moved to her eyes, resting against each one before going on to her eyebrow, the line of her hair, a soft whisper of breath in her ear, his mouth trembling, lingering on her jawline and into the soft hollow at the base of her throat. She arched her body without thought, feeling his lips move across her skin and the arm which had been resting lightly across her shoulders tightened as he turned her towards him. His hand was under her hair, pulling at ribbons and pins, caressing the back of her neck, still gentle, without urgency. She could see the outline of his dark face above hers and the blue glow of his eyes.

For a moment he hesitated, lifting a questioning eyebrow, giving her, she knew, time to draw back, to wait for another time. It has to be done at sometime, his quizzical expression said, and why not now, in the spontaneity of now?

He turned her then, taking her stillness for acquiescence, resting her across his knee. His arms were strong and positive, lifting her up, and his kisses were demanding, opening her lips beneath his own. His tongue teased hers, his hand was smoothing her shoulder, her upper arm, the other holding her since the moment had come and gone when she might refuse.

'Tessa...' His fingers moved slowly, saying there was no hurry, no need to rush this sweet moment, caressing her throat, smoothing her skin until it reached the soft upper curve of her breast.

'Not here, Drew.'

'In your room, then. I have to have you now before you change your mind...'

They stood up awkwardly, then he swung her up into his arms, his lips finding hers, allowing no shrinking away and her arms clung about his neck, her mouth clung to his mouth, afraid to detach herself from the physical junction which was the only one she knew about her cousin Drew.

Her room was warm and sweet-scented, familiar, scattered with the things she had left there before setting off for Longworth Hall. Emma had made up the fire and drawn the curtains, even turned back the bedclothes, and when he placed her on the bed it seemed it had been waiting there for them, for this which was to happen.

Though he was breathing hard now she could see he was making a great effort to hold back for her sake, since was she not virgin, inexperienced in these matters? She wanted to cry out to him to hurry, to get it done, to get it over with. She wanted it behind her, that first time, so that they could be Drew and Tessa again, cousins, friends and, one supposed, lovers.

He gently drew down her dress, exposing her breasts and when she closed her eyes in confusion he put up a hand and cupped her cheek.

'Don't look away, sweetheart,' he whispered, kissing her softly on her mouth and cheek and chin. 'We have nothing of which to be ashamed. Look at me, look at my eyes. See in them what I feel for you.' It was there, his love, his admiration for her as a woman. Not as Tessa Harrison, cousin, but Tessa Harrison, woman, *his* woman. 'I should be patient with you since you have the look in your eyes which says you will grit your teeth and endure it, as women are expected to, but there is no need...'

When he had undressed her completely he stood for several moments exploring with his eyes every part of her body, lingering at her breast and thighs, not touching yet but completely absorbed in the loveliness of her. He began to undress himself and she watched him, diverted by the beauty and fineness of his body, so different from Will's. Will had been broad, heavy, hard, so strong he made Drew

322

seem a lightweight in comparison, but Drew Greenwood was slender, arrow-straight and yet with a fluid grace. Easy and lean as an athlete, smooth-skinned with a fine matt of crisp chest hair which travelled down his belly to between his thighs. Will had been ... Dear God, why should she think...? And in that last moment her mind, amazed, was filled with the memory of him, then Drew bent over her, his candle-lit body eager, his eyes searching hers. She lifted her arms urgently and wound them round his neck, wanting to blot out everything but him and pulled him down to her. His body entered hers and it was done. He groaned and shuddered and called her name as he took possession of her, and it was done.

They lay for a while and she stroked his back, feeling the satiny strength of it and the muscles bunched beneath the skin. A moment ago they had been rigid with need, now they were relaxed and spent. It was as though he had poured into her all his strength, the boyish strength which was Drew Greenwood, leaving him defenceless, weakened, vulnerable, as he had been when he returned from the Crimea. She was the one with undiminished power now, her strength gained from him, her body unbreakable, not weakened as his appeared to be. She wondered if this was all that was to be between herself and her cousin, this ... tenderness she felt, this warm and gentle love, just the same as it had always been, even after what had just happened, for Drew Greenwood. Was she never to know again that lusty delight she and Will had shared, that joy, that abandonment, their bodies clasped together in the sensuality a man and woman can know?

He sighed and sat up, studying her face in the pale glow of the candlelight. He bent to kiss her, cupping her breast with his strong hand.

'You are quite beautiful, my darling.'

'If you say so.' In her body, deep down, was that familiar sensation connected with his fingers which rolled her nipple gently. It began to stir and she felt a great desire to lift her hips, to move them up towards him, but he lay back on the pillow, putting an arm about her and the feeling fled away. She put her head on his chest and when he pulled the quilt up around them she knew they would fall asleep with the greatest of ease, fitting together even in this new environment, as they had always done.

They made love again and again in those months before their marriage, wherever and whenever they could find the opportunity, each time more easily, each time more surely, each time more enjoyably, and she was grateful that he seemed to find such joy in it and in her. Though he did not say the words, she knew he loved her, not just as he had always done, but in the way a man loves a woman. And she was thankful, thankful for that love and for his need of her. It warmed her, gave her comfort and pleasure, made her soft with him, and for him. She would devote her life now to being what he needed, to giving whatever it was he wanted. Not submissive for it was not in her nature, she told herself, but ready, always, to take him in her arms, to love him, to support him, to allow him to support *her*, which was much more important. Robby Atherton was dead now, dead and buried in the grave of her heart, and Drew Greenwood had sprung up to take his place, and the whisper that was Will Broadbent, which came sometimes to ask what of *her* joy, and *her* fulfilment, was scarcely noticed.

# 21

She had seen nothing of Will for two years, not since she had ridden over to Annie's on the day before Robby Atherton was to speak to her mother, so when he rose casually from the chair before Annie's fire as she entered the cottage she felt her breath leave her body in an explosion so violent she thought she was about to swoon.

She was to be married the following Saturday and the invitation, written in Miss Copeland's beautiful copperplate and sent to Annie over a month ago, had still not been answered. She would be awkward, Tessa knew, stubborn and ungracious, declaring herself not the sort to attend a grand society wedding, and absolutely unconvinced that Tessa should marry Drew Greenwood anyway. She had said so a dozen times ever since Tessa had told her she was to wed her cousin.

'He's got thi on't rebound, lass, an' tha should 'ave sense enough ter know it. Tha was ter wed that other chap, tha said, then all of a sudden it were off . . . No, I want ter know nothing about it, lass, so don't look at me like that. What 'appened is thy own affair an' nowt ter do wi' me,' she declared, for Annie had a horror of seeming to interfere in another's life at the same time fiercely defending her own privacy. But she could not resist giving her opinion, nevertheless, particularly when she firmly believed, as she did now, that Tessa was about to make a mistake. And she was not eager to put on her best bonnet, which was her *only* bonnet, and traipse over to the parish church of Crossfold and watch her make it.

Tessa could sympathise with her reluctance to come to Greenacres to join in the celebrations: when one is no more than a lowly mill girl it took courage to place oneself amongst those who consider themselves to be one's betters. She had not dared to offer Annie the 'loan' of a decent bonnet and gown since she knew where that would lead, but if she would just come to the church, see her married to Drew, Tessa would be content and she meant to try to persuade her to do so today.

She had known, though nothing was ever said, that Will still called at Annie's cottage when he was in the district and she had relied on her friend to let her know when that was so that there would be no awkward confrontations. Yet now, in that first moment when she realised that this visit must have been unforeseen, just as Annie had not known that she, Tessa, was going to call, she felt an unexpected surge of incredible gladness.

'Tessa,' he said coolly. 'Are you well?' No more than that, leaving her in no doubt that whatever there had been between them was not only dead but decently buried. He was a man who had, unwillingly, his imperturbable manner seemed to say, lost his head over a pretty girl. That was folly from which he had recovered as one recovers from a heavy cold or a fever, debilitating at the time but not dangerous. So he could greet her quite calmly now, just as though they were no more than acquaintances of Annie's who found themselves together in her kitchen.

'Thank you, yes, and you?' With a great effort she kept her voice just as neutral, her manner just as off-hand.

'I'm well, thank you.'

'I'm glad to hear it.'

'And what brings you over to Annie's so unexpectedly?'

At the back of the room Annie drew in her breath sharply and when one of the children, Tessa could not have said which one, erupted into the scullery from the back of the cottage, Annie moved quickly to the back door and ushered whoever it was out again, whispering something which neither the man nor the woman in the kitchen could hear.

Tessa was stung by Will's familiarity since it was nothing to do with him when or why she visited Annie. So she was not expected, was it any of his concern? Her head lifted imperiously and she turned away from him, tossing her riding crop and cloak to a chair beside the table. She was aware of the silence. She could no longer see him as she stared out of the window to where her mare cropped Annie's few winter plants, but she could feel him there and the dread grew in her, for a small part of her wanted to turn round and touch him. To put out her hand and ... and have him grasp it.

326

Dear God, was she mad? She believed she was for it seemed there was still something in her which called out to something in him despite what had happened since she had seen him last. She did not love him, of course she didn't. She loved Robby and she loved Drew, though in a completely different way, naturally, so why, her suddenly anguished mind asked, was she dithering about in Annie's kitchen allowing herself to become upset at the sight of Will Broadbent?

'My dear Tessa,' he said, amusement in his voice, 'you seem quite agitated. I do apologise if I have . . . startled you.'

'There is no need to apologise.'

'Good, nevertheless you are startled?'

'Of course not. I . . . did not expect to find you here.'

'Nor I you.'

She allowed herself to turn to him then, conscious of the softening in his voice and was just in time to see the strange expression which deepened his amber eyes to a smoky brown, then it was gone and he smiled. He took a cigar case from the pocket of his well-cut jacket, selected a cigar, lit it and when it was drawing to his satisfaction, blew smoke into Annie's kitchen ceiling. His smile deepened as he saw her look at it.

'Aah, yes. As you see I have acquired the . . . er . . . trappings of the business gentleman. The good suit, the cigar, the . . . well, other things.' He gave a sardonic twist of the wide, strong mouth, a lifting of the heavy eyebrows as though to say it was all a performance put on for those who were impressed with such things.

'Congratulations.'

'And to yourself.'

'I beg your pardon?'

'Are you not to be married shortly?' The sudden swerve unnerved her.

'Yes.'

'How splendid. I do like to hear of good fortune. So, it seems we are both . . . doing well.'

327

'It seems so.'

'Oh, indeed. A good marriage is not a thing to be scorned.'

'No.'

'You mean it is not to be a good marriage?' He leaned forward or did she just imagine it? His expression did not change. His face was just as suavely smiling but there was still the remainder of something curiously tense in his narrowed eyes.

'Of course it is.'

'Not like the ... er ... other one?'

'What...?' Please don't, her heart cried out to him. Please don't hurt me, or try to, and in her anguish it did not occur to her to wonder why he should try to do so.

'I do beg your pardon.' He was immensely civil now, all traces of feeling of any sort wiped from his face. 'It has, of course, nothing to do with me. Now,' he turned to Annie who still hovered at the back of the scullery, 'I must be off. I have an engagement this evening which I would not like to miss.' And his manner, and smile, told them both quite clearly that it was with a lady.

He had been gone for several minutes when she felt Annie's gentle touch on her arm. She had been brooding out of the window into the street along which his broad-shouldered back had disappeared and she jumped when she felt Annie's hand, then turned, attempting to smile.

'It seems Will Broadbent has gone up in the world, Annie.'

'Tessa, lass...'

'Don't say it, Annie.'

'Say what, Tessa Harrison?'

'I don't know. You have a look on your face which says you are going to argue with me about ... well, whatever it is you feel must be argued about.'

'Yer can't do it. Yer can't wed Drew Greenwood. Not just because of Will an' what you an' 'im 'ad. But because that cousin o' thine is...'

'Will's nothing to me and I am nothing to Will. Heavens,

it's two years. *Two years*, Annie. I can't just keep drifting from man to man like some aimless butterfly...'

'Nobody ses yer should, but wait ... give it a month or so, lass...' and see what comes of this reunion with Will, her anxious eyes said, but Tessa flung her off roughly.

'I can't.' Her face which, an hour since, had been filled if not with joy then with peace, was now devoid of all expression.

She was married to Drew Greenwood on a white and frosted morning just before Christmas. There was a crunch of new snow underfoot as she walked up the path on the arm of Joss Greenwood and above them the sky was streaked in delicate layers of palest pink and blue. The sun shone hazily through the slight curling mist and when they moved inside the dusty parish church it was scarcely warmer than the crisp air outside.

She wore ivory velvet and carried rosebuds of the same shade from the Greenacres hothouses. Her veil was a marvel of white lace and seed pearls and in her ears and about her neck were the lustrous pearls her bridegroom had given her as a wedding gift. Her wide skirts flowed from her supple waist, whispering across the worn flagstones as her uncle put her carefully beside his own son, and the massed congregation agreed they had never seen a lovelier bride. She looked fragile and mysterious, although of course she was not, for she was tall and had junketed about the high tops and deep valleys of the countryside with her recklessly wild cousins since she was old enough to sit on a horse.

Her family were arranged on both sides of the church since she and her groom were cousins, with their guests in descending order of importance behind them. The Squire with his lady and their family sat in the second pew, naturally – a feather in the Greenwood cap there, by God, with the young Squireen, who was known to be one of those with whom the Greenwoods had made merry, acting as groomsman. Among the mainly commercial congregation were one

329

or two members of the fox-hunting set, those who had taken a fancy to the Greenwood girl, as she was known, over the past few years. She had proved to be not only their equal on the hunting field, but damned amusing as well, with the lofty arrogance they both admired and shared since it was the characteristic which set them apart from the lower orders. And Drew Greenwood had shown the courageous foolhardiness on the battlefield which was the stamp of the pedigreed and ruling class to which they themselves belonged. A rare couple and one they were more than ready to take up.

It was all most gratifying and despite Laurel Greenwood's fierce disapproval of the marriage it was apparent that she considered herself to be getting only her due as she greeted ladies and gentlemen known to be related to the lesser aristocracy. She had been attempting to get her toe in the door at Longworth Hall for three years now, ever since her Christmas fancy-dress ball which had been honoured by the Squire's presence. Surely this meant a further and renewed warmth between her family and that of the leading gentry of the Penfold Valley? The young Greenwoods and the Long-worths were so obviously the best of friends and Laurel had sons and daughters of her own whose future hopes might well be furthered by her acquaintance with the local Squire.

Kit Greenwood, doing her best to signal to her husband that no one would think the worse of him if he sat down, looked quite splendid in one of the new hooped 'cages' or 'artificial crinolines' to support her vast skirt. The bodice of the outfit was separate and worn over it was a 'gilet' or waistcoat, considered a little fast by the ladies of Crossfold where the Paris and London fashions had not yet arrived. It was in a lovely violet-blue, the exact shade of her eyes which had sadly lost their brilliance since the death of her son. Her bonnet, worn at the back of her head, had a dip in the centre of the brim, on the underside of which was a froth of blond lace. She watched her boy, for surely he was still that despite his twenty years, lean against his cousin, his wife now, and as he made his vows his mother was seen to reach for her sister-in-law's hand as though she herself was sorely in need of support. They sat quietly together, the mothers of the bride and groom, perhaps dwelling on their losses as a family, on the past which had led to this marriage, which, if they were honest, neither had wanted for their children.

The wedding breakfast was of such splendour it was talked of for weeks by those, and there were well over one hundred, who sat down to share it: the Squire and Mrs Longworth, Sir Anthony Taylor and Lady Prudence, Nicky Longworth, Johnny Taylor and numerous ladies and gentlemen of their society rubbing shoulders with Abbotts and Jenkinsons and others of the manufacturing classes. Annie Beale had not been persuaded to come. There were flowers everywhere amidst the warm, scented comfort of Greenacres and Drew Greenwood proposing a charming, witty and quite emotional toast to his lovely bride.

It was a moment of great beauty, of great poignancy, when one remembered the son who had been left behind on the battlefield of the Crimean Peninsula, but perhaps with the responsibility of a wife and no doubt a child within the twelvemonth, Drew Greenwood would now buckle to, and become a part of what he would one day inherit.

Jenny Harrison watched them, her daughter and her new son-in-law, her mind not on wedding cake and champagne, on laughter and toasts and kisses, but on what Joss was to say to his son and his new daughter-in-law the next day before they set off on their wedding journey.

They gathered in what had once been the study of Barker Chapman, Kit's father, then in turn hers, her husband's, Jenny's and, occasionally, Charlie's, but never Drew's. Kit, still beautiful despite her fifty-one years; Joss, his face brown with the Mediterranean sun, but lined; Jenny, looking older somehow than her own brother; and Charlie, his pleasant, good-humoured face wondering on what this meeting could

331

be about. Laurel, his wife, making sure of everyone's comfort in the way a good hostess should; making sure everyone understood, particularly Tessa, that she was mistress of this house, at least for the time being.

And Tessa and Drew themselves, sitting close together in the deep leather chesterfield, Drew ready to whisper and giggle, treating the whole event with the light-hearted frivolity he directed towards anything which smacked of the serious. He was eager to be off to the railway station and the start of their grand wedding tour: Italy, France, Austria and wherever their careless search for pleasure took them. They might tarry in Paris since he had a fancy to deck Tessa out in the most fashionable and expensive gowns money – and they had a lot of it – could buy.

Joss smiled at them all, reaching for his wife's hand which was there, as it had always been for thirty years, waiting for his.

'You'll be wondering what all this is about,' he said, 'especially you, Drew.' His son blinked in surprise since he was not wondering at all. He supposed it to be some gathering, a family occasion in which a toast was to be drunk to the health of the bride and groom, wishing his father would get a move on since he and Tessa were to be off within the hour.

'We've been through some rare do's, your mother and me, and we've always managed to overcome them, haven't we, lass? But we're none of us getting any younger and there's still some ends want tidying up, eeh, my love?'

'Rubbish, Joss Greenwood. You might be in your dotage but I'm in my prime yet.' Kit held his hand fiercely, her eyes clinging to his with a passion which was quite extraordinary, even somewhat embarrassing in Laurel's view.

'Aye, well, that's as maybe, but best get things sorted out.' Tessa suddenly realised that what she had always considered to be her aunt's mills, her aunt's house and fortune, in fact belonged entirely to Joss Greenwood since on the day of their marriage, by law, everything she had owned became his, even herself. She had no existence, she did not exist in the eyes of the law except as Mrs Joss Greenwood, and what had once been hers could now be disposed of by her husband as he thought fit.

She felt a warning prickle at the base of her spine and her grip on Drew's hand tightened. The room was so quiet she could distinctly hear the voices of the servants in the breakfast room as they cleared away the table.

'We're not short of a guinea or two.' Her uncle grinned boyishly and his wife shook her head. 'I reckon Kit and I can live very pleasantly, luxuriously even by my standards remembering I was brought up in a weavers' cottage' – he winked at his sister and Tessa could swear she saw a glint of moisture in her mother's eye – 'with what the mills have brought us and the investments we've made. The railways have ... well, I'll not go into details except to say the shares we bought have made a pretty penny. So ...' He paused and though it was of no concern to her, Tessa found she was holding her breath. 'My wife and I have decided to let go, to make over the business to those who deserve it. A partnership. Drew, as our ... our only son will have a three-quarter share but the rest is to go to my sister and brother who, for the past twenty-five years, have kept the whole bloody lot together. They will hold their share, half each of the remaining twenty-five per cent, until their death and then they may leave it to whoever they please in the family, or sell it back to Drew. As the largest shareholder Drew will be general manager but Jenny and Charlie will now be partners in the business. These arrangements were made some time back, before you and Tessa decided on marriage, Drew. There was a proviso which, at the time, was not fully completed and until it is Drew does not become the head of the firm as is his right. Jenny and Charlie are in control as it stands. All the decisions made are theirs alone, but Mr Dalton, the lawyer, is to come here this morning and everything will be put in order, so I would like you all to be present. Naturally, for the time being Jenny and Charlie will continue to advise since Drew has not the experience to do what they have done for so many years. But when the papers are drawn up he and he alone will be in charge of Chapman Manufacturing.'

'*No!*'

They turned as one, all heads moving as one to look at the drained and pallid face of Joss Greenwood's son. He sat beside his wife, his hands wringing hers most piteously. Gone was the look of indolent amusement, of unruffled carelessness, and in its place was an expression so haunted Jenny was reminded of the day he had come back from the Crimea.

'I cannot work in the mill, Father.' He lifted his proud head but in his eyes was the terrified look of a child about to be shut up in a dark cupboard. His bravery on the field was beyond question, both on the hunting field and on the field of war. His courage had been spoken of by several returned officers, acquaintances of the Longworths and the Taylors, but the horror and dread which the one word 'mill' conjured up had, it seemed, unmanned him.

'Then what will you do?' his father asked him, his voice steely.

'Must I do anything, Father? Could we not sell the mills? We could use the money to buy an estate ... land ... farm land ...' His face brightened and the expression of horror began to fade from his eyes. 'I could live as the Squire does, not farming, of course, but looking after the tenants, acting as a magistrate ... a gentleman's life, Father, to which I am particularly drawn ...'

The echo of a conversation – a hundred years ago now, surely? – slipped into Tessa's mind and the day on which it had taken place became clearer with every minute. There had been just the four of them dining that night. Her mother had been there, yes, and this man who was now her husband, Drew Greenwood, and another – his brother, his *twin* brother who was dead but who surely lived on in the man who had just spoken. Her mother was looking towards her

334

as though the thoughts in her head were the same as her own. Drew, as always, had met the confrontation with his aunt that night head on, arguing that what had been in the past should remain there and did not concern those who lived in the present and the future. But it had been Pearce who had sworn he would sell his heritage, sell it without a thought for the men of his family who had made it. Sell it and live as the Squire did, close to the land which bred him.

And now, in almost the same words, Drew had pronounced that that was his hope, that he wanted nothing more than to live the rest of his days in idle luxury, *as Pearce had said*. Where was the Drew Greenwood who had taken up any challenge flung at him? Flaunting and arrogant and sure of himself, was he now, sadly, merging slowly into the weaker, or perhaps gentler character his brother had possessed?

He was still babbling on: '. . . we could sell Greenacres. There are a dozen new manufacturers who would be only too glad to take it off our hands,' he added contemptuously 'and buy an estate where there is a bit of rough shooting, farming land . . .'

'Don't be foolish, Drew.' His mother's voice was more amused than angry, for had anyone ever heard such nonsense and could anyone be expected to take it seriously? Sell the mills? Sell Greenacres! One might as well decide to sell one's own flesh and blood to those who dealt in the slave trade as sell this heritage of theirs, her smile said, and when her husband chose to ignore his son's outburst, she was not surprised.

'You would let others support you then? For that is what you are saying. Your Aunt Jenny and Charlie would do the work whilst you spent the money they earned?'

'Could I not employ a man to do my share? To . . . to do whatever it is you are asking me to do?' Drew was sullen now, his grand scheme which, Tessa was completely aware, would suit his nature better than any other, flung back in his face.

'Jenny and Charlie can do that,' his father's cool voice told him, 'most efficiently too, and there are a score of managers under their directorship, but do you not think it unfair that they alone should take the responsibility of what belongs to you?'

His son twisted about like an animal trapped in a cage which is far too small to accommodate it and for a dreadful moment Tessa thought he was about to spring it and flee, away from his father and mother, away from the prison they were preparing for him, away from his new wife who was all that was holding him together. But her hands steadied his and she drove her unfrightened will directly into his wild eyes, telling him with her own that she was here, that they were together, and the boy who had, for the first eighteen years of his life, been one half of a whole part and had thought he would never survive the loss of the other, sat back and the fear fell away.

'I'm sorry, sir. Forgive me. I was somewhat stunned and spoke without giving the matter any thought. You must not worry about me, about us.' He turned to smile at his Aunt Jenny, then at Charlie and they all relaxed quite visibly.

'Aunt Jenny, Charlie and I will, I'm sure, work out some arrangement convenient to the three of us. After all, the mill belongs to us all and we would not see it go to the wall for the lack of a decent commander, would we?'

His manner was vital and confident, a complete reversal of his terror of a moment ago, letting his parents see that, though he might not have the slightest idea how he was to do it, he would run *his* concern as he damn well pleased. It was a gamble he took for the documents which were to make the mill his were not yet signed. Yet his father appeared prepared to take that gamble, for surely it would make a responsible man of this valiant son of his?

'Then it only needs all our signatures then me and your mother will be off back to that sunshine which, they tell me, is keeping me alive. And you and your bride can be away on your wedding journey which I'm sure you're eager to begin.'

He made love to her that night and indeed every night of their stay abroad with an intensity that told her he was in some desperate straits which only the act of love could assuage – the act of mindless, greedy lust which, though he loved her, was really nothing to do with her, nor him, but the dread of what hung over him and which must somehow be hidden. He groaned and shuddered, giving no thought to her desire, should she have had any, nor her pleasure, should she have had any of that, lying against her, still trembling. His face in the lamplight was drawn, his eyes staring sightlessly to the corners of the shadowed room. When she touched his shoulder he turned again to her, violently, nuzzling his face to her breasts, curling his body about hers, a hurt child seeking comfort and reassurance, protection from the demons which had come to plague him.

'I can't do it, you know,' he said unnecessarily.

'It would be difficult at first.' Her voice was careful.

'You aren't listening to me, Tessa. *I cannot do it.*'

'Then what are you to do, my darling? You heard what Uncle Joss said.'

'Yes.'

'The papers are signed.'

'They are nothing to do with me, Tessa.' His voice had become sullen. 'I didn't ask for this.'

'Then ... will you refuse?'

He flung back the bedcovers and with a rapid stride moved to the table beside the fireplace. His tall, naked body was brown and beautiful in the lamp's glow. He poured himself a whisky, throwing it down his throat in one neat swallow. He had another, then turned to her, his face irritable, his eyes perilous but very sure.

'Oh, no. If I refuse my income will without a doubt be taken from me and I will be forced to manage on some schoolboy's allowance, or whatever they think I am worth. They must give me something since I am the son, but the bulk will go to Aunt Jenny and Charlie, and wouldn't Laurel be pleased about that?' His laugh was harsh.

'Does that matter?'

'It does to me. She is not a true Greenwood.'

'Neither am I.'

'You are my wife and will have what is your right.'

He stood by the fireplace, his body brooding and taut, staring into the fire which still blazed. 'Besides, there must be more than enough for us all. Let us say *my* contribution will be to help them spend it.'

She lay beside him as he tossed and fretted the rest of the night away, her mind struggling to retain the pleasant pictures of her wedding day. She wondered desperately if Joss Greenwood was aware of the box of imps he had opened and set free in his damaged son. She knew he had thought to provide Drew with an incentive to take up his duties by making him head of the firm, whereas he had merely turned his son from an irresponsible, but engaging pleasure-seeker, into a cheat and a liar.

## 22

The machinery in the mill had been running for twenty hours, two shifts of ten hours each, when it was turned off at eleven o'clock on Saturday night. Tomorrow was Sunday, the one day of the week when the mill was quiet, and as the operatives poured out of the gates their wooden-soled, steel-tipped clogs made a merry clatter on the uneven cobbles.

The evening, though dark by now, of course, was still warm with the residue of the heat left over from the day and the navy blue sky was clear and punctured by the light of a million stars.

They were weary, all of them, especially the women who, after a morning of washing and mangling, of cleaning and donkey-stoning the steps of the neat houses they rented from Mrs Harrison, had stood for ten hours on their shifts, spinning, carding, weaving, or toiling in the bleaching and dyeing processes which created Chapman cloth.

But tomorrow was their day off and with the prosperity which had come in the past few years as the textile trade of Lancashire flourished, many of them would be taking a train on an excursion to Preston or Blackburn, Bolton or Oldham where there might be a fair or a circus, a band playing or an open-air troupe of travelling players. Parish Jack, a singer, fluter and fiddler, was a great favourite, appearing regularly in Lancashire cotton towns at 'stirs' and merry-making, in beer-houses and inns. There might be games, a country wake or two, quoit playing, bowling, wrestling, 'bumble-puppy', bull-baiting, all contrived to entertain those who, in the last decade, had the means now to jingle a few spare coins in their pocket.

There were railway day trips to Southport and Blackpool, costing rather more than the working class could afford at two and sixpence a head, but on special days the fare was to be reduced to a shilling for children, one and sixpence for women, and two shillings for a man. With the increased wages the unions were promising them, another ten per cent it was said, it would not be long before they would all be paddling in the sea which few, as yet, had ever seen.

Life had changed since their parents' day when times had been hard. Not that they were easy now but at least families did not starve as once they had. And conditions would continue to improve as their 'Association' fought to achieve an even better standard of living. A pair of self-acting spinning mules which one man or woman could mind had brought about a higher wage trend that was gaining for the minders an aristocratic position within the industry. They had to work harder, naturally, for the higher spindle speeds made for a greater intensity of labour, but in one ten-hour day they earned more than their fathers had in sixteen.

The overlooker in the blow room, a man with the necessary half-crown to spare for such things, was off to Blackpool himself the next day. He had been dwelling on the delight of taking off his boots and dipping his feet in the sea, or even, greatly daring, changing in one of the bathing huts he had heard tell of and immersing his *whole* body in the sparkling wavelets. There might even be some lass with whom he could strike up an acquaintance, leading to who knew what pleasures. He was adjusting the small wheel on the carding machine which laid the raw fibres of cotton parallel, and further cleaned them, when the factory bell began its clangour signalling the end of the shift. Wrapped up in his dreams of tomorrow, the tool he had used for the adjustment was left carelessly teetering on the extreme edge of the machine.

What caused it finally to lose its precarious balance would never be known but when it fell it struck the metal wheel with which the overlooker had been tinkering.

The enormous building was empty by now. The night-watchman had said good night to Mrs Harrison an hour since, and one by one the managers and Mr Greenwood, the last to leave, had nodded to him as he touched his cap to them. He'd go and have a 'brew' as soon as the gate was locked, he told himself, for though the night was warm and a pint of ale would have been more welcome, Mrs Harrison and Mr Greenwood allowed no strong drink in the premises.

Although it was dark in the blow room the outline of the machinery showed up clearly in the light of the stars and the splinter of moon which hung in the sky just above the window. It was quiet and when the spark jumped as metal struck metal, the flare no greater than that of an instantly extinguished match, the sound seemed quite loud. After that there was a hush, almost as though the ghosts which

340

peopled the room – of those workers who had just gone thankfully, wearily, even blithely if they were off on a jaunt the next day – were holding their breath, waiting for what would happen next.

The machinery, once so lethal to small, unwary children, was now properly and securely fenced with wooden casing, miles of it, not just in this room but throughout the factory. The machines were cleaned regularly, of course, for cotton fibres collected inside, mixing, if they were not taken away, with the oil used to grease the parts. There was dust and fly and a collection of flake almost an inch thick in some places and it was to this that the spark jumped.

Like a small but voracious animal it fed on the dust hungrily, disposing of it in seconds before looking round, considerably grown by now from a spark to a flame, for something else with which to feed its appetite. As it grew so did its hunger, and gathering strength it gathered speed.

When the flame reached the soft fibre within the casing it ignited like gunpowder, only a small explosion as yet but loud enough to turn the head of the nightwatchman whose kettle had just come to the boil. He listened intently, prepared to guard against intruders as was his duty, but the sound was not repeated and the hot water was ready to pour on to the tea leaves. He poured it, sniffing the aroma of freshly brewed tea, then sat down and reached for the newspaper which he had found left behind by some manager. It was *The Times*, costing only threepence now the newspaper tax had been abolished. It was not a newspaper he himself would have chosen, *Frazers Magazine*, or *Punch* which both had pictures in them being more to his taste since his reading was not all that good. Still, this was better than nothing and he'd just pick out the headlines whilst his tea mashed.

The fire in the blow room, on the far side of the building from where the watchman drowsed over his *Times*, spelling out words with a calloused forefinger, had devoured the whole room now. If the inhabitants of the cottages in Chapmans Row had turned to look in the direction of the mill they would have seen at least a dozen windows lit up like the hobs of hell, but most of them were tucked up in their beds, getting a good night's sleep in preparation for tomorrow's enjoyment. There was to be a cheap trip to Manchester and Belle Vue Gardens, starting at seven, and they'd need to be up early if they were to get there in time to see the great Fife and Drum Contest, as well as look round the splendid gardens. They dreamed about the visit, those who were to go, as the fire, having devoured the blow room, passed through shaft after shaft, all horizontal and encased in wood. Backwards it surged to the room in which the raw bales of cotton were stored, pouncing on them and causing such an explosion the roof of the building directly above it was lifted twenty feet into the sky; then forwards to the carding room where every drum was stretched tight with cotton and every can filled with the soft rope of yarn which came off the machines.

As the explosion lit up the sky every person within three miles sat up in their beds exclaiming in unison though not perhaps in exactly the same words, but with the same apprehension, 'Good God, what the hell was that?'

Drew and Tessa had been making love, their sweat-slicked bodies entwined on the rumpled bed, the pale moonlight streaming through the drawn-back curtains and open window to touch them with a strange and unearthly beauty. He was at peace for the moment as though the spilling of his seed into his wife's empty womb had released the devils which came more and more often to plague him. Though neither was consciously aware of it, each month both breathed more easily when it became apparent that Tessa was not pregnant. Sometimes Tessa reflected upon it, wondering why she had never conceived and why, now that she was safely married, she did not desire a child. If she cared to dwell on it she supposed the one she held in her arms at this moment was as much as she could manage. Drew, if such a thought were to enter his often confused

342

mind, was aware that he could share her with no one. She was *his* mother, giving him security in a shaking and insecure world, as mothers should he believed, though he had not experienced it with his own. She was the only friend he had for despite his 'pals', the fellows with whom he roistered, he had no others. She loved him unquestioningly and he loved her. Since their marriage he had never been unfaithful to her, despite the many opportunities that had arisen, and he found great satisfaction in that and in the pleasure she now gained in his arms. She had become, in a completely feminine way, the twin he had lost and when their bodies were joined it was as though he and Pearce were returned to the safety of the womb.

'Good God, what the hell was that?'

It took them no more than seconds to fling off the bed-clothes and pull on shirts and breeches. Afterwards Tessa brooded on her own absolute certainty that disaster had struck though at the time she could not identify what it was that had them in such a panic.

'Good God, what was that?'

The words were but a whisper in Jenny Harrison's lamplit bedroom for did she have any real need to ask? Her experience told her. Her years in the cotton trade, her knowledge of mills and their workings had brought with them the fear which lies at the back of the minds of all manufacturers whose buildings are crammed with dangerous machinery, dangerous materials and substances which, if treated carelessly, bring the lot together in disaster, a chain of disasters which was the millowner's nightmare. Of course, it might not be *her* mill, or even a mill at all, but the explosion, for that was what it was, had come from the east and in that direction lay Chapmanstown and Crossfold.

Charlie was out of the bed he shared with Laurel and across the room to the window almost before the echoes of the explosion had begun to resound from hill to hill, those which stood guardian about the Penfold Valley. Even as he anguished on the certainty that disaster had struck *his* mill, for really, when he considered it, he had not actually heard the explosion since he had been deeply asleep, he was struggling into his breeches, hopping from foot to foot in his quite comical efforts to thrust the first one down the leg of his trousers.

'What is it, dear?' his wife asked, not particularly concerned since she had heard nothing.

'I don't know. Go back to sleep. I'll just go and...'

The flames leaped merrily from machine to machine in the spinning rooms on each floor of the mill, racing each other to be first to the weaving shed. Bobbins ricocheted like bullets from wall to wall and just as lethally, exploding into a hundred tiny shards of wood on impact. Beams above the machines, wooden and impregnated with nearly thirty years of oi[l] and cotton flake, caught fire, burned through and crashed down in the space of two minutes.

The nightwatchman, with his mug of tea still in one hand and his newspaper in the other just could not believe it, and stood with his mouth hanging open thinking he must be dreaming. It was no more than ten minutes since he had brewed up and whilst his back was turned, so to speak, someone had fired the whole bloody mill. He watched as the tape-sizing plant where the beams were full of yarn being sized to stiffen and strengthen the threads, became an inferno, the size bringing fresh life to flames which were already twice as tall as the building itself. The heat took his eyelashes and brows and he could smell his own hair beginning to smoulder and he moved then, screaming a warning, far too late, dropping his 'brew' and his newspaper as he raced for the mill gates.

The weaving shed was reduced to an unsteady, smouldering skeleton with a dozen huge tottering beams which once had supported whole floors now sticking up like the fingers on a hand against the brightening sky. The warehouse and despatch room were completely gutted when they arrived in the carriage, driven at a dangerously run-away speed by Drew himself. He was charged up to fever pitch with excitement, his face quite devilish in the lurid flames of the fire. Just for a second, before the horror of the disaster rooted her to the soot-blackened square of ground on which she stood, Tessa was quite appalled by her husband's terrifying intensity. He seemed bewitched, clasping her hand like a small boy who had come across some strange and alarming sight and is unsure whether to be afraid or exhilarated. The fear excited him, and the excitement frightened him, combining to produce a dangerous state of mind in which, it appeared to her, he might dash recklessly into the flames to save some small, quite unimportant item, risking his life to do so. And at the same time she sensed a gladness in him, a delirious relief as though he was overjoyed to see, at last, the destruction of the one thing he hated more than any other on earth.

Then the fury and savagery of the fire took everything from her mind. Her mother stood like a statue in the higgledy-piggledy collection of clothing she had flung on, her eyes following the line of useless water-filled buckets which passed from hand to hand, directed by a frantic Charlie; and then, amid the confused shouts and the realisation of those who operated it that it was a waste of time, her gaze turned to the large hand-pump which had required fifty men to haul it here and pump the water from the nearby river.

Dawn came early for it was not yet autumn and still her mother stood at the top of the brow which led down to the mill, now no more than a blackened, smoking pile, spread over an enormous area of what could only be described now as rubbish. There was nothing identifiable in the stinking debris: the outline of what might have been a spinning mule, melted down in the fierce heat to no more than a lump of metal; a half-burned-through beam, the unexplained mystery of why half of it was barely touched whilst the solid steel had melted.

Scores of silent onlookers stood about with no thought in their minds of going to Preston or Manchester, conscious

345

only of their jobs which had gone up in the flames along with the mill. Men moved about aimlessly through the pools of filthy water, scratching their heads for want of a better occupation, their clogs sinking into the water and the mud as they wondered what to do next. Children watched awed but thrilled, as Drew Greenwood had been, unaware of the consequences which would surely follow this night. And over it all the sun shone benignly from a cloudless sky.

Tessa could not seem to get her stunned and senseless mind beyond the wonder of how much space the mill had taken up. Across the acres and acres of wasteland she could now see the tidy row of cottages, the village church and its graceful spire, the smithy set beside the small row of shops and, to the left, the fields on which the men played cricket and the children ran in the meadow grass. Why, it's open countryside here, her astonished gaze told her, only the mill making it seem like any other small cotton town. There were trees and a park which she had never noticed before, a whole community which had lived under the wing of Chapman industry, nurtured by the thrift and common sense, the foresight and business acumen of women like her mother and men like Charlie.

She stood with her arm about Jenny's shoulders, drawn to her with compassion, their past animosity forgotten, watching as Charlie began to walk in the direction of the ruined mill, his long stride taking him down the slope and through the wide open gateway into the filthy yard. Jenny began to follow and Tessa went with her, both still stunned by the enormity of the destruction. Drew was helping the men push the hand-pump from the area. Pearce, his brother, had loathed – and been afraid of – the factory in his youth. Now Drew, who had been part of him, certainly did not feel the need to poke about in its remains as Charlie seemed intent on doing.

'Charlie,' Jenny's voice was nervous, warning her brother not to go too near.

'Don't fret thissen, our Jenny,' Charlie answered in a

strained, ragged voice, the broad vowels of his Lancashire heritage strong now in his distress. 'I'm nobbut tryin' to see if there's owt in't ...'

'What, for God's sake? Everything's burned to a crisp. What can there possibly be left worth risking getting yourself burned for?'

'Th'office were here, lass. Happen there's a file or two ...'

'Don't be daft, Charlie. Please come back. The wood's still smouldering and your clothes might catch alight.'

'Give ower. The men've cleared a path through theer to mek easier access for't hosepipes. I'll just ...'

'Charlie ... please ...' Jenny begged, then turned to the men who stood in dispirited groups in every corner of the yard. Some had come for miles and some seemed not quite so downcast as others, since it was not their mill which had burned down nor their jobs which were lost.

'Is it safe for him to go in there?' she asked them irritably for, really, her brother was so pigheaded sometimes and would listen to no one. Perhaps if another man told him, one of those involved in the fire-fighting, he might be persuaded to stop poking aimlessly around and come home for a hot bath and a rest. Heaven only knew what he would do with himself, nor she either, until the mill was re-built: the four other mills, the old ones built by Barker Chapman nearly eighty years ago, were small and with only enough managerial work to keep those already employed there fully occupied. But that was for tomorrow. Today must be got through and they were all in a badly shocked state. They needed food and sleep and the sooner they left this desolation the better.

The smoking beam, though as solid as one of the rocks up on Badger's Edge, made from the strongest wood, twelve feet long and at least two feet wide on each of its four sides moved ever so slightly. It stood bolt upright from the dense mass of melted machinery which supported it and though Charlie was at least six feet away and standing quite still as his eyes darted about in search of something he might salvage, a ledger perhaps, a wages book or some record of the work done here only yesterday, it seemed to line itself up with the menace of a wild animal ambushing its prey. It fell so slowly all those who watched were quite convinced Mr Greenwood could easily have side-stepped, and they stood waiting for him to do so, shouting a warning nevertheless, just to be on the safe side. It struck him squarely on the back of the head, falling with a sound like thunder, taking him with it into the muck and filth and water-soaked ashes, the charred wood and melted steel, the stinking ruin of what had once been the best and safest mill in the whole of south Lancashire.

For a moment that seemed to stretch on forever more there was an appalled silence. Then Jenny Harrison began to scream and it was not until her daughter gripped her savagely, pulling her into her own desolate arms – for how could any of them survive if Charlie, dear, dependable Charlie was lost to them? – that she fell into chilling unconsciousness.

The funeral of Charlie Greenwood, little piecer once, in the mill that he had for less than two years owned in partnership with his sister and nephew, was attended by high and low from every part of Lancashire and even beyond into Yorkshire where he had been well known for his clear business head and his reputation for fair dealings. Piecer he might have been, years ago, but when he died, besides being a wealthy man, his wealth now inherited by his distraught widow, he had also been the brother of the illustrious Joss Greenwood, once and for many years Member of Parliament for Crossfold.

The ladies were in black silk with corsage and sleeves ornamented with jet, and skirts with no more than seven flounces, for one did not want to seem ostentatious on such a sad occasion. The gentlemen wore black coat and trousers, mourning bands and tall black top-hats. Black, black everywhere except for the wisps of white cambric and lace, black-edged, which many of the ladies lifted to their eyes though they could not say they had exactly known the dead man.

His sister stood beside Joss Greenwood, erect, composed and quite, quite still, no sign of tears for her dead brother, though her face was paper-white behind her black veil. Her sister-in-law, once Kit Chapman who had built the destroyed mill, wept quietly, more, one felt, for the passing of so young a man than in grief, clinging to her husband's arm, not looking round at the mourners nor the hundreds of operatives who jostled for a place to watch the burying of the man most of them had known only as their millmaster. The remaining four Chapman mills were closed for the day in respect for Charlie Greenwood and the press of spinners and weavers was so great that the hillside on which the church stood was black with them.

His niece was impassive. Her eyes stared stonily at the coffin being lowered into the grave as she supported, or so it seemed to those nearest to them, the sad weakness of her husband and cousin, Drew Greenwood. His behaviour was strange, or perhaps not, when one remembered him as a wild youth. Despite the efforts of his family to persuade him to his proper place in the business, or so it was said in the valley, ever since his father had made it over to him this young and vigorous man had managed to live as though it had nothing at all to do with him. He had never been near the factory, now gone, which was his inheritance, since before he and his equally reckless brother had ridden off to the Crimea. Even marriage to his cousin had not steadied him and at the age of twenty-two he had not, to anyone's knowledge, done a hand's turn in his life and by the look of him drooping at the graveside, his hand in that of his beautiful wife, was not likely to do so in the immediate future.

The mourners had gone and the six adults who remained of Charlie Greenwood's family sat stiffly about the drawing-room wondering how soon they might, without giving offence, be allowed to leave: Kit Greenwood eager to return to the comfortable solitude she and her husband shared in the sunshine of Italy, her son to get his wife upstairs and into the private world he and she wove in their wide double bed and where he felt secure. The graveside had reminded him too sharply of that other one in Scutari, dark and silent and menacing. He needed sweet-scented flesh, pliant and warm, soft-hued with life, the feel of silk and the smell of sensuality to reassure him that he was not dead, and only with Tessa could he find that.

Jenny and Laurel sat side by side on the pale velvet of the sofa, the stark black of their mourning quite shocking against its soft prettiness. For once they were united in their stunned grief, not exactly leaning on one another but both conscious of the sympathy they shared. If she were honest Laurel would admit, only to herself, mind, that her sorrow was strongly laced with the fear of what was to happen to Laurel Greenwood without Charlie to ease the awkward path she trod. What would be her position now in this house where she had been mistress for so long? She could hardly picture her flighty cousin, Mrs Drew Greenwood, wanting to take over but at the same time could she, Charlie's widow, continue as what would now be, with Charlie gone, no more than housekeeper in Mrs Drew Greenwood's home?

Kit clicked her tongue disapprovingly as her husband asked the question she had been dreading. Though she might be his mother, she was not blind to the ... well, shortcomings was a mild way of putting it, of her only son and there was certain to be discord which would only serve to distress Joss Greenwood further. Jenny was fifty-six now – or was it fifty-seven? – and how much longer could she go on, particularly without Charlie? Kit felt she no longer cared. The mills which had once been her whole life could go to the devil, just as long as Joss took no harm from it. Let them get on with it, Drew and Tessa, and run the damn place into the ground. All she wanted was for the few years she and her beloved husband had left to be peaceful.

'Son, you will take Charlie's place now?' his father asked, but it was more of a command than a question, his manner saying quite plainly that, this time, there was really nothing else for it and Drew Greenwood might as well make up his mind to it.

Tessa closed her eyes and waited. She could feel her husband's hands clench over hers and his whole body seemed poised ready for flight. Already the day had placed a great strain on his slender reserve of stability, surely his father could see that? She herself was only too well aware that someone must run the business but surely he knew after all these years that it would never be Drew Greenwood? Never! They had been married for two years almost and in that time she had faced and learnt to accept what he was. Could not they? Providing no one obliged him to do anything other than what he did so well and easily, which was to be a country gentleman with thought for nothing but the care of his guns and horses, the cut of his jacket and the paying of his gambling debts, which he did quite without effort now, he would remain the pleasant, engaging husband she loved. But force him, if it were possible which she doubted, into the mill, and he would simply be unable to face it.

'Tessa...'

'Yes, darling?'

'I am ... do you not think ... there is something ... the stables...?'

'Of course, sweetheart.' She turned and kissed him on the cheek, just as one might a large child who has asked politely to be excused from adult company. 'I know Percy wants to check with you on the condition of your new hunter. But don't be too long for your mother and father are to catch the train to London shortly.'

'No indeed. Excuse me, Mother, Father, Laurel, Aunt Jenny.' He smiled endearingly, his manners exquisite as he stood up. 'I shan't be but half an hour. This damned hunter of mine has developed a cough and I said I would look in to see how he is. At the price one is forced to pay for a decent mount, one cannot afford to neglect it.'

There was a great and sorrowful silence when he had gone as the three who were most concerned contemplated, finally, the awful consequences of the Crimean War on the surviving son of the family. This was the heir; the one who, as was proper, would take up the reins of the business; who should, five years ago, have been compelled with his brother to take up the reins of the business. Tessa wondered at the naïvety of her aunt and uncle who, for some curious reason, had believed up until this very moment that he would. Could they not have seen, years ago, the weakness in *both* their sons? The lack of tough-fibred tenacity which every mill-master, whatever the size of his concern, needs to make a success of it? Joss Greenwood had had it, though he had channelled it into another undertaking. His wife, Kit Chapman had had it, refusing, thirty and more years ago to let a man take over and run her business when her father was killed. And in the veins of their sons had run their blood, the blood of the blunt, outspoken, stout-hearted north-countryman who would fight for his own bit of ground until they buried him in it. Her own mother, no kin of theirs except by the kinship of love, was the same, and so, sadly, had been Charlie. Now there was only Jenny Harrison left to carry on the great tradition and how was she to do it without her much-loved brother beside her? She was approaching sixty, a great age for a woman, and the task of rebuilding the mill at Chapmanstown, of organising into some semblance of order the huge financial commitments, of handling the hundreds of their customers who would now have to look elsewhere for the piece goods and dress goods with which Chapmans had supplied them, the enormous task of painstakingly putting together what the holocaust of the fire had smashed to pieces must now fall on her shoulders alone.

Jenny Harrison lifted her eyes from the pretty Meissen ornament she had been gravely studying and sighed. Her hollow-eyed face was a pale and dusty grey. Her flaunting mass of short curls was covered by her black mourning bonnet and she looked extinguished, the guttering flame of the candle of her life gone out at last. She had lost her brother whom she had loved. They had shared so much, she and Charlie, from the day when as a young boy nearly thirty years ago he had strode out manfully beside her to his place at the mill. He had suffered so much with her, even more than Joss: the bitter hardships, the hunger, the cold, the brutality of the work he was forced to, the desolation of the 'afflicted poor', doing his best despite his tender age to be a man. Now he was gone. She had lost her son, not only the memory of the merry-faced three-year-old who had been taken from her, but the haunted, hate-filled man he had become, who said he would never forgive her for what she had done to Tessa, her daughter, and to him, her son. She would live with that memory until she died with no other to soften it. The two men she had loved more than any other, both gone and, her expression said, she could stand no more.

'I've had enough, Joss,' she said simply, looking only at him.

'Jenny?' Her sister-in-law's voice was unsteady.

'You cannot ask it of me, Kit. If he . . .' she jerked her head in the direction of the door through which Drew had just gone, 'cannot manage, then you must sell it.'

'We cannot sell what has been in the family for almost a century, Jenny.' Kit Greenwood's voice was anguished, her indifference of a moment ago regarding the mills' future apparently fled away.

'Your family, not mine.'

'Dear God, Jenny . . .'

'It's no good, Kit. I'm finished. I can take no more. I want to sit in the sun, as you and Joss do, all day long with no decision to make but which hat to put on or how to fill the hours from breakfast to bedtime. It's gone now, lass, the force, or the need, or whatever it was that drove me on.

Merciful heavens, I'm fifty-seven. That mill's had me since I was a girl and now it's taken Charlie . . .'

Laurel began to sob broken-heartedly, the thought of her future and that of her children looking more and more bleak with every word Jenny spoke. Dear God, if Jenny went, presumably giving her share to Tessa, what would happen to them all? To herself whose world was tottering like a house of cards and to her children who were not only to be fatherless, but homeless and forced to manage on the tiny share she would be entitled to if the other mills were sold?

'Oh, be quiet, Laurel,' Jenny said sharply. 'There's more than enough for you to set up house somewhere and give your boys a decent education, providing you're careful.'

Careful! Laurel sobbed even harder and Kit moved over to her, patting her shoulder carelessly, at the same time keeping an eye on her husband for signs of his distress.

Tessa sat quite still and waited for the blow to fall and when they all turned to look at her, as she knew they would, inside her something shrivelled and died away. She had a life that she enjoyed with a man she loved and who needed her. There was nothing now that she wished desperately to do except to go on in the same pleasant way with no great joys and, more to the point, no great heartaches, with her husband and companion, Drew Greenwood. Her heart began to race madly out of control and the palms of her hands became sweat-slicked and yet were icy cold. Nausea rose to her throat. She knew exactly what they wanted, it was written in three pairs of eyes, since it meant they could all continue to drift through the lives they had chosen for themselves, as she had done since she was a small child. They were to take her freedom away from her. That was what terrified her. They were about to beg her to do her duty, as women of her class and heritage were bred to do. They were telling her they were entitled to her consideration. A sacrifice, then, and was she prepared to make it, three faces begged her to tell them. Her mother seemed to care neither one way nor the other, staring vaguely out of the window as though, now that she had made her stand, she really could not be expected to take any further interest in the outcome.

But could not the mills be sold as Drew had suggested, she beseeched them silently. There must be insurance, a great deal, to be collected for the burned mill. As for the other four, as far as she knew they were prosperous for had she not heard her mother say time and time again that the demands for higher wages by the spinners and weavers must, if it was at all possible, be met since trade was great and expanding? Well, then, four thriving mills. Easy to sell, she would have thought, and surely her uncle, or his wife, who was a clever woman with many contacts in the textile industry, could see to it? There was other property, land in Northumberland she had heard, shares in the railway, in mining and banking which would keep Drew Greenwood in horses and cravats for the rest of his life, surely.

She said so.

Sorrowfully, they replied, that though this was so Joss Greenwood's years in politics had not been without a price. The entertaining alone which was needed to keep a Member of Parliament where he was most likely to be noticed, had whittled away his wife's inheritance. And then there was the villa in Italy and years ago the enormous cost of knocking down Barker Chapman's old property, and building decent cottages in which their operatives might live. The mill at Chapmanstown had cost a pretty penny, expensive machinery, all paid for from the wealth her father had left Kit Chapman. This house was naturally, unmortgaged, but if the profit from the mills were to dry up ... well ...

'Tessa?'

'No, please, you cannot ask it of me. Besides, I know nothing of cotton or the commercial world. I wouldn't know where to start.'

'We would advise you, dearest ...'

'From Italy?'

'We must try, Tessa. Those mills were built by my grandfather . . .'

'Your grandfather, Aunt Kit, not mine. You and I are not related, not by blood. The responsibility is not mine, in any case. And then there is Drew. I must be here when he comes home, always.'

She glared angrily at his desolate mother and father, growing old before her eyes, since they knew only too well now what their son had become. 'You do understand, don't you? I would . . . would willingly help but . . . I am all he has . . .' Her voice petered out, the sharpness suddenly gone, and about her was the air of a cornered animal. When Briggs entered the drawing-room, after first knocking discreetly, she jumped quite violently, her nerves frayed and painful, her head aching so dreadfully she could barely see him.

'There is a gentleman to see you, sir.' He said the word 'gentleman' in such a way it was clear that in Briggs' opinion he was no such thing. 'Are you at home?'

'Who is it, Briggs?'

'A Mr Will Broadbent, sir, come to pay his respects.'

## 23

He looked prosperous, his black coat and trousers immaculate, his mourning bands correct in every detail. He did not even glance in her direction.

'Mr Greenwood, sir.' Briggs announced him to the master of the house but the visitor moved gently to take Jenny Harrison's hand.

'Mrs Harrison. I had no wish to intrude on your grief but I felt the need to come and tell you, and your family, in what high regard I held your brother. He was a fine man and will be sorely missed. I was at the funeral along with a great many men who admired him but I did not speak to you then, not with such a throng.'

Joss was on his feet, his hand outstretched, his face showing his sadness at the death of his younger brother but pleased that this man, a man he did not know, had taken the trouble to go out of his way to show his respect for him.

'We have not met, Mr Broadbent. You are . . . ?'

'I was overlooker, then manager for a short while in Mr Greenwood's spinning room at Chapmanstown. He was a fair master and a good man. I can say no more than that.'

'No, indeed. That is a praise enough and a decent epitaph for there are not many of those, I fear. You are acquainted with my wife?'

Will Broadbent bowed his head in Kit Greenwood's direction, courteous and respectful but in no way humble.

'Mrs Greenwood.'

'Mr Broadbent.'

'And this is my brother's wife and my daughter, Mrs Laurel Greenwood.' Laurel bowed coolly for surely as the widow it should have been to her the first condolences were paid?

'Mrs Greenwood.'

'And my niece, my son's wife, Mrs Drew Greenwood.'

'Mrs Greenwood,' he said for the third time and nobody seemed to find it strange that he did not bow to her. His eyes looked directly into hers and she flinched away from the cool hostility in them; from the height and breadth of him which filled the dainty room; from the terrible blankness of his face which had once been warm with his love and the almost cruel firmness of his mouth which had once covered hers with soft kisses.

She did not speak, indeed she could not, merely inclined her head towards him. He was a stranger after all, known

357

only to her mother in whose employ he had once been, and nothing more was expected of her.

'We were about to take tea, Mr Broadbent,' her aunt said, not unduly concerned with the proprieties at a time like this, or indeed at any other. 'Will you join us?'

'Oh, no, thank you all the same, ma'am. I will not impose on you ... on your ... I was passing the house, that is all, on my way to Hepworth and felt I could not go by without paying my respects. My carriage is at the door and I will be on my way but before I do ... I hope you will not be offended, Mrs Harrison...' His manner had become awkward, his face flushed but his eyes were clear and warm as he turned again to Jenny. 'If there is anything I can do to help you, perhaps some ... well, anything at all.' He straightened his already straight back, beginning to move out of the room. 'You have only to ask, ma'am.'

'That is good of you, Mr Broadbent.' Jenny's eyes grew soft and she lost that faint air of vagueness she had worn since her brother's death.

'Aye ... well, you and Mr Greenwood were good to me, ma'am.'

Tessa's jaws were clenched so tightly together she felt her teeth begin to ache with the pressure. A small shiver of pain shot through her right temple. Her thoughts spun wildly round and round in her head, one following hot on the heels of another, so closely they over-ran and became confused, but one was clear, dominating over all the others, and she clung to it desperately.

She must say something. She must keep him here, at least until she had arranged her chaotic mind into some sort of order. She must not sit here like a painted image over which the ice has set, frozen to her chair, her hands clamped to her lap, her lips sealed and grim. Her uncle was shaking Will's hand again and her aunt was nodding politely as they walked towards the door. Their voices came at her from a great distance, faint and disintegrated, and she knew that if she did not do something now, though God knows what it should be, her life would turn on to a path which would be ill-fitting, like some garment made for another. She stood in the middle of a great and barren expanse with nothing to indicate which was the best direction, the right direction for her to escape from it. She had reached a crossroad but with only one route, a route along which she was being inexorably forced. And Will held the answer to her critical situation. She did not even know why. It was all shadow and illusion, as life itself was, a cruel farce cheating its players contemptuously, the injustice of it scarring them badly, as she had been scarred, as everyone in this room had been scarred, even Laurel whose awkward nature was surely the result of what life had done to her as a small child in the mills. Always it came back to them: the mills. They were the cause of all the turmoil and heartbreak that was in this family. They were the sword which hung over them all, the prison from which none, it seemed, could escape. And she was to be their next prisoner.

Her uncle had his hand on the door handle, ready to usher their guest away to his carriage, to his life, wherever that was, when the door opened inwards and the handsome, apologetic, endearingly smiling face of Drew Greenwood appeared. He had the air of a small boy who knows he has been 'out to play' for far too long and is bound to get a scolding, but could they not see how much he had enjoyed himself and, really, would they begrudge it to him on this sad day? He had been extremely fond of Charlie, as they well knew, and if his heart was distressed was he not entitled to ease it in the comfort of the stable with his beloved hunter? Later, when it could be arranged, it would be in the comfort of his own bed with his beloved wife.

'I beg your pardon.' He sprang to attention with all the grace and good manners bred in him by a succession of nannies, tutors, schoolmasters and, more extensively, his close contact with Nicky Longworth and his friends up at the Hall. 'I was not aware we had guests.' He looked Will up and down, his arrogant superiority showing quite plainly for this man was not their kind, but he smiled and waited courteously to be introduced.

'This is Mr Broadbent, Drew. He was acquainted with Charlie and . . .'

'I worked in his mill, lad.'

'Indeed? My word.' Drew was not at all sure how to deal with Mr Broadbent's bluntness and, never having shaken the hand of a working man before, was not quite certain how to go about it.

'This is my son, Drew.'

'I believe we have met before, Mr Greenwood. It was in the spinning room when I worked for Chapmans.'

'Indeed.'

There was an awkward pause. Will stood quietly, composed, merely waiting politely, as a guest should, to be shown the door but before anyone could move towards it Tessa sprang up, turning all heads in her direction, and rang the bell.

'Really, Uncle Joss, we cannot allow Mr Broadbent to make that long journey to Hepworth – that is near Rochdale, is it not, Mr Broadbent? – without some refreshment, can we?'

Her uncle hesitated and his wife waited, as she always waited, for his answer. Then taking Will by the elbow he began to urge him, reluctantly on Will's part, towards the chair by the small fire.

'No, of course not, Mr Broadbent.'

She had no idea, not the slightest, what she was to say, or do, or on what topic she wished to address him, if there was one. She only knew that this man held the remedy to her desperation; that he was the one to get her out of the corner into which she was backed. Dear God, *how?* she beseeched silently, but no sign of her agitation showed on her impassive face and her eyes did not once lift to his as the conversation flowed slowly, politely, somewhat awkwardly among the company.

They drank tea and ate small cakes and Drew spoke enthusiastically on the virtues of his hunter, on the anxieties of the cough which afflicted the animal and on his chances of taking him to Leicester when the hunting season began.

'You are not to take over the immediate running of your mills then, Mr Greenwood?' Will asked courteously, the first spark of interest pricking his eyes.

'Good God, no. I am no millmaster, Mr Broadbent. I know nothing of spinning or weaving.'

Tessa held her breath. The room was as hushed as a church and she saw from the corner of her eye Will's interest quicken even further.

'If I am not being presumptuous, then who is to take Mr Greenwood's place?' he asked. 'Surely, ma'am,' addressing Jenny Harrison, 'you are not to manage alone?'

Jenny shook herself lightly, as though coming back from some distant place where she had gone to escape the bird-twittering of the drawing-room.

'I? Oh, no, Mr Broadbent.'

'Then . . . ?' He was very polite but clearly confused.

'My sister is to come to Italy with us, Mr Broadbent. She is . . . not herself yet, after the death of our brother, and feels in need of a holiday.'

'I see,' he said, though clearly he didn't.

'The managers will attend to such things as are necessary, I believe. It shall all be left to them.' Drew's voice was careless.

'Indeed, that sounds well enough, Mr Greenwood, but in my experience that is a quick way to ruin. There is only one man to control a business and that is its owner.'

'Really? And you are qualified to give such an opinion?' Drew enquired insolently and Tessa saw Will's face register anger as his hosts' son reached for a cigar, lit it without permission to do so in his mother's drawing-room, then blew smoke slowly from between pursed and smiling lips.

Will's voice was quiet. 'I am a businessman myself. Some years ago I formed a co-operative spinning and weaving concern which I run for its owners who are, of course, the shareholders. As I have a considerable number of shares

361

myself it is in my own interest to ensure the business prospers. I would not care to see it in the hands of men who work solely for a pay packet at the end of each week.'

Of course, he had heard – as who in the Penfold Valley, indeed in south Lancashire had not? – of the reluctance to take up his responsibilities as the Greenwood heir. Had it not been for his uncle, just buried that day, and his aunt who, it seemed, had lost not only her will but her desire for a commercial life, the business would long ago have gone the way of all such mismanaged ventures. Despite the expansion in the textile trade and the ensuing profitable business, it was to no purpose if there was no one to snatch an opportunity when it presented itself, some enterprising player to gamble, to take a chance, to recognise an opening, and that only the man at the top was capable of doing. Seemingly, amazingly, it was not to be Drew Greenwood.

'Then . . . ?' Will began.

Drew's voice was high, haughty, the privileged class answering one of its inferiors who had no right to have spoken up in the first place.

'I can only repeat that the managers at the mills are highly regarded by the family and will continue the running of them as they have been employed to do. I can see no reason to do the work when one employs, and pays, others to do it Mr Broadbent. My wife and I are agreed on it, are we not, Tessa?' He took Tessa's hand possessively in his where it lay passively. Not even Tessa saw the sudden clenching of Will Broadbent's strong jaw.

'I see,' he said coldly, 'then I wish you well, Mr Greenwood, and I must also bid you good day. I have presumed for too long on your hospitality.'

In the polite confusion of leave taking no one noticed that not only did Mr Broadbent avoid Mrs Drew Greenwood's hand, he managed to avoid addressing her at all.

She waited two weeks before she called on him.

'Mrs Greenwood?' Though he was clearly surprised it in

362

no way shattered his icy disdain. His office was small, not at all the splendid affair her own mother had worked in at Chapman Manufacturing and which now, if she could not arrange it to her own satisfaction, awaited her.

It was a cool, blustery day, a shower or two and the wind disturbing the tops of the trees which crowded the floor of the valley in which the mill stood. A small fire burned in the grate at his back and before him was an enormous desk taking up a great deal of space, the rest of the room crammed with shelves in which were hundreds of books of a highly technical nature. On the desk were papers, ledgers, account books, one assumed, pens and pencils, a tray filled with dozens of small wooden cups in which the operative's wage was presented to him. There was a 'piece' or pick glass used to examine cloth construction. The base formed a one-inch square frame, she remembered her mother telling her during one of her attempts to interest her daughter in life at the mill, to count the threads per inch in the cotton. A clock ticked loudly on the wall and as though to remind her that he was a busy man, to state her business and be off, he took out his pocket watch and looked at it. He remained standing behind his desk and did not ask her to sit.

'What may I do for you, Mrs Greenwood?' he asked her coldly.

It was not going to be easy. He was not going to make it easy for her. His steady eyes told her he didn't like her much but he was a man who was not rude to a lady, particularly when she might have come to do business with him, for above all, where she was concerned at least, he was a businessman.

'May I sit down, Will?' She tried a smile but she was nervous and the muscles in her cheeks did no more than twitch. She was in mourning, of course, of the deepest black but her gown was elegant with a wide skirt and flowing sleeves and her large brimmed hat was piled high with black tulle roses. She looked, she knew, slightly frail, pale-skinned, her dark hair smoothed back into an intricate chignon by Emma,

363

her face veil turned up to allow him to see the velvet grey of her long-lashed eyes. She meant to make use of every advantage she possessed.

'What is it, Mrs Greenwood?'

He was telling her he had no time to waste on pleasantries, indeed he had no time to spare for her at all. He was busy with his own concerns, his manner said, and he could see no reason for her to be here in any case. She would be best served to state her case and be on her way.

'I have come to ... well, you know how I am placed, Will, with the mill, now that Charlie is dead and my mother gone to Italy?'

'I had heard, yes.' And he was not particularly concerned.

'I am sure you realise how difficult it is, for the family, I mean.'

'Really! In what way?'

She leaned towards him, smiling her brilliant smile. If he would just invite her to sit down, perhaps drink a cup of tea with him, it would make matters much easier. She had held him once in the palm of her hand, had him eating out of it, as the saying went, willing to do everything she asked providing she did not leave him. He had loved her, wanted to marry her, and there must be some of that feeling left, surely? He would not, could not turn her away without hearing what she had to say, and how much more relaxed it would be if they were to chat, civilly, if not warmly, over a cup of tea. They had parted cruelly. He had spoken bitter words then and she felt herself curl up inside at what she must say but, really, she could think of no other solution and so she must swallow her pride and hope that he had forgotten, or at least allowed the memory of that day to fade. They had met since at Annie's and he had called her Tessa then. They had been ... polite. There had been ... something. Could they not be ... perhaps friends?

But she still felt the need to tread warily, knowing that this man could be dangerous if he chose. She had thought him easily managed, gentle, a peaceful man, a man who would be happy to go through life in a moderate and tranquil way. He was strong, certainly, strong-willed and tough-fibred and would let no man own him, but surely she, as a woman, should be able to reach that core of decency which was the essence of Will Broadbent?

'Though it is some time ago now I have not yet congratulated you on your marriage, Mrs Greenwood. Allow me to do so now,' he continued smoothly, swinging her cruelly off balance with the sudden turn of conversation, 'though as I said when we met previously, I must admit to a slight bewilderment at your choice of husband. When first I heard your name mentioned in connection with matrimony it was linked with that of some landed gentleman from Cheshire. You were to be married to *him*, I was led to believe, or was he too found to be unsuitable?'

It was as though he had cut the ground from beneath her feet opening up a hole, deep and black, which she did not care to contemplate and into which, if she did not take care, she might tumble. Robby Atherton had not been seen nor heard of since the day he had been told of his true parentage. It seemed that her 'parfit gentil knight' had not the heart nor stomach to face her again, either as her brother or her love, and though she had not blamed him, her heart had never quite recovered. He had been forgotten now by the Penfold Valley, as though he had not existed, but not by this man, it appeared.

He smiled and his face took on a musing expression. 'Do you know, Mrs Greenwood, if I live to see ninety I will never understand the ways of the gentry, since I suppose that is what you call yourself, particularly the gentlemen. Now, if I were your husband there is one thing you could be absolutely sure of: under no circumstances would I allow my wife to come begging favours of another man. Because that's what you're here for, isn't it? You want something from me, don't you? You would hardly drive all the way from Crossfold to Hepworth otherwise, looking fragile and wan in your mourning gown, doing your best to seem helpless when you have never been helpless in your life. Really, Mrs Greenwood, it doesn't suit you, this pretence that you are no more than a weak and helpless female. You should try being honest sometime, as I told you once before, I believe. You might find it to your advantage in the long run.'

'Will, please, you have not heard...'

'Nay, and I don't think I want to. It seems the young gentleman whose heart you captured and who was so uniquely suited to your life-style and station in life and whose charms far outshone my own, and for whom you were willing to run to the ends of the earth, barefoot if needs be, no longer found favour in your eyes and that your cousin, the estimable Drew Greenwood, took his place. Really, Mrs Greenwood, one cannot hope to keep up with you. Three men in your bed already and you barely in your twenties...'

'Will, please...'

'No, really, you are to be admired for your tenacity, Mrs Greenwood. I suppose when you consider it, your cousin would be the better prospect: sole heir to the might and wealth of the Chapman concerns whereas a gentleman whose estate would simply devour any money you brought to him might not be such a catch. As for the simple over-looker in your family's mill ... well, need I go on? I only hope your husband has the stamina and backbone to take on not only you, but his inheritance, that is if he is to do so. Or are you, perhaps, to take up your mother's position?'

He grinned wickedly, lifting a sardonic and knowing eyebrow.

She did not wait any longer to be invited to sit down but sank into the nearest chair, the thudding in her chest painful and taking her breath away, echoing in her temples, at the hollow of her throat and the pulses in her wrists. She felt dizzy, weary, as wave after wave of futility and defeat washed over her. She had thought it would not be easy, that she might have to beg and plead a little, make him realise that she had changed – had she really? – that she would make it worth his while perhaps. Would that have worked? But now she could see it was impossible. He hated her, despised her, or not even that. He was indifferent, and that was worst of all. He no longer cared if she survived or not. He was unconcerned with her future or even if she had any, and certainly had no softer emotion lingering in his heart which had once loved her.

'Who's to look after it all, Mrs Greenwood, whilst your husband chases about the countryside on that thoroughbred hunter of his, or tramps the Squire's moor shooting pheasant and grouse, or indeed everything that takes wing? It's been three weeks now and those mills won't be looking quite so profitable, I dare say, not without Mrs Harrison or Charlie Greenwood at the factory gate before the bell goes.'

'The managers ...'

He made a contemptuous movement with his hand and sat down at last, lifting the tails of his splendidly fitting coat. Though his face had none of the masculine beauty of Robby Atherton or Drew Greenwood, nor the etched and lean superiority of Nicky Longworth, it was infinitely more virile with a compelling strength which said that no matter what life cared to fling at *him*, he would never yield to it. His hair was still short and inclined to roam about his head as though he had cut it himself, carelessly, with the first pair of scissors which came to hand, but his smoky amber eyes were steady, firm, his skin brown and smooth. His whole appearance spoke of his rise in life. He was a businessman now, a man of consequence with a new, detached villa on the outskirts of Hepworth, she had heard, set in half a dozen acres of landscaped garden. He had a well-bred bay to ride when he cared to, and a carriage and pair for when he did not. He was an exceedingly attractive and successful gentleman and she wondered idly why he had never married.

'You cannot leave it to your managers, you know. If you do you will go under.' It was said irritably.

'What else am I to do?' She was more composed now, though her heart was still inclined to miss a beat. Now that they had left behind the delicate issue of Robby Atherton and were addressing themselves, she hoped, to the problem of Chapman Manufacturing, Will appeared to be, if not agreeable, at least prepared to discuss what might be done. If she could just get him to listen she was certain she could persuade him to what she had in mind.

'You are recovered now?' He spoke sharply and again his change of direction disconcerted her. Just as she was about to breathe more easily, thinking that she might at last get round to what she had come for, he led her somewhere else, giving her no time to get her thoughts into any kind of order. Recovered? What did he mean? Surely he was not talking about the fever she had contracted over two years ago? He had gone away just before, Annie had said, come up here and started his own venture, far too busy making his own life to bother about hers which had been smashed apart, but then had she herself not been far too busy with the loss of Robby Atherton to bother about *him*? Well, they had both lost something all those years ago but now he had found something to replace it and so had she and she would not spend the rest of her days in the mills which had taken Charlie's life, and her mother's too, in a way, though she still lived. She would find something, someone, she was determined on it, to look after what she and Drew had been left.

'Yes.' She smiled for she must keep on his right side. 'I was ill for a while but I am a tough north-countrywoman and so I recovered.'

'Your . . . friend did not care to stay then, to see you back to health?' His voice was harsh, scornful.

'My . . . friend?'

'Your lover, if you prefer?'

'Please, Will. Must we continually go back to something which happened a long time ago? It's over now and I . . . we must all move on, must we not?'

'I dare say, but now I must ask you to state your business for I've not got all day to sit and gossip.'

368

'No, indeed. You are a man of some importance, I am told and . . .'

'Give over, lass. Let's get to the point. I'm not one of your pedigreed nincompoops who needs to be buttered up before he can be asked to do anything. Speak plain and be done with it.'

She sighed for at last it had come and, as he said, best be done with it.

'I've come to offer you a position, Will.' There, it was out, thank God. She did not like it but the devil drives where the need must, or some such twaddle, and the devil was certainly driving her when she must grovel to this man who had once grovelled to her, well almost. But it was done now and when they had talked of wages and all the other difficult but necessary things – she would leave that to him, having no idea what they might be – she could get on home and tell Drew that he and she could continue to play as they had done, she realised, all of their lives.

'A position? And what might that be, my lass?' He had begun to smile now, his eyes narrowing in amusement, his slanting mouth turning up at the corners. His eyebrows lifted and she could feel the sudden tension in the air, coming not from him but from herself. He was vastly pleased about something, his bold expression said, his whole lounging body said, and again she felt awful uncertainty nibble at her. But what the hell? She was not afraid of him, or his damned insolence. She lifted her head imperiously.

'I would like you to be my general manager, Will. In charge of the mills, I mean. Of course there are only the four smaller ones at the moment but once you get the rebuilding of Chapmanstown under way you would be fully occupied, I'm sure. There will be a lot to see to, arranging with builders and whoever else is concerned with such things, and I'm sure you are right about the men in charge at Crossbank and the others. They will be lying in their beds until nine each day, leaving it all to the overlookers and . . .

well, you will know what I mean. The sooner they are all under the direction of one man the better.'

'Indeed you are right, Mrs Greenwood. I couldn't agree more.'

'Oh, Will, I'm so glad.' She smiled in gratification then became business-like again. 'Now I will leave the question of wages to you since I know you will not cheat me. I have no idea what a manager earns but...'

He began to laugh then. Lifting his head in genuine enjoyment, highly diverted, it seemed, and not at all concerned that he might be offending her. His laughter echoed round and round the room and there was a warm, dancing merriment in his eyes as he turned at last to look at her.

'Tessa, there really is no other woman in the world who would have the damned impudence to come here, after all that's happened between us, and offer me a job as manager in her mill. Does your mind dwell on nothing but what is best for Tessa Harrison, or did it not occur to you that I have my own mill to run, my own business to attend to? I've built this concern up until it's become one of the most productive in south Lancashire, for its size. Oh, not to be compared with Chapmanstown, I'll grant you that, but I'm damned proud of it just the same, and of myself. I've dragged myself up by my bootstraps, aye, and done a few things I'd tell no one about to get here, and not just get here, but to stay _alive_ when I was a lad, and if you think I'm going to jeopardise it all for the sake of a lass who isn't worth a hundred of them in my mill then you must be dafter than I thought.'

'But, Will...' She ignored the insult which she found she did not care about just now. 'You told us it was a co-operative and that means it's not really yours...'

'I own the majority of the shares.'

'I don't quite know what that means.'

'It means that if I left it on its own while I concern myself with your business, mine would suffer and my shares be made worthless.'

370

'But you said yourself that Chapmans needed to be under the direction of one man.'

'Aye, and so it does, but I'm not that man.'

'Please, Will, please. I would pay you anything you asked.'

'*Anything*, Tessa?'

Again his eyes danced with evident enjoyment. 'I really cannot think there would be anything at all which might tempt me. Not now. My life has gone on, you see, leaving you where we last met and what you have done and what I have done no longer matters to the other. I am no longer at your beck and call...'

'Will, please, think it over...'

'I have no wish to think it over, and no need.' His eyes had turned cold again, cold and disdainful. 'You really must become used to the fact that you can't have what you want, whenever you want it, Mrs Greenwood. You mean nowt to me, and neither does that damned business of yours. You and your fine husband can go to the devil for all I care...'

'Will, for God's sake, Will.' Her voice cracked painfully and she stood up, hauling herself to her feet as though she was clawing her way to the surface of a boiling torrent which was dragging her under. Her eyes had turned a brilliant, quite incredible silvery grey, like crystal, in her despair and her breasts rose, drawing his eyes to them. Her face had flushed to rosy pink and the soft flesh of her mouth was moist and swollen. She put out her hands to him in desperation and he felt himself begin to move towards her, his body answering the appeal of hers. 'I'm ready to pay you any wage you ask.' Her voice was husky, just as it once had been in the fierceness of their lovemaking. 'I'll give you shares in the mill, which, I believe ... I have been told, though I really know little about it, will give you a small part of the ownership. Apart from the ones left to Laurel by Charlie it all belongs to Drew and me and he would give anything you name not to have to go in the mill.'

'Would he indeed?' His own voice sounded strange in his ears. His eyes gleamed, an intense speculative gleam which

371

she was not sure she cared for. The lazy unconcern had gone completely, as had his indifference, and she felt the first feather of alarm touch the nape of her neck.

'He ... you will have heard of his brother's death, no doubt?' Her mouth had dried up and she seemed to have trouble forming the words but he merely continued to watch her, allowing her to stumble along at her own pace. 'Well ... they were ... being twins, you understand, they were very close and Pearce's death hit him hard.' Dear Lord, why was she telling him all this unless it was to dissipate the curious tension which had sprung up from somewhere? 'He was himself wounded and it has left him ...'

'You really have no need to explain, my dear. Your husband's ... afflictions are well known to me. Remember we worked ... I use the term loosely, you understand ... together in the Chapman spinning room.'

'So you will help him then?'

'Not him, Tessa, oh, no, not him.'

'Then ... ?'

'You and I ... once ... had a very delightful arrangement, did we not? Do you remember?' His voice was like silk and his eyes had become a warm and appreciative brown and she knew immediately, of course, with what coin he was asking her, no demanding her to pay and she felt the fury explode in her, not just with him and the effrontery of what he implied but at the sudden excitement which stirred in her at the idea.

She had never been so humiliated in her life, she told herself, whipping up her own temper until her cheeks were scarlet with her outrage. His eyes were merry now, maliciously so, and he had the greatest difficulty, she could distinctly see it, in preventing himself from grinning broadly at her discomfiture. Her rage struck even more deeply, a scorching blow which had her savagely struggling not to hit him. If she had held a pistol in her hand she would have shot him in his smiling face and been glad to see the flesh shatter, the blood flow. Her heart was banging and crashing

372

inside her – *why, for God's sake, why?* – far too big for her chest, and deep, deep within her, where no one could see or even know of its existence, the core of her female self, that which had lain dormant for many, many years, began to unfurl and throb, and she hated him, hated him for it.

She lifted her head and though her eyes were hot and baleful with her need to hide from him what was in her, she managed to keep her words cool and contemptuous.

'May I ask what you are suggesting, Mr Broadbent?'

'Come on, my lass. Don't play the innocent with me. I know you better than any man, I would say, and certainly better than that husband of yours. You know exactly what I am saying or do you want me to spell it out to you? Not only do you know, you're excited at the thought, aren't you? You're a woman, Tessa, and though I've had my share before and since, there's been none to match you when it comes to ... pleasing a man, and to taking pleasure from it yourself. I'm sure you know what I mean. I can see it in your eyes right now. So what d'you say? Shall we strike a bargain? You come to my bed and I'll see to those mills of yours for you. You and Drew Greenwood can skylark about to your hearts' content, if you've a mind, and I'll keep your mills running to pay for it, but I'll want a share of the profit, and a share of Drew Greenwood's woman to go with it.'

He grinned, then, with all the time in the world and the unconcern to go with it, reached into the silver cigar case on his desk, selected a cigar, lit it and when it was drawing to his satisfaction, leaned back in his chair and waited.

'*You can go to hell, Will Broadbent*, and the sooner the better as far as I'm concerned. I'd see the mills in ruins before I'd let you touch me again.' She gathered her pelisse about her as she leaped up, snarling and dangerous, ready, should he put out a hand to her, to bite it off at the wrist but he merely grinned more broadly. He took another puff of his fine cigar, his long legs stretched out indolently beneath his splendid desk.

'Just as you please, Tessa,' he said as though it was nothing to him, one way or the other. But when she had gone, sweeping regally from the room, elbowing aside the clerk who would have guided her down the steps to her carriage, he leaned forward in his chair and pressed a trembling hand across his suddenly sweating face.

## 24

'I shall go alone then. If you cannot or will not come with me, which seems to me to be nearer the truth, I shall go alone. You know that Nick has set his heart on this holiday, and on having you there. You are a great favourite, darling, not only with the gentlemen of whom, by the way, I am inordinately jealous, but of the ladies. They seem to find us immensely amusing because of our industrial background and the way, one supposes, we have risen above it. You make them laugh, my love, with your outspoken ways and your quite careless disregard of their belief that they are superior to us. Oh, come with me, Tessa, please. I know we are still in mourning for Charlie, but he wouldn't mind. You know how he was. We have never been stag-hunting before. They say that runs of eighty miles are not uncommon and not a third of the horses which start out are in at the death. What a challenge, eeh? You and I against the others. What d'you say?'

Drew Greenwood paced his wife's sitting-room with all the fire and intensity of a beast which, having been caged, is searching, snarling and dangerous, for the way out. He had just ridden back from the Hall where he had spent the day riding to hounds with the Squire and his guests. He was over-excited as he seemed to be so often these days, Tessa

thought. Either that or bored to distraction, casting around
for something to amuse him, petulant and churlish at times
and at others boyish in his eagerness to tempt her to come
and share his play. But slowly, she knew, he was becoming
increasingly hostile to what he saw as her stubbornness in
the matter of the mills. She felt there was something barely
harnessed within him and if she let go he would not be able
to hold on to it without her, but she must put the factories
into some kind of order before she could resume the pleasurably careless life-style they had enjoyed together before
the disaster of the fire and Charlie's death. No matter what
she said, how she tried to explain to him the need for
someone to be concerned, he still insisted that managers
were employed for that particular purpose and that he could
see no reason for this ridiculous obstinacy on her part. And
he was becoming isolated from her in a quite frightening
way. She who had been his 'steadier' was accused of being
tedious and not half the fun she once had been. He would
not listen to her when she explained patiently that though
they had the managers in whom he set such store to see to
the running of the sheds at Broadbank and Crofts Bank and
the spinning rooms at Crossbank and Highbank, the four
older mills, *someone* was needed to oversee *them* until
order was restored. There was the re-building of Chapmanstown to be considered, insurances, she had been told
vaguely by her mother before she left for Italy, and who was
to do it if she did not? Her own sense of responsibility
towards the accursed business which, after all, belonged
to the Greenwoods, irritated her beyond measure and she
wished heartily that she could do as Drew wished and just
leave the whole damned lot to go to the devil. But something
stopped her. Something only half-understood which had
perhaps to do with old Joshua Greenwood who had died at
Peterloo and all those who had come after him – her own
mother, her Uncle Joss, Charlie. Or perhaps it was her own
stubborn will which would not allow itself to be beaten,
plus the certain knowledge, finally, that Drew would always

375

be just as he was now, never able to be the Greenwood *they* had been, and which, surprisingly, she *was*.

She had said as much to Annie when she had ridden over to her cottage, shortly after she had been to see Will. Drew had gone to the races with Nick and Johnny, sick to death with her long face, he said, and set on escaping it.

'I don't know where to begin, Annie,' she moaned. 'It's like turning a three-year-old loose in a kitchen with instructions to prepare and cook a fifteen-course dinner for thirty people. I have never been in the counting house except to call on my mother and only in the yard to pick up Drew and Pearce and I have never once set foot in a spinning room or a weaving shed. I have heard my mother speak of carding and drawing frames but if you should ask me what they meant and my life depended on the answer I could not describe them. Will you not at least come with me for a day or so to start with? You are a spinner and have some idea as to what I might be looking for. We could walk round the mills together and you could tell me what is happening . . .'

'Yer overlookers could do that, Tessa, much better than me, or one o't managers.' Annie's voice was blunt.

'But I don't want them to know I'm so ignorant. Dear God, Aunt Kit had her father to guide her through it all and Mother had Aunt Kit. Dammit, I've no one.'

Annie hesitated. ''Appen if you was to speak polite-like to Will . . .'

Tessa's face set in an icy mask of contempt. 'I have already offered him the position of manager but he declined. He does not care what I do, he said. I can go to hell in a handcart before he would lift a finger to help me.'

'Yer can't blame 'im, lass. Yer tried him sorely a few years back an' 'e'd not forget in a hurry. Still, I thought 'e might 'ave given thi some hint, some idea where tha might begin. Mind you, 'e said nowt ter me when 'e were 'ere last . . .'

'You've seen him?' Tessa felt her heart lurch painfully.

'Aye. 'E comes over now an' again, like 'e always did, an' we 'ave a chin-wag. Just because you an' 'im 'ad a fallin' out

376

years ago, doesn't mean 'im an' me 'ave to do't same.'

Tessa's face was stiff, she could not have said why since
what was it to her if Annie and Will had remained friends?
She had known, of course, so why did the mention of it
cause this agitation in her?

'You never mentioned him.'

'Would it 'ave made any difference if I 'ad?' Annie, quick
to take offence at the implied criticism and letting it be
known that what she did was her own business, lifted the
kettle from the fire and banged it down on the dresser just
as though the innocent utensil was the cause of her pique.

'No, indeed. None at all.'

'Well, then?'

'Indeed.'

'So what are we arguin' about?'

'We are not arguing, Annie, and certainly not over Will
Broadbent who is not worth giving the time of the day. I
don't want to hear another word about him. I'm going to
get out the carriage tomorrow and go to Crossbank and
show *him* and everyone else who thinks I shall fall flat on
my face that I'm as much a Greenwood as my mother.' She
lifted her head challengingly but in her eyes was the
dreaded anticipation that that was exactly what she would
do, and if she was to fall who would pick her up?

Annie sighed sadly. 'I'm right sorry. I wish I could 'elp
thi, but I can't.' It was said simply, the truth of her words,
the certainty of them very obvious. 'I 'ave me own life ter
sort out now.' Tessa, absorbed with her own problems, did
not hear her. Annie put out her hand. 'Is there no other
way? Could not that 'usband o' thine not 'elp out, or 'appen
yer could sell the mills?'

'I suppose I could try but I don't even know enough to
guess at an asking price. Dear God, if only Aunt Kit or Uncle
Joss or even Mother had remained for long enough to tell
me what to do.'

'From what thi tells me, Mrs Greenwood can't do wi' 'avin'
yer uncle worried. She only cares about 'im an' spendin'

what days they 'ave left together in peace.' In a way, Annie could understand that: a bit of peace must be a wonderful thing to have. Not that she'd ever known any, what with her mam dying and four children to be fetched up somehow, but a thing to be treasured was peace of mind. ''Ow old d'yer reckon they are?' she asked, more to take Tessa's mind from her problems than her own curiosity.

'Who cares?' Tessa's voice was irritable. For God's sake, Annie was really the limit sometimes. She could think of the most foolish things just when sensible advice was needed. What did it matter how old her aunt and uncle were? It was *now* that concerned her and what *she* was to do, if she could only think what that was. Perhaps it might be an idea if she were to go and see ... the bank manager ... or that lawyer chap in Crossfold her mother had dealt with. Would it not be practical to find out about the mill's financial position? That sounded sensible. Its financial position. How much ready cash there was available. Would it be in the bank, hers and Drew's inheritance, and if so could she get hold of some of it? Briggs had already intimated that one or two tradesmen had presented their accounts. No hurry, naturally, since the Greenwoods and Harrisons were valued customers who normally settled their debts immediately they were incurred, not like the gentry who seemed to think next month, next year or even never would be quite agreeable and who could take serious offence, and their custom elsewhere, if pressed.

She felt quite pleased with herself. She stood up and smoothed down the tight-fitting black breeches she wore, smiling a little for she had made a decision and had a sensible plan of action. That was what she would do tomorrow. She would call on the bank manager and the lawyer and then, step by step, one action surely leading to another, she would gradually take a hold on the unwieldly package her mother had left her and which was loosely tied together and called 'the mills'. She'd show them, all of them, meaning, of course, Will Broadbent who had so insulted her with his nasty proposition. She'd show him that she needed no one's help, especially his, to keep the profits flowing from the business which had been the most efficient and productive in the Penfold Valley for almost a hundred years. It only needed that first step to get her going. Everyone had to take it. Her Aunt Kit and her own mother had done it and if they could do it so could she. She'd let no one guess at her complete lack of knowledge or her fear and though they might suspect they would never know for certain. Bluff, it was called, and she would learn to be good at it. Damn him to hell. She'd show him.

'You off then?' Annie asked.

'Yes, I've had an idea. I'll go to see the bank manager. He'll tell me where to begin. Uncle Joss did say something about consulting him and I'd clean forgotten in all the ... well, I'm sure he'll give me some clue where to begin. Thanks for the tea, Annie. I'll be over again soon and if there's anything you need just let me know,' she added for Annie, Nelly, Polly and Gracie had all been thrown out of work by the destruction of the mill. 'By the way, where are the girls? They're usually helping you with something. Don't tell me you've let them escape your tyranny for once?'

'They're workin'. All three o' them.' Annie stood up, moving the pans on the fire, setting the tongs to a more precise angle in the hearth, her face expressionless, her manner defensive, the very air about her rigid with her determination that everything should be in the perfect order she liked. 'And I'm ter be off in a day or two so I'll not be 'ere when yer call.'

'Oh? You never told me you had a job.'

'I'm tellin' yer now an' yer'd best be off or it'll be dark soon.'

'Never mind that. What are the girls doing and where are you going? I thought we'd agreed I'd fit you in at one of the other mills, you and the girls.'

'Oh, aye, an' what about them as was laid off because o't fire? 'Undreds of 'em. Are yer to fit them in an' all?'

'You know I can't do that. There isn't enough work.'

'They know that, an' so do I, that's why I'm off ter...'

'To where?'

'I've found work in Manchester.'

'Manchester! But you can't go all that way. I need you here.'

'What for?'

'Oh, Annie, you know you're the only one with any sense I can talk to. You are ... aware ... of how things are with Drew at the moment.'

'Aye, I reckon the 'ole valley knows.'

'Well, then, I must have someone to ... to discuss my problems with. Is it not possible to find work closer than Manchester? And how are you to get there and back each day? It's nearly ten miles...'

'We're moving. I've sold up an' we're movin'.' Annie's face was gaunt and hollow-cheeked and Tessa wondered why she had not noticed it before, but her voice was tart and quite resolute. 'We've got lodgings in Salford. I've got rid o' most o't stuff ... we 'ad to eat, tha' knows...'

'But you know you had only to ask me...'

'Mebbe so, but we've always managed on our own, like, an' I'll not take charity.' She lifted her chin menacingly as though daring Tessa to try pressing it on her. She was looking for no sympathy. She stated a fact and that was that and there was absolutely no use in Tessa attempting to change her mind. 'The girls are ... pin-heading in Brown Street an' I'm ter do pin-sheeting...'

'Pin-sheeting?' Dear God, what was that?

'Aye, just 'til summat better turns up. Our Jack's in a warehouse in Portland Street. It tekks brass to keep a lad articled. The lawyer in Crossfold kept 'im on as long as 'e could but ... well, 'e's a strong lad an' when things is better 'e can go back. 'Till then us'll manage.'

Tessa fumbled her way into a chair, her face like paper and somehow, though her mind told her it was foolish, this appeared to be even worse than the death of poor Charlie

380

and the chaos she herself was in. She had no one, *no one* in whom she could confide her absolute terror, her sense of being caught in some ghastly nightmare from which somehow she must escape. Only Annie. Only Annie and now Annie was to leave her as well. Drew was ... well, Drew had a contempt for the commercial world so great and so condemning he would beg on the streets rather than submit to it. He was, in the opinion of Crossfold and the Penfold Valley and to himself, if she were to be truthful, too fine a gentleman for the life of a millmaster. He had simply been waiting, they told one another, to get his hands on his considerable share of the Chapman fortune when he would be off, with or without that dashing wife of his, to more exciting climes than Crossfold.

'We are rather rich now, are we not?' He had grinned amiably, daring her to deny it, his vivid blue eyes quite beautiful in the deep, smooth brown of his handsome face. He really is quite flawless, she had thought, from the outside, for she had no illusions about her husband's unstable mind. She herself was wild and just as carelessly imprudent, but where Drew exposed himself to danger with no thought to the consequences, not even aware that there were any, she had, in the past, done it quite deliberately, challenging the gods to stop her. And now the gods had stopped her and she must find a solution without even Annie to give her a hand.

'I didn't know,' was all she could find to say in response to Annie's news. 'I really had no idea.'

'Thi 'as enough on thi mind, lass, wi'out me ter think on. But we couldn't just sit 'ere an' wait fer summat to 'appen. It's same fer us all, them as worked at Chapmans. Mouths ter feed an' no wages ter do it. Anybody with a bob or two put by 'as spent it. Now it's pawnshops' turn, then, fer them as can do nowt else, poor relief. You'd not noticed, what with all you 'ad on yer plate, but I've 'ad ter let me mam's things go.'

Tessa looked about her dazedly noticing for the first time

that the dresser on which Annie's willow pattern had once proudly stood, probably bought at one of the pot fairs which toured the north of England and not worth a great deal but dear to Annie, was empty of all but a couple of chipped mugs, the old kettle and a frying pan with a broken handle – a few things not even the pawnbroker would consider. The room was bare somehow, though she could not have said what else was gone, and when she turned back to Annie her friend began to polish the dresser vigorously, wanting nothing said, nor willing to receive pity and indeed showing quite plainly she would be deeply offended if any was offered.

'There's no need ter look like that, my girl. We'll be all right, me an' the childer.' She always called them that though Jack would be eighteen now. 'It's only temporary, o' course,' she asserted, warning any fates which might be listening that she'd know the reason why should it prove otherwise.

Tessa stood up again, the colour seeping slowly back into her pale cheeks. For a moment she had allowed Annie's news to bring her close to fainting, the awful prospect of not having this sharp-spoken, sharp-faced woman right here where Tessa could find her whenever she pleased, taking her wits. They had been friends, or as close to friends as Annie would allow, for years now, a faintly uneasy relationship since Annie was extremely sensitive to what she thought of as 'decent' and 'proper' and in her opinion persons of a different class did not mix. She was a good listener, becoming involved in all Tessa's troubles, conveying her opinion with grunts of scorn, irritable shrugging of her shoulders, unbelieving shaking of her head, sharp tuttings, an ability to let you know exactly how she felt without saying a great deal. And yet when she did speak she demonstrated her north-country shrewdness, cunning almost, with bite and humour. What was she to do without her?

But she was right, of course. Tessa could not find employment for the hundreds of operatives who had been thrown out of work by the fire until the mill re-opened and only the Lord knew when that would be, but though she might be unable to do anything about the rest she would put this family back to work by the end of the week.

'You get down to the pawnshop and get your things at once,' she said briskly, 'because if you think I'm going to drink out of those dreadful mugs you are mistaken. See, here's a guinea, it's all I have on me. Then get the train to Manchester and fetch those girls back. And Jack. I'll see to the lawyer. Jack's had too good an education to waste it in a warehouse and I'm sure when...'

'You can stop right there, Mrs Greenwood, if you please.' Annie's face was taut with displeasure. Her pale brown hair was dragged back severely into a small bun with not a wisp allowed to escape and the style gave her an added sharpness. She laid her calloused, hard-working hands on the table top – where had her handsome chenille cloth gone? Tessa had time to consider – and her eyes were quite astonishingly vivid in her colourless face. Her voice almost splintered it was so icy. 'We can manage right nicely on us own, if yer don't mind. We've takken no charity, me an' me family, ever, an' we'll not start now. Any road, all't arrangements've bin made an' I'll thank you not ter come 'ere interferin'. You sort out yer own life, my lass, before yer start on mine.'

She sniffed loudly, then turned away as though to imply that there was nothing more to be said on the subject. She'd brook no argument, not from anyone: not from her brothers and sisters who'd set up such a caterwauling you'd have thought she'd asked them to jump off Badger's Edge instead of take up the decent employment she'd found for them, and she'd brook none from this woman who would insist that they were friends. Just as if the likes of her and Annie Beale could ever be truly that. She'd not say she wouldn't be sorry to ... well, to lose sight of her since she'd given Annie many a good laugh on the quiet, but as for allowing her to order their lives, just like they belonged to her or summat, that would never do.

'Annie, please. I really am not offering charity. You will all be working...'

'Aye, an' who'll get t'sack ter give us that work, tell me that?'

'Oh, Annie, please let me...'

But Annie would not be moved. She'd keep in touch, she promised grudgingly, and no, Tessa wasn't to visit them – Annie tried to picture the elegant Mrs Drew Greenwood in the small cellar room she rented in Salford – but first chance she got she'd come up to Crossfold and ... well, it were no good frettin' over what couldn't be helped and Tessa must stop making a fuss over nothing. But when her friend, and she admitted to herself *now* Tessa was her friend, put her arms about her in farewell, Annie allowed the gesture.

Tessa and Laurel sat one on either side of the cheerful drawing-room fire that evening waiting for Drew who had not yet come home from the races. Was that where he had said he was going, or was it off on a day's hunting? She couldn't remember. The episode with Annie had upset her more than she cared to admit and her face was bleak as she sipped the sherry Laurel insisted upon before dinner. Her thoughts were scattered dwelling on the awful disruption in everyone's life caused by Charlie's death. She felt guilty that her own overlying emotion was not one of sadness for Charlie, for his widow and five fatherless children, but for herself who had lost with his death, not only her freedom, her friend who had kept her afloat on more than one occasion when life had seemed quite intolerable, but her husband too, for where on earth was he at this time of night?

'My brother is not to dine with us, then?' Laurel enquired tartly. Her mourning black was deep and sombre, allowing not even a jet bead. She was playing for all it was worth the role her husband's death had cast her in, knowing full well that the deep black gave her an air of fragile vulnerability, a defencelessness which said she would simply break and shatter into a hundred pieces should anyone speak a harsh word to her. She was a widow, a woman for whom the deepest respect and sympathy was expected, and she expected it. She was also a shareholder in Chapman Manufacturing now, or would be when the estate was settled, small certainly, but with a voice in the running of things and she was waiting, unable to comprehend the true state of Drew Greenwood's heedless indifference to the fate of the firm, for him to step into the shoes her Aunt Jenny and her own husband had left vacant. And where was he? And at this time when his disregard for the convention of mourning was really quite indecent. Gadding about still with Nicky Longworth and the other wild-riding young men of his acquaintance, she supposed. It really was too bad and her manner said so.

'He will be here soon,' Tessa replied shortly, not at all prepared for one of Laurel's eternal lectures on the behaviour which was expected at a time like this of a gentleman, which, one presumed, Drew was.

'May one ask where he has gone?'

'One may but I cannot promise to give the right answer.'

'Are you saying you don't know where your own husband is?'

Tessa sighed a long, wavering sigh. "That is what I am saying.' And, really, I could do without your disapproving face and air of displeased resignation, she thought. Indeed, she had begun to worry for though he had been late home on several occasions he had always sent a message to let her know. She did not want to share her anxiety with Laurel, constrained by pride and a reluctance to let her sister-in-law crow, but when Briggs announced that dinner was ready and they moved into the dining-room, the third place set for Drew proclaimed even more loudly his absence.

'I do think he should make more of an effort to be here on time for meals,' Laurel grumbled, picking delicately at the tiny portion of turbot her widowhood allowed her to manage, her manner saying that really, in her state, should she be asked to put up with such thoughtlessness? 'I suppose he is drinking with Nicky Longworth and has not noticed the time, or has probably become so absorbed with whatever those wild friends of his get up to all day, he cannot bring himself to remember that he has a family at home grieving the loss of one of its members,' meaning herself for who but Laurel Greenwood, she seemed to say, mourned her husband?

'I'm sure you're right but there is nothing to be done about it.'

'Really! Well, if he were my husband I know what I would have to say to him.'

'Since he is not your husband perhaps you would keep your observations to yourself,' Tessa hissed. Then, realising that with poor Charlie in the ground no more than six weeks it was hardly the most tactful thing to say to his widow, she began to rise, to go to Laurel who had her black-edged handkerchief to her face. But she had gone too far, it seemed, and Laurel was out of her chair and gliding towards the door, deeply affronted and in no way to be mollified should Tessa even try.

Dear heaven, what had happened to the pleasant, hedonistic, she admitted it now, life she had led in the past with Drew? Her despair was deep as she waved away the poker-faced Briggs and Dorcas with a request for coffee and brandy in the drawing-room, seeing the disapproving twitch of the butler's eyebrows, since no lady drank brandy, but not caring. Her world was disintegrating about her so why should she care that, knowing the servants' grapevine as she did, it would be all over the Penfold Valley by this time tomorrow that, among her other shortcomings, the high-stepping Mrs Drew Greenwood took hard liquor, and on her own?

She stared into the fire having further displeased Briggs by telling him curtly to leave the decanter, she would serve herself and would ring if she needed him. The brandy smoothed its warm descent into her stomach, soothing a little the fluttering butterflies of what she recognised quite plainly as fear. The fumes of the drink reached her head, blurring her sharp thoughts, of Drew and where he might be, of Annie and where she was to go, and of Will.

Will. Dear Lord, why should she give a thought to that perfidious scoundrel? It was he who had brought her down to this. If it was not for him she could even now be with Drew, wherever he was, or at least have him here with her, where he should be, observing the proprieties of mourning for a month or two. It was only because she had been forced since Charlie's death and her mother's flight to Italy to address herself to the wearying problem of the mills, that Drew had ridden off – where did he say he was going? her confused mind asked again – and left her to the tedium of Laurel's false and easy tears. If Will Broadbent had had an iota of compassion in him he would have accepted her offer of manager, *no*, directorship of the Chapman mills thus leaving her to devote herself to the care and constant attention which her husband needed. Will had loved her once, she told herself as she poured herself another brandy, and surely, for the sake of what they had once known and for the simply splendid salary she would have been prepared to pay him, he should have taken her up on her offer. Instead, he had laughed at her, made the most insulting suggestion, humiliated her. God, she could feel the red flames of outrage scorch her body even now for that was what it was that made her so ... so inflammable. Her skin prickled and shivered to her own touch. She was restless and on edge and it was all his fault, the bastard, and if she could get back at him, in any way, by God she would. And all this time he had been going to Annie's, gossiping no doubt the pair of them about Tessa Greenwood and the hard-drinking, rashly gambling, arrogantly riding society she moved in. Well, to hell with them. Both of them. And good riddance. She was going to bed and she didn't care where Drew was either, or what Will Broadbent and Annie Beale had been up to behind her back. She didn't give a damn if he'd taken Annie Beale to his bed as once he had taken her; if he had laid those hard hands and that hard body against the frail but fighting spirit which dwelled in Annie. What was it to her? Damn them, damn them ... she'd show them ...

She knew she was drunk as she stumbled up the stairs to the warm, candle-lit intimacy of the bedroom she shared with Drew, but she didn't care. If it blurred the pictures of Will and Annie ...

She felt her way to the dressing-table, shaking her head, trying to clear it of the ugly thoughts which muddled it. It was nothing to do with her. Annie must be lonely ... and Will ... and how convenient ... She swung back blindly, knocking over an ornament which fell to the carpet with a gentle thud. She felt quite sick and trembling, which of course was due to the amount of brandy she had drunk ... She must get into bed ... where, for God's sake, was Emma ... ?

She awoke in the night, alone for the first time since her marriage, and frightened. Deeply, disturbingly, terrified. Where was he? Merciful heaven, where was he? He was a grown man, strong and vigorous, but wilful and defenceless as a child without her and what accident might have befallen him in his scorn for anything he considered smacked of caution or common sense? She was no saint herself, as anyone in the Penfold Valley would confirm, but deep inside her was that spark of self-preservation, that instinct which told her when she had reached the limit of what might be called foolhardy and could be considered insane, and that Drew lacked. She had restrained him to that limit but on his own, or in the company of only his breakneck friends, where might he have ended up?

She sat up wincing as her head rattled painfully about on her shoulders, then began to thud to the rhythm of her heartbeat. Getting out of bed she moved to the window and stared blindly out into the wavering darkness of the garden, trying to penetrate it for some sign that Drew had come home and was, perhaps, sprawled drunkenly in the drawing-room or at the foot of the stairs. She had not heard his bay or the sound of the dangerously light curricle he drove. It was solidly dark and quiet, the only movement a faint blurring where the bare bough of the tree outside the window shuddered in the wind. It was cold and sinister out there, beyond the walls of the park and the woods which surrounded Greenacres. The wild moorland, the rapid rushing of icy water, the stony hillside was no place for a man, particularly if he was drunk as Drew was bound to be.

He came in with the dawn, trembling slightly from some excess he did not care to speak of, not quite sober but grinning impishly, pleading for forgiveness, slipping naked into their bed, nuzzling into her shoulder. She held his long, lean body in her arms, her cheek resting on the damp thickness of his matted hair, soothing him to warmth and sleep. She felt the tension – caused by what? she wondered despairingly – drain from him, and as it did so her own body relaxed, and her mind, suddenly clear, suddenly impatient with her previous turmoil, knew what she must do, for no one else would.

## 25

She was standing in the middle of the cleared site at Chapmanstown, staring in hopeless bewilderment at the plans the clever young architect was explaining to her when the carriage drew in through the gateway. She glanced at it without much interest. It was probably another of those infernal men from the bank or the insurance company come to fill her mind with incomprehensible figures; to talk of assets and liabilities, of titles and securities and after weeks of being bombarded by such imponderables she felt she really could not take one more.

389

The man who descended from the carriage was overwhelmingly familiar as he stood for a moment beside it seeming to give some instruction to the coachman. When she looked again she was not at all surprised to see Will Broadbent.

He was quite splendid in a well-cut business suit of dark cloth, his shirt front snowy and his greatcoat thrown back from his heavy shoulders in a most dashing way. His tall hat was held against his chest and he bowed before walking towards her with a light tread which came, she assumed, from his experience of being a thief. Now why should she remember that? she wondered dazedly. Then he was beside her, his white teeth startling against his brown skin.

He smiled and his smoky eyes, filled with some secret amusement, ran over her.

'Mrs Greenwood,' he said politely, 'may I say how well you are looking?'

She stiffened and gave him a frigid stare. 'What are you doing here?' she asked rudely and the young architect turned to look at her in surprise. 'I'll just go and...' he began, but she put a hand on his arm to restrain him.

'No, don't go, Mr Talbot. This gentleman will not be stopping.' The memory of her humiliation at his hands made her go hot then cold with anger and she did not wish to be reminded of it nor left alone with its instigator. What was he doing here, anyway, looking so prosperous, with his own carriage and coachman and nothing at all to do with his day, it seemed, but ride over and inspect what she was doing in her own mill yard?

'Are you here on business, Mr Broadbent?' she asked haughtily, her manner implying that, if not, he could take himself off and look sharp about it.

'Indeed I am, Mrs Greenwood, and if we can find somewhere more congenial to discuss it I would be obliged.'

Not by a flicker of his cool eyes nor a muscle of his smooth face did he convey that he even remembered their last meeting. It had been nothing to him; an event of so little importance it had slipped completely from his mind. She was of so little importance to him in his new and distinguished career, in his busy and successful world, that had it not been for the certainty of profit to himself he would not have been here at all.

'I cannot think that you and I could have common business interests, Mr Broadbent, but if you would like to call on my managers at Crossbank or at one of my other mills I'm sure one or other of them could spare you a moment or two.'

She heard Mr Talbot draw in his breath sharply. In the past four or so years Will Broadbent had carved out for himself quite a place in the business community of south Lancashire, creating and enlarging the now-prosperous co-operative over Hepworth way. He was known to have a share in several very profitable schemes and had been successful in more than one gamble to do with the railway, so Mr Talbot had heard. It was Mr Talbot's firm which had drawn up the plans for the mill in which Mr Broadbent was one of the major shareholders and he was a highly respected businessman where businessmen were known to be hard-headed, shrewd and extremely ruthless. Men called on Mr Broadbent these days, not the other way round, which was a fair indication of how well he had done for himself. Now, it was well known that Mrs Drew Greenwood had a high opinion of herself, indeed her fine husband was what could only be called arrogant, but to speak to Mr Broadbent as though he was no more than a weaving-shed overlooker surely smacked of foolhardiness?

Mr Broadbent evidently thought so too, and Mr Talbot watched uneasily, wishing he could slip away and let them get on with whatever it was that was between them, but Mrs Greenwood still had his arm in a grip of steel and short of rudely tearing it from her grasp he was forced to remain where he was.

'I don't deal with managers, lass,' Mr Broadbent said warningly.

391

'And I don't deal with overlookers, Mr Broadbent.'

Mr Talbot watched in growing horror as Mr Broadbent, for a moment, looked as though he would like nothing better than to strike Mrs Greenwood full in her contemptuous face. Then, miraculously, he smiled, a smile of such good humour Mr Talbot thought that he could not have heard exactly what Mrs Greenwood had said.

'Is that meant to insult me, Tessa?' His smile broadened into a delighted grin. He shook his head and, without so much as an 'if I may' or 'do you mind?' he reached out and plucked the plan for the new mill from the architect's hands.

'You go too far, Will Broadbent,' Mrs Greenwood hissed and as she whipped forward to retrieve the plan Mr Talbot stepped back, thankfully, moving to stand several yards away with the site foreman and the master builder in charge who were also present, mouths agape, slack-jawed and wide-eyed, avid spectators of the incredible scene. They were treated to the sight of the imperious and beautiful Mrs Greenwood, wife of the owner of Chapman Manufacturing, dancing at her full height as she stretched up to reach the set of plans which Mr Broadbent held above his head.

'You are being exceedingly foolish, Tessa,' he laughed, 'and undignified too. These men are wondering what on earth can be going on between Mr Broadbent and the exquisite Mrs Greenwood that she has to create such a scene over a piece of paper. Calm down, for God's sake. I only want to study the damn thing.'

'Who gave you the right to walk into my yard and help yourself to the plans for my new mill, Will Broadbent?' she snarled, her eyes narrowed in her angry face. She wanted to stamp her foot and strike out at him, to fly at him with hard, furious fists for he was doing it again, he was humiliating her, but this time in a yard full of curious men.

'Stop it, Tessa, and stop acting like a child in a tantrum.'

'Tantrum, is it? I'll show you who . . .'

'All you are doing is showing these men a side of your nature, which, if you are to go into business, would be best kept hidden and which, if you don't control yourself, will be all over the valley by nightfall. Direct me to your office . . .'

'I haven't got an office,' she snapped perilously.

'Then the foreman's hut will do.'

'You must be out of your mind if you imagine I am about to discuss my affairs with you, and in a workman's hut.'

'Don't do this to yourself, Tessa. Smile and allow me to hold your arm.' He looked about him, one dark eyebrow raised, his eyes beaming with good humour. 'Now, where is the . . . aah, there it is.' He nodded politely to the startled builder. 'May we borrow your office for a moment, Mr . . . er . . .'

'Of course, sir.' The man touched the brim of his tall hat, wondering as he did so why he had called Will Broadbent 'sir', for he himself, as a *master* builder held a position of some importance in the business community of Crossfold.

He closed the door of the small wooden hut behind him and leaned against it. His eyes, almost the colour of treacle in the dim light, were bold now, impudent and full of stifled laughter. She flounced out of his grasp, putting up a hand to her bonnet and adjusting a stray wisp of shining hair.

She had discarded the black of mourning in the month after Charlie's death. She could not have said why she had worn it in the first place except perhaps in deference to her mother, her Uncle Joss and Aunt Kit, who she knew somehow, despite their own unconventional ways, would have been distressed by what the community would have seen as a lack of respect and grief. She felt both for she had loved and respected Charlie as a good and steadfast man who had tried to do his best in the awkward and often trying circumstances created by his wife. But she did wear a dress instead of her breeches and jacket, her instinct telling her she might gain some advantage in this man's world into which she had been flung so unceremoniously, if she appeared womanly. They would be insulted if she careered into the mill yard on her mare, dressed like a lad who seemed more likely to gallop over the moor following the wind, than to do business with them. Today she was in a respectable blue, a deep French blue, demure and ladylike with a touch of sparkling white in the crisp lace at her wrist and throat and beneath the brim of her unadorned bonnet.

But nothing could quell the brilliance of her eyes nor the gloss and burnish of her hair, the satin smoothness of her white skin and her poppy-red mouth which Drew had kissed to bee-stung fullness only that morning.

'Don't go,' he had murmured, his mouth tasting her cherry-hard nipples, his tongue teasing and moist as it travelled down the length of her arching body. She could feel him drawing that glowing thread of excitement from the base of her belly, pulling it taut, making it quiver in anticipation, eager, greedy in its desire to be stretched to its full extent before it snapped in that complete and rapturous climax which she had never yet quite achieved. Each time as it struggled to reach what he reached in his own shuddering orgasm, it slipped away, aching sometimes, and angry, and Drew would fold himself about her, warm and for the moment calm, and she would tell herself that next time it would happen.

'Don't go, stay with me,' he had said this morning and his hands had reached for her as they did every morning when she rose early in order to meet the bank manager, the lawyer, the architect, one or other of the managers at the four working mills. He would turn from her when she tried to kiss his resentment away, pulling the fine lace-edged sheets about his amber shoulders, burrowing his head in the fine, lace-edged pillow.

'Go if you must but don't, for God's sake, expect me to be concerned. If you insist that the managers cannot *manage* without your expertise to guide them, by all means give it to them. I'm sure you are right, Tessa, for you always are, but I am off to Northumberland in the morning with Nicky so don't be surprised if I am not here when you return.'

And increasingly he wasn't!

Now she drew herself up to her full height and the look

she gave Will Broadbent was one of icy disdain. He had dragged her, there was no other word for it, into this ... this shack and she had allowed it since with his considerable strength and indifference to what others might think, he was quite likely to have flung her over his shoulder and carried her here.

'I would be glad if you would state your business, Mr Broadbent, for I have a lot to do today ...'

'Aye, so I heard.'

'I beg your pardon?'

'Your ... doings are the talk of the valley, lass.'

'And exactly what is that supposed to mean?' She had tossed away the 'Mr Broadbent' by now, too incensed to keep up the ice-cool demeanour of a lady confronted by a man who was certainly no gentleman.

'It means that your absurd pretence that you know just what you are about is discussed in every quarter where businessmen gather. They are taking bets at the Cloth Hall on how long you will last and at what price the Chapman concerns will finally be sold. It is very low, Tessa. In one way, they are ready to admire you for doing your best, which is more than can be said for that husband of yours.'

'You keep your foul tongue from my husband's name, you bastard,' she whispered, relieved that the crushing pain of his insult to Drew prevented her from facing the fury of the feared ridicule about herself. How dare they criticise Drew, her dear Drew, who could no more help his nature than they could help being the fools they were. Drew was fine, fine and good, and it was not his fault that he was as he was.

Her face was like a mask, hiding the painful, scalding truth. Oh, yes, she could imagine what they whispered but from no one, *no one* would she allow one word of criticism. He was her cousin, her husband and she loved him as she loved no other person. Let them dare to attack him and she would defend him until she fell wounded, bleeding, dying.

He watched her, allowing no intimation of what was in

his heart to show in his impassive face. Her intensely protective love for the emotionally damaged Drew Greenwood glowed through the shadowed bareness of the wooden hut and he marvelled at it, at the same time despising its undeserving recipient with the masculine aggression of a strong man for a weak.

'Nay, lass, what that lad gets up to is nowt to me, nor you for that matter, but I can't abide to see a decent mill such as Chapman's has been, go under. I admired Charlie Greenwood and your mother. They worked damned hard to make something fine of this business. They were well respected, fair and honest as any man in cotton will tell you. They could drive a hard bargain, mind, especially Jenny Harrison, but always to be trusted. And they treated their operatives fairly. And that's another thing. I can't stand by and see a lot of good folk who could be in decent work, forced to apply for poor relief, and that's what they're being driven to by your ham-fisted methods. These walls should be shoulder high by now, with the prospect of your spinners and weavers being back at their machines by summer. A good mill it was, and could be again. I know because I worked here and it fair sets my blood to boiling to see the way it's going ...'

'Which has nothing to do with you and if you don't remove yourself from my property I shall have you thrown out.' The words could scarcely get beyond her gritted teeth so tightly was her jaw clenched. There were white patches about her mouth and he knew she was holding herself back – just – from springing at him.

'Happen you're right, my lass, but don't let it go. Don't let it slip away from you for the sake of your pride. Get yourself some men together, a board of directors with you as chairman. Men who know what the word 'business' means. Men who know one end of a loom from the other. Men who understand money, and the cotton trade and who can show *you* what to do, or even that husband of yours if you can get him off that bloody horse of his for half an hour ...'

'I've warned you once and I won't do it again.' She was

trembling, so great was her rage. 'Get out of my yard or I'll have you thrown out.'

'Nay, Tessa, you've said that to me a time or two and I'm still here. Remember the first time? You were a slip of a lass, sixteen or so, and you took offence like you always seem to do when someone doesn't move out of your way fast enough. You hit me with your little whip . . .'

'By God, I wish I had it now. Stand away from that door and let me out. When my husband hears about this, as he surely will for I will tell him, he will give you the thrashing of your life . . .'

'Tessa, give over, lass.' He looked highly amused. The very idea of the lightweight Drew Greenwood who did nought from morning until night but gallop about on a bloody horse or shoot at bloody birds taking on Will Broadbent who had learned from the age of five how to take care of himself, was evidently something of a joke.

'Get out of here, Will, or I swear I'll get a gun and kill you myself.'

He became quiet then, his strong face settling into a look of bewilderment. 'Why should you do that, Tessa? What is it in me, and in you, that arouses this . . . this loathing you have of me? I have offered you no injury, ever, and if you are thinking of the last time we met when I made you a certain proposition, which you refused, then I can only say I meant you no insult. Rather the opposite. I admire a man who knows what he wants and goes directly for it, whatever the consequences, so why should I not feel the same for a woman? And you really are a splendid woman. I said so and admitted then that I would be more than willing to resume the . . . the friendship, for want of a better word, we once knew. We were splendid partners then, well matched, if you take my meaning, and could be again. We could give a lot to one another, my dear. So, you see, I am at a loss as to why you seem to find me so objectionable. I mean you no harm. Far from it. You are married now and I hope to be in the same happy state myself one day, so why cannot we be at least polite with one another?' He was grinning, moving forward into the shaft of pale, dusty sunlight which fell through the grimed window of the hut. 'There may be an occasion in the future when we will do business together and you can hardly glare at me as if there was nothing you would like better than to see me dead at your feet. Forget what has happened in the past and look to the future. It could be good for both of us.' There was no mistaking the meaning of his words. 'Don't ignore the advice I'm giving you, Tessa. Don't fight me. Accept it and . . .'

She put up her hands, palms facing him, as though to ward him off, as though he was about to make some physical attack on her. She was white-faced and trembling and for a moment he was alarmed but in her eyes was the blinding brilliance of her rage, making them almost transparent.

'I need neither your help nor your advice and as for doing business with you, *in any way*, I would sooner starve and see my family homeless.'

'Tessa, come now . . .'

'Get out, Will, get out . . .'

Her face which had been so pale became suffused with the deep red blood of her killing rage. She sprang towards him with an incoherent cry which brought the hum of voices in the yard to a sudden silence. Swift as a leopard Will moved to meet her, his arms tight about her waist. She struggled fiercely, her wide-open mouth ready to shrill out the madness of her hatred, but he silenced her, his mouth coming down on hers, capturing those stretched lips, holding them, moving warmly, strongly until he felt them soften beneath his own. She still struggled against him wildly, trying to kick his legs, twisting every way she could against the steel of his arms, her heart pounding in her breast. He held her roughly, hurting her, only his mouth gentle as it moved about her face, then returned to recapture her pliant lips.

'Darling, darling,' he was murmuring and his long, hard body pressed against hers urgently. One hand moved to the back of her head, flinging her bonnet to the corner of the hut, and as her hair came loose his hand was in it, holding her where he might more easily have access to her warm, urgent, demanding mouth.

'Will, dear God...' Her arms were about his neck, clinging to him, terrified that he might slip away, that he might leave her, that the hot sweetness which flowed through her body, so familiar and for which she had waited so long, might be taken from her.

He backed her up against the wall of the hut, their bodies still welded together, the hot need of them burning even through the layers of their clothing. Their mouths clung desperately, honey-sweet and swollen. She was moaning deep in her throat and when his mouth moved beneath her chin, smoothing down the soft flesh of her throat, she arched her back, holding his head to her, offering her breasts to him as she had done in the depths of the bed they had shared five years ago.

They might have gone on, mindless of everything but their bodies' longing, for though both had known love during the years between, they were starving for this. His hands were at her breast, cupping the soft weight and she pressed eagerly against them when from beyond the closed door Mr Talbot cleared his throat noisily.

'Will...' She would have fallen but for his arms about her.

'Darling...?'

'No, no, I'm not...'

'Yes...?'

'Please, let me go.'

'Never, not now.' His lips came down on hers again with all the masculine possession of a man who knows a woman is his.

She was weak, soft and lovely in his arms. 'Mr Talbot...'

'Damn Mr Talbot!'

'My bonnet ... please...'

'Here, smooth your hair.'

399

'Dear God, I can hardly stand. Don't let me go or I shall fall.'

'Not you, Tessa Greenwood. You will never fall for I shall not let you.'

'And how was your day among the industrialists, my love?' Drew smiled sardonically, sipping the pale golden wine with which Briggs had just re-filled his glass. 'Did we make another fortune to add to the one we already have or are we to sell the family silver to buy that hunter I have my eye on?'

'Oh, Drew, you are not to buy another horse, surely? The stables seem full of them already and why you should need another is beyond me.'

Drew turned lazily to Laurel, his lounging manner, his smile, the lift of his dark eyebrow, the curl of his lip, insolent and begging to know exactly what it had to do with her how he spent his own money. He had been in the saddle all day for the hunting season was almost over and he intended to make the most of what remained. After the hunt ball at the end of the month the Squire and his family would be off to some other sporting pursuit in which, naturally, Drew Greenwood would be included. And his charming wife too, if she could be parted from this somewhat astonishing occupation she had taken up with matters of a commercial nature. Like Drew, the Squire was of the opinion that if one was unfortunate enough to be of the industrial world, the world of trade, was it not only sensible and more seemly to leave the distasteful running of the business in the hands of one's employees? There was no need, surely, for the delectable Mrs Drew Greenwood to occupy herself personally with the rebuilding of the mill in which her unfortunate uncle had perished and Drew was to impress on her that they missed her enormously. They would be most distressed if she did not show herself on her superb mare the very next day and in that stunning riding outfit she wore, since the last three months without her had been quite tedious, and he was to tell her so.

'Laurel dear, I do not question the purchases you make and so I would beg you not to question mine.'

'I do not question it, Drew. I am merely pointing out that as you can only ride one horse at a time it seems imprudent to own half a dozen all eating their heads off in the stables.'

'They are all ridden, Laurel, except, of course, those ponies which were brought for Robert and Henry and Joel and which you will not allow them to mount.'

'Robert and Henry are far too busy with their studies and Joel is too young...'

'Rubbish! They must be allowed to play sometimes, Laurel, and as for being too young, Drew and I ... no ... Pearce and I for I am Drew ... Pearce and I ... when we were the same age as Joel were...'

His voice faltered suddenly and his face took on an expression of uncertainty. The wine in his glass slopped over the rim and dripped on to the lapel of his immaculate evening jacket as his hand trembled and he turned at once to Tessa.

'You remember, don't you, darling? We were all up in the saddle long before we were five years old...'

'That may be so, Drew, but my sons are to be millowners' – since you don't appear to be producing any of your own, her tone said – 'and not urchins who are allowed to romp...'

He continued as though his sister had not spoken and when his hand reached for hers, Tessa took it soothingly appalled by the confusion he was in over his own name, the words she had been preparing all day regarding the running of the mill dying away in the back of her throat.

'... and when Tessa was six she was following us out on the moor, weren't you, sweetheart? What times we had, the three of us, didn't we?'

His face had become sweated, just a fine sheen on the glowing brown of his skin as though from some fire within him, and his eyes were the brilliant blue of a sapphire. He gripped her hand fiercely, then, tipping back his head poured the wine, almost in one swallow, down his throat. He held out the empty glass to Briggs without turning and the butler filled it once more to the brim, his own face impassive. This was the second bottle of wine he had opened and they had not yet finished the fish course.

Will Broadbent's face, his hands and lips and ... yes, the emotion he had allowed her to see were pushed savagely to the back of Tessa's mind as she looked into the faltering face of her husband. Her body which had been wild with longing only that morning, grew still and empty.

'Indeed we did, my darling, though I had to fight you every step of the way to let me be part of it. You thought me nothing but a nuisance until I could prove to you both that I could do everything as well as you.'

'You mean the gate?' He pushed his plate away, grinning, the splendid trout on it barely touched, leaning forward to gaze admiringly into his wife's lovely face as he hitched his chair nearer to hers. He had soon given up sitting at the head of the table as Laurel had wished him to do and as was proper for the master of the house, placing his chair next to his wife's at its foot, declaring he could not shout from one end to the other when he wished to address her.

'What a devil you were when you took it into your head to best us, which was most of the time. But I really did think, for a moment only, believe me, that that bloody gate would be your undoing.'

'Drew, please, must you bring such language to my dinner table?' Laurel raised a fastidious eyebrow.

'I'm afraid I must, dear sister. If my wife does not object, which I'm sure she doesn't, do you, my pet? ... there, you see ... then I cannot think it concerns you.'

He indicated to Briggs to refill his glass and Laurel sat up straighter, her face even more rigid with disapproval.

'And if I might just point out, Laurel, whilst we are on the subject, that as mistress of this house, this is my wife's dinner table.'

'Drew, be quiet.'

'No, I will not be quiet, Tessa. I am acquainting Laurel with the fact that she no longer...'

'Drew, how could you?' Laurel's eyes filled with tears and in the background where they discreetly hovered Briggs and Dorcas exchanged glances. 'With Charlie hardly cold in his grave, is it kind to remind me that I must relinquish what has been mine for so long?'

Drew's eyes narrowed and the slightly cruel humour which he acquired when he was drunk, curled his mouth.

'Really?' he drawled, lounging back in his chair, but though he gave the impression of the dashing young man-about-town, cynical, arrogant, carelessly indifferent to anyone's feelings including his own – for had they not already suffered irreparable damage? – he still clung quite desperately to Tessa's hand. 'I cannot recall under what circumstances you undertook to be mistress of Greenacres. My mother, who is the wife of its master, is still alive and now, in her absence and in view of the fact that my father has deeded the property to me, as my wife, Tessa must take my mother's place.'

'I will not stay here to be treated so cruelly.' Laurel rose to her feet, ready to glide from the room as she had done so often since Charlie died and with him the championship which was her due as his wife, and the daughter of this house.

'Laurel, sit down. Drew did not mean to be cruel and, whatever he might say, you *are* mistress here. You know you are splendid at it and that I would be hopeless.' That was true. 'Besides, I am to be fully occupied with the...'

She had not meant to speak of it, really she hadn't. She had seen the lost expression cloud Drew's eyes, the uneasy confusion and even worse which came to plague him. It was mixed with bravado which was meant to let her know he could manage very well on his own if she persisted with

403

her lunatic scheme to run the mills, and yet it told her of his awful fear that, if she did, he might lose his way again without her by his side.

'With what, my sweet?' His voice was deceptively mild and yet again his glass was held out to Briggs who hurried to refill it. 'Let us guess. Come on, Laurel, sit down and we will discuss the ... what is it, darling, that you are to be occupied with? Can it be the charitable works with which married ladies concern themselves, as Laurel herself does, do you not, sister? Or are you to begin making social calls, leaving cards and receiving them, spending your afternoons gossiping about fashion and the perfidy of gentlemen? Are you to accompany your husband as once you did, so pleasantly and with such devotion, or, as I suspect, is it something else entirely?'

Laurel's tears had vanished, dried up mysteriously at the prospect of not only watching the entertaining diversion of Tessa and Drew quarrelling but of discovering what was to happen to her share of the Chapman fortune. As Charlie's widow she owned twelve and a half per cent and surely she was entitled to know how soon she could reasonably expect to get her hands on it when the mills were sold, as sold they must certainly be? Drew was incapable of running them as Charlie and her Aunt Jenny had done, not only by reason of the serious instability of his nature which, though always wild and rebellious, had grown to gigantic proportions since Pearce's death, but by his absolute contempt and antipathy towards anything remotely commercial.

Tessa sighed, wondering why Drew was not able to propel her into the fury which Will Broadbent could awaken in her, nor the hot desire of bodily need, her secret mind slyly added before she could block it. Was the delight of it, the harmony of her marriage, cooled to mere pity and irritation, or were the last few months of frustration to blame for the slight wearing in the fabric of her marriage? The truth of it was she longed, yearned, for someone to whom she could pour out the great wave of her fear and frustration: of her distaste for the days ahead in which somehow she must turn chaos into order, turbulence into the smooth and pleasant life she had once led with Drew. She needed with all her heart to hear someone say, 'Leave it, Tessa, I will see to it for you. There is no need for you to bother your head about it. It is safe with me. Go and play with your husband who needs you more than the mills need you. He will not be able to function without you to hold his hand and lead him through life, so go, go and leave it all to me.' She would have liked nothing better than to wink audaciously at Drew, to joke and tease and take him to bed safe in the perfect knowledge that tomorrow they could do as they pleased, as they had always done. Lie on the rug before the bedroom fire and make love until he was satiated with it. Saddle their horses and gallop the moors until they were exhausted with it. Ride over to the Hall and amuse themselves with their friends, watch Drew drink and gamble feverishly until he was ready to come home, to sleep in her arms, safe in her arms, loved and needed, both of them in their shared brittleness. For that was fast what they had become; easily broken, running away from responsibility, spoiled and worthless, impatient with those who had their feet firmly on solid ground – like Will – restless and forever seeking some diversion to relieve them of that mortal affliction, the affliction of boredom.

Or was she firmly to grasp this nettle which scorched her hands, hurt her quite dreadfully, and if she was, if she was to burden herself with it, the question was *why*?

Will Broadbent's face danced in the shimmering flame of the candelabra which stood in the centre of the table. He was smiling quizzically, the question in his eyes unreadable. *Unreadable*! What had been in his eyes and in his mind was as clear as the light from the candles at which she gazed, and she had almost succumbed to it. Dear God, she had almost given in to the lust he had shown so impudently. He had asked her weeks ago to be his mistress and, clear-headed, she had refused. This morning he had tricked her, confused her, got her into his arms before she knew what was happening, his body telling her exactly what it wanted of hers. But he'd not get it. She was Mrs Drew Greenwood who loved her husband, wasn't she, and Will Broadbent could go to the devil. She despised him and his wild idea of forming ... what had he said? ... a company, a board of directors, perhaps taking on a partner who had business and managerial expertise ... shares, small but shares as an incentive ... what had he said? ... with herself as ... as chairman. She could learn from them and if she learned she would make damn sure they did not cheat her ...

The chair on which her husband was sitting crashed backwards to the floor and across the table Laurel squeaked in alarm as Drew leaped to his feet.

'Goddammit, Tessa, what's come over you, lolling there with your chin in your hand and your mind obviously a million miles away from here? You've barely said a word this evening beyond a remark or two about nothing in particular. Do you know what, Tessa? You have become a bore. Ask yourself when you last made me laugh, or indeed when you yourself smiled at something? You used to be so splendid, always ready for anything, riding with Pearce and me, with Nick and Johnny and the others. They all thought you were the best sport, one of them, and now look at you.'

His voice had become ugly and his eyes were an unnaturally livid blue as he waved his wine-glass towards her, spilling most of the contents on the carpet. At the back of the room Briggs sighed inaudibly for it would not be Master Drew who had the cleaning of it.

'You look ... you look ...' Her husband searched about in his mind for an insult cutting enough to wound her, as he was wounded by her defection. 'You look and sound just like a bloody millowner.'

'Well, that's what I am, darling. That's what we both are and if you won't accept it, then someone must.' She stood up and smiled, not at all put out, it seemed, by his slashing attack, the invitation in her eyes plain enough for everyone in the room to see and understand. 'So why don't we just forget it for tonight? Bring some champagne – see to it, will you, Briggs? – and we'll have a toast, just you and I in our sitting-room. Come. Have you ever made love to an industrialist, my darling? No, well neither have I,' they heard her say as she led her suddenly laughing, suddenly dazzled husband across the wide hallway and up the stairs. 'It shall be a new experience for us both, I'm certain of that.' And surely, her puzzled heart asked, it would drive the image of Will Broadbent's smiling face, his warm lips and hands from her mind forever?

## 26

The young architect, Mr Talbot, accompanied by the builder, Mr Hale, called on her several days later to ask her opinion on one or two alterations to the plans for the new mill. Just small changes, they assured her, but if she was to study them she would see immediately the enormous benefits they would make to the access of raw materials from one department to another, the easy movement of one process to another, the added safety of her operatives and, she would be happy to hear, they would be advantageous to her financially, shaving several hundreds of pounds from the cost.

'Why were these not thought of months ago when the plans were drawn up?' she asked sharply.

'We have had time to ... to go over them more thoroughly, Mrs Greenwood, in relation to the site which was not cleared when they were first drawn up. And with this latest development we also find we shall be able to begin building at once.' Mr Hale twisted his tall hat in his hands, his eyes somewhat inclined to look, not at her, but through her.

'But you said it would be another month at least before you could start the foundations.'

'Indeed I did, but with some reorganisation it is now possible to dig out the footings at once.'

She was inordinately pleased with herself, taking this latest development as an omen that at last things were about to improve. In fact, almost overnight progress surged forward: the mill was invaded by a positive army of brawny Irish labourers, the footings were dug out, the foundations laid and the walls began to grow with a speed which was nothing short of miraculous; and at home Drew was convinced that it was only a matter of time before she would be his constant companion once more. Indeed, he had been so delighted with her plan to form a 'company' of dependable, knowledgeable men to run the mills, he had even promised airily that he might be persuaded to sit on the board with her.

'Providing I don't have to go in the spinning or weaving sheds amongst all that infernal machinery, and providing it doesn't interfere with the hunting season, naturally, I can see no harm in it. Mind you, my darling,' his old mischievous smile, the merry humour he had been blessed with before Pearce's death, warmed his handsome face, 'I cannot promise to understand what they are talking about. Profit and loss was never my strong suit and when it comes to adding one figure to another I am hopeless. I have no head for it, you see, but I'm sure I would recognise it if I was told we had made a profit of a guinea or two. There, that's a bargain then. I shall accompany you to a ... what do you call it? ... a board meeting now and again and you will come with me when there is some excitement at the Hall. My goodness, won't Mother and Father be delighted with me? Their son in business at last? Now that's decided, come here and entertain your husband as he deserves. Take off that gown ... no, no, let me undo the buttons. What a divine creature you are...'

And so, in the weeks which slipped from spring and into summer, as the mill walls grew as high as her shoulders, then ever upwards, forming one storey ... two ... four ... six, her life continued pleasantly enough, balanced quite easily, it seemed, now that Drew was prepared to be patient and share a little of her time with the demands of "the business' as he laughingly began to call the forming of Chapman Manufacturing Company Ltd.

It was really quite amazingly simple when you knew the right way to go about it, she found. Her bank manager, Mr Bradley, when approached, declared himself more than willing to suggest several gentlemen of unquestionable reputation who might be prepared to sit on her board, men who knew the cotton trade and the commercial world in general. Naturally, with the inducement of directors' fees and a chance to purchase some Chapman stock, it could only be in their own best interest to see the five mills prosper. Her lawyer, Mr Dalton, would be delighted to draw up the necessary papers, he said, to ensure that she, her husband and her sister-in-law, and their inheritance, were protected in the most water-tight, *legal* fashion, the major shareholder in the new company being, naturally, Mr Drew Greenwood himself. In fact, he would be pleased if she would consider himself as the company lawyer to ensure that all the legal aspects of running Chapman Manufacturing Company Ltd were completely safeguarded. She was not to concern herself with the complexity of the insurance which had proved awkward but to leave it all to him.

The new mill was quite splendid, six storeys high, oblong in shape and solid, with thirty windows on each of its two long sides and fifteen at each end. There was a chimney, tall and imposing, with the name CHAPMAN MILL in bricks of a contrasting colour, and the whole building had a most pleasing *permanent* look. It would be some weeks before the new machinery could be put in but in the meanwhile those operatives who had not found other employment, and even those who had, were alerted to the forthcoming opening of the mill and the reinstatement of their old jobs.

The next day the company's first board meeting was to be held, but at the bank premises since the brand new board room at the mill would not be ready. Drew had ridden over to the Hall saying ruefully that if he was to be concerned with business tomorrow then he'd better prepare by clearing his head on Longworth Moor with Nicky. She'd smiled to herself reflecting that one would think he was to be involved in the practicalities of running the mill, taking the burden of all that entailed on his own elegant shoulders, instead of spending, as she knew he would, an hour or two yawning at the first and probably the last board meeting he would ever attend.

The meeting was to begin at ten o'clock and as Mr and Mrs Drew Greenwood entered the bank the clock on the tower of the church opposite struck the hour.

'What on earth does one wear for such an occasion?' Drew had questioned languidly as she coaxed him from their bed at seven thirty. He had not come home until the early hours of the morning, for the wild riding gentlemen had celebrated the splendour of the day with innumerable bottles of the Squire's champagne. He had been good humoured then as he sometimes was when he drank, amiable and boyish, but determined, despite his drunkenness, to make love to her. She had submitted to it, unwillingly for the first time since they had become lovers, sensing that it would cause less dissension simply to lie still and allow him his fumbling way. He had fallen into effortless sleep on her shoulder, the deed half done, his naked body heavy on hers, not stirring when she had slid out from beneath him, but the good humour was gone by the morning light.

'Is it really necessary for me to go with you, Tessa?' he asked peevishly, his aching head in his hands, his still-naked body appearing curiously defenceless in its shrunken, flaccid state as he crouched on the edge of the bed.

410

'I'm afraid it is, darling. You are the largest shareholder.'

'Christ, what on earth does that mean?'

'You know what it means, Drew. There will be ... well, decisions to be made ...' she ventured hesitantly, not at all sure herself on the proceedings of a board meeting, so how was she to explain them to Drew?

'Hell's teeth, Tessa, I'm in no state to make decisions.'

'Not decisions exactly. They will ... plan what is to be done at the mill, the board, I mean, but it is all to be voted on. You and I between us have the major holding ...'

'Oh, Jesus, Tessa, don't go on. Just send Briggs to get me into my things and when I'm dressed I'll try to drag myself into the carriage. I promised I would come and so I shall but, believe me, this will be the last time. I had no idea such affairs began at dawn. Dear God, why cannot these people conduct their business affairs like gentlemen, at a decent hour of the day? Better yet, could they not have come to the house?'

'Darling ...' Her jaw ached with the necessity to stop the hot words from pouring out of her mouth and all over him. Dear God, she had seen often enough in the past months that if she lost her temper he would lose his, there would be a stormy exchange and he would refuse to come at all. Dammit, if she could arrange it in some way – she must ask Mr Dalton if it was possible – she would find some means so that he need never attend a meeting again. Once a month, Mr Dalton had said, but the chairman of the board, in this case Drew or his agent, must be present. Could she be his agent – what was it called? Her mother had mentioned it in one of her letters ... proxy, that was it – then she would have no need to trouble Drew with anything beyond putting his signature on whatever papers Mr Bradley and Mr Dalton, the lawyer, presented to her.

Her mother, her Uncle Joss and even Aunt Kit who was not awfully sure that she wished her frail and precious husband to be troubled by the problems of the reorganisation, wrote her long letters of encouragement. Perhaps in her niece Kit Greenwood recognised herself as she had been over thirty years ago when she had taken up the role of 'manufacturer' on her own father's death. Her words of support, of pleading, really, since she did not want to see all that her family had built up crumble away, did their best to let Tessa know she understood her frailty at this time.

'You can do it, Tessa,' she wrote, 'and I promise you that when the challenge, for that is what it is, is taken up and overcome, there is no greater satisfaction to be had. Gentlemen have told us for so long that we are not made as they are, that our minds are not as theirs, that we are inferior to them in all but one thing, that our brains are incapable of dealing with anything more complicated than a menu, but *you* know that is not true, my dear. Your mother agrees . . .'

Jenny did, but her letters were softer, more tender, less pressing. She was the only one to know the desperate unhappiness Tessa had suffered through her love for Robby Atherton. No one's fault, of course, but what mother can resist blaming herself for her children's misery, dwelling interminably on what she might have done to prevent it? 'Don't allow yourself to lose hope, Tessa. *Never* lose hope for it is all we have to get us through the day. Always, *always* the strength to overcome life's adversity is found and I know you to be a strong woman. Take hold, daughter, and you will win through. If there is anything I can do . . .' But Tessa was aware that her mother was saying any help she gave would only be sent *by letter* from the soft, sun-filled world into which she herself had escaped.

She wrote back, letter after frantic letter, begging to be shown the way to 'take hold', to 'meet the challenge', to 'overcome', but though they always replied kindly, optimistically even, she knew that, at their age, they really could not provide the impossible support she begged of them. They had done it once, Kit Chapman, as she was then, and Jenny Harrison, and could not Tessa Greenwood do the same?

In every letter which passed between them not once was it suggested she should turn to her husband.

He grumbled languidly, petulantly the whole time Briggs was dressing him, protesting that his boots hurt his feet, his cravat was too tight, his shirt front far too stiff and how could he be expected to show himself in a business suit, for that was what it was, when he was not a businessman and had no intention of ever becoming one? His head ached abominably and what he needed was fresh air, not the stuffy confines of some damned office. She could see that he was genuinely nauseous, the requirement of being what he hated above anything else, turning his smooth brown face hollow-eyed and pallid. Should she have told him to change into riding breeches, to take up his crop and saddle his horse, to be off on the moorland and up to the tops and that she would go with him, he would immediately be as charming and lovable, as smiling and generous-hearted as he frequently was, sweet-tempered and terribly sorry he had been such a bad-tempered swine. He would be willing to do anything she asked, to go wherever she pleased if only it was not to the mill, which was what this meeting represented.

Mr Bradley and Mr Dalton were in the doorway of the bank waiting to welcome them, holding out their hands to be shaken by Mr Greenwood who complied reluctantly, quite startled, it seemed, by the novel idea.

'The members of the board are waiting for you, Mrs Greenwood, if you would like to follow me,' Mr Bradley told them officiously whilst Mr Dalton went ahead to ensure that doors were opened and a smooth passage was cleared for these important personages. Though neither he nor Mr Bradley would dream of cheating the owners of the Chapman mills since both they and the other members of the board which they were about to form to run the company were all honest, hard-working businessmen, there would be a great deal of advantage to be gained in being associated with such an undertaking. Particularly as Mr Drew Greenwood and his wife and, one supposed, the third member of the family who had a small share in it, Mrs Laurel Greenwood, were all totally inexperienced in the running of the mill and would therefore, one supposed, leave the whole concern to himself and the rest of the board.

'What a delightful day it is, Mrs Greenwood,' Mr Bradley murmured politely, 'quite warm for the time of the year, though one should expect it in July, I suppose.'

'Indeed,' she answered, keeping one hand on the arm of her husband who was inclined to wince away from everything on which his eye fell, from the half a dozen clerks at their high desks who stared at him and his wife with a great deal of impolite interest, he was inclined to think, to the steep stairs he was forced to climb to reach the corridor which led into the board room.

'Is this going to take long, Tessa?' he was heard to say with no attempt to lower his voice, as he followed her up them, and as they moved along the corridor Mr Bradley exchanged glances with Mr Dalton since it was evident that this meeting was going to be even more trying than they had anticipated.

The board room appeared to be filled with gentlemen. They stood in pairs engaged in serious conversation, or sat engrossed in papers about a large, well-polished table, those who were seated springing to their feet as she entered. They were soberly dressed in dark business suits, all of them, important of expression and shrewd of eye, about a dozen of them she could see now, men of obvious worth and standing in the community, whose resolute expressions told her they would be well able to protect the interests of any business in which they had a hand.

Only one smiled and her heart lurched in her breast as she looked into the narrowed eyes of Will Broadbent. She could distinctly feel, and hear, her own breath quicken and the hand which still rested on Drew's arm trembled slightly as the emotive picture of the last time they were together crept stealthily into her mind.

Mr Bradley was leading the way across the smooth Turkey carpet, doing his best to usher the reluctant owner of the

Chapman mills towards the gentlemen who were to sit on his board. Mr Dalton, as Drew moved forward, had Tessa by the elbow, a gentleman paying her the respect a lady deserved despite the strangeness of having one where none had been before. His hand guided her and his voice soothed her since she seemed somewhat alarmed by the seriousness of this meeting and the overwhelming mass of commercial gentlemen to whom she would be unaccustomed. Indeed, he could feel the trembling of her arm as he placed her in her chair and he smiled to let her know she was in safe hands with Mr Bradley and himself.

The glance she and Will exchanged went unnoticed. She had not seen him since the morning in the mill yard, three months ago now, and though she had been expecting him to follow up and take advantage of the incident – for that was all it had been, she told herself, an incident – in the foreman's hut, he had not done so. His embrace had been ardent and her own response to it surprising, but it had meant nothing to her, she had repeated time and time again to herself, and evidently nothing to him either. He had realised, she supposed, that she was happily married and was not the sort of woman to be treated as a convenient release for his own nasty lust. She had been relieved that he had finally accepted her refusal and the last few moments of their encounter, which she must have imagined, she told herself, when he had seemed to imply that there was more to this than the desires of the flesh, were pushed firmly to the back of her mind.

In the ensuing moments of introduction his eyes holding hers let her see quite openly that it was not so. I told you you were not to fall, did I not? they seemed to say, warm and expressive with some deep-felt emotion. You are here with that diminished man you call a husband because of me; because I showed you the way to do it. A few words, no more, were all that were needed to put you on the right path since you are an intelligent woman. These men have been assembled at your command. Let no one tell you differently. They are here to do *your* bidding so show them from the start that you are as strong and forthright as other women in your family have been. Do it, Tessa. It is all yours, so grasp it with both hands and let no man, *no man* pull you down.

'. . . and this is Mr Will Broadbent, Mrs Greenwood. He is a millowner from Hepworth who has been invited to take a seat on the board.' She smiled since she was well aware now that Will Broadbent would not have waited to be invited and the sardonic gleam of humour in his eyes confirmed it. 'He is a man who knows cotton,' Mr Bradley was saying, 'is that not so, Mr Broadbent? . . . and will, I'm sure, be an asset to the newly formed Chapman Manufacturing Company Ltd.'

'Mr Broadbent and I have already met, Mr Bradley.'

'Is that so, Mrs Greenwood?'

Will took her hand and bowed over it but his eyes continued to smile audaciously into hers. They were a lovely pale brown, flecked with amber and gold, the colour they had been, she remembered, when they had made love in his small overlooker's cottage, the colour of love. And she knew, suddenly, as he held her hand just a shade too long, that everything that had happened in the last three months had been his doing: the miraculous suddenness with which the building plans had been re-designed and completed; the increasingly smooth growth of the building itself, the absence of hitches, the wondrous removal of the obstacles and snags which had plagued her in the beginning. Every man on the site from the master builder himself right down to the lowest hod-carrying labourer had worked hard and fast, and in unison, to get her mill up in record time – why did she now think of it as *her* mill, she wondered curiously – and now it was complete and within weeks would be manufacturing the cotton which her family had manufactured for almost a century. Engineers had been employed, sent ostensibly by Mr Bradley or Mr Dalton who had vouched for them. Managers and overlookers found who had been connected with the old mill, all eager and willing to work with, and for, Mrs Drew Greenwood.

And it was all thanks to Will Broadbent who was turning away now to take the reluctant hand her husband held out to him.

The tiny flame of quite giddy joy burned deep within her as the meeting began and she was afraid to look at him. Drew sat beside her, refusing the chair at the head of the table as though the seat might prove to be red hot. On his face was an expression of ill-mannered boredom which she knew hid his painful fear that somehow, while he was not looking, so to speak, he might find himself embroiled in the machinations of the mill again. He barely listened as Mr Bradley began to speak of the advantage in terms of the future development of Chapmans' to be found in the forming of a limited company. He showed some interest when the words 'chairman' and 'managing director' were mentioned for did they not imply that someone, not himself, naturally, nor his wife, was to take over the running of the business? He voted with the rest, as Tessa had told him to, staring quite openly at Will Broadbent who came, of course, from the lower classes, despite his expensive, well-tailored suit, when he was put forward as managing director. It was incomprehensible to him that such a man, a man who had once worked, so he had been told, in one of his own family's spinning rooms, should hold such a position of authority. Still, if the rest of them thought he could do the job who was he to argue? As long as he had enough money in his pocket to continue his own pleasant life with his wife he didn't give a damn who earned that money for him. A Mr Entwhistle, whose wealth came from breweries, Mr Bradley whispered in his ear, as if it made any difference to Drew Greenwood, seconded the motion, and Drew's brief interest flagged. Mr Dalton was proposed as company secretary, seconded by Mr Bradley and Drew put up a languid hand to indicate that he agreed. It was not until his wife's name was mentioned that his unfocused gaze which had wan-

417

dered to the patch of streaked blue sky beyond the window, swung sharply back to the proceedings.

'What was that?' His arrogant, well-bred voice brought the vote taking place to a halt.

Mr Bradley smiled smoothly though it was evident from the expression in his eyes that he had been hoping young Mr Greenwood would remain in the imperceptive doze into which he appeared to have fallen in the last half-hour. He was far less trouble that way. It was necessary for him to be here at this first meeting of the board for appearances' sake if nothing else, and when Mrs Greenwood was made chairman, with the signed agreement of the biggest shareholder, Mr Drew Greenwood himself, giving her the right to chair the proceedings and vote in his place, there was no need for him to attend a board meeting again. And with Mrs Greenwood under the ... ah ... wing, if one could call it that, of that astute businessman, Mr Will Broadbent, Chapmans could once again be the thriving concern it had been under the direction and guidance of Mrs Jenny Harrison and Mr Charles Greenwood. Dear God, the lengths he had had to resort to, the secrecy to which he had been sworn by Mr Broadbent, of course, in order to get this far in the business dealings. He and Mr Dalton, both as close-mouthed and discreet as men of their respective professions had to be, had worked closely with Mr Broadbent on Mr and Mrs Greenwood's behalf and it was not up to him or Mr Dalton to ask why. This was a business transaction; a helping hand to get a thriving business over a sticky patch and to find the means to keep it the profit-making concern it had always been, and for which, naturally, he and Mr Dalton would be suitably rewarded.

'What is what, Mr Greenwood?' he asked patiently, somewhat alarmed by the wild cast in Drew Greenwood's eye.

'You mentioned my wife's name in connection with ... what was it?'

The whole room held its breath as the lovely Mrs Greenwood turned to her husband, her expression one of concern. She smiled at him, a brilliant smile and yet softly reassuring, and there was not one man there who did not envy Drew Greenwood that look. They watched him with expressionless faces but their indignation and impatience could be quite plainly felt. Had it not been for the esteem in which they had held his aunt and uncle and the presence of Will Broadbent who had assured them that there was a profit to be made, it was doubtful if any of them would have agreed to sit on this board. They had expected nothing less, of course, from this young gentleman whose concern it was, since his inflammable nature was well known in the Penfold Valley, but Tessa could see in their cold eyes that in their opinion the quicker the proceedings were got through the better they would like it.

'Mr Bradley is asking for the agreement of the board to . . . well, myself as chairman of the board.' Her voice was patient and the room held its breath.

'*You?*' His face was comical in its amazement.

'Someone has to . . . to chair the board, is that not the correct expression, Mr Bradley?' She turned her charming smile on the bank manager who assured her that it was.

'I don't give a damn about the correct expression, Tessa, nor who the hell does the job as long as it is not you nor myself. Let one of these . . . these gentlemen see to it, for God's sake. That's the whole idea of this arrangement, surely, so let's get the . . . the positions allocated and get out of here.' He turned to Mr Bradley, making a decent attempt to be civil she could see, yet letting it be known nevertheless that he was not accustomed to dealing with tradesmen, which these gentlemen were. 'Can we not just appoint someone, sign a paper or something, Mr . . . er . . . You will know how these things are done, I'm sure, since that is what I pay you for.' His rudeness was inexcusable but only his wife knew that it was caused by fear. 'My wife and I have an important engagement and really cannot remain any longer.'

'Drew . . .'

'No, Tessa, this has nothing to do with us, really it hasn't. A chairman must be employed...'

'That is what we are trying to do, darling.'

'Then let it be done.'

'It must be the major shareholder, Drew. That is how Mr Dalton has arranged it, legally, I mean...'

The gentlemen about the table, except for Will Broadbent who looked as though he might, for some reason known only to himself, spring from his chair at any moment, were grim-faced, clinging, Tessa could see, to their equanimity with the greatest difficulty. And all the while Drew was becoming more restless, his face showing his absolute disdain for these trumpery business dealings. After all, he had only come because Tessa had promised him that it would be just this once, to appoint members to the board and would soon be done with. Now they were taking the liberty of begging his own wife to be employed on it. How dare they even suggest it when it was well known that she was Mrs Drew Greenwood, a lady, and though she had been forced to move amongst them for the past few months, the purpose of this bloody meeting was to ensure that she need do it no longer?

'Don't talk nonsense, Tessa. Any of these fellows could do it. They are all qualified, I'm sure...'

'No, we are not, Mr Greenwood, or we would have no need of you at all.' The quiet voice from the end of the table was Will Broadbent's. Tessa could see the dangerous gleam in his now-darkened eyes and she put out an instinctively protective hand to her husband. Will's jaw clenched perilously when he saw it and she knew she must get Drew away from here at once.

'I think it's time we left, darling, or we shall be late for our engagement.' Her voice was light and airy. 'I think our business here is concluded but I believe Mr Bradley has some papers you are to sign, and myself too, is that not so, Mr Bradley? In fact, I think it might be appropriate if we dealt with that now, if it is convenient, then we can take our leave. There is no other immediate business, is there, gentlemen? We have a managing director . . .' She dare not look at Will lest they see the tiny glow which shone not only in her eyes, but in his, '. . . and a chairman . . .' Without revealing to Drew the chairman's name but letting them know that she would be taking the position herself, she turned to Mr Bradley and smiled.

Drew signed his name carelessly to every paper put before him, ignorant of the fact that, witnessed by a dozen of the valley's leading businessmen, he had just signed away his inheritance to his equally ignorant wife.

'Good morning, gentlemen,' she said breathlessly to each one whilst her husband chafed at the door, a curt nod in their direction all that he considered necessary.

'Good morning, Mrs Greenwood.'

'Good day to you, ma'am.'

As he held her arm courteously, leading her across the room to the protection of her husband, no one but Mrs Greenwood heard Will Broadbent murmur in her ear of his habit of walking the moorland high above Friar's Mere each Sunday.

'Well, thank God that's over. Now perhaps you will come with me to Johnny's Friday to Monday next weekend. You will not believe me when I tell you that poor old Johnny has fallen hook, line and sinker for one of the Henderson girls and has invited her family down from God only knows wherever it is they live, to view his prospects. He means to marry her and she not more than fifteen, so they tell me. Can you believe it? Though why I should be surprised I cannot imagine as I have extolled the virtues of the married state to them all for the past three years. But then they cannot all have the good fortune to be married to the most beautiful and charming woman in the whole of Lancashire, can they?'

The offensive scene in the board room might never have taken place. Indeed, like all the tiresome irritations which came to trouble Drew Greenwood's feverish spirit, it was cast already into a deep hole and covered over with all that was frivolous and amusing and with which he filled his life.

He pulled her to him in the carriage, his boyish face filled with good-humoured satisfaction that at last all that dreadful business was behind him. He could not wait to return to the carefree life they had enjoyed together before Charlie's death and to which now, now that affairs were in other hands more suited to them than his own or hers, they could return.

'I'm pleased for Johnny, and the Henderson girl, whoever she may be,' she answered carefully, not wanting yet to disturb his triumphant belief that she was to be his completely from now on. She knew she would be forced to compromise, to share some of her time with him in his hedonistic pursuit of pleasure; to keep an eye on him, she supposed, but she could not forget that small budding of pleasure she had enjoyed when those men round the board room table had treated her with the respect and care one man will show to another who has power. They would wait to see if she would fail dismally, not displeased if she did since she was a woman, but she'd done damn well so far in her handling of the Chapman venture, they believed. The forming of the company to look after her husband's concerns was good sense since anyone with half an eye could see he was incapable of doing more than pursuing the life of the gentleman he thought himself to be. The mill was to start up again, which none of them had predicted almost a year ago, and she had been clever enough to get some decent advisors, themselves in fact, to guide her along what would be a hard road to tackle.

They had believed *she* had done it. Will Broadbent had given her that. He had let them all believe that *she* had done it and they admired her for it. She had liked their admiration since, until now, both as a woman and a girl she had earned nothing but scorn for her wild ways, her complete lack of judgement, her inability to do more than skylark about the county with her two reckless cousins.

It did not occur to her that at the time she had delighted

in that scorn she earned from all those in the Penfold Valley, whom she in her turn had held in contempt for their conventionality. And she certainly did not connect the change in her attitude with Will Broadbent who had told her that he would be on the path above Friar's Mere next Sunday at noon.

'Well,' her husband said, pulling away from her impatiently, 'are you to go or not?'

'Go where, darling?'

'Hell's teeth, Tessa, will you pay some attention to what I am saying or I shall begin to believe you actually enjoy being an industrialist?' He was laughing now, amused at the lunatic idea that Tessa Greenwood could possibly be entertained by anything other than what she had done so successfully for most of her life. 'Come on, sweetheart, it's all behind us now. You have absolutely no need to go into that mill yard again, and neither have I. Oh, I understand that we may have to attend a board meeting or two, as directors of the company.' He could accept it now that it was over, even believe that he would do it. He grinned endearingly as though to ask if he was not clever at remembering it, 'But that is all and we will celebrate our freedom with our friends next weekend. You must have a new gown, something to turn their heads and make them stare. Cause a sensation as you have always done.'

He made love to her that night, jubilantly, calling her name over and over again, but when she lay sleepless beside his restlessly turning body she knew, despite the triumph which he thought had been his that day, he was still haunted in his dreams by the past.

## 27

She would not go up to Friar's Mere, she told herself, on
that first Sunday after the board meeting nor on any other.
Despite what Will had done for her and her deep gratitude
towards him, she loved her husband dearly and had no wish
to chance the fragile equilibrium which held him, but only
just, to the rationality of his day-to-day living. He had been
uneasy of temper for several days following the meeting as
though considerably unnerved by the narrow escape he and
his wife had had from a life of utter degradation in the mill.
Filled with high spirits one minute and with wild ideas on
how to make Johnny Taylor's weekend memorable, then
cast down in the next and wanting nothing more than his
head on her breast, her arms about him in the complete
privacy of their room. His instability of temperament was
growing beyond even her controlling, she was ready to
admit, and if she were to chance a meeting with Will, even
if it was only to thank him for his help, to tell him how
deeply grateful she was to him for shouldering so much of
her burden, how might it affect her husband should he
come to hear of it?

Sunday came and for the first time in her life she begged
off riding over to the Hall, claiming a headache as an excuse.

'But you go, darling, for I shall only lie here quietly with
the curtains drawn until I feel better.'

His immediate and loving concern almost undid her. He
would stay with her, he whispered softly. He could not bear
to leave her when she was unwell. How many times in the
past had she been beside him when he had been 'afflicted',

the word he used when the nightmares came to terrify him. He would soothe her temples with cologne, her forehead with a cool cloth, hold her head, lie beside and comfort her, kiss her better – smiling – and would not dream of leaving her, no, not if Nicky Longworth and Johnny Taylor came themselves to drag him away.

For an hour he hovered about her, moving restlessly from the bed to the open window, twitching aside the drawn curtains to stare out into the garden, hurrying back to her side each time she moved, begging her hoarsely to tell him she felt better, wondering if he could fetch her anything, until she pleaded with him to go since she really did think she would be better on her own. He was quite visibly relieved.

'Are you sure, dearest? I wouldn't dream of going, you know that, but if you're certain you'd be better alone . . . ?'

'I'm certain, sweetheart. You get along and when you come home I shall be completely recovered.'

'I won't be late, I promise.'

'Stay as long as you like. I'm poor company today.'

'I've never known you have a headache, my love.' He was still hesitant to leave her but dying to be off, disturbed perhaps by the remembrance of another illness in another place.

She heard the wild gallop of his bay's hooves on the cobbles of the stable yard at the back of the house and the pounding on the turf as horse and rider headed off across the parkland towards Longworth Hall. She lay for a while, convincing herself that her 'headache' really did exist and that she would stay and cosset herself, much to Emma's amazement, for the rest of the day. Yet in her heart, which thumped quite madly, and in her mind from which all reason had long since gone, she knew she would be high above Friar's Mere by noon.

'I think I feel a little better, Emma. I might even go out for a breath of fresh air.'

'A walk in the garden would do you good, madam.' The

incredible thought that Miss Tessa, or Mrs Greenwood as she should really call her, was breeding, had leapt into Emma's mind and she was pleased that at last her mistress had acquired some sense. It was well known that ladies in the family way should not climb up on a horse's back and Miss Tessa did look somewhat peaky; a bit pale and strained about her mouth, though her eyes were quite feverishly bright.

For half an hour her mistress allowed herself to be treated like an invalid, just as though she really would rather stay in the seclusion of her home and garden on this day when the sky was streaked with torn clouds and a mist like a silver veil shifted uneasily about the tops. It was not fit to be out in, Emma said cheerfully, even if it was July, placing more coal on the small fire which had been lit. But when she came back from the kitchen with the dainty tray of coffee and toasted muffins Miss Tessa had ordered, her mistress was already in her breeches and riding jacket, her warm cloak over her arm, her hair bundled up into a loose knot and tied carelessly with an emerald green ribbon.

'Send a message to Walter to saddle my mare, Emma. I have decided to go riding after all.'

'Oh, Miss Tessa, please don't.' Setting the tray down Emma moved to take the cloak from her mistress, her face distressed. She'd never forgive herself if Miss Tessa had an accident, out there all by herself, and damaged that precious burden Emma had persuaded herself she was carrying. It was many years since Miss Tessa had gone out alone, in fact not since Master Drew had come home from the Crimea. 'It's not fit to be out in, Miss Tessa. You'd never think it was July. Percy,' who had been Emma's 'intended' for many years now, 'has just told me how nasty it is and the master'd not like it if you was to go out without him. You know how he is . . .' Her voice trailed off lamely. They all knew how he was, those who worked in his house. Doted on his wife, he did, hardly able to bear her out of his sight, and he'd not be best pleased if she was to go galloping over the moor on her own, especially if she was in an 'interesting' condition.

'Do as I say, Emma. I might even ride over to the Hall to join him.'

But when Mrs Greenwood cantered decorously out of the yard and across the stretch of pasture which led to the small wood and on to the beginning of the wild moorland she had three of those fierce dogs with her that she and her husband had bred from the original pack and she was not going in the direction of the Hall.

The mist swallowed the dogs as they raced ahead so that she was constantly obliged to call them back to her. They were fresh and enchanted to be out of the stables, reluctant to come to her whistle, their sleek black shapes slipping in and out of the trailing edges of the mist and cloud which came down to meet her.

He would not be there, of course, since he would not expect her to venture out on such a day. She had not meant to come herself but something had whispered that this was as good a way as any to prove the ethereal nature of his purpose towards her. A dalliance was what he was after, she told herself, with a married woman who would have no claim on him; who would prove no threat to his good name for she would be guarding her own.

He was leaning against a pile of rocks, his face quiet and serious as he turned towards her. He made no move to help her down from her mare and when the dogs circled him, baring their teeth menacingly since they did not know him, he remained still.

'Call them off, Tessa,' he said at last and when she did and they were lying peaceably against the base of the rocks he turned back to his contemplation of the valley which revealed itself as the mist drifted in eddying patches.

'I was hoping you wouldn't come,' he said absently, and she took no offence since she knew exactly what he meant. 'I wanted you to, of course,' he continued, 'more than anything I've ever wanted before. I came up here hours ago,

427

long before there was any possibility of seeing you, and I dare say I would have waited all day.' He began to smile, turning back to where she stood, still holding her mare's bridle, 'So you may be well aware of my feelings for you, Tessa Harrison. Do you feel the same?'

'I have not come . . . lightly.'

'I hoped you would say that.'

'I love my husband.'

'No. You love your cousin, not your husband,' he replied and she knew at last that he spoke the truth. She had always loved her cousins, both of them, and the damaged man who was her husband held a special place in her heart, as did Robby Atherton. But she had loved neither of them with the true, enduring love that exists between a mature man and woman. Girlish love, young love, a bright, shining wonder had been her feelings for Robby Atherton. Compassion and gratitude and need had led her into marriage with Drew. And this man. This true man. What had she to give to him? What was it that he wanted and could she give it to him?

She moved towards him almost unwillingly though her heart was bounding joyfully ahead. She leaned her back against the rocks beside him, her shoulder an inch from his and when he took her rain-wet hand and raised it to his lips she felt the sweetness move in her veins. The gesture was so courtly, so gentle, so sad even, as though he was fully aware of the great and awful gulf which stood between them and she felt the sorrow of what they might have had prick to tears at the back of her eyes.

'Tessa, my Tessa, what are we to do? We cannot pretend, either of us, though I fancied otherwise several months ago, that I want you merely as my mistress. It is more than that. We are back all those years to when you were seventeen and I fell in love with you, and yet look what stands between us now. We have come together again inevitably as I suppose I knew we would for what we had was not something given to many. Its only fault then was that you were too young for it; for the commitment it needed. I was ready but you were no more than a girl and now it is too late, now that we are both ... of a mind ... oh, yes, we are, my girl, so give me no argument. I can see it in your eyes, and in the reality that you are here where anyone will tell you it is madness to be. Why have you come if you don't love me? Not to say thank you as you would have me believe. Why have you risked your marriage, the life you lead and which you seem to find so pleasant, and now, your husband's inheritance for without you it will certainly fail?'

'Will ... for God's sake...'

'What is it, my lovely lass? Are you afraid?'

'Desperately.'

'Not you, Tessa. You are the bravest woman I know, or do I mean the most stubborn?' He turned at last and with a groan pulled her into his arms. His voice was shaking as he tucked her head beneath his chin, holding her so close she could feel a pulse in his throat throb against her cheek.

'I did want to thank you, Will.' Her voice was muffled against his chest. 'I couldn't have done it without you, you know that. I don't even know why you changed your mind. When I first came to ask you for help it took you all your time not to knock me to the floor of your office...'

'I know. I hated you even while I loved you for your bloody nerve in coming. That bright look you gave me, half-afraid, defiant and haughty, for were you not Tessa Harrison who was accustomed to her own way? Yet there was a wariness about you, a readiness, if you like, to run like hell if I turned nasty. But you came just the same and that took courage. God, you were so maddening, with your chin up and your eyes flashing, just as you had always been. It almost broke my heart. It took all my strength not to sweep you into my arms and kiss that supercilious smile from your face.'

She tilted her head and looked up at him smiling. 'I didn't know I looked supercilious.'

'You don't know you're doing it, my darling. It comes so naturally to you. That's why the men in the yard scurry around to do your bidding. You are Mrs Greenwood and your manner tells them that they would be wise to jump when you tell them to. It will stand you in good stead in the months to come.'

'You think I can do it then?'

'I know you can.'

'Even without you there to ... to clear the way?'

He smiled down at her ruefully. 'How did you know I had ... put in a word here and there?' He held her away from him, making no attempt to kiss her, the embrace they had just shared quite without passion. She had never seen him like this before, so introspective, as though he was looking inwards to a man he had not known existed. He seemed surprised at his own actions on her behalf, wrapped in thoughts of the past and of the future in which, his manner seemed to say, there could be no room for Will Broadbent and Tessa Greenwood, at least not together. She was frightened by it for suddenly it was inconceivable that he should go out of her life again for she knew she could not manage, not now, not ever, without his arms about her.

'Will ... ?'

'What is it?'

'Why are we here?' her voice was urgent and he turned to her, surprised.

'I don't understand.'

'Why are we here, Will? Why did you tell me to come? It is this which frightens me, not the mill, though that is bad enough. It would be simpler, far simpler, if we walked away from one another. I don't want ...'

'To love me?'

'Yes ... no ...'

'Then you do love me?'

'I ... we cannot ...'

'Say it. Goddammit, Tessa, say it, but mean it this time.'

'I ... I love you. I love you, Will Broadbent. Can you doubt it now? This is no adventure, as it was the last time.'

'I wish it were, my love, it would be far easier for us both.'

'I dare say.' She moved to stand closer to him, looking up

430

into his stern face. She placed her hands carefully, one on either side of his smooth, freshly shaved cheeks, then her mouth lifted to his as sweetly and softly as a sigh, lingering, tasting the texture of his lips, carrying in her mind the passion of their past but holding back from it.

'Will you stay with me, my darling?' he whispered against her mouth, still not touching her.

'For as long as I can.'

'Aah, Tessa...'

'I know, I know. I have never felt so sad and yet so blindly, rapturously happy.'

'Where...?'

She shook her head and the misted drops of moisture in her hair scattered, some running down her forehead and across her wet cheeks. She blinked as they dewed her eyelashes and he watched with all the fascination and bewitchment of a man under a spell. She was like some water sprite, dewed and shimmering palely in the mist, and yet her mouth was poppy-red and full.

'When?' he said more urgently and she felt the instant unfolding of their desire. His arms drew her to him, a homecoming now, a return to the place where she was always meant to be, and his mouth, wet with raindrops, came down hard on hers, merciless in its aggression. She was his, *his* and he would take her now, put his own special mark on her, his woman, before she could change her mind. 'When, Tessa, when?' His lips parted to take hers and the rain which was falling steadily on them now tasted sweet in their joined mouths.

'I don't know ... there is nowhere...'

'Dear God, how I've loved you, wanted you, all these years, and now the bloody weather...'

They began to smile as they kissed, then to laugh, holding on to one another, the skin of their faces wet and sliding, their hair dripping, their hands which were longing to explore, to touch, to caress what was dear and familiar, cold and wet. The whole loving encounter was becoming

431

impossible, amusing even, so that their laughter released itself high and merry into the grey sky.

After a while they grew quiet, content for the moment to stand within the circle of each other's arms and talk softly of the past, the question of where, or how, or even when they would meet in the future, still unresolved. It would happen, they both knew it. There would be turmoil ahead, they both knew that too, since he was not a man to share another man's woman. He might have believed, in the past, that they could become lovers, live a clandestine life of deceit and lies, of messages passed from one paid hand to another, of hurried meetings and hurried farewells, but Will Broadbent, deny it now as he might, was not a man to live such a life. The day would come when Drew Greenwood's wife, Will Broadbent's *woman*, would be forced to make a choice.

'We could go away, you know,' he said abruptly. 'I have money. We could move away from here. I am not a man without experience. There are other mills...'

'Don't ... don't, Will.'

'You could not bear to leave your husband, you are saying?'

'He could not bear it.'

'He is a grown man though one would not think it to hear him speak. He would survive.'

'No, he would not. He is ... not strong...'

'He looked well enough to me at the board meeting. Somewhat highly strung but then he and his brother were always that. The mills could be run by those men...'

'You told me a little while since that they would fail without me.'

'I only meant that *he* could not do it.'

She held on to him tightly, her face buried against his chest, her eyes tightly closed against the pain and fury in his. So soon, so soon. It had been but an hour and already he was demanding, begging more of her than she could give. They had done no more than kiss and declare their true feelings, hold one another, thanking the gods which had given them this small, shared part of their lives. Somehow she must make him see that they could never, *never* have more. Only she knew what Drew had become, how far down the slippery road his darkened mind had sent him, the death of Charlie accelerating that journey a hundredfold. He was desperately vulnerable, likely to be further weakened by anything which threatened that vulnerability, and knowing this she had come here joyfully to throw herself into Will Broadbent's arms.

'Will, you must listen to me.'

'To hear you tell me how much he means to you?' he said roughly, holding her to him desperately, crushing her, hurting her in his sudden illogical anger. The sweet reason with which he had viewed their relationship was swept away on a flow of savage jealousy.

'You must listen to me. Don't you see we might as well part now, and forever, if you will not see reason?'

'I want you, that is reason enough . . .'

'No, Will.'

There was a great weight on them now, a bewilderment that this had come upon them so suddenly. It was as though a pendulum had swung them, first high on a delirium of delight at finding one another again, falling slowly to the sober realisation of what it would mean to them as they lived that secret life, then high again in possessive, jealous rage. Will was not naïve enough to believe that Drew Greenwood's wife would not make her body available to her husband whenever he required it and in his mind's eye he could picture them, perhaps no more than an hour from now, sharing the sweetness of what he himself was denied. He and Tessa could find a place somewhere, discreet and hidden, he was certain, but for how long! They could meet up here now and again where no one came but the birds and the moorland animals, but for how long? How long would it be before the situation provoked disillusionment, impatience, and a refusal to suffer it any longer?

'Perhaps we should remain ... no more than business acquaintances then?' His voice was cold and he let his arms drop heavily to his side.

'If you think it best.'

'I can see no alternative.' The numb misery in him washed over her.

'Nor I.'

'We had best be on our way then.'

'Indeed.'

'You are ... we are both getting very wet ...'

Their eyes met for that last fatal moment, glazed with pain and the need to hide it, to bury it deep where it could be neither seen nor felt, for it was too much to bear. A moment, an instant, then without coherent thought they flung themselves into one another's arms, crying both of them, that whatever the cost they could not part. His hands were at her face and hers at his, stroking feverishly, then clinging again until their bodies met and strained together.

'I can't wait ...'

'Nor I ...'

'Here ... ?'

'There is nowhere else, my love.'

He tried to spread his cloak and hers upon the wet, spongy turf, using the overhang of the rocks to protect them from the drizzle which still fell, but the garments were already damp before he laid her on the makeshift bed. It was not cold and though the skin of her naked body rose in tingling gooseflesh it was at the delight of the new and erotic sensation as wet flesh met wet flesh. Her breasts lifted ecstatically, the nipples peaked and rosy to his hands and lips. They had waited a long time and they could not hold back, either of them. He entered her at once and that taut thread which had tightened so many times in the past for Drew Greenwood snapped in two releasing in her a languorous breathless pleasure which left her laughing and weeping with her joy.

'Again,' she told him, lifting her body greedily, and he

plunged into her, his own laughter joyous and triumphant. This time the rapture caught them both by surprise as it exploded within them simultaneously.

'Truly, you are perfect,' she breathed when she could at last speak.

'Together we are, my love, my sweet love.'

'Hold me in your arms.'

'Always.'

'Always. You will always love me?'

'How can you ask?'

He wrapped his warm, wet body about hers and drew the damp cloaks about them. His head rested in the curve of her shoulder and as they lay quietly the sun drifted out from behind the wisps of cloud which moved across the sky and the light rain stopped. There was no sound except for her mare as she cropped the grass. One of the dogs yawned noisily and moved into a patch of sunshine and Tessa knew that it was time to leave. She must be home before Drew. She would, of course, tell him she had been for a canter up behind the house but he must not know how long she had been gone.

Will drowsed against her and she studied his relaxed face intently, the hard, flat planes of his cheeks, the strong mouth, half-smiling in sleep, the firm chin unblurred by excess flesh though she knew him to be thirty-five or so. The face of a man who has known hardship and adversity but has overcome it; who has shouldered aside the barrier of class and education and become a man other men respect, a man other women – other than Tessa Greenwood – could love. Only his eyelashes seemed out of place in his man's face for they were long, silky and fine, like those of a sleeping child, giving him an air of defencelessness which was not apparent when he was awake, and which moved her heart to anguished love. His short, straight hair lay spikily on his forehead and she brushed it back with loving fingers. His smile deepened as she dropped light kisses on the corner of his mouth, on his eyes until they opened, and he made love to her again, slowly, softly, gently, without urgency and time simply stopped for her as she fell into the rapture again.

They dressed hastily. She was aware that she must get home before Drew, that it was probably already too late; he was conscious of her anxiety and resented it. She caught his rancour but did not dare to stop and allay it. How could she? It would always be like this and they must both accept it. Don't let him be hurt, her heart begged over and over again, don't let him be hurt *too* much. Don't let me wound him again as I did the last time. But already she knew the pain was there, the pain of letting her go to another man.

He pulled her roughly to him.

'Will you . . . ?'

'What, my darling?'

'Is it too much to ask that you won't . . . ?'

She knew what he was trying to ask, trying *not* to ask for it diminished him in his own eyes, but she could make him no promises and he knew it in his heart. She drew his head down to her shoulder, amazed that this strong man should be so frail.

'I love you, Will,' she whispered. 'No matter what . . . happens between Drew and me, you are the one I love.' She could promise him no more than that.

She thanked God that Drew's horse was not in the stable. Though it probably meant that he would come home the worse for drink, that his earlier solicitude for her had been forgotten, indeed that she had been forgotten, at least she would be saved the complication of explaining where she had been for so long. It was almost six and the intervening hours with Will had drifted by without her noting their passage. Even Walter, she felt, as he took her mare from her must sense the tension in her, the guilt, she supposed, since she had just committed the sin of adultery. Drew in his more reasonable state was aware of her every mood, but if he was drunk, whether merry or surly, it would be easier for her to get through that initial encounter. For the first time, she

436

realised, she was praying that her husband would come home in his cups!

He did, just as the watery sun slid beyond the charcoal grey tops.

'It was a splendid day, sweetheart, quite splendid. We played cards and sampled the Squire's claret and then old Johnny rode over and bored us all to distraction waxing lyrical on the charms of his Alicia. Yes, that's her name, the future Mrs Johnny Taylor, of Hadden Hall. So we plied him with claret and took several guineas off him ... well, I did until Nicky had a run of good luck and ended up the winner by ... now don't look at me like that, Tessa darling. A gentleman must pay his gambling debts ... only 200, sweetheart, and now that the mill is to be back in business and old Bradley is looking after all our investments, we can well afford it. Then, after we had finished the claret Nicky brought up a bottle of ...'

His good humour made him mercifully unaware of her own tenseness and gradually it drained away as she realised that her husband had spent such a pleasant day he had completely forgotten her own reason for not accompanying him.

'... so all in all it should be a splendid weekend. Freddy Piggot is to be there. You remember Freddy, don't you, darling, and that horse-faced sister of his, who, I suspect, is a strong candidate for Nicky? His mama is set on seeing him married and if she can arrange it to her own satisfaction poor old Nicky will be saddled ...' he shouted with laughter. '... did you hear that? Saddled, how very appropriate ... with Freddy's wealthy sister ...'

She listened smilingly, able now to look into his flushed face, to meet his bright and merry eyes. When, after half an hour of lounging by her sitting-room fire, a glass of brandy in his hand and the decanter close by, since the night had turned decidedly chilly, he said, he dredged up from his bemused mind the memory of the morning and her indisposition, he was almost reduced to tears in repentance.

437

'How could I? Oh, my darling, all these hours you have been alone. What a swine I am, and you with a headache ... Will you ever forgive me?'

'I had a ride out ... to clear it.'

'Oh, darling, I'm so glad. You're completely better, really?' With his contrite head in her lap, her hand smoothing his tumbled curls, she sighed, remembering the wiry hair she had caressed that afternoon, studying the face of Will Broadbent as he smiled at her from the dancing flames of the fire.

# 28

It was just over six months since Annie had gone to Manchester and with the new mill to be opened the following week Tessa searched for the scrap of paper on which her address had been scribbled, intending to write to tell her that her job was waiting for her and that she was to come home immediately.

But the memory of their last meeting and Annie's pig-headed refusal of employment at Crossbank or one of the other mills; her absolute determination to do what she thought right and not what Tessa considered best for her, made Tessa leave the note she had begun to write and move thoughtfully to the window. Annie was quite likely to turn awkward if she thought she was being 'ordered' home. She might even be settled happily in her new place and job and be disinclined to return to the cottage – which Tessa had kept vacant for her – and her job at the rebuilt mill. Tessa was not awfully sure what 'pin-heading' or 'pin-sheeting' was. Perhaps it was a splendid job which Annie had found more to her liking and in that case it would need all Tessa's powers of persuasion to get her to come home.

She had missed her. Annie's forthright common sense and practical, realistic outlook on what life could fling at you had often been a lifeline for Tessa in the years they had been friends and she needed her now as she had never needed her before. She was not awfully sure why since Annie was bound to disapprove of her renewed relationship with Will, but there would be comfort in having Annie there in the cottage at Edgeclough, even if it was only to scold.

She had wondered vaguely, now that the mill was to be working again, whether Annie could be employed with something other than her spinning machine. There were hundreds of girls who could do the work Annie had done before the fire. Annie was so bright and sensible, surely she could do something besides mind a couple of self-actors? And her sisters. They were growing up now and were ready, she supposed, for marriage and how much better they would do, back here with their own people. Strangely, she never thought of marriage in connection with Annie. And, of course, there was Jack whose place at Mr Dalton's, the lawyer, had already been arranged and was waiting for him.

No, best get over to Manchester and talk face to face with Annie, make her see what wonderful opportunities were available not only to her, but to her family. Tell her she would be doing them an injustice if she allowed such chances to slip from her grasp. In the most diplomatic way, of course, knowing Annie!

She told no one, not even Will, that she was going. Drew had ridden into Crossfold to see his tailor and would be bound to tarry at the Dog and Gun, and so on a fine day at the end of July she took the train from Crossfold, changing at Oldham for Manchester, arriving at Victoria station as the clock struck noon.

The day was warm and though she wore a light-weight sprigged organdie gown of the palest grey she was immediately aware that not only was the close, smoke-covered pall

439

which hung over the city about to make her perspire in the most uncomfortable and unladylike way, but that her light-coloured gown would be stained and grimy long before she arrived at Annie's. The huge crinoline cage, though cooler than the old fashion of the six or seven petticoats she had worn to hold out the width of her skirt, was awkward to manoeuvre. As she and Emma, whom she had been compelled to bring with her to avoid the attention a lady alone might attract, crammed themselves into a public carriage, Emma was quite appalled by its condition.

'We can't ride in that, Miss Tessa.' Her voice was indignant, but at the same time somewhat apprehensive since, never having travelled in anything other than her mistress's splendid carriage, she was not at all sure of the rough fellow who was to drive them. 'Mr Drew wouldn't like it at all, not at all,' she added tearfully.

'Mr Drew doesn't know so he cannot form an opinion and if we are not to ride in this carriage are you prepared to walk?'

Emma eyed the curious men who seemed to have nothing better to do than lounge about the station yard and stare and the barefoot, filthy-faced urchins, inclined to beg or throw stones, she was sure. Reluctantly she climbed into the carriage.

'Where to, madam?' the driver enquired politely enough, though evidently not accustomed to driving a lady and her maid in his conveyance. When she told him, giving him the name of the street which Annie had written down, she was bewildered when he turned to stare at her.

'*Pike* Street? What, Pike Street what runs by't river?' he asked, his expression quite astounded.

'I do not know where it runs. I merely wish to be taken there.'

'Are yer sure yer mean Pike Street?' he repeated, eyeing her elegant gown, her white, lace-trimmed parasol, her pretty pearl-grey bonnet on which an enormous white silk tea rose bobbed and the dainty white kid boots to which already some quite unrecognisable substance adhered.

'I do and I would be obliged if you take me there at once.'

'Well, you know best,' he remarked cheerfully, turning out of the station yard and into Victoria Terrace which led into Victoria Street.

They proceeded at a steady pace along the pleasant thoroughfare until the carriage turned a corner and there, in the centre of a vast square, stood the imposing building of the Royal Exchange, the very heart of the cotton industry and without which, it was said, the sprawling body of its trade which spread over most of Lancashire, would cease to function. Radiating out from the Exchange like the spokes of a wheel were dozens of streets in which lay the thousands of warehouses, factories and sweat-shops connected with the cotton industry, and all within five minutes' walk of its hub. The Royal Exchange was the focus of buying and selling cotton and on market days, Tessa had heard, its huge halls were crowded from one end to the other with buyers and sellers, not even the least self-respecting of them without his tall silk hat for this was the most important cotton market in the world. She would come here one day, Will had told her, for she must learn everything there was to know about cotton if she was to become the manufacturer her mother and her Aunt Kit had been. All around it, enormous warehouses were crammed with cloth, some of it her own, brought from surrounding towns: Bolton, Bury, Oldham, Stockport, and Crossfold! The excitement began to grow in her at that moment.

The streets became increasingly narrow and twisting the further they went and the buildings were so tall it was almost impossible to see the sky. There were waggons heavily laden with cotton cloth, with piece goods and dress goods, with huge bales of raw cotton and all the commodities on which Manchester had built its reputation as the centre of the cotton industry. Waggons lumbered in and out of wide gateways, the patient, plodding dray horses which pulled them bending their heads with the weight of their huge loads.

'Oh, Lord,' Emma gasped as their own carriage swayed quite dangerously in the frantic rush which seemed to pervade the area. A hurrying multitude crowded about the conveyance and the impassive animal which pulled it, and surely the massed sea of people were in danger of being run down by the dozens of vehicles which crammed the streets, all of which were involved in the many and complex layers of employment the industry produced. Brokers, yarn merchants, dyers, waste dealers, merchants, manufacturers, buyers and sellers, all were hurrying in the direction of the particular street or region which dealt with their own section of the trade. Stockport and Salford were 'making up'; Piccadilly and Portland Street where the great warehouses were situated; Brown Street was 'shirts' and Stride Hill 'underwear'. It looked just as though some careless foot had kicked over an ant-hill, scattering the human ants in every direction, but there was a strange kind of order about it for each ant knew exactly its own destination and business.

'Oh, Lord,' Emma said again, inclined to be even more tearful as rude, inquisitive faces peered in at them, some leering at the sight of two pretty women in a place where the only females were those drabs who worked in one of the hundreds of small factories, sweat-shops most of them, which crowded the cellars of every street, and were allied to the cotton trade.

The bustle of the town centre began to die away as they crossed the river Irwell, turning left to follow what was really no more than a cobbled track running beside the river. It was here that the stench invaded the carriage, faint at first and causing no more than a tendency to sniff and turn one's head in an effort to identify it and its source.

'What is it, Miss Tessa?' Emma whispered.

'God knows, Emma, but whatever it is it seems to be getting worse by the minute.'

They each held a dainty scrap of perfumed lace to their nostrils and Tessa felt her stomach begin to move distastefully as the stink became so strong she could not only smell it, but taste it.

On one side of them ran the river, slow moving, evil looking, with unidentifiable objects floating sluggishly just below its surface. Along its banks great piles of rotting garbage swung in the gentle eddies of river water which had carried it there. The smell was appalling and Tessa had the strongest desire to scratch at herself just as though the deeper they penetrated into the squalid district the more loathsome the miasma of filth grew on her skin.

''Ere we are,' the driver of the carriage told them. He had a look about him which said he would be glad to get away from this place himself. Already attracted by the sight of the carriage, the area was beginning to swarm with what must have been inquisitive children but which looked for all the world like small, scurrying monkeys, grey-coloured, pallid, furtive. He could not imagine what two such elegant ladies wanted here, but a fare was a fare though if they asked him to wait he'd have to refuse. These urchins would pick his cab clean, wheels an' all, if he stood still for more than two minutes.

They were in a courtyard, large and square with immensely tall houses on three sides of it, each floor-level of the buildings contained by an iron-railinged balcony and each connected by narrow stairs up to the sixth and top floor. The courtyard was unpaved and in its centre a huge pool of water had collected in a hollow, unable to run away to the river in which sewage was dumped. Directly in the middle of the water was a broken building with an opening, evidently once a doorway from which not only the door but the frame was missing as well. It was from here that the stench came, an invisible eruption to which those who inhabited the court seemed impervious but which brought stinging tears to Tessa's eyes. Everywhere was filth, mud, rotting carcasses of what must once have been a living cat or dog, and in it the children played, barefoot, almost naked, and men and women lolled, the smoky sunshine and warmth lulling them into a somnolence which gave them the appearance of living corpses.

Emma began to choke and gasp as the foetid air entered her lungs. 'Merciful heaven! Miss Tessa, please ... we can't stay here ... call the carriage ... don't let him go, Miss Tessa. ... We'll be murdered where we stand ... or worse. Please, oh, please, Miss Tessa ...'

Tessa felt the smarting tears clog her eyes but she clung to Emma's arm, convinced that if she did not keep a hold on her the maid might make a run for it. They moved jerkily towards the left-hand side of the courtyard. Her pretty, pale grey gown now had six inches of brown filth about its hem and the ooze of something quite dreadful seeped into her boots. Emma continued to weep loudly.

'Be quiet, Emma,' Tessa said through gritted teeth, 'or I swear I shall strike you. We shall just enquire here for Annie.' She indicated a doorway above which was a sign stating that 'Good Beds' were available, but Emma was beyond caring and continued to cry loudly. The children screamed in play and Tessa wondered how such under-nourished bodies could make such a noise as they threw whatever came to hand at one another. Slime ran down every wall, seeping into the unpaved ground, but a woman leaned casually by the doorway, inured, one supposed, to the horror by its familarity.

'I'm looking for Annie Beale,' Tessa said firmly, her manner letting the woman know that she would tolerate no impertinence.

'Who?' The woman smiled pleasantly, or so she thought, but the sight of the blackened stumps in her mouth made Emma recoil against her mistress's shoulder and reminded Tessa of that day on the moor, long ago now, when the tinkers had chased her.

'Annie Beale. This is Pike Street, isn't it?'

'Aye, it is.'

'Well, then, do you know her? She's about twenty-four

and has three sisters and a brother. She came here six months ago . . .'

'Oh, that one.'

'You know her then?'

''Oo doesn't, stuck-up cow.'

'Where is she then? Where does she live?'

The woman indicated with her head towards a doorway which stood below ground in the third house along the road. Down the flight of area steps which led to it trickled some thick brown liquid, gathering at the bottom and leaking under the fragile door and, Tessa assumed, into the cellar beyond.

She had turned away, her manner brisk and undaunted, wanting somehow to show this woman who eyed her with such amusement that despite her own upbringing she was quite able to cope with the difficulties the woman lived amongst every day.

'She'll not be in,' the woman said.

'Oh . . . ?'

'Well, she'll be at work, won't she, now she's better.'

'Better?'

'Aye, from't fever.'

'Fever?' Emma moaned and Tessa felt the dread move in her.

'What . . . fever?' There were so many. Cholera, dysentery, and dozens with no name but all rife in places such as this and carried indiscriminately to strike down where they were least expected, for they were no respecter of class or privilege.

'We gerrit regular round 'ere.' She smiled more broadly, revealing most of the obscene interior of her mouth. 'Sorts out weak 'uns, they say. Mind you, I've seen a strong, well-set up lad go whistlin' off to't mill in't morning' an ' be lyin' wi' 'is toes turned up by nightfall.'

'Who . . . did Annie . . . her family . . . ?' Her mouth was so dry she could barely speak but the woman continued to grin slyly.

'She'll be at Spicers in Earnshaw Street.'

'And ... the rest ... ?'

'Nay, they've gone.'

'Gone?'

'All on 'em in one day. Seen it 'appen a lot. 'Ole families kick t'bucket an' one left ter tell t'tale.'

Oh, dear God, sweet merciful God ... She felt the ground tilt and for one dreadful moment thought she was about to go down into that foul, slime-coated horror which lay about her, but somehow balancing against the half-fainting Emma she kept herself upright.

'Where ... where is ... Earnshaw Street, if you please?'

'Just up yonder.' The woman turned away, her interest in the visitors at an end.

They walked to Earnshaw Street for there were no cabs to be found in this pestilential jumble of rat-ridden cottages in which ten, fourteen, sixteen persons slept habitually in one room, this area of tottering tenements where the residents lived in rows side by side and on top of one another, where a hundred rooms housed more than a thousand destitute outcasts.

"Just up yonder' proved to be back over the bridge which spanned the Irwell, another rickety building with the name SPICERS PINS over the door, and needing no more than a stiff breeze to have it down, Tessa was convinced. The large room which led directly off the street was filled with small tables at each of which sat four children. None of them appeared to be more than six or seven years old, small, pallid, their eyes quite blank and incurious, and the sound of their wheezy breathing in the foetid air reminded Tessa of the sound of the engines at Victoria station, but that had been cheerful and energetic and this was not. There was a kind of frame fixed before each child on which was suspended what appeared to be a heavy weight. Under each table was a treadle and as the child pressed it with a bare and bony foot, the weight came thumping down with a deafening clatter. They were 'pin-heading', applying heads to the shanks of pins, the heads tightened by a blow from the weight hanging before them.

Annie was not among them.

Emma clung like a child herself to Tessa's hand. She had been brought up in the vicinity of mills and the men and women who worked in them. She was from such a family herself but what she had seen today had sent her senses reeling and she could do no more than follow where Miss Tessa led, praying to her Methodist God to deliver her soon from the horrors she was witnessing today. She winced, sidling even closer to her mistress as a man appeared from behind a machine.

''Ere, what d'yer think you're up to?' he demanded to know, not recognising in that first moment and the dim haze of the work room that Tessa and her maid were 'quality'. 'You've no right in 'ere an' I'll thank yer to be off,' he added roughly, his manner marking him as the owner of the factory and the children who worked there.

'I'm looking for a friend of mine.' Tessa's tone was peremptory. Her eyes were riveted to the sight of one small child, her back bowed in the form of a letter 'C', her head no more than six inches from the table, falling into what appeared to be a deep and comatose sleep. The man gave the child a casual but stinging blow about the ear and her head hit the table top but in an instant her tiny hands were reaching automatically for the pin shanks and her filthy feet for the treadle.

The man scratched his head and Tessa watched Emma do the same. She herself had never felt quite so filthy in all her life. Her skin itched and prickled and she longed to be at home in front of her own bedroom fire, a bath of hot water standing ready to receive her, to soak for an hour in its perfume, but would she feel clean even then?

'Surely there is no need to strike the child like that?' She spoke coldly, using the telling weapon of her class, the only one she had.

447

'There is if I'm ter keep 'em awake, lady. They're no use ter me asleep. Anyroad, what's it ter do wi' you?'

She sighed for there was nothing she could do, not for this child, but she could help Annie, if no one else in this sweat-shop.

'I believe you have a friend of mine working here,' she said haughtily.

'A friend of *yours* madam?' the man said incredulously. 'What, in 'ere?' He eyed her expensive gown and boots, her imperious bearing and the expression on her face which told him she would find her friend or know the reason why.

'Annie Beale. Is she here or not?'

'Annie Beale? A friend of yours?'

'Do you employ her or not?'

'Aye, she's in pin-sheetin' room.'

'Lead me to her.'

'Nay, missus, she's busy an' so am I.'

'Emma.' Emma cowered against her mistress, too appalled and terrified to do more than keep herself upright, just. 'Emma, go and fetch a Peace Officer. I'm perfectly sure these children are all under age, certainly underpaid and definitely undernourished. You will have heard of the Factory Act of 1833, I presume?' The man stood open-mouthed but managed to nod and indicate that he had. 'Then if I am not led to my friend at once I shall report you to the Factory Inspectorate. In fact, I shall probably do so anyway.'

She could hear her mother's voice in her head, saying the words she herself had just spoken about the Factory Act and the Inspectorate, and she marvelled that though her ears had not heard them years ago when they had been discussed, her brain had both noted and retained them.

Annie was the last in a row of girls and young women, all sitting at a long bench with their faces to a grimy, soot-stained window. There was a vice before each one and in the vice was a paper folded previously by the overlooker. The pins made in the outer room were placed carefully, a dozen at a time, in the holes which had been especially punched in the paper, and when the paper was full it was removed and the procedure repeated. The room was damp and packed from wall to wall with similar benches and females, and something else was there too which, though she had never been in such a place before, Tessa recognised as despair.

Annie seemed unable to grasp who Tessa was. When the man tapped her on the shoulder, his truculent face indicating that she was to stand up and shift herself, she did so slowly, her reflexes slack and unco-ordinated. The face she turned to Tessa was grey and narrow, her eyes deep in bony sockets above her cheekbones. Her threadbare skirt and bodice was sweat-stained and sour and her dirty feet were bare.

'Hello, Annie,' Tessa said softly and before the amazed stare of the factory owner and the dozens of women who were his slaves, she drew the drab and unknowing figure of Annie Beale into her own elegant and compassionate arms. She held her for a moment then began to guide her between the benches but strangely, it seemed, Annie did not want to go.

'We're going home, Annie. Home to your cottage in Edge-clough,' Tessa murmured, taking Annie's hand.

'What about them?' Annie's voice was harsh and filled with something Tessa could not identify.

'Who, Annie?'

'Them.' Annie's hand lifted, swinging in a tired arc to indicate all the hopeless faces who were staring dazedly at her and the fine lady who had come so incredibly amongst them.

'What . . . ? I don't understand.'

'Yer never did, lass.' Annie sat down again and drew a sheet of pins towards her.

'You mean you want to take . . . to take them as well?'

The man at her back began to laugh. He had never enjoyed anything so much for years. The idea of this fine madam trailing up Earnshaw Street with this bloody lot at her heels was the funniest thing he'd ever heard. Just wait until he told his missus in that fine villa in Cheetham Hill which 'this lot' had earned for him and his family.

'They're in as bad a state as me, Tessa Harrison.'

'Dear God, Annie, I might have known you'd be just the same. Even with all that's happened to ...'

'I'll not come wi'out 'em.'

'Very well.' The factory owner smirked for he'd have summat to say to Annie Beale when her 'friend' had gone, but his smirk changed to amazement when Tessa turned to the young women at her back and addressed them just as though they were human beings and not the dregs of the streets which he knew them to be.

'I am Mrs Tessa Greenwood,' she said vigorously, 'the owner of the Chapman Manufacturing Company Ltd in Crossfold. Have any of you heard of Crossfold? It is near Oldham.' One or two nodded their heads hesitantly. 'I will give work, decent work, to any of you who can make your way there. Do you understand?' Again a couple nodded their heads and it was to these that she addressed herself. 'I have several mills, spinning mills and weaving and the work is easily learned. Annie here will help you ...' It was then that Annie's new position in life became clear to her and she reached out and clasped her friend's hand.

Really, Mr Briggs remarked fretfully that evening to Mrs Shepherd in the privacy of the housekeeper's small but cosy sitting-room, one wondered what the world was coming to when the gentry – if you could call them that, which he doubted sometimes – brought what one could only term a 'common' person into the house and the mistress of it treated her as though she was her dearest friend: ordering the bath to be placed in front of her own bedroom fire, totally ignoring Miss Laurel's cries of alarm, and the maids running up and down the stairs with jugs of hot water and warm towels, with milk and eggs and soup. And to cap it all sending off a carriage-load of servants, who were, after all, in *his* charge, to some dreadful little cottage in Edgeclough to prepare it for her friend's immediate return, she said. Light the fire, she told them, Mrs Shepherd, and scrub the place from top to bottom. There's some unused furniture up in the attic, Briggs, she said, beds and chairs and things. You will know what is needed, just as though I had the arranging of such like. I want the place to be warm and as clean as a new pin. Mind, when she said 'new pin', Mrs Shepherd, she shuddered quite visibly, though I can't think why. And then off they go, the pair of them, three hours later, in madam's carriage and the whole house in an uproar, and the stables with horses got out, and carriages in and out of the stable yard, and on top of it all Emma having a fit of hysteria, screaming about lice, if you please, tearing at her hair as though she was demented. And as for Miss Laurel, *she* was in a faint after shrieking for the whole valley to hear that if any disease had been brought into the house to harm her children she would never speak to Miss Tessa again. And *he* agreed with her, the master, I mean, though knowing the kind of acquaintance he favours in those low gin shops I hear tell he frequents, I can't imagine why.

'I'll stay with you, Annie,' Tessa said when Annie was settled at her own hearth. 'I'll sleep in the chair by the fire.'

'You'll not.' Annie's face was calm now and her eyes were lucid. She sat in a wing chair, old and somewhat faded, brought over hastily by carriage with several other pieces by the maids, her head resting against its padded back. She was clean, her skin stretched tightly over her delicate bones, pale and thin, but clean, and her own pleasure at the comfort of it showed in the way her eyes lingered on every shadowed corner of the room, on the warm flames licking against her old kettle; in the way she smoothed her hands down the faded but spotless skirt and bodice rummaged from somewhere in Tessa's wardrobe, far too big, but *clean*.

'I'm not taking orders tonight, Annie, you are, and besides, the carriage has gone.'

'I'm all right now, so you can get off home.'

451

'You don't change, do you, Annie?'

'Not where it shows, lass, and I'm not ready to talk ... about ... about them, not yet. 'Appen in a day or two...'

'Annie, oh, dearest Annie...'

'Give over, Tessa.'

'Why didn't you let me know? You know I would have come at once. You make me feel ashamed...'

'Nay, you've nowt ter be ashamed of. Yer've bin a good friend ter me.' It was the nearest Annie could get to a declaration of affection. 'Yer've 'ad enough on thy plate, so I 'eard, ter be botherin' about me an' mine.'

'But it's all done now, Annie. Everything's running beautifully. I've ... we ... we had help...' She looked down at her hands which gripped one another tightly. Her face was soft and smiling and her skin flushed to a lovely rosy hue. 'The mills are a limited company now and there is a board of directors. Will Broadbent ... you remember Will?' She looked up at Annie and her eyes told their own story and Annie knew, of course. But this was not the time to ask questions, even if she had cared to.

'That's why I came to fetch you, Annie,' Tessa went on, not aware that her love for Will Broadbent shone in her flushed face. 'The mill is to be opened next week and your job is waiting for you if you want it. But that's not what I wanted to talk to you about.'

'Yer know I'll do what I've always done an' that's work at mill an' earn me own livin'.'

'But what about those girls from Spicers, and all the other young women who need someone to help them?'

'You'll help them.'

'No, you will.'

'Me? What can I do?'

'You'll think of something, Annie. We could ... open a small factory ... do pin-heading, but in decent conditions...'

'But I'm a spinner...'

'Does that mean you can do nothing else? Would you not

452

like to give a hand to girls who have no one else to help them?'

'Aye.' Annie's face had become quite pink and her eyes glowed.

'But you're to have a rest first, Annie.' Despite Annie's sudden interest it was apparent she was very tired. Beneath the false glow there was a waxy look of strain about her mouth and sad eyes.

'Aye, a day or two, 'appen, then . . .'

'Annie, will you stop being so stubborn? You're in no fit state to . . .'

'I'll decide what sorta state I'm in, if yer don't mind and . . .'

The soft knock on the cottage door made them both jump but even as she moved to open it the image of Will Broadbent slipped into Tessa's mind and her heart began to beat joyfully.

His enormous frame filled the doorway. He was dressed in a rough jacket and cord trousers, the legs pushed into the tops of his knee-length boots. His shirt was opened at the neck and his hair was dishevelled as though he had ridden at speed. He looked exactly as he had done on the day she first met him: a working man with a brown face and hands, a bit rough and ready with none of the smoothness he acquired when he put on his business suit, but clean, dependable, steady, with a curl to his mouth which said he was ready to laugh easily and a soft glow in his eyes when he saw her at the door.

She loved him. Dear God, how she loved him.

'I thought you would be here,' he said, ready, she knew, to take her in his arms, indeed they lifted involuntarily and she almost stepped into them.

'Come in, Will.' The voice from the kitchen was weary and instantly they moved away from the embrace they both longed for. 'Come in, Will, an' tell me 'ow the dickens yer knew I were back. News don't 'alf travel fast 'ereabouts. I'll be 'avin' the Mayor of Oldham knockin' on't door next.'

He knelt at Annie's feet and though she turned red with embarrassment and was stiff and awkward, he drew her slight figure into his arms and hugged her. The gesture was spontaneous, warm with affection, and Annie allowed it. She even smiled and when Will stood up and turned to Tessa her eyes were deep and knowing as he took Tessa's hands in his.

'I might have known this was your doing, Tessa Harrison,' and I love you even more for it, his eyes told her, 'but I'm only sorry I didn't do it myself. I thought she was . . . comfortable . . . with a decent place . . .'

'Don't talk about me as if I wasn't ere, Will.'

'I'm sorry, lass,' he tore his reluctant gaze away from Tessa, 'but I feel that ashamed . . .'

'That's what Tessa said but it were no one's fault. If we'd . . . if the fever, well, wi' first one then t'other goin' down . . . cholera, it was said . . . I couldn't work. Nay, I'm not goin' ter weep again. See, Tessa, give Will a cuppa tea, I'm off ter me bed. 'Appen Will'll see yer back 'ome, lass.' She stood up slowly, her gaunt frame showing the effort required to control her straining emotions.

'I said I'd stay . . .'

'An' I said I want to be on me own, Tessa.' Her voice was sharp and painful, then it softened. 'Just fer a day or two . . .' She could not put into words her need for peace and privacy in which to do her grieving and she begged Tessa to understand. 'I'll be right as rain, lass. I just want ter . . . 'ave a bit o' rest. Come over in a day or two, if yer've a minute ter spare. Now don't come out 'o yer road, only if yer over this way . . .'

'Oh, stop it, Annie. One more word and I'll not come again, ever.'

'I reckon I'd manage on me own if yer didn't.' But Annie was smiling as she made her slow and weary way up the stairs which Tessa's maids had scrubbed, to the warm, herb-scented bed they had made up for her.

'Shall I come up with you, Annie?'

'Nay, my lass. I've bin puttin' meself ter bed since I were a bairn.'

'How did you know she was home?' she asked when Annie had closed the door quietly on her spartan bedroom.

'Oh, it's not easy to move about this valley undetected, my darling. In no time at all the news that Annie Beale was being treated as a valued guest at the home of Mrs Drew Greenwood reached the ears of my head clerk who informs me of anything he thinks might be of interest to me. And knowing Annie as I do, I was pretty certain she wouldn't be happy until she was in her own place, by her own fireside. I came over at once.'

They both smiled at Annie's stubborn pride. Tessa was still dressed in the soiled organdie gown she had put on that morning – was it only such a few short hours ago? – but she had left her bonnet, her parasol and gloves on the bedroom chair where she had tossed them as she had helped Annie inside. Her hair hung about her face and shoulders in damp drifts and there was a streak of dirt across her forehead where she had pushed a frantic hand through it.

'You've had a hard day, Tessa.' The very words she had longed to hear, and who but Will would know her needs, how utterly exhausted she was? How lovely it would be to sink into the chair Annie had just vacated, to kick off her filthy boots and put her feet on the fender, to have a cup of tea put in her hand and pour into some sympathetic ear the dreadfulness of what she had seen that day.

'Sit down, my darling.' When she did his hands were at her bootlaces removing her filthy boots. Then they caressed the arch of her foot, her ankles, smoothing the skin and taking from her weary bones the memory of the recent horrors. The tea was forgotten as he lifted her up and drew her into his arms. Their mouths met for a brief moment and

455

she sighed for Will knew just what was in her heart and troubled mind, as he had always done.

The woman who lay sleepless in her bed above them listened sadly to the silence.

## 29

The formal betrothal between Johnny Taylor and Alicia Henderson was announced at the ball his father gave at the beginning of August, and his weekend guests, amongst them Mr and Mrs Drew Greenwood, were fulsome in their congratulations.

Hadden Hall was a fine old country seat in the parish of Middleton, Sir Anthony Taylor, Johnny's father, being a great landowner in those parts. Like Squire Longworth he had sold a tiny corner of his land to the railways so that the Manchester to Rochdale line might proceed unhindered through Lancashire and had made himself enormously wealthy in doing so.

By chance, as the navvies prepared the track, which was several miles from the Hall, coal was discovered on his land. Fortunately the colliery winding-gear built to get his coal out of his land would not be seen from the windows of his home, so he allowed the necessary work to go ahead, and his income tripled.

Drew and Tessa rode over in their splendid carriage, another following behind packed with their boxes, and with Emma and Hibberson, the footman who was to 'do' for Drew. Behind the second carriage rode Walter on Drew's bay and leading Tessa's mare, for there was bound to be some sort of sport on horseback and though Sir Anthony had a fine stable Drew had declared he would prefer to ride his own animal.

It was a glorious day, the sky across the moors a vast and endless bowl of blue. The summer had been fine with warm, sunny days and a good deal of rain at night and the moorland was a wonderful sight, swathed in the deepest purple heather, the verdant green of the springy turf and the yellow of gorse. The banks of the lanes as they drove through villages and hamlets were covered with harebells, toadflax and hackweed, the occasional field hedge laced with long streamers of honeysuckle and sweet-scented bedstraw.

Drew dragged the clear air deep into his lungs, looking around him contentedly. He put his arm about Tessa's shoulders, indifferent to the eyes of the servants, and drew her more closely to him, smiling down into her face.

'This is better than that damned factory, don't you think, my pet? Just smell the air.' He took another deep breath and obediently she did the same.

'It's lovely, Drew,' she agreed.

'And you look quite glorious, my darling. I shall have to keep a watchful eye on those fellows at Hadden: not one of them would hesitate to steal you from me if they could.'

'Fiddlesticks, Drew, and you shouldn't joke about such a thing. Besides, I might not want to be "stolen", have you thought of that?'

He grinned and bent his head to drop a light kiss on her upturned mouth. He was at peace with himself this morning, and with her. He had made love to her last night, finding nothing lacking in her submissive acceptance, pouring his terrible nightmares from his body into hers, releasing the tension which came to grip him, and sleeping like a child in her arms for the rest of the night. He did not know what his nightmares were any more for it was five years since Pearce had died and six since the horror of the battles he and his brother had fought side by side. In a way his terror had something to do with Tessa which was strange for she was the hand which led him from the shaking quagmire that

457

threatened him. But during the last twelve months she had shown a strange and quite unbelievable attention to the mill, and in that time he had felt his fears begin to grow again. Fears of what? he asked himself in his more lucid moments, and he could not answer. But she was here with him now. The new mill was running smoothly, he had been informed, the directors had it all in hand and he and his wife were to take up their pleasant life again from now on.

'This will be a splendid weekend, sweetheart,' his voice was soft in her ear, 'and there are such good things ahead. D'you know, I think this is my favourite time of the year. The grouse next week and then at the beginning of September the partridge, with hunting to follow. Did I tell you we are invited to Scotland again?'

They were all there to meet them on the imposing steps which led up to the wide front door of Hadden Hall: Johnny Taylor, Nicky Longworth, all Drew's insolently aristocratic friends who welcomed them enthusiastically, young lords at play, not one of them under the age of twenty-five, Tessa thought, and all acting as though they had just been released from the school-room.

'They are high-spirited, Mrs Greenwood.' Sir Anthony took her arm benevolently but his eyes ran appreciatively over the soft swell of her breast inside its cream silk, finely-tucked bodice, her splendid shoulders and slender neck, the bright flame of her lips and the extraordinary colour of her long-lashed eyes. She felt his speculative gaze and knew clearly and suddenly, however he might deny it, that she and Drew would never be completely part of this wild-riding, hell-raking, self-assured and overbearing class of society. Though he might welcome her warmly, Sir Anthony Taylor considered it not at all discourteous to let his glance roam quite openly over her body, to let her see that he thought her charms were there for anyone to admire just as though she was no more than a maidservant in his fine old home. All these years she and Drew had imagined that they were the same as these people, part of their society and accepted by them, whilst in reality they were no more than an amusing diversion. They were welcome wherever they went: both were well-mannered, attractive and charming, with money which Drew lost regularly at cards, and were prepared to join in any mad escapade, showing that wild courage which the privileged class admired, but they were not *of* them.

What had opened her eyes to it, she wondered, as she moved about the elegant bedroom she was to share with Drew, directing Emma in the preparation of the gown she would wear for dinner, the choice of her jewellery, the consideration of how her hair should be dressed. Perhaps she had always known but had chosen to ignore it for what else could she and Drew do with the rest of their lives? They had been brought up as neither fish nor fowl belonging in neither the industrial, commercial world of her mother, her aunt and uncles, nor the autocratic and often noble class to which her cousins had aspired.

But these last twelve months, amazingly, had been the most gratifying of her life, she realised with a shock. Once she had accepted her position in the Greenwood world of business; once she had been shown how to manage that position, to fit herself into it, she had found the challenge quite exhilarating. She had never been made to buckle down to anything or face up to what she really was until Charlie's death and Drew's weakness had compelled her to it.

And she was doing it! What was more, she was doing it well! Now that Annie had returned to the mill and was implementing the scheme Tessa had devised for her and was helping the general day-to-day running of the mill's operatives; now that she had Will to give her his strong hand over the sticky patches and the shelter of his love to protect her, she had the fancy she could make as good a 'millmaster' as other women in her family had done before her.

She moved to the window and stared out across the stunningly beautiful grounds of Hadden Hall. Weekend guests were moving about the stretch of lawn which led down from the terrace to a tree-shaded stream several hundred yards away from the house. The ladies were mostly in white with flower-trimmed parasols and hats, seated beneath wide-spreading chestnut trees, taking tea at tables set with lace cloths and served by housemaids with expressionless faces. Chairs were scattered about for anyone who cared just to sit and watch, and on a flat stretch of lawn cricket stumps were being set up and several young gentlemen, one of whom was Drew, were skylarking. He was brandishing a cricket bat imploring Nicky not to be such a fool and to throw the ball but Nicky and Johnny were ignoring him, launching the ball over his head, backwards and forwards.

'Come on, chaps,' she heard him shout, his voice carrying through the open window, and when they took no notice she had the sudden dreadful feeling that he was about to fling the cricket bat down and stamp off like some small boy in a tantrum. Even from where she was standing she could see the clenching of his jaw and the astonishing flush of hot temper in his smooth brown cheek; then Nicky carelessly threw the ball in his direction, quite unaware of his alarming but fleeting danger, and the moment passed. Drew hit the ball, sending it into the far distance of the trees, his body beautiful in its grace, his beauty stunning in its masculinity. The ladies clapped in admiration and Tessa could hear the murmur of well-bred voices and well-bred laughter.

The meal that night was lengthy and intricate with a great many toasts, not as yet to the wide-eyed bride-to-be and her groom for the official announcement was not to be made until the following night, but to anything these recklessly drinking, carelessly laughing ruling classes could think of and which gave Sir Anthony an excuse to order another bottle from his well-stocked cellar.

Tessa was placed on Sir Anthony's right hand where he commandeered her attention for the whole of the meal. He was said to have been something of a ladies' man in his day and though well past the age for such things, she would have thought, considered himself still to be one! He admired her dark hair which Emma had brushed until it gleamed, placing a white silk tea-rose in the heavy coil at the nape of her neck. He admired her shimmering white gown consisting of nothing but lace and seed pearls, newly designed and made for her by the young assistant to Miss Maymon, just come from Paris and, it was rumoured, so clever she was desirous of setting up in business for herself in the growing and increasingly cosmopolitan town of Crossfold. The dress clung to her, emphasising the loveliness of her high breasts, her small waist and the suppleness of her long-limbed body. The whiteness of her skin was enchanting, he told her, and the velvet-grey of her eyes unbelievable, and all the while his eyes probed the low neckline of her gown.

Once she would have thought this amusing, quite harmless, of course, and therefore not to be discouraged. She would have flirted and laughed, making every gentleman at the table long to be seated with the delicious and witty Mrs Drew Greenwood. She and Drew would have exchanged secret smiles and been highly diverted, falling into one another's arms at the end of the evening in heedless and giddy merriment which would have turned to love-making. They might drink too much of Sir Anthony's fine French champagne, dance every dance, with one another or with any of the dozens of like-minded guests, diverted by anything which kept them from the sin of boredom.

'You are a very pretty woman, Mrs Greenwood,' Johnny Taylor's elderly father told her. His eyes, still on her breasts, informed her that given the chance he had every intention of furthering their friendship and that she, as an industrialist's daughter, should consider herself honoured to receive his attentions.

'Thank you, you are most kind,' she murmured, removing her hand from where his fondled it.

'That husband of yours is a lucky young cub and I shall tell him so.'

What was there to say? 'Thank you again.' She smiled politely, realising that Drew was watching her from some way down the table, the expression on his face quite unread-

461

able. My God, was he angry with her for rebuffing what he considered Sir Anthony's innocent advances, or because he thought she was inviting them? She was never sure these days. His eyes were cool, disinterested almost with that disdainful narrowing which he had learned from the gentlemen with whom he socialised. Then the lady beside him spoke and instantly, courteously, he turned to her and she heard his laugh ring out.

She danced with them all, doing her best to be the Tessa Greenwood they expected. She laughed and flirted, throwing back her head until her lovely hair rippled down her back and they told her it was like old times and, really, they would be very cross if she didn't accompany them on the first grouse shoot the very next week; to Squire Longworth's hunting box in Leicestershire when the season started; to Sir Anthony's castle in Scotland, his villa in Monte Carlo and indeed to every important event in their pleasure-seeking calendar.

It was the same the next day as they boated on Sir Anthony's splendid lake, picnicked under the trees of his lovely woodland, dined in his superbly panelled dining-room and danced the night away in his magnificently appointed ballroom. The announcement was made of the forthcoming marriage of his son to Miss Alicia Henderson and the champagne flowed until not one gentleman was completely sober, nor all the ladies either. Miss Henderson, being only sixteen and just out of the schoolroom was returned, Johnny's duty done, to her mama and the horse-play which the young gentlemen thought appropriate on such an occasion began in earnest.

'Come on, darling. We're going into the billiard room. Nicky has wagered that he and I can drink more champagne in sixty seconds than Johnny and Freddy and we want you to be referee.'

He took her hand, his face flushed, his eyes a quite startling blue. His dark curls tumbled over his forehead and he was excited, feverishly so, enchanted with her beauty and with the envious admiration of the men who had clustered about her all evening. She wore poppy-red in sharp contrast to the pure white of the previous evening, a long, fluted sheath which was stark and simple but extremely daring. Her breasts were almost exposed and suddenly, just as he pulled her to him to let the other fellows see that it all belonged to him, she hated herself, and she hated him.

'No, I don't think so, Drew. I'm going to bed.'

His expression was foolish and behind him his friends became quiet, sensing at that moment something different about Tessa Greenwood which promised to be entertaining.

'Don't be silly, Tessa. Come on, we need your expert champagne-drinking advice. Now then, chaps, I have just had a simply splendid idea.' He turned wildly to the 'chaps' who crowded closer. 'Why don't we drink out of Tessa's slipper?' He bent down, falling on to one knee and lifted the hem of his wife's dress revealing her poppy-red satin slippers, her neatly turned ankles in their sheer white stockings and upwards to her knees and thighs. They all stared, absolutely silent now, for even they knew that this time Drew Greenwood had gone too far.

'I don't think so, Drew. Now, if you gentlemen will excuse me, I shall retire.' Tessa's voice was low, cool and contemptuous.

Leaving her husband lurching drunkenly on the floor at the feet of his friends she moved gracefully towards the stairs and went up them.

He did not come to bed that night though she lay awake listening for his stumbling footsteps. She heard laughter below her window and later the sound of wildly pounding horses' hooves on Sir Anthony's smooth lawn. There were cries from the lake around dawn and women's laughter and a male voice begged someone to 'be a good fellow and help him out of the water'.

She lay in the darkness with her eyes burning in her aching head and her body tossing restlessly, longing for Will and the sane and comforting shelter of his love which would never be wholly hers.

The Drew Greenwoods left at noon the next day. He was haggard and hollow-eyed, she serene and gracious, apologising for their early departure which was unprecedented since Mr and Mrs Drew Greenwood were well known for their staying power and strong constitutions. She spoke vaguely of a family matter and her husband said nothing at all beyond the necessary courtesies. Drew's hunter was inexplicably missing and so was one of Sir Anthony Taylor's fine bays which his own niece, a Miss Victoria Bleasdale of the Northumberland Bleasdales, had ridden only the day before. Miss Bleasdale was still in her room when the Drew Greenwoods made their polite farewell.

'Now, don't you worry about that hunter of yours, Drew, my boy,' their host told him genially, taking his arm across the gravel to his carriage since his guest seemed somewhat frail. 'It will turn up in some farmer's yard and my groom will return it to your ... where is it you live? ... oh, yes ... er ... Crossfold, as soon as it does.' He smiled at Tessa, his manner implying that he fully understood the extravagance of youth, indeed had he not himself once been as rashly imprudent? No mention was made of his own missing bay, nor of his missing niece. He leaned onto the carriage for a last look at Tessa's charming bosom, then stepped back to wave a gracious hand, remarking in an aside to his son that he need not invite that drunken upstart again which was a pity, really, for his wife was most delectable.

Drew waited until they were in their bedroom before he spoke, ordering the maid from the room when she began to open her mistress's boxes.

Tessa sank down on the windowseat and stared blindly into the sun-filled garden. Her mind was cold and empty. She wished someone would tell her what to do, how to deal with the coming crisis, how to calm him, soothe him, convince him that it was all right and that she was not angry with him, that she really did not care that he had probably been unfaithful to her. She would have to care, at least about him, soon. If only he would leave her alone for a while, allow her to steady herself, to gather the resources necessary to paint a tolerant smile on her face, return the fondness, the compassionate fondness in which she held him, to her eyes, the accustomed tone which was needed in her voice. She loved him, and she always would. Still inside him was that core of sweetness he and his brother had shared. Pearce had died with his still intact but in Drew the sweetness was beginning to sour and she no longer knew how to stop it. Well, she did really, of course she did. Had she not been aware for the past twelve months of what was turning her merry, good-natured young husband, her dear cousin, into an unreasonable ... no, that was not the word ... *spiteful* and bitter man? He was afraid, of course, and he really did not know why. He only knew he felt better when she was with him, not just her physical presence but her involvement in all the giddy escapades, the foolish pranks, the recklessly defiant madness he and his well-bred friends got up to.

And last night she had refused so he had insulted her before them all. He had earned himself their frightening disapproval for though he had shown himself to be no gentleman they were.

'Now then, madam, I would like an explanation of your atrocious behaviour this weekend ...'

'Drew, not now, darling.'

'... when we were guests, weekend guests that is, for the first time in the home of one of my dearest friends. You chose to be bloody awkward right from the start, giving Sir Anthony that glacial stare of yours from the moment he took your arm. Oh, yes, I noticed, and so did the others ...'

'Really, Drew, you know that is not true.'

He had begun to stride about the room, unable to contain whatever it was that drove him, his movements rapid and awkward, his arms lifting convulsively with every turn. His intention was clear. He wanted to wound her; to hurt her as he had been hurt for he had made up his mind that the failure of the weekend was her fault, that, and the damned mill!

'Is it not, Tessa? It was not I who insulted Johnny's father when all he wished to do was make himself pleasant. He is an old gentleman who admires a pretty woman. There is nothing wrong in that surely? All it needed to make him happy was...'

'For me to fawn about him and make a fool of myself.'

'Fawn about him?' He stopped his striding to stare at her incredulously. 'Is that how you see it? Is that what you call good manners and breeding of which, I must admit, you were sadly lacking this weekend?'

'Oh, stop it, Drew. You really are making a mountain out of a molehill. Sir Anthony certainly is an old gentleman and should be past such foolishness.' Though she could feel the anger, the indignant outrage growing within her, she attempted lightness, even a smile, since she did not care for the glittering brightness of his eyes nor the hectic flush of his face and neck. 'Come and sit beside me and we will order some lunch. We could go for a ride later, up to Badger's Edge and then, perhaps, an early night.' Her smile was inviting but she was prepared to do anything to calm the conflict which was in him.

'Don't try those whore's tricks with me, you slut,' he hissed.

'Drew, really...' Her eyes had narrowed and her chin rose menacingly. 'First I am frigid and unfeeling in my treatment of that old lecher at Hadden and now I am a slut who practises...'

'You do yourself no good when you insult my friends, Tessa. They have been splendid in their support of me since Pearce ... since...'

'And I have not, is that what you are saying?'

'... and I think it was not asking too much of you at least to be polite to them, particularly Sir Anthony who is no longer young. They are ... or were, though I doubt it now, extremely fond of you but after your refusal to join in the harmless fun they had planned...'

'Don't be ridiculous, Drew. Perhaps it is harmless but do

466

you not find it to be somewhat childish for grown men? All
those "pranks" you get up to . . . ?'

'Which once, madam, you found enjoyable yourself.'

'Indeed , I suppose I must have done, but by God, I am
twenty-three and you are twenty-four years old, Drew, and
surely there is more to life than . . .'

'Oh, of course, one could spend one's day in the company
of those . . . those *oafs* at the mill, I suppose, which you
seem to find infinitely more entertaining than that of
gentlemen.'

'It is gentlemanly, is it, to lift the skirts of one's wife and
reveal her legs for a crowd of drunken, gaping simpletons
to leer . . .'

'You go too far, Tessa.' He took a frenzied step towards
her but her own wild and heedless temper, for so long held
back, had risen to the surface.

'No, *you* do, Drew. I have done nothing of which I am
ashamed. Can you say the same?'

'I hope I am a gentleman since I move in their . . .'

'Don't be so bloody pompous, and besides, I was not
talking of your behaviour before I went to bed, but after.'

'We did no more than we have done a hundred times
when you were with us. We gambled on . . .'

'. . . who would bed the delectable Miss Bleasdale, no
doubt, and guess who it was who won? Did you drink out
of her slipper, you and your playful friends, or perhaps she
still wore them, if nothing else, when you all took a dawn
dip in Sir Anthony's lake?'

'You bitch . . .'

'I see, I am a bitch now, but what does that make you, my
fine honourable gentleman? What is the male equivalent of
a bitch? Well, whatever it is you are welcome to become
one because I'm tired of being your toy, your plaything,
your playmate. I have dragged about this damned country
with you in pursuit of . . . of *fun* . . . is that what you called
it? Harmless fun. Well, I'm . . .'

'Be very careful, Tessa, please . . .'

467

She was too incensed to hear the sudden pleading in his voice as though he was, for perhaps only a moment, aware of how close he was to the madness which was taking him over.

'No, Drew, *you* be careful just for once. Take a good look at yourself and those overbred friends of yours, if you can call them 'friends'. Believe me, should the fancy take them, they would drop you and me like live coals and treat us as the upstarts we are. Vulgar social climbers, that is how they really see us. Common people whose money is new and very ill-bred. We have amused them, Drew, you and I and Pearce...'

'Don't ... not Pearce ... don't you dare to...'

'Dare what? To tell you the truth? I'm only sorry I didn't realise it earlier myself. All these years of playing the fool, wasting our lives on idiots like Nicky Longworth...'

'He is my friend.'

'No, he is not...'

'Then who...'

'I am, Drew, and Pearce was but...'

His face altered subtly before her eyes, changing shape and colour. It seemed to slip and the blood drained rapidly away from it, leaving only the brilliant and raging blue of his eyes.

'Leave Pearce out of this ... bitch ... bitch...'

He raised his arm and she threw back her head challenging, daring him to strike her, not believing he would. Her snarling anger, so long leashed, curled her lip dangerously. When he hit her the blow stunned her, snapping her head to one side, lifting and swirling her loosened hair and knocking her to her knees. She was dazed, blinded as blood flowed from a cut where his ring had caught her flesh. She did not see him raise his arm again and the second blow struck her to the floor.

When she came to he had gone.

# 30

Drew Greenwood did not attend the next day's meeting of the board of directors though his wife was there in her capacity as chairman. Strangely, she wore a close-fitting bonnet with a face veil, unlikely apparel for her elegance was now a byword in the Penfold Valley and the dark bonnet was not as fashionable as it might have been.

The meeting was held in the quite splendid board room of the new Chapman mill. A great deal of worthwhile discussion occurred amongst the directors on the excellent start the new mill had made in its first year of trading. The interest and the dozens of enquiries they had received from men in the cotton industry had been extremely gratifying. They had a full work complement with every position filled, from managers right down to piecers and scavengers. The bales of raw cotton which had been stored in rented warehouses in readiness for the new mill had been opened, blended, carded, drawn out and spun and many thousands of yards of fine cloth had been woven. Providing there was no reduction in the supply of raw cotton which came, as they all knew, from the southern states of America, they would be able to promise a fine profit by the end of the financial year. If Mrs Greenwood would care to look over the figures for July she would be able to see at a glance that what Mr Bradley had forecast at the first board meeting a year ago was already taking place.

Tessa stared through her veil at the neat rows of figures put before her. Mr Bradley's words about the supply of raw cotton and its connection with America rang in her head and more to divert these astute businessmen from her own odd appearance than from any particular desire to know, she asked:

'Should we be worried then about the flow of cotton from America, in view of the possible war there?'

Will Broadbent leaned back in his chair and watched her admiringly. She had got over that first hurdle. Her own shrewdness had connected Mr Bradley's remark with some small doubt on the matter of cotton supply, and these men about the table were pleasantly surprised by Mrs Greenwood's grasp of the situation.

'Well, it's early days yet, Mrs Greenwood, but as you will have read in the newspapers there is some ... shall we call it ... disagreement between the northern and southern states of America. Now there appear to be many reasons why they are at odds with one another, difficult for those not involved to understand, but it seems to be more and more obvious that the cotton-growing states are certainly going to be affected. To what extent is yet to be seen. Already there has been some slowing down of supplies and we have men, agents, looking in the East and West Indies, in Egypt and India for alternative supplies, just in case, you understand.'

'Do you mean to tell me that we have committed ourselves to this new mill and the hundreds of people who work in it and now there could be difficulties in obtaining the raw cotton which keeps us trading?'

Tessa's voice was bewildered but beneath it was a splinter of steel and Will felt his heart move with pride in her. She was no longer the uncaring, furiously riding, defiantly challenging girl with whom he had fallen in love seven years ago. She was no longer the restless, frighteningly high-spirited young woman looking for adventure anywhere it could be found, who had casually thrown his love aside for something her vigorous nature had told her was more exciting, more to the taste of Miss Tessa Harrison. Nor was she the high-flying, imprudently pleasure-seeking woman who had married Drew Greenwood when all else had failed her. Slowly, in the two years since the death of her uncle, she had lifted her head and looked about her; looked beyond her own thrill-seeking world which made fun of those who were sober and hard-working, and had been changed irrevocably by what she had seen. She had not liked what she had been forced to do, forced by some element in her nature inherited, no doubt, from her own positive mother, but by God she was doing it. And she had something else in her, though perhaps she was not fully aware of it yet: it was that she *cared*. She had carried her unstable husband around for years, guided him, distracted him from his obvious frailties, not shrinking from the responsibility he laid on her. She had defended him, become everything he needed to sustain his tenuous hold on reason. Enough for any woman, most would have thought, since he was scarcely fit to be let out alone, but now she had to take on another burden and judging by her steely manner was not to shirk its difficulties.

Mr Bradley put out a placatory hand, then withdrew it hastily since it did not do to pat the arm of the woman who was, after all, his employer.

'Mrs Greenwood, a civil war in America is foreseen by no one, at least not in this country, and even if it were, would you have told us not to re-build the mill?'

Will sat up, straightening out his long, indolent body, waiting for her answer, ready to support her should she need it.

'I really cannot answer that, Mr Bradley, but I certainly would have considered deeply the effect it might have on my operatives.'

*Her* operatives! Will almost smiled.

'As we have, Mrs Greenwood,' Mr Entwhistle, who brewed the finest ale in Lancashire, or so his signs said, put in, 'and I can assure you that in our opinion there is no cause for alarm.'

'You know about such things then, Mr Entwhistle?' she asked sharply. 'I believe you are a brewer.'

'That is so, Mrs Greenwood, but I am also a man who knows business and the world markets and therefore I am certainly in a position to know when I am, or when I am *not* to make a profit.'

'Of course you are, Mr Entwhistle, and I hope you will forgive my ignorance. I apologise if I appeared to be questioning your ability.'

By God, she knows how to handle them, Will exulted. First she puts their backs up with questions they are convinced she would not even understand, let alone ask, then, just as they realise the sharpness of her and are about to bristle, she smoothes them down with a soft word and a smile.

'Nevertheless, I think we should consider that we may have to go on short time, Mrs Greenwood.'

Mrs Greenwood turned politely to Mr Broadbent who had spoken. Her cool, silvery-grey eyes met his through her veil with nothing in them, should they have been seen plainly, but the concerned interest one business associate gives another, nothing in them or her manner – nor his – to reveal that the last time they had been together he had made love to her naked body on his greatcoat in an abandoned hut high on Saddleworth Moor.

'At my own mill,' he continued smoothly, 'which, of course, is smaller than Chapman's and without its resources, we are already running for only four days a week. Temporarily, I hope, but rather than turn anyone off I recommended this policy. Perhaps we may discuss doing the same here, should it be necessary.'

'Indeed, Mr Broadbent, but for the moment we must endeavour to find our cotton wherever we can and perhaps by the next meeting Mr Bradley will be able to report any new market where it can be obtained. And let us hope this war in America will come to nothing though the headlines are that the Union is to be dissolved.'

'I read that report too, Mrs Greenwood.' They smiled

472

politely at one another before turning back to other matters for discussion and for two hours Tessa Greenwood said little as she listened intently to what each member of the board had to report.

Coffee was served at eleven but Mrs Greenwood declined to drink a cup. When they stood up at the end of the meeting she reached for the bank manager's report on the financial trading of the company.

'I will take this with me if I may, Mr Bradley, to study more thoroughly.'

'Of course, Mrs Greenwood. Perhaps your ... husband might care to peruse it. I am only sorry that he was not able to attend.'

'It is the twelfth of August, Mr Bradley.'

'Has that some significance?'

'Come, Mr Bradley. Grouse shooting starts today and it being such a short season my husband was eager to take advantage of it. Now, if you will excuse me, gentlemen, I have one or two things to attend to in my office.'

Will bowed with the rest of them, then, as she was about to leave the room and move along the richly carpeted hallway to her own suite of offices, his voice cut across the polite farewells.

'If I may beg a moment of your time, Mrs Greenwood?'

She turned her head a fraction, speaking over her shoulder.

'I'm afraid I cannot spare even that, Mr Broadbent. I have an employee coming to see me in five minutes regarding a matter which I intend to bring up at the next board meeting. Perhaps in a day or so, if you would care to make an appointment.'

'It really will take no more than thirty seconds, Mrs Greenwood.'

'Mr Broadbent, I ...'

Will smiled urbanely and the gentlemen who still stood in groups about the table, looked round, surprised by the sudden tension in the room.

'I would be immensely obliged, ma'am.'

'Very well, but no more than ...'

'Oh, indeed.'

The moment they were in her office with the door shut firmly at his back, she did her best to avoid him but his left arm held her tightly whilst his right hand lifted her veil. Across her face was a livid red weal and her right eye had a small cut in a raised bruise at its swollen corner.

'I thought so,' he hissed perilously. 'I thought there was some reason why you were wearing that bloody silly hat and veil. He did this, didn't he? That ... that thing who calls himself a man. He hit you, the bastard, but by God he'll not do it again.'

'Will, please ... I hit him back,' she lied.

'And is that supposed to make this more acceptable?'

'He was provoked...'

'Provoked! By what? Your refusal to go with him to shoot bloody grouse, I suppose, or was it your ability to take over and do what he is incapable of doing himself?'

He flung himself away from her, turning about the room in a snapping and uncontrollable spasm of torment. He was beside himself with red-hot anger, and with his own impotence at not having the right to prevent what had been done to her. And yet at the same time he was cold, forcing out each word distinctly, dangerously. His face had gone quite blank and his eyes were empty and bitter. It was as though what had happened had been her fault, something she could have prevented, by distancing herself, she supposed numbly, from what threatened her.

'He was ... he had ... I had led him to believe that I would ... that there was no need for either of us to attend another board meeting ... and then ... we had been ... we were guests at ... I taunted him ... I have been at the mill on many occasions recently, to see Annie ... and others, which he had allowed...'

'Dear Christ, *allowed?*'

474

'It is not as it seems, Will. I should not have said . . . what I did.'

'So he struck you across the face?'

'Believe me, Will, I did not . . . I should not have . . .'

'Do you think I care about that? Do you think that because you say you . . . what was it? . . . provoked him, I can accept this as though . . . ?'

'You must.'

'*Must!*'

'It has nothing to do with you. It is between my husband and myself.' She made herself hold back from the comfort she longed to find in his arms, the comfort of having him hold her, his sympathy, his kisses and the tender concern she badly needed. She had dreaded this. She had hoped at best she could get through the meeting with no one questioning too deeply the strangeness of the dense veil she wore but she might have known that Will would see through not only the veil but her reason for wearing it. He was too aware of her, too deeply involved with Tessa Greenwood and too well acquainted with every inch of her body which only last week he had explored minutely from her hair-line to her toe-nails.

'Is it now, and so I am to stand aside and see the woman I love, a woman whose boots he is not fit to polish, take a beating which would not look amiss on a bloody prize-fighter?'

'Don't exaggerate, Will,' she said coldly, and was alarmed when he made a violent movement towards the door, his fists clenched tightly, his face ominous and snarling. 'Where are you going?'

'Up to the bloody Hall, where else? That's where I'll find him, isn't it?' he wrenched at the door handle just as she reached him.

'Will, you can't, you can't. I won't let you. Can't you see it will destroy him?'

He turned, his chest heaving, his eyes bloodshot, his fists clenching and unclenching. His face was soaked with his

475

own maddened sweat and she knew it was taking every ounce of his control not to strike her, as Drew had done, in sheer, full-blooded frustration. He breathed heavily as the agony of her last words almost felled him.

'Destroy *him?*' he whispered. '*Destroy him?* What in hell's name do you think it's doing to me?'

'You are strong...'

'And better able to bear your cruelty, is that it, my lass? To see you defend a man who ... goddammit ... you so obviously love more than me.' He turned away and crashed his fist against the sturdy frame of the door, then leaned slowly, heavily, against it, defeated, his face pressed close to the dark wood.

'Darling, please, try to understand...' Her voice was gentle, begging for his sympathy.

'Understand what? That I must allow him to do just whatever he pleases to you and then have you defend him for it? Jesus Christ, Tessa, what d'you think I am? Other men have suffered far worse than he has and not become the weak and irrational misfit he is. Why must you give your life, and mine, to keep him from killing himself? That is what he will do one day in his mad ride to destruction and if he does not do it himself, I swear I will do it for him.'

He turned then and with the utmost gentleness put up a hand to her face, almost touching the livid weal which marred it. He smiled so lovingly her heart ached for him and tears blurred her eyes as he placed soft lips on her swollen cheek.

'I love you, Tessa, and despite what I said I know you love me. But he will not hurt you again. It will be the last time if he does.'

Annie found her ten minutes later staring from her window across the cheerful bustle of the mill yard, out to the high moorland which led from the outskirts of Crossfold up to the sky.

'Nay, what 'appened to thi, lass? Yer've not come off that animal o' thine, 'ave thi'?' She studied Tessa's closed face intently. 'I've summat at'ome, a potion I mek that'll tek that swellin' down in a minute. Yer can tek me ower ter Edge-clough in yer carriage an' I'll give thi' a jar.'

'Thanks, Annie.' But Annie knew Tessa had not heard what she said.

'What's up?' she said after several minutes of silence.

'Nothing.'

''Ow did yer come by that black eye?'

'I . . . fell off my mare, as you said.'

'Oh, aye, an' what did Will 'ave ter say about it?'

Tessa turned sharply, wincing as the flesh about her eyes was stretched by the movement. 'What has Will to do with it?'

'I saw 'im comin' out of 'ere no more an' ten minutes since lookin' as though 'e'd like nothin' better than to thrash the livin' daylights out o' someone. Your 'usband perhaps?'

Tessa's shoulders drooped and she sighed deeply.

'Annie, what am I to do? What the hell am I to do? I can hide nothing from you so you are bound to know that Will and I are . . . well, you will know what I mean. But Drew is . . . he needs me so badly. If he should learn of our friend-ship, it would be the end of him and yet I can't give Will up, I can't. Dear God, what can I do?'

'Eeh, 'tis nowt ter do wi' me, lass, an' there's nowt I can say to 'elp thi'. Yer mun walk the road tha's chosen, Tessa Greenwood, an' take consequences an' all. Tha' knows that an' thi' don't need me ter tell thi'.'

Tessa sighed again then turned to smile painfully. 'You're a big help to me, Annie. I know exactly where I stand with you, if no one else.'

'What did tha' want me ter say? Thee an' Will are . . . dear ter me but I can do nowt ter 'elp either of thi'. Yer both welcome at my 'ome any time yer care ter call an' thi'll always find me there, 'appen thi' needs summat. Tha' knows that. I can say no more.'

'I know, Annie, thank you. Now then, how are you getting on with the project?'

Annie sat down in the chair opposite Tessa and shuffled the papers she held, edging them into a careful pile.

'This is't list so far. There's dozens of 'em still turnin' up at factory gates askin' fer me even after all this time. Word's got round. I've fixed 'em up wi' decent lodgin's. Mind, some of 'em 'ave children wi' 'em, but 'appen they can go ter't school while their mams are workin'.' She pulled a face irritably. 'Eeh, Tessa, I can't get mesen set in that there ... office. It's right awkward ter me what wi' that daft beggar as calls 'imself 'ead clerk lookin' down 'is nose. Pompous devil!'

Annie had regained the flesh which she had lost in Manchester but she was still gaunt. Though she was Tessa's age she looked ten years older, craggy as the granite which sprouted on the moorland, and as indefatigable. There was a grimness about her which said that though she had been dealt some of life's severest blows she was still upright and always would be. She looked even more drab and colourless than previously, an over-all impression of grey, in her skin tone, in her pale eyes and her hair which was scraped back into a tiny, uncompromising knot at the back of her narrow head. Her skirt and long-sleeved bodice were also grey, charcoal-grey relieved by nothing but a narrow snow-white collar. Yet despite her austere appearance there was something in her eyes, in the way she looked directly into those of the person she addressed, which gave her hearers a feeling they could not have described. Trust perhaps. A manner which said she would never let them down. A steadfast reliability and strength on which anyone who wished could lean.

For the past eighteen months she had been what Tessa called her 'administrator' – a fancy name for 'overlooker', Annie said bluntly – in the plan which had come to her in the pin-heading factory in Earnshaw Street. At that moment when Annie had refused to leave without the other hopeless and derelict women and children with whom she had worked, the scheme had sprung, completely formed, into her mind. Annie had been compelling her, applying pressure, using their friendship which would not allow Tessa simply to leave her to her fate, to make her see what was happening in the industrial world of which she was now a part. There were thousands upon thousands still suffering the degradation and poverty, the dreadful conditions of their lives in the cotton industry. Most of the cotton manufacturers took little interest in their operatives and made no attempt to improve or ease their plight. They bent their energies and capital to investment and improvement in their mills, not seeing, or if they did, not caring about the squalor around them, nor the men and women who lived and died in it to achieve the profit the masters required. Annie was realistic enough to know that Tessa could do no more than help a few of the multitude who suffered, but by God, her attitude had said on that dreadful day, Annie would make sure she did help those few she could.

Now those same women together with others who had heard of the 'plan' the great lady in Crossfold had set up to relieve women like themselves, were making their slow and often hopeless way – since some of them did not reach it – to the mill where, it was said, decent work and lodgings would be found for those in need. It was not like the poorhouse, they had been told. All their lives they had fought to stay out of that since a woman might be parted from her children there and never see them again. A clean bed was available, nourishing food, a doctor where needed. But what about payment? No, the 'lady' would help there and, providing you genuinely wanted work and a decent way of life, she would not see you starve, nor your children. Mind, she knew a malingerer – and there were those, of course – when she saw one and soon sent them packing, but any woman with no man and with children to support was made welcome. She was one of them, it was said, since she had worked in a factory all her life, and had suffered as they did.

Tessa smiled, wincing again at the pain in her swollen face. 'You can deal with old Rigby, Annie, you know that, so don't complain to me about him. And you must have your own office. These strays of yours must have somewhere to find you.'

''Appen, but it teks some doin' fer women like them ter come up 'ere.'

'You will persuade them to it, if anyone can.'

They talked at length on the progress of the small pin-heading and pin-sheeting factory and of the other employment which was being found, not all in the mills, for Annie's workers. Some had been put into domestic work and indeed anywhere that offered a respectable life, their children admitted to the Chapman school and some, sadly, to a small grave in the churchyard. Annie was busy, her mourning for her own dead family done in private, and her new job with Mrs Drew Greenwood fulfilled some need in her which had shrivelled at Spicers. She was needed now and her gratitude to Tessa, though never voiced since that was not her way, was enormous.

'I'll be off then. I'm ter see a chap about some new fangled pin-headin' machine.'

Tessa was still smiling at Annie's dignified acceptance of her own rise to a position of authority and her evident pleasure in the work she was doing, but when she had gone she left an empty silence, a void into which Tessa's despairing thoughts slowly infiltrated. Though she tried hard to keep them centred on what Annie was doing they would keep returning to the increasingly hopeless situation between herself and Drew, between herself and this mill, and between herself and Will. She was like some favourite toy which a group of defiant children swears belongs exclusively to each one of them, played with and handled, torn and tossed from one to the other until she cared not who had her as long as she could settle peacefully somewhere. Drew was becoming harder to handle with each day, threatening unimaginable terrors if she did not stop going to that bloody mill. Yet the mill, though it had its board of directors, was claiming more of her time and, if she were honest, she was beginning to find it . . . well, a challenge, she supposed, interesting and even exciting at times.

And Will. Where was her relationship with Will, so rapturously renewed, leading them both? He was on a tight rein, a self-imposed rein in his contempt and jealousy of Drew. How long before that rein snapped and when it did, what catastrophe would follow?

She turned as someone tapped lightly on her office door, not even taking the trouble to replace her bonnet and veil. Dear God, what did it matter? The story would be all over the valley by now, how the half-deranged husband of Tessa Greenwood had knocked the living daylights out of her, and each screaming, violent word, carried by the servants' grapevine, would be reported and gloated over in every household.

The door opened and Will stood on the threshold. His cravat was disarranged and his short hair stood up in tousled disorder as though he had ridden hard and at speed.

'I couldn't . . .' His eyes were haunted and his strong face worked with the depth of his emotion. 'I got as far as . . . as Linthwaite but I couldn't . . .'

'Close the door, Will.' Her voice was soft but commanding for there would be curious eyes in the outer office she was certain.

'Yes.' He closed the door behind him and lifted his arms to her. When she ran into them, pressing her poor, damaged face against his chest, he crushed her to him, groaning.

'I can't bear to lose you, my darling. I must accept what we have . . . what *he* has, because I love you. Christ, it tears me apart that . . . I have to share you, but . . .'

'Yes, my love?'

'I can't promise not to . . . to protest,' he laughed weakly, 'if he hits you again, really I can't . . .'

'He won't do it again, Will.'

'How can you know that? He is violent . . .'

'No, frightened. If I can . . . allay his fears he won't . . .'

'Dear God, oh, sweet Jesus . . .' He knew exactly what she

481

meant. They stood for several minutes, drawing strength from one another, then he put her gently from him.

'Perhaps we had better make this look like a business call, lass. Those clerks out there were somewhat alarmed when I stormed past them just now. Call in that head chap of yours and ask him to fetch in the ledgers. Weekly accounting, wages books, order books for the months of August and September, oh, and some coffee. I'm going to give you a lesson in book-keeping. Now, where is that report of Bradley's?'

When Mr Rigby brought in the ledgers Mrs Greenwood had asked for, she and Mr Broadbent were sitting a respectable three feet apart, one on each side of her desk, speculating politely on the possibility of the hostilities in America being averted.

In November 1860 Abraham Lincoln was elected President of the United States of America but by February of the following year eleven of the southern states had seceded from the Union and Jefferson Davis was sworn in as the President of the Confederate States of America. Fort Sumter, an island off Charleston, South Carolina and in Union hands was fired on by the new Confederate troops, President Lincoln called for the mobilisation of Union forces and a state of war was declared between the northern and southern states of America. The 'Brothers War' had begun.

31

Chapman Manufacturing Company Ltd put all its operatives on short time in December 1861 and its largest shareholder, Mr Drew Greenwood, who had come home drunk for the third night in succession that week, was heard to remark to his wife that she could close the bloody mills for good, it was all the same to him.

In the previous month forty-nine mills in the cotton industry had closed down completely and 119 went on short time so that the wages of the millhands fell dramatically or disappeared altogether. The scarcity of cotton, which was after all the life-blood of the industry, had become critical and it was estimated that stocks of raw cotton could last only until the middle of December. There had been a skirmish, it was reported in the newspapers, at a place called Leesburg in Virginia where the northern states of America were defeated, and at Frederickstown in Missouri where this time the South was defeated. What was the cotton manufacturer of Lancashire to make of that? he asked himself as he despaired over the prospect of ever obtaining his bales of raw cotton from America again. How was he to keep his spinners and his weavers at their mules and looms? He stared hard times in the face, and if cotton was not to be shipped from America, where might he obtain it and, in the meanwhile, were his hands to starve?

'There is a rumour that Prince Albert is dead, Tessa,' her husband remarked later in the month, quite cheerfully, since it made no difference to his life, as the war in America made no difference to his life, as the short supply for cotton to his mills made no difference to his life. Tessa was disinclined to believe the report. All kinds of stories circulated among the gossip-mongering society in which Drew moved, of the nobility and their goings-on and even of royal misdemeanours, but this was surely a bad joke on someone's part? The Prince Consort was a young man of only forty-two and in the prime of his life.

But the rumour proved to be true and the nation was plunged into mourning as the bell of St Paul's began its death toll. Grief was universal, pervading every household as if each had lost a dear and respected relative. The funeral was held a week later and the whole of the country came to a halt. Shops and factories were closed, blinds were drawn and flags were flown at half-mast. The Queen, it was said, was out of her mind with grief and shock, and what was to become of them all if Her Majesty did not recover?

January 1862 came in on a wild gale of snow and wind which scarcely abated for three days leaving snow drifts of six feet and more through towns and villages and turning the Pennine moorland into an incredibly hostile stretch of unmarred beauty.

Starvation began to stare into the faces of those who had, over the last few years, come to believe that they were at least adequately provided for. Out of work and having spent what savings they had, those operatives who had been employed as spinners and weavers and in trades allied to cotton pawned their furniture, their Sunday clothes, since they could be done without, and even their bedding in order to feed themselves. By now the shortage of cotton was becoming desperate for the industry, and the *Illustrated London News* printed headlines and pictures of the plight of the Lancashire cotton towns and the great suffering of the people. Men and women were prepared to do anything rather than go on relief. One man advertised that he would shave other men, four for a halfpenny. Another took to 'chair-bottoming' and many sold newspapers, religious tracts or back numbers of penny periodicals. Groups of young girls could be seen gathered on street corners singing, some with musical instruments. They appeared shame-faced, sad and awkward, but their efforts could not last and by the end of April, just a year since the American Civil War had begun, most were thrown entirely upon the Guardian and Relief Committees.

Scenes which had once been commonplace in Crossfold and which were thought to have gone forever, scenes going back to the days when the power loom took over from the domestic hand loom, throwing thousands of men from their ancient profession, returned and multiplied. Sallow-faced, half-naked women lounged about in doorways listlessly watching sickly children in half-hearted play, the two shillings per head or less each family was allowed from relief failing completely to keep them in anything but the poorest of health. They lived on bread, oatmeal and potatoes and had it not been for the tireless work of Mrs Tessa Greenwood and her equally tireless helper, Miss Beale, it was doubtful, so it was said, that they would get through this crisis.

'We have to have some kind of organisation, Annie, and the only way to achieve it, I think, is for you to devote your time to setting up a committee to make sure that those who are in need get at least one decent meal a day. Our own operatives are still able to manage, even on two-thirds of their usual income though how long that will last remains to be seen. They say there are a quarter of a million unemployed, and the cotton which is coming from India is of a poor quality – mixed with an even poorer! They have not the machines to clean away the filth which it contains. Will tells me they are forming a cotton company in Manchester with the intention of raising a million pounds to buy such machinery and send it out there but whether anything will come of it is pure speculation. And even then the price will be exorbitant. They say in Manchester it will be no more than a stopgap measure until the war in America is over but in the meanwhile we must do what we can to alleviate the hardships of those who have depended on us. D'you know, when I was visiting some spinners who were thrown out by the Moorhouse mill there was a woman living in the most appalling conditions in one of those awful courts at the back of Jagger Lane. Everything in the house had been sold except the bed and one cooking pot. Her five children were in the last stages of malnutrition and her husband was in gaol. He had obtained some provisions for them on credit, no more than four and elevenpence halfpenny but when he was unable to pay the debt they took him away . . .'

'An' tha' got 'im out?'

'Oh, yes, and provided them with bedding, clothing, coal,

flour, I believe, and other items of food to see them through until you could get round to them. Here is their name and address.'

'An, what of Chapman mills? 'Ow much longer can tha' keep on four days?'

'I bought up a cargo of cotton last week through an agent in Liverpool. It had got by the blockade out of New Orleans, don't ask me how for they say that only two out of six ships get through. The Union navy has a blockading squadron stationed off each port to prevent ships taking cotton out of the South and returning with essential supplies. Last year we imported 1,261 million pounds of cotton and this year it has fallen to less than half. Eighty per cent of it was from America, Annie, and now we shall be forced to accept the Indian, despite its poor quality.'

The two friends were sitting in Tessa's office, both gazing out on to the strange and empty silence of the Chapmanstown mill yard. It was Friday and last night the machines and engines had been turned off and the boilers allowed to go out. They would not be switched on again until the bales of raw cotton Tessa had purchased arrived at the Chapman warehouses. Only a fifth of those employed in the cotton industry were fully employed, the rest were on short time or with no work at all, and the exact figures were stamped indelibly in the mind of Tessa Greenwood. Once she had been concerned with nothing more complicated than the number of shots it took to bring down fifty birds on the Squire's moor, with how many gowns she should order for the season's hunt balls and how many sovereigns Drew gambled away in one evening, none of which mattered in the least.

Annie seemed to find nothing unusual in the conversation and it was evident that this different aspect of Tessa Greenwood was nothing new to her. Tessa had been chairman of the board of directors of the Chapman mills for two years now, perhaps the most difficult in the history of the company since it was begun so long ago by her husband's great-grandfather. In the last year she had seen so many businesses falter and fall, but not once had she turned her back on her own to return to the pleasures her husband seemingly enjoyed without her.

'I called on Mrs Poynton yesterday,' Annie said, sipping her coffee, her straight back an inch from the back of the chair on which she sat, unlike Tessa who lounged carelessly with the wide skirts of her muslin gown, a lovely shade of soft rose, in a circle about her feet. She wore no bonnet and her hair was piled haphazardly into an untidy coil on the top of her head. She had tied it up herself with a wide velvet ribbon in the same colour as her dress that morning, ignoring Emma's pleas to be allowed to arrange it for her.

'I've no time, Emma, and no, I cannot stop to choose a bonnet. I must be in Crossfold by nine to meet Mr Bradley and then Miss Beale and I are to inspect that old mill in Hardacre Street to see if it is suitable for a school and a kitchen for ... Stop fussing, Emma. No, I can't be bothered with a parasol. If the sun comes out I shall ask Thomas to put up the hood on the carriage. Oh, and Emma ...'

Her voice dropped and Emma leaned forward to hear what her mistress was saying. 'Don't ... don't disturb the master. He is still sleeping and ... well, there is no need to wake him so early.'

Emma nodded respectfully, then turned to look in the direction of the closed door of the dressing-room where Mr Drew slept on most nights now. You could hear him snoring, even through the solid wood of the door. They were the snores of a man who had come home in the early hours of the morning so drunk he really should not have been in charge of that fancy cabriolet he drove. Right across the lawn, Percy said he had ploughed, and through Miss Laurel's roses, leaving a trail of destruction six feet wide and singing so loudly the whole household, including the children in the nursery, had been awakened. Laughing at nothing, he'd been, his horse and vehicle left to droop at the front step and Mr Briggs and Hibberson compelled to carry him up to his bed whilst he begged them to join in some bawdy song he and his wild friends had heard at a music hall in Manchester. He'd sleep the best part of the day, coming down to the small back parlour to sprawl before the fire, avoiding Miss Laurel and her callers in the drawing-room, his lovely blue eyes narrowed to increasingly puffy slits, his mouth hard and ill-humoured, his temper short and unpredictable and, if Miss Tessa was not there, his voice hoarse and his words offensively rude.

Where had he gone, Emma mused as she watched her mistress climb into her carriage, that handsome, good-natured, recklessly laughing young man they had once known? Him and his brother, both of them up to all kinds of pranks but with good hearts and no malice in them, merry as larks providing no one tried to harness them. And now one was dead and the other killing himself, they said, in his search for something even his wife couldn't seem to provide. All his time was spent riding to hounds, shooting grouse and pheasant, drinking brandy and claret until he could hardly see to play cards in the often-dubious company he and his friends kept.

And Miss Tessa toiling all the hours God sent in an effort to keep not only her own mills working and her own operatives from the poor house, but taking in the down-and-outs from the whole of Lancashire, it was rumoured. Her and that Annie Beale.

'Oh, and what was the outcome?' Tessa questioned Annie. 'Will she sit on our committee?'

'Aye, an' that Mrs Bayly an' all. They've promised ter speak to as many ladies as they can about the soup kitchen an' Mrs Bayly knows a Miss Gaunt as she reckoned'd teach school fer nowt. Not just childér but any man or woman as wants ter learn. I've bin round most o't manufacturers an' though some were ready ter show me't door, I managed ter persuade 'em ter remit rents on't workers' cottages. I told 'em if you could do it so could they. Mrs Poynton says as 'ow she knows t'parson at parish church an' all them as goes ter't Sunday school, an' believe me it'll be every bairn in Crossfold an' Chapmanstown by't time I've done wi' em, will be given petticoats an' shirts, blankets an' such fer their mams, an' a bit o' brass 'as bin set aside fer the mendin' of boots. An' Doctor Salter ses as 'ow 'e'll give 'is services free to them what needs 'em.'

'Heavens, Annie, you have been busy.'

'I've nowt else ter do wi' me time.'

'No.' Tessa put a compassionate hand on her friend's arm, then smiled when it was snatched away from her. Annie would never change. As long as she had breath in her body she would use it to help anyone she thought to be in need of it. Many of the ladies of the town moved amongst the destitute cotton workers helping those they called the 'deserving poor', those they considered worthy of assistance by the measure of the respectful gratitude they displayed.

But there were others in utter poverty who were proud, who would not bow their heads for charity and they showed these same ladies the door saying they wanted no busybodies interfering in their household arrangements. And there were others, in order to get more than their entitlement of relief, who included children recently dead in their list of the needy, or who 'borrowed' children to make up their family numbers and so 'diddled' another two shillings per head for each one. There were husbands who were found drunk in bed and starving children in the gutter. Annie saw them all, helped them all, sorted them into some kind of order and intended keeping them there, choose how, until the mills were opened again and woe betide *any* who fell by the wayside when she was in charge!

But they were indebted to her and to Mrs Greenwood as in increasing numbers young men and women, youths, adults who had never been to school in their lives, unemployed hands with time hanging heavy, were encouraged to attend the Working Men's Institutes. There they were taught reading, writing and simple arithmetic for they needed an occupation of some sort to fill their empty days.

Mr Will Broadbent, the largest stockholder in his own mill and therefore the worst hit, was struggling to keep open for a couple of days a week. On the days when the mill was closed, he used the silent and empty rooms to hold classes for his women operatives in sewing and the cooking of cheap and nourishing dishes, and an industrial class for his men in tailoring, boot-making and similar crafts, all of which would come in useful when the present crisis was over and they had returned to their spinning mules.

But in other parts of Lancashire out-of-work millworkers fared a great deal worse. There was widespread bitterness over the 'Labour Test' where the poor who applied for relief had to show their willingness to work. The cotton operatives disliked being classed as ordinary paupers by the Guardians and felt that more lenient rules should govern the granting of relief to decent workmen who were only temporarily unemployed through no fault of their own. They objected to the manner in which the so-called Labour Test was enforced. Men who were indoor workers, badly clothed and close to starvation, were sent out in that first bitter winter on jobs such as stone-breaking, a task which was not only cruel, they said, but often fatal. A man who had worked in a cotton mill required delicacy of touch, and his hands were singularly soft from working in high temperatures and by continual contact with oil and cotton-wool. The stone hammer blistered his flesh and the oakum many were compelled to 'pick' galled his fingers. Flesh and fingers which would soon, please God and the good sense of the people of America, be back at work in the spinning mills and the weaving sheds of Lancashire.

Discussion of the Public Works Bill began in quarters where the relief of the increasingly large numbers of the poor was of particular concern. The hot weather of that summer brought swarms of flies and rats into the alleyways and back streets which meandered through the old part of Crossfold. The cotton famine had caused whole families to move in with another in the same circumstances in order to save rent and, in the previous winter, economise on fuel. Windows had been boarded up and doors padded to retain what little heat there was. Bodies lay close together for warmth and even when the weather became kinder as spring and summer approached, they still squeezed together since they had no chance to do otherwise. Cleaning materials were low on their list of priorities as women watched their children starve and the filth, the mud and raw sewage which seeped through the uneven ground, the overflowing middens and foul pools of dung and rotting garbage became one huge, stinking cesspit. It was a breeding ground for the fevers, typhus, typhoid, scarletina and smallpox which the swarming flies and rats carried assiduously from one house to the next, from one street to the next, from one town to the next.

So what better way, the Public Works Act wanted to know, to keep idle men employed and the fevers at bay, than to put these men to the vexed problem of main sewering? The distressed cotton operatives would be asked to volunteer to do the unskilled manual labour of building not only sewers and drains but reservoirs, good roads, public parks and recreation grounds at labourers' rates of pay. The experience would strengthen their puny frames and improve their skills and without undue exertion they could earn themselves twelve shillings a week and at the same time relieve the Guardians of the task of supporting their families.

'Tis said there's sickness at back o' Jagger Lane,' Annie offered in the long silence which had fallen over the two women.

'What kind of sickness?' Tessa's voice was sharp and she returned her cup to its saucer with a clatter.

'They say tis nowt'. Doctor Salter fetched me from't school this mornin'. 'E knew I were ... well, that I'd 'ad some sort o' fever when I were in Manchester. Reckoned as 'ow I'd survived it then I'd be in no danger now.'

'But what is it?'

'Nay, lass, don't ask me. I'm no doctor.'

491

'Has Doctor Salter no idea?'

''E ses as 'ow its bin a long time since there were an epidemic an' 'im bein' a youngish man, like, 'e's never bin in one.'

'An epidemic? Does he think . . . ?'

'It's bin nearly a year since most of 'em were in full work, Tessa, or 'ad a decent meal except what we give 'em. They're all low, in poor 'ealth, an' the first illness what comes along'll 'ave 'em before thi can say 'pickin' stick'. They'll not call't doctor since they've no brass ter pay 'im. Will ses as 'ow . . .'

'Will?' Tessa felt her heart lurch sickeningly. 'What was he doing there?'

'Nay, Tessa. Tha knows Will, or should do by now. Wherever there's trouble 'e's in't thick of it. Doctor Salter was talkin' of puttin' them what's sick in one o' them empty warehouses in Ashton Lane. Keep 'em apart from t'others until 'e knows what's up wi' 'em. Just ter be on't safe side, like. I said I'd find some women ter nurse 'em. There's a few o' my pin-headin' girls wi' nowt ter do an' they'd be glad of a bit of extra cash.'

Tessa sprang up. 'I'll come and help.'

'No, tha'll not. Will wants yer kept out of it.' Annie's face was impassive, half-turned away and Tessa smiled at the very idea of being 'kept out of it'. These were her operatives, some of them, and she was part of this working community now. Besides, Will had no control over her. If she wanted to go down and inspect the premises she damn well would. He ought to know *her* by now as well. She came and went as she pleased, or as much as she was able with Drew in the often violent moods which came over him. But certainly, despite their love for one another, Will had no authority over her.

'Don't be foolish, Annie. If there is to be an epidemic of some sort in the town then those who are sick will need all the help they can get and I must see what is needed.'

'I know what's needed, lass, an' there's nowt you can do that I can't.'

492

'You mean because of who I am? Because I am Tessa Greenwood and not brought up to hardships as you and Will were?'

'Aye, 'appen that, but most of all because Will wants yer kept out of it.'

'Dear God, what has it to do with you or Will? I'm not a child . . .'

'Then stop actin' like one. Anyway, let's see what's to 'appen first. Get yer gone up to that 'usband o' thine an' see if there's owt' yer can be doin' fer 'im. I 'eard as 'ow 'e caused summat of a disturbance, 'im an' that merry band o' gentlemen 'e rides about with, up at Five Pigeons t'other night.'

'Oh, Lord, what over?'

Annie looked uncomfortable, fiddling in a most unusual way with the enormous reticule she carried around with her and in which she kept all the many and varied items she might need in the course of her active day. No one was quite sure what they were but she could provide anything from a clean rag to wipe a child's runny nose to a safety-pin for a torn hem, a pencil for making a quick note here and there, and even a screw of paper containing tea for some needy woman she visited and who might gain comfort from a brew.

'Nay, don't ask me. 'Tis nowt ter do wi' me, Tessa.' That meant, of course, that it *had* to do with some woman, or Annie would have told her.

It was nearly three years now since Tessa had taken up the burden which she had unwillingly inherited from her mother and Charlie; more than three years since the fire in which Charlie had lost his life. She did her best to share her time between the mills and her husband, going only to Chapmans when it was absolutely necessary for a board meeting or when, as Drew's proxy, her signature was needed on some document, but now the crisis caused by the cotton famine demanded more and more of her time. Secretly she admitted to herself that she found the time she

493

spent there increasingly absorbing and the hours passed in the company of Drew and his friends increasingly trivial.

'We are off to Nicky's for a game of croquet, my love,' he had said to her at lunch-time. 'Why not join us? Johnny and Alicia will be there and Nicky has persuaded Polly Arbuthnot to give that elderly husband of hers the slip. Afterwards we thought we'd ride into Oldham. There's a new song and supper room just been opened, or perhaps the music hall. Who knows? That is the charm of being free, don't you agree? Go wherever the fancy takes us, for that is what makes life exciting, Tessa. Come on, darling, leave those bloody awful figures. In fact, give them to me and I shall dispose of them where they belong. In the back of the fire . . .' He had snatched a sheaf of notes and figures Will had made out for her to study on the variations in trading from month to month since the new mill had begun operating.

'Don't, Drew. A lot of work has gone into those notes. Please, put them back,' she said urgently as he made a movement towards the fire. 'I know you think they are not worth bothering one's head about, any more than the mills and the operatives, but someone has to look after our interests at least until this crisis is over.'

'And then what excuse will you give, my pet? What reason will you dream up so that you might give your undivided attention to the business and not to your husband? Will it be that another catastrophe of desperate proportions will spring up to claim you, d'you think? Or will it be the fascination of making money which seems to have afflicted every member of my family, except myself and Pearce, of course? Really, Tessa, your commercial heritage is beginning to show quite dreadfully. I was only saying to Nicky last week that one can hardly believe that you are the same dashing girl who once rode out with us on more than one escapade. Adventure, that is what we were after, the three of us, you and I and Pearce . . . No . . . I mean . . . Drew. Don't I?'

His voice became uncertain and his eyes narrowed as he looked at something in the far distance of his memory. The papers dropped from his hand and she quickly retrieved them from the carpet where they fell before turning back to him. His taunting manner had disappeared. His shoulders slumped and in his face was the lost and desperate expression he had brought back from the Crimea. He shook his head wonderingly and his voice was soft when he spoke.

'Where has he gone, Tessa?' he said, in much the same way Emma had done only that morning. 'I seem to have lost him somehow.'

'Pearce?' She put her hand to him, her own face as gentle as his.

'No, not Pearce, not Pearce. But ... both of us ... myself ... I cannot seem to function these days now that both of you have left me. I know I do dangerous things but I seem to have no control ...'

She moved quickly to his side, taking his hand in hers, but he turned away to look into the fire. She lifted it, a hard, horseman's hand, brown and strong, to her lips.

'You have not lost yourself, Drew, nor me. I am always here.'

'No, you are not, Tessa, and I'm afraid that ...'

'What, my darling?' In her voice was the depth of her love for him.

'That one day, when I really need you, when Johnny is with his Alicia and Nicky off on some private jaunt with a lady and I have no one, you will not be here when I look round.'

'I shall always be here, Drew, always. You know that.'

'Do I, Tessa? Do I? You were not here this morning when I awoke and called out to you.'

'No, I had to ...'

'I know. Go to the mill, or the school with that woman, or to the soup kitchen ...'

'There are so many of them, Drew, and all needing ...'

'None need you as I do, Tessa. Please come with me this afternoon. Show me ...'

'What ...?'

495

'That you mean what you say. That you love me still. That you are here for me now. Prove it by coming with me.'

And so she had gone dressed in her outrageous black riding coat and cream breeches, her white waistcoat and tall top hat, her boots polished and her mare beneath her. She and Drew raced one another along the wild stretch of track between Greenacres and Longworth Hall and the solitary figure of the horseman who rode quietly, tiredly in the direction of Crossfold was noticed by neither of them as they shouted with delighted laughter in one another's company.

## 32

'I thought you said Will was coming with you. I wanted to speak to him about . . .'

''E couldn't manage it. 'E sends 'is apologies.'

'Apologies? What on earth does that mean? You and he had your meeting with Doctor Salter, I suppose?'

'Aye.'

'And . . . ?'

'And what?'

'Annie, for God's sake stop playing games with me. Has the good doctor decided what is wrong with these people in the vicinity of Jagger Lane?'

'It's come so sudden, like, an' 'e's still not sure. Give it a week or two . . .'

'A week or two? But I thought it was urgent.'

'It could be 'owt, Tessa. Doctor Salter ses as 'ow 'e wants a second opinion so 'e's asked old Doctor Ellison to come an' look 'em over. Not that Doctor Ellison was too pleased ter poke 'is 'ead in them alleys at back of Jagger Lane. But

496

'e's 'ad more experience than Doctor Salter seein' as 'ow 'e's worked in London where such fevers are rife, they say.'

'But what form does it take?' Tessa sat back in her chair and studied Annie's averted face. There was something about her reluctance to meet Tessa's eyes which was most alarming since Annie never flinched away from anyone's gaze. Just the opposite for sometimes her steady eyes seemed to probe right inside Tessa's head just where she didn't want her to see. Now she was staring out of the office window, this time at the busy yard for the cotton Tessa had purchased was at this moment being unloaded and carried swiftly to the warehouse where the bales would be opened in readiness for blending.

'Well, naturally, none of 'em are what yer might call fit. Scrawny and pale from a poor diet...'

'Dear Lord, I hope we can keep our own people working, Annie, and if we can't we must not allow them to fall into the state these are in. Are they all from the Moorhouse mill?'

'No, some are Abbotts. Jenkinsons've turned off 'undreds an' there's some from every mill in't valley.'

'And Jonathan Abbott refused to donate a penny last week when I cornered him at the Cloth Hall.'

'Aye, well, that's as mebbee, but them at back o' Jagger Lane'll need more'n a penny ter see 'em through. There's women wi' babies they can't feed. No milk, tha' knows. There's others've never got over the bronchitis and pneumonia they took last winter. They'll be't first ter go, Doctor Salter ses.'

'Is there nothing we can do to stop it?'

'We're doin' all we can, lass, but 'appen it'll come ter nowt though Doctor ses the symptoms are...'

'Yes?'

'Well, tha'll not want to 'ear what they are.'

'Annie, really. I am no genteel lady who is about to faint away at the thought of sickness, nor am I to shirk the responsibility of doing what must be done.'

'Do thi know, lass, sometimes I can't get over the change

497

in thi'?' Annie smiled and her eyes, so pale and cool more often than not, had a softness in them, a warmth which spoke of her deep affection for this woman. 'Wheer did that 'oity-toity young madam go, the one what used ter come ter my 'ouse an' treat it as though it was 'er own? I'll 'ave a cup o' tea, Annie, if yer please, tha' used ter say, expecting' me ter stop whatever I were doin' an' brew up for thi'. Yer'd sit in't best chair an' keep me from me work, jawin' on about nowt, then, off yer'd go, ridin' like the divil on that animal o' thine, off on some foolish, wasteful jaunt wi' thy scapegrace cousins...' She stopped suddenly, aware that she was speaking of Tessa's husband, then her face hardened. 'Nay, I'm not sorry I said that even though one is dead...'

'Please, Annie.'

'...an t'other's no more than a...'

'*Annie!*'

'Right, lass, I hear thi'. I'll say no more except that tha've turned out champion, Tessa Greenwood. Now, where was I?'

'About to tell me the symptoms of this illness, you fraud, you!'

'Aye, 'appen I am. Well, they start wi' vomitin' an' a loosenin' of the bowels. They shake, Will ses, an' can't stop, an' no one really knows what it is. They say as 'ow it comes from abroad somewhere, India an' such places. It seems ter live in muck an' wi' all them stinkin' sewers an' drains at the back o' Jagger Lane it's a right breedin' ground. Them as is took can't keep owt' down, an' it's a quick death, Doctor Salter says.'

'There have been deaths already?' Tessa's voice was sharp.

'Aye, a few.'

'How many?'

'Well, Will reckons...'

Tessa felt the first dreadful thrill of fear skim along the surface of her flesh and her stomach lurched for no accountable reason. She sprang up from her chair and reached for the parasol Emma had persuaded her to bring this morning.

'I'm going up to Ashton Lane,' she said abruptly, heading towards the door, her every instinct telling her that for some reason she must hurry. Annie stood up too and followed her, her face becoming even paler than usual, her hands reaching out and swiftly capturing Tessa's arm.

'Nay, tha' musn't, lass. Not until Doctor Salter ses tha' might.'

'So it's Doctor Salter who is keeping me away now, is it? I thought it was Will who was giving the orders on where I may or I may not go. What's going on here, Annie?' She threw off Annie's restraining hands, barely stopping in her stride, turning heads in the counting house as she stalked by the clerks at their tall desks, Annie at her heels. Neither of them had taken the time to put on a bonnet and as they reached the yard the sweltering sun struck savagely on their uncovered heads. Tessa called to the stable boy to tell Thomas to fetch round the carriage and all the while Annie was reaching for her, shouting above the clamour of the yard that she was not to go, that Will would be furious, that Doctor Salter would blame her if she brought Mrs Greenwood where it really wasn't necessary for her to go. There were a dozen other good reasons why Tessa should stop right here, or better yet, get on home to her husband.

Tessa swung round to face her, still holding the pretty parasol, making no attempt to put it up to protect her white skin from the sun's rays.

'What are you trying to save me from, Annie? Why is it that suddenly I'm not allowed to visit Ashton Lane? Why can't I see for myself these people who have been struck down by something which may or may not be fever, which may or may not be scarletina, or measles? What is there that ... that Will ... Dear God, it's Will, isn't it? He doesn't want me to ... to see what? Tell me what it is he doesn't want me to see?'

'Nay, lass, don't. I give 'im me word ...'

'To do what, Annie?' All the while the terror grew and grew within her, threatening to crush her heart and freeze the blood in her veins. 'Tell me the truth, Annie. You might as well because, whatever you say, I shall go to Ashton Lane and find out. As soon as the carriage comes I mean to go there, or the infirmary, or wherever Doctor Salter and Will are, and find out whatever it is you're keeping from me.'

'Tha can't, lass. Doctor Salter won't let thi...'

'*Won't!* Doctor Salter has no authority over me, Annie Beale, and neither have you. See, here is the carriage. Now, will you come with me or will I go alone?'

She climbed into the carriage, nodding at Thomas who helped her in, giving him instructions to drive her to the old Clegg warehouse in Ashton Lane. Annie sat beside her, saying nothing, for what was the use?

It was the stench which hit her first, the foetid, appalling air, so hot it lay thickly against her skin. It was dim in that first moment and she could not make out what it was that retched and gasped and groaned and cried out as she moved beyond the open doorway which led from the warehouse yard to the ground floor of the building.

The room was crowded with iron bedsteads, cots, even mattresses laid out on the bare floor. Some sort of attempt had been made to keep the beds separate from one another but to Tessa it seemed that it was impossible to get from one side of the room to the other without stepping on the prone figures that crowded it. There were men and women, children, tiny and silent, others writhing and vomiting, and moving from one to another was Doctor Salter and half a dozen women, some of whom she recognised from her own recently opened pin-heading factory.

'Dear, sweet Jesus,' she whispered. 'What is it...?'

'Now yer 'ere, lass and thy've seen it, yer might as well know. Dr Ellison reckons it's cholera.'

'*Cholera!* Oh, dear God...'

'Aye.'

'But what is being done about it?'

'There's not much can be done 'cept let it run its course. They're tryin' ter keep 'em separate from ... the rest.

500

There's none o't suspects gone to't th'infirmary since week-end. Authorities 've bin informed an' all them 'ouses in't back o' Jagger Lane, where it began, 'ave bin limewashed an' t'bodies an' all.'

'Dear God, why was I not told?'

'What good would that a' done?'

'I could have ... helped ...'

' 'Ow, lass? Tha' knows that 'usband o' thine wouldn't let yer come 'ere 'elpin' out. I wanted to mesen but ... I were persuaded I could do more good in other quarters ... as you can.'

'Where is Will, Annie?'

Annie's disjointed words dried up abruptly and she put a hand on Tessa's arm as she began to move forward into the packed mass of suffering humanity. Flies buzzed lazily over a pool of excrement which dripped on to the floor from the cot of a quiet child and Tessa knew quite definitely that the child was dead. There was vomit on the blankets which covered the shivering, sighing bodies and bluebottles gorged there, but still Tessa pressed on.

'Where is Will, Annie?' She knew if she did not find him soon, if she did not see his tall, dependable, strong and beloved figure bending over some bed she would run, screaming his name, into the warehouse yard. She could feel the panic, the horror, the dread, the awful, awful fear fill and expand her lungs until she knew they would burst. She could feel it rise in her throat, threatening to choke her. She wanted to cry out his name, shout his name at the top of her voice, but Annie had her by the arm, struggling to drag her back from the appalling, writhing misery.

'Tell me where he is, Annie.'

'No, lass, tha' can't. He asked me ter keep thi away.'

'Where is he, Annie? Take me to him or, by God, I'll search every bed in this place until I find him.' And Annie, perhaps with the picture in her mind of the elegant Mrs Drew Green-wood handling every stinking, shivering body in the makeshift hospital in her search for Will Broadbent, led her to him.

He had been put in a corner beneath a window which someone, with a decent attempt at cleanliness had tried to wipe over. He lay on his back, his unfocused gaze on the high ceiling. His short hair lay limply to the shape of his head and his face was grey and withered. A blanket covered him and his large hands plucked at the wool, bony somehow, the flesh already burned away, as it was from the rest of his big frame, by this disease which could kill a healthy man in twenty-four hours. He muttered and mumbled, his head turning towards her as she bent over him, though he didn't know her, then away again as he heaved convulsively in a great spasm of vomiting.

'Will ... Will ... Oh, Lord God ... Will ...' She reached for his hand and from behind Annie tried to stop her from touching him but she sank down beside his bed, oblivious to the stench which came from him, her hands smoothing his forehead and cheeks. 'Oh my dearest, what ... ?'

'Dear God in heaven, woman, what d'you think you're doing? Get away from that man, Annie Beale, and who in hell's that ... ? Goddammit, woman, have you no more sense than to touch that man? Oh, Mrs Greenwood, I beg your pardon, but would you come away from my patient? Do you not realise how ... how unwell he is and how dangerous ... ? You could take the illness with you ...'

Doctor Salter, his young face old and hard and lined, tired beyond endurance, dragged quite forcibly at her shoulder, not caring any more for the niceties of their differing social position in his desperation to get her, not only from the dying man in the bed, but from this hospital. But she struck his hand away, bending, incredibly, to place her lips on the man's brow.

'Mrs Greenwood!' This was not, of course, the time for amazement at Mrs Greenwood's behaviour, though that was incredible enough. He simply could not cope with *visitors*, for God's sake, in the midst of this catastrophe which had

502

come upon the town of Crossfold. 'Please, Mrs Greenwood, this man needs attention...'

She rose crisply, no hint of the soft anguish she had just displayed lingering in her decisive manner.

'Which he shall have, Doctor Salter, but not here.'

'I don't understand you, Mrs Greenwood, and I'm afraid I have not the time to stand and discuss it with you. As you can see, I am an extremely busy man.' He waved his exhausted hand in the direction of the dozens of people who lay about them awaiting his attention.

'Which I shall help to alleviate at once, Doctor Salter.'

'I cannot imagine what you mean, ma'am, so if you will excuse me.' He began to turn away but she had not yet done.

'What nursing does this man need, Doctor Salter? Is there anything special in the way of...'

'No, ma'am. All we can do is try to make their passing a little easier ... more comfortable...'

Her face spasmed in horror and he relented somewhat. 'Go home, Mrs Greenwood. There is nothing you or Miss Beale can do here. It will run its course, this ... fever, and you are needed and can do so much more elsewhere. We are deeply grateful for all the help you have...'

'Thank you, doctor, but I have done nothing. Now, if you could find me some men ... you have men to carry the patients in, I presume?... Good, then if you would be so kind as to fetch them, and my coachman ... no ... very well, I suppose it would not be fair to ask him to risk himself ... some blankets which I will replace, naturally. I shall take Mr Broadbent to ... oh, no, not to Greenacres, there are children there, but to the home of my good friend, Miss Beale. I intend to nurse Mr Broadbent myself, Doctor Salter.'

'Tha can't do this, Tessa,' Annie said, all the way back to the cottage at Edgeclough.

Her face was like stone.

'I am doing it, Annie.' She held his mumbling, tossing head in her lap, drawing the blankets more closely about his heaving shoulders though the sun's heat struck fiercely even through the carriage top which Thomas had put up.

'Tha can't do it, lass. Doctor Salter said...'

'I heard what he said and it appears to me that Will had just as much chance, more, of ... of surviving in your cottage than he has in that stinking...'

'Tha knows what I mean, Tessa.'

'No, I don't, unless it is that you do not want us in your house. I'm sorry, Annie, I had not thought. The fever is infectious, dangerous, I suppose, and Will could bring it with him.'

'Now then, madam.' Annie's voice was sharp and biting. 'Don't tek that tone wi' me. Will ... an' thissen are welcome in my 'ouse whenever tha wants, illness or no. I told thi that years ago, but it's thi 'usband an' family I'm thinkin' on. Tha knows 'ow it'll look ter folk, Mrs Drew Greenwood nursin' a man who was once overlooker in 'er family's own mill. It does look a mite strange, don't tha think?'

'You'll be there, Annie, to safeguard my reputation, if that's what concerns you.'

But it was clear to Annie that Tessa was not really listening to what she was saying. She bent over the delirious man, her face no more than six inches from his foetid breath, her arms holding his head to her breast, supporting him on the carriage seat. Her face was strained and pale and her eyes enormous in her anxiety. She stroked his cheek and murmured his name, soothing him, whispering to him that they were almost there, my darling, telling him that soon he would be in a clean bed and she would give him a sip of soup, broth to keep up his strength, and soon, soon he would better. She had not the slightest notion of what she was taking on, Annie could see, believing naïvely that once they had Will away from that dreadful place, which surely had been doing him no good at all, he would begin to recover. A warm bath, a hot drink and a good night's sleep: wasn't that the remedy for all the illness Tessa Greenwood had yet seen in her life and wasn't that what she would give to her love, Will Broadbent, her attitude said? Annie knew that Drew Greenwood was away from home on one of his frequent visits to his autocratic and privileged friends. Was it shooting, fishing or just some drunken debauch which they got up to with such regular monotony? She didn't know or care. She only knew that when he came home and found his wife had taken the carriage to Edgeclough with the intention of helping to nurse Mr Will Broadbent, a director on the Chapman's own board, he was not likely to be charitable about it.

They got him out of the carriage and up the stairs to Annie's bedroom with the help of Thomas who couldn't stand by and see his mistress and her strange friend struggle with a sick man, whatever he was supposed to have.

'You must go home now, Thomas,' Mrs Greenwood said crisply, 'and tell them I shall stay here for a day or two to help Miss Beale nurse her . . . friend. Mr Broadbent has no one at his own home to . . . to look after him, you see, so we shall keep him here until he has recovered. Now then, here is a list of the things I . . . we shall need. See that I . . . we have them within the hour.'

And Thomas had driven home to Greenacres as though the devil himself sat in his carriage, declaring to the ring of fascinated servants who, thankfully, were not aware of the growing epidemic in the town, nor of Thomas's involvement with one of its sufferers, that Miss Tessa had taken leave of her senses, really she had. There would be holy war when *he* came back from his jaunt to Cheshire and found her gone!

They bathed him first with cooling water, stripping him naked on Annie's plain bed which had known the weight of no man. Together, without embarrassment, they performed the intimate task of cleansing every part of his body as he mumbled and fretted under their hands, knowing neither of them. They dressed him in a nightshirt which had come from Greenacres, watching with dismay as it was stained with the thin contents of his bowels. They changed him, and the bed linen, again and again since he had no control of his bodily functions and they were both obsessed with the need to make him as comfortable as they could. The boiler in which Annie washed her own garments was never taken off the fire and on Annie's clothes-line in the strip of yard at the back of the cottage, sheets and blankets hung limp and unmoving in the humid heat.

'Tha'll 'ave ter leave 'im naked,' Annie said wearily, as she watched Tessa shake out the last dry nightshirt, ready to drag it over Will's head. ''E don't know any difference an tha's only tirin' thissen over what don't matter.'

'But the sheets?'

'Give 'em 'ere. I'll put 'em in't boiler but them's the last. Tha'll 'ave ter spread squares o' linen under 'im until them on't line's dry. We can't keep up wi' 'em, lass, an' 'e don't know.'

And it was true. With every hour which passed Will had sunk deeper and deeper into a frightening state of insensibility. His face was grey, just bare, protruding bones and deep hollows. His cracked lips parted as he dragged in a morsel of air and his breathing barely raised his chest. He no longer muttered or roamed restlessly over the bed. He no longer sweated or vomited. It was as though every drop of moisture his body contained had been wrung out of him. His flesh had gone, melting away like the wax on a candle.

Tessa knelt beside him, watching his face as she had watched it for almost twelve hours, ever since she and Annie and Thomas had manhandled him up Annie's narrow staircase and on to this bed. Only twelve hours and in that time he had lost shape and form and colour with an incredible speed. Even this morning when she had first seen him at the temporary hospital he had still been Will, recognisable, and though ill and delirious a man she would know as the man she loved. Now the face on the pillow could have belonged to anyone. He appeared a skeletal stranger with a grey, mottled face, at first glance already dead, with closed sunken eyes and a ghastly slitted mouth, dry and cracked, which no woman in her right mind would dream of kissing. Even the hair on the apparition looked dead and grey, dusty where the salty sweat had dried on it.

And yet there was something left of Will, something that was just the same. Resting on the dry, cold cheek beneath the closed eyes lay the long and silky lashes she had often teased him about, a soft brown, fine, like those of a sleeping child. In her anguish at the thought that they would never raise again she showered passionate kisses on the wrecked, almost inhuman face of Will Broadbent.

'Will, stay ... don't leave me,' she whispered. 'I cannot manage without you, Will.' The pain overwhelmed her. She had loved him since before she was seventeen; she knew that now. In the nine years which had passed they had lost one another for a while due to her own foolish yearning for something which did not really exist. But for almost three years they had been lovers again in the truest sense of the word. She had bathed in his love, blossomed and grown in it, becoming the complete and loving woman she knew herself to be. Will, strong and lusty, sweet-tempered, good-humoured. Will, unique and irreplaceable. As she watched the disease consume him, dry him out to no more than a husk, the full devastation of what his loss would mean to her struck her a mortal blow from which she knew she would never recover. Robby had been taken from her in the most agonising way but the anguish she had known then had been nothing to what she experienced now.

She could not bear to lose him. She could not face a world without that special blend of gentleness and vitality he gave her. His ardour warmed her female body and his good-humoured wisdom cooled her wild and impulsive nature. His lively, incisive mind sharpened hers. He was positive, daring and filled with his own invincibility and she had known from the moment his amber eyes had smiled whimsically into hers that she could rely on him while he had breath in his body. Though he had laughed at the girl she was, spoken sharply, roughly, she had known instinctively that he was concerned for her, and that concern, com-

507

passion and understanding had shaped her, brought her to this moment of true and selfless love. She loved him beyond any love she had ever known. She always would.

She wanted to pray, if only she could find the words; to ask some God in whom she scarce believed not to take Will from her, and not just from her but from the world which would be the poorer without him. She wanted to, she even tried to as her tears fell on to his beloved face. But as the sun sank in the fiery furnace of the sky below the high line of the moorland and Annie moved quietly to light the candle, her tears dried up, and the words of hopeless prayer dried up.

'I won't let him die, Annie.' Her voice was like a splinter of ice. 'Dammit, I won't let him. Dear God, does he not know how much I love him?'

' 'Appen 'e don't, lass.' Annie's shadow was huge on the wall of the bedroom, moving slowly as she approached the bed.

Tessa turned to her, startled. Her own face had hollowed during the day, with deep purple fingerprints pressed beneath her eyes. She was bathed in perspiration for despite the open window the room was hot and airless and she knew she smelled sourly.

'What d'you mean? Of course he knows.'

' 'E' saw thi and thy 'usband a day or so since . . .'

'Drew . . . ?'

'Thi were up on't tops, 'e said, ridin' together like thi' 'adn't a care in t'world. Laughin', just like tha used to, you an' Master Drew, so wrapped up in one another tha didna see 'im pass thi by.'

'No . . . oh, no, Annie. No, you know that's not true.'

' 'E only knows what 'e saw, lass, an' it took the spirit from 'im. 'E must've 'ad the fever on 'im then.'

'No, I can't bear it.' She put her arms about him, lifting his heavy, lolling head from the pillow, cradling his face against her breast, rocking backwards and forwards in a frenzy of dry-eyed grief. Dear God, she had only gone with

Drew to ease his wretchedness, to reassure him that despite her obligations at the mill and to the people who depended on the Greenwood family, he was still fixed deeply and irrevocably in her heart, that she loved him and always would. He was all that was left of the bright childhood he and Pearce and herself had shared. He was in her care and she would never desert him.

Even for Will!

'Will, oh, Will, my dearest love, how can I tell you what you mean to me? You are the first breath I draw each morning and my last thought at night before I sleep. I awake with you and lie down to sleep with you in my heart. I cannot bear to think of the pain I have caused you and the pain which I know I could bring you in the future, but please, please, my darling, stay with me. Love me, keep me in the safety and shelter of your love...'

Her anguish was almost more than Annie could bear but she stood, transfixed by the love and suffering of Tessa Greenwood, unable to leave her friend to endure that suffering alone. And yet it seemed to be an intrusion to watch it, a violation of the privacy which was a sacred thing to Annie.

But still she stood, and waited.

'Will ... Will, listen to me ...' Tessa bent her head and her tears flowed again, soaking into Will's lifeless hair, washing across his forehead and thick eyebrows, from her eyes to his, dewing his eyelashes. His cheek was turned to her breast, resting there in the peaceful attitude of a sleeping child, and neither woman saw the flicker of his eyelids as the tears of the woman who loved him bathed and soothed their dryness.

'Please, Will, don't let me lose you again ... I love you so much. My need is more than I can withstand ... without you I am useless.' Her voice was broken and desperate. 'There is no one but you in my heart ... only you ...' And she buried her face in his hair and held him to her as she rocked in desolate mourning.

She felt him move then, a mere stirring of his head, a

509

tremor, but when she looked down disbelievingly into his face, his eyes, no more than dark slits, were open and aware. They were wet with tears, whether her own or his it did not matter. Her cry of joy raised Annie's bent head and when she saw the light in Will Broadbent's eyes she turned away and was torn by loud and painful weeping.

## 33

'Don't tha think tha should go 'ome, lass? Will's mekkin' good progress an' tha knows I'll look after 'im as well as tha does.'

'I can't, Annie. I simply can't bear to leave him. Not just yet. I nearly lost him, Annie, do you realise? I nearly lost him for good and I must just stay another day, or two perhaps, to make certain he really is on the mend. My ... husband is not yet home, Thomas says ...' Her manner was defiant as though daring Annie to remark on it. 'Just another day or two, Annie.'

'Nay, tis nowt' ter me, Tessa. Tha mun stay as long as tha pleases, tha knows that, but d'yer not think folk'll begin ter notice where Mrs Drew Greenwood 'as bin fer the last four days? Tha knows 'ow they talk.'

'Let them. Do you think I care what others say? They have always gossiped about me and my family so I am well used to it. Besides, you're so busy at the mill and with the Poor Law Guardians. You know Mrs Poynton and Mrs Bayly are excellent ladies with the best intentions in the world but they don't know, as you do, what is needed and from what I read in that newspaper you brought home, things are only going to get worse. That committee really needs you, Annie.

Local resources will not be able to provide for the mass of destitution which is coming. The American war is not going to end soon, as we had hoped, and relief committees will be desperately needed. So go, Annie, and let me have these few days with Will. As soon as he is able to get down the stairs I'll go home. Now show me again what I must put into that broth and then be off with you.'

It was still hot and sultry and Will had thrown back the sheet from his shrunken body when Tessa carried in the tray of delicacies she and Annie had prepared to bring his strength back. There was a bowl of steaming broth made with shin of beef and a cool egg custard with cream whipped into it. Annie had mixed up a potion of arrowroot rhubarb and honey to prevent any further onset of the debilitating diarrhoea which had drained the life from him, and linseed tea to defend the lining membrane of his stomach. Cinnamon water and syrup of poppies – all mixtures to bind to him the nourishing food which, he complained weakly, Tessa shovelled down his throat whenever he opened his mouth: veal broth, chicken broth, rice, bread pudding. Already the colour was returning to his pallid skin and the brightness to his clear brown eyes. They watched Tessa as she placed the tray upon the small pot-cupboard which stood beside the bed, following her when she moved to the window and pushed it open further in an attempt to allow in a breath of fresh air.

She was dressed in a plain cotton skirt and bodice of Annie's and her heavy hair was tied up in an old cotton duster from which slipping tendrils escaped to lie on her white neck. The dress was too small for she was taller than Annie and fuller in the breast. The buttons on the bodice strained to contain her swelling flesh and her nipples were blatantly outlined against the fabric.

'You look like a country lass, sweetheart, especially in bare feet. Where are your boots?'

'I've stopped wearing them in this heat. Besides, they don't quite match my outfit.' She smiled as she moved back to the bed, fussing with the sheet, pulling it up about his naked body, but he pushed her hand away weakly.

'Leave it, lass. I know it's not heavy but even that weight is too much for me and I'm so hot.'

'Well, get some of Annie's broth inside you and you'll soon get your strength back. No, lie back and allow me to feed you, if you please. Look at you. No more than a bit of old stick and a hank of hair.'

'Give me a day or two, Tessa Harrison, and I'll show you a bit of strength, in fact if you were to lean this way a little more and I was to undo one or two of those buttons ... See, already my power is returning ... look ... My God, woman, you could return a man from the dead. Look at me ...' And indeed his manhood which nestled unobtrusively in the dark curls of his pubic hair was stirring, albeit gently.

'Will Broadbent, you old devil, and here I am waiting on you hand and foot, giving you bed baths ...'

'And lovely they are, my darling. In fact I think I will continue to employ you for that purpose when I return home ...'

'... running here and there at your bidding ...'

'Is that so? Then I bid you get into this bed with me. Take off that fetching costume and lie beside me.'

'Well, really, Will Broadbent, I do believe this illness of yours has been a sham. I think you have been deceiving me and I can only assume it was to get me into your bed ...'

'Get in and I'll show you how ill I am.' But though he lifted his arms to her and his eyes glowed with his love he had not the strength to continue and fell back on the pillow, a slight sheen of sweat coating his body.

'The spirit is willing, is it not, my darling?' she whispered as she leaned over him. She kissed him tenderly, stroking his thin face with gentle hands, his throat and chest, her love for him shining like a bright candle in the dim bedroom. 'But you must be patient. Eat this broth and custard and then sleep. Another few days, my lusty lover, and then you and I will busy ourselves with such things as you have never even imagined.' She continued to kiss him, her mouth sweet and moist, her tongue parting his lips. He groaned in delight and despair.

'You're a wicked woman, Tessa Harrison, a wicked woman. You tell me to be patient and not to become aroused by all the abundant flesh which is erupting out of that ... that thing you have on, and then you kiss me like a wanton and suggest all kinds of delights to come. You have the most beautiful breasts, d'you know that? Of course you do or you would not be displaying them to me. Oh, Tessa, Tessa, soon, my love, soon.' He grinned audaciously, his eyes telling her exactly what he would do to her soon. 'But in the meanwhile give me some of that bloody custard.'

They continued their delightful and loving diversion for another hour, lovers, enchanted with this feast of the love which they had almost lost. It had become infinitely more precious because of that danger and though Will was still weak, they were unwilling to part to allow him the restful sleep he needed to regain his strength. Tessa was content to do no more than sit beside him, to watch him sleep, to hold his hand when he awoke, to laugh softly and whisper the bewitching nonsense which lovers cherish and which she sensed was so important to him now. She could not forget what Annie had told her and though she knew she could not discard her obligation to Drew nor go back to erase the pain she had caused Will on that day on the moors, she was aware that she must treat him and his love for her with infinite care. He was made vulnerable, not just by his illness but by the threat to him inherent in her care and love for her husband. She must protect, shelter and support him until he had regained his full vigour again, as he had always sustained her.

'Sleep now, darling,' she whispered, holding his thin hand to her cheek. 'I will be here when you awake.'

'Promise me.'

'You know I will. I won't move an inch.'

Drew Greenwood rode with a clatter into the stable yard, dismounted and threw the reins to Walter.

'Nice day, Walter,' he said cheerfully. 'A bit warm but very pleasant as I came over the moor. The carriage will be along presently with my boxes. Make arrangements to have them sent up, will you?'

'Aye, sir.' Walter touched his cap before leading the bay away, turning to watch over his shoulder as his master strode across the cobbles and disappeared through the side door of the house. Well, thank God, he himself didn't work in the house, he thought, as he rubbed the horse's nose. There'd be hell to pay in about five minutes, at his guess. He stopped in the doorway of the stable, holding the bay's head, and Percy, who was applying polish to one of a number of saddles, looked up at him as though reading his mind.

'I'd not unsaddle that bay if I was you, Walter,' he said quietly.

''Appen tha right, Percy.'

Drew was whistling as he entered his wife's bedroom, not yet aware of the absolute silence which pervaded almost every room in the big house. Housemaids and parlourmaids, busy about their duties, stopped and looked apprehensively at one another and in the housekeeper's sitting-room Mr Briggs and Mrs Shepherd exchanged significant glances. Even the gardeners turned to look up at the opened windows as though some message was being sent through the still air.

Laurel Greenwood was pouring tea into fine china teacups ready to hand them to the maid who would pass them to her callers. It had been a most trying afternoon for each one had been bursting, positively bursting, that was the word she would have used, to discuss her sister-in-law's scandalous behaviour – was she never to stop scandalising the Penfold Valley? And what would she say on the matter if they should be ill-bred enough to bring it up? She just

514

prayed they wouldn't, though it would have been pleasant to pour out her own outrage at the way in which her sister-in-law continued to flout convention. She lifted her head to listen as her brother's quick footsteps sounded in the hall and the three ladies who were seated with her exchanged glances, vicariously thrilled to be here at this dramatic moment. Surely they were to witness one of the valley's greatest scandals since Kit Chapman had married Joss Greenwood some thirty years ago?

Only in the schoolroom did life go on just as it did every day, calmly and quietly as Laurel and Charlie Greenwood's younger children obediently learned their lessons.

The bell rang in the kitchen and poor Emma who had been backed up against a wall, her face as white as her own frilled apron, gave a small moan. Every maid there sighed in dreadful sympathy since it was not one of them who would now have to face Master Drew.

'Emma, up you go, if you please. The master has rung the bell in Mrs Greenwood's bedroom. Can you not see it?'

'Oh, please, Mr Briggs . . .'

'I'm sorry, Emma.' Even Mr Briggs pitied her for the devastation which was to fall about her ears.

'He'll kill me, Mr Briggs.'

'Don't be silly, Emma. And I'll be here . . . if needed.'

He was striding about the pretty bedroom when Emma opened the door in answer to his shout to come in. A pale little mouse, she seemed, thrown into the arena with a snarling monster which turned on her the moment her head peeped round the door.

'Where is my wife, Emma?' the monster roared. 'Goddammit, it *is* Sunday so she cannot give the excuse that she's needed at the bloody mill. I go away *alone* for a bit of shooting, giving in to her insistence that the whole of the Penfold Valley would grind to a halt without her, so surely it is not too much to ask that she be here to greet me on my return?'

'No, sir, but it's . . . it's Friday, sir . . .'

'Friday! Is it?' He looked confused and an uncertain

515

expression clouded his infuriated blue eyes and for a blessed moment Emma believed that the crisis had been averted. She even allowed herself to move an inch or two further into the room. Miss Tessa had been gone for four days and nights so surely she would be home from . . . Oh, dear Lord . . . from that cottage today and perhaps, if she were to come soon, the master might be persuaded to calm down. But she might have known it could not be so.

'Well, it makes no difference. She knew I was to return today and promised to be here when I did. Confound it, Emma, where in damnation is she?'

'I . . . I don't know, sir.'

'You don't know! Good God, woman, you're her bloody maid! Does she not tell you where she is to go?' He clapped a hand to his brow and turned to the window, staring out over the garden as though she might appear, *should* appear at any moment. 'I suppose she's fussing round those damned peasants she thinks so much about. Making them soup and egg custards and pampering them into believing that it is their right to be fed so royally. Does she never think of her own family, Emma, and what they might need?'

'I don't know, I'm sure, sir.' Emma clung to the frame of the door, ready to dart into the hallway should Master Drew make a move she did not care for. She was aware that Mr Briggs stood motionless at the foot of the stairs and would be up them at the trot should she need him. They were all of them very wary of their master's uncertain temper, sweet and cheerful one minute and running out of control the next. One day, in his remorseless ride towards destruction, he would take anybody with him who got in his way.

Drew turned sharply and the full light of the sun fell about him. He was dressed like a young lord: the finest breeches of pale cream doeskin, well cut and extremely expensive; a shirt of soft cambric, frilled at the front, and long boots called Wellingtons or Napoleons, after those two famous generals who had once worn them. He had discarded his jacket in the dull, throbbing heat of the afternoon and he

516

was bare-headed, but for the first time Emma noticed the puffiness about his eyes, the slight slackening of the flesh beneath his jawline and the discontented droop to his well-shaped mouth. He wore a full moustache now, scorning the long Dundreary side whiskers which were the mode, saying they made him look like an old man. He was handsome still, able to turn any maiden's heart in her breast, but the look of dissipation was clearly etched in his face.

'Where is she, Emma?' he said irritably, his previous good humour completely gone. 'Is she at the mill?'

'Oh, no, sir, not today,' Emma replied then could have bitten her tongue for now she must reveal to her master where his wife was, or find some decent lie to protect her. 'At least, she ... well, I know she was ...'

'Now then, Emma, stop blethering like some old sheep. All I need to know is my wife's whereabouts and then I can go and fetch her home. Surely that is not too hard, even for you?'

'No, sir, but I can't rightly say ...'

'Is she at the blasted Relief Committee thing then? Speak up and come into the room instead of hanging about in the damned doorway.'

'Oh, sir ... please, sir ...' Emma began to weep because, really, she didn't know what to say. It was nothing to do with her and whatever she said she'd be in the wrong. She couldn't tell the master where Miss Tessa was, could she, and yet he'd not be satisfied until he had the truth.

'Now what's the matter, for God's sake? There's no need to blubber, is there? Or is there? What is it?' He strode across the room, his face pinched and suddenly suspicious and Emma shrank away from him, lifting her arm to protect herself for surely he was going to strike her. His eyes had turned the dark and stormy blue which heralded one of his wild tempers and Emma squeaked in terror as he pulled her savagely into the room. 'Where is she, dammit? You're hiding something, aren't you? Covering up for her. Where the bloody hell is she?' He shook her like a terrier shaking a rat and Emma's head flopped about on her neck and her pretty fluted cap fell to the floor.

'Oh, sir ... please, it's nothing to do with me, sir ... please...'

'What hasn't?' His suffused face was an inch from hers.

'She sent a message and Thomas took...'

Drew Greenwood became unnaturally still, his face quite expressionless but in his eyes was a look which his wife, if she had been there, would have instantly recognised. A fox has it when the pack closes in, or a deer which finally knows that he can run no more, that the hunters at his back have worn him down and he can go no further.

'Where is she, Emma?' This time his voice told her he would stand no more prevarication. He had himself under control, but only just. Something had happened whilst he was away and he was quite terrified of it even though he had no idea what it was; something he had dreaded for years, ever since he had come back from the Crimea. No matter how many times he had ridden away from her, hell-bent on danger and damning the consequences, he had always known she would be there, waiting for him, when he came back; loving him always, controlling the outrageous rashness with which he frightened even himself, but which he seemed incapable of overcoming; ready to hold him in her arms until he was steady again.

Today she was not here. Today was the day he had known would come. Today he was finally alone.

'Where is she?' he said quietly, hopelessly. 'Tell me or I'll break your bloody neck.'


They were laughing, the three of them, as they almost tumbled down the awkward stairs into Annie's kitchen. Will was dressed in a clean shirt and breeches but had no shoes on his feet and Tessa had stepped on his toes with her high-heeled boots.

'Watch where you're going, woman, and don't push me,

518

Annie. Give me a minute to get my breath, after all I *am* an invalid and this is my first time downstairs.'

'Dear God, are we to have this wail of self pity every time you move that lazy frame of yours, Will Broadbent? See, lean on me and hold on to the table . . . there, the chair is right behind you . . .'

'Christ, I had no idea I was so weak.'

'An' I'll 'ave none o' that language in my kitchen, if yer please. Now, sit thissen down, lad, an' I'll get thi a glass o' milk.'

'Confound it, not milk again, Annie. I'll have it coming out of my ears at this rate.'

'Never you mind, Will Broadbent. It'll put some o' that flesh back on thi bones an' a bit o' strength in thi legs, then 'appen th'll be able ter see to thissen. Tha'll not be leavin' 'ere fer a week or two yet so just get that down yer an' 'ave less ter say.'

'D'you mean I am to have you bullying me for another week?' But he obediently drank the milk, his eyes on Tessa, his whole demeanour, though striving to be cheerful and determinedly resigned to her going, telling her that he didn't know how he was to manage without her. His heart was in his eyes, loving her, worshipping her, begging her to stay with him, to keep them together as they had been in the last few days though his mind told him she must go. She was dressed in the gown she had worn to the makeshift hospital in Ashton Lane. Thomas was to call for her in an hour and their life was to go on, hers and Will's, just as it had done before his illness. He could remember the desolation which had claimed him only a week ago when he had come across her and her husband as they roistered over the tops. He had thought her to be fickle, empty and fit for nothing but the life she led with Drew Greenwood, a woman who could play with two men and thrive on it, but now he knew the width and depth of her love for him. She had had no need to explain to him what she had been doing up there, where she had been going on that day. There was no need for disclosures between them, nor avowals of eternal love.

His head and his heart were clear now and ready to absorb the full and lovely gift of her complete devotion. What they would do tomorrow, next week, or next year he did not know. She loved him. She had risked her life, her health, her marriage, her reputation for him and in future he would accept from her only what she could give him of herself. His eyes told her so and she smiled, understanding.

'I must go, my darling.'

'I know.'

'I will come as soon as I am able.'

'I know you will. Perhaps . . .' But she knelt before him placing her fingertips against his lips. He kissed them gently and Annie turned away, leaving them to their farewell. Will was looking into Tessa's face and the two women had their backs to the door when it opened, only the sudden shaft of sunlight which streamed across the kitchen telling them that someone stood in the doorway.

Annie was the first to turn and the empty glass she held fell from her fingers to shatter on the stone floor. She uttered no sound but every drop of colour drained from her face, even from her lips. She put out her hand in some gesture of defence, aimed, she was aware, at Tessa and Will, the two people she loved best in the world, but the man in the doorway had eyes for no one but the couple by the fireplace. Tessa had turned, still on her knees and when Drew Greenwood lunged, whether at her or the man she had been kissing, Annie was not sure, she fell back awkwardly against the brass fender. He said nothing, her husband. He was completely silent which was the more terrifying since always before his rages had been loud and explosive, strident with his runaway temper. He kicked her to one side as she tried to scramble to her feet and his hands, strong and brown and lethal, reached for Will Broadbent's throat. They circled it, sinking deep into the loose flesh which had come with Will's illness. Drew's face was contorted, livid and snarling and his eyes were narrowed, a dark and vicious blue. Though Will put up his hands to grip his attacker's wrists he was no match for the younger, more vigorous man. He had been ill and though he was making a steady recovery, his body was weakened, frail still, his enormous strength and power melted away by the fever.

'*Drew.*' Her scream was chilling, high and filled with despair. Like some old, old woman whose age has taken her spirit and whose strength is too frail to lift her, Tessa scrabbled on the floor, reaching with desperate hands to find some purchase on her husband's steel-like legs. She could hear Will's breath choke in his closing throat then it was cut off and the silence contained nothing but Drew's frantic gasping and the drumming of Will's feet on the floor.

'Annie . . .' Still she tried to lift herself, to drag Drew away but he was maddened to brute strength and nothing could break the grip of his fingers about Will's throat. She watched in absolute horror as one of Will's hands dropped slowly to the arm of the chair, then fell to hang limply beside her face.

'Hit him, Annie' she screamed, but Annie was paralysed with shock and Tessa knew, quite calmly now, that she was the only one who could stop Drew Greenwood from killing Will Broadbent. She was the only one who could save his life.

Save him for the second time in a week, she remembered thinking incredulously, then her hand found the heavy brass poker and with her strength renewed she brought it up, then down again and across Drew Greenwood's forearms. She distinctly heard the bones snap and her husband screamed before he fell away, stumbling back against the table, then back again to the doorway through which he had come.

'Tessa . . .' His voice was no more than a whisper. His eyes were on her, huge and clouded, not just with pain and shock but with despair. The rage had gone and the madness, and there remained only a childish uncertainty, a need for her to tell him that she was there, as she had always been there and that he had only to hold out his arms to her and she would fly into them as she had always done.

But he couldn't lift his arms. There was something wrong

521

with them and so she had turned to the man in the chair and was holding him instead.

Blindly he turned into the sullen heat and smoky sunshine and began to run.

The men found him wandering along the track towards Badger's Edge, muttering and already feverish, his useless arms hanging limply at his side.

'Come along, Mr Drew,' Walter said gently, putting a hand on his master's shoulder since they had been told to be careful of his arms which had suffered a serious injury.

'Who is it?' his master said, swinging away wildly, then crying out with the pain of his flailing arms.

'Tis Walter, sir.'

'Walter? What are you doing up here?'

'Us 'ave come ter fetch thi 'ome, sir. Tis gettin' dark an' thi'll not be able ter see thi 'and in front of thi face afore long.'

'No, indeed. I had not noticed ... It has got dark, hasn't it?'

'Aye, sir.'

'And who is that with you?'

'Tis only Percy an' Jack, Mr Drew.'

'But where is my bay, Walter? I cannot return without my bay.'

'Er ... 'e come 'ome a while since, sir. You were throwed.'

'Never, not me, not me, eh Pearce?' and he laughed boisterously over his shoulder into the darkness.

The three men stood about him warily. He had fallen, Mrs Greenwood had said, thrown from his bay in the street outside Miss Beale's cottage in Edgeclough but had immediately regained his feet and run away. It sounded daft to them but who were they to argue? There were some funny things going on these days at Greenacres what with Miss Tessa away up at that mill when not so long since she'd hated the very sight of it, same as him. And what was she doing at Annie Beale's place with Annie no better than a common

522

mill-worker, and in the company of Mr Broadbent who had once been an overlooker?

Still, it was nowt to do with them. They were used to Mr Drew and Miss Tessa and their wild ways and had become accustomed to their strange and unconventional behaviour. Find him and bring him home, they had been told. Look in the direction of Badger's Edge or Friar's Mere for they were the most likely places he would be. And here he was, and poorly by the sound of him.

He wandered along beside them, laughing over something he seemed to hear on the still, warm air. He talked all the time incoherently, and his dead brother's name was constantly on his lips. They tried to help him, even to carry him for he kept straying off the track and was difficult to lead back, but he screamed when they touched him.

It was midnight when they met the carriage on Reddygate Way, just where the edge of town spilled out on to the moors. They managed to get him inside and home to his wife who was waiting on the steps at the front of the house. 'Darling, there you are,' they heard her say, then Hibberson and Mr Briggs were there, and old Doctor Ellison since Doctor Salter was still busy at the warehouse in Ashton Lane which was now a hospital, it was said.

Doctor Ellison strapped up his arms, considerably surprised at the suddenness with which his patient had changed from incoherent delirium to an almost trance-like state, scarcely seeming to notice the pain he must be suffering. And the watery loosening of his bowels was not quite normal, nor the dramatic onset of vomiting. Drew Greenwood's face had become cool and withered, drawn almost, and his pulse was too faint for the doctor's liking.

'We must try to get some fluid into him, Mrs Greenwood, and do go and lie down yourself for a while . . .' His patient's wife looked none too strong herself. 'Let your servants clean up this . . .' He indicated the foul-smelling man on the bed whom his wife was trying frantically to keep clean. 'I shall remain in the house, naturally.'

At some time during the night, Tessa could not have said when exactly since she must have dozed, she found Laurel standing next to Drew's bed, her hand on his brow, her face pale and worried.

'He seems to be cooler,' she whispered when she saw Tessa's eyes on her. 'Do you think it means he is about to come out of this ... this ... ?' She could not seem to find the word to describe the strange state her brother was in.

'I hope so, Laurel,' Tessa said softly and though her pity for him put truth on her lips she could not help but wonder what was to happen when he did.

'Would he drink some of this lemon wine Mary Abbott sent over with her coachman? It is thought to be strengthening and the doctor said he was to have fluids.' Laurel placed the tray on which was a cut-glass jug containing a pale lemon liquid and three glasses on the bedside table.

'He seems to be sleeping and I shouldn't wake him but perhaps I might try some. I'm dreadfully thirsty.'

'I might join you.' Laurel poured them each a glass of the cordial in which ice chinked and as they sipped it they watched over the mumbling, restless man on the bed. They finished the jug between them and the last thing Tessa remembered was the quiet click of the door as Laurel left the room.

The pestilence, carried in the water from which the kind Mary Abbott had brewed her refreshing lemon wine and which was to kill four of her own household began its secret and deadly work during the night.

It was about noon the next day when Tessa began to hallucinate. She distinctly saw her mother in the doorway, her face stern and disapproving, and behind her Charlie told Tessa that it was no use in arguing, someone must mind the mills. She stood up then, leaving the flushed and mumbling figure on the bed, and moved to the window. She was surprised to find it standing wide open since she felt so terribly hot. She really must change her dress for it was wet through

524

with something which had soaked right into the fine cream foulard and it clung to her skin most disagreeably. She lurched back to the bed and placed a trembling hand on Drew's brow but could not make up her mind whether it felt cooler or if perhaps the extreme warmth of her own skin only made it seem so. And she felt so nauseous. She really ought to eat something, she supposed, since she was quite light-headed. When had she eaten last? She couldn't remember. Perhaps if she asked Pearce who had just sat down beside Drew if he would stay with him for a while she would go down to the kitchen ... or should she ring the bell to summon Emma? No, Uncle Joss and Aunt Kit stood in the shadows and ...

It was some time later, she couldn't have said how long, when she found herself on the floor, her cheek pressed into some foul-smelling stickiness on the carpet. Lord, she felt dreadful. So hot and tired. She'd just lie here for a while and then she'd get up and give ... Who was it on the bed who tossed so fretfully? ... Pearce? ... Drew? ... She didn't care really but whoever it was would need a drink. If only Laurel would stop shrieking about the fever and God striking some-one dead for bringing it into the house to threaten the chil-dren ... Who ... who were the children? ... Robert? ... Her head hurt so she could barely think ... and where was Will? Her dear Will ... she wanted Will, his arms about her to help her up and keep her steady ... Will ... Will ...

It was delightfully cool when she awoke, clean and cool. She was in her own bed and though she felt amazingly weak her mind was clear and at peace. She had memories, small and puzzling, like pieces of glass which have shattered and fallen, jumbled, and though she knew what they were, they would not fit into an exact and recognisable shape.

Her mother had been here, many times, weeping. Why? she had thought since it was not like her mother to weep, leaning over her, touching her face and smoothing her hair back from her forehead as she had never known her to do before. And Annie. She could recall awakening to find her in the chair beside the bed, in the dark of the night, the firelight playing on her dozing face, thinner than Tessa remembered her. What on earth was she doing here, she had thought, quite astonished, for Annie had so much to do on the Relief Committee and with the Poor Law Guardians.

And had she dreamed that Emma had been at her bedside, spooning some stuff, milky and sweet, into her mouth, cross with her when she refused to open her lips, begging her to try, to be a good girl and try? Emma had cried, her head on her bent arms on the side of the bed, her face tired, thin and drawn. And Dorcas. Good, sensible Dorcas had been heaping up the fire with coal though it was so hot Tessa thought she had died and gone to hell.

It was like fighting a way through cobwebs, but perhaps the sharpest, sweetest, most disturbing dream had been about Will. He had leaned over her and kissed her. Many times. Warm, comforting, safe. He had never wept like the others but bore her up to a place which delighted her; a place in which he and she had shared moments of truth and beauty. His amber-flecked eyes had smiled and his hands were strong in hers. He had spoken softly to her, bringing her peace and she had slept in the shelter of his arms.

The light from the sky beyond her window was a pale green, the clear aftermath of an evening sunset. She thought she heard the whinny of a horse and the answering call from another. She turned her head and there was Emma, a newspaper in her hand, no longer weeping as Tessa had last seen her, but calm and at peace. Tessa smiled and wondered what her maid was doing reading at her bedside, ready to tease her for it, to make her jump guiltily. And where was Drew in the midst of all this tranquillity? Perhaps it was his bay she had heard a moment ago and soon he would come bursting into the bedroom, striding across the room to lounge indolently at her side, sending Emma shrieking to the kitchen.

But he did not come.

'Where is Mr Drew, Emma?' she asked, but Emma did not lift her head from her absorption in the newspaper.

'Where is Mr Drew, Emma?' she asked again, shouted, she thought, and this time Emma looked up and the most amazing thing happened. Emma stared speechlessly, her mouth open, her wide eyes beginning to leak tears. Tessa felt a small prick of exasperation for, really, there was no need to be so dramatic. It was a simple question needing only a simple answer: "He has gone up to the Hall," or "He is downstairs, shall I fetch him?" But Emma sat speechless and motionless just as though Tessa had caught her out in some dreadful act of which she was utterly ashamed.

'Miss Tessa?' she said, or rather, asked, as though she was not awfully sure. Her hand reached out vaguely in the direction of the bed.

'Of course, Emma. Who else?' The words were tart and came out of her mouth in somewhat of a croak, surprising her. She swallowed and her mouth was dry.

'Oh, Miss Tessa, darling . . .' With a great surge of apparent heartache which she could no longer contain, Emma sank down to kneel beside the bed, weeping as though her heart really was split in two. She sobbed and sobbed, her face buried in the smooth white counterpane, her neatly capped head bobbing with the intensity of her weeping.

Tessa was astounded. Surely there was no need to be quite so distraught? What on earth was the matter with the girl, for goodness' sake? Perhaps she herself was the reason for Emma's mournfulness. Had she been ill? Was that why Emma was weeping so grievously? Whatever it was Emma was dreadfully upset.

'Emma, for God's sake girl, calm yourself, and get me up.'

'Oh, Miss Tessa . . .'

'Never mind, "oh, Miss Tessa". Get me up,' she ordered. This time Emma raised her head, bemused it seemed and quite unable to do more than stare in wonderment at her mistress's face.

'Get me up, Emma, or fetch someone who can. I appear to be dreadfully weak.'

'Oh Miss Tessa, oh, lass, if you knew how we've prayed for this moment. We thought we'd lost you ...'

'Lost me? What the devil are you talking about, girl?' Her voice was irritable and she seemed unable to manage more than a hoarse whisper.

'Miss Tessa, if you only knew ...'

'Knew what, Emma? For heaven's sake, don't stand there blubbering. Go and fetch my husband. Oh, and I'll have some hot buttered muffins, I think, Emma. For some reason I have an enormous appetite.'

They came to tell her then that her husband was dead and had taken his sister, Laurel Greenwood, to the grave with him.

## 34

'I cannot see him, Annie, and that is an end to it. We have nothing to say to one another.'

'Will's got plenty ter say ter thee, lass, an' 'e'll not rest while 'e's said it. Thi' can't treat 'im like this, Tessa, an' I thought thi was fair-minded enough ter see it. It's not Will's fault what 'appened.'

'No, but it's mine and I cannot just take up our ... our relationship as though nothing had occurred. I brought the cholera from Will to Drew and it killed him and not only him, but Laurel. I have made five children motherless and I will never forgive myself. Do you think I can simply go back to being the woman I was before it happened? I know it was not Will's fault that he passed the fever through me to Drew and Laurel, any more than it was the fault of the man or woman who brought it to Crossfold in the first place, but it was me, Tessa Greenwood, who carried it into this house. It was my ... my connection with Will which brought my husband to your cottage and to his ultimate death ... and ... and Laurel to hers. I am not blaming Will, nor punishing him as you seem to think. I am saying, and you must tell him, that I am no longer the woman he loved. I have nothing to give him. I want nothing from him only his acceptance of it. We are two different people now, Annie. I must look after the welfare of my nieces and nephews. I have the mills to run and the people in them who have been thrown out of work by the cotton famine need my support. They need what I can give them. I have nothing left for Will.'

The words were spoken dispassionately but with a firmness and strength which left no doubt that Tessa believed exactly what she was saying. She was dressed in the deepest black of mourning, severe and unadorned. Even her hair, heavy and sliding with glossy health, was strained back from her pale face and confined in a black chenille net. She was thin still from her recent illness, her breasts, once so full and womanly, reduced to the slender proportions of an immature girl. Her grey eyes were shadowed and almost colourless, without expression as she looked out of her study window to the autumn garden beyond.

It was almost the end of October and a cold and early winter was forecast. Gone was the sullen heat of the late summer and with it the illness which had so swiftly struck the town of Crossfold. Two weeks had passed and no new cases had been reported, Annie had told her, and Doctor Salter was to close up the temporary hospital in Ashton Lane since there was no further need of it. Laurel Greenwood and, strangely, several members of the Abbott family had been the last cholera victims to die.

The trees were almost bare now. The late October sun was very bright on the magnificent gold, copper and bronze of the leaves some of which still clung to their branches. Others fell in bright, twisting spirals, covering the grass in a multi-coloured carpet. A couple of gardeners raked them vigorously and continuously, collecting them in piles ready for burning. From beyond the kitchen garden a fine thread of woodsmoke rose into the clear air and the lovely but poignant smell, proclaiming the end of summer and bleakness of winter to come, drifted through the partly opened study window.

In the far distance, way beyond the boundary wall of Greenacres, stretched the endless grandeur of the moorland. The deepest green of summer was changing to the brown of autumn. The heather which was a dense purple in July was taking on its November shades of umber, puce and sienna and above it all the pale, transparent blue of the sky reached out its loveliness as though calling to the woman who stood impassively at the window and who once would have answered with a whoop of joy. Once she would have called for her mare who now stood sadly in the stable and ridden out to meet the beauty which lay all around her.

Annie sat straight-backed in the leather chair beside the glowing fire, the comfort of it in no way tempting her to lean back and relax. It was a pleasant room, completely masculine for it had been designed over eight decades ago for James Chapman, the great-grandfather of the man who had recently been buried. Since those early days two generations of the same family had sat at the splendid desk and now it belonged to Tessa Greenwood whose husband, the fourth generation, had never entered the room unless forced to it. This was the Tessa Greenwood in whose veins no Chapman blood ran; the Tessa Greenwood whose mother had been a 'pauper brat' come from some unknown workhouse with a cartload of others nearly sixty years ago.

It was a snug and intimate room, comfortable with a log fire, the walls lined with books and sporting prints. There were rods and guns, with a chest for fishing flies and a herbarium cupboard for though neither James nor his son Barker Chapman had been sportsmen they had liked the notion of adorning their study as though they were. But mainly it was a working room with functional furniture for the keeping of papers relating to the running of Greenacres and the estate. There were several oil lamps, a drum table, a fine inkstand, winged leather chairs and beside the fire a round table with several of the latest newspapers scattered on it.

Tessa turned away from the window and moved slowly across the room, seating herself on the opposite side of the fire. Her face was expressionless. It was as though the life, the fire, the warmth had been extinguished inside her, leaving behind a passive, unfeeling shell. Still lovely, she possessed an ethereal fragility which was the direct opposite of the tempestuous, undisciplined, carelessly warm-hearted girl she once had been and inside Annie Beale something ached for the loss of that girl.

'Tis no good 'iding, lass. 'E'll get in ter see thi one way or t'other, choose how. Tha knows Will, or should by now. 'E reckons thi owes 'im at least a chance ter say 'is piece an' no matter 'ow many times 'e's turned away by them footmen o' yours, or that chap you 'ave on't gate at Chapmanstown, 'e'll find a way ter do it. 'Appen tha don't want ter see 'im again. That's thy affair an' nowt ter do wi' me but yer mun tell 'im so to 'is face.'

'I cannot see him, Annie.'

'Then tha's a coward.'

'Maybe. Does it matter?'

'It does ter Will.'

'I'm sorry but I cannot help the way I feel. What Will and I had ... did ... was wrong. And now ... I am paying for it, not with my own loss though that was grievous enough for I loved Drew dearly, but through what I have done to Laurel and Charlie's children. Good God, if I spend the rest of my days trying to be to them what Laurel and Charlie were, it would not be enough. I cannot forget that it was what I ...'

'Give over, Tess. Can thi not see it couldn't be thee, or if it was tha could have fetched it from anyone in't mill, or from Ashton Lane ...?'

'But I didn't. It was from Will that Drew and Laurel, and

myself, contracted the fever. And I was the only one to survive.'

'Dammit, lass . . .' The oath on Annie's lips was so completely out of character that Tessa turned her head sharply, tearing her haunted gaze away from the burning logs in the fireplace. Her lips parted in surprise, then the corners of her mouth lifted in a half-smile though the unequivocal expression in her eyes did not alter.

'Annie, really, whatever next! I have never heard you swear before.'

'Never mind that, my lass. Tha's enough ter make a saint swear. Can yer not see what tha's doing ter thissen? Tha's tekkin' on the blame fer summat that's not tha fault. An' not only that, tha's relishing it. Oh, aye, thi are. It meks tha feel better ter blame thissen, though God only knows why. An' yer can tekk that hoity-toity look off thi face an' listen ter me fer a minute fer I mean to 'ave me say.'

Tessa stood up without warning, ready to turn away, to ring the bell for Briggs to show her visitor out, but Annie gripped her arm fiercely.

'What's up, lass? Are thi afraid o't truth? No? Then sit thi down an' 'ear what I have ter say.'

'Very well, but I can assure you it will make no difference.'

'Right, then it'll do no 'arm ter listen.' Annie leaned forward earnestly, her plain and awkward face lit with the strength of her sincerity.

'I bin 'elpin' Doctor Salter clear up the 'ospital in Ashton Lane . . .'

'Dear Lord, Annie! Don't you have enough to do with the Relief Committee?'

'What I do wi' me time is my business. Now listen, lass. I 'ad a word wi't doctor an' though there's not a lot known about the cholera, from what 'e's seen this last couple o' months 'e reckons thy 'usband couldn't 'ave tekken it from Will. *Tha* did for thi were with 'im when the fever were at its worst but 'e ses Mr Greenwood must 'ave 'ad it when 'e come to't cottage. There were no way 'e could've developed it so fast and died

532

so soon. Now I know it comes swift an' tekks 'em off swift . . .
I'm sorry, lass,' she sighed as Tessa's face spasmed in pain,
'but I mun mekk yer see the sense of it.'

'And what about Laurel? Who gave it to her?'

Annie sat back uncertainly and studied the cold, unbelieving face of Tessa Greenwood and it was clear from the
expression in her own eyes that she did not know how to
answer the question. Laurel Greenwood was the last person
on God's earth to put herself in a position which might
bring her into contact with the persons who inhabited the
abominable hovels at the back of Jagger Lane. As far as Annie
knew she had not stirred beyond the confines of her own
home ever since the dread word 'fever' had been mentioned
in the town. Greenacres was situated some distance from
Crossfold and though she had still received callers they too
lived out of town and only mixed with their own kind.

'So you see, Annie, you don't have the answers, do you?'
Tessa continued sadly. 'Someone brought the fever to this
house and killed my husband and sister-in-law and who
could it have been but myself?'

Her days were full for which she thanked, not God – for
how could she possibly believe in Him after what had happened to Drew, to Pearce, to Laurel and to Charlie? – but
the fates which, through these very deaths, filled her days
from five in the morning until midnight with the demands
of her business and her new family. Though less than half
of the cotton imported at the start of 1861 was now coming
into the country, barely enough to keep her operatives at
their machines for more than a day or so a week and sometimes not even that, yet she was at the mill on most days
before the factory bell rang and did not leave until the last
worker had gone. She was in constant touch with her agent
in Liverpool but all that was available was low-grade cotton
from India, Chile and the West Indies and every other cotton
manufacturer in Lancashire was after that.

Many of her competitors had already given up, preferring

to escape whilst they still had a sovereign or two in their pockets rather than lose even those. All the major ports in the southern states in America were stoppered up tighter than a cork in a bottle by squadrons of the Union navy and the flow of raw cotton which escaped the blockade had become no more than a trickle. The distress in the cotton towns was appalling. In Preston, Blackburn, Crossfold, Manchester, whole families were starving and men to whom the word 'relief' was the foulest imaginable, seeing their wives and children reduced to skin and bone, went cap in hand to claim it. Towns once filled with the cheerful clangour of clogs on cobbles, the factory bell and the bustle and noise of steam engines, became populated by wraiths who slipped along quiet, empty streets without a sound as they searched for nourishment for their empty bellies.

In an effort to draw attention to their plight, spinners and weavers, carders and piecers from all over Lancashire somehow gained the strength to march from Stalybridge to London and even, on arrival, to entertain the sympathetic London folk to a concert of brass-band music. Best brass bands in the country, the northerner proudly reckoned he had, and if it gave them at Westminster summat to think on, then the arduous march had not been wasted.

Tessa grew thinner as she shared herself amongst these people who, though they had done their best to be self-sufficient and proudly, fiercely independent, could no longer feed their own children. She and Annie bullied committees into giving further help, if not with money then in relief tickets which could be exchanged for bread and flour, for clothing and bedding, rent and firing for the weather was becoming increasingly colder. They went to every businessman in towns as far apart as Lancaster in the North to Northwich in Cheshire; from Liverpool in the west to Leeds in Yorkshire, to beg help, financial help for distressed operatives. Lord Derby, at the Lancashire County Meetings spoke of the estimated £200,000 distributed by private charities. The landed gentry had rallied to help those in need, even Squire Longworth himself, who had been much affected by the death of his son's close friend and the bravery of his tragic widow, the once magnificent Mrs Tessa Greenwood.

And in the ever-increasing claims on her day she must find some time for the children who had fallen, with the death of their mother, into her care. She discovered that she scarcely knew them. Though they had lived together under the same roof with her ever since the eldest, Robert, was born fourteen years ago, they had been no more than diminutive figures seen walking sedately in the garden in the care of their nanny, well scrubbed and starched little ladies and gentlemen who presented themselves to their mother for an hour each evening in the drawing-room. She dimly remembered a shriek or two of natural childish laughter when their father had been alive but since then it was as though they were small ghosts, misted and silent, moving on the periphery of her disinterested mind, for what had they to do with her?

Robert and eleven-year-old Henry both attended the local grammar school, taken there each morning in the carriage by Thomas and returned the same way in the late afternoon. They were polite, respectful and serious, determined, it seemed, not to allow this tall lady in black who, amazingly, turned out to be their Aunt Tessa whom both remembered as rather fun, to see their confusion. Anne and Jane who came between the boys were small replicas of their mother with her fine, red-gold hair and dainty prettiness. Even at twelve and thirteen years of age they were too taken up with their own destiny in life which, of course, was to be the wives of well-to-do and important husbands, to be much concerned with the woman who had just lost hers.

Only Joel at six years old seemed inclined to be tearful, glad of her interest in him and willing to be her friend. Nanny stood in their midst, the one totally unchanging fixture in their young lives, getting old now and not really needed but still ruling the nursery and the schoolroom where the girls and Joel spent their day.

Tessa, in those first weeks after the funeral, did her best, if not to take her place, at least to stand as substitute for Laurel but she was herself too deep in shock and despair at her loss and too overcome by guilt to do more than visit the schoolroom in the evening before dinner, to smile painfully and ask them how they were. One day, she promised herself, she would take them riding, up on to the high tops where she and her cousins had been as children, teach them to love the rich moorland as she and Pearce and Drew had done. One day when she was . . . recovered – would she ever be that? – when she had put her disintegrated life together again, she would do it. Until then she did all she could to give them a sense of continuity and shelter in their shaken world.

Her grieving in private was terrible and tearing and she knew, deep inside her where no one but herself could see, that it was not for Drew that she mourned but for Will Broadbent. It was six weeks now since she had torn herself from his arms, climbing into her carriage and frantically urging Thomas to take her back to Greenacres. Six weeks since his bloodshot eyes had stared out from the waxen pallor of his face and his bruised throat had worked convulsively as he tried to speak her name.

But he was dead to her now, just as Drew was dead and she must put him away from her, put away his memory as the memory of all those who, though cherished in the heart, are gently laid to rest. She loved him still, that she admitted to herself, but that too would die and in the meanwhile she would wear her widow's weeds, for him as much as for Drew. Somehow she would survive. Somehow.

She became even thinner, like a stick she was, or a black and graceful wand and so withdrawn when she was not at her mills that it was hard to get a word from her, Emma reported tearfully to the rest of the sympathetic servants. She did not weep, not even at the double funeral to which everyone, high and low, in the county came. The Squire and his lady – how gratified Laurel would have been, she had thought – held her hand and begged her to consider their home as hers, and that as soon as her period of mourning was over she was to come and be amongst her friends again. She was an extremely rich and childless widow, the Squire said later to his wife, and might she not now be considered for their Nicky who seemed disinclined ever to settle for one of the lovely young things who had been discreetly put in his line of vision. Perhaps an older, more sophisticated woman might appeal to him. He had always been fond of Tessa and she was most presentable, mixing easily with those of their own class.

She had seen Will that day. Like an emaciated old man, his large frame was gaunt and somehow disjointed inside his loose flesh, his haunted eyes searching her out, his arm trembling in Annie's. He had tried to tell her something with those eyes, or ask her something perhaps, but she had nothing for him, then or now.

She had spent her days in her office at the mill. There had been no cotton for a week now beyond some Indian from Surat, a district in the presidency of Bombay. It was badly packed so that it was dirty, knotty, full of seeds and leaves as well as being short in staple with fibres which broke easily. Carding and spinning machinery had been damaged and at best it was suitable only for coarse cloth and not the fine quality velveteen woven in the Chapman weaving shed.

'I can get no decent cotton, Annie,' she said quietly to the woman who sat across the desk from her. 'How am I to keep them in work? How are they to live? Less than two shillings a head from the Relief Committee . . .'

'An' what tha gives 'em from tha own pocket, lass.'

'Little enough, Annie.'

'Tha's a generous woman, Tessa. To them, an' to anyone that come to thi for 'elp, so why not Will Broadbent? 'E's given thi time ter come ter terms wi' thy grief. 'E's stayed away from thi though it's caused 'im pain. Will tha not see 'im, lass? Talk to 'im?'

Tessa bent her head.

'I can't Annie.'

'Why? In the name o' God, why?'

'We have been through this so often and really I do not think I can stand much more. What is there to say to him that you have not passed on? I cannot go on trying to explain how I feel, what I know I must do, so you must just take my word for it that I know I am right. What sort of woman would I be to ... to ... consort with a man who, unknowingly I admit, killed my husband and sister-in-law? Through me, through me, Annie, and we cannot continue as we were before. It would be ... indecent. No, he must get on with his life in whatever way he thinks fit and allow me to do the same.'

Her face was like a pale, translucent mask, a mask carved from pure, white marble, the lovely bone structure prominently displayed in the fineness of her skin. Her dark eyebrows slanted upwards in stark contrast like blackbird's wings, and beneath them her eyes were the silver streaked grey of the winter lake which was set in the garden at Greenacres. Only her poppy-red mouth had colour, startling and full, the mouth of a sensual woman who knows well the meaning of love. Now it was firm, her jaw clenched challengingly, her expression telling Annie that she was no longer prepared to discuss the man who had once been everything in life to her. She had gambled with the lives of others, not only her own. She had recklessly chanced her reputation, her marriage, her husband's reason, the safety of her family with what she knew to be a killing disease in her love for Will Broadbent. She had given no thought to the danger to others in her own arrogant determination to be with him, to nurse him when she had known that Annie could have done it just as well. And devastation had overtaken her. Now she must pay the price.

'This is the last time I wish to hear his name mentioned, Annie. I will not change my mind. I will not see him and you must tell him so.'

'Tha mun tell 'im thaself, lass.'

'Annie, once and for all ...'

538

' 'E's in t'other room.' Annie nodded her head towards the closed door of Tessa's office, her own face as pale and resolute as her friend's. Then she stood up abruptly pushing back her chair.

Tessa's face lost even its pearly whiteness, becoming ashen, almost grey, and her eyes turned to brilliant, enraged diamonds. She narrowed them like a cat which is ready to attack and her voice was no more than a sibilant hiss.

'How dare you? How dare you interfere in something which has nothing whatsoever to do with you? Who gave you the right to play God in my affairs, Annie Beale? Who gave you the right to meddle, to take it upon yourself to change, or attempt to, the direction in which my life must now go? I cannot forgive this, Annie, and I cannot forgive you. You go too far this time.'

'Tha mun see 'im. 'E needs to 'ear it from . . .'

'Annie . . . Dear God, Annie, what about *my* needs and those of my family? I thought you were my friend, that I could trust you . . .'

'Always, lass, always, so trust me in this.'

'No, no. How did he get in? I gave orders that . . .'

'I fetched 'im.'

'You had no right, no right . . .' For the first time since they told her her husband was dead Tessa's face lost its white, expressionless mask and became distorted with her despair. She turned this way and that, lifting her hands to her head and gripping it savagely. She was like an animal caught in a trap which she had avoided for weeks but from which she could now find no escape. There was pain in her, desperation, fear, and yet a tiny bubble of joy formed which she did her best to quench. This would not do, it simply would not do. She must not see him. She must not. Annie was watching her compassionately, understanding, she realised it now, what it was that terrified her. She held out her hands to her beseechingly.

'Annie, please, Annie, ask him to go.'

'Nay lass, tha mun do that, not I.'

'I cannot see him. I will not. You are cruel...'

The door opened then and he was there. Will. Older than she remembered him, the pain and desolation he had known etched in deep lines from his nostrils to the corners of his mouth. His eyes, so clear an amber as to be almost transparent, were steady as they rested gravely on her and his mouth was clenched firmly, rigidly, as though he was desperately afraid he might speak the wrong words. This was his only chance, his expression admitted and he must make no mistake. He swallowed and she saw his Adam's apple rise convulsively in his throat. Someone, probably himself, had cut his hair and it was short and shaggy across his strong brow. He was still thin and drawn but his jacket no longer hung from his broad shoulders in awkward folds as it had done the last time she had seen him at the funeral.

'Tessa?' He spoke her name, then cleared his throat and she knew he was as afraid as she was but for a different reason. He was afraid that she would not surrender to him and she was afraid that she would.

Neither of them saw Annie slip from the room.

Her fear made her harsh.

'What is it?'

'May we not speak to one another?'

'About what?'

'Surely we have things to ... to discuss?'

'What things?'

He moved further into the room, awkward and stiff as she had never seen him before. Will Broadbent, good humoured, positive, easy with himself and the rest of his world, was replaced by a man who was unsure, doubtful of his own wisdom in coming, afraid to alarm her with his desperate need to know that she still loved him. She must not let him see what was in her or he would not let her go.

She stepped back from him, knowing that if he touched her she would be incapable of resisting him, but he took it for a sign of rejection and his face hardened.

'Tessa, you cannot simply mean to ... to go on as you

540

have done since your husband died? Ignoring the past and what you and I ...'

'Naturally,' she interrupted harshly, 'and why should I not? There are the mills and my dead sister-in-law's children who take up a great deal of my time.' She had a frail grip on herself now but it almost slipped away as she saw him wince.

'I know that. Jesus, do you think I don't know ...' He passed a hand over his face. 'But soon ... or sometime in the future ... surely, when ... when ... Oh, sweet Christ, help me, Tessa, don't let me flounder out here all alone. You know what I'm saying, what I'm asking. I love you so much ... don't ... please don't turn away from me ... let me see your face, your eyes ...'

She had her back to him now, unable to bear any more. She stared, blinded and tortured at the wood panelling of the wall, reeling with the pain of him, holding herself steady, forcing herself inch by slow inch away from the dreadful need to turn back to him, to run into his arms, to hold him, soothe him, comfort and calm his agony with a great outpouring of the love she had for him, but she knew she could not. This man was not for her. Not now. Not ever. She had killed her own husband and her husband's sister for this man and could she live with him knowing that? Could she forget it? Could she ever forgive herself? Did she want to?

'Go home, Will. There is nothing for you here.' Her voice was flat and devoid of all emotion. 'I have nothing for you and I can be nothing to you. I have work to do and have no time for ... diversions.'

She heard him gasp, then there was silence for a long while. She knew he was still there but she dared not turn to face him. She felt the great sorrowing beat of his heart inside her own breast, the pain in his head drumming into hers, the tired and weary ache of his body which was not yet returned to its full strength. Everything he suffered, she experienced too, and she prayed, again to a faceless, nameless god, for the resolution to remain where she was until he had gone. And in her heart a tiny voice, bewildered, angered, persistent, begged to know why she was doing this when all she had to do was turn about to claim the love he was offering her and which she so badly needed. But her heart could not reason. Her heart was warm and unthinking, longing to ignore the cold logic of her mind which told her she and Will Broadbent could never be the same to each other again.

'Diversion, Tessa?' he whispered at last. 'We were more than that to each other. Don't dishonour me or yourself by pretending otherwise. I have loved you truly for the past nine years and I believe you had come to love me in the same way. I came today, as I have tried to come for the past six weeks to offer you whatever you might need at this time of ... grief in your life. I came as a friend as well as the man who loves you. You are free now – let us be truthful with one another – and when a decent interval had passed I wanted to ask you to become my wife. I can give you so much, my lass. We can give one another ... all that we have ... all that a man and woman ...'

He could not go on. The tears ran silently down her face and dripped just as silently on to the black silk of her mourning gown. The absolute quiet moved on and still he stood there but she did not turn to him.

'I came to beg you, Tessa,' he said at last. 'Annie told me how you felt ... the guilt ... but I can see you are not to be moved.' He sounded surprised as though he had expected more of her. 'I was ready to shout and bluster. I was angry, you see, that you had not turned to me. Then I was convinced that I could ... sweep you off your feet, I believe the expression is, that our love would overcome all obstacles. But it doesn't, does it, lass?'

'No, Will, it doesn't.' Her voice was firm and her back which was still turned to him was the same.

'Well, then, I'll not bother you again, Tessa Greenwood. I've waited long enough, I reckon. More than any man should wait for a woman. I'll do what you suggest and make

542

a new life for myself. You see, I want to settle, have sons, a family, and I'll not get it from you, that's clear.'

He was gone when she turned round. Only Annie was there ready to catch her as she fell in a storm of weeping into her strong arms.

# 35

They said in the Penfold Valley that they had never seen a woman mourn the death of her husband as Tessa Greenwood mourned but then the pair of them had been close since childhood, hadn't they, along with that other cousin of hers, Drew Greenwood's twin brother, and was it not to be expected that the loss of the one she married would affect her more than most? And then her sister-in-law going like that at the same time and them children to be seen to was enough to undermine the strongest constitution.

She'd gone a bit crazy, everyone agreed, going at all times of the day, and night too, most likely, high on the moors of Saddleworth, not always riding as one would expect but sometimes tramping in her stout boots with a weaver's shawl thrown about her head as though she had reverted to being the mill girl her own mother had once been. The gleaming stretch of Hollingworth Lake which was actually a reservoir, called the 'weavers' seaport' because it was a place where the millworkers strolled on their day off, seemed to draw her. None knew why for in the days her cousins were alive the three of them had favoured Badger's Edge and Friar's Mere. Sometimes she was seen on the little paddle-steamer which moved across the shining surface of the lake. Mr Talbot, who had designed her new mill four years back and whose wife was particularly fond of a sail on the lake, had seen her, he told Mr Bradley, standing like a figurehead in the bow of the steamer, her shawl slipping about her shoulders, her white face straining upwards to the moorland peaks which surrounded the lake and which contained, though Mr Talbot did not know it being a newcomer to the district, Badger's Edge and Friar's Mere. He had seen her lips move as though she addressed some unseen companion. It was all most spine-chilling really, his wife had remarked, not at all sure she believed him when he told her that this plainly dressed, working-clad woman was the wealthy Mrs Tessa Greenwood.

But worst of all, rumour had it, she had walked into the Five Pigeons, an inn on the moor where the Lancashire and Yorkshire roads met and where radical agitators like her own uncle had gathered in the old days, and asked the landlord for a glass of ale. Bold as you please, she had been, staring round her at the stunned and silent working men, sipping her ale as though she had as much right to be there as they. Going back to her roots, one fool said, but would a woman as rich and powerful as she want to step into the past, they derided him.

'Is there anyone here who knew Joss and Charlie Greenwood?' she had asked, sensibly enough. No one answered for forty years had gone by since they'd been there and she had laughed, shaken her head and made some remark about short memories before striding off again into the autumn afternoon.

Despite her loss and her strangeness she was tireless in her work for the relief of the Lancashire operatives and in her struggle to obtain cotton for her own millhands to spin and weave but during the spring and summer of 1863 she was often to be seen riding her dead husband's bay on the tops of the South Lancashire Pennines. Great wild thing it was and far too much for a woman to handle, they told one another. Those children of whom she was now guardian would be left completely alone if she did not take more care.

She was like a person split in two. She moved about

544

Crossfold and Chapmanstown, watching over her own workers quite fiercely. Sitting on endless committees with that working-class friend of hers from Edgeclough she was the picture of lady-like gentility, her black mourning gown correct in every detail, stark and elegant, her black bonnet discreet and hiding the glossy darkness of her hair. She spoke quietly but her voice was heard and no one starved that she knew about. When there was cotton to be had and her mills were open she was there in her office, dealing with orders and accounts in consultation with her counting-house clerk, her managers and overlookers.

She took an interest in her factory school, even reading aloud for an heroic half-hour or so from the books which she borrowed from the Greenacres schoolroom. In the winter months she brought great cans of hot soup from the Greenacres kitchen and watched with quiet pleasure as eager mouths sipped the tasty nourishment and big eyes, round and attentive over the rims of their mugs, became clouded with satisfaction, minds fed and bellies fed. She sat in on classes where women who were mothers of half a dozen or more spelled out 'cat' and 'mat', their own eyes as gratified as those of their children. They were shown too how to gain the maximum nourishment from the cheapest food, how to sew, not a fine seam or delicate embroidery but sensible, decent garments to keep the children warm in winter.

But there were times when she was doing none of these things, when she could find no man, no woman or child who needed her, no cotton to be carded and spun and woven, when her heart was like an empty, echoing cavern with nothing to fill it but the words she and Will Broadbent had spoken to each other. Then she would fling on her breeches and boots and jacket, tie up her hair with a scrap of ribbon and stride from the house as though the ghosts of all her past were at her heels.

'Let me saddle tha mare, Miss Tessa,' Walter begged her that first time she ordered him to get ready her husband's tall bay. 'Tha cannot mean ter ride Jupiter. 'E be too strong for thi. It tekks a man to 'andle 'im. Anyroad, 'e's not bin out of't stable since ... well, only wi' me for exercise an' 'e's full o' mischief, Miss Tessa. I reckon 'e misses ...' Walter's eyes took on a sad and musing expression for though Mr Drew had been a bugger at times Jupiter was not the only one who missed him. He shook his head and turned back to Miss Tessa who stood waiting, not as imperious and as high-handed as once she had been but determined on her own way just the same.

He took her over that first time, her dead husband's bay, tearing away like a wild beast from a cage. She could do no more than hang on and let him, praying that his hooves would not find a rabbit hole or a loose rock in the dips and folds of the rough terrain; that he would not falter as he leaped across fast-flowing streams and raced along the old trackways which had been there since medieval times, constructed to carry the materials of the booming textile trade to and from manufacturers and markets. Up, up he sped, on to the crest of Saddleworth Moor which had derived its name from the saddle-shaped hill which formed it, crossing the railway line which ran from Manchester to Huddersfield. It was as though the bay, like herself, was searching for something or someone in his mad race into the middle of nowhere with the dogs she and Drew had trained to instance obedience close by his heels.

He swerved suddenly, almost unseating her. It appeared to her that he had heard a call in his own noble head for she could hear nothing but the thunder of his hooves, her own harsh breath in her throat and the high wind in her ears. She thought he would stop then for his lungs laboured and the breath from his nostrils mixed with the steam from his sweating coat, but he went on, almost tearing her arms from her shoulders. North he turned then, back across the railway track, beyond the quarry at Delph until at last they stood, gloriously free both of them, and temporarily at peace in the place known as Badger's Edge.

She was slow to dismount for it seemed the stand of rocks was too emotionally peopled by the men she had loved in the past. They were all there, tall, strong, handsome, laughing up at her in the soft spring sunshine, calling to her to come and join them, to sit and dream with them as they looked out over the softly wooded valley from which no factory smoke rose today. Pearce was there, young as he had been when he had died on the battlefield of the Crimea eight years ago, and his brother, her husband Drew, older but just as merry as he and Pearce skylarked like the young colts they had once been.

There too was Robby Atherton, the man her young girl's heart had loved. He had been forbidden her for in his veins had run the same blood as hers since they had shared the same mother. Warm brown eyes, crisp golden curls lit by the sunlight, slender and fine-boned, he had that air of easy-mannered courtliness she had loved so well. Delightful and charming, but perhaps he lacked the stamina their mother had given to her, Tessa, since concerned with his own devastation he had ridden away with no thought to hers. Sadly she recognised it.

And leaning indolently against the tall, grey-pitted rock, his mouth stretched in a wide smile, his arms folded across his broad chest, his face tipped to the sun, was Will. Will Broadbent, a strong, working-class man, as her own forefathers had been, but with the sweetness and warmth of heart of a true 'gentle man'.

She bent her head and closed her eyes to shut them all out for she simply could not bear the pain of her loss of any of them and her loneliness was quite insupportable. When she opened them again she was still alone but for her dogs and the well-bred, handsome horse she rode and she knew she always would be. She got down slowly and let the reins hang loose. The tired animal was not reared for endurance and had raced for over an hour to reach this familiar place where his master had once come, and she knew he would not roam.

She sat with her back to that same rock where she had sat

so often before, convinced she could feel in the hollow the warmth where masculine shoulders had leaned against the granite. Where was he now, her heart asked painfully? Not Drew, not Pearce, not even Robby, but Will. No one had spoken his name to her for months ever since Mr Bradley had informed the board regretfully that Mr Broadbent had resigned from his position as managing director of Chapman Manufacturing Company Ltd and had put his shares up for sale. They were not worth a lot in today's fragile market but perhaps Mrs Greenwood herself might be interested?

She had answered mechanically that indeed she was, her heart thudding badly out of control but relieved at that moment that the anguish of seeing Will at the now monthly board meetings had been averted. She had heard, like bird twitterings from afar, the discussion and vote on who should take on the position left vacant by Mr Broadbent, and was shaken when she discovered that she was their choice.

'But . . . I cannot . . . really . . .' she had begun to protest. Then, as their faces turned politely in her direction, her cool brain had asked why not? She had been involved in the business in one way or another almost from the day Charlie had died five years ago, and though she knew she was not yet the 'businessman' her mother or her Aunt Kit had been – indeed there was not a great deal of business to be had – she knew in that instant that she could do it. Had she anything else to do with the rest of her life, she asked herself? So she had accepted gracefully, pushing aside the memory of Will's humorous face as it had smiled at her from the shadows in the corners of the dark-panelled room.

It was high summer when she remembered her promise to herself that she would take Charlie's children, as she now called them in her own mind though she could not have said why, up to the moorland tops where she had spent so much of her childhood. They all now had ponies which the girls rode in a decorous, slightly alarmed circle about the paddock, encouraged to do so by her own example and the assurance that it was a proper occupation for a lady to be concerned with. Though they had not said as much, she knew that their minds, which were so like their mother's, saw the exercise as a step nearer to the grand husbands they hoped to win, perhaps from among the gentry with whom Aunt Tessa was acquainted.

Robert and Henry rode to school on their small roans, quite incredulously delighted with the sudden freedom their Aunt Tessa seemed to think was appropriate for them to have, though Nanny was none too pleased and said so repeatedly to Miss Gaunt in the privacy of the schoolroom. But they were bent on careers as manufacturing gentlemen, as their father had been, serious and eager to learn their lessons so that when the time came they would be ready to take up their duties at Chapmans as all the Greenwood men did. They really had no time, they explained politely to Aunt Tessa, to ride in the narrow wooded valleys, across the wooden bridges which spanned tumbling waters, up the old packways and on to the splendour of the tops. Oh, yes, they were certain it would be grand to explore the Druidical remains at Fairy Hole, the Rocking Stone, the Standing Rocks, Dovestone Wood, Badger's Edge and Friar's Mere where Aunt Tessa, Uncle Drew and the scarcely remembered Uncle Pearce had known such 'fun', but they would really rather go into the weaving shed, if she didn't mind. Mr Wilson had promised to explain to them the workings of a new loom he had seen at the London Exhibition last year. Perhaps another time, they said, looking exactly as their father, Charlie Greenwood had done, smiling but very resolute. She had not the heart to dissuade them, wondering at the same time what the ingredient was in them which had been so sadly lacking in Pearce and Drew.

Only Joel showed any interest in the hesitant invitation his aunt extended to him. She was not used to children. She did not compel them to her own preference which might, perhaps, have done them more good in the long run but gave them the choice and only Joel chose to follow her.

They took the dogs. She had Walter saddle her own mare

this time for Drew's bay was too fast for the short-legged cob which Joel rode and when they reached Badger's Edge she dismounted at once, automatically striding to the edge and looking out across the deep clough as though she were alone. In the back of her mind she could hear the boy chattering as he scouted about the rocks, asking questions but apparently expecting no answer, calling up the dogs in a high, excited but unafraid voice.

'It's grand up here, Aunt Tess,' she heard him say, the only person to shorten her name. 'I can see right across the valley . . .'

'Clough,' she said mechanically, her eyes turned away from Badger's Edge, beyond Dog Hill, beyond Whitefield towards Rochdale where . . . where Will . . . But perhaps he had gone now. Perhaps he had left the world of cotton, the broad sweep of the South Pennine moorland, left Lancashire itself and gone to a place where he would not be reminded of Tessa Greenwood and the misery she had brought him. She had not asked Annie who she was quite certain would know, for she wanted . . . hoped . . . that if his name was not mentioned his presence would finally leave her and she would find some peace. One day, surely . . . sweet Jesus, one day the tearing, clawing agony of loss and guilt would ease and she would know, if not peace, then perhaps the oblivion of forgetting.

'Pardon?' the boy said beside her and his bright face smiled up expectantly into hers.

'What . . . ?'

'You said "clough".'

'Oh, yes. The valley. Well, round here we call a narrow valley such as this one, a clough.'

'Why?' She did not as yet know the inquisitive nature of a child, the eternal questions, the ever-ready word "why?"

A small spark of interest stirred her heart and she smiled. She sat down on the sun-warmed rock and he sat obligingly next to her, his small body leaning quite amazingly against hers. His sea-green eyes, pale and just like those of his

550

mother, were trusting and hopeful and she realised that this child had received affection from no adult except Nanny since his mother had died.

'I have no idea,' she answered honestly.

'Haven't you?' He was clearly amazed that a grown-up could admit to a lack of knowledge. In his experience they knew everything and told you so frequently.

'There are quite a lot of things I can tell you, though.'

'Really?'

'Mmm. For instance, a quarry like the one in the far distance is known as a delph. The narrow bridge we crossed ... do you remember ... ?'

'Yes.' He squirmed with delight.

'... that's a hebble and that clearing on the far side of the clough is a royd.' His face gazed up into hers earnestly, then turned in the direction of her pointing finger.

'Why?'

'Because we're in Lancashire.'

'But why?'

She began to laugh and instinctively her arm went about his narrow shoulders and hugged him to her. He wriggled even closer and she knew a moment of unexpected delight at the warmth and contact of her body with that of another human being. A small, defenceless human being who was looking at her as though she was as much a pleasure to him as he was to her.

'Most of the places in Lancashire came by their name because of what was done there, or sold there,' she explained, gaining great satisfaction from his rapt attention.

'Really.' His lips parted in awe and admiration for this clever and very beautiful aunt of his. He had really only just noticed what a very pretty lady she was. The pale, doe-like expression in her face had gone and a flush of rose pinked her cheeks. Her eyes sparkled brilliantly, the sunlight dipping into their silvery depths, and her hair tumbled in a rich, glossy cloak about her shoulders. He could smell her breath as he looked up, his face no more than six inches from hers, and it

551

was nice, not like Nanny or Miss Gaunt who always sucked some nasty sweets, for her throat, she said.

'Oh, yes. Have you heard of Haslingden?'

'Yes.'

'Well, that got its name from the valley of hazels where it was built. Salterhebble came from . . .'

'Bridge?'

'Yes, good boy.' She was delighted with him and his sharp memory and he wriggled again in the glow of her approval, grinning joyously. 'It was a salt-seller's bridge.'

They talked for an hour, leaning companionably back against the stone where she had leaned with this boy's cousins, for that was what they had been since Charlie and Joss Greenwood had been brothers; with her own half-brother and with Will. When they stood up to leave she felt the balm of Joel Greenwood's childish happiness soothe her, and the beginning, perhaps, of an affection they each needed from the other.

The civil war continued, meanwhile, to rage in America where thousands upon thousands of brothers died and their blood soaked into the ground of their own homeland which they defended against one another. The thin supply of cotton dried up completely and all the mills in Lancashire stopped work but it was said that preparations for a great battle were being made and that soon the war would be over and all would be in work again. It was not so and 1863 became 1864 and still it went on, that war which seemed so cruel and pointless to many. Surely the slaves in the South could be freed without men killing one another over it, some said, and if the trouble was that the South wanted to leave the Union, well let them get on with it and then the rest of the world – meaning Lancashire where they did not understand what was happening – could get back to normal. Three years the war had been going on and machinery was rusting up, some of which had not been in use since the end of 1861.

The sympathies of the distressed cotton operatives for the slaves of the cotton South swung dramatically towards the northern states of America when it was made known that since the civil war was the chief cause of the hardship in Lancashire, the people would receive some of the plentiful corn which the splendid harvest had brought to northern America. In January the steamship *Hope* arrived in Liverpool with 1010 barrels of flour from the New York Produce Exchange, 11,236 barrels from the International Relief Committee and later in the month a further 1500 barrels from the Exchange. The food was distributed by the Central Relief Committee and the people of Manchester and Oldham and Burnley amongst many others went to bed with their bellies full for the first time in three years.

The starving cotton families were beginning to take a stand against the grievous suffering with which they were afflicted through no fault of their own and to which there seemed no end. They had been patient long enough, they said, and the war in America which was starving their children was nothing to do with them. Disturbances occurred in the distressed districts, the first noteworthy incident taking place during the distribution of the food sent from America. There was to be a meeting in Stevenson's Square in Manchester and it was intended that the grateful workers should march to Kersal Moor where 15,000 loaves would be given to them. The meeting took place but the operatives declined to allow political speeches to be made about their distress, no procession was formed, the loaves were seized and the operatives went home.

But something had begun that day and serious riots broke out in Stalybridge and neighbouring towns. Dissatisfaction with relief which was to be reduced yet again aroused anger in previously submissive breasts and windows were broken and machines damaged, just as in the old days when the first power looms had come to take the employment from handloom weavers. Special constables were sworn in and the Riot Act read and a company of Hussars was called out to clear the streets. The next day, despite the reading of the Riot Act and the posting of a notice forbidding crowds to assemble in the streets, a mob gathered, stones were thrown, shops invaded and sacked and twenty-nine men were arrested.

The disturbances which took place then and for several weeks afterwards brought the question of emigration to the forefront yet again. Many operatives who could afford to go or were able to obtain assistance had already sailed for America and the colonies, but those employers whose mills were still somehow limping along regarded with alarm the prospect of losing skilled spinners and weavers. What were they to do, they asked one another, when the war was over and cotton came pouring back into Lancashire, as it was bound to do, if their hands whose craft had been handed down from generation to generation and learned during long apprenticeships were no longer available? The northern states of America, where cotton mills were springing up, particularly in New England, were doing their best to attract Lancashire cotton operatives to emigrate and from May 1862 until December 1863, 60,000 persons left the country though only 14,000 of those were from Lancashire. Most of those who had professed a desire to emigrate had been carefully dissuaded from it!

'We'll get through some'ow,' Annie said stoutly as she and Tessa sat with their feet on her kitchen fender, the blast of warmth from the fire reaching up their lifted skirts. It was November and a heavy frost, earlier than usual, had lain a coverlet of white over town and moorland alike and the thoughts of the two women turned pityingly to the thousands beyond their door who had no such comfort.

'Dear God, it had better end soon,' Tessa said and Annie knew she was referring to the war.

'They say t'South'll not 'old out much longer. They've not got resources like t'North. Blockades got 'em by't throat an' their strength's dwindlin'.'

'Like those poor souls out there.'

'Aye,' Annie agreed sadly.

'I never guessed it would last as long as this, Annie, nor how it could affect people so far away. Will we ever recover, d'you think? Will we ever make up all that we have lost? Oh, not in money, but in the improvements which were beginning to come in the lives of the operatives.'

'Millmaisters weren't all as obligin' as thi family, lass.'

'Perhaps not, but a better life was bound to come.'

'An' it'll come again, you mark my words. Will said only t'other day...'

Annie stopped abruptly, cutting off the words on her lips as though they had burned them. She watched the soft flush caused by the warmth of the fire drain from Tessa's face as she sat up slowly in sharp, disjointed movements as though her body were suddenly stiff. She turned her head away and stared blindly into the shadows at the edge of the kitchen, then looked back at Annie. She seemed incapable of speaking though her mouth opened and closed. She stood up jerkily and began to stride about the room, her hands clasping and unclasping. Annie watched her sorrowfully. It was over a year since Will's name had been mentioned between them. Tessa had not asked about him. She and Will had both made it perfectly clear to Annie that neither of them wished to know, ever, what the other one was doing and though she stood between them, friend to both, she had respected their wishes. Now a slip of the tongue had brought Will Broadbent savagely back from the past.

'I'm sorry, lass. I didn't mean ter...'

Still Tessa flung herself fiercely about the kitchen, avoiding Annie's eyes, turning this way and that in her effort to escape the pain the sound of his name was causing her. Her wide black skirt brushed madly against the table, the chairs, the dresser, threatening to dislodge the crockery until finally she stood, as she had stood on that last day in her office, with her face to the whitewashed wall.

'I should have guessed,' she said at last, her voice no more than a whisper.

'Should've guessed what?'

'That you still ... saw him.'

'I told thi a long while since that even if thi an' 'im fell out 'e were still my friend, as thi are.'

'I should have known, of course. I suppose I did know. You were always loyal.'

'I'm ... fond of thi both. I can't choose between thi, lass. It's bin 'ard at times when tha looked as though tha'd never get over it but recently both of thi' 'ave found other ...'

The silence fell again, hard and hurting, and Annie watched as the trembling began in Tessa's shoulders, moving her head wildly and running down her long, graceful back. She folded her arms across her breast, hugging herself tightly as she turned back into the room. Annie had never seen such despair on any face, not even on her own in the mirror when her family was torn from her in the stews of Manchester when the fever struck.

'He ... has ... someone ...?'

'Nay, lass, don't ...'

'Don't ...?'

'Don't ask me ter tell thi what Will's doin'. Not now. Tha made it quite clear a year ago that tha wanted nowt' ter do wi' 'im. Get on wi' tha life, tha said to 'im, an' tha can't blame 'im when 'e 'as done.'

'Annie ...' The shaking of her body became uncontrollable so that Annie stood up, alarmed, reaching out to the woman who surely was breaking apart. She pulled her fiercely into her arms, awkward and clumsy for Tessa was six inches taller than herself, but she held her firmly, murmuring words which said nothing, stroking the smooth and glossy hair which, as Tessa wept, began to fall about her neck and shoulders.

'Annie ... I ... cannot ... bear ... it. I ... just ... cannot ... bear ... it ... without ... him ...'

'I know, love, I know.'

'What ... am ... I ... to ... do?'

'Sit thi down, lass.'

'Annie ...'

'Come on, love, sit down an' I'll give thi summat ter mekk yer feel better.'

'Annie, Annie . . .'

She was quiet at last, the empty glass which had contained one of Annie's 'potions' still clasped limply beween her flaccid fingers. She stared dazedly into the heart of the glowing fire, her colour returned though her hair still fell in shining swathes about her haunted face. Annie watched her, knowing that the valerian which she had put in the elderberry wine would make her sleep soon. But when she woke? What then? Would she want to know, demand to know what Will Broadbent was doing, where he was, and who, if there was someone, had taken her place in his life? Would she be bent on torturing herself as Annie believed women were in circumstances such as this? Well, she would cross that bridge when she came to it for there was no use in looking for aggravation when it damn soon found you on its own. In the meanwhile she would send a message to Thomas at the Dog and Gun where he waited with the carriage for his mistress, to go home. Tessa could sleep here tonight and in the morning . . . well, that was tomorrow.

'Tell me about that little lad, Tessa,' she said softly at last.

'Who?'

'That there Joel tha's so fond of.'

'Annie . . .'

'Nay, not if tha don't want to but I 'eard as 'ow 'e was as able as thissen on that pony of 'is. Ginny Briggs was tellin' me only t'other day she'd seen the pair of thi racin' up ter't top o' Dog Hill an' thi was 'avin' a job ter keep up wi' 'im. What will 'e be now . . . seven . . . eight?'

'He's almost eight.'

'An' a likely lookin' lad. Reminds me a lot o' Charlie Greenwood.'

'Yes.' Tessa's lips lifted in a tiny smile and her unfocused eyes became soft.

Annie relaxed and let her breath ease thankfully from her lungs.

557

'Where shall it be today, darling? You know we won't be able to ride out for much longer, don't you, at least not far from the estate so we must make the best of these last few days. The snows will be here soon, Percy says, and that will be the end of our riding until they melt. Of course, we could go walking...'

'Even in the snow, Aunt Tess?'

'Well, it would be difficult but it is possible.'

'How?'

The boy looked up into Tessa Greenwood's face and his hand which was held in hers, shook it excitedly. He danced along beside her as they went towards the stables, wide-eyed and as unsteady as a colt, small for his age, not like the tall Greenwoods a bit, but endearingly full of charm. He was the only one of Charlie's children to have captured her heart, try as she might to feel other than pity and a deep sense of responsibility for the rest. They had been too old, she had decided, too far down the path on which Laurel's upbringing had set them, knowing exactly what they wanted from life and expecting to get it, as their mother had done. Only this one was Charlie's true child, just like him as a boy, though Tessa of course was not aware of it. Sweet-tempered, generous, affectionate, he yet had a strong core of resolution in him which would not allow the others in the schoolroom to take advantage of his size and youth. There were five years dividing himself and Henry, two dead children between them, but it did not deter him despite his smallness from raising his fists in his own defence against his brothers.

He loved it when she called him 'darling' and he loved her. She didn't call his brothers and sisters 'darling'. She belonged exclusively to him now, he knew that with the selfishness of a child and he basked in her love and approval. He could scarcely remember his father but Aunt Tess kept him alive with tales of her own childhood, her two cousins, and Charlie, who was his father, of course. He loved Charlie because she did and his small world was secure and steady in her loving grasp.

Tessa smiled but on her face was that look of strange sadness Joel had seen now and again though he couldn't for the life of him imagine why she was sad. Of course, he knew she worried about the American Civil War and the shortage of cotton which affected workers in the family mill, but this look had nothing to do with them.

'I can remember,' she began and his delight knew no bounds for she had such lovely 'rememberings', 'one year when it snowed for days. There were drifts twenty feet deep in places right up to the top of the stable door and Walter and Percy had to clear a path across the yard to get to the horses. It was Christmas . . .' She sighed and he tugged on her hand to remind her he was here for sometimes she was inclined to allow her thoughts to wander.

'Oh, yes,' she went on, '. . . Christmas, and I wanted to take a present to someone . . .'

'What was it, Aunt Tess?'

'What, darling?' She was forgetting that as a small boy he wanted to know everything down to the smallest detail.

'The present?'

'It was a bright red knitted scarf.'

That seemed pretty unexciting to him but he wanted to know how to walk on top of the twenty-foot drifts of snow which she described. He had seen it in previous winters lying over the parkland which surrounded his home, so deep Nanny would not allow them out in it saying they would be 'swallowed up'. He waited patiently.

'How . . . splendid.' His voice was polite.

'Yes, well ... I wanted to get to ... Chapmanstown and the snow was so deep, too deep to walk on, so I searched in the cupboard – you know, the one where we keep all the cricket bats and things ...'

'Yes, yes ...'

'... and I found two tennis bats. I had seen pictures in a book, you see, of a man who lived in Canada and walked on top of the snow and the things he had on his feet and ...'

'Yes, what happened, Aunt Tess?'

'I walked to Chapmanstown.' Her voice had become clipped now and her eyes had gone quite funny. He didn't like it. For one awful moment he didn't like it, then she suddenly put her arm about his shoulders and pulled him to her, hugging him, and he knew it was all right again.

He sighed happily but pulled away as they turned into the stable yard. He was nearly eight now and it would not do to let the men there see him holding his aunt's hand.

'Have you decided yet?' she called out to him as they cantered up the back slope behind the house. 'Where shall it be? Friar's Mere, Dog Hill or ...'

'Badger's Edge,' he shouted joyfully into the teeth of the biting wind, for was not that his most favourite place of all? It was where they had gone on their first ride together and though he was only a boy he sensed that it was the place she liked the best. They had sat together through the seasons with their backs to that certain rock since that day when she had first taken him out on his fat pony.

They had watched a skylark soar almost out of sight, a quivering dot in the dazzling summer sky, not lingering at the top of its flight but descending again, dropping and pausing as though it were on an invisible thread. The bird ate the tender stalks of sprouting corn and the farmers hated it, Aunt Tess told him, but it was grand to lie in the sweet-smelling grass up on Badger's Edge and watch it dive from the sky.

They had seen the wheatear, its white patch looking like a dancing snowflake as it spun above their heads into the languid blue of the sky. There had been hedges where wild roses and honeysuckle grew as he and Aunt Tess moved up in the direction of the tops, and in autumn the sharp scent of heather and gorse and peat, the season of mists, of blackberries still warm from summer and swifts flying over his head to warmer parts than the bleak winter moorland which was to come.

But in the depths of that winter, when the moors were cruel and the weather as fickle as a woman's heart, or so Walter had told him though he was not certain of his meaning, they must stay away from Badger's Edge for if the snow should catch them up there they might not be found for days.

It was achingly cold and Aunt Tess had made him put on an extra jumper beneath his warm woollen cape. He had a scarf about his neck and wore gloves knitted by Nanny and when they reached the top they sat shoulder to shoulder for half an hour, the dogs about them, close and warm, gazing out over the steep clough and down to the glint of water which could be seen amongst the leafless trees at the bottom.

'Will we walk on the snow when it comes, Aunt Tess?' he asked presently, his gloved hand smoothing the head of the dog which rested on his knee.

'I dare say,' she replied but her eyes were far away on something he could not see and he moved impatiently. The dog stood up and wandered to the edge of the rocky cliff and Joel watched as the others rose, following with the curiosity of all animals, to investigate what the first had discovered.

'But will we have enough bats?'

'We can look if you like,' she answered vaguely.

'Perhaps Walter could make us some. If you showed him the picture of the man in Canada. He makes all kinds of things with wood and I bet if we were to ask him he could make us some, don't you? We could walk wherever we wanted to then,' he finished, the prospect of a winter shut in with his brothers and sister not a pleasing one.

'Shall we ask him then?' he said after a moment or two.

'What, darling?'

He stood up suddenly, his face reproachful. She wasn't

561

listening to him. She'd gone off to that strange place as she did now and again and he might as well do something interesting as sit here and try to get her to talk. He loved her, really he did, but sometimes she was very irritating, especially when they were having such a good talk about those fascinating 'snow-bats' she had mentioned.

He sighed dramatically, just to let her know he was not at all pleased, then wandered across the stiff, springy turf to see what the dogs were quarrelling over. They were all milling around just as they did when they came across a rabbit hole from which the scent of the animal, safe deep in the earth, titillated their keen noses.

'What is it, Bart?' he asked, leaning into the middle of them, pushing aside two large heads to peer in the manner of small boys at anything which might interest their inquisitive minds. The dogs, big and heavy, were not disposed to be moved from the frozen carcase of the small animal – he was never to know what it was – which some large bird must have dropped and they nudged him, each one's weight four times that of his own.

His thin scream as he lost his balance brought Tessa from the sad reverie into which the talk of Christmas and snow had plunged her and as she leaped to her feet, turning her head sharply she was just in time to see him fall backwards over Badger's Edge.

'Mistress not back yet, Walter?' Percy asked, poking his head round the stable door. Walter was brushing the floor vigorously, his strong shoulders pumping as he propelled the stiff bristles beneath the line of horses' heads which hung over each stall. There were a dozen of them all told, inluding two pairs of matched grey carriage horses. When he stopped, turning to Percy, his late master's bay nibbled his shoulder but he pushed the handsome head to one side, leaning on the brush.

'Nay, what the bloody 'ell's the time? I'd not noticed.'

'Tis gone four an' comin' on dark.'

'She'll be in afore long, Perce. She'd tekk no chances now.' Percy was well aware that Walter meant now she had young Joel to fill the dreadful gap Mr Drew's death had left. A year ago they would have worried for she'd been wild and daft in her grief, but he'd steadied her a treat, Mr Charlie's young 'un.

'Aye, 'appen yer right but she'd best mekk it quick 'cos if it don't snow soon my name's not Percy Barlow.'

'D'yer reckon?'

'Aye. Them clouds've bin bankin' up along't tops fer't last 'our. You mark my words, it'll be comin' down by full dark.'

They worked side by side, settling the animals for the night with soothing murmurs and heavy, affectionate slaps on their rumps. Thomas came in and looked about him, then moved to the carriage horses which were his responsibility, whistling through his teeth as he performed small, unnecessary jobs about the place, secretly as worried as they were, going to the door every few minutes to stare up at the rapidly darkening sky. The lamps were lit and all was cosy in the warm, horse-smelling stable. The men's work was finished for the day. All they had to do was see to Miss Tessa's mare and the lad's pony and as soon as that was done they would go to the warm comfort of the kitchen where there would be steaming mugs of Cook's strong, sweet tea, hot soup to keep them going until their supper, the comfortable laughter of their 'family', for most of the Greenwood servants had been employed at Greenacres for many years. Some, like Dorcas, had even served old Mrs Greenwood and Mrs Harrison, Miss Tessa's mother, who were both now living in the sunshine of Italy with old Mr Joss Greenwood.

There was the pitter-patter of light boots on the cobbles in the yard and holding an old shawl about her head and shoulders, Miss Tessa's maid Emma ran into the stable, her eyes searching anxiously into every corner.

'Miss Tessa's not here then?' she asked, although it was obvious her mistress was not present. Her glance fell on the empty stall which was waiting for Miss Tessa's mare and the

563

next one to it which was also unoccupied and her eyes widened in alarm.

'Don't tell me she's not back, Perce?' She put her hand to her mouth. 'Dear Lord, she should be back by now. It's almost full dark and I felt snow on me face as I crossed the yard.'

Percy looked about him in triumph for had he not forecast this very thing? Then he remembered the seriousness of Miss Tessa's failure to return and he scowled to hide his own misgiving. There was nothing wrong, of course, for Miss Tessa knew them moors like the back of her hand and was not one to take lightly the hostile and furious change-ability of the wilderness which lay about her home. She had been riding out there since she was ten years old and Percy was sure that if she had the slightest doubt that snow might be on the way she'd be headed home in an instant.

Then where the bloody hell was she?

'Where did she say she were off to, Walter?' he asked, attempting to be casual for Emma's benefit since they wanted no hysterical women on their hands at a time like this.

'Nay, don't ask me. She were askin' t'lad, seein' as 'ow it were their last ride afore ... afore the snows. Where did 'e want ter go, she said, but I didn't 'ear 'is answer.'

'Oh, my God ... oh, my God.' Emma began to moan and flap her hands and the men looked at one another over her bobbing cap. 'She's lost, Miss Tessa's lost and that little lad with her. Poor lass ... oh, my poor lass, whatever next? When's it going to end, Percy? It's one thing after another and, really, why one family should have so much heaped on them's beyond me.'

'Give over, Emma,' Percy said roughly, his own dreadful fear only just hidden. 'You'll 'ave her dead an' buried next an' 'er not gone fer more than...'

'When ... when did she go?' Emma shrieked.

'Well, when did she go, Walter?'

Walter shook his head fearfully for Miss Tessa and Master Joel had been up on them moors for over three hours. It was dark now and when the four of them looked out on to

564

the stable yard the lovely dancing snowflakes which were caught in the lamplight were thick and heavy.

He had landed on a small, grass-covered ledge, no more than eighteen inches wide and as far as she could judge about thirty feet down. She was never to know how it had broken his fall and in that first moment she did not even stop to wonder. He lay on his back, one of his arms hidden beneath him, the other hanging dangerously over the edge. His cape had flown out as he fell, spreading behind him, and his face was pale and unmoving against the dark cloth.

She began to scream his name and all around her small birds and animals, disturbed by the dreadful noise, became still, their hearts pounding in terror, and both horses flung up their heads, snorting, Joel's pony pawed the ground, then rolling his terrified eyes, reared up and, trailing his reins, galloped off into the gathering dusk. Her own mare, steadier than a young pony, stood for a moment but as her mistress's screams intensified, tearing the air in terror, she took fright and followed the pony along the track which led to her stable and safety.

'Oh, God ... Joel, darling, can you hear me? Oh, please, Joel, answer me ... Joel, can you hear me, darling? Joel ...' For thirty seconds Tessa Greenwood lost control and was no more than the hysterical, panic-stricken, useless female she herself had always despised. The dogs wheeled about her, confused and afraid but not leaving her, waiting for her command as they had been trained to do, but in those first moments she was out of reach to them, unable to command herself, let alone them.

Still he did not move and she took a deep breath, fighting her need to scream again, to shout for someone to come to help her, to calm her terror, to tell her what to do, to reassure her that there was no need to panic ... anything ... someone ...

But there was no one there, only Tessa Greenwood who must climb down to Joel and carry him up to safety. He was hurt, even from here she could see he was hurt ... not badly, God, please not badly ... and she must get down to him, now, now ... She had no rope, and if he should awake and move ... no, he was not dead ... *he was not dead* ... she would not *let* him be dead ... he could fall further, go over the ledge and down into ... down ... *No! No!* ... she would not let him ...

She flung off her cloak so that it would not impede her, leaving it lying carelessly on the edge and one of the dogs went to lie down on it, guarding it fiercely for it was hers. She did not look down but turned her back on the depths behind her. Her gloved hands ... she should have taken her gloves off for a firmer grip on the rocks ... there was no time to turn back now. There were rocks which were deeply imbedded in the turf at the edge of the drop and with the abyss clutching at her back, dragging her down into it, she clung to them, feeling carefully for a foothold. She found one, then another, each boot planted firmly in some small crevice.

'I'm coming, darling,' she called out again and again as her fingers clawed the rough gritstone rock, glad now of her gloves for her flesh would have been torn to pieces on its sharpness, thanking the fates which had decided that Joel should not fall in the softer shale for had he done so he would have gone straight to the bottom of the clough. Her heart pounded and threatened to break out of her rib cage and she was bathed in the sweat of fear.

'Joel,' she panted, 'I'm coming, don't move, sweetheart.' Her boots slipped on a patch of wet rock and she almost went down. *Wet?* How could it be wet? And then she felt the snowflakes rest lightly on her cheek, then more on her eyelashes and she blinked despairingly. She was almost there, surely? She dare not look down, only up and the edge of the cliff was very high above her head. It was outlined against the dark grey of the sky and from the sky the dread pattern of the slowly whirling snow danced above her, coming to rest on her upturned face.

'No, God, no, not now. Haven't you done enough? Let me at least get down to him. Don't let it snow now, God.' She stared with hatred up into the malevolent heavens as she screamed out His name.

She didn't know how long it was before her booted feet felt the grass which lined the narrow shelf. Even when she reached it she knew she must be careful for it was only as wide as Joel himself and she would have little room to manoeuvre. Somehow, when she had satisfied herself that he was alive ... *and he was alive* ... that he was not badly hurt ... oh, why did he not cry out to her? ... she must get him up the cliff and on to the back of her mare, yes, her mare for she was more placid than Joel's little pony. Please God, help me ... and she began to inch her way along the couple of feet of ledge which separated her from Joel.

Annie was just about to leave the emptying mill yard when Mr Drew's handsome bay clattered through the opened gates. Walter was on his back, his face as white as the snow which had begun to stick between the cobbles and to the rough bricks of the factory wall. She had been in conference with Mrs Poynton and Mrs Bayly, discussing the possibility of those unemployed mill women who had become good, plain needlewomen in the three years they had been at it, making simple garments such as infants' underclothes and selling them to the good-class shops in Manchester or Oldham. There would be nothing fancy but fine cloth and well made, aimed at the middle-class mother, and if she could find a market might it not open up another avenue of work for them, even when the war was over?

She was startled when Tessa's groom loomed out of the growing dark and was ready to be sharp with him but his words stopped hers.

'Tis Miss Tessa an't little lad.' A crowd of men had gathered about them, jostling one another to hear what Walter Hobson was saying. Must be serious for he looked as though he'd seen a bloody ghost.

Annie thought her heart would stop beating and never start again. Though she was only half-aware of it she realised at that moment the strength of the loving bond which lay between her and Tessa Greenwood and how desolate she would be to lose her.

'What . . . ?'

'I'm lookin' fer men to search . . .'

'Search? Dear God, Walter Hobson, speak up man. What's 'appened?'

'Miss Tessa, 'er an' the lad are lost on't moor. Their animals come in not ten minutes since. There's only an 'andful o' strong men at Greenacres, Mr Briggs an' old Jonathan's past it an' . . .'

'Will yer stop babblin' yer fool. Where on't moor?'

'We don't know, lass.'

'*Tha don't know!* 'Ow in God's name are thi ter find 'em then?'

'We don't know that either, lass.'

'Well, don't just stand there. Get these men organised inter groups, then ride on to t'other mills an' fetch all the men there. And on't way shout tha damned 'ead off an' tell every man tha meet ter come ter Chapmans. Able-bodied men . . . that's if there are any left," she said bitterly, 'an' when tha've done that come right back 'ere. There's someone I want thi ter fetch. But first of all give me a list o't places she an' the lad go to. Every damn one, Walter Hobson, an' look sharp or there won't be a soul stirrin' wi' this damn snow comin' down.'

She reached him as the first fine blanket of snow had covered his crumpled figure completely. She could not get past him to reach his legs for she dared not step on his bit of ledge for fear she would tumble him into the depths of the darkness which yawned below him. She laid a trembling, terrified hand on his face, brushing away the snow from it, appalled at its coldness and smallness.

'Joel,' she whispered, scarcely daring to breathe now that

568

she had reached him, desperately needing to find a heartbeat or pulse which would tell her he still lived. Where? His
throat, his temple, where, dear God, where? She wanted to
pull him into her arms, to cradle him, shelter him, warm
him but their position was so precarious might she not
dislodge the pair of them if she moved him in any way? Best
be slow and cautious, examine him as well as she could
with careful hands, since she could hardly see him in the
snow-filled darkness. She began with his face and head,
amazed at the fragility of his childish neck, the small bones
of his head and face, the soft flexibility of his boy's ears.

'Oh, Joel, I love you so much,' she mumbled and for a
moment she was cast back into another place, another time,
with another male figure in her arms. He had been unconscious too, needing her and her strength and she had given
it to him, brought him back with her love. But now she must
concentrate on Joel, keep him alive, warm until help came.
Having come down the escarpment she knew finally, now
that she was here, that she would never get up again, with
or without this child she loved.

She had pulled off her gloves, throwing them unthink-
ingly behind her, not knowing or caring where they landed,
and with her bare hands she gently lifted the boy's head,
supporting it with one as she searched for injuries with the
other. She could feel a large bump to the side, just above
his ear but there appeared to be no blood. Her hands crept
beneath his chin and to her incredulous joy she felt a pulse
throb against her fingers. Oh, thank you, God, thank you,
and she lifted her weeping eyes to the blinding snow for a
moment.

But he was so cold and so was she now that she had been
still for several minutes. If only she had her cloak? It was
made of wool and lined with fur but she knew that she
could not have climbed down here with it draped across
her shoulders. She brushed as much snow as she could
reach from the boy, then carefully eased her jacket off and
placed it across his chest. She tucked it under his chin,

leaning across him to protect him from the steadily falling blanket which was an inch deep all over him, wondering if she might ease him slowly, slowly towards her. If she could lift his small frame ... so slender, so light-boned ... up against her where she knelt, might she not keep him warmer, transmit some of her own body heat to him?

She realised then that she was kneeling on his cape which was spread behind him. If she could get it from about his neck, lift it and place it over his uncovered legs it would at least keep the heavy, wet snow from the lower half of his unprotected body. She shivered uncontrollably, her own shirt wet and freezing to her back, her hair wearing a cap of snow which melted and dripped on to Joel's still face. She knew his arm was beneath him, probably injured in the fall but with a little care and a great deal of good luck she might ...

With a small cry, whether of pain or fear, the boy lurched suddenly into a sitting position, a cry spiralling up into the darkness and completely knocking her from the delicate balance she only just preserved on the ledge. She grabbed at the rock face, at the tufty grass beneath her, at anything which came to her desperate hands in her hopeless struggle to remain on the ledge. Yet even in her fight for what she was well aware could be her own life she was careful not to grab at him. She must not hold on to him for as she fell, and she knew she was about to fall, she must not take him with her.

She made no sound as she went. She had some jumbled idea in her head that she must not frighten him any more than could be helped and her last conscious thought as she slid over the edge into the snow-dancing emptiness of air was that the only man who could save them no longer loved her.

'Tell me, quickly, damn your soul to hell! For God's sake, speak up, man, or I swear I'll strangle you where you stand.' The big hands grabbed Walter by the shoulders and shook him savagely.

570

'I'm tryin' to, sir. Please, I can't say 'owt with thi 'oldin' me up like I was a bloody sack of ...'

'I'm sorry ... please ... I'm sorry. For Christ's sake tell me ...'

'Miss Beale ses yer ter come at once.' Walter's tired face was pale in the lamplight which spilled from the open doorway and across the steps, and the snow was like a shimmering curtain about him. Drew Greenwood's bay drooped behind him. He had been ridden hard and long this night and Walter knew he would go no further but *he* would once he had passed on Miss Beale's message to this big chap. He'd got the list in the pocket of his greatcoat and he was to ask him to pick a place. *The place*. He'd know, Miss Beale had said, and he was to go straight there with Walter and as many men as he could find. There'd only be one chance – though others would naturally search for as long as they could elsewhere – and if he made the wrong choice they'd not find her, not this night and not on any other until the snows thawed. Blankets and ropes and lamps they'd take and whatever this man said was needed, and if he didn't make the right choice Walter would personally choke the bloody life out of him, aye, and swing for it an' all. For a moment a picture came into his mind of a lovely young girl, excited and wild, daring her cousin to cut her long glossy hair. When he had done so, it had lain all over the stable floor like a carpet. After they had gone he had tenderly taken a shining length of it and he had it to this day in a bit of paper in a drawer in his room above the stable.

'Come inside, man, and get warm while ...'

'*Get warm!*. I've no time fer that, beggin' yer pardon, sir. Here's t'list. Tell me where ter go an' I'll be off.'

'Don't be daft, man. We need things. We can't go off half-cocked or we'll be floundering to our deaths, and she'll not live then. D'you not think I don't want to run like a madman up on the moors shouting her name? Jesus ...' His face worked and in his eyes was an expression of suffering such as Walter had never seen before. He himself was right fond

571

of a certain laundrymaid and he supposed he would lay down his life for her if asked but this chap looked ... well, wild ... maddened with some savage emotion which consumed him and lit his eyes to deep brown pits of fire. He'd heard rumours about him and Miss Tessa, hadn't they all, years ago but he'd laughed at them. Now it seems there was something in them after all, looking at this chap's face.

'Now give me that list,' the man said and his voice was choked.

'Right, sir, a cup o' tea wouldn't go amiss whilst tha gets tha coat, like.'

The pain in her shoulder awoke her, that and the sound of someone crying. It was a child weeping its heart out in the most desolate fashion, and a child in pain by the sound of it. God, but she was cold, and wet too, and there was a strange softness, like butterflies' wings, falling on to her face.

'Aunt Tess, Aunt Tess, please come and get me,' the child wept and in an appalling moment of terror it all came back to her. She tried to sit up but the tearing agony in her shoulder pinned her down to wherever she was. Joel ... oh, dear Father, who art in heaven ... take care of Joel ... hallowed be Thy name ... and she tried to raise her voice to tell him she was near but nothing seemed to come out of her mouth and Joel continued to weep.

There was a deep silence when next she regained her senses, soft and gentle and strangely enough she no longer felt cold. In fact, she was most comfortable and didn't mind a bit waiting. What was she waiting for? Who? ... Someone ... she knew she was waiting for someone. She remembered Joel drowsily, wondering if he was as cosy and warm under his white blanket as she was. She hoped so. She called his name softly, up into the veil of snow which fell endlessly out of the sky and knew a small pang of misgiving when he did not answer. Perhaps he had already left? Perhaps he had climbed the rock face and got on his pony and ridden off to Greenacres? A good boy, Joel, and sensible and he'd bring him ... Who? ... Who would he bring? ... Where ... Where was she? ... And how ... ?

The dogs snarled ferociously, a close-packed, snow-covered, almost invisible shape crouched on her cloak and would allow none to approach them as they guarded her, and what was hers.

'Call them off, for God's sake,' the man shouted above the howling of the demented wind.

'Nay.' Walter's voice could scarcely be heard. 'They'll not shift fer anyone only 'er.'

'Then bloody well shoot them.'

'I've no gun, sir.' What did he want with a gun on a night like this?

They watched, the circle of tired men as the big man strode fearlessly through the drifting snow towards the group of savage animals and when they parted for him one or two attempting to lick his hand as though they knew him, the men surged forward to watch in amazement and a legend was born that night.

'She'll be down there. Get ropes.' He wasted no words.

''Ow does tha know, sir?' Walter shouted, his face gaunt in the light from the flickering lamp.

'That's her cloak, isn't it? And those are her dogs guarding it.'

She felt his arms go round her and though her shoulder shrieked in agony she gave a great contented sigh of relief as she moved thankfully into their shelter at last. Where had he been for so long, she wanted to ask him but when she looked up into his dear face she merely smiled for she knew he had come as quickly as he could.

'Will,' she said, laying her head against his chest.

'Aye, who else?'

They were there when she awoke, two anxious faces which both cleared, ready to smile as her eyes opened. The boy had his right arm splinted to his body and there was a

573

swelling above his ear which gave him a somewhat lopsided look but he leaned forward, putting his face close to hers. She could feel his breath fan her cheek and smell its child-like sweetness and knew he was safe, whole and sound. Slightly damaged perhaps, but in the way of children whose recuperative powers are quite amazing, he was ready to engage in whatever she herself was capable of.

'Oh, there you are, Aunt Tess,' he said, just as though she had been out to tea and him waiting impatiently for her return. 'We got you back just as soon as we could but the doctor said we were not to wake you.' He raised his wounded arm a fraction, important and proud of himself for surviving what had, naturally, been an event of great magnitude. 'I've been up all day,' he continued accusingly, 'and waiting here with Mr Broadbent for you to wake. None of the others could come in, of course, though Jane wept and begged to be allowed to look after you but the doctor said you were to sleep.'

Her eyes moved beyond his still pale but excited face to the one which had waited enduringly for as long as she could remember. But there was a hint of impatience in it now which its owner made no attempt to conceal.

'Darling,' she murmured drowsily and both the boy and the man knew the endearment was meant for him.

"How long has it been?'

'Too bloody long.'

The boy stared at Mr Broadbent, evidently much impressed with this sign of his superiority, then turned back to the bed.

'Is your shoulder better now, Aunt Tess?' he continued anxiously, for she was dear to him but a dislocated shoulder could not compare with a broken arm.

The man fidgeted and began to scowl.

'Yes, darling, now give me a kiss and ... well, I have a word or two to say to Mr Broadbent so perhaps, now that you are satisfied yourself that I am recovered, you could go and tell the others.'

The door had barely closed behind him when Will drew her carefully into his arms but she had done with care and steadiness, with self-control and sobriety.

'Kiss me properly, for God's sake,' she demanded huskily against his mouth, which strove to be gentle, and when he did they were both unsteady with the joy of it.

'Damnation, woman, I don't want to hurt you.' He was ready, should she show signs of weakness to place her, reluctantly, back amongst her nest of pillows, but, his expression said, he was even more ready to join her there.

'Hurt me, Will, I beg you, since I have felt nothing, nothing, for years.' And but for the sound of the household beyond the bedroom door he was ready to make love to her right then and there.

'Soon, dear God, soon . . .'

'When we are married, you are saying?' she laughed breathlessly against the hollow of his strong throat.

'And before that, my lass, for I'll not wait. I'll make sure of you this time.'

Again they fell into the sweetness both had denied themselves so often in the decade since they had first met, their flesh melting into that ecstasy which they had found only with one another. Then:

'You will not object to a ready-made family, Will?' She felt a moment of wariness since surely . . . ?

'I mean to add to it,' he said gruffly.

'And the . . . ?'

'Aye, Tessa Harrison, the bloody mills an' all.'

'You would have no objection to . . . ?'

'We'll work side by side, lass, you know that.'

The words put the last mending stitch in the torn fabric of their love, returning it to its durable and everlasting strength, a strength which both of them knew could never be damaged again.